Redwood Dragons

The Complete Series

SLOANE MEYERS

CONTENTS

BOOK ONE: DEFIANCE AND THE DRAGON

CHAPTER ONE

Knox Pars stood as motionless as a stone amidst the thick tree trunks of the redwoods. Even his eyes remained frozen as he stared deep into the forest in front of him, searching for any movements that would give away his prey. He knew better than to be distracted by the rustle of leaves indicating that a bird was flying by, or by the soft scamper of a mouse. No, what he was hunting was much bigger.

He was hunting a dragon.

Knox's body tensed as he breathed in slowly, and deeply. If you hadn't known better, you would have thought that he wasn't breathing at all. His body was a perfectly still mass of muscle. Even in human form, one felt instantly impressed when they looked at him. He was tall, and his piercing green eyes seemed to see right through you. Right now, those green eyes blended in with the deep green of the forest. His dark brown hair blended in with the tree trunks. The redwoods soared high above him, standing watch over the forest as they had for hundreds and even thousands of years. These woods were ancient, and had seen things most humans alive today considered to be the stuff of fairy tales and fantasy legends.

Not Knox. He knew that there was often much more to see than what met the eye. After all, he himself hid a dragon within. He could transform at a moment's notice into a giant, fire-breathing creature that struck fear in the hearts of almost everyone who saw him.

But right now, he was content to stay in human form. This allowed him to slip through the forest undetected, chasing the dragon that had managed to elude him for the last several hours. He was close to catching the bastard, though. Even though he couldn't see the beast, he felt it. He knew that it was hidden somewhere among these old trees. He just had to make sure he saw it before it saw him.

Knox let his eyes roam over the dense forest. Birds sang out, tweeting happy songs in the waning afternoon sunshine. Every now and then the wind rustled through the trees. But otherwise, Knox heard nothing unusual in the sounds of the forest. He was not alone out here, though. He knew it. And he knew he was getting closer.

"Where are you?" he mouthed, not even daring to whisper the words. And then, he saw it. Several hundred feet away, where the trail through the woods rose in a series of sharp switchbacks, there was one spot where the outline of the trees was a little bit too irregular. If you hadn't been well-trained to look for this sort of thing, as Knox was, you would have missed it. But Knox had spent his entire life practicing for moments like this, and now, the slow curl of a smile played at his lips as he saw that the irregular pattern continued just long enough to be the outline of a large dragon.

"Gotcha," he mouthed, again not actually saying a word.

The next few moments were a blur of action. Knox started running toward the steep trail, as silently as was possible for a man as large and muscular as himself. Within a few seconds, a large pop sounded out through the forest, and Knox began to transform mid-run. His head was the first to morph, quickly becoming covered with iridescent dragon scales. His teeth grew until they were so long they would have given

7

chills to even the hardiest of men, and sharp horns grew behind his ears. His body, legs, and arms all followed a similar pattern, changing from soft human flesh to the thick scaled skin of a dragon. His hands and feet became large dragon feet which ended in razor-sharp claws, and wings sprouted from his back. The wings came last, and as they did, Knox let out a roar and rose into the air. His dragon prey had at first attempted to retreat slowly and silently, maintaining its chameleon-like camouflage as it went. But as Knox picked up speed, and the dragon realized it had been found out, it gave up its attempt at stealth. It rose into the air, suddenly starkly visible against the outline of trees and skies as its camouflage completely disappeared and it took on the same iridescent green hue that Knox's dragons scales had. Knox flapped his wings even harder, pursuing the other dragon at top speed. Knox knew the other beast didn't stand a chance. If there was one thing Knox was good at, it was speed. He'd always been the fastest flyer in his crew, and today he was feeling extra energetic. The other dragon made a brave effort to get away, but Knox was soon flying directly over it, reaching his long, clawed feet out toward the other dragon's neck. The other dragon dove suddenly and sharply down to the earth, and Knox followed. As soon as they hit the ground, skidding to a halt between the large redwoods, the other dragon shifted back into human form with a loud pop.

"Damn you, Knox! How did you find me?"

Knox shifted back into human form, doubled over in laughter as he looked over at the other man. "You need to work on your chameleon skills, Myles," he said.

Knox's clanmate, Myles, glared at him for a moment, but eventually cracked a smile. "You're right, I know. I just got nervous when I saw you approaching. I didn't concentrate hard enough."

"I could see your outline," Knox said. "You weren't too bad overall, but if the colors on the edges of your body aren't perfectly lined up with the colors around you, your chameleon camouflage won't work."

Myles sighed. "I need to work on that."

"Yeah, you do," Knox said, but then added kindly. "But good job otherwise. You hardly left a trail of where you had been. Even I had a really difficult time tracking you."

Myles beamed with pride at Knox's praise. Knox was a superb tracker, so this was quite a compliment. Knox was also the best in the clan at using chameleon skills to blend into his surroundings. All reptile shifters could learn to do this, but it was difficult to do it well if you weren't actually a chameleon. Being able to essentially make yourself invisible was worth the hard work of mastering chameleon skills, though. One never knew when one might need to disappear.

"Shall we head home?" Knox asked. "We can do a full debrief there, over beers."

"Now you're talking," Myles said. In the next moment, both men had shifted back into dragon form and were rising high above the Redwood forest, their powerful wings easily propelling their large bodies into the clouds.

Knox breathed in deeply, loving the heady rush of cool air. He had been leader of the Redwood Dragons clan for two years now, but he was still getting used to being the one in charge. Some days, the amount of responsibility that rested on his shoulders nearly overwhelmed him. But on days like today, where he was training one of his dragons on how to sneak through enemy territory undetected, Knox was happy with his role as clan leader. If there was one thing Knox could do well, it was move through woods undetected. William had always said it was Knox's greatest strength. And Knox had enjoyed taking over the training missions that William had spearheaded in the past.

Knox felt a wave of nostalgia wash over him as he thought of William. William had been the leader of the Redwood Dragons before Knox, and it was still hard to believe that the old dragon wasn't around every day. He'd been too old to fight well anymore, and so had handed the number one position in the clan over to Knox. Knox knew William had a lot of faith in him, but he also knew he'd never be as good of a leader as William had been.

William had come from a long line of dragons who had been guardians of the immensely powerful ancient dragon artifacts. William was the last of the ancient Redwood dragons, though, and realized that he needed to figure out who would guard the artifacts when he was gone. Twenty years ago, when Knox had been a young child and had been orphaned during the last great war on shifters, William had rescued him, along with ten other dragon orphans. Knox's clan, the Redwood Clan, now consisted entirely of these ten orphans—himself and nine other dragons. The ten of them were brothers, fighting together to keep the world safe. Myles, Owen, and Vance were the only dragons with Knox in the Redwood forest at the moment, though. The rest of the clan's dragons—Grayson, Weston, Noah, Finn, Holden, and Zeke—were all off in various parts of the world, chasing down dragon artifacts. This was their life: guard the dragon artifacts that had been recovered and were stored in their Redwood lair, and go out to find and recover the artifacts that were still missing—and were often being used by corrupt shifters to do awful things.

These ancient artifacts held supernatural powers that had once belonged to the ancient dragons. Few modern shifters realized what great powers the shifters of old had once held, but the Redwood dragons knew, and they did their best to keep ancient artifacts out of the wrong hands. The Redwoods of Northern California, with their own ancient secrets, were the perfect home base for a group of fantastical beasts like Knox's clan. As Knox rose higher and higher above the forest and turned his great dragon body toward the hidden lair they called home, he felt his heart lighten.

No matter how many worries weighed on his mind as clan leader, he knew he could always relax at their clan headquarters. It was a place of community and safety, only occupied by the ten Redwood dragons. The brotherhood of beasts that retained something of the ancient dragon magic, and were sworn to use it always for good.

It was a good, noble life, and Knox could not have asked for more. Little did he know, though, that he was about to get more, whether he wanted it or not.

CHAPTER TWO

Bree Riley didn't even bother trying to hide the deep scowl on her face. The High Council were all looking at her like she had lost her mind, and she knew they didn't trust her recommendation on the current crisis facing the clan. She also knew that they were fools not to believe her, but one could not simply call the High Council members fools.

"You are young, Bree, and perhaps do not understand the magnitude of what you are suggesting," said Peter, the oldest of the councilors. He had a long, white beard that reached down to his belly, and with his formal pointed hat that was worn to Council meetings, he looked every bit the part of a powerful wizard. And what a powerful wizard he was! Bree knew that, although he was kind, he was not used to being questioned. He had spent his life gathering a deep well of wisdom, and what reason would he see to trust a young Wizard Advocate such as herself? Bree was the youngest and most junior of all the Advocates, and she had only been assigned to work on the dragon stone case because when its existence was first discovered, no one thought it was a big deal. It had been, they all thought, a throwaway project. Bree's research had quickly found otherwise, and now, the wizard clan realized that the powerful stone was actually stones, plural. And those stones, if they fell into the wrong hands, could be fatal to the wizards' ability to practice magic freely and undetected by those humans who believed magic did not actually exist.

"I understand that it's extremely unconventional to suggest that we join forces with shifters," Bree said. "But—"

"It's not just unconventional, it's unheard of!" Samuel, another one of the High Council members interrupted. "Don't you remember your history lessons, child? You are so young that the ink on your Advocate Diploma can barely have dried, and yet you cannot remember what you learned in your wizarding history lessons? The last time wizards attempted to team up with shifters, the entire wizarding race was nearly destroyed! We cannot let shifters know we still exist, or our very existence itself is at stake."

Bree bit her lip, doing her best to maintain a calm exterior even though her insides were flaring up with anger. She may be young, but she was not an idiot. She had graduated in the top of her class from the Advocacy program, and she knew well the stories of how the shifters of old, in their quest for power, had nearly destroyed the wizards. She adjusted her robes and absentmindedly fingered at her blood-red ruby ring. Magic rings were used in place of wands by wizards of modern times. Her family didn't have much money, but her father had given her this expensive magic ring over twelve years ago for her eighteenth birthday, and it had served her well since that time.

"But, your Honors, those were dark times, full of dark shifters. The good shifters themselves were nearly extinguished as well. The evil shifters were in power, and *they* were the ones who tried to kill off wizards. They also tried to kill off those of their own kind, the shifters, who did not agree with them. I understand that the events of those days left a bad taste in the mouths of all wizards—"

A large snorting guffaw arose from the High Council table, but Bree pushed forward, doing her best to ignore it.

"—but we cannot allow ourselves to remain trapped in the past when it would keep us from seeking the help we need today. The dragon stones will be nearly impossible to find and defend if we don't have shifters on our side, helping us. It would behoove us to seek out help from the good shifters before evil shifters discover that the dragon sapphire stone still exists and has been located."

"You are a disgrace to the Advocates," Samuel bellowed out. "How dare you tell the High Council what would behoove us! You—"

"Silence!" Peter bellowed, glaring in Samuel's direction. Bree cringed at Peter's tone, but Samuel did not so much as wince. He glared right back at Peter, defiant. But he did fall silent, and, for a moment, the entire Council room was heavy with the silence. Then Peter spoke.

"Child, your dedication to your work is admirable," Peter said. "We old Council members do sometimes need the zeal of youth to keep us on our toes, and I respect the conviction with which you present your case. But I'm afraid that this is one instance where we must remain firm, no matter how much you disagree with us. The consequences of a misstep here would be too grave."

"But you don't understand," Bree said. "Not reaching out to the shifters would be the misstep. We need them!"

Gasps rang out across the room. None of the other Advocates would have dared to defy Peter in this way. Peter looked taken aback, and, for one awful moment, Bree thought he was going to yell at her. But then his face relaxed, and he chuckled.

"You are a fiery one," Peter said. "But I remain firm in my decision. We will not contact the shifters. This meeting is adjourned."

The room became almost instantly noisy with the hum of excited conversation. Everyone was discussing the unusually tense High Council meeting, and they were all avoiding eye contact with Bree. Angrily, she picked up her folder of work and left the room, nearly tripping over her own formal robes which were a size too big. She'd had to borrow some from her roommate, because she hadn't bought any of her own yet. She'd never expected to be participating in a High Council meeting within months of beginning her work as an Advocate. Usually, such meetings consisted of only seasoned wizards. And, Bree thought angrily, she might as well have not been there today anyway.

No one had taken her seriously. They all looked at her like she was a little girl who knew nothing. But Bree knew too much, and that was the problem. She knew that this was one of those rare occasions when the High Council was wrong, and if they insisted on sticking to their decision, their entire clan was going to be in trouble. Bree's work on the dragon stone project had convinced her of that.

Bree fumed the whole way home, walking as quickly as she could through the streets of Falcon Cross and telling herself to just ignore the curious looks being cast in her direction by the other wizards on the street. She wished more than anything that she had brought her car so she could avoid people, even though the walk home was less than a mile. She liked to stretch her legs when she could, and avoided taking her car when possible. She didn't particularly like working in an office job where she had to sit so much all day, but she did love her work. Well, she had loved it until today, at least. Now she was not so sure. What was the point of all her careful research and detective work if the High Council was just going to laugh in her face?

Bree finally reached home, storming up the stairs to the two bedroom apartment she shared with another Advocate, Lily, who was a year her senior. Bree slammed the door behind her and immediately started peeling off her oversized dress robes. Lily, who had been sitting on the couch with a stack of papers, looked up at Bree and arched an eyebrow.

"I take it things didn't go so well?" Lily asked.

Bree scowled at her, then threw the dress robes across an armchair next to the couch.

"I'll have those dry-cleaned later. Right now I need to think," Bree said, then disappeared into the small bedroom that was hers. She felt slightly better as soon as she closed the door behind her. The bedroom was small, but it was the only place Bree had where she could feel truly alone. She had her own office at the Advocacy Bureau, but her coworkers and supervisors were always popping in and out of there without warning, often opening or closing the door so quickly that Bree's Advocate diploma shook on the wall, threatening to tumble to the ground.

Samuel's words from the High Council played across her mind once again at the thought of her Advocate diploma. He'd sneered at her, telling her the ink had barely dried on her diploma.

He was right about that, at least. Bree had only graduated two months ago, after ten years of grueling higher education. A career as an Advocate was not for the faint of heart. The training was intense, but if you completed it, you were one of the most respected members of the wizarding community. The only ones who commanded more respect were members of the High Council, most of whom had started out their careers as Advocates.

Advocates often worked long hours, doing their best to identify and eliminate any threats to the ability of the wizards to freely use magic. Most of the time, the job was rather straightforward. The largest chunk of time was dedicated to covering up situations where magic had accidentally been used in the view of a non-wizard. This often required creative explanations, but the Advocates were well-trained on how to smooth over even the most bizarre of occurrences. Bree loved being assigned to an Alternative Explanations case. She'd done two already in her time as an Advocate, and they were always entertaining.

Less fun was being assigned to research and report on an identified threat to the wizarding community. When any information came in to the Advocacy Bureau on a potential threat, that threat had to be fully investigated. These came in by the hundreds each year, and usually involved a simple investigation. Most of the time, threats consisted of benign comments by non-wizard humans who didn't actually know magic existed. These humans were always blaming things on weird superstitions without realizing that there was actually some basis to their superstitions. Nevertheless, any time these careless comments were made, an Advocate had to assess the situation and report back on whether there was any credible reason to believe the human actually knew magic existed and might actually intend to stop the wizards from using it.

Rarely, a threat would come from a source other than a human. Shifters occasionally caught wind that magic was much more present in the world than they had thought, and the Advocates had to make sure the shifters were not likely to discover the existence of Falcon Cross or of the wizards. And then, even rarer, were situations when a magical object was obtained by a non-wizard. This was the type of situation that Bree had faced when she was assigned to the dragon stone project.

The project had originally been a minor, unimportant one. That's why, of course, it had been assigned to Bree, the most junior Advocate available. The case had seemed straightforward enough. A powerful dragon stone with magical, supernatural powers had been discovered. The stone had been recovered by a group of shifters, and was now in the safekeeping of the shifter protectors, a group of good shifters who kept bad shifters in check. Bree's task had been to make sure that the stone was indeed safe with the good shifters, and that none of the shifters seemed to have any idea that the world of magic extended beyond this magical stone. The case was pretty cut and dried, and Bree had been quite grumpy when it was assigned to her, although she had done her best not to show it. She knew she was a junior Advocate, and she had to pay her dues doing grunt work before she was given the chance to work on the truly spectacular cases.

It hadn't taken long for her grumpiness to disappear once she started working on the case. The dragon stone was indeed safe. The shifters who held it were known as shifter protectors, and were some of the most powerful members of the shifter world, renowned for fighting evil. Slightly more troublesome was the fact that there appeared to be several other ancient artifacts with magical qualities that the shifters were aware of. These were much less powerful than the stone, but, since they were magical in nature, Bree was obliged to ensure through her research that each individual artifact was well-protected and had not given the shifters reason to suspect that wizards still existed. Things had been going along well until Bree discovered by accident that there was more than one dragon stone—and that, as far as she could tell, the shifters did not know that the additional dragon stones existed.

In fact, as far as Bree could tell, there were four dragon stones in all, but two of them seemed completely lost. Who knew where time had taken those two stones, or whether they even existed anymore. The third stone, an emerald, was, of course, in the possession of the good shifters. And the fourth stone, the dragon sapphire, had recently been recovered by a gem collector in a New York City auction. The gem collector had been delayed several times trying to fly back to his home in Silicon Valley, California, and Bree soon discovered why. A group of men who had once been part of an international drug ring were trying to find the stone. Bree snooped around and discovered that these men had discovered that the stone contained some sort of magical properties, and they were trying to acquire it with the intention of using the magic to become powerful themselves.

Bree had been shocked when she realized what was going on. A full, non-wizard human getting a hold of a magical object with intent to use it for evil was considered a wizarding emergency. Non-wizards were notoriously bad at handling magical objects, and combating the effects of their missteps would require the heavy use of magic, which in turn was likely to cause the wizards to be discovered by shifters or non-wizard humans, or both.

Bree shuddered. If the wizards were discovered, their comfortable way of life would be shattered. Now, they lived in their own community, in a small, out of the way town where no one ever bothered them. They could continue their age-old wizarding practices without fear of persecution or ridicule. But if non-wizards discovered them— or even if the wrong shifters discovered them—their times of peace would be over. The history books were full of warnings about what happened when non-wizards discovered wizards. Witch trials and witch hunts had littered the pages of Bree's history books during Advocacy school. She had hardly been able to believe the awful things that people and shifters had done for fear of magic. Contrary to what the members of the High Council thought, she did take those lessons from history very seriously.

But the High Council wasn't taking *her* seriously. Bree had tried her best to make them see that the dragon sapphire did exist, and that if it wasn't found soon, disaster awaited Falcon Cross. She knew well the aversion the wizarding community had to partnering with shifters, so she had made the case for contacting the shifters as iron-

13

clad as she could. Wizards were great at magic, but they weren't great at fighting without the use of magic. And getting this stone was sure to involve some serious battles. Who could the wizards turn to, other than the good shifters? It was time for the wizards to forget the wars of centuries ago and work together. There was too much at risk for both shifters and wizards if the dragon sapphire fell into the wrong hands.

The High Council disagreed, of course. Bree felt hopeless now as she lay on her bed looking up at the ceiling and wondering how she was going to continue doing low-level Advocate work when she knew that unprecedented disaster was brewing beyond the borders of Falcon Cross.

Hours passed as Bree lay there, mulling over everything in her mind. She tried to think of some way to appeal to the High Council. She tried to think of some different thing she could say, some new point she could make, that would convince them. But she had already thought of everything. She'd laid all her cards out on the table, certain that the right choice would be made. But things had gone dreadfully wrong. All Bree could do was lie on her bed, wondering how long it would take for her entire world to go to shit.

Night had fallen now, and Bree sat up slowly in the dark room. She didn't want to see Lily right now, but the hunger pangs in her stomach had become unbearable. She would grab something to eat from the kitchen as quickly as she could, avoiding speaking to Lily as much as possible. Then she would retreat back into her room. Tomorrow morning at work she would have to face ridicule from all of her coworkers. But, for tonight, she could just spend the rest of the evening pretending that today had never happened.

Bree cracked open the door to her bedroom, and light instantly flooded in from the living room. All of the lights in the common areas were on, but the apartment was quiet. Lily's bedroom door was open, and her room was dark. Bree noticed a sheet of paper on the otherwise empty dining room table, and she went over to look at it. Lily's handwriting sprawled across the page in a short note to Bree.

Hey, Bree. I'm going out to dinner with some coworkers. I figured you'd want some alone time tonight, anyway. If I'm wrong and you want to hang out, of course feel free to call me.

Bree smiled somewhat sadly at the note. Lily was a good friend, and Bree had been unnecessarily rude to her earlier today. Bree sighed. She would apologize later. For now, she was just glad to have the apartment to herself. Lily was right. She did need some alone time.

Wearily, Bree made her way to the refrigerator. She pulled out some deli meat and cheese, then found some bread and began to make herself a sandwich. That was all she had energy to make right now. She felt so hopeless. She might be younger than all of the old wizards on the High Council, but she wasn't dumb. She'd spent the majority of her thirty years on earth studying and learning, and she was damn good at her job. She knew that she wasn't wrong about what she had discovered, or about the need to work with the shifters. But if she couldn't convince the High Council to listen to her, what did it matter how hard she had worked to uncover the truth behind the dragon stones? It's not like she could just up and defy the High Council.

Bree paused suddenly with her hand on a jar of mayonnaise. Or could she?

As an Advocate, Bree knew well the rules and regulations surrounding the High Council. The penalty for defying an official High Council decision was expulsion from the wizarding community after a forced stripping of magical powers. No one in Bree's lifetime had ever been stripped of their powers, but Bree and every other wizard had been warned throughout their lives about how awful the process was. It was supposedly very painful, and the magic spell required to strip someone of their wizarding powers left physical and emotional scars. It was irreversible, and the use of the spell was strictly forbidden except in cases where High Council members performed it on someone convicted of defying a High Council order. The spell was too difficult for most ordinary wizards to perform, anyway. Only a wizard at the level of a High Council member was likely to be successful in using it.

Bree stood frozen in the kitchen staring at the magic ring on her hand. It was the most beautiful, precious thing she owned. The platinum band firmly held the large ruby, which was shaped to a sharp point at the top. That point was where she focused her magic, and the ring had served her well through her years of training to be an Advocate. Not only that, but it reminded her of her father, who had been killed before his time by cancer—that awful disease that not even the world's best wizard could cure with magic. If Bree was stripped of her magic and kicked out of Falcon Cross, she would be forced to give up the ring as well. The thought took her breath away. It would be like giving away a piece of her heart. Like giving away the most beloved memory of her father.

And yet, how could Bree sit silent and do nothing, when she knew in her heart of hearts that she was right? She had worked and reworked her research. She had checked and rechecked her sources, and there was no denying the truth. Disaster was on the horizon for Falcon Cross if the wizards did not act quickly. They needed to join forces with someone as strong as or stronger than themselves, and the shifters were the only ones who fit that need.

What good would it do, to keep her magic and her ring, if the town she loved was destroyed anyway? If she was going to lose everything, she might as well go down with a fight.

Bree slowly made her way back toward her room, her sandwich forgotten and her heart pounding. She couldn't believe she was about to do this, but she didn't see what choice she had. Her father had always encouraged her to be brave, and, perhaps this was what it meant to be brave right now.

Methodically, Bree began to pack a large backpack. She took two complete extra sets of clothes, then stuffed in her file folder of notes that she had presented to the High Council earlier today. She dared not take any electronic data with her. A phone or laptop might be traceable, and Bree definitely did not want to be traced. She packed a few pairs of very warm, woolen socks, some gloves, and a warm hat. She also rolled a hoodie up tightly so it would take up as little space as possible, and then shoved it in next to the other clothes. The rest of the bag she filled with food. She emptied the cupboards in her apartment of dry cereal, granola bars, and some dried fruit snacks. She also made a few more sandwiches. They wouldn't keep long, but at least she could eat them tomorrow before she had to dig into her stash of nonperishable food.

She emptied her wallet of all her credit cards so she wouldn't be tempted to use them and leave a trace of where she was. She kept only her debit card, which she would use to withdraw all of her money from the ATM before leaving town. She had just paid her portion of the rent and bills, which had left her with five hundred dollars total between her checking account and her measly savings account. It might not last her very long out on the road, but it was better than nothing. Five hundred dollars was a lot more than zero.

Bree forced herself to calm down and eat a sandwich now. It wouldn't do to leave on an empty stomach. Who knew how long it would be before she could find some shifters? She had no clear plan, other than to head toward San Francisco. It was the nearest big city, and she knew that there was a big base of unicorn shifters there who worked as shifter protectors. She hoped she could find them, and convince them to help even though they had no idea right now that wizards even existed. So many worries about how this was a feasible plan began plaguing her mind, but Bree forced them away. One step at a time, she told herself. If she was going to do this, she was going to have to do a lot of it by faith.

Bree dressed warmly in dark blue jeans, a long-sleeved black t-shirt, a black sweatshirt, and a black baseball cap. She wore her hiking boots, the pair she'd bought last year with the intention of getting out and getting more exercise. The boots were barely used, but Bree had a feeling that was going to change drastically over the next few weeks.

Bree slipped her ruby ring onto her finger and hoisted the backpack onto her back. Then she turned off all the lights in her room and closed her bedroom door. With any luck, when Lily came home she would assume that Bree had gone to sleep. Lily always left for work before Bree, so she might also assume that Bree was sleeping in or even taking a sick day when Bree didn't stir tomorrow morning. With any luck, it might be tomorrow afternoon before anyone started to truly suspect that Bree was gone. Bree's plan was to drive her car out of town, going for several hundred miles until she was low on gas and had crossed from Oregon deep into California. Then she would abandon her car and continue on foot. Hopefully, the wizards would not catch her trail and would not know where to look for her. Bree shuddered to think what would happen to her if the wizards got to her before she found the shifters and explained the situation. Her only hope now was that she would *not* be caught until after the shifters were desperately needed. The only defense against defying a High Council order was the ability to prove with one hundred percent certainty that the High Council had been wrong. Bree would not be able to do that until there was some sort of action from the men currently chasing down the dragon sapphire. She had to keep the wizards from finding her before then.

Bree took a deep breath and double-checked that she had her ruby ring and car keys. Then she stepped outside and locked the door behind her. The Oregon night was cool, even in June, and Bree shivered when she thought of what cold, hard nights might be ahead of her. The distant sound of laughter drifted from a nearby restaurant, and Bree allowed herself to look around for a brief moment, saying a private goodbye to the town she had grown up in and loved. She felt badly not saying goodbye to Lily, or even leaving a note, but she had to get out of here as quickly as possible.

Her life, her magic, and the lives of this whole wizarding community depended on it.

CHAPTER THREE

Knox laughed as he tipped his beer back. He was seated around a campfire, enjoying a moment of peace after a long, tense day of training missions. It felt good after such a long day to finally have a chance to let loose and relax with his crew. Even two years later, he was still figuring out how to balance being the "boss" with being one of the guys. Knox and the others had all grown up as equals, so giving them directions was strange. They were always respectful of him, but Knox couldn't help wondering sometimes if they secretly harbored resentment toward him for being the one chosen to take over the title of clan leader.

Privately, Knox had expressed these concerns to Noah, the dragon shifter on the crew whom he considered his best friend. Noah had assured him that, while it was natural for anyone to feel disappointed when they weren't chosen for a promotion, no harsh words had been spoken about Knox. The other dragons accepted that a new leader was needed, and they knew there could only be one number one.

Knox resisted the urge to let out a sad sigh. He wished Noah was here right now, sharing laughter, beer, and good food with the crew. But Noah was one of the dragons off on a mission right now. He was working to recover an ancient dragon artifact that had been spotted in Portugal, of all places. The mission had seemed straightforward enough, and Noah had encouraged Knox to go and take the mission. But Knox couldn't bring himself to leave base camp at the Redwoods yet. Knox felt such a great responsibility to all of the dragons here, and he worried that if he left and anything fell apart while he was gone, it would be his fault. Noah told him he was going to have to leave eventually, and Knox knew it was true. But still, Knox procrastinated, and stayed in the Redwoods to run training missions like the one he'd done with Myles today.

Knox glanced at Myles and smiled. Myles had his hands up in the air, gesturing wildly as he told a story of how he'd once escaped from a battle-worn evil shifter only to be attacked unexpectedly by an old lady with an umbrella. Knox, chuckled, and Owen and Vance laughed heartily at the story. Myles had done a good job on the training mission today, and, even better, Myles never took it personally when Knox critiqued him. Some of the other dragons got defensive any time Knox suggested that they might be able to do something a bit better, but Myles always took it in stride. He'd nod his head and say "Got it, Boss," and then he'd make an effort to actually do better next time. If all of the dragons listened as well as Myles, Knox's job would have been a whole lot easier. Of course, no one had ever said this job would be easy.

Knox looked around at the small cluster of cabins that served as base camp for the crew. There were eleven cabins here. Six of them were temporarily empty while their owners were away fighting and searching for ancient dragon artifacts. And one was permanently empty, since it had been William's and he had moved away. The crew had half-heartedly suggested turning it into some sort of storage shed, but no one had been able to bear the idea of transforming William's cabin into a shed. So there it stood, unused and yet somehow making the crew feel as though William's spirit was still among them.

Knox got up from the circle and went to check on the grill that was a few feet away. Burgers and brats were sizzling, and the juicy smell of meat mixed with the smoky smell of charcoal. Knox's mouth watered. One of the biggest downsides to a day of training missions was that breakfast and lunch were often small, cold meals on the run. Knox was looking forward to a nice, hot dinner that consisted of a plate piled high with meat. He was part dragon, after all. He needed plenty of meat to sustain him.

"Grub's ready," Knox called out. Whatever story the crew had been in the middle of telling, they immediately abandoned it as they sprang up and made their way to the grill. They each grabbed a plate and began loading it with food. Knox let them all go first, like a good leader should. Then he filled his own plate and followed them back to the circle around the fire. For a few minutes, everyone was quiet as they stuffed food into their hungry mouths. But as the pace of their eating slowed, everyone started once again talking and laughing.

Knox let his mind drift. He was feeling strangely restless tonight, but he wasn't sure why. Things were going well enough. His dragons were all doing well with their training missions, and the dragons who were out on real missions right now were sending back good reports. By all accounts, Knox was seeing great success as leader of this crew. But he still couldn't shake the feeling that something wasn't quite right.

Knox sighed. Maybe Noah was right. Maybe he had just been sitting still too long. He needed to take a mission and stretch his wings a bit. He had trained his crew well, and he knew deep down that they could hold up well without him. Knox took a long sip of his beer and looked over at Myles, Vance, and Owen. Vance and Owen were arguing now about the best way to start a fire in the woods. Of course, as dragons, they could always shift into dragon form and breathe fire onto a pile of firewood. But it was important to be able to do things while in human form, too, since it was often best on missions to shift as little as possible. Vance and Owen both hated being wrong, and their passionate arguing on the finer points of fire-starting was almost comical. Knox was about to step in and egg them on with an argument of his own, when suddenly it hit him.

Why didn't he go off on a training mission by himself? He could do a survival mission, where he took only very basic emergency supplies with him into the redwoods, and tried to survive as long as he could. He often had his crew members perform these training missions to keep their survival skills sharp, but he had not done one himself since William moved away from the Redwoods. And shouldn't he be training just as hard as his crew?

It was the perfect solution. Knox could work out some of his restlessness, keep his survival skills sharp, and use the mission as a "test" of how things would run while he was gone. If he started prepping everything now, he could be ready to start tomorrow morning. Knox looked up at Vance and Owen, whose friendly argument was escalating as Myles looked on, laughing. Who would he leave in charge, as second? Normally, he would have given Noah that responsibility, but Noah was far away right now. Vance and Owen were more skilled at fighting, than Myles, but they were too hotheaded to make good leaders. Myles always kept calm and rational, no matter the situation. He would be the better choice.

"I'm going on a survival mission tomorrow," Knox announced suddenly. Myles, Vance, and Owen fell suddenly silent and looked up at him in surprise.

"You're going, too? Who are you taking with you?" Vance asked, the confusion evident in his voice. Survival training missions took several days at least, and it was almost a joke among the crew how Knox had been unwilling to leave base camp for more than a day at a time.

"I'm going alone," Knox said, standing to his feet. "And I'm leaving early tomorrow morning. Myles, you'll act as clan leader in my absence. I'm not going to leave you with a lot of instructions. You all know the emergency procedures for taking over as leader in the event of a catastrophe. I want you to all act like I suddenly disappeared without warning and left no instructions. I want to see how you perform with no hand-holding."

"How long will you be gone?" Myles asked uncertainly. Knox knew that it must have come as a shock to Myles that he was to be left in charge. He would have assumed that one of the better fighters, Vance or Owen, would be chosen.

"I don't know," Knox said truthfully. "But that will make it a better training experience for you, too. Let's test ourselves a bit, huh? I know things have been mostly peaceful since William left, but we can never rest on our laurels too much. Complacency kills."

Knox almost wanted to laugh at the surprised faces of his crew members that were staring back at him. They were no doubt thinking he had gone slightly mad with this sudden announcement, but none of them said anything further.

"I'll be gone before the sun rises," Knox said, brushing the dirt off his pants from the log he'd been sitting on.

"And what if we need to reach you?" Myles asked. "What should we do if there's a true emergency?"

Knox calmed his own nerves as he smiled down at Myles. "Handle it," Knox said.

And then, without another word, Knox headed for his cabin to prepare for the closest thing to an adventure he'd had in quite a while.

CHAPTER FOUR

Bree cursed under her breath as the clouds overhead thickened once again, heavy with the promise of rain. It was the third day since she'd left Falcon Cross, and it had rained on and off nonstop the whole time she was traveling.

"Nothing in Advocacy school prepared me for this," she muttered as she found shelter in the hollowed out trunk of an old redwood tree. She wasn't sure where she was, and she had quickly realized how ill-prepared she had been for a solo wilderness trek. Why hadn't she thought to pack a pocket knife? Or a compass? She had plenty of food for the moment, but she was beginning to wonder if it would last her the time that it took to travel to San Francisco. And she was beginning to wonder what, exactly, she was going to do once she arrived there. Her initial excitement at leaving had faded as the days wore on.

But there was no turning back now. She was sure that Falcon Cross was abuzz with news of her leaving, and that if she tried to return she would be stripped of her magic and excommunicated from the wizards. She had to remain strong and focused, not only for her own sake but because she knew that the entire future of Falcon Cross depended on her now. She had to find the good shifters.

The rain started falling, gaining momentum as the minutes passed until it was an all-out deluge. Little rivers of cold water trickled into Bree's tree trunk cave, and she sighed as she picked up her backpack to make sure her food stayed dry. Summer was supposed to be the dry season, but apparently Mother Nature had no respect for seasons.

Bree fingered her magic ring, wishing she dared to use it to start a fire to warm herself. But even though the inside of the hollowed out redwood was a large, empty space, Bree worried that a fire in here would catch the sides of the tree trunk and send the whole tree up in flames from the inside out. So instead, she held her ring out from her body, aiming its sharp point toward the dark, wet world outside the tree, and she cried out *"magicae lucis!"*

Instantly, a flashlight-like beam came shooting from her ring. She aimed it into the forest, sweeping it up, down, and around. It was late afternoon now, and the woods were steadily growing darker as the rain grew heavier. Bree had a feeling she would not be seeing the sun again today.

Her light illuminated the enormous, reddish-brown trunks of the redwoods, standing like eerie sentinels in the forest which felt to Bree like it was alive with eyes. This was ridiculous, of course, but she couldn't shake the feeling that she was being watched. She swept her ring's light beam across the ground foliage, not even sure what she was searching for. Was there an animal out there? Was it possible that a wizard search party had somehow found her and was stalking her at this moment, waiting for the right moment to pounce?

A loud crash sounded from somewhere to Bree's left. She nearly jumped out of her skin as she shrank back into the hollow tree trunk, her heart pounding.

"*Lucis terminantur,*" she hissed, and the light beam on her ring instantly went out. Just before the light died, though, she saw two large squirrels running from a nearby tree. She took a deep breath, trying to steady her breathing. The noise had only been squirrels fighting.

Or had it?

As she strained her eyes to see into the ever-darkening forest, she heard a noise that sounded horrifyingly close to the sound of boots crunching on the leaves and twigs that littered the forest floor. She held her breath, listening as carefully as she could. For a moment, she thought she had imagined it. The only sound she could make out was the falling rain. But then, she heard it again.

Crunch, crunch, crunch.

Someone was definitely out there, and he or she sounded like they were getting closer.

Crunch, crunch, crunch.

Bree held her breath again, willing the sound to go away, but knowing that it wouldn't. When a flashlight beam shone through the darkness outside the tree trunk, Bree nearly squealed in fright. She wasn't cut out for the fugitive life, she thought, catching herself and biting her lip quietly just before she accidentally gave herself away with a frightened noise.

Now, Bree could tell that whoever was out there was sweeping the flashlight across the outside of the tree. They were searching for her.

It must be the wizards, she thought. But how had they found her? She had been careful not to leave a trail. At least in the beginning, she had left no trace of where she had been after she'd abandoned her car in the trailhead parking lot for one of California's state parks. She had gotten lazy over the last day, though. As she grew more miserable, lonely, and tired, she had started to not worry about whether or not she was leaving obvious traces as she stumbled along through the forest. Still, even if she had been leaving a trail today, wouldn't the wizards have had a hard time even finding where that trail began? There would have been miles and miles of forest where she had carefully hidden her tracks.

Crunch, crunch, crunch. The footsteps were right outside the tree now. There was no use wondering *how* they had found her. The reality was that they had. Bree felt her heart beating violently against her chest as she raised her ringed hand high above her head.

"*Magicae invisibilia,*" she hissed as loud as she dared. She felt a rush of energy suddenly pressing against her body, and she knew the invisibility spell had worked. Not that it would do much good against a wizard search party. All they had to do was use a revealing spell and her invisibility disguise would be removed. Still, it might give her a few seconds to try to escape through the tree trunk's opening and make a run for it, although she wasn't quite sure where she could run to get away from a group of wizards.

But just as she was about to slip through the tree trunk's opening, a head appeared there. Bree skidded to a stop, managing to halt her forward momentum just in time to avoid running into the man who had suddenly appeared. Her eyes widened as his own eyes narrowed. He was only inches from her face, and he was peering into the tree, scanning the hollowed out trunk but looking right through Bree.

He was no wizard, and he clearly had no idea that anyone was in the trunk. He was so close that if Bree had leaned forward just a fraction of an inch, her nose would have bumped against his. Her mind screamed at her to back up, but for a moment, she stood frozen. His green eyes held an intelligent expression, and they blended well with the tanned skin of his chiseled face. His short, dark brown hair was soaking and plastered across his forehead. He wore a hoodie, but had not put the hood up against the rain.

Bree could just see the tips of his ears peeking out from under his hair, and she nearly gasped when she saw that they had a slightly elfish shape.

The man suddenly breathed in deeply, his whole face furrowing in concentration as he did. Bree came to her senses and stepped silently backward just as the man leaned deeper into the tree trunk. As quickly as she dared, Bree continued to take steps backward until her back was flat against the tree trunk, just opposite from the opening.

The man stepped into the tree trunk, and suddenly, the hollowed out space that had seemed so large suddenly felt unbearably confining. The man was large—much larger than any wizard or non-wizard human Bree had ever seen. He stood at least a foot taller than Bree, and his giant muscles could be seen even under the thick, soaking fabric of his hoodie. There were still about three feet between where he stood and where Bree stood, but if he reached out, he would feel her there. What would he do, if he realized that there was another person in here? Would he lash out violently at what he would probably perceive as an invisible enemy?

The man breathed in deeply again, his eyes scanning the ground now. Bree winced as she realized that she had left foot prints all over the now muddy floor of the tree trunk hollow.

"Strange," the man said, bending down to put his finger in one of the footprints. When he bent, Bree could see that he had a very large backpack on. She also caught another, better glimpse of his ears. They definitely had an elfish shape. It was slight, but it was there.

The man was a shifter, and one of the mythological varieties. Bree struggled to remember what she knew about shifter classifications. Elfish ears meant either a unicorn or a dragon, but how did you tell the difference? With a furrowed brow, Bree mentally ran through all of her notes from her classes on shifters. Unicorns had iridescent skin, right? And shimmering black eyes.

Bree glanced down at the man's skin. It was mostly covered by soaking wet clothing, but she could see his face, hands and a bit of his forearm. She could not detect the slightest hint of iridescence. And his eyes had been green, not black, with no shimmer to them. Besides that, the elfish shape of his ears was not very well pronounced. From what Bree remembered, unicorns all had very elfish ears, while dragons frequently had only a small elfish shape to their ears, or even no elfish features at all.

The man was a dragon shifter. His deep, confused sniffing made sense now. Like all shifters, he had an excellent sense of smell, and he could no doubt smell that Bree was here, even though he couldn't see her. He stood up straight then, and looked around again. He reached out his arm and started tracing it along the side of the tree trunk's interior. Bree ducked down just in time for him to miss her, and her heart pounded as his hand went over her head.

She was not sure what to do. She was looking for a shifter, but she needed that shifter to be one of the good shifters. If the man had been a unicorn, she would have revealed herself to him right away. Everyone knew that unicorns were good, and nearly impossible to corrupt. But dragons...dragons were fiery beings, and many had been turned to evil over the years. If this man was a corrupt dragon, she might be worse off than if the wizards found her. The wizards would only take her magic. A corrupt dragon would take her life.

The dragon shifter turned in a large circle inside the tree trunk, sniffing deeply and looking up as though he expected to see someone clinging to the trunk and hiding above his head. But, of course, he saw nothing. He ran his fingers through his hair and sighed.

"Strange," he said again. Then, to Bree's great relief he turned and walked back out into the rain. She took a full minute to steady her breathing, and then, slowly, carefully, she walked out into the rain as well. He had not gone far yet. He was walking slowly through the thick, dark forest, looking in every direction and sniffing deeply. Bree almost had to laugh. The poor guy probably thought his nose wasn't working correctly. She had a brief impulse to end her invisibility smell and yell "Surprise!" just to see the shocked look on his face.

But of course, she remained silent. There was something strange about a dragon shifter alone in the woods. Was he running from something, too? And were his reasons for running perhaps not quite as noble as Bree's? She couldn't take a chance that he was an evil dragon, and that's why he was sneaking around out here like a fugitive. But she also didn't want to miss the chance to talk to him if he was one of the good dragons. After all, she was pretty much a fugitive herself, but she was a good person with good motives. Maybe his story was similar.

Bree decided then that she would follow him for a while. If she could stay on his trail, under the cover of her invisibility spell, perhaps she could get a sense of where he was going and why he was out here on his own. If he seemed like the sort of dragon who would not, in fact, kill her, then she would reveal herself to him.

Bree scurried to catch up with the man, who had quickened his pace now. Much to her dismay, he did not seem interested in stopping to take cover from the rain. He was pressing forward with a determined gait, and, unless she wanted to lose him in the dark woods, she had no choice but to follow. She kept up as silently as she could, although occasionally she would accidentally step on a twig and crack it sharply, or make some similar careless noise. Whenever she did this, he would turn sharply, his piercing eyes scanning the forest as he breathed in deeply. Bree could tell he was troubled. Her smell was too strong, and the noises of twigs breaking were too loud to have been caused by a squirrel. He was confused, but he had the sense that he was being followed.

The sky grew darker and darker until it was completely black. The rain continued, and Bree could no longer see the path in front of her at all. She did her best to step softly and not make noise, but it was difficult when she had no idea what her foot was actually landing on. The only way she could continue following the dragon shifter was by following the beam of his flashlight. Even then, it was difficult to keep up. He moved quickly, and with the benefit of light.

At one point, Bree thought she had lost him. The light disappeared, and she could not tell whether he had turned off his flashlight, or had just gotten so far ahead of her that she could no longer see him. She desperately picked up her pace, and wondered if she dared cast a light spell from her ring so she could move more quickly through the darkness. But just as she was about to speak the words of the spell, a beam of light turned on just a few yards away from her. Startled, she froze in place.

The dragon shifter had been waiting silently, intent on catching whoever was following him. He swept his light back and forth quickly across the forest, passing it over Bree without even realizing it. He cursed, then sniffed deeply.

"Come out, coward!" he yelled. "Show yourself. I know you're there. I can smell you!"

Bree shivered but did not move or make a sound. The anger in the shifter's eyes sent chills down her spine, and the light from the flashlight cast long, spooky shadows across his face. Bree wasn't sure if she had ever been so terrified in her life.

She had always been smart, and that's why she had chosen to become an Advocate. The Advocates fought with the strength of their minds, not with the strength of their physical bodies. And Bree was pretty sure that her smarts weren't going to help her very much if the dragon shifter somehow realized where she was. He looked so terrifying right now that she was beginning to think that it must be impossible that he was one of the good shifters.

He can't see you, she told herself. As long as you keep the invisibility spell going, and stay far enough away that he can't reach out and touch you, you're fine.

The dragon shifter swept his light across the forest several more times, then gave a defeated sigh.

"I'm going crazy," he said aloud before giving a nearby tree trunk a frustrated kick. "Losing my edge. William would be ashamed."

Bree wondered who William was, and hoped the shifter would say more. Was William his clan leader? Perhaps this dragon shifter was on some sort of mission for William?

But the shifter said no more. Instead, he turned and continued walking, slowly now. He was sweeping his light back and forth, carefully searching. A few minutes later, Bree realized what he'd been searching for. He found another one of the large redwoods that had a hollowed out area in the trunk, and he crawled into it, using it as a natural shelter. Bree waited a few minutes, then crept up to the opening and peered in.

The shifter looked like he was unpacking for the night. He had taken off his wet clothes and changed into dry ones, and he was now struggling to hang the soaking wet garments on little knobs that stuck out here and there from the tree.

"Don't know why I bother," he muttered. "No way these are gonna dry by the morning, with all the moisture in this damp tree."

He began to rummage in his pack for food, eventually pulling out what looked like a few meal bars. He grimaced as he bit into them.

"Damn rain," he muttered. "Makes it so hard to catch real food. What I wouldn't give for some meat."

He ate two of the meal bars, then lay down on the ground on his back, using his pack as a pillow. Bree felt strange spying on him like this, especially since he kept talking to himself, clearly unaware that anyone else was listening to him voicing his private thoughts. She didn't care that she was getting rained on while she watched, because she was getting a glimpse of who he was and what kind of man he might be.

He muttered things about his crew, wondering aloud how their missions were going. Then he whistled a tune for a while, apparently cheered by the fact that at least he was dry and relatively warm. As he whistled, the rain finally stopped and the sky began to clear. This was lucky, because soon after the man turned off his flashlight, making it extremely difficult for Bree to see into the cave. The moon was coming out from behind the clouds now, though, and from the right angle Bree could just make him out, lying there drumming his fingers on his stomach.

Much to Bree's disappointment, he soon stopped talking. A few minutes after that, the sound of soft snores filled the air. Bree sighed. She wasn't going to learn anything more from him tonight, it seemed. She needed to see if she could find a soft spot nearby to lie down and sleep herself. She didn't dare go into a tree, for fear that she wouldn't hear him when he woke and left. Instead, she would find somewhere as sheltered by the leaves as possible, dry the ground using magic, and hope that it didn't rain anymore tonight.

Bree started to turn away from the tree, but then stopped short for just a moment. She turned back to look into the tree trunk cave, and raised her magic ring to point it at the man's soaking wet clothes which hung from the side of the tree's inner walls.

"*Magicae siccum*," she whispered. Instantly, the clothes dried out. Bree smiled, then withdrew to a soft spot not too far from the man's tree hideout. She pointed her ring at the ground and repeated the words.

"*Magicae siccum,*" she whispered again. The drying spell instantly dried the ground near her ring. She settled down to sleep, using her own pack as a pillow just as the shifter had done. It was not terribly warm, but it wasn't cold, either. Since the rain had stopped and the ground was dry, Bree was almost comfortable sleeping out here.

She stared up at the sky, which was now brilliantly lit by the moon and stars.

"Please be a good shifter," she whispered into the night air, directing her thoughts toward the tree where she knew the man was resting. "I can't keep going on my own much longer."

CHAPTER FIVE

Knox could not shake the awful feeling that someone was watching him, and if his nose was to be trusted, someone was. But no matter how carefully he peered into the forest behind him, beside him, or before him, he couldn't see anyone. He might have thought that whoever was following him was a shifter using chameleon tricks, but the smell was not that of a shifter at all. It smelled like a full human. Knox could not decide what to do.

He was traveling deeper into the forest now than he had planned, getting further and further away from his crew's base camp. But he didn't want to lead the mystery stalker toward his crew. He grew more frustrated with every hour that passed. Something was wrong here. Had his survival skills grown so stale that he could not even catch someone who was following him? Or, worse, was it possible he *was* actually imagining someone?

Two more days passed like this. Knox's food supplies ran low. He purposely had not packed much. After all, what was the point of practicing "survival" when you brought with you more than enough to survive? No, Knox wanted to force himself to hunt and to feel hunger. He needed to set an example for his crew by proving that he himself was capable of everything he was asking them to do. And, if Knox was honest, he was glad to have an excuse to focus on hunting instead of on his phantom stalker.

The rains that had fallen heavily at the beginning of his journey had disappeared now, making it easier and more comfortable to move through the forest. Knox crept silently, watching carefully for any sign of squirrels, the most likely prey he would find out here. But then, unexpectedly, he came across a wounded elk. The great animal was limping, and looked as though it had somehow fractured its leg. The beast sensed danger when it saw Knox, and started trying to retreat, a difficult task due to its injury.

Knox hesitated. This elk would be easy prey, and would supply him a great deal of meat. But he would not be able to eat all of it out here before it went bad, and he hated to waste meat. Then again, the animal was so badly wounded that it was likely going to die, anyway. If Knox did not kill it, one of the mountain lions in the area certainly would.

With a sad tone in his voice, Knox began to sing a soothing song to the elk in an ancient dragon dialect. The elk slowly calmed, and stopped its frantic attempt at retreat. Eventually it sank down in a trance to lie on the soft forest floor, which was covered in thick moss here. The elk closed its eyes, lulled to sleep by the song. Knox crept toward it, still singing. He reached to pull his pocket knife from the holster on his belt where he usually stored it securely when he was moving through the woods. He flipped the blade open, and, when he was close enough to the now sleeping, entranced elk, he quickly slid the knife across the elk's throat.

The razor sharp knife quickly cut through the muscles, veins, and arteries in the majestic elk's neck. The animal never knew what killed it. It gave a quick shudder, and then went still.

"Sorry, old buddy," Knox said. "But I promise you this was a quicker way to die than being dragged down by a mountain lion."

Quickly and with great skill, Knox began gutting and field dressing the elk. As he worked, his sensitive nose still detected the scent of human nearby, even over the scent of dead elk. Knox frowned and looked around, but, as usual, he didn't see anything.

Something had to change. He had to figure out why he was smelling human, or he was going to go crazy. William had always told him that when something didn't feel right he needed to trust his gut. And Knox's gut instincts were screaming at him right now, telling him that he was being followed. But why? And by whom?

As far as Knox knew, there was peace in the shifter world right now. There had not been any unexpected shifter sightings by humans, and there was no reason Knox could think of that a human would be tracking him down. But either he was going crazy, or someone very good at hiding was on his trail.

Knox worked carefully on the elk, all the while keeping a wary eye on his surroundings. His uneasiness grew as the smell of human seemed to even overpower the smell of the elk. His dragon senses were hyper-alert, warning him that he was not alone. At one point, Knox left the elk and walked in a big circle, looking deep into the surrounding forest and trying to find a trace of someone or something. But there was nothing to see, and no sign of any other living thing except banana slugs, spiders, and birds.

Knox returned to his work on the elk, and soon it was time for him to start building a fire. Here, however, his skills failed him. He attempted to start a fire using flint and steel, something he must have done a thousand times over the years. But for some reason, it would not work today.

Knox felt a deep feeling of foreboding. There was no reason for the fire not to roar to life. And there was no reason for him to be smelling a human that he could not see. He set down the flint and steel, and stood. He looked around, his body tense and ready to shift into dragon form at any moment.

"I know you're there," he bellowed. "Show yourself! What is your business with me?"

The only answer was the sound of birds chirping. Knox felt frustrated anger rising in his chest.

"Show yourself!" he called again.

For another moment, there was no answer. And then, for a long moment, the woods went completely silent. Even the birds stopped chirping, and the wind was completely still. Out of this silence came a sudden, sharp yell.

"*Magicae ignis!*"

A sharp hiss sounded, and then, the pile of tinder and firewood that Knox had arranged suddenly went up in flames.

"What the…" Knox said, spinning in a circle, holding his pocket knife in front of him against an enemy he could not see but now had no doubt was real.

"*Invisibilia terminantur,*" came the same voice.

Knox nearly jumped out of his skin when a woman suddenly appeared out of thin air only a few feet away from him. She was dressed in jeans and a hoodie that looked like it had been through the muddiest portion of the forest. She wore a big backpack, and stood tall with her right arm outstretched in the direction of the fire. It was impossible to miss the giant ruby ring on her finger. The stone was enormous, and must have been worth hundreds of thousands of dollars. It looked completely out of place in the wildness of the forest. Knox knew that she had started the fire, but he didn't understand how. She was not a shifter, and definitely was not a dragon. The only possibility Knox could think of was that her ruby ring was a magical artifact, but it did not look like any of the ancient artifacts he had ever seen—and he'd seen well over a hundred ancient, supernatural treasures.

"Who are you?" Knox demanded.

The woman lowered her arm and looked him directly in the eyes. It was only then that Knox noticed how beautiful her dove gray eyes were. Her face was dirty and her light brown hair was messy, pulled into a tangled bun. But she was undeniably beautiful, and there was a look of intelligence in her eyes that Knox had not often seen.

"I'm Bree," she said. "And we need to talk."

"Bree," Knox repeated, letting the name roll over his tongue. It was a beautiful name, fitting for a beautiful girl like her. She didn't seem ready to attack, so Knox slowly lowered the knife he was still pointing in her direction.

"I wouldn't mind some food, either," Bree said, looking longingly at the elk meat that Knox had been preparing to roast.

Knox actually managed a smile.

"Well, I suppose since you started this fire, I'll share my food with you. It's more than I can eat myself, anyway. Let me get the meat cooking, and then we'll talk."

Bree nodded, never taking her eyes off of him as he set up a crude spit to roast the elk. Once it was cooking, Knox motioned to her to sit down. She did so, sliding her backpack off warily and keeping it close, as though she were prepared to run at any moment. Knox noticed that she kept her ring pointed toward him as well.

"What's with the ring?" he asked, raising an eyebrow in her direction. "And don't try to act like it's nothing special. I'm quite familiar with supernatural artifacts."

"Not as familiar as you think you are," Bree said.

Knox immediately felt defensive. Who did this girl think she was? She had clearly found some sort of special stone and had learned how to use it. But she wasn't a shifter, and he would be surprised if she knew much about the ways of shifters.

"And what makes you such an expert on supernatural artifacts?" Knox asked. "For your information, I've spent my life studying them, and chasing after people who try to obtain them to use for their own benefit. If I didn't know better, I'd say you were one of those people now. What claim do you have to that ring?"

"The same claim any wizard has to his or her own magic ring," Bree said, then paused to let her words sink in. Knox tried to process what she meant. Was she saying she was a wizard? But those didn't exist anymore.

Did they?

Knox had heard tales of wizards roaming the earth centuries ago. They had often clashed with shifters. Back when all shifters used to hold more magical powers, it had only made sense that wizards and shifters would have had some inevitable power struggles. But according to the history books, wizards had disappeared hundreds of years ago. There had been a huge battle between evil shifters and an alliance of wizards, and no one had seen or heard of wizards since that day.

"I know what you're thinking," Bree said. "That the wizards are all gone. But this isn't true. The wizards only want you to *think* that they're gone. They're still here, they just keep a low profile. They think that any shifters who discover them would try to destroy them."

"Why are you telling me this?" Knox asked suspiciously. "If you wanted to keep a low profile, following me around for days and then blasting in here using magic to start a fire isn't exactly what I'd call subtle."

Bree sighed, and her face seemed to soften. "No, it's not subtle. And I'm sorry for following you like that. I know it was driving you crazy, being able to smell me but not seeing anything. I had to make sure, though, that you were a good shifter before I revealed myself to you. You see, I'm a wizard on the run. I have some news you're not going to like, but you need to know. I'm risking my life and my magic to tell you this. If I'm caught before I find a shifter to help me, then I'll be excommunicated from my wizarding community. And if I told a shifter who was on the side of evil, well, it would be more than just my life in danger. It would be all of the wizards, all of the shifters, and possibly all of the humans as well."

Knox's head was beginning to ache with a dull sense of dread. He wanted to immediately write this girl off as some sort of dramatic full human who had just been lucky enough to come across a magic ring. He didn't want to believe her that wizards still existed. But he had to hear her out. He was the leader of a clan, and he owed it to his dragons to listen to any possible threats. From what this girl had said so far, it sounded like she was discussing a very serious "possible threat." And if she knew that shifters existed, then she was not just some normal human who had accidentally come across a magical artifact. She knew something important, and he needed to know what it was.

"Well, I can assure you that I am not an evil shifter. In fact, I've dedicated my life to fighting evil. So if you know of evil brewing, I would be a good person to tell."

Knox watched Bree hesitate for just a moment, looking at him thoughtfully.

"I've been watching you for several days, wondering where you were going and who you were," she said slowly. "It was hard to tell what kind of person you were, and I was afraid maybe you were on the run because you had done something wrong. I finally decided to trust you because of the elk."

"The elk?" Knox asked, confused.

Bree nodded. "I saw how humanely you treated it, making sure it was calm before you quickly killed it and put it out of its misery. No one who was truly evil would have bothered with the elk's feelings before killing it."

Knox nodded slowly. Bree was right. He had seen evil shifters torture full animals just for the fun of it, a practice he found reviling. All life needed to be respected, even when taking a life was necessary.

"So now that you've decided to trust me, what is your news?" he asked.

Bree took a deep breath. When she spoke she was staring into the fire instead of looking at him.

"Are you familiar with an ancient artifact known as the dragon stone?" she asked.

Knox's head immediately shot up, and he looked at Bree with a mixture of shock and suspicion. He knew the dragon stone well. It was the most powerful of the ancient artifacts. William had been kidnapped in the process of searching for the dragon stone. Knox had joined forces with a group of shifters in Texas to save William and stop a powerful evil shifter who was trying to steal the dragon stone. The dragon stone was now safely in the hands of the good shifters, fiercely guarded by a large force of shifter protectors.

"I know of it," Knox said. "And apparently so do you. But the stone is under careful guard, and I can assure you it's quite safe."

Knox narrowed his eyes at Bree when he said this. How did she know about the stone, and why was she discussing it with him. Perhaps she was on some sort of underhanded mission to try to find out where the stone was. She didn't look evil, but one could never be sure these days. He had to be careful what he said.

"The *emerald* dragon stone is safe," Bree said. "But there are others. Three others, in fact, as far as I can tell. One of which, the sapphire dragon stone, has been found, and is in danger of falling into the wrong hands."

Bree paused, giving Knox time to react. He looked at her as though she had lost her mind. What was this girl's game? Was she trying to get information out of him about the dragon stone by pretending there was more than one dragon stone? He felt a cold chill of suspicion go through him. Something was off here.

"I can assure you that the shifters holding the dragon stone have researched the matter thoroughly and would be aware if there was another stone. And, I don't mean to be rude, but what reason do I have to believe that you're a wizard? Performing magic using a ring is not enough. Many ancient stones have magical powers, and anyone who found them would be able to use the stone to act like they had magical powers."

Bree sighed, and Knox saw a shadow of frustration pass over her eyes.

"You have to trust me," she said, her voice urgent. Knox saw with alarm that her eyes were filling with tears. He resisted the urge to roll his own eyes. How had his survival mission turned into sitting in the woods with a weepy girl? He didn't believe her tears were real. With every passing moment, he was more and more convinced that she was a spy, sent to find information on the dragon stone by some evil shifter who wanted to steal the stone away. Of course, they would send a beautiful girl to do their work. They would think that a bachelor like Knox wouldn't be able to resist her charms. But Knox had bigger things to worry about than women. He was the leader of a clan of dragons—a clan whose members were often the one thing keeping ancient artifacts from falling into the wrong hands. Apparently, they'd failed with at least one artifact. That ruby ring the girl had was powerful. Knox was well-versed in many types of ancient artifacts, but he had never seen or heard of anything like it. Still, he had to hand it to whoever had come up with the idea of trying to act like wizards still existed. That was a pretty clever move, but Knox wasn't going to fall for it.

"I'm sorry," Knox said, trying to keep his voice calm even though he was sure now that this girl was not here to help him. "Experience has taught me better than to trust people I don't know. You're welcome to share this meal with me, but after that I'll need to get going, and continue on my own mission."

Knox felt somewhat ashamed as he said this. His "mission" was only a training mission. He hadn't done any real missions in quite some time, and he realized now that Noah was right. He needed to do more. His clan didn't need him around every second, and he was growing hopelessly restless. He had not been trained to sit around at base camp all the time. He'd been trained to run straight toward danger. Of course, this girl had no way of knowing any of that. And the less she knew about him, the better.

"You're being a fool," she said. Knox was surprised to see flashes of anger in her eyes now. The tears had passed in a moment's time, and now she was standing tall. "I can show you proof that the sapphire dragon stone exists, and that—"

But she never got to finish her sentence. A sudden, whirring sound filled the air, and Bree whipped around in a complete circle, her eyes widening as she grabbed her backpack and jumped toward where his pack of supplies lay on the ground.

"Shift!" she yelled at him. "Shift, now!"

Something in her voice told him that he didn't have time to question why. He shifted into dragon form, his clothes tearing off his body in shreds as his body transformed. The gust of powerful wind caused by his shifting nearly put the fire out, but Bree didn't seem to notice. She had her hand with the ruby ring on it extended straight from her body, and she was turning in slow circles now, watching her surroundings carefully as the buzzing sound grew louder.

Knox let his dragon go into chameleon mode, melting into the scenery as he tensed up, waiting to see what strange danger was approaching them.

CHAPTER SIX

Bree had grabbed her backpack of supplies the moment she heard the telltale buzzing sound of the drones. Her supplies and Knox's supplies were now both resting on the ground directly by her feet. She could only hope that she was still as good at her shield charm as she used to be.

She knew it would require a great deal of strength to hold the charm against the drones, so she was waiting until the last second to perform it. As the buzzing sound grew closer, she raised her hand with her magic ring above her head.

"Steady," she whispered to herself. "Hold steady. Wait for the right moment."

The buzzing was becoming unbearably loud. The drones were going to be here any second, but Bree waited a few more seconds, nearly waiting too long.

"*Magicae arma*," she finally yelled, squeezing her eyes shut and concentrating as hard as she could. She saw sparks flying from her ring, and a moment later she had the same sort of blurred sensation you get when you open your eyes underwater.

She kept her ring hand high and steady, and she did her best not to think about anything except keeping the shield charm going. The energy from her ring would keep a wall around her and the backpacks, preventing the drones from stealing the packs. They would still be able to see her, but at least they could not take her supplies, which Bree was sure they had been instructed to do.

The drones whizzed around her, trying their best to poke their long, metal arms through the shield charm. They were probably only there for a total of five minutes, but it felt like an eternity to Bree. She was beginning to worry that she wasn't going to be able to hold them off long enough, when, finally, they gave a few angry beeps and turned, whizzing away.

Bree held the shield charm a few more moments, and then let her ring hand weakly fall to her side.

"*Arma terminantur*," she said. The shield charm, which had been fizzling out anyway, died completely. The forest became suddenly clear once again, and Bree felt as though she had surfaced from underneath the water of a swimming pool.

She looked around for Knox, but he was nowhere to be seen. Had he fled? He didn't seem like the type to run away from danger. But she had seen him shift, as she had asked him to do. Not only had she been correct that he was a dragon, but his dragon was enormous. He was much too large to hide from her if he was anywhere close by. Unless he had shifted back to human form already. Bree felt fear gripping her heart again. If he had shifted to human form before the drones left, then they were both in trouble.

But her fears were put to rest when, at that precise moment, a dragon suddenly appeared almost right in front of her. He had thick green skin with iridescent qualities. It gave off hints of pink, purple, and blue, depending on how the light hit it. He had two large wings, and a large dragon head, complete with thick, pointed horns. Bree gasped, as she realized that Knox had somehow managed to blend in with the tree trunks, leaves, and other foliage around them. In all her studies of shifters, she had

31

never heard of any shifters blending into the background like that, except for the very rare chameleon shifters.

"How did you do that?" she asked Knox's dragon. She saw the hint of a smile turning up his dragon lips, which also revealed the sharp dragon teeth lining his mouth. In the next instant a burst of power rushed across the forest. The elk, which was still roasting on the spit, shook from the energy of Knox's shift, and the fire nearly blew out again.

Knox was in human form again, and he was completely naked. Bree averted her eyes, feeling instantly awkward. But even though she only saw his body for a split-second, it was long enough for her to see how impressive he was. Every muscle on his body was sculpted and defined, and he was unmistakably well endowed. Bree felt her cheeks turning pink with embarrassment, but Knox didn't seem at all fazed by the fact that he was suddenly naked in front of her. She could hear him behind her, rummaging through the backpack. She assumed he was looking for clothes, but she didn't dare to look.

"What were those things?" he asked. His voice had a serious, grave tone to it now.

Bree took a deep breath. "Wizard drones," she said. She waited for him to make another obnoxious remark about how wizards didn't exist, but he was silent. She finally dared to turn around. He was wearing a thick pair of hiking pants now, and a pair of replacement hiking boots. He still didn't have a shirt on, and she could not help looking at him now. His chest was broad and strong, and his abs were formed into a perfect six pack. Bree unexpectedly felt her breath catch in her throat. She had noticed from the beginning that he was handsome, but seeing him standing only feet away from her without a shirt made her heart do all sorts of funny flip-flops in her chest. His eyes caught hers, and for one brief, intense moment, she thought she saw a flicker of desire in them. But the moment passed quickly, and he broke eye contact with her as he turned to rummage in his backpack for a shirt.

"Wizard drones?" he prompted.

She forced her mind away from his body, and back to the present crisis.

"Yes, wizard drones. They're a mixture of technology and magic," Bree said. "In times of peace, they're used mostly as guard drones. They patrol the borders near Falcon Cross, the wizard town where I live, and keep a look out for any approaching humans. Usually, no one comes near us. But if someone did, we would take measures to ensure that no magic was used around them. Full humans discovering wizards is one of our greatest fears. It would not take very long at all for things to get messy."

Knox let out a small bitter laugh. He did not have to explain to Bree how well he understood. She knew from her own studies of shifter history how much shifters themselves had been persecuted when humans discovered their existence.

"So I'm guessing that these drones were somehow programmed to look for you?" Knox said.

Bree nodded. "The drones can be programmed to hunt instead of just guarding. I thought that the Wizards might send them after me when I left, but I thought I had managed to get far enough away that the drones would not be able to find me. They have a limited range, and I thought I had escaped that range. Apparently I didn't."

"So why did you ask me to shift?" Knox asked. "Were you expecting them to attack me?"

Bree was encouraged by the fact that Knox didn't seem to be questioning the existence of wizards anymore. For the moment, at least, he was giving her the benefit of the doubt.

"Not exactly," she said. "The drones can defend themselves, but they aren't really weapons. They serve more as information gatherers. They are sophisticated pieces of equipment, aided by magic spells, that can "see" humans, even when the human is using an invisibility spell."

"Ah, so they're useful for finding rogue wizards," Knox said.

"Yup," Bree said. "But they have their limits. They can only see humans, not animals. They are programmed this way because if they were distracted by every animal that crossed their path, they would send a lot of false alarms back to Falcon Cross that we were in danger of being 'invaded.' This limitation means that a shifter who is in human form would be detected, but a shifter in animal form would essentially go unseen by the drones. So as long as you were in dragon form, you were invisible to them."

Knox narrowed his eyes. "That doesn't make sense to me. If wizards do still exist, wouldn't they be concerned about shifters attacking them? After all, there's so much bad blood between shifters and wizards due to the old wars."

Bree shrugged. "Wizards have been very careful to keep their existence hidden from shifters. As long as shifters think we don't exist anymore, we don't have to worry about them attacking us. So the wizard council has been perfectly happy with drones that only see humans."

Knox furrowed his brow, trying to take in everything Bree was telling him. "But if they don't attack, why did they look like they were attacking you? It looked like you had some sort of magic shield up against them that they were trying to penetrate."

Bree nodded. "I was trying to keep them from taking my backpack. And yours, too. They would have taken them both, if they could have. The wizards know that if they can take away my supplies, I'll be forced out of hiding sooner. The drones wouldn't have realized that your backpack didn't belong to me."

"But you held them off," Knox said slowly. "So they didn't have anything to take back to the wizards."

"Well, they didn't have my supplies to take back," Bree said with a sigh. "But I'm sure they transmitted my picture and exact coordinates back to the wizards, confirming that I'm alive and out here. It won't be long before they send out actual wizards to track me down. Then I'll really be in trouble. If they catch me, my days as a wizard are over. Worse, no one believes me that the sapphire dragon stone exists and is in danger of falling into the wrong hands. I presented all of my research to the Wizard High Council, and they did not agree with my assessment of the situation."

"So you just ran away?" Knox asked, looking doubtfully at her. "Assuming that wizards do exist, and their high council disagrees with you, do you really think you know better than them? No offense, but usually high councils are old and wise. You look a little young to be disagreeing with them."

Bree chewed her lower lip for a minute, trying to think of how to respond. Part of her wished that she could just tell Knox off, if he wasn't interested in believing her. She was so tired of being judged for her age. But she needed his help. She needed him to believe her, and his defenses seemed to be wearing down a bit after the drone attack.

"I know it sounds a bit crazy for a young wizard to think she knows better than a high council. But if the high council looked at the research I've done with open eyes, I think they would believe me. The problem is that they won't look at anything I've done that closely since, as you've already pointed out, I'm quite a bit younger than they are. They think I'm just being overdramatic on one of my first work assignments. And they think that telling shifters about wizards would bring ruin to the wizards. They are not only old, they are steeped in ancient traditions and stories, and they refuse to see the world with new eyes."

Knox did not say anything in response to this. Instead, he stared at Bree as though he was trying to see right through her. He still looked doubtful, but something about the drones seemed to have softened him.

"Please trust me," Bree said softly, looking up at him with the most earnest expression she could manage. "I know it's a lot to ask, but the fate of the wizards and the shifters alike depends on our working together. I don't know who you are, or what you yourself are doing out here in this forest, but something tells me that I met you for a reason. Something tells me that you are strong enough and powerful enough to help me."

Knox continued staring at her for what felt like an eternity. Finally, he broke his gaze to glance over at the elk, which was still nicely roasting over the crackling fire.

"If what you say is true, I might be able to help you," he said. "But I must warn you that if it's not, and I find out you are trying to deceive me for some evil purpose, I will have no mercy on you."

Bree shuddered slightly under the intensity of Knox's gaze, even though she had nothing to hide. She had never had anyone look at her so severely, not even the wizards of the high council when she suggested joining forces with the shifters.

"I'm telling you the truth," she said, hoping that her voice sounded convincing.

Knox looked back at her again. "I want to hear more about this sapphire dragon stone. And I think my clan will want to hear, too. But we need to get out of here. If it's true those drones are reporting your coordinates, we need to get you far, far away. How long do you think it will be before the wizards could get here?"

"A couple hours, at least," Bree said. "It will take them some time to get organized. But they'll definitely be hot on my trail by the end of the day."

To Bree's surprise, Knox smiled. "Good. That means we have time to eat this elk. Let's enjoy a hot meal, and then I'll get you out of here and to the safest place I know. We can talk more there."

Bree felt a rush of relief go through her. He wasn't promising her much—mostly just that he would hear her out. But that was a start. And if he knew how to get her somewhere that would be safe from the wizards who were hunting her down, she was willing to go with him.

It was starting to look like Knox was her best chance to save herself and the wizards.

CHAPTER SEVEN

Taking time to eat the elk made Bree nervous. She knew with certainty that it would take at least a few hours for the wizards to get to where the drones had found her. They would need to get themselves organized, and there was no magic spell for teleporting. Depending on how far away they were, it might even be a full day before they got close to her location and started tracking her down in earnest. But that didn't keep Bree from looking around with anxiety every time she heard the tiniest rustle of leaves or cracking of a twig. Her worst nightmare right now would be seeing one of the wizards.

But Bree had to admit that it felt good to have a hot meal on her stomach. She'd never eaten elk before, but she found the flavor similar to beef. She and Knox both stuffed themselves, eating quickly without much conversation. There would be time for talking later. Right now, they both wanted to get out of here as quickly as possible. Knox told her to keep watch while he cleaned up the fire and leftover elk after their meal. Bree got the feeling that he did this so that she would be out of the way more than because he wanted an actual guard. He worked so efficiently that she would have only gotten in the way.

Once everything was cleaned up, Knox told her his plan, and told her a little more about himself.

"I'm actually the leader of a clan of dragons that live further south in the Redwoods. We're known as the Redwood Dragons. It would be a several day hike from here, but if I shift into a dragon and fly, it will only take a few hours. You can ride on my back and hold our backpacks."

Bree's eyes widened for more reasons than one. She wasn't excited about the prospect of riding on the back of a dragon. It seemed a little dangerous, and, while she wasn't necessarily afraid of heights, she wasn't sure how she felt about riding high above the forest with nothing to hold onto but dragon wings. She was also surprised to find out that Knox was a clan leader. What was he doing out here in the middle of nowhere, far away from his clan? Shouldn't a clan leader be with his clan members, leading them? But the biggest surprise to Bree was when Knox mentioned that his clan was the Redwood Dragons. Thanks to her research about the dragon stone, she knew that some dragons from a clan known as the Redwood Dragons had helped the shifters in Texas with recovering the emerald dragon stone. Was Knox speaking of the same clan? Hundreds of questions began swirling in Bree's mind, but she realized that it would take a long time for him to answer all of them. Right now, the most important thing was to get away from here, and quickly. Hopefully, once they arrived to wherever in the Redwoods Knox's clan lived, Bree would have time to ask questions. Besides, the sooner they flew away from here, the sooner her dragon flight would be over. Right now, she definitely just wanted to get that part over with. So she simply nodded at Knox, doing her best to look confident.

"Alright," she said. "Sounds good. Let's get going."

"I'm going to take off my clothes before I shift, so that I don't needlessly ruin another outfit," Knox said. "I'm used to being naked in front of people because of shifting, but I noticed earlier that it made you uncomfortable. Feel free to turn around while I undress if that makes you feel less awkward."

Bree felt her cheeks flushing bright red. So he *had* noticed her discomfort earlier. She nodded quickly and turned around, annoyed at how hot her face had become. Of course, for a shifter nakedness might be totally normal. But for a wizard, nakedness was something that only happened in the bedroom or the doctor's office. And if Bree saw Knox naked, she knew she wouldn't be able to keep herself from thinking about what it would be like to see him in a bedroom.

If Knox noticed her heated cheeks, he made no comment. She heard him shuffling around as he quickly undressed, and then stuffed his clothes into his backpack. A few moments later, a loud rush of wind indicated that he was shifting into dragon form. Bree turned around to see his dragon in front of her, large and powerful. The beast looked majestic, and fit in well with the majestic redwoods that towered overhead. Bree took a moment to appreciate its beauty, but then Knox's dragon was snorting gently at her, gesturing toward his back and indicating that he wanted her to climb on. They needed to get moving.

Bree picked up Knox's large hiking backpack and swung it up onto the dragon's back. Her own backpack was already tightly strapped onto her back. Knox's dragon had bent low to the ground so that she could scramble up his back. She climbed up quickly, then lay low on her stomach so that she was flattened against the dragon's back. She looped one of the straps from Knox's backpack through one of her arms so that it wouldn't fly away, and then she held on as tightly as she could to the scales on the dragon's back. There was not a good place to grip, and she felt somewhat unsecured. But she had little choice. It was either ride his dragon out, or try to hike faster than the wizards who were hunting her down. She knew the wizards would eventually catch her, so she was grateful for the ride, no matter how scary it might be. At least Knox's dragon was big enough that she had a large, stable surface to ride on.

Knox turned his big dragon head around to make sure she was holding on, and then he began flapping his giant wings. The leaves on the trees all around them quivered violently as the force of his wings sent turbulence through the nearby branches, and Bree's heart began to pound as the dragon slowly began to rise. Once Knox was in the air, the ground fell away quickly. He maneuvered skillfully through the thick treetops, rising higher and higher until suddenly he broke free into clear blue sky. He kept rising until the treetops were small and looked like children's toys. The air right near the trees had been turbulent and rough, but once Knox rose into the clouds like this, things were calm. It was almost peaceful, in fact.

Bree relaxed a bit now. As long as there were no sudden bursts of wind, she would be fine. Knox was moving his giant wings at a steady pace, and his body was perfectly straight and still. Bree began enjoying the ride. The world seemed to fall away, along with her worries. For a brief moment, she felt free. She let go of her fear of being found by her wizard clan, or, worse, of not capturing the dragon sapphire before it was too late to stop the forces of evil. Right here, nothing else mattered except the cool wind in her face, and the deep shades of green from the Redwoods below her.

They flew like this for almost two hours. Knox didn't seem to be taking a straight path. He curved around a bit, following the forest, and Bree supposed that he was trying to stay away from populated areas. If full humans saw a dragon flying around, there was bound to be trouble.

Eventually, Bree could tell that they were descending. They slowly got lower and lower, until Knox was flying in downward circles straight toward the treetops. Bree clutched as tightly as she could to his back. She feared the moment that they would enter the trees again. There were so many branches that it wouldn't be hard for her to be knocked off of his back only to go tumbling several hundred feet to the ground.

But Knox once again skillfully maneuvered his way through the trees. He seemed to know exactly where every branch and twig was located. Bree guessed that was because these were his stomping grounds. They must be near his clan's home.

A few minutes later, he landed with a firm but graceful thud on a small open space on the forest floor. Bree realized that she had been holding her breath, and she let it out with a relieved sigh as she slid off of the dragon's back, pulling Knox's backpack with her. She could hardly believe it, but she had ridden on a dragon and survived.

Knox gently nudged her away with his dragon head, and she realized that he was preparing to shift back into human form. He wanted her to move back a bit so that she wouldn't be knocked over by the force. She did so quickly, and soon a rush of powerful energy hit her. She looked away, knowing that he would be naked and once again feeling awkward. He came up to where she stood and took his backpack from her hand. She stared off into the distance, not knowing where to look to make things less awkward. He stepped away and she could hear him dressing once again. After a minute or two, she heard him walking back toward her, but she did not look in his direction until he reached out his hand and gently put his fingers on her chin, turning her face toward him.

His touch sent an unexpected shock of warmth through Bree's body, and she felt her cheeks turning red, betraying her feelings once again. She forced herself to smile and meet those deep green eyes of his.

"You okay?" he asked. His voice was softer than it had been before. The concern in his tone made the warmth flooding through her body feel even hotter.

"I'm great," she said. "You're a very smooth flyer."

He held her chin in his fingers for just a moment, searching her eyes with his own. Then he nodded and dropped his hand. Bree felt relieved. His touch did strange things to her heart, and she had too much on her mind already to be sorting through feelings of desire. And yet, even after he dropped his hand, it took a long time for the warmth in her body to subside. Something had changed between them, and they both knew it.

They had chosen, each in their own way, to trust each other. Bree had decided to believe that Knox was a good shifter, and she had trusted her life to him when she agreed to ride his dragon here. Knox, for his part, had trusted that there was truth in what Bree was telling him, and that she was not some sort of spy setting a trap for him. He had brought her to his clan's home, and Bree knew that signaled a deep level of trust.

At first, his home was not easily seen through the thick forest. They had landed in a small clearing, barely big enough for one dragon to stand in. A crude path led away from the clearing. The path was not very well-worn, but it was still easy enough to see. Knox started walking down this path, and after about a three minute walk they came to a much larger clearing. The tree cover here was thin, although not entirely gone. Whoever had cleared the space here had taken care to leave as much of the forest canopy intact as possible, so that the clearing was still as hidden as possible from above. But the sunlight still came streaming through much brighter here than it did in other places.

Several cabins lined the edges of the clearing. Bree counted two rows of cabins—one row with five cabins and one with six cabins, for a total of eleven cabins. The cabins looked small, as though they couldn't be much bigger than one room each. But they looked sturdy and well-made. In the open space between the rows of cabins was what looked like a common area. There was a large grill, and not far from that there was a fire pit, which was surrounded by long, thick logs that looked like they served as benches. A tall man was sitting on one of the log benches now, with his head bent over a book. He looked like he had been reading intently, but he looked up quickly when Knox and Bree entered the clearing. He smiled, but raised an eyebrow.

"Hey guys, the boss is back," he yelled out. "And it looks like he brought company."

CHAPTER EIGHT

Bree watched a smile break across Knox's face as he waved to the man in the clearing.

"Afternoon, Vance," Knox called out to him. Vance nodded respectfully as he stood. A few moments later, two heads poked out of one of the nearby cabins.

"Afternoon, Myles. Afternoon, Owen," Knox said as he continued walking toward the fire pit in the center of the camp. "I think we need to have a little powwow."

Bree saw all of the men looking from Knox to her and back again. They must not get many visitors, because they were looking at her as though she was an alien. She saw them exchange several meaningful glances with each other.

"I thought you were guarding the camp, Vance," the one named Myles said. "Looks like you weren't watching that well since you didn't warn us the boss was coming in until he'd already landed."

Vance shrugged, but looked slightly annoyed. "You told me to warn you if any unauthorized visitors showed up. I didn't think the boss counted as an unauthorized visitor."

Myles glared at Vance and looked like he was about to say something else, when Knox held up his hand and silenced them.

"Enough, boys," he said. "We don't have time for your usual quarreling. As you've noticed, I brought a visitor with me. A visitor who has news we might all be interested in hearing. This is Bree. We've been flying for several hours, and I'm sure she's hungry just like I am. Let's get some food going, and we'll discuss things over dinner. Any word from the other boys? Is everyone doing alright?"

"Everyone's good, and Noah's on his way back from Portugal," Myles said. "As for dinner, I was making a big pot of chili in my kitchen. That's why Owen and I were hanging out in there. It should be just about done. If someone wants to start a fire out here, I'll bring out the chili. Someone else can grab some beers."

"I'll take care of the fire," Vance said, his eyes dancing. "Since we all know I'm the best at starting one."

There was a roar of friendly protest, and the tension in the air seemed to dissipate as the men laughed and ribbed each other on.

"Can I help with anything?" Bree asked, looking at Knox uncertainly.

"No," he said, smiling back at her. "Just find a seat by the fire pit and relax. You've had quite a day, and you need to rest. You'll feel better once you have something to eat, and then you can explain more about who you are and what you know about the dragon stone."

"Dragon stones, plural," Bree corrected him, not wanting to seem obstinate but thinking it important that he realized the seriousness of the situation.

"Right, stones," he said, his tone neutral. Bree couldn't tell whether he was just humoring her or whether he was actually starting to believe her story about the multiple stones. Either way, he didn't give her a chance to say anything further right then. He shooed her toward the fire pit, and then followed Myles and Owen back to Myles' cabin.

Vance started kindling a fire in the pit, but he did not say anything to Bree. In fact, he avoided eye contact with her as much as possible, and he seemed extremely uncomfortable being left alone with her. Bree got the feeling that there were no other women in the clan, and that any visitors who did come by here were never women.

Thankfully, Vance and Bree were only alone with their awkward silence for a few minutes. Soon, Knox, Myles, and Owen were returning. Knox was carrying a twelve pack of beers in each hand, Myles had on potholders and was carrying a giant soup pot, and Owen was balancing a stack of bowls and spoons. On top of the bowls and spoons was what looked like a loaf of fresh bread and some butter.

Myles set the pot down, and grabbed a soup ladle he had hung from one of the handles. He took a bowl from Owen and scooped out a generous portion, then handed the bowl to Bree.

"Here you go," he said, sounding proud and shy all at the same time. "Best bowl of chili you'll ever taste, if I do say so myself. Knox cracked open a beer and handed it to Bree, and then Owen gave her a slice of buttered, crusty bread. Bree's mouth watered, and she realized then just how hungry she was. The meal of elk had been good, but that had been hours ago, and flying had made her surprisingly hungry even though she hadn't been the one doing the work. She dipped her bread into the steaming hot chili and then bit off a piece.

Myles was right. It was the best damn chili she'd ever tasted. Soon, everyone was sitting around the fire with chili, bread, and beer. Knox took a few bites to ward off his hunger, but he didn't wait long before he started speaking.

"Everyone, as I've already told you, this is Bree. I met her in the Redwoods during my survival mission, and you'll be hearing her story soon. But first, Bree, please allow me to formally introduce everyone. Right here to my right is Myles. This over here is Vance. And that's Owen over on the other side of Vance."

Each of the men nodded politely at Bree as their names were called. They looked at her curiously, but did not ask questions. They were respectfully waiting for their leader, Knox, to explain things.

"This is not even half of my crew of dragons," Knox was saying. "There are six others who are off on missions right now. We are, as I've told you, known as the Redwood Dragons. We're a small clan, but mighty. We've been trained since boyhood in the art of ancient dragon fighting. We are a brotherhood of orphans, found and trained by the last of the great Redwood Dragons who had been charged with guarding ancient artifacts."

Knox paused, and Bree felt her heart starting to pound. This all sounded very familiar, and she was beginning to realize exactly who Knox was. She had heard of him when she heard the story of the emerald dragon stone. How was it possible she had been lucky enough to find the one shifter who best understood the dragon stones and their importance? It had to have been fate. Bree felt truly hopeful for the first time in a while.

"Our lives are dedicated to guarding ancient artifacts as well as finding artifacts that have gone missing and are in danger of falling into the wrong hands. As I'm sure you know, since you know of the dragon stone, an artifact with supernatural power that falls into the wrong hands can be disastrous for all—humans, shifters, and wizards alike."

Bree saw Knox's men shoot him confused looks when he said the word wizard. She also saw Knox glancing down at her magic ring when he spoke of ancient artifacts, and she quietly turned her hand so that it was difficult for Knox to see the ring. He clearly still thought that ring itself was some ancient artifact and not simply a wizard's magic ring.

"Many of our dragons are off on missions to recover artifacts right now. One of the biggest missions we've ever been involved in, a mission I think you know well, was to recover the dragon stone. Or, one of the dragon stones, as you say."

Now Knox's men really looked confused. Vance, who seemed to be a bit hot blooded, could not keep himself from commenting at this point.

"*One* of the dragon stones?" he said. "There's more than one of them? I thought the dragon stone itself was the most powerful of the ancient artifacts, and that we were relatively safe now that it had been recovered."

Knox turned his eyes to Vance. "Bree has brought to my attention the possibility that there may be more than one dragon stone," he said calmly. "But we'll get to that in a minute."

Bree couldn't keep herself from cutting in at this point, though. "Then you *are* part of the same clan of Redwood Dragons that helped recover the emerald dragon stone," she said, her voice filling with awe.

"Yes," Knox said. "Although most of the credit for that mission properly belongs to the shifters in Texas. I guess, if you've studied the history of the stone as much as you claim, you must know the story? The Texas shifters found the stone and kept it out of enemy hands. In the process, William, the former leader of the Redwood Dragons was kidnapped. I went to help rescue him, and after that he retired. He was getting old, and, I suppose he was ready to settle into an easier life than living out here in the forest. He wanted a warm home and a woman, and he got both. He deserved it, too. I've never known a man as honorable as William."

Bree saw all of the men bow their heads in respect when Knox spoke of William. The man had meant a lot to all of them, she could tell.

"I do know the story well," Bree said. "And I must say I'm in awe that out of all the shifters I could have run across, I found one from the clan that was part of recovering the last dragon stone."

"It seems to be a sign of some sort," Knox said slowly. "But you must understand it's still difficult for me to believe everything you've told me. I'm trusting you greatly by bringing you here. I never allow outsiders in our base camp. But if what you're warning me of is true, then we will need each other's help."

This time it was Owen who spoke up. "I am so confused right now," he said. "Can someone please explain what the hell is going on here? There are more dragon stones? And I heard a mention of wizards being in danger? I thought all of the wizards were gone?"

Knox turned to look at Bree. "I think I've given you a pretty good overview of who, exactly, I am. Now it's your turn to explain to my men who you are. After that, I'd like to hear what you know about this supposed sapphire dragon stone."

Bree felt her heart pounding as all eyes turned to her. All of a sudden, she felt the same nervous energy she had felt right before she presented her case to the High Council. This was her second chance to prove to someone that a crisis was at hand. She had failed to convince the High Council. If she failed to convince this crew, she might see her worst fears realized and the dragon sapphire might fall into the wrong hands.

Taking a deep breath, Bree began speaking. She told the whole story, in as much detail as she could. First, she explained that wizards did in fact exist. In an attempt to prove it, she held her magic ring high and performed a few simple spells. She made a flashlight beam shoot from the ring's pointed tip, and then a fountain of fiery sparks. She turned herself invisible and back again. The men looked impressed, but Bree could tell by their faces that they held some of the same doubts that Knox did. How could they know that the ring itself was not just some powerful artifact, enabling her to do magic? Could they really believe that Bree herself was the source of the magic, and that the ring was just the instrument her magic flowed through?

In an act of great trust, Bree allowed each of them to handle the ring. They spoke the same words Bree had spoken to initiate magic spells, but, of course, nothing happened. They looked slightly less skeptical—but only slightly. Sometimes words were not enough to unlock the power of ancient artifacts, and special training was necessary. In that case, it would be possible for a ring to work for one person but not another. In the end, Bree decided she would have to be content with their guarded skepticism regarding whether or not wizards existed. It was the best she could do for now, and she pressed forward with explaining why she had sought out shifters in the first place.

She explained to them her job of Advocate, and what her duties had been in the wizarding community. Then she told them of her assignment, seemingly a throwaway assignment, to make sure that the dragon stone had indeed been recovered and was being held safely away from the forces of evil. She told them how she had discovered that, although the dragon stone was safe, there was actually more than one dragon stone, and one of those stones was in grave danger of falling into the wrong hands. If it did, it would bring ruin to humans, shifters, and wizards alike.

She told of how she had appeared before the High Council, pleading with them and asking them to take the threat seriously. But no one had listened to her, and she had been sent home feeling ashamed. With a trembling voice, she told them of how she had decided to run away and take matters into her own hands—and she explained what the consequences would be for her if she was found. Then, with a rueful smile, she retold the story of how she had trailed Knox for several days before revealing herself and asking for his help. Lastly, she explained what the drones were, and how she could no longer stay where she had been in the far northern portions of the California redwood forests, lest the wizards come and find her.

"So there you have it," she said, looking around at the disbelieving faces of Knox's clan members. "I'm sure, since you all know of the power of the emerald dragon stone, that you can understand how powerful the sapphire dragon stone must be. But if you want details, I brought with me my folder of facts and information on the sapphire dragon stone. It's in my backpack, which, thankfully, the drones weren't able to steal."

There was silence for several long moments. None of the shifters seemed to want to be the first one to speak. They all looked at Knox, perhaps hoping he would be the one to break the silence. But Knox was staring off at the sky, which was now a fiery orange from the setting sun, a thoughtful look on his face. Finally, impatient Vance could not take it any longer.

"Is this all true, Knox?" Vance demanded, his eyes wide as he looked up at his clan leader.

Knox shifted his eyes back to look first at his men, then at Bree. The intensity in his eyes as they met hers unnerved her.

"What she says about meeting me in the forest, and being attacked by drones, is all true," Knox said. "As for the other parts—the existence of wizards and multiple dragon stones—I have no way to verify their truth. But my gut is telling me to trust Bree, and William always told us to follow our gut instincts when all else failed."

"I respect that, Boss," Myles said slowly. "But these are some pretty big claims she's making. It sounds like it could be a trap. What if someone is trying to get information from us on where the emerald dragon stone actually is? We have to be careful. We owe it to the shifter protectors to do everything we can to proceed carefully and make sure that the dragon stone stays safe."

"No offense, Bree," Owen said, looking quickly over at her. "You seem like a nice enough person, but, if you are who you say you are, hopefully you understand that we need to be careful."

"No offense taken," Bree said. She understood that the men were wary. And yet, it took everything within her not to plead with them to see how much depended on their decision.

"I think the best thing for us to do is to have a private meeting, and go over the information that Bree has on the supposed sapphire dragon stone," Knox said. "I wish the other dragons were here to weigh in, too, but we can't wait for them to get back. We need to make a decision soon. Bree, would you mind hanging out in my cabin for a little while so I can talk to the crew alone?"

Bree had been expecting this, and she nodded. "No problem," she said. She stood stiffly, realizing for the first time since she arrived at the dragons' base just how tired she was. She fished out her folder of information on the dragon stones, and handed it to Knox. He handed it off to Myles, then gestured toward the cabins.

"Come on. I'll show you my place."

Bree followed him, feeling strangely nervous about seeing his cabin. She hadn't thought much about where she would stay once she arrived at his clan's headquarters. She had expected the headquarters to be much bigger, and was surprised at how few cabins and shifters there were here. In her mind's eye, she had pictured a big village, like Falcon Cross. A small group might be better, though. There would be less politics involved, and fewer hoops to jump through to get a mission going.

Hopefully a mission *would* be going soon. Bree felt the knot in the pit of her stomach tightening every time she thought about where the sapphire stone might be right now, and how close it might be to falling into the wrong hands.

"This is my place," Knox said as he pushed open the door to a cabin at the end of one of the rows. "It's not big, but it's cozy. Feel free to help yourself to anything in the kitchen if you're still hungry or thirsty, although I'd guess that after all the chili and beer we've had you're probably more tired than anything else. If that's the case, feel free to crash on the couch, or even on my bed."

Bree nodded. "Thanks," she said. "I could use a nap."

Knox nodded too, then stared around the room awkwardly for a moment. "Listen," he said, sounding uncomfortable as he spoke. "I believe you. It's crazy to me to think that wizards still exist, but, hey, a lot of people think that it's crazy that shifters exist. The impossible only seems impossible before you've seen what's actually possible."

Bree chuckled. "That's quite a deep thought."

Knox smiled. "I try. But listen, don't worry about the crew. They trust me, and I'll convince them to trust you."

Bree felt like a weight had been lifted off her shoulders. At the same time, she felt her body heating up again under Knox's gaze. He seemed to feel the heat, too, because he looked at her long and hard before turning to leave.

"Make yourself at home, Bree," he said. When he spoke her name a certain tenderness filled his voice, and the heat in Bree's body intensified. Before she could answer, though, he had turned and left, firmly closing the cabin door behind him.

It was almost completely dark now, but Bree didn't bother looking for a light switch. She bent over to take off her hiking boots, leaving them by the front door, then wiggling her toes as she started walking across the small living room. The cabin was tiny, but it did have a separate bedroom.

"*Magicae lucis,*" Bree said. A flashlight beam came streaming from her magic ring, and she swept the light across the room. The only furniture was a small kitchen table with two chairs, and a couch in the living room. There was not much in the way of decorations, but the place was neat and looked comfortable. Bree made her way to the bedroom, where a giant bed took up most of the small room. It was covered with a large, navy plaid comforter. Bree had not intended to sleep on Knox's bed, but now that she saw it, it looked too comfortable to pass up.

She lay down on it, immediately sinking into the softness with a groan of delight. She was so tired, and it felt like so long since she'd slept in a proper bed. And yet, despite how tired she was, sleep did not come right away.

Instead, she used the light beam from her ring to make little circles of light on the ceiling. She wondered, as she watched the light dancing above her, whether Knox would really be able to convince his shifters to trust her. And did it matter whether everyone else trusted her, as long as he did? He seemed to be firmly in charge here. Hopefully his trust was enough.

Bree thought of Lily, and a deep sadness filled her. She hoped that everything would work out in the end, not just for her sake but for Lily's. Lily had always stood up for her, and it must be heartbreaking now to have a roommate who appeared to be a deserter and treasonous. But Bree had done what she knew in her heart she had to do. Hopefully, one day soon, not just Lily but all of Falcon Cross would understand that.

Bree wondered how long it would take Knox to talk to his clan members. She hoped that it would be long enough for her to get some good rest, because she had a feeling that the days ahead might be even more exhausting than the last few days had been.

With a sigh, Bree lowered her arm, which had been raised so that she could point her magic ring at the ceiling.

"*Lucis terminantur*," Bree whispered. The light went out, and within moments Bree had fallen asleep.

CHAPTER NINE

"Incoming dragon," Myles said. Knox looked up, surprised to see that Myles was correct. Spiraling down through the darkness, lightly outlined by the waning crescent moon, was a formidable dragon shape. Even in the poor lighting, Knox could see the uniquely spiked tail whipping through the night sky. He would know that dragon anywhere.

"Noah," Knox said, his heart filling with joy. "Noah is back. You guys said it was going to be another several days before he got here."

Vance shrugged. "Last time he called he was still in Portugal and was having trouble getting a flight out. Something must have worked out sooner than he thought."

"Well, we'll wait until he lands to discuss Bree and the possibility of another dragon stone," Knox said. "He'll certainly be interested in hearing about this."

A few minutes later, they heard rustling in the forest as Noah made his way down the path toward the cabins. He was in human form, and was carrying a large backpack of supplies. He had already dressed again, and was wearing a pair of jeans and an oversized black hoodie. When he was close enough to see the rest of the dragons sitting around the fire pit, he grinned and waved.

"You're back!" Knox called out to him, rushing up to give him a big bear hug and a hearty slap on the back.

"You're back, too," Noah said, raising an eyebrow at him. "Myles told me you'd gone off on a survival mission, but that wasn't a very long survival mission. I thought you'd still be out there, proving how long you could make it on your own. Don't tell me you got too worried about the crew and came home."

Knox rolled his eyes at Noah's accusing tone. "No. If you must know, I came home because I learned of the potential existence of a second dragon stone."

Knox paused dramatically, expecting Noah to look shocked. But instead, Noah only gave a grim shake of his head.

"So you've heard about it, too," Noah said. "And here I thought I was going to be coming home with news that would astonish you all. It seems someone has beaten me to the punch line, though."

"Wait, what do you mean?" Owen asked. "You've heard of a second dragon stone, too?"

Noah nodded slowly. "Yes. When I was in Portugal, spying on the ones who held the artifact in Portugal I had been sent to find, I heard whisperings of it. At first I didn't believe it was true. I thought that those whispering such things must be misinformed. I thought perhaps they were confused, and had heard some rumors about the original dragon stone that they thought meant it was still missing. But no. The more I listened, the more I realized that what they were talking about was certainly not the same dragon stone that had already been recovered and handed over to the shifter protectors for safekeeping. I did some digging around and found out that what we knew about the dragon stone was only a fraction of what there is to know. I got back as quickly as I could, thinking I would have a tough job ahead of me, convincing you that what I said was true. But it seems that I was wrong. What have you all heard, and who did you hear it from?"

"You might want to sit down for this," Vance said. Noah looked surprised, but then did sit down.

"Pass me a beer," Noah said. "And then someone tell me what the heck is going on here."

Owen passed Noah a beer, and then Knox once again told Bree's story from beginning to end. Noah sipped his beer and listened to the whole thing without once showing any sign of disbelief. That was one of the things Knox loved about Noah. He was good at keeping a poker face, when he wanted to. When Knox had finally finished talking, Noah set aside his now-empty beer bottle and stared into the fire for several long moments. Knox waited, letting him think. He knew his best friend was not taking this situation lightly, and he wanted to give him a chance to process everything he had just heard.

"Wizards, eh?" Noah finally said. "Well I'll be."

Vance, of course, could keep silent no longer. "You don't think it's really true, do you Noah? I mean, Bree did some magic with her ring, but surely that's just a magical artifact."

Noah looked up at the group. His eyes met Knox's and Knox saw that there was no doubt in Noah's eyes that Bree's story was true.

"There have been strange stirrings in the shifter world," Noah said. "I saw and heard a lot of things on my trip abroad. And I've learned better than to doubt the existence of an entire group of people just because everyone has always said they don't exist."

"But what real proof do we have that there are still wizards?" Vance persisted. "It's fine to question things, but a magic ring might just be a magic ring. It doesn't prove that the person who has it is actually a wizard."

"There are rumors that the men seeking the second dragon stone have realized that wizards exist," Noah said slowly. "I don't know how they would know this. The men are, by all accounts, very evil. But they are full humans, and their belief in wizards gives me pause. As for proving that someone is an actual wizard, there is an easy test, you know, to see whether someone actually has magical powers aside from just a magical object."

"There is?" Vance asked, looking surprised. Myles and Own looked surprised, too. But Knox suddenly felt foolish.

"Of course!" Knox said, slapping his forehead. "Why didn't I think of that? We just need to take away her ring or wand and see if she can still do magic."

Knox felt foolish for forgetting this, although to be fair, he had not spent much time studying wizards. They had always been a non-issue, so he hadn't given them much thought. All of his men except Noah were still looking at him in confusion, so he started to explain.

"Wizards can do magic without their rings, or without wands for those wizards who use wands. It makes sense, when you think about it. Their magic is an internal ability. Otherwise all it would take to be a wizard would be a wand or a ring."

"I'm still confused," Myles said. "Why do they carry wands and rings if they can do magic without them?"

"Wands and rings focus a wizard's power," Noah piped in. "They channel all their magic into a single point, making their spells stronger and more effective. For example, a spell to cast a light beam that runs through a magic ring will produce a concentrated beam of light, like a flashlight. That same spell done without the magic ring will still produce light, but it will be scattered."

"So all we need to do is take away Bree's ring and see if she can still do magic," Vance said, finally understanding. "What are we waiting for, then?"

"We're waiting for morning," Knox said firmly. "Bree is exhausted, and my guess is she's already asleep right now. I'm not going to go storming into the cabin, demanding that she hand over her ring and then perform magic tricks."

Knox saw all of his men look at him in surprise. It wasn't like him to be so defensive of someone who seemed to be barely more than a stranger. If Knox was honest, his strong reaction surprised even himself. He was starting to feel inexplicably protective of Bree, and the emotional reaction he was having to her scared him a bit. He was well aware of the heat that passed between them when their eyes met, and he could no longer deny that he was developing some sort of feelings for her. But he could not indulge those feelings right now. He was leader of this clan, and he could not allow romantic emotions to affect his decisions regarding whether he would trust Bree and her stories about the dragon stone. Knox glanced over at Noah. He was grateful beyond words that Noah had returned. Noah was always the voice of reason, and Noah would not hesitate to get in Knox's face and yell at him if he was wrong.

"I think we should spend the rest of the night looking through whatever information Bree brought with her on the dragon stone," Knox said. "That might help us determine whether the second stone actually exists."

"It does," Noah said, sounding weary. "I'm sure of it. Although I'm curious to see how Bree's information lines up with what I heard while I was gone."

"This is unbelievable," Myles said, sounding equally excited and terrified. "I thought after the last dragon stone was found that we'd seen the most powerful artifact we were going to see in our lifetime."

"It appears not," Noah said. "Knox, you look exhausted, and I don't think going through Bree's information is urgent. Why don't you go get some rest? I'll look through everything with the guys, and we'll update you in the morning. You can look through it all yourself then, when you're fresh."

Knox wanted to protest, but he knew that Noah was right. He was so tired now that he wouldn't be very helpful reading through a bunch of stuff. Besides, he trusted Noah to take care of things, and he wanted to trust all of his clan members more. William had warned him that he needed to make sure every dragon in the clan was trained to lead, if necessary. So far, Knox had not been doing a good job of passing on leadership skills. This was a good time for him to show some trust, and let his best friend, Noah, take care of things while he got some much needed rest.

"Alright," Knox said, standing slowly and realizing for the first time just how stiff and tired his muscles were. He gave his men a waving salute, clapped Noah on the shoulder, and then headed for his cabin. He felt a mixture of relief and nerves as he opened the door and stepped into his dark living room. Bree must be asleep by now, but the fact that she was here in his cabin twisted his stomach up in funny ways. He walked silently across the living room and peered into his bedroom. She was sprawled out on the bed, fast asleep and lying on top of the blankets. In the dim light, he could see her chest rising and falling with the rhythm of sleep, and he thought she looked more peaceful now than she had at any moment since he met her. Her right hand was flung across the bed, her large ruby ring gleaming brightly against her skin even though the room was mostly dark. In that moment, any last doubts about the truth of her words slipped away. Knox was always overly suspicious of everyone, and he could smell a lie from a mile away. But after spending hours with Bree today, he had seen nothing but truth in her eyes. He couldn't understand it all, but he knew that somehow wizards still existed. And if Bree indeed was who she said she was, then that gave even more credibility to the rest of her story, and to the reality that the search for the dragon stone had not ended when the emerald stone had been found two years ago. In fact, the search had only just begun. Knox felt a sudden rush of emotion, and his protective instincts took over. If Bree was going chasing after dangerous supernatural artifacts, he sure as hell was going with her.

"My little wizard," he whispered, even though he had no real claim to her. But something told him that fate had brought them together, and that their fates were intertwined. He found himself hoping that their destiny included more than just working together to find an ancient dragon stone. He hoped it meant that their hearts would intertwine as well.

It occurred to him that no one in his clan had ever really had a steady girlfriend. Their lifestyles didn't lend themselves well to a partner. He knew that some of the shifters had enjoyed flings with girls here and there when they were off on missions, but nothing serious had ever come of any of it. Was Knox crazy to think that there might be something more than just lust between Bree and him? Was he even crazier to think it might be possible to date a girl and convince her to move into the woods with a group of bachelors? She was a fugitive now, but that might change. She would probably want to go back to her wizard clan if she could, and there was no way he was leaving his clan.

Knox sighed. There was no sense worrying about things like that right now. He was trying to plan out a life with someone he barely knew, and who might not be all that interested in him anyway. He needed to slow down, focus on what to do about this new dragon stone, and worry about love later.

Moving noiselessly, Knox went to his closet and grabbed an extra blanket he stored in there, then laid it over Bree. Despite his admonitions to himself to let his feelings for her go for now, he couldn't help standing in the doorway for several moments, watching her as she slept, wondering if she might possibly be dreaming of him when she smiled in her sleep.

With a sigh, he finally moved back into the living room and fell across the couch. He was a bit too tall to fit well on the couch, but he was too tired to notice. Within moments of his head hitting the soft cushions, he was asleep.

And he was definitely dreaming of Bree.

CHAPTER TEN

Knox awoke when the first rays of morning sunlight came streaming in through the cabin's front window. He sat up and stretched, trying to work the kinks out of his muscles. It took him a moment to remember why he was sleeping on his couch, and when he did his heart did one of its now-familiar flip-flops.

Bree. She was here, in his cabin, on his bed. Even though he was, of course, being a gentlemen and sleeping on the couch, the thought of her in his bed sent a thrill though his body. Knox stood up and walked over to the bedroom doorway to peek in. Bree was still fast asleep under the blanket he had laid over her last night.

Knox turned and walked across the cabin to look out its front window. He saw wisps of smoke curling up from the fire pit, and Noah and Myles were already sitting out there, mugs of coffee in hand as they leaned over what looked like the folder of papers Bree had brought with her.

Knox left the cabin, closing the door gently behind him so that he wouldn't wake Bree, and then walked toward where Noah and Myles were sitting.

"Morning," Knox said when they looked up at the sound of his approaching footsteps. "Still looking over Bree's information?"

Noah nodded. "It all fits with what I've already heard. There is another stone, that has been missing for centuries. In fact, there are four stones in total. They were all created around the same time as the emerald dragon stone, which is the one that our shifter friends in Texas already recovered. Two of them—a ruby stone and an amethyst stone—are still missing as far as we can tell. They've been missing since the shifter-wizard war that almost destroyed the wizards. But the sapphire stone has been found, seemingly by accident. It was held by a wealthy family in England for a long time—a human family who had no idea what power it held. The last of that family line died, and the sapphire dragon stone, which seems to most to be just a normal gemstone, was put up for auction. A gem collector has the stone now, and is on his way back to Silicon Valley, which luckily isn't far from here. Some ex-drug lords are chasing him down."

"Why haven't they been able to get him, if they're ex-drug lords? I would think they're pretty tough," Knox said.

"It is pretty strange, but perhaps they are afraid to kill the gem collector. There are rumors that if you kill the one who holds the stone, that the stone will turn its wrath on you."

"Is that true?" Knox asked.

Noah shrugged. "No idea. But for now, at least, the rumor is keeping the stone safe. Of course it's very well guarded. Once it gets back to Silicon Valley and is stored in one place, though, it will be easier for the men trying to steal it to do so, since the stone will be in one spot and they can make a solid plan for getting to it."

"How did they find out about the stone and its power in the first place?" Knox asked. "It seems really strange to me that two full humans suddenly know about a dragon stone."

"No one knows," Noah said. "It's quite perplexing. And from what I've heard, it seems like these two guys know that shifters exist. Possibly wizards as well. They're getting information from somewhere, but no one seems to know who. One possibility is that there was some information on the stone in the English family's estate, a journal or something, that had fallen into the wrong hands."

"That seems like a weak explanation," Knox said. "If the English family had information on the stone they probably would have treated it with more care."

Noah shrugged. "It's the best explanation anyone can come up with. Maybe the English family knew about the stone's supposed powers but thought it was a fairy tale or a made up story."

Knox frowned. "Well, I guess it doesn't so much matter how they found out at this point. What matters is that they know, and they're trying to get the stone to use it for evil."

"Exactly," Myles said. "No one knows what they have planned, but these guys have a track record of violent crimes already. Who knows what evil they would do with a powerful dragon stone on their side."

"And we're sure that it is indeed powerful? As powerful as the emerald dragon stone?" Knox asked.

"Well, we can't be sure until we actually see the stone ourselves, I suppose. But there's no reason to think that it's not as powerful as the emerald dragon stone. From the information Bree has here, it looks like the stone was made in the same way as the other dragon stone. An ancient dragon king stored all his magic power in the stone for safekeeping, so that it would help future generations fight evil."

"Didn't they realize that the stones could *help* evil if they fell into the wrong hands?" Knox asked.

"Desperate times call for desperate measures," a woman's voice said.

Knox whirled around to see Bree standing there. He hadn't heard her approaching, and he had to admit that her stealth skills impressed him.

"I suppose you know that better than anyone," Noah said, extending his hand to Bree. "I'm Noah, another one of Knox's dragons. I got in after you'd already gone to the cabin last night, but the crew has told me all about how you left your wizard clan behind, risking your own future as a wizard to do so."

Bree shook Noah's hand politely, then immediately grabbed a mug to help herself to some of the coffee that was keeping warm in a thermos near the fire. She raised her eyes to look at Knox as soon as she had taken a sip.

"So," she asked. "Did your clan members decide to believe that I'm telling the truth, then? Can we get on with actually finding and protecting the sapphire dragon stone?"

"I'm all for getting started," Knox said, looking carefully over at Noah and Myles, but I think that my men would like it if you could prove you're a wizard."

Bree sighed. "You want me to do magic without my ring, I assume? I've been expecting this request, although I had hoped you might come to trust me for my word, instead of forcing me to do party tricks to show that wizards still exist."

Bree's sharp words stung Knox to his core. "I do trust you," he said as calmly as he could. "But I have a clan to think about. And if I'm going to leave them here to go chasing after stones with a supposed wizard, I would appreciate any help I could get in reassuring them that my leaving is necessary."

Bree's eyes shot up to meet his. "*You're* going with me?" she asked, surprised. "I would have thought that now that we were back here and you had a whole clan at your disposal, you'd send one of them so you could stay here and lead."

Knox glanced over at Noah, who was smiling broadly at him now.

"You're finally gonna go somewhere, boss?" Myles asked.

Knox felt his cheeks heat up a bit with embarrassment. It really had been too long since he'd shown his dragons that he trusted them.

"I'm gonna go," Knox said. "This mission will be the most dangerous one out of all the missions that have come up since I started leading this clan. I would never ask any of you to face such danger."

"You know we would, though," Noah said. "We'd face any dangers you asked us to face. We all have the same job here: to protect the ancient artifacts, and keep the shifter world safe by doing so."

"I know you'd all face any danger," Knox said, his chest swelling with pride and gratitude as he looked at Noah and Myles. "But I think it's time for me to take a mission. William, as clan leader, took the last dragon stone mission. It seems only fitting that I, as clan leader, should take this mission."

Knox looked over at Bree and raised his eyes to her, asking her an unspoken question. She understood, even though he said no words. He needed her help to make his clan feel secure. He trusted her completely now. Would she please just show the rest of the dragons that they could trust her, too?

With a sigh, Bree nodded at him. Without a word, she took off her magic ring and handed it to Knox. It felt heavy in his hand. Its weight was greater than you would have expected, even for such a large stone.

"Vance! Owen! Get out here," Knox yelled. A few minutes later, Vance and Owen, both with sleepy eyes and bed-head hair, came stumbling out of their cabins.

"What's up?" Owen asked.

"Come. Sit," Knox said as they got closer to the fire pit. He held up Bree's ring. "I have Bree's magic ring. She's going to perform a magic spell without it, to prove to all of you that she is indeed a wizard, and that wizards still exist."

Vance and Owen nodded, looking somewhat sleepy still, and sat on the same log that Noah was seated on. Knox went to sit by Myles, holding up the magic ring so all could see.

"Alright, Bree. I've got your ring. Let's see what you can do without it."

Knox held his breath for a moment as Bree stared into the small fire that was glowing in the fire pit. She was concentrating deeply, and for a full minute, no one spoke or moved. Then, Bree raised her hands and pointed them both toward the fire, all of her fingers outstretched toward the flames.

"*Magicae ignis,*" she yelled out, her voice loud and authoritative. Almost instantly, red hot flames came shooting from each of her fingers. As they hit the small fire in the pit, it swelled and roared until the dragon shifters had to stand and step backwards away from it. The heat had become too much for them.

Vance rubbed his eyes, looking from the fire to Bree and back again, his face glowing red-orange from the flames.

"My god," Owen said. "It *is* true. There are still wizards."

Knox's heart leapt in his chest as Bree looked over at him and smiled, flames still shooting wildly from her fingers.

"Come on, my little wizard," he said. "Let's go find that sapphire and redeem your name to your clan."

Bree smiled at him and nodded.

"*Ignis terminantur,*" she yelled.

The flames leaping from her fingers stopped instantly, but Knox knew that the fire in his heart had only just begun to burn.

CHAPTER ELEVEN

Bree had checked and double-checked her backpack, and yet she still felt like she was forgetting something. It was ridiculous for her to feel that way, since everything she owned at the moment fit into that backpack. She figured it was just nerves. If this mission went badly, things would go badly for a whole lot of people. Bree hated feeling like she quite literally had the weight of the world on her shoulders, but she figured it couldn't be helped. She had chosen her path when she decided to run away from Falcon Cross. She had decided to be courageous, and now she had no choice but to remain courageous until the end, whenever that might be.

"Ready?" Knox asked, poking his head into the doorway of his cabin. Bree looked up at him, and, as usual, her heart skipped a beat at the sight of him. She had tried to ignore her growing feelings for him, but the more she tried to act like he didn't mean anything special to her, the more he seemed to make her heart pound. She suspected that a big part of her nerves surrounding this journey were due to the fact that he was the one going with her.

"I'm ready," she said. "Ready as I'll ever be, I guess."

He nodded. "Give me a few minutes to give Noah some last minute instructions. I'll meet you out by the fire pit in about five minutes."

"Alright," Bree said. Knox disappeared from view as Bree pulled her backpack onto her shoulders, wondering for the thousandth time that day whether she and Knox actually had a chance at pulling this off. Their plan was basic and haphazard. They were going to rent out an apartment in Mountain View, California, the city in the heart of Silicon Valley where the gem collector lived. They would stalk him, trying to figure out where the stone was and how they could steal it and replace it with a fake sapphire.

Knox had a lot of connections with shady people skilled in things like creating fake replicas of gemstones. Bree didn't ask him for too many details. She figured that when you spent your life tracking down ancient artifacts and guarding those artifacts, you had to play a trick or two now and then. One of Knox's trickster friends was working on a fake sapphire to match the dragon sapphire, and would be handing it off to them when they arrived in Silicon Valley.

The best case scenario would be if Knox and Bree could get the real stone and replace it with a fake stone before the men who were hunting down the stone realized what had happened. This would be difficult to achieve, however. Bree knew that the men were following the stone closely, and would likely make a move to steal it as soon as it arrived at its final location in Silicon Valley. Luckily, Bree had magic on her side, but she wasn't sure that even that would be enough.

Bree walked out of Knox's cabin and into the fresh air and bright morning sunshine. She breathed in deeply, enjoying the smell of the Redwoods that had quickly grown on her. She loved it here at the dragons' base camp. Things felt so peaceful and safe, and Bree had loved having a few days to relish the relaxed atmosphere.

Bree walked toward the fire pit, where Myles, Vance, and Owen were already sitting, waiting on Noah and Knox to finish up their meeting in Noah's cabin. Bree frowned slightly as she saw Vance look at her and then glance quickly away. If one thing had not been relaxed about her stay here in the Redwoods, it had been dealing with Vance. Bree could tell that Vance was still reluctant to trust her, even though she had proven she was really a wizard. He had gone through the information Bree had about the dragon sapphire, questioning it line by line, acting doubtful as to whether the information was actually accurate.

Bree had no doubt that what she knew about the dragon sapphire was correct. She had done extensive research while still in her position at the Advocacy Bureau, and she had found many texts confirming that more than one dragon stone was created. Wizards had helped with their creation, since this had been back in the days when wizards and dragons were still friendly to each other. Perhaps only the wizards still retained the ancient texts discussing the stones' creation, because the shifters didn't seem to have even the tiniest bit of knowledge on any of the other stones. Vance didn't seem to trust wizard information, though. In fact, Bree wasn't sure that he was entirely convinced that wizards were real, despite the fact that she had demonstrated that she could do magic even without her magic ring. She'd heard him muttering something about how many magic objects could be used within a certain distance even if the person using them wasn't actually holding them. He thought the magic ring was still responsible for Bree's magic, even though she had not actually been holding it.

Bree frowned. No matter, she told herself. Knox was in charge here, and he believed her. That was all that mattered. As long as Knox was on board with this mission, things would continue to move forward. Bree sat down on one of the log benches to wait for Knox, avoiding eye contact with Vance as she did.

She didn't have to wait long. Less than a minute later, Knox and Noah came out of Noah's cabin. Noah was laughing loudly, while Knox poked him in the ribs, teasing him about some inside joke or another. Bree smiled. She liked Noah, and she was glad that Knox was so close to him. Noah had been on board with the idea that more dragon stones existed from the very beginning. He had seen things while off in Portugal that had confirmed for him that the additional stones existed, and Bree knew that his faith in the stones had been a major factor in Knox's taking the situation seriously.

"Alright, everyone," Knox said, growing more serious as he approached. "You know the plan. I'm leaving Noah in charge, with Myles serving as his second. I'm asking all of you to be ready to come join us at a moment's notice, if necessary. We are hoping to be able to take the stone without resorting to violence, but if we have to fight, then we will—and we might need your help."

Bree looked around as all the dragon shifters nodded enthusiastically, even Vance. She got the impression that they would much rather be off fighting than sitting around at base camp. That was a comforting thought, since Bree had a feeling that it was going to be difficult to retrieve the dragon stone without instigating some sort of battle. Even if they did get the stone before the other men did, they might have a hard time keeping the men from tracking them down and making a desperate attempt to get it back.

But Bree couldn't worry about that too much right now. She told herself to focus on one thing at a time. The first step was to get to Mountain View. Knox would fly them out of the Redwoods and to a small town near the edge of the forest where a rental car had already been arranged. They would drive the rest of the way, acting like two normal humans instead of a dragon shifter and a wizard. They would go to the apartment that Knox had already rented for them, acting as though they were there to start a new life in the thriving tech industry of Silicon Valley. Hopefully, no one would question them too much.

The plan got fuzzier and fuzzier from there, but Bree figured they would figure it out as they went along. That's what she had done when she left Falcon Cross to wander in the woods. So far, winging it seemed to have worked well for her. She could only hope that the trend would continue.

While Bree's mind had been wandering, Knox had finished his pep talk to his clan. Now, he was undressing and preparing to shift. Bree turned her eyes away. She still felt awkward when Knox got naked to shift, even though he didn't seem to give it a second thought. He had spent his whole life stripping down to shift. But for a wizard, who usually put on robes when something extra magical was about to happen, the idea of randomly getting naked was so strange.

A few moments later, as Bree stared intently up at the tops of some of the redwoods, she heard a loud pop and felt a rush of powerful energy rocking her body. She turned around, and Knox had once again become a dragon, large and fearsome. He flexed his giant wings, giving them a few flaps to work out the kinks. Then he turned his large dragon head toward Bree, giving her a nod to tell her he was ready for her to hop on.

She tightened the straps on her backpack, then scrambled up Knox's dragon back. He had crouched low to allow her to climb up, but it still took some effort to get up. Once she was firmly seated on his back, Noah passed up Knox's backpack for Bree to hold onto. She placed the pack firmly in front of her, then held on to Knox's scaly back as best she could.

Noah gave a nod and then slapped Knox's dragon on its haunches. The shifters all gave Knox and Bree a small salute, and then backed up to give Knox room to fly. Knox raised his dragon head. He let out a large roar, and then, without warning, he let a long stream of fire loose from his mouth. Bree smiled at the sight. It was the first time she had seen him breathe fire, and the sight was both terrifying and beautiful. Of all the shifters she could have found to help her with the task of recovering the dragon sapphire, she was glad her paths had crossed with Knox and his dragons. If anyone could make her mission a success it was them. And Bree desperately needed this mission to be a success.

She had tried not to think too much about what might be going on back in Falcon Cross. But as Knox's dragon rose high above the forest, and everything became still and quiet except for the white noise of rushing wind, Bree found it nearly impossible to keep her mind off of her wizard clan. She wondered how much energy they were still putting into searching for her. Had they doubled up their efforts after the drones? Or had they assumed she wouldn't make it in the wilderness very long on her own.

Bree shuddered to think of what might have happened if Knox hadn't flown her out of the forest after the drones found her. If the wizards had caught her, well…she didn't even want to think about it. She would probably be permanently ex-communicated from Falcon Cross and stripped of her magic by now.

But then, a smile crossed her face. She hadn't been caught, she wasn't stripped of her magic, and she was on her way to find the sapphire stone with a magnificent dragon shifter—a dragon shifter who seemed to have connections with many of the good shifters who would be willing to fight if necessary.

Things might just turn out okay, after all.

* * *

The rest of the day passed by in an unremarkable blur. After flying to the small town where they picked up their rental car, Bree drove the rest of the way to Mountain View. The trip had been horribly planned so that they arrived at the height of rush hour traffic, and Bree found herself bored and flipping through radio stations while Knox slept in the passenger seat and traffic inched along at a snail's pace. By the time Bree pulled into the small apartment complex where they would be staying and the GPS announced "You have arrived," she was ready to pull her own hair out in frustration.

Knox, on the other hand, woke up fully refreshed. He sat up, looked around, and smiled.

"We're here?" he asked.

Bree grunted.

"Wait here," Knox said. "Everything is supposed to be taken care of so that I can just walk into the office and get the keys to our apartment."

Bree nodded, and sat staring idly out the window as Knox bounded off to the office, seemingly unaware of how annoyed she was. He came back less than ten minutes later, a broad grin on his face.

"Got the keys," he said, holding up a small yellow envelope. "Ready to go see our first home together?"

He winked, obviously in a jolly, flirtatious mood. Bree felt quite the opposite of jolly right now. She just wanted to stuff her face with some greasy comfort food and then take a long nap. But she managed to force a smile as she got out of the car and grabbed her backpack, then followed Knox to their second floor apartment.

The apartment was tiny, but Bree had expected this. She knew that housing prices were ridiculously high in this area, and figured they had been lucky to find an apartment at all. Knox seemed to have connections for everything, though, and he had somehow finagled them a good deal on a readily available apartment.

There was only one bedroom, but the place was cozily furnished and the couch was large and soft.

"Don't worry, I'll sleep there," Knox said when he saw Bree eyeing the couch. The thought briefly crossed Bree's mind that she wished they could sleep together in the bedroom, but her cheeks turned pink at the thought and she quickly looked away from Knox so he couldn't see.

"So, what's the plan for tonight?" she asked, more because she wanted to change the subject than because she actually needed to ask the question. She knew that there was no real plan for tonight. Their only goal for today had been to arrive safely in Mountain View without setting off any alarm bells that a shifter and a wizard had just arrived in town. Tomorrow, they would begin in earnest their attempt at stealing the dragon sapphire.

"Dinner," Knox said. "This weather is beautiful, and we're going to find a restaurant with outdoor seating to enjoy the weather and eat some real food."

Bree managed a smile. After several hours in the car, eating mostly snacks from gas stations, she was more than ready for real food. Maybe after eating she wouldn't feel quite so grumpy, either.

"Let's go eat, then," she said. "The sooner the better."

"Do you want to change or shower or anything first?" Knox asked.

Bree frowned at him. "Not really. I just want to eat. Why, do I look like I need a shower?"

"Well, no," Knox said uncertainly, and to Bree's surprise she saw his cheeks turning red. It was the first time since she'd met him that he seemed truly uncomfortable. "But I thought…I mean…I'd heard girls always like to take a lot of time to get ready and they complain if they don't get a chance to get dolled up and…I don't know. I was just trying to be polite. You don't need a shower. You smell great, like the fresh air high up in the sky. And you look beautiful."

His face reddened even more, and he shrugged his shoulders, looking at a complete loss as to what else to say. Bree felt her pulse quickening when he said that she was beautiful, and her face heated up even more. The electricity in the air between them practically crackled, and Bree suddenly found herself awkwardly trying to break the moment.

"We're walking distance from a bunch of restaurants, right?" she said abruptly. "Why don't we just walk down to the main street here and see what we can find?"

Knox looked immensely relieved. "Sounds good," he said. "I've heard there are some pretty good spots there."

Bree forced a smile, but she couldn't quite share the relief that Knox seemed to feel. All she could think about was that her heart was running away with her feelings—and choosing the worst possible time to do so.

CHAPTER TWELVE

Knox peered over his menu at Bree. Her brow was furrowed as she studied her own menu, and her skin was lit up in a warm orange glow by the light of the setting sun. They had found a restaurant with a large bar that boasted typical bar fare like burgers and wings, and Bree had seemed excited at the prospect of a large, juicy burger. The place had a large outdoor seating area and a lengthy beer list, so Knox had been more than happy to choose this place for dinner.

He would have been happy with any place, really, as long as Bree was there with him. He couldn't keep himself from staring at her every chance he got, even though he knew the idea of a romance with her was ridiculous. He lived with a bunch of bachelors in the middle of the woods, and Bree was used to living in a large community. A large *magical* community no less. Sure, he could change into a dragon. But that was the extent of his special abilities. What could a shifter like him offer a beautiful, intelligent wizard like her? Not much, he thought, other than brute strength to help fight another battle to get another dragon stone.

Knox tore his eyes away from Bree to stare at his menu again. His stomach felt like it was twisting up from the painful mix of emotions flooding through him. He hadn't given much thought to finding a lifemate until Bree showed up. He knew that trying to bring a woman home to the Redwoods would be complicated, and no woman had ever been enough to tempt him to deal with those complications.

Bree was different. It was more than just her beauty and intelligence that called to him. There was something more. When she looked at him and their eyes met, he felt like their hearts shared the same heartbeat. Even though in many ways their lives could not have been more different, they had also shared many of the same struggles. They had both lived as humans who weren't fully human, and had to live their lives on the fringes.

Knox wondered if it was actually possible that destiny had chosen a wizard for his fated lifemate. Was that even possible? Could two lives be so different and yet be destined to intertwine? He had always thought that the idea of fated lifemates was a little silly—until now. He'd thought that believing that there was one person for everyone was the same thing as believing in magic. Possible, perhaps, in your wildest dreams, but not likely. But the last several days had changed everything. He'd seen firsthand that magic did still exist, and not only in ancient artifacts but in living, breathing humans. The wizards still walked the earth. And if magic still walked the earth, then was it really such a stretch to think that perhaps love did, too?

"Knox?" Bree asked. "Are you okay?"

Bree's voice brought Knox sharply back to the present. He looked up to see Bree and their waitress both staring at him with funny expressions on their faces. The waitress was holding a pad of paper and a pencil and looking at him expectantly.

"If you need more time I can come back," the waitress said politely.

Knox realized that she was here to take his order, and he felt his cheeks heating up again as he realized that he'd been too caught up in thoughts of Bree to even realize what was going on around him.

"Oh, no, sorry," he said. "I, uh, I'm ready. Give me just a second. Bree, why don't you order first?"

The funny expression on Bree's face deepened. "I already ordered, Knox," she said. "Are you sure you're okay?"

"Oh, right, I knew that," he said, feeling even more foolish as he desperately scanned the menu. "I'm fine. I just have a lot on my mind. Um…give me the Western Burger, with extra cheese. And I'll take another beer when you get a chance. It's been a long day."

He gestured toward his nearly empty beer glass and smiled weakly. The waitress smiled back.

"Coming right up," she said. Knox could tell by her expression that she thought he was a bit of a nut case. Maybe he was. It was pretty nutty to be so caught up in a girl that you completely zoned out from everything going on around you.

After the waitress walked off, Knox forced himself to look up and meet Bree's eyes. She was still looking at him with concern, and the way she raised an eyebrow at him told him that she wasn't going to let him easily get away with saying that nothing was wrong.

"You're quite distracted," she said. It was more of a question than a statement. She was asking him why he was distracted, and he knew it.

Knox took a deep breath, trying to come up with some sort of explanation that would satisfy her curiosity, when a sudden, strange impulse took over him and he decided to tell her the truth.

"Well, you're quite distracting," he said, crossing his arms and leaning back in his chair. Truth be told, he could hardly believe that those words had just come out of his mouth. On the outside, though, he looked perfectly calm and cool.

"I'm…distracting?" Bree managed to ask. Her cheeks had turned pink, telling Knox that she had definitely understood what he meant. He decided he might as well run with the moment, now that he had admitted to his feelings.

"Yes, *you* are distracting," he said, his voice turning husky and low. "How am I supposed to think about finding a dragon stone, or about what could wrong if our plan fails, when the most beautiful woman in the world is sitting right in front of me?"

Bree's mouth fell open as she stared at him, gaping. Her cheeks went from pink to red, and she looked down at her beer without answering him. Knox felt a twitch of fear for a moment. Had he misread her signals? Was she not interested in him, after all? The worst thing in the world right now would be to make things awkward between them. They had an important job to do, and, if everything she was saying about the dragon sapphire was correct, then he really couldn't afford to mess this up.

Then, as quickly as he felt the fear, he pushed it down. He was a dragon, after all. And not just any dragon—he was leader of the Redwood Dragons. They were a fierce bunch, and he had been living small for too long. It was time for him to act like the warrior that he was. Knox lifted his chin high and reached his arm across the table. He put his palm under Bree's delicate chin and lifted it gently but firmly.

"Look at me," he commanded, his voice low and urgent.

She lifted her eyes to his, and he could feel the heat coming off of her face. She blinked a few times, looking uncertain, but he could see the desire in her eyes.

"I know this is bad timing," Knox said. "I know our lives are impossibly different. And I know that inviting a woman to be part of my life would bring some big changes for my clan and me. But I can't stop thinking about you, and how beautiful you are. I can't shake this feeling that you and I are meant to be together. That the reason we crossed paths out in the forest was deeper than just the dragon sapphire. And I cannot go another minute without telling you the truth. I want you, Bree. I think I have from the very first moment I met you, even if I wasn't willing to admit it to myself. You do funny things to my heart. Things no woman has ever done before. And trust me—I've had plenty of women from all over the world interested in me over the years. But I've always had a proud dragon heart, and I wouldn't allow them to conquer it. You're different, though. You're not even trying to win me over and you already have. I've known you less than a month and I already can't imagine life without you."

Knox could feel his heart threatening to beat out of his chest. His blood was running hot all through his body, practically boiling with the desire to strip Bree down and make love to her. He could hardly stand the way she was looking up at him right now, biting her soft lower lip uncertainly as she searched his eyes with her own. He didn't know what she was looking for, but whatever it was she must have found it. She slowly nodded her head before letting out a small, barely perceptible sigh.

"I'd be lying if I said I hadn't had similar thoughts," Bree said.

She didn't say any more than that, but those words, combined with the desire he could now clearly see in her eyes, were enough for Knox. He saw the waitress walking back toward them, and he dropped his hand from Bree's chin to reach into his back pocket for his wallet.

"We'll take our food to go," he said, then handed the waitress a credit card that he had quickly fished out of his wallet. "And please go ahead and close out our tab for us."

The waitress looked slightly confused, but nodded as she set down Knox's fresh beer in front of him. As soon as she scurried away with his credit card, Knox picked up the beer and drank it, letting it all slide down his throat as one long, continuous sip. The hoppy liquid burned in his veins, adding fuel to the fire that was already burning within him. He looked up at Bree, who was watching him intently without saying anything. Her hair, which was pulled up into a messy bun right now, was lit up brilliantly by the fading sunlight. Her skin glowed, and Knox realized with satisfaction that the flush in her cheeks was due to his words.

She wanted him. The most beautiful, wonderful girl he'd ever met wanted *him*. And Knox was going to do his damned best to make sure that she never changed her mind about that. He could feel a stiffening between his legs, and a thrill of electric heat coursing through his body. He let out a low groan as he watched Bree finish the last sips of her own beer.

That waitress needed to hurry up. Knox couldn't sit here much longer, waiting patiently for the chance to get his beautiful wizard home. He felt as though all of the gentle flirting they had done had quite suddenly come to a breaking point. The flood of desire was almost more than he could bear. Knox felt like he was drowning in the best possible way. Neither Knox nor Bree was speaking now. They were only looking at each other with knowing, hungry looks. They had both tried to resist this feeling. They had both told themselves they had no business indulging their own passions when the future of so many wizards, shifters, and humans was at stake. But now that they had admitted to each other that there was something kindling between them, it felt to Knox like an explosion had gone off. He could not hold back much longer. For the moment, at least, all thoughts of the dragon sapphire, of his clan, or of saving the world were gone. The only thing he could focus on was Bree.

Knox felt a rush of relief when the waitress returned with two takeout boxes and his credit card. He gave the girl a generous tip, then grabbed the boxes and stood.

"Let's go," he growled.

Bree didn't need to be asked twice. She stood, and left the restaurant's patio quickly, stepping onto the sidewalk without even a backward glance. Knox fell into step beside her, holding the takeout boxes with one arm and wrapping the other arm protectively around Bree's lower back. He rubbed the side of her hip with his thumb, and once or twice she shuddered with pleasure at his touch. He felt the stiffening between his legs growing, and he didn't have to glance down to know that by this point his desire must be quite obvious to everyone they passed. He could feel his erection pushing insistently against the thick fabric of his jeans, but he didn't feel embarrassed. Why should he be ashamed? Was it a crime to be uncontrollably infatuated with a woman as magnificent as Bree? If anything, anyone who noticed the bulge in his jeans should be jealous. He was the one lucky enough to have won Bree's favor.

The walk back to their tiny new apartment seemed to take forever, but finally, Knox found himself standing in front of their door, fumbling in his pocket for the keys. He felt like he couldn't move fast enough as he pushed the cold metal into the lock and turned it, then nearly dropped the takeout boxes of burgers and fries as he quickly shoved them onto the kitchen countertop. He would eat later. Right now, he had completely forgotten about every hunger pang except one—his hunger for Bree Riley.

As soon as the boxes were out of his hands, he reached both hands up to cup Bree's face in his palms. He pushed her backward against the first spot of open wall he could find. She reached up and grabbed his forearms, holding on tightly as he leaned in to put his lips on hers. Flames blazed through his body as they never had before. He might be able to breathe fire, but nothing in his life had ever compared to the heat of desire that he felt for Bree. She let out a moan, and pushed her hips forward to meet his, putting delicious, unbearable pressure against the spot where his erection was trying to break free right through his jeans.

It was going to be a good night.

CHAPTER THIRTEEN

Bree could hear all the voices in the back of her head, screaming at her that this was a bad idea, that she didn't have time to be making love with anyone right now, and that, worst of all, there was no way on earth she and Knox could make their lives work together for the long term.

Frankly, right now, she didn't give a shit.

The only thing she really cared about was that Knox Pars had his lips on hers and *damn*. He felt like heaven. She'd had to pinch herself back at the restaurant to believe that she wasn't dreaming when he very clearly let her know that she had not been imagining it when she thought he'd been flirting with her. Those looks of desire she'd seen over the last several days were definitely real.

The walk back to the apartment had been torture. She'd done her best to hold it together, but she'd felt the whole way as though she were about to burst from the tingling heat that had filled her more with every passing second. Knox had been stroking her hip, and every stroke had sent a fresh thrill through her. A near constant stream of desire had oozed out from between her legs, until she'd started to worry that she was getting so wet that people on the street would soon be able to tell.

But now, here in this tiny, old apartment, there was nothing left to hide. There was no more pretending, and no more worrying about what-ifs or consequences. There was only desire. Pure, raw, primal desire. Bree melted into Knox's body as he pushed himself up against her. She was trapped so tightly between him and the wall that it was difficult to breathe, but she didn't care. She loved the way he felt against her, and only wished he could be even closer. She wanted their bodies to be one.

Overcome by the passion building inside of her, she reached down to find the hem of his t-shirt. She tore it upward in a desperate motion, not wanting to break their kiss but wanting to feel the bare skin of his chest. Knox pulled back for a split-second to help her pull off the shirt, then quickly resumed the kiss. His tongue was warm and smooth, sliding past her lips to dance with her tongue and to caress the roof of her mouth. Bree put her palms against his chest now, feeling his bare chest for the first time. She had seen it a few times before, since he was always naked when he shifted. But she had always tried so hard to look politely away, and not to notice how wonderful it was.

Now, she allowed herself to fully appreciate it. She let her hands explore, running first across his firm, broad shoulders, then drifting down to his strong, expansive ribcage. She groaned with pleasure as she felt the contours of his stomach, which were shaped into a perfect six-pack. He responded to her groan, pushing his hips harder against hers so that she got a fresh feel of how stiff his erection was. Then he pulled back a bit, breaking their kiss and catching his breath.

He reached for her shirt now, pulling it up and off before reaching behind her back to undo the clasp of her simple, skin-colored bra. Bree trembled as he slid the straps down, slowly and gently removing the garment and leaving her bare-chested in front of him. Her breasts, swollen with desire, rose and fell rapidly as she tried in vain to catch

61

her breath. She reached for the button of his jeans, unfastening it and fumbling as she tried to find the zipper, but he smiled at her and shook his head.

"Not so fast," he said in a husky whisper. "First, I want to do something I must admit I've dreamed of doing since the moment I met you."

And then, he leaned down so his mouth was at the same level as her hard, alert nipples. He closed his teeth over her right nipple, chewing in a firm, steady rhythm that sent a constant stream of tingling heat pulsing through her body. He reached up with his hand to take the other nipple in between his thumb and forefinger, rubbing it with the same rhythm, and causing the pressure in Bree's body to become almost unbearable. She arched her back and moaned, but he gave her no reprieve. And, of course, she honestly didn't want one. His body pleasuring hers was the most intense but most wonderful sensation she had ever experienced.

She could feel that her panties had now become completely soaked, drenched with the juices of her desire for him. He must have known it, too. He reached his hands down to unbutton and unzip her jeans, never taking his mouth away from her nipples. Then he plunged one of his hands down between her skin and the fabric of her panties, reaching past her soft mound and finding her slick entrance with his fingers. He plunged his middle finger into her, causing her to gasp at the sudden heat that filled her once again. Then he used his pointer finger to massage her clit at the same time.

Bree felt like her whole body was going up in the most magnificent, uncontrollable flames. Tingling heat filled her body. Delicious pressure built in her core. Her nipples felt electric, and her legs trembled from the effort of trying to hold her body up while Knox's hand drove itself deep into her body.

Bree tried to hold back, but it was nearly impossible. She could only take a few moments of this intensity before her body gave in. She threw back her head and screamed, yelling out Knox's name as her inner muscles began spasming and clenching around his hand. He straightened up and reached his free arm around her, pulling her away from the wall and close to his body as she trembled and found the greatest pleasure she had ever known simply from the movement of his fingers.

It took quite some time for the tremors to stop racking Bree's body. When the pleasure she felt gradually shifted from spasms to a steady, warm heat, Bree let her body fall limp against Knox's strong form. He held her securely in his arms, and kissed the top of her head. She shivered with delight, all of her senses on overload.

Then, she felt herself go weightless. He was lifting her up in his strong arms, carrying her toward the small bedroom of the apartment. He dropped her lightly on the bed, then started grasping for the lamp. The light was fading fast now, and the blinds were closed in the bedroom, so it was rather dark. But Bree liked the darkness. She felt suddenly self-conscious. It had been so long since she'd been with a man, and Knox's body was so perfect. What would he think of her when he saw her fully, in all her curvy imperfection?

"Leave it off," she pleaded as she heard his fingers reaching the metal of the lamp switch.

He understood well why she had made the request, and he ignored it. A moment later, soft yellow light filled the room as the lamp flickered on.

"I want to see all of you," he said gently, pushing her down so she was lying on her back on the bed. He reached to pull off her shoes and socks. Bree had been so caught up in the moment back by the door that she hadn't even realized she was still wearing her shoes. Knox traced a line across the top of her feet with his fingers, and the motion somehow felt intensely intimate. Next, he reached up to pull off her jeans, which were hanging loosely on her hips since he had already unbuttoned them. She shivered as the cool air of the bedroom hit the bare skin of her legs, but she knew her shivers had more to do with nerves than with the temperature of the room. She felt so vulnerable in that moment. Did he like what he saw?

As if in answer to her silent question, he let out a deep groan as he let his eyes slide over her nearly naked body.

"God, you're beautiful," he whispered in a deep, hoarse whisper. Bree shivered again, this time from delight. Knox moved to pull her underwear off next. He dragged off her simple cotton panties in one impatient movement, leaving a trail of wet juices down her legs from the now soaking garment. Bree felt almost embarrassed by how wet she had become so quickly. She couldn't help it. Knox brought out deep desires in her that she hadn't even known she could feel. Her embarrassment didn't last long, though. He was clearly pleased by how turned on she had become.

"You're so wet for me," he said, his voice hungry with desires of his own. He crawled onto the bed, leaning over her and using his tongue to lick up the line of Bree's own juices that was now running down her leg. He didn't slow down when he got to the top of her thighs, where her legs gave way to her still-dripping entrance. In fact, he sped up, slipping his tongue deep inside of her. Bree squeezed her eyes tightly shut as a fresh wave of tingling heat washed over her. His tongue was soft and warm inside of her, licking up the juices of her desire and searching for the most sensitive spots within her. He wanted to drive her crazy, and he was doing a damn good job of it. He flicked his tongue deep into her, then pulled up slightly and massaged her clit with it. At the same time, he reached his hands up to hold her breasts, one in each hand. He massaged her nipples between his thumb and forefinger while driving her crazy down below with his mouth.

It didn't take long for Bree to lose control again. Any worries over what he thought of her naked body had quickly disappeared, replaced by the realization that she was nearing her second orgasm of the night—and he hadn't even taken his pants off yet. No man had ever made her feel this way. She writhed underneath him, the pressure in her core once again reaching a point that was more than she could take, and then breaking over her in hot, tingling spasms. She screamed out his name once more, her inner muscles clenching around his tongue this time. She could hardly believe it, but this wave of pleasure lasted even longer than the first.

Knox pulled back, smiling. His face was wet from her desire, and he looked as though he might burst from pride. He had made his woman feel incredible, and he knew it. But he wasn't done yet. He stepped off the bed, pushing off his jeans and tight black briefs and allowing his erection to spring free. For the first time, Bree allowed herself to look at him fully in his nakedness. He looked like a god to her, perfect in every way. Every muscle on his body was large and sculpted. His six-pack of abs ended right before a "v" shape in his lower stomach muscles pointed downward toward a fuzzy trail that led to his enormous dick, which right now was stiff and erect, pointing right toward her. The only noise Bree could manage to make was a long, desperate moan. God, she wanted him inside of her. Really inside of her. Not just his hands or his tongue, but *him*. The most intimate part of him.

He did not make her wait long. He slid back onto the bed and slid over her, hovering right above her for a moment and smiling with such affection in his eyes that Bree felt like her heart might burst. He gently kissed her nose, and then her lips.

"You're perfect," he whispered. "Absolutely perfect."

And then, he slid into her. Slowly, but firmly, he filled her. She felt him going even deeper into her than she had thought was possible. He reached to her very core, and she trembled as their bodies became one. He moved in her with perfect rhythm, rocking back and forth and sending new bursts of heat across her being with every thrust. Bree could hardly believe that it was possible to feel as wonderful as she did in that moment. Even though he had already made her come twice in the last half-hour, she felt herself on the verge of exploding once again. Her body tingled and trembled, and she closed her eyes and let the sensation wash over her. She didn't even try to fight it this time. She just let the pressure build until it reached its breaking point, and her body quivered with tremors of delight. This time, her inner walls were squeezing around his erection as she came. The sensation was much more intense than it had been for his fingers or tongue. Each spasm sent fresh fire through her being, and all she could do was lie there, letting the wonder of it pass through her. She did not even have the energy left to scream at this point.

She opened her eyes for a moment and saw that Knox had closed his own eyes at this point. He was moving faster and faster now, nearing his own wonderful release. Before Bree's body had even finished trembling, he let out a long, loud roar. His body stiffened, and he found his release, pulsing into Bree and truly becoming one with her.

It took several minutes for them to both catch their breath again. When they had, Knox slid out of Bree and lay beside her, pulling her into his arms. They could not sleep yet. It was too early. They had cold burgers to reheat and eat, and plans to make for tomorrow. But, for now, they let themselves savor this moment, safe and content in each other's arms.

And in that moment, he was not a dragon and she was not a wizard. They were not two people living two completely different lives, with no idea how they could build a life together. They were just two people, with hearts that had the same heartbeat.

Bree smiled happily and snuggled her face into Knox's chest. What more did you really need than that?

CHAPTER FOURTEEN

Even though the blinds were closed, the bright morning sun somehow found a way to stream into the tiny bedroom of the apartment. Knox's face lay inconveniently right in the path of the large sunbeam, and so he woke very early, even before the alarm clock had gone off. The summer days were long right now, and the sun rose before most of Mountain View's residents had opened their sleepy eyes.

Knox looked over at Bree, whose face was turned away from the window at the moment. She was snuggled deeply underneath the dark gray comforter, which was rising and falling with the rhythm of her sleep. A smile turned up the corners of Knox's lips as he looked at her. He could hardly believe what had happened between them last night. It had been a whirlwind day, and he had never expected it to end with the chance to make love to Bree. But he was eternally grateful for that chance. He felt deep down in his bones that she was his lifemate. Her soul was connected to his, and they had bonded. He would find a way to make things work between them, no matter what the price. She was worth it. If he had to give up his position as leader of the Redwood Dragons to be with her, then he would. He hoped with all his heart that it wouldn't come to that, but he was willing to give up everything for Bree. She made him whole in a way he had never been whole before.

A buzzing from Knox's phone drew him out of his reverie. He looked over to see that Noah was calling him. Knox sat up quickly, surprised. It was still rather early for Noah to be calling. Was something wrong back in the Redwoods? Were his clan members all okay?

Knox grabbed the phone, slipping silently out of the bedroom and closing the door behind him so that he wouldn't wake Bree. He answered the call quickly once he made it to the apartment's living room.

"Noah? Is everything alright?"

"Hey, boss! Yes, everything's fine. Sorry if I woke you, but I've actually got some good news."

"Don't worry. I was already awake," Knox said. "What's your news?"

"I got a call from a guy I met in Portugal. A bear shifter who helped me a lot with my mission over there. I trust the guy completely. He's one of the ones who told me he'd heard rumors of there being more dragon stones, and he's been following the news on the dragon sapphire closely. He learned last night that the sapphire should be arriving in Mountain View today. It was supposed to be coming next week, but the gem collector bumped up the timeline quite suddenly because he got wind that someone might be trying to steal it."

"Looks like the other guys who are after it are being sloppy, huh?" Knox asked.

"Maybe," Noah said. "Or maybe more shifters are learning that the dragon sapphire exists. I talked with Pierce and he's worried that word has leaked out."

Knox frowned. "That's not good news," he said.

Pierce was a unicorn shifter, and one of the shifter protectors. He had helped with the recovery of the emerald dragon stone, the original dragon stone that, until a few days ago, Knox had thought was the only dragon stone in existence. As a shifter protector, Pierce was responsible for the safety of the shifter community as a whole, and he kept a close eye on anything that might threaten shifter safety. Pierce had seen it all, and if he was worried, there was probably reason to be worried.

"Well, if word *has* leaked out, the best thing to do is take care of getting the dragon sapphire as soon as possible. The sooner we can get a hold of it, the less chance there will be of someone with bad intentions getting their hands on it. And I think today might be your best shot at it."

"Sounds like you've got a plan worked out?" Knox asked.

"I do," Noah said. "I've spoken with our contact who was working on the fake dragon stone for you. He's all finished up with the replica, and he's going to meet you at your apartment to drop it off. He should be there in about an hour. Then, you and Bree are going to intercept the armored guard driving the truck with the real stone to the gem collector's house. The gem collector flew in to Los Angeles to try to confuse people, and now he's riding back to Silicon Valley in one of those trucks driven by an armored guard. He's coming up Highway 101, and the bear shifter I spoke with has eyes on the truck. He's going to let us know when it's getting close to you guys, and we'll plan an intercept somewhere on a relatively deserted stretch of highway."

"You're sure you can trust this guy?" Knox asked, although he already knew the answer to the question. Noah would not be listening to the man if he didn't trust him.

"He's definitely trustworthy," Noah said. "He's a good guy, and helped me out a lot on my last mission. He wants to make sure that the good shifters stay in power. He told me his family lost a lot during the last great shifter war, when the evil shifters almost took over. He has a son, and he wants to make sure that his son doesn't have to deal with the same horrors he did during his childhood."

"Okay," Knox said, satisfied by Noah's explanation. It was a common story, shared by many shifters around Knox's age. Knox himself was an orphan due to the last shifter war, as were the rest of the Redwood Dragons. They understood all too well how much could be lost when evil took over.

"So the only hitch in our plan is that we don't really have a plan for how to replace the dragon sapphire without the armored guard or the gem collector realizing what we're doing," Noah said. "Ideally, we'd like to make the switch without them realizing anything had happened. That way we don't have to fight them. This would also keep the bad guys off our trail. If they think the gem collector still has the real stone, they'll keep chasing him instead of chasing after us. Hopefully, by the time they realize that a switch has been made, we'll be far, far away and they'll have no idea who was actually behind the switch. That'll make it much easier to keep the dragon stone safe."

"That would be ideal," Knox agreed. "But it's going to be tough to replace a dragon stone in an armored, guarded vehicle without anyone realizing what's going on."

"I know," Noah said. "But we were kind of hoping that Bree might have some tricks up her sleeve. There's got to be some sort of spell she could cast to distract the guard and the gem collector."

Knox couldn't keep a smile off his face at the mention of Bree's name. "I'll ask her," he said. "I'm not very knowledgeable on the latest wizard trends, but hopefully she knows of something that will work."

"Alright, well, keep me posted on what she says. I'd suggest that as soon as the fake sapphire has been dropped off that you guys start driving south on Highway 101. The sooner you can intercept the armored vehicle, the more chances you might have to make the switch."

"Roger that," Knox said. "I'll go wake Bree up and we'll start getting ready to go.

How are things with the clan?"

"Everything's great," Noah said. "Don't worry about us. The guys here are working on some practice missions, and the guys out on the field are making good progress on their real missions. Everything is running smoothly."

"Sounds like you don't need me at all," Knox said with a laugh.

Noah chuckled. "We do need you. We need each member of our crew. We make a good team together."

"Very true," Knox said, pride filling his chest. His dragons were all special in their own ways, and together the ten of them made a powerful team.

"Alright, well, I'm going to let you go so I can get back in touch with the guy bringing you the fake stone. I'll let you know when I have an exact time that he'll be arriving."

"Ok," Knox said. "Bree and I will start working on a plan for swapping out the stones."

"Sounds good, keep me updated," Noah said.

"Will do."

Knox hung up the call, then looked up and nearly jumped out of his skin when he saw Bree standing in the hallway, leaning against the wall and smiling over at him.

"Hey you," she said with a slight chuckle. "Startled you, didn't I?"

"I'll say," Knox said, shaking his head. "I didn't hear you moving at all."

"Wizards are pretty good at stealth," Bree said. "But unfortunately there's no spell for listening in to the other side of the phone conversation. Sounds like you got an update on our mission?"

Knox nodded. "Yup, that was Noah. Looks like we're going to be on the move today. Which is too bad, because I'd like nothing more than to spend the day in bed with you."

Bree smiled. "Trust me, the feeling is quite mutual. But we knew that we'd be busy. Finding the dragon sapphire is more important than anything else right now."

"Well, today might be the day we actually recover it," Knox said. Then he filled Bree in on everything Noah had told him. Bree furrowed her brow and came to sit at the small kitchen table. Knox followed her with his eyes, taking in how lovely she looked even with her messed up bed head hair, and wrinkled sweatpants and t-shirt. He felt a stiffening between his legs and he knew his eyes were blazing with desire. If only he had met her some other time, when the fate of so many people wasn't resting on their shoulders. He would have loved to forget all his responsibilities for a while and run off with her, soaking in every moment together.

But now was not the time to leave behind responsibilities. And, besides, the dragon sapphire had brought them together. It had brought wizards back into the world of shifters. Perhaps Knox would never have met her if it hadn't been for the stone. All he had to do now was get the stone quickly today, and then he'd have time with Bree. Simple, right?

Something told him that things were unlikely to work out so quickly and easily.

"It wouldn't be that hard to trick them, actually," Bree said. "I could use an invisibility spell to hide from them. Then I could use an unlocking spell to open the truck. The hardest part will be making sure they don't see the truck opening. I can't make the truck door itself invisible because that would be too obvious. So even if I'm invisible myself, they'll still see the door of the truck opening."

"Can't you do some sort of spell to cloud their eyes or something?" Knox asked.

"I could," Bree said. "But then they might get suspicious. They would know that their eyes were clouded over, and unless they were idiots they would guess that it was because someone was trying to steal the stone."

"But you would have switched the stones out by the time their eyes were unclouded and they checked the stone. So they would think everything was fine," Knox said.

"Maybe," Bree said, but her voice was doubtful. "But I'm worried that if they have any hint that something is going on that they would check to make sure the stone hadn't been replaced with a fake. It seems to me that the gem collector is very suspicious already. He wouldn't fly to a different airport and hire an armored vehicle with a guard if he didn't think that someone was trying to get the stone. And if he thinks that someone is trying to get the stone, he'll probably double check to make sure it's not a fake."

Knox shrugged. He supposed that Bree was right. They could not be too careful, as far as Knox was concerned. He wanted this stone recovered today so this mission could be wrapped up and he could focus on other things—like getting back to his dragons and spending time with Bree.

"How long do you think it will take you to do the unlocking spell and switch the stones?" Knox asked.

"It's hard to say," Bree replied. "It depends a lot on how complicated the locks are on the vehicle. But I've always been good at unlocking spells, so unless the locks are crazy different from anything I've seen before, I should be able to make the switch in five minutes tops."

"Will the unlocking spell be noisy?" Knox asked.

Bree shook her head no. "Not any noisier than the door of the back gate of the truck opening. The unlocking spells should not set off any alarms because they aren't actually 'breaking into' the doors. They're actually unlocking them in proper fashion."

"Maybe it's as simple as distracting the guys with conversation, then," Knox said. "If we can catch them before they stop for lunch, then we should be able to easily make the switch. The drive from L.A. to here is long enough that they're bound to want to stop for lunch, or at least a snack, right? When they do stop, I'll just talk to them for a few minutes so they aren't watching the truck, and then you can switch the stones."

"That's probably the best plan," Bree said. "But it does assume that they'll be stopping, and that the back gate of the truck will be facing away from the window of wherever they stop. I'm worried that they might only stop once, and that they'll still be closely watching the truck. The drive isn't *that* long, you know. It's not even seven a.m. now. If they've already left and they drive straight here, they'll be in Mountain View by lunchtime."

"You're right," Knox said with a frown. "We might need to create a diversion of some sort. Like a closed road."

Bree looked up at him and grinned. "Oh that should be easy enough. Although it will require damaging the road, which is probably against the law."

Knox laughed at the mischievous look in her eye. "I'm pretty sure that stealing an enormous sapphire is against the law, too. If we're going to be criminals, we might as well keep going once we've started."

"True enough," Bree said. "Sounds like it's time for me to put some destructive spells to work."

Knox grinned, and just then his phone buzzed. It was a text from Noah.

The guy with the fake stone will be at your door in ten minutes. The real stone is on the move, an hour north of Los Angeles. We are monitoring its position closely.

Knox looked up at Bree. "We better get dressed. The fake stone will be here in ten minutes, and we should be ready to move as soon as possible after that."

Bree's eyes widened as she nodded over at him.

"I can't believe it's actually possible that we might get the stone the first day we're here," she said. "I thought it was going to take much longer than that."

"I did, too," Knox said. "Which is why we got the apartment. But if we don't actually need the apartment, I'm not going to complain. If we get the stone on our first attempt, that would be a dream come true. More time to get to know you."

He winked at Bree, and she blushed, then abruptly stood.

"I'm gonna go get changed," she said.

Knox watched her walk toward the bedroom, his heart beating wildly in his chest.

"Please let this crazy plan work today," he said aloud to the empty room. "I need more Bree time in my life."

He'd never thought he'd be the type to pine for a woman. But oh, how quickly things could change when you found the right woman.

CHAPTER FIFTEEN

Bree squinted at the road ahead of her, wishing she hadn't forgotten her sunglasses at the apartment. The sun was unbelievably bright today, and after several days of being in the relative shade of the Redwood forest, her eyes protested at its unforgiving brilliance.

She glanced over at Knox, who was in the passenger seat with his cell phone glued to his ear, consulting with Noah about the location of the armored car. According to Noah's sources, who were following the armored car at a distance, the armored car had not yet stopped. It was speeding toward Silicon Valley at a consistent pace of ten miles per hour above the speed limit—the perfect pace to go as fast as you could without running a real risk of being pulled over by the police.

Bree glanced down at Knox's lap, where an inconspicuous cardboard box was sitting. The box looked like one of those simple favor boxes you might get at a child's birthday party, but what it held was quite different from plastic childhood trinkets. The box held the fake dragon sapphire, which had been dropped off at the apartment in Mountain View about an hour earlier. Bree had marveled at the replica, which filled the entire palm of her hand and looked surprisingly like a real sapphire. Bree was no expert in gemstones, but even she could tell that this was not some cheap knockoff. The guy who had made this replica knew a thing or two about making fake gemstones. Bree had a feeling that it would have fooled even an expert.

But would it fool the gemstone collector and the armored guard? That was all that mattered for today. They needed to replace the stone quickly and without the gem collector knowing what had happened. Bree glanced down at the giant gem that adorned her own finger—the large ruby on her magic ring, which glinted brilliantly in the sunlight. She felt a nervous twisting in the pit of her stomach as she reviewed in her mind the spells she was planning to use to carve a large fissure in the middle of the highway, effectively blocking traffic, and, hopefully, giving her a chance to steal the real dragon sapphire.

Bree had not done much magic since leaving Falcon Cross. Aside from the spells in the forest to hide from Knox, and then the few spells to prove to the Redwood Dragons that she was a wizard, there had not been much need for magic. Bree felt nervous now, as she thought about using such strong magic spells so far away from the wizard town where she had grown up. She was painfully aware, for perhaps the first time in her life, of just how different she was from normal humans. Sure, she had studied interactions with non-wizards in detail during her time in Advocacy school. But that had all been history and theory. She'd never been in a position where she needed to use magic in front of non-wizards. Casting spells in front of the dragon shifters hadn't been so bad. After all, they were "different," too. They understood what it was like to have special powers. But full humans, well, that was another story. If they saw what Bree was doing, they were likely to throw a fit about it. The last thing Bree wanted to do right now was draw attention to herself like that.

Bree wondered as she drove whether the wizards searching for her had any clue where she was. They obviously had not discovered the Redwood Dragons hideout, and

Bree was thankful for that. But the closer she got to the dragon sapphire, the more she started to worry that she was going to be found out. After all, it was no secret that she was worried about the dragon stone falling into the wrong hands. It would not take a genius to guess that she was in pursuit of the stone. Not only that, but Bree had written a detailed report on the location of the dragon sapphire while she was still working as an Advocate. She had included the fact that it was likely to end up in Mountain View, and she had even reported the addresses for the multiple homes the wealthy gem collector owned throughout the San Francisco Bay Area. The more Bree thought about it, the more she realized that strolling around in plain view in the middle of Mountain View had probably been an enormously foolish idea. She was lucky there had not been wizard spies already there and waiting for her.

Perhaps she had just been lucky, but in any case, Bree told herself that if this mission today failed, she was not going to casually stroll around in Silicon Valley anymore. She had to be more careful.

"Noah said the armored vehicle is less than fifteen minutes away from us right now," Knox said, breaking into Bree's thoughts. "He thinks this is probably a good time to start finding a spot to destroy the road and cause a backup. If we wait too long, we won't leave ourselves any wiggle room if something goes wrong. Besides, we're somewhat in the middle of nowhere right now. It's probably better to wreck the road out here than near a larger city."

Bree nodded, and put on her turn signal to take the next exit. "I'll just flip around to the other side of the highway then, and get going on the spell."

She felt as though her heart was in her throat. She hadn't felt this nervous since she took her final exams for her Advocacy diploma, but even that seemed now like it had been a much smaller deal than this. Bree couldn't afford to screw this up. She had to block the road and stop the armored car at just the right time so they would be caught in a hopeless backup, and she had to do it in a way that no one would see her and know it was her.

Luckily, it was deserted enough on this stretch of highway that no one was likely to see her performing spells, or think anything suspicious of their car parked on the shoulder of the road. Bree drove around so that she was now on the northbound side of the highway and she pulled to a stop on the side of the road just before an exit.

"I'm going to do all the damage right behind us," she said. "Then we can immediately exit and drive on the southbound highway until we can turn around and get on the northbound highway again. We should have no trouble doing that before they close down the entrance ramps. I want to be near the front of the traffic, but not at the very front. I'm hoping to avoid being questioned by the police about whether I saw anything happen."

Knox nodded, glancing down at his phone. "Sounds good to me," he said. "Noah just texted that the armored car is about ten minutes from us now. Let's get this road torn up, and hope that this works."

Bree gave Knox what she hoped was a confident nod, and then she stepped out of the car. Every few seconds, a car whizzed by her. Even out here, on this deserted stretch of land, there weren't very many extended breaks in the traffic. Bree waited until one of the longer breaks and then pointed her magic ring at the road.

"*Magicae inferno,*" she yelled. A white hot flame burst from her ring, much larger than the smaller fire from the *ignis* spell. The *inferno* spell brought about an instant wall of flames that was enough to melt the pavement and send flames shooting several feet into the air. The impressive flames were an important part of Bree's plan. She planned to send a huge fissure across the road next, but she wanted to also cause some sort of destruction that was easily visible, so that cars would not just drive into a fissure at eighty miles an hour.

As Bree had hoped, the cars approaching the wall of flames saw it from a good distance away, and slowed to a halt some distance away from the fire.

"Alright, time to make this little blockage truly effective," Bree said. She pointed her magic ring at the road directly behind the fire.

"*Magicae destruam!*" Bree said. This was a demolishing spell—one which Bree had struggled with all during advocacy school. Today, though, she managed to execute it perfectly. A laser-like beam of light shot forth from her magic ring and suddenly the road behind the fire began to split in two. A huge fissure appeared, making it look like a giant earthquake had torn the road apart. For a moment, Bree stared at the destruction in awe, hardly able to believe that she had pulled off the spell so well. But Knox's voice quickly spurred her back to action.

"Come on, my little wizard," he called from the car, his voice urgent. "We need to get moving."

Bree ran back to the car, jumping into the driver's seat and speeding quickly away from the fire and ruined roadway. Their rental car roared down the exit ramp, and Bree quickly turned around under the nearby overpass. She sped down the access road next to the southbound highway until she came to another overpass, where she turned around again and took the next entrance ramp to get back onto the northbound highway. Already, cars were backing up. Toward the front of the line, she could see drivers starting to get out of their vehicles and talk to each other, many of them scratching their heads as they pointed toward the flames, which were beginning to die down somewhat. The road had melted away, and not much fuel was left for the fire. But the gaping split in the highway just beyond the dwindling fire was more impressive than the flames, anyway. Bree saw the drivers near the front of the line starting to point at the hole, shaking their heads and gesturing wildly. Bree had to hold back a giggle. She wished she could hear what they were saying.

A few minutes later, the sound of police sirens filled the air, and three police cars came roaring up the shoulder of the highway toward the destruction. Bree watched as the policemen surveyed the damage, then started talking to the drivers near the front of the line. Above them, the whirring of a news helicopter could be heard. This mystery fissure in the road had quickly caught the interest of the local television networks.

Knox, who had been on the phone with Noah, suddenly turned to Bree.

"Alright, Noah's source says the armored car is caught up in the backup less than a quarter mile behind us," Knox said. "Are you ready to go switch the stones?"

Bree nodded, although she didn't feel ready. She felt slightly sick to her stomach, thinking of everything that could go wrong. But she couldn't think about all the awful possibilities now. She just had to do her best, and trust that things would work out. Knox pulled the fake dragon sapphire out of the small cardboard box, and handed it to Bree.

"Good luck," he said, leaning over to kiss her.

"Thanks," she whispered, taking a moment to relish how wonderful his lips felt on hers. Oh, how she hoped that tonight they would have the real dragon sapphire safely in their possession, so they could take time to relax in each other's arms. But hope by itself wasn't enough. Bree needed to take action.

"You'll need to take the driver's seat," she told Knox as she put the fake sapphire securely into the front pocket of her light hoodie. "I'll walk back and, if all goes according to plan, I'll get the real sapphire without anyone seeing me. When I get back, I'll perform a repairing spell on the road. No doubt, this will hopelessly confuse the policemen, but it should get traffic moving again before too long. We can escape with the rest of the crowd, and, if we're lucky, no one will realize that the real sapphire is missing for quite some time."

"Sounds good," Knox said. "If you run into trouble or need help, shoot some flames up into the air from your ring."

"I hope it doesn't come to that," Bree said. "But if I'm in dire straits I'll send you a signal."

Knox nodded, his eyes looking worried. "Be careful," he whispered.

Bree gave him a brave smile, then took a deep breath and said *"Magicae invisibilia."*

Instantly, she disappeared from view. She saw Knox shake his head in amazement, then reach out to feel the spot in the driver's seat where she had just been. Of course, his hand ran into her body even though he couldn't see it. The spell made her invisible, not immaterial.

"So weird," he said, shaking his head.

"I know," Bree said. "But no time to play around now. I have to go."

Quickly, she opened the car door and left the vehicle, hoping that no one was watching closely enough to realize that the door appeared to have just opened by itself. She doubted that anyone was paying that much attention to her car. Everyone was gaping toward the front of the backup, where police lights were flashing and helicopters were hovering. Bree started running, unseen, through the stationary line of cars. She wasn't in the greatest of shape, so she was glad when she saw an armored vehicle not too far in the distance. She made for it as fast as she could manage, stopping right in front of it and peering through the front windshield to see, to her relief, that the man in the passenger seat looked exactly like the pictures of the gem collector she had seen when doing her research as an Advocate.

The gem collector was on his cell phone, rubbing his forehead in annoyance and shaking his head as he looked at the long line of cars. The armored guard was on his phone, too, and didn't look much happier than the gem collector. Bree hoped that both of them would be too distracted to realize when the back gate of the vehicle opened. Her heart was beating so fast she felt like it was going to leap out of her chest, but she forced herself to remain calm. She clutched the fake sapphire in her pocket, making sure it was still there and secure. Then she crept around to the back of the vehicle and pointed her wand at the back gate.

"Magicae resero," she whispered. This was the unlocking spell. She heard a click as the door unlocked, and she held her breath as she waited to see whether the guard or the gem collector would turn around. Neither one of them did, and Bree breathed a sigh of relief. But she realized that there was no way the noise from opening the back gate would go unnoticed. It would be too loud, and she needed a distraction. She stepped back from the vehicle and looked around, trying to think of what to do. In the lane next to the armored vehicle, a man was bopping his head to the beat of his radio. The hip-hop music was rather loud, and Bree could make out almost all the words even though all of the man's windows were closed. Bree smiled. Maybe this was her answer. She pointed her magic ring carefully at the man's radio, and spoke.

"Magicae amplificare," she said. The amplifying spell instantly shot the volume of the man's radio to its highest possible level. The man covered his ears, startled, and then tried to turn down the volume on the radio. The volume did not change, and he jumped out of his vehicle, cursing and covering his ears.

Bree knew she only had a few seconds of confusion to take advantage of the moment. She slid the back gate of the armored vehicle open, then jumped in and slid it shut behind her. Finding the stone was easy enough. The back of the vehicle was filled

73

with several soft bags of what she guessed was currency, and then one small black box anchored securely to the side of the vehicle.

"*Magicae resero,*" she whispered, pointing her ring at the box. It clicked open, and she pulled the lid up to reveal a giant sapphire.

"Bingo," she said to herself. She quickly switched out the real stone with her fake one, closed the lid, and whispered, "*Magicae sero.*" The spell relocked the box, and Bree turned to leave the vehicle, but she was too late. The guard and gem collector had turned around now to look through the thick glass between the driver's cabin and the back of the vehicle.

"Reckon I should check on the cargo," the guard said. "That guy is probably just an idiot who messed up his radio, but you know how these things go. The moment you assume something is not a distraction being used to get access to your cargo is the moment you get robbed."

The gem collector had turned around to look too, and was nodding. Bree had never been so thankful for the invisibility spell, but she knew she had no way to get out of the vehicle before the guard came around. Not with the gem collector in the front seat, watching.

"*Magicae sero,*" she whispered quickly, pointing her ring at the back gate of the vehicle to relock it before the guard got there. Then she scooted as close as she could to the back of the vehicle, waiting for him to open the gate himself. As soon as the gate was opened, Bree jumped past the guard, who frowned as he felt a strange rush of wind, but shrugged it off when he looked around and didn't see anything.

Bree stood outside the vehicle for a moment, waiting and watching as the guard checked. Apparently satisfied, the guard turned and left the vehicle, relocking it behind him. Bree shivered at the sight of the large gun the man was armed with, but she told herself to remain calm. He didn't know she was there, and as far as he was concerned, everything was still there in the vehicle. Bree fingered the sapphire in her pocket, which was now the real dragon sapphire. She could hardly believe she had pulled it off.

She realized suddenly that she needed to get going. She was standing there, invisible and staring at the armored vehicle like an idiot. She started to run back toward the front of the line of cars, when she realized that the poor man with the amplified radio was still standing outside of his vehicle, cursing and kicking his tires. Bree raised her ring and pointed it toward the man's radio again.

"*Amplificare terminantur,*" she said. The radio instantly returned to a normal level, leaving the man who owned the car standing there scratching his head in confusion.

Bree ran back to the front of the line of cars, where several more police cars and helicopters had now arrived. The police were trying to figure out a way to direct cars across the steep grass to the access road, since the fissure in the road didn't look like anything that was going to be fixed any time soon. The fire had burned itself down completely by now, leaving melted pavement in front of the giant crack in the road. Bree saw Knox sitting in the driver's seat of their rental car, looking anxiously around and tapping his fingers nervously on the steering wheel. Bree couldn't keep a small smile off her face when she saw the look of concern on his face. She knew that a great part of that concern was because he cared about her, and that knowledge warmed her heart.

She didn't have time right now to sit around watching Knox be concerned for her, though. They needed to get out of here as quickly as possible, and get the dragon sapphire somewhere safe. Bree crept up to the break in the road, still invisible. She raised her magic ring and pointed it toward the heavily damaged roadway.

"*Magicae sarcio,*" she said, a powerful repairing spell. Instantly, the large fissure in the road started closing up. Then the melted areas morphed back into normal pavement. The astonished police officers and onlookers were shouting and pointing. Many of them were backing away from the spot that had just been damaged, as if afraid that it would suddenly come back more damaged than ever. Bree started creeping back toward the rental car, then jumped in quickly next to Knox, who nearly jumped out of his skin when the passenger door of the car opened seemingly by itself.

"Jesus, that invisibility trick is enough to make someone think they're losing their mind," he said, shaking his head as he reached out to poke Bree even though he couldn't see her.

"*Invisibilia terminantur*," Bree said. Within moments, the spell lifted and Knox could see her again.

"Did you get it?" he asked.

Bree nodded, and slowly pulled the sapphire out of her pocket. Knox whistled.

"It looks exactly like the fake one," he said.

"I know," Bree said. "It's crazy. Hopefully this really is the real one."

"I don't see why it wouldn't be," Knox said. "But we'll need to get out of here before we can really examine it. You should probably put it away, in fact. It's not safe to be waving it around with so many other people around."

Bree nodded and put the stone back in her hoodie pocket. She felt strange, knowing that she had such a valuable jewel just sitting there in her pocket like that. She looked back toward the front of the line of cars, and saw that the police were talking to each other, looking confused. They probably were not sure whether it was safe to let people drive over a spot that had been a giant hole only moments before. For several minutes, they consulted. Finally, it looked like they were going to let one lane of cars at a time go on the shoulder of the road. The cars in front of Knox and Bree started inching forward, and Knox started the engine on the rental car again, preparing to follow the line of cars.

"That was pretty impressive," Knox said, glancing sideways at Bree. "I mean, I can breathe fire, but I'm not sure I would have been able to make a strong enough flame to burn a whole roadway in an instant. And then to make that big hole in a matter of seconds…remind me never to piss you off."

Bree chuckled, but she was having a hard time feeling truly happy right now.

"Hey, what's wrong?" Knox asked, sensing her sadness.

Bree sighed. "It's just that getting this stone back was much easier than I expected. Almost too easy, you know? I staked my magic and my reputation in the wizard community on the fact that getting the stone and defending against those who had the stone would result in huge battles that would require help from the shifters. But I basically just walked up to the armored vehicle, took the stone, and walked off. No battle. No need for backup help. Maybe I was wrong. Maybe I should have listened to the High Council, and I do deserve to be stripped of my magic."

"Don't be so hard on yourself, Bree," Knox said, reaching over to squeeze her knee with his hand. "For one thing, you wouldn't have had the information you needed to so easily find the armored vehicle and switch the stones if you hadn't met me. You wouldn't have known the guy who made the replacement stone. And, besides, don't be so sure that there won't be battles coming. The guys who are on the trail of the stone aren't going to give up just because they weren't the first ones to get to it."

Bree frowned. "Maybe you're right," she said. "But I can't help but wondering if I did do the right thing after all, or if this was all worth it."

Knox looked over at her with a big smile, and he squeezed her knee again. The gesture filled Bree with warmth and peace, and she felt at least slightly better.

"You met me," he said. "So I hope it was worth it. And I know you have a good heart. You were trying to do the right thing. I promise you, I will defend you with everything in me. If anyone tries to attack you or take your magic from me, they're going to have to get through me and my dragons first. And, trust me—we might not have magic, but we know how to fight."

"I hope it doesn't come to that," Bree said weakly. But as the car started inching forward again, she had a sinking feeling that it would.

CHAPTER SIXTEEN

Although Knox did not want to say anything to make Bree feel worse than she already did, he had to admit that he was also quite surprised at how easy it had been to recover the dragon sapphire. The whole time they had been chasing down the armored car, he kept waiting for something to go wrong, but nothing ever did. Things worked out as smoothly as they could have possibly hoped for.

It seemed that their long-term plan had been unnecessary, and so had the idea of renting an apartment in Mountain View. Not that Knox was complaining. He'd had plenty of missions that had turned out much more complicated than he'd originally thought they would, so it was good to have things turn out better that he thought, for once.

He wasn't so sure that Bree shared his relief. The closer they got to Mountain View, the more agitated she seemed to be. She stared out the passenger side window of their car, fingering her magic ring and not speaking at all. Every now and then when he glanced over, he could see that she was chewing her lip in frustration. She was not happy, and his heart ached for her. He didn't want to meddle in wizard politics, but it seemed unfair to him that someone who had such a good heart, and had taken great risks solely for the sake of trying to protect her wizard clan, was now worried that she would forever be a fugitive, or be stripped of her magic. Surely, there had to be some sort of loophole. But she didn't want to discuss the matter right now, and Knox decided to respect her desire for silence. There would be time for talking later. Right now, the most important thing was to get the dragon sapphire safely back to the Redwoods.

Knox's plan was to stop in Mountain View to gather up the few things that he and Bree had left there. He had decided not to say anything to the owner of the apartment complex about the fact that they were leaving. Leaving so soon right after arriving might seem too suspicious, and the last thing that Knox wanted to do was to raise suspicions. No, he would just let the owner think that they were still staying there for now.

Once Knox and Bree had gathered up their things, they would drive the rental car back to the town where they had picked it up. Then, Knox would shift back into a dragon and fly Bree back to the Redwoods. It would make for a long day, but they should be able to arrive home late tonight. Knox had already spoken to Noah, who had called Pierce, their good friend and unicorn shifter. Pierce, as one of the shifter protectors, would take charge of the dragon sapphire and make sure that it was taken somewhere that it would be safely guarded. Ordinarily, Knox kept any ancient dragon artifacts that he found in the Redwood forests for safekeeping. But this dragon stone was special. It was not, as far as Knox could tell, originally from the Redwood line of dragons, and so Knox didn't feel right keeping it. He felt it was better to hand it over to Pierce. Once the stone had been handed off, Knox planned to focus on Bree for a while. He hoped that he could convince her to stay with him in the Redwoods, especially if she didn't feel safe going back to her clan. He didn't want to be insensitive to her sorrow, but he wanted her to know that she definitely had a place to go if she felt that she needed a new home.

"I'm worried about being in Mountain View," Bree said, suddenly breaking the silence without warning.

"What do you mean?" Knox asked as he glanced over at her, surprised. They were only about twenty minutes away from their new apartment, and this was the first she had mentioned of being worried about Mountain View itself.

"It's well-known that the gem collector lives there," Bree said. "And my wizard clan knows that I was in search of the dragon sapphire. It's very likely they have spies in Mountain View. I'm surprised they haven't already found me, to tell the truth. I was an idiot to go walking around last night with my face in plain sight."

Knox frowned. "Well, I suppose you might be right," he said. "But we don't have to stay there long. If you want to stay low and hidden in the car, I'll run in to the apartment and get our things. We didn't have that much stuff, so it should only take me a few minutes to gather it all up. We can grab food on the road somewhere, and look at the stone closer then, too. I think it's safe to assume that the stone we got is, in fact, the real stone."

Bree nodded her head. "I'm a fan of anything that gets me out of Mountain View faster," she said. "And I'm positive this is the real stone. There's no reason to think that this one was a fake."

Knox nodded. "Alright. We'll get in and out of Mountain View as quickly as we can."

As they drove closer and closer to the small apartment they had rented, Bree sunk lower and lower in her seat, until she would not have been visible at all to anyone outside the truck. Knox found himself feeling strangely nervous as well. Why hadn't it occurred to him how dangerous it might be to bring Bree here? He had been such an idiot, focusing so much on the dragon sapphire but not thinking about the dangers their search might present for Bree.

"Why don't you do one of those invisibility spells," Knox said as Bree sank so low that she was practically sitting on the floorboard of the car. She looked up at him with a raised eyebrow, and if it hadn't been for the fact that the situation was so serious, he might have laughed. She looked so funny, squashed down there in the bottom of the car.

"I can try," she said, sounding doubtful. "But the wizards searching for me know powerful spells to enable them to see through invisibility spells. There are no spells to give you x-ray vision, though, so as long as I'm actually physically out of sight, they shouldn't see me."

"It can't hurt to stay low *and* do an invisibility spell, though" Knox said.

Bree seemed to agree, because the next words out of her mouth were "*Magicae invisibilia.*" She instantly disappeared from Knox's view, which at least made him feel better. Now that Bree had aroused his suspicions, he couldn't help looking at every car and pedestrian they passed as a possible menace. Were they being watched? Was some seemingly innocent bystander actually preparing to attack them?

"You're staying low, right?" Knox asked. Now that he couldn't see Bree, he had no way of knowing where exactly she was sitting in the car.

"Yup, as low as I can get," came her muffled voice from somewhere near the passenger floorboard.

With a resigned sigh, Knox pulled in to the parking garage of their apartment complex.

"I'll be right back," he said to invisible Bree.

He ran into the apartment and quickly gathered up their things, giving a longing glance to the soft bed in the small bedroom, which they had left unmade this morning in their rush to go catch the dragon sapphire. How he wished that right now he could just stay here, and curl up in that bed with Bree. Although it was still early afternoon right now, Knox felt exhausted, as though he had been up for days.

But it would be a long time before he could cuddle up to Bree. The road ahead of them would take several hours to travel, and the sooner he started, the sooner the journey would be over. Knox took one last look around the apartment to make sure they had not left anything behind, and then he left, holding a large backpack in his arms and locking the door behind him. He wondered if he would ever see this place again, shaking his head at how ridiculous it now seemed that they had bothered to rent an actual apartment.

He got back to the seemingly empty car and threw the backpack in the backseat with a large thud, then slid into the driver's seat.

"You still here?" he asked Bree, groping around in the empty air, trying to feel for her. An invisible hand reached up to grab his, holding it tight.

"I'm here," she said. Knox smiled. Even though he couldn't see it right now, the feel of her hand against his skin was heavenly.

"Then let's go," he said. He fired up the engine and started driving, his eyes once again looking warily around him, trying to see whether any dangers lurked in plain sight. But nothing seemed out of the ordinary. After an hour of travel, they were finally well past the outskirts of Silicon Valley's heart, and Knox was beginning to believe that they had actually managed to leave the area without being found.

"I think we're safe," he said, glancing at the area of the floorboard where he knew Bree was still crouched.

"*Invisibilia terminantur,*" she said, her voice seeming to come out of thin air. But seconds later, the invisibility spell fell away and he could once again see Bree. She stiffly climbed back up into the passenger seat, stretching out her cramped muscles before fastening her seatbelt.

"It's really strange that no one seemed to be watching in Mountain View," Bree said. She was pulling out her hair tie to readjust the messy bun she had pulled her hair into. Her hairstyle had become quite disheveled during her time on the floor.

"Maybe they were still off searching the woods," Knox suggested with a shrug. He did think it was a little strange that no one had been posted to watch the main areas of the city where Bree was most likely to show up. Perhaps, though, they had assumed it would take her longer to get there. Or maybe they had just thought she would never dare to go there so openly. Whatever the reason, Knox felt lucky that they had managed to get in and out of the area with the dragon sapphire and without being caught.

Bree, however, did not seem as convinced. She stared off into the distance through the front windshield with a scowl on her face.

"No," she said. "Something is wrong. There's something ominous about the fact that they weren't here. Something bigger is brewing."

Privately, Knox thought she was being a bit dramatic. Sometimes, things really did just work out well, and when those times came you considered yourself lucky and moved forward. But Knox did not say any of this to her. He merely kept driving and let her mull over her thoughts as she stared out the window. Hopefully, once they were back to the Redwoods and the sapphire was safely handed off to Pierce, Bree would be able to relax a bit more.

They drove at a steady pace, stopping only to gas up and then to grab some food from a drive-through. Both of them were more than ready to be back in the Redwoods, and the only way to get there was to keep moving forward. By the time they got to the small town to drop their rental car off, even Bree seemed to have relaxed somewhat. They were making good time, and nothing out of the ordinary seemed to have happened. No one was following them, and once the car was dropped off, all that was left was to hike a short distance into the woods, let Knox shift into a dragon, and then take off into the sunset sky to make the flight back to the Redwoods base camp.

Knox pulled his backpack on, made sure Bree had all of her stuff, and then began walking into the forest toward a spot he knew would be a good place for him to shift and take off. Before he stripped down to change into dragon form, though, he wanted a chance to actually look at the dragon sapphire. Bree had secured it in one of the interior pockets of her backpack, and she knelt to pull it out now. She gave it a careful look before handing it over to Knox.

"It looks legit," she said. "It's exactly like the fake one we switched it out for."

Knox took the sapphire in his hands and stared at it in wonder. It was firm and heavy, and even in the waning, shaded light of the forest, it seemed to sparkle brilliantly. His mind instantly flashed back to when he had held the emerald dragon stone after its capture in Texas a few years ago. At the time, Knox, along with the rest of the dragon shifters, had thought that the emerald stone was the only dragon stone in existence. Knox remembered thinking that the emerald was heavy, too, and that it seemed to be almost lit from within. This sapphire seemed similar. Although the fake sapphire had been a close replica, the fake had not had the same inner light that this sapphire had. Knox knew without a doubt that the dragon sapphire existed, and that he was holding it in his hands.

He wondered what power he held in his hands. The emerald dragon stone was immensely powerful, allowing a single good shifter to take on an entire army of evil shifters by himself. This was why it was so important that the dragon stones stay in the hands of good shifters. Or, good wizards, Knox thought, looking up at Bree. He still found it hard to believe that whole communities of wizards existed. Even though he had seen Bree in action, and it was clear that she was indeed a wizard, the idea of hundreds more wizards existing in their own clans and towns boggled his mind. After being taught his whole life that wizards did not exist anymore, it was difficult to make the mental switch so quickly to knowing that they were alive and well after all.

But there was time to continue processing all of this new information later. Right now, the important thing was that they did have the actual dragon sapphire, and that they were nearly home.

"It does look legit," Knox said. "Ready to get going? We should get this thing back to base camp where it will be safe."

Bree nodded. "The sooner the better," she said.

Knox quickly stripped down, and Bree helped him fold his clothes and put them in his backpack. She no longer looked away in embarrassment when he took his clothes off to shift, and Knox found it strangely comforting that she was so at ease with him.

When everything was packed up, Knox looked up at Bree to make sure she was okay, and then nodded to let her know he was about to shift. Bree gave him a slight nod of acknowledgment, then waited. With a mighty roar, Knox let loose the dragon within him. A rush of power emanated forth from him, shaking even the trunks of the mighty redwoods. His human skin gave way to thick dragon hide, and his hands became the sharply clawed feet of a dragon. His head became majestic and horned, and he gave it several shakes to work out the kinks that had formed in it while he had been driving for hours in human form.

Bree flung his backpack up onto his broad dragon back, then climbed up after it.

After giving Bree a few moments to secure herself by holding tightly to the iridescent scales on his back, Knox began flapping his wings, lifting himself rapidly up into the air high above the redwoods. The sun was setting in the distance, lighting the tops of the trees with a red-orange glow. Knox breathed in deeply, filling his lungs with the fresh, cool, high altitude air. A small smile curled up his dragon lips as he turned in the direction of the Redwood Base camp.

He was going home, and Bree was coming with him.

CHAPTER SEVENTEEN

Bree breathed a sigh of relief as Knox finally landed near his dragons' base camp. She slid off of him, and waited a few moments as he shifted back into human form and put his clothes back on. They walked together to the cabins, where the fire pit was going strong and Bree saw the familiar faces of Noah, Myles, Owen and Vance, along with some new faces. Everyone rushed forward to greet them, asking dozens of questions at once about the dragon sapphire. Knox laughed and held up his hands, saying that he wanted to get some food and a beer before answering any questions. He did take time, though, to introduce Bree to the new faces in the crowd.

"This is Pierce Dyer, my unicorn shifter friend I've told you about. He's one of the best protectors in the business, and he's going to make sure the dragon sapphire is stored somewhere safe. This here is his lifemate, Aria. She's a wolf shifter, and helps him with his protector work. And over there is Levi Sullivan, a panther shifter and another one of the protectors. I'd guess he's here to help Pierce and Aria get the dragon sapphire safely back?"

The man who had been introduced as Pierce nodded. "Yup. I didn't want to bring too large of a crowd with me and attract attention, but I wanted a couple good fighters with me in case anything goes wrong. I'm assuming, though, that with the dragon sapphire on our side, we'll be pretty safe? If it's anything like the dragon emerald, it should be extremely powerful."

"I would guess it is," Knox said. "But I don't know exactly how it works. We don't have any information on it, like we did on the dragon emerald, so we aren't sure exactly how to activate it."

"I might be able to find some information on that," Bree said. "No promises, but I did find a lot of information on the stone's powers when I was doing my report for the Advocacy Bureau. There might be something in there on how to activate it."

The others nodded, and then started peppering Knox with more questions about the recovery of the stone. Knox retold the story, while Myles started handing out beers and food to anyone who wanted it. Bree was soon happily stuffing her face with a burger and a side of baked beans, content to let Knox speak while she sat silently eating. She had not missed the fact that several eyebrows around the campfire had raised when Knox reached out to protectively squeeze her knee at one point. She supposed that the dragons here didn't often bring women around for dinner, and they must have been surprised at their clan leader's sudden affection for Bree. No one said anything about that, though. Whether it was because they knew better than to question Knox, or because they were just too interested in the story of the dragon sapphire, Bree would never know for sure.

When Knox had finished his tale, he asked Noah to update him on how things had been while he was away.

"Everything's been running smoothly," Noah said. "Everyone out on the field has been progressing well on their missions, and things here have been quiet. The most excitement we had while you were gone was when Pierce, Aria, and Levi arrived."

"Good," Knox said. "I feel a bit ridiculous now for worrying about leaving everyone behind."

Noah shrugged. "Don't feel ridiculous. You care about the clan, and that's nothing to feel foolish about."

Pierce laughed. "Now that he's left you guys once, he's going to be taking off all the time. You guys might even start to miss him."

Everyone laughed, and Bree joined in with a small chuckle, although she didn't really get the joke like the others seemed to. She was about to suggest that everyone go get some sleep when Noah spoke up again, using a serious tone once again.

"Have you guys seen or heard any news since you left Mountain View?" Noah asked.

Knox shook his head no. "Not really. We were just trying to get out of there as quickly as we could, and I didn't really think to turn on the radio. I figured you'd let me know if there was anything especially interesting."

"Well, there was something interesting, although I only saw it about an hour ago, so you might have missed it even if you had been listening to the news," Noah said.

"Was it about the fissure in the road that we caused?" Bree asked, interrupting. She'd been worried about how that would be reported ever since they had left the scene. Any wizard watching the news on that was likely to realize that a wizard had been at work there. Would members of her clan have seen it? Would they guess that she had been there? Had they followed her at all? Bree felt her stomach tightening up with worry once again.

"Well, I wasn't exactly referring to the news on the roadblock, although there was a small amount of coverage on that. Some were saying it was a small earthquake that caused the rift and then a fire, which burned the hole back together," Noah said.

Bree looked at Noah like he had lost his mind. "That doesn't make sense," she said.

Noah shrugged and put his hands up in the air. "Hey, I'm not the one who came up with the theory. I'm just telling you what I heard. There's been a lot of talk about the incident, but no one can explain it away. Which is unsurprising, since no one really knows that wizards exist."

Bree felt uneasy. She hoped, for her sake, that any news coverage on the incident had been small, and had not reached the ears of her wizard clan in Falcon Cross. She had a feeling, though, that her luck was going to run out soon. There were too many coincidences and narrow escapes. How was it possible no one had found her yet. She shuddered, thinking about the pain and agony of losing her magic. Knox put his arm around her protectively, and she felt somewhat better. Would he be enough to protect her from the wrath of her wizard clan's high council? In her mind's eye, she suddenly saw Samuel once again, peering at her over the High Council's table and telling her that she had forgotten all of her history lessons. She shuddered again, and forced herself to turn her attention back to Noah.

"The news I was referring to, though," Noah was saying, "Is that there was an armed robbery attempt on the home of the gem collector who owned the dragon stone."

Bree's face shot up in surprise. "There was? I'm surprised. I thought the guys who were after it were trying to avoid violence."

Noah frowned. "I remember you saying that, and that's why this armed robbery bothers me so much. We thought that the two ex-drug lords who were after the stone would take their time, stealing it by stealth rather than force. The fact that there has been this sudden, violent attack leads me to believe one of two things has happened. Either someone else is now on the trail of the dragon sapphire, and made their own violent attempt to grab it, or the ex-drug lords have decided that the need to get the dragon sapphire is urgent. They might know that you guys were trying to get it, or they might know that someone else was on the trail."

Bree felt like her head was spinning once again. Noah's suspicion that someone else was on the trail of the dragon sapphire worried her. When she had done her report for the Advocacy Bureau, no one else had seemed to know. Had that changed? Was information on the stone leaking out?

"Wait, you said *attempted* robbery," Knox said, frowning over at Noah. "Does that mean that the stone was not actually stolen?"

Noah sighed. "Well, the sapphire was not stolen, but only because the robbers threw it away as they fled. It would seem to me that they realized it was a fake. I don't think the gem collector has realized that yet, but whoever was trying to steal it is bound to be angry, knowing that someone else got to it first. I just hope they don't know that the 'someone' is us."

"We should get the stone away from here and safe into protector hands as soon as possible," Aria said, speaking up for the first time.

"That's very true," Levi agreed. "I hate to break up this party, but perhaps Pierce, Aria and I should all get some rest so we can leave early in the morning and get the sapphire away from here sooner rather than later."

"I don't disagree," Knox said. "But I have to say it's too bad that you'll be leaving so soon after arriving. We're overdue for a proper catch-up."

Pierce grinned. "I'll say we are. You didn't tell me you had a girl."

All eyes turned to look at Knox and Bree, and Bree realized that Knox still had his arm around her firmly and conspicuously. Bree's cheeks turned red as the group all started to laugh.

"Yeah, boss," Myles said, crossing his arms in feigned anger. "You told us you were going off on a dangerous mission. Instead you went chasing after a pretty girl, it seems."

Vance roared with laughter. "Aw, come on, Myles. Don't you know anything about women? Chasing girls is always a dangerous mission!"

Knox opened his mouth to respond, but before any words could come out, Bree saw a look of shock cross his face. The next thing she knew, Knox had pushed her to the ground, and he was lying over her yelling, "Shift! Shift! Everybody shift!"

Pops of energy sounded out all around her, along with cursing, and then a new sound—the whizzing of lasers that Bree knew with certainty were coming from a wizard spell. Bree found herself being lifted in Knox's strong arms, and then he was running like the wind toward his cabin. He pushed her inside, then yelled at her to stay down. Before she could say anything, he had slammed the door behind him. She heard another large pop of energy from outside, indicating that he was shifting into dragon form.

The noise was deafening. Animal roars, human screams, and the buzz of wizard spells filled the air. Bree sat, stunned and unmoving for a moment, plastered against the wall of the cabin with her heart feeling like it was about to beat out of her chest. She fingered her magic ring, wondering briefly whether this would be the last night that she wore it. She felt fear as she had never felt it before, and she squeezed her eyes shut, wishing that she was anywhere but here, or wishing she was brave. Advocacy school had not prepared her for this. She didn't know how to fight, not physically anyway. She only knew how to make arguments with words, and words would do her no good in the violent battle raging just beyond her doorway. She heard a sound like the rushing of a great wind, then saw the night sky lighting up with orange brightness. Knox was breathing fire just outside the cabin, no doubt doing his best to fend off the wizards who were now trying to reach the cabin where Bree was hiding.

Bree felt suddenly ashamed. Here she was, hiding away in a cabin while Knox fought bravely, when the whole reason that they were under attack in the first place was her. There were wizards here, and that could only mean one thing—they had found Bree and were determined to bring her back to Falcon Cross to strip her of her magic for defying the High Council. Bree felt tears stinging at her eyelids. She would not go willingly, that was certain. Perhaps she had made a mistake, but it had been an honest one. She had only ever wanted the best for her clan. How could that be worth inflicting the worst possible punishment on her?

"You've been brave before," Bree whispered to herself. And it was true. It had not been easy to stand up in front of the whole High Council and tell them that they were making a mistake by not contacting the shifters. It had not been easy to run away, knowing that doing so might mean she could never return to Falcon Cross or to the advocacy job she had worked so hard to get. But she had done what she felt she needed to do in the moment. And now, in this moment, Bree knew she needed to fight. She needed to be brave once more.

Slowly, she rose to her feet. She turned to look out the front window of the cabin, expecting to see wizards near at hand, fighting down the shifters to get to her. But what she saw was not only wizards. It was wizards, shifters, and humans—all seemingly in total chaos. There were the dragons, and, of course, the visiting shifters—a wolf, a panther, and a unicorn. Bree had never seen a unicorn before, and she couldn't help feeling amazed at the sight of one, despite the fact that there were so many pressing matters at the moment.

But the shifters that were fighting for the Redwood Dragons were not the only shifters in the fray. As Bree looked out, she saw that there were several other shifters fighting alongside the wizards. Most of them were bears and wolves, with a few lions thrown in here and there. But that couldn't be right, could it? How would the wizards have come after her with an army of shifters when the whole reason Bree was on the run in the first place was that she was the only one who thought it was necessary to let shifters know that wizards still existed? Unless the High Council had had a drastic change of heart, there should not be shifters here. And if they *had* had a drastic change of heart, why were they attacking Bree? Shouldn't they have been coming to tell her that she had been right?

And why were there so many humans mixed among the wizards? That was the weirdest thing of all. The only group wizards feared more than shifters was full humans. There's no way wizards would have willingly asked humans to fight with them. What was going on? Was this group here against the wishes of the High Council?

But before Bree could let her mind wander much further down that trail, she saw, to her horror, that the High Council Wizard Samuel had just jumped in front of Knox. Knox, of course, did not know who Samuel was, or that he was one of the best spellcasters in the country. Knox tried to send a wall of fire at Samuel, but Samuel deftly shot up a shield using a shield spell, and laughed in Knox's face.

"Even dragons are not more powerful than my magic," Samuel yelled. "The sooner you surrender and give us what we want, the better off things will be for you. The longer you fight, the more of your men are going to have to die!"

Bree saw a flash of anger rush across Knox's eyes, and her own eyes teared up a bit with love. She knew in that moment that Knox would die before giving her up. She also knew that she had to stand and fight. She didn't understand why the High Council had suddenly decided to enlist shifters and humans in the fight to get her, but if it was a fight they wanted, she would give them one. If she had to die, at least she would die knowing she had done the right thing. She had helped make sure that the dragon sapphire stayed in good hands. If that was a deed worth dying for, then so be it.

With trembling hands, but a firm resolve, Bree went to the front door of the cabin, swung it open and lifted her magic ring to point in the direction of Samuel.

"*Magicae arma,*" she cried out. Instantly, her shield spell sent up a force field around her. She knew Samuel was a powerful wizard, and it probably would not take him long to break through her shield spell. But she had to at least try to defend herself. Startled by her sudden entrance into the fight, Samuel turned to look at her. When his eyes met hers a shocked look crossed his face.

"Well? It's me you want, isn't it?" Bree yelled out at him, sounding much braver than she felt. "Come and get me, if you dare."

Time seemed to stand still. The moments that followed, before Samuel spoke, felt to Bree like the longest moments of her life.

CHAPTER EIGHTEEN

"Bree?" Samuel finally choked out. He was still holding his arm up, his own shield spell still going strong. But he did not make a move toward Bree, at least not right away. He stared at her as though she was an alien, and Bree suddenly realized that he had not expected to see her here at all.

He was not after her. He was after the dragon sapphire.

Before Bree could process what this all meant, she heard a fresh commotion coming from the west side of the clearing. Suddenly, a small army's worth of fresh wizards burst in, ready to fight with their magic rings raised. For a moment, Bree was even more confused—and she was very distracted. Then she saw that Peter, the leader of the High Council, was leading this new group. His eyes seemed to blaze fire as he looked around the clearing, taking in what was happening. Bree let her guard down for a split-second, and in that split-second, Samuel quickly broke through her shield spell. He quickly grabbed her, pinning her arms to her body, and then yelled.

"Peter! Over here! I've caught Bree! I've caught her. She was gathering all of these wizards, shifters, and humans to do battle against Falcon Cross!"

"What? No! It's not like that," Bree said. Before she could get another word out, though, Samuel roared in pain and let her go. In the excitement of the moment, Samuel had let his own shield spell weaken, and Knox had taken the opportunity to breath fire onto his legs. Now, Samuel was rolling on the ground in agony, trying to put out the fire. In the meantime, a great unrest seemed to suddenly be taking over the group of humans, shifters and wizards that had been fighting with Samuel.

"You never said anything about attacking Falcon Cross," one of the wizards said.

"Yeah, we were supposed to be here to recover the dragon sapphire and then leave to start our own city," another said.

"We better still get our cut of the profits," a rough voice called out. Bree was startled to see that the voice belonged to a man who looked exactly like one of the ex-drug lords who had been trying to steal the dragon sapphire. A horrible realization washed over her. Not only was Samuel here for the dragon sapphire, he had also been in league with the ex-drug lords from the beginning. No wonder he had argued so firmly against involving shifters in a search for the dragon stone.

Bree opened her mouth to yell at Samuel in anger, but before she could say anything, Knox had lifted her with his dragon mouth and had started flapping his wings. He rose high into the air, pulling her above the battle just as things really started to explode. When he reached the top of the forest, he deposited Bree on the highest branch of the tallest redwood, and then swooped back down to the battle.

Bree cursed aloud as she realized what he had just done. He didn't want her in harm's way, so he had flown her up here and left her stranded in the trees. She had no choice but to watch the battle from afar now, and he knew it. Bree desperately tried to think of some sort of spell that would allow her to glide down softly without injury, but she could not remember any good spells with certainty, and she wasn't willing to risk her life by experimenting with spells. If she performed a spell incorrectly before jumping from this high, she would certainly die.

And so, she watched as a massive battle unfolded beneath her. She could not tell from up here who was winning, or who was responsible for the screams of pain that echoed out through the night. Occasionally, she saw a flash of fire from a dragon, or a piercing laser from a wizard. But most of what she could see was just a blur of shadows in the darkness. She wondered constantly whether Knox was safe, and whether the dragon sapphire was still in good hands. She wondered most of all, how it was possible that Samuel, a member of the High Council who was sworn to protect all wizards with his life, had been working with two criminals who wanted to destroy society with the powerful dragon sapphire. Nothing made sense, and she had a feeling that it would take a while to sort everything out, if she ever got a chance. Briefly, she wondered how she would get down from the tree if Knox was killed in the battle. But then she decided that if Knox was killed in battle, she would find it hard to care about anything, anyway.

And then, almost as suddenly as the chaos had begun, it stopped. Bree saw shadows fleeing away from the cabins and into the dark forest, and she saw other figures in pursuit of them. But she could also see shifters gathering around the campfire. Several pops of energy rang out, and Bree could see Knox, Noah, Myles, Vance and Owen all in human form. They were speaking with Peter, who was surrounded by a small wizard army. Bree could not, of course, hear what they were saying. But several times she saw both Knox and Peter gesticulating wildly with their arms. Whatever discussion they were having, it was quite a heated one. Bree fiddled with her magic ring nervously, even though if Peter attacked with any kind of magic spell, there wasn't much Bree would be able to do to stop him. He was far too powerful for her to handle on her own.

After what felt like an eternity, she finally saw Knox nod definitively, take a step back, and then shift back into dragon form. For a moment, she thought that she was about to witness another fight. But then, he suddenly started flying upward, circling back toward the top of the trees where she was. When he reached her, he perched as close to her as he could manage to maneuver his large dragon body, and he motioned with his head for her to climb onto his back. Bree hesitated for just a moment, then climbed on. She knew Knox was about to take her down to meet Peter, and the thought of facing the leader of the High Council filled her with dread. But she knew that Knox would not take her to Peter if he thought there was the smallest possibility that Peter would harm her.

As it turned out, Knox did not fly directly back to the fire pit. Instead, he made his way to the front of his cabin and landed with a soft thud. On the way down, Bree noticed that Samuel was now captured, bound with ropes as well as under the guard of several wizards, who stood with their magic rings pointed menacingly in his direction.

"What's going on, Knox?" Bree asked, looking warily around as Knox gestured for her to go into his cabin. Once inside, he flipped on the lights and started rummaging around in his bedroom for some clothes. He looked tired, but happy, and the muscles on his body seemed even larger than usual. Fighting had brought out the best of him, it seemed.

"I've spoken with Peter, who I understand is the head of the High Council of your clan?" Knox said.

Bree nodded, and, to her surprise, Knox flashed her a huge smile.

"I think you're going to want to hear what he has to say," Knox said as he pulled on a pair of jeans.

Bree frowned, feeling relieved that Knox seemed so sure that everything was going to be okay, but also starting to feel angry that she had been left out of the fight.

"Who do you think you are, by the way, trapping me up in a tree so I couldn't fight?" she demanded to know.

But Knox kept grinning at her, not looking the least bit sorry. He was nearly fully dressed now, and he didn't reply until he'd buttoned up the last few buttons on his navy plaid shirt.

"Sorry about that," he said in a voice that told Bree he wasn't actually all that sorry. "But I didn't want to run the risk of someone catching you, and I didn't trust you to stay hidden. Come on, though. Don't be grumpy. Come hear what Peter has to say."

Knox started walking toward the door, and Bree scurried to follow him.

"Is everyone else okay?" she asked, nervous to hear the answer but needing to know.

"Everyone is fine. Just some scratches, but nothing serious. And the dragon sapphire is safe. Now come on."

Knox quickened his pace but reached back for Bree's hand. She took his hand, feeling instantly safer with his warm firm grip pulling her along. The nerves in her stomach felt like they were going to twist her right in half as she walked up to the fire pit. The Redwood shifters and their Texas shifter friends were all there, and had all dressed again after losing their clothes to their sudden shifts before battle. A few wizards Bree recognized as higher-ups in the Falcon Cross government were standing around as well. But the face she couldn't tear her eyes away from right now was Peter's.

He stood, watching her carefully with a serene but guarded expression on his face. He looked even more terrifying now, on the battle field in a plain gray robe, than he had even in his full dress robes at the High Council meeting where Bree had last seen him.

"Bree," he said, his voice not giving anything away.

"Y-your honor," Bree stuttered. She felt her nerves relaxing just slightly. If he wanted to strip her of her magic, he would be ordering wizards to catch her and bind her, wouldn't he?

Peter closed his eyes with a pained expression on his face now, and then took a deep breath as he reopened them.

"I owe your shifter friends here a huge debt of gratitude. And I owe you quite an apology, Bree," he said.

"You do?" Bree asked hopefully, her heart soaring at the words.

"Yes, I do. Of course, we will have to hold a formal hearing for you, since you disobeyed the High Council. But I think you have more than proven that you had sufficient reason for doing so. Especially since one of the High Council himself turned out to be a traitor. I will be recommending a full pardon for you."

For the first time since the fighting had begun, Bree finally felt like she could breathe. She was still quite confused, though.

"Does anyone want to tell me what's going on?" Bree said, looking around at the faces by the fire. Most of them looked quite somber.

"That Samuel guy was after the dragon sapphire," Knox blurted out, apparently unable to keep quiet any longer. Many of the wizards looked startled by Knox's seeming lack of protocol. It was considered incredibly rude to butt in on a conversation the eldest High Councilor was having. But Peter merely smiled. And, Bree thought, Knox himself was the head of the Redwood Dragons, after all. Yes, they were a much smaller clan than the Falcon Cross Wizard Clan, but they were still a clan nonetheless.

"It's true, unfortunately," Peter said. "Samuel, it seemed, has been trying for some time to acquire the dragon sapphire, using the assistance of the two ex-drug lords you wrote about in your report, Bree. That is why he was trying so hard to strike down any recommendations you made about conducting our own search for the dragon sapphire.

I misjudged him, badly, I'm afraid. I thought he was to be trusted, and usually I am a good judge of character. With him, however, I was quite off the mark."

Bree stood, feeling shell-shocked, and looking over at the spot where Samuel was now held captive. "But, how did he end up here tonight at the same time as you?"

"Pure coincidence," Knox said, impatient with the slow pace at which Peter was explaining everything. "Samuel's men, it turned out, were the ones who attempted to rob the dragon sapphire at the gem collector's home. They quickly realized that they had the wrong gem, but some of Samuel's other men had already been following me because they knew I was in contact with the guy who makes the fake gemstones. They had been following me for days, and knew that I'd had a visit from the guy, presumably to get a copy of the gemstone. But they didn't realize I had switched out the stone because they got sloppy and didn't follow me when I went to chase down the armored vehicle with you earlier today."

Bree could hardly believe that it hadn't even been a full day since she and Knox had switched out the dragon sapphire. It felt like a lifetime ago already.

"But weren't they suspicious of me? If they were watching you they must have realized I was with you," Bree said.

"They thought you were just some girl I was having fun with on the side or something, I guess," Knox said. "They never mentioned you to Samuel, or he would have known who you were, obviously. He had no idea you and I were connected, which is why he was shocked when you showed up here tonight. He thought he would bring his little army of traitorous wizards, shifters, and humans, steal the dragon stone, and suddenly be the most powerful man in the world. The fact that you were here put a serious kink in his plans."

"*We* were here tonight for you, you see," Peter said, picking up the story. "We'd been delayed in finding you, largely due to misinformation Samuel fed us to keep us away from Mountain View so that we wouldn't realize what he was doing with the sapphire. He led us to believe that you had moved on to San Francisco, but when our trail there was completely cold, we sent some scouts back to Mountain View. We figured that, since that's where the sapphire was supposed to be, that we would most likely find you there. And we did. The scouts found you, followed you from afar, and got the location of this hideout. We returned with a full army as soon as possible. In an ironic twist of fate, we got here at nearly the same time Samuel did. We got to see firsthand his treachery, and how he himself had been in league with shifters despite arguing so vehemently against reopening shifter-wizard relations."

"In league with bad shifters," Knox pointed out. "We're not all like that."

"Indeed, I see that now," Peter said. "And if it had not been for the brave fighting of your men tonight, Knox, I'm not sure we could have overcome Samuel's army. We owe you a debt of gratitude, as I've said. And Bree, I owe you an apology. You were right. The dragon sapphire is very powerful and dangerous, and we needed the help of the shifters to recover it."

"So I'm not being stripped of my magic?" Bree asked in a small, hopeful voice. Peter had already indicated that this was the case, but she almost couldn't believe it. She wanted confirmation. Peter smiled at her, and she felt Knox squeezing her hand.

"Like I said, there will need to be a formal hearing, but I can't imagine anyone wanting to strip you of your magic. Now that everything has come to light, I see how right you really were. You did something very brave, Bree. You risked everything to save people who ridiculed you to your face."

"I risked everything to save the clan I love," Bree said fiercely.

Peter smiled. "I know, dear child. And now, your job is done. You've had a long day. You should rest. In the morning, we will provide you with a secure escort back to Falcon Cross, where we will hold a special hearing to clear your name."

"Can Knox come?" Bree asked, feeling bold and standing tall. No shifter had been near Falcon Cross for centuries, but Bree had already decided that she wasn't going without Knox. Peter, however, did not protest.

"If Knox would like to come, he will be our honored guest," Peter said.

Bree looked over at Know and smiled. He nodded at her, affirming that he would go.

"Well, then," Bree said. "I guess I'd better go get some rest for the journey tomorrow. Good night, your Honor."

"Good night, Bree. Rest well," Peter said.

Bree nodded to the rest of the group, and turned to start walking toward Knox's cabin. Knox leaned over to kiss her, then released her hand.

"I'll be right there," he said. "I just need to work out a few logistical details about prisoners and such."

Bree smiled at him and said "okay," then headed for the cabin. The whole day felt like a dream—one that had had the potential to become a nightmare but had somehow turned out like a fairy tale. Just before closing the cabin door behind her, she turned to look back toward the fire pit, where she saw Knox standing tall and mighty, silhouetted perfectly against the orange blaze. She could hardly believe that he was part of her life now, or that someone as magnificent as him loved her. But he did. He really did.

Yes, thought Bree as she closed the door behind her: today had been like a fairy tale.

CHAPTER NINETEEN

Knox woke to the smell of coffee filling his cabin. He sat up slowly in bed, wincing slightly as his stiff muscles protested. The events of the night before came rushing back at him, and he smiled broadly. He was angry that such a big attack had happened on his clan's base here in the Redwoods, but he was happy with how things had turned out. The dragon sapphire was safe, and Bree was safe.

He smiled as he thought of Bree. Inhaling another deep breath of coffee-scented air, he rose and went to the main room of his cabin, where he found her searching through his cupboards for mugs. Her hair was falling in loose waves around her shoulders, and she was wearing the oversized t-shirt of his that she had slept in. Seeing her in his t-shirt, in his cabin, rummaging through his kitchen, turned him on like crazy.

"Hey, you," he said softly.

Startled, she turned suddenly and looked at him with wide, apologetic eyes. "Oh! Did I wake you?" she asked. "I was trying to be quiet!"

"The smell of coffee woke me," Knox said. "But it's okay. We need to get moving early today, anyway. And I don't mind having a few moments with you before the day gets busy."

He crossed the room in a few large strides and put his arms around her. She sighed, and melted into his chest as he kissed the top of her head. He could not put into words how happy he was in that moment. He had wanted this for so long. He had dreamed of a chance to be with her, enjoying her, without worries about the stone or about her being caught. Now, here they were. The stone was secure with Pierce, ready for its journey to shifter protector headquarters. Bree was no longer a fugitive, and would be officially pardoned soon. Everything had worked out exactly as it needed to.

Knox bent down to give Bree a long kiss on her lips. She let out a soft sigh as she returned the kiss, slipping her tongue past his lips and letting it dance in his mouth. Knox felt himself going hard as Bree reached her hands up to wrap them around his broad back, pressing her body against his. He was only wearing sweatpants right now, leaving his chest bare. And he knew she wasn't wearing a bra because he could feel her firm nipples poking through the t-shirt she was wearing, and rubbing against his skin. A thrill of excitement ran through him, and he deepened his kiss, drinking her in as his tongue ran across hers. But just as he started to really get into it, she pulled back and looked up at him uncertainly.

"Do we have time?" she asked. "We have to get ready to leave for Falcon Cross. And I don't want to make the wizards wait when my fate lies in their hands…"

Knox smiled at her tenderly. "We have plenty of time. It's early enough still, and, besides, I think your fate is already decided. The wizards owe you their lives. You saved Falcon Cross by insisting on going after the stone. All that's left is just the formality of pardoning you. Peter said so himself last night."

Bree sighed and leaned her head against his chest. "I guess you're right," she said. "It's just hard to believe that things have actually turned out so well. I was so scared for so long."

"You were so brave," Knox said, using his finger to tilt her chin up so that she was looking directly in his eyes. "It's normal to be scared. But to feel that fear and do the right thing anyway—that's true bravery."

Bree gave him a half-smile then, and Knox beamed back at her.

"I'm so proud of you," he said. Then he leaned down to kiss her again. She did not pull back this time. She returned his kiss even more passionately than before, and it didn't take long for both of them to completely forget any worries about getting ready for the trip to Falcon Cross. The coffee sat patiently waiting in the coffeepot while Knox began pulling Bree back toward the bedroom. The light outside was still the gray-pink of dawn, so the bedroom itself was bathed in muted tones of gray. Bree looked so lovely in this light. Hell, she looked lovely in any light, though.

Despite the full day ahead of them, Knox did not rush. He sat Bree gently down on the bed, then pulled her t-shirt off, leaving her perfect, round breasts exposed right in front of him. He marveled at how full and beautiful they were. So soft, with such hard, alert nipples. He felt himself growing stiffer and stiffer between his legs, until his rock-hard member pushed impatiently against the fabric of his sweatpants. He pushed off the pants quickly, leaving him naked since he had not been wearing any underwear. Then he pulled Bree up into a standing position to quickly pull off her pale pink panties, so that they both stood free of clothes in front of each other. His erection pointed proudly in her direction, ready for its chance to sink itself deep into her. But, for a moment, he just stood there, drinking her in. They both looked at each other, trembling with the anticipation of what was to come, hardly able to believe that they had been lucky enough to find each other.

"Knox," Bree breathed his name out dreamily. That one word was a plea, a request. She wanted him. She needed him. The realization sent a fresh thrill through his body. He pushed her down onto the bed on her back, and his mouth closed over her breasts. She writhed with pleasure and moaned as he took each nipple in his teeth in turn, nibbling firmly, hungrily. He moved back and forth between each breast, pleasuring each in turn, all the while keeping his body firmly pressed against hers, savoring the sensation of bare skin against bare skin.

His erection was poking at the space between her legs, and he could feel that she was soaking wet, her juices of desire dripping down onto her legs and then onto the sheets of his bed. It sent a fresh thrill of pleasure through his body, knowing that she wanted him so badly, and he could hold back no longer. He slid up so that he was right above her slick entrance, then plunged into her. She gasped, and then moaned with happiness, his sudden entrance having taken her by surprise. He moaned himself as he felt her soft warmth enveloping him. She made him feel like he was on fire, but the heat felt so good.

He moved in her, steady and deep, and he closed his eyes with pleasure as he felt her once more writhing and whimpering beneath him. She was not far from exploding, he could tell. And moments later, explode she did. She cried out his name so loudly that the whole base camp must have heard. But Knox didn't care. All he could think about was how amazing he felt as her strong, hot inner muscles clenched around his dick over and over, squeezing tighter with each spasm and sending wave after wave of tingling pleasure across his body. He let the pressure build until it was nearly unbearable, and then, he let himself go, too.

He came into her, a stream of fire shooting through him and into her as he stiffened and roared. The heat and electricity in his body was like nothing he had ever experienced, and he knew for certain in that moment that Bree was his lifemate. They were bonded, and what a special bond they had. He could hardly believe that he was lucky enough to have found a woman who could make him feel like this, a woman so brave and so deserving of his love. With a huge smile on his face, he collapsed gently on top of her, kissing her deeply once again.

There was coffee to drink, bags to pack, and instructions to be given for how the Redwoods base camp should be taken care of while he was away in Falcon Cross. But right now, none of that mattered. All Knox could think about was how amazing he felt, and how beautiful the woman underneath him was.

She was so goddamn beautiful.

CHAPTER TWENTY

An hour later, Bree stood in front of the smoldering fire pit, dressed in a fresh pair of jeans and a simple gray long-sleeved shirt. Her hair was pulled back neatly into a tight bun, and she had even borrowed some makeup from Aria to highlight her eyes and cheeks.

Pierce, Aria, and Levi stood together near the fire pit, too, packed and ready to leave with the dragon sapphire. One of the Redwood Dragons would fly them out of the Redwoods, and then they would head back to Texas. Bree watched as the trio gave big hugs to all of the dragons, and then politely shook hands with Peter and the other head wizards.

"We look forward to a prosperous and mutually beneficial relationship with the shifters in the future," Peter said to Pierce. "Please accept our apologies once again for taking so long to reveal ourselves to the shifters. Even the wisest of wizards can make mistakes, and I see now that I made a mistake in not joining forces with the shifters sooner."

"No apology is necessary," Pierce said. "I understand that in these times caution is often warranted. I'm just glad that we have now been able to join forces."

"Agreed," Knox added as he reached out to squeeze Bree's hand.

"Ready, then?" Myles asked. He would be the one flying the Texas shifters out. They nodded, and a moment later Myles was shifting into dragon form. The Texas shifters climbed onto his back, and a few moments later, Myles was flapping his wings to rise high above the trees. His majestic dragon form was brilliant and green against the bright blue sky.

"Our turn, next," Knox said to Bree, then turned to Noah. "You got everything you need to take care of things here?"

Bree saw Noah grin at Knox. "Yup. Get out of here, boss. You know I've got this."

Knox grinned back at Noah, then gave him a big bear hug. "I know. I should have trusted you much sooner."

Knox saluted the other members of his crew and the wizards, winked at Bree, and then took several steps backward to shift into a dragon at a safe distance. Once he had shifted, Bree climbed onto his back, clutching her backpack. As soon as she was holding on tight, Knox rose high into the air. The wizards would march out, and they had a fleet of cars waiting for them to take them back to Falcon Cross. By nightfall, everyone would have arrived, and tomorrow morning, two trials would be held. One for Samuel, where he was sure to be condemned. And one for Bree, where she was sure to be pardoned.

Bree felt her heart swell with joy as she rose high above the forest on her dragon's back, her magic ring glimmering in the sunlight. Looks like her bravery had paid off in the end.

* * *

The next day, at two o'clock sharp in the afternoon, the trial for Samuel commenced. Bree chose to wait outside the High Council chambers. The last thing she wanted was to see Samuel again, even if he was being sentenced to be stripped of his magic and expelled from the wizard community. Knox watched, and came out to bring a report when the trial was over. Samuel had been condemned and stripped of his magic ring. He was sent to the wizard prison, where he would also be stripped of his magic before being expelled permanently from the wizard community. It was exactly what everyone had known would happen.

"You ready to go in?" Knox asked.

Bree nodded and stood, even though she felt very nervous on the inside. She was wearing a brand new set of dress robes, which Peter had been kind enough to provide for her. Nearly all of Falcon Cross was here, so her roommate, Lily, was wearing the robes Bree had worn last time she was here. Bree was glad to have a pair that fit her properly, anyway.

"You look amazing," Knox said. "Quite intimidating, actually. I wouldn't want to get on your bad side."

Bree looked down at her robes. They were long and a deep ruby red, with strands of golden thread interwoven throughout. The red matched her ruby red magic ring, and brought out the slight reddish hints in her dark brown hair. She felt like royalty, but she was still nervous to step out in front of the whole assembly.

She could not hold back much longer, though. With a deep breath, she took Knox's offered hand and walked into the room, which was packed to capacity. A hush fell over the crowd as Bree walked down the center aisle toward the front, where Knox sat down in his seat on the front row. Bree continued on until she was standing directly before the High Council. Everyone was there except Samuel, of course, whose seat was conspicuously empty. The High Council's dress robes, complete with their tall pointed wizard hats, were impressive, and filled Bree with awe even though she had seen them before.

Bree did her best to still the nervous pounding in her chest, and held her head high as she stood in front of the council. The wizard serving as herald spoke up in a loud voice.

"Your Honors, Bree Riley. Accused of defying a direct order of the High Council, punishable by removal of magic and expulsion from the wizard community."

Even though Bree knew this hearing was just a formality at this point, the words still filled her with terrible dread.

"Thank you," Peter said to the herald, then turned his attention to Bree. "Ms. Riley, what do you have to say for yourself?"

Bree took a deep breath. "Your Honor, I plead not guilty under section seven point three of the High Wizard Code, which states that in cases where it can be proven that the defiance of a High Council order was necessary for the protection of the wizard community as a whole, the defendant shall be found not guilty."

"And why was your defiance necessary for the protection of the wizard community, Ms. Riley?" Peter asked.

"The dragon sapphire was being pursued with evil intent, by those who would have used it to wipe out our entire clan. I know the High Council forbade contact with the shifters, but I respectfully submit that contact with the shifters did turn out to be necessary to fight for and retain the dragon sapphire. When Samuel attacked, we would have lost the dragon sapphire without their aid. And without their help, Samuel might have actually been able to get the sapphire before the good shifters did."

"Thank you for that explanation, Ms. Riley," Peter said. "Based on the information presented here today, it is my recommendation that Ms. Riley be fully pardoned of any guilt for defying an order of the High Council. Are there any here on the High Council who disagree?"

No one else on the High Council spoke, and so Peter let his gavel fall with a might thud. "Bree Riley, you are hereby officially pardoned and reinstated as a full member of the wizard community. Furthermore, as High Wizard of the High Council, I have hereby decided to award you with the Wizard Medallion of Courage, presented to those who risk life and magic in order to do deeds of great service to the clan. You have shown uncommon courage and put the good of the community ahead of your own welfare, and for that, you deserve to be honored greatly."

Bree stood speechless as Peter rose, his deep purple and gold dress robes glittering brilliantly in the light of the High Council room. The herald brought him a black velvet box, which Peter opened to reveal a shining gold medal. The large gold disk hung on a black velvet ribbon and was engraved with the crest of the Falcon Cross clan.

"Bree Riley, in honor of your service to the Falcon Cross clan, to wizards at large, and to our new friends, the shifters, I hereby award you this Medallion of Courage," Peter said.

The crowd in the room went wild. Tears of happiness stung Bree's eyes, and she turned to look at Knox, who gave her a wink and a thumbs up. Bree glanced down at her magic ring and knew that her father would have been so proud of her. Knowing that, and having Knox's approval as well, Bree could not have thought of a more perfect moment.

The High Council officially adjourned the meeting, and Bree was instantly surrounded by wizards wanting to shake her hand and congratulate her. Bree looked up to see her roommate, Lily, fighting her way through the crowd. When Lily finally made it to the front, she threw her arms around Bree.

"I never doubted you, Bree," she said.

"It's true," Peter chuckled. "She threatened to quit her job if we put her on the task force that was assigned to finding you while you were a fugitive."

Bree looked over at Lily with tears in her eyes. "Thank you," Bree said. "It means so much to me that you believed in me."

Lily smiled broadly. "Does this mean you're coming home?"

"Well," Bree said falteringly, glancing from Lily to Peter. "I was hoping actually that I might have permission to go live in the Redwoods with Knox."

Peter raised an eyebrow at Lily, and Knox looked up in surprise.

"You'd do that for me, Bree?" Knox asked, emotion filling his eyes.

"I know it sounds crazy," Bree said. "But in the short time I was there the Redwood Dragons' base started to feel like home to me. I cannot imagine a life away from Knox now, and I would never ask him to leave his crew. If the High Council will allow a wizard to go live with shifters, I would like to move to the Redwoods."

Peter grinned. "The High Council has been discussing the need for wizard ambassadors in the shifter community, and vice-versa. We were going to invite Knox to be a shifter ambassador here in Falcon Cross, but if you want, Bree, we can send you instead to be a wizard ambassador in the Redwoods. I think your training as an advocate would make you perfectly prepared for the job."

Bree's heart leapt at the offer. "I would be honored to take that job," she said.

"It's all settled, then," Peter said. "I'll have someone at the Advocacy Bureau take care of the paperwork and all that, but consider the job yours."

"Thank you, your honor," Bree said, hardly able to believe how her life had changed so much for the better in the last few weeks.

"Thank *you*, Bree," Peter said. "I'm very proud of you. Now if you'll excuse me, I have some High Council matters to attend to, but I will catch up with you again before you leave Falcon Cross."

Bree felt her heart swelling with pride as Peter walked away. Lily let out a long sigh.

"Well, I'm sorry to lose you, Bree. But I'm happy you found love. Knox seems like a great guy," Lily said.

"He is," Bree said, squeezing Knox's hand. "I hope you'll come visit us in the redwoods. You'd love it there."

"I will," Lily promised. "And you'll be coming by the apartment tonight, at least, right?"

"Of course," Bree said. "I'll need a few days to get all my things together, so I'll be around."

"Alright. I'll be seeing you, then," Lily said. "I have to run now to get back to the Bureau, but let's do dinner tonight? With you and Knox both?"

Bree nodded, and Lily gave her a goodbye hug before speeding off. The crowds were thinning now, and Bree found herself alone with Knox.

"You're sure about this?" he asked in a husky voice. "You really want to come live with me in the middle of nowhere?"

"It's not the middle of nowhere. It's the middle of the most magical place on earth," Bree said. "And that's saying something, coming from a wizard!"

Knox smiled at her, and she felt her heart melting at the affection in his eyes.

"Well, I'm really glad to hear it, my brave little wizard," he said. "I know we have not known each other that long, but I already know that I love you."

Bree's breath caught in her throat at the words. "I love you, too," she whispered. "So much. You saved me, in more ways than one."

Knox smiled. "I think we both saved each other. You helped me be brave enough to learn to leave my clan in the capable hands of other dragons. That's important. They all need to know how to lead when necessary. It makes for a stronger clan. And it makes me a stronger dragon, learning to trust others. Which brings me to my next point—I'm planning on doing some missions abroad now and then. Would you be willing to come with me on a few adventures? Provided it works out okay with your new ambassador job, of course."

Bree felt her heart leap with excitement. "I would love to!" she said. "Any mission with you is bound to be an adventure. But, are you sure your clan members are going to be okay with my being around more?"

Knox smiled at her. "They love you, almost as much as I do. They already told me that if I don't find a way to bring you home they're going to riot."

Bree laughed. "Well, then I guess I have no choice but to come with you."

Knox laughed too, and pulled Bree into a big hug, kissing the top of her head.

"Come on, my brave little wizard," he said. "I think you deserve a real date. I saw a nice café on the way to the High Council meeting. Are you interested in sharing a coffee and pastry with me?"

Bree nodded. "Nothing would make me happier," she said.

Knox took her hand, and they walked out of the High Council chamber together. Bree couldn't help but smile at how different things were, leaving the chamber this time as opposed to the last time she was here. Today, she held her head high, she wore a medal for courage, and she was holding the hand of the most handsome man in the world. A handsome man who happened to be a noble dragon, and who happened to love her just as much as she loved him. Life was good—better than it ever had been, in fact.

Sometimes, a little bravery and defiance went a long way.

BOOK TWO: SUMMER AND THE DRAGON

CHAPTER ONE

Vance Pars glanced around the dark Chicago bar as he slowly sipped his whiskey. The place was nearly empty on this rainy Tuesday night, which made eavesdropping a bit more difficult. Luckily for Vance, his dragon hearing allowed him to hear conversations clearly even when he was sitting several feet away from someone.

Right now, he was sitting as close as he dared to a pair of gnarly mountain lion shifters. The two men were a half dozen barstools away, talking in hushed tones and glancing suspiciously up at Vance every now and then. Vance was careful to avoid eye contact with them, but he kept his ears perked to listen to their conversation.

They didn't know Vance was a shifter. He'd used a carefully blended masking scent that made him smell like a full human. His clan mate, Myles, swore by the stuff, but the first time Vance had tried the masking scent, he'd been afraid that it wouldn't work. That was a few weeks ago now, though, and the masking scent had been holding steady for the entire time Vance had been in Chicago. Hopefully, it would only need to hold steady for one more night, and then he could go back home to the Redwoods of Northern California. Most of the time, Vance loved his work, but he hated missions that took him to big cities. He needed space to breathe, and the crowded streets of Chicago were beginning to feel like they were closing in on him.

Vance had been tracking these two mountain lion shifters for two weeks, but this was the first night he'd actually laid eyes on them. The two men were secretive and suspicious of everyone, but since Vance seemed like a normal, disinterested human, he was getting away with eavesdropping—and that eavesdropping was telling Vance exactly what he needed to know. The mountain lions were discussing, in hushed tones, an old spear that was currently on display in the Art Institute of Chicago. The museum's curator believed the spear was just an old Native American artifact, but the mountain lions had learned that it was actually a spear used by the ancient dragon clans. They were planning to stage a robbery of the spear, and then use the spear and its supernatural powers to overthrow the leaders of their own clan.

Vance let a wry smile pass over his lips as he listened, casually taking another sip of his whiskey. It was a story he'd heard dozens of times over the years, in various forms. A shifter would discover the existence of a powerful, ancient artifact, and then decide that they would be able to gain power just by using the artifact. But time after time, Vance and his clan mates had dashed the hopes of would-be tyrants by snatching away the artifacts before those tyrants had a chance to use them. Vance, along with nine other dragon shifters, had dedicated his life to preventing the unauthorized use of ancient shifter artifacts. Much of Vance's time was spent traveling across the country and the globe, recovering artifacts and bringing them back home to his clan's base camp, deep in the Redwood forests. Once the artifacts were safely in the Redwoods, Vance's clan of dragon shifters guarded them fiercely. No artifact had ever been stolen from them once it had been recovered and brought to the Redwoods.

Vance was more than ready to be back in those forests now. It was June, and already the humidity and heat in the city of Chicago was getting under Vance's skin. He was looking forward to the cool, fresh air of home. All he had to do was not screw things up tonight, and he would be back in his own cabin by tomorrow evening.

When the two mountain lions stood and left, Vance forced himself to wait a respectable amount of time before standing and leaving as well. He wasn't worried about finding them. These two, for all their suspicious glances over their shoulders, were terrible about hiding their tracks. They left a clear scent trail everywhere they went, which Vance's shifter nose easily picked up. He sighed as he followed their trail slowly toward the Art Institute. It was getting late, and the streets of Chicago were becoming less and less crowded, especially as Vance followed the scent trial through the business district of downtown. Here, the only signs of life that remained were lights in office windows here and there, indicating that some poor soul was stuck working instead of enjoying the warm night with the rest of Chicago.

Vance moved carefully, doing his best to stay out of sight of the two shifters ahead of him. They seemed like just the type of cowards to call off a mission if they had the slightest hint that someone was following them. The last thing Vance wanted right now was for them to wait another night or two to break in to the museum. If they did, he would have to wait even longer to get home.

Vance didn't blame the men for being nervous. Often, treason in a clan was punishable by death. Any shifter caught betraying his clan was sure to be expelled from the clan, if not killed. Vance's eyes darkened with anger as he watched the men. Traitors deserved to be punished. Loyalty was the highest virtue in Vance's eyes, and he had never understood how someone could betray their own clan members. No amount of money or power in the world could have tempted him to betray the Redwood Dragons. They were his brothers, and he would give his life to defend them in an instant.

Vance sighed. Treason shouldn't surprise him anymore. He saw it on nearly every mission he worked. It still made him angry, though. Vance figured that would never change, even if he recovered a hundred thousand artifacts.

By the time the men arrived at the museum, they seemed to be getting even more careless. Their suspicious glances over their shoulders had decreased, and they were instead becoming giddy with excitement at the prospect of the potential power they might soon hold in their hands. Vance resisted the urge to roll his eyes as he found a spot to hide a short distance away from the back entrance of the museum, where the two shifters were now standing in the open like big idiots.

"Don't screw this up, guys," Vance said. "I want to go home tonight."

The shifters, although perhaps not the smartest guys in the room, had at least made a rough plan for stealing the spear. Vance had overheard them reviewing the plan one last time before they left the bar. They would break into the back door using brute force, then shift into mountain lion form to confuse the guards, who no doubt would be expecting human intruders. In the midst of the chaos, they would quickly make their way to the display on the second floor where the spear was not very well guarded. The museum's security team did not think the spear was one of the higher value items in the Art Institute, and would surely be surprised that a duo of intruders went straight for it during a break-in. Once the spear was recovered, the shifters planned to run out, still in mountain lion form with the spear held between their teeth. They would sprint to a nearby parking lot where they had parked a getaway car, shift back into human form, and speed away. Their human faces would never even appear on the museum's security cameras.

Vance chuckled. They needed to be more careful, if they didn't want their human faces on camera. They were awfully close to the back entrance of the museum right now, and if they moved a few feet in the wrong direction they would be well within range of the cameras. Their plan was a haphazard, brazen attempt to use their shifting abilities to recover the stone. But, again, Vance had seen dozens of attempted robberies like this over the years. Shifters tended to think that the ability to shift gave them the ability to easily steal whatever they wanted. More often than not, their audacious attempts failed, and they were caught by the authorities. That didn't matter that much to Vance, though. He could care less whether or not they were caught. The only thing he cared about was that they got the spear out of the museum before they were caught. Then Vance could swoop down in dragon form and grab it, flying away before anyone realized what was happening.

The shifters had finally quieted down, and were gesturing toward each other silently in the dim light. Vance had a feeling they were about to make a move, and a few moments later he saw that he was right. One of them pulled a black ski mask over his face, pulled a giant axe-type tool with a foldable handle out of his bag, and ran toward the back door they had been staking out. The man unfolded the handle so that he now had a full length axe, and then he started beating against the door with all his might. Even though it was a thick, metal door, the strong shifter was quickly able to break through. Alarms were sounding off like crazy, but the men ignored them as the one holding the axe threw it aside.

Two large pops rang out as rushes of energy burst from the men's bodies, and they morphed into mountain lions. Guards were running toward the door now with guns drawn, but they stopped in confusion as they looked at the mountain lions running into the building.

"What the heck?" one of them yelled out before bounding into the building after the mountain lions. The other guards seemed unsure of what to do, and they looked wildly around outside, trying to find the human who had knocked down the door.

Vance knew it was time for him to shift himself. He was pretty far away right now, but the guards would be doing a thorough search of the area. The last thing Vance wanted was for the guards to catch him and think *he* was responsible for hacking down the door. Vance backed up as quickly as he dared, putting even more space between himself and the museum. And then, with a sudden loud pop and whoosh of energy, he shifted.

Instantly, he grew in size and his hands and feet began morphing into the scaled arms and legs of a dragon, complete with razor sharp claws. His head became the fierce, horned head of a dragon, with sharp teeth, and wisps of smoke rising from his nostrils. Wings sprouted from his back, growing long and powerful. A long tail ending in sharp spikes extended behind his dragon body, which was now completely covered in iridescent scales that went from green to purple and back again in the dim light.

The guards, who had heard the loud pop of energy, started running toward where Vance's dragon now stood. But before they could even rub their eyes to see whether they were actually seeing a dragon in the middle of Chicago or were going crazy, Vance had vanished from their view.

Vance was using a chameleon trick to blend into his surroundings. It was a difficult skill to learn, but any reptile shifter could do it. Being able to disappear into thin air was a highly useful trick, so all of the Redwood Dragons had taken time to perfect it. Vance watched carefully as the guards who had come running ran in confused circles nearby, looking for the source of the loud rush of energy. None of them said anything about seeing a dragon, and Vance figured none of them wanted to sound crazy. After a few moments, half of them went back to the museum while the other half continued searching the outside perimeter. In the distance, Vance could hear the sound of police sirens coming closer. He wished the two mountain lion shifters would hurry things up.

After a few more minutes which seemed to stretch into eternity, Vance heard loud roars as the mountain lions came back into view, one of them holding the spear in his mouth. Chaos ensued, as the guards tried to stop the mountain lions by threatening them with their guns, yelling at them and each other. Policemen were arriving on the scene now, and it was hard to see what was happening in the midst of the dozens of guards and officers who were now trying to trap the mountain lions against the back wall of the building.

Vance knew he had to hurry up and make his move before things got even crazier. He grabbed his backpack firmly with one of his strong dragon feet. Then, as silently as he could, he started flapping his wings and rose into the air. He let his chameleon disguise go, and he became visible against the Chicago skyline. He hated to allow the large group below him to see that there was actually a dragon here, but it couldn't be helped. Maintaining invisibility through the chameleon trick took quite a bit of concentration, and Vance needed to concentrate on other things right now. Like getting that spear.

A shout sounded out as one of the startled police officers noticed Vance's dragon coming toward the fray. More shouts and screams ensued, and the mountain lions themselves looked up, their cat eyes widening when they saw that another shifter had joined them. Vance breathed a huge stream of fire into the air, hoping to confuse and scare the group into inaction, at least for a few precious moments. Then, with a swoop as swift as an eagle's, he dove straight toward the mountain lions. He reached out one of his strong dragon feet, and used his sharp claws to grasp the spear firmly. The mountain lion tried to resist, holding so tightly to the spear with his teeth that he actually rose a few feet from the ground before dropping back down in agony. The second mountain lion roared and tried to leap up to attack Vance, but his teeth and claws merely scraped against the thickness of Vance's scales.

Before anyone else on the ground could react or even process what was happening, Vance had the spear firmly in his grasp and was rising high above the city, turning northeast to fly over Lake Michigan. He glanced back one last time to see how the scene below was playing out. The guards and policemen were pointing up at him, shouting and confused. The mountain lions were slowly slinking away, all but forgotten now that a dragon had been sighted.

Vance was tempted to let out another stream of fire, just for the heck of it. But his clan leader, Knox, was always yelling at him that he needed to be more subtle. So, with a slight puff of smoke, Vance turned his head back to the north and started flying as quickly as he could. He was heading to a suburb north of the city, where the Redwood Dragons kept in touch with a guy who owned a rental car shop. The guy was friends with the owner of a rental car shop near the dragons' home base in California, so Vance knew he could trust him. Vance would get a car and drive home as fast as he could, probably only stopping to refuel and get food. Ordinarily, Vance liked to fly home on a commercial airline. But he would never be able to get the spear he now held through security, so driving was his best option.

Vance turned his head to look behind him one more time. The tall buildings of Chicago's downtown area were starting to grow smaller, and the noise from the city was becoming quieter and quieter as Vance rose high into the air. He was thankful that it was dark, so that his dragon form would not be as obvious against the dark night sky. With any luck, he'd be home within forty-eight hours.

He'd be exhausted, but he'd be home. And he'd mark another "successful mission completion" notch on the bedroom wall of his small cabin.

Vance smiled as he pumped his wings harder and rose higher into the air. He'd worked hard, and he deserved a nice break. It was time for summer to really get started, and there was no place he'd rather spend his summer than the Redwoods of Northern California.

CHAPTER TWO

Lily Tarkett tapped her toes anxiously on the floor of the small rental car office, fidgeting and looking out the window every few seconds. She didn't realize how much she was squirming around until the grumpy store owner sitting behind the counter looked up at her, glaring.

"Wearing out a hole in my floor with those shoes isn't going to make anyone show up any faster, you know?" he said. "But it is keeping me from being able to concentrate on my paperwork over here. Do you mind?"

Lily mumbled an apology and forced herself to still her bouncing feet. It wasn't easy to keep still, though. She hadn't been filled with this much excitement since her first day on the job at the Advocacy Bureau in Falcon Cross. That had been nearly two years ago now, and a lot had changed in those two years. A year ago, Lily's roommate, Bree, had done the unthinkable and defied a High Council order saying that wizards were prohibited from letting shifters know of their existence. For hundreds of years, shifters had been convinced that wizards were extinct, and the wizards had been happy to keep things that way. Wizards had feared that shifters would attempt to destroy them if they became aware that many wizard clans were still alive and well. But when a powerful ancient dragon stone was in danger of falling into evil hands, Bree had claimed that the assistance of the shifters was necessary to save the wizards. She had contacted the shifters, asking them to help her.

It turned out, Bree had been right. Almost overnight, Bree had become a celebrity in Falcon Cross. The High Council had pardoned her for defying their order, and had allowed her to move to Northern California to live with Knox, the dragon shifter she had fallen in love with.

Bree had begged Lily to come visit her in the Redwoods, and now, Lily was finally getting the chance to do so. Lily had been instructed to wait at this rental car office in a tiny town near the edges of the Redwood forest where the Redwood Dragons lived. Bree would be coming with her lifemate, Knox, and another one of the dragon shifters to fly Lily deep into the forest.

All through her ten years of Advocacy School, Lily had been reminded over and over of how dangerous shifters were, and of how extraordinary precautions must be taken to ensure that shifters did not learn that wizards existed. It was almost unbelievable that she was about to spend her summer vacation with a clan of shifters. When she'd booked her plane ticket south, she'd felt almost like she was doing something wrong. A few years ago, a trip like this would have been breaking the law. Now, the High Council in Falcon Cross was encouraging wizards to interact with shifters as much as possible, in order to strengthen and improve shifter-wizard relations. In fact, even though Lily considered this trip a "vacation," she was actually being paid for it. The Advocacy Bureau had given her a paid leave of absence for the entire summer when she requested time off to come see the Lily and the Redwood Dragons.

A flash of movement just outside the window of the rental car shop caught Lily's eye, and she nearly squealed with delight when she saw Bree walking toward the shop, trailed by two very tall, very muscular men. One of the men was Knox, Bree's lifemate. The other one would be one of the other dragon shifters, although Lily wasn't sure which one. She knew there were ten Redwood dragons in total, and she'd briefly met a few of them when they'd been in Falcon Cross on official business. But this particular shifter didn't look familiar, so he must have been one of the ones Lily hadn't met yet.

Lily stood and started gathering her things noisily, earning her another glare from the shop owner, which she ignored. A moment later, the bell above the front door jangled loudly as Bree burst into the store.

"Lily!" Bree cried out, running to envelop her in a warm hug. "I can't believe you're here!"

Lily returned the hug, dropping all the things she had just gathered up. She didn't care. It was so good to see Bree again. Lily couldn't help feeling a bit jealous of her—in a happy way, of course. Bree looked so happy and full of life, and much less stressed than she had during the time Lily had known her in Falcon Cross. Working at the Advocacy Bureau required long hours, and most of that time was spent being stuffed up in a small office. Now, Bree spent most of her time out in the fresh air of the redwoods, and the change had done her good. Lily hoped that maybe by the time the summer was over, her skin would glow as much as Bree's did now.

Knox and the other dragon shifter squeezed into the small office behind Bree. When the shop owner saw Knox, his grumpy demeanor changed, and a smile actually passed over his face.

"Hey, brother," the owner said, standing to heartily shake Knox's hand. "Always a pleasure. How are you?"

"Good man, good," Knox said. "Happy that summer is coming. We don't have many artifacts to track down right now, so I'm hoping for a mostly chill summer with the crew."

"You deserve it," the store owner said, then turned to the other dragon shifter and extended his hand. "And I'll be damned if it isn't Vance himself! I was beginning to wonder if you were ever going to make it back home. You've been gone for months now."

Vance laughed. "Yeah, I had several missions back to back. It was brutal. But hopefully I'm home for the summer now. I'm planning to do nothing but sleep and barbecue for at least a week."

The men all laughed, and just then Vance looked over at Lily and caught her staring at him. She quickly turned back to Bree, but not before she felt a flush of pink heat creeping into her cheeks. Vance was gorgeous, and she could hardly believe she was about to be flown into the redwoods on his back. It had been a long time since Lily had felt a rush of excitement at the sight of a man, but seeing Vance sent an undeniable thrill through her body. Quickly, Lily started gathering up her belongings again, mostly to give herself something to do and to distract herself from Vance's steady gaze.

"How have you been?" Bree was asking, completely oblivious to the fact that Lily's heart had just skipped several beats thanks to Vance. "How are things back at the Advocacy Bureau? I want to hear all of the latest gossip. But, of course, there will be time for that tonight—and time this whole summer, actually. I can't believe you're going to be here for three whole months!"

Bree was talking a mile a minute, going almost nonstop. But Lily didn't mind. In fact, she was glad that she wasn't having to say much of anything herself right now. Her sudden attraction to Vance had taken her completely by surprise, and she needed time to compose herself before she had to ride on his back.

Vance was still talking to the store owner, but Knox had broken away now to come greet Lily.

"Lily, so good to see you. How are you?" he asked, opening his arms for a hug. Lily smiled and gave him a big hug before answering.

"I'm great! It's really good to see you, too. You haven't come up to Falcon Cross as much as I thought you would," Lily said.

Knox nodded. "I know. It's been a really busy couple of months. We had a sudden rush of sightings of old artifacts, so we had to go hunt them all down. But it's looking like it's going to be a pretty quiet summer, work-wise. Should be lots of time for hanging out and having a good time."

A big smile crossed Bree's face. "It's going to be awesome! Two of my favorite people, hanging out all summer long."

Knox's smile widened at Bree's words, and he leaned over to plant a quick kiss on Bree's lips. "It's gonna be good, babe. That's for sure."

Lily felt a small twinge of jealousy. She was so happy that Bree had found such a good man, but she wondered if anyone would ever look at *her* the way Knox looked at Bree. Lily was so busy with official wizarding business these days that she hadn't been on a date in months, and it had been years since she'd had an actual boyfriend. But Lily quickly pushed away her jealous thoughts. She wasn't here in California to have a pity party for herself. She was here to spend time with Bree and to get away from the stress of life in Falcon Cross.

"You guys all ready?" Vance's voice broke in to the conversation. "I know it's early, but we have a bit of a trip ahead of us still. We should get going if we want to make it back to base in time for dinner."

"Oh!" Bree said, clapping her hands a few times in excitement. "Let's get going then. I don't want to miss dinner. It's been too long since everyone was together for a barbecue. Besides, I have some peaches I want to grill for dessert. Have you ever had grilled peaches, Lily? They're pretty much the most delicious thing you'll ever eat in your life!"

Lily and Knox both laughed at Bree and her excitement, while Vance rolled his eyes. But Lily thought she saw the hint of a smile playing at his lips, despite his seeming indifference. He glanced over at Lily again and she quickly looked away, embarrassed that he had caught her looking at him again. What was wrong with her? She didn't even know the guy, so why was he making her blush like a schoolgirl? She hadn't come here for a summer fling, and although Vance was gorgeous, she could already tell that his "too-cool for school" attitude was going to annoy her. When Bree reached for Lily's arm to lead her outside, Bree was more than happy to walk as far ahead of Vance and Knox as possible.

The group headed toward the edge of town, where a small, inconspicuous trail led into the forest. From here, they would hike a few miles until they came to an open clearing, where the men would shift and then fly Bree and Lily the rest of the way to the dragons' base camp. Bree had explained the whole process carefully on the phone last week, and had seemed worried that Lily would protest at the idea of riding in on a dragon. It *was* possible to hike in, but it took significantly longer, and the dragons preferred not to leave trails through the forest that went directly to their hideout. They wanted to keep the place as secret as possible.

Lily had had no qualms about flying in on a dragon. In fact, she found the idea rather exciting. How many other wizards could say they had ridden on a dragon? Lily was looking forward to the experience. At least, she had been looking forward to it until she'd realized that she was going to be riding on a dragon who made her heart feel like it was going to beat right out of her chest with desire.

Bree continued to chatter, but Lily felt distracted and only heard about half of what she was saying. Finally, Bree seemed to notice that Lily wasn't replying much.

"I'm so sorry, Lily," Bree said. "Here I am talking your ear off when you're probably exhausted. Don't worry, though. Riding on the back of a dragon is surprisingly relaxing. You can rest up while they boys fly us to base."

Lily smiled weakly, but in her head she was thinking that it was going to be impossible to relax when she was riding on the back of a dragon shifter who just so happened to be the most gorgeous man she'd ever seen.

CHAPTER THREE

Despite Lily's misgivings, she had to admit that Bree was right about one thing: riding on a dragon was surprisingly relaxing. After hiking a little ways out of town, the boys had stripped and then shifted into dragons. Lily had looked away shyly while Vance stripped, although Bree seemed completely unfazed by it. It was another reminder to Lily of how Bree had managed to integrate herself into shifter life, which still felt crazy to Lily after a lifetime of trying to stay away from shifters.

But any feelings of awkwardness quickly melted away as Lily took in the magnificent sight of Vance's and Knox's dragon forms. The two of them standing next to each other were enough to fill even the most unenthusiastic heart with awe. They both had thick dragon hides that were covered in iridescent scales. Wherever the light streaked through the treetops and hit them, their scales glittered purple, blue, and even pink. They had long, spiked tails that twitched now and then with pent up energy, and their wings looked large even folded up against their bodies. Their heads were the most impressive part, though. They were large, with sharp horns. The tips of their razor sharp teeth could be seen poking through their dragon lips, and every now and then wisps of smoke curled up from their nostrils, hinting at the fact that they had the ability to breathe fire at any moment. They were true dragons, mighty in every sense, and Lily had been filled with a strange sense of reverence as she stared up at them.

That sense of reverence had only increased after she had climbed onto Vance's back and he had flapped his giant wings, lifting her effortlessly through the high treetops of the redwoods. The forest was thick, but he seemed to know by heart exactly where every branch was. He moved through the air like a ballet dancer might move across a stage, powerfully and gracefully. Lily was surprised by how at ease she felt. She had worried that riding up so high would make her scared, but Vance flew so smoothly and his back was so broad that she never worried that she might be thrown off of his back.

And when they finally rose above the treetops and kept going, higher and higher, she felt a sudden sense of privilege. How many mortals had been privileged to ride on the back of a dragon? Perhaps in ancient times, when these mythological creatures had been more prevalent, riding on a dragon had been more common. But today, when most humans thought that dragons had never actually existed, Lily guessed that the experience she was having right now was quite rare.

The air up here was quiet and calm. Lily had never experienced a silence as deep as this, with only the occasional, hushed pumping of Vance's wings to break up the stillness. When Lily glanced behind them, she could see Knox's dragon, with Bree sitting upright on his back and taking in the beauty around them. When Lily looked forward, however, was when she felt like she was truly in another world. Gently sloping, mountain-like hills stretched before her, covered in thick, green redwoods for as far as the eye could see. For the next few hours, Lily forgot about everything, even about the fact that she had an undeniable attraction to the man behind the dragon that she now rode.

All she could see was beauty. Tears of wonder filled her eyelids, and she glanced down at her magic ring, a thick onyx stone, black as midnight. Her clan of wizards used magic rings instead of wands to cast spells, and Lily's ring was a special one. It had belonged to her grandmother, and, although Lily had lost her grandmother years ago, she felt the ring kept her grandmother's spirit close to her. Overcome by the magic of the moment, Lily suddenly had an urge to add her own magic to the moment. Raising her ring high above her head, she yelled out a spell.

"*Magicae scintillula,*" she said. Instantly, shimmering orbs of light that looked like hundreds of shimmering diamonds came shooting from her ring. The sparkling light spheres left what looked like a trail of stardust behind them, and a big smile crossed Lily's face. She'd been doing magic her whole life, but she had a feeling that this was going to be the most magical summer she'd ever had.

* * *

Vance turned his head and a hint of a smile played at his dragon lips. Lily was doing some sort of cool trick that was leaving a trail behind them of what appeared to be shimmering diamonds. She really shouldn't be doing something that attracted extra attention to them, but Vance didn't care that much at the moment. Lily didn't know all the rules about keeping a low profile when in shifter form, and besides, they were out in the middle of nowhere right now. The odds of anyone seeing her little magic show were absurdly low, and Vance had to admit that he was rather enjoying it. The diamond trail sparkling in the sunlight was beautiful.

Just like her.

Vance didn't even try to push away the desire that filled his heart when he looked at Lily. Usually, he kept his guard up around woman. Being one of the Redwood Dragons was a dangerous, solitary life for the most part. Despite the fact that his work took him to many wonderful locations, where he often met beautiful women, Vance knew better than to risk his missions by getting involved with someone. Women were distracting, and they were also good at pretending to be your friend when they were actually spies who wanted to derail a mission. Perhaps Vance was overly paranoid, but he figured it was better to trust too few people than too many.

He couldn't help but wonder, though, if it might be possible to woo Lily. Since she was one of Bree's best friends and from the Falcon Cross wizard clan, he knew Lily wasn't secretly trying to spy on the Redwood Dragons or disrupt their missions. And, of course, she was going to be here all summer. If things went well, Vance would be home most of the summer, too. Was it possible that he might actually have an opportunity to have a girlfriend?

Vance felt his stomach tightening up with nervousness at the thought, which was a strange sensation for him. He was usually brazenly bold, and nothing scared him. But it had been ages since he tried to impress a woman. Did he even remember how? And what if one of the other guys took a liking to her and claimed her first? A wave of jealous anger washed over Vance at just the thought, and he found himself suddenly desperate to find a way to amaze her. He looked behind him, seeing that the stream of shimmering light was ending as she lowered her hand with the magic ring. She caught him looking at her, and a small smile played across her lips. Vance was surprised at how quickly that smile affected him. It sent a thrill through his whole dragon body, and he couldn't keep himself from looking up at the sky and letting out a stream of fire. So much for not drawing attention to themselves. Knox was probably going to chew him out for breathing fire for no reason, but Vance didn't care that much at the moment. All he cared about was impressing Lily.

Vance could see the spot up ahead where he would need to begin descending down into the forest, and he realized he was rapidly running out of time to impress Lily before the other dragons met her. He found a strange feeling of urgency come over him, and he quickly made the decision to show off his flying skills. The only one in this crew who could fly better than him was Knox, and, even then, Vance kept Knox on his toes by constantly striving to improve. Vance felt his dragon chest puffing up with pride. If he flew down at top speed in an acrobatic spiral, Lily was sure to be impressed with his skills. He knew Knox would probably yell at him for that, too. Knox hated how much Vance always tried to show off, but Vance didn't really care what Knox thought right now. He just wanted to prove to Lily that he was the best dragon on the crew. And so, without fully thinking through what he was about to do, Vance reared his head back and gave a giant roar, shooting another huge stream of fire into the air. Then, he dove.

He went slowly at first, giving Lily a moment to realize that they were descending so that she would have time to hold on extra tightly to his back. As soon as he felt her hands digging deeply into his back, he increased his speed. He dove straight down at first, then quickly jerked upward to change his direction. He heard Lily gasp, and he smiled, feeling pleased with himself. He flew in quick, rapidly descending circles, twirling through the air in every direction and showing off his amazing flying skills. He expertly maneuvered through the trees, dodging branches by mere inches, but never so much as scraping the side of his wing against one. When he finally landed with a resolute thud on the forest floor, he felt extremely proud of himself. He stood still long enough for Lily to slide off of his back, and then he let another proud, celebratory stream of fire spring from his dragon mouth. He flicked his tail and stretched his wings, doing his best to show off his dragon form to its fullest before transforming himself back into human form. With a loud pop, he began the transformation back into human form. His tail and wings disappeared, and his body became covered with human skin once again. He shook out his arms and legs as they returned to those of a man, and then he reached to grab his backpack from Lily so that he could get dressed once again.

He smiled as he reached over, hoping she wouldn't be looking away from his naked body in embarrassment as she had back at the beginning of their flight. But his smile faded as he reached for the backpack. She wasn't looking away from him, but she didn't look happy. In fact, her eyes were flashing with anger, and she almost seemed like she was trying to catch her breath.

"Lily? Is something wrong?" Vance asked, instantly concerned. He'd been expecting a round of applause and looks of awe. At the worst, he'd expected her to be feeling shy that he hadn't put clothes back on yet. He had not in the least expected to see her face turning red with rage.

"Lily? What's the matter?" he asked again.

"What the hell was that?" she asked, then threw his backpack at him. "And put some damn clothes on!"

The pack hit him with a surprisingly forceful thud. He took a step backward and tried to quickly fish some clothes out. He was at a loss as to why she was so mad.

"What was what?" he asked as he quickly pulled a shirt over his head, then started looking for pants.

"Why were you flying like a maniac? Were you trying to kill me?"

Vance looked up at her, surprised by the words, and even more surprised to realize that the look in her eyes wasn't exactly rage. It was closer to terror. Just then, Knox and Bree landed next to Vance with a gentle thud. Vance was still looking around in confusion when Lily's gaze shifted over to Bree, and Lily took some of her frustration out on Bree.

"Why didn't you tell me there was going to be a wild stunt show at the end?" Lily asked. She was visibly shaking, and Vance was starting to realize that he had made a big mistake.

"Lily, I'm sorry," he said. "I didn't mean to scare you, honest. I just thought it might be fun to do some tricks. I thought you'd enjoy it." Instinctively, he reached forward to put a comforting hand on Lily's shoulder, but she recoiled like a frightened animal.

"*Magicae arma!*" she yelled. A nearly invisible force field went up, causing Vance's hand to fling backward suddenly.

"Hey!" he said, starting to feel a little angry himself. "I wasn't trying to scare you on purpose. I thought you would *like* doing a little crazy flying."

A loud pop and rush of energy came across the clearing as Knox began shifting back from dragon to human form.

"I had no idea he was going to fly like a madman, or I would never have let you fly on him," Bree said. "I would have gotten Myles, or someone else sane. Come on. Let's go to the cabins. You can sit down and take a breather there."

"*Arma terminantur,*" Lily said. The force field shield fell away, and Bree took a step forward to put her arm around Lily. The two of them started walking down the short path from the clearing, which led to the eleven cabins that served as the Redwood Dragons home base. Bree gave Vance a pointed glare before they left, but Lily did not so much as glance at him. Knox was just finishing getting dressed, and he looked up at Vance and shook his finger at him.

"Not cool, man. Not cool. You scared the living daylights out of our guest before she even arrived at our camp. I'm going to have to go calm her down and make sure she's okay, but don't think you're getting off easy on this. We're going to be having a conversation later."

With that, Knox grabbed his backpack and stormed off after Bree and Lily, leaving Vance standing by himself, confused and angry.

"Someone *sane?*" Vance spat out at to the empty clearing. "I am sane. I know how to fly better than anyone. I'm always careful. And why the hell am I always getting compared to Myles?"

Myles was another one of the clan members, and Vance considered him to be something of a goody-two-shoes. Myles always did everything by the book, never took even the slightest of unnecessary risks, and, in Vance's opinion, was boring as hell most of the time. But Knox loved Myles. In fact, the only person whom Knox loved more than Myles was Knox's best friend, Noah, another one of the dragons.

But what made this instance of getting compared to Myles worse was that Vance hadn't even realized that what he was doing would cause such a big reaction. He had expected to get reprimanded a bit by Knox for drawing attention to himself, but he had never expected Lily to get angry with him. Maybe he should have realized that not everyone would enjoy fast-paced, acrobatic flying, but he loved it so much that it had never occurred to him that it would scare Lily.

"God, I'm such an idiot," he said aloud to a nearby tree. The tree stood silent and unmoving, and, with a big sigh, Knox started walking down the path that led to the cabins. He could feel anger filling him, and he knew he needed to get his emotions under control, but it was hard to feel like he was always getting in trouble just for being himself.

Yeah, he took risks sometimes. That was part of what made him good at his work. He'd risked his own life and health numerous times in order to get ancient dragon artifacts out of the wrong hands. The shifter world was a safer place, quite literally due to the fact that he had swooped in and managed to snatch up powerful artifacts in situations where even his own clan mates had said it would be impossible to complete the mission successfully. Knox always gave him the hardest missions, and Vance always received lavish praise for his work. And yet, he was always getting yelled at by Knox, or by Noah, who served as Knox's second in command. They told him he was too showy. He drew too much attention to himself. Yeah, he was good at taking risks, but he needed to stop taking so many *unnecessary* risks. He needed to be more of a team player, and think about the repercussions his actions might have for the clan, not just for himself.

Vance let out a sigh as the cabins came into view. Bree and Lily were nowhere to be seen, but the rest of the shifters who were at base right now were gathered around the fire pit that stood in the center of the base camp. Knox was with them, gesturing emphatically as he spoke, although Vance had no idea what he was talking about. Vance couldn't see Knox's face, but he could see the other shifters glance up as he came into view. They all had a hint of disdain in their faces, and he knew in that moment that they had already seen how upset he had made Lily. They were glaring at him because he had frightened their guest. All happiness and praise over the fact that he had just recovered a powerful ancient spear was forgotten. Vance let out a long, frustrated sigh.

He was the dragon everyone loved to hate.

CHAPTER FOUR

Vance's mood did not improve over the next several hours. He found himself sulking on the outskirts of the barbecue that night, watching from a safe distance while everyone else laughed and talked with Lily. Not many women came through their little base in the Redwoods, and Vance felt his stomach twisting with jealousy as the other dragons all leaned in a little too close to ask Lily about how her trip from Falcon Cross had been, or about what she was most looking forward to that summer. He gritted his teeth and chewed angrily on his lower lip as he saw Owen gently touching her arm, asking her what her job at the Advocacy Bureau was like. And he did his best to look the other way when Myles laughed a little too loudly at one of her jokes.

But Vance was pretty sure he'd never been so angry or frustrated in his life. He felt he had a claim to Lily. He'd seen her first, after all. Logically, he knew this made no difference. But in his desperation, he grasped at any small reason to call her his. His blood boiled as he watched everyone else enjoying her company, falling all over themselves to get closer to her. And he found himself downing beer after beer as he paced back and forth several feet away from the fire pit.

Knox hadn't spoken to him yet, but Vance knew he'd be getting a lecture before the week was done. Knox hated showoff dragons more than anything, and Vance was the biggest showoff of the group. He would readily admit to that. But he didn't feel like he deserved to be yelled at for scaring Lily. It hadn't been intentional. He had wanted to show Lily a good time. But Vance knew that wouldn't matter. Knox was keenly interested in maintaining good relations between the Redwood Dragons and the Falcon Cross wizards, and Vance wasn't an idiot. He knew Knox viewed his acrobatic flying today as a threat to those relations, but Vance hadn't been trying to stir the pot. He'd only wanted to capture the attention of the most beautiful woman he'd ever seen.

Vance let out a sigh and downed another long sip of beer as Lily laughed at some other stupid joke that Owen had just made. Lily hadn't made eye contact with Vance all evening. Vance had wanted to talk to her and explain things again before the barbecue had been in full swing, but she'd turned and walked quickly in the other direction as soon as she'd seen him coming. Vance frowned as he remembered this. He decided that he'd finally had enough, and turned to walk away from the fire pit, leaving the happy group behind him. He tossed his beer can in the trash, and then slipped into the darkness of the woods.

Instantly, he felt better. He knew some people thought that the forest was spooky at night, but to him, this was when it was most peaceful. He moved almost silently through the woods, breathing in the fresh, woodsy air, and running his hands across the massive trunks of the redwoods.

According to legend, the ancient Redwood Dragons clan had lived in these same forests for thousands of years. The history of this place often brought chills to Vance. Sometimes he could hardly believe that he was lucky enough to be here, running his hands across the same trees that his ancestors had. And yet, sometimes, he felt as though he didn't belong here. It was a nagging feeling that had plagued him his whole life.

After all, he wasn't *really* one of the ancient dragons. His former clan leader, William, had been the last of the Redwood Dragons bloodline. When William realized that he was unlikely to ever have a son of his own, he had gone out and adopted orphaned dragon shifters as his own. That had been during the last great shifter war, so orphans had been relatively easy to find. Vance was one of ten young dragon shifters William had brought here and raised. Now, William had retired and moved to Texas, and Knox was clan leader. And, even though Vance loved Knox most of the time, all the changes in clan politics had intensified the little voice in Vance's head that told him he might be better off somewhere else. When that little voice came up, Vance always pushed it down. But it was getting harder and harder to do.

Vance had been so excited to be home for the summer, but the disapproving looks everyone kept giving him tonight had cooled his excitement somewhat. Was he just too brazen, too rash to be part of this group? And did he really want to spend his entire life alone, without a woman? There wasn't much chance of having a girlfriend as long as he lived out here in the woods, and he had pretty much blown his chance with Lily before they even made it home.

Vance let out a long, frustrated sigh. Lily had awakened desires within him that had been dormant for a long time. He felt almost angry now as he realized that his sudden feelings of discontent with his life here and the summer ahead stemmed from the fact that he would be spending that whole summer looking at Lily, but unable to have her for his own. His dragon was restless within him, and Vance wished he could shift right now and go for a long, soothing flight in the summer moonlight. He didn't dare do that, though. Knox already had enough things to yell at him about. Vance didn't need to add to that list by flying around for no reason and risking being caught.

"Not hungry?" a voice behind him asked, nearly causing Vance to jump out of his skin. It was Knox.

"Jesus, Knox. I know you're the best in the world at sneaking up on people, but do you have to sneak up on your own dragons? You nearly gave me a heart attack!"

"Sorry. It's just habit for me to move so silently," Knox said, but the moonlight revealed the hint of a smile on Knox's lips. Knox was unapologetically proud of his stealth skills.

"Why'd you follow me, anyway?" Vance asked, even though he already knew the answer. "Can't a man get some peace and quiet out in the woods?"

"I wanted to talk to you," Knox said, his voice sounding suddenly weary. "You know you can't keep defying our clan's ground rules about overly showy flying. It's true that this area isn't very heavily populated, but we still have to be careful. If the wrong person sees us and gets too curious, the clan's base camp could be in trouble."

Vance resisted the urge to roll his eyes. He didn't see how his flying style made much difference. Flying was flying, no matter how many flips or barrel rolls he did in the sky. If someone saw a dragon, they would probably freak out regardless of how tamely that dragon was flying. Besides, Lily had set off a long stream of shimmering light behind them. How was that not showy flying?

"Did you also reprimand Lily for her little magic show up in the sky?" Vance challenged.

Knox sighed. "Lily is our guest. It's not my job to reprimand her, but I did explain to her that we try to keep our flying low key around here. She was extremely apologetic, unlike you. Look, Vance, you know I consider you a brother and a dear friend, and I know you're just trying to have some fun. But I can't look the other way when you break clan rules about flying protocol. You've got to stop."

"Or what?" Vance asked, crossing his arms. "You gonna kick me out of the clan?"

A pained expression passed over Knox's face, and, for a moment, Vance felt guilty. He knew that Knox had a lot of responsibility on his shoulders, and that the rules had been set even before Knox's time as leader. Knox was just trying to do his best as clan leader to protect everyone. But, still, Vance didn't appreciate being scolded like a naughty schoolboy when he'd just been having a little fun out in the middle of nowhere.

"Of course I'm not going to kick you out of the clan," Knox said. "But if I can't trust you to play by the rules, you'll be grounded from further missions until I can."

Vance's eyes shot up in shock. "You wouldn't!" he said.

But the look in Knox's eyes told Vance that he would. Vance was tired now and was happy to have a break from missions over the summer. But Vance also knew that he would go stir crazy sitting here on base for months at a time while everyone else was sent off to work on exciting artifact recovery jobs. Deep down, he loved his work, and he didn't want to lose his chance to do the most exciting parts of it.

"You gotta get your shit together, okay?" Knox said, the weariness in his voice growing even more evident. "And for Pete's sake, don't fly like a maniac with a girl on your back. They don't like it."

Vance was about to open his mouth to protest again, but he shut it and thought better of it. Knox seemed like he was just giving him a warning right now, and Vance should just let it go at that. There was no need to explain to Knox why he had been trying to impress Lily. All that would do was earn him some good ribbing from the clan leader, and Vance was not in the mood for that right now.

"Fine," Vance said sullenly. "I'll get my shit together, whatever that means."

Knox sighed, but seemed to accept Vance's half-hearted apology. With a slight nod of his head, Knox turned to head back to camp. Vance watched Knox go, feeling both angry at the clan leader and glad that he himself did not have to take on the responsibilities of boss. Vance knew that Knox did not like the disciplinary portion of being in charge, and he certainly didn't blame him for that. But at least Knox had some sense of control over his life. Vance was feeling more and more like he was just a small, insignificant piece of the shifter world.

Vance was a troubled soul, searching for something but not quite sure exactly what it was that he was searching for. When he saw Lily earlier today, he'd thought for a brief moment that maybe he'd found it. But that hope had been dashed almost as quickly as it sprung up. Vance set his jaw in a determined line and began to turn to walk deeper into the woods, but just before he did, he heard Knox calling back to him one more time. His voice was faraway, but the words came through loud and clear.

"You know, Vance, you have to get a girl to trust you first. Then she'll let you take her on as wild of a ride as you want."

Vance frowned into the darkness, surprised at how much Knox seemed to realize about his desire for Lily, and surprised at how quickly the thought of taking her on another wild ride made his heart beat nearly out of his chest.

CHAPTER FIVE

Lily woke with a start, feeling disoriented as she sat up and realized that her head was pounding. Sunlight streamed in through her window, and she closed her eyes against its unforgiving brightness. Like a flood, everything came back to her, and she smiled despite her wicked hangover.

She was deep in the heart of the California Redwoods, and she would be here for the next three months. She had nothing to worry about, and no work responsibilities to stress her out. For the first time in her adult life, she could truly relax.

Lily swung her legs over the side of the bed and made her way to the kitchen of the small cabin. She started inspecting the contents of the cabinets, hoping to find something that would take the edge off the pounding in her head. She came across a dusty bottle of ibuprofen, with an expiration date two years passed. With a shrug, she popped two of the pills, downed some water, and hoped for the best.

This cabin had once belonged to William, the former leader of the Redwood Dragons clan. But since he'd been gone, the clan had mainly used the cabin for storage. It would serve as Lily's home for the summer, though, and the dragons had made an attempt to clean it up and stock it with basic supplies. Headache medicine must not have been high on their checklist, though.

Thankfully, it seemed that coffee had been a priority, because Lily found a fresh, unopened bag of beans in another one of the kitchen cabinets. Lily started brewing a pot, then sat at the small kitchen table to wait. She had checked the fridge yesterday and knew it was stocked with eggs, yogurt, and fruit, but she felt a little too queasy to eat anything at the moment. Maybe after her coffee.

Lily had surprised herself with how many beers she had downed last night. It had been years since she'd had a proper hangover, but for some reason she'd really let her hair down around the campfire last night. Perhaps it was the excitement of being in a new place, or maybe she was trying to calm down the last bit of nerves left over from her flight into the shifters' base camp. Whatever the reason, Lily had really let loose.

But it had been worth it. Lily could not remember the last time she'd laughed so hard. It's not that she hated her life back in Falcon Cross or anything like that. It's just that she always had so much stress to deal with from her job. Here, she felt like she could just be herself. And the dragon shifters had all been so funny. Bree had warned her that the humor around the campfire could get a little crass. After all, Bree was the only woman in the group. But the men had all been on their best behavior last night, and Lily had never felt uncomfortable.

Well, all of the men except Vance had been on their best behavior. Lily could not believe how rude he had been. First, he had flown like a maniac for their whole harrowing descent down into the forest. Lily had truly thought she was going to die for most of that awful flight downward. And then, he had not even bothered to apologize. The closest he'd come to an apology was mumbling something about how he'd thought she would like the fast-paced flying. After that, he'd ignored her for the rest of the night. Bree had told her not to let him get to her. According to Bree, Vance was constantly showing off or challenging Knox's rules, and causing trouble for the whole clan. Bree said Knox let a lot of Vance's behavior slide, though, because he was one of the best dragons in the group at recovering artifacts. Vance was brazen, yes, but he was also fearless. And sometimes fearlessness was exactly what was needed to get the job done.

At least, that's what Bree had told Lily. Lily had spent her whole working life behind a desk at the Advocacy Bureau. She didn't have a lot of experience with jobs that required fearlessness. Perhaps it was better that Vance had ticked her off at the start. Her silly little crush on him probably would have gone nowhere, considering how different their lives were. Now, any time Lily found herself thinking about how gorgeous Vance looked, she reminded herself of what an asshole he was. It was the easiest way to keep herself from falling for him.

Lily's coffee was done brewing now, so she stood and went to find a mug. She poured herself a generous serving of the strong, black liquid, then crossed the small cabin again so that she was standing by the front window. She smiled as she sipped her coffee and looked out. The forest was just as beautiful today as it had been yesterday. The thick trees with their huge, reddish brown trunks gleamed in the sunlight that filtered through their green tops. Lily could hear birds singing, and now that her headache was starting to subside thanks to the medicine, she could truly appreciate the sounds of the forest. Two of the shifters, whom Lily recognized as Myles and Noah, were sitting near the fire pit, drinking coffee and laughing. Lily decided that she would go join them, and started to turn to find her shoes. But just before she looked away, her eyes caught some movement to the right of Myles, and she saw Vance walking toward the fire pit. She froze, instantly annoyed with him for ruining her plan to go outside. There was no way she was going out there when he was there. She wasn't ready to face him and his snotty attitude again.

But damn, as much as she disliked him, she could not help but admire how wonderful he looked in the morning sunshine. He was wearing a fitted, short-sleeved black t-shirt with a pair of jeans, and the casual look made him look like the kind of guy you could kick back with for hours, talking and laughing. His bicep muscles strained against the sleeves of his t-shirt, and even from here his dark brown hair seemed to shine in the morning light. He kept it cropped close to his head, revealing his slightly elfish ears. It was hard to see their elfish shape from here, but Lily had seen them up close yesterday, and she knew that all dragon shifters had ears like that. She loved the way their ears hinted at the power that lay within them.

A sudden knock on the door startled Lily, causing her to jump and slosh a bit of her coffee onto the floor of the cabin. With a muttered curse, she went to set the mug down and grab a paper towel, calling, "Come in," over her shoulder.

Bree stepped into the room. Lily had guessed it was her, and she felt strangely shy when she saw her friend. There was no way for Bree to know that she had just been admiring Vance from afar, but still, Lily felt like she'd been caught in the act.

"Hey, Bree," Lily stammered out. "I just spilled my coffee like a total klutz. Come on in. How're you doing this morning?"

"I'm great," Bree said, stepping into the room and looking around at the small cabin. "Wow, they really cleaned this place up for you. You should have seen it beforehand. It was filled with all kinds of random stuff. It's probably good that you came to visit, so that they were forced to sort through everything."

"Well, I obviously didn't see it before, but it's nice and cozy now," Lily said as she wiped up the spilled coffee from the floor. "And the bed is so comfy. I slept like a baby."

"Good," Bree said. "I was hoping you would. There's something really peaceful about sleeping out here in the middle of the woods. It's so quiet at night, and you feel like you can really rest."

Lily nodded. "Very true. So what's on the agenda for today?"

"Well, that's what I wanted to come talk to you about," Bree said, looking somewhat guilty. "Knox very unexpectedly got a call about an artifact we need to go recover. We weren't expecting to have any more for a while, and this does sound like a pretty minor mission. But it also sounds like the artifact will be easier to recover if a woman does the job. The guy who currently has possession of it is apparently fairly easy to distract at a bar if you just have a pretty woman sit next to him."

"So Knox wants you to go do the mission," Lily said, quickly catching Bree's drift.

Bree nodded. "He wants to go with me and leave this morning. I'm really sorry to jet off like this right after you arrived, but it should only be a few days. And this most likely will be the only time I have to leave this summer."

Lily gave Bree a genuine smile. "It's totally fine. I can entertain myself easily enough, I'm sure. Besides, I'm still a bit tired from the trip here to the redwoods. I wouldn't mind just relaxing and resting for a few days."

Bree smiled gratefully. "Thank you so much," she said. "I promise I'll be as quick as I can. I've already talked to the guys and they've promised to make sure you're well-taken care of. I even talked to Vance, and told him to just give you some space."

"Thanks," Lily said with a small chuckle, although her heart tightened up in her chest a bit at Bree's words. Lily was feeling a strange desire to see more of Vance, probably due to how wonderful he had looked standing in the morning sun. But she reminded herself that his looks were much nicer than his personality. He was a jerk, and she didn't want to spend her summer pining away for a jerk.

"Myles, Noah, and Owen should all be here the whole time that Knox and I are gone. And one of the dragons you haven't met yet, Zeke, should be coming in sometime today. He just wrapped up a long mission, so I'm sure he'll be in a good mood and be happy to be back. He's really nice, and shouldn't give you any trouble. Still, I'm sorry to leave you alone with all the guys."

"I'm sure I'll be fine," Lily said. "Don't worry about me, really. I'll steer clear of Vance and I'm sure everyone else will take good care of me."

"Okay," Bree said, the gratefulness evident in her voice. "I have to take off really soon, but Myles and Noah are making breakfast at the fire pit. They like to fry eggs and sauté potatoes in a pan over the fire, and I'm sure they'd be happy to share with you. They've also got coffee, although I see you've made some of your own already."

Lily laughed. "Yup, already made and spilled coffee, so the day is off to a good start. But seriously, Bree. You don't need to hold my hand. Stop worrying about me and get going. I'll be fine, and I can't wait to hear all about your adventures when you get back."

Bree smiled. "Alright. Although I don't think this particular mission is going to be very adventurous. It sounds like it'll be a straightforward there and back job."

"Anything is more adventurous than working at the Advocacy Bureau. Although, somehow, you managed to make even that adventurous when you were there," Lily said with a laugh.

"Well, I don't think the Advocacy Bureau appreciated my efforts back then, but they seem to like me now. Working as a wizard ambassador to the shifters is a pretty good gig, I must say."

"I'm so jealous," Lily said. "Life out here in the redwoods seems like a dream."

"Well, nothing's ever perfect in life," Bree said. "But it is pretty sweet. I'll see you in a day or two, then?"

Lily nodded, and gave Bree a quick hug. "Good luck!"

"Thanks," Bree said. "And I wasn't kidding. You should go out to the fire pit and have some breakfast with the guys. Sharing meals with them is a great way to get to know the crew."

Bree gave a small wave, and then disappeared out the front door of the cabin. Lily sipped at the coffee that remained in her mug, and watched Bree disappear across the clearing. Lily did very much want to go eat breakfast by the fire pit, but there's no way she was going out there while Vance was still there. She was still angry with him for his crazy flying antics, which made the way her heart flip-flopped at the sight of him even more confusing.

She watched through the front window as Vance sat beside Myles, apparently making some sort of joke because a moment later the two of them were roaring with laughter. Vance grabbed a plate from the stack that was sitting by the campfire, and piled it high with food. Lily watched, unable to look away even though she wanted to. Owen showed up a minute later, and soon the whole group was eating, talking, and laughing. Lily felt a pang of regret that she wasn't out there, too. She wanted to get to know the clan members better, and she felt silly for avoiding them based solely on Vance. She took a couple of deep breaths, then went to find her shoes. She would walk out there with her head held high, and if Vance didn't like it he could go to his cabin and sulk. There was no reason for Lily to sit here and let him ruin her vacation.

Lily quickly changed out of her PJs into jeans and a t-shirt, laced up her sneakers, and headed out the front door of her cabin before she could change her mind. But she needn't have worried. She stepped out of her cabin's front door just in time to see Vance walking away from the campfire. He was walking toward the forest with an easy stride, and he didn't look back as he disappeared into the large tree trunks.

Lily breathed a sigh that was somewhere between relief and disappointment, and then went to join Noah, Myles, and Owen by the fire pit.

"Hey, sleepyhead," Owen said. "I was beginning to wonder if you were going to sleep the whole day away. Want some breakfast?"

Lily smiled. "I'm starving. I'd love some."

Owen's grin widened and he began scooping out a large plate of food for Lily. She settled in to eat it, and tried to ignore the way Owen looked at her in a little bit too friendly of a manner. Lily supposed it was naïve of her to think that she could come to a shifter camp full of bachelors and not have one or more of them be interested in her. And, truth be told, the idea *had* crossed her mind that a summer fling would be fun. The problem was that all of the guys sitting around the fire pit right now, while handsome, weren't nearly as good looking as Vance—at least not in her opinion. Vance was quite close to what Lily would consider her idea of the perfect male, at least as far as looks were concerned. If only he hadn't turned out to be such a jerk.

"How'd you sleep?" Noah asked, leaning over to hand Lily a fresh mug of coffee. Lily took the mug happily. Even though she'd already had some coffee back in the cabin, she was still feeling a bit groggy.

"I slept great. The cabin is awesome, and it's so quiet and peaceful out here," Lily said, then took a long sip from her mug.

"Yeah, I love the peace out here," Myles said. "There's nothing like coming home from a chaotic mission and being able to just chill out here and enjoy yourself. Coming home never gets old."

"Speaking of missions," Noah said. "I suppose you heard that Knox and Bree headed off on a mission this morning?"

Lily nodded, and then smiled. "Bree told me. She promised me that all of you would take good care of me and entertain me."

The dragon shifters laughed at the sassy tone in Lily's voice, and Owen was the first to speak. "Well, if you want to have a good time out here, I can show you all the best spots in the forest. I know these woods like the back of my hand."

Noah rolled his eyes at Owen's words. "Of course you do," he said. We all do, since we all grew up here. Stop trying to show off."

Owen's cheeks turned slightly red at Noah's words, but Myles threw his head back and laughed. For her part, Lily felt a bit awkward and didn't know how to respond to Owen's offer. The man was clearly dropping hints left and right that he was interested in her, but Lily could already tell he wasn't her type. She tried to avoid answering Owen's offer to show her around the forest by shoving her mouth full of food. Thankfully, Myles chose that moment to ask Noah a question about Knox's and Bree's mission, giving Lily a chance to look at Noah and act intensely interested in whatever it was he was saying. But really, she couldn't stop wondering whether Vance had gone off on a mission, too. Why had he hiked off into the forest alone? Was he going to be gone for several days, too? And why did that possibility make Lily sad? She had to get a grip on her emotions.

"Where did Vance head off to?" Lily asked, trying to sound nonchalant but desperately wanting to know.

Noah shrugged. "He said he was going for a walk. Didn't say where or why, but that's typical Vance. He goes through these phases where he likes to spend a lot of time alone."

"Don't worry, he really is a very nice guy," Myles said. "He'll probably leave you alone for the most part, and if he doesn't we'll get in his face."

Noah and Owen laughed, and Lily laughed weakly along with them. They had taken her curiosity over Vance's whereabouts as worry that she was going to have to see him. But there was only a small part of her that was really worried. The other part of her wanted to know how he was spending his day, and wondering what she might have been doing with him right now if he hadn't messed everything up by flying around like an idiot.

Lily shook her head in frustration as she took another bite of her eggs. What kind of person sat there angry at a man they barely knew while still wondering where he was and wishing to be with him? Lily thought to herself that she was quite a mess, and avoided eye contact with the other shifters, pretending to be intensely occupied with her food. But just then, Myles suggested that they all go down to the swimming hole and spend the day in the water. Lily immediately jumped on the opportunity. If all the guys went, she wouldn't somehow end up alone on an awkward forest tour with Owen. And swimming did sound like fun, even if it was a bit chilly in the forest this morning.

"I'm game," Lily said, and Noah and Owen agreed, too.

"Awesome," Myles said. "I've been itching to swim. Meet you guys back here in fifteen minutes and we'll head out?"

They all agreed, and Lily wolfed down the last bite of her food. She was suddenly looking forward to the day ahead. This would be a good chance to get to know everyone better. Who really cared where Vance had gone?

She'd already let him ruin her afternoon yesterday. There was no sense in letting him ruin any more of her vacation.

CHAPTER SIX

"Wahoo!" Noah yelled, his loud, strong voice echoing through the forest. His yell was punctuated by a large splash as he flew from the rope he'd been swinging on and landed in the large "swimming hole." The place was beautiful, and would have been hard to find if you didn't know where it was. Only one small, barely visible path led here off the main trail, but if you knew where that path was, you were richly rewarded. The small swimming hole was located at the bottom of a large waterfall. Gushing water spilled over a rocky cliff into a deep pool below, and the whole place was surrounded by the gorgeous trunks of redwood trees. The trees in this grove right here were some of the largest that Lily had seen, and she'd had to pinch herself several times to believe that this was really her life this summer.

Right now, she was lying on a towel on the uneven grassy bank of the swimming hole, wearing a t-shirt and shorts over her swimsuit. Even though the sun found its way through the treetops to shine on a good portion of the water, the air here was cool, and the water wasn't exactly warm. Lily hadn't lasted very long in the small pool before deciding to get out and dry off. The dragon shifters all seemed impervious to the temperatures of the pool, however. Lily remembered Bree telling her before that dragon shifters were hot-natured, since they were warmed from within by their fire-breathing abilities. Noah, Myles, and Owen were certainly proving that to be true. They did not flinch in the slightest whenever their bare skin hit the cool water of the pool.

Lily didn't mind that much that the water was cold. She was perfectly happy lying here watching the boys, lazily popping ripe summer berries into her mouth and exulting in the fact that she had nothing to do—no reports due at work, no bosses breathing down her neck and yelling at her that she was behind on all of her projects. Here, there was nothing to do but breathe in the deep woodsy air and relax under the most magnificent trees she'd ever seen.

A few minutes later, Myles came trudging up the steep bank, his swim trunks dripping wet. He reached into the cooler that was sitting a few feet away from Bree, and fished out a beer. Lily smiled. The shifters always seemed to have a good supply of beer around, and they made good use of it.

"Sorry, I'd sit down near you but I'm soaking wet and I don't want to completely drench one of our two towels," Myles said.

Lily laughed. Even though the men had managed to put together two coolers of beer and food in just a few minutes, and had hauled the coolers over the rough path to the swimming hole, they had somehow neglected to remember towels. Lily had happened to bring two, one of which she was sitting on right now. The other one was spread out next to her, and Myles looked at it somewhat longingly.

"I can help you out," Lily said, and then raised her magic ring in the direction of Myles' swim trunks. "*Magicae siccum!*"

Instantly, the drying spell sucked all the moisture from Myles swim trunks, and he stood there as though he had never even jumped into the pool.

"Wow," he said, looking down at his shorts. "That's quite a trick. I forget sometimes that you're a wizard. You seem so…normal."

Lily laughed again. "What is normal?" she asked.

Myles sat down next to her. "Good question. I guess it's sort of strange for a dragon shifter to be talking about normal. We're not exactly what most people would call the 'boy next door.'"

"Well," Lily said, as Owen let out a Tarzan yell and flew into the water with a giant splash. You guys are pretty much typical boys as far as I can tell, except for the fact that you can turn into dragons."

Myles laughed. "Yeah, minor detail there."

Lily chuckled, and, for a few moments, the two of them were silent. There was no sound except the laughter of Owen and Noah as they each tried to dunk each other under the water. These guys really were just like overgrown kids. Lily glanced sideways at Myles for a brief moment. He seemed to be quite down to earth, and Lily decided in that moment that she trusted him. He hadn't made any sort of move on her, and she appreciated that. In fact, he was a complete gentleman—the opposite of Owen, who seemed more than happy to take whatever brazen actions he thought might help him score some sort of deeper relationship with Lily.

"How are things with the wizards these days?" Myles was asking, his face etched with genuine concern. "Bree told us that there was a lot of unrest in Falcon Cross after the High Council made the decision to renew relations with shifters."

Lily frowned, her heart feeling truly heavy for the first time since she'd landed in the Redwoods. For centuries, wizards had hidden their existence from shifters, but things had changed after Knox, Bree, and the other dragons had worked together to save the wizards from a treasonous wizard who was trying to use an ancient dragon stone to overtake the Falcon Cross wizard clan. Since the shifters had risked their own lives and safety to help the wizards, the High Council in Falcon Cross had decided to attempt a complete reconciliation with the shifters. Things were going well so far, but Myles was right—there was unrest in Falcon Cross. Many of the older wizards still did not trust the shifters, and thought that the High Council was making a mistake allowing them to mingle with the wizards. There had been times over the last year that tensions had run impossibly high, but lately things had seemed to be settling down somewhat. Now that it had been a year and the shifters seemed to be remaining loyal, folks were settling down. But Lily didn't feel like getting into the details of all of this right now. She wanted to enjoy the beautiful setting and not think about the stress of the last year. So she wiped the frown off her face and shrugged in Myles direction.

"The last year has brought a lot of changes, and there's always a certain level of discomfort with big changes. But overall things seem to be settling down. I wouldn't have been able to come here for the summer otherwise. My job as an Advocate is really important during times of unrest. I'm young and very junior at the Advocacy Bureau, but I've had a lot of work over the last year just trying to calm down the frantic wizards in Falcon Cross who thought we were all doomed because shifters now know we exist."

Myles laughed, somewhat bitterly. "It's crazy for me to hear that so many distrust shifters. All we really want is to keep good people safe, whether they're wizards, shifters, or humans."

Lily smiled at Myles and the fierce look on his face. He seemed really sweet, and she had a feeling they were going to be good friends. "Well, on behalf of all wizards, I'm sorry that some of the Falcon Cross wizards have been rude and distrustful. For what it's worth, I think your clan is great."

The expression on Myles face softened as he looked over at Lily. "Thanks," he said. "It's good to know you think we're alright. Especially after the way Vance freaked you out for no reason. I'm really sorry he did that."

Lily shrugged and laughed off Myles' comment about Vance, but she couldn't ignore the thrill she felt at the mention of his name. No matter how mad she had been at Vance for his crazy flying antics, she was beginning to realize that she couldn't stop the way her heart was drawn to him. She vowed then and there to work extra hard to keep plenty of space between her and Vance. The less she had to see him, the less she would have to deal with these strange twitches of passion in her chest.

As it turned out, it wasn't actually that much work to avoid Vance. Over the next several days, Lily spent plenty of time with the other dragon shifters. Noah, Myles, and Owen did their best to show her a good time. They took her back to the swimming hole a few times, and they hiked several of the forest paths with her to show her their favorite ancient Redwoods. Every night by the fire pit, they had a jolly barbecue with plenty of good meat and, of course, beer. Lily wasn't even that disappointed when they got word from Knox and Bree that their mission was taking longer than expected, and that it would likely be another week before they made it home. Of course, Lily was looking forward to her friend's return. But she had to admit that even without Bree here, life with the Redwood Dragons was pretty sweet. Lily cared even less that Zeke, the other dragon who was due to arrive home soon, was also delayed. All Lily knew for those glorious days was that she woke with the brilliant sun, breathed in the deep air of the Redwoods all day long, and went to sleep in the perfectly still peace of the forest. Life was good.

Vance was the only sore spot in all of this. Despite her attempts to push him out of her mind, Lily found herself constantly glancing around, wondering where he was. Most of the time, though, no one actually knew where he was. He left to walk into the forest every morning, always slipping into the woods at the same spot. When Lily tried to look around the spot for a path, she didn't see one. He seemed to leave earlier and earlier every day, and Lily found herself waking up earlier and earlier so that she could at least get a glance at him before he took off to start his day. As a few days passed, she found her anger at him fading, and her curiosity growing. Where was he going? What was he doing all day? Surely, he wasn't going into the forest all day just to avoid her? He didn't seem like someone who would hide just because someone else was mad at him.

Lily had always been the type who let her curiosity get the better of her, and, despite her warnings to herself that this was a bad idea, she found herself wanting to follow him, and to see where he was going. So, on the sixth morning after Bree had left, Lily awoke before the sun had fully risen over the horizon. She dressed in layers to ward off the chill of the cool morning and ate a hurried breakfast. Then she wrote a note and taped it to the front door of her cabin, saying that she was going for a walk and would be back later. She was purposely vague. She didn't want any of the other dragon shifters to worry about her, but she didn't want them following her, either. After Lily had finished all of this, she stood by the front window of her cabin, sipping a mug of coffee and looking out into the gray light of dawn. She watched and waited for nearly thirty minutes, and soon the sun had begun to rise above the horizon, bathing the trees in a warm yellow glow. Just when Lily had begun to wonder if Vance had already left and she had somehow missed him, she caught movement to the far left of the fire pit. Vance was walking across the clearing in the middle of the cabins, munching on a piece of toast that he was holding in his hand. He ambled easily toward the same spot where he always disappeared into the forest, and Lily took a deep breath. Here went nothing.

She raised her magic ring high above her head and firmly said, "*Magicae invisibilia!*" Instantly she was shrouded by an invisibility spell. No one would be able to see her as she left her cabin and chased after Vance. She moved quickly, stepping outside and hoping that no one saw the cabin door opening and closing seemingly by itself. Thankfully, base camp was quiet and seemed almost deserted. Yesterday had been a long day of hiking and a late night of barbecuing, so everyone else must have been sleeping in.

Lily saw Vance stepping into the thick trees, and she started running as fast as she could. She didn't want to lose him now, after she'd made all these preparations to follow him. He was moving quickly, and it was hard to keep up with him. She tried to be quiet as she stepped into the trees after him, but it was nearly impossible to avoid all of the twigs, leaves, and other noisy plant material on the forest floor. Every time Lily's foot hit a twig, she winced. The noise of a twig snapping sounded too loud against the relative quiet of the forest. The only other sounds were the birds singing, the rustling of the wind, and the occasional crunch of a twig between Vance's feet. But despite the fact that he was bigger than her, and walking almost as quickly, Vance seemed to move almost silently through the trees. As Lily gained on him, she realized that the majority of the racket in the woods was coming from her. She desperately tried to soften her footsteps, but if she slowed down at all she risked losing track of Vance.

She nearly cursed aloud as she stepped on a particularly loud twig. Vance paused at the sound and turned around with his brow furrowed. He scanned the forest with narrowed eyes, and he paused for so long on the spot where Lily was standing that she thought for a moment that her invisibility spell must have been failing her. But then, his gaze moved on, and Lily let out the breath she had been holding. He looked around for what felt like forever, and he breathed in deeply smelling the air. Lily was tempted to abort her mission right then and there. She knew that dragons, like all shifters, had a sharp sense of smell. There was no way he didn't smell her scent. But, perhaps he thought that it was just a lingering scent from base camp, because a moment later he un-furrowed his brow and turned around with a shrug to continue walking deeper into the forest.

Lily was starting to realize what a bad idea this little trek was. She had no way of masking her scent, and he would certainly realize at some point that he was too far away from camp to still be smelling her unless she was there. She should turn around now, and go back before she completely gave herself away.

But she could not turn back. She was filled with a strange, insatiable need to know where Vance was going and what he was doing. She would be quieter, and follow from a greater distance. Perhaps, if he didn't hear her, he wouldn't turn around and smell for her again. Besides, even if he suspected she was there, he couldn't prove it. He couldn't see her, and Lily could always deny that she had been near him if he asked her later.

So she continued, creeping along behind him and trying not to lose sight of him in the distance as he wound his way through the forest in what seemed like a random series of twists and turns. There was no path here, but Vance seemed to know exactly where he was going—and Lily was determined to find out.

CHAPTER SEVEN

Vance moved through the forest as silently as ever, but his thoughts were unusually troubled today. Lily was following him, that much was clear. He could hear her behind him. She had tried to drop back and make less noise ever since he'd stopped to turn around and look, but he could still hear her now and then. And her smell remained just as strong as it had when he left base camp earlier.

But *why* was she following him? She hadn't spoken to him at all since she yelled at him after they landed the first day she was here. He'd occasionally caught her watching him, but she always looked away quickly. He had convinced himself that she hated him, so it made no sense that she was following him. If she really cared about where he was going, why didn't she just ask? Unless she thought he was doing something wrong, and was following him in an attempt to catch him in the act and report him back to Knox.

Vance's frown deepened significantly at that thought. She didn't seem like the type to tattletale. In fact, from the little bit he'd managed to catch of her personality over the last few days, she seemed quite fun and sweet. Which had only made him more upset that things had gotten off to such a bad start with her. He wasn't about to apologize, though. He hadn't meant anything mean by his flying, and he was still angry that everyone in the clan was treating him like some sort of evil showoff who didn't care about Lily's safety at all. He might be a showoff, but Lily had never been in any danger and they knew it. Vance could have flown down blindfolded and still managed all those flips and turns without hurting Lily. He was a damn good flyer. They were just jealous.

Vance forced himself to push away his irritated thoughts about his clan mates. It wouldn't do to dwell on his anger like this. He didn't want to let poisonous thoughts about his crew fester in his heart. They might not always understand him, but they were his brothers. He loved them, even if they drove him crazy sometimes. Ok, most of the time.

Vance let out a short sigh as he continued making his way through the trees. It wasn't surprising that all of the Redwood Dragons were a little bit different from each other. After all, they had all come from different families. Ten orphans adopted by one dragon might all be one big happy family, but they all had different blood running through their veins. They all came from slightly different dragon stock, and Vance had often thought that perhaps he was the strangest dragon of them all. He had always felt a little too different from everyone else. They all bore the same last name, but Vance was not quite the same as them.

Vance had no way of knowing who his parents were, though. He had asked William, the dragon who adopted him, many times over the years if he could remember any details. William had always been deeply apologetic, but he'd always said the same thing—those had been crazy times, full of death and destruction. William's one focus had been on rescuing orphaned dragons, and he hadn't stopped to make note of who someone's parents might have been, or whether the houses he found the orphaned dragons in had any records of the young dragons' family trees.

Vance understood, truly. He knew that if he had been in William's shoes, desperately trying to rescue young dragon shifters during a violent shifter war, he would not have bothered to stop and check family histories, either. Still, the question of who his parents might have been haunted Vance.

Vance once again forced himself to move his thoughts to something happier. He did not want to spend his entire morning brooding over unhappy circumstances or unanswered questions. He turned his attention instead to the beauty of the forest around him. It was hard not to smile when one thought of that. The forest was full of sunlight today, and Vance loved to watch the patterns the sunbeams made as they filtered down through the deep green leaves of the redwoods. He paused now and then to listen to the songs of the birds, or to relish the soft whoosh the gentle breeze made as it swept through the treetops. A few times, he came across a bright yellow banana slug, and stopped for a few moments to watch as the little creature inched along across the forest floor.

No matter what the details of Vance's past family had been, this forest was home now. The ancient redwoods kept ancient secrets that only they knew, and they had seen thousands of years worth of dragon shifters roaming through their woods. They had been here long before Vance, and they would be here long after him. Somehow, that fact comforted him. He liked knowing that something he had seen and touched would live on after his time here was done. Vance smiled as he breathed in deeply, filling his lungs with the familiar scents of earth, leaves, and wood. And, of course, he could smell Lily. Her scent was fainter now. She must be trying to hold back and avoid detection. But Vance could still smell her, and he could tell that the scent was strong enough that she was still following him.

Vance wondered for a moment what he should do. He didn't mind if she saw where he was going, but he didn't like that she was sneaking behind him. A strange idea popped into his mind just then, and he wondered if perhaps this might be a second chance for him to impress Lily. They had gotten off to such a bad start, and Vance was annoyed with the way she had reacted to him. But he hadn't been able to get her out of his head, despite that. Every time he saw her sitting around the fire pit or laughing with the other guys, he felt his heart twisting up inside of him. Perhaps this was his chance for a do-over with her.

He turned around, smelling deeply and trying to determine precisely which direction she might be following him from. He faced toward where the scent of her was the strongest, took a deep breath to calm his nerves, and then spoke.

"Are you going to show yourself to me at some point, Lily? Or are you going to follow me all day long without saying anything?" Vance kept his voice light and easy, trying his best to not sound threatening.

There was a long pause, and for a few moments, Vance thought Lily was not going to respond to him. But, finally, he heard a long sigh, and then, she spoke.

"*Invisibilia terminantur,*" her voice rang out through the forest. There was a sharp, hissing pop, and suddenly Lily came into view. She was standing a little to the left of where Vance had thought she would be, and she was holding a small canteen of water. Other than that, she had nothing, and Vance wondered for a moment how long she had planned to be out here. It was getting close to ten o'clock, and even if she turned around to walk back to base camp right now, it would be well after noon before she got there. And yet, she had not brought any food with her. He almost wanted to laugh. Falcon Cross was not exactly a big city, but Lily was definitely more of a city girl than an experienced forest-dweller. Luckily for her, Vance always packed plenty more food in his backpack than he needed for the day—just in case.

"So" Vance said, leaning easily against the trunk of a nearby tree. "Where are you heading on this fine day?"

"Uh, I'm just, uh, out for a hike. The weather was good and I thought it'd be nice to explore for a bit." Lily stammered as she spoke, and Vance had a hard time not chuckling at her expense. She was a terrible liar. Which, he supposed, was not a bad thing.

"Bullshit," he said. "Why are you following me, Lily?"

Even though there was still quite some distance between them, he could see her cheeks redden when he asked the question.

"I guess I just wondered where you were going when you snuck off every day. My curiosity got the better of me and I decided to try to find out."

Vance did laugh then. "I'm not exactly sneaking off," he said. "Just because I don't make a formal announcement that I'm leaving every morning, that doesn't mean I'm sneaking. And if you wanted to know where I was going, you could have just asked me, you know?"

Lily's cheeks were bright red now, and she looked extremely uncomfortable. "I didn't think you wanted to talk to me. After, you know, the other day."

"Come over here, Lily," Vance said.

Looking like a child who had just been caught ruining her mother's most treasured possessions, Lily walked slowly toward Vance. For a moment, he forgot what he had been about to say. The closer she got, the more radiant she appeared. Her face was flushed, not just from the heat of her embarrassment but from the effort she had been putting out to keep up with Vance as he hiked. A thin sheen of sweat was on her face, and it made her look like she was practically glowing in the sunlight. Her hair was pulled back into a ponytail, and strands of it had come loose to hang around her face, framing it perfectly. Vance felt a strange sensation come over him as he looked at her, and the air between them seemed to be almost crackling with electricity. Was it possible that, even though their relationship had started off with a fight, that there was still some sort of chemistry between them? Vance took a deep breath, wanting to tread carefully with his words.

"Look, Lily, I know we got off to a bad start, but if we're both going to spend the whole summer here in the Redwoods, we should probably start at least acting civil toward each other. There's no need to act like I don't exist. And I'm sorry if I've acted like you don't exist. We're both grown adults. We can be polite to each other, don't you think?"

Lily shrugged. "Sure, I guess," she said. She did not meet his eyes when she said it.

"And don't try to follow me using your stupid invisibility spell. I can smell you, so I know you're there. I'm not an idiot, either. I know you're a wizard and can make yourself invisible, so it wasn't that hard to figure out that you were trailing me under the cover of a spell."

"Sorry," Lily said. This time she did look up. When she met Vance's eyes, her own eyes had a wary expression in them. Vance was about to tell her that she could continue hiking with him if she wanted, when she suddenly spoke again, and anger was lacing her voice this time.

"Aren't you going to say sorry, too?" she asked, crossing her arms. When she did, her magic ring caught the sunlight, which made the dark onyx stone seem to light up from within.

"Apologize for what?" Vance asked. "For flying you down too fast? I already told you I wasn't intentionally trying to scare you. If you want me to grovel and ask for forgiveness for mistakenly thinking that you'd enjoy a wild flight, then you're going to be disappointed. I'm not the groveling type. If you want to hang out with me, Lily, you're going to have to learn one thing. What you see is pretty much what you get. I am who I am. I might be a little rough around the edges, but I make no apologies for that. If you don't like it, you don't have to hang out with me. I certainly didn't ask you to follow me into the woods."

Lily hesitated, holding Vance's gaze but looking marginally less angry. "You could have killed me," she said. "Plus, it's against the rules to fly in like that. Knox said that—"

"Oh, screw the rules," Vance said, feeling impatient once again. "I follow them most of the time, but, you know what? Sometimes rules were made to be broken. You should know that. Your little friend Bree broke the rules when she came to find shifters and search for the dragon stone against your High Council's orders. And yet, she saved a lot of lives by doing that. I know your job as an Advocate is all about following the rules and making sure all the wizards follow protocol, and that no one does anything that might alert the rest of the world to the fact that magic exists. But if you want to get along well out here in the Redwoods, you're going to have to be a bit more flexible. We don't always follow the rules to the letter. We do what we need to do to get the job done. Perhaps I'm the worst offender. Perhaps I break more rules than anyone else in this clan. But you know what? I've also recovered more ancient artifacts than anyone on this clan. I've saved more lives than anyone else. And as long as there's breath left in my body, I'll be a bit of a rebel. It's just who I am. If you don't like it, you don't have to hang out with me. But I make no apologies for who I am."

Vance crossed his own arms as he finished his rant. He hadn't meant to get quite so worked up or passionate, and he realized that if he wanted a chance with Lily, that he had probably just ruined the last opportunity for that chance that he would get. But he didn't care. He could feel his heart pumping wildly in his chest as he spoke of his accomplishments. He was proud of the difference he'd made in the shifter world through his risk-taking. He knew that Knox was proud, too, even if it was hard to get him to admit it sometimes. If Lily was bothered by Vance's edginess, then she wasn't the right girl for him, anyway. Plain and simple as that.

The two of them stood there for a moment, staring at each other in charged silence. Vance was waiting for the moment that Lily would turn and storm away, disgusted with his refusal to apologize to her, or with his disregard for law and order. But that moment never came. Instead, she looked at him long and hard, and then, without warning, she stepped forward and wrapped his arms around his neck. The next thing he knew, her lips were on his.

CHAPTER EIGHT

Lily wasn't quite sure what had come over her. All she knew was that she was suddenly overcome with an unbearable desire to kiss Vance, and she had acted on it. She had never been the impulsive type. Her whole life back in Falcon Cross had been a series of carefully researched, carefully planned decisions. But something about being out here in the redwoods, alone with the man who was ,objectively speaking, the most handsome man she'd ever met, had somehow cast a strange spell over her. The irony of a wizard feeling like she was under a spell was not lost on Lily, but she didn't think too much about it as she let herself melt into Vance's lips. As she did, she realized she'd told herself so many lies over the last few days about how she was angry at Vance and didn't want to be with him. She realized now that she'd said all of those things to herself so that she could be angry with Vance instead of being angry with herself.

If she was honest with herself, she had acted like a pouty child over the last few days. She could forgive herself for being upset at Vance when they first landed. She'd been terrified, and had reacted out of fear. But once she realized that she had, in fact, been perfectly safe—and that he hadn't been trying to scare her but had actually been trying to show her a good time—she should have calmed down. Instead, she had clung to her anger like a child who was insisting on being right.

Vance had seen right through her bullshit—and had called her on it. Somehow, his in-your-face attitude had turned her on. Lily wasn't used to men who were so rough and raw. All the guys she hung out with back in Falcon Cross worked at the Advocacy Bureau with her. They were all nice enough people, but they lacked a certain masculine fire. They were all super smart and loved to sit around debating the finer points of countless philosophical questions, but they were too polite. They never would have gotten in Lily's face and told her to get over herself, or that rules were made to be broken. Lily had had an epiphany as Vance spoke, and she realized that she'd been living small for far too long. Deep within her, there was a desire to rebel a little, and to live on the edge. For once in her life, she didn't want to do every damn thing perfectly by the book. Maybe this summer was her chance.

All of these thoughts had been swirling in Lily's head as she listened to Vance essentially tell her off. But now, as her lips joined his, it was hard for her to think about anything except how wonderful he felt. She could hardly believe that she was kissing a man who she'd just been arguing with—a man whom she supposedly hated and who supposedly hated her. She had never done anything so brazen in her life. But Vance did not pull away. In fact, he wrapped his arms around her and kissed her back.

His hands were strong against her back, and she couldn't keep a small moan from escaping her lips as she ran her own hands over his biceps. They were strong and firm, and he somehow seemed even taller and more muscular now then he had the first day she'd met him in that tiny rental car office. The heat between them grew, and Lily found herself surprised at how her skin felt like it was on fire everywhere he touched her. Her back burned in the best way possible as he ran his hands across it.

But then, just as suddenly as Lily had started the kiss, Vance ended it. Gently but firmly, he pulled away from her.

"Come on," he said, his voice sounding unusually gruff. "I want to show you something."

Lily tried to push away the disappointment that filled her as the moment between them ended. "Where are we going?" she asked as brightly as she could, doing her best not to sound as deflated as she felt that she was no longer in his arms. Her mood perked up, though, as he reached for her hand, closing his own large palm firmly over her smaller one.

"You wanted to see what I've been up to this week," he said. "So let's go."

He said nothing more. He walked in silence through the woods, and Lily found herself amazed again at how quickly he could move without making a sound. He kept his hand firmly on hers as they walked an irregular path through the trees. There was still no visible trail, but Vance seemed to know exactly where he was going.

The whole time that Lily had been following Vance, he had been moving steadily upward through the forest. Now, though, the incline of the ground became markedly steeper, and Lily found herself sweating and huffing as she tried to keep pace with Vance. She didn't complain, but he seemed to notice that she was struggling, because he slowed his pace down a bit as they ascended. He was forced to drop her hand as the way through the trees narrowed and they had to walk single file. They continued on like this for another hour. Just when Lily felt like she could not possibly walk another step, Vance halted. He looked around for a few moments, as though not quite certain which way he wanted to go. Then he nodded, as though his decision was made, and he grabbed her hand again.

"Come on," he said. "This will be the easiest way up."

The rocks in front of them seemed to be almost a solid wall. Vance seemed to know, though, each spot where the rock jutted out just enough to make a step. Step by careful step, he led her straight up the small cliff, never letting go of her hand. Somehow, even though she knew that this climb was probably even more dangerous than the crazy flight Vance had taken her on, she was not afraid. He held her so firmly, and she knew deep down that he would not let her fall. This time, she trusted him.

Lily had felt for a while now that they were walking among the treetops, but as they climbed the rock wall, they rose above the treetops. They slowly ascended even higher than the tallest of the trees, until they reached the top of the cliff. Lily saw then that the top of the cliff had a smooth, almost table-like top to it. Vance climbed up onto it, and then pulled Lily up with him.

All of a sudden, she felt like she was standing on the top of the world. The view took her breath away, and was almost the same as the view had been when she had been riding in on Vance's dragon back earlier that week. For as far as she could see, rolling hills of redwood forest rose and fell. The deep green of the treetops contrasted starkly with the bright blue of the sky. The sun shone hot on Lily's face, now that all the shade of the forest was below her. But she hardly noticed the heat as she looked around, taking in the beauty that surrounded her.

"Look," Vance said, turning her one hundred and eighty degrees so that she was now facing the opposite direction. He pointed to a spot on the horizon between two of the largest hills.

"That's the ocean," he said, his voice sounding softer and happier than Lily had ever heard it. "I love to come up here and look at it. On cloudy days you can't see it, but in the summertime it's almost always sunny enough to make it out."

Lily strained her eyes to look, and then she saw it, too. The shades of blue between the two hills were different, and, if you knew what you were looking for, you could see where sky turned to sea.

"It's beautiful," she said, then glanced over at Vance "But is this really what you've been doing every single day for the last week? And why make all the effort to climb up here? Wouldn't it be much easier to just shift into dragon form and fly up here?"

Vance laughed. "What would the fun be in just flying up here every day? I like to hike, and sweat a little bit. Besides, flying around in dragon form just for the sake of flying is against the rules, and I wouldn't want to break any rules, you know?"

He gave her a pointed, teasing look, and Lily blushed. There was no animosity in his gaze now, though. His eyes danced merrily as the sunlight hit them and lit up their greenish-gold color.

"This view isn't the real reason I've been coming up here, though," he said, reaching for her hand and pulling her toward the opposite side of the large, rocky surface. "Come look at this. But be very quiet."

Lily nodded, intrigued, as Vance walked with her to the very edge of the cliff. He knelt down and then lay flat on his stomach so that only his head was peering over the edge, and then motioned for her to do the same. She carefully knelt and then lay down, wondering what the point of all of this was.

"Look," he whispered, pointing to a spot just below them where a small part of the cliff jutted out. The wall of the cliff curved at that point, so that most of the little rock shelf was sheltered from the wind by the cliff itself. On the shelf of rock was a nest, with three baby birds in it. They must not have been too young, because they had some adult-looking feathers mixed in with smaller, fluffy baby feathers. The mixture gave them a funny, bedraggled look. They were chirping incessantly, but Lily had not heard them until she bent down, since the angle of the rock wall muffled their cries if you were standing above.

"They're so cute," Lily whispered. "What are they?"

Before Vance could answer her, a mighty rush of wind passed by Lily's right ear. She saw the fierce bird that had zoomed by her continuing on, diving down at lightning speed until it quickly disappeared beneath the treetops. Lily didn't have to ask anymore what it was. She would have known the shape of that bird anywhere. Vance was already answering the question, though.

"They're peregrine falcons," he said. "I thought that Falcon Cross was named for them. Surely, you must have seen them before."

"I must have seen hundreds of them in my lifetime," Lily said. "But I've never seen their babies. They like to nest up high, and I didn't do much climbing back home."

Vance nodded. "Makes sense, I guess. I found these little guys the first morning after you arrived at our base camp. I was angry, and decided to go on a hike to get rid of some angry energy. I've been up here before for the view, but when I came up this time I saw one of the adult birds flying in and looking like they were landing right on the edge of the wall. I was curious and came to look. That's when I found this little rock shelf and the nest. I've been coming to visit them every day since. They've already grown a ton since the first day I found them."

"The parents don't mind your being here?" Lily asked.

Vance shook his head. "They seemed wary of me at first, but I think they've gotten used to me by now. I suppose they don't mind you, since you're with me. Peregrines are smart birds, you know, they have a good sense of who to trust and who not to."

Vance fell silent as he looked down at the birds, and for several minutes, Lily did not speak, either. She watched the young birds, calling out for food. Then, one of their parents came back with a fresh kill, and the impatient calls turned into a sort of happy cheeping as the adult bird fed them. When the adult bird left again to go hunt, Lily finally turned back to speak to Vance.

"It's kind of funny, you know—a big tough guy like you making the hike all the way up here every day to see some baby birds," she said, keeping her voice quiet so that she wouldn't disturb the birds.

Vance looked over at her, his green eyes sparkling so brightly in the sunlight that for a moment all Lily could think about was how much they looked like emeralds.

"There's no reason a tough guy can't like baby birds," Vance said. "Besides, it's not just the babies I've been watching. It's the parents, too. Peregrines are some of the coolest birds around."

Lily smiled. "Well, I am pretty partial to them myself, you know, since I'm from Falcon Cross."

"Did you know their name means 'wandering falcon'?" Vance asked, sitting up on one elbow to look over at Lily. Maybe that's why I like them so much. I've always felt like a wanderer."

"Well, you do wander quite a bit on your missions, from what I'm told," Lily said.

"Yeah, but it's not just that," Vance said. "I've always felt a little bit like I didn't *really* belong anywhere. I mean, I know I belong here, with the Redwood Dragons. It's my home, and these guys are my brothers, as much as we may annoy each other at times. But I never knew who my parents were. I don't know where I came from. I've found myself wondering quite a bit lately about how my life would be different if my parents hadn't died in the war."

Vance got a faraway look in his eyes, but Lily shrugged.

"I don't know," she said slowly. "I get the feeling that there's some part of you that feels as though it's missing something, and you think if only your parents hadn't died, that you wouldn't feel that way. But I don't think it does much good to spend your time wondering about a life that could have been. The life we have is all we're guaranteed for sure, and none of us know how long even that will last. And it seems to me that you have a pretty good family here with your clan. There are a lot of people who would give anything for that."

Vance was silent again for a long time. The sun was directly above them now, beating down its bright rays on their skin. Finally, Vance let out a long sigh.

"You're right," he said. "I need to focus on the good life I have here, and not worry about what I might have missed out on. Sometimes that's easier said than done, though. I guess you could say that I'm a work in progress."

Lily smiled. "We all are," she said.

Vance pushed himself up into a sitting position, and looked down at Lily with an unreadable expression in his eyes.

"So, are we cool?" he asked. "Can we move past the stupid acrobatic flight the other day?"

Lily sat up herself, and gave him a long hard look. He waited patiently for her to answer, but she took her time. She was lost for a moment in admiring how his tanned, chiseled face glowed in the sunlight.

"Yeah. We're cool," she finally said.

And she had a feeling as she spoke that her summer's adventures were only just now getting started.

CHAPTER NINE

"*Magicae effusorium*," Lily cried out, pointing her onyx ring at the spot in the water right in front of Vance. Instantly, the water rose in a powerful, quick wave and hit him square in the face. When it had passed, and he had rubbed it from his eyes enough to actually see her, he let out a roar of feigned anger. She only laughed as he began swimming toward her, rapidly covering the distance between them with powerful strokes of his arm.

"Using spells is cheating," Vance said right before he fell on her and dunked her under. She dragged him under with her, and he let her. The cool water felt good after all the time they had spent in the hot sunshine this morning, watching the peregrines chirp hungrily in their nest. This was the third day in a row that Lily had asked to come see the birds, and Vance was happy to oblige her request. He loved watching the birds himself, and the hike up there was long, which meant he had plenty of time to spend talking to Lily. Now that he was getting to know her, he was certain that he would never grow tired of talking to her.

She was wickedly smart. He'd always thought Bree was smart, but Lily was even a step above her. Vance had soon realized that the wizards didn't mess around when choosing the wizards who would become their Advocates. They only wanted the best and the brightest, and Lily was indeed the best and the brightest. Her intelligence blew Vance away, and she didn't even realize it. He winced at least a dozen times a day when he thought about how he had almost missed out on this chance to get to know her due to his stupid pride.

The other dragons had been shocked the day that Vance and Lily had walked hand-in-hand into the middle of camp, acting as though they'd been in love for years. Noah and Myles had laughed it off and given Vance a good deal of teasing, but Owen had been in a somewhat pissy mood ever since then.

"You always get whatever you want," Owen complained, storming off to his cabin in frustration.

Not always, Vance thought. There were plenty of things he wanted that he didn't have. But, he had to admit, that everything else paled in comparison to Lily. As long as he had her, what else could he really ask for? Besides, Owen would get over it eventually. Vance and Owen were always trying to one-up each other in everything, and Owen was just angry that he'd lost out this time.

Vance hadn't spent too much time worrying about Owen, though. He'd spent every spare second thinking about Lily. After taking her to see the peregrines each day, he'd shown her several of his other favorite spots in the forest. He'd taken her to see the largest redwood he'd ever found, with its massive trunk that had to have been several thousand years old. He'd shown her the hiking trail that went down the edge of one of the cliffs, offering breathtaking views of the redwoods similar to the views up near the peregrines. And, now, he was showing her his favorite swimming spot. The small waterfall here wasn't as impressive as the waterfall at the other swimming hole, which the other dragons liked better. But the water in this pool was luxuriously warm, thanks to a perfectly spaced break in the trees that allowed a good deal of sunshine to stream through to the water's surface. Besides, this small pool was deeper and more secluded, and Vance liked that. He especially liked the seclusion since he was here alone with Lily.

They were both dripping wet now, soaked from their splashing and dunking. Lily's long, dark brown hair hung in wet sections around her face, landing in the water and floating on the surface like a mermaid's hair. Her swimsuit was a bright turquoise color, and Vance loved the way the color brought out the deepening tan of her skin. He felt himself growing hard as he looked at her perfect curves, which were distorted artfully by the water.

He took a step forward, and pulled her into his arms, relishing the way her body pressed against his. He wondered if perhaps today was the day he would finally make love to Lily. He would have loved to have made love to her over and over since the first day they'd gone to see the peregrines together. But Vance had held back, wanting to be a gentleman and unsure of what the proper protocol was. He didn't want her to think he was the kind of guy that was only after one thing, but, surely by now she was realizing that he wasn't. He wanted to spend all of his time with her, and he had for the last several days. But it was getting harder and harder to kiss her goodnight on the door of her cabin and leave it at that. And now, in this moment, with the sun shining brightly in her hair, and the water swirling around her and making her look like some sort of river goddess, he wanted to show her just how badly he wanted her.

She did not seem to notice his hesitation. She leaned into his embrace, letting her head rest against his bare chest and sighing happily. A deep warmth filled Vance's body at the sound, and he wondered yet again whether it was actually possible that she was his lifemate. He'd been told his whole life that there was someone out there for everyone, and that each shifter had a fated lifemate that destiny would bring across their path at the perfect time. But he'd laughed off the notion, thinking that if lifemates did actually exist, destiny had probably overlooked him when pairing people off. After all, he was an orphan, a loner, and admittedly a bit of an ass. He'd never thought that any woman could fit in well with his fast-paced, wild lifestyle. And, in all honesty, he never would have pegged Lily as the type to take a second look at a rebel dragon like him. Yet she had, and they seemed more drawn to each other with every passing second. Was it possible that destiny knew better than him who to send him as a lifemate?

Was it possible that Lily actually was his lifemate?

Vance knew there was only one way to find out. If he made love to Lily and she was indeed his lifemate, the lifemate bond would be formed. They would be inseparable until death. Vance couldn't keep a smile off his face at the thought. Nothing in the world could have sounded more wonderful than knowing that Lily might be his for the rest of his life. Who would have thought that he would fall in love with anyone, let alone a beautiful wizard? But here he was, admittedly falling head over heels. And there in that pool, with the sun flickering down beautifully and the breeze tickling the leaves of the ancient trees, Vance decided it was time to show Lily just how much he cared for her.

He started with a kiss, turning Lily's face gently toward his own and meeting her lips with his. He'd been kissing her as often as he could over the last few days, and her taste was familiar to him now. He could not get enough of it. He slipped his tongue past her lips and drank her in, pulling her body close against his. He let his tongue dance with hers, then ran it over her teeth and the roof of her mouth. He wanted to feel and taste every part of her. She was like a craving he knew he could never fully satisfy. He would always want more, more, more.

She moaned softly as he kissed her, a happy sound that instantly caused him to go even harder. He was quickly becoming rock hard, and he knew she knew it. She pushed her hips against his, pressing her body against his erection. Vance felt a rush of heat in his body. She was inviting him to go further, and he knew it. And suddenly, he didn't care anymore whether they were ready, or whether the timing was right. He was overcome by a deep, primal desire. He wanted her now. He must have her. She was his, and he knew it. His love, his lifemate, his sun and stars. She was everything. She was the family he had always craved. The home he'd never known.

He reached behind her to untie the strings of her bright turquoise bikini, his large fingers fumbling with the delicate strings. She did not pull back or protest. Instead, she looked up at him with wide, hungry eyes. That's when he knew for sure that she wanted him, too. He knew in that moment that they were not leaving this pool until they had made love and become one with each other.

But despite the overwhelming desire filling Vance, he told himself not to rush. He wanted to take his time and savor the moment. He had never felt so desperate to please a woman before. He wanted to show her just how wonderful he could make her feel. He wanted her to beg for more.

He finally managed to slip the bikini top off her. He tossed it aside and let it float away in the water. The pool was small and it would not go far. Right now, he could only think about her perfect breasts, which were full and beautiful as they dipped slightly into the water. Her nipples were hard and alert, pointing toward him and rising and falling gently with her deep breaths. This was the first time he had seen them, and Vance could scarcely believe how perfect and beautiful they were. He let out a low moan of his own as he reached to cup her breasts, one in each palm, feeling their soft fullness in his hands.

She closed her eyes with pleasure right before he dipped his head to find her nipples with his mouth. He ran his tongue over the hard nubs, and then pulled them between his teeth. He moved from left breast to right breast, giving each nipple equal attention. If the sound of Lily's moans was any indication, his actions were driving her wild. He chewed and twisted and pulled, eliciting louder and louder moans from Lily, along with an occasional plea of "Don't stop. Please, don't stop."

Each time she moaned, Vance felt a fresh rush of heat run through his own body. His dick was now a solid rod between his legs, filled with heat and desire and pointing straight toward Lily's body, begging to be let in. But Vance did not give in to its demands just yet. First, he wanted to make sure that Lily was taken care of. He pulled his mouth away from her breasts for just a moment to look into her eyes. He pushed a strand of hair back from her face, kissed her nose, and then dipped his mouth back to her nipples. This time, though, he added his hands to the action. He reached below the surface of the water, slipped his fingers between her skin and the smooth fabric of her swimsuit bottom, and found her soft entrance. He pushed his fingers into her as the clear water of the pool swirled around them. Even though the water here was warm, Lily was hot inside compared to the water temperature. Vance closed his own eyes as he relished her soft warmth. She was softer inside than anything he had ever felt before in his life.

He drove his fingers deeper into her, massaging her inner walls and searching for her most sensitive spots. He knew when he found the perfect place. She shivered as his fingers moved, then whimpered out his name as she writhed in his arms, squirming against the pressure and pleasure of his touch.

He did not give her a reprieve. With his mouth, he continued to twist the hard nubs of her nipples. With one hand, he reached up and held the back of her head, grasping tightly against the slick wetness of her hair. With the other hand, he reached his fingers deep into her and massaged in firm circles, drawing moans from her that were increasingly louder until, finally, she could take no more.

She screamed out, throwing her head back and letting loose all of the pent up passion inside of her. Her inner muscles began to spasm, clenching hungrily around Vance's fingers. He smiled as he felt tremors of delight passing over her body, and he continued to hold her and massage her until her body slowly calmed. He pulled his fingers out of her and stood to his full height. Lily fell against him, limp in his arms but sighing happily.

Vance kissed the top of her head and held her tighter. He would have let her stay there resting for as long as she wanted, but she was not content with just a taste of what he could offer. Not even a full minute had passed before she tilted her head up to look at him and whispered, "More."

Vance grinned at her, and took a small step back so he could bow. "Your wish is my command, my lady," he said.

Then he reached down and pushed off his swimming trunks, slipping out of them and tossing them aside before reaching for the bottom of Lily's swimsuit. She helped him along as he pushed it down and off, and soon, they were both completely naked in front of each other in the sparkling pool of water. Vance reached up to caress Lily's face, and she looked up at him with eyes so full of desire that he felt like her eyes alone could consume him.

"More," she said again, her voice louder and more urgent this time.

He was happy to oblige. He stepped toward her, wrapping his arms around her and positioning his rock hard member right in front of her soft entrance. With one firm, purposeful movement, he slipped inside her.

He saw her eyes fly open as he filled her. He was large inside of her, pushing against her inner walls, reaching deeper into her than he knew she had even thought possible. For a moment, they stood there, looking into each other's eyes while their bodies were connected in the most intimate way. So many things were spoken between them without either of them ever uttering a word. And then, she closed her eyes with a soft moan.

Vance closed his eyes, too. He began to rock his hips back and forth, thrusting gently in and out of her as he took in every wonderful sensation. He never wanted to forget this moment. The music of the birds and the rustling treetops. The sun, warm on his skin. The water, cooling him. And Lily, so soft and so warm, drawing more and more heat from his member as he moved in her. The pressure built until he could hardly bear it. He scrunched up his face, waiting for her to come, and letting the unbelievable heat and electricity of desire flood through him.

She did not make him wait long. With another scream, louder than the one before, she let go. He felt her inner muscles once again, this time clenching over his dick and sending ripples of tingling pleasure across every fiber of his being. As she continued to moan and pulse, he found his own release. He let out a roar, shooting himself into her in a hot stream and letting tremors of pleasure rush across his own body.

He could not have said how long they stood there, wrapped in each other's arms as their passion overtook them. All he knew was that he had never felt anything this wonderful, and his heart had never been so full of peace. As his breathing slowly returned to normal, he felt a comforting heat spreading across his body. It started in his core, and kept going until it reached to even his fingertips and toes. He knew what that heat meant. Lily was his lifemate, and they had formed the lifemate bond. Even as he felt it, he could hardly believe it. How had he, an orphaned dragon shifter, been lucky enough to end up with the smartest, most beautiful woman in the world? Lily was a truly spectacular wizard, whose magic extended beyond just the spells she could cast. She was special, with the rare ability to light up everything around her with something as simple as her laugh. Vance had no idea how they were going to meld their lives into one, but he knew that he would find a way for them to be together, whatever it took.

"I feel so warm," Lily murmured against his chest. "Almost like there's an actual fire burning in my stomach. It's the strangest sensation."

"It's the lifemate bond," Vance said, stroking his fingers through her wet hair. "It means that we are destined to be with each other, and we're bonded together for life."

Lily pulled back to look at him, her eyes wide and shining. "I've heard of that before, but I wasn't sure if it was actually true or if it was just some sort of shifter lore."

"I wasn't sure either if it was true," Vance said. "I thought it wasn't possible for someone like me, with such a wild life, to have a lifemate. But I see now that destiny looks out for everyone. Love really is out there, if you're willing to let it find you."

Lily smiled up at him as he spoke, and the expression in her eyes was so sweet that it made his heart hurt. He wasn't sure what he had done right to deserve someone so wonderful, but now that he'd found Lily, he was never letting her go.

Vance chuckled slightly to himself as he thought of their rocky start. Maybe one of these days, he could convince her to actually enjoy a flight through the treetops with him. But for now, he was still having a damn good time with both of their feet firmly on the ground.

CHAPTER TEN

Lily would not have minded spending the whole day in the water with Vance, making love in between breaks to nibble on the lunches they had packed. But Knox and Bree were finally due back tonight, and Zeke was supposed to finally show up as well. An extra big barbecue had been planned, and the Redwood Dragons were all excited for the party.

Despite her wish to spend more alone time with Vance, Lily was excited, too. She could hardly wait to see the look on Bree's face when she told her that Vance had gone from being her hated enemy to being her love and lifemate. Bree was going to be shocked—hopefully in a good way. Lily knew that Bree had been harboring not-so-secret hopes that Lily would fall for one of the Redwood Dragons, but Bree was going to be shocked when Vance turned out to be the dragon Lily chose.

As Lily followed Vance back to base camp on the winding forest trail, she tried not to worry about where she and Vance were going to live long term. Lily loved it here in the forest, but she hated to give up her job as an Advocate. And she had a feeling that Vance would not want to give up his work with the Redwood Dragons either. But they had a few months to figure things out. Lily didn't want to spoil this perfect day by thinking about logistical details right now. There would be plenty of time for worry at a later time.

When they got back to camp, they found that Zeke had already arrived. Vance introduced him to Lily, and Lily did not miss the way Zeke's eyebrows raised when Vance called Lily "his girl." But Zeke did not question Vance further. He gave Lily a warm smile and told her that he was glad she was here, and that was about it. Zeke said he needed to go take care of some things related to the mission he had just completed, but that he was looking forward to spending time with everyone at the barbecue tonight.

"He doesn't talk much, does he?" Lily asked as Vance walked her to her cabin.

Vance chuckled. "Nope. If ever anyone was the strong, silent type, it's Zeke. He's a really good guy, though. He's almost as good at missions as me."

Lily laughed. "Almost, eh? Sounds like someone's pretty proud of himself."

Vance shrugged and smiled. "I wouldn't want my girl thinking that anyone else was more impressive than me, you know."

Vance puffed out his chest in an over-exaggerated manner and put a comically proud expression on his face. Lily laughed and rolled her eyes at him.

"You look so handsome with your face scrunched up like that," she said, the sarcasm dripping in her voice. "You should make that face all the time."

"Very funny," Vance said. "Speaking of missions, though, I do want to ask Zeke some questions about how his last job went. I'm going to run over and talk to him while you get ready, if that's okay?"

Lily nodded, and Vance gave her a quick kiss on the lips before heading off toward Zeke's cabin. As soon as Lily shut her own cabin door behind her, she couldn't help doing a little happy dance. She could not believe how quickly things between her and

Vance had changed. Only a few days ago she'd thought she hated him. Although, if she was honest with herself now, she wasn't sure that she had ever really hated him. She felt more that she had been trying to convince herself that she hated him because she wasn't ready to face how strong her feelings for him were. Falling in love complicated things.

But it was a good kind of complicated. Lily danced across the cabin to the bedroom, where she stripped off her sweaty hiking clothes and then went to hop in the shower. The summer had barely started, and she was already having the time of her life. She noticed as she looked down at her skin that it had become quite tanned already. All the time she'd spent up on the cliff looking at the peregrines had turned her arms a deep golden color.

As Lily scrubbed soap on her body, she thought about how Vance had told her that peregrines were wandering falcons. Lily had never considered herself much of a wanderer, but being in the redwoods was making her wonder whether she should have spent more time wandering. There were so many places in the world that she wanted to see, but it was hard to get away from her job at the Advocacy Bureau. Not only that, but the High Council of Falcon Cross didn't like it when the wizards traveled too much. Anytime a wizard traveled among full humans, the High Council worried that the wizard was going to accidentally reveal to non-wizards that magic existed. Lily understood that caution was needed, but sometimes she felt that High Council worried a bit too much. Lily, like most wizards, had had it drilled into her since the moment she first wore a magic ring that one must be extremely careful not to do magic near non-wizards. It was second nature to check around for non-wizards before doing magic anywhere outside of Falcon Cross. Lily sighed. At least it was permissible to do magic in front of shifters now. That made life beyond the borders of Falcon Cross a little bit easier.

Lily quickly shampooed and rinsed her hair, then stepped out of the shower to towel off. Bree would be back anytime now, and Lily was in a hurry to speak with her. She wanted the chance to tell her about Vance in private, before the barbecue was in full swing tonight. Lily pulled her hair up into a tight, damp bun after towel-drying it, and then pulled on a pair of jeans and a simple gray t-shirt. She didn't bother to put on any makeup. She had brought some with her from Falcon Cross, but it seemed out of place here in the middle of the forest. Besides that, Lily's skin had taken on such a healthy, sun-kissed glow that she didn't want to spoil it with makeup.

Just as Lily was taking one last look in the mirror, she heard a knock at her front door.

"Lily?" a voice called.

It was Bree. Lily rushed to the front door and flung it open, throwing her arms around her friend.

"You're finally back!" she said.

Bree laughed. "Yeah, finally. As I'm sure you've realized, that mission turned out to be a lot more complicated than we thought it would be. It sounds like you've been keeping yourself busy, though."

Bree raised an eyebrow at Lily, and from the look on her friend's face, Lily could tell that Bree had heard something about Vance and Lily being together. Lily was a year older than Bree, but in that moment she felt somewhat like a younger sister being reprimanded by her older sister. Lily looked at her feet for a moment, suddenly unsure of how to explain things. She'd been excited to tell Bree about Vance, but the doubtful look on Bree's face right now was making her feel strangely uncomfortable.

"You heard about Vance?" Lily asked, hoping Bree would give her some hint about what had happened.

"Yeah. We got in about half an hour ago, and the first thing Owen did was make a sour comment about how Vance gets everything he wants with no consequences or something like that. For a moment, Knox was worried that Vance had been involved in some new mischief—the guy's pretty good at getting into mischief, you know—but then Noah and Myles explained that Owen was just angry that Vance had won you over despite breaking all the rules about discreet flying."

Lily sighed. "Yeah. Owen was interested in me, I think. But he's not my type."

"And Vance is?" Bree asked, sitting on the edge of the small couch in the living room, and cocking her head to one side quizzically as she waited for Lily to respond.

"I know it sounds a little weird, because he and I got started on the wrong foot. But I couldn't get him out of my head, no matter how angry I tried to be at him. I had the chance to talk to him about things and realized that he is actually a really cool guy. He didn't mean to scare me that first day. In fact, he was trying to impress me and just went about it rather poorly."

Bree furrowed her brow thoughtfully for a few moments. When she spoke, she seemed to be choosing her words carefully. "Look, Lily, I like Vance a lot. Despite his tendency to take a few too many risks, he is one of our best dragons. He's undeniably good at his job. But you've always been almost the direct opposite of a risk-taker. Are you sure you know what you're doing, getting your heart all tangled up with his?"

"I'd like to think that I know what I'm doing," Lily said with a half-smile. "But even if I don't, I think it's a little too late to untangle my heart."

Bree looked surprised. "You're that into him already?" she asked. "You've never been the type to move quickly with relationships."

"I am that into him," Lily said. "And he's that into me, too. In fact, we believe we're lifemates. We…bonded."

Now Bree's jaw actually dropped in shock. "Wow. You *are* really serious about this. I mean, don't get me wrong, I'm really happy for you that you've found love. I just never expected it to be with Vance. When I left you seemed to really hate him. And, like I said, you've never been the risk-taking type."

"I know," Lily said. "But, honestly, I've been feeling a lot lately like I've been too careful too many times. I've always played perfectly by the rules, and, sure, it's gotten me far. But I've never felt truly fulfilled or truly happy. I've always felt like there was something more I was supposed to be doing. That's part of why I decided to come out here for the summer. I wanted a chance to get away from Falcon Cross and all the busyness of my job there and have time to think about what I really want from life."

"Does this mean you might end up moving here to the redwoods?" Bree asked, her voice sounding hopeful.

Lily faltered. "I'm not sure how everything is going to work," she said. "I mean you got a job as an ambassador, so that worked out well for you. I'm not so sure that there's going to be work for me here, though. I'm actually quite worried about the logistics of everything, but I'm trying not to think about it right now. We have the whole summer to figure it out. Assuming that things keep going well, I mean. How secure is the lifemate bond?"

Bree's eyes widened as if she couldn't quite believe what Lily was asking. "Lily, the lifemate bond is unbreakable. That's why it's called the lifemate bond—it's for life. If you and Vance bonded, like you say, you'll never truly be able to get away from each other."

Lily paused to consider everything Bree had just told her. She *wanted* to be bonded to Vance for life. She had only known him a week and she already could not imagine life without him. But she was scared, too. What if things didn't work out for them to be together in the end? Sure, she had the whole summer to figure it out, but three months would pass by faster than she thought. What if she and Vance were doomed to always live in different cities, pining away for each other?

Even as Lily had the thought, she knew that would never happen. As much as she would hate to give up her job as an Advocate, she would hate a life without Vance even more. If they could not figure out a way to make their jobs work and be in the same place, then she would give up her job. Simple as that.

But she didn't say all this to Bree. Instead, Lily just shrugged and said, "We'll figure it out."

Bree looked at her long and hard, as if she knew something of the internal struggle that Lily was going through. And Lily supposed that she did. After all, Bree must have had similar thoughts when she was figuring out how to make life with Knox work.

"Enough about me, though," Lily said, eager to change the conversation. "What about you? How did your mission go, other than being more complicated than you thought?"

A look of concern passed over Bree's face. "The mission was okay, I guess. As you know, though, it was indeed quite a bit more complicated than we thought it would be. There are… stirrings in the shifter world. Shifters are on their guard more than usual, and it's turning what used to be a quick mission into a much more complicated affair. Even Knox was surprised by how wary the shifters we were stalking were acting."

"But you did get the artifact you were looking for, right?" Lily asked.

"Yes, this time," Bree said. "But Knox is worried about how difficult missions might become in the long term, if this trend continues. And he's worried about the security of the artifacts in the redwoods. For a long time, no one knew this place existed. But when Samuel tracked the dragon sapphire here and brought an army of wizards, shifters, and humans in, the location was compromised."

Lily's face darkened at the mention of Samuel. Samuel had been one of the High Councilors in Falcon Cross. The High Councilors were powerful wizards who were charged with a duty to govern and protect their wizard clan. But Samuel had betrayed the wizards of Falcon Cross, and had attempted to steal a powerful ancient artifact, the sapphire dragon stone. Samuel had been defeated, stripped of his magic, and exiled. But some of his army had escaped, and there was a looming possibility that they might try to attack again.

"But the dragons here guard the artifacts carefully, don't they? It would take a lot to get past them," Lily said, trying to make her voice sound more confident than she felt.

"Well, yes, things here are well guarded," Bree said. "The dragons keep the artifacts in several different vaults throughout the forest so that no one could easily steal them all at once. The vaults are well hidden and secured. I've also added some protective spells to them so that anyone trying to break in would have a difficult time doing so."

Lily couldn't help but chuckle at the proud note in Bree's voice when she talked about the spells that she had cast. "You always were good at those protective spells," Lily said. You had the highest grade in your protective spells course during advocacy school, didn't you?"

Bree nodded. "I did. But those spells are never foolproof, no matter how strong you cast them. And I worry that there are wizards helping those who want to steal the artifacts. They would know the counter-spells, which would weaken the effectiveness of the protective spells."

Lily sighed. "The fight against evil never ends, does it? It'd be nice to have some peace and quiet for a while."

"It would," Bree agreed sadly. "But I'm told that our current worries are nothing compared to the horrors of the last full-on shifter war. The trouble is that if we can't keep the artifacts safe, there might be another war coming. And with all the artifacts that we have in safekeeping here, a new war would make the last one look like child's play."

Lily shivered. While she worked on her advocacy diploma, she'd studied the history of shifters in great detail. She knew plenty more than she wanted to know about the last shifter war—the war that had left Vance and the rest of the Redwood Dragons as orphans. She could not imagine a war worse than that, and yet, there was no hint of joking on Bree's face.

War might be coming. And, if it came, life as Lily knew it would probably change forever.

"But, surely, now that the wizards and shifters are working together, we can stand against any evil threats that come our way, right?"

Bree looked tired as she spoke. "We have a better chance, now that we're working together, yes. And we have the dragon emerald and dragon sapphire, both of which are very powerful. But the dragon ruby and the dragon amethyst are still missing. No one seems to know where they are, but if they were to be found by the wrong people, they might even out the playing field in a way we don't want it evened out."

Lily's heart went out to Bree. Her friend had been through so much already, and yet her worries were far from over. For the first time, Lily noticed the dark circles under Bree's eyes. She was tired, and faint worry lines were etched into her forehead. Lily went up to her and put her arm around her.

"Try not to worry so much," Lily said. "Knox and the other dragons are doing all they can, and we have a lot of very powerful wizards back in Falcon Cross that would do anything to fight for the cause of good."

"I know," Bree said, forcing a smile onto her face. "It's just hard, when I've finally found so much happiness, to be worried about losing it all."

Lily nodded, her mind immediately going to Vance. "I can understand that," she said. "But we can't let fear of the unknown ruin the happiness we have today. You've been working so hard. Try to relax and enjoy the barbecue tonight. There will be plenty of time to worry about everything else tomorrow.

Bree smiled again, a little more convincingly this time. "You're right. I should go shower and get ready. It's going to be a lot of fun. Zeke can be really funny, when he wants to be. He doesn't talk much, but that makes it all the better when he suddenly jumps into a conversation with a witty comment."

"I can hardly wait," Lily said, "Things are a lot more fun now that Vance and I aren't fighting. The last few days have been some of the most amazing times of my life."

"Good," Bree said, her smile genuine now. "I hope that the positive trend continues for the whole summer. I'll see you at dinner, and you can tell me all about the adventures you and Vance have been having."

Lily nodded, giving Bree a small wave as her friend left the cabin. Lily closed the door behind her and leaned against it, feeling strangely uneasy. Things had felt a little too perfect lately, and Lily had a bad feeling that a storm was coming. This summer was not going to be as carefree as she'd hoped it would be.

But, come what may, at least she had Vance.

CHAPTER ELEVEN

Vance laughed along with the rest of the crew as Zeke described the way he had tricked a lion shifter into handing over an ancient sword without a fight. Zeke was a master at manipulation, and Vance often thought about how he was glad Zeke was on their side. The man didn't say much, and he often held back during barbecues or other social gatherings, but, when he did talk, Vance always came away amazed. Zeke was not only witty, he was smart. He wasn't as good of a flyer or fighter as some of the other dragons, but he made up for it with his intelligence.

Vance smiled as he looked around at the crew. All of the dragons had their own special abilities, and together the crew made a formidable force. Even though they drove him crazy sometimes—and he was sure he did the same to them—they were his brothers. Lily had been right when she told him that he needed to be thankful for what he did have, because when he really stopped to think about it, he realized that he had so much.

Vance glanced sideways at Lily, who was grinning as Noah now gave Knox a hard time about how long he'd been gone on what should have been a simple mission.

"Admit it, you just wanted some extra days for a romantic getaway. You're going soft on us. Bree, what have you done to him?"

Knox and Bree laughed along with the rest of the crew. But as the laughter died down, Knox's face turned serious.

"As much as Noah would like to think I'm going soft, we have a bigger problem than that," Knox said. "I hate to put a damper on the fun we're all having right now, but I think while we're all here, we should talk about the trouble that's been brewing, and what we can do about it."

Vance frowned as Noah spoke. Lily had already told him that Bree had mentioned that there were concerns about the safety of the artifacts that were under the Redwood Dragons' watch. Knox said pretty much the same thing, his face grave as he told the crew that guarding the vaults of ancient artifacts would be top priority until further notice. Vance was not happy with this news. Not only was it disappointing to know that the crew was facing threats from outside, but it also irritated Vance to know that protection of the vaults would have to be stepped up. Vance would much rather be off on a mission, enjoying the thrill of the hunt, then making the rounds to check that all the vaults were well-secured. Vance found guard duty intensely boring. He hoped that he wouldn't be one of the first dragons assigned to make the rounds to the vaults, but as soon as Knox started speaking, those hopes were dashed.

"Vance, I'd like you to go tomorrow to check all the vaults. We'll rotate through so that everyone is taking a turn."

Vance made a face, which earned him a warning look from Knox. Vance sighed and nodded, but he couldn't completely keep the annoyance out of his face. Not only was he going to be bored out of his mind, but checking the vaults would take the entire day, which meant he was going to have to spend the whole day away from Lily. But Vance knew better than to argue with Knox. The man was still annoyed with him over his ostentatious flying, Vance could tell. Besides, he would have to take a turn making the rounds to the vaults eventually. Might as well get it over with. But just as Knox was about to start speaking again, Lily surprised everyone by speaking up.

"Can I go with Vance?" she asked.

All eyes turned to her, and Vance's heart warmed that she was offering to go with him. He would never have asked her to. The trip required hiking through some of the least interesting parts of the forest, and, if the clan was lucky, there would be nothing exciting to see once they were actually at the vaults. Knox seemed to agree with Vance for once, because he was shaking his head at Lily.

"It's not a very exciting task, Lily," he said. "Bree can tell you. She's been there, and there's not much to see."

"That doesn't matter," Lily said "I don't need to be constantly entertained. I was just thinking that if I went I could test the protective spells that Bree cast to make sure they're still working properly."

Vance slapped his forehead. Of course! Why hadn't he thought of that? He'd been so wrapped up in his own miserable thoughts that it had never occurred to him that Lily might actually be useful on the job.

"Well, if you want to go and check the spells, we'd really appreciate it," Knox said. "But don't feel obligated."

"I'd love to help out," Lily said.

And so it was settled that Vance and Lily would go make a round of the vaults the next day. He was no longer dreading the mundane task so much, now that Lily would be going with him. And little did he know that his task would turn out to be anything but mundane.

* * *

The next morning, Vance blinked his eyes a few times when he awoke, confused as to why his cabin looked so strange. He quickly realized that he was not in his cabin, but in the cabin where Lily was staying. He looked over at her to find her still sleeping peacefully, and a smile crossed his lips. They had to be up and moving early this morning, but that had not stopped them from staying up much too late last night. Vance could not get enough of her, and she seemed to feel the same about him. They had made love until the wee hours of the morning, when Lily had finally fallen asleep in his arms, exhausted but happy. He hated to wake her now, but they had to get moving soon if they wanted to make it to all the vaults before sundown.

"Lily," Vance whispered, giving her a gentle nudge with his hand. She sighed happily, then rolled over and went back to sleep. Vance nudged her again, a little more firmly this time.

"Lily, time to get moving," he said.

This time, her eyes actually blinked open, and she looked around with a confused look of her own for a few seconds. Then she turned to him and smiled, her whole face lighting up as she did.

"Hey you," she said. "How'd you sleep?"

"Like a baby," Vance said, planting a kiss on her forehead before sitting up. "Not long enough, though. I could have slept several more hours, but we need to get started on our day. Do you want some coffee for the road?"

Lily nodded and sat up herself. "I think I'm going to need some coffee."

A half an hour later, Vance and Lily were dressed for the day and had packed small backpacks of food. They had eaten a large breakfast, and made sandwiches for lunch and dinner. Along with the sandwiches, they had packed several snacks, including granola bars, oranges, and beef jerky. They were taking plenty of water along, and they each held a large thermos of coffee.

"Ready?" Vance asked. Lily nodded, and they set out, heading toward a trail on the west side of camp that Vance knew all too well. He'd been on vault duty hundreds of times over the years, and he always followed the same loop when checking the vaults. He liked to hike to the ones that were hardest to reach first, so that he could get them done while he was still fresh.

And, once the morning air hit his lungs, he felt surprisingly fresh despite his lack of sleep. The sky was just beginning to lighten, and the other dragons were still in their cabins when Vance and Lily left the camp. For a while, neither one of them spoke much. They were content to take in the beauty of the forest around them, and enjoy the coolness of the morning. Vance knew that they would not be able spend their whole day in the coolness of the forest. Several of the vaults were located at the very top of one of the small mountain hills that dotted the forest. Up there, there were not many trees, and shade was sparse. That would be the most tiring part of their journey. It was all downhill from there, though, quite literally.

After about an hour of hiking, Lily finally broke the silence. "Have the vaults ever been broken into?" she asked. Vance glanced over his shoulder at her. He couldn't help but smile at how beautiful her face looked in the uneven sunlight that was filtering through the trees. She must have been tired, but she did not look it. Her face was glowing and her eyes were bright, and she seemed to be almost enjoying their steep upward hike.

"Vault security hasn't been breached in my lifetime," Vance said. "William, our former clan leader, did a lot to shore up the safeguards on each of the vaults. And, until recently, no one but us seemed to know where our camp or the vaults were. Many of the vaults have been here for hundreds of years, though. In past centuries, there were occasional break-ins. Those break-ins usually signaled the start of a shifter war, because when a powerful artifact was stolen, the shifter who stole it usually tried to use it to gain power for themselves at the expense of others."

"Maybe this is a silly question," Lily said, "But if these artifacts are so powerful and so many people are trying to use them for evil, wouldn't it be better to just destroy the artifacts."

"They're indestructible," Vance said. "Many good shifters over the years have had the same idea and have tried, using every method imaginable, to destroy the objects. No one has succeeded, though, and several have actually died trying. Eventually, most shifters decided that it's safer to protect them than to try to destroy them. Plus, as long as the artifacts still exist, there's still the possibility of using them to defend the good shifters."

"I suppose," Lily said. "It just sounds like, from everything I've heard, that the artifacts often cause more harm than good."

"Sometimes," Vance said. "But there have been times that the artifacts have really saved the day. Anyway, it's not up to me. Knox is the clan leader right now, so it's up to him what we do with the artifacts. He wants them kept in the vaults and guarded, so that's what we do."

Lily seemed satisfied with this answer, and they continued on in silence again for a while. After a few hours of hiking, they emerged at the top of a rocky cliff near the top of one of the mountains, and Vance made his way to what looked like a solid wall of rock. He ran his fingers across it, searching, until he found what he was looking for. In the middle of the wall, blending in so well that it was almost invisible, was a small button. When Vance pushed it, there was a sudden series of beeps, and then a computer chirped, "Fingerprint verified."

Vance pushed the wall then, and the whole thing swung slowly inward, revealing a dark cave behind it. If you had not known it was there, you would never have found it. Vance motioned to Lily to join him, and she gasped as she stepped toward the entrance. Vance couldn't help but smile, remembering that he had reacted similarly when he had seen this vault for the first time as a small boy. This was the oldest vault, and it was filled to the brim with what looked like some sort of strange medieval treasure chest. Swords, spears, helmets, armor, jewels, crowns, shields and more were piled haphazardly in the dank room. When the light from outside hit the piles, they glittered irresistibly. Although this vault was the hardest to reach, it was Vance's favorite. When you stepped in here, you felt like you were stepping back in time—back to the days when dragons ruled the earth. This vault always filled Vance with a certain feeling of reverence. It must have done the same for Lily, because she looked around with wide eyes for several long moments. Vance smiled as she took it in, admiring the way her eyes reflected back the light of the gold.

"It's incredible," she finally said, her voice little more than a whisper.

"I know," Vance said, stating the obvious. There wasn't much else to say.

"Knox is right. It would be a crime to destroy all of this, even if it were possible," Lily said. "It's too bad it has to be hidden away like this."

"I never really thought about it that way," Vance said. "I guess I've always just taken it as a given that a treasure like this had to remain under wraps. You're right, though. It is a bit of a shame."

Lily stepped into the cave, pausing several times as though she wanted to examine every last item. When she had finally seen her fill, she turned and walked back to join Vance at the front of the cave.

"How many vaults are there?" she asked.

"Five in total," he said. "But this one is the oldest and biggest. We add a new vault any time one vault runs out of room, and the fifth vault was just added last year. It's nearly empty now, but I hope to see it filled to the brim during my lifetime."

"You want to fill a whole vault in your lifetime?" Lily asked, sounding surprised. "How many ancient dragon artifacts are out there, exactly? It seems like at some point you would run out of artifacts to search for."

"No one knows for sure, but there are probably thousands and thousands more than what we've found already. They were all made during ancient times, when the ancient dragons were trying to preserve their supernatural powers in these special objects. For centuries, the majority of them were hidden in plain sight, spread all over the world in different locations. Some were in museums. The curators thought they were just plain old ancient items of gold or precious metal. Some were wasting away in ruins of ancient cities. Some were held as family heirlooms by people who had no idea that the heirlooms were as powerful as they are. In the old days, we only found items when a shifter realized that an artifact had power and tried to use it for evil. We'd swoop in and try to steal it away from them. But advances in technology and electronic research have made it easier to find the objects. Unfortunately, a lot of evil shifters know this, too. We don't do much research on our own to find artifacts. We just follow tips on shifters who have found something. We let them do the hard work of finding and recovering an artifact, then we swoop in and take it from them, bringing it back here for safekeeping."

"Don't you worry someone will find and use an artifact before you can get to them?" Lily asked.

Vance shrugged. "We worry about a lot of things. But we're good at what we do, and we haven't lost an object yet. The closest we've come to losing an artifact was with the dragon stones, but even those turned out okay in the end."

Lily nodded, then stepped completely out of the cave so that Vance could shut the door. He used his finger to secure the door again, and the computer chirped perkily as it said, "Vault locked."

"How does that work?" Lily asked.

"It's a state of the art fingerprint reader," Vance said. "It's specially designed to read body temperature, too, so you can't use a fake print that you lifted from somewhere. It has to be an actual, human finger that the print belongs to. The reader is programmed with the prints of all the Redwood Dragons, and now of Bree as well. We can add your print later, too, if you want. But, as you can see, the door itself is hard to see, and the sensor itself is even harder to find. It's pretty unlikely that anyone who didn't know what they were looking for would find it. And even if they did find it, they wouldn't be able to trick the sensor into thinking they had the right fingerprint. On top of all that, the spells Bree put on the vault should offer additional protection. Speaking of which, you said you can test the spells, right? Do you want to go ahead and do that?"

"Yup. But you'll want to come over and stand right next to me first. If she used the spells I think she did, we're going to want to throw up a shield spell first."

Vance cocked an eyebrow at Lily. "Are you sure this is safe?" he asked.

Lily smiled. "I cast one of the best shield spells you'll ever see. As long as you stick with me, you'll be fine."

Vance smiled. Lily was unbelievably sexy when she showed her confident side. She was standing tall and proud, gesturing for him to come stand by her. He happily obliged.

"You'll need to get as close to me as possible, so that the shield covers us both," Lily said. "The best thing to do is stand behind me with your chest pressed against my back, then wrap your arms around me so that your body is pressed up flat against mine."

Vance grinned as he stepped behind her and pulled her into a big bear hug. "Don't mind if I do," he teased, nuzzling her neck.

Lily laughed, but wriggled her arms free. "Very funny," she said. "But I'll need my arms free. Try to behave, and stay inside of the shield. I'd rather not have to drag you back to base camp dead or mortally wounded."

"That sounds ominous," Vance said. He pushed his body up against Lily's back, then held still dutifully and said, "Ready."

Lily nodded, then raised her ringed hand high above her head. Vance let his eyebrows travel upward, and he saw a beam of sunlight glinting off the deep onyx stone.

"*Magicae arma*," Lily yelled. Instantly, what felt like a large force field surrounded the two of them. Everything became strangely blurry, almost as though Vance was viewing it from underwater. Sounds were muffled, too, and Vance knew that Lily's shield spell was going strong. He'd barely had time to look around through the blurriness, though, before Lily was yelling out another spell.

"*Magicae revelabit*," Lily's voice called out, strangely clear since she was inside the shield with Vance. As soon as Lily had spoken these words, Vance felt as though all hell was breaking loose. The force field shield felt like it was being pelted by some sort of large metal objects. Flashes of light could be seen shooting forth from the vault's door, and Vance guessed that they were some sort of laser beam. A burning, acrid smell filled his nose, and he could see what looked like small flames licking against the door of the vault.

Lily was looking around, her gaze moving rapidly from right to left as she took in the action around them. Her ringed hand was still held high above her head, the shield charm shooting thickly around them. When Lily finally seemed satisfied that she had seen everything, she yelled out, "*Revelabit terminantur.*"

Almost instantly, the chaos stopped. The laser beams vanished, the metal pounding ended, and the acrid smell vanished. The ground was still on fire, though, and Lily frowned as she began to lower her hand.

"*Arma terminantur,*" she yelled. Instantly, the shield around them vanished. Vance had a sensation like he was coming up from underwater, and suddenly everything was clear again. The blurriness disappeared, and the sounds of the forest were sharp once more.

"*Magicae aqua,*" Lily said, pointing her magic ring toward the flames. A stream of water spewed forth from her ring and doused the flames, sending sizzling little wisps of steam up from the ground. The earth was charred and black, and Lily frowned as she took in the damage.

"*Aqua terminantur,*" Lily said. The water from her ring stopped flowing, and then she said, "*Magicae sarcio.*"

A bright beam of light shot forth from the ring and everywhere Lily pointed the beam the earth was instantly renewed. The charred earth disappeared and was replaced by soft, healthy soil.

"*Sarcio terminantur,*" Lily said. The white beam stopped, and Lily turned to look at Vance with a furrowed brow.

"That was a repairing spell," she said. "I don't want to leave the forest a mess."

Vance whistled. "You're quite talented," he said.

Lily smiled. "Thanks. So is Bree. She did her job quite well. That's quite a cocktail of protective spells she whipped up. Anyone who does find the vault door and try to break in will be in for a rude surprise."

Vance shook his head in amazement. He felt slightly overwhelmed as he looked over at Lily. She hid quite a lot of power under that calm, sweet exterior. "You are something else," he said. "Come on. Let's go check the other vaults."

They spent the rest of the day hiking through the redwoods together, making the rounds to all of the other hidden vaults. Vance checked each one, using his fingerprints to enter and check the contents. The vaults all appeared untouched and undisturbed, and by the time they left the fourth vault, Vance was feeling a bit more confident about the future of the Redwood Dragons.

"Maybe the evil shifters and wizards found the base camp thanks to Samuel's treason," he said. "But they still don't know where any of the vaults are. These things are nearly impossible to find if you don't know what you're looking for."

At the fifth and final vault, they again found no signs of intrusion. As she had at each of the previous vaults, Lily tested the protective spells that Bree had cast and found them to be in good working order. By the time they turned to leave the fifth vault, the shadows were growing long.

"We might not make it home before dark," Vance said apologetically. "It's difficult to get all of that done in one day. I brought flashlights and headlamps just in case."

Lily scoffed. "Who needs a flashlight?" she said with a grin. "Watch this. *Magicae lucis.*" Instantly a bright beam of light came shooting forward from Lily's ring, lighting up the dusky forest in front of them.

"Oh, come on," Vance said. "Now you're just showing off."

Lily just laughed, and let the bright beam of light sweep back and forth through the dark forest. She was in an exceptionally good mood, and Vance had a feeling that coming on this trek had been good for her. She'd had the chance to feel like she was truly useful to the dragon clan, and Vance had to admit that being on vault duty wasn't so bad when he had Lily with him. He might not even complain next time Knox sent him to make the rounds.

Lily started whistling a merry tune, practically skipping as she moved through the forest with her ring's bright light beam bouncing across the darkening forest in front of her. Knox was leading, but he smiled at the sound of her voice and glanced back at her every so often. They were done with their work, and they were on their way home to a good meal. Besides that, all the vaults were safe still. Life was pretty good, on the whole.

The dusky light was growing darker, and, since he didn't have a magic ring to light the way for him, Vance stopped for a moment to reach into his backpack and find his headlamp. But before he could find it, he heard Lily scream his name, and then yell the words "*Magicae gladio!*"

He looked back just in time to see the beam of laser light shooting from her ring, slicing through the air like a sword and lighting up the area around Lily just enough for him to see an angry tiger running toward her. There were no tigers native to California, and Vance knew instantly that this was a shifter. And not a friendly one, from the looks of it.

Vance instantly dropped his backpack and let out a roar, then began to shift himself. His clothes tore to shreds, and he briefly cursed in his head as he watched fragments of his favorite hiking shirt go flying across the forest in front of him. But there wasn't time to worry about ruined shirts right now. His girl was in danger, and he was going to make this tiger pay for thinking it could bring harm to Lily.

As Vance's body transformed into a dragon, though, he realized with pride that Lily seemed to be holding her own quite well. She was slicing her laser beam sword through the air, holding the tiger back from them by a few feet. The giant cat was growing angrier by the second, snarling, hissing, and growling more loudly with each lunge. Cleary, he had not been anticipating having to fend off an angry wizard.

Within moments, Vance had become fully dragon, and he let out a roar so loud that it must have shaken the treetops of the redwoods nearby. Lily glanced up at him, then stepped aside to let him take the front line in the fight against the tiger. The giant cat never stood a chance. Vance swung a large giant claw at him, slicing the skin on his back into several red, ribboned shreds. The tiger squealed in pain, but still tried to lunge forward and sink his teeth into Vance's shoulder. Vance's dragon skin was too thick for the tiger's teeth to have much effect, but the cat tried one more time, anyway. Vance felt the tiger's teeth sliding off his shoulder's thick scales, and took the opportunity of the cat being close to send another set of slicing claw marks across its back.

The tiger yelped, and must have realized that he was beaten, because he turned to run. Vance was not about to let him get away so quickly, however. This tiger had been hunting them, and Vance wanted to know who he was working with and what exactly he was after. With a giant swish, Vance swung his spiked tail around so that it was directly in front of the fleeing tiger. The beast tripped over it, yelping in pain as it landed on one of the spikes. Vance closed in on the beast, reaching out to grab it with the claws of his dragon hand. The tiger made another desperate attempt to get away, but it was too slow. Vance's dragon had a firm hold on it, and the only thing the tiger did as it struggled was to cause Vance's dragon claws to dig deeper into its skin. The tiger thrashed about, but to no avail. Vance was not letting it go anywhere.

Then, with a loud shout, the words "*Magicae obstupefio*" rang through the air. Vance looked over to see Lily standing with her ringed hand lifted high in the direction of the tiger, which was now immobile under the power of the stunning spell. Vance waited for a few moments, watching the tiger wiggle his head violently. It seemed to be the only part of him that he was able to move. Everything else remained completely still. Vance thought for a moment, and then shifted back into human form.

"How well will that hold him?" Vance asked.

"It's a strong spell," Lily answered. "Don't worry; he won't be able to move unless I release the spell."

"Will he be able to shift to human form while still under the spell?" Vance asked.

"I don't know," Lily said, giving Vance a small, confused shrug. "I've never used this spell on a shifter before."

Vance walked over to where the tiger was lying and bent down near him. "I want you to shift back to human form," Vance said. "If you don't, I'm going to shift back to dragon form and kill you with one long, painful burst of flames."

The tiger growled at him, but then, a moment later, a loud pop sounded off and the tiger suddenly morphed back into human form.

"You two are monsters," the man spat out. He was still immobile from his neck down, and Vance thought for a moment about how strange it looked to see such a large, muscular man lying still and helpless.

"We're monsters?" Vance said. "You're the one who attacked us. Don't complain about losing a fight you started. What are you after, anyway?"

The man laughed, his voice sounding bitter and abnormally loud. "Don't act like you don't know!" he said, twisting his face into an ugly sneer.

Vance felt anger rising in the pit of his stomach. He didn't like being mocked, especially by a nearly immobile man who had tried to kill him only moments before.

"Watch your mouth if you know what's good for you," Vance said. "And just answer the question."

The man rolled his eyes and let out a long sigh. But then, he did answer Vance.

"If you actually don't know that I was sent here to find the location of the dragon stones, then you're dumber than you look," the man said.

Vance scowled at him, his anger rising. "If you think we'd be dumb enough to leave the dragon stones anywhere close to here, then you're the one who's dumber than you look, and trust me—you look pretty dumb."

The man tried to spit in his face when Vance said that, but his aim was poor and he missed. Vance slapped him across the face, his scowl deepening. "Watch yourself," Vance said. "I'm going to take you back to my clan leader so he can question you. We'll see how bold you are then."

Vance reached down to pull the man up, but before he could get him completely off the ground, he heard Lily shriek. As he turned to look at her, he felt the immobilizing spell suddenly disappear, and the tiger shifter landed a giant punch on Vance's face as he regained the ability to use his body. Howling at the sudden pain, Vance reflexively dropped his hands from holding the man, and the man took off running into the woods.

Cursing, Vance turned again toward where Lily was standing, then his eyes widened in horror as he realized that a second shifter, already in bear form, had knocked Lily backward onto the ground. The bear let out a roar, pulling its head back to gain momentum so it could lunge forward and sink its teeth into Lily's neck. Vance heard himself screaming, and he started running toward Lily, but he felt like everything was moving in slow motion. There was no way he could reach her in time, and he felt a helpless, burning rage fill him.

But before the bear could come down fully on Lily, she managed to stick her ringed hand in front of her face and yell out, "*Magicae ignis.*"

Instantly, a stream of fire came shooting from her ring. It hit the bear right in his face and he fell back, howling in pain. In an instant, Vance was once again shifting back into dragon form. As soon as his head had returned to its fearsome dragon shape, Vance let out a stream of fire himself. Anger consumed him as he burned the bear that had just come unbelievably close to mortally wounding Lily. Vance had never been so bent on revenge in his life. The bear turned, trying to run while at the same time trying to paw at the fire that was still burning the fur on his face. But Vance did not let him get far. In an instant, he pounced on the bear, reaching a sharp dragon claw toward the bear's neck and slicing it open. The bear let out one more howl of pain and then fell to the ground in a lifeless thud.

Vance turned and ran in the direction that the other shifter had disappeared. The man was fast, but Vance was faster. Almost no one could outrun his dragon speed, especially not when he was running through these forests, which he knew like the back of his hand. Vance caught up with the man less than two minutes later, just at the edge of one of the larger streams that ran through the forest. The man had changed back into tiger form, and was trying to grab a large backpack in his teeth. The pack was huge, though, likely packed with extensive provisions for a trek through the forest, and the tiger was having difficulty lifting it in his jaws.

Vance was on him in two final, giant leaps. The tiger dropped the pack and roared, trying desperately to fight back. But Vance showed no mercy. His heart was still racing with adrenaline from how close he had come to seeing a bear sink its teeth into Lily's neck, and the primal anger that filled him could not be contained. The tiger yelped in pain as Vance slashed at his throat, and then there was silence.

Vance looked around wildly, sniffing the air to see whether there were any other shifters around. He could not smell anyone else, but he knew he needed to be careful. He knew all too well how easy it was to conceal your scent, if you had the right tools. Vance gave a few flaps of his giant dragon wings and rose into the air so that he would have an aerial view of the area. His sharp eyes darted back and forth across the scenery, searching for any sign of movement. The only life form he could make out between the treetops was Lily. She sat huddled between his hiking pack and hers, with the giant bear lying dead a few yards away from her.

Satisfied that they were once again alone in the forest, Vance spiraled back down to the ground, landing near the spot where the tiger shifter had fallen. He grabbed the tiger shifter's backpack in his clawed hands, lifting it up and flying it back to where Lily was sitting. As soon as he landed, he let go of the backpack and shifted back into human form. Then he ran to Lily, sitting next to her and putting his arms around her shoulders. She was shaking slightly, and her face was wet from tears although she was not crying at the moment.

"Are you okay?" Vance asked, his voice husky with emotion. He hated to see her so frightened and unhappy. This mission together was supposed to have been laid back and fun. He'd never expected that a day of checking on the vaults could have turned so deadly. If he had, he wouldn't have brought Lily with him.

"I'm alright," Lily said. "But I have to say that having a giant grizzly right in front of you is a little unnerving."

Vance could tell that she was trying to keep her voice steady and light, but she still sounded like a frightened child. He felt somehow responsible, even though he could not have known how this day would turn out. He kissed the top of her head and squeezed her tighter.

"I'm really sorry you had to go through that," Vance said. "It looks like Knox is right—something is brewing in the shifter world. Being trailed by two evil shifters while on vault duty is a bad, bad sign. I hope there's some sort of information in the pack I found about who they're working for and what their plans are. We must figure it out and put a stop to this madness. The Redwood Dragons rule this forest. We will not allow evil here."

Vance's voice rose as he spoke, and he felt himself trembling with anger again. Lily felt so soft and warm in his arms, and his heart tightened in his chest when he remembered her screams of terror. But she stirred a bit now, as he held her, and looked up at him.

"We should get back to camp," she said, her voice stronger. "Knox will want to hear about the attacks, and the sooner we can look through those backpacks for information, the better."

Vance pulled back to look at her, pride filling his eyes as he saw that she was quickly gathering her strength. Her shivering had subsided now, and she had a determined expression on her face. She was working hard to overcome the fear that had been washing over her, and it looked like she was finally winning that battle. Still, he didn't want to rush her.

"You sure you're okay?" he asked gently.

Lily looked over at him and nodded. "I got quite a shock, yes. But I'm okay. And I'm more determined than ever to help the shifters protect themselves against the forces of evil. If we all join together, we cannot be defeated!"

Vance smiled. "That's the spirit," he said. "Let me just get these guys buried properly and we'll head back to base. Knox is going to want to hear all about our adventure here. I'd be willing to bet that he's going to make it his top priority to find out who these attackers were, and to plan an offensive attack against them. And I'm going to want to be on the front lines of whatever attack we plan. No one messes with my girl and gets away with it."

And with that, Vance stood and started heading toward the body of the bear shifter. He would clean things up here and then focus all of his attention on finding the leaders behind the attack today. When he did, they were going to curse the day they were born.

No one messed with a dragon and his lifemate. No one.

CHAPTER TWELVE

Lily watched the furrow on Knox's face grow progressively deeper as Vance gave him an account of everything that had happened in the woods that day. The other dragons all surrounded Knox, and they all looked just as concerned as their leader. When Vance had finished the whole story, he set the backpack they had stolen from the dead shifters down in front of Knox, and waited for the mighty leader of the dragons to speak. For several long moments, Knox was silent, his eyes glaring down at the backpack as though it had somehow been responsible for the actions of its owners.

"A storm is coming," Knox finally said. "Looks like we might not have such a lazy summer, after all. Let's see what's in this bag."

Knox reached into his pocket and pulled out his pocket knife, slashing open the top of the bag. It would have been just as easy to unzip the thing, Lily thought. But, she supposed that Knox was angry, and a little bit of brute force probably made him feel better.

Knox started fishing items out of the bag as the rest of the dragons looked on. Most of the contents were basic supplies like food and extra clothing. But toward the very bottom, secured neatly inside a low interior pocket, Knox found a cell phone.

It wasn't your typical cell phone, though. It was thick bulky, like the cell phones of twenty years ago had been. Lily was standing close enough to Knox to see that the phone's screen was monochrome, and that it asked him for a password any time he hit any of the buttons to try to access the menu.

"This is our key to who, exactly, is after us," Knox said. "There's something fishy about this phone."

"How so?" Lily asked, squinting her eyes as she tried to get a better look at it. "It looks like a normal phone to me."

"Of course it does. That's what they want it to look like," Knox said. "But think about this for a minute: when was the last time that you saw a phone this old?"

Lily frowned. "I don't know, exactly. Maybe fifteen years ago? I think these came out when I was in high school, but I can't remember for sure."

"Exactly," Knox said. "No one uses phones like this anymore. I'm not sure they're even compatible with any of the major cell phone service providers."

"Oh…" Bree said, piping in as she suddenly caught on. "The phone isn't actually being used as a phone. It's somehow being used as a way to hold data about whatever missions its owner is being sent on."

Lily saw Knox nodding, his face set in a determined line as he stared at the blinking screen, which was still asking him for the pass code.

"But we don't know the pass code," Vance said, stating the obvious.

Knox nodded. "That's the problem. And I don't want to guess at it randomly. I'd be willing to bet my right hand on the fact that this phone is set to self-destruct if a pass code is entered incorrectly too many times in a row. We have to figure out a way to get the pass code without blind guesswork…but I have no idea how, exactly, we're going to do that."

Lily and Bree exchanged glances, then smiled.

"Are you thinking what I'm thinking?" Bree asked.

Lily nodded. "Revealing spell!" she said with a smile.

"You can do that?" Zeke asked, raising an eyebrow in their direction. "Just make a spell and then you'll know the password?"

Lily grinned. "We might not look like much, but Bree and I are both well-trained wizards. We're a lot more useful than you think."

Zeke chuckled and held up his hands. "Alright, alright. I never said you weren't useful. I'm just surprised that it would be as easy as that. It seems to me like our enemies would have taken precautions against such simple hacks into their systems."

Bree shrugged. "It makes sense if you think about it. Until very recently, most shifters thought wizards were completely extinct. They're probably having a hard time figuring out how to safeguard things against wizard spells. Unless they have a wizard standing over their shoulder telling them which spells could potentially break into an object, they might not even think of the possibilities."

"But they might actually have wizards standing over their shoulders," Myles pointed out. "After all, the army that Samuel raised to try to capture the dragon sapphire had plenty of wizards in it. They might have gone to help the evil shifters with their work."

"Enough talk, you guys," Lily said, feeling surprisingly bold. "They might have wizards, but I doubt any of them are as well-trained in spells as Bree and I. Our spells can likely overcome any protective spells. And, besides, there's only one way to find out if a revealing spell will work on this thing."

She raised her ringed hand, pointed it at the phone, and then uttered the words, "*Magicae revelabit*," in a loud voice.

Everyone held their breath, and for a moment nothing happened. And then, just like that, a series of numbers flashed across the screen by itself. The phone was entering the pass code in of its own accord, and a moment later, the lock screen had disappeared to show a welcome screen.

"Yes!" Vance said, fist-pumping the air. "What did we ever do before wizards?"

Lily grinned over at him, a puff of pride filling her chest. It felt good to hear such strong praise from Vance, and it felt even better when he put his hand possessively on the small of her back. She had often felt somewhat out of place here in the dragons' camp. Bree seemed to have settled in well, but Lily still felt like an outsider. She was still trying to figure out the rhythms and nuances of life in the forest. But, standing here right now, with all of the dragons looking at her in admiration, she felt for perhaps the first time like she truly belonged. The thought made her wonder anew whether there was any way for her to move out here with Vance. Surely, if Bree could work as an Advocate out here, the Advocacy Bureau could find a way to have her work from here, too.

Lily didn't have long to daydream about her future with Vance, however. Knox was already scrolling through the information on the phone, with a deepening frown on his face. He let out a low whistle as he read, his eyes widening in amazement.

"There's a lot on here," Knox said. "I think it's safe to say that the shifter who had this phone did not think that the pass code could be revealed so easily. He never would have put so much information on here, if he had. There are long lists of the names of those who are leading this group. I don't recognize any of the names off the top of my head, but if we research the names we might be able to figure out who some of them are. We can also ask our shifter protector friends whether they know any of these guys. They might be more familiar with them than we are. The name lists are only the tip of the iceberg, though. It looks like there's also quite a bit of information here on different missions. There are reports not only on completed missions but also on missions that are in progress, or missions that are planned. There's a *lot* in here."

"We should make going through it our top priority," Noah said. The rest of the dragons nodded in agreement.

"I'm willing to stay up all night to go through this stuff," Owen said fiercely. "If these fools think they stand a chance against us and our good shifter friends, then they're in for a rude awakening. I'm not going to rest on my laurels until every last one of these fools has been taken down and taught a lesson!"

The other dragons murmured in agreement, but Knox was still frowning.

"I agree with you," Knox said. "But I don't think it makes sense for all of us to stay up all night, exhausting ourselves. This phone screen is small. I can already feel my eyes getting tired from reading it. At the most, two of us will be able to read this at a time."

"Maybe not," Zeke said. "Let me see that phone."

Knox raised an eyebrow and handed the phone over. The group watched curiously as Zeke studied the phone from every angle, frowning and nodding occasionally as he did. Finally, he grinned and looked up at Knox.

"I'm pretty sure I can hook this thing up to the printer in my cabin. I can print us all copies of every last bit of information on here, so that we can all easily read and review it, and even make notes on the pages."

"Zeke, you're a genius!" Knox said. Lily caught Owen frowning when Knox said this, and she nearly laughed. Owen liked to be the best at everything, and he was no doubt angry that Zeke's offer to print out information was overshadowing Owen's valiant offer to stay up all night reviewing that information.

"I don't think we should all stay up, though," Knox said. "We need to make sure we always have fresh, rested dragons on guard, in case our enemies try to attack us again. Zeke, after you've printed everything, why don't you and Myles get some rest. Noah, Owen, and Vance can look over the information with me tonight until we're too tired to think anymore. We'll share what we've learned in the morning, and then the Zeke and Myles can continue going over it, if necessary, while we sleep."

"I want to stay up and help," Bree said.

"Yeah, me too," Lily piped in. After all, they were both Advocates. Sorting through important information quickly was one of their strengths. But Knox was shaking his head no.

"I think it's better if both of you ladies rest," he said. "If anything happens and we do get attacked, we could use well-rested wizards on our side. I have an ominous feeling that the enemy is lurking closer than we think."

Lily was about to protest again, but when she opened her mouth to speak, she was overtaken by a yawn. Vance laughed at her.

"Come on," he said. "I'm sure everyone appreciates your willingness to look over all of this material, but you've had a long, draining day. Your mind will be sharper in the morning, anyway."

Lily wanted to protest again, but the thought of what a long day she'd had reminded her of the battle she had fought out in the woods with Vance. She felt weak at the thought of it, and she decided it might not be a bad idea to go get some rest for a little while.

She let Vance lead her toward her cabin while the rest of the dragons all started talking at once, asking Knox questions about whether he thought the information on the phone was reliable or whether they would be attacked again soon. Lily tried to listen to Knox's answers for as long as she could as they walked away, but it didn't take long for the voices around the fire pit to become too jumbled and distant for her to understand. With a sigh, she followed Vance into her cabin and made her way to the bedroom, where she started taking off her clothes that were dirty and worn from hiking. She and Vance had been in such a hurry to talk to Knox when they got back that neither one of them had bothered changing, and Lily was realizing for the first time what a mess she was. She glanced up at the full sized mirror that hung on the wall of the bedroom, and she saw her dirt-streaked face staring solemnly back at her. Her hair was pulled up into a bun, but it was dirty and greasy as well, and the bun was a mess, with tendrils hanging down at every angle. She couldn't believe how big the bags under her eyes were, and she let out a long sigh. She definitely needed sleep. But she needed a shower even more. There was no way she could happily go to bed as dirty as she was right now.

She looked up to see Vance staring at her, and she suddenly felt self-conscious.

"I look like a wreck," she said apologetically. "I think I'm going to take a shower before bed."

He smiled at her, a sweet tenderness in his eyes as he did. "You're beautiful," he said. "A few streaks of dirt on your face doesn't take anything away from that at all."

Lily blushed and looked down at her feet. "Well, be that as it may," she said. "I'm still going to shower. I don't want to climb into bed like this."

Vance nodded. "You'll feel better, anyway, if you take a nice hot shower. Why don't you go hop in and I'll make you some herbal tea. I know we stocked this cabin with peppermint."

Lily nodded, and Vance disappeared back into the front room of the small cabin to prepare the tea. She quickly finished stripping off her clothes, throwing them in a pile near the door of the room. She let out another sigh when she realized how much work it was going to take to clean all the dirt off. There were no washing machines out here in the Redwoods. Everything had to be cleaned by hand, and those dirt crusted clothes were going to take quite a bit of scrubbing.

Lily would worry about that later, though. For now, she wanted to relax under a nice hot stream of water. She went into the bathroom and turned the showerhead all the way to the hot side, waiting to step into the shower until the water heated up and steam slowly began filling the bathroom.

When she first arrived here at the dragons' base camp, Lily had thought it extremely odd that there was running water in these cabins. They were so remote, and it seemed impossible that pipes reached all the way out here. When she had asked Bree how the dragons had managed this, Bree had shrugged and said. "They have connections."

Lily still hadn't learned what those connections were, but after today she was beginning to feel as though the base camp wasn't quite as remote as she had felt when she first arrived here. Yes, it was a difficult place to reach unless you had the benefit of dragon's wings. Hiking in would take days and days. But difficult was not the same things as impossible, as Lily had clearly seen today. After all, the two shifters who attacked them had made it in. Were there more out there right now, lurking in the shadows just outside of camp?

Lily shuddered, and tried to push the thought from her mind. Everything today had turned out fine, after all. And there were several powerful dragons here at camp. It would be difficult to surprise them at their base, and even more difficult to overcome them. Even wizards would not be enough to guarantee victory. After all, the dragons had Bree and Lily on their sides, and Lily was a damn good spell-caster if she did say so herself.

With a long, resigned sigh, Lily started shampooing her hair and then lathering soap all over her body. The hot water felt like heaven, and Lily smiled as the dirt and grime of the day was washed off her body. She was glad, now, that Knox and Vance had both insisted that she get some rest. The idea of falling into a nice soft bed was more and more appealing by the second.

And yet, Lily was not ready to sleep just yet. She let the hot water continue to run over her long after the dirt and soap was all washed away. The steam felt soothing, and Lily had not realized until just that moment how much she needed to feel soothed. The day had not been an easy one. The beginning had not been too bad. Hiking around with Vance and testing the vaults had been fun. But the attack in the woods had shaken her to her core. She had been in such shock that she had not been able to even process at first the fact that she had nearly died. A few more seconds, and the bear's teeth would have been at her throat. She was lucky that her reflexes had kicked in, and that she'd been able to ward off the bear with a fire spell. Not only that, she was lucky Vance had been with her, too. She wasn't sure she would have had the strength to continue pushing back the bear on her own, even with her powerful spells. Vance had demolished the bear in the nick of time, and Lily shuddered again, thinking of what might have happened if he hadn't been there to step in. Lily had certainly not expected to come so close to death during her summer vacation, but she had to admit that she felt a little proud. She was hanging with dragons, and she was still alive. Not many wizards she knew could say that they had done battle with a dragon by their side, and Lily chuckled thinking that, if nothing else, no one could ever again say that she was just a boring, unadventurous Advocate.

Just as Lily was about to turn off the water and start drying off, Vance appeared and stood next to the shower. He himself was still quite dirty, although it looked like he had washed his hands and face.

"Tea's ready," he said with a smile. "Looks like you've been able to relax a bit in here."

Lily smiled back at him. She regretted now that she had treated him so harshly for the way he had flown her in to the Redwoods that first day. She knew now that she had never truly been in danger. Vance was not the type of man to take risks with someone else's life, and he was fiercely protective of those who were on the side of good along with his clan. She studied his handsome face as it gazed back at hers, and she was overcome with happiness at the knowledge that he was hers. In many ways, they were still getting to know each other, and yet, she felt almost as though she had known him all her life. There had always been a part of her heart that had belonged to him, and now that she had found him she felt truly at peace for the first time in her life. As she watched him, she was filled with the desire to hold him close and to feel his arms around her. She needed sleep and he needed to get back to the fire pit to consult with Knox. But all of that could wait, Lily decided. They had not truly had a moment of calm together since the attack in the woods, and they needed one.

"Come here," Lily said, beckoning him toward the shower with her finger. "You're dirty, too. Let me clean you off."

A smile broke out across Vance's face. "If you insist," he said. He stepped back to kick off his clothes, leaving them in a dirty heap on the bathroom floor. Then he gently crowded into the shower to join Lily under the steaming water. As the water washed over his hair and skin, Lily reached for the shampoo that she had just been using. She squeezed a little bit out onto her hands, and then began massaging it into his hair. He closed his eyes and moaned in pleasure as she worked, and Lily felt a delicious thrill of desire run through her own body as she watched him responding to her touch.

When she had finished working all the shampoo into his hair, he threw his head back under the water to wash away all of the lather. Lily watched him as he did, admiring his body openly. The water had washed away much of the dirt now, and she could clearly see that his deeply tanned skin was covered with angry red scratches. Here and there she could even see a deeper gash. The fight in the woods had not left him completely unscathed. Yet somehow, the marks only made him appear even sexier to her. They reminded her that he was a warrior, and that he had fought for her.

His biceps flexed as he rubbed the water through the top of his head, and Lily let her eyes slide over his broad shoulders and chest, down to his perfectly sculpted six pack. She took in his powerful thighs and calves, and then let her gaze move back to his large dick, which was standing erect now between his legs. She shivered with delight at the sight of it, and at the knowledge that he was already turned on and ready for her. She moved her eyes back up to his face for a moment to see that he was done washing his hair. He was studying her now, with a heat in his expression that took Lily's breath away.

Without a word, she reached for the bar of soap. She stepped behind him and moved the soap in tiny, firm circles across his shoulders and back, working up a soapy lather as she slowly began inching downward. She lathered up the small of his back, then rubbed the bar against his firm ass with determined strokes. He sighed with satisfaction at the movement, and she felt another thrill go through her own body.

She continued down, rubbing circles through any of the grime of the day that still remained on the back of his legs. She was bent low, her hair falling in long, wet tendrils around her face. Here, crowded into the shower with Vance, the rest of the world felt so wonderfully far away.

Lily stood and moved around to Vance's front. He had his eyes closed, and he kept them that way as she began to clean his chest and arms. She moved with slow deliberate motions as she descended once again, cleaning his ribs, stomach, and hips. She did not touch his erection yet. She was saving that for last. With purposeful movements she continued on toward his legs, lathering up the front of his thighs, his knees, and his calves, and delighting in the way he would occasionally let out a soft moan.

When she was finally satisfied with her work on his legs, she stood once again, and turned her attention back to his dick, which was standing stiff and hard as a rock. With steady hands, she moved the soap between his legs, and then began rubbing it across his erection. With one hand, she held his thick shaft firmly. With the other, she moved the soap in firm, small circles. She felt him trembling as she worked, taking her time and rubbing across first the top and then the bottom so that no spot on his manhood was left untouched.

When she was finally satisfied that she had teased every spot she possibly could, she set the soap aside and took his erection in both hands. She moved her hands back and forth across it, rubbing away all the soap and feeling herself tremble every time Vance shuddered. His moans grew more frequent and intense, and Lily smiled when she thought of how his pleasure was coming from her.

He had been content for some time to let Lily have her way with him, but now, he seemed to want more. He reached up and grabbed Lily's breasts firmly, one in each hand. The motion surprised her, and a squeal of surprise and delight escaped her lips as his strong palms covered her breasts. His thumbs flicked across her nipples, and she could feel hot moisture oozing from between her legs—moisture that was definitely not coming from the shower itself. Lily's body was responding to Vance's touch, and he was responding to hers. Desire was building, hot and impatient, in both of them, and Lily began to feel as though she might explode from the intensity if she did not find a release soon.

Luckily, Vance seemed to share her desperation. With strong hands, he reached down to move her own hands away from his erection. Then he pushed her up against the back wall of the shower. The water did not reach there, but the steam was strong and floated by Lily's face in curling wisps. Lily closed her eyes again, breathing in deeply and enjoying every sensation that was filling her. The moist air, Vance's firm hand, and then, his erection reaching and poking against her soft entrance.

He moved quickly, hungrily. He took her face in his palms, and slipped his tongue into her mouth just seconds before he slipped his large shaft between her legs. She squeezed her eyes tighter as he filled her, pushing against her inner walls and bringing a whole new warmth and fire to her body. The medley of wonderful sensations washed over her. The heat, the moisture, the pressure. It was all almost too wonderful for her to bear. She could hardly believe that she was lucky enough to experience this.

His hips moved against hers as he thrust into her. There was an urgency in his movements now, as though he needed her to know how badly he wanted this, too. The rapid movements caused the pressure in Lily's core to grow, and the flames burning inside of her intensified. Her body began to tingle, and she squeezed her eyes shut even tighter as the wonderful mixture of sensations washed over her.

It did not take long for him to push her over the edge. She cried out his name as she found her release, and her body began to clench and spasm, squeezing his dick hungrily as it continued to move inside of her. She trembled as the tingling, sweet sensation spread to the furthest reaches of her body. This moment was the most consuming thing she had ever experienced. She was his, and he was hers.

He felt the strength of their bond, too, she could tell. He groaned as she continued to spasm around him, and then he stiffened and gave one final, giant thrust as he came into her. She could feel him, pulsing inside her, matching the rhythm of her own pulsing body. They stood there, intertwined and panting as their bodies trembled from the intensity of the moment they had just shared. Lily did not know how long they stood, but she knew it was several minutes, at least. Still, when he finally pulled out of her, it was too soon. She wanted him to stay inside of her forever.

She looked up at him and smiled at the sight of him, his wet hair sticking every which way as he looked down at her with his emerald green eyes. She was surprised by the intensity his expression still held. He looked troubled, and she reached up to push back the wet locks of his hair.

"What's wrong?" she asked. She felt her heart tightening with worry. Was it her? Was he having second thoughts about being with her? But she'd thought that what they'd just shared had been so wonderful. She had felt a deep connection with him, as though their very hearts were one. Had he not felt that, too?

But he soon put her fears to rest. He reached up and stroked her face, and when he spoke, his voice was heavy with emotion.

"You are the most wonderful, beautiful thing that has ever happened to me," he said, and to Lily's surprise his voice cracked as he continued. "I can't believe I almost lost you today. I never could have forgiven myself."

"It wasn't your fault," Lily said gently.

But Vance shook his head. "The most important job of my life is to protect you," he said. "I love you, Lily. Truly and deeply."

Lily felt tears stinging her eyelids, and she was thankful that the water from the shower disguised them.

"I love you, too," she said. "For always."

She laid her head against his chest, and her heart leapt with joy when she heard him repeat the words back to her.

"For always," he said.

CHAPTER THIRTEEN

Vance blinked against the bright sunshine, wondering for a moment why his head was pounding so much as he sat up slowly in his bed. Had he had too much to drink last night? And why was he in his own bed, not Lily's? Surely she had not made him go back to sleeping in his own bed after he had experienced the joy and warmth of sharing a bed with her?

But no, as he rubbed his bleary eyes and the morning came into focus, it all came rushing back to him. He had not had too much to drink. In fact, he hadn't had a single beer last night. His head was pounding because he was so tired. He wasn't sure exactly what time it was right now, but it was still early from the looks of the morning sunlight that was beating relentlessly on his face. He had not gone to bed until the early hours of the morning, which was also why he was sleeping in his own cabin instead of Lily's. He had not wanted to wake her, and he didn't trust himself to be able to slip in quietly next to her.

From outside, he could already hear the sound of voices around the fire pit. Knox was already out there, even though he hadn't slept any more than Vance. Vance wondered, in fact, whether Knox had been able to sleep at all. The information they had read through last night had been troubling, and Vance knew that life was about to change for all of them. The easy, breezy summer they had hoped for would not be happening. Not this year, anyway.

Vance quickly got dressed. He would go see Lily, and then make his way to the fire pit, where he knew Knox was planning to update everyone in the crew on what they had learned. When Vance opened his door, though, he was startled to see Lily already standing there, her fist raised.

"I was just about to knock," she said, laughing. "Did you hear me coming?"

"No, I didn't," Vance said. "I was too wrapped up in my own thoughts. But I'm glad you're here. I was actually on my way to get you and tell you that we should go to the fire pit. Knox is going to want to talk about the information we found on the phone."

Lily's face turned serious. "Your voice has a bit of an ominous tone to it," she said.

"Well, it's not exactly the best news in the world," Vance said. "Come on, you'll see what I mean in a few minutes."

Vance led Lily to the fire pit, where Noah was serving fresh coffee from a thermos. Myles was grilling breakfast steaks, and Knox and Bree were speaking in worried, hushed tones. Vance accepted a steak and a mug of coffee, and he and Lily were silent for a few minutes as they both drank coffee and ate. Not long after, Zeke and Owen showed up. Knox looked up when they arrived, and decided that it was a good time to start speaking.

"Morning, everyone," Knox said. Vance thought that Knox's voice had not sounded so weary for quite some time. His eyes had dark circles under them, and his voice was gravelly from lack of sleep. But his expression was still bright and hopeful and Vance found himself thinking that, despite the differences they had sometimes, he really was happy to have Knox as his clan's leader. As far as dragons went, Knox was one of the best, and Vance felt lucky to have Knox in charge of the Redwood Dragons.

A chorus of good mornings sounded back at Knox, and then there was silence for a few moments while he collected his thoughts. Vance glanced at Lily's face and saw the concern etched into it. The somber mood of the group was affecting her, and Vance's heart went out to her. This was definitely not going to be the summer getaway she had hoped for. He reached for her hand and gave it a gentle squeeze, and she looked over at him and smiled bravely. Vance felt his heart melting a bit. She was doing her best to stay positive, and he could only hope that she would still be able to smile after hearing what Knox had to say.

"As you all know, I went through all the information from the phone with a couple of the guys last night," Knox said. "What we learned means that we are probably going to be spending our summer fighting, instead of relaxing as we had hoped."

Knox paused again, and Vance looked over at Lily. The morning sun was shining on her dark brown hair and giving it a brilliant, warm glow. Her skin looked fresh and tanned, and her eyes were bright. But they were filled with worry, and, as much as Vance wished he could tell her not to worry, he knew that there was plenty to worry about.

"These are stapled copies of all the information that was in the phone. There should be a copy for everyone," Knox said, as he reached for a pile of papers and started passing them around. "The two shifters that attacked Vance and Lily were scouts. As far as we can tell, they were sent to scope out the situation, and see where we hide our valuable artifacts. They were supposed to report back on any likely hiding spots for the dragon stones, and on what type of security systems we have in place. Of course, the dragon stones are not hidden anywhere near here. They've been sent to the shifter protectors in Texas for safekeeping. But our enemies seem to think we kept them nearby. This is good, in a sense. It will buy us some time. It's bad, however, because it means that our Redwoods hideout is at risk of attack."

"You really think they'd be dumb enough to attempt another attack on our base camp, after the last attack here went so poorly?" Owen asked.

Knox shrugged. "They might think they are better prepared now. And maybe they are. They've been gathering numbers and training fighters. And they are just stupid enough to be dangerous. They are so hungry for the dragon stone that they are willing to take great risks to get it. Unfortunately, that means we need to be prepared for a full-scale attack."

"But haven't you guys always known that there might be an attack here?" Lily asked. "I mean, that's not exactly earth-shattering news, right?"

Vance saw a tired smile pass over Knox's face. "You're absolutely right, Lily. We are always at least somewhat expecting an attack. But this is different. We know for certain that it's happening, and it's happening soon. Not only that, but we know that we're going to have to spread our resources out beyond just this base camp."

"Why?" Myles asked, frowning. "Our base camp is the most important place in the world to us. If we think it's going to be attacked, shouldn't we end all of the other missions and bring all of our dragons home to defend us here? Surely, there isn't an artifact out there more important than defending our home. After all, our home is where all our artifacts are kept after we recover them."

"Well, we're definitely going to put all our missions on hold for the time being," Knox said. "But our resources are still going to be spread thin, because our base camp here isn't the only place our enemies are planning to attack."

Vance watched Lily's face carefully as Knox broke his next piece of news. He knew that she was not going to be pleased.

"There is an attack planned on Falcon Cross," Knox said. "It seems our enemies hold a bitter grudge over how poorly their last attempt at capturing the dragon stone went. They have planned an attack on the wizard town as retribution. The information we have doesn't make it clear when or how they will attack, but we cannot be too careful. We must assume it will be soon."

Lily sucked in her breath, and Vance saw her looking over at Bree for confirmation. Bree nodded sadly.

"It's true," Bree said. "We've already called the High Council in Falcon Cross this morning, to tell them what we've learned."

"What can be done, though?" Lily said. "If the army coming now is anything like the last army that attacked here, it's big and powerful. Can a few dragons really hold their own against such a large group? And what about Falcon Cross? We have fighters, but they haven't seen battle for a long time. Things could get a little gnarly."

"Our enemies have a big army, true. But we have dragons," Vance said, his chest puffing out.

"And not just the dragons here," Bree said. "We know dragons in Texas who are willing to fight with us, too. Things are far from hopeless for us. But we need to be prepared."

"Which is why it was actually a good thing that those fools yesterday attacked us," Vance said. "They lost the best thing they had going for them—the element of surprise. We will be vigilant now, and we'll be ready for them when they come."

Knox nodded, a proud smile on his face.

"We will indeed be ready," Knox said. "I've come up with a plan. Unfortunately, this plan requires us to split our forces. As much as I would like to keep all of the Redwood Dragons together, we have too many different places we need to protect. First, we need to make sure that the dragon stones in Texas are safe. Bree and I will be visiting the shifter protectors there so that we can consult with them, and so that Bree can cast some protective spells over the dragon stones. Second, we need to protect Falcon Cross. Noah will be leading a group there, which will include Owen, Myles, and Zeke. The rest of the dragons will stay here to guard our base camp and our vaults. That means Finn, Grayson, Holden and Weston will be coming home from their missions to join Vance here. In fact, I've already talked to them and they're already on their way home."

"Who will be in charge here?" Vance asked. He was surprised that Knox was going away and sending both Noah and Myles to Falcon Cross. Usually, when Knox was gone, Noah or Myles was left in charge. Knox trusted their leadership more than anyone else's, and, although Vance sometimes had his own quarrels with them, he had grown used to their leadership styles. He wasn't interested in learning how to deal with another leader, and despite his best efforts to keep a neutral expression, he felt a scowl creeping onto his face. Knox, however, was smiling.

"You will be in charge, Vance," Knox said.

Vance choked on his coffee. This had been the last thing he would have expected. Knox knew he was a very effective dragon when it came to recovering artifacts, but Knox also didn't like the way Vance always took risks.

"Me?" Vance asked, unsure what else to even say.

"Yes, you," Knox replied. "I know that you and I have had our differences, and that I'm not always pleased with your fondness for taking risks. But you are one of our bravest dragons, and I have a feeling that a certain amount of risk-taking might be necessary to survive the months ahead. If you want to be leader while I am gone, the job is yours."

Vance blinked a few times, his heart swelling with pride. He could hardly believe that Knox was trusting him in this way. Not only that, but Vance wanted to get back at the shifters who had attacked Lily. Since, according to the phone data, the shifters were planning to attack the dragons' base camp here in the redwoods, staying here would give Vance the best chance of getting to fight those bastards. He would not hesitate to take down every last one of them.

"I would be honored to lead while you're gone," Vance said to Knox. "But there's just one thing."

"Yes?" Knox asked, looking at him expectantly.

"I'm only staying here if Lily can stay, too," Vance said, squeezing Lily's hand tightly as he spoke. "She is my life now. If I must fight, I want to do so with her nearby, so that I know I can protect her and keep her safe."

Knox looked over at Lily. "Lily? What do you want to do? If you want to stay here, then you are more than welcome to. It will not be easy, and there are certain to be attacks. But then, the same could be said of Falcon Cross. Dark days are ahead."

Lily raised her chin high. "I want to be wherever Vance is," she said, a hint of stubbornness in her voice. "His heart is my home now. If he stays here in the redwoods, then I want to stay, too."

"I think that's a great idea, actually," Bree said, speaking up again. "Since I'm going to Texas with Knox, we won't have a shifter ambassador here. Lily could take over that post for me, and make sure things are running smoothly with wizard-shifter relations. It's going to be more important than ever in the coming days."

"That's true," Noah said. "And I think having someone around here who can cast spells is going to prove to be useful as well."

"It's all settled, then," Knox said. "I'll go to Texas, Noah will take a group to Falcon Cross, and Vance will lead a group here, with Lily by his side. There's just one more thing."

Knox paused, and Vance waited patiently for him to continue. Since he had heard most of the plan-making last night, Vance had a pretty good idea of what Knox was about to say. He wasn't wrong.

"We're going to need to take the offensive on finding the remaining two dragon stones. If Bree's research is to be trusted, and I think we all agree that it is, then there are still two dragon stones out there—a dragon amethyst and a dragon ruby. No one has seen or heard anything about them for a long, long time, but we need to start looking. If they are still out there to be found, we have to find them first. That's why I'm going to task the dragons who remain here in the redwoods with researching where these stones might be. Anyone else who has time to jump in, though, should feel free to help out."

"Sounds like we're all going to be mighty busy over the next few months," Noah said.

"Maybe years," Bree said with a sigh. "These things have a way of taking a long time to resolve."

"Well, whatever the case, at least we know we've got some action to look forward to," Knox said with a twinkle in his eye. "Now, I'd like everyone to look through these printouts of information and see if there's anything else in them that we missed that might be a problem. Vance, walk with me for a minute. I want to talk to you."

Vance stood to his feet and followed Knox away from the fire pit. He could feel everyone's eyes on him, but he did not look back, not even at Lily. He had never been singled out like this by the clan leader, and still could hardly believe it was happening.

He, Vance Pars, was going to be in charge of base camp. Turns out his risk-taking hadn't completely ruined his chances of glory after all.

Knox walked into the redwoods, following one of the better-worn paths. For a while, no one spoke. Vance waited patiently for Knox to speak, admiring the towering redwoods in the meantime. Finally, Knox stopped, then turned to look at Vance. He put a strong hand on his shoulder.

"Listen, Vance, I know I've been hard on you for being too showy, and taking too many risks. I've had to be firm, as leader of this crew. It's important that we don't make it easy for people to find our hideout."

"I know," Vance said, bracing himself for the lecture on being careful that he was sure was coming. But when Knox opened his mouth again, it wasn't to lecture him, but to praise him.

"I put you in charge for a reason, Vance. As many headaches as you've caused me over the last few years, I've seen what you're capable of. I want you to take as many risks as you need to while I'm gone. I trust you, and I think it's important that you know that. I know you have the clan's best interest at heart. So do what you need to do to keep this place and our dragons safe."

"I will," Vance said, his heart filling with pride.

"I know you will," Knox said. "Now let's head back. I'll tell you everything you need to know about leading the clan while we walk, but then I'll need to pack. So will the dragons going to Falcon Cross."

Vance nodded, and kept pace with Knox as he walked and talked. When they reached camp once again, Vance felt confident that he knew everything he needed to know to lead the Redwood Dragons. Knox seemed to think so, too, because he clapped him on the shoulder again and then gave him a thumbs up.

"Good luck, Vance. I know you'll do great. Oh, and, just one last thing."

"What's that?" Vance asked.

"Nice job on the girl," Knox said with a grin. "Lily's quite a catch. You did well, and Bree is right—we'll need a wizard around here. Keep Lily safe."

"I will," Vance said. And as he said it he saw Lily watching him from across the clearing. She smiled, and he felt his pulse quicken with happiness. Hard times might be coming, but it didn't matter. He could handle whatever the world threw at him, now that he had a soft hand to hold at night.

* * *

The next twenty-four hours were a blur of activity. Dragons arrived back from their missions, returning home to defend their base camp and vaults. Other dragons prepared to leave for Falcon Cross, where Lily knew preparations for war were being made. Vance was busy doing security briefings with the dragons who would be left behind, making sure they all were alert and ready for a potential attack.

Lily should have been worried, with all the nervous energy in the air. But she felt strangely calm. Deep down, she realized she had always had a premonition that this summer was not going to go as planned. Now, war was on the horizon, but Lily was not afraid. She had Vance by her side, and she was excited about taking on a new role as a wizard-shifter ambassador. The winds of change were in the air, and life as Lily knew it would never be the same, but she did not mind. She felt truly alive and happy for the first time that she could remember. Vance must have noticed that she felt that way. Just before the dragons left for Falcon Cross, he found a moment alone with her.

"You're glowing," he said. "I mean, you always look beautiful. But there's something different about you today."

Lily smiled. "I feel I have a purpose, now. And knowing that I have a part to play here in the redwoods and that we are going to be together... well, it takes a load off of my mind. I feel like everything has worked out well. Of course, I'm not happy that our enemies are threatening us. But what is life without a little adventure?"

Vance laughed. "I wholeheartedly agree with you. Just don't get mad at me if some crazy flying is involved in the next few months."

Lily laughed, thinking of how angry she had been at him the first day they met. That seemed like so long ago now, even though not even a full month had passed.

"If you want to fly crazy, then go for it," she said. "Just make sure you don't do anything truly stupid. I love you, and I want you to always come home to me in one piece."

Vance's eyes softened as they looked at her. "I love you, too," he said. "And don't worry. I'm very fond of being in one piece. I'm also fond of you being in one piece, and I don't trust anyone else to protect you the way I will. So I'll make sure not to do anything stupid. I want to be around to protect you. And to see our babies grow up."

He blushed a bit as he said the last part, and quickly looked away. Lily bit her lip and then smiled. They hadn't discussed babies, but somehow there was an unspoken agreement between them that they wanted babies. Lily could not imagine a better father for her children, and she allowed herself to daydream for a moment about how perfect a little dragon wizard would be. Although, if those little dragon wizards got even a fraction of their father's love for adventure, Lily was going to have her hands very full.

Her hands were full, now, because Vance's hands were filling them. He squeezed her palm tight in his own as they bid farewell to the dragons bound for Falcon Cross, then watched them as they rose high into the air a few minutes later.

The sun was setting, and it outlined the flying dragons in bright orange and red hues. This was the end of the summer she had thought she was going to have, but that didn't matter. It was the beginning of her life with Vance, and she had never been more excited for that adventure to begin. She looked over at him now, and saw him standing tall and proud. He was officially leader of the redwood base now, and would retain that title until Knox returned.

But no matter what the future held, he was always first in her heart. He looked at her and smiled, and she smiled back without hesitation. She'd found the love of her life, and he loved her back. Nothing else mattered.

Even though Fall was still months away, this was without a doubt the best summer she'd ever had.

BOOK THREE: THE COMMANDER AND THE DRAGON

CHAPTER ONE

Zeke Pars breathed in deeply, relishing the way the cool evening air filled his lungs. It was quiet out here, high above the forests of Oregon. The only noise hitting his ears was the soft whooshing of wings as he and his fellow dragon shifters flew toward their final destination. Zeke peered through the darkness, trying to make out anything that might look like a town. But despite his keen eyesight, the only things he could see were the dark shapes of the trees below him. In the pitch black of this moonless night, the forest here appeared nearly indistinguishable from his home forest in the California Redwoods. All he could see for miles and miles was darkness and trees.

Zeke sighed as he thought of home. He hadn't been able to spend much time there lately, and he wasn't sure how long it would be before he had another chance to fly home. But with danger lurking ever closer for the wizard town of Falcon Cross, Zeke knew it was important for as many dragon shifters as could be spared to help guard the town. The wizards were the Redwood Dragons' allies, and deserved protection.

Ten dragons made up the Redwood Dragons clan, but only four of them were traveling to Falcon Cross tonight—Noah, Owen, Myles, and Zeke. Zeke was bringing up the rear, watching as his dragon clan mates sliced through the air ahead of him, turning their heads this way and that, searching for any telltale signs that Falcon Cross was nearby. The group should be getting close, but they had already been warned that the city would be hard to spot. It was kept well hidden by magic spells, since the wizards did not want any surprise visits. Zeke knew that Noah, who was leading the group, had been given specific instructions to search for a uniquely shaped grove of trees. That grove of trees would indicate that Falcon Cross was nearby. Supposedly, once the dragons flew low enough to break through the invisibility barrier of the wizards' spells, the whole town would suddenly come into view. Noah had been to Falcon Cross before, but it had been before the invisibility spells had been cast. It had been simpler times, when such strong precautions had not been as necessary.

Zeke's dragon lips turned down into a frown as he watched Noah continuing to search. He knew that Noah must be having just as much trouble seeing in the dark as he was, and no doubt was feeling frustrated. The group had been traveling for three days now, moving slowly despite the urgency of their mission. They had flown an indirect route, doing their best to avoid any areas that were populated by humans. Shifters and wizards alike feared discovery by humans, and now, with tensions between good and evil higher than ever, the dragons did not have time to deal with frightened humans.

They had enough to deal with in their own clan, Zeke thought as he continued to watch Noah, who had slowed his pace slightly. Zeke had a feeling that Noah was lost, but Noah was unlikely to admit to it. Not this early in the game, at least. Noah was a good leader, but he did not like to admit defeat. He would fly in circles for hours before admitting that perhaps he had gone off track. And, with all of the bickering within their group over the last three days, Noah certainly did not want to add the inability to find Falcon Cross to his list of disappointments.

173

Noah was second in command of the Redwood Dragons, underneath Knox, who was the clan's alpha dragon and first in command. But Knox had gone to Texas to take care of protecting two powerful dragon stones that were hidden there, so Noah was leading the group to Falcon Cross—and leading this group had not been an easy task. Owen and Myles had constantly bickered, and Owen had questioned nearly everything Noah had to say. When Noah tried to assert his authority, Owen had challenged him as much as he dared. Owen did not take kindly to submitting, especially to a dragon who was only serving as a second place leader. Noah did everything he could to keep the peace, but several fights had broken out over the last several days, and dealing with the fallout from that had put the group severely behind their anticipated arrival in Falcon Cross.

Zeke, as usual, had not participated in the bickering. He preferred to keep to himself and keep quiet, speaking up only when he felt he had something particularly useful or witty to say. Perhaps Zeke should have tried to help Noah more, but, then again, perhaps his interference would have only made things worse.

Zeke sighed again, a long, loud sigh that sent a stream of hot smoke from his nostrils and into the night air. Noah was circling around, making a one-hundred-and eighty degree turn to head back in the direction from which they'd come. They were lost, and, as much as Zeke didn't want to hurt Noah's already wounded pride, he wished the man would just stop for the night and look again in the light of morning. Zeke had hoped to be lying in a real bed tonight, but at this point he had grown so exhausted he just wanted to lie in *any* bed, even if that bed was a sleeping bag on the forest floor.

Just as Zeke was turning, flying a wide arc to change directions along with the rest of the weary dragons, a flash of light to his left caught his eye. Immediately, all of his muscles tensed and his heart began to pound. He let out a low warning roar loud enough for the other dragons to hear, and, quick as lightning, they formed a circle in the air, their giant fire-breathing heads facing outward toward whatever threat might be lurking in the night sky. This defensive circle was a well-practiced move, but Zeke had never had to give the warning signal for it in a real, live emergency before. He was pleased at how well his clan mates all responded under pressure.

There wasn't time to sit back and congratulate himself right now, though. Something was following them in the darkness, and they needed to figure out what it was. Zeke strained his eyes, searching, and he knew the other dragons were doing the same. For a few moments, everything was dark and silent, and Zeke began to wonder if he had imagined the flash of light and called a false alarm. He almost hoped so. There was darkness like never before lurking in the shadows of the shifter world right now. Zeke was not particularly eager to meet up with it here, in unfamiliar territory, while weary from several days' travel. Still, he would fight fiercely if he must. He knew he had the power of several dragons on his side, and he did not fear what the enemy might throw at him.

In the next instant, though, he immediately relaxed his stance as he saw where the light had come from. A hissing pop sounded off just after the words "*Invisibilia terminantur,*" rang through the air. Several lights appeared, attached to the rings of several different wizards, who were zooming through the air on what appeared to be glorified broomsticks. Zeke recognized them as Falcon Cross military wizards from the insignia on their uniforms. He wasn't sure whether he should be happy or angry. He wasn't thrilled that the wizards had made him think an enemy was about, but he had to admit that he was glad to know someone had joined their group who would know how to get to Falcon Cross. He'd be sleeping in a real bed tonight, after all.

The wizards whooshed into a haphazard formation, hovering in the air in front of Noah, whom they somehow seemed to know was the lead dragon. Often, non-dragons thought all dragon shifters looked alike when in dragon form, but the leader of this group obviously recognized Noah despite his dragon shape.

"I'm Raven Morey of Falcon Cross," the leader said, giving a deep bow at the waist, as though she were standing on solid ground and not perched precariously on a skinny stick a few thousand feet in the air. "Our commander, Mac Somers, told me to keep an eye out for you and help lead you into the city if I spotted you. It can be nearly impossible to find if you don't already know where it is."

Noah nodded his large dragon head, although Zeke thought he heard a small sigh escape Noah's lips. Noah probably wasn't happy about being rescued, and by a woman, no less. Still, he hid his wounded pride well, and Raven didn't even seem to notice when Owen let out a small snicker at Noah's expense.

"My apologies for frightening your crew," Raven said, turning slightly in her seat to glare at one of the wizards behind her. "Allan apparently needs to revisit invisibility spells 101. You should not have been able to see his light until we were right next to you."

"It's not my fault," Allan protested. "It was Benji's sloppy flying. He ran into me and nearly knocked me off my broom. I was a bit more preoccupied with not falling a thousand feet to my death than with maintaining my invisibility spell."

"You're the one who was flying sloppily," one of the other wizards, presumably Benji, said in protest.

"Enough," Raven said sharply. "You can explain yourselves to Mac when we get back to headquarters. For now, we need to get these dragons out of open air and safely down to the city. Are you all decent at rapid aerial descent?"

Noah nodded, keeping a polite, neutral expression on his face even though the question was almost comical. The Redwood Dragons were some of the best flyers around, and could move their giant bodies through their air with incredible speed and agility.

"Alright then, let's go," Raven said, then winked at the dragons. "And try to keep up."

Zeke would have laughed out loud if he'd been in human form. He had a feeling that if the dragons were leading the way, the wizards would be the ones having trouble keeping up. Maybe, when things had calmed down and they weren't all facing imminent danger, he should challenge these guys to a race and show them what dragons were capable of.

For now, though, getting to Falcon Cross and out of the open air was top priority. Raven gave some sort of hand signal to her crew, and in the next instant, the wizards were all flying downward at a sharp angle. Zeke could see them leaning against their brooms, their chests nearly touching their broomsticks as they made themselves as aerodynamic as possible. The lights from their magic rings flickered like glittering beacons in the dark night, making it possible for the dragons to easily follow them.

Noah dove after the wizards first, followed closely by Owen and Myles. Zeke once again brought up the rear, preferring to hold back a bit and make sure that the group was protected from behind. A few seconds after the other dragons had begun their descent, Zeke dove, too. He zoomed through the air, relishing the sound the wind made in his ears as he picked up speed. The roar of the wind grew as he flew, and the cool air felt refreshing on his hot dragon scales. Wizards and dragons alike flew downward nearly two thousand feet through open air, looking like unidentifiable streaks in the night sky. Then, just before the leading wizard would have crashed into the treetops, she pulled up her broom to straighten out her flight path. She was now flying in a straight line just above the trees. Across the forest, a series of "whoosh, whoosh, whoosh," sounds rang out, as each wizard and dragon abruptly halted their downward flight path and switched to straight, level flying.

Zeke's dragon lips turned up in a smile as he flew. It had been a long time since he'd flown this fast, and he had forgotten how much fun it could be. Up ahead, he saw Owen shoot a short burst of flames out of his mouth, and he knew that the other dragons were having just as much fun as he was. For a few minutes, they flew like this, zooming over the trees. And then, with incredible agility, the wizards changed direction again to dive down below the treetops.

Another sequence of "whoosh, whoosh, whooshes" rang across the forest as the wizards and dragons all flew into the thick forest. Zeke had to admit that this change of direction was going to be difficult for him. He did not know the trees here well, like he did at home. In the dark, it was going to be difficult to maneuver through the unfamiliar branches while maintaining the speed he would have liked to maintain. He had no choice, though, but to do his best to keep up. With determination, he watched carefully to see the exact spot in the tree cover that the group was disappearing into. Just after Myles dove down, Zeke dove as well.

He slowed slightly, expecting to be greeted by a tangle of branches that he would need to maneuver. But a strange thing happened once he flew below the treetops. Suddenly, the forest that had been in front of him moments before seemed to melt away and disappear. In its place was what appeared to be a giant village. Lights flickered in windows here and there, city streets were lit by glowing lamplight and by the headlights of the occasional car that passed by, and the faint sound of a dog barking could be heard from somewhere below.

Zeke's eyes widened in wonder as he realized that the wizards had not been kidding when they said that Falcon Cross was hiding in plain sight. The spell they had cast over the entire town to make it look like just another part of the forest was undeniably effective. If Raven and the other wizards had not come to help out the dragons, they probably would have been up there searching all night for Falcon Cross.

Now, the wizards were landing softly on a grassy area at the outskirts of the village. Zeke slowed his pace slightly so that he could take a moment to observe what the village looked like. Although the other dragons in the group had seen Falcon Cross before, this was Zeke's first time. He had never been in any wizarding village before, in fact, and he wanted to take it all in.

There wasn't much that looked different from a normal, human village. The houses and trees seemed ordinary enough. The layout was pleasing, with lots of open space and no sense of overcrowding. The most remarkable thing about the village, really, was that you would not be able to see it from above at all due to the wizards' spells. Despite the open sky above him now, with stars twinkling brightly, Zeke knew that anyone flying over this spot would only be able to see thick trees. Zeke shook his head slightly in amazement as he slowly continued his downward spiral toward the spot where the rest of the group had already landed. He landed with a soft thud next to them, and shook out his giant dragon wings a bit before folding them against his dragon body. Noah, Owen, and Myles were still in dragon form, and Zeke would wait until Noah shifted back to human form before shifting himself. Zeke looked over at Raven, who had dismounted from her broom and was smiling over at the dragons.

"Welcome to Falcon Cross," she said.

Zeke let out a happy puff of smoke from his nostrils. They had finally made it.

CHAPTER TWO

Zeke looked at himself in the mirror one last time. He tugged on the corners of his suit jacket, and shifted uncomfortably from one foot to another. He knew that the reflection looking back at him was his own, but he didn't feel like himself. He never did when he had to wear a suit. Occasionally, he had to dress up to blend in when he was on a mission and trying to recover an ancient dragon artifact. If he was spying on someone in a situation that required a suit, he wore a suit. But when he had the choice, he preferred a more casual look. His day-to-day wardrobe consisted almost entirely of relaxed hoodies, t-shirts, and jeans.

He wasn't spying on anyone tonight, but tonight's occasion, unfortunately, still required him to wear a suit. The Wizard High Council of Falcon Cross was throwing a banquet in honor of the Redwood Dragons, and all of the wizards would be wearing their finest dress robes. Dragons, of course, did not have dress robes, but they could wear suits. Noah had told the crew, in a tone that said they'd better not argue, that everyone would need to wear suits tonight.

Zeke had not even brought a suit with him, but there were several good tailors in Falcon Cross who had been more than happy to alter suits to fit all of the dragons. Zeke had to hand it to the guy who had worked on the suit he was now wearing. The suit fit as though it had been custom-made for Zeke from the start. Zeke grinned at his reflection. He did look pretty handsome, if he said so himself. But he still wished he didn't have to go to this silly banquet.

Zeke was not fond of most social events, especially ones involving hundreds of people where he was the guest of honor. He preferred to keep a low profile and keep to himself, but he knew that would be virtually impossible tonight. Any wizard worth anything in Falcon Cross was clamoring for the chance to meet one of the dragons. Owen, at least, was excited for the event. He'd told Zeke that he hoped there would be plenty of pretty female wizards there tonight.

Zeke rolled his eyes just thinking about Owen's words. Here they were, on the verge of another great shifter war, and all Owen could think about was girls. If Zeke had it his way, they would be diving right into making plans with the wizards for how to best protect Falcon Cross. The village could quite literally be attacked at any moment, so it didn't make sense to Zeke that the dragons would be partying the night away. Zeke had said as much to Noah, but Noah had brushed aside his concerns.

"You'll find that there will be a lot of formal events while you're here in Falcon Cross," Noah had said. "It's the wizards' way. Pomp and circumstance is important to them, and we need to do everything we can to respect their traditions while we are guests in their town. I know you aren't big on parties, but do your best to at least act like you're having a good time. We have to keep shifter-wizard relations on the best terms possible. After all, we need each other. It's important to have allies at a time like this."

And so, reluctantly, Zeke had agreed to attend the banquet. Zeke looked at his watch and groaned. It was time to get going, and he was already looking forward to the

177

end of this banquet. The day had been busy, between searching for suits and getting a tour of the village. Zeke could hardly believe it had been less than twenty-four hours since he landed in Falcon Cross. He hadn't had a chance to truly rest, and it didn't look like he was going to get one for another several hours at least.

Zeke looked at his reflection in the mirror one last time and realized that he was scowling.

"Game face, Zeke," he told himself. "Remember to look happy. Noah is right. You need the wizards."

Zeke walked out of the bedroom and out the front door of the small house he was staying in. The wizards had provided a small house for each of the dragons, all of which were within a few blocks of each other. This had been an unexpected surprise for Zeke, who had figured they would be put up in a hotel room, or at the very least that all the dragons would be staying in one big house together. Having his own place was going to make being away from home so much better. Raven had been the one to show him to the house last night, and she had apologized over and over for how tiny it was. Zeke had just laughed and said it would do just fine. The houses might be small, but they were palaces compared to his tiny one-bedroom cabin back in the Redwoods.

Zeke walked down the street, heading for Noah's house. All of the dragons had agreed to meet there, and then head to the banquet together. Peter, the leader of the Wizard High Council, wanted to introduce them at the beginning of the banquet, so it was best if they all arrived at the same time.

When Zeke got to Noah's place, the rest of the crew was already there, standing around in the front yard waiting for him. A large, black SUV was parked in front of the house, with a driver who was patiently waiting to take them to the banquet. Noah, Owen, and Myles were all dressed just as sharply as Zeke, in well-tailored suits that seemed to gleam in the late afternoon sunlight. What a sight the four of them must make! They all stood taller than the average human or wizard, and they all had large muscles that were evident even through the fabric of their suit jackets. Noah looked up as Zeke approached.

"Ready?" he asked Zeke.

Zeke nodded. He resisted the urge to make a comment about how he just wanted to get this over with. Instead, he smiled as convincingly as he could and made his way to the waiting SUV. Noah sat in the front passenger seat next to the driver, and Myles climbed into the third row of the SUV's seats. That left Owen to sit next to Zeke. Owen was in an obnoxiously good mood, bragging about how much food he was going to eat and how he was going to impress all of the girls with his dance moves.

Zeke turned away from Owen's rowdy jabbering to look out the window of the SUV, which was beginning to pick up speed. He watched as the houses slowly gave way to a more business-centered area of town. He noticed a grocery store, a pharmacy, and a few restaurants. One of the restaurants looked like a pub, and Zeke made a mental note to check it out when he got a chance. He was forced to travel a lot for his work, and one of his favorite things to do when he arrived in a new city was to immediately find a local pub to frequent. Somehow, having a place that was "his spot" made him feel more at home.

Falcon Cross was a charming town. All of the houses and buildings looked like they had come straight out of an old European village. Most were made of stone, and Zeke almost thought they looked like miniature castles. Some of the streets were paved with cobblestones, which added to the old world feel. Zeke's assessment from the air last night had been correct, too—there was a plenty of open space here. Buildings were spaced generous distances from each other, and there were several green places around the city center, filled with wild flowers or just lush green grass. Even now, on a weekday afternoon, Zeke saw several wizards lying out on the grass enjoying the sunshine. Zeke was a loner by nature, but if he was ever going to live in a city, this was the kind of place he would want to be. Everyone seemed so happy and carefree.

Zeke frowned. And yet, he knew that this happiness was fragile. No one knew for sure who was behind the plans to attack Falcon Cross, but from the intelligence the dragons had received, there was quite an army being built. An evil army. Zeke knew that Knox would not have sent dragons away from the Redwoods to protect Falcon Cross unless he thought the threat here was serious. After all, the Redwoods were where many ancient dragon artifacts were being stored. It was important to protect the place at all costs, and yet Knox had sent nearly half the clan here, to help the wizards.

Owen let out a particularly loud guffaw, and Zeke looked over at him in annoyance. How could he act so immature, when so many things of actual importance were happening in the world right now? Zeke was loyal to everyone in his clan, and would have protected them all with his life. But he liked Owen significantly less than the rest of the crew. The man was extroverted, ostentatious, and loud—about as different from Zeke's quiet introversion as you could get.

The SUV pulled up to the building where the banquet would be held, and Zeke looked up at it through the window in awe. The building was shaped like a large dome, and was decorated with gold and ruby accents. It was different from the rest of the town's architecture, but it was made of the same stone as the other buildings, which allowed it to still fit in well. A long series of steps led up to the front entrance, and right now those steps were filled with wizards dressed in their finest. A few of the younger wizards, who did not yet have dress robes, were wearing evening gowns or suits. Most of the wizards, though, wore long, flowing dress robes. The robes were thick and often shimmery, and came in every color imaginable. As Zeke climbed out of the SUV, he noticed robes in shades of red, blue, purple, black, green, yellow, and even a few orange. The steps of the domed building looked like a colorful rainbow of wizards. Many of them had pointed wizard hats, too. The shimmering hats bobbed up and down as the wizards made their way into the building.

To his dismay, Zeke quickly realized that he and the other dragons all stood out unmistakably in the crowd. Not only were they not wearing robes, but they were much taller and more muscular than average. It would be impossible to miss the group of them as they walked together into the hall of the high council. And, indeed, as they started walking up the steps, led by Noah, every wizard stopped and turned to look. Some whispered and pointed. Others cheered. Still others reached out to shake their hands as they passed, offering words of gratitude to them for coming to Falcon Cross. Zeke had never felt so on display in his life, but he reminded himself to keep a pleasant expression on his face.

"Make way, make way!" yelled out a familiar voice. Zeke looked up to see Raven pushing her way through the crowd. She was wearing a simple but luxurious looking black velvet dress robe. It had a high collar, and the only decoration on it was the Falcon Cross military seal embroidered in gold on the top left. She grinned as she approached them, and Zeke saw Owen puffing out his chest a bit and adjusting his suit jacket. It took all of Zeke's willpower to keep himself from rolling his eyes.

"Mac sent me out to see if you guys were here yet," Raven said. "You're supposed to come to Peter's private chambers to meet with him and await the official start of the banquet."

Noah nodded, and the group started following Raven, who kept yelling out, "Make way! Make way!" at the top of her lungs. This, of course, drew even more attention to them, but at least the crowd was quickly parting now as Raven marched forward.

When they walked through the entrance to the High Council Hall, Zeke found himself once again filled with wonder. The floors were all made of gleaming wood, and the walls were made of some sort of stone that seemed to shimmer. Light poured in from outside thanks to large windows lining the domed ceiling. Sunbeams caught the gold embroidery on several banners that were hanging from walls in evenly spaced gaps, making the banners shimmer as well.

The front entrance was crowded with wizards, but after a few moments of walking they reached a large wooden door. Raven pointed her magic ring at the door and said, "*Magicae aperio,*" and the door swung open by itself with a loud creak. The dragons followed Raven through the door, and when they were all through, Raven turned around and once again pointed her ring at the door. This time, she said "*Magicae cludo.*" The door swung closed of its own accord, and a loud thud sounded in the hallway.

After the bustle and noise of the entrance foyer, this hallway seemed almost eerily quiet. The only noise was the soft clicking of everyone's shoes as they walked. The hallway was decorated similarly to the entrance foyer, but there were many more doors here. Raven confidently moved forward at a brisk pace, then stopped in front of one of the doors and knocked on it.

"Raven Morey, here, your Honors," Raven called out. "I have the Redwood Dragons with me."

"You may enter," a voice boomed from behind the door. Raven stepped forward and opened the door, this time using her hand instead of magic. She stepped aside to allow the dragons to enter the room, and then closed the door behind them.

The room was set up like a large office. A desk of deep, rich wood stood in one corner, along with a high-backed velvet red chair. Two wooden chairs stood across from the desk chair, presumably for visitors. Across the large room, though, a large wooden table stood. It was ornately carved and had eight similarly carved chairs surrounding it. Peter was sitting at one of these chairs, a smile on his face as he greeted his visitors. Zeke had never met him before, but he looked exactly as Zeke had pictured him. His dress robes were a deep sapphire blue, interwoven with threads of shimmering silver. He wore a tall, pointed wizard hat of the same hue, and he had several golden cords and tassels draped around his neck. His long, white beard reached down to his stomach, reaching nearly as low as his hat reached high. His magic ring was the largest Zeke had seen yet, and it was made of a dark blue sapphire.

His magnificent, imposing appearance was softened somewhat, however, by the twinkle in his eyes and the broad smile of his lips.

"Welcome, welcome," Peter said, rising to shake their hands. "Thank you so much for agreeing to come to this banquet tonight. I know you're tired from your travels, and I know you have a lot of official business you want to get done, but this celebration serves an important purpose, too."

Peter looked at Zeke while he said this, and Zeke wondered whether Noah had mentioned how he had complained about the banquet. Zeke suddenly felt ashamed of himself for complaining that someone else wanted to throw a party in his honor. That really had been poor manners. But Peter looked away just as quickly as he had looked at Zeke, and Zeke let out the breath he hadn't even realized he'd been holding.

"As you can see, most of the wizards in Falcon Cross are excited that you're here," Peter continued. "They are all eager for a chance to meet you, and seeing you in person at this banquet will solidify their trust in you. It's important that they trust you, since you are going to be working closely with our military. There are also, however, wizards who still do not trust shifters. These are mostly the older generation of wizards, who have been told for decades and decades that shifters are not to be trusted. It's hard for them to switch allegiances so quickly, which is understandable. Seeing you here tonight is a small but significant step. When they see you interacting with the High Council and other wizards in a peaceable manner, it will help them to learn to trust you. It's a slow process, but a necessary one."

"You boys all be on your best behavior," Noah said, with a pointed glance at Owen. "Don't screw up this opportunity to make a good impression."

Owen said nothing, but the annoyance on his face was impossible to hide. Zeke took a strange satisfaction in watching Noah reign in Owen a bit. *Somebody* had to keep a handle on that wild child.

"Just be yourselves, and I'm sure everyone will love you," Peter said diplomatically. Zeke managed to catch himself before he snorted out loud. He was pretty sure the older generation of wizards would not be amused if Owen acted the way he normally did at a party. Zeke looked up and caught Myles' eye, and he saw a hint of amusement there, too. He had to look away from Myles before they both started laughing.

"The order of events for the evening is fairly simple," Peter said, seemingly oblivious to Zeke's and Myles' barely contained laughter. "In a few minutes, we'll head to the Great Hall, which has been converted to a giant dining room for the event. There is a raised platform at the front of the room, where the VIPs will sit. The entire Wizard High Council will be there, as well as the heads of major organizations. Among others, you'll see the head of the Advocacy Bureau, the head of the Society for the Preservation of Magical History, and, of course, Mac, our military Commander-in-Chief. You will all sit up there with us as our guests of honor. I will kick off the evening's festivities by introducing you and toasting to shifter-wizard relations. We will have dinner, and then, there will be live music and dancing. Noah, if you would like to make a speech at some point, that would be great. Don't feel obligated if you don't want to, but I do think the wizards would like to hear from you."

"I'd love to say a few words," Noah said.

Peter's smile broadened, and he glanced at his watch. "Alright, then, I think that's it. Unless anyone has questions, I think we can go ahead and head to the Great Hall."

No one had questions, so the group left Peter's office and started heading toward the middle of the building, where the Great Hall was located. Raven went ahead of them, and started rounding up all the wizards and telling them to find their seats in the Great Hall.

The Great Hall was more impressive than anything Zeke had seen so far in Falcon Cross, which was saying something. The large, circular room was located in the center of the building and let in an enormous amount of sunlight—almost the whole ceiling here was made of windows. It had the same shimmery walls that the rest of the building had, and even more banners than the hallways. Each banner bore a fanciful insignia, but Zeke only recognized one: the Falcon Cross Military Insignia.

The large open space of the room had been filled with dozens of circular tables covered in dazzling white tablecloths. Silver place settings were arranged in front of each cushioned chair, and large carafes of water and wine were positioned at the center of each table next to colorful floral arrangements. At one side of the room, there was a raised platform, just as Peter had said. Here, there was one long table with somewhere between fifteen and twenty chairs and place settings. Floral arrangements and carafes of wine and water were spaced evenly across the length of the table, and Zeke could see that several members of the High Council had already taken their seats and were already indulging in a glass of wine.

Peter led them toward the table, and when they got closer Zeke saw that there were place cards at each setting. He found the one that read Zeke Pars in elegant script and sat down, reaching immediately for one of the water carafes. This crowded room and the prospect of being introduced to everyone in it had made his mouth go dry. He hadn't come to Falcon Cross to be treated like a celebrity. He'd come to work with the military here to protect from attacks. From what he understood, there was a lot of work to do. The military here had been trained as guards to watch out for humans who might accidentally discover Falcon Cross and the existence of wizards. They were mainly trained to deal with minor threats from oblivious humans, not with major threats from angry shifter or wizard armies.

As Zeke looked around, though, he saw that he was the only one who seemed concerned about the fact that everyone was partying instead of watching out for enemies. Noah and Myles were talking and laughing with a few of the other High Council Members. Owen was laughing with a pretty blonde, of course. The woman was wearing, of all things, a sparkly, hot pink dress robe. Zeke had seen quite a few showy robes since arriving at the Great Hall, but this one was on a level of its own. The woman who was wearing it seemed to have a personality as bright as her robe, too. She kept throwing back her head to let out a loud laugh, which caused her long blonde curls to bounce around her shoulders. Her skin glowed in the sunlight that was streaming through the windows above, and she was objectively the most beautiful woman Zeke had ever seen. Zeke felt an unmistakable twinge of jealousy as he watched Owen reach over to lightly touch the woman's arm. Zeke frowned and quickly looked away. It shouldn't matter to him whom Owen was flirting with. Of course, in Zeke's opinion Owen should be focusing on the work they had come here to do, not on flirting. But if Owen was going to insist on acting like a flirting buffoon, what did it matter to Zeke who his girl of choice was?

Still, Zeke couldn't help stealing one more glance in the direction of the girl and Owen. A fresh wave of jealousy washed over him, but before he could even look away again, Peter was loudly calling for order, using a magic spell instead of a microphone to magnify his voice. The room began to quiet and people began to find their seats. Zeke watched Owen look around for his nametag, and he felt a small measure of satisfaction that the girl in the hot pink robes would have to go take her seat on the main floor. For a little while, at least, Owen would be prevented from flirting with her.

But then, to Zeke's horror and amazement, Miss Hot Pink Robes did not find her way to the main floor. Instead, she sat down at one of the seats in the head table and reached for a carafe of wine to fill her goblet. Zeke was dumbfounded. *She* was the leader of one of the big wizard organizations? What kind of organization would possibly thrive with a giggly, flirty girl at its head? Zeke strained to see her place card, but she was too many seats away and he couldn't see it very well from this angle, anyway.

Just then, Myles took his seat next to Zeke. Zeke glanced at him, and, trying to appear as nonchalant as possible, he pointed at the woman in the hot pink robe. "Who's that?" he asked, keeping his voice light.

Myles looked in the direction his finger was pointing, and raised an eyebrow in surprise. "Oh, you haven't been introduced? I wish I'd known. I would have introduced you two. That's Mac. You know, the Commander-in-Chief of the Falcon Cross Military."

Zeke blinked a few times, wondering if he'd heard Myles correctly. "Mac? Mac is a silly, giggling female who wears sparkly hot pink?"

Myles gave Zeke an annoyed sideways glance. "There's nothing wrong with laughing or wearing hot pink, you know. Just because you always want to be grumpy at parties doesn't mean everyone else has to be, too. But yes, that giggling female in the hot pink robe is Mac. Short for MacKenzie. And she's the commander of the Falcon Cross Military."

Zeke looked over at Mac, who was currently using her shiny silver goblet as a mirror to reapply her lipstick.

"God, we are in so much trouble," Zeke said.

CHAPTER THREE

MacKenzie "Mac" Somers finished touching up her lipstick and glanced out across the crowd for a moment before turning her attention back to Peter, who was growing more insistent now that everyone needed to take their seats. He shouted for order several times, with only marginal success. Mac had to remind herself that rolling your eyes at the Head Wizard of the High Council was strongly frowned upon. But Peter was too goddamn polite sometimes. He knew if he *really* yelled, that people would know he meant business and shut up right away. That's what Mac would have done. But Peter insisted on taking the long route, shushing and admonishing over and over until finally, after what seemed like an eternity, every wizard in the room had found their seat and stopped talking.

"Good evening, to wizards and shifters alike," Peter said, the broad smile on his face growing even broader as he spoke. Mac felt her heart softening toward him. He might be too polite, but he did make an excellent leader for their wizard clan. He was jolly and kind, just like you'd expect an ancient wizard to be. But he was also shrewd, and had managed to keep the clan safe with very few mishaps over the years. He was also the most powerful wizard that Mac had ever seen. She'd seen him give a demonstration at the military training academy on several different occasions, and she was always impressed with his grasp of even the most difficult magic spells. The man was a legend in wizard circles, and Mac knew they were lucky to have him here in Falcon Cross.

"I'm so pleased you could all join us for this banquet tonight," Peter continued. "A few short years ago, this banquet would have been impossible. We still lived in a time when wizards feared shifters, and shifters were not even aware that wizards still existed. But now, here we are, together as allies. As you all know, grave times are upon us. We face threats from the outside as never before. But, thanks to the generosity of the dragon shifters, we can all rest a little easier at night. They have graciously agreed to come stay in Falcon Cross to help us defend the city for as long as we need them here."

A chorus of cheers and applause rose from the crowd, although Mac saw that a few wizards were frowning. She knew there were still some holdouts who believed that the shifters were going to turn on the wizards at any moment. Mac had to admit that she had been skeptical of the shifters at first. She had been slow to believe that they were trustworthy and on the side of good. But after working with a few of the dragons, several of whom were here tonight, she had changed her mind. She had never met a group of men as smart, strong, and loyal as the Redwood Dragons. She trusted them, and she knew that Falcon Cross desperately needed their help. The wizards needed any help they could get, really. Mac was proud of the soldiers in the Falcon Cross military, but she was not a fool. She knew they had been trained for times of peace, not of war. It was time to change that, and if anyone could help her with that task, it was the Redwood Dragons.

"Please stand as I call your name, so that everyone here can see who you are," Peter was saying. Mac turned her attention back to Peter, and then watched as the dragons stood in turn. First was Noah, the leader of the group that had come to Falcon Cross. Noah had visited Falcon Cross on several occasions, and Mac had a good working relationship with him. Then came Myles, the quiet one. Mac had also met Myles before, on one of his previous visits to the wizard village. She liked his easygoing, carefree attitude. Then there was Owen—loud, boisterous Owen. Mac sighed. She could already tell that it was going to be difficult to reign in Owen. He was even more brazen than usual right now, and he was even venturing so far as to flirt openly with her. She was going to have to nip that in the bud. Owen was a good man, on the whole, but he was definitely not Mac's type. She preferred her men a little less rowdy. Finally, Peter introduced Zeke, the new one.

Zeke was the only dragon here whom Mac had not met before, and she couldn't help but stare as he stood when Peter called his name. Peter rattled off a few pieces of information about Zeke, talking about the number of ancient dragon artifacts that he had recovered, and some of his special achievements in acrobatic flying, but Mac barely heard a word of it. She was too busy staring at him.

All of the dragons were tall and handsome, but Zeke was on a whole different level. Mac was not sure how she had not noticed him when the dragons were walking into the room earlier, but she was noticing him now. His dark hair was cropped close to his head in an almost military style, but he had allowed a hint of dark stubble to grace his cheeks. His eyes were dark green, and intense. He looked around as though he could see through everyone in the room, and Mac found herself grateful that he did not turn and look at directly at her. She wasn't sure she was prepared to handle a gaze like that. He did not smile as Peter spoke, but he didn't exactly frown, either. He kept a neutral expression on his face, and nodded politely in thanks when Peter finished his speech and the room broke out into applause. He sat down quickly, and turned his attention back to his wine goblet. Mac smiled. This guy must be the complete opposite in personality from Owen.

Zeke, Mac said to herself, letting the name roll around in her mind for a moment. It was a good, strong name, and just unique enough to be truly fitting for a shifter, she thought. Mac had always wished that her name was a bit more exotic. MacKenzie seemed too ordinary for a wizard. Perhaps that's why she had decided to shorten it to Mac. She liked how Mac was a bit of an unexpected name for a girl.

Noah had taken the stage now, and was giving a short speech about how the shifters were all very glad to be there. Mac wasn't paying attention at all anymore. She was staring at Zeke, knowing that she was being way too obvious but unable to tear her eyes away from him. She had never been the type to fawn over a man—a fact which surprised many. For some reason, people seemed to think that any girl who loved sparkles and hot pink would automatically be the type to be boy crazy. But no, Mac had never been boy crazy. She'd dated sparingly, preferring to pour her energy into her career instead of into finding a husband. And, in many ways, that decision had paid off. She was the youngest Commander-in-Chief in the history of the Falcon Cross Military—and the most accomplished. She'd achieved more in her short tenure as commander than many previous commanders had managed in their entire careers. It hadn't taken long for the wizards of Falcon Cross to respect her, despite her affinity for all things frilly and girly.

And yet, one look at Zeke was enough to make any single woman go a little boy crazy. Mac couldn't deny that her heart was pounding a bit faster than normal as she gazed over at him. He was looking respectfully up at Noah, but Mac noticed the way his fingers drummed tensely on the tabletop. She was familiar with that sort of finger-tapping, because she'd done it herself many a time. He wasn't pleased with sitting still, she knew. He wanted to plan and take action now, not sit around and eat banquet food and give toasts. Mac smiled. Zeke might be handsome, but he had a lot to learn about the ways of wizards. Magic folk loved their feasts, even in times of war.

Noah finished his speech, and Mac dutifully clapped even though she hadn't paid attention to a word of it. Then, out of nowhere, dozens of drones appeared, their long drone arms balancing heaping plates of food. They buzzed about with such speed that it was almost hard to see them. Soon, the plate of every person in the room had been filled with a variety of gourmet food, prepared specially by the top wizard chefs for this special feast. There were roasted vegetables with caramelized onions, buttery mashed potatoes, and perfectly grilled steaks. Each table was also provided with bread baskets full of steaming hot rolls, and a large community bowl of salad. Mac felt her stomach growling as she looked down at her plate. She'd been so caught up in staring at Zeke that she hadn't realized how hungry she had become.

She dug into her food, nodding politely as Alfonso, the man sitting next to her who served as the head of the Advocacy Bureau, started talking about one of the latest cases his Advocates were working on. It had something to do with a wizard forgetting a magical pair of boots in a hotel room while on vacation. The hotel staff had been beside themselves with terror when the boots started walking around on their own and parroting off directions to the closest airport.

"They were those newfangled GPS boots. You've heard of them? You cast a directions spell on them and then you can ask them for directions to just about anywhere. I guess the last place the guy asked for directions to was the airport. Then he somehow forgot them in the room."

Alfonso shook his head in disgust and speared a roasted carrot with his fork, munching it thoughtfully for a moment before continuing.

"It's getting worse, you know?" he said. "In all my years at the Advocacy Bureau, we've never had so many incidents of forgotten magical objects in such a short amount of time. Wizards are getting sloppy. I'm glad we have the shifters on our side and all, but I think a lot of wizards think now that it's okay if shifters know about us, that it's okay if humans know, too. Nothing could be further from the truth."

Alfonso slammed the table with his fist, and Mac jumped. She had only been half-listening again, and she was finding it hard to get worked up about the day-to-day problems of the Advocacy Bureau right now. She was too busy glancing over at Zeke out of the corner of her eye.

"Job security, I guess," she said to Alfonso. He "hmphed" and then went back to shoveling food into his mouth.

A little while later, the drones came back and cleared away all the dinner plates and food. They also refilled all of the wine and water carafes, which was quite a big job since most of the tables now had empty or nearly empty carafes. When that was done, the drones returned with dessert. In front of each person, they deposited a small plate with a slice of chocolate cake on it. Mac smiled as the first bite of cake hit her tongue. The head chef had really outdone himself with this meal. It was the moistest, richest chocolate cake she had ever tasted. She savored every bite, and was even thinking about asking for a second helping. But before she could flag down one of the drones, she heard the soft music that had been playing abruptly changed to a fast-paced pop song.

"Alright, Falcon Cross," the DJs voice came across the room loud and clear, thanks to an amplifying spell. "I hope you've all had enough to eat, because now it's time to *dance!*"

Cheers went up across the room, and several wizards made a beeline for the dance floor. Mac snuck a glance over at Zeke, thinking that she would love the chance to dance with him, but before she could even begin to work up the courage to go ask him, she felt someone firmly grabbing her hand and pulling her up from her seat. She looked up to see that Owen was right next to her chair.

"Come on. Let me have the first dance of the night," he said his eyes twinkling. He started tugging her toward the dance floor before she could collect her thoughts enough to protest, and a cheer went up from the High Council table when they saw her and Owen together.

"Nothing's better for shifter-wizard relations than a good round of dancing," one of the High Council members joked.

Mac gritted her teeth and sighed. There was no way she could say no now. Owen, who seemed oblivious to her hesitation, practically skipped toward the dance floor that was on the opposite end of the room. Once they got there, Mac had to admit that he was a surprisingly good dancer. She knew he'd spent most of his life living out in a remote area of the California Redwoods, so she wasn't sure where he had learned his moves. Whoever had taught him, though, had done a damn good job. Mac found that she was actually having fun, but she still couldn't keep herself from stealing a glance back toward where Zeke was sitting. The Great Hall was large, so she couldn't see his expression from here, but she could at least see that he was still sitting down and not dancing with anyone else. But if she thought her glances were inconspicuous, she was wrong.

"I'm not gonna have a chance with you, am I?" Owen said, letting out a long, exasperated sigh. Mac forced herself to bring her attention back to the present, and tried to figure out what Owen was talking about.

"Huh?" she managed to say. She could feel her cheeks turning bright red, and she knew she'd been caught staring at Zeke.

"You've barely looked at me for the last several minutes," Owen said. "But you've certainly spent a lot of time staring in the direction of where Zeke is sitting."

"I...uh...um," Mac said, and then shrugged. She was out of breath from dancing, which was a little bit annoying since Owen didn't seem to be breathing heavily at all. She felt flustered, and she had no idea what to say to his undeniably accurate observation.

"I'm always playing second fiddle," Owen said with another sigh. "Anytime I'm even remotely interested in a girl, it always turns out that she's already interested in one of my buddies. I have the worst luck with these things."

Mac looked up at Owen, and for the first time since she'd met him, she saw not just an annoying, boisterous dragon, but a pained, lonely man who just wanted someone to settle down with. Her heart went out to him a bit, but that still didn't mean that they were right for each other.

"Look, you're a great guy," she said. "But we aren't right for each other. We'd drive each other crazy. I know one day you're going to find the perfect girl who can really keep up with you. And when you do, it's going to be amazing."

Owen gave her a wry smile. "Thanks for letting me down easy," he said.

Mac laughed. "I mean it," she said. "You're going to make some girl really happy. Just not me."

"You want Zeke to be the one to make you happy, eh?" Owen asked.

Mac blushed. "I mean...I have to admit I think he's really attractive. I don't know anything about him, though. Unlike you and Noah and Myles, he's never been to Falcon Cross before. What's he like? Do you think he would dance with me?"

Owen winced. "Well, I hate to say it, but it might be my turn to let you down easy, now. Zeke isn't much of a dancer. He's not much of a partier, in fact. And he's the epitome of the strong, silent type. I'm not sure I've ever heard of him being interested in a girl, but I have to say that I would be shocked if he went for a girl as bubbly as you. He's pretty much the opposite of a social butterfly."

Mac felt her heart sink a bit, and it must have shown on her face, because Owen hurried to explain further.

"It's not that you aren't awesome," Owen said. "It's just that he's kind of a loner. And he's already pissed off that we're partying right now instead of working on tactical stuff."

Mac frowned. "He isn't entirely wrong about that, you know. We do have a lot of work to do, and we can't spend a lot of time on having fun, unfortunately. But one of the most important jobs that we have to do is to convince the wizards who are still doubters that the shifters can be trusted. And throwing a banquet like this is a good way for everyone to get to know each other. When the wizards see that the shifters are down-to-earth, normal people, and that they honor our traditions of feasting, it will go a long way toward convincing them to trust you guys. Trust me on that one."

Owen put his hands up in a sign of surrender. "Hey, you don't have to convince me. I was happy to come to a banquet tonight. Zeke is the one being all grumpy about it."

Mac glanced back at where Zeke was sitting. He was by himself now. Everyone else was up and mingling, or on the dance floor. The song that had been playing ended, and some couples were leaving the dance floor.

"I'm going to go talk to him," Mac said to Owen, a note of determination in her voice.

"To Zeke?" Owen said. "Good luck."

Mac grinned. "I love a good challenge," she said, and then winked at him. "Thanks for the dance. And if you're interested in a finding a girl, don't give up yet. There are lots of pretty wizards here who would kill for the chance to dance with one of the dragon shifters."

Owen smiled back at her. "Thanks. I'll keep that in mind."

Mac made her way back toward the platform, where Zeke was still the only one sitting. She took the seat next to him and did her best to ignore the annoyed look that fleetingly passed across his face.

"You're Zeke, right?" she asked.

He nodded, and stared straight ahead while taking a long sip from his wine goblet. Owen had been right. Zeke was definitely going to be a tough nut to crack.

"I'm Mac," she said. For a moment he didn't say anything, but then he seemed to remember his manners and he turned to look at her, extending his hand to shake hers.

"Nice to meet you, Mac," he said, a pleasant smile suddenly appearing on his face. "I understand you're the head of the Falcon Cross military?"

"That's correct," Mac said, suddenly struggling to speak. Up close, he was even more handsome than he had been from far away. His eyes were intense, and appeared to be flecked with gold. His ears had the slightest hint of an elfish bend to them, giving away the fact that he had dragon shifter genes. His tanned skin glowed in the red-orange light of the setting sun, which was streaming in brilliantly through the windows above. When he locked his eyes on hers, the room around her seemed to disappear, and she could only see him. Her heart started beating faster, and her whole body felt like it was several degrees too warm. She stared at him and tried to think of something else to say, but the words wouldn't come. She wondered if she was having an effect on him like he was having on her, but his eyes gave nothing away.

Finally, he looked away, and stared off at the crowd again. The party was in full swing now, with a packed dance floor and wizards laughing and talking everywhere. Even Peter was getting into the party spirit—he was off to one side of the room showing off his impressive command of what the wizards affectionately called "party trick" spells. Right now, he was shooting colorful streamers from his magic ring. Not only did the streamers appear to come out of thin air, but they also turned into balloons in midair. After floating upwards for a few seconds, they popped loudly into a shower of sparkling confetti. Mac smiled as she watched the confetti cover the laughing group of wizards who had gathered to watch.

"So, Mac," Zeke said, suddenly breaking the silence. "Since you're the commander of the military, how do you feel about all this partying when we're on the verge of war?"

The challenge in his voice was evident, and Mac had a feeling that no matter what she said, he was not going to approve of it unless it was a total denouncement of the banquet. But Mac didn't think that the banquet was a waste, and she wasn't going to lie to Zeke about that. She tried to choose her words carefully.

"Even in times of war, perhaps *especially* in times of war, it's important to hold on to a sense of community. Wizards believe that celebrating life and its joys and festivities is something too sacred to sacrifice, no matter what the circumstances. And, by being here tonight, you and your fellow dragons are showing us that you hold celebrations sacred as well. Believe me, this will come in handy when times are tough on the battlefield. Remembering that you drank wine and danced with someone makes it easier to be willing to fight together on the battlefield—even if you must fight to the death."

Zeke frowned, but did not argue with Mac's statements. He looked over at her again and his expression actually even softened for a moment. Emboldened by this, she gathered up all her courage and asked the question she had wanted to ask since she first laid eyes on him tonight.

"Do you want to dance?"

Zeke looked at her so intensely that Mac once again found it difficult to breathe. For a moment, she thought he was going to agree, and her heart began pounding so fiercely that she began to fear it might break right through her ribs.

But then, Zeke shook his head.

"I don't dance," he said simply, his eyes kind but leaving no doubt that there was no room for negotiation on this.

Mac didn't know what to say. She had somewhat expected this answer, and yet she was overcome by how crestfallen she felt. Before she could come up with a response, though, Zeke was standing to his feet.

"See you in the war room tomorrow, MacKenzie," he said. Then he gave her shoulder a gentle squeeze before walking off the platform, and across the room to where his leader, Noah, was standing and talking to a group of wizards.

Now Mac was the one sitting alone on the platform. She sat there for a long time, rubbing her shoulder which felt like it was on fire with electricity where he had touched it, and relishing the thought of how beautiful her full name had sounded coming from his lips.

CHAPTER FOUR

The next day, Zeke once again found himself riding in a big, black SUV with his fellow dragons. This time, however, they weren't heading to the Great Hall. They were heading to the Military Headquarters of Falcon Cross. Zeke was feeling much more excited about today's agenda than yesterday's. He was ready to jump in and start planning a defensive strategy for the village. Plus, as an added bonus, today's meetings did not require a suit. He was dressed comfortably in a pair of jeans and a navy polo shirt. He looked presentable, but he felt much more himself than he had in his suit last night.

Last night had seemed to go on forever. Zeke had done his best to act like he was having a good time, and he figured he'd done a halfway decent job of that. He'd spent most of the night shadowing Noah, shaking hands with the same people Noah did and making small talk with the same people Noah chatted with. Zeke figured that if he followed Noah's lead, no one could fault him for not participating enough.

Zeke glanced over at the seat across from him in the SUV, where Owen was sitting and staring out the window. Owen had on a pair of dark sunglasses and was rubbing his forehead. No doubt he was slightly hung-over and exhausted from the evening before. If Zeke had worried about participating too little in the party, perhaps Owen should have worried about participating too much. Owen had done enough drinking and dancing for all four of the dragons combined, and he was paying for it today. Zeke was tempted to tease him about how rough he was looking today, but in the end he opted to keep his mouth shut. Owen was already on edge, and if Zeke annoyed him he would probably be in an even worse mood. And Zeke wanted everyone to be in good shape for the meeting today.

If Owen thrived on parties, Zeke thrived on work. Zeke had spent most of the early morning running through different topics that he wanted to cover in their meeting today. He only hoped that Mac would turn out to be a more serious commander than he had judged her for last night. He knew that the rest of the crew liked her, and that they were annoyed with him for judging Mac because of her sparkly, hot pink robes. But could they really blame him? How was he supposed to take anyone in hot pink robes seriously?

Zeke had to admit that, when Mac actually came over to talk to him, she came across as much more serious than he had thought she would. She seemed thoughtful and she had an intelligent look in her eyes. Still, he couldn't quite understand why she would want to present herself as a bubbly girly girl instead of a serious commander.

Zeke found his pulse quickening slightly as he remembered the moment Mac had sat down next to him last night. He had been completely unprepared for how beautiful she was. When he had seen Owen talking to her earlier in the evening, he'd thought she was good-looking, but he hadn't realized just *how* good looking. He'd been so preoccupied with her flashy dress robes that he hadn't noticed how smooth and perfect her skin was, or how soulful and lovely her deep blue eyes were. She was undeniably gorgeous, and she affected him in a way that few women did. Average beauty had long ago lost its charm for Zeke. He had traveled the world, and he was a good-looking man, so there had been no shortage of women pursuing him. But he wasn't interested in anything ordinary. If he was going to shake up his life to allow a woman into his heart, she would have to be both exceptionally beautiful and exceptionally intelligent. Something told Zeke that Mac was both of those things, if only he could look past the glittery front she insisted on maintaining.

Zeke frowned as this thought crossed his mind. Was he really sitting here musing about Mac's potential as a romantic partner? Maybe Owen wasn't the only one around here who needed to get a grip. Zeke was here to work, not to fantasize about a woman. Especially not a woman who seemed to be nearly as obnoxiously outgoing as Owen.

The SUV pulled up in front of Military Headquarters. This building was fenced and gated, and the driver of the SUV came to a stop at the gatehouse to show the guard his I.D.

"I'm here to drop off the shifters," the driver said, a note of pride evident in his voice. The guard peered at the driver's I.D., and then stuck his head into the driver's window a bit so he could look in at the shifters.

"We're happy you're all here," said the guard. "Goodness knows we need all the help we can get when it comes to fighting."

Zeke frowned. He'd heard some variation of that sentiment quite often since the rumors of war first started, and he was beginning to worry. Was the army here really as bad as everyone made it out to be? Perhaps Mac wasn't as intelligent as she'd appeared, after all. She seemed smart enough, but, then again, she'd seemed a little too dedicated to all the frivolous wizard traditions and customs—like the feast last night.

Zeke didn't have long to ponder the matter, though. After a short drive up to the entrance of the building, the SUV pulled to a stop to allow the dragon crew to disembark. Zeke looked up at the large stone building as they made their way up the front steps. It was made of stone, and, although it was much less ornate than the High Council headquarters had been, it still looked impressive, with its high walls and oversized wooden doors.

Raven was waiting for the crew at the top of the steps, and she gave them a small wave as they arrived.

"Come on in," she said. "Mac is waiting for you. She'll meet with you first to give you an overview of the military here, and then after lunch I'll give you a tour of the building."

Zeke was growing tired of tours at this point, but he didn't want to complain. The rest of the crew already thought he was enough of a downer for his attitude about the banquet last night. The little bit of the building that he did see as Raven walked them to Mac's office didn't seem like anything special. It was mostly a long hallway interspersed with several office doors. On the walls hung framed portraits of numerous wizard military heroes. Zeke noticed with wry satisfaction that none of them were wearing hot pink.

If he had been expecting Mac to be wearing hot pink and sparkles again, though, he was in for a big surprise. When Raven opened a door marked Conference Room 1C and motioned for them to enter, there was not a drop of pink to be found. Instead, standing at attention at the head of the conference room table, was a very different version of MacKenzie Somers from the one Zeke had seen last night.

This Mac wore her blonde hair in a high, tight bun. She was not wearing a drop of makeup, as far as Zeke could tell, but he thought with awe that her natural, glowing skin looked even more beautiful than her makeup covered face had last night. She seemed taller than he remembered her, which didn't make sense since he was pretty sure she had been wearing heels last night. Perhaps it was because the way she stood, so proud and straight with such a stern expression on her face, made her such a daunting presence.

She was wearing a military dress robe that was midnight black in color. On the left chest of the robes, the Falcon Cross military insignia was embroidered into the robe using silver thread. There was no pink to be seen on her today, and the only sparkle was the glint of metal from the numerous military badges that were pinned to her robe, signifying her high rank and multiple achievements. Zeke could hardly believe that someone so young had been so highly decorated. He figured it could only mean one of two things—either the wizards gave away military awards for every little thing, or Mac was actually a lot more fearsome than he'd originally judged her to be. Given the stern expression on her face right now, he was inclined to believe it was the latter.

"Good morning, gentlemen," Mac said as they entered the room. "I trust you all slept well. Feel free to find a seat anywhere you'd like."

Zeke raised his eyebrows in surprise when he heard Mac speak. Her tone was different than it had been last night. It was more formal, and had an unquestioning note of authority to it. He had to admit that if he hadn't seen her all dolled up in pink and sparkles last night, he would never have thought to question whether she was serious enough for the job of military commander. But those hot pink dress robes and her flirtatious giggling were impossible to forget.

Zeke sat down in a chair near the middle of the long table, and the rest of the crew sat not too far from him. They were all comfortably spaced out, and yet reasonably close to where Mac was standing, waiting for them to settle in. A large stack of papers and a laptop sat on the table in front of her, and she shuffled through the papers for a moment before she began speaking.

"Our first order of business, I think, should be to get a good sense of what our resources are. We should discuss both the size and training of the wizard army, and we should also talk about what particular expertise all of you bring to the table. I know you are all excellent fighters and can all breathe fire, but I'd like to know if there are any special talents unique to any of you that I should know about. Once we all know each other's strengths and weaknesses, we will be able to better plan for whatever the enemy might throw at us."

"Well," Noah said, "We're definitely all good fighters, as you've said. And yes, we all breathe fire. We are also all excellent flyers. We've been well trained in acrobatic flying, and should be able to out-fly anyone the enemy can send our way. But we do all have specific strengths, too. I'm probably the best of the bunch at one-on-one combat. I can take on up to ten opponents at once, and not blink an eye, depending on how strong each of those opponents are, of course."

Zeke saw Mac raise an eyebrow at this, and he felt a little puff of pride in his chest. What Noah was saying was impressive, but he was also being modest. Noah could usually take on fifteen opponents at once. The man was the fastest dragon at one-on-one fighting that Zeke had ever seen. Of course, there had not been many opportunities for fighting at that level during their lifetime, but Noah had worked hard to keep his fighting skills sharp. Like all of the Redwood Dragons, Noah had lost both of his parents in the last great shifter war. One of Noah's ways of dealing with the grief had been to learn how to fight better than anyone else. Noah had sworn that if there was ever another great war, he would be well-prepared to defend those he loved. It looked like that next great war was on the verge of breaking out, but Noah was ready.

"As for Owen," Noah continued, "He's the guy you want when you need to raise your troops' morale. The man knows people, and he can get just about anyone riled up about just about anything. If you feel like your soldiers need encouragement and motivation, just ask him to say a few words to them. They'll be raring to get on the battlefield in no time."

Zeke saw Owen sit up a little straighter and smile as Noah praised him. Noah's words were true, of course. Owen might be obnoxiously outgoing and a little too quick to party sometimes, but the man could get anyone to follow him into battle. He had a knack for saying exactly the right thing to motivate people to action.

"Now Myles is your stealth man," Noah said. "He's got the chameleon trick down cold. You know the chameleon trick?"

Mac shook her head no, so Noah explained.

"It's basically a disappearing trick. Of course, chameleon shifters are best at it, but any reptile shifter can learn to do it. All of us here have learned it, and can become invisible by blending into our surroundings. But Myles is the best of the group at it. He can disappear so quickly and silently that you'll swear he just disappeared into thin air. Not only that, but he's good at moving silently through even the most difficult terrain, and he's a damn good spy. If you need some intelligence work, he's your best bet."

Zeke knew he was next, and so did Mac. He saw her glance over at him, and when her eyes met his, his heart did a sudden, unexpected flip-flop in his chest. He caught himself just before he sucked his breath in a little too loudly, and he did his best to keep a neutral, unaffected expression on his face. But he could not pretend that he had not just felt a shiver of desire run through his entire body.

Get a grip, he told himself. *You know she's not your type. And besides, you guys are going to be working together to lead a military. Romance isn't exactly conducive to a good working relationship.*

Zeke looked away toward Noah, acting like he was supremely curious to know what his leader was going to say. In reality, he already had a good idea of what it would be, and he was right.

"Zeke here is what I like to call our secret weapon," Noah said. "Don't let his quiet, unassuming attitude fool you. He's one of the smartest people you'll ever meet. He can help you come up with brilliant strategies for both offense and defense. He'll plan attacks so brilliant that your enemies will be defeated before they even know what hit them. He'll set up defenses so well-thought-out that it would take an army ten times the size of yours to defeat you. In a nutshell, he's the guy you want as your right-hand man, to advise you on what your next move should be. We are all here to serve in whatever ways you best think we can, of course. But my strong recommendation is that you leave the grunt work to me, Myles, and Owen, and keep Zeke close by for the big strategy decisions."

Zeke felt his chest puffing up a little more at Noah's praise. He had expected Noah to recommend him as a strategist, but he hadn't expected him to praise him quite so highly. He was almost a little embarrassed at how forceful Noah's words had been, but at the same time, Zeke knew damn well that he deserved the praise. He had worked hard to learn how to devise strategies of all sorts, but military was his expertise. Zeke had gone out of his way to read and learn from the notes, memoirs, and biographies of hundreds of great military commanders, both shifter and human. He had self-taught himself how to be a warrior, and, although he hadn't had many chances to use his offensive knowledge yet, he had proven many times over that he was excellent at defensive strategies. He had devised ways to keep the dragons' ancient artifacts safe, and he had planned new ways to keep their hideout in the woods safe. Not only that, but he had proven his ability to think outside the box on his many missions to recover ancient artifacts. He had often recovered artifacts much quicker than anyone thought possible, simply by using unconventional methods to swoop in and get the job done.

Zeke finally forced himself to turn his gaze back to Mac. She was studying him intently, and he could see that she was fighting some sort of internal war with herself. She was wrestling with whether or not to appoint him as her right-hand man, he could tell. She was hesitating for some reason, and he wondered why. Did she feel threatened by him? Was she worried he was going to sweep in and take over all her authority? Or, perhaps, she didn't believe Noah that he was really that intelligent. Sometimes, because he didn't say a lot, people thought that Zeke didn't know a lot. But nothing could be further from the truth. Just because he was the strong, silent type didn't mean he couldn't be smart, too. Zeke frowned slightly, feeling a familiar twinge of annoyance. He hated it when people judged him for not being outgoing and loud, as though being quiet and introspective was some sort of fatal flaw.

But even now, as he waited for Mac to respond, he said nothing. Whatever battle was raging in her own head, she must have finally decided in his favor. After several long moments, she simply nodded as she squinted at him.

"Alright," she said. "Sounds like you and I will be working quite closely together. And trust me, there's a lot to do."

Zeke still did not say anything. Instead, he merely nodded back at Mac, who gave him another long, hard gaze before turning back to the rest of the group.

"First, let me explain to all of you exactly how the Falcon Cross Military works," she said. She picked up one of the stacks of paper in front of her and started passing around stapled copies of what looked like the slides from a PowerPoint presentation. "After I'm done with that, you can all tell me what you know about the threats of attack that our enemy has made. We'll probably be here all morning, so I hope you're comfortable. Raven went to get some coffee, water, and an assortment of breakfast pastries, so at least I know you won't be hungry. Now let's dive in."

With a sigh, Zeke picked up his pen and reached for one of the blank legal pads sitting in a stack in the middle of the table. He wrote "Notes" across the top in bold, black script, and then sat back and waited for Mac to begin her presentation. He wasn't sure he had ever been quite so curious about how, exactly, a commander was running an army. This was going to be interesting.

CHAPTER FIVE

Mac clicked through to the last slide of her presentation, which had the simple words "Any Questions?" on it. She turned to look at the four dragon shifters in the room, hoping that she had covered everything she needed to cover, and that they had understood it reasonably well. Noah, Myles, and Owen were staring down at their notebooks with furrowed eyebrows. Zeke was leaning way back in his chair with his pen in his mouth, staring at the ceiling. She wasn't sure whether he was thinking or bored, but she decided that for the sake of her own pride she would assume that he was thinking.

While Zeke and the other dragons "thought," Mac mentally went over everything she had just told them. She wanted to see whether she had left out anything important. She knew that some of it had been repeat information for the dragon shifters who had previously visited Falcon Cross. But it never hurt to review, and, besides, she'd wanted to make sure that Zeke was on the same page as everyone else.

She'd started out by giving them a brief history of the Falcon Cross military. The wizards in her clan were, by nature, peaceful individuals in general, and so for a long time the clan had not even had a military. But several centuries ago, there had been a harsh civil war among many of the wizard clans, and Falcon Cross had finally been forced to admit that they needed an army. It was a good thing they had formed an army then, too, because not too long after the wizard war, there had been a wizard-shifter war, which had nearly wiped out the wizards. In fact, the shifter world had believed for a long time that wizards were completely extinct. This was purposeful. The wizards, not just in Falcon Cross but in other wizard clans as well, had retreated into well hidden villages to live by themselves, far away from any shifters. They had worried that if the shifters knew that any wizards still lived, there would be more bloodshed and then the wizards really would be extinct.

Mac had explained that Falcon Cross was much smaller in those days. It had taken several centuries after the wizard-shifter war for the Falcon Cross clan to be built up to the numbers it was at now. And even though the clan had grown quite a bit, the military had not kept pace with that growth. It was a small army, since during the long centuries of peace, most wizards had decided that their time would be better spent pursuing other professions. Falcon Cross had never had a mandatory draft. They hadn't needed to, since there had been no wars to fight. The clan had lived alone in its isolated village, happily keeping to itself, and the rest of the world had no idea that it existed. The small military that remained had focused mostly on guarding the perimeters of Falcon Cross to make sure that no non-wizards got in. The army had not been idle. They had made great strides toward improving their ability to hide from potential discovery. But it had been hundreds of years since they had actually fought in battle, and that was worrisome.

They had participated in war games with other wizard clans, and had performed well at those games. But the war facing Falcon Cross right now was no game. How could a small army, used to times of peace, possibly prepare for the threat of a large, well-trained army that was bent on destroying them?

Mac hoped with all her heart that the dragons would have answers to that question. She knew that they would need to recruit more soldiers, and train both those soldiers and the soldiers they already had on how to actually fight. But she wasn't sure that she was the best person to teach those soldiers how to fight. All of the recognition and awards she had received had been for the great strides she had made in peacetime defensive strategies. She felt horribly unprepared for the fight ahead.

"I don't have any questions right now," Noah said, breaking into Mac's thoughts. "I think that our best bet might be to discuss the threat that we're facing, so that we're all on the same page. Then we can work together to come up with solutions. Does everyone else agree?"

Everyone else nodded, and so Noah launched into his discussion of what the dragon shifters knew about the coming war. Mac stood with her pen ready to take down as many notes as possible. She had already spoken with Knox, the leader of the Redwood Dragons Clan, about what the dragons knew of the threatened war. But she wanted to make sure she had the most complete and up-to-date information possible as they began training her army.

"Less than a week ago, we had some unexpected visitors in the Redwood forest," Noah began. "We were already aware that trouble was brewing, but we didn't know at the time how great the extent of that trouble was. While Vance, one of our dragons, was on the way home from conducting a routine security check on some of our vaults, he and his girlfriend were attacked by two shifters. There were no red flags or warning signs that there would be an attack like this, but the shifters were extremely violent and nearly killed Vance's girlfriend. Thankfully, their attack was ultimately unsuccessful, but unfortunately both attackers were killed in the fight, so we couldn't question them. Vance brought the attackers' belongings back to our base camp, though, and when we searched them we found a cell phone that was actually being used to store information on missions that the attackers had been participating in."

Noah paused for a moment and took a sip of his coffee, while Mac wrote furiously, desperately trying to keep up with her handwritten notes.

"It wasn't clear from the information we recovered who, exactly, is in charge of the army the attackers were a part of. What is clear, however, is that the army is large, reasonably well organized, and very capable of doing some serious damage to both good shifters and good wizards alike. The army consists of humans, shifters, and wizards, and whoever is leading the army has made plans to attack not only Falcon Cross, but also the Redwood Dragons hideout and the group of shifters in Texas who are responsible for guarding the dragon emerald and dragon sapphire."

Mac looked up from her notes. "So, I'm assuming that this army is after the dragon stones, since they've chosen to plan attacks on the three places where the dragon stones are most likely to be hidden."

"That's right," Noah said. "The two attackers who came to the Redwoods were serving as scouts, trying to find information on where the stones might be hidden. They thought that the stones were hidden in our vaults there, where we store numerous powerful dragon artifacts. It's a reasonable assumption, but of course it's wrong. The two dragon stones that have been recovered are in Texas under the watchful eye of the powerful shifter protectors."

"Do you think they are planning to attack the Redwoods first, since that's where they sent scouts first?" Mac asked.

"You're *assuming* that they sent scouts there first because the scouts that went to the Redwoods were discovered," Zeke interrupted. "But it's possible that other scouts have been here or to Texas, and they just haven't been found."

His tone had not been challenging at all. Nevertheless, Mac found herself feeling strangely defensive.

"If scouts had come anywhere near Falcon Cross, my wizards would have discovered them," she insisted. "We may not be the best warriors, but we know how to watch out for intruders. Someone would have to be incredibly talented *and* lucky to get past our guards."

Zeke shrugged. "If you say so," he said, then turned to look back at Noah expectantly, waiting for his leader to continue. His refusal to argue with Mac made her feel even angrier. He might be handsome and a good strategist, but who did he think he was, to come in here and question her ability to guard her village like that? She knew how things worked around here much better than he did, and she had half a mind to remind him of that. She might have, too, if Noah hadn't started talking again at that moment.

"It probably doesn't matter that much whom they attack first," Noah said. "Any attack on any of these three locations is likely to be a brutal blow to our forces. Like I said, we don't know who is leading this army, but we know that the army is large and well-organized. Our main objectives are to lose as few lives as possible to their attacks, and to protect the dragon stones at all costs. We cannot, under any circumstances, let our enemies know that the dragon stones are hidden in Texas. The more we can keep them in the dark about where the dragon stones are, the better. I don't even want to think about what would happen if those dragon stones fell into the wrong hands."

Mac felt a shiver of terror run through her as she thought about the evil someone could do with the dragon stones. There were many powerful, ancient artifacts in the world, most of which could do great damage if they were in the wrong hands. But the dragon stones were more powerful than almost all the other artifacts combined. If someone used them for evil, it would unleash a terror on the world like nothing ever seen before.

And, to complicate things further, the two stones that were in Texas were not the only dragon stones. There were two others, a dragon ruby and a dragon amethyst, that were still missing. No one knew where they were, and Mac worried that someone evil would find those stones before the good shifters and wizards could recover them. She knew that the Wizard Advocacy Bureau was working on trying to discover the stones' location, and the shifters were doing the same. But the stones had been lost for centuries, and seemed to have vanished without a trace. No one was having much luck finding anything that seemed even remotely helpful in discovering where the stones were.

"I assume there's still no word on the two missing dragon stones?" Mac said, just to make sure.

Noah sighed, and the frustrated look in his eyes told Mac all she needed to know before he even spoke.

"No word," Noah confirmed. "We can't figure out where to even start looking, really. My only comfort is that it's unlikely that our enemies have any more information than we do. We have some very smart wizards and shifters working almost around the clock on the problem, so hopefully we can figure it out before the other guys do."

Mac nodded. "So I guess, all we really know at this point is that there's a big army poised to attack us. But we don't have any idea when that attack will be?"

Noah shook his head no. "There was no indication of time frames in the information we received, which worries me even more. It could be any day now, and Falcon Cross is woefully unprepared for an attack of that magnitude. No offense, Mac. I know you're a great commander, but you've trained your army for times of peace."

"No offense taken," Mac said. And she really wasn't offended. She had done a damn good job as commander. The brewing war was an exceptional, highly unexpected situation.

"That's why we should have started working last night, instead of having a party," Zeke said.

Mac glared at him, and was about to make a sharp comment about how he clearly didn't understand how to motivate wizards, but Noah beat her to it.

"Enough, Zeke," Noah said, his voice sterner than Mac had ever heard it. "We've already thoroughly discussed why the banquet was necessary, and I don't want to hear about it again, okay?"

Zeke gave Noah a sulky, impatient look, but did not retort again. Mac held her breath for a moment, uncomfortable with the heavy tension in the air. But the other dragons didn't seem affected by it, so Mac decided to move on.

"Maybe I'm missing something here," she said. "But since we have the dragon stones, and they *are* incredibly powerful, why don't we just use them to defeat our enemies? It doesn't make sense to me to keep them hidden when we could bring them out and quickly gain the upper hand."

"It's a fair question," Noah said. "And one that I've asked myself. But the shifter protectors who hold the stone think that it's better to hold off on using them if possible. Anytime we take them out of hiding, there is a small chance that they could be stolen. We would rather keep them under full protection until it's absolutely necessary to use them."

"When is it absolutely necessary, if not now?" Mac asked, feeling somewhat incredulous. "It sounds like we're facing the most serious threat we've ever seen before."

"It sounds like it," Noah said. "But we aren't exactly sure. We want to wait and see what the armies actually look like before making a decision on whether to use the stones."

Mac frowned. "If we wait, and it's as bad as we think or worse, we could lose a lot of lives that the dragon stones might have saved."

"I know," Noah admitted. "I sort of agree with you that it might be better to pull the stones out now. But the shifter protectors are adamant that we keep them under close guard and keep their location secret as long as possible. Our best bet in the meantime is to plan how to build up our fighting forces."

Mac's frown deepened. She was beginning to see that meshing the fighting styles of several different groups was not going to be easy. The wizards, dragon shifters, and shifter protectors all seemed to have slightly different ideas of what the best ways to fight and defend themselves were. There were going to be some clashes of wills, she was sure of that. But they all had to learn to work together. It was the only chance they had of survival. Their forces were small, but if they worked together they had a chance of coming out of this thing victorious. For now, at least, she knew Noah was right. Their energy was better spent building up their army instead of trying to argue with the shifter protectors about the dragon stones.

"Alright," Mac said. "Well, I'm going to take these notes to my office and start working on a plan. Raven will be taking you all on a tour of the building, and then you can all spend the rest of the afternoon and evening coming up with your own ideas and contributions for our battle plan. Let's meet here again tomorrow morning to flesh out the exact details. If we combine the best of everyone's plans into one coherent strategy, I think we'll have a pretty good starting point. And, of course, if you have any questions or want to get a hold of me in the meantime, feel free to call me or just swing by my office. I'm happy to brainstorm or help however I can."

"Sounds good," Noah said, standing to his feet. The other dragons stood to their feet as well, and they all shook hands with Mac and wished her luck before filing out into the hallway where Raven was already waiting. Zeke was the last to leave, and he held Mac's hand just a beat longer than necessary before leaving the room. He met her gaze with his own, and his eyes were intense but his expression was unreadable. Mac felt her heart racing, and she was sure that her cheeks must have been turning pink from the heat she felt there. She tried to think of something to say to defuse the intensity of the moment, but she suddenly felt nervous and words failed her. Before she could gather her thoughts, Zeke had released her hand and was turning to join the group of dragon shifters that was already following Raven down the hallway.

Mac shut the conference room door behind her and leaned against it, trying to catch her breath. She had to get a grip. She was commander of an army, for crying out loud. She couldn't afford to lose her heart to someone right now. There was no time for romance, especially a romance with a man who was supposed to be helping her make a plan to ensure her army could stand up to whatever threat the evil shifters and wizards were sending their way.

Besides, Mac was pretty sure by this point that Owen had been right. Zeke was a tough man to crack. He did look at her with a certain intensity, but she wasn't entirely sure whether that intensity could be attributed to romantic feelings or not. If she looked at his behavior as a whole, she didn't have much reason to think that he had feelings for her. He had made several snide comments about the lack of good fighters in Falcon Cross, and Mac couldn't help but take those comments personally. After all, she was the commander of the army. If there weren't good fighters, she was most to blame. She knew she had good reasons for not training a legion of warriors before now, but still...something about Zeke made her second guess everything she'd ever done during her military career.

And then, with sudden, starting clarity, Mac realized why she was so upset by every remotely negative comment Zeke made. She wanted to impress him, and it hit her hard when he was not impressed by something she had done. It stung when he criticized the state of the army she had led for the last several years, not because she didn't already know that there was room for improvement, but because she wanted Zeke to view her with admiration and respect. She wanted to impress him, but she could already tell that he was a hard man to impress.

With a sigh, Mac stood up and walked across the room to start gathering her papers up. She had to get rid of the silly idea that there might be some sort of romance brewing between her and Zeke. He wasn't here to find love, and neither was she. They were here for a war, and she needed to keep that at the forefront of her mind. Besides, his interest in her was likely nothing more than a work interest. Yes, he had seemed to pay a lot of attention to her in the meeting today, but of course he would. She was the speaker half the time. Mac needed to get her things, go to her office, and focus on work.

She straightened up her back and headed out of the conference room, keeping her head high as she strode purposefully toward her office. She had a lot of strategies to flesh out, and no time to waste on extracurricular pursuits. She was commander of a whole goddamn army. She needed to act like one.

Yet despite all of her stern admonitions to herself, she couldn't keep Zeke's face from constantly flashing across her mind's eye as she sat down in her office and tried to focus on the task in front of her.

CHAPTER SIX

Zeke breathed a sigh of relief when the last of his clan mates finally left for the day. He hated days like this, where he was forced to spend pretty much every second around other people. Even though he loved his crew, and the wizards in Falcon Cross were all extremely nice, he needed some alone time. Now, he could finally get it.

After meeting with Mac, the dragons had gone on a long tour of the military facility. Despite his initial skepticism, Zeke had found himself quite impressed with the place. The wizards may not have trained for war, but they had all the necessary resources. They just needed to focus and work hard over the next several days and weeks, and Zeke knew that big strides could be made toward a more fearsome army.

Zeke frowned. Assuming of course, that they actually *had* weeks or even days. He had a feeling that an attack was coming sooner rather than later. The enemy must have realized by now that the scouts they had sent to the Redwood Dragons' forest had been killed. It had been at least four days now since those scouts had had any kind of contact with their leaders. Zeke had no way of knowing how often they were supposed to check in, but he knew that by now even the most easygoing of commanders would be growing uneasy. And if the enemy was growing uneasy, he might accelerate any plans for attack. If Zeke had been in the enemy's shoes, and had lost scouts in enemy territory, he would have been extremely worried about losing the element of surprise. Zeke had a sneaking suspicion that there would be an attack within the next couple of days.

This worried him. If the army was as large as he feared it would be, then Falcon Cross was in trouble. Zeke and his clan mates were good fighters, but they could not work miracles. At a certain point, they would be too outnumbered to resist. It was imperative that the army in Falcon Cross be built up as much as possible, as soon as possible. And Zeke had very specific ideas on how that should be done—but he had a sinking feeling Mac wasn't going to agree with him.

He had to admit that he liked her a bit better today than he had yesterday. Seeing her dressed in uniform and standing in front of a room of shifters to boldly give a presentation had made him feel a little better about the fact that she led the army that stood between the enemy and the destruction of Falcon Cross. Still, she wasn't experienced with fighting real wars, and neither were her soldiers. Not only that, but he had realized during the meeting this morning that she had a stubborn streak almost as bad as his. Odds were good there were going to be some serious sparks flying between them—and not the good kind of sparks.

Oh, there had been some of the good sparks, too. He couldn't deny that looking at her did funny things to his heart. Really, though, what man could look at a woman like that and not feel *something*? She was drop-dead gorgeous, and she kept looking at him in a way that made him feel like she was sizing him up as a man. But there wasn't time to kindle those sparks right now. He had more pressing matters to take care of then wooing a girl. Besides, odds were good Mac was going to hate him after they had the conversation about her army that he knew they needed to have. She wasn't going to like his advice one bit, but he hoped that for the sake of Falcon Cross, she would take it.

Zeke fingered at the edge of his notebook, furrowing his brow as he thought. He should go talk to her one on one sooner rather than later. The sooner they got the initial conversation over with, the better. They could be angry at each other if they had to be, but they needed to start moving on their plans. The clock was ticking. Besides, perhaps Mac would surprise Zeke and be more willing to listen to him than he anticipated. He wouldn't know until he tried.

Zeke stood and gathered up his things. He would head to Mac's office and see if she was still there. It was not yet five p.m., so she likely would be. The work day was far from over for any of them, really. Zeke's clan mates had only left so that they could at least work from the comfort of their own homes—but they would still be working. Mac would be working, too, and since she was the commander here, she should be staying in the office until at *least* five p.m. If she didn't, Zeke would be pretty unimpressed with her.

Mac was indeed in her office. As he approached her closed office door, he could hear the soft sounds of instrumental jazz drifting from behind the door and into the hallway. On the wall next to the door was a black nameplate that had "MacKenzie Somers" printed on it with gold lettering. Zeke shook his head, thinking for perhaps the twentieth time that it was odd how she went by "Mac." He thought MacKenzie was a beautiful name, and he wished she didn't shorten it. Then again, Mac had a nice ring to it, too. It was a good, strong nickname, and seemed fitting for a military commander.

Zeke raised his right fist and rapped lightly on the door a few times, but there was no answer. He tried again, a bit harder this time, and a few moments later the music stopped.

"Come in," Mac's voice called from behind the doorway.

Zeke pushed the door open and was instantly greeted by a vanilla-cinnamon smell. He quickly saw that the source was a candle that was burning on top of one of Mac's bookshelves. Several white wooden bookshelves lined the walls of the room, but there was plenty of open wall space, too. And the appearance of those walls shocked Zeke a bit as he walked into the room. They were hot pink, the same color that Mac's dress robes had been. The hot pink stood out sharply from the white bookshelves and from the wood of Mac's desk, which was also painted white. Mac's desk chair itself was white leather, as were the two visitor chairs that sat across the desk from Mac. A large glass window took up almost the entire back wall of the office, and Mac's desk was situated so that her back was to the window. Her desk was cluttered, but not hopelessly so. It looked like she'd been working hard all day.

Beside Zeke, to the left of the entrance door, a wooden coat rack stood. It was also painted white, and held a simple black jacket and a hot pink scarf. At least the jacket was normal enough, Zeke thought. He felt his eyes widen as he looked around the small room. He told himself to be polite and not react to the unconventional decorating scheme that Mac had used in the office, but he couldn't help himself. Before he knew it, he was opening his mouth to speak.

"Why don't you lobby to change all the military uniforms to hot pink?" he asked, his voice dripping sarcasm.

Mac, who had looked up from the paper she'd been bent over when he walked in, raised an eyebrow at him. "I've thought about it," she said. "But a lot of men can't handle wearing pink. They get their manhood all threatened by the color, which really makes me think that they aren't as masculine as they claim to be. If your manhood is threatened by a color, then maybe you're not as tough as you seem, after all."

Zeke frowned at her. "It's not about feeling threatened," he said. "Wear pink to the banquets if you want to, but this is a military office. It's unprofessional."

Mac frowned right back at him. "I'm not wearing pink right now. I'm wearing my official military uniform. Is that not impressive enough for you? And who cares if I want to decorate my office with shades of pink? It's my personal space. Most of the time, if I want to have a meeting, I book a conference room. I rarely have visitors here. And you're the first visitor who's been rude enough to comment on the color of my walls. Didn't your mother teach you any manners?"

"My mother died when I was five," Zeke said flatly.

Mac's face immediately fell. "Right. Sorry, I forgot," she said, her voice sounding less antagonistic than it had before. She looked incredibly uncomfortable, and Zeke actually felt a little sorry for her.

"It's alright," he said. "I didn't come up here to discuss my mother. Nor did I come up here to discuss the color of your walls. We need to figure out what we are going to do about training up the Falcon Cross army, and I have some suggestions."

"Alright," Mac said, her voice sounding wary. Even though she had agreed to take Zeke on as her strategist and right-hand man, Zeke could easily see that she was still not sold on the idea. And, he supposed, coming in here and starting off their conversation by criticizing her love of the color pink had probably not been the best way to start things off.

He took a deep breath and gazed over at her, knowing that he needed to choose his words carefully. She looked back at him steadily, and he saw a deep determination in her eyes. She might not fit his conventional idea of a commander, but Zeke had to admit that she had some good qualities. She was smart, she worked hard, and she wasn't afraid to get in your face. Besides, as far as he could tell, she *had* done a good job of leading the Falcon Cross army. She was quite young to achieve the position she had achieved, and she might not have a lot of experience with war, but she had done a good job with what she had.

Her frown deepened as she leaned back in her chair and crossed her arms, giving him a cold, calculated look. "Well?" she prompted. "What are your brilliant suggestions. Let's hear them."

Zeke took one more deep breath. He had a feeling she was going to disagree with him, but he needed to just spit it out.

"We shouldn't try to grow the army," he said. "We don't have time to waste on recruiting right now. The enemy might be attacking us at literally any moment. The best thing we can do is spend every spare second we have on training the soldiers you already have to fight better."

Mac's eyes widened with incredulity. "Are you serious? I thought you were supposed to be the gifted strategist of the group. Were you listening at all today? Did you hear how small the Falcon Cross army is compared to how big we think the enemy's army is? This is a crisis. We need more soldiers, and the sooner we can recruit them, the better."

"Numbers aren't enough," Zeke countered. "We could be attacked at any moment. It's highly likely that an attack is coming within the next few days, in fact. Every second we waste on recruiting is a second that could have been spent on beefing up the training of the soldiers we already have. Even if we could recruit a thousand more soldiers, it wouldn't do us any good. We don't have the time to train them. Our best bet is to train the soldiers we have. Look at my clan, for example. There are only ten of us, but we have managed to hold off armies much, much larger than our clan. We have worked hard to learn how to fight well, and—"

"And you're dragons," Mac pointed out.

"So?" Zeke said, frowning. "What does that have to do with anything?"

"Oh, come on," Mac said. "Everyone knows that dragons are powerful fighters, and can take on much more than the average shifter. Besides, you can breathe fire."

"Wizards can shoot fire from their magic rings," Zeke pointed out.

Mac sighed, sounding tired. "Yes, we can. But we usually do so in order to start a campfire or something along those lines. We just aren't even close to as skilled as dragons are at battle, no matter how many spells we know."

"Which is why you need to invest all your time in training the wizards you do have," Zeke said, feeling his frustration starting to rise.

"Which is why we need to raise as large an army as possible," Mac countered. "We can raise an army faster than we can train one. Even the worst fighter can at least do a little bit to hold off the enemy."

"You're out of your mind!" Zeke said, shocked that she would even say that. "You realize that sending someone unequipped to fight into battle is about the same thing as sending them to their death, right?"

Mac's frown deepened as she looked over at him. "Wizards all know how to fight," she said. "Perhaps they're not very good at it, but they know the basics. And in this instance, I think that the basics will have to be enough. I won't have my clan's village be overrun by the enemy while perfectly good wizards are sitting at home doing nothing because they didn't understand how serious the threat that faces us is."

"Do *you* understand how serious the threat facing us is?" Zeke asked, his voice starting to rise. "You're sitting here worrying about the size of the army that will attack us, and yet you've done nothing to actually further our defenses. Since I arrived in town, I've been to a banquet, had a brief presentation on the history of the Falcon Cross army—"

"—it wasn't that brief," Mac protested.

"And I've had a lovely tour of military headquarters," Zeke said, ignoring Mac's comment. "It seems to me as though no one around here is placing any priority on actually preparing the army."

"Least of all you!" Mac said, rising to her feet and slamming her fist on the table. "You came waltzing into Falcon Cross like you're our savior and know what's best for us, but you don't understand how the wizarding world works at all! You think that feasts are a waste of time, but I already told you that wizards need to feel like they know and trust someone before they will go to battle with them. You can't seem to wrap your head around the fact that the feast actually was an important and necessary step in building up our army. Morale is higher than ever in Falcon Cross after the banquet. And then, today at the meeting, you sneer and sit there with this cool look on your face like you've got war all figured out and no one else in the room does. Well let me tell you something, Zeke. War has a lot of variables. And I may be a peacetime commander but I do know my troops much better than you. If you want to help us, then we need to work together instead of nitpicking over every little thing. And you've got to trust me a little more."

"I do trust you," Zeke said, somewhat surprised by how forceful Mac's tirade had become. "But—"

"No buts!" Mac said. "Either you trust me, or you don't. And for fuck's sake, can you stop criticizing me about the pink already? You sit here and complain about how we're at war and we're wasting time, and yet half of the things you've said to me since we've met have been to complain about how I like pink. Who cares? I don't think that the color of my office is going to matter much when the enemy troops come swooping in. What's going to matter is that we have an organized army and a united front. I may not be perfect, Zeke, but I'll tell you one thing: I love my wizards. I hate evil. And I'm going to do my damned best to make sure that evil stays away from my wizard clan. Now are you with us, or not? Do you trust me, or not? Are you going to shut the fuck up about the color pink, or not?"

Mac slammed her fist on the table one more time as she finished her angry diatribe. For several long moments, the office was completely silent except for the sound of Mac's breathing. Her face was flushed red with anger, and her eyes flashed with such passion that Zeke wouldn't have been surprised if literal flames had started burning in her pupils.

In that moment, she was exceedingly beautiful. It was not the right time or place for him to be thinking about her in that way, but he could not stop himself from noticing how perfect the angles of her face were, or how smooth her skin appeared, or how full her curves were under the fabric of her uniform.

"I asked you a question," she insisted, her voice still filled with rage. Zeke met her eyes with his own, and he suddenly felt ashamed of himself. He was here to help, not to stir up discord between the wizard military and the dragon shifters. She was right, in a sense. He did not understand the ways of wizards. And unless he was willing to try to understand, all of his military knowledge and expertise would do no good here. He wished in that moment that he could have a do-over of the last twenty-four hours. He had been treated like an honored guest, and he had returned the courtesy by criticizing everything he possibly could. He needed to apologize, but how?

And then, in a flash of inspiration, he knew what to do. He stood, and walked a few steps across the office to where the coat rack stood. He took the pink scarf off the rack and wrapped it around his neck, throwing the tail of the scarf over his shoulder with a flourish. Mac looked at him in surprise and confusion

"What the..." she asked, her words trailing off as though she was unsure even of what question she should be asking.

Zeke stood tall and straight, the pink scarf no doubt looking comical on his broad shoulders and muscular neck. He took a deep breath, and then, reminding himself that it took a real man, a strong man, to apologize, he began speaking.

"I'm sorry, Mac. You're right. I've been rude and insolent, and I'm sorry for that. But just as much as you love your wizard clan, I love my dragon clan. I may have an awful way of showing it, but I just want the best for Falcon Cross, because the best for Falcon Cross right now is the best for good shifters and good wizards everywhere. My clan thrives when your clan thrives. You are our allies, and that means something to me. Dragons value loyalty above all else, and I will fight fiercely and loyally to protect you, to protect your wizards, and to protect the side of good. I trust you. And I'm with you. And you're right—who cares what color the walls are. Or our clothes for that matter. If you want me to wear pink every goddamn day I'm here then so be it. All I ask in return is that you trust me, too, and that you at least hear me out when I have something to say. I know I have an outsider's perspective, and that there are things I just won't understand. But sometimes an outsider's perspective is good, too. It helps you see the blind spots you otherwise would have missed. And I think that, together, we can make an unbeatable team that will lead Falcon Cross to victory in whatever war is coming. So what do you say? Truce?"

He held out his hand for her to shake, and, for a moment, she just stared at it. She looked back and forth between his hand and his eyes, and he thought she was going to refuse his peace offering. But then, her eyes changed, and she nodded. Slowly, she raised her hand to meet his. Their palms clasped together, and he shook her hand firmly. Their eyes met, and in that moment, there was a rush of heat and electricity between both their hands and their eyes. Zeke was overcome with an urge to kiss her, but he resisted. He did not want her to think that he'd had ulterior motives when he apologized.

Yet as he started to pull his hand away, she gripped it tighter. Then, almost before Zeke could realize what was happening, she was leaning over the desk that separated them, and her lips were on his lips.

A fire like Zeke had never known rushed through his body. He pulled his hand away from Mac's grip and then reached to climb over the desk, scattering her papers as he did. She only laughed, her eyes dancing as he pushed her up against that ridiculous hot pink wall of hers and kissed her deeply. He slipped his tongue past hers and drank in the taste of her. His skin tingled as she ran her hands across his back and pressed her hips against his. Every fiber in his being was filled with a desperate need for more of her, and from the soft moans that were escaping her lips, it seemed she felt the same.

They kissed like this for several minutes, and despite the warning bells going off in Zeke's mind that this was a bad idea, and that he needed to focus on the war and not on kissing Mac, he could not pull away. She was like a drug that had instantly hooked him, and he only wanted more.

When she finally pulled away to catch her breath, they were both flushed and panting. She looked up at him and grinned, a mischievous expression crossing her face.

"I thought you said we couldn't afford to waste a single second on fun," she said, crossing her arms dramatically.

Zeke laughed. "Well, you told me that wizard-shifter relations need to improve. I was only doing my part."

Mac threw back her head and laughed, and the sound of it filled Zeke with a fresh wave of warmth.

"Come here, you," he said, then reached to pull her closer. But before he could find her lips again, the lights in the office suddenly went out, and the loudest siren Zeke had ever heard was blaring through the late afternoon air.

"Is that…" he started to ask.

"It's a warning siren that our invisibility shield has been breached!" Mac shouted. In the dusky light of her office, Zeke saw her running to grab her broomstick. She glanced back at Zeke, her eyes filled with an expression of dread, and he knew his own eyes must be mirroring back that same dread. The army wasn't ready. The wizards hadn't received additional training yet. There had been no new recruits who could help fight. But it didn't matter. The enemy was here now, and they had no choice but to fight back the best they could.

"The war has begun," Mac said grimly. She pointed her magic ring at her window and shouted, *"Magicae aperio."* The window slid open, and then, with a look of grim determination, Mac mounted her broom and flew out into the sky above Falcon Cross.

Zeke jumped up onto the windowsill and let out a roar, then shifted into a dragon. His human form gave way to his giant dragon body, which he knew would not fit inside the frame of the window. He jumped before he had fully finished shifting, freefalling for several seconds before his wings finished appearing so that he could flap them and make his way high into the sky to join Mac and the gathering wizard army.

The fight for Falcon Cross had begun.

CHAPTER SEVEN

Mac spun in a giant circle on her broom, trying to assess the situation. She scanned the growing group of wizard soldiers, hoping to see one of her scouts who could tell her what was going on. Despite the fact that the Falcon Cross army had performed innumerable drills on what to do if the invisibility shield was breached, all of the wizard soldiers Mac saw looked panicked and most were not properly in formation. She had to get this under control, and fast.

She rose high into the air, so that she was flying above everyone else, gritted her teeth and said, "*Magicae amplificare.*" The amplifying spell would allow her voice to carry throughout the whole village of Falcon Cross, which would hopefully allow her to bring some order to this chaos.

"Wizards! Into formation," Mac yelled. "Remember your training, and prepare to defend our home!"

Her voice seemed to bring a bit of calm to the wizards, and they all began moving to their designated spots, forming ranks and preparing to fight whatever enemy was coming their way. But what enemy was that? Mac looked all around and could not see any unfamiliar faces. Her wizard army was there, of course. There were soldiers in the air on their brooms and also on the ground, finally in formation and ready now to take on whatever was about to be thrown at them. And the dragons were here—Mac could see all four of them up in the air, circling high above even her. Their mighty wings beat at the open sky and an occasional blast of fire streamed from one of their mouths as they swung their heads back and forth, no doubt searching for the enemy as well. But everything was quiet. Even the sirens had faded now. Had it been a false alarm?

And then, finally, Mac saw one of her generals streaking through the air toward her. It was Raven, and Mac hoped that she had some news on why the alarms had gone off when there did not appear to be any enemies nearby.

"*Amplificare terminantur,*" Mac said, ending the amplifying spell on her voice so that she could talk to Raven without the entire village hearing her.

Raven came screeching to a halt right in front of Mac, breathless, sweaty, and flushed.

"What's going on, Raven?" Mac asked, concern filling her voice. Raven looked worried, and Mac immediately lost any hope she'd had that this was a false alarm.

"There are thousands of them," Raven said. "And they've got us surrounded. I don't know how they did it, but they seemed to have figured out where we are. They penetrated the invisibility spell, which set off the alarms. But they only partially penetrated it. They can see us now, so they know for sure that they've found us. But the protective shield tied to the invisibility spells is still holding strong. They haven't managed to penetrate it yet, but any moment now they will."

Mac's heart started beating faster. "They must have wizards with them, then?" she asked.

Raven nodded. "Yes. They have hundreds of wizards, all of whom are doing their best right now to cast counterspells on the protective spells. They also have hundreds of humans and hundreds of shifters. It's a large army, probably twice the size of ours."

Mac considered this information. "The humans should be easy enough to get rid of. Their defenses won't be very useful against our spells or the dragons' fire. But the wizards and the shifters will be more difficult, especially since we're outnumbered."

Raven nodded, her eyes looking worried. "All we can do is the best we can do," she said. "We've trained well, but we've never had to deal with an actual attack. I'm worried about how well the soldiers will perform under pressure. And—"

Raven never got to finish her sentence. In the next instant, a loud, deafening roar sounded off as the protective shield around Falcon Cross was penetrated. Suddenly, hundreds and hundreds of enemy soldiers were pouring into the city. Mac watched in horror as she saw them beginning to brutally attack the wizards on the Falcon Cross front line. Mac took in the situation, trying to assess how powerful the enemy wizards were and what kind of shifters they were up against. As expected, the enemy humans were falling like flies. But the enemy wizards and enemy shifters were putting up an incredible fight.

Mac scanned over the enemy lines. The wizards seemed about equally matched with her own army in skill, which was bad news since they outnumbered her wizards. They were gaining ground by sheer strength of numbers right now. The enemy shifters were moving forward against her wizards, too. There were some impressive beasts—grizzlies, lions, tigers, wolves, and mountain lions. But as Mac flew in a circle high above the battle, she noticed the one thing that would actually give them a chance to win: there were no shifters that could fly. Not only that, but the enemy wizards did not appear to be able to fly, either. Mac didn't see any brooms, and all of them seemed to be keeping firmly to the ground despite the fact that half of the Falcon Cross army was hovering above them in the air, waiting for the enemy to rise into the air so that they could engage them in battle.

"*Magicae amplificare*," Mac said, once more amplifying her voice so that she could speak to her crew. Once the spell was effective, she yelled out, "Aerial attack, Formation B!"

This was a planned scheme of attack that was to be used in the event that an enemy unable to fly attacked Falcon Cross. Mac had never expected that the great army coming at them would not have anyone in it able to fly, but she was not going to complain about this stroke of luck. She watched as her somewhat dazed troops sprang into action. They formed into predetermined groups and then fanned out, flying in rapid, zig-zagging patterns above the attacking enemy. The Falcon Cross soldiers in the air began pointing their magic rings downward, yelling out defensive spell after defensive spell. Enemy wizards and enemy shifters began to fall. The enemy did its best to aim spells up at the attacking Falcon Cross wizards, but the Falcon Cross soldiers were expert flyers, and their rapid zigzag movements made it difficult for the enemy to hit them.

And, of course, there were the dragons. As soon as the dragon shifters realized what was happening, they flew down to join in the aerial attack as well. They flew in large circles over the enemy shifters, breathing out huge streaks of fire and burning to a crisp dozens of shifters with each pass. Wisely, the dragons did their best to stay away from the enemy wizards. Dragons were large beasts, and so a spell had to be extremely strong to affect them. But that didn't mean they were immune to the spells the attackers were throwing out, and they did their best to avoid them and focus on taking out the enemy shifters. At this point, there did not appear to be any more enemy humans. They were all either dead or they had fled in terror. Slowly, but surely, the enemies forces were diminishing, and Mac felt her heart filling with hope.

"*Amplificare terminantur,*" Mac said, once again ending the amplifying spell on her voice. She flew high above the fray, her sharp eye keeping a lookout for weak spots or breaks in the ranks of either side. At one point, she saw that a group of lion shifters had managed to completely break through the barrier of Falcon Cross wizards on the ground. The lions started rushing into the city, where they would have easily been able to kill off any civilians they found.

"Oh, no you don't!" Mac said through gritted teeth. She dove downward, flying at lightning speed toward the ground, and pulling up right in front of the lions. "*Magicae afflictio,*" she yelled out. The spell hit one of the lions square in the middle of the head, and he let out a loud yelp of pain before falling to the ground in a lifeless heap.

"*Magicae afflictio! Magicae afflictio!*" Mac yelled over and over, aiming her magic ring at each lion in turn. One of the lions roared in anger and lunged right toward her. Another of the lions had the opposite response, and turned to flee in terror. It didn't matter. Mac hit them both with the same spell, and they both crumpled to the ground in heaps, never to roar again.

Mac glanced around to make sure that all the lions had been killed, and that the Falcon Cross line of soldiers preventing the shifters from entering the main village had been closed and reinforced. Satisfied that the line was holding and all was well, she turned her broom to fly upward and once more assess the situation from the sky. But before she could gain any upward momentum, she felt the breath go out of her as she was hit forcefully from behind. The blow knocked her off her broom, and she hit the ground with a large thud. A searing pain shot through her shoulder, but she ignored it as she rolled onto her back with her face upward. She looked around desperately to see where the attack had come from, but all she could see was houses, trees, and nearby parked cars. Then, suddenly, a lion sprang into her field of vision. She barely had time to register in her mind that there was a lion running toward her before he was right in front of her. He hurdled up into the air when he was a few feet away, making a giant leap toward her with his teeth bared and ready to clamp down on her neck.

Weakly, Mac raised her ringed hand. She wore her ring on her right hand, and it was her right shoulder that was currently causing her blinding pain. But she grimaced and forced herself to keep moving. She had to get her ring up and a spell out of her mouth before the lion reached her, or she would be dead. Everything seemed to move in slow motion, and for one horrifying moment, Mac realized that she wasn't going to be quick enough. She couldn't believe that this was how she was going to die, knocked off her broom in battle and eaten by a lion shifter.

But then, in the middle of the lion's leap, he was suddenly knocked sideways by a giant stream of fire. A roar of pain rose up from the lion's mouth as he rolled on the ground a few feet away, engulfed in flames. At the same time, a whoosh of wind rushed by Mac's face as a giant dragon form rushed by her face. After the dragon passed her, he slowed and then turned around, landing on the ground and running over to her to make sure she was alright.

Mac found herself looking up into Zeke's eyes, only right now they were part of a dragon head instead of a human one. Zeke looked her over, searching to see if she was severely wounded. Satisfied that she was not, he gave her a wink with his deep green eyes, and Mac could have sworn that his dragon lips turned up in a smile. Then, with a puff of smoke, he hopped up into the air and pumped his wings, once again flying high up into the sky. Mac shook her head in amazement. He almost seemed like he was having fun.

Mac wasn't exactly having fun at the moment, but she wasn't going to complain about that too much. She was happy to be alive right now, and she needed to get back up into the sky to continue directing her troops. She stood to her feet and ran over to where her broom had landed on top of a small bush. Pulling the broom off the bush, she hopped on and then launched herself back up into the sky. She winced slightly at the pain in her right shoulder, but did not let it slow her down anymore. The pain was already diminishing, and, besides, a sore arm was nothing when she could have been dead.

When she got back into the air, she could see that the tide of the battle had turned significantly in favor of the Falcon Cross wizards. There weren't many enemy soldiers left to fight, and the Falcon Cross soldiers were quickly finishing off those that were. A few of the enemy soldiers had turned, and were cowardly running back into the forest. Several of the Falcon Cross wizards on brooms were flying after these deserters, zapping them with spells in an attempt to not let anyone get away. Mac was pleased to see this. If they could manage to keep any escapees from going back to the enemy leader to report, so much the better.

The dragons were still circling, although they were flying much slower now as they looked carefully for any remaining foes. Now and then they would find an enemy solider and finish him or her off with a burst of fire, but as the minutes passed, they weren't finding any more enemies to destroy.

Finally, the noise of battle ceased completely. The wizards on the ground looked around warily, ready to meet any straggling enemy soldiers. The wizards in the air looked this way and that, searching for any more attackers. But there were none. The enemy had been defeated in total, and an eerie silence settled over Falcon Cross as the Falcon Cross soldiers looked around in disbelief, almost unable to believe that they had actually done it. This had been the first real battle they had ever seen, and they had won it.

The battle had not been without cost, though. From her vantage point high above the city, Mac could see that many of the lifeless bodies on the ground belonged to Falcon Cross wizards. Her heart caught in her throat. She was famous for being the youngest Commander-in-Chief Falcon Cross had ever seen, and it was true that she was talented and had accomplished a great deal in her short tenure. But today had reminded her that she was still relatively young, and still had not faced many of the harsh realities of life.

Mac hated to think of who might be among the dead soldiers. Each one of them was special and unique, and none of them deserved to die. With a sad, resigned sigh, Mac started spiraling downward on her broomstick. She landed in the grassy area in the middle of Town Square, and did her best to choke back the traitorous tears that were threatening to spill over. It would not do for her army to see her cry. Now, more than ever, she needed to be strong for them.

Mac looked around for Raven, and saw that her most trusted general was already flying downward toward her. At the very least, Mac thought, she knew that Raven had made it through the battle. A glance upward into the sky told her that all of the dragons were fine, too—although that wasn't much of a surprise. It wasn't easy to bring down a dragon, especially when you yourself couldn't fly. Mac's heart tightened with gratitude as she saw Zeke's dragon flying in a large arc above her. It was good to know that he was safe. She needed him now more than ever. She had a feeling that not only was he going to offer invaluable strategic advice for her army, but he was also going to offer emotional support. Right before this battle had begun, Mac had seen how caring Zeke could be when he wanted to be, and she needed more of that right now. It was not going to be easy to face all of the deaths that had just occurred in Falcon Cross.

Raven came to a soft landing in front of Mac, and hopped off her broom.

"Are you alright?" Raven asked, concern filling her voice. "I saw you take a pretty big hit from a lion down there. It's a good thing Zeke was nearby and saw it, too. That lion was angry."

Until that moment, Mac had forgotten all about the pain in her shoulder. She had been too filled with emotion to even notice it. But Raven's question brought the searing pain back into sharp focus. Mac winced, and realized that she was probably going to need some pretty strong pain meds over the next few days. For now, she just did her best to smile bravely over at Raven.

"I'm fine," Mac said. "Just gonna be a bit bruised and sore, I think."

Just then, a black SUV with the official Falcon Cross crest on it drove up to the edge of town square. Mac watched as Peter, the head of the wizard High Council, stepped out of the vehicle and started walking quickly toward her. He was wearing black robes and a matching black hat, the simple yet elegant uniform that most of the High Council members wore to work on a daily basis. Dress robes were too delicate to be worn every day, so this was how Peter usually looked when Mac saw him.

Peter's face was paler now than Mac had ever seen it, and yet there was still an air of confidence and calmness in the way the High Councilor moved. He swept up next to Mac and Raven and looked at them with a grave expression on his face.

"Is the situation contained?" he asked.

Mac raised a surprised eyebrow. She was surprised that Peter would have come out into the open if he wasn't one hundred percent sure that the danger was over. He was too precious for Falcon Cross to lose him. Then again, he never had been the type to shy away from danger. In fact, a few years ago when the wizards had gone to attack the Redwood Dragons and bring home Bree Riley, the wizard advocate who had discovered the location and importance of the dragon sapphire, Peter had insisted on leading the attack. Many had argued with him, and told him that he would better serve Falcon Cross by protecting himself. And yet, he had gone to the Redwoods. And, of course, he had managed to come back in one piece. Perhaps Mac shouldn't really be all that surprised that Peter was out here when the battle had just settled down.

"Yes, the situation is contained," Mac said. "The attacking army has been completely defeated. But I haven't heard a report yet on what the damages were. I think Raven was just about to share?"

Mac looked expectantly over at Raven, who nodded solemnly. "Well, happily I can report that we appear to have totally demolished the attacker's army. As far as we can tell, not a single person escaped. This is good news for us, since it will prevent any word of mouth information about the battle from reaching their leader. Unfortunately, it appears that many of the humans in the attacker's army were wearing cameras, which were transmitting images of the battle back to someone, presumably their leader. So whoever is leading them saw what happened and, unless he's an idiot, will realize that the army's biggest weakness was its inability to fly."

"So they are going to send back a new army, full of shifters and wizards who can fly," Peter said.

"Potentially, yes," Raven said with a sigh.

"We'll have to prepare for another attack," Mac said. "I'm sure there are many more coming. But for the moment, at least, things are calm. What about the death toll for Falcon Cross?"

Mac felt a lump in her throat as she asked the question. She almost didn't want to know, but she knew that she would have to face the cold, hard numbers eventually. When Raven spoke, though, Mac realized that the moment to face those numbers had not yet come, of course.

"We don't know the Falcon Cross death toll," Raven said. "The battlefield is a mess, and the bodies of the attackers and of our Falcon Cross soldiers are all hopelessly mixed together. We have wizards working on the situation, but it's going to take a while to clean up."

Mac watched as Peter stroked his face thoughtfully. He seemed to be contemplating something, although Mac couldn't imagine what. She was too shell-shocked right now to take a guess at the inner thoughts of a High Councilor. But then, Peter spoke.

"They got in by breaking through the invisibility shield, correct?" he asked.

Raven nodded. "We're not sure how they discovered where we are, but they had a lot of wizards with them. Once the location was discovered, the wizards got to work on breaking the protective shield that surrounded Falcon Cross. Unfortunately, they were able to do so much quicker than we thought they could have, and they attacked in full force once they were in."

"And why didn't anyone see them in the forest when they were approaching the city?" Peter asked, a sharp note of disapproval in his voice. Mac and Raven both cowered a bit at his tone. He was not pleased that security had been breached, and if anyone was to blame it was Mac and Raven. Mac was commander of the whole military operation after all, and Raven led the groups of guards that often patrolled the city. Mac hadn't even had a chance to talk to Raven yet, so she wasn't sure herself what had happened.

"The enemy wizards cast powerful invisibility spells," Raven said. "They were able to hide their entire army that way, and we didn't see them until it was too late."

"I thought we train our army, especially our scouts, on how to recognize when someone was hidden behind an invisibility spell," Peter said, the disapproval still evident in his tone.

"Well, we do," Raven said. "And we have some very highly-trained wizards who have been able to recognize every invisibility spell thrown at them in all of our war games with other clans. But these wizards had some kind of spells I've never seen before. I honestly don't know how they did it."

Raven looked like she was at a loss for words, but Peter was stroking his chin thoughtfully. "Dark magic," he finally said, a frown evident on his face even behind his thick white beard.

"Dark magic?" Raven repeated.

Just then, another black SUV drove up. This time, when it stopped, all of the dragon shifters piled out. They were back in human form now, and all wearing jeans and t-shirts. Several of them had scratches or gashes in various spots on their face and arms, but overall none of the seemed to have been wounded too badly in the battle.

Mac's eyes met with Zeke's, and the care and concern filling his gaze as he looked over at her was enough to make her heart do a flip-flop. She felt a rush of heat and desire go through her being as he walked toward her, looking down at her and asking in a husky voice.

"Are you alright?"

Mac nodded. "I've got a pretty sore shoulder, but other than that I'm fine, mostly thanks to you. Thanks for saving my life."

Zeke's lips turned up into a smile. "It was nothing," he said, his voice raw with emotion. "I never would have forgiven myself if anything happened to you."

Mac smiled weakly back at him, unsure of what to say and feeling a bit weak in the knees from all the emotions flooding through her. It wasn't Zeke's responsibility to protect her any more than it was anyone else's, but Mac felt incredibly turned on by how much he cared for her.

211

If anyone else had noticed the moment passing between them, they didn't say anything. Raven was busy catching the dragons up on everything she had just told Peter and Mac, and Mac noticed that Peter's frown was deepening as Raven went through the story again.

"It sounds to me like the enemy is using some very ancient dark magic," Peter repeated when Raven had finished.

"Dark magic?" Noah asked, looking from Peter to Raven to Mac and back again. "That doesn't sound good."

"No, it's not," Peter said. "If our opponent, whoever he or she might be, is using dark magic, then things are only going to get worse from here. Dark magic consists of ancient spells known for their incredible power—and for twisting the souls of whoever uses them."

"Twisting souls?" Zeke asked, sounding both confused and skeptical. Mac was already shuddering, though. She had studied dark magic briefly during school, and she already knew much of what Peter was about to explain.

"Dark magic is very powerful," Peter said. "The spells can accomplish many things that ordinary spells cannot. But that power comes at a price. Every time a wizard casts a dark magic spell, that spell eats away at the person's soul. You see, spells that powerful require more fuel than just a magic ring and a talented wizard's ordinary magical abilities. They draw on the very fabric of a wizard's being."

"I don't understand," Owen said. "Are you saying that a wizard practicing dark magic is literally losing his or her soul?"

"That's exactly it," Peter said. "And let me tell you, a soulless wizard is a frightening thing to behold. They care about no one and nothing except for themselves. They will destroy anyone and everything in their path. They don't follow the human or wizard rules of decency. We have many forbidden spells in the wizarding world. Just like humans have laws prohibiting things like murder, wizards have laws prohibiting different spells that would cause harm. A soulless wizard will not only disregard the laws, he will also twist the prohibited spells to make them as awful as he possibly can. Eventually, dark magic will kill the wizard that uses it, but not until that wizard has left great damage in his wake."

"Why would anyone use magic that they know is going to kill them?" Myles asked.

Peter gave a sad shrug. "For some, even death cannot dim the allure of power. Those people are often the most dangerous and destructive, and I fear that we are dealing with that kind of enemy now."

"What can we do about it, though?" Raven asked. Mac could tell she was trying to look brave, but her voice quavered when she spoke.

"For the moment, what we can do is to clean up the town and bury our dead," Mac said. She forced herself to speak in a strong, authoritative voice. This had been a long hard, day, and she wanted nothing more right now than to go home and curl up in her bed and cry. But there would be time for that later. Right now, it was important that her soldiers saw a confident, brave commander who was in control of the situation. She looked over at Peter, and he seemed to be looking at her with approval, so she continued.

"While the town is being cleaned up, I will be working with Zeke to develop a clear strategy for how we will prepare our army. We were lucky this time. Our enemy for some reason did not think it was necessary to send any soldiers capable of flying. I can almost guarantee that next time we will not be so lucky. Raven, I think the very first thing you should do is to recast the invisibility and protective shield spell. We've seen that it doesn't stop our enemies, but at least it slows them down and gives us a warning that they are coming."

"Actually, I'd like to cast the protective spells this time," Peter said, speaking up.

Mac looked over at him in surprise. Raven was exceptionally good at protective spells, and Peter knew that. Even Peter himself was unlikely to improve upon the invisibility spell that Raven had cast. Raven looked a little bit hurt, but Peter put his finger in Raven's face and shook it a few times.

"I know you're a damn good spellcaster, Raven Morey," Peter said. "So don't think I'm trying to say otherwise. But I know advanced protective spells that are much more powerful than your ordinary invisibility and protective shield spells."

Mac was taken aback. "Then why didn't we use them already?" she asked. It didn't surprise her that Peter knew spells she had never heard of. He was always pulling some random spell out of his pocket that no one in Falcon Cross had ever heard of before. But she couldn't think of any reason that he would not have already used a more powerful protective spell to defend his village, if he knew one.

"The spells I know are so powerful, in part, because they focus on one thing," Peter said. "In other words, they are shield spells, not invisibility spells. They protect amazingly well, but they are not able to hide our location."

"But, isn't that dangerous?" Raven asked. "Just having Falcon Cross out there in the open like that?"

Peter smiled at her. "Well, we can hide if we want to, but our enemy has already discovered our location. Even if they don't have the exact coordinates, they know the general area. So rather than continue trying to hide from them, we should build up our defenses even more."

Mac nodded slowly. "Makes sense," she said.

Peter smiled. "Glad you agree with me, Commander," he said. "I'm off to cast the spells now, and then I'll be holding an emergency meeting with the High Council. We'd like an update on military plans by tomorrow afternoon, if possible."

"Of course, your Honor," Mac said.

And just like that, Peter nodded and turned to go back to his SUV.

"Is there anything else you need from me?" Raven asked. "If not, I think I should go help with the cleanup efforts."

"No, I don't need anything else right now," Mac said. "Go ahead and get started on cleanup. It won't be a fun job, but the sooner we get it over with the better."

"We'll go with you," Noah said. "If we shift into dragon form we can make quick work of moving the bodies, especially the ones from the enemy that you're going to just want to bury in a communal grave."

"We'd really appreciate your help," Mac said. "Although, Zeke, you should stay behind with me. We have some planning to do."

Zeke nodded solemnly. In the next instant, Raven climbed onto her broom and zoomed away. Noah, Myles, and Owen shifted into dragon form and joined Raven in the air, flying off toward the outskirts of town where Mac knew several wizards would already be hard at work on the cleanup efforts. Once Raven and the dragons were out of sight, Mac turned wearily to look at Zeke. His eyes were searching hers again, filled with concern that warmed her to her core. She wished she could collapse into his strong arms, but this was not the time or place for that.

"Come on," she said, motioning toward the black SUV that had brought the dragons over and was still waiting patiently near the curb. "Let's head back to my office. We have a lot of work to do."

He nodded and turned to follow her toward the SUV. A sad sigh escaped Mac's lips as Zeke held the door of the SUV open for her. If only they were heading back to her office to resume their makeout session. But no. Instead, they were heading back there to await a death count and to try to figure out how to prevent even more carnage.

CHAPTER EIGHT

The blows to the Falcon Cross army were not as bad as they might have been. Mac had lost about fifty wizards. While this was a big blow to the morale of the Falcon Cross clan, it was a bit of a relief to Mac. She had braced herself for numbers in the hundreds, and considered anything below fifty to be a resounding success. One big memorial service was held three days later, commemorating all of the soldiers who had so bravely died in the war, and the families of those who had passed also held individual funerals for their loved ones.

The mood in Falcon Cross had changed. Before the attack, the wizards had all been going on about their business as usual. Most had still been jolly, and had not taken the threat of war all that seriously. It was hard to imagine war, when you had never seen one, and even your grandparents or great-grandparents had never seen one. There had been peace in Falcon Cross for so long that everyone had forgotten what it was like to be faced with the heartache and terrors of war.

Now that many of their own number had died, though, the wizards were somber. They went through their days nervously, always glancing over their shoulders as though an attacker might suddenly appear and try to kill them, too. They spoke in whispers, and Mac had a feeling that much of that whispering was directed at her. She knew that many were not happy with the way the way the battle had turned out, although it had actually turned out much better than it could have. Falcon Cross had been extremely lucky that none of the attackers could fly. Next time, they might not be so lucky.

Mac frowned now, as she sat in her office sipping slowly at a steaming hot mug of coffee. It was nearly eight o'clock in the evening, and the sun was setting slowly somewhere behind the trees. The light coming in through Mac's office window was fading, but she didn't bother yet to get up and turn on her office lights. She sat, sipping her coffee and thinking.

Were the people of Falcon Cross right? Was she to blame for the fact that wizards had died? She had done her best to lead them, but perhaps, as Zeke had accused her of in the beginning, she had not worked as hard or as quickly as she should have. She was young, and although the people of Falcon Cross had once celebrated how precocious she was, this week they had whispered that she was too youthful and inexperienced to be leading an army.

Mac frowned. The truth of the matter was that *everyone* in Falcon Cross was too inexperienced to be leading an army. No one here had seen war. The closest they had come had been the battle for the dragon sapphire in the Redwoods a few years ago, but even that had been a relatively small skirmish, and none of the Falcon Cross wizards had actually died. No, Falcon Cross was completely oblivious to what a real war felt like. The wizards may have studied wars, and played war games, and practiced defensive drills—but none of it was real. Things had just gotten very real, and the whole town was reeling. It had been a week since the attack, and Mac still felt like she was in a fog. Perhaps she shouldn't have been as shocked at how awful it felt to actually fight a battle and see your soldiers killed, but there was no way to put the emotions into words. It was something that, unless you had experienced, you could never truly understand.

The dragons understood, Mac thought. True, they had all been young when the last great shifter war had occurred. But they had still experienced the pain of it. They had all become orphans in the war, and Mac figured there wasn't much that could be more painful than suddenly losing both of your parents at once.

Thinking of the dragons made Mac think of Zeke, as she so often did these days. They had not kissed again since the night of the attack, even though Mac had seen Zeke constantly over the last week. The two of them had reached a compromise on how to best build the Falcon Cross Army. Zeke had agreed that some recruiting efforts were needed. The army that attacked had been huge, and it was clear that it had only been a portion of the enemy's forces. The information they had managed to glean from searching the belongings of the dead enemy soldiers revealed that the army that attacked had been a preliminary force, sent to weaken Falcon Cross. Mac guessed that an army at least three times as large as what they had faced still remained to be defeated.

Owen had been placed in charge of recruitment, assisted by Raven and Myles. They were doing a great job so far, and the Falcon Cross army was growing daily. Noah, along with one of the top Falcon Cross soldiers, Benji, was working on training the new recruits as quickly as possible. Mac and Zeke were spending nearly every spare second strategizing or overseeing the advanced training that was being done for many of the wizards who had been soldiers for years and already had basic training down cold.

Zeke was exceptionally talented at everything related to war. He knew how to make battle plans, how to see the weak spots in a training regimen, and how to whip the Falcon Cross soldiers into the best shape of their lives. He was leading daily extended workouts with some of the troops, and, although Mac did not participate since she was too busy with other official business to add more on to her daily workouts, she did like to "coincidentally" walk by the field where the workouts took place when Zeke was leading them. He usually wore a pair of black gym shorts and no shirt, since the summer sun often beat down mercilessly from above. Mac couldn't keep herself from stopping to admire the way he looked, with his perfect six-pack glistening with sweat, and his huge biceps flexing as he put the soldiers through their paces. He was truly the most gorgeous man she had ever seen.

And she had kissed him, Mac thought, putting her fingers to her lips for a moment to touch the spot where Mac's lips had once met hers. She had relived that kiss dozens of times over the last week, always wishing that the attack had come at any time other than that exact moment. What would have happened if they had not been interrupted? Mac felt somewhat ashamed that she could even think that way. After all, wizards had died. How could she sit here and bemoan the fact that a kiss had been interrupted? And yet, she could not get that kiss out her head.

It was the wrong time for romance. She had known from the first time she saw Zeke that he was special, and that she was hopelessly attracted to him. Even when he had acted like an asshole in their meetings, she hadn't been able to shake the feeling that he was somehow connected to her. And when he had kissed her, she had felt an electricity between them like nothing she had ever experienced before. But electricity and happiness and romance would have to wait now, wouldn't it? The whole wizard and shifter world was on the brink of war, as far as she could tell.

A knock on her door brought her attention sharply back to the present. She hadn't been able to manage much solitary work time over the last several days. Even when she closed her office door and turned her office lights off, working only by the sunlight that came in through her window, people knew she was here. There was always a question about something, and Mac knew that she needed to be as available as possible for her army during this difficult time. Still, she had thought that by now, when it was well past eight o'clock and most people had gone home, that she would have finally had a chance to think and work in peace. Apparently, that was not the case.

"Come in," she said wearily. Sitting up straight and pushing back a stray strand of hair that had fallen across her cheek. She needed to at least look put together and professional, even if she didn't feel that way at the moment.

But when the door opened and she saw who it was, she instantly relaxed.

"Zeke!" she said, a smile breaking out across her face. "I thought you said you were leaving for the night."

"I said I was leaving," he said. "I didn't say it was for the night. I had an errand to run, and I've run it. Now I'm back to do some more work. If you're going to burn the midnight oil, then so am I."

Mac sighed. "I feel like no matter how much I do, there's always more to get done. It's like we're in this race against time, except we don't actually know how much time we have. The next attack could be in ten minutes or ten days or ten weeks! Who knows?"

Zeke stepped into the room and closed the door behind him. He flipped on the lights, and Mac could see that he was holding a large brown paper bag. He sat down across from her, making himself at home in one of her office chairs and stroking his chin thoughtfully for a few moments.

Finally, he glanced at her coffee mug and raised an eyebrow. "When's the last time you ate?" he asked.

Mac scrunched up her brow thoughtfully. "Um, eleven, I think?"

"And was that a full meal or a snack?" Zeke asked.

Mac sighed. "It was a granola bar. But a really big one."

"Mac, you have to eat something. I know you're busy, but you can't survive on coffee and granola bars. You're not saving time by skipping meals, because you won't be able to think as clearly or work as efficiently."

"I know," Mac said, but she knew she didn't sound convincing.

"And you shouldn't be drinking coffee this late, either," Zeke said, glancing at her mug. "You're going to be up all night if you keep that up, and you do need to sleep at least a little bit."

Mac frowned. "Who made you the food and sleep police?" she asked, trying to keep her voice light. She knew he was right, but she was having a hard time focusing on eating and sleeping when so many other things were troubling her mind. Sleep was the most difficult task of all right now. Every time she closed her eyes, all she could see was the screen at the memorial service that had displayed the names of the wizards who had died in the attack. But she didn't want to tell Zeke that. She didn't want to appear weak in front of him. Even though they were on good terms now, she was still reluctant to let him see any weakness. She was a commander, after all. She wasn't supposed to lose so much sleep over the normal results of war.

But Zeke seemed to be able to read her thoughts, because he crossed his arms and frowned at her.

"I know you're upset about the wizards who died," he said.

Mac looked up at him in surprise. "How do you know that?" she asked, her voice a challenge.

"I can see it in your eyes, Mac," he replied. "Look, it's okay to be sad. No one expects you to be unaffected by the deaths of your soldiers and clan members. But you have to take care of yourself. You have hundreds of soldiers who are still alive who are depending on you to lead them. Don't hide behind work as excuse to wallow in your grief. I'd be willing to bet that you haven't gotten much actual work done in the last several hours, anyway."

Damn it, Mac thought. Why did he have to be right? She had been working hard, true. But the last several hours had been slow going. She was distracted and couldn't focus, and a good deal of that distraction was probably due to the fact that she was tired and hungry.

She didn't have to answer for Zeke to know that he had hit the nail on the head.

"So, will you eat with me, at least? Even if you insist on finishing that coffee you should have some food."

"Alright," Mac said with a sigh. "Just let me pack up my stuff I guess. We'll probably have to go get takeout somewhere, unless you have food at your house. I haven't done groceries in days, so unless you want to eat cereal my place probably isn't the best bet."

"Do you like tacos?" Zeke asked.

"Of course," Mac said, and laughed genuinely for perhaps the first time that day. "Who doesn't love tacos?"

"That's what I figured," Zeke said, and reached down into the paper bag he had brought in with him. "Which is why I brought us some."

"What? There are tacos in that bag?" Mac said. "How did I not smell them when you walked in?"

"Probably because they're sealed up tightly in this insulated carrier," Zeke said. He pulled an insulated bag out of the paper bag and set it on Mac's desk. As Mac pushed away some of the many piles of papers that covered her desk, Zeke unzipped the insulated bag. Instantly, the smell of tacos, rice, and beans filled the room. Zeke carefully pulled out the food and started arranging it on the desk. There were several tacos with both soft and hard shells. Zeke had chosen several different kinds of meat, too. Mac saw fish, chicken, beef, and shrimp. Her mouth watered as the delicious aromas hit her nose.

"Alright, I asked for them to put the toppings in separate containers, because I wasn't sure what you would like," Zeke said as he began to arrange the containers on the desk. "We've got lettuce, tomatoes, cheese, sour cream, guacamole, onions, cilantro, rice and beans. Oh, and chips and salsa, of course. They're from Maria's Magical Taqueria. I was told that it's the best place in town."

Mac's eyes widened. "Zeke, this is amazing. And yes, Maria's is *the* place for tacos here in Falcon Cross. I love her food!"

He beamed at her. "I thought you might like it," he said. "Now dig in."

Mac didn't need to be told twice. She quickly dressed a beef taco, loading it down with all her favorite toppings, and then took a giant bite. As soon as the food hit her tongue she realized just how hungry she had been. She ate greedily, stuffing her face in a very unladylike manner. She was too tired and hungry to worry about whether Zeke thought she was being a pig right now. She had a feeling that he didn't care at all, anyway. He was busy stuffing his own face. They didn't talk much as they ate. Both of them were too busy eating their fill. Zeke had purchased a ridiculously large number of tacos, and yet they nearly polished off the whole spread.

"Feel better?" Zeke asked.

Mac nodded. "Much better. Thank you. Seriously. I should have just taken a break and eaten something hours ago."

"So what about trusting me one more time and going home to get some sleep. No offense, but you look exhausted."

Mac started to protest, but when she opened her mouth she yawned. Zeke gave her a pointed look as if to say, "I told you so."

"Fine," Mac said. "I'll go home and take a short nap, but I really do need to get some more planning done tonight."

Zeke frowned. "I can't imagine that anything you have to do can't wait until tomorrow morning, but I guess a nap is better than nothing. Did you drive in today?"

"No, although I wish I had," Mac said. "I'm so tired now that the idea of climbing on a broom and riding across town sounds exhausting. I guess the sooner I get it over with the better, though."

She stood to start gathering up the trash from their meal, but Zeke stopped her.

"Just get together whatever stuff you want to take home with you tonight," he said. "I'll clean up this trash. Then I'll give you a ride home. I borrowed one of those black SUVs this morning."

"Zeke, no, you don't need to do that," Mac said. "The houses they have you guys staying in are the complete opposite direction from my house. I'll be fine on the broom, I'm just whining."

"This isn't up for debate," Zeke said. "I'm taking you home. You're way too exhausted to be riding around on that silly broom."

Mac looked up at him, ready to protest again, but the look in his eyes stopped her. His expression was filled with deep concern, and she could see flames of desire burning in his gaze as well. Mac's own body filled with heat as she held his eyes for a moment.

He still wants me, she thought. I wonder if he's been thinking about me as much as I think about him.

There were so many things she wanted to say to him, and so many things she wished she could ask him about what was happening between them. But this was not the right time. He was right. She needed to rest. Maybe tomorrow she could be more focused and work quicker. Maybe then she would have a little bit of time left over to spend with Zeke, talking about something other than military strategies.

CHAPTER NINE

Mac woke with a start as the vehicle came to a halt. She blinked a few times, confused about where she was.

"We're here," said a familiar voice.

Mac looked over to Zeke sitting in the driver's seat, looking at her with an amused expression on his face. When she looked out the passenger side window, she saw that they were parked in front of her house. That's when it all came back to her. Zeke had shown up unexpectedly at her office, brought her dinner, and then insisted on driving her home so she could at least take a nap. But had she really fallen asleep on the fifteen minute drive to her house?

"I guess I was a bit more exhausted than I thought," Mac said, starting to gather up her things from the floor of the car. "Sorry for zonking out on you. I guess I didn't provide much in the way of conversation on the drive over here, huh?"

Zeke chuckled. "It's quite alright," he said. "I'm just glad that you got some rest. Now I know that you at least slept fifteen minutes today."

His gorgeous green eyes sparkled as he laughed, reflecting the streetlights up ahead. Mac was overcome yet again by how handsome he was, and she wished more than anything that he would kiss her.

Not the right time, she told herself again. She felt a bit sullen, though. She had spent so much of her life feeling alone, and now that there was finally someone who sparked desire in her, she had to wait. She could see from Zeke's eyes that he still felt something for her. The passion in his gaze was unmistakable. But he was holding back, and she should too. They had a war to fight. He knew better than to keep kindling the flame between them during a time like this. She should know better, too. She was Commander, after all!

"Just let me get my broomstick from the trunk," Mac said abruptly, forcing herself to move. If she sat here staring at him any longer, she wasn't going to be able to resist the urge to kiss him. She reached for the handle of her door and started to climb out, but then Zeke killed the engine and reached for his door handle as well.

"I'll help you," he said.

Mac almost said something about how she didn't need help. She was perfectly capable of opening the trunk and grabbing her things on her own. But then she realized that if Zeke helped her it meant she got to see him for a few extra moments, and she kept her mouth shut.

When they reached the back of the vehicle, she let him raise the gate of the trunk and retrieve the broomstick. He handed it to her before shutting the gate again, and she took it with a small sigh. Time to say goodbye.

But neither of them said goodbye. Instead, they stood there, looking into each other's eyes and trying to make sense of the mixture of duty and passion that was warring within them.

"MacKenzie," Zeke finally said, his voice soft as he spoke her full name. God, she loved it when he spoke her name like that. He raised his right hand and stroked the side of her face with the back of his palm. Electric heat shot from his hand to her face, then spread rapidly through her body. Her legs trembled a bit, and she felt a sweet, tingling desire rising up in her core.

"Zeke, we…we shouldn't," Mac said weakly.

"No?" he asked in a husky tone. He never stopped stroking her face.

"There's… there's a war going on. And we have work to do and…" Mac's voice trailed off. All of her reasons suddenly seemed unimportant. There was a war going on, yes. And of course she had work to do. But she was desperately lonely. She had been for so long. She'd been searching for someone who could make her come alive, and now, in the oddest of ways, she had found that person. Was she really supposed to pretend that she wasn't consumed with an overwhelming desire for him, just because a war was raging beyond the borders of Falcon Cross? Mac met Zeke's eyes, silently pleading with him to tell her that this was all somehow okay. That they could be together despite the duties they both held to take care of the troops.

"I've learned a lot about war in my relatively short time on this planet," Zeke said. "And one thing I've learned is that love doesn't stop for war. In an odd sort of way, love can keep you grounded when everything else is falling apart around you. There is promise in a spark of passion. Promise that maybe someday, life will once again be filled with simple joys."

Mac looked up at Zeke, unsure of how to respond. She desperately wanted what he was saying to be true. She wanted permission to love him, even though they were in the midst of the biggest crisis that Falcon Cross had ever faced. But she could never forgive herself if she didn't give defending this city everything she had. She couldn't bear the thought of more wizards dying, even though she knew it was a likely outcome no matter what.

But when she looked at Zeke now, she could see that the fire in his eyes was only burning brighter. He wanted her, as much as she wanted him. Was it really so wrong to give in, and enjoy a few moments of peace? Weren't they allowed a few moments where life felt normal?

Zeke seemed to think so. Without saying another word, he gently, slowly, bent over and kissed her lips. He gave her plenty of time to pull away if she was not comfortable, but she knew the moment that he started moving toward her that she was all in.

When his lips finally touched hers, an explosion of heat and passion ripped through her body. He filled her with an incredible warmth, and any fears or doubts that had plagued her mind instantly fell away. All of her worries disappeared, and the whole world seemed to just melt away. There was only him.

His kiss was slow, deep, and desperate. He drank her in as though he was a man who had been in a desert for weeks, and her kiss was water. Both of his hands moved to her face, cradling it in his palms. They stood there in the moonlight for several long, delicious minutes, both giving in to the desire that had gone unsatisfied over the last week.

When he finally pulled away, Mac found that she was breathless. Her face was flushed and hot, but she had never felt so wonderful in her life. There was a stirring deep within her. Her very core was filled with a tingling sensation. Her body was responding in a way it never had before to any man. She felt connected to him on a deeper level than just physical. It was almost as though her soul wanted him.

She looked up at him, searching his eyes with her own. Did he feel it, too? Did his soul come alive at her touch the way hers did at his? It was hard to truly read his expression now. His eyes were a mixture of emotions, and the moon had slid behind the clouds. Zeke's back was facing the streetlight, leaving his face dark. Mac strained to see the story his eyes might hold. He did not keep things a mystery for long.

"Do you want me to stay?" he asked her. His voice was deep and full. There was no mistaking his meaning. Mac realized suddenly that she liked this about him. When he wanted something, he made it clear. When he felt strongly about a subject, he spoke his mind. There were times that this could come across as harsh, of course. Before she had understood his personality, she'd thought he was just being an asshole in all their meetings. But now she saw that he was just a man who knew what he wanted and went for it. There was a certain comfort in that. Mac liked knowing that, with Zeke, what you saw was what you got.

"Stay," she said, her own voice soft and barely more than a whisper. Zeke smiled tenderly at her, then reached with one hand to pick up her broomstick that had been leaning against the SUV. With his other hand, he grabbed one of her hands and started leading her up the walkway to her front door.

As they approached, Mac raised her ringed hand and said, "*Magicae aperio.*" The door swung open by itself, and Mac and Zeke walked through it, with Zeke holding the broomstick. As soon as he had set the broomstick down, he closed the door firmly behind him and turned to look at Mac. She felt almost like she was seeing him for the first time. He stood so tall, and made such a commanding presence in her small entryway. The size of his muscles was evident from the way the fabric of his shirt strained against his arms, and she knew from watching him during the workouts he led that his stomach and leg muscles were just as impressive as his arm muscles.

It was his eyes that really got her, though. They were such a deep shade of emerald green, and the expression in them was so intense. He seemed to see right through her as they stood there, both knowing that they were on the edge of something big. They both knew that they were about to cross over the point of no return. In fact, Mac thought that perhaps it was already too late for her. She was beginning to suspect that, despite all her efforts to convince herself otherwise, she was hopelessly in love with Zeke.

Zeke took a step forward, then another, then another. The tension in the room made the air so thick and heavy that Mac felt like she was standing underwater. With every step he took toward her, she could feel her heart rate increasing. With her eyes, she begged him to kiss her, to hold her, and to make love to her.

When he reached the spot where she was standing, he bent his head down toward her and kissed her softly. His lips moved slowly and deliberately, and he reached his arm around her back to draw her in closer to him as he kissed her. Mac let out a soft moan as her body pressed against his. She could already feel his erection, straining against the fabric of his jeans. He felt huge, but Mac was not surprised by that. Zeke was tall, and a man's man. Of course he would be well-endowed.

He pulled back from the gentle kiss for a moment, and looked deep into her eyes once more. Mac wasn't sure what he was searching for, but he seemed happy. She gave him an encouraging smile, and he let out a low growl of satisfaction.

And then, in the next instant, the gentle kisses were gone. Zeke seemed to be overcome with a sense of urgency and a sudden, insatiable hunger. He let out a loud roar, pushed Mac up against the wall, and kissed her with a fervor like nothing Mac had ever seen. His hands were against the side of her face, gripping her with his palms and pulling her face firmly against his while he drove his tongue deep into her mouth. She moaned as the heat of his presence filled her, thinking that there was nothing quite like kissing a dragon. His tongue felt like it was on fire, and she realized suddenly that she should have expected him to be hot. He could shoot flames from his mouth when he was in dragon form, after all.

He kissed her for several minutes, sending wonderful shivers of delight up and down her spine with every skillful movement of his tongue. But soon, mere kissing was not enough for him. He pulled away and looked at her, his eyes wild with desire. He was breathless and panting.

"Where's your bedroom?" he asked in a husky voice.

Mac pointed to the hallway on her right. "Second door on the right," she said. Her own voice sounded strange to her. It was high-pitched and almost musical, but she wasn't quite sure why. All she knew was that Zeke affected her like no one else ever had.

"Come with me," he commanded. His gruff, authoritative tone turned her on. She liked it when he was a bit rough with her, and right now, he was being rough. He was making it clear that he wanted her, and he wanted her *now*. He grabbed one of her hands firmly and led her down the hallway toward the bedroom.

Once they were inside the room, he made short work of removing her clothes. She wasn't wearing her military robes today. She had opted for less formal wear instead, and this morning had chosen a form fitting button down shirt with the Falcon Cross military insignia on it. Zeke tore it off in one single movement, sending buttons flying across the room. Mac didn't care. Buttons could be sewn back on. Right now, she was reveling in the fact that the most gorgeous man she had ever seen was desperate to make love to her.

He finished pulling her now-buttonless shirt off, and she wriggled her arms out of the sleeves as he did to help him. Then he reached behind her to unclasp her simple black bra, quickly sliding it off and throwing it across the room. He stepped back for a moment to admire her breasts, letting out a long, low growl of appreciation as he allowed his eyes to slide hungrily over the soft, full mounds and hard, alert nipples. He stepped forward again, and drew one of those nipples into his mouth, sucking and chewing on it with intense pressure. Fresh waves of heat shot through Mac's body as Zeke teased and pleasured her nipples. She could feel tiny beads of sweat forming on her forehead as her dragon set her on fire.

He was only getting started, though. After acquainting himself with her nipples, he moved his hands down to the button of the black dress slacks she was wearing. He unfastened it and unzipped the zipper. Then he pushed the pants down, grabbing her underwear at the same time so that both garments were removed in record time. Mac didn't even remember kicking off her shoes at the door, but she must have because they were no longer on her feet. She was so focused on Zeke right now that it was hard to think about or remember anything but him.

Zeke looked her up and down several times, taking in her naked curves and grunting with approval. Mac breathed a sigh of relief as he did. He was clearly pleased with what he saw. After a few moments of letting him look at her, Mac grew bolder and stepped forward to reach for his shirt. She gave him a devious look as she pulled it up and over his head, and he growled in response. Mac continued on, dropping her fingers to find the button on the waistband of his jeans. He had taken off all of her clothes, so it only seemed fair that she return the favor. As she fumbled with the button and zipper of his pants, he reached his hand down to feel between her legs. Mac was dripping wet by now, which brought another growl of approval from Zeke. He stuck his finger deep inside her slick entrance, stroking at her inner walls and making it impossible for her to focus on taking off his pants. She gave up on the task for a moment, moving her hands instead so that they rested on his hips as he reached his own hand deep inside her. He stroked firmly and with a steady rhythm, causing pressure and heat to build rapidly in her core. She could feel the juices of her desire oozing out over his hand as he searched and found her most sensitive spots.

She trembled as she felt her pleasure reaching a breaking point. He must have been able to tell that she was nearing the edge, and he increased the speed of his finger until Mac could hold back no longer. With one loud, long scream, she cried out and gave in. She was on fire, and spasm after spasm rocked her body. She was filled with a fire even hotter than before, and she cried out his name again and again as the sweet release passed over her. He only grunted again, then lifted her in his arms and carried her to her bed, where he laid her gently down on her back. As she sank into the soft comforter, he reached for the button and zipper on his jeans, which she had never gotten a chance to undo. He took care of it for her, pushing his jeans off, and leaving only tight black briefs, which didn't leave much to the imagination as far as the size of his dick was concerned. His erection was stiff and long, poking insistently against the fabric of his underwear.

In another moment, the briefs were gone, too, and Zeke stood naked before her. His dick pointed proudly in her direction, its thick shaft throbbing with the anticipation of what was to come. Mac's body had stopped spasming, but at the sight of Zeke's erection she felt a fresh wave of wetness between her legs. He was huge, and she could not believe that he was about to be inside of her.

Zeke's eyes looked at her with that same intense hunger Mac had seen all evening. He crossed the room in two quick steps, the powerful muscles in his thighs rippling as he moved. He climbed onto the bed, and pushed Mac, who had sat up slightly, back down so that she was flat on her back. He looked at her and smiled so sweetly that Mac had to fight to keep tears of happiness from filling her eyes.

"Are you ready for me?" he asked. His voice was low and gravelly, filled with unrestrained desire.

"Yes," Mac whispered. "I'm ready."

With swift, skillful movements, Zeke positioned himself so that he was hovering above her, his swollen, stiff erection positioned just above the spot where her legs joined together. He looked directly into her eyes, smiled sweetly, and then closed his eyes just before sliding deep into her.

Mac gasped as he filled her. Her own eyes flew open in surprise at how large he was. Just the sight of his dick had not been enough to prepare her for what it would feel like once it was actually inside of her. She could feel burning hot pressure pushing against every available centimeter of her inner walls. The pressure only grew as he started to thrust, sliding slowly in and out of her and sending hot electricity throughout her body. Mac had barely recovered from her last release, but she could feel herself already building to the point of erupting again. It was impossible not to be overcome by the pleasure, with Zeke's enormous manhood pushing insistently against her most sensitive places.

And so, although Mac tried to hold back for as long as she could, she soon found herself screaming out Zeke's name again at the top of her lungs. Moments later, her release came again. Spasms of pleasure rocked her body as her inner muscles clenched around Zeke's dick. Sweet, hot tingles spread from her core and radiated to the furthest reaches of her fingers and toes. She had never felt more alive than in that moment, with her whole body responding to the passion and desire of her dragon.

Zeke moved faster now, thrusting harder and more urgently as the pressure within him began to build. He gave a few short growls, and then, with one giant, stiff thrust and one long, loud roar, he found his release as well. He came into her, his body racked by shivers of delight as he gave himself fully to Mac. For several long moments, they were both silent and still as they let themselves fully experience the pleasure filling their bodies. Finally, Zeke slid out of Mac and moved to lie next to her on the bed. Mac glanced over at him and smiled, wanting to say something but unsure how to put words to the joyful emotions that were filling her.

Zeke reached to offer her a blanket, but she waved him away.

"I'm so warm," she said. She lay on her back, still catching her breath as her chest rose and fell, her breasts rising and falling to the rhythm of her breathing. She was still wearing her magic ring, and a beam of moonlight that was shining in through the window reflected off the deep purple of the stone. With her ringed hand, she reached for Zeke's hand and held it. He stroked at the ring, and it struck Mac in that moment how strange it was that only a few years ago shifters hadn't even known wizards existed, and wizards had been forbidden to speak to shifters. Now, here they were, two individuals with different powers and abilities, but the same desire: to see good triumph, to live in peace, and to find love and happiness.

Mac had so much she wanted to say to Zeke, but she didn't know where to start. And besides, she was so tired. The fatigue that had been following her around all day was closing in on her again. She told herself to get out of the bed and put some clothes on so that she could work for little bit longer before going to sleep, but it was so hard to move when the bed was so comfortable, and Zeke's hand was so strong and warm.

Mac told herself that she would give herself five more minutes to lie there, and then she would get up and keep working. But her willpower was no longer stronger than her exhaustion, and in less than a minute she was asleep. She did not even stir as Zeke gently tucked a blanket over her before going to get some work done himself.

In fact, Mac would not stir again for the next ten hours.

CHAPTER TEN

"Holy shit!" Mac said.

Zeke was in the kitchen, but he heard her loud and clear. Her exclamation was followed moments later by the sound of her scrambling out of bed, banging around in her bedroom—presumably looking for clothes—and then stumbling out into the kitchen, where Zeke was seated calmly at a barstool next to the kitchen's island.

"It's past eight o'clock already!" Mac announced loudly as she entered the room. Zeke felt his lips twitch up slightly in amusement.

"So it is," he said. "And good morning to you, too."

"You don't understand," Mac said, her voice sounding peeved. "I should have worked all night, or at least gotten up at five a.m. to get a head start on the day. Now I've done nothing, *and* I have a status meeting with military leadership in less than an hour!"

Mac looked flustered, confused, and slightly angry. Her hair was a mess, flying in every direction, and she was wearing a wrinkled, oversized t-shirt that was printed with some sort of Christmas graphic. She looked so funny that Zeke wanted to laugh, but he forced himself to keep a serious face. She would only be angrier if he laughed at her.

"The meeting is postponed," Zeke said calmly. "Come sit down and have some coffee. There are also bagels. I went and picked some up because you weren't kidding when you said that there's no food in your house."

Mac threw her hands up in frustration. "Postponed? The meeting is postponed? Who postponed it? I'm the commander! I'm the one in charge of the meetings."

"I postponed it," Zeke said, keeping his voice steady and as neutral as he could. "I'm sorry if I overstepped my bounds, but I didn't want to have to wake you. I'm not sure I could have if I tried, anyway. You were sleeping like a rock. A literal rock, Mac. You were so dead to the world that if I hadn't been able to feel your breath by putting my finger under your nose, I might have thought that you were actually dead. Now sit down and eat a bagel."

Mac opened her mouth like she was about to protest again, but then she clamped it shut and sat down at the barstool next to Zeke. She was quiet for a long time, but eventually reached for a bagel and the cream cheese that was sitting in front of her. Silently, she spread the cream cheese on her bagel, then ate the whole thing before she spoke.

"I guess I did need sleep," she admitted. "Still, it should have been my decision to postpone the meeting."

"Mac, I don't want you to think I'm trying to take over your job, but you have to start being a little more sane," Zeke said. "There's no big difference between having the meeting at nine this morning or at three o'clock this afternoon."

"That's when you scheduled it for?" Mac asked.

Zeke nodded. "It's rescheduled for three. Let me tell you, though, there is a big difference in whether you sleep and eat properly. You may be a wizard, Mac, but you're still part human. You still need to take care of yourself. If you're not thinking clearly because you're exhausted, you're not doing anyone any good."

"I wasn't that tired," Mac said. "Anyone can survive on low sleep for a little while."

"Oh yeah? And can you honestly tell me that you're not thinking much clearer now, after a proper night's rest?" Zeke challenged.

Mac looked down and didn't answer.

"I think your silence is answer enough," Zeke said. "Things are a little less foggy now, eh?"

"Fine," Mac said. "You're right. I needed to sleep. But now that I have and I'm awake, I need to get back to work."

Her voice sounded distressed, and Zeke reached over to put his hand over her hand. He squeezed her small hand tightly, and she looked up at him with tears threatening her eyes.

"I just don't feel like we've done enough to prepare, but I'm not sure what more we can do," she said. "We're recruiting and training new soldiers, and spending every spare moment training the soldiers we already have. I've already seen incredible improvement in their fighting abilities, but I just don't think it's enough. I know we're going to lose more wizards, and possibly lose Falcon Cross itself. I can hardly bear to think about it. I keep thinking that if only I had prepared for war sooner, none of this would be happening. I was such an idiot to assume that times of peace would continue on forever."

"No one can fault you for not knowing that a peace that had continued for centuries was going to end," Zeke said. "All of the commanders before you assumed that, too. And there's no use beating yourself up for not doing more when you're already doing everything that you can do. It will only drain away more of your energy."

Mac put her head in her hands and made some sort of response, but it was so muffled that Zeke couldn't understand what she was saying. He reached over and gently lifted her face away from her hands, then held her cheeks in his palms.

"Listen," he said. "You're not alone in this, okay? You've got some great people working for you, and I'm here with you, too. Whatever we have to face, we'll face it together, alright?"

Mac sighed, then nodded. Zeke leaned in and gave her a gentle kiss on the lips, and she sighed again.

"I wish I'd met you during happier times," she said. Her voice was soft and her face was flushed, indicating that her body was responding favorably to his touch. Zeke would have liked nothing better in that moment than to take her back to the bedroom and show her just how much he cared for her. But he knew that they really did need to get started on their day's work. He would have to wait to make love to her again, although he could feel the telltale stiffening between his legs as his body responded to the sight and feel of her. He could not help the fact that desire rushed through him like a flood anytime she was near.

For now, though, he just smiled at her. "There will be happier times again one day," he said. "But for now, at least, having you in my life makes these trying times more bearable."

Mac smiled at him then, her first genuine smile of the morning. "Well said," she replied, then stood. "I'm going to shower and change quickly, and then head in to work. Want to go together in the SUV?"

Zeke nodded. "I'm ready when you are."

Less than twenty minutes later, Mac reappeared in the kitchen, freshly showered and once again wearing a button down shirt with the Falcon Cross military insignia on it. She had put on some light makeup, and had her hair pulled back in a tight, neat bun.

She looked worlds happier than she had last night, and the bags under her eyes were no longer visible. Zeke stood, and began folding up the papers he had been reading.

"Ready?" he asked.

She nodded, and they made their way out to the SUV. Mac brought her broomstick with her, so that she could use it to come home later if she wanted to. She told Zeke that it was a good idea to have it on hand in case there was an attack and she needed to fly on a moment's notice. The military had spare broomsticks, but Mac said it was always more comfortable flying on your own broomstick that you were used to.

Once they were on the road, Mac became quite talkative. She started running through all the different potential defensive strategies they had been using to train the Falcon Cross wizards, and also told Zeke about the training they were offering to any civilian wizards who wanted to feel better prepared to defend their homes in the event that the wizard defenses were breached and the enemy started infiltrating the village itself.

"I just don't know where the best place is for us to focus our energy," she said. "We have limited time, although we don't know exactly how limited. There's no way we can possibly train the wizards on everything I would like to have them trained on before the next attack happens, so I need to prioritize. That's hard to do, though. I don't want to make the wrong choice and focus on teaching the wrong strategies that we don't end up using."

"That's what the meeting this afternoon is about, right?" Zeke asked.

"Right," Mac said. "All of the military generals are going to discuss what we think is most important, and make a plan of action. You're coming to the meeting too, right?"

"I'll be there," Zeke said. "Although, I've been thinking a lot over the last several days about how to best train the army, and I think I have an idea that makes a lot of sense. I'm curious what you think."

"Okay," Mac said. "Lay it on me."

"Well, first of all, let me ask you something. I've noticed that many of your wizard soldiers seem to be pretty talented at flying on their brooms. How much training have they had on acrobatic flying?"

"Oh, tons," Mac said. "Flying is a skill that's been quite developed in the wizarding world over the last several centuries. After all, flying is one skill that is useful both during times of peace *and* times of war. So even though we haven't seen much warfare, we've worked hard to develop our flying skills."

"I think this is the key to victory for Falcon Cross," Zeke said.

"Okay," Mac said slowly, but Zeke could tell she wasn't really following him. "I know flying is important, but it was only as useful as it was during the last battle because the enemy didn't realize that he needed to send flying wizards and flying shifters. We've already discussed how we won't be so lucky at the next battle. I promise you he's working hard right now to assemble an army that can fly. In fact, that's probably the only reason he's delayed attacking again for this long—he wants to make sure he's rounded up everyone on the side of evil who can fly."

"Exactly," Zeke said. "Mac, don't you see? He's struggling to round up an army of shifters and wizards who can fly!"

"So?" Mac asked, still sounding confused.

"So, he probably didn't have a whole lot of soldiers who could fly. My guess is that whoever is behind this war is working overtime right now to try to get together a group that can fly."

Mac frowned. "So, that's buying us time. That's good. But you sound like there's more to your theory than that."

Zeke nodded. "I've noticed that not all of the wizards around here fly. And the two wizards I know well—Bree and Lily, who live at the Redwood Dragons base—have never said anything about broomsticks or flying. So I started asking around, and I learned, to my surprise, that the majority of wizards don't learn to fly."

"That's true," Mac said. "Flying is not an easy skill to learn, so most wizards don't even attempt it. And the High Council discourages civilian wizards from learning to fly. They don't outright prohibit it, but they place strict rules on civilian flying. Broomsticks must be registered, and there are strict penalties for performing a flying spell without authorization."

"Flying spell?" Zeke asked.

"Flying spells are how the broomsticks fly," Mac explained. "Broomsticks may look wooden, but they have cores made of a special stone material that conducts magic well. When a wizard wants to fly, they must cast a flying spell on their broom. These spells are strong, and the stone core of the broomsticks makes them even stronger. They're not invincible though. If a broomstick is damaged, say, in battle, a wizard could fall to their death."

Zeke shuddered. "I guess that's another reason the High Council wants to regulate civilian flying."

Mac nodded. "There are lots of rules. The High Council wants to make sure that no one is flying around on an unsafe broomstick, or with a weak flying spell. And any civilian who does learn to fly must not fly beyond Falcon Cross airspace. The last thing we want is for a wizard flying around on a broomstick to be spotted by a human. It's incredibly difficult to maintain an invisibility spell while flying. That's a lot of magic to manage at once. Only the most talented wizards can do it."

"This is great news, Mac," Zeke said, his voice rising with excitement. "I think our enemy has not been able to find many evil wizards who can fly. He might be able to train the wizards he already has, but they'll be well behind the curve of your wizards, who have been flying for years already. And it's not easy to find shifters who can fly. There are dragons, but most of them are firmly on the side of good. Dragons are very difficult to corrupt with evil. There are eagles as well, but they are even rarer than dragons, and are also very difficult to corrupt. My guess is that whoever our enemy is, he's going to be searching for bat shifters. Bats can be good flyers, but they are relatively easy to defeat with dragon fire."

"So you think we might actually stand a chance in this war, due to our flying skills," Mac said, turning hopeful eyes toward Zeke as he pulled into the long driveway of military headquarters and rolled down the window to show his I.D. to the guard.

"Morning, Zeke," the guard said. "Morning, Commander Somers."

Zeke and Mac returned his greeting, and then Zeke continued driving down the long driveway.

"I think we stand a damn good chance. And I think we should put all of our emphasis on beefing up the flying skills of our wizards as much as possible. We should spend every spare minute training the new recruits how to fly. And the veteran soldiers should work on improving their flying skills so they can easily outmaneuver anyone in the sky."

Zeke saw hope in Mac's face for perhaps the first time since the attack on Falcon Cross.

"You just might be right, Zeke," she said, her voice rising with excitement. "I'll talk to Raven. She's one of our best flyers, and can train the veteran soldiers. Benji and Allan can work with the new recruits. If we can outfly the enemy, we can defeat him. Or at least keep him from destroying Falcon Cross."

"That's what I think, too," Zeke said, reaching over to squeeze Mac's knee affectionately as he pulled to a stop in one of the parking spaces near the side of Military Headquarters. He killed the engine, and looked over at Mac, who was practically glowing with happiness in the morning sunlight. He smiled, thinking that the determination that he'd seen in her eyes the first night he'd met her had finally returned.

"This is huge, Zeke," she said, covering his hand with her own. "Thank you. I've been so busy stressing out about all the little details of what to teach the soldiers that I didn't take time to see the big picture. We can do this! Falcon Cross can be victorious."

In response, Zeke leaned over to kiss her. This kiss was soft, slow, and sweet. They knew they didn't have time to do anything but work right now, but Zeke didn't care. These stolen moments with her were the most glorious moments of his life. He had never been an overly optimistic person, but he couldn't help but believe that everything in this war was going to turn out okay.

He hadn't mentioned it to Mac yet, but he already knew she was his lifemate. When they had made love the night before, he'd felt the telltale burning in his core—the heat of the lifemate bond. Until last night, he'd all but resigned himself to the fact that he would be alone for life. What woman would want to spend a lifetime with an introverted dragon who was always traveling for work? Even when he was home, he spent his days secluded in the Redwood forests, far away from civilization. There weren't too many women who would fall in love with a man like him. Yet somehow, despite the fact that she knew everything about him—all of his flaws and shortcomings—Mac still wanted him. She had still given herself to him. How had he gotten so goddamn lucky?

Zeke didn't have time to ponder the question right now. Mac was already pulling away and reaching for the handle on the passenger side door.

"Looks like I need to go talk to Raven and plan out some flying lessons," she said. "See you in the meeting this afternoon. I already know the generals are going to love your plan."

She closed the door behind her, gave him a little wave and blew him a kiss, and then bounded up the steps of Military Headquarters.

Zeke smiled as he watched her go. If only this war could be over quickly, so that he and Mac could figure out how to settle down into normal life together. With a long sigh, Zeke opened his own door and climbed out of the SUV. He had a feeling that this war was going to last longer than any of them had anticipated.

At least, though, he would be fighting with Mac by his side. She might have a thing for sparkles and pink, but she was the toughest girl he'd ever met.

Falcon Cross was in good hands.

CHAPTER ELEVEN

Unfortunately for Zeke, he barely saw Mac for the rest of the day. He was busy conducting workouts for the new recruits, now focusing on building strong leg and arm muscles, both of which Raven had told him were very important for broomstick flying. He had broken away for the meeting at three o'clock, which had been a resounding success as he had hoped. Everyone loved the idea of building up the wizards' flying skills, and lessons had already begun in earnest for the wizard soldiers.

Now it was nearly eight p.m., and Zeke was finally tearing himself away from his desk. Mac had set him up with a temporary office in Military Headquarters, and right now the desk in that office was covered with papers, most of which Zeke had scribbled notes on. He had done everything he could to help plan strategies and training for the Falcon Cross army. Today, he had switched his focus to aerial defensive tactics. He had seen some of the advanced Falcon Cross flyers today, and he was impressed. He knew that with just a little bit of training, they would be able to handle just about anything that the enemy could throw at them.

"We just need a little bit more time," Zeke said aloud to his empty office. "Just a little bit more time."

If they were attacked tonight, well, they would do the best they could, and hopefully it would be good enough. But the longer the enemy held off, the better. Zeke leaned back in his chair and rubbed his forehead. The problem was that no one seemed to have any idea where the enemy was, or what he was doing. Zeke had met with Noah, Owen, and Myles today. Noah kept in touch with Knox to keep up to date on any news regarding the war. But whoever was fighting against them had been eerily quiet. In Texas, where Knox was helping the shifter protectors, and in the California Redwoods, were Vance was protecting the Redwood Dragons' base, things had been completely calm. No attacks had been made, and no enemy scouts had been sighted.

It was too quiet for Zeke's liking. Something big was brewing, and Zeke worried that the enemy would be back in Falcon Cross within the week. Undoubtedly, the enemy's pride had been wounded by the crushing defeat his last army had suffered. He would want to repay the wizards for that.

Zeke sat up straight and stretched his arms out. There was no sense in sitting here any longer and worrying. He should take the advice he had given Mac, and go get some good food and rest. He wondered if she was still here, in fact. He'd found a small gift for her this afternoon when he went into town for lunch. If she was still here, then he would give it to her now. If not, he was going to be disappointed that she hadn't said goodbye, but he would be glad that she was taking his advice to eat and rest.

Zeke grabbed the small paper bag that contained the gift, and left his office, heading for the stairwell that would lead him to Mac's office. When he got there, though, the office was dark. The lights were off, and the door was open, but Mac's broomstick was gone, so she must have headed out already. Zeke closed the door behind him with a sad grunt and headed back to the stairwell. He had so hoped to see Mac again tonight. Maybe he should text her to see if she'd had dinner yet. If not, maybe they could eat together.

Zeke was surprised by the way his chest tightened up whenever he thought about Mac. He had never been the type to overthink what a girl might be thinking of him, but he couldn't seem to keep himself from worrying about where Mac was right now, or why she hadn't stopped by to see him before she left. Perhaps she didn't feel as strongly about him as he did about her. Perhaps last night had been more of a fun diversion for her than a life-changing bonding moment, as it had been for Zeke.

Zeke knew that no matter how Mac felt about them, there was no going back for him. There would never be another girl for him. They were bonded, even though she probably had no idea what a lifemate bond was. For Zeke, at least, the rest of his life would be spent loving and protecting Mac, as much as she would let him.

Zeke frowned, suddenly wishing that he had gone to Mac's office earlier so he could catch her and talk to her before she left. He hadn't wanted to bother her too much because he knew she had so much work to do—she'd spent the whole morning and much of the afternoon in the war room with her generals, mapping out plans. Zeke had not gone because he'd thought that she had it under control, and that he would be of more use helping out with the new recruits. But now he was feeling sullen at just how little he had seen Mac today.

He was so bad at this whole romance thing. In pretty much every other area of his life, he was the epitome of confidence. He knew what he wanted and how to get it. But this was new for him. This was a girl. A girl he loved.

Love. He rolled the word around in his head, and smiled. He did love Mac, which was strange to think about because he'd only met her a little over a week ago. But she had already captured his heart. Zeke determined right then and there that the next time he saw her, he would tell her that. After all, they were in the middle of a war. Tomorrow was not guaranteed to anyone. He needed to use the time he had now to say the things that were on his heart.

Zeke pushed open the door of the military headquarters building, and started walking down the long steps toward the lone SUV. He was glad that the wizards had let him borrow one so he could come and go on his own time instead of having to bother a driver with his odd schedule. He was indeed one of the last people here tonight. He knew there were still guards, and there was always at least one general on duty these days, just in case there was an attack at odd hours in the middle of the night or late evening after others had all left for the day. But those wizards must have all ridden their broomsticks to work, because there were no other cars in the parking lot right now.

As Zeke reached the bottom of the steps, his ears perked up. He could have sworn he heard music coming from the direction of the training fields. His hearing was very sharp, thanks to his dragon genes, and it sounded almost like the sort of music you would waltz to. Intrigued, Zeke decided to investigate. He walked quickly toward the back of military headquarters, where the training fields were located directly behind the building. He knew those fields well by now, since that's where he led the workouts for the soldiers during the day. He was curious why someone would be playing music out there, but as he walked closer and closer to the back of the building, the sound got louder and louder.

When he rounded the corner of the building, his eyes widened in surprise. On the field in the very center of the training fields, there was a tote bag that he recognized as Mac's, and a sweater that he knew also belonged to her. The music appeared to be coming from somewhere in the tote bag, and Zeke knew enough about wizardry by now to guess that Mac had some sort of portable music player in there that she had cast an amplification spell on so that she could hear the music in the air.

And she was very much in the air.

High above the training fields, Mac was on her broomstick and performing some of the most beautiful aerial moves he had ever seen. She looked like a ballerina in the air, timing her twists, flips, and turns perfectly to the music that was emanating from her bag. Zeke was mesmerized. He'd heard the expression "poetry in motion" used to describe dancers, but he had never seen anyone who moved quite so poetically.

Mac continued on for several minutes, not missing a beat as one song ended and the next song began. She did not notice Zeke far below her, sitting next to her tote bag now and looking up at her, watching her soar through the air. The next song must have been the end of her playlist, because when it ended the music faded away. Mac slowed, then turned her broomstick downward to return to earth. Zeke watched her, and saw her eyes widen in midair when she spotted him. She landed next to him with barely a thud, and stepped off her broomstick hurriedly, laying it next to her tote bag.

"How long have you been here?" she demanded. Her cheeks were flushed bright red. Zeke wasn't sure whether it was from the exertion of flying or embarrassment that he had caught her flying.

"For about two songs," he said. "That was quite some flying up there. You almost looked like you were dancing."

"Well, I used to do aerial broomstick dancing in high school and college," Mac said, sitting down next to Zeke and pulling a bottle of water out of her tote bag. She took a long sip of water, guzzling down about half the bottle before replacing the cap.

"Is that an actual sport or something?" Zeke asked, confused.

Mac laughed. "I forget sometimes that you didn't grow up around wizards. Yes, it's a sport. Quite a popular one, too. All the wizard high schools have teams, and many of the wizard colleges. I went to military academy, and they, of course, had a very competitive team. "

"Let me guess, you were captain of the team?" Zeke asked.

Mac blushed but didn't answer.

"You were!" Zeke said. "You've pretty much always been an overachiever, haven't you? Captain of the sky dancing team, youngest military commander ever. What's next, Mac?"

Mac crossed her arms defensively. "It's called aerial broomstick dancing, not sky dancing. And overachiever sounds like such a negative word. There's nothing wrong with putting your whole heart into what you're doing. And that's just what I've always done."

"I noticed," Zeke said wryly. "But I'm a little surprised to see you out here sky dancing, excuse me, *aerial broomstick dancing*, when just this morning you were yelling at me for allowing you to actually get a decent amount of sleep. Don't get me wrong, I'm glad to see you relaxing a bit. I'm just surprised."

Mac frowned. "Well, I'm not actually relaxing. I mean, it is kind of fun. But practicing these moves helps me to practice the moves I need to be a good fighter in the air. 'Sky dancing,' as you call it, may look like a silly sport on the surface. But it requires extreme proficiency in many moves that are very similar to the moves you need to fight a battle up on your broomstick. I wanted to run through a few of my old routines to make sure I'm staying sharp. I might even try to teach some of the extremely advanced moves to our best flyers. If we keep working at this, we're going to have the best damn army of flying wizard soldiers this world has ever seen."

Zeke smiled at the pride in Mac's voice. "I think that's an excellent idea. And, for the record, I really do think it's okay if you want to do something to relax a bit. You've been pushing yourself way too hard over the last week. I'm glad you at least slept last night, even if you are mad at me for moving the meeting time."

Mac smiled sheepishly. "It's alright. I'm not mad. And I have to admit that you were right. I did really need to catch up on sleep. I got more done today than I have in a long time."

"That's good to hear," Zeke said, reaching for her hand. He stroked it with his thumb for a few moments, and then dropped his voice to a low, husky tone. "I missed you today, you know. I wanted nothing more than to sneak up to your office and shut and lock the door behind me so we could have a little fun. But we were both so busy."

Mac's cheeks started to flush again at Zeke's words. "I would have liked that very much," she admitted. "I can't tell you enough how much I wish things were peaceful right now."

"Well, wartime or not, I'm glad you're in my life. We just have to make the best of what we have right now. I actually did head up to your office to find you, by the way. I wanted to see you before I left, but I guess you were already out here."

Mac nodded. "I've actually been out here for quite some time," she said. "It's probably about time I headed out. If I don't get a proper dinner and some rest, you're going to be on my case about it."

Zeke laughed. "You've got that right," he said. "Before you go, though, I have something for you."

"You do?" Mac asked.

Zeke nodded, and handed her the small paper bag that had the gift for her inside. She pulled out a small, square-shaped package that was wrapped in sparkling pink paper. Mac laughed and winked at him.

"How'd you know that pink was my favorite color?" she teased.

He rolled his eyes at her. "Just open it," he said.

She carefully tore at the paper, and opened it up to reveal a cashmere pink scarf. It was a deep hot pink shade, brilliant with just a hint of shimmer to it. The salesperson had led Zeke to it right away when he said he was looking for a scarf for Mac. Everyone knew she loved pink, and this scarf was perfect for her.

"Zeke," she said, almost at a loss for words. "Wow. Just, wow. It's so soft. And so beautiful. Thank you so much. But what's the occasion?"

Zeke smiled, pleased that she seemed to like it as much as he'd hoped she would. "The occasion," he said, "Is that I'm replacing the pink scarf that was in your office until I shifted into a dragon while wearing it."

Since Zeke had still been wearing Mac's scarf when the attack on Falcon Cross started, it had been torn to shreds as he hurriedly shifted into dragon form. He knew that Mac would not have dreamed of complaining about the loss of her scarf—not when so many people had lost their lives. But Zeke had noticed the glaring absence of the scarf on the coat rack every time he visited Mac's office since then, and he had decided to do something about it.

"You really didn't have to do that," Mac said. "It wasn't your fault that you had to shift all of a sudden like that."

"I know I didn't have to," Zeke said. "But I wanted to. I know you loved that scarf, and I did my best to replace it with something that you'd love just as much."

"I think I might love it more," Mac said as she stroked the soft fabric of the scarf. "It's so beautiful, and it was a gift from you."

She looked up at him, and her eyes were filled with sweet desire. Zeke wished that they were somewhere secluded and alone right then, instead of in the middle of the open training fields. He would have loved to tear her clothes off and take her right then and there, showing her how deeply the passion inside of him burned for her. But he had to content himself with leaning over to kiss her on the lips. Even with the knowledge that they were in full view of anyone inside of headquarters, it took all of Zeke's self-control to keep from ripping her shirt off the same way he had in her bedroom last night. The sun was sinking behind the horizon, and the sky was lit up brilliant oranges and reds that cast a warm glow over Mac's skin. She looked so beautiful in that moment that it made Zeke's heart hurt.

He took a deep breath then, and decided that he wanted to make this moment extra special for Mac. Perhaps they could not make love under the setting sun, but that did not mean that they couldn't be close to each other. Zeke reached his hand into Mac's tote bag and pulled out her tiny music player, then pressed play. The player must have still had an amplification charm on it, because immediately the notes of a beautiful waltz filled the air, loudly and clearly.

Mac gave him a quizzical look as he stood and offered her his hand. "What are you doing?" she asked as he pulled her toward him.

"I'm asking you to dance with me," he said.

Mac raised an eyebrow at him. "I thought you told me that you don't dance," she said.

"I don't," Zeke said. "But for you, I will. For you, I'd do anything. Now, may I have this dance?"

Mac smiled at him, and her eyes filled with happy tears. "Yes," she whispered. "Of course."

And so they danced. Underneath the pink and orange sunset sky, they moved in perfect rhythm to the music of the waltz. Although Zeke had claimed he didn't dance, he actually knew how to waltz perfectly. He'd had to learn several years ago while on a mission to recover an ancient dragon artifact. In order to fit in with a group he needed to spy on, he'd learned to dance, since they all liked dancing. The mission had been a difficult one for him, which perhaps was part of the reason why he never wanted to dance. Dancing had always brought back bad memories of that mission. But perhaps, he thought as he twirled around with Mac, it was time to make some new memories.

When the first song ended, they did not stop. They danced to another song, and then another, until the sun had completely disappeared and the sky turned to the gray-blue light of twilight. The music died then, mid-song, and Mac sighed.

"The battery must have died," she said. "I could cast a spell to revive it, but I suppose since it's getting dark we should be going, anyway. Although I don't really want to. I could dance with you here all night. For someone who claims not to dance, you're pretty damn good at it. Where'd you learn to waltz?"

"Long story," Zeke said. "How about I tell it to you over dinner?"

Mac grinned. "Sounds good. A certain bossy dragon shifter did tell me that I have to eat proper meals."

Zeke grinned back at her, then leaned down to nuzzle her nose. "You know I'm right," he said. They both laughed, and then Mac started to pull away from his embrace to go gather her things. But Zeke pulled her back before she could get away.

"Wait just a second," he said, his voice filling with emotion. "There's one more thing I want to tell you."

"Oh?" Mac asked. "What's that?"

Zeke took a deep breath, looked her straight in the eye, and said. "I love you, Mac."

Mac's eyes widened and started to fill with tears again. "I love you, too," she said. "I wanted to tell you last night, but I felt silly for saying it so soon. But as soon as we made love, I knew. It was the strangest thing. It was like my whole body was filled with this wonderful warmth, and I just knew."

Zeke's heart filled with joy. So she had felt it, too. "That's the lifemate bond," he said.

"Lifemate bond?"

"Shifters believe that destiny has chosen one person for us all, to be our partner for life. Our lifemate. When we find that person and make love to them, it forms the lifemate bond. It's a similar idea to the concept of soulmates, except much stronger than that. It's an unbreakable bond, and it lasts for your entire life."

"Wow," Mac said. "That's intense."

"I know," Zeke said gently. "But I can't think of anyone I'd rather spend my life loving and protecting than you. I hope you feel the same way about me, but even if you don't, there will never be anyone else for me now. I'm bound to you. My life from this day forward is yours."

Zeke held his breath, waiting for Mac to respond. A few tears had spilled over her eyelids now, and were leaving wet, salty trails down her cheeks. But a smile broke across her face then, and her skin glowed by the light of the moon, which was growing stronger with every passing second.

"I feel the same way," she said. "I can't think of anyone I would rather spend a lifetime with than you."

Then she leaned forward and tilted her face upward toward him. He leaned into her kiss, his skin burning as the heat of desire filled him. She looked so beautiful right now, with tendrils of her hair falling loosely from what had been a tight bun this morning. The flying had left her with a sexy windblown look, and Zeke wished again that they were alone out there on the field. She had closed her eyes, and he closed his then, as he drank in the wonderful sensation of her lips on his. He wrapped his arms around her, and she wrapped hers around him. Despite the constant threat of danger from the enemy, life in that moment was perfect.

And then, suddenly, the perfection was broken by a long, loud siren. Flashing red lights started spinning on every corner of the Military Headquarters building, and Zeke felt his heart drop. He knew what that siren meant.

"We're under attack again," Mac cried, breaking free from Zeke's arms and running for her broomstick. Up above them, the sky was already filling with wizards, who were zooming upward on their brooms at top speed.

Mac pushed a stray strand of hair back from her face as she picked up her broomstick and swing her leg over it. She paused to look back at Zeke, her face set with a grim determined look.

"Here we go," she said, and her voice sounded like a mixture of nerves and grit.

Zeke rushed over to her, took her face in his hands, and kissed her on the lips one more time.

"Be careful up there, okay?" he said.

Mac nodded. "You too," she said. And then she kicked off the ground, zooming upward into the air to join her army.

Zeke let out a roar, and began to shift into dragon form. It was time to fight for the hometown of the woman he loved. He'd be damned if he let the evil forces win.

CHAPTER TWELVE

The sky around Mac had erupted into utter chaos. Wizards from both sides of the battle were zooming back and forth, casting spells at each other and doing their best to throw shields up before any spells hit them. Bat shifters were everywhere. They weren't that hard to take down, and Mac must have already zapped nearly fifty of them out of the sky with blasts of laser light from her magic ring. But they seemed to just keep coming. They were ugly, pesky things, and more than one of them had landed a sharp bite on Mac's arms or legs.

She ignored the pain and kept flying, doing her best to keep tabs on which way the tide of the battle was turning. Everything was so frenzied up here that it was hard to tell, but it seemed that things were moving steadily in favor of Falcon Cross. High above her, she could see the dragons circling and shooting flames from their mouth at evil wizards and shifters alike. Below her, on the ground, hundreds of ground forces were also engaged in the battle. Their enemy had not been content to rely solely on the wizards and shifters who could fly, and it had been a smart move on his part. Mac's army was stretched thin trying to keep all of the moving parts of the enemy army at bay.

Mac had not intended to be right in the thick of the fighting as she was now. She preferred to be higher up, above it all, so that she could see everything clearly and give instructions to her wizards. But the enemy had swept in so quickly that Mac had been caught up in the rush of soldiers, and was now fighting at the very heart of the battle. She wondered, as she threw attacks left and right from her magic ring, why Peter's protective shields around Falcon Cross had fallen so quickly. They should have held longer. Falcon Cross should have had more of an advanced warning, more time to prepare for the onslaught while the enemy tried to break through the shield. But no, the protective shields had quickly fallen. Something was off here. Peter was one of the best spellcasters alive today. His spells should have been more effective.

There wasn't much time to worry about it now, though. Mac danced across the sky, much the same as she had less than an hour earlier to her music. Only this time, she was twisting and weaving through deadly laser beams and angry bats. She slowly rose higher and higher, trying to make her way to a spot above the fighting where she could see exactly what was happening.

The noise of battle rang incessantly in her ears. Screams of anger mixed with screams of pain, and the zinging of both attacks and shields from magic rings filled the sky with an electric hum. Mac flew through it all, adding the noise from her own attacks and shields to the cacophony. She did not scream, though—not in anger and not in pain. She used all of her energy to focus on moving higher and higher above the ground.

The mass of moving bodies slowly thinned out, and finally, she broke free from the fight. She tilted her broomstick upward and rose high into the air, rising even above the spot where the dragons were circling. When she looked down, she smiled. From up here, she could see that the Falcon Cross army was going to win this battle. The bats had nearly all been killed at this point, and the evil wizards in the air were almost all gone as well. Even though Mac had not yet had a chance to implement her new training program that would focus on flying, her wizards had easily outflown most of the evil wizards.

"*Magicae amplificare,*" Mac said, putting an amplifying spell on her voice so that she could talk to her army. She looked around carefully for a few more moments to make sure that she had a good grasp of how the battle was playing out, and then she spoke.

"Squadrons two, four, six, and eight, shift your focus completely to attacking the ground troops," Mac said, her voice booming across the sky. "We've almost completely wiped out their aerial army, and the ground army should be easy to take down. Onward, for magic, and for Falcon Cross!"

"For magic and for Falcon Cross," came the roar of her soldiers replying back to her in unison. Then, the squadrons Mac had called out turned their broomsticks downward, flying lower until they were right above the ground troops. When the Falcon Cross wizards began aerial attacks in earnest on the enemy's ground forces, it was only a matter of minutes before the ground forces began running back, attempting a hasty retreat. The other Falcon Cross squadrons, which had continued their aerial defense of the city, were buoyed with courage by the sight of the retreating ground forces. They attacked the enemy's aerial forces with a renewed vengeance, aided by the dragons who were taking down several enemy soldiers each minute with their carefully aimed streams of fire. Mac smiled and fist pumped the air. Victory was theirs once more. In just a few more minutes, the battle should be all but over.

"*Amplificare terminantur,*" Mac said, ending the amplifying spell on her voice. She had spotted Raven down below, and wanted to go talk to her. Mac wanted to take some hostages alive for questioning, and they needed to act quickly if they were going to do so. The enemy forces were retreating rapidly now.

Mac turned her broomstick downward, holding tightly to the handle as she prepared to fly downward. But just as she started to gain momentum, she heard a sickening crack, followed by a burst of evil laughter. Mac had not seen the burly enemy wizard sneaking through the air toward her. She had let down her guard as she mused about taking hostages. That had been an almost fatal mistake.

For the next several seconds, everything seemed to move in slow motion. The enemy's deadly laser beam had, thankfully, missed hitting her by a few inches. In a stroke of luck, she had turned to fly downward at the exact moment the enemy wizard had attempted his sneak attack. Thanks to her sudden and unexpected shift in direction, the laser had struck the back of her broomstick instead of her. She had escaped instant death because of this, but she was not safe yet.

The force of the laser sent her broomstick hurtling backwards, and a giant crack had formed in the handle of the broom. Worse, the laser beam had interfered with the flying spell on her broom. Mac had been holding on tightly to her broomstick since she had been preparing to fly downward. Otherwise, she would have been knocked clean off of it by the blow. But it didn't matter much that she had managed to hold on, because her broom was no longer flying. Mac was hurtling downward through the air now, clinging to a broken broomstick that no longer held a flying spell on it.

"*Magicae sarcio!*" Mac yelled, trying to aim her magic ring at the crack in the broomstick to repair it. But it was nearly impossible to aim and perform the repairing spell correctly while flopping around through the air. She felt fear gripping her heart, but she forced it down and told herself to focus. If she panicked now, she would be dead for sure. She had to repair the broomstick and recast the flying spell before she hit the ground and met a thunderous, splattering death.

"*Magicae sarcio! Magicae sarcio!*" Mac tried over and over, but it was impossible to bring any semblance of control to her movements up here. She had been thousands of feet in the air, which had given her some time. But now she could see the ground moving closer and closer. Soon, she would be falling through what was left of the aerial forces. Perhaps she could manage to grab onto someone else's broomstick as she fell. If she got one of her wizard's brooms, that would be best. But even if she only grabbed an enemy's broom, and had to fight him or her for it, that would be better than flopping around wildly and trying unsuccessfully to fix her own splintered broomstick. Mac tried to turn herself so that she could see below her better, but the force of the wind against her body as she fell made it hard to control her movements.

"Don't panic, don't panic," she told herself, even though she could feel panic rising in her chest. And then, suddenly, her downward motion came to a halt with a mighty thud. She had landed squarely on a dragon's back. The dragon turned to look at her, his concerned eyes searching to see if she was okay. It was Zeke, and Mac knew in that moment that it had not been a coincidence that she had fallen onto him. He had flown over to save her, and he had been successful. He let out a puff of smoke and a low growl, and Mac understood. He wanted her to tell him that she was alright. Was she?

Mac took a quick inventory of her body. She was fine. The laser beam had missed her entirely, and, falling through the air, while terrifying, had not been physically harmful. Mac looked back at Zeke, her eyes wet with tears at the realization that he had just saved her life yet again.

"Thank you. I'm okay," she mouthed, unable to make herself speak for the moment. Then, she regained her wits. Where was that bastard that had knocked her off her broom? He was going to pay. Mac looked up, and saw him high, high above them. He had been watching her fall, no doubt laughing and delighting in her impending doom. It was fully dark now, but the moon was brilliant tonight, and Mac could clearly see him, flying in small circles and no doubt angered by the way she had been picked out of the sky by one of the dragons.

"Zeke, just hold steady for a moment. I need to fix my broom!" Mac yelled. Zeke nodded his giant dragon head, and flapped his wings gently to hold her steadily in the air. Mac pointed her magic ring directly at the splintered portion of her broomstick.

"*Magicae sarcio,*" Mac yelled. The broomstick instantly snapped back together, looking good as new thanks to the powerful repairing spell. Mac picked it up and examined it carefully to make sure that there was no remaining damage, and saw happily that there was not. Once she cast a new flying spell over it, the broomstick should fly just as well as before.

"*Magicae volant,*" Mac yelled as she pointed her ringed finger at the broomstick again. Instantly, the broomstick began to buzz with energy, and Mac knew the flying spell was taking effect. She hopped onto the broom, and did a few turns in midair right above Zeke, just to make sure that it was truly working. Satisfied that it was, she nodded to Zeke, and then turned the broomstick upward.

With lightning speed, she tore away from Zeke, flying upward to where the wizard who had nearly killed her was still hovering. He had been watching her, and when he saw her coming toward him on her newly repaired broom, he turned and started to flee.

"Coward!" Mac yelled, even though she knew he couldn't hear her. She leaned down against her broomstick, making herself as aerodynamic as possible. The enemy wizard dove downward, perhaps thinking that there would be more safety if he returned to where the fighting was and had some of his fellow soldiers to help him. But the battle was nearly over now. Here and there, a few skirmishes were still taking place, but for the most part, the din of fighting had ceased. Mac frowned as she realized that she'd never had the chance to go tell Raven that she wanted some of the enemy soldiers kept alive for questioning. That had been the fault of this cowardly wizard, who had knocked her off her broom.

"No matter," Mac said to herself through gritted teeth. "Since he kept me from telling Raven I wanted hostages, he'll get to be the hostage."

Mac had nearly caught up with the enemy wizard now. He was flying low and fast, but she could tell he was not an overly skilled flyer. He overcorrected his flight pattern whenever there was an obstacle in the way. This haphazard flying had slowed him down considerably, and Mac could have easily taken him out with a well-aimed laser beam shot from her magic ring.

But if she shot him down, he would likely die, which of course would make it impossible to question him. No, she had to figure out how to bring him to a stop without killing him. Mac furrowed her brow in concentration, trying to decide what to do. Then she had an idea that she thought would work well.

She leaned forward on her broomstick, pushing it to its maximum speed. Because she was much more skilled at zooming around obstacles than the enemy wizard was, she was able to easily overtake him. As soon as she passed him, she came to a sharp stop and swung around one hundred and eighty degrees so that she was facing him. His eyes filled with terror when he saw her—he had been so intent on dodging the stationary objects in front of him that he had not even noticed that she'd passed him. He came to a screeching halt and tried to switch directions to get away from her, but he didn't get very far.

As soon as his speed was slow enough that Mac knew a fall wouldn't kill him, she aimed an attacking spell at his broomstick. His broomstick cracked loudly, and he screamed as he started falling toward the ground. He was about twenty feet above a large row of bushes, and he came crashing down directly onto it, yelping in pain as he hit the stiff branches with quite a bit of force.

"*Magicae obstupefio*," Mac yelled, pointing her ring directly at him. The stunning spell rendered him motionless from his neck down. He cursed Mac and then started yelling for help, but there was no one left to help him. The last remaining enemy soldiers were fleeing the city now, with Falcon Cross soldiers in hot pursuit. Mac pointed her broomstick down toward the stunned man and flew down to land beside him with a gentle thud.

"You picked the wrong wizard to mess with," Mac said, stepping off her broomstick. "You're going to pay dearly for knocking me off my broom."

The man said nothing, but looked at her with eyes full of rage. It didn't matter how angry he was, though. He had lost in his little race against Mac, and his fellow soldiers had lost the battle against Falcon Cross. He had no one to help him, and Mac had already seen what a coward he was. She had a feeling it wouldn't take too much pressure to get him talking. She felt a rush of hope and excitement. Perhaps he could even be persuaded to tell them who this mysterious enemy they were fighting against actually was.

Mac looked up then to find Raven, but she didn't have to look far. Raven had already spotted Mac, and was just coming in for a landing a few feet behind Mac.

"We've won again," Raven said, her voice breathless and excited. "The enemy forces are completely gone or dead. Well, except for this one you've got right here, I suppose. But we did it again, Mac! We beat back the enemy even though his forces are much larger than ours. Can you believe it?"

Raven let out a whoop, and before Mac could even answer her, the dragons were also coming in for a landing beside her. Large bursts of energy rang out as they all shifted back into human form. They were all starkly naked, since their clothes had been ruined when they shifted into dragon form. Mac merely averted her eyes from the lower halves of the bodies, but Raven giggled and then coughed uncomfortably.

"Oh, grow up, Raven," Mac said, then pointed her magic ring toward each of the dragon shifters in turn. "*Magicae obscuro. Magicae obscuro. Magicae obscuro. Magicae obscuro.*"

The lower halves of Noah's, Owen's, Myles' and Zeke's bodies were instantly shrouded in a thick, obscuring cloud so that their nakedness was not visible.

"Happy?" Mac asked, looking at Raven. Raven turned bright red, but Owen, who apparently thought his new "cloud cover" was hilarious, threw back his head and laughed. The other dragons, however, seemed more interested in the enemy wizard, who was still lying on the bushes, unable to move.

"You're planning to question him?" Noah asked

Mac nodded in confirmation, and the enemy wizard cursed again.

"You won't get any information out of me!" he said, his voice filled with contempt. But no one was impressed by his declaration.

"We'll see about that," Myles said, stepping over and yanking the man off the bushes and throwing him over his shoulder like a lumpy sack of potatoes. "Where do you want him, Mac?"

"We have some prison cells inside of Military Headquarters," Mac said. "One of the wizards guarding headquarters can show you where they are."

"Owen and I will go with you," Noah said. "Zeke, I suppose you'll want to stay with Mac to get a debrief on the battle."

Zeke nodded. "I think we'll need to update the High Council, too, right?"

Mac nodded wearily. As the adrenaline from the battle faded, she was beginning to feel exhausted. But there was still much to be done tonight.

"Come on, Raven," Mac said. "Come with Zeke and me. We'll need your insights on the battle to properly update the High Council. They'll be pleased that we managed to take a prisoner. I'm sure they'll want to start interrogating him right away tomorrow. The sooner we can identify our enemy, the sooner we might have a chance at actually ending this ridiculous war."

Raven nodded, and fell into step behind Mac and Zeke, while the other dragon shifters started heading for military headquarters with the prisoner. Even though they were in plain view of Raven, Zeke reached for Mac's hand and squeezed it, then held on tightly. Mac looked up at him and smiled. Perhaps progress was slow, but progress was indeed being made. Together, they were beating back the enemy. There was no one Mac would rather have by her side for this fight.

CHAPTER THIRTEEN

The rest of the night was a blur for Mac, but a relatively happy one. She was shocked in the best way possible when she learned that there had been no new fatalities in Falcon Cross. There were some critical injuries, but everyone was expected to pull through and make a full recovery. The enemy, of course, had not been so lucky. Once again, the Falcon Cross army had handed their evil opponents a resounding defeat. And, although no one could be sure what the future held, all of the High Council members agreed that their enemy was likely to hold off for some time before attacking again. He would, undoubtedly, want plenty of time to recover and to build up an army that actually had skill in flying. This meant that the Falcon Cross army would have some breathing room to build up their own flying skills, and to perfect the town's defenses.

Peter, the lead High Councilor, was troubled by the fact that the shield around the town had been broken through so quickly. He'd said that only wizards trained in dark magic would have been able to break through a shield that quickly, which confirmed his suspicion that whoever their enemy was, he was practicing dark magic. This did not bode well for the future, and Peter said that they would need to post extra guards all around the Falcon Cross borders. Peter was pleased that a prisoner had been taken, too. All of the High Council agreed that they needed to find out what kind of enemy they were dealing with as soon as possible, if they wanted to survive. The last few battles had turned out well, but there was an ominous feeling in the air. These relatively easy times would not last forever.

But for the moment, at least, Falcon Cross was safe. Mac had gone home happy with that knowledge. Zeke had come home with her, and she had been glad for his comforting presence after the stressful battle. He'd gone with her to the training fields to pick up her bag and her new scarf, which had been left behind in a hurry when the fighting started. Mac had smiled ruefully as they gathered up her things.

"Seems like every time we kiss, another attack comes," Mac teased. "Maybe I should stay away from you."

Zeke had grinned at her, and pulled her into his arms for an extra big kiss. "Don't think you're getting rid of me that easily," he'd said.

By the time they got home, it was nearly three in the morning, and Mac had been exhausted and starving. Zeke had poured them both huge bowls of cereal, and after eating their fill they had gone to bed together, instantly falling asleep in each other's arms.

Mac awoke the next morning to the smell of coffee. Zeke's side of the bed was empty, but she could hear him whistling from down the hallway. A smile played across Mac's face as the events of the night before came rushing back to her. Falcon Cross had seen another victory, and her sexy dragon shifter was here with her, in her home. For the first time in several weeks, Mac felt at peace. She still had a lot of work to do today, of course. But she didn't feel as frenzied as she had for the last several weeks. She felt calm, and hopeful. Surely, with time on their side—and a prisoner to interrogate, big breakthroughs were ahead.

Mac sat up and was about to head to the kitchen, but she stopped when she heard the sound of Zeke's footsteps coming down the hallway. He appeared in the bedroom's doorway moments later, a steaming hot mug of coffee in his hand.

"Hey," he said softly, crossing the room and sitting on the edge of the bed next to her, then handing her the coffee mug. "I came to see if you were awake yet, and to bring you coffee. I thought I heard stirring in here."

Mac took the coffee mug gratefully and took a long sip. "You heard me stirring?" she asked, somewhat incredulous. "How? I've barely moved."

Zeke grinned. "Dragon hearing. It's quite exceptional. You'll never be able to sneak up on me."

Mac groaned as he laughed, but she couldn't keep a smile from turning up the corners of her lips. She loved discovering all the unique abilities that Zeke had, thanks to the fact that he was part dragon. She took another long sip from the coffee mug, and then set it down on her nightstand. A quick glance at her clock told her it was nearly nine-thirty. Ordinarily, she would have panicked that she was in bed so late on a work day. But today, she felt she deserved the sleep. Besides, she'd gone to bed so late, and she didn't have any meetings this morning.

"Have you talked to anyone in the office today?" Mac asked. She *was* quite curious what the other dragon shifters were saying about the battle last night, and whether they agreed with Peter's assessment that the enemy was unlikely to attack again anytime soon. Zeke seemed to know without her saying this out loud that that was what she really wanted to know.

"I've talked to Noah," Zeke said. "He agrees that the enemy will likely hold off on attacking again in the near future. But he warns that we should not use this as a reason to sit back and take a breather. There are dark forces at work here, and we need to do everything we can to figure out exactly what those forces are, and to be prepared. Noah is actually meeting with the heads of the Advocacy Bureau this morning to put together a special task force who will be researching dark magic and the most effective ways to combat it."

Mac's eyes widened. "Wow. That's pretty serious. The Advocacy Bureau is infamous for staying away from research into dark magic. They believe that it's best left alone, even for academic reasons."

Zeke nodded. "Noah told me that. But he said that the High Council has decided that, given the recent events, we need more wizards here who are skilled in defeating dark magic. In times of peace, it was alright to stay away from the subject. But now, we need to be prepared."

Mac nodded. "I'd have to say I agree."

"Of course, the other way we are hoping to combat our enemy is by talking to the prisoner we took yesterday. They're holding him at Military Headquarters right now. They plan to begin interrogating him today, as soon as you arrive."

Mac started to get up. "Oh! I should get going. I don't want to keep people waiting, and we do need to get started on interrogating him as soon as possible."

Zeke pushed her back down, though.

"Relax, Mac," he said gently. "Everyone understands that you needed to rest last night. It won't make much of a difference for the interrogation if you take your time to enjoy your coffee and have some breakfast. Another hour won't change things much. And it's better if you're in a rested, relaxed mental state when the interrogation starts. Things might get challenging if this guy resists as much as he claims he will."

"I don't think he'll resist much," Mac said. "He's a coward. But you're right; I do need to be rested and calm when the interrogation starts."

Mac forced herself to take a deep, calming breath, and then she reached for her coffee mug again. She took a nice long sip, before setting it back down and looking up at Zeke. "This coffee is great. Thank you," she said. "And I guess I also owe you a thank you for saving my life. Again."

Zeke smiled tenderly at her. "Anytime, babe," he said, then leaned in to kiss her.

Mac pulled back slightly. "I'm a mess, Zeke. I just woke up and my hair is everywhere. And I probably have coffee breath and—"

"You've never been sexier," Zeke interrupted, moving forward again to kiss her. This time, Mac let him. His kiss was slow and sweet, and she felt a deep happiness filling her as he slipped his tongue past her lips and let it dance with her tongue. He pushed her backward so she was lying on her back on the bed, and then he lay on top of her, continuing to kiss her deeply. Somehow, he managed to distribute his weight in a way that kept Mac from feeling like he was squashing her. His body felt so good against hers. He was so strong, and Mac could feel his erection, already poking at her through the fabric of his plaid pajama pants. He didn't have a shirt on, and she let her hands run over the sculpted muscles in his back as he kissed her.

All thoughts of work, war, and interrogation fell away. Right now, in this room and in this moment, there was only Zeke. He was all she needed, all she wanted. She drank him in, relishing the way his hands felt as they held her face.

He kissed her for a long time, and she cherished every second. By the time he finally pulled away, Mac was soaking wet with desire. From the looks of the huge, stiff erection poking through his pants, Zeke was also feeling the passion in the room. Ordinarily, Mac would have been filled with worry about work. She would have protested this morning makeout session, saying she needed to get to work. But today was different. Things were reasonably settled at Military Headquarters, and Mac needed this time with Zeke. She needed to find the comfort that his arms could bring. She needed to feel him inside of her, and to be one with him. The last few weeks had been so stressful, and filled with so much uncertainty. She wanted to feel the certainty of Zeke's touch now, and to know that they belonged to each other.

Zeke was swinging his legs off the side of the bed now. He stood and quickly removed his pajama pants, kicking them off and across the room. He wasn't wearing any underwear, so his rock hard dick sprang free, proudly facing toward Mac, who wanted nothing more than to have it inside of her again.

Mac sat up and pulled her nightshirt off, throwing it over onto the pile where Zeke's pants had landed. She wasn't wearing a bra, so her breasts were now fully on display for him. He let his eyes rove over them, and growled with approval. The way he looked at her, so caring and passionate all at once, turned Mac on. She felt a tingling, growing electricity in her very core, and the feeling only grew stronger as Zeke started walking toward her. He climbed back on to the bed, and reached for her panties. In a firm, quick movement, he pulled them off of her, leaving her naked and dripping wet before him.

With all encumbrances out of the way, Zeke moved so that he was straddling Mac's body. She lay on her back, looking up at him with wonder, trying to memorize what it looked like to have his face there right above her face. He smiled at her, and then, he closed his eyes as he gently entered her.

Mac closed her eyes, too, as he filled her. She loved the way he pushed against her inner walls, his slow, steady movements causing the pressure within her to build, little by little. She could hear his breathing turning rapid as the pressure built within him, too. He felt like fire inside of her, but his was a heat that she wanted. She wanted him to burn her up, every minute of every day, just as he was right now.

He leaned down so that his mouth was right by Mac's ear as he moved in her. As he rocked his hips back and forth, pushing deeper and deeper into her body, he whispered in her ear.

"I love you, MacKenzie."

She moaned. His breath was hot, and his voice ragged. The sound and feel of it drove her wild. Her body tingled, and responded to his every touch. He moved his hands across her skin, his strong, rough fingers sending shivers across her soft curves. And always, always, he kept rocking his dick back and forth inside of her.

Mac could have stayed in that moment forever, but, at last, the pressure grew too overwhelming. She felt her body exploding with waves of ecstasy as her release came, sending sweet, electric heat through her body. Her inner muscles spasmed, clamping down around Zeke's giant erection over and over, hungrily claiming him as her own.

He followed closely behind her, letting out a roar as he stiffened and then found his own release with one last, giant thrust into her. His dick pulsed as he came into her, and their bodies were truly one. Mac gasped for air, overcome by the intensity of the moment. She opened her eyes, and looked up at the face of her dragon, overcome by how wonderful he was. She had never felt a love like this, and she wasn't sure how it was even possible to feel so close to another human being. But she did. She felt like his heart and hers were sharing the same heartbeat, and she had never been so happy.

After they had both caught their breath a bit, Zeke kissed her nose, and then slid out of her to lie next to her on the bed, cradling her in his arms. She nuzzled her face against his chest, not caring anymore that her hair was a mess and she had no makeup on. All she cared about was that she was safe here in his arms. She wanted to enjoy that feeling, and so she pushed away every thought of all the things she had to accomplish today.

For the moment, everything except Zeke could wait.

CHAPTER FOURTEEN

Zeke felt a strange nervousness in his chest as he walked down the long hallway toward where the interrogation of the prisoner would be taking place. On the outside, he looked completely stoic, as always. But on the inside, his troubled thoughts churned like an unsettled sea. He was looking forward to the chance to learn more about their enemy, but he had a deep feeling of foreboding as well. He had a feeling that any answers they received today were likely to bring more questions as well.

The attacks had been strange. They had been sudden and violent, but they also did not seem to be well-thought out. Their enemy, whoever he might be, was powerful, but too angry to work in a truly calculated way. Zeke feared for the day when that changed. If their enemy took the time to truly plan out a strategy, the good shifters and wizards would be in trouble. The first step, though, was to get more answers. Mac seemed to think that this guy was cowardly enough to talk, and Zeke hoped with all his heart that she was right.

Thinking of Mac instantly lightened his mood. He looked over at her now, walking next to him, and he couldn't help but smile. She looked impressive today. She was once again wearing her midnight black military dress robes, complete with her impressive array of military medals and badges of distinction. Her long, blonde hair had been flat-ironed so that it was completely straight, and she wore a dark black wizard hat on her head. The Falcon Cross military insignia was embroidered on the front of the hat with silver thread, and beneath the hat, Mac's face was set with a determined expression. She was here to get answers, and Zeke had no doubt that she would get them.

He had seen, during his short time in Falcon Cross, that while there might be a part of Mac that enjoyed pink, sparkles, and frills, she was one of the toughest women he had ever met. She worked hard, giving her all to the city and clan she loved so much. And she did not shy away from danger. When faced with deadly enemies in battle, she flew fearlessly toward the fray. His heart swelled with pride at the realization that she was his. What more could he ask for than a brave, beautiful woman, with a healthy side of spunk? All those years that he'd thought he would never find a lifemate of his own, it was because he hadn't realized that women like Mac actually existed. But she did exist, and she was his. He vowed in that moment never to take her for granted.

Zeke and Mac were followed by several of the Falcon Cross generals, as well as by several members of the High Council. It was an impressive show, and Zeke felt somewhat out of place. Noah, Myles, and Owen had been invited to join the group as well, and Zeke was thankful for their presence. The dragon shifters were all dressed in their suits once again, and they made an impressive sight. But it was still hard to top how impressive the wizards appeared as they walked down the hallway in some of their finest robes. The group as a whole looked fearsome, and the prisoner must have agreed, because when the large double doors to the interrogation room were opened, Zeke saw his eyes widen in fright. Zeke's dragon nose could literally smell the fear coming off the man's body. Perhaps Mac was right. This might not take very long at all.

The interrogation room was set up somewhat like a courtroom. The prisoner was sitting in a box similar to a witness stand in an ordinary courtroom. He was chained on both his hands and feet, and a guard stood next to him. The guard's magic ring glinted menacingly in the bright lights of the courtroom, and the prisoner had of course been stripped of his own magic ring. He had no hope of escape.

Long benches that were raised like stadium seating faced the witness stand. As the wizards and shifters walked in, they silently took their seats on these benches, looking solemnly over at the prisoner, who appeared more and more fearful by the moment. As soon as everyone was seated, a wizard who would be serving as the record-keeper for the interrogation stood and spoke to the prisoner.

"You are here today as a prisoner of war. Falcon Cross abides by the international wizarding rules of war, which require us to provide you with humane living quarters and food, but allow us to use reasonable force to question you in relation to any ongoing war. We will ask you a series of questions. Should you choose to answer peaceably, you will be granted safekeeping and comfortable keep here in our prisons. Should you refuse to answer our questions, you will be subject to the full extent of interrogation methods allowed by international wizarding law."

The record-keeper sat down, then, and Mac stood to walk to the front of the room. She paused a few feet away from the prisoner, and cleared her throat. Before she could say anything, he spat in her direction and said.

"You'll never get anything out of me!"

Mac smiled at him, but there was no warmth in her smile. It was a cold, calculated smile, and it left no doubt in the prisoner's mind that she meant business.

"We will get something out of you," Mac said. "The question is how much pain it will cause you. I hate to bring pain on a fellow wizard, but I need information you have in order to protect the wizard community as a whole. If I have to cause you pain to get that information, I will."

Zeke watched the prisoner carefully. The fear was plainly evident in the man's eyes, but still, he spat again and glared at Mac.

"You won't get anything from me," he declared, crossing his arms across his chest as best he could with the chains that were binding him.

"We'll see about that," Mac said. "But let's start with something easy. What is your name?"

The man said nothing, continuing to glare at Mac.

"Alright," Mac said with a sigh. "Don't say I didn't warn you. Peter?"

Peter stood, and walked over in front of the witness stand. As lead High Council member, he preferred to perform any torture spells on prisoners. That way, he knew that no one was overdoing a spell or breaking international wizarding law with regards to how much pain wizards were allowed to inflict on prisoners.

"*Magicae calor*," Peter said, pointing his ring at the prisoner. The guard next to the prisoner stepped back so that he was out of reach of the heat spell. Almost instantly, the prisoner began to sweat as a glowing bubble of hot air surrounded him. Mac had told Zeke about the different spells that were used to try to convince prisoners to give up information. The *calor* spell surrounded the target with air as hot as the hottest deserts in the world, making them extremely uncomfortable. Still, it was one of the mildest torture spells, and often did not convince prisoners to talk. The wizards always started with it, though, because they didn't like to cause more pain than necessary. They hated torture, and did not enjoy using it. But as Mac had said, in this case it was necessary to protect the lives of the wizard community at large.

The prisoner proved to be even more of a coward than Mac could have imagined, however. Faced with a room full of powerful wizards and shifters, and sweating under the intense heat of the *calor* spell, the man caved.

"Fine! Fine! I'll tell you my name," he said. "Just make the heat stop!"

"*Calor terminantur,*" Peter said. Instantly, the glow of hot air around the man vanished.

"My name is Seth," he said, his voice raspy as he gasped in gulps of cooler air. "I was a wizard in a clan located in the northeastern United States, the Pine Mountain Clan. I left to join his Lordship's army, because he promised me a better life, where I would actually have power and people would listen to me. Back in Pine Mountain, I got bullied a lot and no one ever seemed to appreciate me."

Seth's voice had a bitter tone, which was accentuated by how raspy the heat had made his voice.

"Get Seth a glass of water, please," Mac said to the guard. The guard crossed the room to where a small table was set up with water glasses and water pitchers. The water was intended for the Falcon Cross wizards, but Mac was showing the prisoner a bit of kindness in hopes that it would keep him talking without resorting to more torture spells. As soon as the glass was handed to the man, he drank thirstily, as someone who had gone days in a desert without anything to drink. When he finished, Mac took a few steps toward the witness stand, and continued her questioning.

"And who, exactly, is his Lordship?" Mac asked, spitting out the words "his Lordship" as though they left an awful taste in her mouth.

Seth hesitated, and the smell of fear emanating from him increased. Peter rubbed his magic ring threateningly, making it clear that more torture spells were coming if the man did not answer Mac's question. But, of course, Seth was not only afraid of the wizards in the room. He was also afraid of his Lordship, whoever that was. No doubt, Seth's evil leader would not take kindly to Seth talking about him. If Seth talked, and the enemy army found out, he would face certain death if the enemy got a hold of him.

"Can…can you protect me?" Seth asked in a quivering voice.

"If you tell us everything you know," Mac said, "Then we will protect you with the full force of the Falcon Cross army. You will stay in our prison as long as the war is going on, but you will be treated well, and we will guard against any attempts by the enemy to get to you. Odds are, they don't even know you're alive at this point, anyway. But we will protect you no matter what, if you talk."

Seth sat in silence for several moments, considering Mac's words. As he thought, Peter spoke up as well.

"Seth, you will be as safe here as you would be anywhere else. I know that there is some dark magic being used by enemy forces, and I am the best wizard in the world at combating dark magic. Of course, nothing is ever guaranteed, but here you have the best chance of surviving the havoc that is coming. If you help us, we will offer you our protection. In addition, when the war is over, and depending on your behavior, we will consider rehabilitating you and letting you join our wizard community—provided, of course, that you show a change of heart to work for the side of good."

"But what if you lose the war?" Seth asked.

Peter sighed. "If we lose the war, then I fear for the future of us all. Dark magic eventually destroys everything in its path, even the one who thought he controlled it. For the future of wizards and shifters alike, we must not lose this war. You can help us, Seth. You can make a real difference now. You don't have to settle for just being a cog in the enemy's machinery."

The whole room seemed to be holding its breath as Seth considered Peter's words. Zeke watched, wondering if it was possible that this man, this cowardly man, might be the key that finally unlocked the mystery of their enemy and his sudden rise to power.

After what felt like an eternity, Seth finally nodded.

"Alright," he said. "I will speak. As long as you promise to protect me as much as you can."

"On the honor of Falcon Cross," Mac said, "If you tell us who our enemy is, my army will do its best to keep you safe."

Zeke watched in amazement as Seth nodded, took a deep breath, and then began to speak.

"His name is Saul Malum. At least, that's what he tells us. Most of us just call him 'your Lordship,' per his request. He's a dragon shifter, but no one knows exactly where he came from. There are rumors that he was in Europe during the last great shifter war. He would have been a baby, or at least a young child at that point. Some say that he was taken in by a lone wizard after he lost his parents in the war. He's very interested in magic. Very knowledgeable about it, too. I've never met a non-wizard who knows so much about magic."

"I suspect my hunch was correct, then, that he's been dabbling in dark magic," said Peter. "This is a very dangerous thing for anyone to experiment with. But it is especially dangerous for a non-wizard. This Saul is liable to destroy himself, and the rest of the wizard and shifter world with him. Humans won't go unaffected, either. Saul must be stopped!"

There were murmurs of agreement. Zeke looked over at Noah, who had a troubled look on his face. Zeke had a feeling he knew why. When Noah started speaking a few moments later, he said exactly what Zeke had expected him to say.

"Dragons are nearly impossible to corrupt," Noah said. "Unicorns are the only creatures more difficult to draw over to the side of evil. The fact that Saul is a dragon, who is now following evil, is cause for great worry."

"If a wizard did indeed raise him, and managed to corrupt him, it must have been a very dark wizard," Zeke agreed.

Mac frowned, and turned back to Seth. "Do you have any other information at all on where he came from?"

Seth shook his head no. "I don't know anything else, I swear. He keeps his background a secret for the most part. But I do know what he's after."

"Let me guess. The dragon stones?" Mac asked.

Seth looked somewhat disappointed that Mac already knew this, but he nodded his head vigorously nonetheless. "Yes. He knows that two—the emerald and the sapphire—have been found already. He keeps attacking Falcon Cross because he wants to steal them back. And he has plans to attack the shifters in Texas and in the Redwood forest as well. But he's also got an army of shifters, wizards, and humans working on finding out where the other two stones are."

"The amethyst and the ruby." Mac said with a sigh. "Peter, we have to find those before he does."

"I agree," Peter said. We cannot allow them to fall into the wrong hands. The trouble, though, is that no one has any idea where to even begin looking for them. The trail is completely cold. We've had Advocate Wizards working on research for quite some time, and they've come up with nothing."

"We've had the shifters back in the Redwood forest researching as well," Noah said. "But they've also come up empty handed."

"That's not surprising," Seth said. "Saul's army of researchers hasn't found anything, either, and they've been searching for a long time."

"Well," Myles said, speaking up for the first time since the interrogation started. "I guess we're in a race against time here. We have to find the dragon stones first."

"And we have to protect the stones we have," Owen said, piping up as well. The wizard generals of Falcon Cross murmured their agreement with Owen.

Zeke saw that Mac was frowning again as she turned back toward Seth. "Do you know if Saul has more plans to attack Falcon Cross?"

"I'm not sure what his plans are now," Seth said slowly. "He thought that by teaching us to fly we could overcome your army by sheer numbers. But he didn't realize how much better at flying you all were. I didn't expect it either."

Sam's voice had taken on a rueful tone. Zeke saw a shadow cross over Mac's face. No doubt she was remembering how Seth had almost killed her during the battle yesterday evening. But she quickly schooled her features, returning her face to a professional-looking, neutral expression.

"Where is he getting his army from?" Mac asked "I don't understand how he has so many soldiers still, when we've killed off so many."

Seth shrugged. "I don't really know. Most people are pretty hush-hush about where they came from. I only know that he has some recruiters, who go looking for shifters or wizards who are feeling outcast from their clans. His recruiters are really good at convincing you that joining his Lordship's army will change your life for the better."

"You can stop calling him your Lordship now," Owen said sharply.

Seth grimaced. "Sorry," he said. "Force of habit."

"But you have no idea when he might attack again?" Mac asked, persisting with her question and ignoring Owen's interruption.

"No, sorry," Seth said. "He's pretty unpredictable, and doesn't make plans too far into the future. He might focus his attacks elsewhere for a while after suffering two major defeats here in Falcon Cross, but it's hard to say for sure."

Mac and Peter started conferring together then, speaking in low tones that no one else could hear. Finally, Mac stepped back and looked at Seth. "Thank you, Seth. That will be all for now. As promised, you will be under our protection as long as this war is going on. We will treat you well, and I hope that you'll be willing to answer any further questions we may have for you in the future."

Seth looked relieved that the questioning was coming to an end.

"Sure," he said. "Thank you."

The guard took him then, leading him back to his cell and leaving the wizards and shifters alone in the room.

"Well," Mac said, turning to face the group. "That went as well as could be expected, I think."

"Does this change our plans at all?" Raven asked.

"I don't think so," Peter said, speaking up. "We will continue to focus on flying lessons for the wizard soldiers, and we will ramp up our efforts to find a trace of the other dragon stones. Perhaps some of you dragon shifters can help with that. From what Seth said, I think we have a little time before another attack on Falcon Cross. Saul will want to rebuild an army of flyers, not just of ordinary soldiers. And he'll want to make sure those flyers are better trained this time. That will all take quite a bit of time. We are safe, for the moment at least. But we cannot rest on our laurels. We need to work harder than ever now. I'm also going to assign a group of Advocates to see if they can learn anything possible about Saul. At least now we have a name to go on, and we know he's a dragon shifter. It's a start."

Murmurs of agreement rose from the group, and for the next hour some detailed plans of action were discussed. Zeke listened with interest, taking some notes of his own to review with Mac later. He had a good feeling about things now. After all, they already had two dragon stones. If they had to, they could use them against this mysterious Saul. And they had just as good a chance of finding the other two stones as Saul did. On the whole, things were looking up. The good shifters and wizards had a long way to go, but they would get there eventually. They just had to be patient and keep moving forward with the information they had.

Mac seemed to agree. A few hours later, Zeke went to meet her in her office, and she was all smiles, with her new pink scarf wrapped around her neck as she worked. She greeted him happily, and motioned for him to sit down.

"You're in a good mood," Zeke observed. Mac's smile widened, her whole face lighting up with happiness.

"Well, today's been a good day," Mac said. "We found out who our enemy is—even if it is very basic information. And we have a plan. We know we need to work on our soldiers' flying skills, and we know we need to find the missing dragon stones. There's a shit-ton of work to do, but at least we know we're heading in the right direction."

Zeke grinned at her. "Are those the *only* reasons it's been a good day? Because my day started out pretty good before I even got to the office, if you know what I mean."

Mac's face blushed bright red as his words reminded her of their lovemaking session that morning. "Zeke Pars, behave yourself! I can't take you seriously when you tease me about our extracurricular activities."

"And I can't take you seriously, MacKenzie Somers, when you're wearing that ridiculous pink scarf," Zeke said.

Mac's blush deepened, but she rolled her eyes. Zeke knew she loved it when he used her full name. No one else ever did, which made it all the more special when he said it.

"You bought it for me," she protested.

"True enough," Zeke said, winking at her. "On second thought, you should wear it to your next interrogation session. No prisoner will be able to withstand the torture of looking at something so pink."

"Oh, stop!" Mac said, crumpling up a paper into a ball and throwing it at him. He laughed, and then rose slightly from his chair so that he could lean over her desk and plant a big kiss on her lips. She sighed, and returned the kiss. When Zeke pulled away and sat down again, he couldn't help but notice that her face was actually glowing now. He loved that his kisses did that to her. And he loved how much fun they could have together, even in the most trying of times.

"I'll never stop teasing you," Zeke said, a broad grin covering his face. "But I'll also never stop loving you. No one else could ever make my heart soar the way you do. And despite the hard road ahead for shifters and wizards, I know my life will always be full of love and laughter from now on. Life with you is good, Mac—pink, sparkles, and all. I wouldn't change a damn thing about you. You're perfect."

Mac sighed again. "You're perfect, too. I couldn't have asked for a better partner to take on this challenge with. Things won't be easy, but nothing worthwhile ever is. And I have a feeling we're going to have a lot of fun along the way."

"Agreed," Zeke said, his heart feeling fuller and happier than it ever had. "And how about we start off that fun with a proper dinner out tonight? With any luck, we can make it through one meal without being interrupted by a battle."

Mac laughed. "Sounds good," she said. "I know I'm not going to get away with working too hard and forgetting to eat while you're around, anyway."

Zeke laughed, too. He grabbed Mac's hand as they left the office, and held it tightly as they walked out of Military Headquarters to go find a restaurant. Even in the hardest of times, destiny and love had a way of finding you.

As Zeke looked over at Mac, he knew he'd never been so happy to be found.

BOOK FOUR: DETERMINATON AND THE DRAGON

PROLOGUE

The sky above the California Redwoods gave off no light. Clouds hid the stars and a small sliver of the moon from view, and the air stood eerily still. Nothing moved in the darkness, in fact, except the deep green eyes of a lone dragon shifter.

Weston Pars sat tensely on the log near the fire pit, peering right and left into the blackness of the forest. The fire in the pit had long since died, flames giving way to glowing embers which eventually gave way to cold black coals. By all outward appearances, this was just another normal night at the Redwood Dragons' base camp. The clan members—the five who were here on base at the moment, at least—had grilled burgers and brats for dinner, enjoyed a beer or two (or three), and then made their way to bed in their respective one bedroom cabins. Weston had taken the first watch, from midnight to three. He was assigned to wake Holden at three in the morning to take over the watch, but Weston was beginning to think that he might need to wake the dragons earlier than that.

Something was very wrong.

He couldn't see or hear anything out of the ordinary, but he had a gut feeling that he was being watched. When the hair on the back of his neck stood on end, he tensed up even more. Someone was out there. Someone evil. And Weston had a pretty good idea of who it was—he'd bet his right arm that Saul's army had returned.

Weston remained as still as a statue, careful not to let his facial expression change. If the enemy's army was watching him, he did not want to give away the fact that he knew they were there. He'd rather they kept their guard down, thinking they had the element of surprise, for as long as possible. Weston breathed in deeply, filling his lungs with forest air and using his keen dragon's sense of smell to search for any unusual scents. If there were intruders out there, he should be able to smell them from a good half mile away. Weston breathed in all of the normal, woodsy odors. Tree trunks, leaves, soil, rocks, and moss, among other things. But then, his nose picked up another scent. It was a strange, sweet smell, reminding Weston of sugary frosting like the type you find on grocery store sheet cakes. But there were no grocery stores for miles, and no hiker would have lugged a sheet cake out into the redwoods. As soon as Weston smelled that sweetness, he knew for sure: enemies were afoot.

Masking scents had become ever more popular lately. They were sold by scrupulous and unscrupulous shifters alike, but they all had one thing in common: they replaced the smell of shifter with another smell, usually something that seemed benign and ordinary. And, in many settings, the smell of sugar certainly would have been nothing to raise an eyebrow at. But here, in the middle of the dense forest, where cakes were rare, it was a dead giveaway that someone was out there, using a masking scent.

Weston casually reached into his pocket, feeling for his cell phone and pressing the button on it that linked to the cell phones of Vance, Holden, Grayson, and Finn. Grayson had rigged a vibrating alarm signal between all of the phones, so that any dragon could set off a vibrating alarm on all five cell phones at once by pushing and holding down the home button of one of the phones for five seconds straight. Weston felt his own phone begin to vibrate in his pocket after five seconds, and he released the home button before casually pulling his hand back out of his pocket. The phones would continue vibrating for the next thirty seconds. Hopefully, that would be long enough to wake the rest of the clan.

Weston resisted the urge to look toward the cabins. He could not in any way act like he knew that anything was amiss. Whatever attackers the Redwood Dragons were about to face, their best hope for victory was to lure those attackers into a false sense of security. Weston did his best to appear on the outside like he had no idea that anyone was waiting for him. On the inside, though, he was tense, and ready. His dragon roared within him, screaming to be let out.

Steady boy, steady, Weston thought to himself. He had to wait until just the right moment. The sickly sweet smell of sugary cake was growing stronger. The enemy was getting closer. Weston's heart began to beat faster as adrenaline filled his body. This attack had been a long time coming, he knew. He was ready to actually have the chance to fight, instead of just preparing to fight as they'd been doing for the last month.

For another few minutes, the forest remained dark and silent. Nothing seemed to stir, but Weston was not fooled. The sugary smell grew stronger still.

And then, a sudden roaring sound came from the forest as the enemy army rushed forward. The invisibility spell they had been under broke as they moved forward too quickly to maintain it, and Weston saw hundreds of angry eyes coming toward him from the once dark forest. There were wizards, shifters, and humans, illuminated by the lights of torches, flashlights, and magic rings. The humans would be easy enough to dispose of, despite the swords they carried. Full humans moved much too slowly to be any real threat to a dragon. The shifters would be more of a problem. In the split-second that Weston took to do an inventory of the situation, he saw lions, bears, tigers, bats, and panthers. And, of course, the wizards would be able to do substantial harm with their magic rings, if they could aim their curses quickly enough to hit the dragons. Which only meant that Weston and the other dragons would have to be quicker than them.

Weston had observed all of this in a fraction of a second, but he did not pause for long. He had been prepared to shift at a moment's notice, and now, he did. He let out a long, angry roar as his human body began to give way to the body of a dragon. His clothes tore to shreds as his body quickly grew too large for them. His human flesh hardened and morphed into the thick hide of a dragon. He was covered with iridescent scales that glinted in the light of the torches and flashlights, shimmering in shades of green, blue, and purple. His head grew several sizes, growing horns as it became a dragon head. His teeth grew long and sharp, and smoke rose from his nostrils. Wings sprouted on his back, and his arms and legs became fearsome dragon legs, ending in razor-like claws.

He was not the only one. The rest of the clan had indeed been warned by the vibrating alarm. As Weston's body was completing its transformation into the body of a dragon, so were the bodies of four other dragon shifters. Just moments after the enemy army had charged the Redwood Dragons' base camp, five dragons were rising into the air, pumping their wings furiously and already breathing out streams of fire.

The enemy army had expected the shifters to morph into dragons, but they had not expected it to happen so quickly. Thanks to Weston's calmness, they had been fooled into thinking the dragons were not ready.

Fools, thought Weston as he rose higher into the sky. Dragons are always ready.

Weston joined the rest of his clan as they shot out stream after stream of well-aimed fire. Shifters, wizards, and humans alike screamed in terror and pain, and the smell of burning flesh filled the air as the enemy soldiers met with the fury of the dragons' fiery breath. Wizards attempted to aim attacking spells at the dragons, but the dragons moved quickly and were difficult to hit. It was nearly impossible for the wizards to see, anyway, in the midst of the chaos. Fire was everywhere. Some of the redwood trees had gone up in flames, and part of one of the dragons' cabins was beginning to burn.

The growing fire seemed to terrify the army, and Weston heard someone shouting something about forest fires and how they destroyed everyone in their path. A good portion of the attacking army retreated after that. But some stayed, mostly wizards. They continued to fight, sending blinding laser beams through the air, trying to hit one of the dragons in a vulnerable spot. A few of the laser beams made contact with Weston, but his thick hide was difficult for the spells to penetrate. Once, one of the beams hit him on the underside of his tail. That one stung, and he let out a roar of pain as the heat from the laser beam melted his skin.

The battle raged on for about ten more minutes. By then, so many of the attackers had either been killed or fled that the remaining enemy soldiers thought better of continuing the attack. They retreated, calling curses over their shoulders as they left. Weston and the other dragon shifters chased after them, their streams of fire bringing most of them down in lifeless heaps before they could get very far away.

When the last of the enemy soldiers were gone, Weston turned back toward base camp. Vance, the dragon shifter in charge here at camp, had already shifted back into human form. He'd run into his cabin to call for his lifemate, Lily. Vance had instructed her to remain hidden during the battle for safety reasons, but now, the dragons needed her help. There were fires everywhere, many growing rapidly in size. Lily was the only one who could put them out in time. Weston watched as she raised her magic ring and pointed it at one fire after another.

"*Magicae superaqua. Magicae superaqua. Magicae superaqua,*" she said over and over. The spell caused huge gushes of water to shoot from her magic ring. She used the water like a fire hose, quickly putting out the flames.

When her work was finally done, the shifters stepped back and surveyed the damage. One cabin was badly burned, and would need some repair work. Much of the ground around base camp was charred, and several nearby redwoods had suffered fire damage as well. Additionally, there was some water damage to another cabin due to the flood of water from Lily's ring. But, overall, things weren't too bad. The dead bodies of enemy soldiers lay everywhere, and here and there a discarded flashlight still shone its light across the ground where it had been dropped, illuminating the mess of burned bodies and scorched earth. Plenty of clean up and repairs would be needed, but for now, the dragons were just glad that the enemy had been beaten back.

Weston sighed. They had known this attack was coming, but it still felt a bit surreal that the war had finally reached the dragons' base camp, deep in the redwoods. Their enemy was growing more and more restless, and Weston felt sure that worse battles were to come. Vance seemed to agree. He let out a long string of curses and then looked over at the rest of his clan.

"We need to warn the others," Vance said. "They'll want to know that Saul is on the move again."

CHAPTER ONE

Myles Pars blinked his eyes open in the darkness, disoriented for a moment by the fog of sleep that attempted to cling to him. He sat up slowly, wondering where that annoying buzzing sound was coming from. Then, in an instant, he was fully awake as he realized it was his phone vibrating. A glance at the glow of his bedside clock told him it was 3:25 in the morning, and the only people would be calling him this early were his clan members—and only if something was wrong.

Myles grabbed for his phone, knocking it off the nightstand in his haste, and cursing as it went tumbling loudly to the ground and slid beneath his bed. He groped around for it in the darkness, finally closing his palm over it and pulling it back up from the floor. A glance at the caller I.D. showed him that the call he'd just missed was from Noah, and Myles felt his stomach tightening with nerves. Noah was the dragon shifter in charge of the group of Redwood Dragons that was currently residing in the wizard town of Falcon Cross to help the wizards defend their village from Saul's attacks. Noah was second in command of the Redwood Dragons' clan, answering only to Knox, the alpha leader and first in command of the clan. If Noah himself was calling at this time of the morning, then things must be serious.

Myles saw the voicemail indicator showing a message from Noah, but he did not bother to listen to it. Instead, he called Noah back right away.

"Myles," Noah said as he picked up the call, not bothering with pleasantries like saying hello. "The Redwood base camp was attacked a little over an hour ago. Vance just called me to let me know. The dragons there managed to hold off the attackers, but a lot of damage was done to the trees around base camp, and to one of the cabins."

"Is everyone alright?" Myles asked, now fully awake.

"All our clan members are fine," Noah said, his voice sounding weary. "Just minor scratches and such. But we're worried that the attack indicates that Saul is returning."

Myles frowned, his heart dropping in his chest as Noah spoke. Myles was glad to hear that none of his clan members had been harmed in the attack, but the attack was not good news. Saul was an evil dragon shifter who was leading an army of corrupted shifters, wizards, and humans on a quest to gain control of the dragon stones. The dragon stones were four powerful ancient stones that contained within them the power of the ancient dragon shifter kings. Myles had spent his life trying to recover ancient shifter artifacts that contained ancient powers, but the four dragon stones were by far the most powerful of the ancient artifacts. Saul knew this, and he wanted all four of them for his own. Saul's goal was, quite literally, to rule the world.

Luckily, with the help of dragons from Myles' clan, two of the dragon stones had already been recovered by good shifters—the dragon emerald and dragon sapphire were in Texas, under the watchful guard of the shifter protectors. Saul didn't know where the dragon emerald and dragon sapphire were, but he knew that the good shifters had them, and the good shifters had lived under the threat of attack by Saul's army for the last several months. Saul had attacked Falcon Cross, where Myles was staying right now, but had ultimately been unsuccessful and had retreated. That had been about seven months ago. Now, it was January, and things had been quiet for quite some time.

But the quiet had not been peaceful. The Redwood Dragons and the wizards of Falcon Cross knew they were in a race to find the last two dragon stones—the dragon amethyst and dragon ruby. If those dragon stones could be found by the side of good before Saul could find them, then Saul would not stand a chance against the good shifters and good wizards. The only problem was that no one had any idea where to even start looking. No one had seen the remaining two dragon stones for several hundred years, and trying to uncover clues as to their whereabouts was a painstaking, frustrating process. Myles had been working closely with the wizard advocates of Falcon Cross for more than a half year now, carefully researching and trying to discover where the stones might be. But he felt no closer to an answer now than he had half a year ago.

He knew that Saul's army had been trying to find the dragon stones, too. Was it possible that Saul had some clue as to the amethyst's or ruby's whereabouts, and that's why he had suddenly grown bold and attacked the Redwood Dragons? And would there be more attacks, possibly on Falcon Cross as well?

"We'll need to step up our efforts to find the other dragon stones," Noah said, breaking into Myles' thoughts. "That's why I called you in the middle of the night. There's nothing you need to do at this exact moment, but I would bet you're going to wake up later this morning to a flurry of emails from Alfonso about the dragon amethyst and dragon ruby. He's going to get even more demanding than he already has been, and he'll probably be adding some people to the research team. I just don't want you to be blindsided by everything that's going on."

The frown on Myles' face deepened. Alfonso was the head of the Advocacy Bureau, and he frequently clashed with Myles over the best way to conduct the search for the dragon stones. Myles didn't enjoy being micromanaged by Alfonso, and he also didn't like it when Alfonso added new people to the research team. The team searching for the dragon amethyst had swelled to such a great number now that Myles frequently found people were wasting time arguing over what research had already been done, or how best to move forward on research. All of this took away from actual research time, and made it difficult to make any real progress.

"Thanks for the heads up," Myles said. "I suppose there's not much I can do to keep Alfonso from adding more people to the team. And I'm glad that everyone back at base camp is alright, but this does not bode well for the future."

"No, it doesn't," Noah agreed. "I fear that our months of quiet are over. War is on the horizon, Myles. Saul might be reckless, but he's been building his army over the last half year. His soldiers are better trained than they were last time he attacked Falcon Cross, and he has more of them. As obnoxious as Alfonso can be, try to remember that the man is under a lot of pressure. Everyone holds him responsible for the fact that the other dragon stones have not been found yet, even though, as you know, finding them has proven to be a nearly impossible task."

Myles merely grunted in response. He knew that Noah was right, but it was hard to give give Alfonso any grace. The old wizard *was* under a lot of pressure, and he frequently took out his frustrations on his research team. Myles had grown terribly weary of always being yelled at by the man, especially when many of the problems the research team was experiencing were due to Alfonso's overstaffing of the team in the first place.

"Do your best to be nice," Noah said, a hint of warning in his voice. "You know that we need to do everything possible to keep wizard-shifter relations good."

Myles sighed. "Understood," he said, even though he didn't want to acknowledge that Noah had a point. The dragon shifters and the wizards needed each other. Neither group could fight this war on their own. The enemy was too powerful, and there was too much at stake if evil triumphed.

"I'm going to call the other guys," Noah said. "I'll check in with you tomorrow to see how things are going at the Advocacy Bureau, alright?"

"Alright," Myles said, then watched the screen on his phone as it switched from the call timer to a flashing "Call Ended" message. He set the phone down on his nightstand and put his elbows on his knees, then put his head in his hands.

Something had to give, and soon. Myles had been focused on the search for the dragon amethyst for months now, but the only thing he knew now that he hadn't known six months ago was that Alfonso could be a real jerk when things weren't going well. Odds were good that, after the news of the attack last night, Alfonso was going to be in an extra-jerky mood. This meant that he would be yelling at everyone in his path, and no one would get anything done.

Myles lifted his head and glanced at his clock again. It was just after three-thirty now, and he knew he should go back to sleep. He didn't have to be at work for several more hours, and he was going to need a lot of energy for the day ahead. But he already knew that he wouldn't be able to sleep anymore tonight. His head was swirling with worry over what the days ahead would bring, and he was filled with anger and indignation over the fact that Saul had attacked his clan's home base back in the redwood forest. Although Myles would likely be staying in Falcon Cross until this war ended, his heart was still back in the California Redwoods.

"That bastard," Myles said aloud through clenched teeth, his blood boiling as he thought of Saul. "He had no right. He's going to pay."

Myles stood, then, and made his way toward his closet. There was no sense in wasting time lying in his bed and staring at the dark ceiling in anger. He would get dressed and go in to work now. That would at least give him a few hours of peace and quiet to work before Alfonso got there. It might be the only hours of real work he was able to get done today.

Less than ten minutes later, Myles was in a black SUV, driving toward the Advocacy Bureau. The SUV was one of many owned by the Falcon Cross government, and Myles and the other dragons had made frequent use of the vehicles during their time in Falcon Cross. The large SUVs had plenty of room for Myles' tall dragon shifter form, and he loved the comfort of sitting in the soft leather seats.

Now, he turned up the radio and turned the vehicle toward the big stone building that served as the Advocacy Bureau. Despite his tense mood, he found himself humming along to the songs coming over his loudspeaker. Darkness and silence enveloped Falcon Cross right now, and Myles couldn't help but feel a little better, knowing that he was at least going to have a few hours of uninterrupted work today. With any luck, he could actually make some progress on his search for the dragon amethyst.

Myles' upbeat outlook did not last long, however. As he rounded the corner of the hallway in the Advocacy Bureau where his office was located, he saw that the door was open and the light was on. His heart sank. Was it possible that Alfonso was already here? But why would he be in Myles' office, when Myles wasn't scheduled to actually come in to work for several more hours? Myles found himself tensing up as he walked down toward the office. Something was strange here. He breathed in deeply, but he did not smell Alfonso's familiar scent, which usually reeked of a particularly strong cologne. Instead, his keen dragon nose picked up that there was some other wizard in there—a female wizard.

The door in the office was slightly ajar, and Myles slowly pushed it open as he approached. He saw then that it was indeed a woman in his office. He had never seen her before, he was quite sure of that. She was the most stunning woman he had ever seen, and if he had met her before, he would have remembered the way her curly dark hair shone. She had smooth porcelain skin, and striking violet eyes that would have been impossible to forget.

And yet, beautiful or not, she was still in *his* office, shuffling through his papers. His office was large, and had originally been meant for two people. There was a spare desk that until now had been unoccupied the entire time Myles had worked in this office. She was occupying it now, though, sitting there and looking up at him with a smile as though there was nothing strange about being in someone else's office unannounced at four in the morning.

Myles scowled at her, his mood darkening once again. Could he not get one minute to work in peace in this damn place? He crossed his arms, and kicked the office door fully open as he stepped into the room. His large form towered over her as he stood above where she sat at the desk.

"Who the hell are you?" he asked, his angry tone matching his angry words. But she did not seem fazed by his obvious fury. She looked up at him, a smile on her face that reached all the way up to her eyes.

"I'm Harlow. Harlow Watkins. Your new officemate."

CHAPTER TWO

"My *what?*" Myles asked, his face starting to turn red with anger..

Harlow grimaced a bit on the inside, but she did not let the smile leave her face as she looked up at the man glaring down at her. He hadn't given her his name, although he'd demanded hers. But she didn't need a formal introduction to know that this giant of a man was Myles Pars. You could easily pick out the dragon shifters in a crowd in Falcon Cross. They were the tallest, most muscular, and most handsome men Harlow had ever seen. And, now, seeing Myles up close for the first time, Harlow was stunned to see that he was perhaps the most handsome of the bunch. Even the scowl on his face could not hide the handsome features of his tanned, chiseled face. His green eyes flashed with anger, but they were still the deepest green Harlow had ever seen. His reddish brown hair was mussed up in a way that surely was accidental, and yet looked almost artistic—the way a model's hair might be purposefully messy for a photo shoot.

"I'm your new officemate," Harlow repeated calmly. "Alfonso wants me on the dragon amethyst project, and he wants me to work closely with you. He said it wouldn't do for me to stay in my old office, clear across the building from here. He wants us close to each other so we can brainstorm and discuss our work as needed."

Harlow watched as the expression on Myles' face darkened even more. Harlow had been told that Myles was the most easygoing of the dragon shifters, but he was not living up to that reputation right now. In fact, he looked like he might explode with rage at any moment. Harlow supposed she couldn't blame him too much. She imagined she would have been a bit put out if she showed up to work early in the morning only to find a stranger sitting in her office, acting like it was completely normal to take over half an office with no warning whatsoever.

In truth, Harlow was feeling a bit annoyed herself right now. She came in to work around four in the morning nearly every single day. That gave her about four hours to work before other wizards started arriving for the work day. Of course, she didn't enjoy getting up so early every day. But it gave her the opportunity to actually be productive for four hours straight, something that was quite literally impossible once her coworkers arrived. Alfonso was always scheduling meetings these days, most of which were pointless. Not only were the meetings completely pointless, but many of the wizards felt the need to discuss the meeting topics to death both before and after the meetings as well. It's a wonder anyone got anything done at all these days, with all the time wasted on talking. It was somewhat ironic that, in the wizards' most desperate time of need, the Advocacy Bureau had nearly ground to a halt due to all the fretting over the war.

Harlow remained one of the few wizard Advocates who worked more than she talked. She'd always been driven, but the task of finding the dragon amethyst had filled her with a fire like never before. She wanted nothing more than to find that stone before Saul and his evil army could find it. This sort of thing was the reason she had become an Advocate in the first place. She'd wanted to take a job where she knew she'd spend her days using her powerful intellect to help protect the wizards of Falcon Cross.

262

And her hard work lately had paid off. She'd made some startling discoveries of shifter and wizard activity in Devil's Melt, a remote area of Montana. She had a hunch that this unexplained activity had something to do with Saul's search for the dragon amethyst. After she'd shared her findings with Alfonso, he'd promoted her and moved her over here next to Myles, telling her to use whatever resources necessary to find out what was going on in Devil's Melt. Alfonso was desperate for any breakthrough at this point. He was under a lot of pressure from the Wizard High Council to make some real progress on the search for the dragon amethyst, but real progress had been maddeningly elusive.

Until now, Harlow thought. She was onto something, and she had high hopes that things were about to turn around for Falcon Cross. Myles didn't seem interested in hearing about why she was in his office right now though. *Their* office, really. It was just as much hers as his now, since Alfonso had assigned her to it.

"This is unacceptable," Myles said, his voice rising with every word he spoke. "I already can't get anything done around here. Then I come in extra early hoping to—gasp!—get some work done, and I find some random chick in my office claiming to—"

"Random chick?" Harlow interrupted, feeling a bit indignant. "That's highly unprofessional!"

But Myles ignored her and continued on his tirade.

"You're sitting here claiming Alfonso sent you and that you're going to help me with the search for the dragon amethyst? The only help I need is some goddamn peace and quiet to get some actual work done."

"I can assure you, if you want peace and quiet, you'll get it from me. I only want to get work done as well," Harlow said.

Myles glared at her but didn't answer. After a few seconds of scowling, he stomped over to his desk and sat down, slamming his fist on his desk angrily for emphasis. He did not look at her again as he fired up his computer, its blue glow giving a strange tint to his angry red face as the machine came to life. Harlow resisted the urge to let out a long, annoyed sigh.

Well, we're off to a not so great start, she thought in frustration as she turned back to her own computer. At least, though, if he wasn't speaking to her, she might still get some work done this morning before the Advocacy Bureau came to life with its usual buzz of pointless talk and gossip.

* * *

A whole week later, Myles still wasn't talking to Harlow. His original anger had softened somewhat, and he nodded a courteous greeting to her when he arrived at work every day. But that was the extent of their conversation, and Harlow was beginning to think that Alfonso's bright idea of sitting them next to each other so that they could collaborate wasn't so bright after all. You couldn't collaborate with someone who wouldn't even talk to you.

And yet, Harlow couldn't bring herself to dislike Myles. There was something about him that she found soothing, in fact. Perhaps it was the way he absentmindedly hummed country tunes as he worked, without even realizing it. Or maybe it was the way he stayed so serene during meetings, even when the whole room was in an uproar of disagreement over the best strategy for searching for the dragon stones. Myles seemed to Harlow like a bit of calm in the middle of the storm that constantly hung over the Advocacy Bureau these days.

She had a feeling, though, that despite his unflustered appearance, things were not so calm below the surface. Every now and then, she saw him frowning with a strained look on his face. She knew that, despite his brave front, he felt the same pressure and worries they all did. Perhaps he felt it even more than she did. Harlow knew that his home in the redwood forests had been attacked. The dragon shifters there had managed to hold Saul off, for now. But there were not many dragon shifters remaining in the redwoods, since nearly half of Myles' clan had come to Falcon Cross to help the wizards. The dragons' home was at risk, and Harlow knew it must not be easy for Myles to sit here in Falcon Cross, working on what seemed like a dead end assignment for Alfonso, a boss who seemed only capable of criticism these days.

But Myles never complained. His anger the first morning they met was the closest thing to complaining that Harlow ever saw from him. As the days passed, Harlow saw that Myles actually wasn't that different from her when it came to his job. He did his best to keep his head down and work hard, ignoring the office drama as much as possible. Harlow found that she actually enjoyed having an officemate, when that officemate was quiet and didn't distract her from her work. Although, to say that Myles didn't distract her at all wouldn't exactly be true. Even though he didn't talk to her, she found herself a bit obsessed with stealing glances at him. He was too good-looking not to. He had an adorable way of scrunching up his face and biting his lip when he was thinking deeply that Harlow loved to see. She frequently found herself mentally drifting away from her work as she wondered what it would be like to kiss those lips. It was a ridiculous fantasy, really. Myles had made it pretty clear that he wasn't interested in being social, even as friends. So why in the world would Harlow waste her time thinking about him in a romantic way? She promised herself a thousand times that she would stop being so ridiculous, and a thousand times she broke that promise. It wasn't her fault she'd been assigned to share an office with pretty much the sexiest man alive.

And yet, Harlow did manage to get quite a bit of actual work done. On the eighth work day after she'd moved into Myles' office, Harlow stumbled across some information that took her breath away. In Devil's Melt, the remote area of Montana where Harlow had found shifter and wizard activity, she had managed to hack into what was supposed to be a secure mobile phone connection. She had been recording the line for a few days, but nothing exciting had come of it at first. Whoever owned the line didn't seem to use it much, and Harlow hadn't been paying very close attention to it. The few garbled conversations she picked up had been discussing food supplies, which indicated to her that some sort of long-term project was taking place. But the details of who was behind that project or what it was about had been unclear. Harlow had, of course, suspected that Saul was behind the project, and that its goal was to find the dragon amethyst or ruby. But without some sort of actual proof, Alfonso had been reluctant to bring the matter up to the High Council. He'd already faced embarrassment over several false alarms, and he did not want to add more to the list.

On this day, though, as Harlow absentmindedly listened to the recordings from the line, she suddenly heard garbled words coming through that confirmed her suspicions. She hadn't been expecting much from the recording, so when a discussion about the dragon amethyst started playing over her headphones, she sat up so quickly to grab for a pen that she knocked several file folders of papers off her desk. Out of the corner of her eye, she saw Myles give her an annoyed look, but she ignored him. She was too busy trying to hear what was being said on the recording.

Saul's upset at our lack of progress, said one voice, its tone weary and resigned.

I know, a second voice said. *But what are we supposed to do? Even with a rough knowledge of the stone's location, this is still like searching for a needle in a haystack.*

There was a short period of time where the recording was so garbled that Harlow couldn't make out what was being said, no matter how hard she tried. Then, the first voice became clear again in the middle of a sentence.

...but that's our only option. We have to keep moving forward, no matter how cold and hungry we are. Saul will kill us if we go back without the amethyst.

But what if it's not here? the second voice asked. *I'm at my wits end trying to keep these roads clear for the food supplies to get through. I'm decent at fire spells, but it seems like no matter how fast I melt the snow, more falls. I wish Saul would let us fly some food in. We have enough wizards who know how to fly now.*

I know, the first voice said. *But he's adamant that he won't use a single flying wizard for anything other than battle.*

That's so stupid. If we find the dragon amethyst, it'll be worth thousands of flying wizards in a battle. It's so goddamn powerful.

I know. But you know how Saul is. Once he makes up his mind about something...

The recording broke off into more unintelligible garbling. Harlow listened to the garbling for a few minutes, straining to hear anything else useful. Just when she was convinced that the rest of the recording was going to be hopelessly unclear, a few more sentences came through.

Well, according to those records Sam found, the amethyst is somewhere in this goddamn wilderness. We've already searched most of Devil's Melt with no luck, but that doesn't mean it's not there. We need more to go on than just a single sentence saying it was transferred from "dragon's claw to the forest's claw" in Devil's Melt.

Yeah, I know. What kind of bullshit riddle is that. I mean...

The recording became garbled again, and remained that way for the last few minutes of the conversation. Harlow replayed the recording several times, trying to make out any additional words, but she could not hear anything else no matter how hard she tried. Still, even with the limited information she had, this conversation was a huge step forward. She looked over her notes once again, growing more and more excited with each sentence she read.

For one thing, this proved that her hunch had been correct: the shifter-wizard activity in Devil's Melt was definitely related to Saul. Not only that, but the recording proved that their reason for being in Montana was to search for the dragon amethyst. It sounded like they'd found some significant information about the stone's whereabouts, although they obviously didn't have an exact location. Harlow drummed her fingers on her notebook as she reviewed the information. Someone had found records of the amethyst. And damn it, if someone else had found records, then that meant Harlow could find them, too. She needed to double down on her efforts to search. Perhaps if she used the name of the town in Montana where Saul's cronies were hiding, she might have better luck.

Harlow sat up straight and started to pick up the receiver of her desk phone to call Alfonso, but then she thought better of it and set the receiver down. It was almost five p.m., and people were already starting to leave for the day. She could stay late, and burn the midnight oil working on this problem. Maybe, if she was lucky, she would find something more on the dragon amethyst with the new information she had gleaned from the recording. She was starting to think that she could find some more information on the amethyst if she just tried a few different searches from a few new angles. If she was right, then in the morning, she might have a lot of useful information to show to Alfonso.

Harlow smiled at this thought. If she could get Alfonso a real win, not just a false hope that petered out into nothing, Alfonso would be greatly indebted to her. He would probably promote her again, and she would get to work on even more interesting cases. Visions of Advocate awards and accolades filled Harlow's imagination. She had poured her heart into her career, and she had been successful to a certain degree. But this was her chance to truly move up the ladder. If she had found a way to track down the dragon amethyst, no one could deny that she deserved every award she got.

In a sudden frenzy of excitement, Harlow started pushing aside the piles of paper on her desk to make room for a new, blank notebook. She turned to her computer, ready to do some serious research and, hopefully, find some new, groundbreaking information on the dragon amethyst. Another two hours passed by in a blink as she lost herself in her work, and she barely noticed when Myles rose to leave for the day. She might not have seen him leaving at all, if he hadn't paused at the door to turn and say goodnight.

"Working late, huh Harlow?" he asked.

Harlow looked up in surprise. He usually left with a simple but pleasant "Good Evening," so the fact that he had stopped to say anything else at all caught her off guard. And once she was looking at him, she couldn't help but notice for the thousandth time how gorgeous he was. His green eyes were watching her intently right now, full of curiosity. She realized with a certain sense of satisfaction that he was actually interested in knowing what she was working on. And, suddenly, she was overwhelmed with a desire to tell him about the recording and the possibility that she might have found a new, more effective way to search for records on the dragon amethyst. She'd been keeping all of this inside for the last two hours, and she was beginning to feel like she might burst with excitement.

"It's definitely Saul's people in Montana," she blurted out. "I'm sure of it now."

In response, Myles raised an eyebrow, then walked back into the room, sitting in the rickety guest chair that stood in front of Harlow's desk.

"Oh?" he asked. The curiosity in his eyes was growing, and Harlow found herself even more excited now that she had someone to share her excitement with. Over the next few minutes, she told him about the recording, explaining in detail everything that had been said. She explained that she thought some of the information had given her a better idea of how to effectively search for the records of the dragon amethyst. When she was done, she held her breath, waiting for him to respond. He furrowed his brow and bit his lip in that adorable way he did, and Harlow found herself doing her best to ignore the little flip-flop of excitement in her stomach when he looked up at her with his expressive eyes.

"Can I hear it? The recording I mean," he said. "I'd like to listen to it for myself, too, if you don't mind."

"Sure," Harlow said, grabbing her headphones and handing them over to him. She pulled up the audio file while he was putting the headphones on, then pressed play as soon as he was ready. For the next several minutes, she sat there in silence as he listened, still furrowing his brow and biting his lip. When the recording was done, he pulled the headphones off and sat in silence, thinking. Harlow was dying to know what he thought, but she forced herself to be patient and wait while the eternal seconds ticked by. Finally, he looked up at her and grinned. It was perhaps the first time he had given her a genuine smile, and she thought her heart was going to stop in her chest from the thrill of it. She was quickly realizing that it was a lot easier to ignore how intoxicating Myles was when he was sitting on the other side of the room and not talking to her. Now, she couldn't ignore the way her heart was racing right out of her chest as he sat here in front of her and looked directly into her eyes.

"This is huge, Harlow," he said, looking pleased. "I think you're right. I think if you search using some of the location names they've mentioned, and perhaps even phrases from the riddle one of them discussed at the end, you might be able to make headway on our search. I'm assuming you've told Alfonso about this?"

Harlow hesitated, which was enough of an answer for Myles.

"You haven't?" he asked, incredulous. "Alfonso would be furious if he knew you didn't come to him with this recording the moment you discovered it."

"I know," Harlow said, admitting to herself for the first time that perhaps waiting until tomorrow to tell Alfonso about the recording hadn't been the best idea. "But it was pretty late when I discovered it, and I thought it might be better to spend the evening testing out my theories on how to better search for the dragon amethyst. That way I could give him a more complete analysis of the situation tomorrow."

Myles just laughed. "He's going to be mad when he realized you knew this today and didn't tell him, regardless of your reasons. You know that, right?"

Harlow shrugged weakly. "Too late to change my mind now."

Myles face turned serious again. "I can stay late and help you, if you want. We could probably make great headway if we both work on this tonight."

Harlow hesitated again. Part of her wanted Myles to stay. She would never have thought she'd feel that way, but the way he had taken a sudden interest in her work, combined with the way he looked at her with deep concern, made her feel warm and cared for. It had been too damn long since she felt warm and cared for, and she never wanted the feeling to go away. But another part of her worried that if he stayed here tonight, she wouldn't be able to get any real work done. How was she supposed to focus with a man as handsome as Myles looking over her shoulder?

Of course, she couldn't explain all of that to him. Thinking quickly, she came up with another excuse.

"I think it's probably better if you go home and rest," she said. "Alfonso might have some followup research he wants one of us to do tomorrow after I tell him about the recording and about whatever information on the dragon amethyst that I might find. It's probably better if one of us is fresh, you know?"

Myles gave her a long, hard look, and she suspected that he saw straight through her excuses. She braced herself, expecting him to argue with her, but in the end he did not. He just smiled at her, and nodded.

"Alright," he said. "If that's what you think is best. But let me give you my cell number, just in case."

He leaned forward and tore a small scrap off one of the papers on Harlow's desk. Then he grabbed one of her pens and started writing something down. He stood as he set down the pen and handed her the paper.

"Here. This is my cell number," he said. "If you decide you do want any help tonight, or if you just want to run something by me, then give me a call. Don't worry about what time it is. I'm happy to come in at any time of the day or night. And make sure you get at least a little bit of sleep yourself, alright? You know Alfonso is probably going to make you recount your research in painstaking detail. You don't want to be a total zombie."

"Alright," Harlow said, reaching to take the paper from his hands. His fingers brushed against hers, and lingered there just a moment longer than necessary. Harlow was startled by the heat and electricity that shot from his hand to hers, and she looked up at his face, searching his eyes for some sort of acknowledgement that he had felt it, too. But his expression gave nothing away as he backed away from her toward the door. He gave a small wave and a smile, then turned to leave.

"Goodnight, Harlow," he called over his shoulder, his voice much warmer than it had been any time before. He disappeared down the hallway in a matter of seconds.

"Goodnight, Myles," Harlow whispered, even though there was no way he would hear her.

She looked down at the paper in her hand, with his number written in messy scrawl. She felt a little shudder of excitement go through her body as she recalled his fingers touching hers, and she thought, with a happy smile, that perhaps sharing an office was going to turn out alright for both of them in the end.

CHAPTER THREE

Harlow woke with a start as a strong hand firmly shook her shoulder. She sat up quickly, looking around at the office she shared with Myles and wondering why she had been asleep at her desk. She never took naps at work. There was always too much to do, and not enough hours in the work day.

"Morning," an amused voice said.

"Morning?" Harlow asked, looking up for the first time to see that both the hand and the voice that had woken her belonged to Myles. She also realized that bright sunlight was shining in through the eastern-facing window in the office. That's when she realized with horror that she had fallen asleep at the office last night. It was indeed morning, and she had never made it home last night. She'd been so caught up in her research that she'd pushed herself to the point of literal exhaustion and passed out at her desk.

"Oh, shit," she said as she looked down at her wrinkled clothes. "What time is it? I have a meeting with Alfonso at nine."

"It's eight," Myles said, then held out a cup of coffee to her. Harlow realized for the first time that the room had filled with the smell of breakfast sandwiches and coffee. Gratefully, she took the coffee and then the breakfast sandwich that Myles offered to her.

"Cream or sugar?" he asked holding out a handful of coffee condiments that had been in his takeout bag.

Harlow grabbed one of the creamer packets, quickly added it to her coffee, and then took a long, greedy sip of the hot liquid. She began to revive a bit, and her face turned red as she realized that her makeup and hair must be a complete disaster right now. But if Myles thought she looked terrible, he did not comment on it.

Instead, he sat down once again in the guest chair in front of her desk. He pulled out a breakfast sandwich of his own to munch on, taking a gigantic bite as soon as he had peeled the paper back.

"I'm starving," he said in a voice muffled by food.

"Me too," Harlow said as she began to unwrap her sandwich. "How'd you know I'd been here all night?"

Myles swallowed his bite of food and smiled. "I didn't," he said. "I figured you'd be here already, since you always get to work so early, but I had no idea you'd been here all night. Find anything good in your research?"

Harlow groaned. "I found a lot of good stuff, actually. I was planning to present it to Alfonso at our meeting today, but I don't know how I'm going to get it all together in time for the meeting. I had intended to go home and come back in really early this morning to finish preparing for the meeting. Falling asleep at my desk and waking up an hour before the meeting looking like a hot mess was never part of the program."

Myles laughed. "Oh, come on. You don't look that bad. Just wash your face and put your hair up in a bun or something. That'll only take a few minutes and then you'll have at least half an hour to get yourself organized for the meeting. Alfonso isn't going to

269

notice what you look like."

"That's what you think," Harlow said, her feelings of panic starting to grow. "He's yelled at me before for coming to a meeting with a wrinkled shirt, and the shirt wasn't even all that wrinkled. Look at me right now! My shirt has more wrinkles than a baby elephant. And there's also no way I'm going around without makeup. I'll scare everyone senseless looking like that."

Myles stopped laughing and gave Harlow a funny look. "I bet you're beautiful without makeup on," he said, his voice sounding strangely husky. Harlow felt her heart starting to race again, and she did her best to take a few deep breaths and calm down. The last thing she had time for right now was to get all flustered by Myles' comments. She needed to focus on figuring out a way to postpone her meeting.

"That's very kind of you to say," Harlow replied, struggling to keep a normal tone in her voice. "But I really can't go to a meeting looking like this."

She wolfed down the last few bites of her sandwich, then stood to leave. "Thanks for the sandwich. I'm going to go home and think of an excuse for being late while I drive. I'll be back once I've had a chance to shower and change."

"You're not even going to tell me what exciting things you found in your research?" Myles asked, looking disappointed.

"I'll tell you later. I really have to run now," Harlow said as she gathered up stacks of paper on her desk and started stuffing them into her purse. She was just about to grab her keys when the door of the office swung wide open and Alfonso stepped in, looking red-faced and angry.

"Harlow, you better hope for your own sake that you have some information of use at our meeting today. If you don't come up with some ideas for finding that damn amethyst soon, I'm going to demote you. Why did I bring you over here and give you this posh office if you're not even going to get any work done for me? Hasn't Myles helped you brainstorm on better ways to research? Am I the only one working around here?"

"Sir, I—" Harlow started to say. She could feel her face turning red with embarrassment as Alfonso berated her in front of Myles. She never got a chance to finish speaking, though, because in the next instant Alfonso had interrupted her to talk to Myles.

"You son," Alfonso said. "Why don't you join Harlow at the meeting today? Perhaps you can make some sense out of this mess we're in and help us find the amethyst. Lord knows we could use more help, since the staff we have isn't making any progress."

"Well, sir—" Myles began. But he was interrupted as well.

"Just come to the meeting, Myles," Alfonso said. "And, you, too, Harlow. Don't you dare be late. And do something about that wrinkled shirt. I won't have you showing up like that to my meetings. It's unprofessional."

With that, Alfonso left the room, muttering as he slammed the door loudly behind him. Harlow could feel tears springing to her eyes, and she did her best to hold them back. She did not want to cry and look weak in front of Myles. But in the end, the emotions of the morning were too strong for her to push away. She hadn't slept well and there was a crook in her neck from the odd angle it had been in when she zonked out at her desk. The physical pain from moving her neck and the emotional pain of being yelled at, combined with her overwhelming exhaustion, made the perfect storm. She burst into tears.

Harlow felt ashamed, and immediately tried to regain control of her emotions, but she was too overwhelmed. She stammered out an apology to Myles, turning away under the guise of grabbing a tissue from the shelf behind her desk. She had been so excited for the meeting with Alfonso today, because she had so many new research findings to share. How had things spiraled downward so quickly? Harlow hiccupped out a sob despite her best efforts to hold it in, and a fresh wave of embarrassment washed over her.

But the next thing she knew, she felt strong arms pulling her close. Myles had crossed the space between them and had pulled her against his chest, holding her tightly and telling her not to let Alfonso get to her.

"He's just a jerk who doesn't know how to treat his best employees," Myles said. "You've worked really hard and put a lot of effort into searching for the dragon amethyst. You deserve to be proud of yourself."

Harlow hiccupped again, but her sobs started to die down. She felt an incredible warmth rushing through her body as Myles patted her on the back, each pat sending fresh shocks of electric heat from his hand to her body. Her heart was racing once more, and for a moment she forgot about everything except how wonderful Myles' body felt against hers.

Her mind was racing as quickly as her heart now. What did he mean by this gesture? Was it just a friendly act, or was he indicating that he had deeper feelings for her as well. Harlow wanted to pull back in confusion, but she could not bring herself to move. Not when Myles' arms felt so deliciously strong as they circled her. In the end, it was Myles who pulled back. His eyes were intense as they gazed down at her, but Harlow had troubled reading exactly what his expression meant. It probably didn't help that her vision was still blurred by the moisture of tears.

"You can borrow one of my shirts," Myles said. "I always try to keep extra one on hand in case I unexpectedly need to shift and end up ruining my clothes."

Harlow actually laughed out loud at that. "Myles, I don't know if you've noticed but you're a couple sizes bigger than me. I'd be swimming in your shirts!"

But Myles wasn't joking. "It will work," he said. "You're wearing skinny black jeans right now. Just wear one of my shirts over them, like a tunic. I've seen girls do it, so I know that's a thing. You'll look wonderful, and if Alfonso complains about your appearance he can go stick his oversized head in a pile of cow shit."

"Myles!" Harlow said, surprised at the way he had just insulted the head of the Advocacy Bureau. Usually Myles was careful about his manners, especially when referring to authority figures. But he just shrugged and grinned down at Harlow.

"Well, it's true," he said. "The man *does* need a bit of an ego check."

Harlow couldn't help but grin, and, for a moment, the tension in the room broke. Myles crossed the room and reached into a duffel bag under his desk, pulling out a shirt and tossing it to Harlow.

"There, that should work. I'll leave you alone for a few minutes so you can change. I'm going to be working in one of the conference rooms, but you have my cell number now. Call or text me if there's anything I can help with. Otherwise, I'll see you at the meeting."

With that, Myles disappeared out the office door. Even though she was short on time, Harlow stood there for several moments, trying to process everything that had just happened.

"He hugged me," she said aloud in wonder. "He actually hugged me."

Harlow took a couple of deep, ragged breaths to try to steady her emotions. So far, this morning had not gone at all the way she'd thought it was going to, but it looked like it might turn out okay, after all.

With a hint of a smile playing at her lips, she reached down to take off her dirty, wrinkled shirt and replace it with Myles' fresh, clean shirt. She had a feeling she was going to like the way it looked on her.

CHAPTER FOUR

Myles glanced casually at his watch, still laughing loudly at the bad joke that Alfonso had just told. There were only two minutes until nine o'clock, and Harlow still wasn't here. Myles hoped she was going to make it in time. He didn't want to see Alfonso's reaction if Harlow was late. The man was laughing at the moment, but he was clearly on edge.

Myles was a bit on edge himself, but for a different reason. He didn't know what had possessed him to cause him to suddenly wrap his arms around Harlow, but, damn, it had felt good. He'd spent the last week trying to stay angry at Harlow for taking over his office, but he'd been failing a little more at that task every day.

The more he got to know Harlow, the harder it was to find fault with her. She worked harder than any of the other Advocates he'd encountered, keeping her head down and her nose to the grindstone. Myles could easily see why Alfonso had wanted to promote her. She got shit done in a time when many of the other Advocates seemed to have mentally checked out and decided that a search for the dragon amethyst or dragon ruby was an impossible task. In the short time he'd worked with Harlow, Myles could already see that she didn't believe in the word "impossible," and he respected her for that.

She also hadn't been nearly as annoying as he'd feared she would be in the beginning. In fact, she hadn't been annoying at all. She never wasted his time with mindless small talk, and she kept her desk and side of the office neat and clean. Myles had no real complaints about her.

And since Myles could not find a reason to dislike her, he found it really hard to overlook all of the reasons he did like her—one of which was her incredible beauty. He knew it was a bit vain to focus so much on a woman's looks, but how could he not? Anyone who saw her had to admit that she was a sight to behold. Her generous curves, shiny hair, and smooth skin were enough to make him look forward to coming in to his office every day, even if he had to share that office. Perhaps *especially* if he had to share that office.

And yet, as much as he was growing to like Harlow, he had never intended to hug her today. It had been a gut reaction. The moment he had seen tears springing to her eyes, he had desperately wanted to do something to make her feel better. Now, as he pretended to be amused by yet another one of Alfonso's jokes, Myles wondered what Harlow thought of the way he had embraced her. Her tears had subsided at his hug, so that had to be a good sign, right? But had she taken his hug as a romantic gesture? And perhaps more to the point, did he *want* her to think of it as a romantic gesture? Was he really growing to care for Harlow that much?

As if to complicate his thoughts even further, Harlow chose that moment to rush into the room, looking more beautiful than ever. Alfonso stopped laughing and looked down at his watch, which must have read nine o'clock on the dot, because Alfonso hmphed and made a comment about how she was barely on time. Myles frowned rather pointedly at Alfonso. He hadn't thought Alfonso was that bad of a person at first. For the first few months, Alfonso had been reasonably kind, and frequently seemed jovial, even. But lately, his mood was increasingly sour, and he seemed to find endless opportunities to criticize his staff. From what Myles had heard, this rude, demeaning behavior had started after Saul's attacks on Falcon Cross. Alfonso was under a great deal of stress, and he was taking it out on his staff.

Big mistake, Myles thought as he watched Harlow rush into the room. Harlow was the kind of person who would work her ass off for you, but he knew that even she would have a breaking point. Lately, Alfonso seemed determined to find that breaking point. He took every opportunity to criticize Harlow, and if he wasn't careful, he was going to lose one of his best employees.

Right now, however, Harlow looked like she had decided to fight another day. She had a determined look in her eyes as she sat down in one of the seats across the table from Alfonso. Myles could not stop staring at the way his shirt hugged her curves. It surprised him how much of a turn-on it was, and he was thankful that he was sitting under a table so that the stiffening between his legs was not visible to anyone. The shirt Harlow had was one of his green plaid button-downs, a warm flannel shirt that was perfect for this cooler January day. As Myles had suspected, the shirt looked like a tunic on her. It draped beautifully across her ass, looking stylish over her skinny jeans. At least, Myles *thought* it looked stylish. He wasn't exactly a fashion expert, but he had seen many of the girls wearing long shirts like this over their leggings or skinny jeans, and he thought it looked really cute. He had never liked the look quite as much as he did right now, though. Harlow looked absolutely stunning. She had pulled her hair back into a neat bun, and no one would have known that less than an hour ago it had been a complete tangled mess. Not that Myles had minded the mess. He'd thought it looked quite sexy, in fact. But, of course, for this meeting the professional-looking bun was more appropriate.

The best part about her appearance right now, though, was that she had taken Myles' advice and simply washed her face completely clean of makeup. Myles had never seen her without makeup, and, as he'd suspected, she looked beautiful without it. Her skin glowed from the inside out, and, without a bunch of eye makeup on, her naturally beautiful blue eyes could shine through. Myles was smitten, to put it mildly. He had to force himself to look away from her to focus on Alfonso as the man started talking.

"Nice of you to join us, Harlow. I hope you have something useful for me."

Myles felt his blood boiling. Alfonso had no reason to speak to Harlow in such a rude manner. It certainly wasn't Harlow's fault that the search for the dragon amethyst had gone so slowly. Harlow had been working harder than almost anyone on the issue.

But Harlow did not look bothered by Alfonso's tone. Instead, excitement shone in her eyes as she opened a file of papers.

"I think I have something very useful," she said. She pulled out a few sheets of paper stapled together, handing one copy to Alfonso and one to Myles. When Myles looked down at his copy, he saw that Harlow had typed up a transcription of the recording she had managed to capture where two of Saul's men were discussing the amethyst.

"What's this?" Alfonso asked, frowning down at his paper in confusion.

"This," Harlow said dramatically, "Is the key to us finding the dragon amethyst."

She went on to read through the entire transcript, putting special emphasis on the parts where Saul's men talked about finding records of the dragon amethyst's location. When she'd finished reading, she looked up at Alfonso with a big smile on her face.

"This sounds promising," Alfonso said slowly, his voice much less antagonistic than it had been before. "But it doesn't give us that much information, really. So we know that Saul's people have found something indicating the stone is in Montana. But without something more specific than that, we aren't likely to find anything. The dragon amethyst isn't just going to be lying around in the open, and Montana is a big state. Even if you narrow it down to certain areas of Devil's Melt, it's still, as the guys on the recording said, like searching for a needle in a haystack."

Myles was surprised by how quickly the tone in Alfonso's voice had changed, even though the information on the amethyst offered only a tiny glimmer of hope. Myles gave his head a small shake of wonder as he watched Alfonso studying the transcript with a furrowed brow. He almost looked like the kind, wise old wizard he had been before all of the desperate but fruitless searching for the dragon stones had begun. The man was under a lot of pressure, but still—that was no reason for him to treat his people as poorly as he did.

Harlow seemed oblivious to Alfonso's mood at the moment, though, regardless of whether it was good or bad. Instead, her voice was filling with more and more excitement as she spoke.

"It's true that this alone isn't much to go on," Harlow said. "At least not by itself. But I used clues from this conversation to try some new searches for the dragon amethyst. I was hoping that with the new information I had, I would be able to use different search angles to uncover clues I hadn't been able to find before, and I wasn't disappointed."

Harlow started digging into her folder for another paper, and Myles perked up his ears. This information would be new to him, and he was keen to know what Harlow had found last night. She seemed to think that it was big, whatever it was, and he held his breath without even realizing it as he took the paper that she passed across the table to him. Was it possible that the Falcon Cross wizards were finally getting a break in their seemingly endless search for the dragon amethyst?

He let out his breath as he looked down at the paper, scrunching up his face in confusion. There was a long list of what looked like county courthouses, a few public libraries, and several university libraries.

"What's all this?" Alfonso asked, apparently as confused by the long list as Myles was.

"This," Harlow said, "Is a list of all the places where Saul's army has been able to find records that described the dragon amethyst and where it is hiding. I'm not sure how they initially were able to find all of these places, but they've amassed quite an extensive list of places, as you can see."

"So have you found stuff on all of these organizations' databases, too, now?" Alfonso asked, his voice rising even more with excitement.

"Well, no," Harlow admitted. "We have a problem. You see, none of the records were electronic. They were all too old to be digital, and the libraries and other places had not gotten around to scanning and digitizing them yet."

"Meaning there was only one physical copy of each record, which Saul's army has already acquired," Myles said, starting to catch on.

"Exactly," Harlow said. "Saul's people have visited each and every one of these locations, and, it seems to me, they have stolen the physical records. I found news articles on every single one of these places, talking about break-ins and robberies, all around the same timeframe a few months ago. It doesn't take a genius to figure out that Saul's people must have gone in and taken the records."

"This is bad news for us," Alfonso said with a sigh, still staring down at the list. "If Saul has the only copies of these records, and he's had them for months, then we're screwed. His people have already been searching for a while, and they already know a lot about where the amethyst might be. We'll have to figure out a way to steal these records back, but that will be difficult. I'm sure they're well guarded. And we're in a race against time. Any day now they could find the stone."

"Well, we're not necessarily screwed," Harlow said. "On the one hand, it could be a positive thing for us that they've stolen all these records. Look at it this way: they've done the hard work of gathering them all up for us. Now we just have to swoop in and take them. And Saul might have a large army of shifters and wizards working for him, but they aren't exactly the brightest bunch. I'm sure that their progress at finding the amethyst has been slow. We have some really smart people here at the Advocacy Bureau. I know that if we can just get our hands on those records, we'll be able to figure out where exactly we need to go to find the amethyst."

"If our people are so smart, and Saul's are so dumb, then why did they find all of these records before us?" Alfonso asked.

Harlow shrugged. "Maybe luck. Maybe the fact that he has such a large number of people working for him. I'm willing to bet that the number of people he had researching this problem was at least three times the number we had."

Alfonso crossed his arms. "Well, I hope for all of our sakes that you're right, Harlow, and that we can get these records back and quickly decipher them. Good work. It looks like you've finally found a significant clue, and goodness knows we needed a breakthrough. I'll go talk to the High Council and let them know. I suppose we'll need to alert Mac over at Military Headquarters, too. We'll want to send in some of our best soldiers to get these records from our enemy."

"Uh, yeah, speaking of that. There was one more thing I wanted to say," Harlow interrupted.

In an instant, Myles saw the confident excitement fade from Harlow's face. Whatever she was about to say was something that Alfonso was not going to like, and she knew it. Myles' heart went out to her. She had worked so hard, and she looked so nervous now, standing there tensely as if she feared Alfonso might verbally attack her again at any moment.

"Well?" Alfonso prompted. "What is it?"

"I don't think you should send soldiers in to take the records from the enemy," Harlow said. "They will be looking for soldiers, and I don't think that brute force is going to be very effective at getting these records back. The job is going to require a great deal of stealth."

"Hmph," Alfonso said, stroking his chin in thought. "I suppose you're right about that. I'll talk to our department of spies here at the Advocacy Bureau and see who our best man or woman is. We have some really talented spies here who should be able to outsmart Saul's men."

"Actually," Harlow said, her voice unmistakably shaking at this point, "I was going to tell you that I think you should send me."

The silence in the room was overwhelming. Alfonso and Myles were both staring at Harlow with gaping jaws. If Myles hadn't known better, he would have thought that Harlow was joking. But no, she would not joke around in a meeting with Alfonso. She knew better than that.

And then, Myles felt a rush of fear come over him at the thought of Harlow heading off into the thick of Saul's villains. Harlow was smart, and Myles had no doubt she would be able to sort through the records on the amethyst stone easily once the Falcon Cross wizards acquired them. But she was not trained as a spy. She was one of the very best research advocates, true. But that did not give her the skills needed to go sneaking into the thick of the enemy's camp.

"Harlow, no," Myles said before he could stop himself. "It's too dangerous. Saul's army will surely have all kinds of traps set up for spies. We need someone specially trained in stealth. And besides, it's so dangerous. You know that the High Council suspects that Saul's people are using dark magic. You don't want to get caught up in all of that mess."

"I'm not afraid of dark magic," Harlow said, her eyes filling with anger as she glared over at Myles. "And just because I'm not formally trained as a spy doesn't mean that I don't have stealth skills. All Advocates have to take basic stealth coursework during Advocacy school. And, in this case, I'm the best one to sneak up on Saul's men. I'm the one who discovered where they are, and I've been following them closely ever since I discovered them. I've been tracking their movements and listening in on their phone conversations. I know how they work. I'll be able to sneak in on them better than anyone."

Myles could practically see the smoke coming out of Harlow's ears. She was angry at him for not sticking up for her, and he felt his stomach clench up unhappily as he realized that all of the progress they had made toward being on friendly terms with Harlow had just evaporated in an instant. But he'd had to say something. He couldn't bear the thought of her waltzing into a trap laid by Saul's men. Harlow was better off staying here and leaving the dirty work to the specialized spies. The Advocacy Bureau could not afford to lose her brains, and, Myles realized with a sudden pang of fear in his chest, he could not bear the thought of losing his officemate. She was quickly becoming much more than just an officemate to him, and there was no use trying to deny that fact to himself. He wanted to say something more to convince her that going to Devil's Melt to search for the records was a bad idea, but before he could open his mouth, Alfonso was speaking up.

"It's very noble and brave of you to offer to go," Alfonso said, slowly standing as he spoke and beginning to gather up the papers in front of him. "But Myles is right. It's going to be a very dangerous job, and one that's best left to our professional spies. Thank you for all your hard work, Harlow. And my apologies if I was harsh on you earlier. The last few months have been quite, uh, stressful. But I shouldn't be taking that stress out on you."

But Harlow ignored Alfonso's apology, her eyes still angry and filled with frustration. "I'm not trying to be noble or brave," she said, clenching her fists at her side. "I'm trying to tell you that I can do this job better than any of your spies. I get how Saul's guys in Devil's Melt work! I can sneak in on them better than anyone, and recover those records quicker than anyone else. You said it yourself, sir. We're in a race against time. Every second matters."

Alfonso gave Harlow a patronizing smile, which only caused her face to grow redder with rage.

"I appreciate your willingness to help," he said. "But I'm sure our spies can handle this. That's my final word on the matter. Now, if you'll excuse me, I need to go talk to the High Council. Thank you again for all your hard work, Harlow."

With that, Alfonso whisked out of the room in a flash, not even bothering to say goodbye to Myles, who was now left uncomfortably avoiding eye contact with a very angry wizard.

"You!" Harlow said, pointing a finger emphatically in his direction. "I thought you had my back! Thanks for taking sides with our mean old boss instead of with me."

Harlow started shoving her papers back into her bag, tearing the edge of one in her haste and rage. Myles took a deep breath, desperately trying to figure out the right thing to say.

"Harlow," he said gently. "I'm sorry for taking Alfonso's side, but I do think in this instance he's right. This is going to be an extremely dangerous mission."

"I'm not afraid of danger," Harlow spat out at him as she hiked the strap of her bag over her shoulder and started making her way toward the door. She turned just before she left the room to get in one last jab at him.

"I'm surprised that *you* of all people are so worried about danger, anyway. I thought dragon shifters were supposed to be fearless."

With that, she left the room, slamming the door so violently behind her that one of the framed paintings on the wall shook. Myles let out a long sigh and leaned back in his chair. He stared up at the ceiling for several minutes, absentmindedly looking at the smooth white surface while he pondered the situation.

He was disappointed that his refusal to support Harlow's desire to go to Devil's Melt had caused a rift in the newfound peace between them. But he was happy with the way things had turned out. Someone else would be sent to recover the records, and, eventually, Harlow would forgive him for not backing her up today. At least he hoped she would. But regardless of how long it took her to stop being angry with him, he was not sorry for speaking up. This mission would be extraordinarily dangerous, and he couldn't bear the thought of Harlow being in mortal danger.

She'd been wrong when she said dragons were fearless. Oh, dragons were brave, to be sure. They were, perhaps, the bravest of all the shifters. But they weren't completely fearless. They feared losing the people they cared about.

And if there was anything the last twenty-four hours had taught Myles, it was that he cared for Harlow much more than he wanted to admit.

CHAPTER FIVE

Myles avoided his office for the next several hours, choosing instead to work alone in one of the giant, empty conference rooms. He thought it might be nice to give Harlow some space, since they hadn't exactly left the meeting on good terms. He hoped that she would see his letting her use the office alone as an olive branch of sorts, although he had a feeling it was going to take a lot of olive branches for her to forgive him for not supporting her point of view in front of Alfonso.

Thankful that he had his laptop with him, Myles opened it up and settled down to work. He reviewed the information Harlow had handed out at the meeting with Alfonso. He had already looked at the transcript of the recorded phone conversation, and at the list of organizations where records had been found. Harlow had attached some more papers to the back of the list of organizations, however, and Myles started looking through those papers now. He whistled in admiration as he saw that she had organized into detailed notes all of her observations on the shifters up in Devil's Melt. She hadn't been tracking the group for very long, and yet she'd already managed to learn a lot about them and how they worked. She had names for a few of them, and descriptions of personalities for others whose names she still hadn't been able to learn. She had made a timeline as best she could of the actions Saul's crew had undertaken since arriving in Devil's Melt. She had a rough map of the areas they'd searched, and notes on what search methods they had used in each of those areas.

Myles spent a good two hours studying Harlow's notes. When he was done, he leaned back in his chair and once again stared at the ceiling, this time letting his mind drift off to everything he still needed to work on researching himself. He was supposed to have been working closely on the amethyst research with Harlow, but both of them had branched off on their own after she first moved into his office. Myles regretted that now. He should have been kinder to Harlow from the beginning, instead of acting like a spoiled brat who couldn't handle sharing his office. What was done was done, though, and he could only hope that Harlow and he would still have opportunities to work together in the future.

While Harlow had been doing her research, Myles had been researching incidents of unexplained magic to see if any of them might lead back to the dragon amethyst. The Advocacy Bureau kept a record of incidents where magic was used around humans but no wizard was ever found to be responsible. Most of the time, these incidents were chalked up to a lucky wizard managing to get away with the unlawful use of magic near humans. But Myles suspected that some of these instances were due to humans inadvertently finding and activating ancient magical objects. It was a long shot, but he'd thought that maybe one of those objects might turn out to be the dragon amethyst, or perhaps even the dragon ruby.

So far, he hadn't had much luck with finding anything that might be the dragon stone. He had, however, found some traces of unexplained magic that seemed to have hints of dark magic to them. Myles was not an expert in dark magic. In fact, he barely understood the basics. But he knew that Peter, the head wizard of the Falcon Cross

High Council, suspected that Saul and his army were dabbling in dark magic. If this was true, then traces of unexplained dark magic might help them discover more about what Saul's army was doing.

Myles knew that dark magic slowly sucked away at the soul of the person using it, which was part of what made it so dangerous. Once all sense of humanity and decency was lost, someone using powerful dark magic spells was capable of committing horrible crimes against humanity. Eventually dark magic would destroy the person using it. But the Falcon Cross wizards were worried that Saul was going to cause irreparable damage to the shifter and wizard worlds long before his use of dark magic caught up with him and destroyed him from the inside out.

Myles hoped that his own research would help the Falcon Cross wizards at least understand what types of dark magic Saul's army was using. This would help them be better prepared to face it, a skill that was going to be important for any spies that the High Council sent to Devil's Melt to try to recover the records of the dragon amethyst.

Myles knew he wouldn't be able to finish organizing all of his research today, but he figured it was better to go talk to the High Council sooner rather than later. Who knows how soon they would want to send out a group of spies? Myles wanted to be sure he at least presented a rough report of his findings before any Falcon Cross wizards left the village for Devil's Melt.

With a determined grunt, Myles sat up in his chair again and began gathering up his papers and laptop. He'd need to go by his office first to get a few things. Hopefully, if Harlow was there, she would be at least a little less angry with him than she had been earlier. Myles couldn't help but smile. He wasn't exactly holding his breath that she'd forgive him completely, at least not this quickly. He'd seen over the last few days how stubborn Harlow could be when she felt strongly about something. And she obviously felt strongly about the fact that she was the best one for job of going to steal the amethyst records. Luckily for Myles nerves, Alfonso felt strongly the other way. Myles was glad he wasn't going to have to spend the next several weeks worrying about whether she was getting caught up in a dark magic attack by the enemy.

A few minutes later, Myles knocked gently on the door to the office he shared with Harlow. He didn't need to knock, strictly speaking. After all, it was his office, and had been his first. But he thought that Harlow might appreciate not being startled, and he wanted to do everything he could right now to be nice to her.

There was no answer from inside, however. Myles knocked again, louder this time. But there was still no answer, so he finally pushed the door open. To his surprise, the office was empty and dark. He flipped on the lights, and saw that Harlow's desk was neat and tidy, and her laptop and purse were not there. It almost looked like she'd left for the day, which shocked Myles a bit. Of course, Harlow certainly deserved to go home early today. She'd worked hard all night, and had presented information in the meeting this morning that had the potential to give Falcon Cross a chance to find the dragon amethyst before Saul. But in the time he'd shared this office with Harlow, Myles had never seen her go home early. She was always here before him in the morning, and she always left after him in the afternoon—and that was saying something, because Myles worked long hours himself. But Harlow was the hardest worker he knew.

Myles frowned. Maybe she was even angrier than he thought about not being allowed to be the one to retrieve the amethyst records from Devil's Melt. With a grunt of frustration, Myles crossed the room and sat down at his desk to quickly gather together what information he could about the dark magic traces he'd been researching. He told himself that he'd have to worry about Harlow later, even though that was much easier said than done. He couldn't get her beautiful face out of his mind. How had he spent so much time in this office with her without trying to get to know her?

He couldn't worry about it now. His first priority at the moment was to get his research on dark magic to the High Council. Then he could leave for the day, and, perhaps, start figuring out a way to convince Harlow to speak to him again.

Myles worked quickly, and a few minutes later he was walking out of the Advocacy Bureau with a folder of roughly organized papers in his arms. As he walked out to his SUV, he found himself scanning the parking lot to see if Harlow's car was still there. But her little red coupe was nowhere to be seen, confirming that she had indeed left for the day.

Feeling strangely dejected, Myles climbed into the SUV he was borrowing and fired up the engine. He made the short drive over to High Council Hall, mentally rehearsing what he would say to Peter when he got there. After parking, he checked his reflection in the mirror and smoothed back his hair. Even though he had worked closely with Peter over the last several months, Myles still always felt a sense of awe when he was in the great wizard's presence. Many said that Peter was the greatest wizard in the world, and, although Myles hadn't met many wizards outside of Falcon Cross, he found it hard to imagine that any wizard out there could be more impressive than Peter. Luckily for Myles, Peter held a great respect for the dragon shifters, and had insisted that they feel free to come to him any time they had concerns, big or small. Myles was taking Peter up on that offer now, and had a feeling that this concern fell more under the category of "big." Myles knew enough to know that dark magic was no laughing matter.

Myles walked up the long, impressive stairs that led to the entrance of the High Council Hall. This building was another part of Falcon Cross that never ceased to amaze him. Its tall dome stood proudly against the deep blue sky, and could be seen from almost anywhere in Falcon Cross. Its smooth stone sides shimmered in the bright early afternoon sunlight, and Myles could not help pausing for just a moment to admire the building's beauty.

Only for a moment, though. He had an important message to carry to Peter. Myles started taking the front steps two at a time, his strong legs carrying him easily up to the building's front door. Myles swung one of the heavy doors open and stepped inside, relishing the rush of warm air that immediately hit his skin. Even though, as a hot-natured dragon, the cold January air didn't bother him as much as others, today seemed to be a particularly chilly day. Myles was glad to be inside.

He made his way toward Peter's office by memory, walking swiftly down the hallway past the majestic banners hanging from the walls that were emblazoned with different crests and insignias from many Falcon Cross institutions. Myles recognized a banner embroidered with the Falcon Cross military insignia on it, and another with the official seal of the Advocacy Bureau.

He turned from the main hallway into another smaller hallway, and toward the door of the office that was right next to Peter's office. This was where Peter's secretary, Jill, worked. She would know if he was in the middle of something important at the moment, or if he was not that busy and it was okay to knock on his door and interrupt him.

"Good afternoon," Jill said pleasantly as Myles walked in. "How can I help you?"

"I'm here to see Peter," Myles said as he closed the door behind him. He was about to explain his errand further to Jill when he saw something that stopped him in his tracks. Jill's office was set up with a large waiting area full of comfortable plush chairs. And right now, in one of those chairs, sat Harlow.

Myles had not noticed her car parked outside, and she had been the last person he'd expected to see when he walked into this room. She looked up at him now with a scowl on her face. Her expression was a mixture of anger and guilt.

"What are *you* doing here?" she asked, crossing her arms.

"I could ask you the same thing," Myles said, raising an eyebrow at her. It was highly unusual for a wizard to come speak to Peter without an appointment, and Myles was relatively sure that Harlow would have mentioned it to him this morning if she had an appointment with Peter. Harlow didn't answer him right away, but the guilty look in her eyes intensified. Myles eyes slid downward toward the folder resting on the chair next to Harlow. The folder was stuffed with papers, and looked similar to the folder Harlow had brought to the meeting with Alfonso this morning. Suddenly, everything clicked in Myles' mind.

"You're going to ask Peter if you can go to Devil's Melt, aren't you?" Myles asked, his eyes widening. "You're going behind Alfonso's back to try to get Peter on your side."

"Yes, I'm going to ask Peter if I can go to Devil's Melt," Harlow said, standing to her feet and sticking her chin stubbornly into the air. "Because I'm the best wizard for the job. I know how those men operate. I've memorized all the details of the searches they've done—as many details as I've been able to recover, anyway. I'll be able to retrieve the records faster than anyone else, and I'll understand how to avoid detection by them better than anyone else."

"Harlow, it's not safe," Myles said, his voice rising a bit. Why did she have to be so stubborn? He knew that arguing with her was only going to make her even angrier at him, but he couldn't stop himself. How could she not see how deep into evil Saul's army was? It wasn't just about sneaking in unnoticed. It was about sneaking in unnoticed and getting out without crossing any of the dark magic spells that had been cast. And, if Myles' research was a good indicator, there were quite a few of those spells waiting to curse anyone who tried to cross the enemy. But before he could start in on a rant about dark magic again, Harlow beat him to the punch.

"And don't start trying to warn me about dark magic," she said, coming to stand right in front of him and pointing a finger in his face. "I'm a wizard, remember? I know more about dark magic than you seem to think I do. And I'm not going to let evil spells scare me away from fighting for the side of good."

The bright ceiling lights above them reflected off her magic ring, which was a deep green tourmaline surrounded by tiny, rough diamonds. It was one of the most beautiful magic rings Myles had seen, and for a moment it distracted him. The thought crossed his mind that it was perfect for Harlow—a beautiful and unique ring for a beautiful and unique wizard. His heart clenched up when he realized how deeply he cared for her. He had watched a few of his clanmates find lifemates recently, and he'd been happy for them, sure. But he'd never really understood how they could feel so deeply about someone that they would actually want to spend their lives with that one person. He was beginning to see a glimpse of what they'd been feeling. When he looked at Harlow, he had the strange sensation that he was coming alive for the first time. He desperately wanted to hold onto that feeling, and onto her.

"No one is saying that you're scared, Harlow. But, come on. There are people specially trained to deal with these things. They can go look at all your notes and research and learn from it. You have to trust that they know what they're doing, and that Alfonso has his reasons for wanting to send them instead of you."

"They won't understand my research and notes as well as I do," Harlow said, her voice rising. "And since when have you been on Alfonso's side. The man has been a stressed out asshole lately. I can't take anything he says or does seriously."

"Harlow, Myles, please," Jill interrupted. "Keep your voices down. Peter can probably hear you shouting from his office next door."

"Indeed I can," Peter said.

Myles and Harlow whipped around to see that Peter was standing in the doorway of Jill's office, a somewhat amused expression on his face. Everyone in the room, including Jill, had been so distracted by the argument at hand that they had not even noticed when Peter walked into the room.

"Your Honor. I'm…I'm sorry," Harlow stammered, embarrassed. "I didn't realize how loud we were being."

"I'm sorry, your Honor," Myles said, although he did not feel embarrassed at all. He'd had a reason for raising his voice, and he was not going to feel badly for wanting to protect Harlow.

"It's quite alright," Peter said. "I had just finished up with my last meeting and was about to come over here to ask Jill whether I had any new messages or visitors. And it appears that I have two visitors! What a lucky wizard I am."

Peter's eyes sparkled merrily as he spoke. Myles had always liked that about him. The old man was wise, and fierce when he needed to be. But he cared deeply for the citizens of Falcon Cross, and always treated them with kindness. He looked even happier than normal today, in his long white wizard robe that matched the white of his long white beard. He wasn't wearing his wizard hat right now, so his long white hair was fully visible as well. His giant magic ring sparkled impressively on the finger of his right hand, and Myles couldn't keep himself from staring at it for a moment. That ring had helped its owner perform some of the most powerful spells the wizarding world had ever seen, and the sight of it filled Myles with almost as much awe as the sight of Peter himself.

"Well?" Peter prompted. "Were you two here to see me? Or did you come just to talk to Jill? I won't hold it against you if you did. She is a great deal prettier to look at than me, after all."

"Oh stop it," Jill said, blushing from Peter's praise. "These two are both here to see you, of course. About a matter of some importance, it would seem, from the volume of their voices. The young lady was here first."

Myles saw Peter glance over at Harlow, and then back at him. Harlow opened her mouth to say something, but before she could get any words out, Peter was turning back toward the door and gesturing back at Myles and Harlow.

"Why don't you both come along together," Peter said. "It sounds like the two of you disagree on something related to dark magic, from what I heard of your shouts a minute ago. Perhaps I can help you sort the situation out."

Harlow glared at Myles, then marched after Peter. Myles followed, feeling somewhat triumphant. He felt confident that if he was in the room when Harlow spoke to Peter, there was no way that she would be able to convince the old wizard that sending her to Devil's Melt was a good idea.

Looks like Harlow would be staying home safe and sound after all.

CHAPTER SIX

Harlow forced herself to remain silent as Peter leaned back in his giant office chair, stroking his long beard and considering the arguments that both Myles and she had made. She desperately wanted to jump in and say something else in support of her cause, but she had already said everything she had to say. Any words she spoke now would just be repetition of what she'd already said, and Peter would not appreciate her interrupting his thoughts.

Harlow snuck a glance over at Myles, and the scowl on her face deepened. He looked completely serene as he watched Peter with a steady gaze. He looked so sure of himself, confident that he had won this argument. Harlow hated him for his smug expression, mostly because she knew that smug expression was likely justified. Myles had come in here with some impressive research about how deeply into dark magic Saul had ventured. Harlow had to admit that the truth of it was quite frightening. But that didn't change the fact that she thought she was the best one to go steal the records about the dragon amethyst. No matter how deadly the task proved to be, she was the best one for it. She just hoped that Peter would somehow see that, despite Myles' loud insistence otherwise.

"Hmm," Peter said, and Harlow perked up, thinking he was about to make a decision. But he did not speak again, and settled back into thinking. Harlow took a deep breath, and continued to wait. She tried to distract herself by studying the impressive Falcon Cross banners that hung from the ceiling, but it was no use. Her mind was focused on only one thing: what would Peter's decision be.

Harlow had never been in Peter's office before, and, in fact, had never been this close to the great, old wizard. It felt a bit surreal to be sitting across from him now. She knew Myles had met with him several times. All the dragon shifters had, since they were honored guests in Falcon Cross. But it was highly unusual for a junior wizard like Harlow to be sitting in the office of any of the High Council members, let alone the head of the High Council himself. Harlow had needed to work up a great deal of courage to be able to make her way to the old wizard's office, and even more courage to boldly tell him that she should be the one to go to Devil's Melt. And, despite all of that courage, Myles had likely ruined her plans with all his apocalyptic talk about dark magic. Harlow glanced at him again, the anger in the pit of her stomach growing with each passing second.

She had to admit he was damn good looking. And, for a brief period of time this morning, she'd even thought she might be attracted to him. But that feeling had passed quickly enough when he had argued against her in the meeting this morning. Everyone told her that Myles was the most respectful, easygoing man they knew, but Harlow hadn't seen that side of him. He seemed rather strong-willed to her, and set on getting his way.

His way, which just so happens to be the complete opposite of what's actually best for Falcon Cross, Harlow thought. She scowled at him, but he was still staring at Peter and didn't see her. She was still wearing the shirt Myles had given to her this morning, and she wished more than ever that she'd taken time to go home and change. She didn't want to wear his shirt. She didn't want to share his office. She didn't want anything to do with him. He was gorgeous, and that was about the only thing he had going for him. Looks alone weren't enough to make a good friend, coworker, or office mate.

"Well, I've made a decision," Peter announced, suddenly sitting up straight and smiling happily over at both of them as though he'd just heard that they won the lottery. Harlow felt her heart start racing in her chest again. Meanwhile, Myles had his hands folded calmly in his lap, waiting for what was sure to be a decision in his favor. Harlow frowned. Why did he care so much what happened to her, anyway? He had plenty of other things to worry about, like his own clan members.

"I'm going to allow you to take this mission, Harlow," Peter said. Harlow had already opened her mouth to protest what she was sure was not going to be a favorable decision for her. When she heard Peter's words, she almost didn't believe them at first. Her mouth hung open, frozen in place from her shock. It was Myles who spoke first.

"*What*!?" he asked, his voice making no attempt to hide the fact that this was not the decision he had hoped for.

"I'm going to let Harlow take this mission," Peter repeated calmly. "I believe, Harlow, that you are fully aware of the dangers. And there are many dangers. The threat of dark magic is not something to be taken lightly. But you've sat here and listened to Myles describe the horrible possibilities that he's discovered in his research, so you're well aware of what might be facing you. It's very brave of you to still want to go and attempt to retrieve the amethyst records. I only have one caveat for you. You must understand that, should you choose to accept this mission, I cannot guarantee your safety. Devil's Melt is a long ways from here. As far as I know, there are no good wizards within one hundred miles of there. If you run into trouble, it will be up to you alone to use your wits and magic skills to get to safety. There won't be time for any kind of rescue mission. If you understand that, then I will allow you to take the mission with my blessing. I do believe that, as you have said, you are the most qualified person to quickly retrieve the records. If you are willing to do this for Falcon Cross, we will be very much in your debt. I just want to be sure that you understand that it is not in any way required of you to go, and that it will be very dangerous if you do go."

Harlow sat for a moment in silence, dumbfounded by Peter's words. Excitement and adrenaline filled her body as she realized that this was actually happening. Peter, the head High Council wizard, was giving her the mission to go and retrieve the amethyst records. Peter's word was the final say in Falcon Cross. No one, not even Alfonso, could tell her no now.

"Thank you, your Honor," she finally managed to stammer out. "Thank you so much. I do understand the dangers, and I'm willing to face them for the sake of Falcon Cross. I won't let you down, I promise."

"Your Honor, this is ridiculous!" Myles interrupted. "It's not just a dangerous mission if she goes, it's a suicide mission! She'll never come out alive. You're sending her to her death!"

"Enough, Myles," Peter said before Harlow could even open her mouth to respond. "My decision is final. Harlow will go to Devil's Melt to retrieve the amethyst records."

"Thank you, your Honor," Harlow said again, then stood. "I won't take up any more of your time. You've been most kind."

Harlow knew better, but she couldn't resist shooting Myles a smug look as she turned toward the door. So what if Myles didn't think she had what it took for this mission? Peter believed in her, so nothing else mattered. She would show them all what she was capable of.

Myles face had a tortured look on it. He almost appeared nauseated, which surprised Harlow a bit. He was taking his defeat much harder than she'd thought he would. Once again, she thought of how wrong everyone seemed to be about his "easygoing" nature.

She turned away from him as she reached for the door handle. He could be upset all he wanted. It wouldn't change a thing. She had a mission to plan and pack for. But then, just as she started to open the door, he said four words that stopped her in her tracks.

"I'm going with her."

Harlow turned around to look at him with ice in her eyes. "You're not invited," she said through clenched teeth. Who did he think he was? Just because he was an oh-so-special dragon shifter didn't mean he could join whatever old mission he wanted to.

"I don't care whether I'm invited or not," he said, standing up now. His height seemed more intimidating in that moment than it ever had before. "It's not safe for you to go alone. I could never live with myself if something happened to you and I wasn't at least there to try to stop it."

Harlow rolled her eyes. "As much as I appreciate the sweet sentiment," she said. "I don't need a bodyguard. You'll only slow me down."

"Actually, Harlow," Peter said, standing to his feet now as well. "I think it would be a good idea for Myles to go with you. Dragons are quite good at stealth, believe it or not."

"Or not," Harlow hissed under her breath. Her momentary elation had turned to anger and despair as she looked over at Peter, whose face was looked as jolly as it ever did. He had already made his mind up to allow Myles to go, and she knew it. Still, she couldn't help protesting. She had to at least try to make Peter see that Myles was not needed on the mission, and would only compromise it by being one more person who might ruin their stealth game.

"Your Honor," Harlow said, doing her best to keep her voice neutral and calm. "I do appreciate his offer to help. Truly. But this mission will rely not on strength in numbers but on the ability to sneak into the enemy's lair. More people will only make secrecy harder to maintain. I know the risks and dangers, but I think it's better for the mission that I go alone."

The moment Peter smiled at her, his hands clasped loosely in front of him in a calm, stoic way, Harlow knew all the protests in the world would do no good. Myles would be coming with her.

"You are right, Harlow, that this mission does not depend on strength in numbers. If it did, I would not hesitate to deploy the whole of the Falcon Cross army to ensure its success. Recovering these records is that important. And yes, it requires the utmost abilities in stealth. But I promise you that Myles, and all of his clan members, in fact, are very skilled at this type of thing. And although I can tell that you were hoping to work solo, there may come a day very soon where you will be glad for the company of a dragon. They are more useful than you might think. Myles will go with you."

Peter still looked as jolly as ever, but the determination in his eyes told Harlow that his decision was final. As much as she wanted to continue to argue and protest, she knew it was no use. As it was, she had already stepped out onto dangerous ground by making her first protest. It had been hammered into her brain since she was a little girl that you respect the decisions of High Council members without question. Who was she, a junior employee at the Advocacy Bureau, to question the head of the High Council?

And so, despite the anger and frustration boiling just below the surface, she forced herself to keep a calm, pleasant expression on her face.

"As you wish, your Honor," she said. Then, without another word or look aimed in Myles direction, she turned and left the room.

To her surprise and embarrassment, hot tears started to fill her eyelids as soon as she stepped into the hallway. She walked briskly, keeping her eyes open wide and unblinking in an attempt to will the tears away. She just had to make it to her car, and she could fall apart as much as she wanted to. The last thing she wanted was to let anyone here in High Council Hall see her cry. Not when she had just been entrusted with what might be the most important mission of her life. She had to be strong, and get her emotions in check.

Just why those emotions were bubbling up so uncontrollably within her was not entirely clear to Harlow. She was not the crying type, and yet, this was the second time today that she was feeling traitorous tears welling up in her eyes. Myles was affecting her in strange ways, she decided. Having him along on this mission was going to be a disaster.

Just then, she heard the sound of pounding, running footsteps far behind her in the hallway.

"Harlow, wait!" a voice called. It was Myles. "Harlow, please, just wait for a moment."

Harlow felt the frustration in her core rise to an impossible level. Why couldn't he just leave her alone? With an angry grunt, and without even looking back at him, she broke into a run herself.

She had to get away from Myles Pars.

CHAPTER SEVEN

Myles pumped his legs faster and faster in a desperate attempt to catch up with Harlow. He was an incredible runner, but she was pretty fast herself—and she had a significant head start on him. He gained steadily on her, but he wasn't sure he'd be able to catch her before she got to her car. If she made it behind the wheel before he could get to her, there was no way he could catch her. He could run fast, but unless he shifted into dragon form and flew, he could never hope to outpace a car.

He ignored the strange looks everyone gave him as he sped through the Great Hall's entrance. Harlow and he must have made quite a curious sight: an angry speeding wizard and a determined, pursuing dragon shifter.

Everyone in town had an opinion on the dragon shifters. Most people viewed them with a mixture of awe and reverence, looking at them as saviors who had come to save Falcon Cross from Saul, the most formidable enemy the wizarding village had seen in centuries. But there were still those here who remained skeptical of the dragon shifters, and Myles was sure that if any of those group were watching him now, they were no doubt shaking their head in disgust at him, assuming that whatever strange argument this shifter and wizard were having, it was all his fault.

But *was* it all his fault, Myles wondered as he continued to chase Harlow, his legs burning as she disappeared out the front door of the building several seconds ahead of him. He did his best to speed up even more, but he was already going as fast as his legs would carry him. She might be furious with him for inviting himself along on his mission, but she had been the one to insist on taking on this ludicrous mission in the first place. He was somewhat angry with her for going behind his back to talk to Peter. Alfonso would surely be furious, too.

The thought crossed Myles' mind that he didn't have a right to be angry with Harlow. After all, they might be office mates and they might both be working on the amethyst project, but that was where their relationship ended. If she wanted to go get herself killed in the middle of Devil's Melt, what concern of it was his, really? There were hundreds upon hundreds of wizards here in Falcon Cross. Why did it matter so much to him what happened to one particularly obstinate wizard?

Myles was just beginning to admit to himself the reason. He was falling for her, and he knew it. He had tried to ignore the growing desire for her that seemed to rise and swell from deep within him, but it was no use. He'd been falling for her since the day he met her, no matter how much he tried to deny it. Perhaps that's why he had been so tense around her. His clan had dubbed him the champion of calm, thanks to his easygoing nature. But the last few days, he'd been anything but calm. He'd been on edge, and even though he tried to blame it on the stress of work, he'd known he was lying to himself. He'd been stressed out over work before, and never reacted like this. It wasn't work driving him crazy. It was Harlow.

Myles burst through the front door of the Great Hall just in time to see Harlow rounding the corner of the building to the left. With a grunt, he started flying down the long steps, hoping that her car was not parked too close. If he had just another minute or two, he thought he could catch her. His heart beat wildly in his chest, both from the effort of running and from the emotions filling him as he considered what, exactly, his feelings for Harlow might mean.

It was not possible that she was his lifemate, was it? He had never felt this strongly about a woman, and yet, he'd never had a woman push him away as much as Harlow had. She had briefly seemed to soften toward him this morning, but that had ended the moment he agreed with Alfonso that Harlow should not go to Devil's Melt. And, after the meeting with Peter today, Myles would be surprised if Harlow deigned to talk to him for quite some time. To say that she was displeased that he would be coming along on the mission was an understatement.

But what else could Myles have done? He would have been useless if he stayed here, spending every waking moment worrying about Harlow and wondering if she'd been hurt or killed. There was a deep, almost unbearable need within him to protect her. How could he do that if she was off in Devil's Melt, facing down the threat of Saul's men and dark magic all by herself?

Myles had rounded the corner of the building now, and he could see Harlow racing toward the spot where her little red coupe was parked. He ignored the burning protests of his leg muscles and pushed forward with everything in him. If he was lucky, he would make it just in the nick of time to stop her. For a few moments, all he focused on was running. He was getting closer and closer to Harlow, and she seemed to be growing tired, and slowing slightly.

She had to slow even more to pull her keys out of her pocket and open her door. Despite Myles' best efforts, she managed to shut the door behind her and lock it a split second before he got to her. He was not going to be deterred yet, though. He was determined to talk to her. In a flash, he jumped up onto the hood of the car, and positioned himself right in front of the driver's window.

"Just let me talk to you for a minute!" he yelled. "I know you can hear me in there."

In response, she merely started honking her horn like crazy. When he still didn't move, she fired up the engine. She looked at him with fury in her eyes and honked one more time, then started driving. Myles held on tightly. If she thought he was going to be scared off by being on the hood of a moving car, she was wrong. He'd been in situations more dangerous than this hundreds of times during his missions to recover dragon artifacts. He could handle much worse. Besides, she wasn't going to be able to drive very fast with him sitting right in front of her and blocking her view out the front window. She tried to move forward, revving the engine a bit in an attempt to scare him, but he didn't flinch.

"Just let me talk to you," Myles yelled again.

"Just leave me alone!" she said. She looked like an angry hornet, but still, Myles stupidly persisted.

"I'll leave you alone if you talk to me for a minute," he said.

In response, she laid on her horn, long and loud. The two of them must have made quite a scene, and were drawing even more stares now than they had been when running through the Great Hall. Myles did his best to ignore the growing crowd, but he was starting to worry that this little display he was putting on might not be the best idea. He was pretty sure he wasn't winning any new dragon shifter fans right now. And yet, it was so hard to tear himself away from Harlow. If she would just hear him out, perhaps she would come to understand that he was only insisting on coming on the mission because he cared about her.

"You're not gonna win this battle," a laughing voice to his left said.

Somewhat startled, Myles looked over and saw an old wizard standing on the nearby sidewalk. The wizard was wearing traditional wizard robes in a deep purple color. He also wore a traditional wizard hat in the same shade of purple, its long pointy top reaching high above his head. The man's eyes twinkled with unbridled amusement and he let out a soft chuckle as he looked over at Myles' predicament.

Myles was tempted to tell the man to mind his own business, but he couldn't bring himself to yell at an older man. It had been drilled into him too deeply to respect his elders. So, instead, he settled for asking, "What do you mean?" through clenched teeth. The man's smile widened.

"I mean, son, that you need to be able to recognize when a woman needs space. I'd say this young lady is giving you clear indications that she doesn't want to talk to you right now. You need to honor that. Pushing a woman to talk to you when she really doesn't want to is only going to make you both frustrated. Trust me on that. I've had a few years' experience. The way to her heart isn't to push her so hard that you push her away."

The man winked at Myles, and Myles found himself growing even more frustrated.

"I appreciate the advice, sir," Myles said, doing his noble best to keep his voice from filling with rage. "But this is about a matter of state business. It's not about trying to win her heart."

"Oh?" the old man said, the amused expression never leaving his eyes. "You could have fooled me."

Myles felt a strange sensation in his stomach when the old man said those words. It was almost as if the words had been a punch in the gut, and Myles knew why: it was because they were true. With a frustrated growl, Myles hopped off of Harlow's hood. They would have to have a conversation at some point, but now was not the time. Not with a crowd of people gathering to watch, and an old man giving Myles advice on how to win a girl's heart.

After Myles hopped off the hood, Harlow gave a short, triumphant honk of the car's horn. As she started to pull away, she rolled down her window slightly and shouted at him.

"You had no right!" she said. "This is *my* mission."

Myles sighed as he watched her drive away.

"It wasn't about whether I had the right or not," he whispered after her. "Can't you see that? It was about the fact that my heart gave me no choice but to throw myself into the ring to protect you."

There was, of course, no answer from her rapidly disappearing tail lights.

* * *

Four days later, as their small commuter plane touched down on the runway of Devil's Melt Municipal Airport, there had still been no answer from Harlow. Not really, anyway. She had taken on an air of absolute professionalism, and would speak to him whenever it was necessary for them to communicate regarding their plans for the mission to get the amethyst records. But if there was not a professional reason for her to be speaking to him, she would not talk to him. A thinly veiled anger hung behind her eyes, and Myles' patience itself was beginning to grow thin. He even thought a few times that perhaps he'd been wrong about her, and she was more of a spoiled brat than an intelligent, strong woman.

It was, however, difficult to actually ignore her intelligence or strength. She had plenty of both. Yesterday, on the eve of their journey, Peter had taken time to practice a few defensive spells with Harlow. An invitation like that from the leading High Council wizard himself was considered quite an honor, and it showed how seriously Peter took this mission. Myles had been invited to watch, so that he would better understand how the spells worked if Harlow needed to use them out on the field. As Peter put Harlow through her paces, Myles had been impressed all over again with her abilities. Peter did not go easy on her—after all, Saul's army would not go easy on her. She needed to be prepared. But Harlow had risen to the occasion. She had moved with lightning speed, rapidly deploying shield spells and deflecting spells to counter every attack Peter threw at her. Her magic ring had seemed to glow as she practically danced across the room, her face scrunched up in perfect concentration. Myles could not have torn his eyes off of her if he'd wanted to.

But he didn't want to. He wanted to watch her forever. She was beautiful beyond anything he'd ever seen. And somehow, he'd managed to piss her off. He was the guy that everyone got along with. *Everyone.* So it frustrated him to no end that the one person he most wanted to be on good terms with seemed to hate him.

Myles forced his mind into the present moment as the small plane's brakes brought it to a grinding halt on the short runway. It turned to taxi toward the hangar, where a car would be waiting to take Myles and Harlow to their hotel. At six seats, the plane wasn't the smallest one Myles had ever been in, but it was close. It was used primarily to shuffle tourists from the nearest major city into Devil's Melt. The pilot had told Myles that the plane made the trip several times a day during the summer. In the winter, it was not uncommon for a whole month to go by with no trips to Devil's Melt. Not many tourists made their way to this sleepy northern Montana town in the middle of the desolate cold.

The pilot let Myles sit in the copilot seat, and tried to pry him with questions about what his business was in Devil's Melt. Myles kept things as vague as he could, passing it off as research for a report on the seasons of Montana. Myles had thought this was somewhat of a lame excuse, but the pilot had seemed to buy it, and had started prattling on about what his favorite seasons were and why. Now, as Myles and Harlow deplaned from the small aircraft, the pilot shook their hands and wished them luck, letting them be on their way with little fanfare.

Myles drove the rental car to the hotel, and Harlow rode the whole fifteen minutes in silence with him. Myles had to stifle back a sigh as they made their way into the snowy parking lot. He was doing his best to ignore Harlow's icy attitude, but it was getting harder and harder the more they were alone together.

Huge snowflakes began pelting the windshield as Myles pulled the car to a stop, and he raised his eyes to look at the cold, gray sky. It had been snowing off and on ever since Myles and Harlow had landed in Montana, and Myles had seen a blizzard forecasted for that evening. He'd hoped that they'd be able to get started on their mission early tomorrow morning, but it didn't look like that was likely to happen. Not with such a huge storm rolling in.

Myles checked them into the hotel, which was quite a sleepy place at the moment. In the summer, it would fill up with tourists and the bright neon "No Vacancy" sign out front would be illuminated almost nonstop from June to August. Now, however, Myles and Harlow appeared to be the only people here. Their car was the only one gracing the parking lot, and the man at the check in had seemed very excited to hear that they would be renting out two rooms instead of just one. Myles had almost laughed at the thought of asking Harlow to share a room with him. If he'd tried that, she might have actually broken her icy silence—in order to say a few choice words to him.

Their rooms were next to each other on the first floor, conveniently right in front of where Myles had parked the car. Without bothering to ask if she needed help, Myles grabbed Harlow's duffel bag from the trunk and carried it into her room for her. She followed him, said a curt thank you, and then waited expectantly for him to leave the room. He hesitated, glancing at his watch to see what time it was. He was starving, but right now it was only three in the afternoon. Too early for dinner.

"Did you need something?" Harlow asked. Her voice was not exactly cold, but it didn't have much warmth in it either. Her eyes looked tired, and Myles realized that she was probably exhausted from the preparation for this trip, as well as from traveling.

"I know you probably want to rest a bit, but I thought perhaps we could meet in an hour or so to discuss our plans. And then maybe we could grab dinner? I know I'm not your favorite person right now, but you do have to eat. And we have to work together so we might as well make the most of it."

"We have to work together because you insisted on coming on this trip," Harlow said, crossing her arms. "I'll be civil, but I'm not interested in fraternizing with you. I don't want to be all chummy and go to dinner together and such."

Myles sighed. "Fine," he said in a weary tone. "No dinner, then. But I do think we should get together to discuss our plans now that we're here. How does an hour from now sound?"

"It sounds fine," Harlow said. "I'll see you then. Now, if you don't mind, I'd like to rest for a bit."

Myles nodded and moved to leave the room. His heart felt heavier than it had in a long time. He realized that he'd hoped that being out here by himself with Harlow would somehow improve things between them, but so far it seemed to be having the opposite effect. He walked into his own room and closed the door behind him, looking forlornly out at the snow swirling around the window. He had to remind himself that his motivation to come on this trip was not so that he could become best friends with Harlow. It was to protect her from the harm that was coming their way as soon as Saul's people had the slightest inclination that they were here.

Myles got up and went to open the backpack he had brought along with him, pulling the laptop out of the bag and setting it on the small hotel room desk to power it up. He was tired, but he already knew he wouldn't be able to take a nap with so many troubled thoughts swirling through his brain. He might as well get some work done.

He immediately immersed himself in reviewing all of Harlow's notes on the locations where Saul's men had already been in their search for the dragon stone. Myles had marked these locations on a map of the area as best he could, hoping to be able to make some sort of guess as to where the group would be going next. The first thing Harlow and Myles needed to do was to track down the group. Then they could work on sneaking into the group's camp to find the amethyst records. Figuring all of this out was no easy task, since the group seemed to be moving fairly quickly across the region. There was the possibility that Saul's men had some sort of stationary base camp where they received and kept supplies. Many of the conversations Harlow had managed to record and eavesdrop on had implied that this was the case, but Harlow had never been able to find out exactly where such a base camp might be located.

Myles suspected that it was somewhere near here, the city of Devil's Melt Proper. It would make sense, because this would be the easiest area to fly in supplies. It bothered him a bit, though, that the pilot who had flown in Harlow and him hadn't mentioned any other flights. Surely, even if the pilot had not been the one actually flying supplies in, he would have noticed the extra winter activity at the airport. It was possible that Saul's men were subsisting on hardly any supplies, but Myles wondered if perhaps the pilot knew more about what was going on around here than he let on.

Harlow and Myles could not be too careful.

Myles continued working, becoming so engrossed in his work that he barely noticed that almost a full hour had ticked by. He checked and rechecked the map, and studied Harlow's notes, hoping to glean some new information that he had not seen before. But nothing he read shed any new light on their situation, until he looked at the map one last time before going to meet with Harlow. As he looked back and forth between Harlow's notes and the map that she had marked up, he noticed a discrepancy between the marks on the map and the location descriptions from the conversation transcripts. Frowning, he corrected the marks on the map, and suddenly everything made sense.

With the incorrect markings, the map had seemed to show an erratic pattern of searching by Saul's men. But with the corrected marks, it was easy to see that Saul's men were moving in a definite pattern—a pattern that made it potentially possible to predict where they would be heading next. Excitedly, Myles double checked his work just to be sure. It was easy to see how Harlow had made the mistake. Some of the locations were very similar, and she was under a lot of stress and hadn't slept well for days. But Myles was sure now that he was right, and the new pattern made it look like Saul's men should be coming right back by Devil's Melt Proper very soon.

Myles jumped up to go take the paper over to Harlow and show her, his heart beating with excitement. Perhaps finding Saul's men wouldn't be as difficult as he'd originally thought it would be.

Before Myles could even get his shoes on, though, there was a knock at the door. Myles opened it to find Harlow standing there, looking annoyed.

"I thought you were coming to my room," she said, stepping into Myles' room. "Did I misunderstand?"

"Uh…I don't think we ever said, actually," Myles said, glancing again at his watch and seeing that it was now several minutes past the time when Harlow and he were supposed to meet. She hmphed and sat down on the edge of the hotel bed, seeming to be in an even worse mood than she had been earlier. Myles smiled, though, thinking that the news he was about to share with her might cheer her up.

"Anyway, the meeting place is not that important," Myles said. "I made a big discovery, Harlow. You're not going to believe it but it turns out the map we've been using to study the location of Saul's army contains flaws."

"Flaws?" Harlow asked.

Myles nodded his head vigorously. "You accidentally misplaced a mark on one of the locations, which had thrown the whole map off. I caught it and corrected the error, and now you can see a definite pattern in the way Saul's men are moving. Here, look."

Myles thrust the map at Harlow, and she took it, staring down at it with a doubtful look.

"Look," Myles said, pointing to a spot on the map. "The black line is the path we originally thought Saul's men were taking. This red line is the corrected path. See how it's more of a predictable pattern? And look, if they continue following the pattern, they should be coming by here very soon. We might be able to catch up with them sooner than we thought."

Myles looked up at Harlow as she took in the lines on the map. He'd expected her to be excited once she realized what the map showed, but her frown only deepened as she looked down at the map.

"This can't be right," she said. "I checked over this several times."

"I know you did," Myles said. "And most of the map was correct. It was just this one little error you made that threw the whole thing off. It was an easy error to make—especially with all the work you've been putting in lately. See how the location descriptions are really similar? But this one is actually the correct one."

Myles pointed to the red, corrected line that he had drawn on the map and waited patiently for Harlow to see what he was talking about. But after looking at it for several long moments, she shook her head and handed it back to him.

"I don't see what you're saying," she said, crossing her arms. "The original line still looks correct to me."

Confused, and feeling slightly embarrassed, Myles looked down at the map again, trying to see whether he had indeed been wrong to think that the original markings on the map were wrong. But no, as he looked over the map and notes again, he was sure that he was right. He looked up at Harlow, whose arms were still crossed, and eyed her somewhat incredulously. Was she legitimately refusing to see the truth? Myles knew she was not a dumb person. There's no way she was actually just not understanding what he was saying to her. Maybe she felt bad that she had made a mistake?

"Harlow, no one is going to fault you for making an error like this," Myles said. "I didn't bring it up to rub it in your face. I brought it up because now that I see it, I think finding our enemies here will be much easier than we originally thought it would be. This is good news. I thought you'd be happy about it."

But Harlow's eyes flashed with anger as she looked up at Myles. "I don't need you to give me good news," she said. "I don't need you to do anything for me. I just want you to leave me alone. You didn't want me to come out here in the first place. Are you just looking for proof of my failures now?"

Myles was taken aback. And then, he started to feel angry himself. He'd tried to be nice, but this had gone too far, and he had reached his breaking point.

"Bullshit, Harlow," Myles said. "You're a smart girl, and a very hard worker, but if you aren't willing to be a team player then what does it matter? This search for the dragon amethyst is so much bigger than just you and me. The future of the shifter and wizard worlds is hanging in the balance here, in case you hadn't noticed. I'm sorry if it hurts your pride that you made a mistake, but I think you'd better swallow that pride and think about the bigger implications here. This isn't just about you."

Myles had risen to his feet, and he was practically yelling at this point. He didn't care anymore, though, about sparing Harlow's feelings. Perhaps he'd been too impressed with her beauty and intelligence to see how whiny and self-centered she actually was. He still cared about her safety, and he would still do his best to protect her while she was here on this mission. But he was done walking on eggshells around her. She needed to grow up.

To his surprise, she didn't yell back at him. She stared at him in shock for a few moments, then stood slowly to her feet and laid the marked up map down on the desk.

"I need to go," she said quietly. "I think we'd better reschedule our little work session for later."

Myles would have yelled at her again, except for the fact that her voice had broken slightly when she spoke. She was obviously working very hard not to cry at the moment. He wasn't sure whether he wanted to yell at her some more or take her in his arms.

Damn it, Myles, he thought to himself. Didn't you *just* tell yourself that you were done tiptoeing around her feelings?

He didn't have much time to ponder that question, though, because in the next instant she started running for the door, bursting into tears as she did. Before he could think about what he was doing, Myles grabbed her arm and held her back.

"Stop," he said, putting his body between hers and the door. He had his back to the door, and so was standing face to face with her now. She refused to look him in the eye as tears started spilling down her face, and Myles knew in his gut that these were not the tears of a whiner, or of a weak woman. These were the tears of someone who felt deep pain. But why, exactly? This must be over more than just a simple mistake on a map. Slowly, Myles reached his hand underneath Harlow's chin and tilted it upward so that she was forced to meet his eyes.

"What's really going on here, Harlow?" he asked. She sighed, shuddered, and then cried some more. Myles waited patiently, not letting her look away. If it took all night, he would stay here until she talked. There was a blizzard outside and nowhere for them to be, really. He could wait. They both needed to clear the air between them if this mission was going to be a success.

And failure was not an option.

CHAPTER EIGHT

Harlow desperately wanted to get her emotions under control, but the more she told herself to get it together, the more she seemed to fall apart. She wished Myles would let her escape, but he had made it clear from the way he was blocking the whole door with his body that he had no intention of letting her go anywhere until she told him why she was crying.

The way he'd put his hand under her chin wasn't helping things much, either. His touch had filled her with an intense warmth, and her heart was doing funny things in her chest. The realization that she still felt some sort of passion for him, despite the fact that they'd barely been on speaking terms for most of the time they'd known each other, only added to the confused mess of emotions swirling within her.

She felt ashamed that he'd found such a blatant error in her maps. She'd tried so hard to make everything perfect, and she had failed. Not only that, but her failure had been discovered by Myles, the one person who she wanted to prove herself to more than anyone else.

But why? Why did it matter so much to her what he thought of her? Was it really because she wanted to show him that she didn't need his help? Or was it that she felt something deeper for him and was afraid to admit it to herself? Harlow didn't even know herself anymore. But as she looked up at Myles, her chin trembling from his fiery touch, she decided that perhaps the best way to sort through this was to at least tell Myles what little she did know for sure. And so, she took a deep breath and began speaking.

"I love Falcon Cross so much," she said. "I've never told you this, but I'm an orphan, just like you."

Harlow saw Myles raise an eyebrow in surprise. He and all of the Redwood Dragons were orphans. They had lost their parents in a shifter war a few decades ago, and had all been rescued and raised by the same older dragon shifter.

"I had no idea," Myles said, his voice softening somewhat. "I'm sorry. Sometimes I forget that my clan is not the only one that has suffered great tragedy."

Harlow gave a little wave, as if to wave away Myles' apology. "It's ok," she said. "My parents died a long time ago, so even though I still miss them, of course, the wound is not fresh. It was a freak accident, where a magic spell went wrong and killed my mom. My dad tried to save her, and the spell affected him in the process. I was part of a different clan at the time, and after the accident, no one would talk to me. They all thought I was cursed. I escaped, and ended up in Falcon Cross after meeting some Falcon Cross scouts in the forest. The scouts were kind to me, as were all the people of Falcon Cross. They took me in as their own, and I'm forever in their debt. Who knows where I'd be today if not for them."

Myles was quiet for a moment, staring at her and taking in everything she'd just said. Finally, he simply said, "Wow."

Harlow bit her lower lip, trying to keep it from trembling, but it was a difficult task. The emotion flooding through her was not easily contained. But she forced herself to take a deep, shuddering breath, and then continued.

"I owe my life to Falcon Cross, and that's why I decided to become an Advocate. Advocacy school required a tremendous amount of work, but it was the best way I knew of to serve the clan I love, and repay them just a little bit for everything they've done for me."

"Advocacy is a noble profession," Myles said. "It's one of the most prestigious jobs in the wizarding world. Even I can tell that, and I'm still pretty new at learning about the ways of wizards. But what does this have to do with being so upset about my coming with you on this mission? Or with being devastated by making a simple error on a map."

Myles dropped his hand from her chin now and leaned backward against the hotel door, looking expectantly at her as he waited for her reply. The fact that he had stopped making contact with her body made it easier to concentrate, but Harlow couldn't help but feel a rush of disappointment that he was no longer touching her. She pushed away the feeling and pressed on with her explanation.

"I've worked my ass off as an Advocate because I wanted to prove that saving me was worthwhile. I wanted to show the people of Falcon Cross that they made a good decision when they saved me. I've had a lot of success in my career—"

"Yeah, you have," Myles interrupted. "For someone as young and junior as you are at the Advocacy Bureau, you've been given quite an impressive array of assignments. Alfonso might be acting like a jerk lately, but he knows you're a damn good worker. He wouldn't have given you all of those assignments if he didn't think so."

"I know," Harlow said reluctantly. "But even though I've worked hard and been successful, I still haven't managed to do anything *that* amazing. I want to do something spectacular. Something that will really show once and for all that I'm an invaluable member of Falcon Cross."

"So you wanted to find the amethyst records by yourself, to prove you could do it," Myles said, finally catching on.

Harlow nodded. "I thought that if I could do this one thing all by myself, that everyone in Falcon Cross would think of it every time they see me from now on. Instead of seeing the orphaned girl who had to leave her own clan for fear of a curse, they would see the top Advocate in Falcon Cross, who saved the village from the dangers of Saul's army getting to the dragon amethyst first."

"But then I insisted on coming, so you had to share the spotlight," Myles said quietly. Harlow could see understanding dawning on his face.

She nodded miserably. "And worse, you found an error in my work. Sure, like you said, it was an easy error to have made. But it proves to me that I did need you, or at least I needed *someone*, on this mission to help me. I can't, in fact, do it on my own."

"Harlow," Myles said, his voice surprisingly soft as he said her name. The sound of it sent a rush of heat through her that was almost stronger than the heat from his actual touch had been. "No one is expecting you to do everything on your own. And I promise you, no one in Falcon Cross thinks that you need to prove anything to them. I guarantee you that when they look at you they don't see a cursed orphan. They see a smart, capable Advocate who has already done great things for her clan."

"How can you know that?" Harlow asked sadly. "It's a nice thing to say, but you barely know me. You haven't been around that long."

"I didn't have to be around very long at all to see that you are someone special," Myles said. "I've heard nothing but good things about you. Everyone at the Advocacy Bureau talks about how smart you are, and what an asset you are to the team. I had no idea that your background involved becoming an orphan and being ostracized from your clan. You know why? Because it doesn't matter. No one cares where you came from. They don't look at you as someone who is less than them, or has something to prove. They look at you as one of the best Advocates, because you are."

Harlow looked down at her feet, not saying anything for a long time. She didn't know what to say. Was it possible that Myles was right? Did the people of Falcon Cross think of her as one of them, and not merely as an outsider to be tolerated? Had she been worrying for nothing, and, worse, treating Myles poorly for no reason? She wanted to believe that what he was saying was true, but it was hard to know what to think right now. She wiped at the wet streaks on her face where tears had been falling, and finally looked up at the dragon shifter in front of her. He was waiting patiently, his deep green eyes looking at her with such an intensity that she felt sure he must be able to see right through her.

"I...I guess I owe you an apology," she said. "I don't know if I can fully accept yet that people don't see me as an outsider. But this whole situation has made me realize that I might be more sensitive about it then I should be."

"You're definitely more sensitive about it than you should be," Myles said, his eyes actually lighting up a bit with amusement.

Harlow sighed, but cracked a smile. "Okay, okay. I've been too sensitive about what people might think of my past, and as a result I lashed out at you and treated you like crap when you offered to come on this mission to protect me. I'm sorry. In fact, for the most part, I've treated you like crap since the first day I met you. I don't suppose we could have a do-over?"

Myles grinned. "We can definitely have a do-over," he said, then stretched out his hand. "I'm Myles, nice to meet you."

Harlow felt a rush of relief and happiness as Myles smiled down at her. "I'm Harlow," she said, smiling sheepishly as she took his hand. "Nice to meet you, too."

"Harlow," Myles said with a wink. "Now that's a nice name. I have a feeling we're going to be friends."

Harlow laughed. "I hope so," she said, and started to pull her hand back from the handshake. But Myles gripped her hand tighter, and pulled her closer to him until their bodies were only inches apart.

"Do you trust me?" he asked, his voice suddenly husky.

Harlow blinked a few times, doing her best to ignore the way heat was flooding her body, radiating out from the hand that Myles was tightly holding.

"I...I..." she stuttered.

"Listen to me," Myles said. "You're damn smart. I know that. I know you have what it takes to find these records. But Saul's army is dangerous. I'll promise to trust you on where to search and how to sneak in for the records, if you trust me to protect you. Don't push me away and act like you don't need me. You do need me. We need each other if this mission is going to be successful.

Harlow felt like she couldn't breathe. Confessing her fears and shortcomings to Myles had felt like a very intimate thing to do, and now, with him standing so close to her and looking at her with unmistakable heat in his eyes, it was all she could do to squeak out an "okay." Myles looked deeply into her eyes, searching. She did her best to meet his gaze, and to say with her eyes the things she could not seem to say aloud with her mouth.

I do trust you, Myles. I need you. I know I can't do this alone, no matter how hard I try.

They stood there for several long moments, their breathing ragged and the air between them heavy with electricity. Harlow saw Myles eyes drop to her lips, and, for a moment, she thought he was going to kiss her. Her heart beat faster at the thought, and her entire body filled with so much heat that she felt like she was on fire. But then, he looked away, and stepped out of the doorway. The moment was over.

"I know we planned to work now instead of getting dinner, but you look tired, and I'm starving. Why don't we see what we can find for food and then call it a night. I know we need to work quickly, and that we're under a lot of time pressure, but I think we'll both be a lot more useful if we get some rest first and start fresh in the morning.

Harlow wasn't about to argue with that. "Alright," she said. "Just let me go change and grab my purse."

Myles nodded, his eyes looking out the window toward the darkening sky and thickly swirling snow. "I'll go ahead and warm up the car," he said. "Meet me there when you're ready?"

Harlow nodded, and scurried off to her room, wincing at the frigid air that hit her face when she opened the door to Myles' hotel room and stepped outside. She had brought plenty of thick winter clothing with her, but she hadn't bothered to put any of it on for the short walk from her hotel room to Myles' room. Now, she almost wished she had, even though the rooms were so close that she only had to be outside for a few seconds. The weather here was brutal, and, she had a feeling the work they were here to do was going to prove to be brutal as well.

And yet, in the space of a few minutes, she had gone from feeling alone out here to realizing that Myles might turn out to be a good friend after all. He'd asked her to trust her, but what he didn't understand was that she had already trusted him by sharing her fears with him. She felt strangely at peace, now that she had confessed her concerns.

But she felt nervous, too. The idea of being alone at dinner with Myles sent a fresh round of butterflies fluttering about her stomach. Try as she might, she could not seem to fully shake the heat and excitement that had begun coursing through her body the moment Myles had first touched her chin.

Perhaps this mission was going to be even more of an adventure than she'd originally thought.

CHAPTER NINE

Myles peered at the sticky, laminated menu that he held in front of him. The food seemed to be fairly standard fare for a diner in a tourist town. Nothing looked extraordinary, but all the basics were available. Burgers, chicken fried steak, salads, and similar dishes were on offer, and Myles scanned over the options several times before settling on a cheeseburger and fries. He hoped the meal would be decent, but it's not like he had any other options. This was the only open restaurant in town, and even the lone grocery store he had driven past on the way here had appeared closed. When Myles had asked their server about it, the girl had shrugged.

"It belongs to Old Man Jenkins," she'd said, as though everyone in the world knew who Old Man Jenkins was. "In the winter, sometimes he shuts it down for a few days at a time just because he doesn't feel like working. If you live here during the winter, you learn to never let your pantry get too empty. You never know when Jenkins will disappear."

This wasn't good news for Myles, who had wanted to grab some fresh food before heading out to try to track down Saul's crew. He crossed his fingers that Old Man Jenkins would be in the mood to work tomorrow, but with the blizzard growing fiercer every second, Myles wasn't holding his breath. The non-perishable food he and Harlow had packed in their duffel bags would probably have to do.

The server was coming back with their drink order now—an iced tea for Myles and a Long Island Iced Tea for Harlow. Myles had raised an eyebrow when his dining companion had ordered such a strong drink, but she had merely shrugged in response.

"The liquor keeps you warm," she'd said.

Myles had let it go, but he had a feeling it wasn't warmth she was looking for as much as something to calm her nerves. She'd been a bit on edge since their conversation in his hotel room earlier, which struck him as a tiny bit odd. He would think that having come clean with her worries about her past would have given her a sense of relief, but the woman sitting in front of him right now, nervously tapping her fingers on the table in front of her, looked anything but relieved. Perhaps she was starting to worry in earnest about facing down Saul's men, Myles thought.

Myles himself was uneasy when he thought about Saul's men. Myles hadn't realized until they landed in Devil's Melt a few hours ago just how deserted the place was during the winter. Any outsiders stuck out like a sore thumb, which means that Saul's crew would have also stuck out like a sore thumb if they came through here. And yet, no one in town had mentioned another group coming through at any time this winter. It seemed to Myles that, as much as the townspeople here liked to talk about how remarkable it was that he and Harlow were visiting in the winter, they would have commented about it if another group had come through here this winter. But they hadn't said a word, which meant one of two things as far as Myles was concerned: either Saul's men had come in a different way and the townspeople had never seen them—a highly unlikely scenario since there were no other airports for hundreds of miles; or, Saul's crew *had* been here, but had paid off the townspeople not to talk about them.

And, Myles thought with a furrowed brow, if the townspeople were on Saul's payroll, they had likely agreed to let Saul's crew know right away if any more strangers came through. Myles frowned. Everyone in town seemed incredibly interested in knowing where he was from and why he was here in the middle of the winter. This could just be natural curiosity, or it could be an attempt to get information to feed back to Saul's men. Myles feared the latter.

There was not much he could do about it at the moment, though. The winds were howling so insistently outside right now that Myles was beginning to worry about whether he and Harlow would even be able to make it back to the hotel tonight. Moving away from town to hide somewhere else was out of the question, at least until this weather cleared a bit. Even a dragon was not strong enough to fly through snow like this. So, Myles contented himself with staring absentmindedly at his menu, and glancing suspiciously up at the server every now and then. At least, if Myles and Harlow were stranded by the blizzard, Saul's men would be stranded, too. Myles and Harlow would be safe in Devil's Melt Proper—for the night, at least.

Their server was taking her sweet time returning to their table, so Myles shifted his attention back to Harlow, who was sipping at her Long Island tea and still drumming the table with her fingers. Her menu was lying flat on the table in front of her, and she was studying it intently, as though it were notes for a final college exam. She seemed oblivious to the fact that Myles was staring at her, and so he indulged his desire to stare.

She was as lovely as ever in the dim light of the diner. Her hair was pulled back in an absolute mess of a bun right now, and she had bags under her eyes from lack of sleep. But even her exhaustion could not hide her beauty, and Myles felt his heart swelling in his chest as he watched her.

They'd had a tumultuous beginning to their relationship, and for a moment he'd thought that they wouldn't be able to salvage a true friendship out of the mess of anger between them. But it had only taken a few sentences of explanation for Myles to understand why Harlow had been acting the way she had. She felt like an outsider, a feeling that Myles was only too familiar with. He had grown up as an orphan, too, and although he'd been lucky enough to be taken in by a wonderful clan of other orphans, he'd always had a sense of not quite belonging. Perhaps that was just his lot in life, to never quite feel at home.

He hadn't asked Harlow how old she'd been when her parents had died, or how long she'd been in Falcon Cross, but it was obvious that she also didn't feel quite at home. Myles had been shocked to learn that one of the best Advocates, and a wizard who had been allowed to take the mission to search for the amethyst records, still felt like she had something to prove. And yet, he understood in a sense. Even though Myles knew his clanmates loved him deeply, he still struggled sometimes not to worry about how well he was fitting in. And that was with an entire clan of misfits! He could only imagine how much harder it would be if his clan mates were not orphans just like him, but rather had been in the clan long before he came along. Myles heart softened even more toward Harlow as he considered this. She'd not had an easy road.

That didn't exactly excuse the times that she'd acted rudely toward him, but it did help explain things a bit. And besides, Myles knew he was not without fault here. He'd said and done some things that qualified as rude and unfriendly, too. Perhaps, the idea of a "do-over" and pretending that they were starting their friendship from scratch was the best idea Harlow had come up with yet. Looking at Harlow now, Myles heart ached to get to know her better, and to reach beyond her somewhat guarded exterior to see what was in her heart.

Were there any feelings for him in there, he wondered? He could not deny that, even in the times that he'd been angry at her, he'd wanted her. He hadn't been able to shake the feeling that they were connected somehow, and he had a suspicion that there was more to it than just physical desire. Her very soul seemed to call to his, and yet, how could that be? It was not feasible that this beautiful, intelligent wizard, with an independent streak a mile wide, might be his lifemate, was it? Was it possible she might really need him, despite her insistence that she could do everything on her own? Even now, after she'd agreed to trust him and admitted that she did need help, her eyes still had a determined, independent look in them. Myles felt a strange mixture of emotions filling his heart, but he wasn't sure how to define them. The thought came to his mind that perhaps this mixture of emotions and desire was what love felt like, but he pushed the thought away. Myles wasn't scared of much, but the word love frightened him a bit.

Their server came and took their food orders, then, and Myles was thankful for the brief distraction. After the server walked away, though, Myles and Harlow were left without even menus to look at. They were somewhat forced to look at each other, and Myles found himself strangely at a loss for words. They couldn't talk about their mission right here in the middle of the restaurant. There was far too much risk that someone would overhear. And their whole tumultuous friendship had revolved around work, so Myles wasn't even sure what sorts of hobbies or other interests Harlow had that she would enjoy talking about. After a few moments of awkward silence, he finally decided to just ask her.

"So, what do you like to do for fun?"

She looked up at him with a bit of a relieved smile, and he gathered that she had been trying to figure out how to start a conversation, too. It was almost like they were on a first date or something. Myles felt his heart clench up in his chest again at the thought of taking Harlow on a date. Maybe, when this was all over, if they managed to stay friends through this perilous mission, he'd get the chance to take her on a real date. For now, he'd have to settle for a work dinner at a deserted diner in the middle of nowhere.

"I don't have much time for fun these days. Work keeps me quite busy. But when I do have the time, I like to bake. I can make a mean cupcake, let me tell you."

Myles grinned. "I'd love the chance to test one out," he said.

Harlow laughed. "Well, if we ever get out of this godforsaken snow-hole, maybe I'll make some for you. But I'm warning you, they're very dangerous for the waistline. They're so good that it's really hard to stop eating them, and the reason they're so good is they're loaded with calories."

Myles laughed. "Sounds like they're worth it. I'll just have to do a couple extra workouts here and there."

"Oh they're definitely worth it," Harlow said with a grin. "And then my other big hobby, which is much lower in calories than my baking obsession, is magic painting."

"Magic painting?" Myles asked, confused. "That sounds like some sort of arts and crafts project from elementary school."

This brought a loud peal of laughter from Harlow. "It's a lot more complicated than anything I ever did in elementary school, trust me."

Myles saw her glance down at her magic ring, then glance around to make sure their server wasn't too close. Smart girl, Myles thought. She wants to make sure no one here overhears her talking about being a wizard. Satisfied that no one was close by, Harlow continued with her explanation.

"It's a special artistic technique that uses magic spells to produce a stream of paint from your magic ring. It's sort of difficult to do, because you have to aim the streams of paint carefully. If you move your hand too quickly or don't keep it steady, the stream of paint will go where you don't want it to on the canvas."

"It sounds sort of like spray-painting," Myles said.

Harlow smiled. "I guess you could call it spray painting. We just work on big canvasses instead of on concrete walls. Some wizards are really good at it, and have made pretty impressive paintings that look as detailed as a painting made with an actual paintbrush. I'm not quite there yet. Actually, I'm pretty far from there. I only recently took up magic painting, and work makes it hard to get to the classes. I'm determined to continue, though, even if I have to take it slowly."

"There's nothing wrong with taking your time," Myles said. "The circumstances we're in right now are rather unique. Work won't always be this busy. At least, I hope it won't."

Harlow nodded. "I know. I keep telling myself to be patient. I haven't even told you the best part about magic painting yet, though. You see, because the paint is produced by a magic spell, it's magic paint, of course. The spell gives the paint special qualities that allow it to move, even after it's dried on the canvas."

Myles frowned. "It moves on the canvas? I'm not sure I understand."

"It's like a moving picture," Harlow explained. "For example, if you painted a horse in a field, you could paint it in such a way that it would appear to be running across the field. You have to be careful that you apply the paint in the right way, or it won't look right—I've had some pretty funny mess-ups where an animal appeared to be cut in half when it was moving or something like that. But when you do it right, the effect is really cool. I have one painting I made of a sailboat that looks like it's flying across the water, sending sea spray up behind it. I'll have to show it to you when we get back. If we get back, I mean."

Harlow's eyes darkened a bit, and Myles couldn't resist reaching across the table to give her forearm a gentle, reassuring squeeze. "We'll make it back," he promised. "Don't give up before we've even started."

Harlow gave him a brave smile and nodded, but he could see that she was troubled. Myles was troubled, too, if he was honest. The strange looks he kept getting from their server made him uneasy. He was beginning to feel more and more like the looks were stemming from something stronger than just general curiosity. Saul's men were no fools, and Myles began to feel with certainty that he and Harlow were being watched.

He did his best to act as normal as he could during the meal. He laughed and joked with Harlow, keeping their conversation as light as he could. She asked him about his hobbies, and he told her that he studied martial arts in his free time. She seemed surprised by this.

"I would think a dragon wouldn't need to bother with things like martial arts," she said. "After all, when you can turn into such a fierce beast and breathe fire on someone, why would you need to know how to do fancy fighting on the ground?"

Myles just laughed. "It's always good to know as much as possible about how to fight," he said. "I've been on many missions where it benefitted me greatly to not have to shift into dragon form. Besides, I really enjoy learning the techniques and discipline involved in martial arts. The joy of learning is reward enough for me."

"How did you learn, though, if you lived out in the middle of the Redwoods your whole life?" Harlow asked. "There aren't any karate schools out there, are there?"

Myles laughed. "Well, no. You're right about that. The Redwood Dragons' base camp is on the outskirts of civilization, a good distance from any town. But our old clan leader, William, was a fourth degree black belt and taught all of us dragons through pretty much our whole childhoods."

"Oh, wow," Harlow said. "So all of the dragons must be pretty good at martial arts, then."

"Yes, we're all talented fighters, in many disciplines," Myles said. "But I'm one of the best, because I continued on with training even after William left. I'm not as good at fighting in dragon form as some of the other dragons. I've always struggled a bit with controlling my large dragon form as well as the others can. But I can beat almost any of the Redwood Dragons in hand to hand fighting while in human form. The one exception is my clan mate Finn. Finn has continued training in martial arts, too, and he's an even better fighter than I am. I can still beat him at the chameleon trick, though."

"Chameleon trick?" Harlow asked.

"It's the ability to blend perfectly into your surroundings, kind of like a chameleon. All reptile shifters can do it, although chameleon shifters are naturally the best at it."

"Wow. I had no idea you could do that," Harlow said. "It's almost like you guys can all do an invisibility spell, too."

Myles laughed. "Yup, it's sort of like that. Although your magical abilities far outstrip mine, obviously. I'm constantly in awe of what you wizards can do."

Harlow shrugged. "I guess I can see how it would be strange, if the world of wizarding was new to you. But it all seems so normal to me."

"Yeah, well, you grew up as a wizard, surrounded by wizards," Myles said. "I've spent most of my life thinking that wizards no longer existed. It was quite a shock to my system when I found out they did."

Harlow grinned. "Surprise," she said, with another shrug.

Myles smiled at her, then grabbed the last bite of food off his plate. "We should get back to the hotel," he said. "The storm is getting worse, and besides, I don't like the way our server keeps staring at us. We've been talking in fairly quiet voices, so I don't think she's overheard much of what we said, but she seems to be taking an unhealthy interest in us nonetheless."

Harlow frowned, but, to her credit, did not automatically turn around to look at their server. She sat with restrained curiosity instead, her face darkening once more. "Let's get out of here," she said through clenched teeth.

Myles nodded, and motioned for their server to ask for the check. They had already stayed here too long, but he hadn't wanted to leave. He hadn't wanted dinner with Harlow to end. Even though it had only been in a small, sleepy diner, and it hadn't been an official date at all, something about sitting across from her and sharing a meal had felt so wonderful and intimate. He wished they could have continued on with dessert, and maybe another Long Island Iced Tea for her. He would have liked to order a coffee to sip leisurely, warming his body and his soul as he enjoyed her company for a bit longer. But those sorts of unhurried evenings would have to wait. Perhaps, once they got back to Falcon Cross, they could spend more time together, and explore the feelings that were slowly beginning to burn between them. Myles found himself fascinated by Harlow more with every passing minute. Now that she had opened up to him about why she acted as stubbornly as she did, he was intrigued. He wanted to know even more about her, and he wanted to show her that she was perfect just the way she was. But for now, duty called. And that duty required them to focus completely on recovering the amethyst records.

When the check came, Myles paid it all in cash. He never used a credit card when he was out on a mission, if he could avoid it. He had a whole slew of credit cards and I.D. cards with fake names on them, to help him avoid detection when he was out searching for ancient dragon artifacts. But the best way to pay, when possible, was to use cash. It left no trail, not even a fake one.

Myles and Harlow quietly left the diner, walking outside into snow so thick that you could only see a few feet in front of you. Myles' brow creased with worry. It would be slow going getting back to the hotel, and he hoped that things didn't get worse before they arrived. It was already going to be next to impossible to see the road in front of him.

At least, Myles thought as he climbed into the vehicle, this weather would make it impossible for the enemy to find them.

For now.

CHAPTER TEN

Harlow lay in the surprisingly comfortable hotel bed, shivering. She had turned the heat up to what she thought was a generous temperature right before she climbed into bed, but the coldness in the room seemed to be growing, not decreasing. She pulled the thick blankets closer around her and listened to the howling of the wind, willing herself to fall asleep. But sleep was not coming easily tonight. The mixture of the cold room and her unsettled mind made it impossible to drift off.

Harlow's swirling thoughts bounced back and forth between her feelings for Myles, the difficulty of locating the amethyst records, and the dangers of dark magic. Each subject weighed heavily on her mind, and after tossing and turning for over an hour, she got up to check on the thermostat. The room was steadily growing colder, and she was beginning to wonder if she had accidentally turned the heat off instead of higher.

She cursed as she stubbed a toe on the foot of the bed in the darkness, then hobbled over to flip the light switch on. When she flipped it, however, nothing happened. She cursed again as she flipped the switch back and forth with no result. Frowning, she felt around in the darkness for her duffel bag. When she found it, she dug around in it until she found the small flashlight that she knew was in there. She turned the beam on, flooding the small hotel room with a sudden burst of light. She swung the beam around, and saw that there was a lamp on the nightstand by the bed. She walked over and turned the switch on the lamp, but nothing happened. She walked over to the lamp on the desk and tried to switch it on, but again nothing happened.

Harlow swung her flashlight beam toward the thermostat on the wall, walking over to look at the digital display. The screen was completely dark. She pushed a few buttons, but nothing happened.

"Power's out," she announced dejectedly to the empty room. No wonder she'd been so cold. She went to the window and peered out, but the darkness was so thick out there that she might as well have been looking at a black wall. There were no streetlights, or at least none that she could see. Perhaps the power outage had affected the streetlights too, or perhaps the snow was too thick to allow the light of any streetlamps to shine all the way to her window. Harlow shivered as she shined her flashlight into the darkness, pressing it against the window so that the light would shine outward instead of being reflected back into the room. The light revealed that the snow was still swirling, thicker than ever.

With a frustrated grunt, Harlow stepped away from the window and looked around her room. She was already wearing thick flannel pajamas and woolen socks, but it wasn't enough to keep the cold at bay, even when she had been huddled under the thick comforter. She frowned and used her flashlight to look over her cold weather gear. If she put on her thick outdoor clothes she would probably be okay, but she wasn't sure how comfortable she would be. She could heat her room using a magic spell, but she needed to get some sleep. She wouldn't be able to keep the spell going while she slept, which meant she would soon be waking from cold again. Harlow glanced toward the dark window again, and decided that she needed to try to get to Myles' room. Perhaps

306

he had power. If not, he was probably freezing, too. Perhaps if they huddled together in one bed and shared their body heat, they would be warm enough to actually get some sleep. Harlow's face blushed bright pink at the thought of snuggling up close to Myles in bed. Try as she might to tell herself that she was thinking about lying next to him strictly to keep warm, she couldn't deny that there was a small part of her that wondered what it would feel like to have his body pressed against hers. The more she tried to push thoughts of desire for Myles out of her mind, the more they seemed to fight their way in. She stood up straight and abruptly walked over to put her outdoor gear on. The longer she thought about it, the more confused she was going to make herself. She needed to get over her own feelings and just go over there, like a grown adult, and see if Myles' had heat or not. She might not even need to sleep in his bed, if his room still had power and heat. Each of their rooms had two double beds, so she would just take the other bed if the room was warm.

Harlow quickly bundled up against the cold outside, then went to the door, took a deep breath, and opened it. The blast of cold that greeted her was far more intense than even the frigid cold of her hotel room. Angry snow swirled around her, forcing its way into her room and into her eyes as she struggled to pull her hotel room's door shut behind her. She felt a momentary rush of fear as she realized just how dark and snowy it was outside. Even if she held her hand up a few inches from her face, it was difficult to see. She frowned and took a deep breath to steady her nerves. She had her magic ring on. If she needed to shoot out a blast of fire to melt the snow in front of her, she could. She'd either have to take her glove off to do it, or ruin her glove, but at least she knew she had the option.

Harlow placed her hand against the exterior wall of the hotel room, and started slowly walking in the direction of Myles' hotel room door. The door was the very next one, and not far at all. She should reach it soon, and then, hopefully, Myles would be able to hear her knocking.

Harlow struggled along determinedly until she felt the knob of the next door with her thickly gloved hand. It wouldn't do much good to knock with her hand right now. The thickness of her gloves would completely muffle the sound. Instead, she kicked with her heavy boots, keeping a steady rhythm as she pounded against the thick door. Kick, kick, kick. She waited a few moments, but the only response was the swirling of the snow outside around her. So she tried again. Kick, kick, kick.

Again, she waited, and again, there was no answer. Shivering and muttering, she struggled to pull her glove off her right hand, where she wore her magic ring firmly on her finger.

"*Magicae amplificare*," she yelled out, then started kicking again. The amplifying spell made the noise of her kicking several times louder. Only a few moments later, the hotel room door swung open and Myles dragged her in. He was wearing pajamas, but looked wide awake and alert. His eyes darted back and forth, looking behind her and trying to see what threat might be lurking in the dark, swirling snow. But, seeing nothing, he slammed the door shut behind her and deadbolted it.

"Harlow? What in the world are you doing?" he asked.

She shivered in response and tried to shake some warmth into her ungloved hand, which had turned stiff and blue with alarming speed once exposed to the elements.

"*Amplificare terminantur. Magicae therma*," she said, first ending the amplifying spell and then starting a heat spell. Instantly warmth emanated from her ring, quickly thawing out her frozen hand. Once that had been taken care of, she looked around the darkness of the room, and realized that, although it was warm compared to the temperature outdoors, it did not feel much warmer than her room had felt. Then she saw Myles flipping the light switch for the main light in his room, with no response from the lamps.

"What the…" he said.

Harlow was pulling off her heavy woolen face mask so she could speak more clearly. "The power's out," she said. "I wasn't sure if it was just my room or yours as well. It must be the whole hotel."

"Probably the whole town," Myles said, his frown looking exaggerated in the long shadows created by Harlow's flashlight. "Blizzard must have caused an outage."

"How did you not feel the cold in here?" Harlow asked, looking doubtfully at Myles' pajamas. They didn't seem to be any thicker than the ones she'd been wearing. "I couldn't sleep because of the chill."

Myles shrugged. "It's my dragon genes," he said. "They keep me pretty warm, and my internal temperature automatically begins to rise if the air around me is too cold."

"You mean you have an internal heater?" Harlow asked, her jaw dropping slightly. That sort of thing would come in pretty useful for him on their mission. She was quickly seeing that winter in Northern Montana was no joke.

"I guess you could call it a heater," Myles said. "If you think about it, it makes sense. I can breathe fire, after all. That requires my body to be able to produce quite a bit of heat."

Harlow nodded slowly, then a fresh shudder of shivers ran across her body.

"You're freezing," Myles observed, stating the obvious. Harlow would have rolled her eyes at him if she hadn't been shivering so violently.

"I couldn't sleep in my room," she said. "It was too cold. I thought I'd come over here and see if you by chance still had power, but it seems you don't."

She didn't mention that she had also thought that perhaps they could huddle together to keep warm. Now that she was standing directly in front of Myles, who was decidedly not shivering and looked unbearably handsome in his flannel pajama pants and long-sleeved gray t-shirt, Harlow found herself feeling quite shy. She couldn't bring herself to actually make the suggestion. Luckily, she didn't have to.

"You should sleep in the same bed as me," Myles was saying firmly, already taking her hand and leading her further away from the hotel door. "Don't worry, I'm not trying to make a move on you or anything. But if you huddle next to me, the warmth of my dragon genes will keep you plenty warm. It's too dangerous for you to try to sleep without heat tonight. The temperature outside is well below freezing, and I doubt it's much warmer in here. Take off your outdoor gear and come warm up with me."

Harlow nodded, shivering too violently now to even reply. His tone had been quite businesslike, and he didn't seem embarrassed at all to be making the suggestion that they snuggle together. Perhaps he doesn't think of me as strongly as I think of him, Harlow thought. She tried to push down the disappointment that filled her, but she could not ignore it completely. If a man cared for a woman at all, even a little but, wouldn't he be at least somewhat excited at the chance to sleep next to her? Harlow thought so, and she began to question then whether she had seen really seen anything in his eyes yesterday when he looked at her, or if she had just imagined it.

Myles helped her out of her thick winter clothes, and then pushed her gently toward the bed. After double-checking to make sure that the door was locked, he climbed into bed beside her slipping easily under the thick comforter. He slid his arms around her, and pressed his body up against hers. Instantly, Harlow was covered in his warmth. Her shivering slowed, and then ceased, until she actually began to feel comfortable again.

Myles body was strong, and having his muscled arms around her made her feel safer than she ever had before. He was spooning her, so she couldn't see his face to try to read his expression. She wasn't sure that she would have dared look into his eyes right now, anyway. Was he feeling anything for her besides friendly concern, and, if not, did she really want to know? She wasn't sure how her heart would react to the knowledge that he didn't have deeper feelings for her.

Then again, she wasn't sure how her heart would react to the knowledge that he *did*.

Harlow closed her eyes tightly, telling herself that she couldn't worry about it right now. All she could do at the moment was enjoy this time with his arms around her. If this night was the only one she had to fall asleep in his arms, then she wanted to enjoy it to the fullest. There were, she thought, not many things you could do with a friend that were more intimate than sleeping together, actually sleeping. It showed that you trusted the person, and they trusted you, and Harlow realized with a bit of surprise that she did fully trust Myles. She wasn't sure that she could have said that twenty-four hours ago, but a lot could change in a day, it seemed.

Despite Harlow's worries that her anxious thoughts wouldn't let her sleep, that was the last thought she had had before drifting off into dreamland.

CHAPTER ELEVEN

Harlow opened her eyes to find them staring straight at Myles' sleeping face. One of his arms was loosely draped over her hips, and his chest rose and fell slowly with the rhythm of sleep. She blinked in surprise, but the disoriented feeling only lasted for a few moments. It all came back to her quickly—the power outage, her brief walk through the blizzard to Myles' room, and then his insistence that he could keep her warm through the night thanks to his dragon.

His dragon, Harlow thought, a little thrill of excitement rushing through her body. She was sleeping next to a dragon. How many wizards could say they had done that? Not many, to be sure. She knew that a few of the other Redwood Dragons had paired up with wizards from Falcon Cross, but that still left very few wizards who could claim to have been this close to a dragon. The realization made Harlow feel special, and she couldn't help but smile. Myles chose that exact moment to wake up, opening his eyes to find Harlow smiling at him. She blushed, but a smile instantly crossed his face as well.

"Good morning, sunshine," he said, his voice rough and gravelly from several hours of non-use. "Sleep okay? Warm enough?"

Harlow nodded. "You're pretty great at keeping a bed warm," she said, trying to keep her voice light and teasing. His smile deepened, and, to her surprise, he snuggled closer to her and squeezed his arms tighter around her.

She felt a thrill of pleasure rush through her. It was an excited, giddy feeling that was becoming more and more familiar the more time that she spent with him. Her heart rate increased as he nuzzled his nose against her ear. She couldn't see his face anymore, but his body was pressed so tightly against hers that she was pretty sure his expression must be one of desire. She found herself holding her breath, wondering what he would do next. Until now, they had done a good job of keeping up the pretense that their reasons for being in the same bed were purely practical. But he was moving quickly beyond the boundaries of practical, and he was making no apologies for it. He draped one of his legs over her legs, and pushed his hips against her hips, and that's when she felt it.

He was large, and hard as a rock. He pressed his stiffness against her, causing her heart to beat impossibly faster than it already was. She trembled in his arms, trying her best to calm her nerves but hopelessly failing at the task. How could she be calm in a moment like this, when the most handsome man she had ever seen, the dragon whose bed she had shared last night, was making it clear exactly what effect she had on him?

They lay like this for several minutes. Harlow was completely still except for her breathing, which came in faster and faster breaths as her mind began to truly comprehend the fact that Myles desired her. She knew that she had longed for this in some way since the very first time she'd laid eyes on him. Even when she'd hated him, she'd been unable to completely get the nagging thought out of her mind that his body joined to hers would feel like heaven. Now, she had gone completely over the edge. Their friendship had been growing exponentially since their standoff last night before dinner, and that friendship was quickly deepening into something greater. Harlow closed her eyes and allowed herself to relish the way Myles felt with his hips pressed against her. She could feel herself growing ready for him as the juices of desire began filling the space between her legs. She wanted him, but how far would he take things this morning? And if he did make a move to take things all the way, was it really a good idea? Wouldn't a new romance distract them from the task at hand?

Harlow didn't have much time to consider this question, although she could have considered it all day and still come up with the same answer. After the small taste of him she'd had, she would never be satisfied until she had tasted all of him. Luckily, he seemed to agree.

He pulled back from nuzzling against her ear, and brought his face right in front of hers.

"Harlow," he said softly. It was the only word he said, but somehow it held so much meaning. Harlow smiled at the sound of her name on his lips, and then, before she knew it, his lips were on her lips.

He kissed her softly at first, and she closed her eyes as she took in the mixed sensation of his smooth lips and prickly chin. She didn't mind the roughness, though. It made him feel like a man's man, and the stubble looked damn sexy on him, too.

After a few moments, he slipped his tongue past her lips, and the urgency in his kiss increased. He massaged her tongue with his, drinking in her taste as he ran his tongue across not only her tongue but her teeth and the roof of her mouth as well. He held her firmly against his body as he kissed her, his hips pressing against her as his hands gripped her by the small of her back. Harlow could feel the heat in her body rising, and the wetness between her legs growing. Her rational mind screamed at her to stop, telling her that they needed to talk about this first, and that she shouldn't sleep with someone before discussing with him their feelings for each other. But Harlow pushed away the thoughts. She didn't care right now about logic or reason. It didn't matter what her head tried to tell her. Her heart knew. She was falling for Myles, hard and fast.

He sucked her tongue deep into his mouth, then nibbled on it gently, sending fresh tremors of excitement through her body. His motions stemmed from an intensity of feelings within him, she could tell, and yet he moved with an easy familiarity. They were together in this moment, united by a common quest but forgetting all about the duties of that quest for now. In this room, there were only the two of them. They were everything to each other.

Myles slid his hands around from behind Harlow and found the hem of her flannel pajama shirt. He slid his fingers up between the fabric so that they were touching Harlow's skin. He was warm, but she still could not keep from shivering at his touch. He drew tiny circles around her belly button, causing her to gasp and wriggle in delight. Then he moved upward toward her breasts, which were bare beneath her shirt since she never slept with a bra, and had been too preoccupied with other worries to think about putting one on last night before coming over to Myles' room.

Now, she was thankful for that oversight. She moaned slowly as he covered her breasts with his hands, one in each palm. His hands pressed against the fabric of her shirt as he began to massage slowly, and Harlow once again squirmed with pleasure under his touch. Heat seemed to shoot from his hands into her breasts, and then radiate through her entire body. She trembled as he moved his hands so that now it was just his fingers over her nipples. He grabbed one hard nub between each of his thumbs and forefingers, first massaging gently, and then, gradually beginning to twist with movements that were increasingly strong.

Harlow had lost all sense of time and space. Everything around her had disappeared except Myles. She shuddered with impatient relief as he finally slid his hands out from under her pajama shirt and began to actually unbutton it. He worked quickly, and she gladly wriggled out of the sleeves to help him remove the shirt completely. He pushed the blankets back just a bit, so that they only covered her lower half. Her chest and stomach were bare against the cold air of the room, but he did not leave her cold for long. With a swift movement, he flipped her onto her back and then lay over her, so that his body warmed her. He put his hands on her shoulders, warming them as he slid his head into position right above her breasts. He used his teeth to pleasure her nipples now, massaging them with his tongue before nibbling and then biting down hard. She arched her back, pressing against him and moaning again. Her body was growing warmer with each passing second, as the fire of his touch consumed her.

After several minutes of this, Myles slowly rolled off of her. Harlow opened her eyes to look at him, wondering what he was going to do next. He only smiled at her in answer, and then slipped out of the bed to stand beside it. He pulled off his shirt with one smooth movement, exposing his broad chest and chiseled abs. Harlow took in his appearance with appreciation. His chest had just the right amount of hair, not too much and not too little. He looked perfectly masculine and strong and she let out a long, satisfied sigh. He wasn't done yet, though.

He pushed off his pants, and boxers, stepping out of them and then standing to his full height so that Harlow could see his long, thick manhood in all its glory. He was rock hard, and enormous. Even though she had felt him beneath the sheets, she had still not been prepared for how large he would look once he was fully on display. She let out a happy gasp and bit her lower lip with anticipation. He smiled, pleased at her response, and stood there for another few moments to allow her to admire him. His legs were strong and thick with muscles, and Harlow loved the way they accented the stiff erection between them. If Harlow had ever wondered what the body of a god might look like, Myles would have been a fairly good example. He was magnificent.

When he was satisfied that she'd had enough time to look, Myles climbed back onto the bed. He dove under the covers then, finding the waistband of her pants and underwear and pulling them off together. The movement left a long, wet trail down her legs. She was soaking with anticipation now. Her whole body was filled with a tingling sensation of electricity as she waited for Myles to resurface from underneath the blankets. He slid so that his body was over hers, and then crawled back up so they were chest to chest and face to face. Harlow could feel his stiff shaft as it grazed up her leg, stopping just below the entrance between her legs, which was now throbbing with anticipation.

His skin had a strange, almost otherworldly color in the gray-blue light of dawn. The curtains had not been fully drawn last night, and they let in a tinted, snowy light now. Myles' face hovered above hers, and he smiled softly, looking into her eyes as he did, searching to see whether she wanted more.

Harlow wanted all of him. And she desperately wanted to tell him that, but when she opened her mouth to speak, the words seemed to stick in her throat. She looked up at him, trying to form a coherent reply, and silently pleading with him to understand, but she could not seem to organize her thoughts.

"Shhh," he said, putting a finger to her lips. She smiled at him, grateful that he seemed to know exactly which emotions she was trying to convey. No more words were necessary between them. Myles closed his eyes, and Harlow followed suit. Then, with a slow, steady movement, he entered her.

He pushed against her inner walls, stretching her and rubbing her in the most delightful way as he filled her. Every nerve ending in her body seemed to respond as she filled with radiant heat and tingling electricity. If she'd thought he seemed large by the way he felt between their clothes, or the way he had looked when he stood next to the bed, it had been nothing compared to how large he felt once he was actually inside of her. She was helplessly, wonderfully full of him.

He began to rock his hips back and forth then, slowly sliding in and out of her. The movement sent fresh shockwaves of pleasure through Harlow's body, and she could feel the pressure in her core building, growing to a nearly impossible level. Her senses felt hyperaware in that moment, and she could hear the ragged sound of his breathing as he took her. Her own breathing was rapid and desperate. She gasped for breath as every passing second left her more and more delirious with the ecstasy of becoming one with Myles. She never wanted this moment to end, and she did her best to hold onto the wondrous, tingling, pressure-filled sensation as long as possible. Finally though, she could hold back no longer, and her release came crashing over her.

If she'd thought that the anticipation had been wonderful, then this was truly rapturous. The tingling pressure gave way to hungry spasms, as her muscles clenched around Myles over and over. She moaned as the tingling sensation reached a climax, causing her whole body to shudder with happiness. Wave after wave of hot pleasure washed over her, and she cried out loudly, yelling Myles' name out as he gave her the most beautiful feeling she had ever experienced.

She still did not open her eyes, but as the wonder of the moment consumed her, she could hear his breathing growing more ragged and desperate still. He moved rapidly within her, thrusting with greater and greater force until, finally, he stiffened and let out a roar. Harlow could feel him pulsing within her as he filled her, and at the same time she was filled with an intense heat. The warmth was greater than anything she had ever experienced, outshining even the electric heat of passion that had filled her when Myles first began kissing her. She squeezed her eyes shut even tighter, trying to take in all of the wonderful sensations that filled her. She felt more at peace than she ever had before, and she wanted that peaceful feeling to last forever.

When, at last, the pulsing of their bodies had slowed, Myles gently slid out of her and landed beside her on the mattress with a rough thump. He pulled the comforter up over them and then drew her close to him, wrapping his arms around her and once again enveloping her with his strength. They were both sweaty, sticky messes, but Harlow had never been so happy. She knew that they needed to get up and get moving, but she couldn't bring herself to pull away from the warmth of his arms yet.

Just a few more minutes, she told herself, closing her eyes as she buried her face in his chest. As soon as her eyes were closed, though, she felt the exhaustion of the last few days catching up with her once again. After coming to Myles' room last night she had slept soundly, but not long enough. Here, in the comfort of Myles' arms and the afterglow of their lovemaking, it didn't take long for her tiredness to catch up with her. Within moments of shutting her eyelids, she was asleep.

CHAPTER TWELVE

Myles sat at the hotel room's desk, watching Harlow as she slept and wondering whether he should wake her or let her sleep. They needed to get moving soon, but he also knew she needed to rest. She'd been carrying around a great amount of worry over whether this mission would finally prove to everyone that she was a worthwhile citizen of Falcon Cross. That worry had weighed on her, draining the life and energy from her. He could see the weight beginning to lift from her now. Confessing her fears to him had helped tremendously, he knew. Having someone around that you didn't have to hide your true self from was surprisingly energizing. His hope was that she would slowly regain her mental and physical strength, and rest was a crucial part of that.

Rest could not be had at the expense of safety, however. Myles glanced down at the map on the desk in front of him, and then at his watch. It was nearly ten in the morning now, and he dared not hang around here much longer. The storm had cleared early this morning, and the power had come back on about an hour ago. The clearing weather no doubt meant that the server at the restaurant, if she was indeed a spy, had been in contact with Saul's men by now.

Myles rose and walked over to the hotel window to look out. The room was warm again, thanks to the restored heat and power, but the window was still cold as he pressed his face against it. All he could see was thick, deep snow. It was everywhere. The rental car was nearly buried, and snow had blown against the sign near the front of the parking lot which announced the name of the hotel to everyone driving by. None of the letters on the sign were legible at the moment. The roads were in poor shape, too. The snow had covered everything so completely that it was hard to even see where the parking lot ended and the road began. Everything looked like a large, white blur.

He frowned, and turned to walk back to the desk. The roads would be plowed, but slowly. There was one big plow truck in town, as he understood it. The guy who owned it worked slowly, and sometimes would not even bother plowing if the forecast predicted that another storm was coming soon. It might be days or possibly even a week before the roads here were clear again, and even then, Myles knew that once he got a little ways out of town, the roads would once again be unplowed and covered with thick snow. He was beginning to regret even bothering to procure a rental car. It wasn't going to do him much good in this wintry wonderland. He'd thought it would be helpful in town, but he knew now that they couldn't stay in town. It was too dangerous. The storm might have kept Saul's men away temporarily, but he had no doubt that they would be coming soon. The impassable roads themselves would not stop their enemy. Saul's men had been here long enough that they would have already figured out a way to travel despite the snow. Unless Myles and Harlow wanted a messy confrontation in the middle of town, they would have to do the same.

Myles looked down at the map on the desk again, and traced with his fingers the small black "X" he had drawn there just this morning. That particular "X" marked the spot where he planned to go hide out with Harlow. According to his careful reading of topographical maps, there were caves there. Myles figured they should be able to find a deserted cave and use it as an inconspicuous base. Keeping the cave warm would be a challenge, but Myles figured they'd just have to figure out a way to build a fire and keep things toasty. Staying in this hotel, as lovely as its creature comforts were, was no longer an option. Besides, as they had seen last night, having a hotel room did not guarantee that you would have central heat. The wilderness out here was not too kind to men and his manmade comforts. A cave hideout might offer just as much shelter as this dingy hotel.

Harlow stirred, and Myles looked over at her sleeping form, which was huddled below the blanket. She murmured something unintelligible in her sleep, but then settled back down. Myles grinned. Despite the numerous worries plaguing his mind right now, he could not help smiling at the sight of her. He almost could not believe that she had let him make love to her—not after the rockiness of their relationship as colleagues over the last few weeks. But all animosity between them seemed to have evaporated away after their talk last night. He'd felt a special connection to her after she'd been vulnerable enough to share her fears with him. That connection had seemed to grow deeper and stronger over the course of yesterday evening, and once Myles had her in bed next to him, it had been nearly impossible to ignore the way his heart thumped when she was near.

And now that they had made love, he knew why he had been so drawn to her from the very beginning: they were lifemates.

Lifemates, he thought, looking over at her with a lump of emotion in his throat. He wasn't quite sure how to describe the emotions he felt. There was a mixture of excitement, disbelief, and deep, deep love. He'd thought that there was something special about Harlow since the day he'd laid eyes on her, but he hadn't dared to let himself consider the possibility that it was because they were destined for each other. She was too much for him on so many levels: too beautiful, too stubborn, too proud, too intelligent… the list could go on. He had so many reasons he could have given for why she was not right for him. And yet, she *was* right for him, because she was his lifemate. He had felt the bond when they made love. They were forever connected. Myles sighed happily at the thought. He hoped that Harlow would be okay with the fact that she'd bonded with him. She seemed into him now, but how would she feel once she realized that they were bonded for life?

Myles would not have to wait long to find out. At that moment, Harlow sat up slowly in the bed, rubbing at her eyes and looking around with a slight hint of embarrassment on her face.

"I fell asleep again?" she asked. "What time is it?"

"About ten," Myles said, standing to go sit nearer to her on the foot of the bed. "And don't apologize. You needed the rest."

Harlow still blushed, though, and looked down at the comforter that was wrapped warmly about her. That's when she seemed to notice that the power had returned.

"It's warm in here again," she said. "Did the heat come back on?"

Myles nodded. "About an hour ago. Which means that about an hour ago, our friendly server from the restaurant last night was probably able to call Saul's men and inform them that we're here in town."

Harlow's eyes widened. "You should have woken me," she said. "We need to get out of here!"

"We do," Myles agreed. "But I was trying to balance your need for rest with my worry over how long it will take Saul's men to get to us. The roads are impassable by car, so they'll have to use some other means. I would guess, though, that they're well-prepared for weather like this. They probably have snowmobiles or some other similar

315

method of snow-friendly transportation."

"How are *we* getting out of here, if the roads are impassable?" Harlow asked. "We don't have access to a snowmobile, as far as I know."

"Well," Myles said slowly, watching her face to gauge her reaction. "How do you feel about riding on a dragon?"

"Riding on a dragon?" Harlow repeated dumbly, looking at him as though he'd gone somewhat out of his mind.

"Yes, riding on a dragon," Myles repeated. "I could shift into dragon form, and you could ride on my back, holding all of our bags securely up there. It's not hard to do, I promise. In dragon form, my back is so large that it's quite stable. You wouldn't need to be constantly holding on for dear life or anything like that."

Despite Myles reassuring words, Harlow still looked troubled. "What other options do we have?" she asked in a tone of voice that told Myles she clearly hoped that there would be some other good options. He was going to have to disappoint her.

"We don't really have any other options," he said. "We could try to find a snowmobile ourselves, but given the fact that many of the townspeople here are likely reporting to Saul's men, I have a feeling we aren't going to be able to find anyone willing to rent us a snowmobile. Either we fly out with me in dragon form, or we wait here for Saul's men to show up and do our best to fight them."

Harlow looked dejected. "I guess I'm going to have to ride a dragon, then," she said in a resigned tone."

Myles reached over and squeezed her hand. "It's not that hard, I promise. I'll make sure to keep you safe."

Harlow nodded and tried to give him a brave smile, but it was unconvincing. Myles stood and went to sit next to her on the bed, wrapping his arms around her tightly. "I promise I won't let anything happen to you," he said. "Try not to worry too much. Most people end up thinking riding on a dragon is fun, once they get over their initial nerves."

Harlow smiled a little bit more convincingly, but she still looked more nervous than Myles had ever seen her. He hated to have to do something that made her so uncomfortable, but they had little choice in the matter.

"I think we can be out of here within fifteen minutes," Myles said. "Perhaps half an hour if you'd like to take a shower. I'm not sure when we'll have access to a shower again, so if you want to take a quick one go ahead. I'll start packing up while you do that. I've already brought all of your bags over from your room, so you won't need to trudge through the snow to get to your stuff."

Harlow nodded gratefully. "I'll take a shower, then," she said. "Don't worry, I'll be quick."

Harlow rummaged in her bag for some fresh clothes, then disappeared into the bathroom to shower. Myles quickly started packing up his things, which didn't take very long at all. They'd only been here one night, and he had barely unpacked anything. Putting away the maps that he'd been studying was the most time consuming part. A few minutes later, Harlow had finished her shower, and he heard the whir of the blow dryer as she dried her hair. Not long after that, she emerged from the bathroom, dressed in jeans and a thermal long-sleeved shirt—and looking a bit more relaxed than she had when Myles first suggested that she ride on his back in dragon form.

"Let me just pack away the things I just used in the bathroom, and then we can get going," Harlow said. Myles nodded, and used the time to double-check that none of his things had been missed under the bed or chairs when he packed. He watched Harlow out of the corner of his eye, wondering if he should say something to her about the lifemate bond, or even just about how wonderful it had been to be with her last night. He wasn't sure what to say, though, or how to say it. Every time he opened his mouth, the words seemed to stick in his throat. After several minutes of internal struggle, he finally decided that it was better if he waited until they were safely at their next hideout before he tried to explain things to her. The conversation might get long, and he was becoming hyperaware of the ticking clock on the wall. Each second that passed by was a second closer to Saul's men finding out where they were.

Myles felt weird saying nothing at all, though, so he settled for a quick check to make sure Harlow wasn't regretting anything that had happened the night before. He walked over to where she was zipping up her duffel bag, and turned her so that she was facing toward him. He put a hand on each of her shoulders, and looked deeply into her eyes.

"Hey. How are you feeling?" he asked, feeling somewhat awkward. "I hope you know that I didn't just invite you into my bed to take advantage of you. I really did want to keep you warm. But making love to you was a wonderful, unexpected benefit. I don't think I've ever been happier."

Harlow smiled up at him somewhat shyly. "I feel great," she said. "Truly. I'm really happy, too."

Myles pulled her into an embrace, stroking the back of her neck and gently kissing the top of her head. "I'm so glad to hear that," he said huskily. "I wish I had time right now to tell you all of the things I'm feeling, but we have to move. I want you to at least know, though, that you mean the world to me, and you've made me such a happy man. I promise, this is only the beginning of wonderful things for us."

Harlow nuzzled her face against his chest in response, and Myles kissed the top of her head again. He could have stayed there in that moment forever, but the clock on the wall was still ticking, reminding him that Saul's army would be closing in on them soon.

"Ready, kid?" he asked Harlow, tousling her hair affectionately. She nodded. Her face still looked nervous, but it was starting to show some hints of determination, too.

Myles picked up their bags and started walking toward the room's door.

"Time for the ride of your life," he said, winking back at her as she started shrugging into her thick winter coat. He couldn't help pausing for one extra beat as he looked at her standing there in the muted light from the gray, snowy world outside. She was the most beautiful creature he'd ever seen, and he'd never felt so damned lucky in his entire life before that moment.

CHAPTER THIRTEEN

Harlow had never experienced anything quite so exhilarating. Myles had been right: once you got over your initial worries about riding on a dragon's back, you realized that it was pretty damn fun. She hardly even noticed how frigid the air was as they sliced through the gray winter sky. It was hard to notice anything up here except how spectacular the view below her appeared, and how magnificent the beast she rode on was.

Myles' dragon was beautiful. She'd seen the dragon shifters in dragon form before, but never up close. Several months ago, when Saul's army had made a series of attacks on Falcon Cross, Harlow had watched through her office windows as the dragon shifters circled high above the city, breathing streams of fire out to take down their enemies. That had been a fearsome sight, but it still had not been as awe-inspiring as seeing a dragon up close.

Up close, Harlow could see all the marvelous details that were impossible to notice from far away. She ran her hands over Myles' thick dragon hide, admiring the way his green scales shimmered even in the dull winter light. When the light hit them the right way, they took on iridescent shades of pink, blue, and purple. Harlow thought that she had never seen anything so beautiful.

Myles had not been exaggerating, either, when he said that his dragon form was large. Harlow had seen during the battles that the dragons were giants, but, again, seeing them up close gave a different perspective. She'd had no concept of just how large they actually were. Even with Harlow, two duffel bags, and another large backpack on Myles' dragon back, there was plenty of spare room. As Myles had said, this did make his back a very stable place to sit while he flew. Harlow had been worried before takeoff, but she had not felt nervous since they actually launched into the air. Myles was a steady flyer, and his back felt completely safe to her.

His long neck and fearsome dragon head stretched far in front of her, and his long, spiked tail stretched behind, whipping through the air with ease. But it was his wings that really took her breath away. Calling them massive would be an understatement. Each wing stretched out from his body at least twice as long as the length from his head to tail. They skin on the back edges of the wings were thinner, which made the iridescent effect of his scales even more pronounced. His wings looked like a true work of art to Harlow. She watched, mesmerized, as they rose and fell with powerful grace, propelling them quickly away from the town and toward the spot Myles had chosen for their next hideout.

It had been a big step for Harlow to let Myles take complete control of where they would relocate to next. She was slowly learning to trust him, and to trust that she did not have to do everything on her own, or make every decision by herself. Myles had studied the maps very carefully for several hours while she was sleeping, and he was convinced that there were caves out here they could hide in. He was also convinced that Saul's men would not be too far from the caves, based on the predicted travel path he had made the night before. If Myles' observations were correct, then Harlow might

318

have a chance within the next few days to sneak into the enemy's camp and steal the amethyst records. If they could manage to finish their mission that quickly, everyone back home was sure to be pleased. The wizard High Council might even recognize them with an award, and Harlow wasn't going to lie—she wouldn't mind being recognized a little bit for all her hard work.

But the best thing about going home would be that she would be able to spend time with Myles in a normal, safe environment. She was glad to be with him now, of course. She was happier than ever that he had won the argument over whether or not he would accompany her on this mission. But the middle of a snowy wilderness, with enemy soldiers close at hand, was not the best place to kick off a new relationship.

Relationship. Harlow frowned as she considered the word, and wondered what kind of relationship she and Myles had. They had fought, then worked out their differences, then made love, and then…they had not really discussed things. There had been no time, of course. They'd needed to get away from the hotel. Still, Harlow felt anxious whenever her mind turned to considering what it was that Myles might want. Would this just be a fling for him? A fun diversion while he was off on a mission? Or was it something deeper? Something that meant something.

He'd said this was only the beginning. But the beginning of what? Did Harlow dare to hope for something truly permanent?

Her fretful thoughts were interrupted by the realization that they were beginning to spiral downward. Myles was moving in wide, graceful circles, slowly losing altitude so that Harlow never felt frightened by too sharp of a downward angle. Below them, dark black rocks jutted out from the snow here and there. Harlow assumed those must be the tops of the caves, although it was hard to say what anything was for certain right now. Last night's snowstorm had covered the landscape quite completely.

A few minutes later, Myles came to a smooth landing right in the middle of the black rocks. From this vantage point, it was clear that these were caves, although their entrances were almost completely blocked by snowdrifts. Myles looked back at her, and gave her a gentle nudge with his dragon head. Harlow understood that he wanted her to dismount, so she grabbed the bags and threw them off his back, then slid down and off herself, landing with a soft thud in the snow. She sank in all the way to her waist, and found herself struggling to move forward even a few feet. Myles, on the other hand, seemed to be able to walk around fairly easily, thanks to his giant dragon legs. He swung his head to and fro, inspecting the different cave entrances. Harlow presumed that he was trying to decide which cave would make the best hideout for them. The caves didn't seem all that large. Many of them were not much more than shallow rock shelters, barely big enough for two humans to stretch out inside.

Myles finally settled on one of the medium-sized caves, and swiped at the snow in front with one of his giant front legs. Snow went flying in a powdery white shower, and Myles continued swiping like this until much of the entrance was cleared. The inside of the cave was quite full of snow, too. It had probably been piling up there all winter, since the weather had not been warm enough to melt snow for quite some time. Myles decided to do a little melting on his own, though. He let out a loud roar, and then shot a stream of fire from his large dragon mouth. The flames gave off an intense heat that Harlow could feel even from several yards away. The warmth felt good, and she watched in fascination as even the top layer of snow near her began to melt from the nearby heat. After a few short minutes of fire-breathing, Myles had reduced the inside of the cave to a sopping wet puddle. He continued to breathe fire on the water, until it boiled. Harlow frowned, unsure of what he was trying to do. He didn't seem to be getting the results he wanted, either, because after a few moments he stopped and backed away from the cave. With a loud roar and a huge rush of energy, he shifted back into human form, completely naked from head to toe.

"Goddamn, it's cold out here. Even for a dragon shifter," he said. "Toss me my duffel bag."

Harlow reached to the spot a few feet away from her where the duffel was, and with some difficulty dragged it toward her. She picked it up high above her head, and then it hurled it toward Myles with all her strength. It landed just a few feet away from him, and he reached out to grab it from the snowdrift it had landed in. He quickly opened it and began to rummage around for clothes, cursing the cold as the snow bit at his bare skin. Harlow waited until he was dressed and had stopped cursing before speaking.

"What were you trying to do, breathing fire on all the water in the cave?" she asked as she started laboriously trudging through the snow toward him.

"I was trying to make the water hot enough to boil away, so that the cave would be dry for us," Myles said, wiping at his brow, which was covered with thick snowflakes. "But there's too much of it. It'll take hours. There was so much snow in there that melting it turned the cave into a literal pond. I think we might be better off just choosing another cave, and clearing the snow away completely by hand instead of melting it. We can't very well set up camp on top of a pond."

Harlow grinned when she heard what Myles had been trying to do. "You need to dry out the cave? Oh, that's easy. Allow me," she said. She stumbled the last several feet through the thick snow, right up to the edge of where Myles' snow melting efforts had indeed turned the ground into a sopping wet mess. She pulled the glove off her right hand, and then raised her magic ring to point it at the water.

"*Magicae siccum*," she said. Energy radiated from her ring, and the water in the cave began to evaporate rapidly. After only a minute of this, the inside of the cave was bone dry. Harlow looked triumphantly over at Myles, who blinked a few times in amazement as he looked at the cave.

"Right," he finally said. "I forgot you could do magic."

"Minor little detail," Harlow teased. "Now let's get our stuff into the cave and see if we can warm up a bit. I'm freezing."

"Here," Myles said, tossing her his duffel bag. "Take that inside and I'll go grab the other bags."

He trudged through the pathway Harlow had made when she walked over, grabbed the other bags, and then trudged back. He deposited them on the cold hard earth that made up the floor of the cave, and then began rummaging around inside the cave, trying to gather up the large, loose stones that were scattered here and there.

"We'll have to make a fire pit," he explained. "It's not exactly ideal to have smoke going up into the air, telling anyone nearby where we are, but we can't freeze to death either."

"By 'we' you mean 'me,' don't you?" Harlow said, raising an eyebrow at him. "Your dragon genes seem to keep you warm enough to deal with this weather. Well, at least they keep you warm enough when you're not butt naked in the snow."

Myles chuckled. "Fair enough. But we have to keep you warm, too. And as much as I would love to just wrap you in my arms constantly to heat you up, that's not very practical. So we'll have to build a fire. Hopefully, Saul's men won't be close enough to notice the smoke in the sky. And if they are, well, then we'll just have to fight them. Things might come to that anyway."

Harlow grinned. "You're forgetting something again," she said with a twinkle in her eye. Myles looked over at her and narrowed his eyes suspiciously.

"What?" he asked.

"I can do magic, remember?" Harlow said. Then she raised her ringed hand and said, "*Magicae therma.*"

Almost instantly, the room began to fill with a welcoming warmth. Myles stared at her, dumbfounded.

"That's a pretty useful trick," Myles observed. "I didn't realize that spell could warm a whole room. But why didn't you just use that in your own room when the power went out last night?"

"Because I can't keep the spell going while I'm asleep," Harlow said. "Which means that when it's time to go to bed here in the cave, we'll either need to build a fire, or you'll have to snuggle close to me while we sleep to keep me warm."

Harlow winked at him for added emphasis, and he let out a low growl noise.

"Come here, you," he said reaching toward her to pull her close. His lips covered hers, and he wrapped his arms firmly around her. He pressed hips against hers to let Harlow feel the stiffening between his legs.

"So that's a 'yes' to snuggling me?" Harlow asked in a teasing voice when Myles broke off the kiss for a moment to catch his breath. He growled again, and started in to kiss her again. But he stopped before he reached her lips, suddenly taking on a thoughtful expression.

"You know," he said, his voice soft. "I would like to fall asleep next to you every day for the rest of my life, regardless of whether the temperature around us is hot or cold."

Harlow swallowed hard, her eyes widening as she looked up at him. "That's...that's quite a long time," she said.

"I know," Myles said. "Well, I mean, hopefully it will be a long time. I'm going to do my best not to get killed on this mission."

He laughed at his own joke, but Harlow frowned. "Don't joke about dying. It's not funny."

Myles reached out and brushed a stray strand of hair back from her face. His finger left a trail of heat across her face, and she closed her eyes for a moment, relishing how wonderful his touch felt.

"Hey," he said, his voice even softer now. "I'm not going anywhere anytime soon, okay? And I mean it when I say I want to spend a lifetime with you. I know you probably think I'm crazy for saying that so soon, but it's true."

Harlow felt her heart beating faster as she stared up at Myles. His deep green eyes looked down at her with an intensity that was becoming quite familiar now. She was learning that dragon's didn't really half-ass anything. When they decided to do something, they were all in. And, apparently, that included falling in love.

"How can you know for sure?" Harlow asked. "You barely know me?" She asked the question not to cast doubt on the truth of his words, but because she was genuinely curious. She thought she felt similarly, but he was right. It *did* seem crazy to know, after one time of sleeping together, that you wanted to be with someone forever. Especially when, until the day before, you thought you hated the person. But Myles said he knew, and, if Harlow really searched her heart, she knew, too. She never wanted to leave Myles' side. He might drive her a bit crazy sometimes, but he was exactly the calm, steady influence that her sometimes unsteady heart needed.

Myles took a deep breath, and smiled a bit ruefully down at her. "It's a bit of an involved explanation, actually," he said.

"I've got time," Harlow replied.

Myles nodded, took another deep breath, and then launched into his explanation. "In the shifter world, we have what are known as 'lifemates.' We believe that every shifter has a destined lifemate—someone they are fated to spend their whole life with. It's similar to the human concept of a soulmate, except it's even a bit stronger than that. I'm not sure if wizards believe in soulmates or not?"

Harlow shrugged. "Some do, some don't. I've always thought the concept seemed a bit farfetched."

Myles chuckled. "Well, then, you're probably going to think the idea of lifemates is *really* farfetched. We believe that, throughout your whole life, destiny and fate are working to bring you together with your lifemate at the perfect time. Some shifters might suspect that someone is their lifemate from the moment they meet them. With other shifters, it might take some time. But the one thing that all lifemates have in common is the lifemate bond. As soon as two people who are fated lifemates make love for the first time, the lifemate bond is formed. Once that bond is formed, the two will never truly be able to break ties from each other again. The threads of their lives are irreversibly connected."

"That doesn't sound that farfetched to me," Harlow said, her voice barely more than a whisper. "Because I feel like that's exactly what happened between you and me. I would never have known to explain it as a lifemate bond, but after we made love I felt different. I felt...connected to you, in a way I've never felt connected to anyone before."

"Did you feel your body fill with warm glowing heat, right in your core?" Myles asked, his own voice a whisper as well.

Harlow nodded. She felt suddenly lightheaded, and was so overcome with emotion that she found it difficult to speak.

"I felt it, too," Myles said. "That warm glow is the lifemate bond. It bound us together for life, Harlow. Of course, you can make your own decisions about what future you think we have together. But for me, I know with certainty that there will never be anyone else. No matter what you decide you want, I'm yours for life. My existence from now on will be dedicated to making you happy, to protecting you, and, hopefully, to building a life together."

Harlow felt her heart beating rapidly in her chest as she looked up at Myles, drinking in the love that she saw in his gorgeous dragon eyes. "I feel the same, Myles," she said. "I am yours for life, come what may. I can't wait to see what adventures lie ahead of us."

Myles smile deepened, and he leaned down to kiss her again. Harlow closed her eyes, and let his love wash over her. So much uncertainty clouded the horizon, and there was no way to know whether the good shifters and wizards would be victorious. But tomorrow would take care of itself, Harlow decided. Right now, at least she knew she had a dragon shifter who cared for her, wrapping his arms around her. She could not ask for more.

CHAPTER FOURTEEN

Myles would have loved to spend the rest of the day wrapped up in Harlow's arms, but he knew that lazy days of lovemaking were not his lot at the moment. He hoped things would be different once he and Harlow made their way back to Falcon Cross, but for now, they must focus on the task at hand.

Myles and Harlow studied their maps and made plans, each of them assuming a businesslike air as they considered their options for finding and overtaking Saul's men. Myles was convinced that the enemy must be nearby, but Harlow was not so sure.

"We're assuming that they're moving forward in their search in a logical pattern," she said. "They might not be doing that. Especially if they do know that we're here. If they know they're being watched, they'll want to keep things as confusing and unpredictable as possible for us."

She had a point, but Myles still thought the odds weighed in favor of the men being close by.

"You heard them on the recordings, talking about how they were running short on supplies," Myles said. "They would not want to waste resources by searching in a haphazard pattern. Besides, if they know that we're here, they might try to stay close by so that they can search for us. The townspeople would have told them we are only two people. They probably think they can handle two of us. And if they surprise us, they might be right. Which is why we have to find them before they find us."

"Right But this snow is going to make scouting out the area on foot nearly impossible," Harlow said. "Do you think you could do a bit of aerial reconnaissance? If you shift into dragon form, you'd be able to quickly cover a large area by flying around. You could check the locations where we think our enemies are most likely to be hanging out at the moment, and see if your hunches were correct."

"I could do that," Myles said slowly. "But there's just one problem."

"What?" Harlow asked.

"They'll see me circling. We'll lose any remaining element of surprise we might have had. They'll know that I know where they are, and they aren't complete idiots. They'll know that an attack is imminent, and they'll be prepared for it."

"Can't you do that chameleon trick so they can't see you?" Harlow asked.

Myles frowned and shook his head no. "It's really hard to maintain chameleon status when you're flying. You're moving too fast to keep up with every little change in the shade of the sky or the shape of a cloud. I've tried so many times, and no matter how hard I work at it, you can still see my outline against what should be empty sky."

"Just your outline? If you can mostly hide, and only show a dragon outline, perhaps they won't notice it," Harlow said hopefully.

Myles chuckled. "Well, it's hard to miss a dragon shape in the sky, even if it is a subtle one. But I guess it might be worth a shot. Our only other option is to search on foot, and that will take far too long. Plus, it will leave a trail in the snow, which we really don't want to do."

"I think aerial reconnaissance is the best option," Harlow said. "Sure, they might see you, but we've already discussed how they probably know we're around here somewhere. They must know we're searching for them, so they are probably worried about an imminent attack, regardless of whether they see your dragon form or not. I think flying around to find them does us more good than harm."

Myles considered her words carefully. "You're probably right," he said finally. "But there's just one other thing. I hate the idea of leaving you here alone. What if they find our hiding spot, and I'm not here to help defend it."

Harlow rolled her eyes. "Oh, come on, Myles. What are the odds that they will find this place? We flew in, so we didn't leave any trail on the ground for them to follow. And we didn't see anyone ourselves on the flight, so it's pretty unlikely that they saw us flying in. I'd say we're pretty safe here. Besides, I do know how to fight. Of course, I would greatly appreciate your help if we are attacked, but it's not like I'm some damsel in distress who will be completely helpless if you leave me here alone."

Myles sighed. She was right, even though he didn't want to admit it. These caves were well off the beaten path, and quite well-hidden. Odds were good that Saul's men didn't even know they were there. Myles had only found them by very carefully studying a topographical map, and even on that map the caves weren't marked well. He'd been careful not to leave a trail when they came in, too, so he doubted they'd be followed. And it was true that Harlow was a pretty good fighter. He'd seen her sparring with Peter before they left Falcon Cross. She had some serious skill as a fighter, especially for a wizard who spent most of her day sitting at a desk. The Advocates were generally known for their brains, not their brawn.

"Alright," Myles finally said. "I'll go. But you have to promise me you won't build any fires while I'm gone. Or do anything else that might draw attention to the hideout."

Harlow rolled her eyes at him. "I'm not as stupid as I look," she said.

Myles grinned at her. "Well, then, you must be a genius, because you actually look quite smart." He leaned in to kiss her, and she playfully tried to swat him away. He laughed and pinned down her hands so he could steal a kiss, but only a short one. It was time to get to work.

Less than an hour later, Myles was stripping naked in preparation to shift. He always took off his clothes before shifting when he could, because otherwise they'd be torn and ruined in the shift. He wasn't looking forward to stepping out into the snow in bare feet, but, thankfully, he would not have to be naked in the cold for very long. The cave was toasty warm right now thanks to Harlow's heat spell, and he would only have to be outside for a few seconds before he'd be in dragon form. Once his skin had shifted to dragon hide, he'd be plenty warm enough.

He looked up at Harlow, who was watching him with a cheerful expression on her face. She was optimistic that his flight would go well, and that she would be perfectly safe while he was gone. But Myles wasn't so sure. He had a bad feeling in the pit of his stomach that he couldn't quite shake. He did his best to brush it away as just general nerves, but still the anxiety lingered.

He didn't have much choice in the matter, though. Sooner or later, he'd have to leave Harlow alone if he wanted to do aerial reconnaissance. Taking her with him would make maintaining invisibility even harder. He couldn't keep her invisible, so she'd have to attempt to hold an invisibility spell over herself while he flew. From what she told him, invisibility spells were extremely difficult to hold while flying. Between the two of them, they were bound to mess up their attempts at staying invisible, compromising their mission unnecessarily. No, Myles knew it was better to leave her behind. But that didn't change the fact that he hated doing it.

"I'll try to be back by nightfall," he said, trying to act as cheerful as Harlow looked.

No sense in letting his worries seep over and bother her, too. "Don't worry too much if I'm not, though. If I'm worried someone has seen me, I might need to lay low and sit still for a while until they've given up watching. Whatever you do, don't try to come after me alone. If for some reason it's been several days and I haven't come back, get in contact with the military in Falcon Cross and ask them for assistance."

Harlow opened her mouth to protest at this, but Myles held up his hand. "If the enemy was able to take me down alone, odds are they'll be able to do the same for you. Promise me you'll get backup help if that happens."

Harlow frowned at him, but eventually nodded. "Okay. Fine," she said. "But please stay out of trouble."

"I intend to," Myles said, then winked at her. "You try to do the same."

Harlow rolled her eyes dramatically, but Myles could see the worry behind the silly front she was putting up.

"Hey," he said, drawing her into his arms. "Everything's going to be just fine, okay? Just relax and maybe go over some more of the maps while I'm gone. I'll be back before you know it."

"Okay," she said, burying her face in his bare chest. He took a moment to enjoy the feeling of her skin against his skin, and then he reached down to guide her chin up so that she was looking at him. Her eyes were deep pools of violet, shimmering with too much moisture as she tried bravely to resist the urge to cry. Myles could not help but be overcome by the depth of his feelings for her as he looked down at her beauty, and at the concern that she so clearly held for him. Before he could think too much about it, he found himself speaking out words he'd been holding back out of some sense of not wanting to rush things.

"I love you, Harlow," he said. And he did. Why shouldn't he tell her? He'd already told her that he wanted to spend his life with her. Surely, she must know that this meant he loved her?

The tears in her eyes did spill over then. Two tiny droplets, one from each eye, fought their way past her eyelid and left a wet, salty trail down her cheek. And then, her lips turned up in a small smile.

"I love you, too," she said. "So very much."

Myles smiled too, and then he planted a quick kiss on her forehead before turning to leave the cave. He stepped out into the snow, wincing as the cold hit his toes. But moments later, a rush of energy reverberated back into the cave as his body began to transform once more into a dragon. The feeling of cold fell away as his dragon body, with its thick hide and fiery center, overtook his weaker human flesh. He turned his giant dragon head to look back at Harlow one more time, admiring her beauty before turning his head toward the sky. He pumped his wings a few times, rising quickly into the air, and then did his best to turn his scales into chameleon form.

He must have looked strange, a blurry, gray outline of a dragon slicing through the sky. He wasn't perfectly blended into the gray clouds, but he hoped he was blended well enough to avoid the notice of too many people. He could only hope for the best. He turned his eyes toward the ground now, sweeping his gaze back and forth as he began searching for anything that might give away a base camp of some sort. If he found another camp out here, it was almost certain to be Saul's men.

Ready or not, here I come, Myles thought as a small smile turned up his dragon lips.

With any luck, their enemy would not, in fact, be ready.

CHAPTER FIFTEEN

Harlow threw the large map across the room in frustration. She'd been staring at it without really seeing it for the last twenty minutes, at least. Focusing on anything other than her worry about Myles was proving to be nearly impossible. She knew that he was capable of taking care of himself. She'd seen him fight before, during the Falcon Cross battles, and she knew he could hold his own against angry shifters and wizards. His razor claws, sharp teeth, and fire-breathing abilities made him a fearsome foe to meet.

And still, she worried. How could she not? If Saul's men somehow did find him and chase him down in the sky, they would almost certainly use dark magic on him. And even a dragon would struggle to stand his ground against the horrors of dark magic spells.

Harlow chewed her lower lip anxiously as she stood and made her way to the entrance of their little cave hideout. It was far too early for Myles to be on his way back yet, but she couldn't keep herself from staring up at the sky, straining to see whether the outline of a dragon was visible anywhere. She looked for several minutes, but there was nothing to see but the gray clouds, which were starting to thicken again. Another snowstorm was brewing, and Harlow hoped it wouldn't be as intense as the last one. They needed at least halfway decent weather if they were going to be able to track down Saul's men and sneak up on them.

Harlow let out a long sigh, and then turned to walk back into the cave. She needed to do something useful, but map-reading wasn't going so well for her. Perhaps she should try to review the transcripts of the conversations she had recorded. She'd been over them several times before, but there were still things being said in the conversations that didn't make sense to Harlow. Perhaps it was some sort of code language, meant to confuse anyone listening in. Harlow was determined to discover its meaning. She started walking toward the backpack, which held most of the transcripts. But she never made it there.

In an instant, she found herself sprawled out face-first on the cold, hard floor of the cave. A searing pain shot through her back, and she yelped as something hard rammed into one of her shins.

"*Magicae obstupefio*," a voice called out. It was the most sinister-sounding voice Harlow had ever heard, and she felt a chill run up and down her spine at the same time that she felt an invisible, tightening pressure pushing against all of her limbs. The stunning spell left her unable to move anything below her neck, and she felt panic setting in as rough hands pushed her over onto her back.

She was looking up into the ugliest face she had ever seen. A dark-haired wizard with beady dark eyes was staring down at her. His long nose ended in a sharp point, and his face was twisted with lines that deepened whenever he let out one of his evil laughs—which he was doing right now. He was accompanied by several other wizards, all of whom had similar expressions of wicked triumph on their faces.

Harlow knew there was no way she would be able to break out of the binding spell. It was too strong for even the best of spellcasters to combat. It was difficult to cast a strong counterspell when you didn't have free use to move your ringed hand.

Her ring! Harlow realized with a start that the first thing her captors were likely to do once they finished laughing was to steal her magic ring. Without it, Harlow's magic would be weak and unfocused—virtually useless. She felt fury rising within her as she thought of their grubby, evil hands touching her beautiful magic ring. But then, she remembered a spell she had learned a long time ago, during the first years of Advocacy school. It was an invisibility spell that only affected a very small area—an area about the size of most magic rings. The spell was generally used in situations where you wanted to fool other wizards into thinking you were not a wizard. If you acted like a normal human, and hid your magic ring, it was possible to sneak into wizard territory and perform magic spells before the other wizards knew what had happened. Harlow had never heard of anyone using it while immobilized by a binding spell, but she figured it was worth a shot. The upside of the ring invisibility spell was that you didn't have to move your ringed hand to perform it properly. In fact, it worked best when your hand was held perfectly steady.

Was it possible that she could hide her ring from her captors? Would they realize she had performed the ring invisibility spell, and take her ring off anyway, or would they just think they'd caught her in a moment where she wasn't wearing her ring? Harlow took a deep breath as she looked up at the men around her, who were still laughing loudly at her expense. It was now or never. She had to successfully perform the spell before they got around to looking for a ring on her hand. If they noticed it before she made it invisible, they would know for sure that something was going on.

"*Magicae abscondo*," Harlow said. She spoke as loudly as she dared, which was not very loud. She hoped her voice had enough force in it to make the spell effective, but she could not take a chance that the men would hear her over the sound of their laughs. If they knew she was performing spells, they would get suspicious, and the game would be over.

Thankfully, the men were still laughing too hard to notice that any words were coming out of Harlow's mouth. Harlow did not feel any sort of energy as she said the words of the spell, and she thought with a sinking heart that perhaps the spell wouldn't work when she was immobile. She lifted her neck as high as she could, trying to find an angle where she could see her right hand. It took quite a bit of strain, but she finally got her eyes high enough, and she looked at her paralyzed right hand, which was frozen against the side of her right leg. And what she saw sent a rush of joy and relief through her whole body.

There was no magic ring visible on her finger. Harlow could steel feel the stiff metal of her ring's band pushing against the skin of her finger, but when she looked at her hand all she saw were bare fingers. The spell had worked. Her ring was invisible.

The leader of her group of captors saw her straining her neck upward, and mistook the purpose of the movement as an attempt to escape. He let out another long, obnoxious laugh.

"Ain't no good trying to get away from us, Missy. That binding spell is impossible to break. You might as well relax your neck, or you'll be adding a stiff neck to your list of woes. And trust me, that list is going to get very long before we're done with you. Now, first things first, let's strip off your magic ring. I don't want no funny business from you."

The man knelt down and grabbed Harlow's hand with a rough jerk. Harlow held her breath, thinking that if his hand happened to brush against the ring while he was grabbing at her, then he would know that she had cast a spell to hide the ring. His laughter died down as he looked down at her hand, confusion etched in his face, and for one eternal, awful moment, Harlow thought that he had realized what was going on. But then, in the next moment, he dropped her hand, letting it fall limply beside her again. His guards looked at him in confusion, and he only added to their confusion by throwing back his head and starting to laugh again. He laughed so long and hard that Harlow began to wonder if he was actually a touch insane. Finally, he stood, wiping away tears of laughter from his eyes.

"What an idiot you are," he said, looking down at Harlow. "You hide out in the most obvious spot around, and, not only that, but you don't even bother to wear your magic ring while lounging around in this cave by yourself. No wonder you were so easy to capture."

The man burst into a fresh wave of laughter, and his men, now that they understood what he was laughing at, joined in.

What an idiot YOU are, Harlow thought as she glared up at the man. *My ring is on my hand right now, you're just too blind to see it.* She also made a mental note to tell Myles, if she ever got out of this mess, that his supersecret hideout had not turned out to be so secret after all. Saul's men were clearly familiar with this little clump of caves.

Not only were they familiar with the caves, but they knew that Harlow wasn't out here alone. Once the leader had managed to stop laughing again, he gave Harlow's right side a hard kick with one of his boots, and pointed his own ringed hand in her direction.

"Now," he said. "We'll find your ring later. I'm sure you must have stowed it in one of the bags here. But first—I know you are not out here alone. Tell me where your accomplice is."

Harlow merely glared at him in response, which made him angry.

"It's no use trying to hide it," he said. "We have eyes everywhere in town. They're the ones who tipped us off that these caves were here, and they told us about you and your little boyfriend. I know he must be around here somewhere, and I mean to find him. You can either tell us willingly now, or I can torture the information out of you."

The man raised his ringed hand threateningly, but Harlow still did not open her mouth. She glared back at him, and he let out a long dramatic sigh.

"Fine, I guess we're going to do this the hard way," he said. "*Magicae pressura.*"

Harlow felt a horrible pressure fall suddenly over her entire body. It weighed down on her, heavier and heavier until she could barely breath. She gasped for breath, and was filled with an intense urge to try to wriggle and get herself out from under the pressure. But, of course, she could not move her body to actually wiggle. And besides, you could not simply wiggle away from this spell. It would follow you, crushing you until you were utterly suffocated. Harlow felt panic rising within her, and the man sneering down at her must have been able to tell, because a wicked smile crossed over his face as he suddenly lifted the spell.

"*Pressura terminantur,*" he bellowed out. Instantly the spell ended and the pressure that had been weighing down on Harlow lifted. She gasped for breath as her captors all sneered and laughed at her.

"Now," the leader said, glaring down at her. "Are you going to talk? Or was that little taste of torture not enough for you? Believe me, that was amateur hour. I've got plenty of spells that would make that last spell look like child's play."

Harlow had no doubt that he did. She knew enough of dark magic to know that she did not want to experience the worst of what this man had to offer. She had no illusions that telling them where Myles was would be enough to completely save her from their spells. But giving them some information might buy her time. If they would just leave her alone for a little while, she might be able to figure out some way of freeing herself from their hold. And perhaps, given enough time, Myles might figure out where she was and come rescue her. Harlow took a deep breath, and did her best to put on a defeated expression. Let the idiots think they had beaten her down. They would see her true spirit soon enough.

"Well?" the leader asked, his voice filling with excitement. Harlow knew that her sad, defeated face was having the desired effect. The man thought she had finally given up.

"He went to town for supplies," Harlow lied, allowing her voice to crack as though she was trying to keep from crying.

The man smiled then, looking triumphant as he turned to one of his minions. "Radio our guys on base," he said. "Tell them to send a group into Devil's Melt Proper to snag the other miserable wizard wretch. Once we've got them both, we'll let Saul know that we've taken a few captives. He might be interested in interrogating them."

Harlow shuddered at the thought of being interrogated by a master of dark magic, and she tried to push away the panic that was rising again. She had time. It would take a while for the group sent to Devil's Melt Proper to realize that Myles wasn't there. In the meantime, she might be able to figure out a way to escape. Or perhaps Myles would figure out where she was.

She was in great danger, she knew, but panicking would not help anything. She needed to remain calm and think rationally about what to do.

The leader barked a couple of orders at his men, and the next thing Harlow knew, she was being hoisted up on one of the men's shoulders, her immobile body flopping helplessly as he carried her to a snowmobile that had a trailer of sorts attached to the back. He threw her unceremoniously onto the trailer, causing her to wince as her body hit the stiff hardness of the trailer's floor. Then, the other men threw in the duffel bags and backpack that had been in the cave. They were taking everything that had been in the cave, and Harlow felt a wave of frustration pass over her as she realized that they were going to see all of her notes from the last several months. They would see all the maps that she and Myles had marked up, and they would find the transcripts of their radio and phone conversations that she had printed out. They would know how much she knew, and once they did, they would certainly be even more watchful of her. They were not going to make it easy for her to escape, that much was certain. At least, though, Myles would know the minute he got back that she'd been kidnapped. If they'd left the bags, he might have thought she'd gone for a walk or something. But with the cave cleared out, he would have no doubt that something had gone amiss, and Harlow was certain he would come searching for her right away. She just hoped he wouldn't be too late.

The clouds had darkened considerably, and snow had started falling once again. It started as a few small flakes, but within minutes those few flakes had turned into a thick, swirling whiteness. Harlow felt her heart tightening with despair. The snow would quickly cover any tracks the snowmobiles left, leaving no trail for Myles to follow. She hoped that, at least, the weather might make him come back to the cave sooner than he had originally intended.

Harlow's captors threw several thick blankets over her, ensuring that she was completely hidden in the back of the trailer. No one who saw the snowmobile zooming along would think that there was a person lying paralyzed in the back of the trailer. Even Myles would not think much of it if he saw her from above as he flew back to the cave. He would just think that he'd spotted the enemy carrying supplies around. By the time he got back to the cave and realized that Harlow had been kidnapped, Harlow was sure it would be too late for him to attack this group out in the snowy wilderness. By then, her captors would no doubt have reached the relative safety of their base camp, wherever that was.

The snowmobiles roared to life, and then, a few moments later, Harlow felt the trailer start to move as the small group began their trek across the cold, snowy landscape. She closed her eyes and did her best to rest. She refused to sleep, and risk the possibility that the spell hiding her magic ring would break as she slept. She needed that ring now more than ever. But she did try to at least relax a bit. She would need as much energy as she could once she arrived at the enemy's base camp.

She had no doubt that there would be plenty more dark magic awaiting her there.

CHAPTER SIXTEEN

Myles swung his giant dragon head back and forth, straining to see through the rapidly thickening snow. He hadn't had much luck on his reconnaissance mission thus far, and with the weather worsening as it was, he knew he should just head back to the cave and try again another day.

A few strings of choice curse words streamed through his head as he finally turned to fly back to the hideout. He had left this morning full of high hopes that he would quickly find Saul's men, and then fly back to Harlow with the triumphant news so that they could begin planning their break-in. But after a few hours of flying, he was beginning to realize that he had underestimated how difficult it would be to spy on Saul's men.

For one thing, he was quite sure by now that they must be using some sort of invisibility spell on their hideout. He'd hoped that this wouldn't be the case. After all, invisibility spells were extremely difficult to maintain, especially for an area as large as an entire base camp. But all of the natural hideouts Myles had found and checked had been empty. Saul's men must have decided that it was worth it to devote a good deal of their wizard manpower to maintaining an invisibility spell, and hiding out in the open. They were somewhere close by, Myles was sure of it. Snowmobile tracks crisscrossed the landscape, although try as he might Myles wasn't able to follow any of them to one particular spot. He could not find anywhere that he could say with certainty held an invisible hideout.

Dejectedly, he flapped his wings against the growing wind and snow. He would have to try again another day. Perhaps Harlow would have some insights on how to find a hideout that was under an invisibility spell. Heck, she might even know some spells that would reveal a hidden hideout. Perhaps he should just bring her along next time. He hated to risk being seen, but it didn't do any good to fly around aimlessly, hopelessly searching.

The snow was so thick now that Myles nearly passed right over the cave hideout without seeing it. A small dark spot of rock caught his eye at the last second, and he switched directions abruptly to begin circling downward. Maintaining his direction was difficult. The wind howled and pushed insistently against his wings, but he managed to stay somewhat in control until he landed with a rough thud several yards away from the cave they had chosen as a hideout.

It was dark in the cave, which surprised him. He would have thought Harlow would have a lantern going so that she could study the maps some more. Maybe she was sleeping, though. Myles supposed that a day stuck in a dark cave by yourself would probably get pretty boring after a while. He might have tried to sleep some of the hours away himself if he'd been in a similar situation.

Myles almost hated to shift back into human form right now, because he worried that the noise and energy of shifting would wake up Harlow. But he didn't want to sit out here in the snow any longer, either. He was plenty warm enough in dragon form, but the swirling snow beat at his eyes in a rather annoying way. Besides, Harlow would probably be happy to see that he was back. He knew she had been quite worried about him, even though she'd done her best to hide her anxiety.

With a low roar, Myles began to shift back to human form. His body began to shrink back to human size, and his thick dragon hide slowly morphed back to human skin. His arms and legs lost their dragon shape, and the claws on his hands and feet disappeared. His tail and wings disappeared, and his head lost its horns as it returned to its human shape. Almost instantly, Myles began to shiver. The snow where he was standing came up to his waist, completely enveloping his lower half in its frosty temperatures. The top half of his body wasn't faring much better. The snow beat against it so thickly that he might as well have been standing up to his forehead in snow. Muttering more curses, he began to make his way through the thick snow banks and toward the cave.

By the time he made it into the dark cave, his teeth were chattering. Unfortunately, Harlow didn't seem to have any kind of heat spell going in here, either, because the inside of the cave wasn't all that much warmer than the outside. He looked around in the darkness, not seeing anything much and trying to figure out where the duffel bags might be so that he could at least get some clothes on. Finally, he lost patience and didn't care if he woke Harlow up.

"Harlow," he yelled. "Harlow, can you get up and help me? I need my clothes, and I wouldn't mind a heat spell and some light. My ass is turning into a block of ice."

There was no answer except the howling of the wind outside.

"Harlow?" Myles yelled again. His eyes were starting to adjust to the dim light of the cave, and his frustration was starting to turn to panic.

"Harlow!" he yelled. There was still no answer, and now, he could clearly see that the cave was empty. He turned in wild circles kicking around at the floor as though he might somehow just not be seeing the bags. He completely forgot about being cold as he tried to make sense of the situation. Was it possible he was in the wrong cave? No, this one was the exact shape and size of the hideout he had left earlier today. And it was completely free of snow on the floor. New snow was beginning to accumulate near the entrance of the cave, but the rest of the space was bare and dry. This was the cave from which he and Harlow had cleared the snow.

Only Harlow wasn't here. And neither were their bags. Myles heart filled with terror as he began to comprehend the awful truth.

"They found her," he said aloud. "They found her and took her, along with our bags."

There was no other reasonable explanation. Harlow would not have just left, leaving him no clues to her whereabouts. If she had to leave in a hurry for some reason, she would have left him some sort of sign. And she probably would have been kind enough to leave him some clothes, too. Myles looked down at his hands, which were ice cold by now. His human form, although strong and full of internal warmth, was just not able to combat temperatures this severe without at least some clothes to protect him.

Myles gave a big grunt of frustration, and then headed back outside, where he quickly shifted back into dragon form. Just moments after the transformation was complete, he felt better. His body, now protected by dragon hide, felt warm again. He blinked his dragon eyes a few times, looking around as he tried to spot any signs of struggle. He breathed in deeply, trying to catch the scent of any strange intruders. But he could not see or smell anything. The snowstorm had wiped away all evidence that any living being had been here. All he could see and smell was snow and rock. He whirled around in several large circles, desperately searching for clues. How had they found her? How had they taken her away? Where had they gone?

There were no clues, no answers to his questions. Myles let out a roar, and breathed a long, angry stream of fire from his mouth. But venting his frustration did not help him feel better. He would not feel better until he found Harlow, and got her away from those despicable excuses for soldiers that made up Saul's army.

Myles could sense the panic rising in his chest. Saul's men practiced dark magic, and he knew that they were the kind of evil people who would take great pleasure in using dark, evil spells on Harlow. The first thing they would have done, too, would be to strip her of her magic ring. She was out there right now, in an invisible hideout and completely helpless against some of the worst evil that humanity had to offer. How could he have been so stupid, to leave her here alone? His primary objective on this mission had been to keep her safe, and he'd failed at that. He'd gotten so caught up in the excitement of the search for Saul's men, that he'd let down his guard and let Saul's men come right to their hideout to kidnap Harlow.

Myles let out another roar and began to flap his dragon wings, lifting himself up into the air again. He had to find her. He had no idea how he was going to figure out where Saul's army was hiding under an invisibility spell, especially in the middle of this damnable snowstorm. And he wasn't sure how he was going to break into that hideout once he found it. There were sure to be plenty of evil wizards and shifters, guarding both the base camp and Harlow herself.

But he had to find a way. He must launch a rescue effort, and he must not fail.

The love of his life was depending on him.

CHAPTER SEVENTEEN

Harlow shivered in the darkness. She was still under the blanket on the snowmobile's trailer, although the snowmobile hadn't moved in nearly half an hour. For a while, she'd heard voices around her as the men had discussed where they should keep her on the base, and whether they should tell Saul now that they had her, or wait until the other group got back from town with a second prisoner.

Harlow had wanted to laugh out loud. They sounded so certain that they were going to capture Myles. They were going to be awfully disappointed, since Myles was nowhere near Devil's Melt Proper. Harlow hoped that they searched the town for a long, long time, though. The more time they wasted, the more time Myles had to come rescue her before they got really angry at her for lying to them.

There were no more voices around her now. Everyone seemed to have walked off, and Harlow began to wonder if they had somehow forgotten about her. Her shivering was growing steadily stronger. The blanket didn't offer much warmth, and the temperature outside seemed to be dropping. If someone didn't come get her soon, she very possibly might die of frostbite and hypothermia.

Just when Harlow was ready to give herself up as lost, she heard voices coming back toward the trailer. A few moments later, the blanket was thrown back suddenly, and Harlow winced at the sudden brightness. The sky was relatively dark, thanks to the late hour and thickening storm. But even the snowy grayness was bright compared to the blackness of the thick blanket.

She felt rough hands pulling her up. Her body was still immobile under the binding spell, but she could feel aches in her stiff muscles. It seemed doubly cruel to have aches in muscles that you couldn't even move. As her eyes adjusted to the light, she managed to focus her gaze on the men surrounding her. There were some who must be shifters. They were tall and muscular, as shifters usually were, and they did not have magic rings on their fingers. Others in the group were not quite as tall or muscular as the shifters, but they did boast brilliant magic rings on their fingers. Evil wizards, Harlow thought. Saul's minions, who were no doubt eager to test out their dark magic skills on some poor victim like herself.

No one said a word to her as they hauled her like a large sack of potatoes toward a large tent. Harlow looked up at the sky and saw that it looked slightly blurry. Either her vision was playing tricks on her due to the long hours spent in darkness under the blanket, or there was a poorly done invisibility shield over this base camp. Harlow was willing to bet it was the latter, and that realization filled her with despair. Myles would have difficulty finding any sort of base camp in this weather, let alone a base camp shrouded in an invisibility spell.

For the hundredth time that day, Harlow reminded herself not to panic, but heeding her self-admonitions was getting more and more difficult as the hours passed. She was beginning to feel like a fool for ever thinking that she was capable of coming on a mission like this by herself. Perhaps Alfonso had been right, after all. Perhaps this should have been left to the professional spies. It didn't matter now, though. What's done was done. She had chosen to take this mission, and she had gotten herself into this predicament. It was up to her to get herself out of it.

The men entered the large tent, and Harlow instantly felt warmth washing over her body. She was grateful for that, at least. The men walked briskly through the tent, which appeared to have been divided into several dozen rooms. They finally stopped in front of one of the open door flaps to a room and ducked inside. Harlow strained to look around, and saw that they were in some sort of small sleeping quarters. The small room had a bed just large enough to sleep one adult, and a small wooden trunk. That was it for furnishings. The man who had been holding Harlow dropped her roughly onto the bed, then to her utmost surprise, pointed his magic ring at her and said, "*Obstupefio terminantur.*"

The invisible energy that had bound Harlow's body dissipated immediately, and she found herself able to move once more. She sat up in the bed and rubbed at her stiff arms, looking warily over at the men who had just brought her into the room.

"Lucky you, the boss wants to talk to you," the man who had just dropped her said. "Clean yourself up. You'll find clothes and a hairbrush in that little trunk, and one of our wizards should be here any moment now with a basin of water for you to wash off your face with. Make yourself look presentable. It would serve you well to impress the boss, trust me. And don't try any funny business. My men are guarding the room on all sides. If you try to escape, we'll make you curse the day you were born."

With that, the men disappeared from the room. A few seconds later, the door flap opened and a short, plump wizard walked in carrying a basin that sat attached to the top of a tall pedestal. The woman nodded courteously to Harlow, then set the basin pedestal down in the middle of the room. She pointed her magic ring at it and said "*Magicae aqua.*"

Instantly, the basin filled with water. The woman bowed slightly, then turned and left the little tent room without another word. Harlow sat motionless for a full minute after the woman had gone, but then roused herself and stood. She had no idea who this "boss" was or why the guards thought it was lucky that he wanted to talk to her, but she couldn't imagine that anything good would come of this. She figured, though, that if she'd been instructed to wash and dress, she might as well do so. She needed to pick her battles here, and there was no sense in angering anyone over something as minor as getting dressed.

Harlow opened the chest to find to her surprise that it contained wizard dress robes in a deep ruby red color. She couldn't imagine why the "boss" would want her to wear dress robes, except perhaps to make fun of her. With a sigh, she started stripping out of her street clothes. If he wanted to make fun of her, let him. The more time he wasted on silly antics, the more time Myles had to find her and rescue her.

Harlow slipped into the dress robes, which fit surprisingly well. Whoever had guessed at her size had done a good job. She found the hairbrush in the trunk and brushed out her long dark locks. Then she went to the basin and splashed a small bit of water on her face. The water was surprisingly warm, and Harlow sank her hands down into it once she realized this. The heat of the water slowly chased away the chill in her fingers. Once she was ready, Harlow was not sure what to do next, and she sat down on the small bed to think. She fingered at her magic ring, which was still invisible, and thought about what spells she might use to get herself out of here.

She had to plan things carefully. There were way too many wizards out here for her to overcome by herself. She would have to use stealth, but even then, she needed a clear plan. If she merely used an invisibility spell and left, she would be in the middle of a snowy wilderness with no supplies and no idea which direction to walk in. Perhaps she could find a way to steal a snowmobile and make a break for it that way. That would require some finesse, though. She'd have to put a silencing spell on the snowmobile, along with an invisibility spell, or her captors would realize what was going on. Snowmobiles don't just start riding away of their own accord.

Then, suddenly, with her mind fixated on invisibility spells, Harlow realized that it might be possible to damage the invisibility shield that surrounded this base camp. She stood, excitement filling her as she tried to think of a counterspell that would work. She didn't need to damage the whole shield. Just enough so that Myles would be able to see the camp if he flew over it. The invisibility spell had not been cast very well, by the looks of it, so it shouldn't be too hard to make a dent in it. Harlow squeezed her eyes shut as she thought, trying her best to come up with an idea that would work. After a few moments of thinking, she opened her eyes and snapped her fingers.

"Got it," she said. But she would need to be in open air for it to work, not under the roof of the tent. She was about to open the door flap to her little tent room to ask if she could be allowed to have some fresh air, when the flap was opened by one of the guards.

"Come on," he said. "We're going to see the boss."

"Is he in this tent?" Harlow asked, trying to keep her voice casual.

The guard rolled his eyes at her. "Of course not. The boss don't hang out with the common folk. He's in his tent. Let's go."

Harlow could not have been happier at this news. It meant she would be outside for a few moments while they transferred her, giving her a chance to perform the spell she had in mind She quickly fell into step behind the guard, and the other guards who had been waiting in the hallway joined her. She took a deep breath to steady her nerves as they stepped outside. She was going to have to cast this spell stealthily, so that the guards didn't realize what she was doing and figure out that she still had a magic ring. She was frantically trying to come up with a good diversion, when fate decided to hand her one.

A sudden, loud explosion sounded off in the otherwise stillness of the snowy base camp. Harlow found herself knocked to the ground along with several of the guards. Screams rang out across the yard, but Harlow did not bother looking to see what was going on. This was her chance, but she knew she only had a few seconds to act. While everyone else was disoriented, following the instinctive urge to look around and see what had caused the explosion, she would be carving out a hole in the invisibility shield.

Harlow pointed her ringed hand toward the sky as unobtrusively as she could, and yelled out, "*Magicae oblitero.*"

She could feel the energy shooting out from her hand, and she knew the spell was working. She moved her ring in a large circle as she pointed it toward the sky, hoping to cover a large area with the spell. Nervously, she glanced around at the guards, but none of them seemed to have heard her scream out her spell. There had been too much other shouting going on. Harlow glanced up toward the sky, hoping and praying that the magic repelling spell had worked.

It was a defensive spell, normally used to surround yourself with an invisible force field of sorts. That force field repelled any and all magic spells, which kept anyone inside of it safe from attacking wizards. It wasn't a very strong shield, and so was usually used only as a way to buy time when trying to get away from an attacking wizard. It would not hold very long in a battle—as soon as a wizard realized the spell was there, several counterspells could easily break down the force field, allowing magic to work in that area once again.

But it didn't matter that the force field was easily destroyed, as long as Saul's army didn't realize it was there. They had no idea that she had her magic ring still, and so they would not be expecting her to have been able to cast any spells. The force field would keep any magic spells from working in the area where Harlow had cast it, including, of course, invisibility shields. If Myles flew over this area, he would be able to see the enemy's base camp through the large, gaping hole in the invisibility shield. Harlow bit her lip as she looked up, silently praying that he would fly by here soon. She wasn't sure what plans "the boss" had for her, but she had a feeling they weren't good.

Rough hands pulled her up, then, and everything around her came back into sharp focus. She looked around, remembering suddenly that she had no idea what had caused the explosion. A glance over her left shoulder showed her the problem. A snowmobile had exploded, and had caused the snowmobile next to it to explode as well. Both vehicles were up in flames now, and were surrounded by angry, shouting wizards.

"Stupid ass showoffs," muttered the guard who had pulled her up from the ground. "Always trying to one-up each other on their spells. I told them that one day they were going to do some real damage with all their antics. Boss won't be happy about losing two snowmobiles for no reason, no siree."

The other guards grunted and muttered words of agreement, and Harlow couldn't help looking back over her shoulders again to stare at the wizards gathered around the burning snowmobiles. They were all yelling at each other, too wound up in the moment to even bother with using a water spell to put out the fire. The scene was almost comical, and reminded Harlow of a clown show she had once seen where the clowns ran around in frantic circles while a fire blazed behind them. She wanted to laugh, but she didn't think her captors would take too kindly to that, so she kept her mouth shut.

The guards were pushing her toward a large tent now, which Harlow assumed belonged to the boss. Several shifter and wizard guards surrounded the structure. They nodded courteously to the guards who were escorting Harlow, and stepped back to allow them to pass. Harlow felt her stomach clenching tightly with anxiety as she followed the guard in front of her into the tent. All of Peter's warnings about dark magic came flooding back to her mind, causing a cold sweat to begin to break out onto her forehead. Would the "boss" try to use dark magic spells on her, to try to force her to talk? Harlow had vowed she would never give away information about her clan or the dragon shifters, and she meant to stick to that vow. But she wasn't looking forward to facing down dark magic by herself. She had her ring, true. But there were too many evil wizards and shifters here for her to fight on her own. She was only one wizard, and she could only do so much.

Swallowing the lump in her throat, Harlow allowed one of the guards to take her arm and lead her deeper into the tent. There seemed to be an outer chamber and inner chamber in the structure. The outer chamber was full of plush-looking couches and chairs and tables constructed of rich wood. The tables were covered with platters of delicious-looking food, and pitchers of water and wine. Harlow felt her mouth watering, and she realized that it had been hours since she'd eaten anything. In the back of her mind, she wondered why Saul's men, whose conversation she had recorded, had complained about supplies running low. They must have fixed their supply problem, because from the looks of the spread here, there was plenty of food. Or, perhaps, the supply problem only existed because the boss took all of the best food for himself.

Harlow didn't have long to ponder the question. She was being pushed through a tent flap now into the inner chamber. She stumbled a bit from the force of the guards arms on her back, but managed to catch herself before she completely fell over.

When she looked up and looked around, she was taken aback by the richness of what she saw. The tent walls in here were covered with velvet drapes the same shade of ruby red as the dress robes that Harlow was wearing. Dozens of large candles filled the space, casting ambient light across the whole room. Harlow questioned the wisdom of lighting so many candles inside a structure like a tent, which might catch fire easily. But she supposed the boss didn't care much. He could probably just get a new tent.

Speaking of the boss, Harlow was pretty sure she had just come face to face with him, and she gasped at what she saw.

CHAPTER EIGHTEEN

"Samuel!" Harlow exclaimed, unable to hold back her shock.

The man in front of her, an old, white-haired wizard wearing dress robes of ruby and gold, with a tall wizard hat of the same color, rose to his feet and bowed.

"Indeed," he said. "I'm Samuel. I'm pleased to see that the citizens of Falcon Cross have not forgotten me entirely. And you must be Harlow."

Harlow was speechless. Samuel had been one of the High Council members in Falcon Cross, until he had committed treason and had been stripped of his magic and excommunicated. How had he ended up here, commanding an outpost of Saul's army? The stripping of magic was irreversible, and would have left Samuel as nothing more than a helpless old man. And yet here he stood, obviously in charge and revered by all of the shifters and wizards in this base camp. Harlow's eyes inadvertently made their way down to his right hand, where she saw to her surprise that he wore a magic ring of dark, black onyx.

Samuel saw her gaze as it landed on his ring, and he smiled a sinister, evil smile.

"Oh yes, my dear. I'm wearing a magic ring. And as you might have guessed, I wear it so I can do magic."

With that, he raised his ringed hand and screamed out, "*Magicae ignis.*" Flames shot from his ring, coming dangerously close to hitting the very flammable roof of the tent. Despite her resolve not to speak any more than necessary, Harlow could not help herself.

"But…but you were stripped of your magic. The process is irreversible," she said.

"*Ignis terminantur,*" Samuel said. The flames stopped, and he turned toward Harlow with a look of extreme satisfaction on his face.

"I was indeed stripped of my magic," he said, his voice dripping with bitterness. "But such a procedure is not, as you have always been told, irreversible. There are ways to restore magic. They are painful procedures, to be sure. But not so painful as spending the rest of your life with no ability to do magic."

He dramatically turned, sweeping his long dress robes in a giant circle as he did. He walked to a large, high-backed arm chair that looked suspiciously similar to a throne, and sat down. Behind the "throne" hung several traditional wizard accoutrements: a few broomsticks for flying, an old-fashioned wand, which most modern wizards had given up in favor of the more practical magic rings, and a long sash that was embroidered with ancient runes. Harlow knew wizards of old had often worn these sashes because they believed the sashes enhanced their magical powers. She'd always been told that was just a legend, and there was no truth to it. But then again, she'd also been told that magic could not be restored once it was stripped away. And yet, here in front of her was a man who had been stripped of magic and could still perform magic spells.

Samuel leaned back in his chair, with his hands resting regally on the armrests. He eyed Harlow curiously, sizing her up. She wanted to ask how, exactly, his magic had been restored, but she refrained. She did not want to give him the satisfaction of acting any more interested than she already had. It didn't matter, though, whether she asked. He had apparently decided to tell her anyway.

"You see, Harlow, there are powers in magic greater than you have ever been allowed to know," he said. "And my liege and leader, Saul, has become an expert at such powers. It was, you see, Saul who gave me back my magic. He is a great man and I owe him my full allegiance."

"You owed your full allegiance to Falcon Cross!" Harlow spat out, disgusted by Samuel's show of bravado. But Samuel, who seemed unperturbed by Harlow's anger, merely laughed.

"Oh, to be sure, I swore allegiance to Falcon Cross. But the wizards in Falcon Cross let me down. They would not touch the most powerful magic, the magic that could have allowed our clan to rule the world. Instead, they insisted it was too dangerous. They held us back from true glory. Falcon Cross could have been great, Harlow. Instead, it will be subject to Saul, the truest master of magic there ever was."

"Master of *dark* magic, you mean," Harlow said, her tone disgusted. But Samuel only chuckled again.

"Oh, child. You must get over this aversion to 'dark magic,' as you call it. There is no dark or light in magic, only powerful or weak. Join us. Choose the side of power."

Harlow's eyes widened. "You're delusional," she said. "Dark magic destroys those who use it."

Samuel raised an eyebrow at her. "So you've been told. Just as you've been told that magic can't be restored, or that only those who are born as wizards can use magic. But Saul was not born a wizard, and yet he uses magic. It's time to question what you thought you knew."

"What are you talking about?" Harlow asked. She was confused. She'd been told that Saul was a dragon shifter. And shifters could not use magic—not as far as she knew. Samuel was right. Harlow had always been told that only those who were born as wizards could use magic.

"Saul was born a dragon shifter, yes," Samuel said as though he were reading Harlow's mind. "But he has also been given the ability to use magic. He met a wizard who practiced, as you call it, *dark* magic. That wizard performed a spell on him that turned him into a wizard, and he has since become an expert in dark magic. Forget your precious Peter back in Falcon Cross. Saul is the most powerful wizard you will ever meet."

Harlow was speechless again. Her whole being was filled with horror at what Samuel was telling her. It seemed impossible, and yet, it must be true. Peter himself had said that dark magic could do strange things that normal, good magic could not. Although, as she looked up at Samuel's twisted, evil face, Harlow had no doubt that at least *one* thing she'd always been told about dark magic was true: it turned the person who was using it evil, and sucked away their soul. Perhaps dark magic was powerful, but it would certainly destroy anyone who used it. Not to mention that most of the dark magic spells were used to inflict pain on others, which Harlow was not interested in doing. Harlow looked up at Samuel with hatred in her eyes. She could not believe that he used to be someone she looked up to. He seemed unaffected by her glares, however, and continued to smile down at her.

"You're probably wondering why I've brought you here," he said, drumming his fingers on the armrest of his chair. "The reason, my dear child, is to ask you to join us."

"Join you and Saul?" Harlow asked, incredulous. "Never!"

Samuel started laughing again. Harlow generally didn't like to harm people if she didn't have to, but she had never wished so badly that she could punch someone in the face. Her stomach turned every time Samuel called her "dear child," as though they were somehow akin to family. She wanted nothing to do with this man and his evil plans.

Samuel stood then, and nodded to the guards, which seemed to be some sort of signal. Two of the guards left the room, and came back a few minutes later carrying a large wooden trunk between them. They deposited the large trunk right in front of the chair where Samuel had been sitting. A woman had followed them in, a young wizard dressed in ruby robes that were similar to the dress robes Harlow was wearing. She stood by the trunk with her hands folded neatly in front of her, attentively watching Harlow. Samuel nodded at the woman, and she produced a large set of keys which she promptly handed over to Samuel.

"It's this one, your Honor," she said, bowing slightly and pointing to one of the keys. Harlow felt her stomach turn again as she heard Samuel referred to by his old title of "your Honor." There was nothing honorable about him, and that young wizard was severely mistaken if she thought Samuel deserved a title like that. For his part, Samuel clearly enjoyed the title, because he gave a slight bow back in the woman's direction.

"Thank you, Isabelle," he said, then moved to unlock the trunk. When he had pushed back the lid, he pulled out first Harlow's duffel bag, then Myles' duffel, and then the backpack they had been using. After that, he pulled out a large, leather briefcase that appeared to be stuffed with papers. Harlow blinked a few times, straining her eyes to see what kinds of papers they might be. But Samuel was all too happy to tell her.

"The amethyst records, Harlow," he said with a huge, stupid grin on his face. "I believe you're familiar with them?"

Harlow did not answer him. She glared in his direction, trying to put up an unimpressed façade. On the inside, though, she was frantically trying to figure out a way to get the records. Perhaps if she ran and grabbed them quickly, then grabbed a broomstick from behind Samuel's chair to cast a flying spell, she could escape before they had time to react. She would just need a little bit of a head start.

But no, Harlow thought as she looked around the room. There were way too many of them, and only one of her. There was no way she could escape before someone hit her with some sort of spell. Besides, she had only flown on a broomstick a handful of times, and she was awful at it. Broomstick flying was heavily regulated in Falcon Cross, and it had never seemed worth it to her to put in the time to learn how to do it properly. She had never regretted that decision as much as she did right now. Her very core seemed to ache as she looked over at the amethyst records. That was what she had come for. They were right there, just a few feet away from her, and she had no way to steal them away.

"I've read though all your notes, and I've seen your maps," Samuel was saying, and Harlow turned her attention back to him as he spoke. "I must say, I'm impressed with how much you managed to figure out. The Advocacy Bureau certainly doesn't know what a treasure they have in you. Let me guess, you're completely underestimated and unappreciated there?"

Harlow said nothing, although there was some truth to what Samuel said. She supposed he knew, from years of living in Falcon Cross, that many times being an Advocate could feel like a thankless job.

"Leave Falcon Cross, Harlow," Samuel said. "Come join us. We will teach you the most powerful spells in existence. We could use someone of your abilities and intelligence. You'll be appreciated, and find glory and fame here. Just say the word, Harlow. Swear your allegiance to me and to Saul, and we'll return your magic ring and make you an honored member of our company."

Harlow started a bit at the mention of her magic ring. She realized suddenly that if Samuel had gone through all her things, he would have realized that there was no ring in the bags. Hadn't he become suspicious, wondering what had happened to it? Wizards might take their rings off now and then, but they never strayed far from where they were.

Samuel must have seen the startled expression on Harlow's face, because he started laughing again. Harlow cringed at the evil sound of it.

"Oh yes, dear child," he said. "We found the ring. Did you really think hiding it in a secret pocket would save you from us finding it? I must say, for all the intelligence you've shown, that was quite a fatal mistake. You'd have been better off just leaving it in plain view on your finger so you could use it when you were attacked."

"Secret pocket?" Harlow asked dumbly. She didn't have any secret pockets, and she certainly hadn't put her ring in any of them. In fact, she could still feel her ring now, its metal encircling her finger under a shroud of magic invisibility.

"Oh yes," Samuel said haughtily. "There's no use pretending you don't know what I'm talking about. Isabelle told me that she found the secret pocket and the ring when she searched you upon your arrival here. The ring is in safekeeping now, in our most secure, most closely guarded trunk. Isn't that right, Isabelle?"

"Exactly right, your Honor," Isabelle said. Harlow gaped at Isabelle in confusion, but the woman's face remained impassive. Harlow was beyond confused. She had never even seen Isabelle before this moment, let alone been searched by her. What game was she trying to play, lying to Samuel so casually?

"So you see," Samuel continued, although Harlow was watching Isabelle instead of him now. "Your ring is there for the taking. All you have to do is join us, and Isabelle will go retrieve it for you. Instead of being a hopeless prisoner, you can be a hero, using your formidable intelligence to help us find the dragon amethyst."

Isabelle's expression remained completely impassive as Samuel spoke. But then, in a movement so short and subtle that Harlow almost missed it, she saw Isabelle's eyes flit downward. For a split-second, Isabelle's eyes landed on where Harlow's ring was resting quite invisibly on Harlow's hand. Then, Isabelle looked back up at Samuel attentively.

She knows, Harlow thought, a sudden flicker of hope filling her heart. *She knows I have my ring, and she's purposely keeping that knowledge from Samuel.* Harlow had at least one friend here, even if Myles did not manage to find her. Emboldened by this knowledge, Harlow stuck her chin out defiantly in Samuel's direction.

"I still believe in honor, and in fighting for good," she said. "I would die a thousand deaths before I would join you."

For the first time since Harlow had arrived in the tent, she saw anger cross over Samuel's face.

"Well, perhaps that can be arranged," he said, then pointed his magic ring at Harlow. "*Magicae fulmen.*"

Instantly, a searing pain shot through Harlow's entire body, and she felt her feet leaving the ground. She found herself suspended several feet above the floor of the tent, with constant shocks of pain shooting through her. It felt like someone was sending painful electric shocks through her over and over again. As hard as she tried to resist giving him the satisfaction of knowing he was hurting her, the agony was too much to bear, and she opened her mouth to let out a loud, painful scream. Her scream was followed by a long, evil laugh from Samuel.

"*Fulmen terminantur,*" Samuel said. Harlow fell to the ground with a thud as the spell ended. She winced as the fall nearly knocked the wind out of her, but the pain of the fall was nothing compared to what the pain of the spell had been. She panted for air, panic rising in her chest. That was just one measly spell. What else was Samuel planning to do to her? She knew from her studies that dark magic knew almost no bounds. She braced herself as Samuel began circling her, his eyes flashing with rage. No matter what, she told herself. I must remain strong. I would rather die than betray my clan.

"Was that enough?" Samuel asked, sneering. "Are you ready to join us, or are you going to be a glutton for punishment."

Harlow did not answer him. She closed her eyes tightly and resisted the almost overwhelming urge to try to use a shield spell. She could not let him know yet that she had her ring. She needed to save it for an opportune time, when she might actually have a chance of escape. There were too many guards here now. Any spells she used would be cancelled out by counterspells in a matter of minutes.

"Fine," Samuel said, raising his ringed hand again. "Have it your way."

Harlow felt her stomach clench up at the anticipation of another round of painful shocks, but the shocks never came. At that moment, screams suddenly rose up from somewhere outside the tent, followed by a loud roar. Samuel paused with his hand in mid-air, looking up in confusion and looking over at his guards with questions in his eyes. The screams grew louder and more frantic, and the guards turned away from Harlow and toward the door, the wizards among them raising their ringed hands to defend against whatever threat was out there.

Harlow was frozen in place, wondering if now was a good time to try to make a break for it, when she finally managed to make out the one word everyone outside was screaming over and over.

"Dragon! Dragon! Dragon!"

CHAPTER NINETEEN

Myles was fighting blindly, roaring and breathing out giant streams of fire in every direction. After seeing the hole in the invisibility shield which revealed this camp to him—surely, Harlow's work—he'd intended to make an attempt at sneaking in. But the guards watching the camp had seen his blurry dragon form flying across the sky. They'd been pretty trigger happy, too, immediately shooting up a laser-beam attack from their rings. Myles had easily dodged the attack, but in doing so had completely given up on his attempt to maintain his chameleon-like cover. Once he was visible, he figured the best thing to do was just attack everyone. He slashed with his claws, bit with his teeth, and breathed fire out onto everyone in his path, all the while keeping a careful eye out for Harlow.

He didn't see her anywhere, though. Several of the tents were on fire now, and he saw dozens of wizards and shifters pouring out of them. His dragon eyes darted back and forth, but there was no sign of her. She was here, though, he knew it. And he would find her. He had sworn to protect her, and he would get her out of here or die trying.

A few seconds later, his eyes caught sight of an unusual number of extra-large guards running out of a particularly large tent. His eyes narrowed, and he instantly knew that something special was in that tent. Otherwise, why would so many elite guards be there? Myles let out another stream of fire on the group of snowmobiles to his left, setting off a series of gas explosions. Then he took off running toward the large tent. He breathed fire onto the side, sending the tent up in flames. He ignored the spells that wizards were casting at him right and left, and most of them just bounced off his thick dragon hide. A few shifters who had transformed into animal form were trying to attack him as well, but he easily swatted away even bears and tigers with his powerful dragon arms.

Moments later, when he ran through the burning hole in the tent wall, he found himself in a large room face to face with several of the evil wizards, who had formed a protective circle around Harlow. The only wizard who was not guarding Harlow appeared to be guarding a large trunk. Myles turned his dragon head toward the circle, and let out a warning roar.

One of the wizards, who appeared to be the ringleader of the group, laughed, and shook his magic ring menacingly in Myles' direction.

"Not much you can do, sulfur-breath. If you burn us, you'll burn the girl, too, and I take it you're not so keen to do that. She doesn't have a magic ring anymore, so she won't even be able to put up a shield against your fire."

Myles hesitated, his eyes glancing down to Harlow's right hand where she usually wore her ring. She saw his eyes searching, and suddenly yelled out. "*Abscondo terminantur.*" Instantly her ring appeared on her hand, seemingly out of thin air. Before any of the other wizards could react, she yelled out "*Magicae arma.*"

Then she nodded at Myles, and he knew what the nod meant. She had a shield up, it was now or never. He had to act before the other wizards caught on to the fact that

344

Harlow did, in fact, have her ring.

He aimed for the leader first. The man tried to speak out a spell of some sort, but he was too slow. His haughty boasting had been his downfall, and he screamed in pain as he went up in flames. Several of the wizards near him caught fire, too, but many of them jumped away in time, scrambling out of reach of the red hot fire. Myles saw Harlow frozen in place, looking at the leader. Her face had contorted into a look of horror, and Myles whipped his tail around to prod her gently. She needed to get moving. They were not even close to safe yet. The touch of his tail seemed to spur her into action. She jumped to her feet and ran straight toward the wizard who was guarding the trunk. To Myles surprise, that wizard did not raise her ring to attack Harlow. Instead, the wizard reached down to pick up a leather briefcase, and held it out to Harlow.

Myles did not have time now to figure out what was going on with the briefcase and the other wizard. More guards and shifters were swarming into the room, and it was everything he could do to hold them back. He stood in one spot and slashed with his arms and tail, while breathing fire at each new wave of attackers. He took out many of them, but he could not keep this up forever. He was growing tired, and they needed to get out of here. He glanced back at Harlow, to see her consulting with the same wizard who'd been guarding the trunk. They were standing next to two broomsticks now. The other wizard was gesturing emphatically to Harlow, and Harlow was violently shaking her head "no."

That pause to glance back was Myles' downfall. While he was looking away, a wizard managed to hit his wing in a vulnerable spot with a vicious spell. Myles let out a roar of pain, and before he could fully recover, another wizard hit his wing in almost the same spot. Myles responded by sending off his largest stream of flames yet, and the tent was now a huge mass of flames, smoke, and burning bodies. For a moment, the avalanche of attackers stopped, blocked off by the rising flames. But any relief Myles might have felt was short-lived. When he tried to move the wing that had been hit, it would not respond properly, and sent horrible pain through his entire body. He fought off a wave of panic. This did not bode well for his ability to escape from this hellhole.

He looked back at Harlow, then, and saw that she was running toward him.

"Shift!" she yelled. "Shift back into human form so I can talk to you for a minute."

He did, causing the whole tent to shudder from the force of his shifting. In human form, the wound on his wing looked like a huge gash down his left side. It ran from his ribs to his hips, and it hurt ten times worse in human form than in dragon form. He saw Harlow's eyes look at the gash in shock, but he waved off her concern.

"I'm alive. No time for bandages right now. We have to get out of here," he said. "I don't have any clue, how, though. I can't fly. My wing is damaged too badly. Maybe there's a snowmobile still in working condition that we could use."

Harlow's face was white as the snow that covered the Montana landscape. Myles saw the other wizard Harlow had been talking to approach them just then, and he bristled. Harlow shook her head.

"Don't worry. She's a friend. I'll explain everything later, but we can trust her. Her name's Isabelle."

"I told you, it's Izzy to my friends," the woman said. "And listen, Harlow, you need to fly him out of here on a broomstick."

"I can't," Harlow said, panic rising in her voice. "I can barely control a broomstick when it's just me on it, let alone with a passenger!"

"We don't have a choice," Izzy said. "We can't outrun them on a snowmobile. They'll just get on another one and catch us. And if we don't leave now, we're going to be overcome by the guards soon. In fact we probably have less than a minute before they break through this fire wall and get back to attacking us."

Myles could feel himself growing lightheaded from loss of blood. He was naked from shifting, and shivering violently. The warmth of hot blood flowing down the entire left side of his body almost felt good.

"Harlow, you go," he said. "I'll stay and keep them at bay while you fly off."

"No! They'll kill you!" she said, her eyes filling with tears.

"They'll kill us all if we stay," Myles said. The agony in Harlow's eyes told him that she knew he was right.

"So be it," she said grimly, and ran toward the broomstick. Myles' own eyes filled with tears as he watched the love of his life for what he knew would be the last time.

She grabbed the broomstick, pointed her ring at it, and yelled, "*Magicae volant.*" The broomstick buzzed with energy from the flying spell, and Izzy did the same with a second broomstick. Harlow swung the leather briefcase over her shoulder, and Izzy grabbed the duffel bags and backpack, binding them all together with a magic spell so they were easier to hold.

Harlow mounted her broomstick, and wobbled wildly for a moment before gaining some semblance of balance. Myles raised his hand to wave goodbye and blow her one final kiss. But then, to his surprise, she raised her own hand—her ringed hand—and pointed it straight at him.

"*Magicae pluma,*" she yelled out, casting a weightlessness spell over him. Then she zoomed toward him and scooped him up as though he were light as a feather, positioning him in front of her on the broomstick and wrapping her arms tightly around him.

"No way am I leaving you! Hold on tight," she said. The broom wobbled, and Harlow flew straight backwards, crashing into the tent wall where the broomstick had been hanging a moment ago. Myles dimly saw a thick, long wooden wand hanging on the wall, and he reached out and grabbed it. He couldn't do magic, but he could sure as hell do some damage clubbing someone over the head with this thing.

"You're using your feet too much," Izzy yelled at Harlow. "Just very slight movements are all it takes. If you move too violently you make the broom shoot forward or backward like a rocket."

"Alright," Harlow said, although her voice made it sound like she thought it was anything but alright. "Let's go."

Izzy nodded, then let out a wild yell and shot straight through the fire wall Myles had created. Harlow followed suit, moving her broomstick so fast that Myles barely felt a flash of heat as they passed through the flames. On the other side of the fire, dozens of enemy soldiers were waiting. They tried to grab at Harlow, who was having trouble controlling the direction of her broom. Myles used all of his remaining strength to swing the wand he had grabbed. He moved it left and right in wide arcs, knocking out several soldiers with sheer force. Izzy was already rising high above them, shouting encouragement to Harlow while aiming spells to help ward off attackers.

Finally, Harlow managed to break free. The broomstick shot straight up into the air, and other then a few wild zig-zags, held mostly steady for the next few minutes. Izzy continued to call encouragement to Harlow, who seemed to fly smoother with each passing minute. Myles supposed that being further and further away from the enemy camp was helping calm her nerves quite a bit, too.

He realized with a sudden start that they had probably just left the amethyst records to burn, and his heart clenched with sadness. They had failed at their mission, and had no new information on how to retrieve the dragon amethyst. Myles felt another wave of lightheadedness wash over him as Harlow picked up speed. He was still bleeding profusely, and his spirits were not improved by the realization that the amethyst records were gone, likely destroyed forever.

At least, though, Harlow is safe," he thought, looking down at her arm that was still wrapped around him. He smiled at the sight, and then gave in to the exhaustion and lack of blood.

He stopped fighting the waves of pain and nausea, and everything went mercifully black.

CHAPTER TWENTY

Myles blinked his eyes open as bright sunbeams fell across them. It took a few moments for everything around him to register. He was lying under a thick blanket that felt strangely familiar. The window that was allowing sunbeams into the room offered a view that he'd spent most of his life waking up to: the heart of a California Redwood forest. Myles smiled dreamily and settled deeper into his pillow. It was good to be home.

Then, just as quickly as he settled down, he sat up with a start. The movement caused a sharp pang of pain to cut into his left side. Home? Why was he home in the Redwoods? And how in the world had he gotten here? The last thing he remembered was leaving an enemy camp on Harlow's broomstick, with a deep wound on his side.

Myles reached down to pull up the left side of the long-sleeved t-shirt that he was wearing. Yup. There was a huge, ugly gash down his side. Someone had stitched it up nicely, and it did look well on its way to healing, but there was no doubt that he'd suffered a nasty wound.

And all for nothing, he thought bitterly. The amethyst records still hadn't been recovered. But at least Harlow was safe? Or was she? His heart clenched up at the thought of Harlow. She'd been in much better shape than he had when they left the enemy's camp. Was she here in the Redwoods, or had she gone back to Falcon Cross? Surely, she would not have left him without saying goodbye. Then again, he had no idea how long he'd been unconscious. It had surely been a long time, since he was all the way back in his cabin at the Redwood Dragons' home base.

Myles stood up slowly, worried that his side would cause him pain again. But as long as he didn't make a sudden, sharp turn in the wrong direction, the wound on his side didn't seem to cause him too much trouble. He walked out of the small bedroom and into the living room of his cabin, where, he found, to his great joy, that Harlow was asleep on the couch. She had a book on her chest and looked as though she had fallen asleep in the middle of reading.

Her face appeared a great deal more peaceful than it had the last time Myles saw it. Her smooth skin glowed in the morning sunlight, and an expression of pure calm was on her face. She must have been dreaming about something happy, because the corners of her lips were turned up in the slightest of smiles. Myles could have watched her sleep all day.

She seemed to sense his presence, though, because a few moments later she opened her eyes. It took a couple seconds for her to focus her vision on Myles, but as soon as she realized he was standing there, she shot straight up from the couch, causing the book on her chest to go tumbling to the floor.

"Myles! You're awake," she said, rushing over to him. She was just about to wrap him in a giant bear hug when she stopped, her eyes filling with concern.

"Wait, how do you feel? Does your side hurt?" she asked.

Myles smiled. "It's alright. It doesn't really hurt that much, as long as I'm careful not to twist too far one way or the other. I certainly don't think a hug from my girl is going to do any harm."

Harlow grinned, then, and threw her arms around him. Myles buried his face in her soft hair and held her tight. She felt so small in his arms, and he was overcome with emotion thinking of what might have happened to her if he hadn't been able to find the enemy's base camp in time. Thinking about the enemy's camp reminded him of the giant hole in the invisibility shield.

"Harlow," he asked, pulling back to look at her face. "That big gap in the invisibility shield around the enemy's camp…was that your doing?"

Harlow's grin widened. "Yup," she said. "Those idiots never realized I had a magic ring, and I used it to make a gap in the shield so you could find me. I knew you'd come for me."

"Of course I came for you," Myles agreed, brushing back a strand of her hair. "When I got back to our hideout and you weren't there, I felt like such an idiot. I never should have left you alone out there."

Harlow shrugged. "It was my fault. I should have been watching for intruders more closely. But it doesn't matter anymore, anyway. Everything turned out just fine."

"Did it though?" Myles asked with a sigh. "I mean, I'm glad we both made it out okay. And I'm happy to be back home in the Redwoods, even though I have no idea how we got here or why we came here instead of going back to Falcon Cross. But we still don't have the amethyst records, and now we'll likely never get them. In fact, they were probably destroyed in all that fire. This is a big blow to the side of good in this war."

Harlow gave him a funny look. "But, you're wrong," she said. "We *do* have the amethyst records. I didn't realize that you didn't know that."

Myles' eyes widened. "We have the records? Seriously? How?"

Harlow laughed. "There's a lot I need to catch you up on. Here, sit down on the couch and I'll do my best to fill in the missing details."

Myles slowly walked over to the couch and sat down. He couldn't quite believe what Harlow was telling him. How was it possible she had the records? She'd been a prisoner up until the moment he rescued her, and there had been no time to go searching for the records before they escaped. Then, suddenly, it hit him.

"That leather briefcase!" he said, remembering the briefcase that Harlow had swung over her back just before they escaped. "Was *that* full of the records?"

Harlow nodded happily as she sat down next to him. "Yes. And we've got it here now."

Harlow proceeded to tell him all about how she had been captured, and managed to hide her magic ring. She explained how she had quickly made a hole in the invisibility shield, and how the ringleader of the enemy camp had been Samuel, an old High Council member from Falcon Cross. She told Myles about how Samuel had tried to get her to join the enemy's side, and about how he had started to use dark magic on her when she refused. She had just started to explain how she had realized that Izzy was an ally, when she was interrupted by loud shouts from outside.

Myles looked up, startled. "What's going on out there?" he asked, quickly rising to his feet. Harlow jumped up too, looking even happier than she had a few moments ago.

"Oh!" she said. "That must be Peter and the squadron from Falcon Cross!"

"Peter is here?" Myles asked, somewhat shocked. He was still confused how he himself had gotten here. And he had no idea why Peter himself would come all the way to Falcon Cross. Myles let out a long sigh. "It seems I missed even more than I thought."

"Come on," Harlow said. "Put on a hoodie or something and then we'll go out and greet Peter."

She started to head toward her own hoodie, which was hanging on a coat rack by the front door, but Myles caught her arm and stopped her. When she turned to look at him, his heart caught in his throat. He was still confused as heck about nearly everything, but the one thing he knew for certain was that he would never get tired of looking at Harlow's face. She brought to life parts of him that had been dead for a long, long time. Just looking at her filled him with a sense of hope for the future. For a few beats, he held her eyes, drinking in how lovely she was.

"Wait," he finally said in a soft voice. "Before we go out there, can you at least explain to me how I got here, and why Peter is here, so that I don't feel totally out of the loop. Heck, I don't even know how long I was unconscious before waking up!"

"Three days," Harlow said in a voice just as soft, wiggling her arm free from his grasp so that she could hold his hand instead. "We flew like the wind to get here—the whole way on broomsticks. I haven't spent much time flying on broomsticks, as you may have noticed, so it was rough going at first. But I got better after the first hour or two. Izzy led the way, and her encouragement kept me going."

"But how did you even know where the Dragons' camp was?" Myles asked. "It's not exactly easy to find and you've never been here before."

Harlow shrugged. "I called Falcon Cross. Once we were far enough away from Saul's men, we stopped to check on your wounds. Izzy's a doctor, apparently. She stitched you up really well, and said you were lucky to be alive. She also said you're healing up way faster than she would have thought you would."

Myles nodded. "It's the shifter genes. Shifters tend to heal faster than the average human."

"I don't doubt it, after watching you the last couple days. Anyway, while she stitched you up, I got in touch with the Advocacy Bureau. They gave me the coordinates for base camp here, and said it was better for you to come here and recuperate at home. They said it was because they thought you'd rest and heal better here, but I think the real reason was they didn't want Izzy in Falcon Cross until they had a chance to vet her."

Myles frowned thoughtfully. "They don't trust her? Or, maybe a better question would be, do they have a reason not to trust her?"

"They are wary of her," Harlow said. "I think she's trustworthy, but Peter is concerned because she was in the enemy's camp for so long. He worries she's a spy. But she helped save my life. If she hadn't lied to Samuel to make him believe that I didn't have a magic ring, I wouldn't have been able to defend myself when all hell broke loose."

A knock at the door interrupted Harlow's explanation. Myles went to open it, and found Finn, another of the Redwood Dragons, standing there. Finn's mouth dropped when he saw Myles out of bed.

"Myles! You're up! How do you feel?" Finn asked, reaching to pull Myles into a big bear hug, and giving him a few slaps on the back for good measure.

"I'm great, man," Myles said, returning the hug. "It's good to see you, Finn. It' s been way too long."

"I know, brother. Way too long. So long in fact that you went and found yourself a girl."

Myles raised an eyebrow at Finn. "So everyone knows about Harlow, eh?"

"Hard not to notice," Finn said, winking in Harlow's direction. "Harlow has hardly left your side. She's been taking good care of you, and the way she looks at you makes it obvious that it's because she's in love."

Myles glanced over at Harlow, who shrugged and was blushing.

"Seems like I owe you one, Harlow," he said.

"Nah," she said. "I think we're even at this point. We kind of saved each other."

"Harlow told us all about your dramatic escape from Saul's men," Finn said. "Wish I could have been there to take out a few of those bastards. But anyway, there'll be more time for talk later. I came to get Harlow because Peter is here, and wants to see her. Izzy is going to be giving her testimony, and Peter will be deciding whether to accept her into the Falcon Cross clan. Peter wants Harlow to witness the testimony. You should come too, Myles, since you're awake. After all you witnessed the whole battle at the enemy's base camp. Peter probably wants to hear about what happened there."

Myles nodded. "Alright," he said. "I was just coming out with Harlow, actually. I'm still somewhat confused about what happened, but I think I'm starting to piece it together."

"Come on," Harlow said. "I'll be explaining things to Peter, and so will Izzy. You'll start to figure it all out bit by bit."

Myles grabbed his hoodie as they left the cabin, putting it on to ward off the slight chill of the February air. The Redwood forest was cool, but it felt practically balmy after the frigid weather in Montana. He breathed in the deep, woodsy scent in the air and smiled. He had enjoyed his time in Falcon Cross, and he had a feeling he'd be going back very soon, but damn it if it wasn't nice to be home for a bit. He looked up at the trees, smiling as he took in the view of the ancient tree trunks, many of which had been there for over a thousand years. This place was ancient and mystical, and he loved it.

In addition to Finn, the other members of his clan who were currently living at the Redwoods' base—Vance, Grayson, Holden, and Weston—were standing around the fire pit in the middle of the base camp. Peter was there, with a large group of wizard soldiers. Another of the Redwood Dragons, Owen, was standing next to Peter. Owen was currently living in Falcon Cross, but must have flown out here with Peter so that there would be a dragon in the convoy.

Myles walked toward the fire pit, but before he could even reach one of the benches to sit down, he was mobbed with hugs from the dragons and wizards alike. Everyone was happy to see him feeling better, and asked him questions at a rapid pace until Peter called for order.

"Come now, everyone," Peter said in a booming voice. "There'll be plenty of time to harass Myles later, perhaps over a lovely barbeque for dinner. For now, let's get on with hearing the testimony of Miss Torres."

Myles looked over to see Izzy, whose last name was presumably Torres, sitting on a bench across from him, looking determined but slightly pale. He caught her eye, and gave her a friendly, encouraging smile. She smiled back, although she still looked nervous.

The rest of the group sat down, either on the log benches or on the ground, as Peter began the meeting. First, he congratulated Myles and Harlow for successfully retrieving the amethyst records. Then, he asked Harlow to recount the events that led to the capture of the amethyst records, so that everyone would know the story. Harlow obliged, telling again the story she had already told to Myles of her capture, and of how Samuel had tried to get her to convert to the side of evil. Peter's face was grave as he listened to her discuss the enemy's use of dark magic, but he did not interrupt Harlow. Harlow made sure to tell everyone about how Izzy had tricked Samuel into thinking that Harlow didn't have a magic ring. Harlow also told of how Izzy had helped her figure out how to fly a broomstick out of the enemy's camp, and how Izzy had stitched up Myles. At the end of Harlow's story, Peter turned to Izzy. His expression was serious, but not unkind.

"Well, Miss Isabelle Torres," Peter said. "From what Harlow has said, you were extremely helpful in getting the amethyst records, helping Harlow and Myles escape, and ensuring that Myles' wound was stitched up. We are grateful for your help. But despite your good deeds, the fact remains that you were in the enemy camp, and supposedly working for Saul. Can you explain why this was the case, if you truly do not want to follow the side of evil?"

Izzy stood slowly. Myles watched as she took a deep breath and looked around the circle, her face pale. When she spoke, though, her voice was strong.

"I know my situation must seem odd," she said. "After all, why would someone who wants to help the side of good be working for the side of evil? The answer, friends, is that I was not given much of a choice. My wizard clan, a small clan on the East Coast, was raided by Saul's men. They killed anyone who did not agree to swear allegiance to Saul. Perhaps I should have let them kill me, but then, I thought, I will be no help to anyone if I'm dead. I thought that perhaps, if I played along with Saul's men, that I would eventually have the chance to escape, or to at least sabotage some of their operations. As you know, I was able to do both of those things a few days ago."

Izzy paused to look around, and Myles looked around, too. The faces staring back at Izzy looked skeptical. Harlow must have noticed this, because she grabbed Myles' hand and squeezed it very tightly. Myles squeezed back. He knew Harlow was nervous for Izzy. In Harlow's mind, Izzy had helped save both of their lives and had played a significant role in getting the amethyst records. Harlow thought Izzy deserved to be an honored member of the Falcon Cross clan, and Myles tended to agree. But it wasn't up to Myles to decide. Peter would have to be the one to make the final judgment call.

"I did not tell the enemy's men that I was a doctor. I have decent broomstick flying skills, and because of this, I became one of the guards for the amethyst records. Samuel wanted wizards who could fly well as guards, since they've had so much trouble with the flying wizards in Falcon Cross. I tried for a long time to think of a way to escape and take the amethyst records on my own, but it always seemed impossible. There were too many other guards. But then, Harlow was captured. I didn't know who she was, but I knew she was on the side of good, and that was enough for me. When Samuel asked if I'd found her magic ring, I said I had. I realized that if he didn't know where it was she must still have it, hidden under some sort of invisibility spell."

"Smart girl," Peter said approvingly. It was the first overtly positive thing he'd said about Izzy, and Myles felt Harlow squeezing his hand tighter with excitement. Perhaps Izzy was winning Peter over.

"When Samuel called me in with the amethyst records, I had my first chance to see Harlow. I was impressed with how well she resisted the enemy's attempts to use dark magic on her."

It was Myles' turn to squeeze Harlow's hand. He hated to think about how she'd been tortured. His blood boiled in anger, and he swore for the thousandth time that he would destroy Saul and his army, no matter how long it took.

"When Myles came roaring in as a dragon," Izzy continued. "I knew this was my chance to escape, and to take the amethyst records with us. Samuel had been a fool to bring them out in the open as he did, but he always was a bit of a fool. He was trying to show off to Harlow what he had. The rest of the story, you've already heard from Harlow. I helped her use a broomstick, and led her away from the enemy's camp. Then I stitched up Myles' wound. I also gave the amethyst records over to Harlow. I hope that this proves to you my loyalty to the side of good. I'm not sure what more I could have done to show you that I do not want to work for Saul. I was there by force, and got away as soon as I could. It was one of the darkest times of my life, and the only thing that kept me going was the hope of eventually escaping."

Izzy finished speaking, and for several minutes, everyone was silent. The silence stretched uncomfortably long, but no one spoke as Peter paced back and forth, stroking his beard thoughtfully and considering Izzy's case. Finally, he stopped pacing and nodded. He had made his decision.

"Isabelle Torres," he said, his booming voice filling the whole clearing between the redwood trees. "It is my opinion as the lead High Councilor of Falcon Cross that you are loyal to the side of good, and should be allowed to join the Falcon Cross Clan. You were only working for the enemy under circumstances of extreme duress, and, when presented with the opportunity, you not only escaped yourself, but also helped our friends here escape. Not to mention, you helped us acquire the amethyst records, which we believe will allow us to find the dragon amethyst. This is a huge victory for the side of good. It would be my great pleasure to welcome you to Falcon Cross."

Izzy's eyes filled with tears as cheers broke out in the small crowd. Peter went to embrace his new clan member, and the cheers grew louder. Myles looked over at Harlow and saw that tears were filling her eyes as well. He wrapped his arms around her and kissed the side of her face.

"Looks like you've found yourself a new lifelong friend," Myles said.

Harlow looked up at Izzy, who was now being mobbed with congratulations by the whole group. "Looks like we all have," she said, and then snuggled deep into his embrace.

Yes, Myles thought. It was good to be home.

CHAPTER TWENTY-ONE

The rest of the day was no less exciting than the beginning had been. Plans were made to fly the amethyst records back to Falcon Cross the next day. Myles and Harlow would join the squadron, with Harlow once again flying with Myles on her broom. She was getting much better at flying, and Myles' wound was still too fresh for him to fly in dragon form. His human form was much better, but it would be a few weeks before his dragon wing was back to normal.

Harlow wasn't glad that his wing was injured, but she was happy that he was making a good recovery. And she was looking forward to flying together on her broomstick—this time without worry of being shot down by an enemy's dark magic spells. Ordinarily, invisibility spells were hard to maintain while flying, but Peter knew how to do a very complicated spell that would shroud the whole squadron in a constant cloak of invisibility, as long as they flew reasonably close together. It should be a safe, uneventful trip home. First, though, the whole group had a chance tonight to rest. And after the busy day they'd had, Harlow knew everyone was looking forward to that chance to rest.

There had been lengthy discussions on what was in the amethyst records, and how best to start preparing a mission to find the dragon amethyst. Harlow knew that, once the records were back in Falcon Cross, the Advocates would begin analyzing them while the military began preparing a search party. Things would need to move quickly. Although they had managed to steal the records, Saul's army might remember much of what was written in the records. There was still no guarantee that the enemy would not find the dragon amethyst first. Time was of the essence.

When all of the more somber discussions were done, though, there had still been time for an evening barbeque. Wizards loved celebrations, and the dragons had thrown them a huge party. There had been plenty of food, drink, and merriment. Even in these dark times, one could still find time to enjoy a good meal with friends.

Harlow was full and happy as she walked with Myles back to his cabin. She savored the way her hand fit so perfectly in his, and marveled for the hundredth time at how quickly he had stolen her heart. She had spent so much of her life trying to prove that she belonged, but she realized now that all of that struggling had been unnecessary. Myles had helped her to see that she did belong, and that she did have a place in Falcon Cross. Not only that, but she had never felt so at home as she did in his arms. Even though a war was raging around them, Harlow felt strangely at peace.

"I was wrong, you know," Harlow said to Myles as they walked into his cabin. "I *did* need you. If you hadn't been there to storm the enemy's camp in dragon form, I don't know what would have happened."

Myles shut the cabin door behind him, and smiled at her, taking her into his arms. "Well, we never would have known where to look for the amethyst records if not for you. And you did your part to help me rescue you by making the hole in the invisibility shield. The truth is, Harlow, we need each other. Not only for this mission we just completed but for every part of life from now on. We're lifemates, remember? Destined to be together. You complete me, and I complete you. And I wouldn't have it any other way."

Harlow smiled up at his deep green eyes, and her heart had never felt so full. The smile he returned told her that he felt the same. He held her gaze for a moment, and then, he closed his eyes and bent to kiss her. She closed her eyes as well, drinking in the warmth that flowed from his body to hers. There was no feeling in the world that compared to the joy she felt when she was in the arms of her dragon.

Myles kissed her deeply, slipping his tongue into her mouth, tasting her, and tickling the roof of her mouth. Their tongues danced together as they both held each other close with desperate arms, as though holding on for dear life. Harlow could feel her whole body responding to his touch. She grew warmer and warmer as he rubbed the small of her back with his hands. Her breasts tingled beneath her clothes as he pressed his chest against hers, and she could feel his erection, stiffening and growing between his legs as they kissed.

Between her own legs, heat and moisture was building. She felt pressure and heat building as her body prepared itself for him. Her extremities tingled with electric excitement, and her stomach kept flip-flopping with excitement. With every second that passed, she grew more desperate to have Myles inside of her. She craved him with a hunger like she had never known. He was right. They did complete each other.

After several minutes of increasingly passionate kissing, Myles reached a point where he seemed unable to hold back any longer. He grabbed the bottom of Harlow's hoodie and tore it up and over her head. Then he quickly followed suit with her shirt, leaving her standing in front of him in her bra, breathing heavily from the anticipation that filled her. She returned the favor by tearing his hoodie and t-shirt off as well, but she paused as he reached to pull her close again. She had just seen the ugly red line down his left side, and it had given her pause.

"Are you okay?" she whispered, gently tracing a line right next to the gash. "I don't want to do anything that's going to hurt you or slow down the healing process."

Myles let out a low growl. "I'm fine," he said. "It looks much worse than it feels. And if you want to speed up the healing process, then kiss me again. Your touch is like medicine to me."

The seriousness in his eyes told Harlow that he wasn't joking, and she smiled widely as she happily moved forward to oblige him. He groaned happily as her lips covered his again, then lifted her easily up off the ground to carry her into his bedroom. Harlow wrapped her legs around his waist, marveling at how easily he moved. He was right— the wound on his side did not seem to be bothering him at all.

Once they reached the bedroom, he dropped her on the bed and reached to pull off her shoes, and then her jeans. He kicked off his own shoes and jeans, and Harlow could see his erection pushing against the fabric of his briefs. She closed her eyes and sighed happily at the sight. It still took her breath away that he was hers. He was so perfect in every way, and yet he had chosen her. He had seen past her shortcomings and faults, and truly believed in her. And for that, she would be forever grateful.

Myles seemed to move with a deep sense of urgency now, as though a beast had been awakened within him. He slid onto the bed and reached behind her back to unclasp her bra, sliding it off and tossing it aside to leave her breasts bare before him. He cupped them both in his hands, pushing them close together so that her nipples were only inches apart, and then he moved his tongue back and forth rapidly across both nipples. She felt the hard nubs stiffen, and the tingling pressure in her body increased as he sent little shockwaves of pleasure throughout her body with every flick of his tongue. Her panties were soaked now from the intensity of her desire for him, and she moaned as she felt his erection pushing against the wet garment through the fabric of his underwear

The room felt like it was one thousand degrees. Heat and ecstasy filled her, and she felt herself burning up in the most delightful way. She was beginning to feel a sense of urgency herself. She could not wait much longer to have him inside of her. When he pulled back to strip out of his underwear, she pulled off her panties as well, kicking them across the room and leaving her whole body naked and trembling before him. He grinned down at her, eyeing her appreciatively from head to toe.

"Looks like someone is getting a little impatient," he said. Harlow was in no mood to wait while Myles teased her.

"Fuck me, now!" she ordered. His eyes filled with fresh fire and heat at her words, and he growled again.

"I'll teach you to order me around," he said, a mischievous smile crossing his face. He climbed over her, positioning his erection just above her slick entrance, and then rammed into her.

Harlow shouted out as he filled her. He was impossibly large, stretching her inner walls and rubbing hard against her most sensitive spots. She arched her back against him, trying to find relief and wanting more all at the same time. His fire filled her with every thrust, sending hot electric tingles throughout her whole being. She thrashed underneath him, moaning and sweating as he brought her closer to the edge with every passing second. Finally, she could not hold on any longer. With another loud scream, she gave in.

Her release came in rapid, violent waves. Her inner muscles clenched around his erection hungrily, sending wave after wave of the most wonderful ecstasy coursing through her body. She felt like she was drowning in a sea of passion, and she did not want to be saved.

He followed quickly behind her, roaring and stiffening as he thrust into her one last time. His muscular arms twitched with an overwhelming fervor as he filled her, pulsing into her. For several long, wonderful moments, they rode the waves of bliss together. They were truly one, and everything else seemed to disappear.

Harlow felt a happiness bordering on giddiness. She never wanted the moment to end, but, even as Myles slid out of her and lay next to her on the bed, pulling her into his arms, she knew that the moment never would truly end. The fire she felt in her heart, the flames that Myles had started there, burned constantly within her. They were bonded together, and as long as they both lived, their hearts would always burn as one, no matter how close or far apart they were.

Harlow snuggled closer against Myles' chest, safe in his arms. He kissed the top of her head and drew her closer, tightening his embrace around her. A few minutes later, she felt his breathing shift into the steady rhythm of sleep. She sighed happily as she gave in to the pull of sleep herself, and a small smile played at her lips as thoughts of Myles took over her dreams.

CHAPTER TWENTY-TWO

The next morning dawned sunny and bright. Just after sunrise, a group of wizards and dragons rose unseen into the clear blue sky. The invisibility shield Peter cast was a powerful one, shrouding the large group in secrecy and keeping them safe from the prying eyes of curious humans—or the sinister eyes of any enemy soldiers who might be watching.

If anyone had been able to see the group, however, they would have been in awe at the sight. Two mighty dragons—Owen and Finn, circled gracefully around a group of wizards in dark traveling robes, their broomsticks all in perfect formation and their magic rings glinting in the sunlight. This was not a group you wanted to mess with.

They picked up speed as they rose above the tops of the mighty redwoods, leaning close against their broomsticks to urge them on toward Falcon Cross. Toward home. Peter rode at the front of the group, with the amethyst records secured comfortably in his traveling bag. As soon as they reached the wizards' village, plans would begin in earnest to use the information in the records to send out a search for the dragon amethyst. In fact, Finn had been invited to come back to Falcon Cross to help in the search, since he was known as one of the best dragons in the Redwood Dragons clan at tracking down hard-to-find artifacts. In return for his help, Peter had left several wizards back in the Redwoods, to assist with defending the Redwood Dragons' home base.

As for Harlow, she sat on her broomstick with Myles, who sat behind her this time. His arms wrapped comfortably around her as they rode, and she smiled every time she looked down and saw his strong hands resting on her stomach. Every now and then, he would plant a kiss on the back of one of her shoulders, sending a little thrill of happiness through her whole body. When she glanced to her right, she saw Izzy flying next to her, also with a huge smile on her face. Harlow imagined that, after months of being trapped by wizards who practiced dark magic, Izzy must feel like she'd been given a second chance at life now that she was free.

Harlow herself felt like life was starting fresh. She'd realized that the people of Falcon Cross did indeed love her. She had a new friend in Izzy—someone she already knew would be a friend for life. And she had Myles.

Her heart beat faster in her chest when she thought of him. They had been through so much in their short time together, and she knew that many more wonderful adventures lay ahead. Things would never be dull with a dragon for a lifemate, and Harlow wouldn't have it any other way.

As if he sensed that she was thinking about him, Myles squeezed her tighter and planted another kiss on her back. Harlow smiled, then leaned into her broomstick a little more to pick up speed. They were going home, together.

Their mission had been a success, in more ways than one.

BOOK FIVE: DESTINY AND THE DRAGON

CHAPTER ONE

Dragon shifter Finn Pars shifted restlessly from foot to foot, only half-listening to what Peter, the old wizard standing at the podium was saying. The wizards loved pomp and pageantry, and would use any old excuse to give a speech. Finn had expected that he would have to listen to a long discourse before he and the rest of the search party were allowed to leave, but knowing that ahead of time didn't make it any more bearable.

Finn watched with a bored expression as Peter droned on. Peter served as the head wizard of the Falcon Cross High Council, and was renowned as one of the most powerful wizards alive. But Finn still had difficulty tolerating his speeches. Finn was a dragon, after all. Dragons thrived on action, not on words. Finn respected Peter and everything the old wizard was capable of, but at the moment, all Finn wanted to do was get moving.

Finn looked over to his left, where the rest of the search party stood. There were four of them total, a small number considering the size of the task that lay before them. But the High Council of Falcon Cross had agreed that stealth mattered more than anything on this quest, and therefore had limited the members of the search party to the bare minimum.

Owen, Finn's clanmate and fellow dragon shifter, stood directly to Finn's left. He was twiddling his thumbs and squirming restlessly, just like Finn. Owen was perhaps the most hotblooded of Finn's clan, the Redwood Dragons. Owen had been raring to go on this search since the day the amethyst records had been found. The amethyst records gave clues to the potential location of the dragon amethyst, a powerful ancient stone that held within it the possibility for the good shifters and good wizards to gain the advantage in the war against evil which they were fighting. Owen had been forced to wait, though, as the records were carefully studied and the best potential search path was discovered. Now, months later, the search party was being sent off. They just had to wait for Peter to finish his speech.

Finn's eyes shifted to the two wizards in the search party. Raven Morey was a Falcon Cross native, and had been a part of the Falcon Cross military for a decade, at least. She was an excellent soldier, skilled at stealth, magic fighting, and broomstick flying. Her impressive array of talents made her an important member of the search party.

Next to Raven stood Isabelle Torres, better known as "Izzy." Izzy had recently arrived in Falcon Cross, after escaping from the enemy's army herself. Izzy was trained as a doctor, and, since the search party might encounter some dangerous situations, Peter had thought it would be good to send her along. Izzy's firsthand knowledge of how the enemy worked might come in handy, too. And, like Raven, Izzy was skilled at broomstick flying. She would easily be able to keep up with the rest of the search party.

Everyone in the group was wearing dark black uniforms. On the left chest of each uniform, gold thread had been used to embroider in the Falcon Cross military insignia. Normally, the dragons didn't wear wizard uniforms, but Peter had offered them to Finn and Owen, and the two dragons had thought it rude to refuse. Finn had to admit that the group looked quite fearsome in their matching uniforms. Finn and Owen stood tall and muscular, and Raven's and Izzy's magic rings glinted in the sunlight. Anyone who tried to mess with them was sure to face painful consequences.

What a group, thought Finn as he looked them over with pride. Two of the best dragons and wizards there were. This was going to be fun. If Peter ever finished his speech, that was.

Almost as if the old wizard could hear Finn's thoughts, he chose that moment to give the closing remark of his speech. Cheers went up from the crowd, and Finn felt the blood pumping faster through his veins as excitement filled him. This was it. After months of preparation, they would finally have the chance to head out into the world and take their chances on finding the dragon amethyst.

Noah, the dragon who was second in command of Finn's clan, came to shake hands with each of the search party members as they began mounting the broomsticks. Even though Finn and Owen could have flown if they shifted into dragon form, it would be easier to maintain invisibility if they rode on the broomsticks behind the wizards. Dragons could somewhat hide themselves by using chameleon-like tricks, but it was difficult to do while flying. Raven and Izzy were both talented at invisibility spells, and were sure they could keep the whole group invisible as they flew through the sky. Since they were riding as passengers, Finn and Owen would both be wearing giant backpacks. Those backpacks were stuffed with as many supplies as could possibly be crammed into them. There was food, water, clothing, flashlights, and, of course, maps and notes on where the dragon amethyst might be. Finn tightened the straps on the backpack a bit before climbing up onto Izzy's broomstick.

Finn didn't mind the chance to ride on a broomstick. It sounded like fun, and, besides, he wasn't going to complain about being forced to sit behind a beautiful woman like Izzy. And, from the stupid grin on Owen's face right now, Finn guessed he was pretty happy about sitting behind Raven, who was definitely easy on the eyes as well.

"Take care of yourselves," Noah was saying. Peter had joined Noah next to the broomsticks, and was shaking hands as well now. Finn was always surprised at how strong of a grip the old wizard had. For an old man, he was quite powerful.

Finn nodded respectfully toward both Noah and Peter, as did the rest of the search party. And then, Izzy and Raven both shouted, "Ready?" at the same time.

Finn and Owen gave them a thumbs up, and the two wizards shot up into the air. An honor guard of wizard soldiers rose all around them to see them out of the city. The military dress robes of the honor guard glittered purple and gold in the sunlight, and Falcon Cross banners fluttered behind them. Finn had to admit that, despite his impatience with the speeches, he was enjoying the impressive show of might the wizard military was putting on.

Trumpets sounded from somewhere below as Izzy and Raven rose higher and higher, eventually leaving even the honor guard far below them. Finn breathed in deeply, relishing how cool and fresh the air up here was.

He looked down to see that the village of Falcon Cross had already disappeared from view. The small city was protected by an invisibility shield. Once you rose above the shield, you could no longer see the buildings and streets that made up the wizarding town. Instead, your eyes were fooled into thinking that all that was below you was more treetops, just like the other hundreds of treetops that stretched out for miles.

With a happy sigh, Finn tore his eyes away from the trees below him and looked instead toward the horizon in front of him. Finn was no stranger to searching for powerful hidden objects. He had spent his life searching for ancient dragon artifacts.

The Redwood Dragons clan consisted of a group of ten dragon shifter orphans, all of whom had been rescued during the last great shifter war by one great dragon, William. William had raised them as brothers, eventually retiring and turning the reigns of clan leadership over to Knox, who now served as the clan's first in command. The clan had been spread out into different groups lately, though, thanks to the rising war between good and evil. Knox had gone to Texas, to help a group of shifters there guard the two dragon stones that had been recovered—the dragon emerald and the dragon sapphire. Four dragons remained in the Redwoods, guarding the dragon clan's home base along with several wizards. And the other five dragons had gone to Falcon Cross to help protect their wizard allies. Now, though, Owen and Finn were once again on the move, leaving Falcon Cross behind as they searched for yet another powerful dragon stone.

There were four dragon stones in all, and the two that were still missing *must* be found by the good wizards and shifters. Those stones were so powerful that, if they fell into the wrong hands, they could be used to destroy everything good in the world. Finn gritted his teeth together as he thought of the awful possibilities if their search failed. Izzy drove her broomstick higher into the air, and Finn vowed to himself that he would find the dragon amethyst or die trying. If the good wizards and shifters could find this amethyst, only the dragon ruby would still remain unaccounted for. And once the amethyst was safe, all efforts could be concentrated on the ruby. Victory was so close that Finn could almost taste it. Failure was not an option.

The most important mission of his life had just begun.

CHAPTER TWO

It didn't take long for Finn's excitement to fade into dull boredom. Despite the great adventure that lay ahead of the group, flying over hundreds of miles of wilderness got boring after a while. Finn found himself constantly glancing upward, willing the sun to move faster across the sky. Once sunset came, the group would stop for the night. Finn could hardly wait to get off this broomstick and give his sore ass a rest. Not to mention, he was starving. The group had not stopped for lunch, and the feeling of fullness his breakfast had given him had long since worn off.

So it was with great happiness that he realized several hours later that the wizards were slowly descending. They were over a thick forest, although Finn had no idea where exactly they were. For a while, he'd tried to keep track of roughly how many miles had passed, but after a few hours of flying he'd grown bored even with that. Once they landed, he would pull the GPS out of his backpack and take a look. His best guess was that they were somewhere over central Idaho by now. Falcon Cross was in Oregon, but the wizards flew like the wind. It wouldn't take them very many days to reach northern Montana, where they were heading. It would be a week at the most.

Izzy leaned down against the broomstick, pointing the front end of it toward the treetops as she began to speed up her descent. She and Raven both zoomed expertly below the tops of the tall pine trees that dominated the forest, somehow avoiding all of the unevenly placed branches despite the rapid speed at which they were flying. Finn's arms clung tightly around Izzy's waist, and he did his best to lean in the same direction she did to help her as she steered. He marveled at the wizards' flying skills. They may not have been born with wings, like dragons were, but Finn was pretty sure they were at least as good as the dragon shifters at zooming through the skies. Before another minute had passed, Izzy was coming to a smooth stop on the forest floor.

"Seems like as good a place as any to stop," she said, nodding back toward Finn. "Go ahead and hop off."

Finn stiffly climbed off the broom, rubbing his ass as he did. He laughed as he noticed Owen doing the same thing.

"It's even worse than a bike seat," Owen complained when he realized why Finn was laughing. "I swear to god I'm not going to be able to walk straight for a week after today."

Raven gave Owen's arm a playful punch. "I thought you guys were tough dragons," she teased. "But you can't even handle a little old broomstick?"

Owen scowled at her, although his eyes were dancing merrily. "Easy for you to say. You've had years of practice on that stupid wooden stick."

Raven just laughed, and gave Owen another punch in the arm. Finn couldn't keep a smirk from crossing his face when he saw the two of them interacting. He swore they looked at each other like two teenagers in love, although he was sure if he accused them of liking each other they would have vehemently denied it. Izzy had no qualms about pointing it out, though.

"Enough flirting, you two," she said, crossing her arms and frowning sternly in their direction. "Let's get our campsite set up before we completely lose daylight."

As Finn had suspected, Izzy's accusation caused a flurry of protests from Owen and Raven. Finn chuckled as he watched Izzy rolling her eyes at the two supposed lovebirds, then he turned to head into the woods.

"I'm going to find us some dinner," he said. "I should be back soon."

His departure was barely acknowledged amongst the heated discussion of whether Owen and Raven had actually been flirting or not. Finn moved silently through the woods, breathing deeply as he tried to locate any potential food sources. His shifter genes gave him heightened senses of smell and hearing, and he was hopeful that those heightened senses would allow him to find some meat to eat. The group had plenty of meal replacement rations in their bags, so they certainly wouldn't starve if he couldn't snag something tonight. But it had been a long day of travel, and he would have paid a lot of money for some fresh food right now.

Since there were no stores out here to sell him food, though, he had to rely on his own hunting abilities. He crept silently through the forest, hardly disturbing its stillness as his eyes darted to and fro, and his nose and ears smelled and listened. Luck must have been on his side, because less than two minutes later, he spotted a deer about twenty-five yards away from him. It was a buck, placidly nibbling on one of the pine trees.

Bingo, Finn thought. As silently as a shadow, he reached down to his side where his pocket knife was holstered against his military uniform. He moved forward toward the deer, careful to stay downwind from it, until he was within sprinting distance. Then, he ran forward as fast as his legs would carry him. Even in human form, Finn's legs were impossibly muscular. He moved forward with the speed of a cheetah, quickly going from a near standstill to a full-on sprint.

As soon as he started running, the deer heard him. It started to bound away, but it was too slow. This was no ordinary human that hunted it. This was a dragon shifter, and the deer had barely had time to realize that it was under attack before Finn had leapt onto its back and sliced its neck with the knife. It took several moments for the loss of blood to take down the deer, and Finn held on tightly that entire time. When the deer finally expired, Finn loosened his grip and moved to begin field dressing the animal.

Not long after, he walked triumphantly back to the campsite, where a warm fire was now blazing in front of several thick blankets that had been spread out on the ground. The group had not brought tents with them, since they were packing as lightly as possible, but Finn didn't mind sleeping under the stars. It was May now, and, although the temperatures were dropping as nightfall took hold, the weather was bearable. Additionally, the uniforms that each of the group members wore had been treated with climate control spells by the wizards. The spell worked even better than a winter coat. Finn had not felt chilled for even a moment since they left Falcon Cross, and he knew that the temperatures in the sky had been quite cold.

"I brought dinner!" he said, holding up the deer as he neared the fire. The other three, whose heads had been bent over a map, looked up and noticed him for the first time. Owen let out a whoop when he saw the deer.

"You always were a kickass hunter," Owen said. "I'm so glad I'm not going to have to eat a meal replacement bar for dinner tonight. Those things taste like cardboard."

"They're not that bad," Izzy said. "I kind of like the peanut butter flavored bars."

Owen made a face at her. "You're crazy," he said. "Are you sure Saul's army didn't burn off your taste buds or something?"

Izzy made a face at him and went back to studying the map. Finn made a face at

Owen too, a face that told him he better not tease Izzy like that. Owen scowled and rolled his eyes at Finn, but then went to start building a spit to roast the deer meat on. It was a good thing, too, because if Owen had tried to press the subject, Finn would have really let him have it. Even though it had been months now since Izzy escaped the enemy's camp, Finn could tell that the horrible memories still haunted her.

And no wonder. Saul, the dragon shifter who led the enemy's army, had become obsessed with dark magic, as had all of his underlings. In fact, Saul had used dark magic to turn himself into a wizard, something that was normally impossible for anyone who had not been born a wizard. As the enemy's army became steeped deeper and deeper into the realm of dark magic, the awful possibilities for pain and destruction grew greater and greater. Who knew what awful things Izzy had seen? Even worse, before her escape she'd been forced to pretend that she supported Saul and his army. She'd had to stand by and act like she enjoyed watching the destruction they caused. Finn shuddered. No wonder she clammed up whenever someone mentioned her time in the enemy camp.

With a sigh, Finn turned to help Owen with the deer. But Owen, seeming somewhat repentant after his callous comment to Izzy, waved him away.

"Nah, Finn, I'll take care of this," Owen said. "You caught it, so you deserve to relax for a bit. I'll take care of cooking it."

Finn nodded, and went to sit by the two wizard women. Owen wasn't the type to say he was sorry, but Finn recognized his insistence on cooking as the closest thing to an apology that he would make for teasing Izzy. Finn was only too happy to accept Owen's offer to cook, since he wanted to take some time to look over the maps and figure out where, exactly, their journey today had taken them.

"We're right here," Izzy said, pointing to a spot on the map before Finn even had a chance to ask about their location. "We made good time today, I'd say."

"You ladies did a great job flying," Finn said, winking at them. "You flew almost as fast as a dragon would have."

The two wizards rolled their eyes at him, but he could see that they were still pleased by his backhanded compliment.

"If we keep up this pace, we should make it to Devil's Melt within two days," Raven said. "Of course, we'll probably have to slow down somewhat as we get closer, to make sure that our invisibility shields are working at one hundred percent. The faster we go, the more chance there is of the shield not working properly. And enemy soldiers are sure to be watching the area around Devil's Melt like hawks."

Finn nodded absentmindedly as he studied the map. Devil's Melt was the area in Northern Montana where Izzy had been held in the enemy camp against her will. It was from there that the amethyst records had been stolen from the enemy and brought back to Falcon Cross. The enemy knew that it was only a matter of time before a search was sent out for the dragon amethyst using the information on its location that had been in the records.

Finn frowned as he contemplated what dangers they might face once in Devil's Melt. The group would try to stay under the cloak of invisibility as much as they could, but it was still possible that the enemy would figure out they were there. If that happened, Finn and the rest of the group from Falcon Cross would have to fight. Normally, Finn didn't mind fighting. In fact, he somewhat enjoyed a good chance to take out his frustrations on an enemy. But he wasn't sure how well the four of them would do against the large contingent of Saul's army that was likely still in Devil's Melt. Even though Saul's men had lost the amethyst records, they knew that the dragon amethyst was nearby. They were certainly still searching, and they would be eager for the chance to recapture the records to continue that search. Finn sighed and let out a frustrated curse.

"If only we'd gotten to the records before them," he said. "It would have been nice to search Devil's Melt without having to constantly worry about Saul's army. Can you imagine how quickly we would have found the stone if we didn't have to worry about staying invisible and watching our backs?"

Raven shrugged. "You're right, but there's no sense in dwelling on it. We just have to do the best we can with the circumstances that we have. And hey, at least the enemy figured out for us that the amethyst is in Devil's Melt. Otherwise we might still be searching with no direction whatsoever."

"Yeah, well, I'm still not convinced the stone is in Devil's Melt," Izzy said, a note of frustration in her voice. Raven and Finn both looked at her in surprise.

"What do you mean?" Finn asked. "Do you think someone else got to it first? Surely, no one could have found it without these records. And we know that Saul's army didn't find it even when they had these records on hand."

Izzy shook her head. "No, it's not that I think someone else found it. It's just that I think everyone is too focused on Devil's Melt. When the wizard Advocates in Falcon Cross were looking over the records, they didn't even consider that the stone might not be there anymore."

Raven and Finn both looked at Izzy like she'd lost her mind, but she just shrugged back at them.

"Look," Izzy said. "I was with Saul's army for a long time. They searched high and low in Devil's Melt, and they had all of the information in the records at their disposal. But they still didn't find anything. I think it's possible that the information in the records isn't as straightforward as everyone thinks. The dragon amethyst used to be in Devil's Melt, that's for sure. But just because it was there at one time doesn't mean that it's still there. It could have been moved, and I think some of the riddles in the records indicate that it has been."

Finn frowned. "It seems weird to me that all of our wizard Advocates would miss the fact that the stone's been moved. And, besides, if you really think the stone has moved, why didn't you say something to the Advocates when they were planning out this mission?"

Izzy shrugged. "I did say something. I told them to consider other locations, but they insisted on keeping their blinders on and pointing us toward Devil's Melt. So, here we are. On our way to Montana to search for a stone that might not even be there. Of course, I hope for all of our sake's that I'm wrong and that the stone is there. But, if we don't find it, don't say I didn't warn you."

Finn frowned as he stared back down at the map. A troubled uneasiness seemed to rise in the pit of his stomach. What if Izzy was right? What if the dragon amethyst had been moved, and they were heading to Devil's Melt—straight into enemy territory—for no reason? Finn had always trusted the wizard Advocates. After all, they were some of the smartest people he'd ever met. Not to mention, Myles and Zeke, two of his own clan members, had been heavily involved in planning this mission. He knew all of the dragons in his clan were extremely intelligent. But even smart people made mistakes, and Izzy was right. The focus had been on Devil's Melt since the beginning, and no one had seemed to question it.

When Finn looked up again, Izzy was watching him with a slightly raised eyebrow. He knew that she could see the doubt in his mind now, too. But what could they really do, except press forward with the mission they'd been given?

"Well, if it's not there, then at least we'll have tried," he said. But his tone was unconvincing. No one wanted to waste time searching in an area where the stone would not be. And no one wanted to risk running across the enemy and his dark magic without a good reason.

Raven opened her mouth as if she was about to say something, but before any words could come out, she froze, and a troubled look crossed over her face. Finn followed her gaze, and soon saw the problem.

Standing across the small clearing that formed their campsite, was a woman who was not part of their party. The woman was dressed in hiking garb and had a giant hiking backpack on her back that likely held a tent. She waved as she approached the campsite, her smile making it look as though she thought she'd just arrived at some sort of wilderness party.

"Uh-oh," Finn said. "Looks like we've got company."

CHAPTER THREE

Finn felt everyone around him tense up. He sniffed deeply, trying to see if the woman was a shifter. But he could tell by her scent that she was a full human. And she did not appear to have a magic ring on, either. She wasn't a wizard, as far as he could tell. It was possible she really was just an ordinary hiker who had happened across their campsite, but they couldn't be too careful. And besides, they should have put an invisibility shield around their campsite to protect against both Saul's army and against random passersby like this.

"Which one of you two was responsible for the invisibility shield?" Finn asked through gritted teeth, keeping his voice low so that the newcomer couldn't hear him.

Raven shrugged. "We hadn't bothered yet. We figured since we were way out in the wilderness, there weren't likely to be any humans out here. And there's no way Saul's army followed us here."

Finn looked over at Raven in shock. "Are you freaking kidding me right now?" he asked in a hissing whisper. "I thought you were supposed to be one of the best soldiers in the Falcon Cross army, and yet you don't even see the necessity of putting up a protective shield? You should never assume that we haven't been followed. And, as you can plainly see right in front of us, there's always a risk of hikers finding us."

"Calm down, Finn," Izzy said, keeping her voice low as well. "Perhaps we should have put a shield up, but there's likely no damage done. This woman seems harmless enough."

Izzy nonchalantly pointed her magic ring toward the woman and whispered, *"Magicae revelabit."*

Finn blinked a few times, waiting for some sort of magical phenomenon to occur, but nothing happened. The newcomer was talking to Owen now, and pointing toward the deer that was roasting on a spit over the fire. Owen looked back at Finn with a helpless expression on his face, as if to ask what the hell he was supposed to say to this random woman. Finn ignored Owen for the moment, and turned back toward Izzy.

"What spell was that?" he asked.

"A revealing spell," Izzy whispered calmly. "It can be used for a variety of things, one of which is to reveal whether there are any kind of magical spells around someone. I wanted to see if this woman was hiding a magic ring, or had any kind of magical shields around her. But there was nothing. I'm pretty sure she's just a plain old human who happened to stumble across our campsite."

"What are we supposed to do about her?" Raven asked.

Izzy shrugged. "Invite her to dinner."

Finn balked at this suggestion. "No way," he said. "We can't let random people hang out with us. You can't know for sure that she isn't some sort of spy."

Izzy gave him an impatient sideways glance. "Look, Finn, if we try to tell her she's not welcome here, we're going to sound a lot more suspicious than if we just act like we're a normal, friendly group out camping in the woods. We have plenty of food. Let's just invite her to dinner and then tomorrow morning make sure we head off in the opposite direction of whichever way she's heading."

Finn sighed. He hated to admit it, but Izzy was right. "Fine," he said. "But let's also make sure that tomorrow we put up an invisibility shield when we stop for the night."

Finn glared at Raven, who scowled back at him in annoyance. Raven didn't like to admit she was wrong, but this time she was. She was just lucky that there weren't any enemy soldiers nearby.

"You probably should go ahead and put up a shield now," Izzy said, giving Raven a kind smile. "Just in case there are any enemy soldiers around."

"Well, there aren't any," Raven said stubbornly. "But if it makes you feel better, then whatever."

She stood and went to the outer edges of the campsite. She began whispering and gesturing with her ringed hand. Finn saw the hiker, who was still standing by Owen, looking curiously over at Raven. Owen was glaring at Finn now, still unsure of what to do. Quickly, Finn stood and walked over toward the fire. He put a huge, jolly smile on his face and acted like he'd never been as happy to see anyone in his life as he was to see this woman right now.

"Well, well, Owen," Finn teased. "Who's your pretty new friend?"

Finn was startled to see as he drew closer to the fire how pretty the woman actually was. Her eyes were almost the same shade of deep green as his own, and her dark brown hair—pulled into a haphazard bun—had even more of a reddish tint to it than his. Her skin was smooth and flushed from the fresh air, but he could still make out several freckles on her nose and cheeks. Her smile broadened as Finn approached, and he couldn't help but notice how soft and full her lips were.

Owen looked relieved that Finn was taking charge of the situation. "Her name's Anya," he said. "Anya Steele. She's been hiking out here for the better part of a week, but she said we're the first people she's come across."

Finn caught the underlying message in Owen's words: this girl was alone, and the area around here was relatively deserted. Hopefully, Anya would be the only stranger they came across.

"Well, if you'd like some company, you're welcome to stay for dinner," Finn said, gesturing toward the roasting deer. "As you can see, we have plenty of food."

Anya looked relieved. "I'd love to, if you really don't mind," she said. "I do love the solitude of hiking alone, but it does get a bit lonely at times."

Finn smiled. "We don't mind at all. Please, make yourself at home."

Finn caught Owen's questioning eye, and gave him an almost imperceptible shrug as if to say, "What choice do we really have?"

Raven must have finished her invisibility spells, because she came walking over to the fire now as well, followed closely by Izzy.

"Hi," Raven said holding out her hand to Anya. "I'm Raven."

"Anya," Anya said, reaching to shake Raven's hand.

"And I'm Izzy," Izzy said. "What are you doing all the way out here by yourself?"

Anya smiled. "I'm actually hunting for plants," she said. "I'm a botanist, and I've been out here cataloging what types of plants grow out here. Apparently, most people don't think chasing down plants is very exciting work, because I usually have to make these trips on my own. Or maybe people just don't like giving up all their creature comforts to camp in the woods for weeks on end. What about you guys? What are you doing out here?"

Finn froze at the question, but Izzy handled it beautifully.

"We're camping for weeks on end," Izzy said with a laugh. "We spend a lot of time in the city back home, but we all love nature. So we decided to use our vacation time this year to escape to the woods."

"That's great," Anya said sincerely. "I couldn't stand spending all my time in the city. How have you liked the woods so far?"

"It's great," Izzy said with enthusiasm. "We'll be sad to go back."

Anya nodded, then raised a curious eye toward Izzy's shirt. "What's with your clothes?" she asked. "I thought you guys were out here doing some sort of work, since it looks like you're wearing uniforms."

Finn felt his stomach tightening with nerves once again, but once again Izzy didn't even flinch at the question. She got a somewhat sheepish look on her face, and then laughed.

"Well, if you must know, Raven here thought it would be fun to pretend we were part of some sort of survival expedition, complete with team uniforms. Silly, I know, but I guess when you spend all your time in the city you come up with crazy ideas like that. It's a bit weird, but we humor Raven. And besides, the uniforms are surprisingly warm."

Izzy laughed and gave Raven a friendly punch. Raven glared at Izzy but said nothing. Anya, for her part looked confused and a bit doubtful of Izzy's explanation, but finally just shrugged.

"Sounds like fun," Anya said. "So how much longer will you be out here?"

Izzy waved her hand dismissively at Anya. "A bit," she said. "But our trip is boring compared to yours. I want to hear more about what you do. How did you get into botany?"

Anya smiled. "Well, okay," she said. She started talking about how much she'd loved plants even in high school, but Finn didn't stay around too long to listen.

"Let's go refill our water bottles at the stream while the girls talk," Finn said to Owen.

"The stream?" Owen asked, confused. "What stream?"

Finn gave him a pointed, exasperated look.

"Oh, right, the stream," Owen said, then grabbed his water bottle and walked off into the trees with Finn.

"Damn it, Owen, you don't make it easy to lure you away from the crowd," Finn said once they were out of earshot.

"Sorry. I was distracted," Owen said. He still sounded distracted, in fact.

"By what? How pretty Anya is?" Finn teased. Owen was a well-known womanizer.

"What? No, I hadn't even noticed," Owen said. For once, Finn believed him.

"Yeah, you wouldn't have," Finn said. "Not when you've been staring at Raven nonstop since we left Falcon Cross."

This statement earned Finn a glare, and Finn laughed.

"Did you bring me out here just to make fun of me?" Owen asked.

Finn shook his head, still laughing. "Nah, I was just going to explain to you the plan regarding Anya, so that we're all on the same page."

Finn told Owen that Izzy had determined Anya was not a wizard, and that she had thought it best to be friendly to Anya tonight. He explained that they would make sure to go separate ways first thing tomorrow, and that Raven had put up an invisibility shield, just in case.

Owen nodded when Finn was finished speaking. "I guess that all makes sense," he said. "I still don't have a stranger at the campsite, but what can we really do under the circumstances?"

"Agreed," Finn said. "There's one more thing, too. It doesn't have anything to do with Anya, but I thought I'd mention it to you since we have a moment alone. Izzy is worried that the dragon amethyst might not actually be in Devil's Melt."

To Finn's surprise, Owen didn't look surprised at all. "Yeah, she already told me that," he said. "She's convinced that if it was there then Saul's army would have found it long ago."

"She told you? When?" Finn asked.

"Yesterday afternoon," Owen said. "She was trying to get me to talk to Noah or Peter and have them postpone the mission until her suspicions could be investigated further. But she'd already talked to Noah and Peter, and they didn't think her claims had merit. I tried to talk to them again, but they remained firm in their decision."

Finn raised an eyebrow in Owen's direction. "Why didn't you tell me?" he asked.

Owen shrugged. "I didn't have a chance, really. Things were so busy with all the preparations to leave. And it doesn't really matter, does it? If Noah and Peter don't think Izzy's claims have merit, then the mission is going to continue forward as is, regardless of what we think."

"What *do* you think?" Finn asked, trying to read into Owen's guarded expression.

Owen was silent for several long moments. Finally with a sigh, he spoke.

"I think Izzy is right," he said. "I don't think we're going to find anything in Devil's melt except enemy soldiers."

With that, Owen turned and started walking back toward the campsite, leaving Finn alone to muddle through his confused thoughts. Izzy and Owen both thought the dragon amethyst had been moved? They weren't the kind of people to make big claims like that with no justification. Then again, Noah and Peter were quite smart. If they thought the dragon amethyst was still in Devil's Melt, they must have their reasons for thinking that, too.

With a sigh of his own, Finn walked back toward the campsite. He didn't have much choice right now other than to continue forward with the mission as it had been planned out. That was the only choice any of them had, really. They were honor bound to follow the commands of their leaders, and their leaders were all telling them to go to Devil's Melt. And yet, Finn couldn't help thinking that perhaps Izzy's suspicions were correct. Sometimes, you had to question everything you thought you knew before you found the truth. And Finn was beginning to suspect that the wizard Advocates, despite their intelligence, had not, in fact, questioned *everything*.

Finn's eyes caught Anya's gaze as he walked back toward the fire. Her beauty was breathtaking, especially in the warm glow of the fire, and he almost wished he'd met her under different circumstances, where he would have been able to get to know her for a span of time longer than one night.

Such was the life of a dragon, though. He was always on the run, always on the move. There was always work to be done, and, if Izzy's and Owen's suspicions were correct, the work required of him now was going to take much longer than any of them had originally thought.

With a sad sigh, Finn took the roasted deer meat that Owen offered to him. He found a seat that gave him a direct line of sight to Anya. If he could only enjoy looking at someone so beautiful for one night, then he was going to make the most of that night, at least.

CHAPTER FOUR

Anya tossed and turned in her sleeping bag under the open stars. Sleep eluded her, despite her best efforts to calm her mind. She had decided not to set up her tent tonight, since her four new friends sleeping around her didn't seem to have a tent with them. She figured her sleeping bag and clothes were warm enough. She would just join them in their open-air slumber. Except there was no slumber for her. They were all actually sleeping, and she was not.

She counted stars for a while, trying to trick her mind into drifting off to sleep. Sleep still did not come, but Anya enjoyed marveling at how brilliantly the stars shone. She'd spent months at a time out here before, but she never got tired of how beautiful the night sky was hundreds of miles from any city lights.

She'd also never seen other hikers this far into the wilderness before. Not recreational hikers at least. Once, she'd come across another group of scientists, and another time she'd met a national park ranger. But that was it. There was something fishy about the group that slept around her.

Perhaps that was why Anya could not sleep. Her four new friends seemed harmless enough, but Anya still felt wary. Their story did not add up. Why would anyone come this far out for a vacation, especially if they were normally city dwellers? Most city dwellers who were going on a big hiking trip for the first time stayed much closer to civilization, just in case. And, although this crew seemed well-prepared for the wilderness, with food, water, and water purification tablets, among other supplies, there were still some things about them that seemed quite strange. For one thing, the two girls were wearing giant gemstone rings. Who wore such expensive, showy jewelry for a hiking trip? Most of the serious hikers Anya knew left even their wedding rings at home. And whatever the rings on these girls' fingers were, they didn't seem to be wedding rings. They wore them on their right hands, for one thing. And the two men in the group were obviously not in a relationship with the women, although the one named Owen didn't do a very good job of hiding how infatuated he seemed to be with Raven.

The one named Finn didn't seem to have much interest in Izzy, though. Those two definitely were not an item. Anya was surprised to find that this knowledge made her happy. Why did she care what Finn's relationship status was? Sure, he was quite handsome. Perhaps the most handsome man she had ever seen, in fact. And his eyes did crinkle up in the most adorable way when he laughed. But she was unlikely to ever see him again after they parted ways tomorrow. Besides, she wasn't entirely convinced that he wasn't a dangerous man. Actually, she wasn't convinced that any of these four were actually who they said they were.

Anya glanced over to her left and frowned at the gently rising and falling chests of her new friends. They all still wore those ridiculous uniforms, and she wondered for the hundredth time what the real story behind the uniforms was. The insignia on the uniforms was unlike anything she'd ever seen before. It reminded her of something you might see on a medieval knight's banner. Were these four really delusional enough to want to wear uniforms and pretend to be on some sort of survival team? That made no sense to her.

"They're hiding something from me," Anya whispered into the cool night air. A few feet away from her, Finn turned over. For a moment, Anya held her breath, thinking that perhaps he wasn't sleeping after all and had heard her whisper. But no, there was no way he could possibly have heard her. It had barely even been audible to her own ears. A few moments later, she heard Finn's breathing return to the steady rhythm of sleep, and she relaxed.

She felt a bit foolish for worrying about the group of them, when she really thought about it. Surely, if they were dangerous people, they would have harmed her by now. And if by some chance they were just an odd group trying to live out some sort of survival fantasy in the woods, then they might be nerdy—but that didn't make them bad people. Anya furrowed her brow. Perhaps they were really scientists, and were working on some sort of secret project that they couldn't talk to others about. That must be it. It made the most sense to her. Although, the giant rings still confused her.

Anya sighed, and closed her eyes again. She needed to sleep, otherwise she wasn't going to be able to hike very far tomorrow. Not that it mattered. She didn't have anywhere in particular she needed to be. She was on her own schedule out here, and she had the survival skills necessary to last indefinitely on her own. To tell the truth, she hadn't been one hundred percent honest with her new friends, either. Oh, she hadn't exactly lied to them. But they'd seemed to think that she was out here gathering information as a botanist for some big important employer, and she'd let them think that. People often looked at her like she was a little crazy if she told them the truth.

The truth was that she was out here on her own, indulging her own curiosity about plants and enjoying the solitude. She'd worked as a botanist for a big pharmaceutical company before, in their "natural remedies" department. But her heart hadn't been in it, and after her father, a botanist himself, had passed away, leaving her a huge inheritance, she'd quit. Now, she had enough money to be financially independent. She didn't need a job, but she did need nature. She needed plants. She needed time away from the hustle and bustle of "normal" life. She came on these trips often. She was writing a guidebook on the flora out here, but it was a fun project, not a moneymaker.

She was happy with her life, overall. She liked living mostly off the grid, and when she missed people too much she bounced back to her small hometown for a bit until she once again craved alone time. Sometimes, though, she wondered if she could really keep up this life forever. She was young, and should have had a lot of friends and perhaps a family of her own. At least that's what society told her she should be doing. But instead she traipsed through the woods alone. Would she regret this one day? Would she wish she hadn't turned herself into a nomadic hermit, and had actually settled down?

With another sigh, Anya tried to push these worries out of her head. No wonder she couldn't sleep. Too many damn questions and worries running through her mind. She decided to try to distract herself by running through a mental catalog of all the plant specimens she'd collected today. This plan seemed to work, because within a few minutes, Anya had drifted off to sleep as well, finally at peace. She would not, perhaps, have felt so peaceful if she had been able to see that Finn turned toward her once again when he heard her breathing soften into a dreamy rhythm. He opened his eyes, which glowed slightly in the darkness like the eyes of an animal as he watched her. In her innocence, Anya had thought that all four of her new friends were sleeping. She didn't realize that one of them would always be on guard, watching for any unusual movement in the night sky.

She slept soundly for about fifteen minutes before she was awoken with a start by a giant roar. And, in fact, even when she awoke, she thought she must still be asleep, and having some sort of strange dream.

Finn and Owen were tossing their large backpacks to Izzy and Raven, shouting something about Saul's soldiers that didn't really make sense to Anya. Light flashed from the giant rings on the women's fingers. Izzy and Raven shrugged into the backpacks and then grabbed what looked like broomsticks from behind a large tree. Anya giggled in her dreamlike state, thinking how silly it was to have broomsticks out in the middle of the woods. Everything was so bizarre that she was sure it was all a figment of her imagination. She watched the supposed dream with amusement, not realizing that she was conscious enough to actually have the thought that her subconscious had managed to come up with some strange things.

In the next instant, she realized that this was definitely a scary dream, a nightmare of sorts. Izzy and Raven screamed out some words that sounded suspiciously like Latin to Anya, but they weren't words she understood. The only Latin words Anya knew were the scientific names of plants. Izzy and Raven swung their legs over the handles of the broomsticks, the same way witches did in all the Halloween stories that Anya had ever read. Then, to Anya's astonishment, the broomsticks rose up off the ground. The two woman were flying, hovering several feet off the ground and moving in quick circles. Anya could see their eyes by the light of the moon, full of fear. It did not occur to Anya to be afraid. She was watching this with interest, and a bit of annoyance. It was only a dream, but still, she did not appreciate her mind being filled with frightening images.

Anya glanced back at Finn and Owen, and her eyes widened in shock. She saw that they were stripping their clothes off until they were buck naked. Even though it was only a dream, Anya looked away, embarrassed. She turned her gaze back toward the flying women, but moments later the men were standing next to the women, shouting words Anya couldn't quite make out to them as they stuffed their clothes into the backpacks on the women's backs. Anya slowly stood, and began to walk toward the group. She wanted to hear what they were shouting about. As she walked, she heard a sudden, loud roar. Startled, she looked to her left, to where the noise had come from. Her eyes widened again as she saw several large lions charging toward them over and over. But each time the lions charged, they seemed to run into some sort of invisible barrier. Behind the lions, there were other beasts. Tigers, bears, and leopards charged as well. And behind them, there was a large group of people, all floating on broomsticks in much the same manner that Izzy and Raven were floating. From their hands, laser-like beams of light shot out. But the lasers seemed to be stopped by some sort of invisible wall as well. Anya strained her eyes to see whether these people were wearing giant rings like Izzy and Raven. She couldn't see from here, but the light shooting from Izzy's and Raven's hands had looked similar to the light the other people were shooting. They must all have some sort of rings that shot light.

Anya chuckled again at the absurdity of her dream, and then turned to look back at her four friends. She walked toward them, and could hear now what they were shouting.

"How the hell did they find us?" Owen asked as he finished stuffing his clothes into Raven's backpack, and then pulled the zipper shut.

"Probably has something to do with the fact that we had no invisibility shield up when we first arrived," Finn said, his voice sounding bitter.

"Now's not the time for arguments, guys," Izzy warned. "They're going to break through our protective shield any second. We have to get out of here."

"What about Anya?" Finn asked as he finished stuffing his clothes into Izzy's backpack.

Anya saw the four of them all turn to look at her. Even though she was fully clothed, she suddenly had an odd sensation like *she* was the one naked. She felt exposed as they all stared at her.

"We have to take her with us," Izzy finally said.

"But—" Owen began.

"No, Izzy's right," Finn said. "The enemy is going to think she's part of our group. If we leave her here, they'll kill her."

Anya saw Owen look over at Raven, who gave a small, sad nod.

"Alright," Owen said in an unhappy voice. "She comes with us. This mission is off to a great start, isn't it?"

No one answered his sarcastic remark. They seemed to be pressed for time, and kept looking nervously toward where the beasts and other people on flying broomsticks were still trying to break through the invisible barrier.

"I'll take her," Finn said. "Let me fly in front, and you guys guard my rear. Izzy and Raven, as soon as we're up, do your best to throw an invisibility spell over us. I know it won't be perfect when we're moving so fast, but maybe in the dark it'll be enough to allow us to lose them."

"Roger that," Raven said. "You guys ready to leave the protection of the shield? It's not gonna hold much longer, anyway. They've got too many wizards throwing counterspells at it."

"Ready as I'll ever be," Owen said. "Let's get this over with."

Anya watched them curiously, trying to understand what was happening, but none of it made sense. She supposed that was the thing about dreams. They never quite made sense. Although, usually, you didn't realize a dream didn't make sense while you were in it. You had to wait until you woke up for that.

Anya suddenly had the horrifying thought that she wasn't dreaming. She shook the thought away just as quickly as it came. There was no way this was real. People don't just fly around on broomsticks, she thought. And there are no lions or tigers in the forests of Idaho. Still, she decided to try to pinch herself just to be sure. But just as she reached for the skin on her arm, she was thrown backwards. She hit the ground hard, but sprang back up quickly. She had reflexively put her fists up in front of her, ready to fight whatever enemy had just knocked her over. But what she saw when she stood up caused the blood in her body to run cold.

There in front of her, covered in some sort of strange, glowing energy, were Owen and Finn. Except they weren't exactly Owen and Finn anymore. They were changing right before her eyes, their human forms giving way to some sort of animal shape with a dark, scaled hide. Their hands and feet became sharp, clawed reptilian feet, and wings and tails sprouted from their ever-growing forms. Anya took a step backward in fear and awe. This was definitely a dream if people were turning into animals. But what kind of animal, exactly, were they?

She didn't have to wait long to see. As their transformations completed, their heads became fearsome dragon heads, complete with teeth so large that each one was the size of Anya's arm. She took another step backward, trying to understand how there were suddenly two dragons in front of her where Owen and Finn had just been. The dragon that had been Owen a moment ago suddenly pointed his head up and shot a long stream of fire into the sky. This seemed to be some sort of signal, because Izzy and Raven nodded and began rising higher into the air on their broomsticks.

"Alright, Finn," Raven yelled. "We're ready. Grab Anya and fly like the devil. We'll be right behind you."

"Wait, no," Anya started to say. Even in a dream, she wasn't sure how she felt about being carried around by a giant dragon. But Finn—er, the dragon that had been Finn until a few moments ago—didn't stop to see how she felt about it. He started flapping his wings, rising almost instantly into the sky. As he rose, he reached out his giant, clawed feet, stretching them toward Anya. She let out a scream as she realized that he was going to grab her with those claws, but no one paid any attention to her protests.

Her eyes squeezed shut in horror as the impossibly large claws closed around her torso, but, to her surprise, she felt no pain. She opened her eyes again and saw that the dragon had somehow managed to pick her up without puncturing her. She felt a momentary rush of relief, but that relief did not last long. She realized that she was rising higher and higher into the air, and the dragon was beginning to pick up speed as he feverishly flapped his huge wings. She wanted to scream again, but the sound stuck in her throat. She was too overcome by terror.

She looked behind her, and saw the other dragon following. Behind him were Izzy and Raven, rising on their broomsticks and flying backward so that their faces were turned toward the mess of animals and broomstick people below. They held their right hands high as if ready to attack, but they had no weapons that Anya could see. The only thing they had was those ridiculously huge gemstone rings they wore. The rings, though, seemed to be some sort of weapon. Anya supposed you could knock someone out with one of those things if you hit them square in the face with it. She almost would have laughed at the thought, if she hadn't felt so frightened at the moment.

Suddenly, she heard a rushing noise as though she were passing through a jet of water. The rushing noise only lasted a few moments, and then, suddenly, everything else sounded louder. The roars of the animals below became unbearably loud, and the shouts of the people on broomsticks seemed to have been amplified several times. Anya couldn't make out everything they were shouting, but it sounded like they were yelling, "They left the shield!" over and over again.

Anya didn't have much time to listen or try to figure out what they meant by that, though, because in the next instant, a huge battle broke out. The small legion of people on broomsticks rose in the air toward them, somehow shooting out laser beams of light. Izzy and Raven seemed to be shooting out laser beams as well, yelling things in Latin again while they swooped and twirled through the air on their broomsticks. The dozens of laser beams clashed in the air in a dazzling array of sparks that might have been beautiful to watch if Anya hadn't felt so terrified.

The dragon that had once been Owen was joining in the chaos, breathing out huge streams of fire toward the people chasing them. He moved unbelievably quickly for such a large beast, and Anya watched in horrified awe as his fire sent person after person tumbling from their broomstick in a ball of flames. Finn did not participate in the battle. Instead, he flew forward ever faster, his wings never slowing as he pumped furiously against the cold night air. Anya glanced down at his large claws that encircled her, and she shuddered. A single claw could have easily pierced through her entire body, and yet, he was somehow able to hold her tightly without hurting her.

Anya shook her head back and forth vigorously a few times, trying to wake herself up. She'd had enough of this strange dream, and if this sort of nightmare was the price for sleeping, she didn't want to sleep. She'd rather go back to the calm and sanity of lying sleeplessly under the silent night sky, with her new friends lying next to her in normal, human form.

But no matter how hard Anya shook her head, she couldn't make herself wake up.

In desperate frustration, she reached once again to pinch herself on the arm. If she couldn't bring herself out of this nightmare, at least she could prove to herself that it was just a dream. But when she pinched her arm, she was startled by how sharp the pain was. Eyes widening, she tried again. Again, she felt a very real, very sharp pain when she pinched herself. Anya looked back at the battle in the air again, her whole body filling with a sickening sense of dread. It was not possible that all of this was real, was it? And yet, if it wasn't real, then why couldn't she wake up?

Anya felt hot tears starting to roll down her cheeks, and then, overcome by the madness around her, she felt everything going black.

CHAPTER FIVE

Finn glanced over his giant dragon shoulders, relieved to see that everything behind him was dark. The moonlight illuminated the outlines of Izzy and Raven as they swooped back and forth on their broomsticks, still watching behind them for any sign of straggling pursuers. And he could also see the outline of Owen's dragon, silently slicing through the night sky with his giant dragon wings. But other than that, the sky was empty. Their small group had managed somehow to outrun the much larger contingent of wizards who had somehow found them in the middle of nowhere.

Finn furrowed his brow as he continued to pump his dragon wings rhythmically. They needed to stop, and soon. He could feel Anya hanging limply in his large dragon claws, and concern filled him. More than likely, she had passed out from the shock of everything she had just seen. But there was always a possibility that she'd been hit by a stray attack from one of the enemy wizards, even though Izzy and Raven had done a good job of holding them off. Still, Finn was hesitant to stop so soon. He wanted to put more distance between his group and the enemy wizards.

They were far enough ahead that they should be safe, but, then again, Finn had thought they were safe back at their original campsite. How had Saul's army managed to find them despite their invisibility barrier and protective shield?

Finn frowned. They had been without an invisibility shield for a short amount of time after they landed, true. And there was always a risk when flying that invisibility shields or chameleon effects were not properly covering the moving wizards and dragons. But Finn did not think that the Falcon Cross group had had any major slipups. They should have been safe from discovery. As evidenced by the attack tonight, though, they hadn't been as safe as they'd thought.

Finn's frown deepened. There was only one explanation. The enemy's dark magic was growing stronger. Dark magic counter spells were stronger than normal counter spells. The enemy was using such spells to see through invisibility barriers and break through protective shields, and their techniques were only growing stronger.

Finn glanced over his shoulder once more, and made his decision. They would stop now. They were safe, for the moment at least. He had no idea how much longer that safety would last, but while it did, their best use of time was to regroup. They needed to check on Anya, who hopefully would revive quickly once they stopped, and they needed to figure out how to move forward from here. They had to find a way to get the dragon amethyst, but there was no question in Finn's mind that going into Devil's Melt right now would be a death trap. Their invisibility spells weren't working properly, and the area was sure to be heavily guarded.

Slowly, Finn began circling downward. He almost felt as though his heavy heart was dragging him downward, its weight pulling him toward the cold, dark earth. He slipped silently through the treetops, managing to avoid all of the thick branches despite the darkness and his size. Behind him, Owen made it through silently as well. And, of course, Izzy and Raven did not make any noise either. They were much smaller than the dragons, and just as skilled at flying.

Not that their flying skills were doing them much good, Finn thought bitterly as he landed on the forest floor. If their invisibility spells didn't hold against the enemy's counter spells, it didn't matter how skilled they were. They would still be found out, and, in Devil's Melt, where they would be hopelessly outnumbered, they would quickly be killed.

Finn gently uncurled his long, fingered claws to release Anya onto the ground. She didn't move, and he felt fear gripping his heart as he bent his dragon head to look at her. He might not know her well, but she'd been quite friendly to him and his friends. He hated to see anyone harmed in the cross fire of this war, but especially an innocent human who was as nice and beautiful as Anya.

Anya's eyes were closed, and Finn could not tell while in dragon form whether she was even still alive or not. With a low growl and a rush of power, he began shifting back into human form. His thick dragon hide morphed back into tanned human skin as his tails and wings disappeared and he once again took on the shape of a human male. Beside him, Owen was shifting back to human form as well. Izzy and Raven had just landed, and were hopping off their broomsticks. Finn saw Izzy looking over at Anya's still form with concern, and within moments of jumping off her broomstick, Izzy had shrugged out of the backpack she'd been carrying and was running toward their new human friend.

"Was she hit?" Izzy asked, not even looking up at Finn as she asked the question. Izzy's doctor training had kicked in, and she was already checking Anya for vital signs. Raven was running over with the backpacks, and began digging in one of them for Izzy's compact medical kit. Owen had grabbed the other backpack and was rummaging in it for clothes. Finn had not even considered the fact that he was still naked, but he realized as he watched Owen that getting dressed was probably a good idea. If Anya *was* still alive, it was better that he and Owen were fully dressed when she regained consciousness. The poor girl had already suffered enough shocks.

"I'm not entirely sure whether she was hit," Finn said as he began pulling his clothes out of the backpack from which Raven had just pulled Izzy's medical kit. "I didn't feel anything that felt like a hit, but we were moving so quickly and everything was so chaotic that I'm not entirely sure I would have felt a jolt even if one of the enemy's lasers did hit her."

"She's still alive," Izzy said, her eyes moving rapidly back and forth as she took an inventory of Anya's status. "And she doesn't seem to have any injuries. I think she just passed out from shock. Someone hand me one of our sleeping bags so I can warm her up. Raven, can you elevate her feet a bit?"

Izzy continued to work quickly, doing her best to make Anya warm and comfortable. Finn let out a sigh of relief as soon as he knew for sure that Anya was still alive, but then he turned his attention fully to getting dressed. There wasn't much he could do to help Izzy. If he tried to assist, he would most likely just get in the way. Once he was dressed, he watched carefully as Izzy worked, barking orders to Raven. Anya's face looked pale, an effect enhanced by the silver light of the moon that filtered down through the treetops. Even so, it struck Finn how beautiful she was. His heart unexpectedly clenched up, and he turned away to look at Owen, searching for any distraction that would take his mind off the strange feelings that bubbled up inside of him when he saw Anya lying there so still.

"Do you think they're still following us?" Finn asked Owen, even though he already knew the answer. Of course they were being followed. Perhaps not by the same group of wizards and shifters that had just attacked them, but Saul had an enormous number of soldiers at his disposal. Finn was quite certain that more troops had already been dispatched to chase them down. And the shifters who had been at their campsite were probably still following them on foot somewhere in the dark forest.

"Yeah," Owen said, answering the question even though they both knew the answer was unnecessary. "They're on our trail, no question about that. The only question is how long it will take them to catch up. Speaking of which, I don't think Raven's put up an invisibility shield yet. Raven!"

Finn saw Raven turn her head sharply at Owen's urgent tone. Her eyes looked tired, but her reactions were still quick.

"We need a shield!" Owen said in a frustrated tone. "You guys need to stay on top of that!"

"Sorry that I was trying to help revive the human who is now hopelessly tangled up in this mess," Raven said as she rolled her eyes at Owen. But despite the sarcasm and annoyance in her voice, she hopped to her feet and held her magic ring in the air, drawing large arcs around them as she started to cast protective shield and invisibility spells.

"*Magicae arma. Magicae invisibilia,*" she said over and over, drawing arc after arc with her ring while Izzy continued to bend over Anya. Finn turned to Owen with a raised eyebrow.

"Don't be so hard on Raven. It's not really her fault that we were found, you know," Finn said.

"Not her fault?" Owen said, incredulous. "How can you say that? The enemy must have found us because we didn't have an invisibility spell put up at our campsite immediately after we landed. That's the only way they could have seen us. Not only that, but because we didn't have a spell up, Anya found us and we now have to deal with her. That's not going to be easy—think of everything she saw back there! Shifters, wizards, and protective shields. Not to mention that she was carried out of there by a dragon. I've seen enough of full humans to know that she's going to be pretty freaked out when she wakes up."

"I agree that Anya is going to be freaked out when she wakes up," Finn said. "But I wouldn't blame Raven for that. I don't think Saul's men found us because we forgot to put up an invisibility shield for a few minutes—"

"Because *Raven* forgot to put up a shield for a few minutes, you mean," Owen interrupted.

Finn sighed. Owen could be so stubborn when he had decided that someone was to blame for something. And, of course, it was never Owen himself to blame. It was always someone else.

"We all are responsible to make sure proper precautions are taken," Finn said. "If a shield should have been put up earlier, than we're all to blame. But, anyway, I don't think it matters when the shield went up. Even if it had been right away, Saul's soldiers still would have found us."

"Why do you say that?" Owen asked, narrowing his eyes at Finn.

Finn shrugged. "We flew that whole way under a cloak of invisibility, and we stopped off in a very remote area of the woods. What are the odds that Saul's soldiers happened to be flying by there during the small window of time that we didn't have our shields up? Not very high, I'd say. I think they're tracking us in other ways. They know tons of dark magic spells. I don't think even Izzy realizes how powerful their dark magic abilities have become."

Owen was quiet for several moments, but his silence told Finn more than any words. Owen was always talking, so the fact that he had nothing to say about this meant he realized that Finn was right. There was no denying the fact that they had underestimated the enemy. Saul and his army had become more powerful than any of them had dared to imagine.

"If this is true," Owen finally said, his voice slow and tight, "Then this pretty much dooms our mission. I mean, there's no way we can get into Devil's Melt and search for the dragon amethyst if they know we're coming and can see us. There's too many of them. They'll slaughter us."

"I know," Finn said. "We'll have to reevaluate our plans. But our first priority right now is to make sure Anya is taken care of. The Advocacy Bureau back in Falcon Cross is going to throw a fit when they realize that we let a human see shifters, wizards, and magic in action."

Owen grunted in annoyance but said nothing further. The Advocacy Bureau was a wizard agency in Falcon Cross that, among other things, made sure that full humans did not discover that wizards and magic existed. There were all sorts of wizard rules and regulations to ensure that wizards did not accidentally use magic around humans, and, if any wizard discovered that a human had seen magic, that wizard was required to report the incident immediately. Finn wasn't sure what all the rules were, but he imagined that the Advocacy Bureau was going to find a few rules that had been broken tonight. There was no way they were going to shrug off the fact that Anya had seen everything she did tonight.

Finn kicked at a tree root in frustration. He understood the importance of working closely with the wizards. This war was serious business, and the more help they all had the better. But he wasn't used to dealing with so much government bureaucracy. Before his clan had teamed up with the Falcon Cross wizards, it had just been the ten of them, working on missions in whatever way they saw fit. There were no big government agencies telling them how to act. Finn didn't like this new way of working, where he was always worrying about what the Falcon Cross agencies were going to think. He tolerated the agencies, for the sake of maintaining peace with their wizard allies. But there was no way in hell he was going to put up with being treated like some sort of disobedient child just because a human had gotten tangled up in their mission. Sometimes, shit happened. Things like this were bound to occur now and then. Besides, the shifters and wizards all had much bigger things to worry about right now. Like how the hell they were going to manage to get the dragon amethyst before Saul's army did.

Finn's thoughts were interrupted by a happy shout from Izzy. He looked over to see that Anya's eyes were blinking open. He felt his heart leap in his chest with a mixture of happiness and trepidation. He was happy she was alive, but he wasn't sure the group was going to like the way she reacted.

Anya sat up slowly, and Izzy urged her to move even more slowly.

"You've had quite a shock, Anya," Izzy was saying in a gentle tone. "Take your time sitting up."

"I...I think I had a strange dream," Anya said. She looked around at the wizards and shifters, furrowing her brow in confusion. She took in their surroundings, and slowly seemed to realize that this section of forest was not the same section of forest where they had all spent the earlier part of the evening.

"Where are we?" Anya asked, a note of fear and suspicion creeping into her voice. "And how did we get here?"

Finn exchanged glances with Owen and Raven. Izzy had her eyes fixed on Anya's face.

"Well, we, uh, had to leave our other campsite behind," Izzy said, grasping for words.

Finn stepped in then. He knew that Anya was going to have a hard time processing everything she'd just seen. Hell, it was hard enough for humans to process just the fact that shifters existed. Add wizards into the mix, and Anya's head was certainly going to be spinning with disbelief by the time he was done explaining things. But Finn had found, in the few times in his life when he'd had to inform humans of the existence of shifters, that straight, frank honesty was usually the best policy. The more you tried to soften the truth or dance around it, the more confused people got—and once they were confused it was even harder for them to believe the fantastical truth you were telling them.

"Anya, listen," Finn said, coming to sit down on the cold forest floor next to Anya. "You've been caught up in some things that are probably hard for you to understand. And you've seen some things tonight that are probably hard for you to believe, but you weren't dreaming."

Finn paused and gave Anya a moment to respond. She merely narrowed her eyes at him, so he took a deep breath and then continued, gesturing toward Owen.

"Owen and I are what are known as shapeshifters. We have the ability to shift back and forth between human and animal form. There are actually quite a few types of shapeshifters in the world. You saw a few others tonight—there were lions, bears, and tigers attacking our campsite, if I remember correctly. But Owen and I are dragons. We have dragon genes inside of us, and can turn ourselves into dragons at will."

Finn paused again, and this time, Anya spoke.

"That's preposterous," she said. "People can't just change into animals at will. Especially not animals that don't actually exist. Dragons aren't real."

Finn glanced over at Owen, who gave a slight shrug as if to say, *what do you expect her to say?* Indeed, Finn thought as he looked back at Anya. *What did I expect her to say?*

A common human reaction to the existence of shapeshifters was to deny that they could actually exist. Another common reaction was to freak out and think shapeshifting was contagious. If the growing fear in Anya's eyes was any indication, she was struggling with whether she should laugh in his face or run from him in terror. He decided to try to explain further.

"I know it sounds crazy," he said. "But dragons do exist. They used to roam the earth as freely as any other animal, but they were one of the first species on our planet to become extinct. They survive now only in shifter form. And, yes, Anya, shifters do exist. Certain people can change into animals at will, and I'm one of them. I know you saw me change into a dragon a little over an hour ago. I'm able to do that because of a genetic mutation that mixes human DNA with dragon DNA. It's not contagious, so don't worry about that. It's just a genetic trait that some humans happen to have."

Anya looked back and forth from Finn to Owen with suspicious eyes. "I must still be dreaming," she said.

"You're not dreaming," Finn said gently. He wasn't sure why, but he felt an overwhelming urge to take her hand in his. He listened to the urge, hoping that somehow his touch would be enough to make her believe that what he was saying was true. Her eyes shot up warily to meet his when his fingers closed over hers, but she did not pull away. He took this as a positive sign and continued speaking.

"Most shifters aren't dangerous," Finn said. "Owen and I certainly aren't. Not to you anyway. There are, as you might have guessed from what you saw tonight, some shifters who aren't very nice. Those shifters were trying to attack us, and we had to get you out of there. But don't worry. You're safe now. We aren't going to hurt you."

Finn watched Anya's eyes as she continued to watch him and Owen carefully. Her hand was so soft, but so cold. He wanted to rub her fingers to warm them, but he was afraid that if he moved, she would startle and pull away. All he wanted right now was for her to calm down. The truth, of course, was that he didn't know for sure that she was safe. None of them were guaranteed safety right now. But at least he knew that as long as he was alive, she was safe. He wasn't going to let anyone harm her.

After a lengthy silence, Anya looked over at Izzy and Raven, who had been listening intently to Finn's explanation.

"Well, even assuming that you and Owen really are dragons, what are they?" Anya asked, gesturing toward the two women with her chin. "They didn't change into animals, but they, uh, acted quite strange."

"They're wizards," Finn said. "They can do magic. I know you noticed their magic rings, because I saw you staring at them last night. Those rings aren't just pretty pieces of jewelry. They work in a way similar to a magic wand, allowing Izzy and Raven to focus their magic and perform powerful spells."

Anya gave him a deadpan stare. He would have laughed at how incredulous she looked, except it really wasn't funny. Not to her, anyway. She'd just had her world turned completely upside down. Everything she thought she knew about what was possible was wrong. Perhaps one day she would be excited by these revelations, but that day was not today. Probably not tomorrow, either, if she was anything like all of the other full humans to whom Finn had explained shapeshifting.

After another long silence, during which Finn and the rest of the Falcon Cross group held their breath, Anya finally burst out into laughter. She threw her head back and laughed so long and hard that tears started streaming down her cheeks, and she pulled her hand away from Finn's so that she could wipe them away. She kept laughing as she looked around at her new friends, shaking her head in bemusement.

"Okay, okay. Very funny, guys," she said. "You got me. For a second there I thought you might actually be telling the truth, and that shifters and wizards actually existed. I have to say, you guys put on a pretty good show. How did you do it? How'd you make it look like you turned into dragons and were flying on broomsticks? And why'd you do it? That's a lot of effort to play a trick on someone you've only just met."

Anya laughed even harder, wiping away more tears from her eyes as she nearly doubled over from the hilarity of it. Finn, Owen, Izzy and Raven did not laugh. They looked back at Anya with somber, awkward expressions on their faces, until Anya realized that they were not laughing with her. Her laughter died in her throat as she looked back at them with widening eyes, finally fixing her gaze on Finn.

"You're not joking, are you?" she asked in a small voice.

Finn shook his head no. "It's all true," he said. "Shifters and wizards exist. And it just so happens that we're in the middle of a huge battle between good and evil right now."

Anya looked over at Raven, then, with a mixture of fear and awe in her eyes. "Show me," Anya demanded. "Show me some magic. Prove you can do it."

"Uh…" Raven said, looking helplessly from Izzy to Finn and then to Owen. Finn knew that the prohibition against using magic in front of humans was deeply rooted in Raven's psyche. It was Owen who stepped in to reassure her. He put a gentle hand on her shoulder as he spoke.

"It's okay, Raven," Owen said. "She's already seen plenty of magic. One more spell isn't going to make the Advocacy Bureau freak out any more than they already will."

Raven took a deep breath and nodded, then raised her ringed hand. "*Magicae scintillula*," she said.

Instantly, a huge shower of glittery, sparkling light shot out from Raven's ring. Finn smiled as he watched it. He loved it when the wizards did tricks that were pretty much for pure show instead of for any truly useful purpose.

Anya stared at the shimmering show for a few moments, though, and then promptly passed out again. Izzy let out a groan of frustration, and looked accusingly at Finn as though the entire situation was his fault.

"Well, *that* went well," Izzy said as she moved to check on Anya. Finn merely shrugged and grinned, much to Izzy's annoyance.

He'd seen worse reactions to the revelation that shifters existed. Anya would come around.

CHAPTER SIX

Anya opened her mouth to scream, but she could not force any sound to come out. She was being tossed wildly around in the air as the dragon who grasped her with his claws flew faster and faster. Behind her, she could hear the whizzing of laser beams and the rushing sound made when a river of fire spewed forth from a dragon's mouth. She strained her eyes to try to make out the figures flying behind her. But the darkness was too great. She couldn't see anything beyond the tip of the tail that belonged to the dragon that held her. As she continued to strain her eyes, the darkness seemed to press in on her even more. Eventually, she could only see to the base of the dragon's tail, not the tip. Then, she could only see the muscular tops of the legs that held her. The darkness grew, and she could only see the claws that surrounded her body, terrible and sharp, yet somehow not piercing her. Finally, all she could see was her own hand, inches in front of her face. Then, everything was black, and Anya screamed again. The darkness was alive, encircling her, blinding her, and suffocating her. The next time she tried to scream into the inky blackness, her voice caught in her throat, and terror overwhelmed her heart.

"Anya!" a loud voice spoke her name, and firm hands shook her shoulders. With a start, Anya opened her eyes. She winced at the bright light of day that greeted her, and struggled to focus on the fuzzy face in front of her. After a few moments, Anya finally saw that it was Izzy. One of the wizards.

The wizards, Anya thought, feeling somewhat sick to her stomach. A glance to her left revealed that Finn and Owen were still there, too, watching her with grave expressions on their faces.

"It's alright," Izzy said in a soothing voice. "You had a bad dream."

Anya blinked a few times, trying to process what Izzy was telling her. She'd had a bad dream. It had all been a dream. Wizards and shifters didn't really exist. Anya sat up slowly, feeling somewhat foolish.

"It was the craziest dream," she said, shaking her head and trying to shake off the feeling of dread that pursued her even in her waking state. She looked around at the forest, thinking she would be back in the campsite she'd been in the night before. It all had been a dream. The attack, and the subsequent explanation. What kind of strange things had she been reading lately to fill her subconscious with the ideas of shifters and wizards?

But as she looked around, she realized that she was not in the same campsite she'd been in the night before. She was somewhere else entirely. She glanced suspiciously down at Izzy's hand, and saw that a giant gemstone ring still graced the woman's fingers.

"Is that…is that ring…special?" Anya asked in a small voice. She didn't want to say the word magic out loud. Saying it out loud would make everything real. She desperately wanted Izzy to look at her in confusion right now, wondering why Anya was suddenly so interested in her ring. But Izzy's face softened into an expression of sympathy, not confusion.

"It's my magic ring, Anya," Izzy said. "You didn't imagine all of that. Shifters and wizards do really exist, and you saw a battle between some of them last night."

Anya jumped rapidly to her feet, wanting to run but not knowing where she would go. It wasn't exactly that she was afraid of Izzy and the others. They didn't seem like they wanted to hurt her, and, if they did, it probably wouldn't do her much good to run anyway. No, it wasn't that Anya was afraid. It was just that she was overwhelmed by everything she'd just learned was true. It couldn't be possible, and yet, looking around at the serious faces staring back at her, Anya knew it was true. Shifters and wizards existed. And by some strange, freaky coincidence, Anya had gotten herself tangled up in their war.

Anya felt a rush of dizziness as her body adjusted to the sudden change of position, but once that initial dizziness had passed, she did take off running into the forest. She ignored the shouts of protest behind her and kept running. Her pace was slow and her movements were clumsy, but she pressed forward anyway. She ignored the branches that scratched at her face, and only stopped for a moment to wince in pain when she stubbed her toe on a thick tree root.

She ran until her sides cramped up fiercely, and she could no longer force herself forward. She collapsed onto the forest floor then, finding herself in a mossy cool spot and relishing the way the soft moss felt between her fingers as she lay there, gasping for breath and trying to make sense of all the nonsensical details that swirled in her thoughts.

She looked behind her, but everything was silent. They had not followed her, then. She wasn't sure whether she should be happy or angry about that. After all, here she was in the middle of the forest by herself. She had no supplies and no idea where she was. She had some decent wilderness survival skills, but it was still going to be a struggle to get out of here and back to civilization.

Anya sat up slowly and looked around, wondering if she should go back. But a stubborn anger and pride rose in her chest. If they didn't care enough about her to make sure she made it out of the forest safely, then she didn't want their help, anyway.

High above her, a bird began singing a happy song, as though nothing in the world was wrong. Bright sunlight lit the ground with a mottled pattern as it made its way down through the leaves and branches, and here and there Anya could see insects buzzing happily along. The whole forest seemed unaware that Anya's whole idea of reality had just been smashed to pieces. The enormity of everything she had just learned weighed on her, and she fought the urge not to cry. She might have lost that battle and let the tears fall, too, if it hadn't been for the sudden appearance of one of the dragon shifters.

"You should take it easy, you know," he said. "You've had a couple nasty bumps to the head, and if you pass out again while running around like a maniac, you're liable to get another one."

Anya started and looked up. It was Finn. She hadn't heard his approach at all, and she'd been too busy feeling sorry for herself to notice him walking through the brush toward her mossy oasis.

"If you don't want me to pass out again then you shouldn't sneak up on me like that," Anya said. "You almost gave me a heart attack appearing out of thin air like that. Wait, *did* you just appear out of thin air? Can you do that?"

Finn chuckled. "No, not really. I can't do magic like the wizards. I do have the ability to act like a chameleon when I'm in dragon form and blend into my surroundings. But I can't do it while in human form. I snuck up on you using good old fashioned stealth skills. I didn't mean to walk so quietly, though. It's just a habit borne of years of practice living out in the woods."

"Hmph," Anya said, not knowing how else to respond. She felt embarrassed that he had nearly caught her crying, and she still hadn't conquered the anger she was feeling toward him and his whole little crew for the way they had dragged her into a mess she'd never wanted to be a part of.

He took her non-response as an invitation to sit down, and plopped himself beside her on the mossy ground. He had a distinctive woodsy smell that was somehow separate from the smell of the woods around her. It was a deeper, richer scent. It reminded her of a redwoods forest she'd visited during her childhood. Her father had taken her to see San Francisco, and they'd split their time between the city and the nearby forests. Anya still remembered those hikes as some of the most gorgeous she'd ever been on, and she couldn't keep a smile from crossing her face at the memory.

"You smell like California," she said aloud before she could really stop herself to think about what she was saying. Finn looked over at her in surprise.

"I'm from California," he said. "But I haven't been home for several months."

Anya shrugged. "Well, you remind me of some forests I visited there a long time ago."

Finn chuckled. "Redwood forests?" he asked.

It was Anya's turn to look surprised. "Well, yes," she said. "I guess you must live near them?"

Finn smiled as he picked up a stick and began absentmindedly tracing circles in a nearby spot of bare earth. "I live in the Redwoods, actually," he said. "I have a cabin out there with...uh...with some other guys like me."

"You mean with other dragon shifters?" Anya asked.

Finn sighed. "Yes. With other dragon shifters. I wasn't sure whether I should say the word 'shifter' or not. I thought you might take off running again if I did."

Anya looked down at her hands. She caught the note of accusation in Finn's voice, but she wasn't going to apologize for running.

"You have to admit that it's a lot to take in," she said.

"It is," Finn admitted. "And I'm sorry you got caught up in our world. Truly, I am. I know that most humans find it somewhat upsetting to learn that shifters exist, although I have to say it's hard for me to understand why. It's not as though you've ever been harmed by a shifter or a wizard. They've always been there, even though you were ignorant of their existence."

Anya pondered this for a moment. "I suppose you're right," she said. "I don't think I'm upset because I'm worried of being harmed, though. I'll admit that fear did cross my mind. You can't exactly blame me for wondering, when faced with a pair of giant fire-breathing dragons and their wizard sidekicks, about whether or not I was safe. But once I realized you guys didn't seem interested in harming me, I had time to focus on a deeper, darker fear."

"Which is?" Finn prompted.

"Well...what else is out there that I'm unaware of?" Anya asked. "And how can I be certain of anything anymore? My whole life I've believed in science. I trusted my senses, and that what I could see, observe, touch, and test was true. Now I learn that magic exists, and that humans can change into animals. I feel as though everything I knew was wrong."

To Anya's surprise, Finn smiled at her. "Well, I don't think you have to throw in the towel on science just because shifters exist. Like I told you, there's a perfectly good scientific explanation for it. It's a genetic mutation, and my DNA is partially composed of dragon genes. You can observe my changing into a dragon and back again just like you can observe anything else in the scientific world. Now, as for magic, I'll admit that it's a little harder to comprehend. There's not always a good explanation for what the wizards can do. But you can still see and observe the effects of magic, so it's sort of scientific. The real problem, though, is when you say you're worried you'll never be certain of anything anymore. None of us can ever be truly certain of anything, Anya. We can only do the best we can with whatever information we have at the time. You can never know everything, so stop worrying about that and just enjoy the ride."

Anya furrowed her brow and thought about what Finn had just said. It made sense. After all, even science brought surprises. New animals or new scientific phenomena were always being discovered. Even in the world of botany, new breakthroughs were made all the time.

"I guess you're right," she said slowly, looking over at him. The sunlight was shining directly on his face right now, and she noticed for the first time a large scar across his left cheek. It was a faint white line, but it was clearly visible when the harsh light of direct sun was on it. It only added to his rugged, fierce appearance, and Anya suddenly found herself wondering who this man was. She knew his name, and that he was part dragon, but little else. She'd been so overwhelmed with the sudden realization that shifters and wizards existed that it hadn't occurred to her what a fascinating life Finn must have had. Had it always been filled with danger? Why was there a war going on in the world of shifters and wizards? Anya's curious scientist side began to take over as she realized that she had just encountered a situation perhaps even more exciting than finding a new species of animal. She had essentially discovered a new species of mankind. In fact, two new species: shifters and wizards. Her anger and trepidation gave way to fascinated curiosity, and she turned shyly to look at Finn again.

"Can I ask you some questions?" she asked. "About shifting and stuff, I mean."

Finn grinned at her and leaned back onto his elbows, settling into the soft moss as if he were settling into a soft couch for a long chat with friends. "Sure," he said. "Ask me anything."

Anya felt like a kid who'd just been told she could choose anything she wanted in a candy store. Where should she even start with all of her questions? She decided to start with the one that had been nagging at her the most since she'd first seen Finn and Owen morph into dragons.

"Does it hurt?" she asked.

"When I shift, you mean?" Finn asked.

Anya nodded.

"Not really," Finn said. "It mostly feels like there's a lot of pressure pushing down against your limbs. It's not exactly comfortable, but it isn't painful. And it's over very quickly, anyway. If I haven't shifted in a long time, it's actually a relief to let myself morph into dragon form. My dragon DNA gets restless if I don't let my dragon out now and then, so I try to shift at least once a month. Lately it's been a lot more, though."

"Because of the war?" Anya asked.

Finn nodded. "We've all been trying to keep our dragons in top shape, just in case we have to shift and fight at a moment's notice. Which, as you saw, is a very real possibility."

"What is the war about?" Anya asked. "And is it only shifters and wizards? There aren't going to be attacks on humans, are there?"

"Well, if my side wins the war, there won't be attacks on humans. If we lose, though, I fear for all of us."

"That's rather cryptic," Anya said, frowning.

"I suppose it is," Finn said. "I didn't mean for it to be, but it's a lot to explain and I'm not quite sure where to begin."

"I've got time," Anya said, leaning back in the moss on her elbows the same way that Finn had. He looked over at her and she was surprised to see how close their faces were now. His face crinkled into a smile, and, for a moment, time seemed to stand still. It had been ages since Anya had felt a true rush of desire, but she knew she was feeling one now. Finn's smile went deeper than just his face. It reached his eyes, and he had somehow put his very heart and soul into that smile. If asked, Anya would have been hard-pressed to explain what she meant by that, but she somehow knew it was true. Her own heart and soul seemed to respond to the smile, and for a split-second she was overcome by the absurd notion that she should lean over and kiss his smiling lips. Something was passing between them, and she knew he felt it, too, by the way his eyes locked with hers and saw right into her.

But just as quickly as the moment happened, it ended. He looked away, staring up at the treetops as though they were the most interesting things he had ever seen. Anya felt like time began to move again. She could once again hear the birds singing and the rustle of the leaves. The forest around her came back into focus, and she could see things other than just Finn's face. She desperately wanted to recapture the emotion she had felt only moments before, but Finn seemed determined to press forward with his explanations.

"The truth is," Finn said. "Wizards aren't the only source of magic in this world. In fact, centuries ago, dragons used to hold magical powers as well. Over the years, the dragons' power weakened. Eventually, the dragons began to store their powers in different physical objects in an attempt to preserve those powers."

"How is that possible?" Anya asked. She felt as though the more she learned about the shifter and wizard worlds, the more confused she became.

"I don't know how to explain it, other than to say that it just works somehow. I've never had magical powers myself, so I've never been faced with the task of storing them in an old stone or pot or something," Finn said. "Perhaps it's easy to do, perhaps it's not, but at the end of the day, the ancient dragons somehow found a way to do it. As a result, there are hundreds of ordinary looking objects scattered across the world that actually contain immense power. My clan, the Redwood Dragons clan, until recently spent most of our time searching for these objects. We recover them and take them back to our base in the Redwood forests for safekeeping. We believe that the world as a whole is safer when these powerful objects are kept in the hands of good shifters."

"Makes sense," Anya said. "No matter what form power comes in, it's always devastating when in the hands of the wrong people."

Finn nodded. "Well, it turns out that there are four ancient artifacts that are exponentially more powerful than any of the other ancient artifacts. They are actually four gemstones—an emerald, a sapphire, an amethyst, and a ruby. Until very recently, we didn't even know that these stones existed. They were created in secret by the ancient dragon kings, who put all of their power into the stones. The ancient dragon kings knew that they would not be able to stand against the forces of evil that were warring in the world at that time, so they preserved their power in hopes that a future generation might find the stones and use them for good. Well, for hundreds of years the stones remained hidden. A few decades ago, though, there was another big shifter war, and some of the good dragons discovered the existence of the dragon emerald. The dragon emerald was recovered, and put in safekeeping, where it remains to this day."

"What about the other stones?" Anya asked, finding herself being drawn into the story. She was imagining an ancient world full of powerful dragons and wizards, similar to the fairy tales she'd always read as a child.

"Well, that's where the trouble starts," Finn said, a shadow passing over his eyes. "Not long ago, the wizards learned that the dragon sapphire had been located. They worked with us to recover the sapphire, and that's actually how they became our allies. But we weren't the only ones who had heard word of the dragon stones. A power hungry dragon shifter named Saul started building an army with hopes that he could find and recover the remaining two dragon stones, the amethyst and the ruby. He's managed to gain a lot of ground and get a frighteningly large number of people to follow him. His army includes wizards, shifters, and even humans."

"There are humans who know about all of this and are fighting a war over it?" Anya asked, incredulous.

Finn nodded sadly. "Saul knows how to win people over. He promises power and wealth, and that anyone who follows him will be leaders in the new world regime he plans to establish once he finds the other dragon stones and uses their power to make himself king of the world."

Anya could not help giving a snort of laughter. "King of the world? Really? Sounds a bit dramatic."

But Finn wasn't laughing when he gave her a sideways glance. "Perhaps it sounds a bit dramatic, but that doesn't mean it's not possible. These stones are powerful. Each time we find one, it is more powerful than the one we found before. If any of them were to get into Saul's hand, it could spell disaster for the entire world. Including humans."

Anya frowned. "It still seems a bit extreme to think that someone could take over the whole world using a couple of small gemstones."

"It doesn't seem extreme to me," Finn said. "Because I understand how powerful these gemstones are. The ancient dragon kings were more powerful than any ruler alive today. That power is preserved in those stones, and Saul would have no qualms about using it to cause great terror and destruction, all so that the whole world would fear him and obey him. You asked what this war is about, Anya. Well, the short answer is that it's about power. Saul is an evil man, and he's hungry for power. I shudder to think what will happen if he gets that power."

"What makes him so evil?" Anya asked. She felt a strange, growing sense of dread filling her as Finn talked. The tone of Finn's voice made it sound like Saul wasn't just your ordinary, power-hungry dictator. There was something more to it than that.

"That's also difficult to explain, but I'll try," Finn said. "In the world of magic, you see, there is good magic and dark magic. Good magic is just your normal everyday magic, and it's what most wizards practice. There are, of course, some very powerful spells. But most wizards use those spells for good, and the wizarding community has a lot of rules and regulations about what is allowable in terms of magic use. Too many rules and regulations, if you ask me. But, anyway. That's 'normal' magic, if you will."

"Okay," Anya said. "So I'm assuming this Saul guy doesn't practice normal magic?"

"No, he doesn't," Finn said. "He practices dark magic, as do all of his minions. Dark magic is very, very powerful. You can do some truly awful things with it. The problem is that dark magic spells require bits of your soul to be effective. If you want to practice dark magic, you have to be willing to literally give up your soul."

Anya shuddered. "That sounds pretty awful," she said.

"It is," Finn said. "The longer someone practices dark magic, the worse off they become. They grow more powerful, for a time. But you can only sell your soul for so long before doing so destroys you. No one can practice dark magic and survive. It kills everyone it enslaves. And the longer someone is practicing dark magic, the more impossible it becomes to bring them back to the side of good. I would imagine Saul is a lost cause by now. He's worse even than a normal dark magic wizard."

"Why is that?" Anya asked.

"Because he's not actually a wizard. He's a shifter," Finn explained. "Ordinarily, only those who are born as wizards can practice magic. But shifters can gain magical abilities, too. After all, centuries ago many shifters *were* born with magical abilities. The only problem is that, in this day and age, the only way for a shifter to get magical abilities is through dark magic. The spell to give a shifter magical abilities is itself a difficult spell for even the most accomplished of dark wizards. Whoever performed the spell on Saul is probably dead by now. But he certainly left behind quite a legacy. Saul is destroying everything in his path, and if we don't stop him he might destroy the whole world before dark magic destroys him. I know it probably sounds like I'm being dramatic once again, but it's the truth. We're on the edge of a world war unlike anything anyone has ever seen before."

Anya frowned. "If it's as dire as you're saying it is, then why don't you try to get more help? Talk to the humans about it! Get some governments involved. Or use the dragon stones you already have. You said they're exceptionally powerful, right? Why can't you use their power to defeat Saul?"

Anya watched as Finn looked up at the sky. He watched the treetops without really seeming to see them. When he finally spoke, his voice sounded sad, and he did not look at Anya.

"I wish it was that easy. But we cannot risk it. We don't know who we can really trust, and Saul's powers of persuasion have proven to be very strong. Our best hope of victory is not to raise an army, which might betray us and be swayed by dark magic, but rather to take away the source of Saul's potential power. We must find the dragon stones before he does. If we have to use the other dragon stones to hold him off, we will. But only as a very last resort. We cannot risk them falling into the wrong hands. Of course, we may soon reach the point of last resort."

"Why do you say that?" Anya asked.

Finn looked back at her then, and he looked into her eyes long and hard. He was searching for something, but what?

"You can trust me," Anya said. "I may not have reacted in the best way possible to the news that shifters and wizards exist, but I'm not an evil person. I believe that good is worth fighting for, and I would never betray you to an evil shifter-wizard or his army."

Finn must have believed Anya's speech, because he nodded and even cracked a small smile.

"I suppose, if you weren't trustworthy, I would have already told you too much," Finn said. "I guess I made the decision to trust you the moment I explained to you how shifters and wizards exist. And I think it was the right decision. Hopefully you don't prove me wrong."

Finn looked up at Anya and winked, and the warmth on his face sent a funny little thrill through her body. It was so strange, she thought, to be sitting here having a conversation with a man who looks completely ordinary and yet can change into a dragon at a moment's notice. She still felt like she was dreaming, but the dream was starting to feel less and less like a nightmare and more and more like an adventure.

"You made the right decision," Anya said, winking back at him and feeling deliciously flirtatious as she did. "I'm completely trustworthy."

Finn laughed, but only for a moment. His face sobered up again as he began speaking. "Owen, Izzy, Raven, and I are supposed to be on a mission to find the dragon amethyst right now. We have a bunch of old records that point to a place in Montana known as Devil's Melt as the location of the stone. The only problem is that we stole these records from Saul's army, so Saul knows that the stone is somewhere in Devil's Melt, too."

"So it was his army that attacked you last night, right?" Anya asked. Things were slowly starting to make more sense.

"Yup, that was his army," Finn said. "But we aren't sure how they knew where we were. We expected that Saul would be closely watching for us near Devil's Melt. But we were hundreds and hundreds of miles away from Devil's Melt last night. We should have been relatively safe, because we had been traveling under invisibility spells. They shouldn't have had any idea where we were. Which means either they have dark magic that can see through invisibility shields, or they have spies in Falcon Cross."

"Falcon Cross?" Anya asked. "Where's that?"

"Oh, right," Finn said. "I forget you're still new to this group. Falcon Cross is in Oregon. It's the wizarding village where Izzy and Raven are from. Some of my clan of dragon shifters are there right now, helping out with various military operations as we attempt to hold off Saul's army and find the dragon stones. Falcon Cross has become a sort of command central for this war. If there were spies there, that would be a devastating blow. But I don't really think there are. If that were the case, they probably would have attacked us much sooner. I think it's more likely that the enemy's dark magic abilities are growing. Our invisibility shields are strong, but the enemy is getting through them anyway."

"So could they see us right now?" Anya asked, feeling suddenly worried and exposed. She peered into the thick brush of the forest, half-expecting to see evil eyes staring back at her. But nothing stirred except the occasional squirrel or bird.

"Yeah, they could definitely see us right now, if they were here," Finn said. "But don't worry. They're not here. They might have some pretty strong spells, but they still suck at flying. We outflew them last night, and are far enough away now that they aren't likely to look for us out here. We're far enough away in the wrong direction, I should say."

"The wrong direction?"

"We flew south instead of north," Finn said. "They're expecting us to fly toward Devil's Melt, where the amethyst is. And that was our original plan. But there's no way I'm heading into Devil's Melt without some sort of reinforcement. If they found us in Idaho, they'll definitely find us in Montana. I don't know if you noticed, but the campsite we're at now is different than even the first spot we escaped to last night."

"I hadn't noticed," Anya admitted. "I was so confused when I came to the first time that I didn't pay much attention to what the forest looked like."

Finn nodded. "No big surprise there. You had a lot to think about. But just to catch you up, I'll tell you what happened. After you passed out for a second time last night, we decided that we needed to keep moving. We were still relatively close to the area where we were attacked, and we didn't want to chance another attack. So Izzy put a sedation spell on you and put you on her broomstick. Then we flew all through the night as far south as we could get. We're somewhere in Utah right now. The good news is that we're probably off the radar of Saul's army, for the moment at least. The bad news is that we're far, far away from the dragon amethyst with no idea how we're going to manage to get to Devil's Melt and find it. Our only option at this point might be to get the dragon emerald and dragon sapphire and use their powers to protect us while we search for the amethyst. But that decision won't be mine to make. Oh, and, we're also really far away from where we originally found you. I'm really sorry about that. We'll find a way to get you home, I promise. Last night, though, the priority was to get away from Saul's men. If we'd left you behind and they found you, they would have killed you."

"And what if I don't want to go home?" Anya asked.

Finn looked up at her in surprise. "Well, no one's forcing you to go home. I just assumed that you'd want to. And I also thought you might be a bit pissed that you innocently went to sleep at a campsite in Idaho, then woke up in Utah surrounded by shifters and wizards."

Anya felt her heart beating faster as she looked at Finn. She could hardly believe she was about to say what she was going to say, but she knew she didn't have a choice. She still didn't understand everything, but she understood one thing: this Saul guy could not be allowed to win. If what Finn was saying was true, then a lot of good people were at risk right now—shifters, wizards, and even humans.

"Listen, Finn," Anya said. "The attempts your clan and these wizards are making to do things on your own are admirable, really. You're sacrificing a lot, and now that I know that, I'm truly grateful. But if you think I'm going to go quietly back to my old life now and act like nothing out of the ordinary happened, you're wrong."

"What are you trying to say, Anya?" Finn asked, narrowing his eyes slightly as he looked at her.

Anya squared her shoulders. "I'm trying to say that I think you just found the first human soldier for the army against Saul."

CHAPTER SEVEN

Finn should have seen it coming, but he didn't. Anya's words took him completely off guard, and he stuttered as he tried to formulate a response.

"Anya, that's...that's very noble of you. But I'm not sure you understand the dangers involved here. You could die. Saul and his men would think nothing of torturing you and killing you."

"I'm not afraid, and I'm not stupid," Anya said. "I've heard everything you've been telling me, and I realize that there are risks involved. But it sounds like it's a little late for safety, anyway. What happens if I go back home now and you guys aren't able to get the rest of the dragon stones? I'll still be in danger. The whole world will be in danger if Saul has that kind of power. Not only that, but I'll have to live with the knowledge that I might have been able to do something to stop Saul."

"No offense, Anya, you seem like a smart girl," Finn said gently. "But what could you do? You don't have any magical powers, and you can't change into a fierce animal. The humans who have joined Saul's army are the first to be slaughtered whenever there's a battle."

"And who do you think Saul will use as pawns if he finds the other dragon stones? The humans will be the first to go, I guarantee it. I'm not going to go home and sit around waiting and hoping that the world doesn't come to an end. Let me help you. I may be small, but that doesn't mean I'm not fierce. I have more heart than most people twice my size, I promise you."

Finn was surprised by how insistent Anya was being. Usually, humans ran the other direction from shifters as fast as they could. When you added in the fact that he had just told Anya that the whole world was in danger of imploding on itself, Finn had expected her to be running as fast as she could away from the Falcon Cross group. Perhaps there was more to this fiery little character than met the eye. He took a moment now to look her over again. Her hair was even messier than it had been last night. The bun she'd been wearing it in had come out in the chaos of flying. Her hair hung in long tangled waves around her shoulders, but even in that state it was beautiful. The color perfectly set off her green eyes, and her smooth skin glowed in the light of the sun. A few freckles dotted her nose, and here and there she had a scratch on her face from running so frantically through the bushes. She was a mess, but a beautiful mess.

He knew she was doing funny things to his heart. There was no sense in denying the infatuation that washed over him every time he looked at her. But thinking that she was a beautiful woman and acting on those thoughts were two different things. He could not afford to fall for her, no matter how much faster she made his heart beat. She might be brave and eager to help, but she was still human. He could not in good conscience bring a human into this war. Not after seeing what had happened to the humans who were part of Saul's army. Humans were nothing more than easy targets in this fight, and he didn't want to turn Anya into an easy target.

Besides, it wasn't his decision to make. Any new clan members had to be approved by the clan leaders. Unless one of the High Council wizards or the lead dragons approved Anya, it didn't matter so much what he thought. And he told Anya as much.

"Anya, I'm not the one who decides who is allowed to go on our missions or fight in our armies. I can't give you permission to join us, and I can guarantee that those who do make those decisions will be wary of taking on a human. They don't even like to allow new wizards or shifters to join us, for fear that a spy might get in."

"You must have some sway with them, though," Anya persisted. "Come on, you guys dragged me into this. You owe me a chance to prove that I can help. Tell them that I deserve to be part of this."

"Anya," Finn started to say again. He was trying to find the words to explain to her that he didn't think he had that much sway and that, even if he did, he wouldn't want to use his influence to convince his clan leaders to allow Anya to be part of a war that might get her killed. But before Finn could get any more words out, he was interrupted by Owen, who showed up in the forest just as silently as Finn had not even half an hour ago.

"You guys better come back to the campsite," he said gravely.

Finn jumped to his feet, instantly alert. "Is something wrong? Did they find us again?"

"No, I think we've given Saul's army the slip, at least temporarily," Owen said. "But Peter and Knox are here. They want to discuss what to do about Anya."

"*Knox* is here?" Finn said, feeling truly shocked. Finn had not seen their clan leader, Knox, in quite some time, since he had been busy helping to guard the dragon stones in Texas. If anything, Finn would have expected Noah, the second in command dragon, to show up. Even that would have been surprising to Finn, but perhaps he should have known something like this would happen. The wizards worried obsessively about humans discovering magic. Of course they would be over the top worried about a human seeing an attack by Saul's army. Knox was probably coming to reassure Peter that everything was alright. Finn relaxed a little bit at that thought. Knox was levelheaded, and could talk some sense into the wizards. And it would be good to see his clan leader again. Finn felt excitement filling his heart as he turned to Anya.

"Come on," he said. "The guys who can make a decision about whether to let you join the war are here."

Anya stood and nodded, looking pleased. She wouldn't look so pleased if she understood how hard it would be to convince them, Finn thought. Still, he felt a rush of happiness at her smile. He turned abruptly to walk in front of her, telling himself to get it together. He already knew how this story ended. Peter and Knox would listen to Anya beg for a chance to fight alongside the wizards and dragons. They would nod sympathetically, but ultimately decide that it was too dangerous for a human. Perhaps they would offer her extra protection as an incentive for her to go peaceably back to her home. But in the end, Anya would have to go home. Finn was sure of that. There was no sense in letting himself feel anything for her. And yet, he couldn't help feeling like his heart was breaking a little as he watched her walking in front of them now. She was moving quickly, as if in excited anticipation. She thought she would be able to convince them to let her stay, but she truly didn't know what she was asking for.

Finn glanced over at Owen, who had his mouth set in a grim line. Owen must be worried that we're going to get chewed out for letting a human see us, Finn thought. Finn wasn't too worried about that. He didn't care all that much anymore. He'd been chewed out plenty of times in his life. What was once more? He was just happy that there was someone else here now to show Anya that she was asking for the impossible. Finn decided to talk to Owen about Anya, who was now far enough ahead of them that she wouldn't hear what the men were saying if they kept their voices low. Maybe talking would loosen Owen up a bit and wipe that worried scowl off his face.

"She's one of the most accepting humans I've ever met, you know?" Finn said. "I mean, yeah, she tried to run off at first. But after she calmed down and I explained more about shifting to her, she actually seemed quite curious. In fact, when I told her about the war and why we were attacked last night, she actually wanted to join our army. Can you believe that? I mean, there's no way Peter and Knox will let her, but it's pretty brave of her to even ask, don't you think?

Owen did not seem impressed by this news, though. In fact, his scowl deepened. "Peter's not going to be happy that you told her everything about the war. Did you explain about the dragon stones, too?"

Finn nodded. "Yes, but what was I supposed to tell her? We were attacked by people who obviously want us dead. There aren't many easy ways to explain that, other than the truth. What's with you, anyway? Usually you're the first one to roll your eyes at the wizards and all their overly cautious rules. But you're almost acting like you yourself think that I shouldn't have said anything to Anya. Are you actually still worried that she's a spy or something?"

Owen stopped walking for a moment and let out a long, annoyed sigh. Anya was quite far ahead of them now, rapidly heading back toward their latest makeshift campsite.

"I don't think she's a spy," Owen said. "But Peter is freaking out about a human discovering magic, and the war."

"That's nothing new," Finn said. "They're always freaking out about that sort of thing."

"No, but I mean, really freaking out," Owen said. "Finn, they want to wipe her memory."

Finn's jaw actually dropped as he looked over at Owen. He opened his mouth to try to speak, but the only thing he could manage to say was, "*What?*"

Owen nodded in confirmation. "Peter's not alone. He brought one of the most senior wizard Advocates with him—to perform the spell if they do decide to wipe her memory. That's why Knox came all the way out, too. He's trying to convince Peter that a memory wipe is unnecessary and a bad idea."

"It *is* a bad idea," Finn said vehemently, finally finding his voice. "Why would Peter risk all the complications just to keep one human from knowing about wizards? One human who wants to help us, no less."

Owen merely shrugged and said nothing. There wasn't much to say, really. Finn knew Owen agreed that it was a bad idea, but if Peter decided that it was necessary, there would be no stopping him. The old wizard was one of the wisest, kindest people Finn had ever met, but he was also one of the most stubborn. When Peter set his mind on an idea, it was virtually impossible to convince him to change it.

Finn felt his heart dropping as he considered the possibility that Anya's memory would be wiped. Finn didn't know much about magic, but he knew about memory wiping. Izzy had explained it to him one night when telling him about the horrible things that Saul's army had threatened to do to her when she had been their prisoner. Memory wiping was not itself a dark magic spell, but it was rarely used among good wizards due to its risks. Dark wizards, of course, generally didn't care about bad side effects.

And the potential side effects were many. The memory-wiping spell was a difficult one, and only the most talented wizards were allowed to even attempt it. Peter himself would defer to a senior wizard advocate if the spell was to be performed, because the senior Advocate would actually have a small amount of experience with performing the spell. Occasionally, if a human saw too much magic and was threatening to expose the wizards to the government, the wizards would decide to have an advocate wipe that human's memory. Over the years, a few cases of memory wiping had been carefully documented, and most of them had not ended well.

In one case, the wizard casting the spell had erased too much of the human's memory. The human had not been able to remember anything at all for the last ten years before the wipe. The human had no recollection of his job, his wife, or even of his newborn baby girl. The poor guy had been forced to go to therapy because the human doctors thought he was suffering from some sort of mental illness. In another case, the spell had destroyed the human's ability to make new memories, and the human could not remember any new experiences he had for more than a few seconds. And there was more than one case where the person had just gone completely, irreparably crazy.

Finn shuddered. He barely knew Anya, but he already cared about her a great deal. He couldn't imagine what it would feel like to see her go crazy, or forget about her life from the last ten years. She didn't deserve that. No one deserved that. Finn knew the wizards were just trying to protect themselves, but it seemed like such a violation of basic human rights to wipe someone's memory for no reason other than that person had accidentally crossed paths with a wizard.

And, of course, if Anya's memory was erased, she would not remember him. Somehow, that realization cut deeper than all his other worries. The thought of never seeing her again, and having her not even remember meeting him, took his breath away. Finn watched Anya's rapidly disappearing back as she raced through the woods, not knowing that she was racing toward potential doom.

"I'm not going to let them do this to her!" Finn growled, anger filling his voice.

"You can't interfere," Owen said, although he sounded sad when he said this. "I don't always approve of the way the wizards do things, either, but we have to respect their traditions and reasoning. They're our allies, you know. We need them. Knox will do his best to talk sense into Peter, but you have to stay out of it and let Knox take care of it."

"Bullshit!" Finn said. "I've had enough of this bullshit. Yes, they're our allies, and we do need to respect that they sometimes have different ways of doing things. But that doesn't mean that I have to stand by and let them do something that's clearly wrong. Anya is a good person. She wants to help us. She isn't going to rat us out to the enemy, and there's no reason to risk destroying her life and memory because we're too afraid to admit that *we* screwed up by allowing her to see our campsite in the first place."

Owen, who was usually quite a fiery personality, merely shrugged in response, then let out a resigned sigh.

"Well," Owen said. "If you want to say something to change Peter's mind then you better hurry up and go say it. I get the impression that he was in quite a big hurry to get this 'threat' taken care of."

Finn's eyes darkened and he quickened his pace as he followed Anya back toward the campsite. "Anya's not a threat. She deserves better than this, and I'm going to fight to make sure she gets it."

Out of the corner of his eye, Finn saw Owen's eyes widening a bit in surprise. But Owen did not question Finn. He seemed to sense that, for some reason, Anya mattered deeply to Finn.

And she did. Finn himself wasn't sure exactly why, but Anya mattered a lot. Perhaps more than anything had ever mattered to him before. The thought both troubled and excited him, but he didn't have time to wonder about it now. First, he would go save Anya's memory. Then he would sort through his feelings for her.

CHAPTER EIGHT

Anya stumbled into the clearing feeling full of adrenaline and hope, but she stopped short at the sight that greeted her. Izzy and Raven were there, of course, but neither one of them would meet Anya's eyes. They were dressed in robes now instead of in the uniforms they had been wearing when Anya first met them, and they had brushed out their hair and washed their faces. Anya marveled at how much the simple change of outfits made them look so much more like the wizards she now knew that they were.

The truly impressive sight, though, was the three men standing near Izzy and Raven. Even though Anya had never seen them before in her life, she knew right away that two of them were wizards and one of them was a shifter. They were important men, here on an important mission. The three of them together made an awe-inspiring, almost fearsome sight, and Anya found herself dropping her eyes uncomfortably to her feet, unsure of where to look or what to say.

One of the wizards was an older man, with a kind face that was deeply etched with laugh lines. He wore a dark red robe, and a matching wizard hat that rose high above his head in a perfect point. He had a long white beard that reached down to his belly, and looked more wizardly than even his magnificent hat. He'd had his hands clasped in front of him when Anya entered the clearing, but now he stretched his right hand out to shake Anya's. She looked up at him as he spoke.

"I'm Peter," he said. "Head wizard of the Falcon Cross High Council."

Anya wasn't sure what a High Council was, but it wasn't hard to figure out that this man was someone worthy of respect. She glanced down at his giant magic ring and admired the way it glittered in the morning sunlight.

"I'm Anya," she said. "Anya Steele."

The old wizard nodded and smiled kindly, and then gestured toward the wizard next to him. "This is Kirk Bryant," Peter said. "He's what's known as a wizard advocate in our clan. It's a job that requires a lot of different skills, but the main purpose of the job is the protection of our wizard clan from outside threats."

Anya wondered as she politely shook Kirk's hand whether she was one of those "threats." She had a feeling that she was, and despite the smile on Peter's face, she could feel the wizard sizing her up. She looked over at Izzy and Raven again, hoping for some sort of reassurance. This time, Izzy met her eyes, and gave a small shrug. Anya wasn't quite sure how to interpret the shrug, but she didn't have time to think about it. Peter was gesturing toward the man who looked like a shifter. The man must have been a good foot taller than the wizards, at least, and he was twice as muscular. He had the same green eyes and reddish brown hair that Owen and Finn had, but his hair was cropped much shorter, allowing Anya to see his ears. She was surprised to see that they had a slight elfish point to them, and she wondered if Owen and Finn had ears like that, too. Their hair was too long to see the tops of their ears very well.

"This is Knox," Peter was saying, and Knox stretched out his hand to shake Anya's hand. But before Knox could say anything to Anya, a loud whoop echoed across the clearing.

"Knox! You're really here!"

It was Finn. Knox looked away from Anya as they broke off their handshake, and Anya saw a huge smile spread across the man's face. She glanced back and saw that Finn was jogging across the small clearing toward Knox, a huge grin on his face as well.

"Finn," Knox said. "It's been too long."

And then the men practically collided with each other. They slapped each other's backs as they hugged and both spoke at a mile-a-minute pace. Anya couldn't help but smile at the sight. It didn't take a genius to figure out that these two were close friends. Owen came back into the clearing a few moments later, and walked over laughing.

"Hey, what's going on with this bromance, guys?" Owen asked. "I didn't get a big hug when Knox first saw me!"

"Aww, is someone jealous?" Knox teased. "Come here, Owen. I'll give you some love, too."

Owen tried to duck away, but Knox was too quick and grabbed him around the neck. Knox rubbed the top of Owen's head vigorously, turning his hair into a complete mess while Owen shouted in protest and Finn laughed. The smile on Anya's face widened. Perhaps these men were dragons, but she had no fear of them. They were good people, who cared about friendship and honor. What more could you ask for in a person?

Anya turned and caught Izzy's eyes again, but the woman still was not smiling. She looked nervous, and Anya could not understand why. Anya knew that the newcomers were here to decide whether she could remain with the group or not, but, surely, Izzy would not have such a worried look on her face only because of that, would she?

Or would she? Anya's smile faded a bit. Perhaps Izzy and Raven did not like her, after all. Maybe that's why they had looked so upset when Anya came back to the campsite. Were they afraid that Peter would let her stay with the army? Because surely he would let her stay, once he saw how dedicated she was to the cause of good. She might not know much about wizards or shifters yet, but she knew right from wrong, and she wanted to do everything she could to fight for the side of right.

Anya turned to look at Finn, who was still laughing and catching up with Knox. But Finn stopped laughing when Anya caught his eye, and he seemed to remember that the moment was actually quite serious.

"Oh, right," he said. "Um, Anya, have you been introduced to Knox? He's the leader of my clan."

"We've been introduced," Knox spoke up. "Although we were somewhat interrupted by your arrival, Finn. Anya, it's nice to meet you. I'm the clan leader of the Redwood Dragons, as Finn told you. I hope my boys have been treating you well?"

Anya wanted to laugh and make some sort of smart remark about how she supposed they had, since Finn had saved her life by carrying her away using dragon claws. But she caught the serious expression on Izzy's face once again and decided that this wasn't the time for jokes.

"They've been treating me very well," she said, and left it at that.

Anya looked to Finn, trying to see in his eyes if there was some indication of whether he thought this little powwow was going to go well for her, but he wasn't looking at her anymore. He was looking at Peter who was starting to speak again.

"Anya, I'm not sure whether anyone has explained to you why you're here?" he asked, then looked at Anya expectantly.

"Well, yes," Anya said, taking a deep breath and standing as tall and straight as she could. "From what Finn has told me, I know that it's highly unusual for a human to discover the existence of wizards and shifters. And I know you don't want humans to interfere with your war, so you're here to decide whether to send me back home or to allow me to fight with you. I know you might not think I have much to offer, but you're wrong. Just because I can't shift into an animal or can't do magic doesn't mean that I can't help you. I'm very smart, and I'm a very hard worker. I'm sure there are a lot of things I can do that will make a difference for you."

Anya wanted to keep speaking, but she had seen a confused look cross over Peter's face. She took a deep breath and forced herself to be quiet. If he had questions for her, let him ask them. She would clear up any doubts he had about letting her join the war. At least, she hoped she would. She looked at Finn again, trying to catch his eyes and plead silently with him to take up her cause. But Finn was staring intently at Peter, refusing to meet her eyes.

Anya felt her heart dropping. Was he really going to refuse to support her in this? She looked around at the other faces, but no one was meeting her eyes except Knox and Peter.

"I see," Peter said, a slight frown on his face. "Well, Anya—"

"Peter, I think we should give the girl a chance," Knox said, interrupting. All of the wizards except Peter looked at Knox in shock. Anya got the impression that they weren't used to seeing anyone interrupt Peter, not even the head of the Redwood Dragons clan. Peter seemed unfazed though. He merely raised an eyebrow in Knox's direction and gave him his attention.

"Oh?" he asked, waiting for Knox to explain further.

"Look, I know the wizards have their ways of doing things, and we dragons try to be supportive as much as we can. But I cannot stand by and support taking such drastic measures on a girl who has no idea what's about to be done to her, and has given no reason for us to doubt her," Knox said.

Anya was confused. "Drastic measures?" she asked. She did not like the sound of that. Something told her that Knox wasn't just talking about sending her home. What were they going to do to her? And why didn't they trust her? But, for the moment, she got no answers. Instead, Peter and Knox looked at each other, both with steely expressions. Anya glanced at Finn again, but he was still carefully watching Peter.

"Knox, we have to be more careful than normal. We're in the middle of a war. You must understand our history! Wizards who are discovered by humans have been persecuted throughout history. Perhaps Anya accepts us, but it's too risky for her to know of our existence. If she tells anyone else, then we are doomed for sure. We cannot defend ourselves against a human witch hunt at the same time we are defending ourselves against Saul's army."

Anya saw a flash of anger in Knox's eyes as Peter spoke.

"You think my boys and I don't understand what it feels like to be persecuted?" Knox said. "Trust me, humans are just as fearful of shifters as they are of wizards. I know what it's like to be persecuted just for being who you are. But we can't live our whole lives in fear. Humans are a very real part of our world, and we can't freak out every time one of them learns of our existence. We could probably use a few humans on our side, in fact. Look at Saul! He's using humans. We should, too. They think about things in slightly different ways than we do. That could be really useful. And besides, what's to stop Saul from telling the whole world that wizards and shifters exist? He's just crazy enough to do that, you know? And if he did decide to do something insane like that, it would probably help us to have a couple humans already on our side, you know?"

Peter stroked his long beard, considering what Knox had said. Anya could feel her heart pounding. She was sure that there was something here she was missing. Peter was talking about her like he wanted to get rid of her completely. Was he suggesting they kill her? Surely not? How could these wizards claim to fight on the side of good if they were murdering people? And yet, Peter's remarks had sounded quite serious. There didn't seem to be a way to explain them except to think he wanted to get rid of her permanently. Fear gripped Anya's heart as she watched Peter thinking, but she forced herself to remain still and keep a calm expression on her face.

"I understand your point, Knox," Peter finally said. "And I do value your opinion, as our closest ally. But I cannot simply allow a human who has seen so much to go back to her home. There is too much risk. I need some sort of assurance or promise that she will keep our secrets safe."

"I'm not going to go blabbing about you to anyone," Anya said, feeling exasperated. "In fact, I'm not even asking to go home. I'm asking to stay with you and fight with you."

"Give the girl a chance," Knox said. "She's fired up to help our soldiers. Let her."

"I can only bend wizarding law so far," Peter said, with a glance at the wizard advocate. "The only way to allow her to stay is for someone to vouch for her. And you know what that means, Knox. Anyone who vouches for her is agreeing to suffer the same punishment as her if she betrays us. May I remind you all that the punishment for betrayal is death?"

Peter crossed his arms as though that settled the matter. He looked around at the group with a resigned expression that seemed to say that he hated to do what had to be done, but had no choice in the matter. Anya held her breath, looking around at all of the somber faces, none of which were looking at her. Her eyes finally rested on Finn, who was still staring straight ahead at Peter. She felt a rush of anger at his silence. How could he just stand there and let them question her sincerity like that. True, he hadn't known her very long. But he had trusted her enough to tell her everything about the war already. Surely, he could trust her enough to speak up for her.

Anya felt her heart dropping with despair as the silence weighed heavily around her. Perhaps she was hoping for too much. She'd thought that she and Finn had shared some sort of moment back in the woods, but she was beginning to think she'd been wrong. There was nothing special between them. He seemed to like her well enough, but he wasn't willing to risk his life for her. After all, that's what Peter was asking him to do, wasn't it? Pledge his life as a guarantee that Anya was trustworthy enough to be accepted into this army. Peter knew that no one here would want to do that. No matter how much they might like her—and Anya had no way of knowing how much they really did like her—speaking up for her would mean putting their own lives on the line for a stranger.

Anya supposed she couldn't really blame Finn for not wanting to do that. He'd only just met her, and all he had to judge her character on was words, not actions. Still, she looked over at him, willing him to look at her and see the sincerity in her eyes. He did not look at her, though. Anya's heart dropped further, and for the first time since Finn had chased her down in the forest, she truly felt afraid. She was all alone here in this group. She wanted nothing more than to help them, and yet, none of them trusted her.

She saw Finn clench his jaw, and she noticed the muscles in his arms tensing up. He took a few deep breaths, as though trying to steady his nerves, but he did not speak. Anya had all but given up hope when, suddenly, he turned to look at her.

As soon as she saw his eyes, she knew that she was safe. There was a heat in them that warmed her to her very core, and a fierceness that told her he would not let them harm her. Before he even spoke the words, her heart knew they were true.

"I will speak for her," he said. His voice hung heavy in the air, seeming to echo through the silence. Peter looked up in surprise, as did Knox. All eyes in the group focused on Finn as he stood tall and began to speak.

"I will speak for her," he repeated. "She wants to join the cause of good. Let her. She has shown us nothing but grace since the moment we were attacked. She could have immediately tried to go to the police in anger, but she didn't. She could have lashed out at us for not telling her from the beginning that we were shifters and wizards, but she didn't. She could have treated us like monsters or freaks, but she didn't. She has tried to understand us and to understand where we are coming from. She deserves to have the same courtesy extended to her."

Anya saw Peter look back and forth between her and Finn, an unreadable expression in his eyes.

"Finn, it's very noble of you to offer this," Peter said. "But you understand what you are saying, right? Speaking for Anya means that if she betrays us, you're treated like a betrayer as well."

"I know what I'm saying," Finn said, his voice sharp and determined. "And I'm willing to say it because I believe in Anya. Has this war turned all of our hearts so cold that we cannot recognize truth and honor when it is standing right in front of our faces? It's time for us to trust more, and to stop letting fear guide our actions. All of Saul's actions are borne of fear. Why would we want to be like him? I say, if the humans wants to help us, let them. And so, I will speak for Anya. Let her join us."

Finn looked back at Anya then, his eyes filled with intensity, but also with tenderness. Anya was overwhelmed with gratitude for the vote of confidence he had just given her. She knew that for as long as she lived, she would never forget this moment: this moment when a dragon shifter believed in her against all odds.

"Thank you," she mouthed to Finn. She wanted to say so much more. She wanted to tell him that he would not regret this. She would not let him down. She would fight for his honor as well as her own. But now was not the right time. Now, she needed to be still and wait for Peter's response. She looked at the old wizard, wondering how someone who looked so somber could have a face so full of laugh lines. Perhaps he wasn't always this pessimistic, she thought. But right now, she felt like she hated the old man and all of his assumptions about her. Who did he think he was, to think she deserved death just because she'd accidentally discovered the existence of shifters and wizards? But before Peter could respond to Finn, another voice spoke up.

"I will speak for her as well."

Anya looked over in shock. It was Owen. He had come to stand right beside Finn, and the two of them together made an impressive sight. Anya felt her eyes welling up with tears as she realized that she had two friends here, at least.

"I have only seen good from Anya," Owen said. "And dragons believe in good. We *must* believe in good, now more than ever. Anya may be human, but she has a true heart. I will not stand by and see her abused with a memory-wiping spell."

Anya barely had time to wonder what Owen meant by "memory-wiping" spell before Knox was moving to stand beside Finn and Owen.

"I will speak for Anya, too," Knox said. "I may not know her at all, but I know my men. They would not vouch for someone without believing that person to be worthy of their protection. If my men are willing to risk their lives for this woman, then I am as well. I respect the Falcon Cross wizards as our allies, but in this instance I think honor should outweigh tradition. With all due respect, Peter, there is no honor in performing a memory wipe on a human who is swearing to you that she wants to help you and your people."

Anya's head was spinning. Memory wipe? Was that what it sounded like? Had the wizards' plan been not to kill her, but to wipe her memory? Anger filled her at the thought. Who did they think they were, to destroy her memories? Her memories were who she was. They might as well kill her if they were going to do that! Perhaps this Peter guy was a hot shot wizard, but Anya wasn't going to treat him with respect if he thought her memories were disposable. She would tell him exactly what she thought of his "protective measures."

But before Anya even had a chance to open her mouth to vent her rage, she saw Izzy moving forward out of the corner of her eye.

"I will speak for her," Izzy said, standing beside Knox. "It's high time that wizards stopped living in fear of all humans. And a good place to start would be with letting Anya, who has begged to help us in this war, be part of our army."

Raven moved forward next, standing next to Owen. Anya saw Owen look over at Raven and take her hand as she looked up at Peter with her chin stubbornly pressed forward.

"And I will speak for her," Raven said. "There isn't much more to say than what my friends here have already said. I agree with them that we should trust Anya, and I vouch for her as well."

Anya stood in awe as she looked at the line of wizards and shifters who stood together, elbows all locked now. Her eyes filled with tears, and she struggled to keep from letting them spill over. The show of solidarity on her behalf touched her deeply, though, and she found it difficult to keep her emotions in check.

She looked back at Peter to see that his face had broken into a broad smile.

"Well, it seems I have my answer, then. Kirk, no memory wiping spells will be necessary today."

Kirk was the only one who looked disappointed about this.

"But, Peter," he said. "The girl has seen so much!"

"So she has," Peter said. "But as I said, our wizard law allows for humans to keep their memories intact when another clan member is willing to vouch for them. Judging by the line of people standing in front of me right now on Anya's behalf, I would say her memory is quite safe."

Kirk didn't look happy about this decision, but he did not protest again. Peter turned to look at Anya then, and gave her a warm smile.

"Anya Steele, welcome to the Falcon Cross army. I hope you won't hold our hesitant welcome against us. We have our laws that we must follow, but it seems that you have managed to overcome even the strictness of the laws. Anyone who can garner this much support must be a true friend of the side of good. We will start looking for a suitable job for you right away."

"She belongs with us," Finn said, speaking up in a loud, determined tone. Peter looked up with surprised curiosity, and Anya glanced questioningly over at Finn as well. He stepped forward, standing a few feet in front of the others as he spoke.

"She belongs with us," Finn repeated. "I've always scoffed at the idea of destiny, but I can't help but think that destiny brought her across our path for some reason. Our dragon amethyst mission needs to be completely reworked, and I have a feeling that Anya can help us with that. Perhaps we just need some outside eyes to take a fresh look at the situation."

Finn met Anya's eyes, and she saw that the fire in them was burning even hotter than before. She wanted to go to him, to fall into his arms and thank him. He was, after all, the one who had stepped up first. He had risked his life for her, and inspired others to do the same. She owed him her everything. But she did not move, not yet. She waited for Peter to respond, holding her breath as she did.

"Well," Peter said, "This is a specialized mission, and it's highly unusual for us to add someone to a mission like this after it has already started. But, it would seem that the whole dragon amethyst search team is rather fond of Anya, so I leave it to you all as a group to decide. The vote must be unanimous, but if you all want Anya on the team, then I will allow her to join you."

Peter looked over expectantly, waiting for the group to make its decision. None of them hesitated for so much as a second.

"Finn's right," Owen said. "She belongs with us."

"I agree," Raven said. "She should be on our team."

"No objections from me," Izzy said, "We could use all the help we can get."

Anya saw Finn's smile broadening as he looked at his friends. Her own heart filled with warmth and gratitude. They wanted her on the team, and she would do her best to make sure their faith in her was rewarded. She didn't know how she was going to do it yet, but she was going to make a difference in the search for the dragon amethyst.

"Looks like you're in, Anya," Peter said. "Welcome to the dragon amethyst search team. For the sake of wizards, shifters, and humans everywhere, I pray you are all successful."

"We will be," Anya said, not caring whether the others thought she was foolish and overly optimistic. "We will be."

And she knew in her bones that it was true.

CHAPTER NINE

Finn sat on the hard ground a short distance from the fire with his knees drawn up in front of him. He had his arms wrapped around his legs and he held a cold beer in one hand, which was quite a treat out here in the wilderness. Knox had brought a stash of beer with him, which had made the dragons and wizards even happier to see him. Knox was a good leader, always taking care of his crew in any way he could, even if that just meant bringing some cold beers out to the woods.

And the beers *were* cold, thanks to the chilly weather. The calendar might say that it was spring, but some sort of weather system was moving through the area and causing the temperatures to drop rapidly. Finn decided he had one reason to be thankful that he wasn't in Montana right now. The weather there was likely even worse.

Still, Finn thought as he watched the crackling flames, he did wish he was in Devil's Melt, despite the weather. He wished he was searching for the dragon amethyst. He wished he was doing *something*.

He was tired of sitting around fires. Even with Knox here, talking and joking, Finn felt restless. It was good to see his clan leader, but he would have enjoyed a meal around the fire pit back home much better. Finn wanted this war to be over, and to be home in his own cabin again. No one else in the circle seemed to share his restlessness tonight, though. Peter and Kirk were laughing as Raven told them a story about falling off her broomstick during an official military flying presentation. Owen was, of course, sitting a little too close to Raven. Izzy was in some sort of earnest conversation with Knox, and Anya was listening in, nodding and smiling. Everyone seemed happy and at ease, but Finn could not find it in himself to relax right now.

There was a goddamn war going on, and the enemy was growing stronger with every passing day. Finn could not keep himself from constantly glancing at the sky, wondering whether they were being followed and whether their invisibility shields would hold. He hoped they were safe for the moment, since they were so far from Devil's Melt in the wrong direction. But if the last twenty-four hours had taught him anything, it was that he could never be sure of safety.

His eyes fell on Peter again, and he scowled despite himself. The old wizard was known as wise, kind, and generous, and yet he had wanted to wipe Anya's memory. There were some things about the wizarding world Finn would never understand, and he worried that the alliance between the wizards and shifters was growing weak. Knox seemed to think everything was fine, but Finn wondered how two groups with so many differences could truly align themselves as one against a threat as powerful as Saul.

Finn supposed that they had no choice in the matter, and that was why they were making things work. After all, neither of the groups were likely to win on their own. They needed each other. Finn saw Raven throw back her head and laugh, and watched as Owen reached over to squeeze her shoulder.

"I guess some of us need them more than others," he said under his breath.

Several of his clan members had now found their lifemates among the wizards of Falcon Cross. Knox had been the first, when he had stumbled across a wizard named

Bree in the middle of the Redwoods. Now, Vance, Zeke, and Myles had also found wizard lifemates. From the way Raven and Owen were acting, Finn had a feeling that Owen might not be far behind.

Finn smiled. He did like Raven, and he thought her spunky personality fit Owen quite well. In fact, all of the wizards whom his clan members had chosen as lifemates were wonderful people. But even though he approved of some of the individual wizards, he didn't have to approve of the wizards' barbaric, outdated laws.

Finn let his eyes move over to Anya again. She was still listening to Izzy and Knox's conversation, although she had a slightly confused look on her face right now. Finn almost wanted to laugh. The poor girl had been thrown suddenly into quite a different world, and her mind must be spinning as she tried to take it all in. She was a smart girl, though. She'd catch up quickly.

Finn felt his heart twist up in his chest in a funny way as he watched Anya. The warm firelight enhanced her beauty, and he found himself admiring the radiant appearance of her skin under the reddish-orange glow. He still couldn't say exactly why it had mattered so much to him that her memory be saved. He wanted to think that he had spoken up for her based solely on his belief that memory wiping was a horrid practice, but he knew his reasons went deeper than that. He felt something for her, but he was having a hard time admitting it to himself.

He had never been the "falling in love" type. He'd never had a serious girlfriend, even when he'd been on long missions that kept him in the same location for months on end. He'd always found it easier to keep his heart closed off and not feel anything for anyone. And who could blame him? Being a Redwood Dragon wasn't an easy life. He and his clan members lived in the middle of nowhere, isolated out in the heart of the California Redwoods. They had no families, except each other. They spent their days doing dangerous work, chasing down powerful ancient artifacts. What kind of woman would want a part in that?

Finn had always thought that no woman would. But now, in the span of less than a year, four of the ten Redwood Dragons had managed to find lifemates. Perhaps Finn was feeling a bit jealous that they had someone to love and protect, and that's why he had chosen to stick up for Anya. Yes, that was it. It wasn't that he wanted Anya in particular. It was just that he wondered what it would be like to love someone. Or, heck, maybe he was just jealous that they got to get laid whenever they wanted. He loved his solo life, but could anyone blame him for sometimes wishing that he had someone warm next to him in bed?

Especially someone as gorgeous as Anya.

Finn frowned and tried to push away the thought. He hadn't saved Anya so he could get laid. He wasn't that shallow. He lifted his beer can to his lips to take another long drag and distract himself, then realized that the can was empty. Frustrated, he threw the can aside and stood to his feet. No one paid any attention to him as he paced back and forth in front of the fire for a few moments. They were all busy with their own conversations, and that was just fine with him. He wasn't in the mood to talk right now.

In fact, he wouldn't mind some time to himself, and he decided that now was as good a time as any to steal off into the woods for a solo walk. Maybe filling his lungs with some fresh, woodsy air would help calm him down. He took one last glance over his shoulder at the group around the fire. Knox looked up, seeming to sense that something was wrong. Finn's eyes met with his clan leader's eyes, and Knox raised an eyebrow at him, questioning.

Finn shrugged, and motioned to the woods. Knox gave a small nod, understanding even though no words were spoken. Everything was fine. Finn just wanted some space.

Finn slipped into the dark forest, every step taking him further from the light and noise of the fire. He breathed in deeply, savoring the scents and silence of the forest at night. The only sound now was the low hum of nocturnal insects, but that blended into the background so well that it could hardly be counted as noise.

After about a minute of walking, Finn felt a slight pressure on his body, and his ears filled with a noise like rushing water. He had reached the boundary of the invisibility and protective shield that surrounded the camp, but he did not hesitate to walk through it to the other side. After a few seconds, he was past the boundary and everything was quiet once again. He wasn't worried about straying from the shield tonight. Despite his constant worry about enemy soldiers following them, Finn knew that it was unlikely that they were here tonight. And if they were, then so be it. He wouldn't mind shifting into dragon form and burning up a few evil wizards right about now. Finn was in no mood to be messed with.

After about fifteen minutes of walking, Finn came to a small stream. He smiled as he sat down on the grassy bank and listened to the soothing babbling of the water as it gurgled around rocks and made its way onward. There was a break in the tree cover here, and the moon shone down brightly, leaving traces of silver in the swirling water. The simple beauty of it calmed Finn's nerves, and after a short while he even found himself humming the melody of one of his favorite country songs. This moment would have been absolutely perfect, if only the threat of war wasn't hanging over his head.

And if only Anya were here, too.

The thought popped into his head unbidden, and he pushed it away as quickly as he could. What was his problem tonight? He'd saved her because it was the right thing to do. It didn't mean that he was going to start some sort of romantic affair with her. Heck, she probably wasn't even interested in a romantic affair with a dragon. She was the most beautiful woman he'd ever seen, and he was pretty sure she could get any guy she wanted. Why would she choose a dragon shifter, with all the baggage that entailed?

Finn laid back on the ground so that his face was toward the sky, and began counting stars. He tried to focus on the little twinkling lights instead of on the unfamiliar feelings swirling in his core. If he thought about Anya too long, he began to stiffen between his legs. He could not allow himself to indulge thoughts of sleeping with her. The very idea was crazy. He had to work with her, now. He couldn't have his dick standing at attention every time she was nearby.

"Twenty, twenty-one, twenty-two," he said, counting and desperately trying to think of anything but Anya. "Twenty-three, twenty-four, twenty-five."

"Counting stars?" a voice asked. Moments later, Anya's face was right above his, blocking his view of the stars and sending a fresh rush of hot blood to the stiffening member between his legs.

"Jesus Christ," he said, sitting up so quickly that Anya barely had time to move her head and avoid being rammed in the face by his forehead. "I didn't hear you coming at all."

Anya fell back onto the ground beside him, laughing. "Now you know how it feels," she said. "Serves you right."

Finn looked over at her, his heart pounding from a mixture of nerves, anger, and passion. He wasn't angry at her. He was angry at himself for being so wrapped up in his thoughts that he had completely stopped paying attention to the forest around him. He had dragon senses, after all. There was no way Anya could have snuck up on him like that if he'd been alert to his surroundings instead of counting stars. Thank god it had only been Anya, and not enemy soldiers. After a few seconds, though, the initial shock wore off and he began to see the humor in the situation. He even managed a small chuckle.

"I guess I sort of deserved that," he said. "Although, I did stick up for you earlier today. I would have thought that would have been enough for you to not get back at me for sneaking up on you."

Anya giggled. "Fair enough. But, truth be told, I wasn't actually trying to sneak up on you. I was walking at a completely normal pace through the forest, stepping on twigs and everything. You were just so lost in thought that you didn't hear me stomping around."

Finn ran his fingers through his hair, somewhat troubled. "I was that out of it, huh? Good thing it was just you and not one of Saul's soldiers stomping around out here."

The smile froze on Anya's face when Finn said this. "Do you think there might be enemy soldiers around?" she asked. Finn could tell she was trying to look brave, but her eyes looked fearful. He supposed that after the ordeal she'd been through last night, she was hoping for at least one night of peace and quiet.

"I don't think Saul's army is out here," he said. "They wouldn't know to follow us this far south, and, honestly, they might not care to bother us as long as we're so far from Devil's Melt. Their main concern is making sure we don't get the dragon amethyst. There isn't much danger of us finding it out here."

Anya nodded, her face relaxing a bit as Finn reassured her. "I suppose it's going to get pretty gnarly once we head back toward Devil's Melt," she said.

Finn laughed. "Yes, gnarly is a nice word for it. I'm not sure when we'll be heading back, though. We need to find a way to make ourselves invisible despite their dark magic defenses. Either that or we'll need to take a whole freaking army in there. It's not an ideal situation. We would have been much better off if we'd been able to maintain some element of surprise, but we weren't able to do that. We'll just have to work with what we've got. Peter and Knox have been discussing the situation all day, but I'm not sure they've come to any conclusions."

"Knox seems like a good leader," Anya said, looking over at Finn uncertainly, as though worried he might contradict her.

Finn felt his chest swelling with pride. "Yes, he is. A very good leader. We're lucky to have him at the head of our clan."

"He's not at all like Peter, is he?" Anya asked, her voice wary.

Finn exhaled deeply before answering. "Peter is not a bad guy. In fact, some think that he's one of the wisest, kindest men that ever lived. The problem is that he's stubborn, and that the wizards still have some very strict, very outdated laws in effect. Instead of changing these laws, the Falcon Cross wizards seem intent on following them to the letter. It drives me crazy, but there's not a lot I can do about it. We need the wizards as allies, so we have to be respectful of their ways to a certain degree. Today, though…they wanted to go too far. I wasn't about to let them harm you like that. That's why I stood up for you. I hope you don't throw me under the bus now."

Finn gave Anya a lopsided grin. He wasn't worried about her betraying the side of good in this war. He might not know her well, but it wasn't hard to see that there wasn't a single evil bone in her body. He wasn't sure that she would be as helpful as she claimed she could be to their cause, but at least she would not betray them. He still thought she'd be safer if she went back home and stayed out of the way of the war, but she seemed determined to tag along on this journey. He worried for her well-being, but he had to admit that the thought of seeing her every day excited him.

He was growing excited between his legs again, too. He looked quickly away from Anya's face, trying to distract himself by watching the water of the stream again. He was thankful that it was nighttime, and he hoped that Anya would not be able to notice his erection by the light of the moon.

Anya wasn't paying attention to the space between Finn's legs, however. She was looking at the water herself, a frown etched across her face.

"I won't let you down," she said. "I meant it when I said I wanted to help fight Saul's army in any way I can. But I have to admit that, as much as I like Izzy and Raven, the wizards' ways of doing things trouble me. I mean, they seem nice enough, but they can't really be that nice, can they? Not when they were just standing there while Peter discussed harming me. It sounded like he wanted to kill me just for being human."

Finn swung his head around to look at Anya in surprise. "Kill you? They weren't going to kill you!" he said. "They were going to wipe your memory, which is still pretty awful in my opinion. But they weren't talking about actually murdering you. Even wizards aren't that backwards."

"Oh," Anya said in a flat tone that told Finn she was still very confused. "I heard them talking about memory wiping but I wasn't sure what that meant. And everything they said at the beginning made it sound to me like they were just going to kill me to get rid of the problem."

"Oh, Anya," Finn said, his heart going out to her as she looked back at him with uncertain, questioning eyes. He was realizing now just how terrified she must have been, standing there being judged by wizards and shifters whom she thought were plotting to take her life. He reached for her hand tentatively, and to his relief, she did not pull away. She looked at him with wide eyes, and he had to resist the urge to pull her into his arms. As it was, the warmth flowing between their hands felt intoxicating. He took a deep, steadying breath, and then began explaining.

"They were not planning to kill you, but they were planning to use a magic spell that wipes your memory clean. It's one of their stupid, backwards procedures. Whenever a human has seen magic or discovered that wizards exist, their standard procedure is to wipe the human's memory clean back to the point where the human encountered the wizards."

"That's awful!" Anya said. "That's a violation of human dignity. They can't just wipe someone's memory because they screwed up and let someone see magic. Besides, why are they automatically assuming that all humans are horrible people who are going to persecute them just because they're wizards? Not everyone is so unaccepting!"

The more Anya spoke, the more fired up she became. Anger flashed in her eyes, and she squeezed Finn's hand so tightly that he was sure she must be leaving red marks. He didn't care, though. She was beautiful when she was angry. In fact, she was beautiful when she was happy, and when she was sad. She was so goddamned beautiful, no matter what. He had given up trying to keep hold back his arousal. Everything about her right now was turning him on, although, she still seemed not to notice. She was too consumed with rage at the wizards, and rightly so, he thought. Even though they had not intended to kill her, they had intended to violate her.

"I agree. It is awful," Finn said. "And it's why I chose to stand up for you today. Not only do I think wiping someone's memory is an unacceptable practice in itself, but the memory-wiping spell is very difficult to perform. It's easy to mess up and wipe too much, or to cause the person to go crazy, or a host of other problems. I wasn't about to let them do that to you."

Anya was silent for a moment, staring at the stream with a brooding expression on her face. She still held Finn's hand, and he tried to memorize the way her palm felt in his. He wasn't sure whether he would ever have a chance to hold her hand again, and he did not want to forget this moment. He wasn't willing to admit to himself yet that he had any deep feelings for Anya, but he could not deny that his whole body wanted her. If she hadn't been so distraught at the moment, he might have attempted to make a move on her then and there. If he thought she would have him, he would have rammed the space between her legs so forcefully that she would have trouble walking the next day. He wondered as he watched her, whether there was anything wrong with indulging in pure, carnal passion. Did she feel the electricity between them, too? Was she as desperate to find relief in someone's warm arms as he was right now?

Her face gave nothing away. She stared at the stream still, but she didn't seem to really see it. He held his breath and waited. For what, he was not sure. In that moment, he knew that, although she was not a wizard, she had captured him under her spell. For several minutes, she remained silent, and he remained captivated by the mere sound of her breathing. Then she turned to him and gave him a small smile.

"I came out here to thank you for saving my life," she said. "But I guess I should be thanking you for saving my memory. I'm not sure which would be worse to lose."

Finn let out the breath he hadn't even realized he'd been holding. "Well, I'm glad you didn't lose either," he said. "And, by the way, don't worry about Izzy and Raven trying to do any weird magic on you. They're young, and very progressive wizards. They don't agree with the methods that a lot of the older wizards use. They respect Peter, because the old wizard has done a lot for their clan, but they know that sometimes he is too set in the old ways for his own good."

Anya nodded, then turned her gaze back to the water. "I like them a lot," she said. "And they stood up for me, which is saying something."

Finn smiled. "They'll continue to stand up for you. We all will. You're part of our team now, and we're a close group."

Anya nodded again, and looked at Finn as if expecting him to say something else. She still held his hand, even though the moment of urgency that he had grabbed it in had long passed. They stared at each other, and Finn felt an overwhelming urge to kiss her once again. He pushed it away, but he could not tear his eyes away from Anya's gaze. Was he imagining things, or were her eyes filling with heat just as his were? Hot blood flowed through his body, urging him to throw Anya down on the ground then and there, and show her what a dragon body was capable of doing. But he held back. This was madness. His life had no space for a woman, especially a human. He could not let himself fall for Anya, but he was afraid that if he didn't tear his eyes away from hers, he would tumble over the edge. And yet, he continued to look at her.

Their eyes remained locked until Anya dipped hers to look between his legs. The moon had freed itself from the occasional clouds and shone brilliantly now. There was no denying his arousal. It was there, saluting her and beckoning to her. Finn never took his eyes off her eyes as she looked at his manhood, considering. He felt his breath coming faster and ragged, and the more he tried to slow it down the more he lost control. He could feel a deep primal urge overwhelming him. He knew he needed to look away, but he could not.

He was still captured under her spell.

She finally raised her eyes to his again, and the heat in her gaze was now unmistakable. She watched him as he held his breath, and then slowly, torturously, she slipped her tongue past the part in her lips and ran it across her lower lip. Finn's thighs trembled, and he wanted to roar at the top of his lungs before ripping off her clothes and accepting the invitation she was offering him. Still, he managed to hold back.

"Anya," he said, his voice ragged and hoarse. "I cannot fall in love. I cannot promise you a life with me. I'm a dragon, with a wandering dragon heart."

Anya smiled at him then, a wicked sultry smile. "Who said anything about love?"

she asked, licking her lips again.

"You're not doing this just because I saved your memory, are you?" Finn asked. It was growing more difficult to speak, and the fire within him was growing higher, getting harder to hold back. "You don't owe me anything, you know that. I did the right thing to do, with no expectations of repayment of any sort."

Anya threw back her head and laughed then. The musical sound seemed to echo all around Finn, and the rod between his legs felt like it was made of throbbing steel. It begged to be allowed to take her, but still he restrained himself. He would not do this unless she really wanted it for her own pleasure. He could make no promises of a future to her, and he required no recompense for his speaking up for her.

"Oh shut up and kiss me," she said when she finally stopped laughing. "I'm not doing this because I feel like I owe you anything. I'm doing it because I've never seen anything quite so impressive as what's between your legs right now, and I'd be a fool to let this opportunity pass me by. Who knows when I'll be alone with you in the woods again."

That was all Finn needed to hear. He did roar, then, as he pushed himself over on top of Anya, flattening her underneath him on the cool forest floor. His erection pushed against his clothes and poked at her, seeking a release from the pressure building within it. Anya let out a squeal of delight as his body covered hers, but her squeal was quickly silenced by his kiss.

Her lips were soft beyond belief, and her mouth tasted faintly of orange, perhaps from the slight citrus notes of the beer they had been drinking around the fire. He slid his tongue against hers, attempting to taste every last millimeter of it. He kissed her deeply, running his tongue across the back of her mouth. She moaned, and lifted her legs up to wrap them around his hips.

The night no longer felt cold. In the heat of his passion, Finn was burning up inside as he never had before. He kissed Anya with an urgency, as though he were a man in the desert dying of thirst, and her kiss was water. He was so hot that he would not have been surprised to have opened his eyes and find that he was in a desert. He felt as though her were lying under the heat of a midday sun. It seemed impossible that he was actually under the moonlight of a cool forest night.

Anya seemed to feel the same urgency he did. She wrapped her arms around him, too, pulling him closer as he kissed her and thrusting her hips against his. She rubbed against his stiff erection, increasing the pressure and making him feel as though he was going to explode from the inside out. He growled, and nipped at her ear. She yelped in delighted pain, and sank her teeth into his neck, nibbling and sucking and claiming his body as hers. They were, in that moment, slaves to the carnal desire that rose within them.

It had been a long time since a woman had caused a stirring between Finn's legs, and he had never felt an arousal this strong. He tried out of some sense of decency to slow things down. In the back of his mind, he reminded himself that women liked it when you warmed them up first. Wasn't he supposed to be teasing her, and drawing the experience out? He couldn't think clearly anymore, with all the blood in his body rushing to the rod between his legs.

"Oh, fuck it," he said aloud. She was warm enough. In fact, if her skin was an indication of her internal temperature, she was burning up just as much as he was. He tore at her shirt hungrily, pulling it up and over her head. She reached for his shirt as well, returning the favor. They rolled across the ground, a tangle of arms and legs and fabric as garment after garment came off. They left a trail of clothes and pressed grass in their wake, kissing urgently even as their hands tore away at the cloth between them.

Despite the cool temperature of the night, Finn was sweating. He could see that Anya was sweating, too. The moonlight glistened off the glow of sweat that covered her forehead, and he found himself turned on even more by the sight of it.

"Burn for me, baby. Burn!" he roared.

She responded by pulling him closer again, biting down on his lower lips and thrusting her hips against his. He roared again, the pressure nearly too much to take. The only piece of clothing between them now was her underwear. He could feel it as his dick pressed against it, obnoxiously blocking his way into Anya. The fabric was soaked through with her juices, and they began to coat his erection. It was not enough. He wanted more. he must have more.

He slid down to her hips, and tore at the panties with his teeth. She wriggled and squirmed to assist him, and in moments he'd managed to slide them down and off her legs—miraculously without tearing them in his frenzy.

He paused for a moment, just a moment. He wanted to take in her beauty. Just as he had memorized the feeling of her hand against his, he wanted to memorize the way her body looked in the moonlight right now, naked and glistening, her full breasts rising and falling with her rapid breathing. Her hair was a mess, a beautiful mess. He saw her eyes, wild with hunger, and he knew they mirrored his own eyes. This was reckless. They should not be here together, making love under a full moon with no protection while so many other pressing matters waited for them back at the campsite. And yet, neither one of them could stop. They were on this reckless ride together, giving in to the strongest desire either of them had ever felt.

"I'm going to ravage you," Finn said, his voice a low growl now. The response in Anya's eyes told him very clearly that she wanted to be ravaged.

He did not delay any longer. He slid over her, his broad chest brushing against her alert nipples, his taut, muscular stomach just above the soft curves of her feminine abdomen. He swayed his hips, letting the top of his dick probe, gently searching until it found what it was looking for: the soft, wet spot where her body would open to him.

He took a deep breath, and then rammed into her. Her eyes flew open and she squealed in surprised delight as he filled her. He was large inside her, pushing against her inner muscles and stretching her to conform to his shape. His eyes slid shut from the sheer pleasure of the sensation. She was so silky wet, and so hot. God, she was so hot inside. Her heat enveloped his erection, setting fire to the most sensitive part of his body. He thrust deeper into her, pushing until she covered his entire shaft, and then he thrust his hips forward. At first, he never even pulled out of her as he thrust. He just rocked his hips, groaning as the impossible heat of her body spread across his entire being.

Then, he began to move with a greater urgency. He slid in and out, coming down hard with each thrust. He rammed into her, showing no mercy as he filled her again and again, stretching her and reaching so far inside that he thought he might actually be hitting bone.

Her arms were around him, and her hands were on his back. She held on tighter with each thrust of his body, panting for breath with her eyes squeezed tightly shut. She screamed out as she came, and dug her fingers into his bare back as her body began to shudder. It was the most wonderful scratching sensation he'd ever felt. He wanted nothing more in that moment than to have her nails permanently etched into his back.

Her insides were so slippery with desire, and yet she held his dick tightly, clenching down on it over and over as her inner walls grasped at him hungrily. He felt the pressure building within him, and he let out a low moan as he felt himself ready to burst. That moan turned into a roar as he exploded into her. Fire shot from his body into hers, and he shuddered as he felt his body giving itself to her. He thrust several more times, giving up every last bit of his energy to extend the incredible tidal wave that was washing over him.

When at last both of their bodies had stopped pulsing, he slid out of her and collapsed next to her on the cool grass, trying to catch his breath. He felt a strange, burning sensation in his core that he had never felt before, and his heart filled with wonder. If he didn't know better, he would have thought that he was experiencing the lifemate bond. It had always been explained to him as a warmth that occurred after making love with your destined lifemate.

But it wasn't possible that this human he barely knew was meant to be his life partner, was it? Finn looked over to see her smiling at him. Her naked breasts still rose and fell from her rapid breathing, and her sweaty skin glistened in the moonlight. No, he thought, it was impossible that a creature so wonderful was his. He pushed away thoughts of love and lifemates, afraid to even consider the possibility for fear that he would be disappointed. Women like Anya didn't fall in love with men like him—wild men with nothing holding them back from adventure and risk.

With a short sigh, he pulled Anya into his arms. He didn't know what the future held, but he knew that he had this moment right here with Anya. And if that was all he ever had with her, he would still be the luckiest man alive.

She snuggled close against his chest, searching for his warmth. His dragon genes were kicking in as the heat of lovemaking mellowed out. His body was hot at its core, even in human form, and he pulled Anya even closer to warm her against the cool night. Behind him, he felt the cloth of his shirt. He reached for the discarded garment and draped it over Anya to warm her further.

"Finn?" she murmured sleepily.

"Yes?" he asked.

"Your ears. Are they elfish like Knox's? I forgot to look."

The question surprised Finn, and he smiled. "Yes. All dragons have a bit of an elfish look to their ears. Some more than others, but we all have it to some extent. A remnant of the days when dragons still had magic powers."

"Mmm," she said, her head still buried in his chest. "I thought so."

A few minutes later, he felt her breathing slowly mellow out into the gentle rhythm of sleep, and, despite his own attempts to remain alert, he soon followed her into dreamland. He no longer needed to count stars to remain calm. He was more at peace now than perhaps any other time in his life, despite the knowledge that Saul's war still raged around him.

CHAPTER TEN

Anya woke with a start as Finn sat up suddenly, his eyes wide and alert. Clouds once again covered the moon, filling the forest with darkness and spooky shadows.

"What is it?" she whispered, her heart beginning to pound.

Finn put a finger to his lips, indicating that she should be quiet. She nodded, but it took a great deal of self-control to keep herself from asking more nervous questions. He was peering into the forest with green eyes that almost seemed to glow, and she instinctively knew that he had heard something. Perhaps it was just a wild animal. In that case, Anya was not worried. She knew Finn could easily shift into dragon form and take down any wild animal that might be roaming through this forest.

But what if Saul's soldiers had tracked them down once again? Anya knew enough by now to realize that she and Finn would be pretty vulnerable out here on their own, away from the protective shield that surrounded their campsite. She began to feel foolish for venturing out here on her own.

She did not regret sleeping with Finn—not even a little bit. The moments of passion that they had shared had been some of the most intense, wonderful moments of Anya's life. But perhaps they should have gone back to the others afterward instead of so foolishly falling asleep out in the open. Not only were they unprotected, but there was no fire to warm them out here. Anya was realizing more with each passing second just how cold she was. Her toes and fingers felt like ice, and now that she was not pressed against Finn's body, the rest of her own body was quickly freezing over as well.

Finn breathed in deeply, smelling the air. His brow furrowed further at whatever it was he seemed to smell, but before Anya had much time to worry about it, a twig snapped to her left, then another and another. Her heart pounded in her chest as she looked desperately into the dark forest, sure she was about to come face to face with Saul's army.

Finn was jumping to his feet, too, and she thought he was about to shift, although she wasn't sure how much good one dragon could do on his own against Saul's army. But Finn didn't shift after he stood. Instead, he walked quickly over to where Anya's clothes were still strewn across the ground, and grabbed them up. He tossed them to her with a look of exasperation on his face and said, "You're going to want to put these on."

Anya wasn't sure why it mattered whether or not she was naked if she was about to get killed, but she shrugged and started pulling on her shirt. At least it gave her something to do, which helped calm her nerves slightly. The snapping of twigs was growing louder, and Anya suddenly heard a familiar voice shouting out.

"I think they're over here. Their trail goes this way!"

It was Owen. Anya's heart leapt with hope. If he was out here then perhaps the others were, too. They could help fight.

But Finn still wasn't shifting. Instead, with an annoyed grunt, he was pulling on his pants. Anya's frown deepened. Why would he be putting clothes on if there was a threat at hand? The pants would only be ruined when he shifted.

415

A few seconds later, she had her answer. Owen, Peter, and Raven came bursting through the trees. Raven had some sort of flashlight beam coming out of her magic ring, and she swept it across the clearing until it landed directly on Anya, who was suddenly extremely grateful that Finn had told her to put on her clothes.

"What the…" Anya said, at the same time as Raven. Finn didn't seem confused at all, though. He pulled Anya close by his side, and she noticed as he did that he still was not wearing a shirt.

"They're searching for us," he said in a low voice. "We've been asleep out here for who knows how long, and we left no word of where we were going. They've probably been worried sick. And now they're going to be annoyed as hell that we were just out here having fun."

Raven's flashlight was still trained on Anya and Finn, the bright light making it impossible for Anya to see Raven's face. She could see Owen's and Peter's faces, though, and their looks of concern were slowly changing to expressions of bemusement.

Raven realized what was going on a split second before Owen did, and hurriedly lowered her light. Owen, however, had no such sense of propriety, and he burst out laughing. Anya felt her cheeks turning red as everything slowly made sense to her. She and Finn had been caught together in the woods hurriedly throwing clothes on. There was no denying what they had been doing out here. She looked up at Finn, who was letting out a long sigh of exasperation and glaring at Owen. But Owen was not about to stop laughing, he was doubled over now, poking Raven in the arm and pointing over at them as if catching two grown adults making love together in the woods was the funniest thing he'd ever seen.

Raven continued to avert her eyes, looking embarrassed. At least, she looked embarrassed as far as Anya could tell from the dim, shadowed light of her flashlight, which now faced downward toward the ground. Peter did not laugh, and he did not look embarrassed. He did seem mildly amused though.

"I see," Peter finally said, nodding slowly. "It all makes sense now."

"For the record, I didn't speak up for her because I wanted to mate with her," Finn said. "I wasn't planning on this at all. It just sort of happened."

This confession only caused Owen to howl with laughter even more, and even Raven cracked a smile. Anya's cheeks were burning so hot now that they must have been bright red, and she was thankful for the darkness. She was sure Peter was about to give them some sort of lecture, or, worse, say that she would not be allowed to stay with the group if she was only here to bang Finn. But Peter said none of those things. Instead, he turned and started walking back through the forest.

"Come on back to camp, Finn, and bring your girl with you. Oh, and put a shirt on. I don't care if you're a dragon, it's still too damn cold at night for you to be prancing around half naked. The last thing I need is one of you guys getting pneumonia."

Finn groaned, but said nothing as he pulled his shirt on over his head. Owen continued to laugh, but Finn ignored him now. Anya felt Finn grabbing her hand and firmly pulling her toward the forest in the direction Peter had gone. He walked briskly, so that in a few moments they were several yards ahead of Owen and Raven. Ahead of them, Anya could see another light beam bouncing through the woods, and she assumed that Peter must have turned his ring into a flashlight now, too. Finn and Anya had no light, and no way of making one, but Finn did not have any trouble walking through the dark forest. He never stumbled, and held Anya's arm firmly so that she did not fall, either.

"You're pretty good at walking in the dark," she observed. She felt like she needed to say *something* to break the silence. This whole situation had turned out to be one of the most awkward moments of her life, and it unnerved her a bit that Finn wasn't talking at all. After she spoke, though, he seemed to realize that he should say something.

"Dragon eyes," he said. "I have really good night vision, even when I don't have a flashlight."

"Sounds useful," Anya said lightly, then gripped his arm fiercely as she nearly tumbled face first over a tree root she hadn't seen.

"Yeah. Quite useful," Finn said, then grunted. "Listen, Anya, I'm really sorry that they stumbled across us like that. I should have known better than to stay out there by ourselves, especially naked. It's not a good idea to be away from camp for so long with Saul's army on the move, and if I would have stopped to think for two seconds I would have realized that our crew would eventually come looking for us."

"Our crew," Anya repeated in a low voice, liking the way the words sounded on her tongue.

"Huh?" Finn asked, thinking she had been saying something to him.

"Oh, nothing," Anya said. "I just realized that you called everyone 'our' crew. Which made me realize that I'm included in that, too. I have a crew. It's been a long time since I've had a crew. It feels good."

Even in the darkness of the night, Anya could see the smile that lit up Finn's face.

"Of course you have a crew now," Finn said. "I'm glad that you're focusing on that instead of being mad at me that we got caught naked in the woods."

"Well, technically we weren't naked when they caught us. I was already dressed, and you had your pants on. But, yes, it was still obvious what we'd been doing. I don't have any right to be mad, though. I knew as well as you did that our friends were nearby and might come looking for us. I was just too caught up in the thrill of the moment to care. I must say, though, that Owen's laughter is getting obnoxious."

Finn snorted. "Don't worry about him. I'll make a nice comment or two about Raven and get him to shut up. He still won't admit that he likes her."

"Really?" Anya said, surprised. "I didn't realize he wasn't admitting to it. It's so obvious."

Finn shrugged. "He's always been a player. I think he's nervous about settling down. He wants to maintain his bad boy, ladies man reputation."

Anya laughed. "Well, if he wants to maintain a reputation as a player then he needs to do a better job of hiding his feelings for Raven."

"Agreed," Finn said with a chuckle. They walked in silence for a few more moments, until Anya could see the soft glow of the campfire up ahead. She was about to comment on how they'd kept the fire going all night, when Finn spoke first and interrupted her thoughts.

"You know, people are probably going to treat us like a thing now," he said.

Anya felt a strange, nervous emotion run through her. "And?" she said, trying to keep her voice even. "Does that bother you?"

Finn looked over at her, his face barely visible in the darkness. He paused for a moment, considering. "No," he finally said. "It definitely doesn't bother me. Does it bother you?"

Anya bit her lip to keep from smiling. "No," she said. "No, it doesn't bother me either."

"Good," Finn said. Then he took her hand as they walked into the campsite together. Anya did smile then. She wasn't sure exactly what all of this meant, but she was pretty sure she liked it.

Her smile weakened a bit as they walked into the campsite. She'd heard the rushing sound that indicated they'd walked back through the protective shield, and she saw Knox and Izzy sitting around the fire, looking tired as they spoke with Peter. Anya felt a sudden rush of guilt. She'd been so caught up in the moment with Finn that it had never crossed her mind that people might worry about her. She wasn't putting up a very good first impression of how well she was going to help this team, and she felt her stomach clenching up with worry again. Would Knox and Peter scold her? Would they go back on their decision to allow her on the team? Did Owen, Raven, and Harlow even still want her on the team? Anya walked toward the fire pit holding tightly to Finn's hand, trying to find a measure of comfort and security in the warmth of his palm.

"What the hell, Finn," Knox said, looking up as they approached. Anya steeled herself for a long lecture, but then to her surprise, Knox burst out laughing.

"If you were gonna go bang around in the woods, you could have at least warned us not to expect you back anytime soon. I'm glad you had fun, but we've been worried sick about you while you were off with your girl here."

"I'm not sure I'm his girl," Anya started to say, not wanting Finn to think that she was making assumptions about them. But her voice was drowned out by the loud laughter of Owen, who had just come back into the campsite with Raven.

"I thought you told me you'd never fall in love, Finn," Owen said. "In fact, I remember you telling me once that you were definitely staying away from humans."

"Easy, guys," Finn said. "I'm sorry I made you all worry but do you have to give me such a hard time at two in the morning?"

"Three in the morning," Knox corrected. "And yes, of course we have to give you a hard time. What kind of friends would we be if we didn't?"

Anya felt her cheeks turning bright red again. She felt like her whole life was on display right now, and she wanted to say something in her and Finn's defense, but she wasn't sure what.

"No one said anything about falling in love," she blurted out in protest, looking up at Finn in desperation. He raised an eyebrow, seeming somewhat surprised by this outburst. But Peter spoke up before Finn could reply.

"No one had to say anything, Anya. It's obvious from the way he looks at you. I'm just surprised I didn't see it before. I should have known the moment he first spoke up for you."

Peter's eyes danced merrily in the light of the fire, and the rest of the crew seemed to be just as amused, now that their worries about Finn and Anya being in trouble were gone. Anya opened her mouth to try to protest again, but Finn shook his head.

"It's no use," Finn said. "Their favorite pastime is giving people a hard time over finding love. Even the slightest hint of romance, and they start in on nonsense like this. The best way to get it to stop is to ignore it."

"Oh, you can ignore all you want," Owen said. "I'm not stopping anytime soon."

Finn turned to Owen to say something to him, but Knox held up his hands for silence before any more words could be spoken.

"I think that's enough for tonight. It's late, and we all need rest. Finn, I'm going to chew you out properly for this in the morning, but right now I'm too tired to yell. Let's all hit the sack. The last thing we want is to be caught off guard by the enemy when we're exhausted."

Finn didn't wait to hear what anyone else would say to that. "Come on, Anya," he said, grabbing her hand and pulling her toward his sleeping bag. "Knox is right. Let's get some rest."

Anya went with him, feeling self conscious that everyone was going to see her sleeping right next to him, but also feeling glad that she would be next to him and be able to share his warmth.

She was hopelessly confused about his feelings for her at this point. He'd made it sound like their time together in the woods was purely a chance for some physical fun. But now, he was acting like it had meant something more to him. Truth be told, Anya hadn't intended to do anything more than have a bit of fun, either. But after experiencing what it was like to be close to Finn, she wasn't sure she'd ever be happy being away from him again.

She lay down next to him, snuggling into his oversized sleeping bag and relishing the way the heat of his body washed over her. He wrapped his arms around her, and she felt her heart beating faster from the electricity of his touch. All around them, the rest of the group was settling down into their own sleeping bags as well. Anya had so many questions for Finn, but she was afraid to ask them. How could she talk to him without everyone else listening in?

She tilted her face toward his, her eyes filled with questions. She opened her mouth to ask him why he wanted her next to him, but he put a finger to her lips.

"Shh," he whispered in her ear. "We'll talk more tomorrow. For now, let's just enjoy being together tonight."

Anya sighed. She wanted to enjoy the night, but how could she when she was feeling so strangely desperate for him, and so worried that tomorrow they would be back to acting like just friends. As if Finn sensed her worries, he looked down at her and smiled.

"The first of many nights together, I hope," he added.

Anya bit her lip as a huge grin spread across her face. She wasn't sure what adventures lay ahead of them, or where, exactly, Finn thought this was going. But knowing that he thought it was going *somewhere* was enough for the moment.

Anya pressed her body closer against her dragon's warm body and allowed sweet sleep to envelop her.

CHAPTER ELEVEN

When Anya woke up the next morning, she was surprised to find that Finn had already left the warmth of the sleeping bag. Feeling slightly disappointed, she sat up slowly and looked around the small campsite, but he was not there, either. In fact, the only other person she saw was Izzy, who was sitting close to the dwindling fire with her head bent over a stack of papers.

Anya quietly lay back down for a moment, feeling nervous and not quite ready to face Izzy on her own. In the bright morning light, the events of last night seemed even more embarrassing. How had she ended up having wild sex with Finn, getting caught with him in the woods half naked, and then still joining him in his sleeping bag in front of everyone as if she didn't care what anyone thought? Anya's cheeks flushed bright red, and she was glad no one was watching her at the moment.

Did she care what anyone thought? Did it matter to her if Izzy thought she'd been reckless last night? Anya wanted to make a good impression on her new friends, and she knew she and Finn shouldn't have strayed so far from the campsite for so long. But surely, that was their only transgression. They were both adults, after all. What was to keep them from sleeping together if that's what they both wanted to do?

Anya frowned up at the treetops high above her, which were swaying gently in the breeze. From what she had seen of the group that was searching for the dragon amethyst, they were a tight knit crew. She worried that they would feel possessive of Finn, and annoyed that she had swept in and started taking up a special place in his heart.

Anya wanted to believe that she was being ridiculous. After all, they were all adults here, right? And last night everyone had seemed to be in a relatively good mood once Finn and she were found safe. Owen had seemed especially happy for the chance to tease Finn. The group would have some fun with it and then move on, right?

Anya hoped so, but she still felt nervous to go talk to Izzy and face the truth of the situation. Lying there in Finn's sleeping bag, Anya had never felt so human and small. Until she met the dragons and wizards she was now sharing a campsite with, she'd never had a reason to feel ordinary. She was smart, after all, and had lived a fulfilling life as a botanist. But now she felt unremarkable, like being smart wasn't enough. In fact, perhaps she was wasting time worrying about what the others would think of a relationship between Finn and her. Perhaps Finn had come to his own conclusions in the light of day, and had realized that he didn't want to waste time on a mere human. Maybe that's why he had gone off somewhere with the others. Maybe he didn't want to be there when she woke up in his sleeping bag.

Anya sighed and sat up again. The longer she lay here brooding, the more her mood was going to worsen. She might as well get up and go talk to Izzy instead of imagining a bunch of reasons why Finn wasn't going to want to be with her anymore. Anya had never been an insecure person when it came to men, so this rush of emotions was new to her. But it was hard not to feel a little bit unsure of yourself when you were imagining how you measured up in a dragon's eyes.

Izzy raised her head from the papers she was looking at when she heard Anya stirring.

"Hey," Izzy said kindly, smiling at Anya. "Sleep okay?"

There was no hint of animosity or derision in Izzy's voice, and Anya relaxed a bit as she slid out of the sleeping bag and stood to make her way over to Izzy.

"I slept alright," Anya said. Every muscle in her body seemed to protest, but she forced herself to walk without wincing. Much of the soreness was from her energetic romp in the woods with Finn, or their subsequent nap on the cold, hard forest floor, and Anya didn't want to give Izzy any reason to tease her.

But Izzy did not seem interested in teasing at all. After Anya sat next to her on the log that was serving as a makeshift bench, Izzy flashed her the warmest smile Anya had ever seen on the wizard's face.

"You're probably wondering where everyone went," Izzy said. "Peter and Knox took them on a scouting mission to see if there are any good places for some sort of semi-permanent headquarters out here. The plan is for us to hunker down and stay put until some sort of plan can be worked out for getting safely into Devil's Melt. They would have taken you along but Finn insisted that you needed rest. You've had quite a time of it the last couple of days, after getting caught up in our battle and discovering the existence of wizards and shifters."

Anya nodded, trying to look nonchalant but feeling an immense sense of relief that Finn seemed to have had a legitimate reason for leaving her behind. Anya's stomach felt like it was churning right now from the strange mixture of emotions that filled her. She knew she needed to calm down, but it was hard to do. She hadn't expected to feel so strongly for Finn after sleeping with him. She'd thought she would have a bit of fun, and that if they liked each other's company they might continue to develop a bit more of a relationship. But she'd truly had no expectations other than a night of fun. Finn had made it clear that he didn't want to fall in love, so Anya had put up a wall around her heart to prevent herself from falling in love, too. At least she'd attempted to put up a wall. She'd apparently failed miserably, because Finn was all she could think about now. She wanted to hold him in her arms right now, and she wanted him to love her back. And she wanted the rest of the group to be okay with her and Finn being together.

Izzy seemed oblivious to the mess of thoughts running through Anya's head, although Anya had a feeling that this had more to do with Izzy's being polite than with Izzy's actually not realizing how turmoiled Anya felt at the moment.

"I was left behind to guard the campsite," Izzy said, continuing on with her explanation. "Saul's army isn't anywhere near here, as far as we can tell. But still, we have to be careful. Especially since we have the amethyst records here. We have copies of them back home, of course, but we still don't want Saul's men to steal back this information. It's the key to finding the dragon amethyst, although it's not a very easy key to use. It contains a lot of riddles and information about the dragon amethyst being formed and then stored in Devil's Melt, but there aren't a lot of specific details about where, exactly in Devil's Melt."

Anya peered over at the papers in interest. "That looks like quite a messy assortment of information."

Izzy sighed. "It is. It makes sense that it would be a mess, though. Whoever compiled this information would have wanted to keep the dragon amethyst safe, and so they tried to keep things as vague and convoluted as possible. Maybe a little too vague and convoluted. We can't seem to make any progress on figuring out where in Devil's Melt the stone is. The riddles are all too confusing. And we can't go to Devil's Melt without some sort of concrete search plan in place. It's too risky. Every moment that we spend anywhere close to the area is a moment of mortal danger. The enemy's dark magic is growing too strong. Our shields are less of a protection against them with every passing day."

"But with every passing day you're risking them finding the dragon amethyst instead of you," Anya observed. "And if their dark magic is growing stronger every day, then the longer we delay in going to Devil's Melt, the harder it's going to be."

Izzy sighed. "You're right, of course. But we can't go in blindly just because we know that time is of the essence. It would be a suicide mission. And yet, I worry that by the time we formulate a plan, the only option is going to be sending in an army and trying to take complete control of Devil's Melt. Our army is strong enough to win that battle, I think. But it would result in a lot of bloodshed. Of course, if Saul gets his hands on the dragon amethyst, there will be plenty of bloodshed. I'm sure of that."

Anya watched Izzy put her head in her hands. The young wizard's whole body was hunched over in frustration, and Anya's heart went out to her. Anya felt guilty, too, for sitting here worrying that Izzy was going to spend the morning teasing her about Finn. What a fool Anya was for thinking that anyone here was so wrapped up in her romantic life. They might have some fun teasing her when an opportune moment arrived—like catching her in the woods with Finn. But they weren't sitting around thinking about how to give Anya a hard time. They had much more important things on their minds.

Anya should be focusing on those important things, too. She wasn't sure yet how, exactly, she was going to help. But sitting around brooding about Finn wasn't doing any of them any favors. She had to get started on this mission somehow.

Anya glanced at the pile of papers surrounding Izzy. Perhaps reading up on the information they did have would help her. At least she would be on the same page as everyone else as far as knowledge of Devil's Melt went. And besides, Izzy had made it sound like a lot of the information was in riddle form. Anya had always been good at riddles. Perhaps she could solve a few of them for this crew.

"Can I look over the records?" Anya asked, pointing toward a particularly large pile of papers that sat at Izzy's feet. "I'm not doing anything else important right now, and who knows, maybe a fresh set of eyes will help."

Izzy's face brightened at the suggestion, as though she had wanted to ask Anya to do that very thing, but hadn't known how to suggest it. "It would be great if you could look through everything," Izzy said. "Are you sure you're up to it, though? Finn will kill me if he thinks I'm pushing you to work instead of rest."

Anya rolled her eyes. "It's not like it's that taxing to sit here and read. And besides, I've rested plenty. I don't think I could sleep anymore now if I tried."

Izzy smiled, although she still looked uncertain. "As long as you feel up to it," she said. She started to slowly gather up some papers to hand over to Anya. "This stack of papers here is probably the best place to start. It's a lot of background information on the stone and on its arrival in Devil's Melt, as well as a lot of general information about the Devil's Melt area. I know reading through all of this can feel a bit dry, but I think doing so gives you a good foundation when you start reading some of the other documents that have riddles and other less straightforward information."

Anya nodded. "I can handle a bit of dry reading," she said. "I did plenty of that in university, trust me."

Izzy laughed at Anya's little joke, but then sobered up a bit.

"Anya, are you sure you want to come with us?" Izzy asked. "Don't get me wrong, I like you a lot and I'm happy to have you come along. But don't you have a life back in Idaho that you want to get back to? Surely, your friends and family must be wondering where you are? And it sounds like you had a promising career in botany. What will happen to your job?"

Anya snorted. "I had a life in Idaho, but I'm not sure it's one that I want to go back to. It was a fairly lonely life. My dad passed away, and I don't have any other family. I work for myself, doing freelance research on plants in the Idaho area. And I don't have a lot of close friends. To me, it makes sense to come on this mission and help as much as I can to get the dragon amethyst and keep the whole world out of danger. I know you all think that I don't truly understand the danger I'm getting myself into, but I do understand. I know I might not make it out of this alive. But the truth is I would rather risk everything on an adventure than play it safe and keep living a normal, boring life like everyone else I know."

Izzy grinned. "Alright, then. As long as you know what you're getting into."

"I like to think I know," Anya said slowly. "Although, I have been a bit surprised by some of the wizard laws. Like threatening to wipe my memory even though I promised to protect you all. That doesn't seem just."

Izzy's face darkened. "So you do know what was going on with that meeting."

"Finn told me," Anya said. "He doesn't seem to be much of a fan of the wizard's memory wiping techniques, either."

"Nor should he be," Izzy said, a frustrated tone filling her voice. "I'm really sorry about that. I don't agree with the practice of memory wiping, but some of our elder wizards really hang onto it. Peter is a wise old wizard, but he likes to follow wizard law to the letter. Please try not to let it get to you. And don't let it ruin your opinion of wizards on the whole. We're very nice people, I promise. Even Peter himself is a wonderful man. But wizards still have a hard time sometimes knowing how to live in harmony with humans. We've been persecuted quite badly over the years, and we're still trying to figure out how to reconcile the pain of the past with the reality of the present. We're a work in progress. And trust me, if it were up to me, memory wiping would be abolished completely. But changing wizarding law is a long, long process."

Anya smiled at Izzy. "You don't have to apologize to me. You didn't write the laws. And you stood up for me, at great risk to yourself."

Izzy winked at Anya. "Yeah, so please don't go deserting us. It would really suck if I had to be killed because I spoke up for you and then you turned out to be a traitor. Although, truth be told, I don't think Peter would actually follow through with executing a bunch of his top shifters and wizards. Even he doesn't follow the law that closely."

"Well, I have no plans of deserting you or turning into a traitor, so you have nothing to worry about, anyway," Anya said. "So, now that that's settled, let me get down to business and start reading through this stack."

Izzy started to hand the stack of papers over to Anya, then paused again.

"So, wait," she asked, somewhat shyly. "Are you and Finn really a thing?"

Anya hesitated, unsure of how to answer. Part of her wanted to say yes, but she wasn't sure if that was the correct answer. She'd been agonizing over this very question all morning, but she didn't want to admit that to Izzy. So she just smiled coyly and shrugged.

"You'll have to ask Finn," Anya said. Then she grabbed the papers from Izzy's hands and settled in to read without another word.

* * *

Several hours later, Anya looked up blearily, rubbing her eyes and realizing for the first time that she hadn't eaten anything all day. The hunger pangs in her stomach were becoming more insistent, now, and would not be ignored. But Anya didn't have her own bag of supplies anymore. Her things had all been left behind when Saul's army attacked, and right now Anya was alone. She didn't feel comfortable digging through her new friends' backpacks, but if Izzy or the others didn't get back soon, she might do it anyway.

Izzy had wandered off about forty-five minutes ago, saying she was going to look for a stream. She promised not to go further than the protective shield, and told Anya to yell at the top of her lungs if anything suspicious happened. But everything had been quiet and still since Izzy left. Even the air was motionless—the usual breeze that rustled the treetops was noticeably absent. It almost would have been peaceful, if not for the fact that Anya worried about how fast, exactly, Izzy would be able to get back to her if Saul's men did attack. Anya wasn't much of a fighter, especially not when faced with wizards shooting laser beams and fierce shifters baring their teeth. Anya quickly pushed away such thoughts. Izzy had promised to stay close by, and, besides, the rest of the crew would be back any minute now. Everything would be fine.

At least she hoped it would. To take her mind off her worries about being attacked with no defenses, Anya decided to get over her discomfort and start searching for food in one of the bags. Surely, no one would fault her for grabbing a small snack when she'd been left here alone in the middle of the day.

Anya opened one of the packs and started searching for something edible. The pack she had opened had a lot of clothing in it, a flashlight along with several batteries, and another folder of papers that must have been more information about the amethyst. Anya pulled out the stack of papers so that she could reach further into the bag, and her persistence was rewarded. She came across a stash of meal bars.

"Bingo," she said, grabbing one of the bars and then carefully replacing the clothing, flashlights, and batteries. She started to put back the papers, then paused. It was only a small folder. Perhaps she should look through this one. She had been reading through a long history of the dragon amethyst, and she wouldn't mind switching it up a bit. Anya left the folder out and closed the backpack once again, then took her meal bar and the folder over to sit on the log bench again. The fire had long since died out, and Anya stared for a moment at the charred, crumbling logs while she slowly munched. Her mind was far away though, lost in another time and place as she thought of all she had read today.

The dragon amethyst had a long, convoluted history, and reading through the information Izzy had given her made it clear to Anya that big chunks of that history were missing from the records. Enough had survived, though, to piece together a rough idea of where the mysterious stone had come from.

One of the ancient dragon shifter kings had been banished to the cold of what was now northern Alaska after his clan had been defeated by an army of evil wizards. The wizards had thought that if they locked him up in a cold prison in the snow, heavily guarded by their most powerful wizards, that they would be able to break his spirit and take his magical powers for their own. But the dragon king had known they would try this, and so, the night before they had captured him, when it was clear there was no hope of victory for his clan, he had created the dragon amethyst.

He'd needed a wizard to help him. Thankfully, one of his longtime friends and most trusted advisors was a wizard. The wizard assisted him in draining all his magical powers and storing them in the dragon amethyst, thereby preserving his clan's greatness for all time. After the stone was created, the dragon king had sent the wizard away into the night, under a strong invisibility shield, to hide the dragon amethyst. The dragon king hoped that, one day, some surviving members of his clan might find the stone and reestablish their clan's former glory.

The dragon king's hope of a future uprising of his clan was never realized. The dragons were on the decline, and the age of evil wizards was rising. Over the next several centuries, shifters and wizards would battle back and forth, destroying many great clans in the process. Through it all, the legendary dragon stones, including the dragon amethyst, were nearly lost to history.

Luckily, the wizard who hid the dragon amethyst made some records of his journey, which were carefully copied by scribes and handed down through the centuries. The surviving records were found about one hundred years ago by a group of young lion shifters who, hungry for power, made fresh copies of the records and hid them across the country in inconspicuous places, such as the records of county courthouses. The lions had been killed off in another clan war, however, and the records had almost been lost to history again until Saul's men managed to find them. But then, a dragon and wizard from Falcon Cross had managed to steal the records from Saul. The problem, though, was that even with the records, the location of the dragon amethyst was far from clear. The records were incomplete, and full of riddles that didn't seem to make sense. According to Izzy, Anya hadn't even gotten to the most confusing portions of the record yet. But Anya was already confused.

With a sigh, Anya put the last bite of her meal bar into her mouth, chewing slowly as she mentally reviewed everything that she had learned about the location of the stone. The wizard who had hidden it had originally taken it to what was now northern Canada, where the dragon king was to be banished. Perhaps the wizard had hoped that the king might be rescued, and then have his power restored by taking possession of the dragon stone. But the dragon king had never been rescued. Bereft of his power, he had been beaten down and quite likely killed by his enemies while in captivity, although no actual records of his death existed. The wizard who held the dragon amethyst had started taking the stone south, then. His intentions had been to take it to a dragon clan that was in the southern part of the north American continent, but he had never made it that far, either. The wizard had made it as far as Devil's Melt, which at the time was mostly a deserted, snowy wasteland. There, the wizard had died of pneumonia, and there the records of the dragon amethyst seemed to stop.

There were a few other notes from dragon shifters who knew of the stone and had come searching for it over the centuries, but no one had ever found it. At least, there was no record of anyone ever finding it. Perhaps someone had, and had never made a record of it. Or perhaps the records had been lost to history.

Anya frowned. The more she learned about this quest, the more she thought it didn't make sense to risk all of their lives by heading into Devil's Melt. The records showed that many searches had been done there, thus showing all of the places that the dragon amethyst was not. But, in Anya's opinion, the fact that the records they had left off with the dragon amethyst being hidden in Devil's Melt was no solid indication that the stone was still there. Why was everyone convinced that it was? Was she missing something, here? Perhaps she just had not read enough of the records yet. There might be something more in the later records and riddles that proved the stone was still in Montana.

Thinking of later records reminded Anya of the folder she had pulled from one of the dragon's backpacks. She turned to it now, opening it to glance over it and see what information this random folder might contain. When she opened it, though, she was disappointed to find that the papers in the folder were mostly handwritten notes by Raven. The notes seemed to have been taken during a meeting back in Falcon Cross, because the handwritten script across the top said, "Meeting with F.C. Advocacy Bureau re: Amethyst location." It must have been a long meeting, because Raven had drawn several doodles along the margins of the paper, including a couple doodles of her own name. The notes from the actual meeting were haphazard and messy, and didn't make much sense to Anya. She flipped through the pages anyway, chuckling a bit at Raven's hand-drawn artwork and looking for any information that might stick out as important.

Nothing caught her eye though, until the last page. There, Raven had written "Dragon Claw to Forest Claw?" in bold, capital letters, and underlined it several times. Anya furrowed her brow. Something about the phrase rang a bell in the back of her mind, but she could not think why. She didn't have long to consider it, either, before Izzy walked back into the campsite, nearly causing Anya to jump out of her skin in surprise.

"Sorry I took so long," Izzy said. "But I found a great spot where the stream curves really close to the campsite and is deep and clean. It's a nice place to freshen up and take a bath of sorts. The water is pretty warm, too, I guess because it pools up a bit there and the sun shines on it through the trees. You should go check it out. Relax for a bit."

Anya laughed. "I must look like I need to relax right now. You scared me witless just now. How do all of you walk so quietly? I didn't hear you at all until you were right beside me and started talking."

Izzy looked sheepish. "Sorry. Habit, I guess. But really, you should go for a swim and clean up before the rest of the crew gets back and all want dibs on the stream. Speaking of which, I'm a little surprised they aren't back yet. It must be after noon already, and I don't think they took any food with them."

"Yeah, speaking of which, I hope you don't mind but I raided one of the bags for a meal bar. I was starving," Anya said.

Izzy slapped her forehead. "Sheesh, I should have thought of that. Of course I don't mind. I should have told you before I left to help yourself to whatever you wanted. I wasn't planning on being gone so long, but still. I don't think you even ate breakfast! I'm so sorry!"

Anya shrugged. "It's alright. I had so much on my mind that for a long time I didn't even realize myself that I was hungry. I'm better now, and I might take you up on a swim in the stream. My head is spinning from everything I read this morning, so I could definitely use a break."

Izzy nodded. "It's a lot to take in. How far did you get?"

"I read through most of what you gave me. I think I probably had about ten pages to go when I stopped for lunch. But then I got distracted by a folder of notes I found while looking for food. It looks like it was just some of Raven's handwritten notes though."

"Oh, right," Izzy said, with a dismissive wave of her hand. "Those must have been from our meeting with the Advocacy Bureau before we left. One of the Advocates, Harlow, said that when she was spying on Saul's soldiers in Falcon Cross they seemed to be obsessed with the phrase 'from dragon claw to forest claw.' I was with Saul's soldiers for a while and never heard them say that, but Harlow was spying on the field scouts and said that they said it a lot. She thinks it's important, but I'm honestly not sure why. It's just one more riddle that doesn't make sense to me."

"Hmm," Anya said, furrowing her brow.

"Why?" Izzy asked, suddenly curious. "Do you think it sounds important, too?"

"I don't really know," Anya confessed. "It reminds me of something I've heard before but I can't think what. And my brain is so fried right now."

"You've read a lot this morning," Izzy said, looking down at the stack of papers piled next to Anya. "You should really go and take a swim and let your mind rest. Maybe you'll have some new insights after a break."

Anya nodded and wrinkled her nose. "Yeah, you're right. Besides, I wouldn't mind rinsing off. I haven't had anything close to a bath in at least a week. Even for a wilderness lover like myself that's a bit much."

Izzy laughed. "I know what you mean," she said. "That's the biggest reason I wanted to find a branch of the river that came close to camp."

"Is it safe to go by myself?" Anya asked uncertainly, looking toward the sky as though some of Saul's evil soldiers might suddenly appear out of thin air.

"Perfectly safe," Izzy said. "Saul doesn't know we're here, and, even if he did, the portion of the river I found is close enough that it's still covered by our protective shield. Even with all their dark magic, it still takes Saul's soldiers a bit of time to break through our shields. I would know there was an attack going on long before anyone could get to you."

"Alright," Anya said, feeling somewhat reassured. "I'll go, then. How do I get there?"

Izzy gave her quick directions to the spot she'd found, and even found her a fresh set of clothes from one of the backpacks.

"It's a Falcon Cross military uniform," Izzy said. "I hope you don't mind wearing it, but we don't have many extra clothes so it's all I can offer. You can wash your own clothes in the river and put them back on once they dry."

"I'd be honored to wear a Falcon Cross uniform," Anya said. And she meant it. Despite her misgivings about the wizards and their outdated laws, she was happy to be part of this group. Izzy and Raven had stood up for her and been nothing but kind to her, and Anya was finding herself growing excited at the prospect of actually making a difference in the search for the dragon amethyst. She still wasn't sure how she was going to do that, but she was determined that she would.

"Do you want anything else to eat," Izzy asked as she handed over the uniform. "We have more meal bars, and some trail mix and stuff like that."

Anya shook her head no. She was a bit hungry still, but not overwhelmingly so. And, right now, she wanted some time to soak in the water and think. She had a feeling that whoever Harlow was, she was right. There was something about the dragon claw and forest claw riddle that held the key to finding the dragon amethyst. Anya was determined to figure out the secret, and water had always helped her think more clearly.

With resolve in her step, Anya waved to Izzy and started walking toward the stream. She was going to prove that she had something to offer, even though she was only human. Perhaps she might even impress Finn a bit.

Anya smiled at the thought and quickened her pace. She hoped that Finn would be back at camp by the time she was done with her swim. She was intending to have some riddles solved by then.

CHAPTER TWELVE

The water swirled around Anya, the warm ripples soothing both her body and mind. She was naked and on her back, with only her face, breasts, and small bit of her torso poking above the surface of the small pool. She closed her eyes and imagined that she was floating on a cloud, far away from the worries and troubles of her present life. For a moment, her imagination did carry her away. But her mind would not be silent for long. The chaos in her head insisted on pushing its way through, no matter how hard she tried to act like it wasn't there.

Izzy had been right about this section of the river. The river had carved out a bit of an inlet into the forest here, and the water inside of it was still, peaceful, and warm. It felt heavenly, and getting rid of the dirt and grime that a week in the wilderness had caused felt positively luxurious. Anya had taken her time, using her bare hands to scrub water across her skin until there was not a speck of dirt left on her shimmering wet body. Once she was clean, Anya had pushed onto her back to float, and she had been like that for nearly half an hour now. The skin on her fingers and toes had crinkled into a raisin-like texture, but Anya paid it no mind. She was at peace to think about the riddles of the amethyst records here, and that's what she was doing. Thinking, thinking, thinking. She rolled the words 'dragon claw' and 'forest claw' over and over in her mind. But still, no answer came to her. She was growing slowly frustrated. She knew that those words meant something to her, but she could not remember why.

She was close to giving up and heading back to the campsite, when the sound of a twig snapping startled her out of her aquatic reverie. Another snap came, and another, and Anya sat up as quickly as a lightning bolt, keeping her body below the surface of the water even though the river was so clear here that one could easily see anything below its glassy top. Her cheeks started to turn red as she looked around to see who was coming. For a moment, she had a flashback to what it had felt like to be caught lying naked with Finn in the middle of the woods. Who was about to come upon her naked now? Surely Izzy would have warned the men in the group that Anya was taking a bath out here.

But as Anya's gaze darted wildly around, it finally settled on the person responsible for the snapping twigs, and she relaxed. Finn. Her physical nakedness in front of him did not cause her embarrassment, although, perhaps, her emotional nakedness did. The insecurities she'd felt on his account came rushing back in an instant, and she felt exposed. She dipped her eyes slightly as he approached the edge of the river, his boots crunching the ground with exaggerated noise.

"Was I loud enough this time?" he asked, a grin on his face as he came closer. "I know you don't like it when I sneak up on you."

If he was aware of the discomfort she was feeling right now, then he did a damn good job of hiding it. He sat on the edge of the river and began to take his boots and socks off. He rubbed his feet as he did, his eyes wincing a bit in apparent pain as he tried to get the circulation going.

"I thought there was an elephant coming," Anya said, trying to grin as well. She didn't want him to see the pain and confusion in her eyes, so she tried her best to hide it completely. He wasn't so easily fooled, though. He gave her a searching look as he rolled up his pant legs and then dipped his feet in the water.

"I'm sorry I wasn't there when you woke up today," he said, his voice cautious. "You were dead to the world this morning, and Peter and Knox wanted to head out on a scouting mission at the crack of dawn. I thought it was better to just let you sleep."

"It's fine," Anya said, her voice sounding unnaturally high despite her efforts to sound normal. She smiled warmly, but Finn was still watching her carefully, as if trying to see into her very soul.

"No, it's not fine," he said. "We made love in the forest the night before, and I told you we'd talk about it when we woke up. But then I up and disappeared on you. I'm sorry. I hope it didn't cause you too much anguish."

Anya was surprised by the tenderness in his voice. He might be a tough dragon, but he still had a soft heart. At least, when it came to her he seemed to have a soft heart. She looked away from him to try to hide the emotion in her eyes. She focused on the treetops above her and shrugged.

"You told me before we slept together that you couldn't fall in love. What we did wasn't about feelings or a relationship. It was about the fact that we both had an itch to scratch and we scratched it. There's no need to apologize for being gone when I woke up in the morning."

Finn let out a long sigh, then stood and started to take off his clothes. Anya watched him from the corner of her eye, avoiding his gaze but not able to keep from stealing glances at his muscular body as he stripped. Within a minute, he had removed all of his clothing and dumped it in a pile on the ground next to Anya's pile of clothes. The next thing she knew, he had slipped into the small pool and swum over to her. When he reached her, he tilted her head upward toward his.

"Look at me," he ordered her, his voice deep and gravelly. Anya tried to look away, but he held her chin firmly.

"No, look at me," he said. "I want you to see my eyes when I say this. I thought I couldn't love a human. I thought there could never be anything more between us than just a couple of friends having fun. But I was dead wrong. I think I only said those things because I was scared to admit the truth to myself. And the truth, Anya, is that I've known since the moment I met you that you were someone special. I was attracted to you instantly, and, at first, I thought it was just because you're the most beautiful woman I've ever seen. I thought it was just a case of insane lust due to your incredible beauty."

"Sweet talker," Anya joked, her voice light as she tried to pass of Finn's words as flirtatious flattery. But he wasn't having any of that.

"No, I'm serious, and you know it," he said. "You're perfection, Anya. I've seen a lot of beautiful woman before, but never someone as beautiful as you. And I thought that if you were willing to have a bit of fun, well, then why not? We're two grown adults after all. But you know as well as I do that after we slept together everything changed."

"Did it?" Anya asked, her voice small and trembling as she looked up into his eyes. His hair was glistening with water droplets from the short swim over to her, and little trails of water ran down his tanned face. He blinked as one of the water trails hit his right eye, but he never moved his hands away from Anya's body to try to brush at his face. He kept one hand firmly on her chin, and the other firmly on her hip. She could feel his dick, standing erect and poking at her stomach as they both stood there, naked in the water. Her eyes pleaded with him, although she wasn't quite sure what she was pleading for. He smiled at her, then, and the warmth of his smile felt like it melted her very soul.

"You know it changed," he said, bending his head down to nuzzle her nose with his nose. "There was a connection between us that went beyond just the physical. The moment I locked eyes with you while inside of you, I knew that there was no turning back for me. I had fallen in love, just like that. Do you hear me, Anya? I love you. I wanted to tell you last night, but I was trying to come up with some sort of romantic speech and felt woefully inadequate. Then, when the crew found us and dragged us back to camp, I didn't want to try and explain my feelings for you with a bunch of nosy ears listening in. I thought I would steal away with you this morning and just tell you how I feel, even if my attempt at a romantic speech turned out to be far from perfect. You can imagine my frustration when I was forced to go scouting instead. But here I am now, finally alone with you and finally telling you how I feel. I love you."

Anya could hardly breathe as she looked up at him. "But...you're a dragon. And I'm a human. And..."

Anya trailed off, afraid to say the words she wanted so desperately to say. Finn waited, never taking his eyes from hers as he waited for her to complete her sentence.

"And I love you, too," she finally said.

The broadest smile she had ever seen spread across his face. He pulled her in close for a kiss, his tongue quickly slipping past her lips as he wrapped his arms tightly around her. The water swirling around them felt cool now. It was no match for the heat of Anya's body as she filled with desire for the man who held her. Finn, too, was burning up. She could feel his skin, hot to the touch even below the surface of the water.

Something in the back of her mind tried to tell her that this was crazy. Her rational side tried to insist that they were going to be caught and teased again, that they didn't know each other well enough to throw around the word "love," and that a dragon and a human could never make it together in this world. Anya pushed away each objection as it came. Perhaps dragons and humans were worlds apart, but that didn't change the fact that their worlds had just collided.

Finn raised his hands to her breasts, enveloping their round fullness with his large, strong palms. He massaged them as he continued to kiss her, continued to drink her in. She felt a trembling between her thighs as her body responded to his attention, yearning to have him inside of her. Heat filled her, radiating out from his palms and his tongue and setting her whole body on fire. It's hot business, loving a dragon, Anya thought. Then she giggled, amused by her own thoughts.

Finn pulled back from their kiss for a moment and raised an eyebrow. "What's so funny?" he asked.

Anya looked into his emerald green eyes and gave a small shrug, trying to look coy. He growled in return, a mischievous glint in his own eyes as he pulled her back into his kiss. This time, he dropped one hand from her breasts and let it slip below the water, searching until it found the soft warmth between her legs. She moaned slightly as his finger explored inside of her, rubbing against the most sensitive part of her body and sending streaks of hot fire radiating out from between her legs.

She closed her eyes as he drew circles on her inner walls. Her mind was beginning to quiet now. It was impossible to think of other worries when Finn was driving her crazy like this. Her thoughts became mercifully consumed with him and only him. Sweet, pressure-filled heat flooded her, and every nerve ending in her body began to tingle with electricity. The electricity grew, until she felt that surely anything she touched would be shocked by the powerful passion that filled her. Finn thrust another finger inside of her, and the wide span of the two fingers pushing against her was too much to take. She felt herself going over the edge, and in the next instant she let out a yelp of surprised pleasure as spasms began to rock her body. She trembled, falling against Finn's body as she shook, his heat and electricity taking her to heights she had never been before. He kissed the top of her head, then gently nuzzled her ear. He kept his fingers inside of her as her insides clenched around them, and wrapped his other arm firmly around her bare back.

She had never felt so safe. She had the strange sensation that she was falling apart, but in a good way. She let the feeling wash over her, and, when it had subsided, she rested her head on Finn's shoulder. He held her there, stroking her mess of tangled wet hair and seeming to enjoy just being together. Anya could still feel his erection pressing against her lower stomach, but he was not in a hurry. He was drinking in this wonderful moment, just as she was.

To her surprise, after a minute or two of this, he spoke.

"Humans don't really know of the concept of lifemates, do they?" he asked.

Anya tilted her head back so she could see his face. "No, I guess not. I've never heard that term before."

Finn nodded slowly. "I think it's just a shifter thing," he said. "The wizards don't really know of it, either."

"Lifemates," Anya said, repeating the word. She liked the sound of it. She could somewhat guess what was meant by the term, but she asked anyway. "What are lifemates?"

Finn's smile deepened, causing his eyes to crinkle up merrily as he looked down at her. "It's sort of like the idea of a soulmate, but more intense. In the shifter world, we believe that each person has someone they are destined to be with. From the moment of your birth, fate and destiny are working together to bring you across that person's path. When you do meet them, you're almost always instantly attracted to them— although I have heard of instances where two lifemates initially did not like each other. But, in any case, things usually start out feeling like your run-of-the-mill, normal infatuation with someone you're attracted to."

"And then?" Anya asked, feeling slightly breathless as Finn looked happily down at her.

"And then," he said, "You end up sleeping with that person. You might think it's just having a bit of fun together, which is what I thought we were doing last night. Or maybe I knew it was more, but I was afraid to admit it to myself. Whatever the case, as soon as you make love to your destined lifemate, you form a bond with that person."

"What does that mean?" Anya asked, her breathlessness increasing. She had a feeling she knew where this was going, but she forced herself to wait and let Finn talk.

"Well, once you're bonded to your lifemate, you can never truly be separate from them again. Oh, sure, you might be apart physically, but your very souls are intertwined. Your destinies are one. You feel it when they feel pain, even if they are far away from you."

"But how do you know that you're bonded?" Anya asked. Her heart felt like it was going to pound out of her chest now.

"You just know," Finn said with a shrug. "I mean, you can feel the physical effect of the bond when it's happening. It feels like a hot warmth at the very core of you. But the bond itself is so much more than that physical sensation. It's a deep knowing, an understanding, that you and this person are meant to be together. It's a connection of your souls, if you will."

"I...I felt a warmth when we made love last night," Anya said. "I'd never felt anything like that before and I wasn't sure what to make of it. But I've felt different ever since. I've had this strange sensation that almost makes me feel like I've found a new home, and I haven't been able to think of anything but you."

Finn brushed a wet strand of hair back from her eyes. "That's the lifemate bond," he said softly. "I felt it, too. And it's why I can tell you that I love you, even though we've only known each other a few days. I don't need more time to know the truth. We're bonded. We're lifemates. I swear to you, Anya, I will spend the rest of my life protecting you, and fighting to make you happy. I don't know how all the details will work out. I know I'm a dragon and you're a human and we have different lives that we have to figure out how to entwine into one. But I promise you, we will figure out how to do that. Because I know now that I cannot live a day without you, and that there is nothing in the world that I want more than to be with you. I hope that you feel the same, because whether or not you do, I'm a lost cause. There will never be anyone else for me but you, Anya. I love you, with every fiber of my being."

Anya bit her lip, but could not keep the silly grin from spreading across her face. "I love you, too," she said. "I told myself that there was nothing serious between us, but there's no use trying to deny it. I don't know how this will all work either, but I know deep down that it will work. We're meant to be together."

Finn smiled tenderly at her, his eyes heating up again. "You're really something special, you know that?" he said in a husky voice. "I've never met anyone so enchanting."

He pulled her close to him again, putting his lips on hers and thirstily kissing her again. Anya immediately felt a thrill of excitement run through her body. The space between her legs, which had barely stopped throbbing from the attention of his fingers, started tingling again. The heat and electricity that had been fading a bit instantly surged back, and she moaned happily as his tongue danced in her mouth. He put his arms around her, pulling her close to his chest so that her hard nipples were pressed against his rough skin. The rubbing sensation sent a fresh wave of hot desire through her, and she squeezed her eyes shut even tighter, trying to take in all the wondrous sensations that being with him caused. It was an overwhelming symphony of pleasure, and she could not imagine feeling happier than she did in that moment.

But she was about to feel happier, because in the next instant she felt his dick pushing at her, seeking her soft warmth. The water swirled around them in warm circles as Finn moved his hips until he was perfectly positioned right in front of her. And then, with one long, ragged sigh, he slid into her.

Anya felt like fireworks were going off inside her body. He stretched her inner walls and filled her in the most intoxicating manner, and even the very slightest movements that he made hit sensitive nerve endings and sent shocks through her. She pressed her hips forward to meet his, filled with wonder at how impossibly far into her body he reached.

He rocked his hips back and forth in a steady, thrusting motion that caused the fire burning in Anya's body to slowly build, hotter and hotter. She felt the pressure within her building to the point of explosion again, and her breath came in an increasingly rapid rhythm. Just before she reached the climax of her passion, she opened her eyes. She wanted to memorize the way everything looked in this moment. Finn's face was inches from her own, his eyes squeezed shut in perfect concentration as he moved in her. The water droplets in his hair still glistened in the bright sunlight. Behind him, the deep green of leaves was accented by the rich brown of tree trunks. The sky above them was robin's egg blue, and the water swirling around their hips was clear as crystal. Anya looked down to see the skin of Finn's chest pressed against her breasts. The sight of her own full breasts pressed against his muscular body turned her on, and she shuddered from the fresh wave of electric passion that rushed through her.

Finn felt her shudder, and opened his eyes to look at her. She looked up at him, and lost herself in the deep green of his gaze. His eyes seemed to burn as he looked at her, and the intimacy of looking at each other while their bodies were connected was too much for her to take. She could hold back no longer, and let out a stifled scream as she came again, hard and fast. Her inner muscles squeezed his dick tightly, and her mouth opened wide as she gasped for air, trying to catch her breath as the glorious waves of passion washed over her. She never closed her eyes, though, and neither did he.

He continued to look at her, seeming to see right into her soul as he thrust again and again, his powerful hips claiming her for his own. And then, while she was still trembling from the aftershocks of her own pleasure, he stiffened and thrust into her even harder than before. She could feel his steel shaft throbbing inside of her as he gave himself to her. The movement prolonged her own throbbing, sending a fresh rush of heat through her body.

Their eyes never moved. His gaze remained locked with hers, and in that intimate moment, she felt like she was seeing into someone's soul for the first time in her life.

His was a dragon soul. Perfect, noble, and hers. She did close her eyes then, leaning against him with a soft whimper of happiness. She had never imagined that happiness could reach so deep into the very fabric of one's being, but she knew in that moment that Finn had made her the most joyful woman alive.

CHAPTER THIRTEEN

Finn lay on his back on the mossy riverbank, completely naked as he stared up at the azure sky above him. He smiled as his fingers curled around Anya's, still unable to believe that she was actually his. The last thing he had expected when he had flown out of Falcon Cross last week was to find a lifemate in the midst of the search for the dragon amethyst, but he sure as hell wasn't complaining. No wonder his clan members who had found love were always so happy. If he'd known that finding your lifemate felt so amazing, he would have been searching for Anya long ago.

Of course, he probably wouldn't have found her until now, anyway. That was the funny thing about destiny. You could try to control your fate all you wanted to, but somehow things happened when they needed to happen. Trying to speed up the process only resulted in frustration.

No matter what the reason that it had taken this long for Anya to cross his path, Finn was just glad she had crossed it. She made him feel complete as a man, a feeling he hadn't even realized he'd been missing. And, of course, it didn't hurt that she was the most beautiful, intelligent woman he'd ever met. He could not possibly have hoped for anyone better.

Finn could have lay there forever, but he knew they needed to get back to the campsite. If they stayed out here too long, one of the others would come looking for them again, and they would have to endure a fresh round of teasing. Not that Finn minded all that much. After all, there were worse things to be teased about than winning the affection of a woman like Anya. With a sigh, Finn sat up and let Anya's fingers slide from his. She looked over at him with a quizzical expression, shadowing her eyes with the palm of her hand so she could see him. She was still naked, too, and he paused for a moment to admire the way her curves glowed in the afternoon sunlight. But only for a moment.

"We should get dressed and get back," he said. "Peter and Knox are going to want to discuss what our next steps are. I've already stayed away much longer than I should have. I was sent to fetch you, not to make love to you. Although, I'm sure they figured we were going to have a little fun."

Finn winked at Anya, and a pink blush crept up into her cheeks. She groaned.

"Are we that obvious?" she asked.

Finn laughed. "It's hard not to be out here, with everyone in such close quarters at the campsite. It's pretty clear what we're doing if we sneak away together."

Anya sighed. "I suppose you're right. All the more reason to find the dragon amethyst as soon as possible so we can spend some time together without everyone being in our business. What are the next steps, by the way? Do Peter and Knox have a plan?"

"Not really," Finn said, and he could not keep the hint of frustration from his voice. "We covered a lot of ground, flying around the area to see whether Saul's soldiers had followed us at all. But nothing looked suspicious. They either didn't see us come this way, or they just don't care that we're here. But I don't see what the point was in scouting out this area, anyway. Peter and Knox want to set up a temporary headquarters, but it doesn't do us much good to sit here, even if we are safe. The dragon amethyst is still under danger of falling into the wrong hands, and we still have no idea how we're going to get it. We're wasting time right now, and we don't have time to waste."

Finn saw Anya frown and furrow her brow, then shake her head slightly.

"You're going to think I'm crazy for saying this," she said. "But I don't think the dragon amethyst is in Devil's Melt."

Finn raised an eyebrow in her direction. "Why do you say that?" he asked.

Anya shrugged. "Just a hunch," she said.

"A hunch?" Finn said, unable to keep the frustration from his tone. "Anya, we've had a lot of really smart people looking over the amethyst records, and they all agree that the amethyst must be in Devil's Melt. Saul's men obviously think so, too. Unless you have a solid reason for that hunch, I'd say it doesn't do us much good."

"Well..." Anya said slowly. She looked like she wanted to say more, but then she clamped her mouth shut. Finn didn't tell her that Izzy and Owen also thought the dragon amethyst wasn't in Montana. Unless someone could give him a solid idea of where else it might be, he didn't see the point in turning their focus away from Devils Melt.

Finn pulled his clothes back on, and tossed Anya the Falcon Cross military uniform that was lying on the ground beside the river. Izzy must have given her that to wear so that she would have fresh clothes. Anya dressed in silence, but her brow never unfurrowed. When she was finished pulling on the uniform, Finn let out a whistle.

"That looks good on you," he said. Anya blushed, but looked pleased.

"It was nice of Izzy to lend it to me," she said. "Although I think it actually belongs to Raven."

Finn laughed. "Nice of Izzy to give away Raven's clothes, eh?"

Anya smiled, and her face relaxed a bit. She gathered up her other clothes, which were still hanging on nearby tree branches to dry.

"Shall we head back?" she asked. "I can hang these by the fire later to finish drying."

Finn nodded. "Yeah, let's get back to camp."

They fell into step beside each other, both lost in their own thoughts for a few minutes. Finally, Anya broke the silence.

"Speaking of Raven, I read some of her notes from a meeting about the dragon amethyst."

"Oh?" Finn asked. Izzy had told Finn that Anya had spent the morning looking over notes about the dragon amethyst, but he didn't really expect Anya to have any new insights. There was a lot of information to go through, and most of it was only background information. It didn't offer much in the way of clues as to where the amethyst might actually be.

"Yeah, it looks like she was really interested in a riddle about a dragon claw and forest claw. Do you know which one I'm talking about?" Anya asked.

Finn could not keep himself from laughing. "Oh, I know that riddle," he said. "One of the wizard Advocates, Harlow, is obsessed with it. She's convinced it's the key to finding the dragon amethyst, but I don't know why. It doesn't seem to me that it's any more important than any of the other riddles. And if you spent as much time reading through our amethyst records today as Izzy said you did, I'm sure you saw that there are a lot of damn riddles. And most of them don't make any damn sense."

"There are a lot of riddles," Anya agreed. "But I think Harlow's right. I think the claw riddle means something important."

Finn did his best not to let out a sigh of exasperation. After all, he'd told the rest of the crew that it would be good to have a fresh set of eyes on the amethyst records, and Anya was providing that fresh set of eyes. He should let her have her say.

"Why do you think that?" Finn asked, trying to keep his tone neutral. But Anya only shrugged, adding to Finn's frustration.

"I dunno," she said. "It just reminds me of something. But I can't think what."

Finn chewed his lower lip to keep from making a smartass comment. He knew Anya was smart, but she wasn't showing it right now. This war would not be won on hunches and feelings. They needed concrete answers on where the amethyst was.

They walked in silence for another minute or two, and had almost reached the campsite when Anya stopped short and snapped her fingers.

"Oh my god," she said. "I know where the amethyst is."

Finn stopped short, too, then. "What? Where? And how do you know?"

"It's not in Montana at all," Anya said. "It's in the California Redwoods."

Ordinarily, Finn would have snorted in laughter at a suggestion like that. He'd been born and raised in the California Redwoods, and knew those forests better than almost anyone. If you'd asked him just twenty-four hours ago, he would have told you that he was certain that there were no dragon stones in the redwoods.

But twenty-four hours ago, he'd also been sure that he would never truly love a woman, especially not a human. Yet here he was, head over heels for his beautiful, human lifemate. And even though his head screamed at him that she didn't know what she was talking about, his heart whispered to him to listen to her. He chose in that moment to listen to the whisper.

"How do you know that?" he asked, his heart pounding as he waited for her answer. He did his best to suspend disbelief. Was it truly possible that she knew where the dragon amethyst was, and that it had been hiding right under their noses this whole time?

"I remember now why I thought the riddle sounded so familiar," Anya said, her voice growing more excited with every word she spoke. "My father was a botanist, too. He loved nature, and especially plants, and he took me on a lot of trips with him to see different forests and expose me to many different kinds of vegetation. Once, when I was very young, we went to see the Redwoods in northern California. I mean the ones in the very north of California, almost at the border of Oregon. I know we hiked and camped for days, although I don't remember a great deal from our trip. I do remember that my dad seemed to always be looking for something, although he didn't say what it was he was looking for."

"Was it the dragon amethyst?" Finn interrupted, unable to believe that he had somehow run across a human whose father had known about a dragon stone. But Anya was shaking her head no.

"I don't know that it was the amethyst," she said. "I'm not sure he knew that such things existed. But he was looking for what he called the 'forest claw.'"

Finn felt the hair on the back of his neck standing on end as Anya spoke. She was onto something, and he knew it. The excitement in her face was causing her skin to practically glow, and Finn reached out and took her by the shoulders, unable to stand still any longer.

"And did he find it?" Finn asked. "What was the forest claw?"

Anya was nodding vigorously. "He told me later that he'd only heard rumors of it, and he wasn't sure that the rumors were true. But he did find it in the end. The forest claw is a large redwood root that sticks out from a cliff into open air right in front of a waterfall. The root is shaped like a giant claw. It almost looks like a dragon claw, in fact. Behind the waterfall is a hidden cave. I never saw the cave. My dad climbed up the rocky cliff next to the waterfall and disappeared behind it into the cave. He wouldn't let me go with him, because I was so young and he was afraid I would fall from the cliff if I attempted the climb. But I'll never forget his face when he came back from looking at the cave. I asked him what he had seen, and he shook his head in wonder and just said, 'Anya, it's true. The place is magical. Actually magical. I thought the guy who told me that was out of his mind, but it's true.' That's all he would say. I don't know how he knew about the place, or who the man was that told him where to find it. I was so young, so everything from that trip is a bit fuzzy in my memory. My dad did take a picture of me in front of the forest claw waterfall, though. He framed it and it hung on his wall until the day he died. He always said it was one of his favorite pictures of me, but he never actually referred to the scenery as the forest claw after we left the redwoods, which is why I'd forgotten where I'd heard the name."

"Do you know how to find the spot again?" Finn asked. He was trying to remain calm, but his heart was pounding faster with every passing second. He knew deep in his soul that Anya was right. Somehow, this forest claw waterfall was the key to finding the dragon amethyst.

"I don't have any idea how to get there," Anya said. "But my dad kept meticulous notes anytime he was exploring a forest. When he died I couldn't bear to throw them out, so I still have them all. They're in a small storage unit back in Idaho. If we find the notebook from that trip, I'm sure we'll be able to find the spot again."

Finn squeezed Anya's shoulders and then pulled her tight against his chest. "Anya, Love, I think you might have just won this war for us," he said.

He felt Anya shrug. "Well, don't get too excited yet," she said. "We have to see first whether we can find the spot again. And even if we find the spot, who knows whether there will actually be an amethyst there or not. There are still a lot of things that might not work out the way we want."

But Finn was having none of Anya's modesty. "Are you kidding me?" he said, pulling back to look at her. "You just described a magical place known as the forest claw. And our smartest wizard Advocate is convinced that the forest claw is the key to finding the amethyst. I have a feeling this is the big break we've been looking for."

Anya looked back at him with eyes that still held uncertainty. She was opening her mouth to say something when Finn heard footsteps approaching them through the forest. He turned, tensing up as he faced the direction the sound was coming from. He relaxed when he saw that it was only Owen, pushing through the thick brush to get to them.

"Hey you two lovebirds," he said with a grin. "Are you coming back to camp or what? Peter and Knox want to hold a powwow, and they're getting tired of waiting on the two of you."

"Oh, we're gonna hold a powwow alright," Finn said. "Wait until you hear what Anya's just told me."

Owen gave Finn and Anya both a quizzical look, but then pointed the way toward the campsite.

"I'm all ears," Owen said.

"As you should be," Finn said. "Anya accidentally stumbling across our group might just be the best thing that could have happened to us."

Finn grabbed Anya's hand and pulled her toward the campsite. He saw her cheeks turning pink again as she blushed under his praise, but this only made her lovelier. His heart was full as they walked back to the rest of the group with what he hoped was the answer to their prayers.

CHAPTER FOURTEEN

Anya took a deep nervous breath, and did her best to give Peter and Knox a convincing smile.

"So there you have it," she said. "I believe the forest claw my dad found is the same one mentioned in the riddle. If I'm right, then the amethyst might be there. Or, at least, they're might be some further clue there as to where it actually is."

Peter and Knox looked at each other, seeming to speak to each other without using words. But Anya could not read much into their expressions. They were silent for an unbearably long time, and when they finally looked back over at her, she still was not able to tell whether or not they were pleased. She held her breath and waited for them to speak, but when they did speak it was not her they addressed. Peter looked over at Finn, Owen, Izzy, and Raven, raising a quizzical eyebrow in their direction.

"And what does everyone else think of going searching for the forest claw?" Peter asked.

Finally given permission to speak, everyone spoke at once. Anya could not easily make out individual words, but the general consensus was clear. The whole group thought that searching for the forest claw was a good idea. The chaos only grew louder until Knox raised his hands for silence.

"Hold on, everyone! One at a time," he said.

"I think it's a good idea," Raven said, quickly speaking up. "It sounds promising, and, besides, what else are we going to do? The only way we're going to be able to get near Devil's Melt right now is to take the whole Falcon Cross army out there. I say looking for this forest claw waterfall is worth a shot."

There were murmurs of agreement, and everyone else in the group made some sort of similar statement. Knox nodded.

"Makes sense to me," he said. "Not only that, but I'll be honest, I'd like to get back to Texas and see Bree. I'm missing my girl something awful right now. I wish I hadn't left her behind."

Anya looked over at Finn and bit her lip with excitement. She had wondered how she was going to make a difference in this war, and now, it looked like she might have her answer. Finn smiled at her and took her hand, then looked toward Peter, who was stroking his long white beard. Anya was trying very hard not to hate Peter right now. Despite what everyone had said about the old man being kind and wise, she couldn't quite forget that he had wanted to wipe her memory. If he denied her the chance to search for the forest claw, she wasn't sure she could ever forgive him.

But, finally, he looked over at Knox and nodded, having made his decision.

"I agree with all of you," Peter said. "I think looking for the forest claw is a good plan. Devil's Melt is a hornet's nest right now. If we have another option that might lead us to the dragon amethyst, we might as well take it. And for the sake of good shifters and wizards everywhere, I hope that Anya is right. I hope this magical waterfall cave will lead us to the dragon amethyst. In fact, if this is the course of action we want to take, we should move as quickly as possible. If the stone *is* there, then we want to get to it before anyone else gets wind of what we're doing."

"We can fly out tonight," Owen said. "If we fly like the wind all night we should be able to get to Idaho sometime early tomorrow. Hopefully, Anya can find the notes she needs quickly, and we can be on our way to California by tomorrow night."

"Holy shit," Izzy said, her eyes widening. "Do you guys realize that it's possible we could have the dragon amethyst in our possession within a matter of days?"

"I hope I'm not wrong about all this," Anya said, feeling suddenly self-conscious. The whole group was about to put a huge amount of effort into a plan she was responsible for. She hoped with all her heart that something useful came of this. Finn gave her a reassuring smile.

"We have to try," he said. "The worse that happens is we don't find the dragon amethyst. Getting out there and doing something is better than sitting around here hiding from Saul."

There were murmurs of agreement all around, and then Knox stood up, brushing dust and leaves from his pants.

"Alright, everyone. Start packing up," Knox said, then looked over at Finn and Owen with a grin. "Looks like you boys are heading home to the Redwoods."

Finn and Owen could not keep silly grins from spreading across their faces, and the effect was contagious. Anya found a smile spreading across her face as well.

"Please let this work," she whispered under her breath. "Please, please, please."

* * *

Early the next morning, as the first gray streaks of dawn rose over the sleepy town of Broad Brook, Idaho, five people flew unseen across the morning sky. Under a cloak of invisibility, two wizards, two dragon shifters, and one human arrived to search for a notebook they hoped would provide the key to finding the powerful amethyst that could protect or destroy humanity, depending on whose hands it was in.

Anya was riding on a broomstick with Izzy, and wore one of the group's large backpacks on her back. Owen and Raven rode on another broomstick, and, behind them, Finn flew in dragon form, keeping himself as well hidden as he could using a chameleon trick. Broad Brook was Anya's hometown, located in the furthest southwest corner of Idaho. It was so strange to her to see it from the air like this, hovering just a few hundred feet above the houses on a thin wooden broomstick. The moment felt surreal to her, but, unlike the first time Anya had flown with this group, she now knew that this was not a dream. The wizards and dragons that surrounded her were very real. Anya could not have been happier with that knowledge. She glanced back toward where she knew Finn was flying through the air unseen, and she smiled. She'd only just met him, but life with him had already been an adventure.

Izzy started slowly descending as they flew further into the heart of the little town. Out of habit, Anya glanced nervously around at the open sky. There had been quite a bit of worry that Saul's soldiers might be watching this area, and that the group's invisibility protections wouldn't work against him. But, so far, their journey had been quiet and uneventful. The enemy was not watching this far south, it seemed. Not yet, anyway. Anya shuddered at the thought of the unsuspecting little town being watched by such an evil being. Then she gritted her teeth in determination. She was going to do everything she could to make sure he never had possession of this place.

A few minutes later, Izzy finished her descent and came to a soft landing in front of a storage unit facility. Behind them, Anya heard Raven and Owen landing, and then Finn. A loud pop sounded through the air, and then Finn was suddenly visible again.

His chameleon disguise disappeared as he morphed back into human form. Sharp hisses rang through the air as well, indicating that the invisibility shield around the groups on the broomsticks had been cancelled. Anya had been so caught up in looking over at the storage units that she hadn't even heard Izzy or Raven terminating the shields, but suddenly she could see Raven and Owen again, and she knew they could see her.

"Looks like we weren't followed at all," Finn said as he started to pull clothes out of the bag that Anya had just dropped on the ground. Anya shook her head slightly in amazement at how nonchalant he was about being stark naked in front of anyone. No one else in the group batted an eyelash at his nudity, but Anya was still getting used to the fact that shifters had no clothes on once they returned to human form. It's a good thing she'd never been the jealous type, because Izzy and Raven were seeing her man in all his glory right now, and she was pretty sure that many woman before them had, too, just by virtue of his shifting.

"No, we weren't followed," Izzy said, raising her eyes to the sky. "But we should hurry. They might be patrolling through this area, even if they aren't constantly watching it. We can't be too careful."

Finn had finished dressing then, and he nodded. "Agreed. Let's get moving. Anya, I'm assuming you have a code or key or something for this place."

"Yes, a code," Anya said. "The main gate is this way. Come on."

Anya led them toward where a giant car gate allowed vehicles to enter the facility. Next to it was a door for pedestrians with an attached codebox. Anya entered the code from memory, and the door beeped before allowing her to push it open. The group followed her to the front of the building, where she entered another code to allow them into the building itself. Long hallways of storage units stretched in front of them, but the one Anya was looking for was not far. She turned down the second hallway to the right, and stopped at the fourth unit on the left.

"This is it," she said. She took a deep breath and punched in the code to open the unit. Another soft beep sounded, and then, she was able to push up the garage-type door to step inside. The flood of memories that hit her was staggering. Her father's things were everywhere—things she probably should have sold or donated when he'd died, but she could not bear to part with them. She saw his old hiking pack, a folded up tent, his snowboard, and a host of other mementos of the active, outdoorsy life he'd loved. She steadied herself against the rush of emotions stirred up by the sight, and moved toward the back of the unit, where she knew she would find the boxes and boxes of journals and field notes that he'd left behind.

Seeing all of his possessions made her miss him like crazy. She knew if she wasn't careful she could lose herself for hours in here, and she didn't have hours to waste right now. She had to push down her feelings for the sake of this mission, and quickly find the journal she was looking for. Luckily, she had organized his notes in roughly chronological order before boxing them up. This made finding the boxes from the time of her early childhood relatively easy. She opened the first box and forced herself to ruthlessly flip through them, not stopping to read in depth or reminisce. She promised herself that when this was all over, she would come back and give herself as long as she wanted to look through these. But, now, she had something very particular she needed to find.

The rest of the group waited patiently while she searched. They'd offered to help flip through the volumes, but Anya's dad had written in such messy script that she was worried none of them would be able to read it properly. She was used to the haphazard scrawl, and quickly made her way through it. Even though she was the only one working, it didn't take long. Within fifteen minutes, she'd found what she was looking

441

for.

"Bingo," she said. She'd opened a journal to find a picture of her as a child, standing in front of the forest claw waterfall. The edges of the photo were yellowed, but the main portion of the photo was well preserved and gave a good visual of the waterfall and the forest claw tree root. Anya passed the picture back to Finn.

"This is it," she said, her voice trembling with excitement. "And I bet this journal has all the notes on where and how he found it."

Finn took the picture from her and squinted at it while the others crowded around him. Anya, meanwhile, turned her attention back to the notebook in her hands. She flipped through quickly, her excitement growing with each page that she turned.

"This is definitely it," she said. "These notes pretty much give step by step instruction on how to find the waterfall."

Finn handed the photo off to Owen, then leaned over Anya's shoulder to look at the notes. "I can't read a word of that chicken scratch," he said.

"Don't worry," Anya said. "I can. Looks like our next stop is the California Redwoods."

CHAPTER FIFTEEN

Finn never would have admitted it to anyone, but his muscles ached something awful as he climbed into his sleeping bag. The amethyst search party had been hiking for three days straight, pushing themselves to go further than they should have each day. Finn knew that he was not the only one hurting, but no one suggested scaling back their efforts. Everyone in the group was determined to get to the forest claw waterfall and see what secrets it held. Still, he was glad when darkness had fallen and they all decided to stop for the night.

They'd eaten a hearty dinner of roasted rabbit, thanks to Owen's hunting skills—which had yielded them the fresh rabbit to eat. They'd replenished their nonperishable food supplies before leaving Idaho, but it was still nice to have meat when it could be found. And it was relatively easy to find out here. Overall, this trek had felt almost like a vacation expedition. Spirits were high and the weather was good. There was still no sign of Saul's soldiers, and Finn was beginning to truly relax. If they were going to be followed, they would have known it by now.

"I think we're getting close," Anya said, breaking into his thoughts. She was lying next to him on her stomach, her elbows propped up so that she could read her father's journal by flashlight. Her brow was furrowed in concentration as her eyes scanned the page. Finn smiled, thinking how adorable she looked when she was this earnest about something.

"You should put that away and get some rest," Finn said. "You must have read through the whole thing at least a hundred times already, anyway."

Anya gave him a sheepish look. "I know. But I can't help it. It's so mind boggling to think that a trek I went on with my dad so long ago might be the key to finding the dragon amethyst. Besides, it's been a while since I'd seen his things. It reminded me of how much I miss him, and seeing his handwriting makes me feel closer to him. There's just something about a handwritten page that seems to connect you to someone you lost, you know?"

"I don't know," Finn said, regret in his voice. "When my parents died, everything we had was destroyed. I have nothing to remember them by, not even my own memories. I was too young when they died."

Anya's face twisted contritely. "I'm sorry," she said, starting to put away the journal. "I shouldn't have been so insensitive. I only meant—"

"No, don't apologize," Finn said, reaching to pull her into his arms. "I've made my peace with the situation. And, in some ways, perhaps it's easier to not remember them. I saw the pain in your eyes when you looked through that storage unit. You loved him very much, I can tell."

Anya nodded, and buried her face into Finn's chest. "I did. He was an amazing father. I've felt lost ever since he died. That's one reason I'm so happy to have found this group. It's nice to feel like a part of a family again, even if it's not a traditional family."

Finn squeezed Anya tighter, enjoying the way her soft warm body fit perfectly in his arms. "Well, I'm glad you like it, because I'm not letting you go now that I've found you."

Anya sighed happily at his words, and then was silent for so long that Finn thought she had fallen asleep. But then she murmured softly into his chest.

"I think we'll reach the forest claw tomorrow," she said. "According to my dad's notes we should be getting close."

Finn looked down at Anya to reply, but her eyes were closed, and she was breathing rhythmically now. It seemed that was the last thing she'd said before falling asleep. So Finn remained quiet, but he felt a fresh wave of excitement wash over him. If tomorrow they could find the dragon amethyst, then not only would their mission have been a success, but they could go home. He and Anya could spend some time together in a real bed, instead of just a sleeping bag. Finn realized that he wasn't quite sure where "home" would be now, but then he decided it didn't matter that much. He'd love to head back to his cabin in the Redwoods, sure. But, at the end of the day, home for him now was wherever Anya was. He smiled at the thought before giving in to the rhythm of sleep himself.

Finn felt as though he had barely closed his eyes when he was opening them again to find bright morning sunlight streaming down onto their little campsite. Every muscle in his body ached, and he groaned aloud, wondering how it was possible that it was already time to get up and get going.

"Come on, sleepyhead," Anya said, apparently feeling much more refreshed than he did. "It's time for breakfast. And the sooner we get going the sooner we can find the forest claw. We're really close now!"

With another grunt, Finn forced himself to sit up and get moving. After a quick breakfast, the group cleaned up the campsite got moving. Anya and the others chatted amiably as they hiked, but Finn still felt groggy. He remained silent for the most part, looking around and taking in the beauty of the forest around him.

This stretch of redwoods was further north than the redwoods where his clan lived, but the scenery was similar. Towering, reddish brown tree trunks reached hundreds of feet above him, their beautiful wood offset perfectly by their deep green leaves, and by the green brush that covered the forest floor. He breathed in, relishing the familiar scent of a redwood forest, a smell he had grown up with. The earthy notes filled his nostrils along with the coolness of the morning mist, which had not yet been burned off by the steadily rising sun. Even when the sun reached its height at noon, it would be cool here under the shade of these ancient trees.

They trudged along for the better part of two hours, Finn lost in the beauty of the forest around him while the others continued to chat on and off. Then, suddenly, Anya gave a shout. Finn's head snapped to attention, and he saw the others running toward her, looking in the direction where her finger was pointing. Finn rushed over, too, ready to shift and fight if it was an enemy she was pointing at. But it was no enemy. Instead, just on the other side of a huge redwood trunk that Anya was standing next to, the sound of rushing water could be heard. And, if one squinted, you could almost make out a waterfall up ahead.

"That's got to be it," Anya said, fumbling in her excitement as she tried to open the notebook she'd been carrying. "Yes, look! Look at this!"

Finn peered over her shoulder to see she was pointing to a crude map her father had drawn. He couldn't read anything on the map though, so he just shrugged and nodded.

"I'll take your word for it," he said.

Owen, Izzy, and Raven were peering down at the map with similar quizzical looks on their faces, and Anya let out an exasperated sigh.

"Oh, come on you guys," she said. "According to the map, it's right there!"

She was pointing to an indecipherable smudge on the map as thought it were the plainest thing in the world, and Finn couldn't help but snort in amusement.

"We'll take your word for it," he said again, laughing.

Anya rolled her eyes, but smiled good-naturedly as the others started laughing.

"Come on," she said. She started walking forward briskly, and the others scrambled to keep up with her, still chuckling. But they weren't laughing anymore a few minutes later when they turned the corner around another big redwood trunk. Now there was a clear path through the brush, and the waterfall was on full display. It was rushing a great deal more than it had been in the picture Anya's father had taken decades earlier, but the rock wall next to it looked the same. And there, spread across the front of the falls, plain as day, was a giant root of a redwood in the shape of a claw.

Finn stared in disbelief. This was exactly what they had hoped to find, and yet, now that it was right in front of him, he could hardly believe his eyes. The scene was beautiful, with glittering, cascading water providing a white backdrop for the deep reddish wood of the forest claw root. At the bottom of the rocky cliff from which the waterfall fell, there was a large pool of swirling water. The pool grew narrower the further away it got from the waterfall, until it turned into a stream that flowed away into the depths of the forest. The view from where they stood was nothing short of majestic, but it wasn't just the natural beauty that had grabbed a hold of him. There was a certain magic in the air, too. He couldn't quite explain it, but he knew they had just found something significant.

As he looked over at the four faces next to him, he knew he was not the only one in awe. The whole group looked at the waterfall with reverence, as though they had never seen anything quite so stunning. And perhaps none of them had, thought Finn.

"We found it," Anya finally said, stating the obvious. Murmurs of agreement came from all around her. Then, the loud cawing of a bird somewhere above them seemed to break them all out of their trance.

"Come on," Finn said. "Let's go check it out.

It took them another half hour to reach the bottom of the falls. The brush grew thicker and more overgrown the closer they got to the water. But, finally, they made it to the edge of the pool. Anya stood in the same spot where she had stood all those years earlier for her father to take her picture, and looked around with tears glistening in her eyes.

"I can't believe I was here with him," she said, blinking quickly to try to control her emotions. All she succeeded in doing, though, was causing a few tears to escape her eyelids and roll down her cheeks. Finn wrapped his arms around her from behind and kissed the top of her head as the whole group stared at the waterfall.

"It's crazy, isn't it?" Izzy said. "You were here so long ago, and now you're here again, hopefully to find the dragon amethyst. It's almost like destiny intended it."

"I think destiny intended a lot of things," Anya said, reaching to squeeze Finn's hands, which were clasped across her stomach. Finn's whole body warmed at her touch, and he kissed her head again.

"Well, enough staring at the place," Owen finally said, breaking the spell somewhat. "Let's see if we can find the cave that's supposedly behind all that water."

Finn let go of Anya and walked over to the foot of the rock wall with Owen. Spray from the falls quickly made their hair and clothes damp, and the whole wall was a slippery, wet mess.

"It's not going to be an easy climb," Finn said. "Maybe Owen and I should go it alone and you ladies can wait down here for us."

"Are you crazy?" Izzy said. "I'm not some dainty princess who can't climb a wall just because of a bit of water. I want to see what's in that cave."

"Yeah, I already missed out on the cave once when I was a kid," Anya said. "This time I'm going in."

Finn saw Owen glance over at Raven. "I suppose that means you're coming, too?" Owen asked with a resigned sigh. Raven merely grinned in response.

"Alright," Finn said. "Looks like we're all going. Be careful, please. I know Izzy is a doctor, but I'd still like to avoid having any broken bones for her to treat if we can."

"Wait, why can't the wizards just fly their broomsticks up?" Anya asked. "That seems safer than trying to climb."

"Aw where would the fun in that be?" Raven said with a wink. "Besides, it's difficult to hover on a broom, especially with water spraying all around you. I think climbing might actually be the better option."

Anya looked doubtful, and Finn had his own doubts as well, but he said nothing. He figured it was better to let the wizards be the judge of where it was safe for them to ride a broomstick.

"Come on," Owen said impatiently. "Enough dilly-dallying already. I want to see what's up there."

"Me too," Finn said, then jumped up to start climbing. "Race you to the top, Owen."

Owen grunted and jumped up beside Finn. "That's a race you know you're gonna lose, brother," he said.

Finn was too busy looking for his next rock hold to answer, but from below him he heard Raven's voice, dripping with sarcasm. "What happened to being careful, boys?" she asked. "I swear to god if one of you falls and hits your head because you're being stupid and racing, I'm going to kill you."

"Hey, it's all good," Izzy said. "If they kill themselves off that just means more food for us."

Peals of laughter rose to Finn's ears, but he did not respond. He was too busy concentrating on the task of climbing. He could feel his body growing warm from the effort, and he was probably sweating, but it was hard to tell since he was already so soaked from the waterfall's spray. He glanced below him now and then to make sure that the women were alright, especially Anya. He felt nervous to have her climbing up this steep, slippery cliff, but he knew he could not deny her this opportunity. She was, after all, the whole reason they were here. Besides, she had a lot of experience in the great outdoors. He had to trust that she knew what she was capable of and would not push her limits too far.

Finn kept an eye to his right as he climbed, looking for anything that might indicate a hidden cave. But all he could see behind the falling water was a sheer rock cliff, worn smooth by centuries of water pounding against it. He continued to climb, and had nearly reached the halfway point, when he finally saw a break in the rock wall. Just below the spot where the giant forest claw tree root stretched across the waterfall, there appeared to be a ledge. Finn felt a rush of adrenaline and excitement, and he sped up his climb, quickly pulling ahead of Owen. The closer he got, the more sure he was that he had found the cave. The entrance was not as large as he would have thought, but it was plenty big enough for him to know it was a cave, at least. Owen finally saw it, too, and gave a shout of triumph. Their little race was forgotten now. All they cared about was that they had found the cave.

Getting to it was a bit tricky. The wall behind the waterfall was smooth, with no footholds. Finn had to stand on the portion of the cliff that was not worn down and reach as far as he could just to grab the bottom of the cave floor. Once he had a grip on it, he hoisted himself up. For a moment, he was dangling by one arm, and he felt a slight bit of dizziness as he made the mistake of looking down. But then, he managed to grab the ledge with his other hand, too, and pull himself up. The cave was dark, much darker than he expected. The waterfall muted all of the light from outside, and it looked like the front of the cave was relatively small, anyway. It looked like there was a tunnel leading away from the main entrance, but he would explore more in a minute. First, he wanted to make sure everyone else got in safely.

Owen was already swinging himself up in much the same manner Finn just had, and Finn took a moment to grin at him and say, "I won the race, bro."

"You had a head start," Owen said, rolling his eyes.

"Tsk, tsk. Sore loser," Finn said, still grinning.

"Oh shut up and let's get the girls in here," Owen replied. Finn laughed, but nodded.

"Grab my feet so I don't fall out," Owen said, lying flat on his stomach with his arms hanging over the edge of the cave entrance. Finn did as he asked, bracing his own feet against the side of the cave's wall and holding onto Owen's feet.

"Grab my hands. I'll pull you up," Owen yelled out the entrance. A moment later, Finn felt Owen lurch forward a bit as one of the women grabbed his hands. Finn held on tightly, and a moment later, Izzy's face appeared in the cave entrance. He couldn't see her expression very well, but he could tell her eyes were wide with wonder.

"This place is really well hidden," she said.

Finn didn't have time to reply before he felt Owen grabbing another one of the woman, and a moment later Raven appeared. Finally, Anya was pulled up, breathless and soaking wet like the rest of them, but looking very happy.

"We found it!" Anya said, excitement filling her voice.

"We did," Owen agreed. "But what is it, exactly? I can't see anything in here. It doesn't seem to be much more than a rocky hole behind a waterfall."

"*Magicae lucis*," Izzy and Raven said at the same time, then laughed. Their magic rings instantly lit up with flashlight-like beams, which they swept across the rocky space. The front portion didn't look like much, but there was indeed a tunnel.

"Come on," Finn said, pointing toward the tunnel. "If there's anything of interest in here, it'll be in that tunnel."

Anya bit her lip, looking worried. "I hope this was all worth it," she said.

"Hey, chin up, lady," Raven said, giving Anya a friendly squeeze on the shoulder. "We might find something amazing in that tunnel, and, even if we don't, at least we tried."

Finn gave Anya's shoulder a reassuring squeeze as well, and then followed Izzy's flashlight down the tunnel. It was long, narrow, and dark, and Finn was glad the wizards could light the way. He'd been so excited to climb up here that he hadn't even thought to bring an actual flashlight. Finn felt like they were walking forever, but in reality it was probably only about a minute before Izzy gave a shout. Finn wasn't quite sure whether her shout had been one of excitement or terror, but he rushed forward to see what she was looking at and rushed right into a gigantic, open room. What he saw in that room rendered him speechless.

By the light of Izzy's ring, he could see the outline of a dragon skeleton. The bones must have been here for centuries, undisturbed except perhaps by Anya's father and whomever it was that had told Anya's father about this place. On the wall behind the dragon skeleton, someone had etched some writing into the wall. And in the dragon's bony skeleton claws, a giant amethyst rested.

"What in the world…" Owen said as he came into the room. Raven's light also fell on the shimmering purple stone and the dragon skeleton. For a moment, no one spoke or moved. Finally, Anya broke the silence.

"Is that…is that the dragon amethyst?" she asked.

"I would think so," Owen said. "Finn, can you read what's written on the wall? It's in an old dragon dialect. You're better at reading those then I am."

Finn walked over to the wall and squinted his eyes at the ancient characters etched into the stone. By the light of Izzy's ring, he slowly read and translated the message.

"Here lies Cyril, the noble dragon king, may he rest in peace. And may his powers, held in this noble dragon amethyst, remain untouched by evil hands for as long as those who are good still walk the earth."

"It's true, then," Raven said, her voice barely more than a whisper. "This is the dragon amethyst. We found it. We actually found it."

Finn nodded, reaching for Anya's hand. The moment almost did not seem real. They had sought this stone for so long, and had expected to do great battles to get it. And yet, here it was, lying quietly in a cave in the middle of a forest, where it had been for ages.

"Are these bones from the dragon king who made the amethyst, then?" Anya asked.

"Yes," Izzy said. "I don't know how he ended up here. Perhaps the wizard who helped him with the stone brought him here to die in peace. He would have been weak, with all his powers gone and his enemies torturing him. But it appears that, at least, he was able to die with dignity. May he rest in peace."

"Should we try to move him?" Owen asked, looking over at Finn. "Bury him, perhaps?"

Finn shook his head. "No. I think this is as fine a burial as he could have asked for. We should leave him here, undisturbed. I hope his old bones rest easier, too, now that the amethyst will be safely in the hands of good shifters and wizards."

Finn looked over at Anya, who was staring mournfully at the bones. "Did your dad ever say anything about the man who told him of this place? I'm curious who he was, and how he knew of it."

Anya shook her head. "My dad didn't tell me much. Only that the man was one of the wisest, kindest men he ever met. There's a picture of him here in the back of the notebook, actually. His name was Wyatt, I guess. That's what's written on the picture. But there's no last name."

"Funny," Owen said, leaning over to look at the notebook, which Anya had pulled out of her jacket pocket and opened. "Finn, wasn't Wyatt your father's name?"

"Yeah," Finn said with a shrug. "But that's just coincidence. There's no way it's the same Wyatt."

"Um…" Owen said, looking at the picture then. "I wouldn't be so sure. Look at this picture. This is the spitting image of you, Finn."

Finn suddenly felt hot all over. With a feeling of slight trepidation, he leaned over to look at the picture that Anya was now holding up to Owen's face. He had no idea what his dad had looked like. He had been so young when he was orphaned, and all of his family's possessions, including photographs, had been destroyed in the war. But when he looked at the photo in Anya's hand, his heart clenched up tightly.

A man, who indeed was the spitting image of Finn, was standing in front of a giant redwood trunk, arms stretched up to the sky and a huge smile on his face. There was no denying the relation. On the back of the photo, in neat cursive, was written simply, "Good luck and all the best. Sincerely, Wyatt."

"Anya," Finn said, looking back and forth between her and the photo. His eyes were growing blurry from the tears that had started to fill them. "This…this is my father."

"Are you sure?" Anya asked, her eyes widening. "I…I can see the resemblance, now that I really look at the picture. I hadn't paid much attention to it until just now."

"It's my father, I'm sure of it," Finn said, his voice choked with emotion. "His name was Wyatt, and this picture looks exactly like me. It has to be him. I…I can't believe this. I've never seen a picture of him before. I thought any record of him was gone. Yet somehow, he knew your dad. My father knew the father of my lifemate."

Finn looked at Anya's eyes, which were filled with tears now, too. She pressed the photo he was holding against his chest. "You take it," she said. "Keep it. It's yours."

Finn nodded, then pulled her in close. He didn't care that everyone was standing right there watching, he closed his mouth over hers, kissing the girl who had been connected to him for decades, without their even knowing it.

When Finn pulled back from Anya, he saw Izzy walking gingerly over and picking up the dragon amethyst. She looked at it with reverence, and then smiled up at the rest of the group.

"It seems like this stone is truly magical," she said. "It's been working its magic here for a long time, and it brought us here together. This is a good sign. The war is turning. Good will prevail in the end. I can feel it in my bones."

Finn wiped at his eyes and smiled. "Wait 'till Peter and Knox hear about this," he said, grinning at Anya. "Maybe Peter will finally have to admit that the laws about memory wiping need to be changed. It would have been disastrous if we'd wiped your memory."

"I dunno," Izzy said with a grin on her face, too. "I agree that the memory wiping laws need to change. But I think that you and Anya would have still found each other regardless of whether your memories had been wiped. Destiny obviously wants you two together."

"Fine by me," Finn said, sweeping Anya in for another kiss.

"Alright, lovebirds," Owen piped in. "That's sweet and all, but save the kissing for later. We need to get this stone out of here and to safety. I suggest we take it out of here and then fly it back to the Redwood Dragons base camp. That's not too far from here, and once we're there we'll be able to contact Knox and Peter and see where they want the stone."

"Good idea," Finn said, his heart swelling with happiness as he held Anya tight. "Come on, Anya. I'm going to show you my home."

CHAPTER SIXTEEN

The sky was dark by the time the dragon amethyst search party approached the Redwood Dragons' base camp. This had been easy enough to arrange, given how long it had taken to get the dragon amethyst out of the cave, and how long it took to fly home from the northern redwoods. The group would have waited for darkness anyway, though. They worried that Saul was watching the area near the Redwood Dragons' cabins, and they did not want to have to fight another battle right now. They were tired, and ready for some well-deserved rest. Luckily, their invisibility shields and chameleon tricks worked extra well in the darkness, and the trip was as uneventful as they could have hoped for. The most exciting part was when they reached the spot near the cabins where they needed to descend into the forest.

"Hold on tight," Izzy said over her shoulder, giving Anya just enough warning to grab onto Izzy tightly before Izzy pointed her broomstick straight down and started zooming toward the treetops at full speed. Anya squeezed her eyes shut, sure that they were going to crash into the thick branches. But Izzy managed to expertly maneuver through the obstacles and land safely in a small clearing with no more than a small thud. Anya stumbled off the broomstick, dizzy and disoriented, but Izzy seemed completely stable as she gently swung off herself. A rush of wind passed by Anya's ear, then, and seconds later she saw Finn's dragon come into view as he dropped his chameleon-like disguise. A few seconds after that, she heard another hiss as Raven ended the invisibility spell that had been disguising her and Owen. The whole group had landed safely.

"Welcome to the Redwood Dragons lair," Owen said to no one in particular as he jumped off Raven's broomstick, clearly excited to be home. A rush of energy rang out, and the dragon that had been Finn began to morph back into human form. Anya started sliding the backpack she was wearing off her back, knowing that he'd be naked and wanting clothes once his transformation was complete.

She strained her eyes to see, but wasn't able to make out much of anything in the darkness. There was no moon tonight, and the forest here was thick and dark. While her eyes were still adjusting to the darkness of the forest floor, she heard a shout of excitement from somewhere over her left shoulder. Startled, she turned to look and saw that two men who were very tall and just as muscular as Owen and Finn were coming crashing through the trees, swinging flashlights.

"What the hell, guys!" one of the men said, but his tone was jolly. "We had no idea you were coming here tonight. For a minute there I thought we were about to be attacked by Saul's stupid army again."

"Vance!" Owen said to the man, then pulled him into a big bear hug.

"And Grayson!" Finn said to the other man, turning to give him a hearty slap on the back as well.

The next half hour was a flurry of talking. Anya was introduced to the dragon shifters who were guarding the Redwood Dragons' base. In addition to Vance and Grayson, there were Holden and Weston. There was also Vance's lifemate, a friendly wizard named Lily. Several other wizards from Falcon Cross were here to help guard the camp, and Anya's head was soon spinning from the introductions, and from the noise of everyone talking at once as they explained to the Redwood Dragons how the dragon amethyst had been found. Anya wasn't sure she had ever seen a more excited group of people. As soon as he'd heard the story, Vance went to call Peter and Knox. Not long after, he came back with the news that Peter was sending a large group of wizard soldiers from Falcon Cross to assist with transferring the dragon amethyst to Texas, where the shifter protectors were already guarding the dragon emerald and dragon sapphire. Peter also extended a personal invitation to Anya to come to Falcon Cross as an honored guest. Anya wasn't exactly keen on visiting the town of the wizard who'd wanted to wipe her memory, but she said nothing to the others. She didn't want to offend Izzy and Raven.

Finn guessed at the meaning behind her hesitation, though. Not long after, the whole group was sitting around a firepit and enjoying freshly barbequed food. Anya was savoring the hot meal after weeks of surviving on wilderness cooking and meal bars. She had just bitten into a juicy burger when Finn crossed his arms and looked at her with a raised eyebrow.

"You're not really thinking of declining an invitation to be the guest of one of the most powerful wizards alive, are you?" he asked. "It's a great honor."

"The man tried to wipe my memory," Anya protested around a mouthful of burger.

"And I'm pretty sure he realizes now that he was very wrong to even think of that," Finn said. "Give him a chance to say he's sorry. And go see Falcon Cross. It's a really cool place. It's not every day you get to see a wizarding town."

Anya grunted noncommittally, but she knew Finn was right. She should go. Peter could not question her loyalty now that she'd found the dragon amethyst. But thinking of going to Falcon Cross brought up a bigger question for her. Where would she live now? She wanted to be with Finn, but she had a feeling he wouldn't want to go live in a fully human town in Idaho. She didn't really feel at home there herself. And now that she knew that dragons and wizards existed, how could she ever hope to go back to living as if they didn't?

"And what about you?" Anya asked, meeting Finn's deep green eyes. "Are you going back to Falcon Cross?"

He understood what she meant by the question, and smiled. "If you go to Falcon Cross, I'm going with you," he said. "And I do have some unfinished business there to take care of. But my heart is here, in the redwoods. I'm planning to come back to my cabin here as soon as possible. And when I do, I'd love to have my beautiful lifemate join me in that cabin. I know you love the outdoors, Anya. This is a beautiful place to live, and there's no shortage of plants for you to explore."

Anya smiled, her heart filling with joy. "I think I'd be really happy here," she said, looking up at the dark night shadows of the trees that towered above them. "And hopefully now that the dragon amethyst is found, your clan can live in peace here."

"I hope so," Finn said, but he sounded wary. "The war isn't over yet, though. Finding the dragon amethyst gives us a huge advantage, but we still have to find the dragon ruby before we're completely safe. Peter might want my help with that, too."

Anya nodded. "I guess I'd expected as much. Seems there will be more adventures ahead then, huh?"

Finn laughed. "Well, regardless of whether we're sent to search for the dragon ruby or not, I have a feeling that life is going to be one giant adventure from now on. I've done a lot of crazy things in my life, but being with you is my biggest, best adventure yet. I can't wait to see what the future holds. Our pasts are connected, Anya. I know that means our future is going to be incredible."

"I couldn't agree more," Anya said, smiling happily as she took another bite of her burger. Finn reached over to squeeze her hand, and the familiar warmth of his body flooded through her. She knew the road ahead of them still held challenges, but they would face them together, and that was all that mattered. Right now, she just wanted to relax and enjoy the good food and good company. Spirits were high around the campfire. The dragon amethyst was theirs, and they all knew that this was the beginning of the end for Saul.

Later that night, when Anya slipped into Finn's cabin with him, she was exhausted, but happy. After he shut the door behind them, he dug in his bag for a moment until he found the photo of his father that Anya had given him. Without a word, he went and hung it on the refrigerator door. His eyes glistened with tears as he stepped back to hold Anya's hand. It was strange to see such a big, tough guy on the verge of crying, but Anya appreciated that he was comfortable enough with his emotions not to hide them completely. And he had a right to feel emotional. This was, after all, the only link he had to the father he never knew.

Without a word, Anya went and found the picture of her in front of the dragon claw falls—the one her dad had taken so long ago. She hung the picture up by the picture of Finn's dad and smiled. The two old photos fit well together.

"I think our dads would have been really happy to see us together," Anya said.

Finn smiled. "I think so, too. I wonder if they knew, somehow, that fate would bring us together."

Anya took Finn's hand again, and he pulled her into his arms.

"I like to think they knew," Anya said. "And I like to think that, if there is a heaven, they're both up there sharing a beer and looking down on us right now."

Finn held her tighter. "I like to think that, too," he said.

His arms fit perfectly around Anya, warming her. She looked up at the pictures on the refrigerator, and, for the first time in a long time, she felt like she was home.

BOOK SIX: ESCAPE AND THE DRAGON

CHAPTER ONE

"Shh!" Owen Pars said, holding his finger over his lips and trying to appear stern while he looked over at the dark-haired silhouette sitting a few feet away from him. But his warning only made Raven chuckle harder. Her shoulders shook with laughter, and her giggles came out in odd sounding snorts as she tried to stifle them with her hands. Owen could hardly keep from laughing himself as he watched her.

"Don't make jokes like that if you don't want me to laugh," she whispered when she finally regained enough control to speak. "You're the one over here doing ridiculous impressions of people. Have you ever thought about becoming a standup comedian after the war's over? You'd be hella good at it."

"Hella?" Owen said, raising a playfully mocking eyebrow. "Since when do you say 'hella'? Seems you're integrating into northern California quite well."

He saw her shrug her shoulders in the darkness. "When in Rome..." she said, letting the cliché trail off without finishing it.

Owen smiled into the darkness, imagining the way Raven's eyes must be sparkling with merriment right now. Even his sharp dragon eyes couldn't see through the inky blackness inside the cabin, though. The windows all had shades drawn over them, blocking out what little moonlight might be filtering down through the redwoods and into the small clearing where the Redwood Dragons Clan lived.

"You shouldn't be here," Owen said. "Vance would kill me if he knew that you were in here distracting me from my job."

Raven snorted again. "There's not much to distract you from. You don't really have to watch things that closely right now, you know? This cabin is surrounded by wizards, and there are two dragon shifter guards watching over the whole base camp itself. If anyone is going to try to break in here and steal the amethyst, you'll know they're coming long before they get here."

"I suppose so," Owen said. "But then how did you get in here without them seeing you?"

"I snuck in earlier, before they closed and locked the door of the cabin. No one paid much attention to me then because they thought I was just another part of the crew guarding the place."

"No one ever suspects you of anything, Raven," Owen said. "That makes you pretty dangerous."

"Ah, well, that must be why you hang out with me," Raven teased. "You like living on the edge."

"I never said I *like* hanging out with you. I only tolerate you because I'm a nice guy."

Raven snorted loudly again. "Hah! Now I know you're lying. No one's ever accused you of being a nice guy."

Owen shushed Raven again, and swiped at her in the darkness, trying to playfully punch her in the arm. She somehow managed to see that he was coming and wiggle out of his way. This, of course, triggered a fresh wave of laughter from her.

455

Owen rolled his eyes, but couldn't help but smile. If he had one guilty pleasure in his life right now, it was flirting with Raven. The woman drove him crazy, but in a good way. She was one of the few wizards who did not seem frightened by the fact that he was a dragon shifter, and she was one of the only women he'd ever met who could match his sarcastic wit strike for strike. He had spent a lot of time with her over the last several months as they searched for the powerful dragon amethyst. Sometimes, they argued like cats and dogs, but at the end of the day they always made up. They "got" each other, and Owen had never met another woman he could truly say that about. In another life, he might have tried to convince Raven to be his lifemate.

But they weren't in another life. They were in this life, the only life they had, and the life they were fighting desperately to save from the enemy's ever advancing evil army. Owen didn't have time for romance, and he didn't think it was appropriate to romance a fellow soldier, despite the fact that many of his clan members had done so.

Owen took in a deep breath and let it out in a long sigh as Raven's laughter finally died down. For a few minutes, they were both quiet, and he sat in the comfortable silence with her, thinking of what strange events had brought him to this point in his life, where he sat in a dark room with a beautiful wizard, guarding a giant amethyst.

Owen had lived out here in the Redwoods for as long as he could remember. He was one of ten dragon shifters in the Redwood Dragons clan, all of whom had been rescued after they were orphaned in the last great shifter war. William, the dragon shifter who had rescued them, had led the clan for several decades, but had now retired to a simpler life in Texas. Ironically enough, Knox, who was the dragon shifter currently in charge of the Redwood Dragons, was in Texas right now, too. Knox was helping a group of shifter protectors in Texas to guard two of the dragon stones—the dragon emerald and dragon sapphire. The dragon amethyst, the stone Owen was currently guarding, would be heading to Texas tomorrow evening, once a large group of wizard soldiers from Falcon Cross arrived to escort it over. The dragon stones were powerful, ancient artifacts that held the powers of four ancient dragon kings. Now that the amethyst had been found, the only missing stone was the dragon ruby. If the ruby could be found by the good shifters and wizards, then their enemy Saul would have no hope of taking over the world for evil, as he was trying to do.

"It kind of sucks, doesn't it?" Raven asked, breaking into his thoughts. "We should be allowed to go with the soldiers who are escorting the amethyst back to Texas. After all, we found it."

"Sort of," Owen said. "Anya is the one who really found it."

Anya was the lifemate of Owen's clanmate, Finn. Anya had figured out where the dragon amethyst was hidden, and together with a small search team that included Owen and Raven, she'd recovered the stone.

"Details, details," Raven said. "Our search team found the amethyst. That means we should get to take it to Texas."

Owen shrugged. "I guess so. But, honestly, aren't you tired of traveling around, anyway? I'm actually a bit relieved that Peter is sending other soldiers to take care of transferring the amethyst. We get to stay here in the redwoods for a bit and eat real food every meal. Not to mention we get to sleep in a real bed."

"You're not sleeping in a real bed right now," Raven pointed out.

Owen rolled his eyes. "No, but I will be tomorrow night, once the amethyst is gone and someone else is guarding it."

Raven made a hmph sound. "You're getting soft in your old age, Owen," she said. "Since when would you rather sit in the comfort of your own cabin than take on a mission?"

"My old age?" Owen asked, laughing. "I'm pretty sure you're the same age as me, so if I'm old, then you're ancient, too."

"Nonsense," Raven said. "I'm timeless."

Owen opened his mouth to make another sarcastic remark, but he never had the chance to get the words out. A sudden, loud roar from outside stopped him before he could speak. He looked at Raven in horror, and, even though he couldn't see her expression in the darkness, he was sure her expression mirrored his own. For one long second after the warning roar had sounded off, everything was silent. And then, all chaos broke loose.

The sharp zing of laser beams cutting through the air was so loud that it could have been heard for miles. Voices screamed mostly unintelligible words as the attacking wizards sent off spell after spell from their magic rings. Curses from the good wizards and shifters filled the air as they began to fight, trying to overcome the surprise of an attack that they'd had virtually no warning was coming. Huge pops of energy exploded through the air as the dragon shifters began to shift into dragon form. Owen himself began shifting, his clothes tearing off into dozens of shreds as his human body transformed into the larger, fearsome body of a dragon. He glanced at the small chest in the middle of the cabin, which held the dragon amethyst. He had been charged with protecting the stone, and he would fight to the death to keep it safe. Saul's army could not be allowed to take possession of it.

Saul's army, Owen thought in confusion as he scooted his dragon belly so it covered the chest where the amethyst was held. How did Saul's army know we had the amethyst? Surely, that's why they're attacking. But we arrived here less than twelve hours ago. How did they already assemble an army? Were they waiting for us? And how did they see us coming in through our invisibility shields?

Owen had so many questions, but there was no time to think about answers right now. The main priority had to be protecting the dragon amethyst. Next to his giant dragon form, he saw Raven stepping forward, holding her right hand high in the air. The hand was balled into a fist, and her magic ring was glowing slightly. All traces of laughter were gone from her face as she prepared to fight.

"*Magicae arma!*" she yelled out. Nothing visibly changed in the room, but Owen knew enough about wizards and magic to know that Raven had just cast a shield spell around them. The spell would help hold off attackers, but only for so long. There had been shields around the entirety of the dragons' base camp, and clearly those shields had been penetrated. The enemy's dark magic was growing stronger, allowing them to break through even the most robust of shields. And, it seemed, the enemy was able to easily see through the invisibility shields that Owen's wizard friends had been using. Owen growled, a low, frustrated rumble rising in his dragon throat. He didn't even know why they bothered to put up invisibility shields anymore.

Outside, the sounds of battle grew louder. Owen wished he could be outside, breathing streams of fire onto the attackers and showing them what happened to evil bastards who dared attack his clan's cabins. But he forced himself to stay still and quiet. He breathed in and out in slow, methodical movements. His place was here, in front of the dragon amethyst, keeping it safe. He wished that he knew how to use the amethyst's powers. There had been no plans made to use its powers, since the leaders of the dragon and wizard clans thought it best to keep the stone hidden and unused as much as possible. But, surely, this situation was an exception. If the stone's powers had to be used to keep it out of the hands of the enemy, then Owen figured his leaders would understand. The only problem was that Owen wasn't sure how, exactly, to activate those powers.

The noise outside was deafening, but Owen and Raven held their ground, silent and waiting. Shrieks of pain filled the air, and Owen could only hope and pray that none of those shrieks belonged to someone he loved. He glanced at Raven, but could not see the expression on her face in the darkness. She was wearing her Falcon Cross military uniform, which kept the lines of her silhouette crisp and smooth. Owen's heart clenched up a bit as he looked at her. If the battle made it into this room, that would mean that things were going very poorly for the Redwood Dragons and their wizard friends. And it would mean that he and Raven were in mortal danger. Despite the fact that he'd watched Raven face plenty of mortal dangers in the time he'd known her, he couldn't keep himself from feeling fear at the thought of losing her. A low growl rumbled up from his belly, and his whole body tensed as he waited, knowing that at any moment he might be called upon to defend both the amethyst and Raven.

"Easy, dragon," Raven's voice said softly, cutting through the tension in the air and wrapping around his heart like a soothing embrace. "You'll get your chance to fight."

Owen's dragon lips curled up in a smile. She thought his growl was an impatient desire to fight. Which was no surprise since, ordinarily, Owen loved a good battle. But right now, his growl was a frustrated one. He wanted her safe. He wanted the amethyst safe. And damn it, he wanted one night where he could relax and didn't have to shift and fight. Just one night. Was that too much to ask? This constant battling was getting old.

The shrieks of pain grew louder, and Owen could smell the acrid scent of smoke filling the air. More than likely, one of the cabins was burning. Perhaps more than one. He just hoped that the cabin he was in right now did not catch fire. The heat in the small room was increasing, but the smell of smoke was not close enough for this cabin to be the one that was burning. The air in the room hung heavy and stagnant, and still he waited.

The fifteen minutes he spent in there, motionless with Raven by his side, felt like an eternity. Owen was a man suspended in time, waiting for the clock to start ticking again. He felt removed from the battle raging beyond the walls of the cabin. He heard the fighting but it did not reach him. It could not touch him.

And then, the door to the room he was in opened, and reality came rushing back. He aimed his dragon mouth toward the doorway, ready to let out a long stream of fire, but Raven yelled at him.

"Wait!" she said. "It's one of ours."

A moment later, a sharp hissing noise filled the room as another woman's voice called out, "*Invisibilia terminantur.*"

The invisibility shield that had been surrounding the intruder fell away, and Owen saw Lily, the wizard lifemate of his clanmate Vance, standing in the room. Her hair was a sooty mess, and her clothes were torn and burned in several spots. Deep scratches covered her face and arms, but none of the injuries looked life-threatening. She looked at Raven in surprise, but did not comment or ask why Raven was with Owen and the amethyst. There was no time for explanations right now. Instead, Lily turned to look at Owen, speaking to his dragon in a hurried tone.

"You have to get out of here, and take the amethyst with you," she said, panting for breath as she spoke. "We're far outnumbered and losing the battle. Vance says it won't be much longer until we're forced to retreat."

Owen felt like he had just been punched in the gut. The thought of Saul's army taking over his home made his skin crawl. He wanted to roar in anger, and rush out to meet the attackers with a fresh wall of fire, burning as many of them as possible. But he forced himself to hold still and wait as Lily continued to speak.

"Vance is going to make a big show of retreating, leading everyone north away from the cabins. When he does, you need to fly as fast as you can in the opposite direction, taking the dragon amethyst with you. Keep yourself hidden using your chameleon skills as best you can, and fly as far and as fast as you can away from here. When you're sure you're not being followed, stop and contact Falcon Cross. They'll be able to send help."

Owen slowly shook his head no. This was madness. He was only one dragon. If Saul's army found him alone, there was no way he would be able to defend himself against them and keep his hold on the dragon amethyst.

"We have no other choice," Lily said when she saw him shaking his head. "These are Vance's orders! You have to follow them. The enemy is too strong, and even if we retreat they might catch us and overpower us. No one here knows how to use the dragon amethyst, so we can't rely on it for protection. And if they take it from us, all our efforts to find it will have been in vain. You have to go, now! Our best hope is for you to escape with the amethyst without them realizing it."

Owen started to shake his head again, but then a large howl of pain went up from just outside the cabin, and he saw, through the doorway Lily had just entered, that the front door of the cabin was splintering. The enemy was breaking in. They were running out of time. Lily looked back, panic filling her eyes.

"I'll hold them off as long as I can," she said. "Now *go!*"

Lily ran toward the front of the cabin without waiting for an answer, jumping over the piles of assorted supplies that the Redwood Dragons kept in here. This cabin had been used as a supply shed of sorts for a long time, but it looked like they were about to lose all of their supplies. Heck, it looked like they were about to lose all of their cabins, for that matter. Owen took a deep breath, forcing down the anger that filled him, and told himself to concentrate on the task at hand. Vance had ordered him to escape with the dragon amethyst, and Vance was in command of the dragons' base camp right now. Owen had no choice but to follow his orders. He looked up at the ceiling, trying to gauge how best to burn a hole in it so that his dragon could escape.

"I'm going with you," Raven said. He looked over at her to find her standing there with her hands on her hips. For a moment, he wanted to protest. Vance's orders had been for him, and the road ahead of him might be very dangerous. It's possible he would die trying to escape from Saul's men. Then again, it sounded like staying here was going to be quite dangerous as well. And if he and Raven were going to die, it would be a comfort for them to die together, at least. Besides, having a wizard along who could help him fight might not be such a bad thing.

Owen smiled a dragon smile at Raven, and nodded his assent. Then he turned to look back at the ceiling, ready to burn it down. But Raven held up her hand to stop him.

"Allow me," she said. "Stand as flat against the wall as you can. The ceiling's going to cave in once I cast this spell."

Owen tried to flatten himself against the wall, but it wasn't much use. His dragon form was too large to get out of the way, so he just braced himself and gave a small nod to Raven. She flattened herself against the wall and raised her magic ring in the direction of the ceiling, then began casting spells.

"*Magicae invisibilia. Magicae disseco,*" she yelled out.

The first spell Owen easily recognized as an invisibility spell. She was casting it over the roof in hopes that Saul's men would not notice that the cabin was being destroyed from the inside out. The second spell Owen had never heard before, but it seemed to be some sort of cutting spell. Raven moved her hand in a large circle as she pointed her ring toward the ceiling, and some sort of energy seemed to emanate from her ring, slicing right through the cabin's thick wooden roof. Within moments, a giant circle of the ceiling came crashing down around them, splintering as it hit Owen's dragon back. The crash only added to the noise coming from the front room of the cabin, where Lily and several other wizards were in a heated battle with several of Saul's soldiers. Raven's invisibility shield must be working, though, at least for the moment, because none of the soldier's in the front room seemed to notice Owen, Raven, and the amethyst—or the fact that the roof back here had just caved in.

"There aren't any broomsticks in here, so I'll ride on your back," Raven yelled, running to scoop up the giant amethyst. She tucked the large stone securely into the front pocket of her uniform, and then ran over to jump on Owen's back. She raised her ring and cast several invisibility and shield spells, and then wrapped her arms as best she could around the base of his thick dragon neck.

"Alright, I've done all I can," she yelled through the smoky chaos. "Hopefully those shields will hold us at least until we get beyond the view of Saul's army. Use your chameleon skills, too, just in case."

Owen nodded. He had the ability to change his dragon form to match his surroundings, camouflaging himself in much the same way a chameleon would. It was difficult to maintain this type of camouflage while flying, but he would do his best. Hopefully, between his chameleon skills and Raven's invisibility shields, they would be able to get out of here unnoticed.

Owen glanced over at Lily, who sensed that they were ready to go. She paused for a moment and raised her magic ring to send thousands of sparks into the air. This must have been some sort of signal that she and Vance had agreed upon, because moments after the sparks started flying, Owen heard Vance roaring loudly, calling for a retreat.

More chaos ensued as the dragons and good wizards started flying after Vance, due north. A roar of triumph went up from some of Saul's soldiers, and they began pursuing the retreating army. The wizards who had been fighting Lily in the front of the cabin cheered, and abandoned Lily to join in the excitement of the chase. Owen took a deep breath, trying to steady his rapidly beating heart. It was now or never.

He pushed off his hind legs, springing as high into the air as he could through the giant hole in the cabin's roof. As soon as the momentum of his jump had pushed his wings past the hole, he began flapping furiously. He turned his face toward the south, catching only a small glimpse of Vance, the retreating army, and the dragons' base camp. But that small glimpse was enough to tear at his heart.

Nearly all eleven of the Redwood Dragons' cabins were up in flames. Several of the redwood trees that surrounded the cabin were burning as well. Dead bodies were strewn across the open space between the cabins, and, while Owen could not tell from up here whom the bodies belonged to, he knew that many of them were Falcon Cross wizards. He could see the telltale black and gold of their military uniforms by the light of the flames that were burning his beloved home base to the ground.

Owen's stomach turned as he realized that his boyhood home, the place he had grown up, had been destroyed and was being overtaken by the most evil soldiers he'd ever encountered. Every fiber of his being filled with anger, and he wanted nothing more than to turn around and burn as many of them to a crisp as he could. But he forced himself to keep his eyes trained on the dark, southern horizon. The dragon amethyst was more important than revenge right now. He had to do his best to keep it safe.

He could feel the weight of Raven's body on his back, and her arms squeezing comfortably around his neck. Her presence soothed him, and he was glad in that moment that she had snuck in tonight to see him during his guard duty. Maybe, just maybe, the two of them working together could figure out a way to get the amethyst to safety.

Owen nearly laughed as he realized that Raven had gotten what she wanted, after all. She was going to be part of the team escorting the dragon amethyst to Texas, and, so was he—whether he liked it or not.

Let's do this, he thought with a sigh, pumping his wings as quickly as he could and slicing through the air in the opposite direction of the only home he'd ever known.

CHAPTER TWO

Raven's muscles ached, and every cell in her body tried to seduce her into closing her eyes and sleeping. But she ignored the aches, and fought to stay awake. She sat upright on Owen's dragon now, looking all around them as he moved steadily through the sky. She was watching for anything suspicious, but there was no sign of any enemy soldiers in the sky. As far as she could tell, their escape had been successful. Saul's soldiers had been so excited to see Vance's retreat that they hadn't noticed the chameleon dragon and invisible wizard rising into the sky.

The thought of Vance and his retreat filled Raven with sadness. She knew the retreating group would have flown as quickly as they could toward Falcon Cross, where reinforcements would be ready and waiting to help them hold back Saul's army. But Falcon Cross was a long ways from the Redwood Dragons' base camp, and Vance's army would have been exhausted and weak. She didn't want to think about what would happen if Saul's soldiers managed to overtake them, but she couldn't keep her mind from wandering in all sorts of horrible directions. Her only hope was knowing that Saul's soldiers had never been as good at flying as the Falcon Cross wizards or the Redwood Dragons. Hopefully, Vance and his army had been able to keep up their pace long enough for Saul's men to lose them. Raven knew Saul's soldiers would stay on their trail all the way to Falcon Cross, but if they lagged behind just enough, Vance would make it. He had to make it. There were too many people Raven cared about in that army. She couldn't bear the thought of them falling into the hands of dark wizards and evil shifters.

The first gray light of dawn was beginning to streak over the horizon, pushing back the darkness of one of the longest nights of Raven's life. She watched the ground below them with interest. She had no idea where they were, but she knew that they were quite far from the redwoods. Owen had flown with lightning speed, and the scenery below her looked nothing like the lush green of a redwood forest. Everything was dry, rocky, and sandy. The only plants were the small, dry shrubs typical of desert climates. And even though the sun itself had not yet peeked over the gray horizon, the air felt almost unbearably hot.

As the sky continued to lighten, and the pinkish orange sun finally made its way into view, Raven could see that there was some sort of small town ahead. It appeared like a small oasis in the middle of the desert, with one long highway stretching away from it in either direction. She felt Owen adjusting his direction slightly, and heading for the town. She could tell that he was tired as well. His pace had slowed quite a bit from when they first left the redwoods last night, and the flapping of his wings was gradually growing weaker and weaker. He was using the last of his energy to get them to the little town.

But what then? Raven thought. They had no supplies, and no money. Owen didn't even have clothes. All they had was the dragon amethyst and each other. Raven smiled at the thought, despite her weariness. Each other. If she had to be in as precarious of a position as she was right now, there was no one she'd rather have with her than Owen.

He'd been her favorite dragon since the very first day a group of the Redwood Dragons had arrived in her hometown of Falcon Cross. He was just as stubborn and witty as she was, and she'd known from day one that they were going to be great friends.

What she hadn't known, though, was how her heart would fall for him. In retrospect, perhaps she should have seen it coming. After all, he was as handsome, muscular, and noble as they came. He could be obnoxious and strong willed, sure, but that only made Raven love him more. She hated it when a man acted all wishy-washy and weak. She'd take a fighter over a peacemaker any day. The only problem, of course, was that Owen was a fighter, as was she, and that meant that they were spending all of their time these days fighting against Saul's army. There was no time for romance, or exploring feelings for each other. All their energy had been focused on one thing and one thing only: bringing an end to Saul and his regime of evil.

Owen was getting closer to the small town now, and descending as he did. Raven finally allowed herself to lie down on his back for a moment to rest, although she would not close her eyes for fear of falling asleep. She let herself enjoy the way Owen's strong dragon back moved beneath her, gently rolling her side to side as his wings made their final efforts of the night. He landed with a soft thud just as the sun finally broke over the horizon in all its fullness. Next to him was a small cluster of rocks which would offer some shade, which Raven could already tell would be a necessity as the sun rose higher and higher into the sky.

Owen lay down on his belly to allow Raven to slide off his back. Once she her feet were on the ground and she had taken several steps back from him, he began to shift. A rush of energy pushed her backwards a bit as his transformation began, but she did not fall. She knew enough by now to brace herself whenever one of the dragons was shifting. She didn't pay much attention to the change as Owen's body began to lose its dragon shape and return to its muscular human form. She was digging in the pocket of her shirt, double-checking to make sure that the dragon amethyst was still there, safe and secure. She knew that it was, and yet, it made her feel better to see it with her own eyes. She stared down at the shimmering purple stone, and sighed. So much trouble, for such a seemingly ordinary gemstone.

Owen had completely returned to human form now, and she looked up at him to see that his eyes were as tired as her own. He was completely naked, of course, but this did not faze her. She'd seen many of the dragon shifters naked numerous times, since they lost their clothes every time they morphed into dragon form. She had to admit, though, that she always noted with satisfaction that Owen had the largest dick of them all. They were all huge, but he seemed just a bit huger. Not that it mattered. She had no claim to him. Still, he was her favorite, so she liked seeing that he was the "best."

"Any idea where we are?" she asked, closing the pocket the amethyst was in and forcing her thoughts away from his dick.

Owen rubbed at his tired face with open palms. "Somewhere in Nevada, I'd guess," he said. "But I have no way of knowing for sure."

"We'll have to get supplies," Raven said, her voice flat. Owen nodded, his expression looking just as flat. They both knew that the only way they were going to be able to get supplies right now was to steal, and neither one of them relished the idea. They preferred to do things the honorable way, but since the only thing of value they had on them was an amethyst that they must keep and protect at all costs, they didn't have much of a choice.

"I suppose I'll have to do the honors," Raven said with a sigh.

Owen nodded. "Sorry, I hate to make you be the one to sneak around, but I think it's better that way. You can use invisibility spells and I can't. You know the chameleon trick only works when I'm in dragon form. And I'm naked, which you might not mind so much but I have a feeling that anyone who caught me would be pretty upset to find a random naked man slinking around."

Raven couldn't resist a smile. "Hey now, don't get so cocky. What makes you think that *I* don't mind seeing you naked?"

Owen smirked and thrust his hips forward, accenting what lay between his legs. "You've never complained before."

Raven just rolled her eyes at him, but her smile broadened. It felt good to flirt with him for a moment. It made their current situation seem a bit more normal. A bit more like just another day at the job. And that was all it was, wasn't it? Just another day on the job. They'd faced challenges worse than this before. Raven hadn't had to steal for the cause before, but she was willing to bet that if any of the humans in this town knew why she needed supplies, they'd be more than happy to help her. The problem was that if she told them the truth, they would probably think she was crazy. Humans seemed to have a hard time believing that there was an evil dark wizard dragon shifter out there trying to take over the world. So, stealing it was. All Raven could do was make a note of what she took and send payment for it as soon as she was able.

"I suppose I'll go ahead and get this over with," she said, glancing toward the town. The spot where Owen had stopped looked like it was about a half mile outside the small town's borders. Not very far, but Raven was so tired right now that the thought of walking even a half mile made her groan with pain. She wished she had a broomstick so she could fly in, but she didn't, and she wasn't likely to find a broomstick of the wizard sort out here.

"Sorry you have to be the one to go," Owen said. He looked at her with a tenderness that was a bit out of character for him, and Raven felt her body heating up under his gaze. She quickly waved her hand in the air, as though waving away his concern.

"It's no big deal, really," she said. "Besides, I didn't have to do any of this. I chose to come with you last night of my own free will. I wanted to help."

Owen nodded. "Still," he said. "I know stealing isn't an easy thing, even when it is necessary for the greater good."

"Let's just call it borrowing," Raven said. "I have every intention of paying these people back."

"Well, then," Owen said with a grin. "I hope you can 'borrow' a big breakfast for me. I'm starving after all that flying. Try to find some real food. None of these gross nonperishable meal bar things we always have to eat when we're out on missions."

Raven laughed. "I'll see what I can do. Any other requests for what you'd like me to 'borrow'"?

"Some clothes would be good. A backpack, perhaps? And some basic supplies like a flashlight, water…you know the drill."

Raven nodded. "I'm on it," she said. "I'll try to figure out where we are, too. Hopefully I'll be back within a few hours."

"Alright," Owen said, settling down beneath the rocks. "I'll try not to party too hard while you're gone."

Raven rolled her eyes, and then turned toward the town. "*Magicae invisibilia*," she said, waving her ring over her head with a flourish. She felt the small rush of energy that told her she was now covered by an invisibility shield, and she started walking forward with a sigh.

"Oh, and Raven?" Owen said.

"Yes?" Raven asked as she turned back to look at him. He couldn't see her anymore and was looking slightly to her left as he spoke.

"If you need help from me, send up those sparks in the air like Lily did last night. I'll shift and come get you."

"Alright," Raven said. "Although I really hope that won't be necessary."

She glanced up at the ever-brightening sky as she began walking toward the town again. As far as she could tell, none of Saul's army had followed them. She wasn't sure she had ever hoped so badly that she was right about something.

It took her about fifteen minutes to walk the half mile, which was quite a slow pace for her. But every time she lifted her foot to take a step, she felt like she was lifting a heavy, leaden block. Her muscles protested with every movement, stiff and cold from the long night of flying. She mentally added a sleeping bag to her list of things to 'borrow.' She would have given almost anything right now for a soft spot to lie down.

Near the border of the town was a small green sign that read "Sandview, Nevada. Population 4,903." Raven had never heard of the place before, but of course this did not surprise her. It looked like it was barely enough of a town to warrant being a small dot on a map. The place was sleepy, with not much activity happening this early in the morning. Raven wondered what time it was as she walked down the quiet main street, until she saw a bank up ahead with a large clock out front. Six-thirty in the morning.

Raven took in her surroundings, trying to figure out where her best chance of finding easily accessible food and supplies would be. A small gas station on the main drag was a likely spot for food and basics like flashlights, batteries, and water bottles. But she also needed a backpack of some sort, and some clothes. She would either have to break into someone's home and search for what she needed, or find a store that sold clothes and backpacks. Somehow, stealing from a store seemed less intrusive than stealing from an individual. After all, the items in a store were up for grabs, and Raven could pay for them later, as soon as she had access to money once again. Call it a self-designed layaway, she thought. But she still felt guilty as she continued walking down the street, looking for a store that might have what she needed.

It didn't take long to find a place. A few blocks down from the bank and gas station was a store that boasted the best prices in Nevada on outdoor goods. Raven had a feeling the sign was exaggerating a bit about the prices, but it confirmed to her that they were, indeed, in Nevada. She walked up to the front door of the store, and saw that it did not open until ten a.m. With a frustrated grunt, she took a step back and looked around. She wasn't sure that breaking in was the best idea. The place might be alarmed, and, even though she was under an invisibility shield, she still needed to be careful not to do anything to raise suspicion. She couldn't open a door when someone was watching, or take items off a shelf in full view of someone. People would become alarmed if doors and objects seemed to be moving by themselves. And if she broke into a store, people would be carefully looking around for anything suspect. No, she definitely didn't want to set off any warning bells.

But she didn't want to wait until ten a.m. to start gathering supplies, either. She wanted to get back to Owen as quickly as possible so that they could start planning their next steps. Not to mention, if Owen was half as hungry as she was, he was probably anxiously waiting for some food.

Raven looked around at the deserted streets. What choice did she have, though, other than to wait? There was no one out and about now, but breaking into a store was bound to draw attention. She squinted in each direction, but the only signs of life were a few cars parked in front of a diner down the road, and one car at the gas station she'd walked past. With a resigned grunt, Raven turned to start walking toward the diner. Perhaps she could sneak some food while she waited. At least she would not be hungry, then. There wasn't much she could do about Owen.

As she started walking, though, she was suddenly startled by the sound of a man's voice. Looking to her left, she saw that he was walking down the narrow alley between the outdoor goods store and the bookstore next door. He was on his cell phone and not paying much attention to his surroundings, although Raven knew he could not see her, anyway. She watched him with curiosity, wondering where he was heading. He wore a pair of khaki pants and a black polo shirt, which looked sort of like a work uniform to her. Was he going to open one of these stores? Perhaps it would be a store with something useful for her. She flattened herself against the front window of the outdoor store to let him pass and see where he would go. A few moments later, he stopped in front of the door of the outdoor store and started fishing in his pockets. Raven's heart skipped a beat. She could hardly believe her luck when he pulled out a set of keys and started fumbling to open the front door. This was her chance. She could sneak in behind him and "shop" in relative ease with no customers or other employees in the store. She slowly tiptoed until she was right behind him, hardly able to contain her excitement as he turned the key in the door.

"Yeah, man, well, I'll have to catch you later," the man was saying. "I'm at work now. Ralph wanted me to straighten up the stock room before we open today. He suspects that our district manager is coming through in the next day or two for a surprise inspection."

There was a pause as whoever was on the other end of the phone conversation said something. During this pause, the man managed to find the correct key and open the door. He moved immediately to an electronic alarm box behind the front door and started entering a deactivation code, letting the door swing slowly shut behind him. While he was distracted by the code box, Raven quickly slipped in beside him, giving the door just a slight nudge to keep it open an extra second so she could enter the store. She held her breath and watched the man, hoping he hadn't noticed anything odd. The man paid her no mind, though. He was too distracted by his phone conversation and by entering a code into the code box. After a few more comments to the person on the other line, the man hung up and started walking toward the back room, grumbling under his breath about how he was always the one who had to come in early.

Raven waited several minutes to make sure the man had really gone, and then she started walking around the store. The place was small, but well stocked. The shelves overflowed with every sort of camping gear you could hope for. Near the front of the store, a display of brochures tempted tourists with "exciting expeditions" and "thrilling tours." Raven grabbed a few of the brochures and flipped through them, trying to get a better sense of what kind of place Owen and she had landed in. Although they were in some sort of barren desert right now, it seemed that this town was not too far from a national park that offered all sorts of hiking, camping, and various other outdoor activities. It was the end of May, and Raven suspected that the town was probably just gearing up for the busy summer ahead. Perhaps that's why the shelves here were so well stocked.

Whatever the reason, Raven wasn't complaining. She put back the brochure she'd been holding and started to get to work. The first thing she needed was some sort of backpack in which to hold all of the items she gathered. She quickly found the largest hiking backpack the store carried, and pulled it off the shelf. Its absence left a gaping hole in the display, and she winced at the sight as a fresh wave of guilt washed over her.

"It's for the greater good, remember," she told herself. "And besides, you're going to pay them for it as soon as you can."

The words did little to ease her guilty conscience, but she had no choice other than to continue. Now was not the time to hesitate. For all she knew, Saul's men might be tracking them down while she stood here in this store, seemingly safe in the middle of nowhere. This thought made Raven work quicker. She silently gathered up a large sleeping bag, flashlights, batteries, water bottles, water purification tablets, granola bars, shoes and clothes for both her and Owen, a GPS unit, and other various supplies. By the time she was done, the bag was bursting at the seams. She had a feeling that if anyone watched the security camera of the time she'd been in the store, it would look pretty funny. She kept an invisibility shield over the backpack itself, but there would be several instances of items seeming to suddenly disappear off of shelves of their own accord. With another sigh and a whispered apology to whoever owned this store, Raven swung the heavy backpack onto her back and made her way toward the front door. The man had not reset the alarm, although he had dead bolted the door. Raven looked down the street in either direction to make sure no one was close enough to notice the door opening by itself. The street was growing slowly busier, but the area near the store was clear. She quickly unlocked the deadbolt and slipped out. Then she started walking away from the store as quickly as her aching muscles would allow.

She still hadn't eaten, and her stomach growled loudly in protest. Walking was truly torture now, as her exhausted body buckled under the weight of the bag she'd stolen. She forced herself to keep moving, heading back toward the edge of town, back toward Owen. More restaurants were opening now, and a cute little café next to the bank was bustling. Raven quickly decided to risk going in and stealing some food. It would be a little tricky to grab a meal with so many people around, but Owen's words about wanting real food echoed in her mind. She wouldn't mind some real food, either.

She set the backpack down in a spot as out of the way of the sidewalk as she could find, making sure that an invisibility spell still covered it. Then, she slipped into the café doors behind the next couple that entered. She had a hard time not running into anyone, and a few times someone bumped into her and turned around to apologize, only to stare in confusion at empty space. Raven just kept moving. She made her way to the kitchen, where the cooks were whipping up omelets, bacon, breakfast potatoes, pancakes, and other goodies. Raven grabbed a large paper bag that she supposed was meant to house to-go boxes, but she didn't even bother with the boxes. She just started going down the line in the kitchen, quickly putting plate after plate into her bag, one on top of the other. The bag soon became heavy under the weight of all the plates and food, and Raven whispered "*Magicae corroboro*" under her breath to reinforce it with a strengthening spell. For a moment, no one noticed that plates were suddenly disappearing off the line into thin air. Since the bag was so close to Raven, it was covered by her invisibility spell and no one could see it. But when Raven reached for a full thermos of coffee, she pressed her luck too hard. One of the servers saw the thermos move and disappear.

"What the…" the server said. The cooks looked up then, and quickly noticed the impossibly empty serving line.

"Hey, where'd all the food go?" one of them asked.

Raven didn't stick around to see what they did next. She ran straight back into the crowded dining room, quickly pushing her way through the startled customers who were crowding around the door as they waited for a table.

"Hey!" they yelled, turning to give each other accusing looks as they tried to see who had jostled them. Then, several of them saw the front door open by itself. Raven slipped outside as quickly as she could, but stopped to turn around and watch the scene in the restaurant unfolding. The server she'd seen, as well as one of the cooks, were at the front of the restaurant now, talking to the hostess and gesturing wildly toward the kitchen. The hostess and several of the customers were pointing toward the front door, miming it opening and closing. The server and hostess quickly came to the front door and stepped outside, looking around wildly as though the perpetrator of this strange phenomenon might suddenly come into view. Raven, who stood several feet away from them unseen, held her breath and waited.

"It was the weirdest thing," the server said. "The coffee thermos just disappeared. And the food, too, it seems. And then you're sure the door opened by itself?"

"I saw it with my own eyes," the hostess said. "Do you think…"

"No," the server said emphatically. "Those are just stories. There aren't really any ghosts out in the desert here."

"But then how do you explain what just happened," the hostess said.

The server looked confused for a moment, but then shook her head and shrugged. "Probably some kids, trying to scare everyone into thinking the ghost stories are real. "Come on. Let's not give them the satisfaction of a show."

With that, the server turned around and walked back into the café. The hostess followed, but not before looking warily over her shoulder. Raven let out the breath she'd been holding, and walked to where her backpack was hidden. She swung it onto her shoulders and groaned at the weight. Pointing her ring back toward it, she whispered, "*Magicae pluma.*" Instantly, the bag became as light as a feather. Raven usually avoided spells which made things weightless. She felt it was better to always build up her muscles by bearing the weight of whatever load she was carrying. She was in the military, after all. She had to stay in shape. But right now, her pride and military ideals were taking a backseat to the exhaustion flooding through her body.

"*Magicae pluma,*" she said again, pointing her ring at the bag of food, which instantly grew lighter as well. With a happy grunt, she started walking. Cheating and using the spells just this once was no big deal. She knew the feather spells also made invisibility spells less effective, but she wasn't worried about that at the moment. She still hadn't seen any sign of Saul's army, and her invisibility shield would still work well enough against the oblivious humans in this town.

Feeling somewhat better, she picked up her pace. The sooner she got back to Owen, the sooner they could both eat. Her stomach had grown so empty that she felt nauseous at this point. She walked back by the gas station she'd passed on the way in, thankful that she already had everything she needed and didn't have to stop. She did notice, though, that someone had left the newspaper stand open. She glanced left and right, but saw no one. So she grabbed a newspaper and quickly continued on her way. It would be interesting to see what the local town considered news. Perhaps reading the *Sandview Scribe*, as it was called, would give her a better understanding of where Owen and she had landed.

She stuffed the newspaper into the bag with the food, and kept walking. It only took her about ten minutes to get back. Her pace had quickened at the promise of sitting down to rest and eat, and she used her last burst of energy to walk quickly back to Owen.

She found him asleep underneath the rock. Already, the sun was beating down mercilessly on the desert landscape, but beneath the shade of the rock it was still relatively cool. Raven sat down and began unpacking the food, careful not to make too much noise. He needed rest, and she had no intentions of waking him just to eat. If he got hungry enough, he would wake up and have some food. In the meantime, she would eat on her own.

She pulled the dishes of food out of the bag, and attempted to rearrange them so that the food, which had become quite mixed up during the walk back, looked at least somewhat organized. She made one giant, heaping plate for herself, then put the rest back into the bag to await Owen.

"*Magicae therma*," she said softly, pointing her magic ring at the food. Heat emanated from her ring and warmed the food, until it was just as piping hot as it had been when she pulled it off the line in the café's kitchen. For the next several minutes, Raven munched on bacon, eggs, breakfast potatoes, and pancakes. She wished she had some syrup, but even without it the pancakes were delicious. That café deserved its popularity. All of the food was excellent. She drank one of the disposable water bottles she'd taken from the outdoor goods store, then she found a thermos she'd grabbed and used its top as a mug to pour coffee into. The dark black liquid was strong and smooth, and between the caffeine and the food, Raven felt decently revived even though she hadn't slept all night.

Owen still slept, seemingly dead to the world. Raven watched his chest rising and falling, and, for a few moments, she allowed herself to enjoy just watching him. He looked so peaceful in his sleep, with all the worried creases that normally accompanied his waking expression smoothed away. Raven chewed her lower lip sadly, thinking about how much she would like to spend time with him just for fun, and not because they were running around trying to defeat Saul. Then again, she shouldn't complain too much. After all, she probably would have never met him if it hadn't been for this war. War, which tore so many things apart, had brought them together. Raven smiled at this thought. She supposed that, even in the midst of the worst of times, there was always good to be found.

Owen showed no signs of waking any time soon, and Raven did not feel particularly tired at the moment, so she decided to read the newspaper she had taken. Besides, it was probably best if one of them was awake and on guard, just in case. Just because she hadn't seen any signs of Saul's men didn't mean there was no danger of being found. Raven had learned during this war to never underestimate your enemy.

Raven took another sip of her coffee, then flipped open the newspaper, ready for some light reading. But the headline she saw made her blood run cold.

"You've got to be kidding me," she said. But she knew this was no joke. It was all there in black and white—plain as day, if you knew what to look for.

CHAPTER THREE

Owen blinked his eyes open, and, for a moment, felt completely disoriented. He was staring at the top of a large rock, and he felt beads of sweat all over his body despite the fact that he was fully naked. He turned his head to the right and saw a vast stretch of desert in front of him, interrupted only by a small town that looked to be about a half mile away. That's when it all came rushing back to him. The battle, the retreat, escaping with Raven and the dragon amethyst.

Raven! Where was Raven? She had gone into town to get supplies, and he had fallen asleep like an idiot, with no one standing guard over him.

He sat up quickly, nearly banging his head on a low portion of the rock he was sitting under. He saw with relief that Raven had returned. She was sitting several feet away from him, leaning against the opposite side of the small rocky wall and reading a newspaper. Her face looked pale, as though she had just seen a ghost. Next to her, he saw a large hiking backpack, and a brown paper bag that smelled suspiciously like breakfast food. His stomach growled loudly, and Raven looked up.

"Hungry?" she asked. She was smiling, but her voice sounded tired, not teasing like it normally did.

"I could definitely eat," Owen replied. "What time is it?"

"Not even nine yet," Raven said. "I haven't been back that long, actually."

"Not even nine?" Owen said. "Wow, it's really hot for being so early in the morning."

Raven nodded. "Yeah, well, you were right. We're in Nevada. In a town called Sandview, which is apparently the one oasis in a large stretch of desert. But tourists come here for the nature, which keeps the town running. And, it would seem, tourists aren't the only ones who come here. Look at this."

Raven shoved the newspaper in his direction, and he took it from her wearily. He would much rather eat than read a newspaper right now, but whatever she'd seen here she clearly thought was important. It only took him a moment to understand why. At the top of the *Sandview Scribe*, a large, bold headline read "Ghosts in Sandview: Has Dark Magic Returned?"

"What the heck?" Owen said, looking up at Raven.

"Keep reading," she said. "It's really weird, and I'm not quite sure what to make of it."

Owen's eyes returned to the page, and he read aloud slowly. "The rumors of ghosts in Sandview persist, as once again on Friday evening, the town lost power with no explanation. Not only that, but after the power was restored, several items were missing from local stores. Additionally, items continue to disappear from store shelves without explanation. Readers of the *Sandview Scribe* will remember that several 'robberies' recently have left police baffled. Items are stolen from stores, but security cameras do not show anyone taking the items. Instead, the items seem to move out of the stores by themselves. This strange phenomenon has led many to believe that ghosts are involved. Although some laugh at such an absurd suggestion, others in Sandview remember that this town has a history of paranormal activity."

Owen paused his reading and looked up at Raven with wide eyes. "Items disappearing from shelves by themselves? That sounds like someone stealing under the cover of an invisibility spell."

"I know," Raven said, gesturing toward the large backpack sitting next to her. "It sounds a lot like what I did today to get this stuff. Which makes me think…"

"There are wizards in Sandview," Owen finished for her. He felt his heart beginning to pound. This did not seem like good news. If this was a normal wizarding town, Raven would have heard of it. There weren't that many wizarding towns in North America, and Raven and the other wizards knew by heart where most of them were.

"And if there are wizards here," Raven said, answering the question Owen had before he could ask it, "Then that almost certainly means that they are Saul's wizards. No good wizards would be hiding out here, let alone stealing things, without a good reason. And as far as I know, we're the only ones with a good reason to steal things."

"But why would Saul be out here?" Owen asked. "This is the middle of nowhere. Surely, if he wants to steal from stores, there are more convenient places to do so."

Raven's face looked grim. "Keep reading," she said.

Owen turned his face back to the page. "Those who know the history of Sandview remember that several decades ago, an unexplained increase in the number of bats in nearby Sandview Canyon Caves took place. Around the same time, unexplained thefts took place at local stores, much like the recent thefts. The bats killed several townspeople, and the thefts were never explained. Many have claimed that some sort of evil spirits or ghosts were responsible for both occurrences, but, of course, no proof of ghosts has ever been found. Recently, the bats in Sandview Canyon Caves have been increasing in number once again, leading many to believe that the ghosts have returned. Keep reading the *Sandview Scribe* for updates on this developing situation."

Owen looked up at Raven again, his eyes dark. "I know why the bats are increasing," he said.

"So do I," Raven said. "I've been briefed on the history of shifter wars, and I know all about cloning bat shifters."

Owen raised an eyebrow at Raven, somewhat impressed. "I didn't know you knew that much about shifter history," he said.

Raven nodded. "When the Falcon Cross wizards and Redwood Dragons first became allies, Knox briefed the military leadership in Falcon Cross on shifter war tactics. He told us about the last dark shifter, Rocco, and how he cloned bats. Apparently, Saul knows about the cloning trick, too. At least, I'm assuming it's Saul's people out here. God forbid there's another enemy lurking that we don't know about yet."

"No, I'm sure it's Saul," Owen said. "The fact that there are wizards sneaking around under invisibility spells means that whoever is behind this is working with wizards. It has to be Saul."

Owen closed his eyes for a moment and rubbed his forehead, trying to stave off the headache that was beginning to pound behind his temples. Not long ago, an evil shifter lord named Rocco had tried to fight the Redwood Dragons and their shifter friends in Texas to gain control of the dragon emerald. Rocco had nearly succeeded, too, thanks to his large army of bat shifters. Rocco had learned how to clone bat shifters, quickly raising a giant army that was almost impossible to defeat. Thankfully, the good shifters had discovered Rocco's hideout and taken him down before he could grow his army large enough to get to the dragon emerald. But it seems that Rocco's bat cloning technique had not died with him. Saul was apparently building an army out here, quietly cloning bats which he no doubt planned to use to try to steal the dragon stones.

"I need to eat something," Owen said when he finally opened his eyes. "I can't think straight and I'm getting a headache from lack of food."

"Oh, right," Raven said. "Sorry, I got really caught up in the ghost headlines. Here, let me warm some food up for you."

Raven pulled a couple plates of food out of the brown paper bag, and assembled the food onto one giant, heaping plate. Then she pointed her magic ring at the plate and said "*Magicae therma.*"

"A warming spell," she explained, handing the food to Owen. "It will make the food taste like it's hot off the stove. And here, I have some coffee, too."

She poured some coffee into a thermos lid and handed it to Owen. The liquid was strong and piping hot, and just one sip of it did a lot to revive Owen.

"This is quite a spread," he said, feeling grateful. "How did you manage to get all this?"

Raven groaned. "Don't ask," she said. "It wasn't the smoothest operation ever, and I think I perpetuated the ghost rumors in the process."

Owen laughed, but then they both were silent for a few minutes as he ate hungrily and Raven took the newspaper back to read over the article again.

"If this is true, then we're in a lot of danger," she finally said. "We should get away from here as quickly as we can, before they realize we're here. The last thing we want is to have to fight a huge army of bat shifters to keep the dragon amethyst safe."

"I'm not so sure about that," Owen said as he slowly chewed on a crispy slice of bacon. "It might be good to stay here for a bit and spy on Saul's operations. He must not think any of us know about the bats. That's why he's cloning them out here in the middle of nowhere. If we can spy on him, maybe we can figure out a way to sabotage his cloning efforts."

Raven looked at him like he was out of his mind. "Are you insane?" she asked. "You know his dark wizards can overcome my invisibility spells. We're out here by ourselves, just the two of us, against who knows how many dozens or even hundreds of wizards—not to mention hundreds of bat shifters. If we don't get out of here before they find us, we're doomed."

"But they're not going to find us," Owen said, his voice growing excited as he spoke. "Don't you see, Raven? They can break through your invisibility spells, yes, but they have to do so on purpose. They don't suspect that any of us are out here, so it's unlikely they're spending much time going around trying to break invisibility spells just in case. As long as we don't give them any reason to suspect anything, we can stay here undetected and spy on them. We might get some truly valuable information!"

"No way," Raven said. "One false move, just one wizard suspecting something, and they'll break through my spells in a heartbeat. We'll be toast."

"So we won't give them a reason to suspect anything," Owen said. "This is the perfect opportunity to sabotage Saul's efforts in a big way. And it's a damn good way to get back at them for what they did to my home last night."

"I agree that they deserve vengeance for what they did to your home," Raven said, crossing her arms. "But this is not the way to get vengeance. We were given one, important job: get the dragon amethyst to the shifter protectors in Texas. We need to stick to that job and not get sidetracked."

"No, *I* was given the job," Owen said. "You tagged along on this mission uninvited. Which is fine, but since it was my mission, I think I should get to make the rules."

As soon as the words were out of his mouth, Owen knew they were a mistake. Raven's eyes flashed with anger.

"Really? You think you would have been better off on your own or something? May I remind you that I'm the one who went into town and got all of this stuff for us? I'm the one who is keeping us under an invisibility spell right now. You wouldn't even have clothes without me! Speaking of which, why don't you put some clothes on and cover up that obnoxious dick of yours. Just because you're a shifter doesn't mean you can parade around naked all the time."

Owen smirked. "I think I'll stay naked for the moment. It's too damn hot for clothes."

Raven rolled her eyes. "No it's not. I'm wearing clothes."

"Feel free to take them off."

Raven huffed and turned her back on Owen, grabbing the newspaper and burying her face in it. For several minutes, she fumed silently while Owen polished off his plate of food. He knew the best thing to do would probably be to apologize or offer some sort of olive branch, but he wasn't really in the mood to say sorry. Even though his stomach no longer growled with hunger, he was still feeling tired and cranky. He hadn't slept very long, and every muscle in his body ached from his long flight out here. Sure, Raven's magic skills were useful, but she couldn't deny that his dragon skills were useful, too. It irked him that she was acting like she was so much more special than him.

Damn women, he thought to himself, lying back down to take another nap. They always think they're right.

He purposefully lay on his back so that his dick was clearly visible, just to annoy her. He had no problem being naked in front of her, and he was getting a bit too much satisfaction from her irritated reaction to his refusal to put on clothes. With his stomach full, and his body warm from the heat of the day, he quickly drifted off to sleep.

He wasn't sure how long he slept, but it must have been nearly all day. When he woke up again, the sun was low in the western sky. He looked up to find that Raven was gone, and he felt a mixture of panic and frustration rising in his chest. Had something happened to her? Or had she just gone off without telling him, in which case he was going to give her a piece of his mind. Owen sat up and quickly jumped out of his shady rocky haven, looking all around. For a moment, he saw no sign of Raven, but when he turned around, he saw her sitting on the top of their little rock hideout. Beads of sweat glistened on her forehead, and her face was set in a half frown.

"Good morning," she said, her voice dripping with sarcasm as she looked up at the late afternoon sun. "I trust you slept well."

Owen frowned. She was angry that he had slept all day. Well, let her be. He wasn't going to apologize for getting some much needed rest.

"I slept like a baby," he said, raising his arms up above his head in an exaggerated stretch, being sure to push his hips forward to emphasize that he was still very naked and his dick was still very much in plain view. Raven rolled her eyes but said nothing. Damn. He wasn't sure he'd ever seen her quite this pissed off.

"Didn't you sleep?" he asked casually. If the dark circles under her eyes were any indication, she had not been sleeping all day as he had. She looked exhausted. And yet still as beautiful as always. Even tired and angry, she was a vision to behold.

"Only an hour or so," she said. "I was busy."

The implication in her voice was clear. She was busy. Someone had to get shit done, and he was slacking. Owen resented her attitude. He'd flown all night, and if she really wanted to get out of here, the only way was for him to fly them out. He wouldn't have been able to fly again without sleeping a good long time, like he'd done. But Owen didn't say anything. He just looked at her with an annoyed expression on his face, daring her to say more.

With a sigh, she hopped down from the rocks to stand next to him. "Are you ever planning on putting clothes on again?" she asked.

"Nah, I kind of like feeling uninhibited and free," he said, shaking his hips a bit for emphasis. This earned him another eye roll from her.

"Well, I suppose it's not worth putting clothes on. After all, you must be just about ready to shift and head out of here. We should travel by night, and it will be dark soon."

Owen heard the challenge in her words. If she wanted to fight, then he was up for the challenge. He wasn't going to be bossed around by a girl, even one as beautiful as her.

"We're not going anywhere yet, Raven," he said, his voice rising slightly. "I'm in charge of this mission, since I'm the one who was ordered to take the amethyst. And I say we need to stay at least a day or two and see if we can figure out what's going on with these bats."

Raven looked tired, but her eyes flashed with anger nonetheless. "We cannot stay here, Owen. Don't you understand? Getting the amethyst to safety is more important than ever. God, why are you so goddamned stubborn all the time? If you really want to spy on the bats, then come back in a few days, after the amethyst is safely with the shifter protectors in Texas. And it doesn't matter that Vance sent you on this mission. He only sent you because you happened to be the one guarding the amethyst at the time of the attack. You're not in charge of anything, least of all me. You can't make me stay here."

"Then go," Owen said, gesturing toward the desert with a flourish of his right arm. "Be my guest. See how far you get on your own."

Raven looked up at him with a pained expression on her face. He knew it was unfair of him to suggest that she leave. Even if they disagreed on how to run this mission, or who was or wasn't in charge, they were still on the same team. They still needed to look out for each other. But damn it, he wasn't the one being so goddamned stubborn—she was. She needed to back down a bit. So he crossed his arms and waited for her to make some sort of apology and say they could stay another night or two.

He should have known better. With an angry toss of her head, Raven walked into the cave and started pulling the giant hiking backpack onto her shoulders.

"Fine," she spat out at him. "I'll go. And *you* can see how far you get on your own. It's not so easy with no supplies and no invisibility spells. I hope you're enjoying being naked as much as you claim you are, because it's gonna be difficult to get clothes without me."

With that, Raven turned and started marching across the desert, due south. Owen watched her for a few minutes, expecting her to eventually turn around and come back, but she kept marching. After ten minutes had passed, and she was starting to become just a speck on the horizon, he realized that she was serious. She was leaving without him, even though she was probably going to die trying to walk across the desert. Who knew how far it was to the next town, and then to the town after that? Even if she survived, it would take her an eternity to reach the shifter protectors this way.

"Damn it, Raven," he said. He had no right to be angry. She was only repaying his stubbornness with her own. And yet, he *was* angry. Furious, even. Throwing all caution and fear of being discovered to the wind, he let out a roar and shifted into dragon form. He made a weak attempt at using chameleon skills to hide himself from any of Saul's soldiers who might be around and watching, but he was so angry right now that he couldn't concentrate properly on camouflaging himself against the sandy desert ground. With a grunt and a huff of smoky breath, he flapped his wings and rose into the air, heading toward Raven. In dragon form, it took him less than a minute to catch up with her. She looked up at him as he flew toward her, her deep blue eyes nearly black with rage. He ignored the daggers she was sending him with her gaze, and reached down his giant dragon claws to pluck her right up from the desert floor. Then he turned and started flying back toward their little rocky shelter.

"Put me down," she yelled, wriggling her body so violently that he was afraid one of his claws might accidently puncture her skin. "Put me down or I swear to God I'll kill you."

Owen ignored her until he reached the rocks again, then he dropped her, making sure that she was about a foot above ground when he did, so that she'd tumble a bit. As soon as he landed himself, he shifted back into human form with a loud pop and rush of energy.

"There," he said. "You're down."

"What the hell is wrong with you?" Raven yelled. She was sliding the backpack off her shoulders, her face red and seething with rage. "How dare you!"

"What the hell is wrong with *you?*" Owen yelled back. "You're usually the one up for anything, but you're not willing to take a golden opportunity to spy on Saul's men? I thought you were more adventurous than that!"

"You ignorant bastard!" Raven screamed, rushing toward him. She raised her hand and slapped her open palm against his left cheek with a surprising amount of force. He felt a red welt almost instantly forming on his face.

"What the hell, Raven? You're lucky you're a woman. Otherwise, I'd beat you to a pulp right here and now."

"Go ahead and try!" she said, raising her other hand and slapping him hard across the other cheek. She continued yelling at him, punctuating each word with a fresh slap. "You. awful. ignorant. idiot. stupid. stubborn. dragon!"

When she finally stopped, she stood in front of him with her hands on her hips. Her face was bright red and she was breathing hard. Her eyes were dark with rage, and she had a look on her face that just dared him to speak. So he did.

"Anything else?" he asked with a sneer.

Slap!

His face smarted, and he was sure it was bright red from the force of her hand against his cheek, but he would not give her the satisfaction of knowing she had caused him pain.

"What's wrong with you, Raven?" he asked, his voice low and angry. "It's not like you to run in fear from the enemy, or to complain about needing to follow the rules to the letter. You've never been one to argue about who is or isn't in charge. What gives? Is this war finally getting to you? Do you need a vacation or something? A couple months off from work."

She closed her eyes briefly, and when she opened them, she looked so angry that he thought he was about to be slapped again. But she kept her hands on her hips, and then spoke in a low, even tone.

"You know I love a good adventure just as much as you do, Owen," she said. "But this isn't about adventure anymore. It's about survival."

"Oh, come on, Raven. It's been about survival for the last six months, at least. Don't act like all this danger is anything new."

"I went into town again while you were sleeping," she said.

Owen raised his eyes in surprise. "And?"

"I tried to contact Falcon Cross. I tried to contact the shifter protectors in Texas. I even tried to contact your home base in the Redwoods, as a last resort. I called every number I could think of that someone we know might answer."

Owen felt a strange sensation fill him, almost like bile was rising in his throat. "And?" he asked, not sure if he really wanted to know what Raven was about to tell him.

"And I got no answer, Owen. No answer from anyone. Do you understand what that means? There's no one monitoring the emergency phones in Falcon Cross. The Redwoods base is definitely taken by the enemy. And the shifter protectors…they are not answering either. Everyone is either in a huge battle right now, or already defeated. We have no way of knowing what's going on, but I can tell you for sure that whatever it is, it's not good."

Owen could not speak. He felt his heart twisting up in all sorts of strange ways as the full meaning of Raven's words hit him. A thousand emotions rushed through him at once, and he nervously ran his fingers through his hair as though that motion could somehow keep him from drowning in the ocean that was washing over him.

"Don't you understand, Owen?" Raven said. The anger had gone out of her voice now. She sounded sad, like her heart was breaking with every word she spoke. "It's entirely possible that everything—and everyone—we love has fallen to Saul. All we have left is each other. I cannot lose you, too. I know that if we stay here in Sandview we might be able to learn all kinds of valuable things about Saul's operations. And, yes, normally I'd be up for the challenge. But not now. Not when everything is so uncertain. You're all I have, Owen. Don't ask me to stand here and watch you risk your life unnecessarily when I've already lost everything."

Owen looked at Raven, who stood in front of him with her eyes filling with tears. Behind her, the sun was setting further, lighting up the sky in a brilliant display of pink and orange. In that moment, all of the anger went out of Owen as well, and a different emotion filled him. A different fire began burning in his veins, and he knew it was time to stop dancing around the truth. If what Raven feared was true, and they truly were all that was left of the good shifters and wizards, then they probably were not going to last long on their own. And if his days were so numbered, then there was only one thing Owen knew for sure: he wanted Raven to know, before he ran out of time, that he loved her.

He'd loved her from the beginning. From the very first moment he saw her. He'd tried to deny it. Tried to hide behind his reputation as a ladies' man to keep from admitting the truth to everyone, even to himself. But he could not hide any longer. Not when the devastating possibility of having lost everything loomed so heavy over his heart.

He opened his mouth to try to speak, but he did not know where to begin. How do you put into words the emotions that make your heart beat? It's an impossible task. And so, instead of speaking, Owen took a step toward Raven. He put his arms out and pulled her, trembling, into his embrace. And then, he put his lips on hers.

She did not pull away as he kissed her. She melted into him, and let him say with his kiss the words he could not find to speak: *I'm sorry. I love you. You're my everything. Hold on to me, and we'll make it through this somehow. We'll make it through this together.*

She kissed him back, her kiss telling him secrets of its own: *I'm sorry, too. I love you, too. I've wanted this for so long. Everything is still going to be okay, as long as we're together.*

Together.

Owen held her tighter, and felt relieved that, no matter what was going on out there, Raven and he were together.

476

CHAPTER FOUR

Owen's lips were softer than they appeared. Raven could not stop marveling at this fact as he kissed her underneath the setting sun. She'd wanted him to kiss her for what felt like an eternity, and, although she wished the kiss had come about under a happier set of circumstances, her heart still leapt for joy at the realization that she was finally getting what she had secretly wished for.

Perhaps her wish had not been so secret, to tell the truth. She had endured a great deal of teasing from her colleagues about what was or was not going on between Owen and her. They were infamous for flirting, for stealing a touch or a handhold here and there. But they had never spoken plainly to each other or anyone else of their feelings. They had always denied that they cared for each other in any way except as fellow soldiers in the fight against evil.

She'd been so angry with him a few minutes ago, but the fight had gone out of her with each slap she'd given him across the face. She was a bit ashamed of losing her temper, but she'd had reasons to feel rage, after all. So had he, she supposed. They'd both been right, and they'd both been wrong. Now, together in each other's arms, she had the sense that they'd both forgiven each other.

He was stubborn to a fault, just like her. She'd always loved that about him. And somehow, the fact that they had both denied their feelings for so long made this moment seem all the more real. They had fought hard for it. Perhaps they had waited too long, but at least they knew that this kiss, and the confession of love behind the kiss, was not something they had taken lightly.

Raven's heart felt troubled. The possibilities haunted her of what might have happened to the group retreating from the redwoods, or to the wizards at Falcon Cross, or even to the shifter protectors in Texas. She had spent the day in anguish, alternating between being too angry to look at Owen and wanting to wake him up so she could cry in his arms. Now that she was in his arms, though, she no longer felt like crying. She felt strangely comforted.

Despite the great dragon strength that lay within him, he was gentle with her. His arms around her were strong but loving, and even the movement of his tongue as it slipped between her lips felt like a caress. She squeezed her eyes shut even tighter and willed herself to forget about everything except Owen. There would be time enough to worry, to search, and to grieve about whatever faced them ahead. But this moment, here with Owen, was a chance to lose herself in the simple happiness of having another human being who cared about her. His embrace reminded her that, despite how bleak the world might seem right now, all was not hopeless. All was not lost. Love could still find a way to shine in the darkest night.

And, ironically enough, it was night now. The last rays of the sun were sinking behind the horizon, and the sky was changing from an orange-pinkish glow to a somber, darkening gray. But Raven did not feel afraid or sad. She felt happy, and strangely at peace. Owen was here. She still had him.

He broke off their kiss for a moment and looked up at the sky, then pulled her gently as deep into their little rocky hideout as they could go. She had spread the sleeping bag she'd taken out across one half of the floor of the shelter, and Owen laid her gently on it now. Once she was comfortably on her back, he returned to kissing her. There was a deeper urgency in his kiss now, though, as if the hunger inside of him was growing with each passing second. He pressed his body against hers, and she felt his erection, stiff as steel against her legs. She envied him his nakedness. She wanted to be naked, too. She wanted her skin to feel his skin. She wanted there to be nothing between them, nothing holding them back.

But he was moving slowly, and taking his time. Raven told herself to relax and enjoy the moment. After all, she had waited for this moment for so long. He placed his palms on her cheeks gently, holding her face as his tongue danced with her tongue. His hands were so warm. She'd noticed that about him before, in the few times when they'd dared to hold each other's hands. He was always so warm, as though the dragon that burned within him could not keep itself fully contained. And she loved that warmth. Even here, in the hot desert, she loved his warmth. She wanted more of it.

Raven felt like she was lost in an ocean, stranded with only Owen to keep her company. And he was enough. She let everything else fade away, and concentrated on the wonder of his kiss. He was a sweet relief, a reprieve from the seemingly never-ending hardships that faced her these days. She wanted this moment to be something they enjoyed together. Something that took them far away from heartache, war, and pain. And she wanted more of him. His kiss intoxicated her, but it wasn't enough. She craved more.

As if he heard her thoughts, he moved his hands to the buttons on her shirt. She was wearing a simple button down hiking shirt that she'd taken from the store this morning. Even though she'd only had it on a few hours, she knew the shirt had become sweaty and dusty. She was a sweaty, dusty mess herself, but she didn't care. She wasn't embarrassed by her dirt-streaked face or messy, tangled hair. She and Owen were past the point of putting up appearances around each other. They'd spent too much time in the trenches together during this war to worry about a little dirt or sweat. They knew each other well, and they wanted each other. Had wanted each other for so long. And now, finally, they were giving in.

Owen's fingers made quick work of unbuttoning the shirt, and even quicker work of unclasping Raven's bra and sliding it off her shoulders. As soon as the top half of her body was naked, he lay next to her on the sleeping bag and pulled her on top of him. He moaned softly as her sticky, sweaty skin pressed against his. His hands went to her breasts, cupping their sides. Her hard nipples were pressed firmly against his chest.

"I've wanted to feel you like this for so long," he whispered huskily.

Raven could not reply. All she could do was look at him, drinking in the deep green of his eyes. She had looked into those eyes so many times before, but this time was different. This time, he wasn't hiding his feelings or holding back the passion that he felt. This time, he let her see into his soul, and she liked what she saw.

He burned with passion, a deep flaming passion. He burned for her. She reached up with wonder to trace one finger across the side of his cheek.

"My dragon," she whispered.

He growled then, and pulled her face close, kissing her again. His lips covered hers with a deep urgency, and she let herself fully experience the moment. Everything else fell away. There was only him, and her, and their bodies pressed against each other. This was all she had ever wanted, but she hadn't been able to admit that to herself until this moment.

A fiery, burning passion rose within her own body. She grew hotter and hotter, even though the air around them was cooling as the night continued to take hold. The darkness grew, but Raven did not notice it. She was too busy noticing how her very core seemed to be on fire. She trembled, as a tingling electricity filled her everywhere that Owen's skin touched hers. He had his arms wrapped around her now, and his hands on the small of her bare back. Those hands that she had gaze at so many times, wishing, hoping for a moment like this.

Her legs trembled, and the space between them grew wetter with each passing moment. Her whole body was responding to Owen, begging for more of him. She wanted him inside of her, but he was not rushing. He took his time, slowly caressing her back as he continued to kiss her deeply.

When he'd had his fill of kissing, he gently rolled them over so that she was on her back once again, and he was on top of her. He moved to unbutton her pants, and she trembled involuntarily as his fingers brushed against the bare skin of her stomach. He noticed, and smiled up at her. All of the anger and frustration was gone from his eyes now. She was finding it hard to even remember in that moment why they had fought. What did it matter? What did anything matter, as long as they had each other?

Owen unlaced Raven's shoes and pulled them off, then tugged off her now unbuttoned pants, along with her panties. Raven felt the desert's cool night air blowing over her naked body, and she closed her eyes to relish the sensation. After the hot, sweaty day she'd endured, this gentle breeze felt like heaven. And so did Owen's body, which was once again pressing against hers. Only this time, there were no clothes between them. There was only skin against skin, and Raven shuddered with pleasure at the feeling.

She could feel his stiff erection pressing against the bottom of her stomach, leaving a small smudge of his moisture on her. She herself was so wet and slippery between her legs now that she could feel the juices of her desire beginning to drip down and onto the sleeping bag below them. She'd never felt so gloriously turned on before. Owen could have slid into her in that moment, and she would have welcomed him gladly. But he did not. Still, he waited. It was almost as though he never wanted this magical moment between them to end.

He moved his lips over her stiff nipples, flicking at them with his tongue. He alternated between nibbling, licking, sucking, and biting. Raven could not keep track of where his mouth and hands and body were. She was consumed by his dragon fire. Her own body was burning up at its very core, the fire and electricity rushing over her in hot waves. Her thighs trembled where his thighs pressed against her. She told herself that she should return the touch. She should kiss him, too. She should caress his back or nibble his ear. But she could not. She was too overcome now by him and his touch to move. She arched her back and moaned, letting herself fully experience the wonder of his body pleasuring hers.

The wonder had only just begun, though. When he'd had his fill of her breasts, Owen pushed himself up on his arms and moved back slightly so that his stiff, throbbing erection was directly above her slick, trembling entrance. He paused there, and Raven opened her eyes wide to look at him, questioning.

"You know, if we do this then there's no going back," he said, his voice a hoarse whisper. "We can never again pretend that there's nothing between us, or that we don't have deeper feelings for each other. Are you sure you want to do this now?"

Raven smiled up at him. His tanned skin was glistening with beads of sweat. His reddish-brown hair stuck out in every possible direction as he looked at her with smoke and fire in his eyes. His broad chest rose and fell with rapid, excited breathing just above her breasts, which were also rising and falling from the effort of her own breath.

He had never looked so handsome.

"I think we've already passed the point of no return," she said.

That was all he needed to hear. In the next moment, he was sliding into her, filling her so naturally it was as though he had always belonged there. Raven felt his stiff, thick shaft pushing against her inner walls, making room for itself as it went deeper and deeper into her. The movement sent shocks of tingling electricity through her. Her whole body felt like it was a tangled mess of heat, pressure, and tingling. Owen moved slowly, but even still, the sensations that filled Raven were almost too intense to bear. She squeezed her eyes shut and clenched her fists, arching her back so that her hips thrust forward to meet him. She felt that she could not take any more, but she wanted more nonetheless.

He moved in her, slowly, methodically, purposefully. There was no sound now other than their breathing, and the soft brush of skin against skin as he rocked his hips back and forth, in and out, in and out. With each thrust, the pressure built and the heat intensified. Raven had never felt anything so glorious. The electric tingling had become so intense that she felt like she was seeing stars. And then, the crescendo came.

Her whole body felt like it exploded into a million wonderful pieces. She gasped as her inner muscles spasmed, clenching around Owen's erection over and over. Each spasm of her body sent another wave of tingling and electricity through her body. The pressure that had been building inside of her released into a heat unlike anything she'd ever felt. She could not move, could not even moan. All she could do was lie there, breathing in the most intense, wonderful moment of her life. She let her eyes flicker open to see Owen, his own eyes still closed, squeezed shut with concentration as he rocked his body against hers. She watched his face as he moved in her, pressing against the spasms that still rocked her body. And she thought in that moment that this, *this*, was what was meant by "making love."

Owen's release came then in a sweet, shuddering wave. He stiffened, squeezed his eyes shut tighter, and then moaned softly as he pulsed into her.

When their bodies had finally stopped trembling, he slid off of her and lay next to her. He wrapped his arms around her and they both lay there for a long time in silence. No words were necessary. They had things to discuss and plans to make and issues to resolve, but right now, all that mattered was being together. Raven snuggled closer against him, and closed her eyes, feeling at peace for the first time since they'd made their hurried escape from the redwoods.

Her breathing evened out, and she was finally able to fall asleep, finding in the arms of her dragon the rest she so desperately needed.

CHAPTER FIVE

The soothing sound of Raven's rhythmic breathing filled the tiny, rocky shelter, but Owen still felt tense. He was glad that she was getting some rest, but he himself could not sleep anymore. He'd slept all day, and now, he was wide awake and restless. His eyes glowed dimly as they scanned the horizon, searching for signs of bats or wizards or anything else unusual. But nothing stirred in the darkness. It was quiet.

Too quiet.

Owen tugged absentmindedly at the neckline of the simple gray t-shirt he was wearing. He'd finally put some clothes on, and he was surprised at how well Raven had guessed his size. Then again, perhaps he shouldn't have been surprised. They'd spent so much time together now that they knew each other well. Owen smiled. After tonight, they knew each other about as well as two humans could.

He'd felt the lifemate bond forming as they made love. He'd long suspected that Raven might be his lifemate, but he'd never allowed himself to dwell on the thought for very long. He'd long been known as a player, and the thought of being with one person for the rest of his life had always frightened him. But Raven was different. The only thing that scared him about her was the thought of not being with her for the rest of his life.

Owen glanced over at her sleeping form, and his smile deepened. He hoped she would sleep for a long time. She needed the rest. He knew she had wanted to get away from this town and to Texas as quickly as possible, but, even if they did head straight for Texas like she wanted, one more night wouldn't make much difference. And whenever they did leave, he needed her awake and alert. Having a wizard ready to fight on his back would make him feel a lot safer as he flew. If Saul's soldiers caught wind that a dragon was flying around with the dragon amethyst, they would focus all of their attention on him, trying to bring him down and steal the stone before he could reach the safety of the shifter protectors in Texas.

Owen turned to look toward the shadowy town of Sandview that sat in front of him. Only a handful of lights were on in the town, likely from the gas station or one of the motels. The quiet felt eerie and unnatural, even for a sleepy village in the middle of nowhere. Owen's eyes turned toward the sky, searching. There was no moon tonight, although the stars did twinkle brightly in the desert sky.

He didn't know what, exactly, he thought he would see. If any of the dark wizards were around, they would almost certainly be hiding themselves under invisibility spells. They wouldn't want to make a big show of things in front of all the unsuspecting townspeople. Owen stared at the sky for several more minutes, anyway, and then turned to look for some food in the backpack. He didn't want to overly deplete the supplies Raven had stolen. They had a long road ahead of them, after all. But he was so hungry right now that his stomach felt like it was twisting itself in knots. He would eat just one meal bar to take the edge off.

Owen found a peanut butter flavored bar and tore it open. He bit half the bar off at once and started munching while he dug around in the bag, looking for some water. He found a bottle, but finished eating his meal bar before he drank any. Even then, he only allowed himself a few sips. If he and Raven did somehow become stranded, water would be even more precious than food.

When he was done drinking, he carefully replaced the cap on the water bottle and put it back in the backpack. Then he went back to his spot at the front of their little hideout to resume his watch. He sat down with a contented sigh and looked up at the sky, but his heart stopped the moment he did.

The stars had disappeared entirely. Where the soft orbs of light had been twinkling only minutes before, there was only inky black. And, Owen realized with horror, that inky blackness was moving. The black sky seemed to undulate, ripples of darkness swelling, rising, and falling.

"What in the world?" Owen whispered, rubbing his eyes. Was he imagining things, or was this some trick of dark magic? But even after rubbing his eyes and opening and closing them several times, the dark waves still persisted across the night sky. Owen tensed up, wondering whether he should wake Raven. If there was dark magic afoot, he would need her help fighting it. A lump formed in his throat as this thought crossed his mind. If there was dark magic afoot, he and Raven didn't stand much of a chance trying to fight it on their own. Their only hope was to avoid discovery. Owen knew that Raven had cast invisibility spells and protective shields over their hiding spot, but those would not last long if the dark wizards were casting counterspells. Owen chewed his lower lip nervously, hoping that perhaps the wizards were not suspecting any enemies to be out here, and weren't actively trying to disarm any invisibility spells.

Owen glanced back at Raven, who looked so comfortable and peaceful curled into their sleeping bag. He hated to wake her, but he would rather wake her now than have her startled out of her sleep by enemy soldiers. He gritted his teeth and looked up at the sky one more time, and then, suddenly, he realized why the blackness seemed to be moving.

"Bats!" he exclaimed in wonder. There must have been hundreds of thousands of them. Their black bodies were so numerous as they flew above the town that they were blocking out the stars. Owen quickly crawled over to the sleeping bag and started shaking Raven awake. He wasn't going to hesitate any longer. She had to see this.

"Raven," he whispered in a loud hiss. "Raven wake up."

She blinked her eyes open, disoriented. She focused on his face and smiled, but then sat upright wide awake when she saw the concern in his own eyes.

"What is it?" she asked. "What's wrong?"

"Come look at this," he said, and motioned toward the front of their rocky shelter. She crawled after him, and her gaze followed his finger upwards as he pointed toward the sky. He saw confusion in her eyes, the same confusion he had felt only minutes before.

"They're bats," he said. "Thousands and thousands of bats."

Understanding dawned on her face, and horror filled her eyes.

"So many of them," she whispered in awe.

"I know," Owen said. "It's incredible."

"What are they doing?" Raven asked, never taking her eyes off the sky.

"Circling the town. Although I have no idea why. It seems odd, doesn't it, that they're in plain sight? You would think that Saul and his army wouldn't want his bats parading around for all to see."

"You'd think," Raven said. "Maybe he wants to scare the people in Sandview for some reason?"

"But why?" Owen asked, a deep sense of dread filling him. "Is he trying to force them into his army?"

Raven didn't answer, other than to shrug in frustration. She continued staring up at the sky, and Owen turned his eyes skyward again. No sooner had he looked up, though, that he heard Raven gasp, and his own heart filled with fresh horror.

The bats were no longer alone up in the sky. Zooming underneath them now, were hundreds of wizards flying in on broomsticks. They all had beacons of light shooting from their magic rings, and the closer they flew to the town the brighter the sky became with their lights, until it might as well have been daytime.

"I'd say Saul is definitely trying to scare the townspeople for some reason," Raven murmured. "The bats are bad enough, but having wizards fly in with no invisibility spells? That's guaranteed to terrify any full human."

The show wasn't nearly over, though. A thundering sound suddenly filled Owen's ears, and he looked behind him to see hundreds of lions, bears, tigers, wolves, and panthers running across the desert toward them.

"Shit!" he said, pushing Raven back into the rocky hideout. "Get back. Out of their way."

They moved just in time, both sitting with their backs flattened against the wall as the shifters ran past them and headed full speed ahead toward the town. Owen had never been so thankful for an invisibility spell. The shifters never so much as gave Owen and Raven a second glance as they ran past, unaware that they were running right past the coveted dragon amethyst.

When the last of the shifters had passed them, Owen exhaled, and turned to Raven with a grim expression on his face.

"We have to get out of here," he said. "You're right, babe. Hanging around here is definitely not a good idea. That's way more wizards, bats, and other shifters than I want to take on."

"Not to mention a dragon," Raven murmured, her eyes wide as she continued to stare up at the sky.

"Dragon?" Owen choked out. He followed Raven's gaze, and his own eyes widened. Overcome by curiosity, he crawled back toward the front of the rocky shelter to get a better view. If he'd ever in his life before this thought that his blood ran cold, he'd been mistaken. He'd never felt a chill go through him like the one that filled him when his eyes saw Saul. And Owen had no doubt that the dragon he was seeing right now was Saul.

Illuminated by the lights of hundreds of his dark wizards, the ugliest dragon Owen had ever seen flew slowly across the night sky. Saul's dragon was a dark red, and there was no shimmer to his scales, like there was to every other dragon Owen had ever seen. The red scales did seem to glow under the wizards' light though, making Saul look almost like his whole body was covered in blood. His translucent wings had scars so huge across them that Owen could see them from even here on the ground. Each wing had four points to it, with a sharp black spike extending from each point. Saul's tail extended behind him, horned with spikes of the same dark black color as the spikes on his wing. His dragon feet ended in the longest claws Owen had ever seen, and Owen shuddered just looking at them. In one of his feet, he carried a giant wizard's wand. It was more of a staff, really, but it looked like a mere wand when held by the giant claws of Saul's dragon. The end of the staff had a glowing orb of light on it that looked both beautiful and sinister at the same time. And his head. Oh his head. It was gigantic, even for a dragon, with large, gnarled horns extending several feet into the air above it. He swung it back and forth, and Owen cringed when he saw Saul's eyes.

They glowed solid red. He did not seem to even have any pupils—just two orbs of swirling, horrifying red. He searched the sky, the ground, the town…Owen did not know what he was looking for, but he knew he did not want to be found by this evil dragon right now, with no army to reinforce him. Owen had never been a praying man, but he was praying right now, pleading with whatever higher powers might be out there that his invisibility shield would hold. He felt Raven reach over and squeeze his hand tightly, and he knew she was praying, too.

"He looks more awful than I could have even imagined," Raven whispered in horrified awe.

Owen nodded. "Is that a wizard staff he's holding?" he asked.

Raven nodded. "I don't know of any wizards that still use wands or staffs these days. I thought everyone had switched to magic rings. But I suppose a ring would be lost in shifting. That must be why he uses the wand."

"It's so unnatural," Owen said with a shudder. "A shifter who's also a wizard."

"Agreed," Raven murmured, never taking her eyes off the horrifying sight that Saul made as he moved slowly across the sky, his giant, scarred wings flapping lazily while bats and wizards on broomsticks swirled around him. Owen watched, too, continuing to hold Raven's hand. Ordinarily, shifters could not do magic. Only those who were born wizards were capable of casting spells. But dark magic allowed anyone to become a wizard, and Saul, who had been born a dragon shifter, had become a wizard as well using dark magic. His transformation was not without its costs, though. Every time a wizard cast a dark magic spell, it cost that wizard a piece of their soul. This slow chipping away of the wizard's soul would twist and corrupt the wizard, making him or her ever more evil, until finally the use of dark magic would kill the wizard. Saul undoubtedly had given up a great deal of his soul to reach the point he had, and at some point the dark magic he loved would kill him. In the meantime, though, his evil actions were threatening the peace and safety of good wizards, shifters, and humans everywhere.

Owen followed the outline of the great dragon as he approached Sandview, and then, to his great shock, an evil, booming voice suddenly filled the air.

"People of Sandview," Saul's dragon said as it flew directly over the heart of the small town, "Look up and see the power of Saul, the mightiest dragon king there has ever been."

Saul's booming laughter filled the night sky, and Owen and Raven looked at each other in shock.

"He's speaking!" Raven exclaimed. "In dragon form! I didn't know that was possible."

"I didn't either," Owen said, just as shocked as Raven was. "I've never heard of a shifter being able to talk while in animal form."

"It's some sort of dark magic spell, I guess," Raven said. "Paired with an amplification spell. That's what's making his voice so loud."

"I offer you all a choice, as I have offered many other humans," Saul said, continuing to circle slowly above the town as he spoke. "I need more humans in my army. Join me, and you will be part of the most powerful army that has ever existed. You will be granted great power, honor, and wealth. Defy me, and you will face certain death."

To punctuate his death threat, Saul breathed a huge stream of fire into the air. But the flames weren't an orange-yellow color, like normal flames were. Instead, they were an unnatural, blood red color. Even from this distance, screams of terror could be heard from the citizens of Sandview. Raven and Owen exchanged another glance of horror.

"We have to get out of here," Raven said. Owen did not argue.

"Let's pack up the sleeping bag and get going," he said. "Our best chance is probably to sneak out quietly while Saul and his army are preoccupied with terrorizing the people in Sandview."

It went without saying that, if Saul and his evil army became aware of the fact that Owen and Raven were sitting just outside town with the dragon amethyst, all attention would be turned to killing them and stealing the amethyst away.

"What about the people in Sandview?" Raven asked. She sounded like she felt as sick to her stomach as Owen did right now.

"There's nothing we can do for them," Owen said sadly. "The two of us alone aren't strong enough to stop an army of this size. Even if we knew how to activate the dragon amethyst's powers, I'm not sure it would be enough. The best thing we can do for them, and for all humans, really, is to get the amethyst to safety."

Raven let out a long sigh and nodded. "Alright. Let's make a break for it."

She looked at the sky, and then added, "And let's hope that break is successful."

"It will be," Owen said through clenched teeth. "It has to be."

CHAPTER SIX

Raven's heart pounded in her chest as she strapped on the large hiking backpack, in which all of her and Owen's supplies were securely packed. She cinched the straps as tightly as they would go against her body, and then gave Owen a small nod.

"Alright," she said. "It's now or never."

"And we're invisible right now, as best you can tell?" Owen asked. He was standing in front of her completely naked, ready to shift into dragon form. They were both doing their best to ignore Saul's dragon, which was still circling above Sandview and yelling out booming threats at its horrified citizens.

"I've cast the strongest invisibility shield I possibly can," Raven said. "We don't have a protective shield around us, because I've focused all of my magical power into the invisibility shield to make it as strong as possible. I think we both agree that staying invisible is our only hope of survival, anyway. A protective shield won't last half a minute against an army of this size."

Owen nodded. "Alright, then. Let's do this."

He stepped forward and gave her a soft kiss on the lips. Warmth flooded from his body to hers, and the heat felt like a reassuring hug wrapping around her. She could use all the comfort she could get right now. She was a seasoned warrior, and had made it through several battles in the last year. But she knew that if Saul's soldiers saw them, all her military training would not save her. She took a deep breath to steady her nerves, then looked down at her magic ring. It was glowing with a soft light, reassuring her that her invisibility spells were in effect. All she could do was hope that they held long enough for Owen to fly them out of this hornet's nest.

He had taken several steps backward now, so that he would have space to shift into dragon form without knocking her over. She met his eyes and gave him a brave smile. He smiled back, his eyes sad. They both knew that their lives, as well as the fate of the dragon amethyst, hung in the balance.

"Hey," he said, taking another couple of steps backward. "You know I love you, right?"

Raven's heart leapt happily in her chest. "I know," she said. "I love you, too."

His smile deepened, and then, a rush of energy hit her like a wall of water. He began his transformation into a dragon, while Raven nervously watched the sky. Her heart clenched in fear, thinking of what would happen to her and Owen if any of Saul's soldiers saw them right now.

But the invisibility shields were still doing their job. No one so much as glanced in their direction, as far as Raven could tell. All eyes were still on Saul, as he circled and made terror-filled threats against the citizens of Sandview.

When Owen had completely shifted into dragon form, he bent low to the ground so that Raven could climb on. She checked the straps on her backpack one last time, and then hoisted herself onto her dragon's broad back. He glanced back at her, checking to make sure that she was secure. She gave him a thumbs up sign, then grabbed firmly onto the thick scales on his back. Reassured, he began pumping his wings, and moments later they were rising into the dark sky, leaving behind their rocky hideout.

Raven held her breath, her heart rate increasing as they rose higher and higher, and the view of Saul's army became clearer and clearer. Owen took a long, circular route around Sandview, which kept them well clear of the mass of bats shifters and wizards that crowded the airspace near Saul. But they were so high that Raven could still see the streets of the town in the distance, and she was surprised to see that they were full of people. She would have thought everyone would hide inside at the sight of a dragon, but perhaps the sheer incredulity of a dragon's existence was enough to keep them gawking. She wondered if they would give in to Saul's demands, and join his cause. They probably would, she thought bitterly. And could she really blame them? What choice did a small town of humans have against a fire-breathing dragon who practiced dark magic? She felt especially sorry for those people who were in Sandview as tourists. They'd come to enjoy a relaxing vacation, and instead had discovered a sinister dragon. Raven wondered whether Saul would allow them to leave and go back to their homes. She guessed not. He wouldn't want them spreading rumors about him, or trying to get help from the government to squash his army.

And could his army be squashed? Raven glanced doubtfully over the mass of bats and wizards in the air, and then surveyed the horde of shifters on the ground. She was beginning to wonder if even the dragon stones would be enough to stop them. She'd been told by all the experts that the dragon stones were immensely powerful, and could take on even the strongest of armies. But the more Saul's army grew, the harder it was for her to imagine defeating him using just a couple of gemstones. She hoped that the stones were truly more powerful than they looked. Otherwise, the small army working for the forces of good was going to find itself quickly overcome by Saul and his horde.

They had passed the airspace crowded by Saul and his soldiers now. Owen's wings sliced silently through the air, lifting them higher and higher until Saul's army looked like toys. Owen was picking up speed, and Raven finally began to think that they might actually make it out of here unnoticed. She scanned the airspace all around them, looking for any strange blurry spots that would indicate someone was hiding under an invisibility shield. She saw nothing unusual, although the darkness hung so heavy that locating a possible invisibility shield would have been difficult even for her well-trained eyes. She could only hope that the darkness was keeping their own invisibility shield strong and undetectable as well.

Raven had no doubt that Saul would have scouts hidden for miles all around the town of Sandview. He'd want plenty of guards watching out for trouble while he made his ridiculous speech to its townspeople. So far, Raven hadn't seen anyone, but that only made her more nervous. Saul's soldiers were definitely out here. But where? And were they being lazy and doing the bare minimum of watching out for visible threats, or were they constantly casting counterspells in an effort to detect invisibility shields? Raven could only hope for laziness, but she worried that she might be hoping for too much. She crouched low on Owen's back as he flew, searching the horizon with her magic ring ready. If they were attacked by a large group of guards, there wouldn't be much she could do. She was a well-trained fighter, but still—she and Owen were only two people. One dragon and one wizard could only do so much.

The further Owen flew, though, the more Raven started to relax. Saul and the city of Sandview were growing smaller and smaller on the horizon, and surely they were nearly past the danger zone. Raven would be surprised if Saul had posted guards much further out than this. She took a deep breath and let it out in a long, relieved sigh. They were going to make it. They had actually managed to sneak out of there right under

Saul's nose.

Raven sat up and smiled, then reached to pat Owen on the shoulder in celebration. But as her arm stretched out in front of her, she felt a sudden, sharp pain shooting through it. She recoiled, jumping backwards so quickly that she lost her balance and fell over on her side completely. If Owen's broad dragon back had been any smaller, she would have fallen off and gone catapulting downward toward the earth, and certain death.

But even though she'd managed to not fall off of Owen's back, she still couldn't be sure that she wasn't facing certain death. Another sharp pain hit her, this time in her side, right below her right hip. In the next moment, she finally saw them. A group of about twenty wizards closing in on her. They must have been casting strong counterspells, because Raven's invisibility shield was not fooling them. They picked up speed as they headed toward her, and their own invisibility shields began to fail. Even the dark magic spells of these dark wizards were not enough to hold an invisibility shield at the speeds the wizards were traveling.

Raven quickly abandoned her own useless invisibility shield, and focused all her magical energy on a protective shield. Within moments, these dark wizards would be in close enough firing range to do some truly serious damage.

"Magicae arma!" she yelled out. A force field of protective energy surrounded her and Owen, and just in time, too. A split-second after the shield went up, several huge blasts of laser fire from the dark wizards magic rings came rushing toward Raven and Owen. The laser beams collided with the protective shield and set off a huge shower of sparks. Those sparks were the first thing that alerted Owen to the fact that they were in trouble.

Raven saw Owen turn his giant head backward toward her, his eyes quickly checking to make sure that she was alright. Once he knew Raven was okay, he looked behind them, where the attacking wizards were now in full view. Raven saw his dragon eyes beginning to glow green with anger. Unlike Saul, Owen could not speak while in dragon form, but Raven was pretty sure that, if he could have, he would have been spewing out a stream of curses right about then.

"Just fly!" Raven yelled at him. "Our only hope is to fly faster than them and escape. I can't hold this many of them off for long, and I'm worried that there are more out here who will join in the chase once they realize what's going on."

Owen let out a low roar, and Raven could hear the frustration in the noise. But he didn't have time to express himself much beyond that roar, and he knew it. They needed to fly, and fly like the wind. Owen turned his head forward again, and started pumping his wings even faster than before. He'd been holding back his speed a bit so that Raven could maintain their invisibility shield, but now, with the hope of maintaining any kind of stealth completely gone, he threw all of his energy into flying as quickly as he could.

And oh, how he could fly! Raven felt the wind that whipped at her face growing steadily stronger as Owen's pace increased. Behind them, the dark wizards, who had been so gleefully laughing at her and throwing out magic attacks, were starting to look angry. Raven couldn't keep a smug smile off her face. Dark magic might be powerful, but it did have its limitations. There was no dark magic spell that miraculously made you better at flying. Flying was a skill that could only be learned through a great amount of time and effort, and Saul's soldiers were all much less experienced at flying than the Falcon Cross wizards or Redwood Dragons. Owen had spent his entire life practicing his flying skills, and it showed. Even Raven's hair was unable to stand up to his speed. Her long locks came loose from the bun she had pulled them into and whipped around her face in a tangled mess.

She did not bother trying to shoot off any magic attacks at their pursuers. At this speed, the odds were pretty low of hitting one of them with a blast strong enough to knock them off their broomstick. Raven focused all of her magical energy on the protective shield she had cast around Owen and her, hoping that it would hold long enough for them to get out of range of the dark wizards. Their chances of that seemed good. Owen pulled ahead of the group a little more with each passing second.

"Come on, Owen," Raven whispered under her breath. "You can do this. You can get us out of here."

As if he could hear Raven's silent encouragement, Owen seemed to pick up speed. He sped forward at an impossible speed, and Raven would have let out a cheer of victory if she hadn't been so busy concentrating on keeping her balance as she crouched on Owen's back. The dark wizards behind them were starting to grow smaller and smaller in the distance, and Raven breathed a sigh of relief. They were going to make it. Escape was theirs.

And then, disaster struck.

Raven heard the whizz of a broomstick right above her head just before she saw it. She attempted to throw an attack out at the wizard, but she was too late. She couldn't get the laser beam out of her ring fast enough, and before she could even finish the words to the spell she was trying to cast, she found herself completely frozen. She was surrounded by what looked like a blue force field, and even her lips could not move. She'd seen stunning spells hundreds of times before, and experienced a few of them herself, too. But all of those stunning spells only froze someone from the neck down. She'd never seen or heard of a spell that could freeze someone completely, even freezing up their face.

Raven told herself not to panic. She was still on Owen's back, even though she was frozen. If he could just keep flying and get them out of there, then she would have time to figure out a way to do a counterspell that might release her. She just had to remain calm and hope that Owen could get her out of there before they actually caught her.

That hope didn't last more than a few seconds, though. Raven felt a sudden jolt, like the kind you might feel if you were in a vehicle that suddenly braked to a screeching halt. She couldn't move her neck to look around, but it didn't matter. She was positioned perfectly to see that she was now suspended in her blue ball of energy in midair, and no longer on Owen's back. Not only that, but she now saw, as she faced forward, that a fresh wave of wizard guards was ahead of them. There must have been another line of guards still to come, and the guards that had been chasing Owen and Raven had somehow alerted them that a dragon and wizard were heading their way. Raven felt her heart sinking in her motionless, suspended body. There was no way they were going to get away now. There were too many enemy soldiers, and Raven could not help Owen at all. She was a helpless, motionless ball in the middle of the sky. She wanted to cry, but the stunning spell had frozen even her tears, it seemed. She could do nothing but watch in horror as Owen rapidly slowed his flight. He had realized that she was no longer on his back, and that he was facing a wall of wizards both in front of and behind him.

Raven wanted to scream at him to keep going, and to save himself. But she could not scream right now, and even if she could have, he would not have been able to hear her. They had been fools to think that they could get away from Sandview unnoticed. Saul's army was too massive. They should have known that there would be enough guards to practically form a small army themselves.

Owen had seen Raven's predicament, and he was in full-on fight mode now. He was breathing fire in every direction and slashing with his claws, taking down wizard after wizard in his rage. He moved steadily toward her, spinning in a circle as he flew and doing his best to hold at bay the wizards that surrounded him in all directions. He was doing a pretty impressive job of it, too. The large size of his dragon body was deceptive—he could maneuver with incredible speed. And his thick dragon hide protected him from the constant laser beam attacks that the dark wizards were sending out from their magic rings. Slowly, but surely, he was making progress toward her.

Raven could not move her lips, but she silently prayed for strength and good luck for him. Was it possible that maybe, just maybe, they might make it out of here yet? She wanted to hope for escape still, but she wasn't sure she dared. She was sure that there were hundreds of wizard guards ready to fly over and join the fight if they realized what was going on.

Owen continued to fight, and the air around Raven grew hot as he got closer. The flames he was shooting out of his mouth were lighting up the sky and filling it with heat. Even though she couldn't move her body at all, she could feel her heart beating wildly in her chest. She had been in a lot of frightening situations in the last year, but this one felt like the worst. Her normal coolheaded demeanor was abandoning her now, and she could feel panic rising in her chest. And then, just when she thought things couldn't get worse, they did.

The blue force field around her, which had been holding her up in midair, suddenly dissolved. She felt herself go weightless as she fell through the air. The stunning spell that had held her frozen in place dissolved as well, and she could move again. This didn't do her a lot of good, though, since all she could do now was flail helplessly against the wind created by her fall. She opened her mouth and screamed, but she had no idea whether Owen could even hear her, or if he'd be able to get to her in time.

Ironically enough, it was one of the enemy soldiers who saved her. She felt the whizz of a broomstick as it rushed by her, and she felt a strong, rough hand grabbing her out of midair.

"Gotcha. Saul's gonna want you alive, Darling," the wizard said. Then he pointed his magic ring at her and yelled "*Magicae suspendo.*"

Raven once again found herself suspended in midair, surrounded by a blue force field. But this time, the wizard who caught her didn't use a stunning spell on her, so she was able to move. She looked up above her, where the battle was raging on. The wizard who had caught her and put her back inside a force field trap was zooming upward on his broomstick to join in the fray. Raven tried to point her magic ring upward and shoot out a magic attack, but she soon found that her magic wouldn't work inside the force field.

"Freaking dark magic," she said through gritted teeth. She felt helpless as she watched Owen high above her, taking down wizard after wizard with his streams of fire. He was holding his own against them remarkably well, but it didn't matter much. The wizards kept coming. In the distance, Raven could see the light beams from dozens of magic rings. More wizards had been alerted to the fact that a rogue dragon shifter and wizard had intruded on Saul's territory. It was only a matter of time before Saul himself heard about this, if he hadn't already.

Raven tried to yell at Owen, to tell him it was useless and that he should just attempt to escape. But the force field that had trapped her seemed to block sound, too. She couldn't hear the noises from the battle above, and no one paid any attention to her screams, leading Raven to believe that no one out there could hear her.

And then, suddenly, the force field disintegrated again, and she was once again falling through the air, flailing and screaming to no avail. This time, not even the dark wizards seemed to notice her. They were too busy swarming around Owen, trying to take him down. Raven felt panic rising in her chest again as she picked up speed, falling faster and faster toward the dark earth below. She had to be less than a minute away from impacting with the earth, and she whimpered, unable even to scream.

Stop panicking, she told herself. Think. You have to think. How can you save yourself?

And then, in an instant, she had a flash of brilliance—a crazy idea that just might work. She pointed her magic ring toward herself and yelled out the spell that made objects as weightless as a feather.

"*Magicae pluma*," she said. She felt a shock of energy go through her, and then, her rapid fall abruptly stopped. Instead of hurtling toward the ground, she was floating now, just like a small feather. It took her a full minute to get her breathing back to normal, and to realize that she was not moments from certain death, after all. The bile that had been rising in her throat gradually subsided and she was able to think clearly.

Owen must have killed both of the wizards who had tried to hold her inside of the force fields. When a wizard died, any spells that they had been using immediately ceased to operate. That's why the force fields, and the stunning spell, had ended so suddenly. Raven was surprised that none of the dark wizards seemed to have noticed now that she was missing. She was, after all, the one holding the dragon amethyst. They must not know that she and Owen were actually carrying the amethyst. That was the only explanation. And, if that was true, it was best if things stayed that way. If Saul or any of his soldiers suspected that the amethyst was so close, the whole throng back by Sandview would be after Owen and Raven in an instant.

Raven couldn't see anything on the ground clearly in the thick darkness, but she had to be getting fairly close to it. Owen and the battling wizards looked very far away. Raven had a feeling that he didn't even know where she was, which no doubt made him quite unhappy. She tried to think of the best way to get his attention. Just as she landed on the warm, sandy ground, she hit upon an idea. Raising her magic ring high above her head, she took a deep breath and prayed that this would work.

"*Magicae scintillula*," she said. Instantly, a large shower of shimmering sparkling light shot upward from her ringed hand. She held her hand steady, and waited.

A few moments later, as she'd hoped, Owen saw her. She knew that he'd seen her, because she saw him start to dive downward toward her by the light of the dark wizards' rings. She held her hand steady, praying that he would reach her first, before any of the dark wizards. Her heart beat faster the closer he got.

"Come on," she whispered. "Fly, Owen, fly."

She watched as he got closer, outpacing the wizards despite their best efforts to catch him. Her heart leapt with joy as she saw him approach her with his feet and claws outstretched, ready to scoop her up.

He plucked her expertly from the ground, wrapping his razor sharp claws around her perfectly so that he held her firmly without harming her. He barely slowed down as he swooped by, and the sudden forward momentum made Raven somewhat dizzy. She took a couple deep breaths to steady herself, and then yelled out, "*Scintillula terminantur.*"

Instantly, the dazzling sparks that had been shooting out from her ring disappeared.

"*Magicae arma*," she yelled out, concentrating on putting a protective shield around her and Owen. Owen's dragon hide protected him fairly well, but he did have a few vulnerable spots. The last thing she wanted right now was for him to get hit in one of those spots and go down. And she herself was vulnerable, an easy target as she hung suspended by Owen's claws.

Owen was flying faster than Raven had ever seen him fly before. The battle, and nearly losing her in it, must have energized him. His body above her was straightened into a perfectly streamlined shape. He looked like a bullet as he zoomed through the air, only his flapping wings breaking up the aerodynamics of his form.

Raven glanced behind them, seeing to her relief that the dark wizards were losing ground. Owen never looked back, and never slowed. He just flew forward as if his life depended on it. And it probably did. Raven knew that if they were caught, Saul would likely torture them for information and then kill them. He would quickly discover that they held the dragon amethyst, and steal it to use for his own evil purposes. This would be a great blow to the good shifters and wizards, and would be an ultimate failure on the part of Raven and Owen. Their task had been to get the dragon amethyst safely to the shifter protectors in Texas. As long as Owen could outrun the group behind him, they might still have a chance of doing that.

They were far enough away from Sandview now that Raven hoped there were no more guards ahead of them. If she was right, and their enemies were all behind them now, then it looked like they were going to make it. Raven felt her heart pounding in her chest, as it had been for most of the last hour. She felt helpless as she watched Owen above her, putting all of his energy into flying. She couldn't do much to lend a hand, other than pray for strength for him. She didn't know whether praying would help all that much, but she prayed, anyway. Anything that had the slightest chance of improving their odds of escape was worth a try.

Raven didn't know if it was her prayers, Owen's flying skills, or just dumb luck, but at some point it became clear that they were, in fact, going to escape. The lights from the dark wizards' rings grew smaller and smaller, and eventually disappeared. No new enemies appeared in front of them, and Raven felt herself relaxing somewhat as they flew. The only sound she could hear now was the whooshing of the wind as it flew past her ears in a steady stream.

Owen was not relaxing. He was flying as fast as ever, speeding through the sky. Raven had a crick in her neck from the odd way her body was positioned in his claws, and she wanted to tell him to stop and take a break. But something about the way he was flying kept her from actually making any kind of move to stop him. There was an urgency to his movements that she had never seen before, and she had seen him in some very urgent situations. He flew for hours, never slowing down, until she wondered at how it was even physically possible for him to maintain such a pace for so long.

Finally, just when Raven thought she couldn't handle the discomfort of the flight any longer, she felt him slowing and descending. She could see that they were approaching the outskirts of another small town in the middle of nowhere, and he must be planning to stop here for the night. She breathed a sigh of relief. She could hardly wait to get her feet on solid ground again.

And she hoped with all her heart that this small town didn't harbor an army of bat shifters, like the last small town they'd been in had.

CHAPTER SEVEN

As soon as Owen had landed, and had set Raven down softly on the ground, he collapsed into a panting, aching heap. He did not even have the energy to shift back into human form right now. All he could do was lie there, breathing heavily and feeling slightly embarrassed that he was appearing this weak in front of Raven.

Of course, he should not have felt embarrassed at all. He had just flown faster than he ever had in his life, and for quite a great distance. He had thrown all his energy into getting as far away from Saul as he could, as quickly as possible. For the moment, at least, it looked like his efforts had succeeded. He was safe. Raven was safe. And, perhaps most importantly, the dragon amethyst was safe. He had no idea how long this feeling of safety would last, but he would enjoy it while it did.

He hadn't realized until he stopped how exhausted he felt. As he looked around now, trying to take in his surroundings, he realized that everything looked slightly blurry. His eyes were too tired to focus properly on anything, and so he shut them. He knew that up ahead there was a small town. He guessed that they were somewhere in Colorado, but he couldn't quite be sure. When morning came, he and Raven could regroup and figure out where they had landed.

The thought of Raven made him shudder with relief. There'd been a good stretch of time tonight, when he was fighting the dark wizards, when he'd thought he was never going to see Raven alive again. Remembering those moments made his heart feel like it was literally twisting into knots inside of him. He opened his eyes again for a moment, just to make sure that she was really there with him, really okay.

She was just shrugging out of the giant backpack that she wore, moving stiffly as she let it fall to the ground. Owen knew she probably felt exhausted, too, even though she'd only been a passenger on this flight. Rushing through the sky for hours while hanging from a dragon's claws was not the most comfortable way to travel.

Raven did not complain, though. She rushed over to him as quickly as her stiff muscles would allow her to, and wrapped her arms around his large dragon head.

"Owen! Owen, are you alright? I was so scared for a while there. I think we're okay now, though."

Owen could not answer. All he could manage was a soft sigh, and then he closed his eyes. Sleep began to overtake him. He tried to fight it, but its pull was too strong and his exhaustion was too great. The last thing he remembered hearing before he lost consciousness was Raven's voice as she cast protective spells over them.

"*Magicae invisibilia. Magicae arma. Magicae…*"

* * *

When Owen opened his eyes once again, the sky was lit up by a bright pink sunrise. He lifted his head, and was surprised at how heavy it felt. That's when he realized he was still in dragon form. He blinked his eyes a few times, trying to shake off the disoriented feeling that filled him. It had been a long time since he'd fallen asleep in dragon form, over a decade perhaps. He couldn't figure out why he was in dragon form at first, but then the events of the night before came rushing back to him. He lifted his head further, looking around for Raven. He curled his dragon lips up in a smile when he realized that she was curled up next to his dragon belly, her chest rising and falling as she slept peacefully beside him. He took a few moments to enjoy her beauty. The dawn made her skin glow with a warm, rosy tint, and her shiny hair fell around her face and shoulders in thick waves. He sighed, wishing that he could lie here with her all day, enjoying her company, instead of worrying about Saul's army or the dragon amethyst.

But it would be some time before he could hope to have the luxury of a carefree day again. As slowly and quietly as he could, he scooted his dragon body away from her and stood. He walked a good distance away to shift back to human form, hoping that he was far enough away that he wouldn't wake her when he shifted. But before his body was even done turning back into human form, she was standing to her feet, watching him carefully. He walked back toward her, shrugging apologetically.

"Sorry. I thought I was far enough away to shift without waking you."

She smiled. "I think I woke up when you moved. You were so warm, and then you were gone and I felt chilled."

Owen pulled her into his arms, nuzzling the top of her head. "Better?" he asked.

"Much," she said, her voice muffled against his chest. They stood like that for a few minutes, holding each other tightly and wondering at the fact that they were both alive, and free, and still had possession of the dragon stone. After several minutes, Owen finally pulled away and started to dig in their backpack for some clothes.

"Any idea where we are?" Raven asked him as he dressed.

Owen shook his head no. "Have you looked at the GPS unit you stole?"

"The GPS unit I took with good intentions to pay later," Raven said, giving him a cross look. "And yes, I've looked at it. We're somewhere in southwest Colorado, it seems. You flew really far last night."

"That doesn't surprise me," Owen said as he rubbed his upper arms. "I haven't been sore like this for a long time."

Raven sat down on a small rock and frowned. "I tried to contact Falcon Cross again, but there's still no response. I'm trying not to panic, but I'm worried about everyone back home."

Owen walked over to sit beside her. "Don't get too worried just yet," he said. "Saul had quite a large army with him in Sandview, and I don't think an army that huge could have gotten from Falcon Cross to Sandview so quickly. I don't think there's been an attack on Falcon Cross. My guess is they're having some trouble with their lines of communication. Perhaps Saul is trying to keep our different groups of shifters and wizards from communicating with each other."

"We shouldn't even try to contact them, then," Raven said, looking even more worried now. "If he's hacked into their communication systems, he might be able to trace us whenever we call, and figure out where we are."

"It's possible," Owen said. "Which is why we shouldn't hang around here long. We should keep moving. If you called Falcon Cross this morning, Saul's army might already be on our way to try to attack us."

"Great," Raven said, putting her head in her hands. "I should have thought of that. We aren't much of a match for his army on our own, as you've seen."

Owen shrugged. "No, we're not. But we are faster than them. And I'm not sure whether they know that we have the dragon amethyst. If they don't realize that we have it, they might not be that interested in chasing us down. There's not much point in sending a whole army after two rogue soldiers."

"That's true," Raven said. "But I wouldn't be surprised if they did know we have the stone. If they caught up with the army retreating from the Redwoods, they would have realized that someone escaped with the stone in a different direction than the army."

Owen and Raven were both quiet for a few minutes. Neither one of them wanted to think about the possibility that their friends had been caught by Saul's army during the retreat from the Redwoods. But it was a very real possibility.

Finally, Raven let out a long sigh and broke the silence. "So what now?" she asked.

"Now, we make our way to Texas," Owen said. "Our original mission was to get the dragon amethyst to the shifter protectors there, and I think we should continue to work toward that goal."

"We haven't been able to get a hold of the shifter protectors in Texas, either," Raven said. "What if they aren't there anymore?"

"I think they're still there," Owen said. "They're just having trouble with their lines of communication, too. And, honestly, if they aren't there any more, then we're doomed. That would mean Saul's army had managed to capture them despite the fact that they have both the dragon emerald and dragon sapphire."

"True," Raven said. "That does seem unlikely."

She kicked at the dusty ground with her foot, and then let out another long sigh.

"Well," she finally said as she looked up at Owen. "I guess we should get going, then. No sense hanging around here, where Saul's army might be able to find us."

"How are our supplies?" Owen asked.

Raven shrugged. "We're alright for the time being, I think. We have plenty of food, and it should easily last us until we get to Texas as long as we keep flying at a relatively quick pace."

Owen nodded. "I think we should go ahead and start flying, then. If we need to stop for supplies later, we can. But the most important thing now is to get away from here before Saul's people find us. I would imagine they're also not too happy that we discovered his little bat shifter project out in Sandview."

"No, probably not," Raven said. "Let's eat a quick breakfast and get going, then."

Owen and Raven both wolfed down meal bars, and then Owen started stripping off his clothes again in preparation to shift. He had just taken off his shirt when Raven looked up at him and gave him a sad smile.

"It kind of sucks, doesn't it? Having to be on the run and worry about all this dark magic shit. I'd much rather go home and spend time hanging out with you, enjoying life."

Owen winked at her as he started unbuttoning his pants. "Soon enough, Love," he said. "Don't give up hope just yet. Saul might have seen a few victories, but the war is far from over. We'll beat the darkness yet, trust me on that."

And with that, Owen tossed the last of his clothes to her, and began shifting into dragon from. It was time to get the dragon amethyst to safety.

CHAPTER EIGHT

Owen flew nonstop until dusk, but he kept his pace much slower than it had been the night before. For one thing, he didn't want to wear himself out completely. He needed to save some of his strength in case Saul's army did manage to find and attack Raven and him. For another thing, flying during daylight was more dangerous than flying at night. Keeping his pace slow allowed Raven to cast a more effective invisibility spell over them. So far, the spell seemed to be working, because they hadn't been attacked and hadn't seen any sign of enemy soldiers.

When darkness started falling, he decided it was a good time to stop and rest. He was hungry, and they had made good progress today. Owen felt he deserved a break, and he found a somewhat rocky spot to stop and rest. The scenery had once again become flat and desert-like, and there weren't many well-sheltered places around. Hopefully, the darkness and Raven's invisibility shield would be enough to keep them safe tonight, and allow them a good night's rest.

"According to the GPS, we're pretty much on the border of Texas and New Mexico right now," Raven announced as soon as Owen had shifted back into human form. She had already spread out their sleeping bag, and was now pulling some of his clothes out of their backpack. She tossed him a shirt and a pair of pants, then sat down on the sleeping bag next to the backpack.

"That's good," Owen said. "We should be able to make it to the shifter protectors sometime tomorrow."

"Assuming they're still there," Raven said.

"They're there," Owen said as he pulled on his pants. Raven looked at him skeptically, and he supposed he couldn't blame her. He had no sure way of knowing that the shifter protectors, and his own clan leader, Knox, were all still there and alright. But he felt deep in his heart that they were, and that was assurance enough for him.

Raven shrugged and started digging in the backpack for some food. "I hope you're right," she said. "And I hope this is the last night for a while that I have to eat a meal replacement bar for dinner. I'm so sick of these things,"

"Me too," Owen said. "But at least we have food and don't have to try to sneak into another town right now. I think it's better to keep ourselves as low profile as we possibly can. With any luck, we'll be feasting on Texas barbeque tomorrow night."

"Hopefully with a side of cold beer," Raven said as she tossed Owen one of the meal replacement bars.

"Now you're talking," Owen said with a grin. He came to sit down by Raven, and the two of them munched hungrily for a few minutes. Owen looked up at the sky, which was almost fully dark now. The stars were already shining brilliantly, and he smiled as he watched them twinkling.

"It's beautiful, isn't it?" Raven said, following his gaze.

Owen reached his left hand over to rest on Raven's right knee. "Very beautiful," he said. "There' nothing quite like looking up at a night sky when you're miles away from any big cities. Well nothing except…"

496

He let his voice trail off, and Raven looked at him with one of her eyebrows raised in a questioning expression.

"Except?" she asked.

He grinned at her and then, in one swift move he pushed her over onto her back so that he was on top of her.

"Except making love under an open night sky, miles away from any big city."

Raven rolled her eyes at him, but he could see by the moonlight the flush of excitement that was starting to creep its way into her cheeks.

"You're ridiculous," she managed to say, but her voice sounded breathless and full of anticipation. She wanted him. He was sure of it.

"Am I, now?" he said, then bent his head forward so that his lips met hers. He felt a familiar heat filling his body as he kissed her, and he closed his eyes so that he could fully enjoy the sensation. To his surprise though, Raven pulled her face away and tried to wriggle out from under him. He opened his eyes again to find her shaking her head at him.

"Owen, this isn't a good idea."

His heart dropped, and the hair on the back of his neck actually stood on end from the sense of alarm that filled him. He sat up slowly, trying to keep his breathing even.

"Why not?" he asked. He didn't like the feeling of dread that her words gave him. He wasn't used to being rejected by women, and especially not by a woman who less than a day ago had told him she loved him. A thousand different scenarios flooded across his mind, each more troubling than the next. Was their romance really going to be that short? Or was she trying to play one of those games women play where they act like they're rejecting you just to make you want them more? Owen frowned and crossed his arms. He wasn't going to play a game like that, and he would have thought Raven was better than that. Or maybe she just thought they shouldn't be together because they were colleagues? Because he was a dragon and she was a wizard? Because their friends had all teased them that they liked each other and they had been vehemently denying it for months?

"Why not?" Owen repeated. His voice sounded strained and raspy, which surprised him. He was not in control of this situation, or his emotions, and he didn't like that. But how could he be expected to control his emotions when the woman he loved was sitting there telling him that they shouldn't sleep together? Oh, god. Was it the sex? Had she not liked the sex? He thought he'd done a good job of pleasuring her, but then again, some women were good fakers.

"Raven," he said, hating the way the frustration he felt was so obvious in his tone of voice, but unable to stop himself from talking. Raven wasn't looking at him now, though. She was scanning the sky, her eyes passing back and forth over the glittering stars with an intense focus.

"They could be anywhere," she said. "Saul's soldiers could be anywhere, and we don't know for sure how well our invisibility shields are holding. If we start fooling around and stop paying attention, we're giving them an open invitation to swoop in and attack us while we're completely unaware and completely helpless."

Owen felt his breath go out of him in a rush of relief. So that was all. It wasn't that she didn't like *him*, or didn't want *him*. She just thought it was dangerous to make love under the stars when Saul's soldiers might be hiding in those stars, waiting for an opportune moment to attack.

She was right, of course. But he didn't give a damn about safety at the moment.

He gave a low, hungry growl, and then pushed her back onto the sleeping bag. "If they're watching, let's give them something to watch," he said. He reached to start pulling off her shirt, tearing it off her body so quickly that it was gone almost before she had a chance to realize what he was doing.

"Owen!" she squeaked out in protest. 'This is a bad idea. The invisibility shield…"

"It hasn't failed us yet today," Owen said. He tore off her bra, and then her pants and then removed the clothes from the lower half of her body in a matter of seconds. His dragon was roaring within him, hungry and desperate. He had to have her. So what if they were in a risky situation? He'd spent his whole life living on the edge, but nothing had ever made him feel quite as reckless as Raven's beautiful face. He jumped to his feet to take off his own pants, and in a few moments he was just as naked as Raven was.

"Owen," she said, protesting again. But her protest was a little weaker this time. She looked up at him with wide, hungry eyes. Her naked body looked exquisite in the moonlight, and he saw a flash of silver as the moonlight shimmered off the wet spot that was now growing between her legs. Her mind might be trying to hold her back, but her physical body could not resist him.

And he could not resist her.

"It's dangerous," she whispered in one more feeble attempt to hold him back.

"I know," he said. But he did not slow down as he moved above her. She closed her eyes then, and he knew she was giving in to the desire that was holding them both captive. The primal urging inside of him, the burning love, the electricity in the air between them…it was all too much for him to hold back out of fear of attack. Let the enemy dare to interrupt this moment. Owen would kill anyone who got in his way right now. He would not be stopped. The desire was too strong.

He opened his eyes one last time, and saw Raven reaching up toward him. Her arms wrapped around his neck, and he felt her hips arching up to met him as he rammed into her. The moment they connected felt like an explosion. Heat rushed through his body, setting every last bit of him on fire. He closed his eyes and let the inferno take him.

The pressure built in his body as he rammed hungrily into her, over and over. He could be a gentle, tender lover when he wanted to, but there was nothing gentle about his movements right now. The hunger that filled him at this moment did not allow for tenderness. It was a blind, raging hunger that could only be satisfied by one thing.

Her.

She was perfection, he thought, as he slid in and out of her. Her slick, soft warmth enveloped him. He had never known a passion this intense. His body felt like it was entirely composed of electricity, with every nerve ending crackling and buzzing. Somewhere in the back of his mind, his consciousness tried to warn him to stay alert. There were enemies afoot, and he could not completely let down his guard, even in a moment like this. But focusing on anything other than Raven proved impossible, especially when she arched her back even further and pushed her hips up against him as she exploded. She screamed out in ecstasy, and he opened his eyes to watch her as she came.

Her nipples were hard and her breasts full, bouncing softly in the moonlight as her body shuddered beneath him. Her inner muscles clamped around him over and over as she tossed her head back and forth, as though trying to contain the sensations that filled her. Her face was scrunched up tightly, and Owen felt a thrill rush through him at the sight of it. He had done this to her. It was his body, his movements, his love that had made her feel this way. This knowledge turned him on like nothing else, and he felt the pressure between his legs growing to an impossible climax.

Once again, he squeezed his eyes shut, and then he was completely gone. The inferno within him centered itself between his legs, and then he stiffened as he completely lost control and came into Raven. His dick throbbed, pushing back against her inner walls, which were still clenching around him. They were lost together in the pure bliss of being one with each other. The moment had come so hard and fast, but sleeping with her was anything but quick and casual. This perfect pleasure had resulted from a buildup of months and months of desire. And even as the trembling in his body slowed down, and his panting evened out to a more reasonable, even breathing, he knew that making love with her would never feel anything less than extraordinary. She was too good and too sweet, and her fire burned him too fiercely. They were made for each other.

With an exhalation that was somewhere between a shudder and a sigh, Owen finally pulled out of Raven to lie next to her. But before his sweaty body had completely disconnected from hers, he saw her eyes widen, and she shrieked.

"Owen! They found us!"

The words registered in his mind only moments before a loud, thundering explosion sounded off, filling the night sky with streaks of fire.

CHAPTER NINE

Raven was on her feet in milliseconds, but getting her bearings took longer. The noise in the sky above her was deafening, and the flames were blinding. She wasn't sure how long the dark wizards and shifters had been there, but it could not have been too terribly long. The protective shield she'd set up was still holding. For now.

It would not be much longer before they broke through, though. The explosions and flashes of fire were coming from the attacks on the shield, and Raven knew enough of Saul's army by now to know that a protective shield would not hold them back for long.

Owen was already on his feet, shifting into dragon form with an explosive rush of energy. Raven ran for the backpack, cursing the fact that she was naked. There was no time to pull clothes on, though. She might only have a matter of seconds, and the most important thing was to keep the dragon amethyst safe. But how?

She swung the backpack up onto her shoulder and looked doubtfully up toward the sky. How, exactly, she and Owen were going to fight off an army of this size was beyond her. Above her, just outside the transparent protective shield, she could see what looked like hundreds and hundreds of wizard wands, lit up constantly by the magic spells the dark wizards were casting. By the light of the wizards' wands, Raven could see hundreds of glittering, evil eyes. The bat shifters were here, their awful screeches filling the air as they swirled around the wizards, hungry for the chance to attack.

Raven looked over at Owen, feeling the true grip of fear for perhaps the first time in her life. They were facing certain death. There was no way one dragon and one wizard could hold their own against an army of this size. Raven felt like crying, but she forced back the tears. She would not allow Saul's soldiers the satisfaction of seeing her weep. Instead, she looked over at Owen, whose giant dragon form was standing tense and ready, and she mouthed the words, "I love you."

In response, he shot a stream of fire straight up into the air—his way, she knew, or returning the sentiment. And then, all hell broke loose.

A sickening crack sounded across the sky as the protective shield broke. Raven let the protective shield spell go, focusing all her magic energy instead on what would be her last battle ever, barring a miracle. She gritted her teeth as she watched the hordes of dark soldiers beginning to hurl downward toward her. If she was going down, she was at least going to take out as many of them as she could.

"Steady," she whispered to herself. "Steady. Wait until they are close enough to hit."

Next to her, Owen also stood still, tense and holding in his fiery breath until the enemy soldiers were within range. It didn't take long. Saul's soldiers had been high up in the air, but as the shield broke, they dove downward with incredible speed. The bats were slightly faster than the wizards, and arrived first.

"*Magicae appugno*," Raven yelled, holding her magic ring high above her head, and slicing it through the air as she yelled the attack spell over and over. "*Magicae appugno, magicae appugno.*"

Burning laser beams shot out from her ring, killing every bat they came in contact with. Piles of dead and dying bats started falling around her, shrieking as they fell from the sky. The wizards were arriving now, and, although they were more difficult to take down due to their shield spells, Raven still managed to fell quite a few of them. Beside her, Owen was doing his part to kill off enemy soldiers, roaring as he breathed a constant stream of fire in the direction of the advancing horde.

But their defense did not last for long. Even Owen's thick dragon hide could not protect him against such a large onslaught of enemy soldiers. Raven heard him yelping in pain as some of the dark wizards' attacks managed to hit him in vulnerable spots. Raven herself felt sharp pricks of pain as the wizards hit her with their attacks, or the bats managed to sink their teeth or claws into her.

She continued to fight bravely, but she felt her strength waning. Her arm grew weak and tired, but she forced herself to keep slicing it through the air, her hoarse voice yelling out, "*Magicae appugno, magicae appugno,*" over and over. The skies grew darker, and soon she could not see the stars anymore. Then Owen was separated from her, blocked from her view by a wall of dark wizards and shifters. Raven did not allow herself to think about the fact that this was the end. She only allowed herself to focus on killing as many of Saul's soldiers as she could.

Just focus on the next soldier, and then the next, and then the next, she told herself. And so she did. She knew Owen was still alive and fighting, because every now and then she saw a stream of fire rising into the throng. The fire was getting further and further away from her, however, and the minutes between blasts were growing longer and longer. He was fading, just like her.

Finally, one of the dark soldiers dealt Raven a blow too great for her to withstand. She felt herself losing her balance, and tumbling to the ground. She had fought bravely, and had done her best. But all was lost now. If they didn't already know that the bag on her back held the dragon amethyst, they would soon find out. They would take it back to Saul, who would gloat over the fact that he had managed to capture back the powerful stone.

Raven felt a fresh blast of laser fire hitting her. The blow had struck her backpack, splitting it open with such force that Raven was knocked sideways, and the contents of the backpack went flying in every direction. Her naked body rubbed against the rough ground as the enemy closed in for the kill. She closed her eyes as bat teeth sunk into her flesh and last beams stung at her. She squeezed her hand shut into a fist, then, and was surprised to find that her fingers were closing around something round and hard.

She did not have to open her eyes to know it was the dragon amethyst. Somehow in the chaos, the stone had landed right beside her hand, and the dark soldiers had not yet realized it had been in the bag. Raven squeezed her hand even tighter around it, wishing that she could hide it from them forever. But she knew it was no use. Her strength was fading, and once they had killed her, they would quickly realize what she held in her hand.

If only I knew how to use this stupid thing, she thought. If only I knew how to activate its power.

But she did not know. No one had figured it out yet, and she had no time left to learn. The world around her was growing gray, and quieter. Sound and color was fading away as her strength left her. She tried to her turn her thoughts to Owen, but all she could seem to focus on was the cool, purple stone in her hand.

I wish I knew how to activate your power, she thought again. And then, somehow, in the midst of the buzz of battle, she thought she heard it whisper back.

Help is yours, if only you would ask.

I'm hallucinating now, Raven thought. I'm making things up now.

But the whisper seemed to come again.

Help is yours, if only you would ask.

Raven felt like she was going crazy, but what did she really have to lose at this point. She might as well indulge her pointless fantasy, and pretend in her final moments that all hope was not actually lost.

"Help me," she whispered, directing all her thoughts toward the stone. "If you can really hear me somehow, then please, help."

Nothing happened when she whispered these words, and Raven finally allowed a single tear to escape her eyelids. Her very last hope was gone. Not even the dragon amethyst would save her now. She squeezed her eyes shut, doing her best to think only of Owen. Owen, whose gorgeous, tanned face with its handsome, chiseled features would now live only in memories. If she had to die, at least she was dying with him. They'd had a good run together, even if it had been unfairly short.

Not long after she closed her eyes, however, she felt a sudden jolt of energy go through her right arm, which was holding the dragon amethyst. The force was so powerful that it lifted her whole body several feet off the ground. She slammed down to the earth again, eyes open wide in shock as she looked around to see wizards and bats shrieking in pain. Most of the wizards had fallen off their broomsticks, tumbling to the earth with their hands covering their faces as they yelped in pain.

"Did I do that?" Raven thought as she looked around. "Or, perhaps more accurately, did the dragon amethyst do that? Did it really respond to my request for help? Have I unlocked its power?"

A fresh wave of hope surged through her as she looked around. Saul's soldiers seemed to have forgotten her in their anguish. They were turning around in confused circles, shrieking in pain and trying to escape from some sort of unseen attack. Raven looked down at her hand in wonder, slowly unfurling her fingers to look at the amethyst, which was now glowing slightly in her palm.

"Please, help me," she repeated again, not sure what she expected to happen, but feeling insanely curious. This time, the rush of energy came almost before she had finished speaking the words. She felt another jolt, and her whole body was once again hurled several feet in the air as the dragon amethyst reacted to her words. The energy from the stone seemed to radiate out from her in one big, circular blast. This time, once the blast settled, the shrieking had stopped, too. The second blow from the dragon stone had sucked all of the remaining life out of the dark wizards and bat shifters. Raven slowly stood, looking around for any signs of movement and not seeing any. The blasts of laser fire had ended abruptly, replaced by a cool gentle breeze that felt like heaven against her naked, sweating skin.

Raven's eyes scanned the seemingly endless sea of dead wizards and bats, biting her lip to hold back the tears of relief that wanted to flood through her. But the feeling of relief was short-lived. Her heart nearly stopped in her chest when she saw, amidst the wizards and bats, the lifeless form of a giant, green dragon.

"Owen!" she screamed, and started running toward him, tripping over the thick mass of death that lay in between them.

* * *

Owen had been in plenty of hairy situations in his life, but he had never been in a situation where he was so sure he was going to die. The mass of enemy soldiers around him was so thick that he couldn't see two feet in any direction. He had long since lost sight of Raven, and he wasn't even sure whether she was still alive or not. If she wasn't, then he didn't much want to live, either. He couldn't imagine a world without Raven.

But he had no way of knowing for sure whether they had killed her, and somehow the knowledge that she might still have breath left in her body kept him going. Every now and then, he would gather his strength as best he could and shoot a stream of fire straight up into the air, hoping that she would see it and know he was still here, still fighting. If she still lived, he wanted her to know he was thinking about her—would be thinking about her, until his dying breath.

And that dying breath was coming, he knew. His energy was fading, and many of the bat shifters seemed to have figured out where the vulnerable spots in his dragon hide were located. They were clawing and biting at him, and he could feel trickles of blood starting to ooze out of his body. His very life force was fading away.

He fought as hard as he could, for as long as he could. He wanted to kill as many of the enemy soldiers as possible. But, finally, he could fight no longer. His dragon legs gave way, and his mighty dragon body fell to the ground with a giant thud. He heard a gleeful cheer rising from the soldiers that surrounded them, but he did his best to ignore it. He closed his eyes, and focused all his thoughts on Raven. In his mind's eye, he saw her beautiful face. He wanted her to be the last thing he thought of before he died.

No sooner had he closed his eyes than he felt a giant rush of energy rock his entire body. He heard shrieking all around him, almost as though the wizards and bats were in pain. Another rush of energy seemed to shake the very earth he was lying on, and then, everything went silent.

After the chaos of the battle, the silence felt soothing, welcoming. The air around him, which had been so hot in the midst of battle, felt cooler now. He felt almost like a breeze was brushing against his dragon hide. Was this what dying felt like, he wondered? It wasn't as bad as he'd thought it would be. He squeezed his eyes tighter and let the cool breeze wash over him. The quiet was so strange after all of the shrieking of battle.

But then he heard a noise in the midst of the silence. It sounded like someone stumbling around over a great deal of obstacles. Then he heard a shout.

"Owen! Owen!"

The voice sounded suspiciously like Raven's, and his eyes flew open in confusion. What he saw confused him even more. He did not appear to be in any sort of afterlife, as he'd thought. Instead, all appearances seemed to indicate that he was still on the battlefield. Dead wizards and bat shifters surrounded him by the hundreds, and here and there flames were still burning from where laser beams had set something on fire. And then, Owen saw her.

Raven.

She was wearing one of his t-shirts, but it was so large on her that it almost looked like a dress. She didn't have on any pants or shoes, but she was dragging along what looked like the remains of the backpack they'd been carrying since they left Sandview. Her right hand was balled into a fist, but between her fingers he could see something glowing purple. The dragon amethyst, he thought. She was holding the dragon amethyst, and it was lit up somehow.

Confused, he sat up slightly. Every muscle in his body protested at the movement, and a sharp pain shot through his left side. But the fact that he was moving seemed to bring great relief to Raven, who had nearly reached him by this point.

"You're alive!" she shrieked. "Oh, thank god, you're alive!"

She crossed the last few steps to reach him and then threw her arms around his dragon neck in a giant hug.

Alive? Owen thought. I'm alive? How is this possible? He looked around again, taking in the silent battlefield. There were far more soldiers dead then he and Raven could have ever hoped to have killed on their own. Was he dreaming? Or was he really still alive somehow, with their enemy defeated. He wanted to ask Raven so many things, but he couldn't speak while still in dragon form. Gently, he pulled back from her and stepped backward several feet, tripping over lifeless wizards and bats as he did. Raven let him go, instinctively understanding that he wanted space to shift back to human form.

Owen closed his eyes and let the human side of his DNA take over. He felt his body growing smaller as the great size of his dragon form shrunk down into the form of a man. His thick dragon hide gave way to softer human flesh. His wings and tail disappeared, and the horns on his head shrunk away as his ears lost their dragon shape. In less than a minute, his transformation was complete. He stood before Raven in human form, and he saw tears spring to her eyes as he watched her.

"Owen," she breathed out, then ran to him and threw her arms around his neck again. He wrapped his arms around her, too, rubbing the small of her back and letting her weep for a moment as he tried to gather his thoughts.

"Am I really alive?" Owen asked.

Raven stepped back to look at him and laughed. "Yes. You really are alive. This is all really happening."

"But…how?"

"The dragon amethyst," Raven said. "I asked it for help and it responded. I'm still not sure exactly what happened. All I know is that I was lying on the ground, thinking all hope was lost. Then one of Saul's soldiers tore my bag open, and the dragon amethyst landed next to my hand. In desperation, I just asked it for help. And it actually responded! Some sort of energy or force field came rushing out of it, first stunning and then killing all these soldiers."

Owen looked around at all the dead wizards and shifters on the battle field. There must have been thousands of them. "This is a mess," he said.

Raven shrugged. "I can clean it up," she said. "I know a magic spell that should do the trick."

Owen rubbed his forehead. He was still trying to process the fact that he was alive, and their enemies were dead. Well, at least the enemies that had attacked them tonight were dead. Saul still had plenty of soldiers to send after them. Once news of this battle reached the evil dragon wizard's ears, Saul would probably send a fresh wave of attackers after Owen and Raven. This thought is what finally spurred Owen to action. He didn't have the luxury of time to sit around and ponder everything that had just happened to him.

"If you can clean this up, then do it. We need to move."

Raven hesitated for just a moment, but then nodded. She pointed her ring toward a pile of the dead bodies and started saying, "*Magicae eradico. Magicae eradico.*"

The bodies started disintegrating into wisps of dust, which were quickly blown away by the cool night breeze. Owen didn't like treating dead soldiers like this. Even enemy soldiers deserved a proper, respectful burial. But they didn't have much of a choice at the moment. If he and Raven left any evidence of battle here, it would only make them that much easier to find—and make Saul all the more determined to find them.

Owen turned away and focused on repacking Raven's backpack. She had repaired it with one of her magic spells already, but the items it should have contained were scattered all over the place. Owen carefully put their food, clothes, and other supplies back into the bag, leaving out a set of clothes for Raven so she could get dressed again when she was done obliterating the enemy corpses. He would not bother getting dressed, since he would be shifting into dragon form again soon.

The last thing he wanted to do right now was to fly more. His body was exhausted from flying all day, and from the battle he had just endured. But the battle had made it clear that they needed to move. The sooner they could get to Texas, the better. Owen guessed they had about twelve hours of flying left before they arrived in Persimmon Springs, the town where the shifter protectors were keeping the dragon stones. That was a long stretch of flying, but at least he would have a chance to rest once he got there. One more big push, and then he could indulge in a day or two of relaxation.

At least, he hoped he could relax a bit. He still didn't know what had happened to Vance and the others who retreated from the Redwoods. And he couldn't say for sure whether Falcon Cross was still standing. All he could do was pray for the best, and hope that there was still time to turn this war around.

For the better part of an hour, Owen watched Raven as she walked the field, swinging her magic ring in wide arcs and saying "*Magicae eradico. Magicae eradico.*"

When, at long last, her work was done, she turned and walked back to him with a somber expression on her face.

"All done," she said, stating the obvious. "Now let's get out of here."

She was tired, too. The dark circles under her eyes gave away her exhausted state, although she tried to hide it.

"Come on," Owen said. "Let's get out of here and get to Persimmon Springs so we'll be safe."

Raven laughed bitterly. "I'm not sure we'll ever truly be safe again," she said. "We should have known better than to make love in the middle of field with a war raging around us."

Owen thought he detected a note of accusation in her voice, which angered him slightly.

"You didn't put up *that* much of a fight," he said, crossing his arms. "Seems like you really wanted to have some fun, too. And besides, it wouldn't have mattered if we'd both been prepared and keeping watch instead of having sex. There were too many soldiers for us to fight or outrun on our own, regardless of whether they caught us by surprise or not. The dragon amethyst is the only reason we're still alive right now, and whatever else we were doing didn't make a lick of difference. You know that."

Raven shrugged, but the bitter look never quite left her eyes. Owen sighed and pushed the backpack in her direction.

"Put this on," he said. "I'm going to shift, and then we need to get out of here. We don't have time to dilly dally."

They didn't have time to argue, either, and they both knew it. Raven glared at him, but then started pulling the backpack straps over her shoulders. Owen resisted the urge to roll his eyes at her as he walked several feet away to shift. He didn't think she had a right to be pissed at him, but he would let it go for now. They could sort out who was at fault for what after they'd reached Persimmons Springs. For the moment, Owen was just glad that they were both still alive. He'd very much like to keep things that way, and that meant moving, and fast.

A rush of powerful energy shook the ground as Owen once again transformed himself into a dragon. He bent low so that Raven could climb on his back, which she grudgingly did. And then, they were off again, flying through the dark night sky toward the small town of Persimmon Springs.

Owen hoped with all his heart that the shifter protectors were still there. If not, then not much hope remained for the good shifters and wizards.

CHAPTER TEN

Raven had felt exhausted plenty of times before in her life, but she was realizing with every passing minute that she had never truly known what being tired felt like before now. Every bone in her body ached. Every muscle screamed in protest as the motion of Owen's wings rocked Raven back and forth. Even her skin seemed to throb with pain. She wished that she could just collapse onto Owen's dragon back and sleep, long and hard. But she fought to keep her eyes open. She had to watch out for enemy soldiers. She forced herself to scan the horizon, looking east and west, then north and south. She did not want to be the victim of a surprise attack again. Perhaps Owen was right, that the fact that they were surprised hadn't made much difference to the outcome of the battle. Still, Raven was a seasoned soldier, and she felt ashamed that she had let her guard down so much. She did not want to make that mistake again, and so she continued turning her head in every direction, watching for any sign of incoming soldiers.

But she saw nothing, and sleep fought incessantly to take hold of her. Just as the first gray-pink streaks of dawn were starting to appear, she finally gave in. Her eyes slid shut, and the sweet, soothing blackness of sleep overtook her. She slept dreamlessly, unaware of anything going on around her. She did not feel it when Owen started to slowly descend toward the earth, circling downward until he came to a soft landing right in front of a giant, white farmhouse. It was only when he nudged her head with his dragon snout that she regained consciousness.

Blinking in confusion, she opened her eyes to find the morning sun shining brilliantly down on the world. Gone were the soft, muted grays of sunrise. It must have been about nine in the morning now, from the looks of it.

Embarrassed that she had fallen asleep, she sat up quickly and slid off Owen's back, looking around in search of some sort of familiar landmark.

"Where are we?" she asked Owen, even though she knew he couldn't answer her while in dragon form. But he was already shifting. As soon as she was off his back, a familiar rush of energy filled the air around her, indicating that he was beginning the transformation back into human form.

"Persimmon Springs," Owen said, as soon as he was done shifting. "This house serves as home base for the shifter protectors here, but I'm not sure if they're here. I'm hoping that—"

Owen never got to finish his sentence, though. Suddenly, the front door swung open, and a flood of people came running out, all screaming at once.

"Owen! You're here! You're still alive! And this must be Raven? God, we were so worried. Do you still have the dragon amethyst? Did any of Saul's soldiers follow you? We've been sitting on pins and needles hoping for some word from you!"

"Whoa, whoa, whoa!" Owen said, laughing. Raven thought she saw a hint of tears springing to his eyes, but she couldn't be sure. "We have the dragon amethyst. But one question at a time. And I get to ask some questions, too. I have a lot of them!"

Raven looked around at the group, surprised at how large it was. She recognized

Knox, who was the leader of the Redwood Dragons clan. Next to Knox was Bree, who was Knox's lifemate. Bree was famous in Falcon Cross, since she had been the one to discover the dragon sapphire and to forge an alliance between the dragons and wizards. Raven was about to introduce herself to Bree when an older, pleasantly plump woman came pushing through the crowd.

"Out of my way, everyone. Out of my way!" the woman said. "You all settle down and let these two come inside and get something to eat. They look like they're starving, and I daresay they'll be much happier talking to all of you at the breakfast table, over plates of eggs and bacon."

"Ma, you stepped on my foot," one of the men protested.

The woman waved him off. "Shouldn't have been standing in my way," she said. Then she grabbed Raven's hand. "Come on, my dear. Let's get you some food. I'm Hazel, but everyone around here just calls me Ma, and you should too. I keep this place running, and let me tell you, it's quite a job with all these whiners and complainers always getting in the way. You'd think I never did anything for them, and—"

Raven glanced back at Owen helplessly as Ma dragged her toward the house. He just shrugged and smiled, then started following them. The rest of the group came as well, and soon they were all seated around a kitchen table, where heaps of delicious breakfast food covered every spare inch. Raven saw scrambled eggs, crispy bacon, biscuits, breakfast potatoes, toast, jam, and fresh fruit. Carafes of water and juice stood next to a large thermos, which Ma quickly pointed to and identified as coffee.

"Now eat up, my dear." Ma said. "Don't be shy. You're just in time for breakfast, and we always have plenty of food around here."

Raven didn't need to be told twice. Owen, who was seated next to her, had started introducing her, telling everyone her name and that she was a military commander in Falcon Cross. But Raven hardly paid attention, barely raising her hand to give a small wave of acknowledgement to everyone at the table. The smell of food had made her realize that she was so famished she could hardly think straight, and she piled her plate high with a little bit of everything.

After a few bites of food, however, the fog in her mind began to clear. She looked up and made eye contact with a few of the other people at the table, who were all staring at her with amused looks on their faces.

"Uh...I guess I was hungry," Raven said. Everyone laughed, and Owen leaned over to plant a kiss on her cheek.

"Have you heard anything I've been saying?" he asked. Raven looked at him and saw that his eyes were dancing with merriment. She felt happy, suddenly. They had left the battlefield in the middle of an argument of sorts, and they probably both owed each other an apology. But right now, they were happy and among friends, with plenty of hot, delicious food in front of them.

"Sorry," Raven said, giving him a sheepish grin. "I wasn't paying much attention."

Owen rolled his eyes playfully. "I guess I'll start over, then. I was introducing you to everyone. You know Knox and Bree already, I'm assuming?"

Raven nodded, and smiled at the couple, who smiled warmly back.

"The rest of the group work as shifter protectors, guarding the dragon stones and looking out for the welfare of shifters in general. There's Levi and his lifemate Olivia. Levi is a panther shifter. Next to Levi are the three Texas dragon brothers and their lifemates—Theo and Maddie, Zane and Molly, and Drake and Kaiya. They're Ma's sons, although of course, everyone is Ma's kid around here. You met Ma already, but her that's her lifemate William sitting next to her. William was the leader of the Redwood Dragons clan before Knox. He rescued all of us orphan dragons and raised us to be the men we are. He lives out here now, retired and deserving every moment of peace he can get."

"Not much peace around here, with so many noisy kids," Levi commented, turning to shush a young boy who looked like a perfect miniature version of him. That was the first Raven noticed of the "kids' table." Behind the main table, about a dozen children of various ages sat at a smaller table.

"Oh, let them be noisy," Ma said. "There's no sound so wonderful as a rambunctious child."

"Huh," Theo said, crossing his arms and looking at his mother. "That's not what you said when us boys were little."

Everyone laughed, but Ma just shrugged. "I'm allowed to change my mind," she said.

Raven chuckled, too, but her head was swimming. "That's a lot of names to remember," she said.

"Oh, that's only about half of us," William said, smiling at her. "There's also Pierce and Aria, Griffin and Avery, and Max and Cassie. They're off on guard duty this morning, or taking care of other chores. I can't keep up with what everyone's doing. But anyway, there's a whole big crew of us. And we're awfully glad to have you join us."

"Agreed," Knox said, speaking up for the first time. "We were worried when we hadn't heard from you that you'd been captured, and that the dragon amethyst was lost."

"We tried to contact you, but we couldn't get through," Owen said. "We were worried that something had happened to all of *you*."

"I told you guys that the communication lines aren't working properly," Levi said. William waved him to silence, though.

"We'll figure all of that out in a minute," William said. "Right now, I want to hear about how you two got here from California."

The fog was still lifting from Raven's brain, and she suddenly realized that no one had said yet whether everyone in Falcon Cross was alright. She assumed they would have told her by now if something was terribly wrong, but still, she wanted some reassurance.

"Wait!" she said. "What about the wizards? And Falcon Cross? Is everyone okay there? And did the group escaping the Redwoods make it out okay."

Owen gave her a funny look. "You really have been out of it, huh? That's the first thing Knox told us. Everyone in Falcon Cross is alright, and Vance and the others made it safely to Falcon Cross itself without being caught. Unfortunately, the Redwoods base camp is in enemy control now."

Raven took a shuddering breath. "Can we get it back from them?" she asked.

Knox spoke up. "Well, we hope to eventually. But it's not a priority right now. We need to focus our manpower on finding the dragon ruby, and keeping the other dragon stones safe. There are other vaults near the Redwoods base camp that are full of powerful ancient artifacts, and we're worried about the security of those vaults. Hopefully, Saul's men don't find them. But even if they do, the dragon stones are more powerful than all of the artifacts in the vault combined."

"You're telling me," Owen said. "The dragon amethyst saved our lives." And then he told the group the story of the battle the night before, and how the amethyst had activated just in time. He also told of what they had seen outside of Sandview, and how Saul was building an army of bat shifters. Owen gave as many details as he could remember of the events that had transpired since he had escaped from the Redwoods with Raven. He only left out how he and Raven had finally admitted their love for each other, but Raven supposed it wasn't necessary for him to explain this to the group gathered around the table. It was obvious to anyone looking at Owen and Raven that they were together now.

Together, Raven thought, and she smiled. She'd loved Owen for so long, and it was nice to officially be his. Even if he did act like a stubborn jackass now and then. When he was finally finished speaking, the table was silent for quite some time.

"Wow," Levi finally said. "Sounds like we've underestimated Saul a bit. He's following in the footsteps of many evil wizards before him with the whole bat shifter army thing."

William nodded gravely. "He definitely isn't sitting back and taking it easy. But let's not despair too much. For one thing, he's lost the element of surprise, now that Owen and Raven discovered his hideout in Sandview. For another thing, we have three of the four dragon stones. If we have to use them, we can. And, as Owen and Raven saw, the stones can be very effective at beating back even a large enemy army."

Raven sat up straighter. "Why don't we use the stones to go destroy Saul's army right now?" she asked. "Let's just end this thing!"

The table fell silent, and the shifter protectors looked at each other with worried expressions.

"What?" Raven asked. "What's the problem? Why can't we do that?"

"The problem," Theo said, "Is that we don't want to take any chances on the dragon stones that we do have being stolen away. We've discovered some information on the dragon ruby, and it seems that the ruby is the most powerful of the dragon stones by far. If Saul's soldiers are able to get to it first—and they're searching like crazy right now—then we need to make sure we have all three of the other stones. It's our only chance for victory. We're not out of the woods yet."

"Not even close," Levi agreed. "We need to focus all our energy on finding the dragon ruby and keeping the dragon stones that we do have safe."

Raven studied the faces surrounding the table. Everyone wore a grave expression, and the mood was somber. She felt somewhat deflated herself. She'd told herself that if she and Owen could just get the dragon amethyst to Texas, and to safety, that the war would be all but won. But it seemed they had a lot of work to do yet. Even the children had fallen silent now, seeming to sense that the adults were all unhappy about something.

Finally, though, Ma's cheerful voice broke through the gloom. "The first thing y'all need to focus on is finishing up this food. Then you can worry about chasing after rubies. You're not going to get very far on an empty stomach."

Everyone laughed, and the tension was broken. No one at the table right now had an empty stomach, since they'd been eating nonstop for the last forty-five minutes or so. But they all obliged Ma and started picking at the last pieces of toast and fruit. For the moment, things seemed happy again.

But Raven was not fooled. The undercurrent of despair could still be felt in the room, and she knew that Owen and she would not be able to rest easy just yet.

CHAPTER ELEVEN

Despite the ominous cloud that had hung over the breakfast table while discussing the dragon stones, Raven found the farmhouse in general to be a happy place. After eating, Ma sent her and Owen off to get some much needed rest. They both collapsed into the warm softness of the giant king bed that filled the room they'd been given on the second floor. No one even bothered trying to give them separate rooms. It didn't take a genius to realize that they wanted to be together.

Raven had opened the window before they fell asleep, enjoying the fresh air that came seeping in through the screen. Several hours later, she awoke to the sound of laughter drifting up through that same window. She stood slowly and stretched, then walked over to look down at the source of the laughter. The kids were all outside, running and playing with William, who was surprisingly agile for his age. A smile crossed Raven's face as she watched. There might be a war going on, but children still found ways to be joyful. She was so enthralled with the scene below that she didn't hear Owen getting up as well. She jumped, slightly startled, when he put his arms around her from behind.

"He's so good with kids," Owen said as he kissed the top of Raven's head.

"William?"

"Yeah. He's the one who raised all ten of us in the Redwood Dragons clan. We were orphans, with no real future, and he made us into a family."

"Family," Raven repeated, savoring the sound of the word. The group of shifter protectors here in Texas might not all be related by blood, but it was clear that they all considered themselves a family. Raven had seen the same sense of family among the Redwood Dragons. Even though they were separated by war and duty right now, they were all a family. She wondered what it would be like to be part of a family like that.

"I wish we could stay here for a while," Raven said wistfully. "It would be nice to have some time to just 'be,' you know? To not have to worry about war or fighting or protecting dragon stones."

"I know," Owen said, squeezing his arms tighter and kissing the top of her head again. "One day. Soon. I promise."

Raven sighed. "How can you promise that? We don't know when the dragon ruby will be found, or how long it will take to finally bring Saul to his knees."

Raven felt Owen shrug. "I just have a good feeling about things. That battle with the dragon amethyst was a sign, I think. Even though the enemy is strong, the forces of good are stronger. We'll always find a way to overcome them."

"I hope you're right," Raven said.

"I'm always right," Owen said, and Raven rolled her eyes as she turned around to face him.

"Oh? Like when you said we could make love under the stars in an open Texas field with no danger of being attacked by the enemy?"

Owen laughed. "It turned out alright in the end, didn't it?"

Raven gave him a look that said he was being ridiculous, and he laughed again.

"Okay, okay. Seriously. I'm sorry that turned out the way it did. I owe you a do-over."

Raven feigned annoyance. "And what makes you think I want to sleep with you again?" she asked.

To her surprise, the joking expression left Owen's face, and his eyes turned serious.

"I don't know what you want, Raven. But I can tell you what I want. I want to spend the rest of my life with you. You know about lifemates, right?"

Raven's heart started pounding. She nodded. She'd heard about lifemates from the other wizards who had started relationships with the dragon shifters. The shifters believed that each person had someone they were destined to be with for life. When you found that person and made love to them, the lifemate bond was formed, binding your hearts and souls together for the rest of your lives. According to the shifters, the lifemate bond was unbreakable.

"Do you think I'm your lifemate?" Raven asked, finally finding her voice. Her heart was pounding so loudly now that she was sure they must be able to hear it downstairs.

Owen smiled at her. "I know it. I'm bonded to you, Raven. You're my destiny, my fated lifemate. I love you more than anything, and I want to spend the rest of my life with you. Will you have me? Will you marry me? I know I should have a ring when I ask that question, and I promise I'll get you one. But I can't wait any longer to tell you how I feel."

Owen got down on one knee in front of Raven, and she covered her mouth in shock as he continued smiling up at her. "Marry me," he said. "Say you will."

Raven felt tears springing to her eyes. She nodded enthusiastically, causing the tears to spill over her cheeks. "Yes!" she said. "A thousand times yes!"

Owen stood up then and pulled her into his arms, spinning her around with a whoop. There was a lot wrong with the world at large, but in that moment, Raven's world was perfect.

* * *

Owen wanted to shout from the rooftops that the most wonderful, beautiful girl in the world had agreed to be his. Unfortunately, he couldn't take much time to enjoy the moment just then. Before he and Raven had gone to sleep, Knox had told him that Raven and Owen were wanted back in Falcon Cross immediately. Plans were already in motion to start a search for the dragon ruby, and Peter, the head wizard in Falcon Cross, wanted Owen and Raven to be a part of the planning committee. There was no time to lose, and a late night flight back to the West Coast had already been arranged.

No rest for the weary, Owen thought as he stood in the living room of the farmhouse a few hours later, bidding all of the shifter protectors goodbye. Raven was putting up a brave front, but he knew she was sad to be leaving her new friends so soon after meeting them. Ma seemed to sense Raven's sadness, and gave her an extra long hug.

"Now don't you worry," Ma said. "Our door's always open, and this war will be over soon enough. You can come back for a nice long visit, and I'll cook you so much food you'll have to buy bigger sizes in all your clothes."

Everyone laughed, even Raven, who was wiping at the tears in her eyes. Owen took her hand and gently led her outside, where Levi's truck was waiting to drive them to the airport. The drive was long, and made mostly in silence. Everyone in the vehicle was lost in their own thoughts, until they got to the airport and had to say goodbye once more, this time to Levi.

"Take care, man," Levi said, giving Owen a big hug and a couple of hearty slaps on the back.

"You too," Owen said.

Raven gave Levi a big hug and a tearful goodbye, and then it was time to head into the terminal. They didn't have any luggage to check, and they quickly made it through security. Raven was trying to put up a brave front, but Owen could tell she was sad, and tired. They'd had quite an exhausting couple of days, and he was glad that they were flying home on a commercial airline instead of attempting the flight in dragon form again. Taking the dragon amethyst on a plane would have been risky, but they had no dragon amethyst now. They just had each other, and the amethyst was safely under the protection of the shifter protectors they had just left behind.

They had a bit of time before their flight took off, and they waited at the gate together, holding hands as they sat in those ridiculously uncomfortable blue plastic chairs. Every time Owen looked over at Raven, he was filled with a deep sense of love and happiness. He wished they had more time now to just be—to just relax and enjoy each other's company. He wanted to do something special for her, but there was no time.

Or was there? Suddenly, he had an idea.

"Hey, I want to check on something," he said to Raven, trying to keep his voice casual, and praying that he could pull this off. "I'll be right back."

Raven looked mildly curious, but shrugged and let him go. He went to talk to the agent at the gate, and a few minutes later was pulling out his credit card and taking two updated tickets from her. Everything was set. Just as he made it back to the seat where Raven was waiting, the gate agent spoke into the loudspeaker to announce that it was time to begin boarding.

"Come on," Owen said, reaching out to offer his hand to Raven. "This is us. Time to board."

Raven looked up at him but didn't move, except to shake her head.

"It's still too early. They're only boarding first class right now."

Owen smiled, and continued to hold out his hand. "I know. Time to board."

Raven looked at him like he was the slowest person alive. "We're not first class," she said, rolling her eyes.

"Yes, we are," Owen said. He reached for her hand, pulling her off the seat, and then gave her one of the new tickets the gate agent had just handed him. "I got us a little upgrade."

Raven's eyes widened. "What? But...how?"

Owen shrugged, pleased. "I just went up there and asked to upgrade our tickets. I wanted to do something special for you. I know we haven't had the type of weekend you might expect when getting engaged, but at least I can make sure you have a luxurious, comfortable flight home."

Raven stared down at the words on her new ticket like they were written in Greek. "I've never flown first class before," she said.

"Me neither," Owen replied. "So we'll get to experience it together. Come on."

Raven grinned and finally let him pull her toward the ticket agent. Their seats on the plane were huge, with plenty of legroom. Raven groaned happily as she sat down. "This is more like it," she said. "Maybe I'll actually get some rest on this flight after all."

She closed her eyes happily, but did not actually fall asleep. Thirty minutes later, when the plane had finally taken off and reached cruising altitude, her eyes popped back open.

"Do you think they're going to send us with the search party for the ruby?" she asked.

Owen shrugged. "Who knows. I don't think they have many leads yet. I know Holden and Weston from my clan have been working hard on searching, but it still might be a while before we're ready to send off an actual search party."

"Excuse me," the flight attendant interrupted as she approached them. "Are you Raven Morey?"

Raven looked up at her. "Yes, that's me."

"Good. We have a special treat for you," the flight attendant said with a smile. "I'll be right back."

Raven looked accusingly at Owen, but he just smiled coyly at her. About a minute later, the flight attendant returned with a miniature cake, just big enough for two people. It was smothered in chocolate frosting, and the word "Congratulations" was written on top with pink frosting. The flight attendant put the cake down on Raven's tray table, along with a plastic cake knife and two plastic plates and forks. A second flight attendant followed behind the first, and set down two plastic cups of champagne.

"Congratulations on your engagement, Ms. Morey," the first flight attendant said. "Enjoy your cake and champagne."

"Congratulations," echoed the second flight attendant. "And let me say, this man is a keeper. Any guy who arranges for chocolate cake for his woman is a winner in my book."

Raven looked over at Owen with a wide grin on her face. "I guess I'll keep you," she said.

Owen laughed as the flight attendants walked away. "Well, you haven't tasted the cake yet, so maybe you should reserve your judgment. And I had a lot of help from the gate agent. Finding a cake in an airport at the last minute isn't exactly easy. But I wanted to do something special to make this occasion memorable and romantic for you. It's not every day you get engaged."

Raven's smile melted his heart. "Thank you," she said. "Seriously, thank you. You didn't have to do anything, but this is so sweet of you."

Owen felt a puff of proud satisfaction. She liked his surprise. He'd done well, and he'd made his woman happy. What more could a man ask for? "Cheers," he said, holding his plastic champagne glass up to Raven. "To the many adventures we've already had, and the many more to come."

"Cheers," she echoed. They clicked their glasses together, and took a long sip of the bubbly liquid. Then Owen cut into the cake, putting one slice on each of the little plastic plates. Raven quickly dug into hers, closing her eyes in satisfaction as the sweet confection hit her tongue.

"Well," Owen asked. "How does it taste?"

"A heck of a lot better than a meal bar," she said.

Owen laughed, then took a bite of his own piece of cake. The chocolate was moist and rich, and, Raven was right—after too many meal bars, this little piece of cake was heaven.

"Still," he said, looking over at Raven and using his thumb to wipe a smudge of chocolate off the left side of her mouth. "I wouldn't trade any of our meals together for anything. Even the meal bar dinners. It's all been part of the adventure."

Her smile told him that she agreed. He leaned in and kissed her then, savoring the sticky sweetness of her chocolate covered lips. Life in the middle of a war on dark magic might be crazy, but he wouldn't trade it for anything.

Not when he got to share that life with Raven.

BOOK SEVEN: STEALTH AND THE DRAGON

CHAPTER ONE

Holden Pars tapped his fork absentmindedly on his plate. He had eaten all but the last few bites of his breakfast skillet, but had hardly tasted the food. He'd been too busy discussing with Violet, who sat across from him now, the likelihood that Saul had any spies in Blackstone.

Holden looked around the small restaurant, which had been unimaginatively dubbed "The Blackstone Diner." Lack of creative name didn't seem to hurt business here, however. Every table in the joint was full, and several waitresses in grease-stained aprons rushed around with coffeepots, order pads, and plates piled high with eggs and bacon.

Everyone here seemed ordinary enough. No one smelled like shifter in here, and Violet had assured him that there was no magic in the air, which meant there were no wizards around. So why did Holden still feel so uneasy?

A large roar of laughter came from one of the corner tables, where several men pounded the table and knocked over one of their coffee mugs in their excitement. The noise had startled Holden, but the men seemed harmless enough, if a bit overly boisterous. He suspected that, in the last hour alone, those men had consumed what should have been a week's worth of caffeine. A harried waitress rushed over to clean up the spilled coffee, brushing away their apologies with a polite smile. Holden admired the girl's poise. If he'd had to deal with a rowdy crew like that, he'd have lost his shit on them a long time ago. But she seemed to take it all in stride, albeit a tired stride. The dark circles under her eyes gave away the fact that she hadn't slept much the night before.

"She's pretty, isn't she," Violet said, following Holden's gaze. Her words sounded almost like an accusation, and their meaning was clear. They were here to deal with the threat of Saul's army, not to ogle pretty waitresses. He flushed, embarrassed that he'd been caught staring at the waitress, although he had no reason to be ashamed. He hadn't been admiring the waitress's appearance, although, now that Violet pointed it out, the girl *was* quite pretty. Woman, not girl, Holden thought. The waitress looked to be about Holden's age, after all. She had curly red hair that she had tried to pull back into a neat bun, with mixed success. Her green eyes sparkled from across the room, and, despite the exhaustion in her face, her features were pretty.

Holden looked at Violet and shrugged. "She's not bad-looking," he said. "But I was looking more at those men then her. They're awfully boisterous."

Violet gave a slight nod. "Yeah. But they're harmless enough. No shifters or wizards in that crew."

Holden nodded, too. "I guess there's not much else to see in here, then. Should we get going? Or did you want one more cup of coffee before we venture out?"

Before Violet could respond, the front door of the diner swung open, and a tall, red-faced man stormed in, dragging a sullen looking boy behind him. The boy must have been about twelve or thirteen. His face still held traces of lingering boyhood, but his deep green eyes held all the defiance of a full-grown man. His mop of dark black

517

curls shook furiously as he struggled to get away from the grasp of his angry captor.

"I didn't do anything!" the boy yelled.

The man holding him ignored him. "Where's Elise?" he growled.

No one responded. The whole diner fell silent as the man back and forth across the room, venom in his gaze. "I said, where's Elise?" he repeated.

Everyone seemed to be collectively holding their breath. Holden glanced sideways at Violet. She was watching the scene with mild interest.

"I swear to God, I'm going to beat up all of you in here if someone doesn't tell me where Elise is. This good-for-nothing boy of hers—"

"You ain't beatin' up no one," interrupted one of the men from the table in the corner. "How many times do we have to tell you? Boys are gonna be boys, alright?"

"This is more than boys being boys! This kid is out of control."

"You listen here," said the man at the table standing now. "You let go of that boy or—"

"It's alright, Ralph," another voice interrupted. "Let me deal with him."

Holden raise his eyebrows in surprise as the waitress, who had been bent low to the ground to wipe up spilled coffee, rose to her full height. Her dishrag hung by her side, sopping wet from the dark black coffee she'd been trying to clean up.

"You need to get this kid of yours on a leash, Elise," the angry man snarled.

"What did he do this time?" the waitress asked. She was the "Elise" the man was looking for. Holden looked back and forth between Elise and the boy. He could see the resemblance now: the same green eyes, and the same face shape. Even their curly hair was similar, albeit different colors.

"I didn't do anything, mom!" the boy yelled, trying unsuccessfully to swing his arms and punch his captor. The angry man was too strong for him, though. He grabbed the boy's arms with his one free arm, and gave a violent shake with his other arm. The boy's whole body shook, and he yelped in pain.

"Hey!" the man named Ralph shouted, coming to Elise's defense again. "You leave him alone."

"Ralph, please," Elise pleaded. But the men at Ralph's table seemed to be itching for a fight. They rose as one, shouting and running toward the man who held the boy captive. Fists started flying, and plates of food shattered on the floor as the brawling men ran into tables. Half the restaurant patrons were shrieking in terror, and half were cheering as though they were watching some sort of sporting event. Elise yelled loudest of all, imploring them to stop. A man who had the look of a manager came out from the back of the restaurant when all the noise started, and threw up his hands in frustration.

"Elise! Not again!" he yelled. But his voice was lost in the din, and even Elise didn't seem to hear him anymore. She was screaming hysterically now, and trying to fight her way through the tangle of flying fists and kicking legs. Holden wanted to yell at her to stop. She was going to get a broken nose, or worse, if she pushed her way into that mess. But then he saw the source of her hysteria. The boy had been caught up in the chaos. No one was paying him much mind anymore, not even the angry man who had first dragged him into the diner. But the boy was hopelessly trapped, whimpering as he held his arms protectively over his face to ward off the punches that were flying in every direction.

Holden sprang into action. He jumped from his seat and ran toward Elise, ignoring Violet's cries of protest. With firm hands, he grabbed Elise by the shoulders and pulled her back from the edges of the brawl.

"No!" she yelled, struggling against him. "No! My boy! They're going to beat him to a pulp!"

"Listen to me!" Holden yelled, shaking her shoulders. "Look at me, and listen!"

Elise looked at him, and abruptly stopped her hysterical crying. An expression of surprise crossed her face. "Who are you?"

"A friend," Holden answered. "I'm going to get your boy out of there. Go wait outside the front door for me. I'll bring him to you and you can get him away from here, alright?"

Elise hesitated a moment, squinting her eyes and, Holden guessed, trying to decide whether she could trust this stranger. But after she looked back at the brawl again, she turned back to Holden and nodded. She must have known she didn't stand much of a chance of rescuing her boy herself.

"Okay," she said in a shaky voice. "Please hurry."

Holden nodded, then released her shoulders. She scampered toward the front door of the diner, and Holden dove into the mess of fighting men. He used one arm to shield his face and head, and another arm to push aside anyone who stood in between him and the boy, who was now curled up in a ball on the floor in the very middle of the brawl.

The men were all brawny, and no stranger to fist-fights from the looks of things. But Holden still had no trouble pushing them aside. His dragon strength coursed through his arms as he fought his way to the boy and scooped him up, easily holding him in one arm despite the fact that the youth was more of a teenager than a boy. The dueling men seemed to not even notice Holden and the boy. They were so caught up in the fight that they didn't seem to even know what they were fighting about anymore. They shouted and hurrahed and yelled out unintelligible threats, taking joy in the thrill of the battle without caring what that battle was actually about.

"Let me go!" the boy screamed suddenly, and tried to punch at Holden and wriggle away. "Let me go! I didn't do anything!"

Holden tightened his grip around the boy in response, continuing to drag him through the fray.

"Hush, boy. I'm trying to help you!" Holden said through gritted teeth. Getting out of the throng of fighting men was proving more difficult than getting in had been. Holden only had one free hand now, and trying to ward off flying punches while pushing through the angry men was too much of a task for just one hand. Holden did the best he could, wincing as an angry fist landed square on the left side of his neck. That was going to be sore later. He tried to keep his head low as he inched through the mob, cursing at the boy in his right arm who was still desperately trying to get away from him.

When he finally broke free, he dragged the wriggling boy toward the front door and pushed it open with a violent kick of his foot. Elise immediately ran toward the boy, pulling him into her arms and looking him over to make sure he wasn't seriously injured.

"I could just kill you, Nick!" she said, her voice a half yell and half sob.

"Well that would make all of my effort just now kind of pointless," Holden quipped. But Elise and the boy ignored his little jest.

"I didn't do anything mom, I swear," the boy said.

Elise boxed his ears and then turned to Holden. "How can I ever thank you?" she said.

Holden shook his head, which was starting to pound from where it had been struck a few too many times in the last few minutes. "No need. Just get him away from here before that crew inside realizes he's gone."

Elise bit her lip and nodded. "Come on, Nick," she said in a firm tone. "We're going home. And then you're going to tell me what you did, because I know you. I know you did *something*."

Nick scowled at his mother, but didn't say anything as she started dragging him away. Holden held a hand up to gingerly cover his right cheek, which was swelling slightly from a punch. He watched through squinting eyes as Elise marched off without looking back. But Nick, the boy, turned back just before they rounded a corner and went out of sight. And Holden's eyes widened at what he saw an instant before Nick disappeared from view.

It had been brief, but unmistakable. There, in the bright morning sunlight, Holden had seen Nick's eyes glow like an animal's. And there was only one explanation for that.

"Looks like there are shifters in this town, after all," Holden whispered as he stared at the now empty street.

CHAPTER TWO

"Hold still, damn it!" Violet hissed as she tried to apply the warm compress to Holden's swollen cheek.

"You're making it worse," Holden said, trying to wriggle out of her reach. But she was too quick for him. She grabbed his arm and pulled him firmly down into the chair. He could have easily overpowered her with his dragon strength and pulled away. But he decided he was better off submitting to her attempts to doctor his face. She was already pissed enough at him as it was. No sense in making things worse. And, despite his protests, he had to admit that the warm compress did actually feel good, after the initial shock of unexpected heat had passed.

"You're lucky I'm helping you, let alone speaking to you, after that stunt you pulled in the diner. What happened to keeping a low profile?"

"No one noticed me. They were too busy hurling punches at each other. And what do you suggest I should have done instead? Let that boy's mom get beat up trying to rescue him? Or leave the boy alone in that brawl to get his teeth knocked out?"

Violet sighed, and sat down on the couch next to Holden.

"No, I guess not," she said, deflated. "But we're not off to a very good start. No wizard or shifter spies in this town, and no one here seems to know anything about Sandview. Either all the townspeople in Blackstone are really good at playing dumb, or we're wasting our time by being here."

"I don't think we're wasting our time," Holden said. Violet didn't answer, other than to slouch lower into the couch cushions and groan. She rarely agreed with his assessment of things, and, ordinarily, Holden would have egged her on, asserting his opinion until she was blue in the face from the frustration of trying to defend her own position on the subject. But Holden was too worn out for games like that at the moment. This day had stretched on forever, and he wanted to sink into bed and sleep right now. But eight p.m. seemed a bit too early for a respectable adult to go to bed. He should try to make it until at least nine.

He hadn't told Violet yet about what he'd seen in Nick's eyes. It wasn't like Holden to keep secrets from her, but he wasn't sure what, exactly, to tell. Nick had shifter eyes, but the boy had not had the scent of a shifter. There was something strange about that, unnerving. Holden wanted to tell himself that he'd been seeing things when he saw the glowing eyes, but he knew deep down that he hadn't. They had been there, bright and real as the lamp that sat in front of Holden right now.

"So what's the plan for tomorrow?" Violet asked, breaking into Holden's thoughts. "More pointless scouting?"

Holden sighed. "Your attitude stinks, V. You know that, right?"

He felt her shrug her shoulders. "I didn't spend a decade of my life in Advocacy school just to sit around in a sleepy small town looking for enemies that aren't there. We have to go to Sandview if we want to make any real progress on this mission."

"Peter and Knox both think it's too dangerous, and I can't say I disagree with them," Holden said.

"What, are you chicken?" Violet teased.

"No. I'm just not stupid," Holden said. "You know that if Saul is, in fact, still in Sandview, that place is being guarded like a fortress. We'd never get into that town alive, no matter how many invisibility shields you cast."

Violet's humph told him that she had no credible counterargument. Holden leaned his head back and looked up at the ceiling, staring at the swirling patterns of white without really seeing them. A few weeks ago, one of his own clanmates had discovered that their enemy, Saul, was taking over the nearby town of Sandview. "Nearby" was, of course, a relative term. Sandview was about fifty miles away, but Blackstone was one of the closest cities to the isolated town of Sandview. Saul was building an army of bat shifters and dark wizards there, and Violet and Holden had been sent to learn just how much progress Saul had made on his army, and where his weak spots might be. Going directly to Sandview was too dangerous. Saul knew his secret location had been compromised, and he undoubtedly had his guards on high alert. The dark wizards knew how to see through invisibility spells, which meant there was no chance of sneaking in undetected. So Peter, the head wizard in Violet's hometown of Falcon Cross, and Knox, the dragon shifter who led Holden's dragon clan, had instead chosen Blackstone as the best place to start their mission.

Holden had expected to find a few of Saul's men in Blackstone. After all, if he were Saul, he would have worried that the nearby towns would provide gateways to his main base in Sandview. But Saul seemed not to share those worries. Either Saul didn't have any guards posted in Blackstone, or his guards here were doing a damn good job of hiding.

"*Magicae levitate*," Violet said, pointing her magic ring at the coffee table in the middle of the room and causing it to rise several inches off the dingy beige carpet.

Holden rolled his eyes. "Stop showing off," he said.

But Violet just laughed. "You're just jealous that you can't make things levitate."

"Of all the magic spells I could be jealous of, that one's pretty far down the list," Holden said.

Violet shrugged. "It's one of the better ones, I think. Look, the more you concentrate the higher you can make the object go."

Holden watched with mild interest as Violet scrunched her face up, focusing her eyes on the coffee table as it continued to rise into the air. Her magic ring glittered a deep purple in the lamplight. Holden wondered what type of stone it was. Amethyst, perhaps? In any case, the purple color matched Violet's name. The coffee table's ascent slowed even more the higher it rose, and Holden found his gaze wandering around the room instead. He and Violet were renting a small, furnished two-bedroom apartment for their time in Blackstone. The place looked like it hadn't been renovated in about twenty years. When they'd first arrived yesterday, it had also looked as though it hadn't been cleaned in twenty years, either. Violet had taken care of that, using a cleaning spell to quickly get rid of the dirt and dust caked onto every available surface. Still, even though the dirt was gone, numerous stains remained. Holden wrinkled his nose in disgust as he looked at a faint brown splotch on the kitchen wallpaper. Was it a food stain? He didn't even want to know how long it had been there.

A sudden, loud knock at the door startled Violet, and the coffee table came crashing back down to the floor.

"Damn it," she said. "I was just starting to really get some height."

Holden, however, was more worried about who might be at the door than about a broken spell. Although he knew he'd done the right thing by saving the boy this morning, Violet was right. Getting involved in that mess wasn't exactly the best way to keep a low profile, which had been one of the strictest orders they'd received when setting off on this mission. Holden put a finger to his lips to tell Violet to be quiet, and then tip-toed to the door to see who it was. He hoped he hadn't gotten himself embroiled in some sort of local feud. To his relief, there was no one there but a young boy, bouncing nervously from one foot to another and holding a cardboard box full of candy bars. Holden relaxed a bit. A kid this size couldn't hurt him, and it looked like the kid was just making the rounds in the apartment complex to sell junk food for a school fundraiser.

He was right. When he opened the door, the boy stammered something about Blackstone community pride and supporting the town's future by helping the local schools. Holden didn't really want a candy bar, but he took pity on the boy and pulled out his wallet.

"How much? I'll take two."

The boy's face brightened, and he gladly took the four dollars Holden gave him for the two chocolate bars. He stammered out such a long-winded thank you that Holden almost offered him another two dollars just to continue on his way. But Holden had a soft spot for kids—something about their innocence always warmed his heart—so he smiled kindly at the boy until the stammered thank you was complete. Then he closed the door behind him and went back to the living room.

"Think fast," he said, tossing the bar at Violet. She looked up with what would have been barely enough time for a normal person to register that some sort of object was about to hit them in the face. But Violet wasn't a normal person. She was a wizard, with damn good reflexes. Her hand shot up and caught the bar a split-second before impact. Frowning, she looked down at it.

"Chocolate caramel peanut delight," she read off the label.

"Some kid was selling them for a fundraiser," Holden said, tearing open his bar and taking a huge bite.

"This is the last thing my waistline needs," Violet protested.

Holden rolled his eyes. "Your tiny waistline can easily handle a candy bar," he said around a mouthful of chocolaty caramel goodness. "Try it. It's actually not bad."

Reluctantly, Violet opened her candy bar and took a bite. She made a face and set the bar down on the coffee table. "I hope you didn't pay good money for that," she said.

"Two dollars," Holden said with a grin. "And the money goes to a good cause. If you don't eat that, I will."

"Help yourself," Violet said, leaning back against the couch. "I'm not wasting calories on something that tastes like cardboard."

"Honestly, V," Holden said. "I don't know why you obsess about your weight so much. You're perfect."

She sighed. "Thanks. It's just part of being a woman, I guess. I've always felt like everyone is judging me on my appearance."

Holden wanted to say that he thought that was all in her head, but he figured he didn't know much about what it was like to be a woman. So instead, he just said. "Well, I mean it. You're perfect."

Violet threw a throw pillow at him. "Stop trying to sweet talk yourself out of the fact that you caused a big scene this morning."

"I'm not sweet-talking, and I didn't cause a big scene," Holden protested.

"Really? Have you checked in with Knox and Peter today? Did you tell them about the incident?"

Holden glared at Violet. "I didn't tell them. There's nothing to tell. I don't think anyone even noticed me."

Violet shrugged in a way that indicated she clearly didn't think the brawl had been a non-incident, but she said nothing further. Instead, she picked up the remote and turned on the television, absentmindedly flipping through channels. Holden munched on his candy bar in silence, brooding as he stared at the noisy, busy screen.

The truth was that Violet might be more right than she knew. The fight might not have been a non-incident, after all. If Nick was a shifter, then there might be other shifters in town. But if that was the case, why couldn't Holden smell them? He frowned as he picked up Violet's abandoned candy bar and started digging into that, too. He knew that shifter masking scents had become quite popular lately. In the shifter world at large, masking scents were being sold that would cover the smell of shifter with some other mundane smell. Popular choices were the scent of cake, the scent of coffee, or the scent of grass.

But Holden didn't think that Nick had been wearing any sort of masking scent. Masking scents were always a bit overpowering, and there hadn't been any particularly strong scent on Nick. Holden had worked hard to be able to detect the warning signs of a potential masking scent—its overpowering nature, its overly artificial odor—but nothing about Nick had rung any warning bells. Holden rubbed his forehead. Perhaps there had been new developments in masking scents that he wasn't aware of? He sat up straight, then. If that was the case, his clanmate and best friend, Weston, would know.

"I need to make a phone call," Holden said, standing and starting to head for the bedroom that was his. Violet gave him a mischievous look.

"Finally gonna call Knox and confess to your bad behavior this morning?"

"You're insufferable," Holden said, and then crossed his eyes at her. Her laughter followed him to the bedroom until he shut the door firmly behind him. Normally, he took all of Violet's teasing in stride, and she his. They worked well together because of that. But today, her teasing was hitting a little too close to the truth, and that was bothering him. He pulled out his cell phone and hit speed dial.

"Hey, buddy," Weston answered on the second ring.

"Hey," Holden replied, his nerves calming somewhat at just the sound of his friend's voice. "How're you holding up in Falcon Cross?"

"Oh, alright," Weston replied. "They're keeping us all busy doing research to locate the dragon ruby."

"I figured," Holden said. The dragon ruby was one of four powerful ancient dragon stones. Each of the four stones held tremendous power, and three of the stones—the dragon amethyst, the dragon sapphire, and the dragon emerald—had already been recovered by the good shifters and wizards. But the dragon ruby was rumored to be more powerful than the other three stones combined, so finding it was a top priority. If it fell into Saul's hands, he would surely use it for evil. Holden didn't even want to think about the kind of destruction he would cause.

"What about you? How are you holding up? And how's Violet?" Weston asked. Holden could tell that Weston was trying to keep his voice casual when he asked about Violet, but Holden wasn't fooled. He'd known Weston almost his whole life, and he could tell when the man felt nervous about something. As much as Weston tried to hide it, Holden suspected the man had a thing for Violet. Holden was glad that his own interest in Violet was merely platonic. It would have been tough on his friendship with Weston if they'd both been in love with the girl. Although, really, Holden didn't have much interest in a romantic relationship with anyone. The idea of loving someone terrified him. He'd lost his parents as a young boy, and, ever since then, he'd thought that perhaps it was better to be close to as few people as possible. That way, you had less to lose. Less chance of heartache. Weston didn't seem to have any such qualms, though. He was always chasing after some pretty girl or another. Violet was more than likely just a passing obsession. On any other night, Holden might have tried to tease Weston and squeeze a confession of love out of him, just to drive his friend crazy. But tonight there were too many other urgent matters to consider.

"I'm good. Violet's good. We had an uneventful day for the most part," Holden said.

"For the most part?" Weston asked.

Holden smiled. His friend knew him well. "Yeah, for the most part. But there was one thing that happened early in the day that's been bothering me. I can't seem to get the incident out of my head, but it doesn't make any sense to me. I was hoping you might be able to help me figure it out."

Damn it, thought Holden. *I just called it "the incident," too. Good thing Violet can't hear me right now.*

"Shoot," Weston said. "I'll see what I can do."

"We were at a diner here in town. Seems to be a popular place with the locals because it felt like half the town was there. Violet and I had just about finished eating breakfast when this guy storms in, furious and dragging a boy by the collar. The boy looked like he was about twelve or thirteen. The kid's mom is apparently a waitress at the bar, and the man had come looking for her, to tell her to get her boy under control."

"What had the boy done?" Weston asked.

"You know, I'm not actually sure," Holden said. "The man never said. Before he could get into too much detail, a huge fight broke out in the diner. A bunch of the customers must be pretty loyal to the boy's mom, because they started throwing punches at the man who'd dragged the boy in. Soon, half the restaurant was involved in a giant brawl, and the boy was caught up in the middle of it. He wasn't fighting. He was just in the middle of this mess of fighting men and couldn't get out."

"Let me guess," Weston said. "You rushed in to pull him out of there and save him."

Holden sighed. "I guess you know me well."

"So much for keeping a low profile in town."

"Now you sound like Violet."

"Well, she has a point."

"I don't think anyone saw me," Holden said. "They were all too busy getting off on beating each other up. But, anyway, the point of this story is that when the boy was scurrying away from the restaurant, he looked back at me and his eyes were glowing. Like an animal's. But he didn't smell like a shifter, and he didn't smell like a masking scent. In fact, he didn't really smell like anything. I don't know what to make of it. I know what I saw in his eyes, but if he's a shifter then I should be able to smell something. It's been bothering me all day. I was wondering if maybe there was some sort of new and improved masking scent out, something that completely covers up any smells. I thought if there was you might have heard of it?"

There was such a long pause on the other end of the line that for a moment Holden thought he might have lost Weston. But the other man finally spoke.

"I see," Weston said. "And what does Violet make of all this?"

"I...didn't tell her yet," Holden admitted. "I'm not sure what to tell, and I want to figure out what I'm dealing with. If there are other shifters in town and I'm just not smelling them, that could be a big problem. We searched all over the place for any shifters or wizards in this town, but, so far, we haven't found anything. It's hard for me to believe that Saul has no spies here, though, which makes me think there's something I'm missing. If there's a new masking scent that keeps you from smelling shifters, then we're screwed. Saul's soldiers would know I'm here and could attack me before I even knew what was coming."

Another long pause.

"I wouldn't necessarily be surprised if Saul didn't have spies in Blackstone after all," Weston said when he finally spoke. "He makes strange decisions sometimes that don't make a lot of sense. Not only that, but he's fighting on a lot of different fronts. He's trying to build up his bat shifter army, trying to protect the Redwoods base camp he stole, trying to keep an eye on Falcon Cross and the shifter protectors in Texas, and trying to find the dragon ruby. He's spread pretty thin, so he might not bother putting spies in nearby towns. He might be content with just having guards surrounding Sandview itself."

"Okay, well, even assuming Saul doesn't have spies here, can you explain why a boy would have shifter eyes but not smell like anything? Is there a new type of masking scent that does that?"

"Not that I know of," Weston said. "But, let me ask you this: you said the boy didn't smell like anything. Do you really mean that? Like nothing at all? Not even like human flesh, or the clothing he was wearing?"

Holden furrowed his brow. "That's right," he said, trying to remember. "Nothing at all. Not even clothes. It was the weirdest thing. He was standing right in front of me, and I could *see* him but I couldn't *smell* him. And I don't have to tell you that dragon shifters have some of the sharpest noses around."

"Damn," Weston said, his voice sounding slightly awed. "Sounds to me like the kid's a ghoster."

"A ghoster?" Holden had no idea what that was, but he didn't particularly like the sound of it.

"Yeah, a ghoster. I thought they were all extinct, but it's the only explanation," Weston said.

"Okay," Holden said slowly. "And are you going to give *me* an explanation on what the hell a ghoster is?"

"They're also known as the invisible shifters," Weston said. "A while back I was assigned to a mission in a town that had been a famous ghoster town back in the day, and that's where I learned about the phenomenon. Basically, there used to be a large group of dragon shifters that had the ability to produce pheromones that masked all scent. They could give off these pheromones at will, and thus be 'invisible' as far as smelling them was concerned. This ability was referred to as ghosting, and it made them quite dangerous in the days when dragon shifters still ruled the earth. They could sneak up on other dragon shifters and cause all kinds of havoc. But as far as I know there haven't been any cases of ghosting in a long time, and the general agreement in the shifter world is that the ghosters are extinct. But I can't see many other explanations for what you just told me."

Holden took a few moments to process everything that Weston had just told him. "You're sure that's what it is?" he finally asked.

Weston laughed. "I don't know for sure. Nothing is ever certain these days, it seems. But from what you told me, it sounds like a classic case of a ghoster."

"Great," Holden said with a groan. "So it sounds like Saul has discovered that ghosters exist, and is using them as spies. That's gotta be why it appears as though there aren't any shifters in this town.

"Eh, I wouldn't be so sure that Saul·is behind this, or that there are others in town.

It sounds like the boy isn't in control of his shifter side, which makes me think that he's not a soldier or spy. He's just a kid who has special abilities that he doesn't know what to do with. Think about it. A spy wouldn't have let you see his churning animal eyes. Animal eyes while in human form is a sign of an underdeveloped or undercontrolled shifter side. You know that."

Holden paced back and forth in his bedroom, considering. Weston was right. Holden had been so caught up in the strangeness of the boy having no scent that he'd glossed right over the fact that the boy's animal eyes likely indicated a very restless, very uncontrolled shifter side.

"Still," Holden finally said. "If he is a shifter I have to look into him a little more closely. I can't be too careful, and I don't want any of Saul's cronies sneaking up on me because I wrote them off as nothing more than troubled little boys."

"Sure," Weston said. "Go check on him. I bet you anything you're going to find out that there's no dad in the picture. The kid probably had a shifter father who isn't around, and his mom probably doesn't even know he's a shifter—or, at the very least, has no clue how to deal with it. I've seen this before so many times. Shifter kids who don't know they're shifters. They just know they're different, and the older they get the more restless and angry their inner shifters become. It's always a sad situation, to be sure. But it's not likely that the kid is any real danger to you or your mission."

"Does the fact that he's a ghoster make him more dangerous than a normal shifter?" Holden asked.

"Well, ghosters aren't super strong or aggressive, if that's what you're asking. The only thing that makes them more dangerous than a normal shifter is their ability to sneak around without their scent giving them away. Damn. I'm so jealous that you're there. I wish I could come see this kid for myself. I spent so much time hearing about ghosters of the past when I was on that mission in an old ghoster town. What I wouldn't give to see a real live ghoster now."

"Well, come on out here and join our mission," Holden said. But it was only a joke, and they both knew it. As much as Holden would have loved to have Weston here, too, everyone had their specific assignments these days, and Weston's was back in Falcon Cross.

"I wish I could, man," Weston said. "But Peter's got me spending my days with my eyes crossed in front of a computer, trying to research where that damn dragon ruby is."

"No luck yet?"

"No, we haven't made any progress. I'd much rather be out on a field mission like you."

"Well, it hasn't been very exciting so far," Holden said. "But maybe learning more about this ghoster kid will liven things up."

"I hope so. Keep me posted on what you find out, alright?"

"Will do."

Holden bid Weston good night and hung up the call, but he didn't go back out to the living room. Instead, he lay on his bed and stared up at the ceiling, mulling over everything Weston had told him. The idea of a shifter who could not be smelled was both fascinating and terrifying. All shifters had incredible senses of smell, and relied on that sense of smell to keep them safe. A shifter who could not be detected by smell would be at a serious advantage.

Holden suddenly sat up, wondering if there was any more to learn about ghosters than what Weston had told him. He walked over to a small duffel bag of reference books that he'd brought with him just in case he needed to research anything while on this mission. Violet had teased him relentlessly about being a bookworm, and asking if he knew that most people just looked things up online these days. But Holden had ignored her and brought the books, anyway. Now, he was glad that he had. Despite Violet's teasing, ancient shifter history wasn't exactly something you could learn about just by running a few Google searches. Holden did have a book, though, that he thought might hold some answers, and he rummaged through his duffel bag looking for it.

"Ah ha," Holden said when he found what he was looking for a few minutes later. He pulled out the thick volume, which had the title *An Exhaustive Encyclopedia of Shifters through the Ages* embossed on its cover in gold lettering. Holden sat cross legged on the floor and started flipping to the section for the letter "G." He flipped through the pages, ignoring the illustrations of fantastical beasts mixed with mundane, ordinary animals. Finally, he found it.

"Ghosters!" he said aloud when he turned to the page with that word written across the top. But the entry was brief, and did not give any more information than what Weston had already told him. Holden read through the text several times, as though each new reading might magically reveal some new tidbit of information. But no matter how many times he read it, the text remained the same.

Ghosters were a rare variation of dragon shifters, prominent during the age of the dragon kings. They were called ghosters because of their ability to completely mask their scent, thereby sneaking up "unseen" by the noses of other shifters. Ghosters were in high demand by the dragon kings, who often assigned them to positions as spies or assassins. There have been no confirmed instances of ghosters since A.D. 1035, and ghosters are believed to be extinct in modern times.

Underneath the text was a drawing of a dragon, but the picture did not look like anything special to Holden. It was just your everyday, garden-variety dragon as far as he could tell. With a sigh, Holden shut the book. The mental image of the young boy's eyes from that morning, glowing and troubled, haunted him. He wanted to know more about who the kid was, and who his dad was. Weston was convinced that the boy didn't work for Saul, but that was easy for Weston to say—he was safely back in Falcon Cross, in no danger of being spied on.

Holden drummed his fingers on the cover of the book, wondering where he should start with his investigation of the boy. He glanced up at the clock on the wall. It was 8:45 now, almost late enough for a self-respecting adult to go to bed. But he wasn't tired anymore. His conversation with Weston had given him a second wind, and he wanted to do something now to learn more about the young ghoster in this town. But what could he do at this hour?

Almost as soon as he asked himself the question, Holden had an answer. He could go to the diner, of course. He doubted the boy's mother would be there now, since she'd worked the morning shift. But perhaps someone there would be willing to tell him more about the woman or her son. It was as good a place as any to start.

Holden quickly pulled on a light hoodie, then went out to the living room to pull his shoes on. Violet raised an eyebrow at him.

"Where are you going?" she asked. She had finally turned off the television and was flipping through the pages of the novel she'd bought at the airport bookstore before their flight to Nevada.

"A walk," Holden said. "I need some fresh air."

"Want me to come with you? We could discuss our plans for tomorrow. We still haven't decided what we're going to do."

Holden shook his head no. "We can talk more when I get back. Right now I just want to clear my head a bit."

Violet looked for a moment like she might protest, but then she shrugged and sat back against the couch. "Suit yourself," she said.

Holden stuffed his keys and wallet into his pocket, gave Violet a small wave, and then left the dingy apartment. He felt a bit guilty for not including Violet in his little excursion. After all, he had a plausible explanation now for what he had seen earlier today. It would have been a good time to loop her in on the situation. But something still held him back, and he wasn't quite sure what.

A few blocks down the road, he finally realized what it was, and that realization startled him a bit: he hadn't told Violet where he was going because he was secretly hoping that the boy's mother, Elise, would be working at the diner tonight after all. And he was slightly excited at the thought of getting to talk to her alone.

CHAPTER THREE

Elise Merritt scrubbed the countertop vigorously, running her dishrag in circles to scrub away imaginary dirt. The countertop was so clean at this point that you could have eaten straight off of it, with no need for a plate. But Elise kept cleaning, anyway. It gave her an outlet for all her pent up, nervous energy.

Her mind wandered to the verbal lashing she'd endured in her boss's office just a few hours earlier.

"This is the last time I'm warning you, Elise!" he'd yelled. "You keep your brawls out of my diner or you go find a new job."

Elise cringed at the memory of how he'd jabbed his pointer finger right into her chest. She'd tried to protest that she couldn't keep grown men from fighting, and that if it wasn't her son they'd be fighting over something else. That was true enough. Blackstone's locals loved nothing more than an excuse for a fistfight. She'd been shocked by it when she'd first ended up here three years ago, but she was used to it now.

Her boss insisted on blaming her for the fights, anyway. He needed someone to blame, and lately most of the fights had revolved around Nick somehow, so naturally they were all Elise's fault. Elise stopped scrubbing the counter and bit back tears as she thought of her little Nicky, who wasn't so little anymore. She was at a loss on how to help him. He was a good boy deep down, she knew that. She wasn't just being a biased mother when she said that. He truly had a kind, soft heart. But something seemed to torment him, and she didn't know what it was. It had gotten worse lately, and Elise lived every day in fear that he was going to piss off one of the men in town bad enough for them to truly hurt him.

Elise bit her lip in an attempt to hold back the tears that wanted to spill over her eyelids. It wouldn't do to cry while on the clock. The diner was empty now, except for her and the one cook in the back, but you never knew when someone might come walking in the front door. There was still a little over an hour until closing time, after all. If someone caught her crying and told her boss, she'd have to endure a fresh round of yelling from him. To distract herself from her emotions, Elise decided to make a fresh pot of coffee. The one sitting on the burner behind the counter had probably been there for a few hours, and, even though it wasn't likely that someone would come in requesting coffee at this hour, it wasn't a complete impossibility. Making a fresh pot gave Elise something to do, at least, and she threw herself into the task as though her life's purpose was to make the best diner coffee in the world.

She dumped out the old coffee and grounds, then rinsed the pot and filter before putting in a new filter, new beans, and fresh water. She had just pressed the bright orange "Brew" button when she heard the bells above the front door jingling.

Ah ha! she thought smugly. *A customer. I bet they're going to be just desperate for a cup of coffee.*

But the smug smile froze on her face when she turned around and saw who it was. Standing just inside the doorway, and looking straight at her with eyes even greener

530

than her own, was the man who had rescued Nick this morning.

"You!" she said. It was the only word that she could manage to get out in her surprised state, and it seemed to amuse him.

"Me," he replied, a hint of a smile playing at his lips. He walked up to the counter and sat down at one of the barstools. "This place is a lot less busy now than it was at breakfast."

"Uh, yeah. Breakfast is our busiest time. And it's too late for dinner for most people right now. I don't even know why the boss keeps the place open so late. We don't do much business after nine p.m., unless there happens to be a home game during football season. But it's not football season now. But of course you know that. Or maybe you don't, I guess. I shouldn't assume you know about sports just because you're a guy."

Elise forced herself to stop talking. She was rambling on about nonsense to the man who had saved her son from serious harm. What a blubbering idiot she was. But something about his eyes unnerved her. She felt open and exposed, like he somehow knew something about her that she didn't even know about herself. She had overcompensated by opening her mouth and letting whatever words popped into her head come tumbling out. Taking a deep breath, she forced herself to smile calmly.

"Anyway," she said. "Did you want something to eat?"

He shook his head. "I'll just take some coffee, if you don't mind."

Elise grinned, feeling triumphant. "Of course. I've just made a fresh pot. Cream or sugar?"

"Just black, thanks," he said.

Elise turned to grab a mug. She had to wait another minute still for the coffee to finish up, but she did so with her back to the man. She needed a minute to recover her composure. For one thing, she hadn't noticed this morning how handsome he was. She'd been so distraught about Nick that she'd missed details—like how tall the man was, and how muscular. Like how perfectly his green eyes sat in his chiseled, handsome face, or how his dark hair set off the deep tan of his skin. She took a deep breath as she poured his coffee, then smiled as confidently as she could as she set the mug in front of him.

"I owe you a big debt of gratitude," she said. "Thank you for what you did this morning, for my son."

The man took a sip of his coffee before answering. "You don't owe me anything," he said. "I only did what any decent human being would have done."

Elise raised an eyebrow at him. "Well, I suppose this town is a bit lacking in decent human beings, then, because you're the only one who attempted to help."

The man laughed and shrugged, then held out his hand. "I'm Holden, by the way."

Elise took his hand and shook it. "Elise. But you probably already know that." She glanced meaningfully down at her nametag, and he laughed again. God, that sound was so wonderful. She wanted him to laugh again and again and again, but she couldn't think of anything else funny to say at the moment, so she settled for small talk instead.

"What brings you to Blackstone?" she asked. "We don't get too many outsiders around here. Most of them go to Sandview instead. It's a bit bigger, and closer to the national park."

She thought she saw a worried expression cross his face when she mentioned Sandview, but he smoothed it away so quickly that she thought perhaps she had just imagined it.

"I'm working on some research," he said.

Elise frowned. "Research? What could you possibly be researching that would require a trip to Blackstone?"

Holden paused for a moment, tilting his head to one side as though assessing her. She wasn't entirely sure he'd seen whatever it was he was looking for, but finally, he shrugged.

"Would you believe me if I told you that I'm working on a documentary about small towns?"

Elise rolled her eyes at him. "No."

He laughed. "I thought as much. Well, then, all I can tell you is that if I tell you I'd have to kill you."

She laughed, too, then. "You hardly seem like the killing type."

He shrugged, and took another sip from his coffee. He looked at her over the rim of his mug with a mischievous glint in his eye. It occurred to Elise that perhaps she should be frightened. After all, here was a man she didn't know, who wouldn't tell her what he was doing in town and was making jokes about killing her. That sounded awfully creepy when you thought it through, but somehow Elise just knew that he was harmless. At least, he was harmless to her, she thought, taking a peek at his bulging bicep muscles. She had a feeling that he could do some pretty serious damage in a fight, if he wanted to.

"Well, Mr. Mystery Researcher," Elise said, putting her hands on her hips. "Can you at least tell me how long you're planning to be in town?"

He shrugged again. "However long it takes," he said.

"To finish your research on small towns?" Elise said with an accusing raise of her eyebrow.

"To finish my research on small towns," he agreed with a wink.

Elise laughed. She liked this guy. He had an easy way about him that made you feel instantly comfortable, like you'd been friends for years. "Well, just be careful. You might end up intending to be here a few months and then staying for years. Don't ask me how I know."

Elise couldn't keep the bitterness out of her voice when she said this, even though she'd been intending the comment to be something of a joke. She should know by now that there was nothing funny about being stuck in Blackstone, going nowhere.

"Oh?" Holden prompted. He wanted to know more, but she wasn't sure she was ready to divulge her life history to this stranger. He was a handsome, funny stranger, sure. But she'd only known his name for a few minutes. No need to confess all her secrets right away. So she tried to turn the moment back into a joke.

"Yeah, well, I got stuck here for a while, but I think it might be just about time to move again. I'm wearing out my welcome at this point, I think."

"Because of your son?" Holden asked. Elise froze as her eyes met his. Was that why he was here? To ask questions about her son? She suddenly didn't feel so friendly anymore.

"It's just time, I think," she said in a neutral tone. "And, anyway, I'm quite rudely taking up your time with idle chitchat. Are you sure you don't want to order some food?"

The hint was clear: this conversation is over. But he ignored it and pressed on regardless.

"Moving somewhere else isn't going to solve the problem, Elise," he said. But despite his gentle tone, Elise's anger flashed.

"You have no idea what kind of problems I have or don't have," she said. "Now, did you want to order something or not? I have work to do."

Holden sighed and leaned back in his barstool. For a moment, Elise thought he was going to end the conversation there. But then, he leaned forward again and looked at her earnestly.

"I think you'd be surprised at how much of an idea I have of your problems," he said.

Elise crossed her arms protectively over her chest. "Look, Holden, I appreciate what you did for my son today, I really do. But I don't want to discuss my problems, okay? Can we please just drop this?"

But he wasn't going to drop it. He had a look of determination in his eyes that looked strangely familiar. Elise was startled when she realized why. It was almost the same way Nick looked when he'd set his mind to something.

"Let me guess," Holden said. "Nick has always been a good kid, but has always been a little bit different, too. You've noticed he seems to have abnormally exceptional senses of hearing, smell, and sight. He's also strong, freakishly strong for a boy his age. Not only that, but he's restless. He paces, and seems agitated for no reason. This agitation started when he was a young boy, but it's gotten worse as he grows older. That's why he's always getting into trouble with the men in town, isn't it? When he's restless, he seems almost out of control, and he lashes out destructively, ruining property and harming people. You're worried that the townspeople aren't going to put up with him much longer. And he's probably been on the receiving end of quite a few disciplinary measures at school, I would guess. Oh, and, let's not forget his eyes. The way they glow and churn sometimes? You've noticed that, too, I presume?"

Elise took a step back, looking at Holden in horror. He had just described Nick perfectly, but how? She'd hidden Nick's strange abilities and restlessness from everyone, and, until this moment, she thought she'd done a decent job of that. Sure, people thought he was a little terror and a menace to the town, but no one knew how strong he was, or how restless. Or about his freakishly good senses.

"Who are you?" she whispered to Holden. "Why are you really here in Blackstone?"

Holden must have realized that he was frightening her, because the expression on his face softened somewhat. "I'm a friend, I promise. I can help you, and Nick. Let me ask you something. How well did you know Nick's father?"

Elise frowned at Holden. The question was somewhat rude, and a part of Elise wanted to tell Holden to mind his own business. But another part of her wanted to believe that he might somehow be telling the truth when he said he could help Nick. She took a deep breath, and decided to take a chance on trusting this man. After all, what could he do? Tell everyone in town that her son was a freak? Elise was on the verge of having to move away, anyway. What did it really matter what people thought of her anymore.

"I…I didn't know him very well. In fact, he was just a summer fling," she admitted, then rushed to add. "I know that Nick needs a better male role model. He needs a daddy to help show him right from wrong, and how to behave like an honorable man. I'm doing the best I can myself, but it's not enough. But what can I do? There aren't many good men in town for Nick to look up to. And I thought I was doing the right thing by keeping Nick a secret from his dad. I thought he'd be better off raised by me alone. Now it's too late."

Elise realized she was rambling again, and she forced herself to stop talking. Holden tilted his head to one side, looking at her curiously. No doubt, he was trying to make sense of everything she'd just said, and was having a hard time of it.

"Why is it too late?" he asked. "And why did you think Nick was better off being raised without his dad?"

There was no judgment in Holden's tone. Just a gentle, prodding curiosity. Elise started talking again, attempting to explain in a clearer manner, and hating the way her voice shook as she spoke.

"Nick's father was…a bit wild, for lack of a better term," Elise said. "I met him when I was waitressing at another diner in another small town. That was about thirteen years ago, but it feels like a different lifetime."

"So Nick is thirteen?" Holden asked, sounding surprised. "I had pegged him more as an eleven-year-old."

"He's twelve," Elise said. "Don't forget it takes nearly a year to make a baby."

"Oh, right," Holden said, a sheepish blush crossing his face. "I always forget about that part."

Elise laughed. "Typical. Why would a man concern himself with the minor detail of nine months of uncomfortable, painful pregnancy?"

"Sorry," Holden said, looking even more sheepish. But Elise waved her hand in a manner that said not to worry about it. She didn't want to get distracted by a silly discussion on pregnancy, no matter how amusing Holden's contrite face might be. She would lose her nerve to talk about Nick's father if she didn't keep going.

"I was a bit younger then, and my head was full of the kind of dreams you have when you've just become an adult and tasted your first little bit of freedom. You think anything is possible, and that the world is literally yours for the taking. You think it's just a matter of time until you hit your big break and everyone realizes how amazing you are. You think you're going to be someone and do great things."

Holden was smiling at her with recognition. "Yeah," he said softly. "Those were the days, weren't they? And then real life comes and hits you smack in the face."

Elise laughed, somewhat bitterly. "Exactly. And real life hit me in the face not long after I met Nick's father. His name was Joey, and he was something else. He blew into that sleepy diner one morning and swept me off my feet before I'd even had a chance to ask if he wanted coffee. He was a charmer, and about as wild as they come. He told me I was far too pretty to be wasting all my time shuffling eggs and coffee around every morning, and convinced me to take the next morning off to come see his favorite, secret hiking spot."

Holden laughed. "He sounds like he was kind of a cheese ball."

Elise shrugged, but smiled at the memory. "He was, I suppose. But he was a daring cheese ball, who turned every day that summer into an adventure. He was always pushing the envelope, and I was just young enough to follow him on every crazy scheme he came up with. It was a good summer, and when I think about some of the adventures we had, I'm amazed I made it out alive. But I did. I made it out alive, and pregnant."

"But you never told him," Holden said, prompting.

"No," Elise said. "When I realized I was pregnant, I had horrible visions of him taking our child on the kind of adventures he'd been taking me on, and I realized that perhaps there was a bit too much recklessness in him. I didn't think he was ready to settle."

"He must have left, though, before you were too far along?"

"Right. He decided, in a fit of patriotism, to sign up for the army toward the end of the summer. I was surprised. The army, with all its discipline and rules, seemed like a terrible fit for someone like him. But the fact that he was leaving gave me a good excuse to break up with him. I told him I didn't want a long distance relationship. He begged me to give him a chance to make it work but I stood my ground."

"That sounds like more than a summer fling. It sounds like he really loved you," Holden said.

Elise averted her eyes from Holden's, and hung her head a bit. "I suppose you're right. And I'm ashamed of the fact that I never told him about Nick, or the pregnancy. I was young, and stupid, and I thought I was doing the right thing. I thought Joey was too wild to be around a child. But now I realize it wasn't fair of me to keep his son a secret from him. And, god, how I wish Joey was around to help with his boy. Despite my efforts to keep his father away from him, Nick is turning out to be just as wild, it seems. I don't know how to deal with him. But his dad died in combat out in Iraq, never even knowing he had a son. Nick was barely three years old at the time."

Elise tried to hold back the tears, but a few of them managed to spill out anyway. Holden said nothing. He just looked at her kindly and waited for her to continue. Elise struggled to regain her composure, and wiped away the little trail of water the tears had left on her face.

"After he died, I tried to find a family to contact. But he didn't seem to have any living relatives, not even distant ones. The man was strange. Like he'd come from another world and never quite settled into ours. He had no one here but me, I guess. And I let him down. And now I'm letting his son down. Nicky is a good boy, but—"

Elise stopped speaking abruptly when the door to the diner opened. The bell jingled noisily in the otherwise silent restaurant, and a big, burly man walked in. Elise took a shaky breath and blinked quickly, willing the rest of her tears to dry off without spilling. When her vision cleared, she saw that it was Ben, one of the local guys who had been involved in the fist fight this morning. Ben eyed Holden, and Elise would have been willing to bet a month's wages on the fact that Ben was contemplating whether he could start another fistfight right then and beat Holden down. Elise also would have bet a month's wages on the fact that Holden would win in a fight with Ben. Ben might be big and strong, but Holden was bigger, and stronger. Ben seemed to recognize this fact, too, because he finally walked across the room and sat down a few barstools away from Holden.

"This man bothering you, Elise?" Ben asked, looking with concern at Elise's face, which was no doubt red right now from the effort of suppressing her tears. Elise felt Holden tense up across the counter from her.

"No, Benny, not at all," Elise said, forcing a bright smile. "We were just chatting, small talk and such. Can I get you anything?"

Ben looked doubtfully over at Holden, but finally shrugged and nodded. "Coffee would be great," he said.

"Coming right up," Elise said, turning to grab a mug and thinking that she really was glad she'd made this fresh pot, after all. She kept her back to both men as she slowly poured the coffee, giving herself an extra moment to compose herself even more. After stalling as long as she dared, she turned around with a bright smile and went to set the mug in front of Ben.

"Here you go," she said. "You take it black, right?"

Ben nodded, and picked up the mug to take a long sip. Elise allowed herself a quick glance back at Holden, but she did a double take when she found herself staring at an empty barstool. Where Holden had been just moments before, there was only an empty mug, under which he'd tucked a ten dollar bill. Far too much for a mug of coffee and a tip, but he hadn't stayed around for his change. In fact, she hadn't even heard the bells above the door jangle. She wondered if perhaps he'd just slipped off to the bathroom, but as the minutes ticked by, and Elise listened to Ben's mindless chattering without really hearing it, she finally had to admit to herself that he was gone.

She wrapped her arms around her waist and shivered, wondering why she suddenly felt so cold and alone. She'd see him again though, wouldn't she? After all, he'd promised to help her. To help Nicky.

Holden seemed like a man of his word. Then again, if there's one lesson life had taught Elise all too well, it was that things weren't always what they seemed.

CHAPTER FOUR

Holden walked several paces behind Violet, trying to pay attention to what she was saying but failing miserably. They'd been walking for what felt like days to him, although a quick glance at his watch told him it had only been two and a half hours. The late June sun was hot, and his t-shirt was plastered to his back with sweat. He wanted to tell Violet that this search was pointless. They'd looked through all of the small rocky caves at least twice already, and there was nothing to see. But Violet refused to give up yet. She said she just had a feeling that something was out here, and she was determined not to leave until she found it.

"*Magicae revelabit*," she said over and over now, sweeping her ring back and forth as she searched one of the small caves for hidden magic spells. She'd already searched this cave, but she knew that, and Holden didn't bother to point it out. He didn't have a better idea of what to do with their time right now, and at least the search was keeping her occupied. She hardly seemed to notice that he wasn't listening closely to her chatter, and this gave him time to think.

He had to tell Violet about Nick. After the conversations he'd had with Weston and with Elise, Holden knew with certainty that Nick was a shifter. A dragon shifter, he was betting, and a ghoster as well. Holden had been relieved to find out that Elise had not met Nick's father in Blackstone. In all likelihood, Nick was, in fact, the only shifter in Blackstone. With each passing day, Nick was becoming more convinced that Weston was right—Saul hadn't wanted to waste any of his troops on guarding the tiny little town of Blackstone. Perhaps he'd sent some scouts through, just to make sure that no shifters were hiding here. They would have missed Nick, since he didn't smell like a shifter at all, and would have reported back to Saul that the town was only occupied by humans.

Holden scratched at the stubble on his chin as he followed Violet to the next cave. Outside of Blackstone, there was a portion of rocky terrain sticking out like an island in the middle of the otherwise barren desert. The rocks were so dark in color that they were almost black, which was where the name Blackstone had come from. No one could say why the rocks were so black, but the townspeople were all irrationally proud of the rocks, as though they themselves had created these wonders of nature. The rocks formed a large expanse of miniature caves, and Violet had become fascinated with the little caves, convinced somehow that there were shifters or wizards hiding there. But a very thorough search had revealed nothing, and still, she persisted.

Holden watched as Violet again began sweeping her magic ring across the cave, checking for any hidden magic spells. She would not find anything, he knew. But he humored her, letting her continue her work without interruption. His mind drifted constantly back to Elise, and Nick, and the long-dead Joey, who had fathered the boy. From what Elise said, it sounded like Joey had been an orphan, just like Holden. Holden's clan, the Redwood Dragons Clan, was actually made up completely of orphans. Ten of them had been rescued by William, an older dragon shifter, when the last great shifter war had left them without parents. William had raised the ten dragons as brothers, and now, as adults, they were a fearsome clan, a force to be reckoned with. They had joined forces with the Falcon Cross wizards to face down Saul and protect good shifters and wizards from dark, evil magic. Holden had never been as glad for his clanmates as he was now. The war had been hard, and he wasn't sure how he would have managed to stay calm and sane if he'd have to face all of this evil alone. Knowing his clanmates were with him, and always had his back, had kept him calm, and sane. Holden wondered about Joey. The man had probably had no one. Most of the shifter orphans from the war had been left to drift through life alone, unguided and always wary of what people would think of them if their shifter secrets were discovered. No wonder Joey had been a wild man, as Elise had said. Holden figured he would have been reckless, too, if he'd been in Joey's shoes, with no one to love him and nothing to lose.

Holden frowned, wondering why a man like Joey had joined the army. Perhaps he'd fallen in love with Elise, and had been searching for a way to bring stability into his life. Perhaps he'd wanted to prove to her that he could be a responsible partner. If that had been the case, it was all the more tragic that he'd never known he had a son. Holden didn't think Elise had made the right choice in keeping Nick a secret from Joey, but he wasn't going to judge her too harshly. She seemed to have realized that she'd made a mistake, and hell if Holden hadn't made some pretty shitty mistakes in his own younger days.

Holden felt a sudden, strange thrill rush through his veins as he thought of the way Elise had smiled at him at the diner last night. If Joey had fallen in love with that girl, Holden would not have blamed him one bit. She had a smile that could have tamed even the wildest of hearts. Holden felt badly for leaving without saying goodbye last night, but he knew he wouldn't have been able to talk to Elise about her son anymore once the other man entered the diner. And he also knew that the longer he'd stayed sitting there, the more confused he'd become about why his heart wouldn't stop beating like crazy. He wasn't looking for a woman. Sure, Elise was beautiful, but opening his heart to someone was not an option. All that ever came of loving was heartache and loss. Holden knew this all too well from the loss of his parents. The thought of losing one of his clanmates scared him badly enough. He could never handle living every day in fear of losing a lifemate.

"Holden!" Violet hissed at him. The urgent tone of her voice broke into his thoughts and brought him back to the present. He turned to look at her, and the worry written across her face instantly sent his senses into high alert.

"Didn't you hear that?" she asked, her voice not much more than a worried whisper. She was standing with her back to the cave's wall, looking out at the entrance with her magic ring raised in a defensive stance.

Holden strained his ears, but heard nothing. He breathed in deeply, trying to smell any suspicious scents in the air. He smelled nothing, but that didn't necessarily mean much, as his recent discovery of ghosters had taught him.

"I don't hear anything," he said, turning to look at Violet with questioning eyes. She merely pressed her fingers to her lips, indicating that he should be quiet. Holden waited, breathing as softly as he could and staying alert for any unusual noises. He was about to give up, when he heard it. From somewhere in the maze of small caves, a voice screamed. The sound was a bit faint, indicating that whoever was screaming must be on the opposite side of the caves from where Holden and Violet were standing. But there was no mistaking the pain and agony in that scream.

Violet looked at Holden with a grim expression on her face. He had a pretty good idea what she was thinking, because he was thinking it, too. This secluded, rocky outcrop would be the perfect place for Saul's soldiers to bring prisoners for torture. And that scream sounded quite tortured.

"We have to go find out what's going on," Violet whispered. Holden merely nodded, then motioned to her with his hand. He started creeping in the direction of the sound, taking care to stay as hidden as possible against the walls of rock. Out of the corner of his eye, he saw Violet raise her magic ring above her head.

"*Magicae arma*," she said in a low voice. A buzz of energy surrounded them as the protective shield spell she'd just cast went into effect. He wanted to tell her to use an invisibility shield, too, but he knew it was pointless. None of the invisibility shields the Falcon Cross wizards could cast had been able to hold up to the enemy's dark magic. It was better for Violet to focus all of her energy on the protective shield in hopes of keeping them safe if the enemy was out here, waiting to attack.

For several minutes, everything was quiet. Holden and Violet crept forward at a slow pace, wary and watching. Holden was beginning to think that the source of the scream, whoever it was, had either been silenced permanently or given a reprieve from torture. But then, in a loud, sudden burst, another scream rang out, and another. The sound was pure terror, and almost inhuman. Holden looked back at Violet to see her holding her hand over her mouth, her eyes wide with disbelief.

"What are they doing to that poor soul?" she asked, forgetting even to whisper in the face of such a horrendous sound.

Holden didn't answer right away. Instead, he listened as the screams grew more desperate and urgent. Then, suddenly, he knew exactly was he was hearing.

"That isn't Saul's men. There's not torture going on here," he said, starting to run. "I know what that sound is."

"Holden, wait! What the hell are you doing?" Violet's panicked voice called from behind him. But he didn't slow down. He kept running toward the sound of the screaming, which was now constant and sounded almost like a roar. When he rounded the corner of one of the rocky caves about a minute later, he found just what he'd expected.

There, on the hot, rocky ground, writhing in pain, was Nick. The boy's face, twisted in pain, looked so much like Elise's face that Holden felt like his heart was twisting up in his chest. Holden had a vague realization that Violet had run up behind him. He glanced back at her and saw her standing there uncertainly, holding her magic ring up as though she was unsure whether the boy on the ground presented a threat or not.

"What...what is going on?" she asked in a shaky voice. Even though she didn't know the reason, she could tell that something was very wrong here.

"The boy's a shifter, but he doesn't know it yet. His inner shifter is trying to get out and it's freaking him out. I'll explain in more detail later. Right now I have to help him."

Holden quickly went to kneel beside the boy, who was shaking and screaming. His eyes were green and churning, and he thrashed his hands wildly at Holden.

"Get away from me! Get away from me!" Nick screamed.

"Nick, I'm Holden. I'm a friend, I promise. I can help you."

Nick thrashed out again, but as he did his human hand suddenly turned dark green and then morphed into the long, clawed hand of a dragon. This sent him into a fresh panic, and he screamed even louder, as though someone were standing over him ready to kill him. The hand seemed almost liquid for a moment, shifting back and forth between dark green dragon skin and pale peach human flesh. Nick's face was pure horror, and he looked like he was about to throw up.

"Get away from me! No one is supposed to see me like this!" he yelled.

Holden continued to kneel calmly beside him. "Like what?" Holden asked. "Like this?"

Holden held up his right hand, and allowed it to shift into dragon form. His own hand's transformation was much smoother than Nick's had been. Holden kept his eyes on Nick's face, watching the boy's eyes widen as he stared in shock at the fierce, clawed dragon hand that now appeared where a human hand had been only moments before. The change had shocked Nick into silence, and the boy sat, panting and sweating, with his own hand limply hanging by his side, half human and half dragon.

"What...how...who are you?" Nick choked out, looking suspiciously at Holden.

"I'm Holden. I'm a friend, and a dragon shifter just like you. I can help you."

"I'm not a dragon shifter!" Nick yelled, scooting backward away from Holden until a few feet separated them. "I don't even know what that is."

"You cannot change who you are, Nick," Holden said. His use of the boy's name seemed to get his attention. "But I can help you control it."

There was a pause in the conversation as Nick screamed in pain again, falling to the ground and writhing. Violet stepped forward, uncertain but worried.

"What's wrong with him?" she asked, fear in her voice. "He sounds like he's dying. We have to get him to a doctor!"

"He's not dying," Holden said calmly, motioning for Violet to back up. "He's just got an inner dragon who has never been let out. Until he shifts, the pain will continue to get worse, and the attempts of his body to shift will get harder and harder to resist."

Violet still looked uncertain, but she backed away. Holden's respect for her went up a lot in that moment. He already respected her, as his partner on this mission, but he knew it wasn't easy for her to trust him right now. Not with a boy writhing on the ground in mortal pain. He felt a pang of guilt that he hadn't trusted her more and told her about Nick from the first moment he realized the boy's secret. But he'd had his reasons, and he didn't have time for feeling guilty right now. Nick needed his help.

Nick had stopped screaming for a moment, his inner dragon taking a short reprieve from trying to get out. But Holden knew it would not be long before the dragon tried again. He'd never seen a shifter child this old who hadn't shifted before, but he'd heard awful tales of how situations like this caused extreme pain, and often uncontrolled violence on the part of the shifter child. No wonder Nick had been wreaking so much havoc in Blackstone. He was a boy on the edge.

"Can you really help me?" Nick was asking now, his voice a desperate plea. "Can you help me control it?"

"Yes," Holden said, his voice firm and confident. "But you have to trust me. Can you do that, Nick? Can you trust me, and do exactly as I say? I promise I am a friend. I'm here to help you."

Nick didn't answer, but Holden thought he saw a slight nod, and that was enough of an answer for Holden. He walked over to Nick, slowly and deliberately, and took the boy's hands. Nick trembled but did not pull away.

"Stand up," Holden said, pulling the boy up as he spoke. "Stand up and hold onto both of my hands tightly. Then close your eyes and just breathe, in and out, in and out."

Nick did as he was told, whimpering and trembling. Holden waited until he felt Nick's palms beginning to tighten about his own, indicating that Nick's dragon was once again trying to fight its way out of him.

"Alright, Nick, I know this hurts a bit and feels strange, but I promise you I'm going to take care of you. Keep your eyes closed, and breathe in and out as steadily as you can. Focus all your energy on your breathing. Don't think about anything else, and don't open your eyes. You're going to feel almost as though a rush of electricity is shooting through you. Ignore it, and the pain, as best you can. Just breathe, Nick. Just breathe."

Nick's grip on Holden's hands tightened even more, until Holden felt as though the boy's small hands were going to crush his much larger palms. But still, Holden held on. The boy kept his eyes closed as he'd been told, but after a few moments he began to scream again.

"Breathe, Nick! Just breathe! Don't think about anything else. Keep breathing, and keep your eyes closed."

Nick continued screaming, but he did seem to be making an attempt to steady his breathing, despite his screams. After another few moments, his grip on Holden's hands loosened, and the boy's hands and forearms started shifting into dragon claws once again. Nick screamed, and started to try to fight the transformation. His hands began to turn human once again, and Holden knew he needed to step in.

"Nick, don't resist it. Just breathe. Focus on the energy you feel in your core, and just breathe."

Nick's hands turned back to dragon claws. A popping sound echoed across the nearby rock walls as Nick's shoes flew off his feet in shreds, giving way to the giant dragon feet that were breaking free from Nick's human form. As soon as those shoes came off, Holden knew that Nick was going to see this transformation through. For the first time, the boy would see himself as the dragon that he was.

The rest of the dragon came forth in a rush of power and energy. Nick's t-shirt and shorts tore away, and desperate human screams became the loud, primal roars of a dragon.

"Get back, Violet," Holden yelled over his shoulder. "And keep that protective shield up. He's going to be disoriented and a bit wild when he's all done shifting."

Violet did as she was told, flattening herself against one of the rock walls as Nick finally became fully dragon. He was enormous, with the deepest green dragon hide and scales that Holden had ever seen. His head had two sharp horns, and his long tail was magnificently spiked. Two wings had sprouted from his back, and Nick seemed unsure of what to do with them. He flapped them a few times, stumbling about as he stretched out his dragon body. Holden knew Nick must be feeling disoriented. The dragon ran straight into one of the rock walls, which seemed to freak him out. He roared, and took off running in the other direction, flapping his wings and swishing his tail, until he ran into another of the large rocky walls. The dragon coughed a few times, and then breathed out a stream of fire. This seemed to surprise him, and he ran in fright until he bumped into another rock wall. Holden held back, letting Nick's dragon thrash about in confusion for a few minutes. Violet watched with wide eyes, and was surely glad for her protective shield in the next moment, when Holden's large, spiky tail swished directly at her. It stopped when it came into contact with the protective shield, and swished in the other direction.

When Nick's dragon finally started to calm, Holden walked up to him, speaking slowly and firmly.

"Alright, Nick. You did really well for a first shift. Now it's time to get you back to human form. Nod your head if you can hear me and understand me."

Nick's giant dragon head bobbed unsteadily up and down, and Holden gave him an encouraging smile.

"Good," Holden said. "Now, I want you to hold very still, close your eyes, and breathe in and out steadily once again. As you do, concentrate on your dragon claws, and imagine them becoming human hands once again."

Nick's dragon eyes blinked shut, and his dragon chest shuddered a bit as he attempted to steady his breathing. Holden was silent, waiting and hoping that Nick was doing as he'd been asked, and was concentrating on his human form. It took a few minutes, but Nick seemed determined to master this, and Holden waited patiently. Then, his patience was rewarded. A sudden pop of powerful energy rushed across the space between them, and Nick began shrinking in size. His thick dragon hide once again turned to human flesh, and his tail and wings disappeared. In less than a minute, Nick was in human form again, lying on the ground shaking and sobbing. But his sobs no longer sounded tortured or filled with pain. They sounded tired, and relieved.

Holden went to the boy and scooped him up in his arms.

"Shhh. Shhh," he said. "It's all over now. That's the worst it will ever be. You're going to be fine."

Holden looked over at Violet, who was still standing against the rock wall, uncertain of what she should do.

"Can you cast some sort of sleeping spell on him?" Holden asked. "He needs to rest."

Violet nodded and rushed over. Holden figured she was glad that there was some way she could help out. She raised her magic ring above his head tenderly.

"*Magicae dormeo,*" she said in a soft voice. Almost instantly, Nick's sobbing ceased. His eyes closed, and he went limp in Holden's arms. The boy's breathing changed to the steady rhythm of sleep.

"I'll clean up this mess, too," Violet said, pointing her ring at the shreds of clothes that had torn off of Nick's body when he shifted. "*Magicae eradico, magicae eradico.*"

As Violet spoke, the spell she was using caused the torn clothes to disintegrate to dust. When she was done, she looked up at Holden with a suspicious expression.

"You didn't seem all that surprised to find a shifter here," she said, her tone somewhat accusing. "I get the feeling that there's something you're not telling me."

Holden sighed. "Yeah. There's a lot I'm not telling you, and I owe you a big apology for that. We need to get this boy to his mother, though. Can you cast an invisibility spell so that we can head into town without being seen? We can take him to our apartment and find him some clothes, and then we can try to track down where his home is located."

Magicae invisibilia," Violet said in response. The energy of the invisibility spell buzzed around them. The spell might not hold up well against dark wizards, but it would keep Violet, Holden, and Nick completely concealed as they walked into town. And it was a good thing, too. Holden didn't want to imagine what the people of Blackstone would say if they saw him walking in with Nick in his arms, asleep and completely naked.

"Thanks," Holden said. "Let's go, and I'll explain everything."

And he did. As they walked back toward town, Holden told her everything. He started with the moment he had realized Nick might be a shifter—the moment he'd seen those green, churning eyes. Then he told her about his conversations with Weston about ghosters, and with Elise about Nick's long-lost father. When he finally stopped talking, Violet was silent for quite some time, her brows knitted in thought. Holden worried that she was angry, but her face gave nothing away. When she finally spoke, thought, her voice sounded more sad than angry.

"You should have told me," she said. "You know I wouldn't have laughed at you. I would have tried to help you from the beginning."

"I know," Holden said. How could he explain to her that one of the biggest reasons he'd kept silent was that his feelings for Elise confused him? He was determined not to let his heart get tangled up with Elise's, and yet he feared that it already was. Besides, he had a feeling he was going to be seeing a lot more of Elise. Nick needed his help, and Holden wasn't going to leave the boy hanging. That likely meant spending a lot more time around Elise. Holden looked down at the boy sleeping in his arms, and then sighed. The boy was likely going to be in a state of shock when he woke up. Holden could only hope that he could calm the boy in time to keep him from lashing out at someone in town or destroying someone's property. Holden felt as though each day here seemed to bring something new to worry about. Elise. Nick. Ghosters. Violet's anger. It had been much easier when all he'd had to think about was whether Saul had any men here.

But Violet spoke again, then, and her words made it clear that she didn't hold any sort of grudge against him. "You're a good man, Holden, taking care of the boy like this. He's really lucky you're here."

Holden smiled gratefully at her as they arrived back at their apartment complex and started walking toward their building. "Thanks, V. I only hope his mom agrees with your opinion on that."

Holden feared Elise was not going to react well to the news that her son was a dragon. One thing was certain: the next few hours were going to be full of difficult situations.

"I didn't sign up for this," Holden muttered to himself as Violet fumbled in her pockets, looking for the keys to their apartment. "I'm supposed to be chasing down dark wizards, not babysitting young shifters."

And yet, Holden already felt himself excited by the idea of training Nick in the ways of shifting. The kid had had a rough start at life, but he had a ton of potential, too. He was plucky and determined, and Holden thought they were going to get along just swell—provided that Elise allowed him to help. The thought of Elise tied Holden's stomach in knots again, and he pushed away those thoughts as he walked into the apartment and deposited Nick on the couch while he went to look for some clothes.

There was only one way to find out what she thought about shifters, and that was to go talk to her about this whole situation. It was time to get this show on the road.

CHAPTER FIVE

Elise tensed up when she heard the doorbell ring. She hadn't seen Nick for hours, but she had a feeling that whoever was at her door right now was here to complain about him. She let her hairbrush drop on her bathroom counter with a frustrated sigh, and made her way to the front door. She was almost ready for her shift at the diner, and she could not be late again. Her boss was already angry enough with her over the fight yesterday, and he was looking for any excuse to chew her out. Elise didn't think he'd fire her. She was his best waitress, and this was a small town. He'd have a hard time replacing her with someone who could keep up the pace she did. Still, she didn't want to see how far he would go when he was angry. If she lost this job, she'd be screwed. She had no savings, and was barely getting by as it was.

Elise took a deep, steadying breath. She couldn't let her worries get away with her like that. She was a survivor. She'd made it through tough times before, and this would be no different. She had to stay strong for Nick. He had a good heart deep down, Elise knew that. She just had to help him through whatever was tormenting him right now. She wished he would open up to her and tell her what was bothering him, but he refused to talk about it. He refused to talk about much of anything, actually, and that hurt Elise more than anything. They used to be close, and he used to freely tell her all his worries and fears, but he'd clammed up lately, hiding in his secret world of pain. Elise had been hopeful for a few brief minutes last night that the new guy in town, Holden, might actually know how to help Nick. But then Holden had disappeared, and Elise hadn't seen or heard from him today. Elise wasn't holding out much hope that she was ever going to see him again.

The doorbell rang again, and Elise quickened her step, biting her lower lip to try to calm her nerves. She stood on tiptoe to peer through the peephole, bracing herself for what she would see. But what she saw was not at all what she expected, and she gasped. She'd assumed she'd find one of the angry men who was always yelling at her about Nick's bad behavior, but the only man she saw was Holden. And in Holden's arms, Nick lay limp.

Elise's heart dropped all the way to her feet and she flung the door open. "Nicky!" she gasped, her voice catching in a sob. She started toward him, but Holden stepped quickly away so she couldn't touch him.

"He's fine, Elise. Just sleeping. He needs to rest, and I need to talk to you," Holden said.

Elise ignored him and stepped toward Nick, putting one hand on his wrist to feel for a pulse, and placing the other hand lovingly on his forehead. Holden started to pull away again, but he stopped when another voice spoke up.

"It's alright, Holden. He won't wake easily while he's under the sleeping spell."

Elise whipped her head to the left, looking for the source of the voice. A slender woman with deep purple eyes and silky, chestnut hair stood there, twisting absentmindedly at a large purple ring on her finger that matched the color of her eyes. Elise had been so distraught by the sight of Holden that she hadn't even noticed the

544

woman standing off to the side.

"Who is this?" Elise asked, a note of accusation in her voice. Her stomach was twisting up uncomfortably. The woman seemed pleasant enough, but she was dazzlingly beautiful, and Elise had a feeling that no man on earth would be able to resist the woman. Jealousy burned in Elise's core, not because she begrudged the woman her beauty but because she had a sinking feeling that this woman was with Holden. Elise had not admitted it to herself until then, but she'd been nursing a tiny crush on Holden. She should have known better than to think a man like him wasn't taken already. He was too handsome, too kind. Too much of a catch.

"This is my partner, Violet," Holden said. "She helped me get Nick here without being seen. But we're going to be seen if we stand out here any longer. Can we come in?"

Elise resisted the feeling of despair that tried to sweep over her when Holden said Violet was his partner. She took a deep breath and stood as tall as she could, reminding herself that the most important thing right now was taking care of Nick, not worrying about losing a man she'd never had a claim to in the first place. Still, jealousy is a hard beast to keep down, and Elise felt it roaring up within her when Violet placed a hand on Holden's arm and leaned over to whisper something in his ear. Holden nodded, and Elise was sure she saw tenderness in his eyes when he looked up at Violet.

Swallowing hard, Elise forced herself to stand as tall as she could, and pointed toward the door to Holden's left.

"This is Nick's room," she said. "You can put him down on his bed in there."

Holden nodded, and moved toward the room. Violet followed, opening the bedroom door for him so he could walk in easily. Elise wanted to scream at her to go away, and that her help wasn't needed. But Elise had no real reason to dislike Violet, so she bit her tongue. The woman seemed nice enough, and did seem to be genuinely concerned for Nick, which was what mattered right now. Elise had been relieved to feel a pulse when she'd checked Nick's wrist a minute before, but the limpness of his body and the way he slept so deeply worried her. She didn't see any bruises or scratches on his body, which hopefully meant he had not been in a fight. But she did notice that the clothes he was wearing were not his clothes. The t-shirt and gym shorts he had on looked about five sizes too big. It was a wonder they didn't fall off.

"What happened?" Elise asked in a shaky voice, sitting beside Nick on the bed after Holden had gently laid him down.

"It's a long story, which I'll tell you in a minute, but we should go to the living room to talk," Holden said. "Don't worry, he's fine. But he's been through quite an intense ordeal, and he needs to rest for a bit. Violet will stay with him while we go talk, if you want."

Holden was looking at her expectantly, waiting for her to agree to leave her son's side. Elise didn't want to leave Nick, but Holden was right. Nick did seem fine, albeit exhausted. And Elise was burning with curiosity. She wanted to know what the devil had happened to her son, and she could tell that Holden was not going to talk about it until they'd left Nick's side. She wasn't sure how she felt about leaving Violet behind to watch him, but the woman did seem capable, and kind. Elise had no right to hate her just because she'd gotten to Holden first. Who knows, maybe Holden wasn't really Elise's type anyway. After all, she'd barely met him. His gorgeous looks might set her heart to racing, but that didn't mean he was actually a good match for her. With a sigh and one last look at Nick, Elise rose.

"Alright, just let me call in to work and then we can talk."

Holden nodded, and followed her out of the bedroom, closing the door behind him. Elise called the diner, thankful that one of the hostesses answered instead of her boss. She told the girl that she was sick and wouldn't be coming in. There was no way she was blaming her absence on Nick. She knew her boss would not think that taking care of your child in an emergency was a valid reason to miss work. The hostess was sympathetic and told Elise to feel better, but Elise knew her boss was going to blow a fuse when he heard she was missing. So be it. Elise had no choice but to stay home right now. Nick needed her.

She hung up the call and turned to walk to the couch in the living room. She was surprised to see that Holden had started brewing a pot of coffee. The gurgling of the pot and the familiar aroma that filled the air felt strangely comforting, and Elise plopped down onto the couch with a tired sigh.

"Where are your mugs?" Holden asked. Elise pointed to the appropriate cupboard, and Holden grabbed two mugs to fill with the strong, black liquid.

"Cream or sugar?" Holden asked.

"Just black for me," Elise said. "And if I remember correctly from the diner last night, you take yours black, too."

"Good memory," Holden said, then flashed her a dazzling grin. Elise felt her heart skip a beat, and she thought sadly that Violet was a very lucky woman. But she pushed away the jealousy that was trying to rise again as Holden came over to offer her a cup of coffee. She didn't have room in her life for a man, anyway. What man would want to get involved with a waitress who was barely making ends meet and had a son whose behavior was completely out of control?

"So what happened? What did Nicky do this time?" Elise asked once Holden had finally settled down into the couch as well. Holden took a long, slow sip before answering, and Elise felt dread filling her. She did not feel encouraged by the fact that it was taking Holden so long to come up with the right way to answer her.

"Nick has been through quite an ordeal today," Holden said slowly. "I'm going to explain it all to you, but be prepared to be a little bit shocked, okay? Don't worry, he's fine. In fact, he's going to feel much better once the dust settles a bit. But what I'm about to tell you will probably sound crazy at first. Just trust me, okay?"

Elise wanted to say that he was asking a lot of her. He wanted her trust, but she barely knew him. He'd taken off last night without a goodbye, and then today he'd shown up unannounced with her son hanging like a deadweight in his arms, warning her to be prepared for a shock. The circumstances didn't exactly inspire trust, but Elise found herself nodding her head anyway.

"Okay. I trust you," she said. What choice did she really have? She just hoped that whatever had happened with Nick today wasn't going to cause any long term damage.

Holden took another sip of his coffee, and then asked a question that made Elise think for a moment that he'd lost his mind.

"Have you ever heard of shapeshifters?"

Elise blinked a few times, not sure that she'd heard him correctly. "Of what?" she asked.

"Shapeshifters," Holden said, keeping eye contact with her. "You know, people that can shift into animals at will?"

"Uh, yeah. I guess I have. I've read some stories that had shifters in them." Elise had no idea what any of this had to do with Nick, and she rubbed her forehead roughly, wondering if this was all some sort of weird dream. Nothing made sense to her at the moment.

"Okay," Holden said. "Well shapeshifters aren't just found in stories, Elise. They really exist. In fact, I am a shapeshifter. A dragon shifter. I can change from human to dragon and back again at will."

Holden paused, looking at her closely and waiting for her to react. Elise wasn't sure whether to laugh or cry. The man she'd thought she was falling in love with just a few moments ago had just proven he was crazy. And that meant that she was unlikely to get any real help for Nick from this guy. Elise bit her lip in that way she did when she had no idea how to respond to a difficult situation. She finally opted to make a joke of it.

"Oh, come on, Holden. Be serious."

"I am serious."

He held up his hand, then, and flexed his strong arm muscles before taking a deep breath and squeezing his eyes shut. Moments later, to her utter astonishment, Elise watched his human arm morph into a much larger, iridescent green limb that looked suspiciously like a dragon arm. Her mouth hung open, and stayed that way even as Holden opened his eyes and allowed his arm to return to human form.

"This isn't real," Elise said. "There's no way. I'm dreaming all of this."

"It is real," Holden said calmly. "And the reason I'm telling you about it is that your son is a dragon shifter as well."

Elise's stomach tightened uneasily. "What did you do to him?" she asked in a strained voice.

"I didn't do anything to him," Holden said, still calm. "Shifting is genetic, which is why I asked so many questions about Nick's father. It's not something that's passed along through, say, a bite, like a werewolf."

Elise's heart was pounding. The room felt like it was starting to swim in front of her, and she could hardly hear what Holden was saying.

"What did you do to him?" she said again, desperate. She stood up and started running toward Nick's bedroom. Suddenly, she felt that leaving him in there with Violet, whom she barely knew, had been a horrible idea. She reached for the bedroom door, but before she could grab it, strong arms grabbed her and held her back.

"Elise, listen to me. Try to stay calm, okay. I know this is a lot to take in, but please, trust me. You said you would."

Holden turned her so she was facing him, and she looked up at him with wild eyes. She hadn't known when she said she'd trust him that he thought he was some sort of shapeshifter. Or maybe more than just thought—she'd seen his arm transform. Was this some sort of cruel trick he was playing, or was he actually able to transform into a dragon? How was this real? How was this actually happening?

"Nick is fine. He's safe, and he's sleeping. He needs the rest. I can explain everything to you, and I can help him. I already have helped him some, in fact. But you have to calm down and let me talk."

Elise took a few deep breaths. Holden smelled woodsy, like a deep forest. Ordinarily, she would have swooned to have a man like him with his arms around her. But right now, all she could think was that he might be crazy and her son might be in there with a crazy woman.

"Is Violet a shifter?" Elise asked.

Holden shook his head no. "She's a wizard. A good one. She's making sure Nick sleeps well and is protected right now."

Elise blinked. "A *wizard*? You two really are out of your minds."

She started to struggle against Holden's grip again, but he held her firmly. "Elise, listen to me. You've seen Nick's eyes churning and glowing, right? You told me you had."

Elise stopped struggling and narrowed her eyes at Holden. "What does that have to do with anything?"

"He has dragon eyes. That's why they glow and churn. It's his inner dragon trying to get out. His eyes have been doing that for a long time, I know. You noticed it way before I ever arrived in town, so you know I didn't turn him into a shifter. He's been a shifter his whole life. It's just that he's getting old enough now that his animal side was tired of being held back constantly."

Elise felt weak, like her knees were going to give out. Something in the tone of Holden's voice told her that he was serious, and that she needed to trust him. And he was right. She *had* noticed the strange glowing and churning in Nick's eyes for quite some time now. She'd had no idea what it meant, but if Holden had an explanation, maybe she should hear him out. What could it hurt to let him talk? If he was crazy she could politely send him on his way. But if he wasn't, and everything he was saying was true, if that strange trick with his arm wasn't actually a trick…then Elise needed his help. Desperately. She forced herself to remain calm, and turned toward the couch again. Holden let her go, and then came to sit beside her.

"Tell me everything you know," she said. Holden looked at her with great kindness in his eyes, took a deep breath, and then started speaking.

"As I said, shifting is a trait you're born with. Shifting is embedded within a person's DNA, and is passed down genetically from parent to child. That's why I asked so many questions about Nick's father. I wanted to know if he sounded like someone who might have been a shifter."

"And did he?" Elise asked.

Holden nodded. "He fits the profile, for sure. The wild, reckless behavior is typical of shifters, especially ones who don't have a family. Shifters are stronger than average humans, and heal quicker, so they can take more risks. And many shifters lost their families in a war that took place when I was a boy. I won't bore you with the details, but my guess is that Joey, Nick's dad, lost his family then, too. Perhaps when he found you, he was only looking for a good time. But he must have fallen in love with you. Maybe he thought joining the army would show you he could settle down and be someone you'd want to be with long-term."

Elise choked back a sob. "And I pushed him away, saying I didn't want a long-distance relationship. And I kept his child from him! Oh, god. I feel sick. But why didn't he tell me he was a shifter?"

Holden shrugged. "It's hard to say. Shifters are often persecuted for being different, so we usually try to hide our abilities. I suspect that Joey was trying to figure out the right time to tell you and never quite found it. Then, as you know, he was killed unexpectedly while in Iraq. He just never got the chance."

Elise sat back against the couch. The swimming sensation in her head had intensified. "But, Nick hasn't…I mean…how has he been a shifter all these years and I've never seen him turn…turn into a dragon?"

"Well, it's kind of complicated, but the simple explanation is that Nick himself didn't know he was a shifter, and he had no one to tell him, or to teach him how to shift. Usually, with shifter kids, their parents will tell them about their abilities from the very beginning. They'll teach them how to shift when they're just toddlers, and by the time the kid is Nick's age, they'll have learned quite well how to control their shifting abilities. But since Nick thought he was just a normal human, he's been continuing on through his childhood as though he was a normal boy. Except he's not a normal boy."

"No," Elise said softly, interrupting Holden. "He's not a normal boy. He never has been."

Holden smiled. "I hope you can take heart in the fact that your son is indeed very special. The stubbornness and bad behavior you've seen from Nick over the last several months has come as a result of his dragon being cooped up inside for too long. Very young children don't seem to suffer much in the way of ill effects when they don't shift. But as shifter children get older, and their inner animals get stronger, well, let's just say a cooped up dragon is very unhappy. Because Nick never let his inner dragon out on his own, that inner dragon started to grow more and more insistent, trying to push its way out. This internal unrest has been tormenting Nick, causing him to act out in unpleasant ways."

Elise put her head in her hands. "If only I'd told his father about him. I was trying to protect him. I didn't want him to grow up to be wild like his dad. I'm such an idiot."

Holden reached over and gently pushed Elise's hands away from her face. He hooked his thumb under her chin and raised her face to look at him. "Don't beat yourself up over it. You didn't know. How could you? Besides, it's all in the past now, and you can't change it."

Elise still felt like she was reeling. As crazy as everything Holden was saying sounded, she knew it was true. And her only worry now was Nick. "Can you help him?" she asked, her voice pleading. "You said you could?"

Holden smiled at her, and the tenderness in his eyes made her breath catch in her throat. "I can help him. I found him out in the Blackstone caves earlier today. I was out there with Violet when we heard screaming. We ran over and found Nick in quite a state. His dragon was trying to shift, and he was trying to hold it back. Of course, he didn't know that that's what he was doing. He just knew he felt awful and that the awful feeling was growing harder and harder to control. I walked him through how to shift, and he turned into a dragon. Then I helped him back to human form. I'll keep helping him, assuming he's willing. I can show him how to control the shifting, and the first shift is always the hardest, anyway. The worst is behind him."

Elise tried to process everything Holden was telling her. Her Nicky was a dragon, and had to learn to control his dragon side. The idea seemed preposterous, and yet, everything Holden was saying made sense. Nick had grown progressively more stubborn and unhappy in the last year. He'd often apologized to his mother for his actions, yet he seemed unable to stop them. Was it really possible that all of his ghastly behavior had been caused by an inner dragon?

"Will this help with all the, uh, acting out that Nicky does?" Elise asked, almost not daring to hope for it. But Holden's gentle smile reassured her once more.

"I think you'll find that your boy is quite a different person when he wakes up. He'll be more at peace than he's been in a long time, and I'm willing to bet that many of the bad behaviors you've been dealing with will cease to be a problem."

Elise let out a relieved breath. "Does it hurt when he shifts?" she asked. She was afraid to hear the answer, but she needed to know.

"Usually, no," Holden said. "But if a shifter has gone too long between shifts, it can be a bit painful. I won't lie to you, Elise. When he shifted today, it no doubt hurt like hell. But next time it won't feel like much more than a little bit of pressure. As long as he shifts about once a month, at minimum, he'll be fine."

Elise nodded. "Does he know now that he's a shifter, then?"

Holden tilted his head sideways. "Well, he knows he turned into a dragon. I imagine he'll need a bit of an explanation when he wakes up."

"Can you...explain things to him?" Elise asked. "I think you'll do a much better job of that than I would."

"I'd be honored," Holden said, and Elise breathed out a sigh of relief. This day had been strange, but if everything Holden was telling her was true, and her son's problems had all stemmed from the fact that he was a shifter and didn't know it, then that meant better days were ahead. Nick could learn to control his shifting, and be free from the inner torment he'd been feeling. It seemed almost too good to be true, and yet Elise knew in her heart that it was.

"And he's a…a dragon?" she asked. "I thought dragons weren't even real. Then again, I thought shifters weren't real until today. Are there other types of shifters? Other animals, I mean?"

"Nick's a dragon," Holden said, nodding. "Dragons are very real, and they used to roam the earth freely, but they're now extinct, except in shifter form. To answer your other question, though, there are many kinds of shifters. Bears, lions, tigers, and wolves are some of the more common. But really, just about any animal you can think of might exist in shifter form somewhere. Shifters are more common than you think."

"And wizards?" Elise asked, glancing toward the bedroom door, behind which Violet sat with Nick.

Holden chuckled. "You have had a day of it, haven't you? Discovering the existence of shifters, wizards, and dragons, all in one go. I don't know how common, exactly, wizards are. Their clans tend to keep to themselves and stay even more hidden than shifter clans do. But they do exist, and Violet is one of them. I hope you don't mind, but she put a sleeping spell on Nick. He needed to rest, after everything he'd been through."

Elise considered this. "Is it dangerous?" she asked.

"The sleeping spell? No, it's harmless. Helpful even, since it allows him to rest."

Elise rubbed her face with her hands, trying to rub away the feelings of confusion that filled her. She had a lot of questions, still, but right now, she mostly wanted to see Nick. She knew there would still be a bit of a bumpy road ahead of her son, but she was glad they had answers to what had been tormenting him. And she was even a little bit proud, now that the initial shock was over. Sure, some people might consider shifters to be freaks of nature. But she thought it was pretty damn cool that her son could transform into a dragon.

She looked up at Holden, who was studying her carefully, concern etched into his handsome face. He could change into a dragon, and he certainly was no freak. He was one of the kindest, most caring men she'd met in a long time. Too bad Violet had found him first. Elise forced herself to push away any lingering romantic thoughts about Holden. He belonged to another woman, and, from the little Elise had seen of that woman, she seemed like a kind person. Besides, Elise worried that any kind of romance would cause emotional trauma for Nick. It was better that she stay single for the sake of her son.

"Can Violet wake Nick up?" Elise asked. "I'd like to talk to him, if you think it won't be too taxing?"

Holden nodded. "She can wake him up. He's been sleeping for a bit, so hopefully he feels alright now. I should warn you, though, he's probably going to be ravenously hungry when he wakes up. Shifting takes a lot of energy, and the first time even more than normal."

Elise laughed. "Well, that's bad news for my refrigerator. Nick already has one of the biggest appetites I've ever seen. Does your girlfriend have a spell that can make food magically appear?"

Holden looked confused. "My girlfriend?"

"You know, Violet?"

"Oh," Holden said, laughing. "I don't think she can make food appear out of thin air. And she's not my girlfriend."

"But you introduced her as your partner," Elise said. Now she was the one who looked confused.

"Right. She's my *work* partner. But we're just friends. Trust me, there's nothing romantic going on between us. My buddy Weston has a thing for her, and he'd kill me if I looked at her that way. Now come on, let's go see if we can wake up your boy and explain to him what's going on."

Elise followed Holden to the bedroom without another word, but she bit her lip to try to hold back the smile she felt pulling at her lips. She'd completely misunderstood the relationship between Holden and Violet, and she couldn't deny that this fact made her quite happy.

Despite her best efforts to hold it back, the smile broke free, anyway.

CHAPTER SIX

Holden watched with mild amusement as Nick poured the last of the box of cereal into his bowl, then splashed milk over it. The box had been completely full when Elise pulled it from the pantry fifteen minutes ago, but Nick had made short work of eating the entire box. Holden knew that the boy's eating was a mixture of true hunger and of just the need to do something with his hands. Nick had a lot to think about.

Holden had explained everything to Nick that he had just explained to Elise. He told the boy about how his father had almost certainly been a dragon shifter, and about how, under normal circumstances, the man would have taught Nick how to shift. Holden explained that the uneasiness and turmoil Nick had been feeling was due to a restless inner shifter, and that those feelings should ease up now. Holden also told him that the pain he'd felt today when he shifted was abnormal, and that shifting would not hurt in the future, as long as he shifted at least once a month. He even explained what ghosting was, and that this was a very special talent to have, even for a shifter. If the boy was impressed by this fact, he didn't show it. Nick's face remained expressionless during Holden's entire speech. Finally, Holden promised to teach the boy everything there was to know about life as a shifter, then asked if he had any questions.

Nick's only question had been, "Can I have something to eat?" And so, Elise had given him the only food she had in the house right then, a box of cereal that was now completely devoured. Nick was scraping the last of the sugary flakes from the bottom of the bowl at that very moment. No one spoke. Everyone seemed to be waiting for someone else to break the silence, which had grown tense in the last few minutes. Holden knew that Nick would have many more questions as the days passed. He knew that adjusting to life as a shifter would not be a completely smooth ride. But he would let Nick ask the questions when he was ready. The worst thing right now would be to push the boy. Everyone else in the room seemed to understand that as well, because they all kept silent, too, following Nick's lead.

It was a full minute after the last of the cereal had been scraped from his bowl that Nick finally looked up. He looked directly at his mother, and, with a trembling voice, he spoke.

"I'm so sorry, Mom."

Holden watched as Elise's eyes widened. She rushed around the table to her son's side, taking him in her arms. "You don't have anything to be sorry for," she said, choking back her own tears. "I'm the one who should be sorry. I should never have kept you a secret from your dad. I thought I was doing the right thing, but I was wrong. So very, very wrong."

"No, mom. That's all fine. I understand. I mean I'm sorry that I'm...that I'm an animal. I knew something was wrong with me, and I tried to hide it. But it got stronger and stronger and I couldn't hold it back any more. I'm so sorry. It must be a huge disappointment to know that you have a monster for a son."

Nick's body shuddered, and Holden could tell that the boy was struggling not to cry. Nick lost that struggle, though, when Elise took the boy's face in her hands and raised it so they were looking at each other eye to eye.

"You are *not* a monster," Elise said, a fierceness in her voice unlike anything Holden had ever heard. "Do you hear me? I love you more than life itself, and I'm so damn proud of you, and nothing could ever change that. Especially not the fact that you're a shifter. You have a gift, Nick. A special talent. Anyone who can't see that and thinks that you're a monster is missing out on knowing one of the most amazing people this world has ever seen. That's what you are, Nick: amazing. And don't you ever forget it."

Nick was sobbing now, and Holden decided it was time to give the mother and son a moment of privacy. He motioned to Violet, who understood and followed him out onto the apartment's tiny patio.

"Wow," Violet said. "What a day."

"You're telling me," Holden said, wearily rubbing at his eyes, which felt like they ached from exhaustion. It was a strange sensation, to feel like your eyes themselves ached. But from the looks of it, Violet was feeling about the same level of exhaustion right now.

"You should go home," Holden told her. "Get some rest. Besides, one of us needs to call headquarters in Falcon Cross and check in, and I don't think we should do it from here."

Violet raised an eyebrow in surprise. "You're not telling Elise and Nick about the war? I noticed you hadn't made any mention of Saul or his army, or of the dragon stones."

"No," Holden said wearily. "Maybe I should, but I feel like I should give the boy a little bit of time to get used to the idea of shifting before I spring on him the fact that there's a huge war going on in the shifter world."

Violet nodded, although she didn't look entirely convinced. "Alright. Well, I'll head home and touch base with headquarters. They'll be interested to know that we found a shifter in town, and a ghoster no less. Even though Nick doesn't have anything to do with Saul's army."

Holden shrugged. "Yeah, it almost doesn't even count as news that we found a shifter here, given the circumstances. But tell them anyway. At least they'll know that we've been trying to search, even though we haven't had much success."

"Right," Violet agreed. "And what about you? How long are you planning to stay here?"

"A few more hours, maybe? I want to make sure the boy is alright before I leave. He's had quite a shock."

"And you want to make sure his mom's okay, too, don't you?" Violet asked. The teasing note in her voice was unmistakable, and Holden groaned. Was it that obvious that his heart was doing flip-flops over Elise? Well, no matter. He wasn't going to act on any of his feelings. For him, love was a strictly forbidden emotion. But Holden didn't want to have a heart-to-heart about his complicated emotions, especially not with Violet, who took great pleasure in running to the ground every possible opportunity to tease him.

"Oh lay off it, V," Holden said, trying to keep his voice light. "You know Elise and Nick both need a bit of steadying right now. I'm going to calm them down a bit more and then come back to the apartment."

"Alright," Violet said, the knowing smile never leaving her face as she made her way to open the patio door and head back inside. "Happy steadying."

She winked at him, and before he could respond, she was in the apartment, telling Elise and Nick that she needed to go, but that they were welcome to call her any time they needed anything. She gave each of them a hug, and then disappeared out the front door.

Holden walked slowly back into the room, where Nick was absentmindedly tapping his spoon on his empty cereal bowl.

"Still hungry?" Holden asked.

Nick looked up at him and gave a sheepish shrug.

"I'm hungry, too," Holden said. "What if we order a pizza, my treat?"

Holden looked at Elise for approval, and she nodded, looking relieved.

"Pizza sounds fabulous," she said. Holden figured she was glad to avoid a trip to the grocery store tonight. She'd had quite a day, too, and probably didn't want to venture out and chance meeting anyone she knew.

Thirty minutes later, they were munching on extra cheesy slices of pepperoni pizza. Nick's appetite seemed to finally start settling after the third slice, and he looked over at Holden curiously.

"Violet is really nice," he said. "And I can't believe she's a wizard. It's so cool that magic is real."

Holden nodded. "The wizards have been a great help to the shifters. We've been...working on some things lately, and they've stepped in to help wherever they could."

Holden saw Elise narrowing her eyes at him. "Are these 'things' you're working on the reason you're in Blackstone?" she asked. "Do they have anything to do with the 'research project' that you refused to tell me about?"

Holden did his best to laugh off her comment. "You're quite nosy about my work, you know?" he said breezily. "It's really not that interesting."

Elise frowned at him, but took the hint that he didn't want to talk about it. She went back to eating her pizza slice, but Holden had a feeling that this would not be their last conversation about his "research."

For now, though, Holden needed to focus on warning Nick to be careful. The conversation wasn't an easy one to have. How do you tell a boy to be proud of his shifter abilities, and then a few breaths later tell him it's safer to hide them? Holden knew it would be much easier to explain if he told Elise and Nick about the shifter war, but he didn't want to worry them with those details. Not yet, anyway. They both needed a bit of time to recover from the shock of the day before he sprung even more life-changing news on them.

"Nick, listen," Holden said, looking across the table to look the boy directly in the eye. "Shifting is a wonderful gift, and the more you learn to control your inner dragon, the more you're going to love being a shifter. But you do need to be careful about revealing your shifter abilities to others. Unfortunately, there *are* people out there who view shifters as monsters or freaks of nature. Those people are only too happy to bully shifters and treat them like criminals. Their actions are unjustified, but unfortunately there are more people like that out there than you might think."

"So you want me to hide who I am?" Nick asked. His voice held a clear note of belligerence. Holden supposed he couldn't blame him. After telling the boy all day that shifting was special and that he had nothing to be ashamed of, Holden was now telling Nick to hide his shifter side. The message was confusing, but Holden was doing the best he could. The issues were so complicated.

"I'm not telling you to hide who you are," Holden said. "I'm just telling you to be careful about who you show your shifter side to. Be sure you only show people you trust, okay?"

"Okay," Nick said, sounding mildly appeased as he reached for another slice of pizza. Holden breathed out a small sigh of relief, thinking he'd handled the matter reasonably well. But when he looked over at Elise, he could see in her eyes that she was not as appeased as her son seemed to be. Holden had a feeling that she'd be asking him more questions later, and he was right.

A few hours later, after the pizza had been demolished and a few board games had been played, Nick announced that he was exhausted and needed to go to bed. It was only nine o'clock, and Elise seemed surprised that her son was voluntarily going to bed before ten p.m. But Holden was only surprised that Nick hadn't gone earlier. Shifting for the first time took more energy than Nick had ever spent in a day before, Holden was sure of that. Holden bid Nick goodnight and waited in the living room while Elise, who was still worried about her son, went to make sure he settled into bed alright. Holden could have slipped out before Nick went to his bedroom, but he didn't want to leave Elise yet. He told himself it was because he wanted to make sure that she was okay after the day she'd had—and he did. But he would be lying if he said that his growing desire for her had nothing to do with his decision to stay.

"You're a fool, Holden," he whispered to himself as he sat on the couch, twirling the fringe of a throw pillow around his fingers. He didn't want to fall in love, but he couldn't tear himself away from this apartment. Not yet. Not before he had one more chance to look into Elise's beautiful, deep green eyes.

A few moments later, those deep green eyes appeared in front of him again. Elise sat in the armchair across from the couch, positioning herself on the edge of the seat as though she didn't plan to be sitting for very long. Holden felt a bit disappointed that she hadn't chosen to sit on the couch next to him. He was being a fool. She didn't look at him as anything more than someone who could help her son. There was nothing between them, and, even though it was better that way, Holden's mood sank at the realization, anyway.

"He was out before his head even hit the pillow," Elise said, shaking her head. "I don't think I've managed to get him to bed this early since he was a preschooler."

Holden smiled. "Well, enjoy it while it lasts. He'll probably be tired for the next day or two, as his body adjusts to shifting. But after that, I'm sure he'll be back to wanting to stay up late."

Elise nodded, but didn't say anything else for a few moments. Holden decided that perhaps he'd overstayed his welcome, and that it was time to go. He pushed back the strange feeling of disappointment he felt at the prospect of leaving Elise, and forced himself to stand.

"I should get going, I suppose," he said. "You probably want to get some rest, too."

"Sit," Elise said, her voice stern. Holden looked at her in surprise.

"What?" he asked, not sure he'd heard her correctly.

"I said sit," she repeated. "Nicky might be done with his questions for the day, but I'm not."

Holden raised an eyebrow and sat back down. "Alright," he said, curiosity filling him. "What else did you want to know?"

"I want to know what you're not telling me," Elise said, crossing her arms. "Why are you really here in Blackstone? Every time the subject comes up, you try to make a joke out of it and avoid the truth. But people don't come to Blackstone on vacation. There's a reason you're here, and I want to know what it is. If you're going to be spending a lot of time with my son, I want to make sure you're not involved in something dangerous or shady."

Holden let out a small sigh. She was right to question him, of course. And he admired her straightforward attitude. But he wasn't sure how much he should tell her. Violet and he were under strict orders not to discuss the war with any humans, but

Elise was the mother of a shifter, so she wasn't exactly your average human. Her son might be caught up in the shifter war if things went badly, and Holden supposed she had a right to know that.

"It's sort of complicated to explain," Holden said, stalling for time.

"Just do your best," Elise replied, leaning back into her chair now, as though she were settling in to catch up with an old friend. Holden knew in that moment that he had no choice. Elise's face was set in such a determined line that he was sure she wouldn't let him leave until he'd confessed his mission in its entirety.

"Alright. I'll do my best," he said, although he still wasn't sure quite how to begin. He figured he should just start talking, and hope that his explanation came out reasonably coherent. "It's true that most shifters are good, like I told Nick. But there are, unfortunately, shifters who are evil. Just like there are good and bad people, I suppose."

Elise nodded, waiting for him to continue.

"Well, one particularly evil shifter recently decided to start a war. His name is Saul, and he's a dragon shifter who also has wizard abilities."

"There are shifters who are also wizards?" Elise asked, her eyes widening in genuine surprise.

"Well, ordinarily, no. But there is a branch of wizardry that is known as dark magic. It consists of evil spells that cause great harm, and that actually eat away at a wizard's soul, so much so that a wizard who continues to use dark magic will eventually be killed by it. One of those dark magic spells allows a wizard to give magical abilities to a non-wizard. Some dark wizard did that for Saul, so he's now a dragon shifter practicing dark magic. And he's leading a giant war. He's gathered together an army of evil shifters, evil wizards, and even some misguided humans, and he's trying to take over the world."

Elise laughed out loud. "That sounds pretty dramatic," she said. "I don't think one army of shifters and wizards could literally take over the entire world."

"Well," Holden said sadly. "I wish you were right about that, but I'm afraid you're not. You see, there are several powerful ancient artifacts that bestow supernatural powers on their owners. The ancient dragon shifters *did* have magical powers, and they stored them in several different types of objects. The most powerful of these ancient artifacts are the dragon stones. There are four—an emerald, a sapphire, an amethyst, and a ruby. Each of these stones holds enough power to take down an entire army. The good shifters, whom I work for, have recovered all of the stones but the ruby. We're keeping the stones in safekeeping, away from Saul and his army."

"Well that sounds promising," Elise said, frowning.

"It does, but it's not enough," Holden said. "The dragon ruby, which is the stone we still haven't found, is rumored to be more powerful than all three of the other stones combined. It could wipe out entire armies easily, and quite literally allow Saul to take over the world."

Elise was quiet, blinking at him in disbelief.

"I know it sounds absurd," Holden said. "But it's true."

"So, what can be done about it?" Elise asked.

"Well, I'm part of an alliance of wizards and dragon shifters that are trying to find the dragon ruby before Saul does. The reason I'm in Blackstone, though, is that Saul has taken up headquarters in Sandview."

"Sandview?" Elise repeated, a tinge of fear in her voice. "That's pretty close to here."

Holden nodded. "Yup. Blackstone is the closest town. Violet and I were sent to scope things out after some of our fellow soldiers discovered that Saul is raising an army by cloning bat shifters there. Don't ask me how the whole cloning thing works. I don't understand the details, I just know that it's allowed Saul to quickly raise a giant army. He's also been terrorizing the people of Sandview, although we aren't sure how much. Part of our job is to find out, and to figure out a way to stop Saul's operations. It's too dangerous to go directly to Sandview, though, so we were sent here first to get our bearings."

Elise had a crease of worry running across her forehead. "If things in Sandview are so dangerous, than Blackstone must not be all that safe, either. We're not that far away."

"Well, that's part of what's complicated," Holden said. "Saul doesn't seem to be paying much attention to Blackstone. And that's probably because there are no shifters here. Or, at least, he *thinks* there are no shifters here. I'm sure he sent scouts out here to check, but since they couldn't smell that Nick is a shifter, they assumed there were no shifters, and they left."

Elise caught on quickly. "So as long as they think there are no shifters here, they'll stay away. Which is why it's so important that no one realizes that Nick is a shifter."

"Exactly," Holden said.

Elise pondered this information for a few moments. "Why didn't you tell him about the war?"

Holden frowned slightly. "I thought he'd been through enough already today. I didn't think it made sense to burden him with more worries, especially when there isn't really anything he can do to help the war effort. He's too young to fight, and, besides, he needs to learn to control his dragon better before he'll be of any real use in a shifter fight."

Holden saw the panic crossing Elise's face. "Is this common? Shifters warring and fighting?"

"It happens every couple of decades," Holden said. "But it's not a constant thing. And besides, dragon shifters are the strongest of the shifters. Nick will have the upper hand in any fight he might find himself in. His ghosting will protect him, too. Shifters rely on our sense of smell to find other shifters in a battle. A shifter who can't be detected by smell is very dangerous—and very safe from unwanted attacks."

Elise still looked worried, but she nodded her head as though Holden's words had reassured her. "So that's really why you told Nick not to go around telling everyone he's a shifter."

"That was the main reason, yes," Holden said. "It is true that there are plenty of people out there who treat shifters horribly for no good reason. But those people, while annoying, aren't usually dangerous. The real danger now would be if Saul's army discovered that shifters were in Blackstone. I think that, eventually, we'll need to tell Nick what's going on. But I wanted to give him a day or two to adjust to the fact that he's a shifter before telling him that there's a potential world war on the horizon."

Elise let out a long sigh. "I think that's probably a good idea."

Holden felt his heart twist up in that funny way that was becoming all too familiar. He could tell that Elise felt exhausted, and worried, and he wished there was some way for him to shoulder her pain for her. Without giving himself time to think about what he was doing, he rose and went to kneel in front of the armchair she was sitting in. He grabbed her hands in his, marveling at the way his large, rough hands covered her smaller ones completely. She looked at him and bit her lip, which he could already tell was a habit of hers. He would have loved nothing more than to bite her lip himself, among other parts of her body, but he forced himself to stick to holding her hands.

"Listen, Elise. I know this is all a bit scary for you. And I won't lie to you. There is a lot of dangerous stuff going on. But I promise you, I'll do everything in my power to protect Nick. I'll watch out for him, and I'll train him how to use his shifter abilities to keep himself safe. I can't guarantee you that no harm will come to him. I wish I could, but life just doesn't work that way. What I can guarantee you is that as long as there is breath in my body, I will fight to make sure no harm comes to Nick."

Elise swallowed hard, but she couldn't keep a few tears from squeezing their way past her eyelids. She nodded, and gave Holden a lopsided smile. "Okay. Thank you."

They looked at each other in silence for a few moments after that. It would have been the appropriate time for Holden to let go of her hands and make his way home. They'd said all there was to say tonight. But he did not let go of her hands, and she did not try to pull away. Instead, they sat there, eyes locked. Holden felt a fire beginning to burn inside of him. He told himself to move, to get out of that apartment right away, before his heart betrayed him. But he could not tear his eyes away from Elise's. And then, before he could stop himself, he was leaning forward, and she was tilting her head toward him.

Their lips met softly, silently. There was no noise in the living room of that tiny apartment except for the ragged breathing of two people who knew this was probably a bad idea, but, for that one tiny moment, didn't care.

Holden held that soft kiss as long as he dared. And then, with a small sigh, he rose and made his way to the door.

"Tell Nick I'll stop by tomorrow, alright?" he said, turning as his hand reached for the doorknob.

Elise nodded at him, her curly red hair bouncing on her shoulders as she did.

"Good night, Elise," Holden said softly. And then, he was out of the apartment before she had a chance to respond. He ran all the way back to the apartment he was sharing with Violet, wondering what the heck he'd been thinking and whether it was too late to keep himself from completely falling for Elise.

CHAPTER SEVEN

Elise dreamed strange dreams that night, filled with dragons and wizards and magnificent, dazzling rubies. She tossed and turned so much that by the time she woke up, all of her blankets and sheets had fallen to the floor of her bedroom in a tangled mess.

She sat up slowly and glanced at the glowing numbers on her alarm clock, which told her it was still twenty-two minutes until the five o'clock alarm would start blaring at her. She rubbed her eyes, trying to rub away the last vestiges of sleep. Her stomach flip-flopped with a mixture of fear and excitement as the events of the previous day came back to her in a rush. Her son was a dragon shifter, and one with a special talent for ghosting. Holden could help him learn to use his shifter abilities properly. But there was also a war going on that might threaten the safety of the entire world. A powerful dragon ruby was missing, and Holden and Violet were part of an alliance of wizards and shifters that were trying to find the ruby. Violet was a wizard. But she was not Holden's girlfriend. Holden had kissed Elise last night.

He kissed me! Elise thought, her mind settling on this one thought.

Elise touched her lips gingerly, as though afraid to rub away the memory of the kiss. The kiss had taken her by surprise. She'd been admiring Holden since the first moment she'd met him, but she'd never expected him to actually notice her. She'd figured a guy like him would have plenty of options for women—women who were far more beautiful than her, who had their lives together and weren't scraping to make ends meet by always working double shifts at a small town diner. Oh, and women who didn't come with the baggage of a twelve-year-old son.

Elise fell back against the mattress and stared up at the ceiling, which looked gray in the faint gray light of early dawn. How could she have been so stupid, to let herself fall for Holden? And then to let him kiss her like that? She'd been caught up in the moment, that was all—swept off her feet by the fact that he had so generously promised to protect her son. But she had to make sure that the next time she saw him, he knew that their kiss had been a one-time event. It was precisely her need to protect her son that had kept her from ever having a serious romance after Nick's dad left for the army. The last thing Elise wanted was for her son to finally have a male role model in his life, only to have that man disappear again. As soon as Elise started getting close to a guy, she would clam up and come up with an excuse to break things off. She couldn't bear to think of the pain in Nick's eyes if he finally thought he had a dad, only to have that dad desert him.

Which was why Elise could not allow things between her and Holden to grow romantically. Holden had offered to protect and help Nick. Elise wasn't going to mess that up by starting a relationship with the man, no matter how goddamn sexy he was. If Elise never dated Holden, there was no chance of her eventually having an awful breakup with Holden. There was no chance of Nick viewing Holden as a father figure only to have Holden leave because of Elise.

Elise sat up again and swung her legs over the side of the bed. She was destined to be alone, at least until Nick was grown, and that was all there was to it. There was no sense in feeling sorry for herself. She had a lot to be thankful for, after all. She had a job, and a place to live. That was more than a lot of people could say. And she had a wonderful son, who gave her the inspiration she needed to keep moving forward. Life was hard now, but every sacrifice Elise made, she was making for Nick. He was worth it. Because of her hard work now, he would have a better future.

A little less than an hour later, as Elise cracked the door open to Nick's bedroom to whisper goodbye before heading off to work, she did her best to remind herself that she was doing this all for him. He slept soundly, not even stirring when she looked in. With a sigh, she closed the door again and left the apartment, locking the front door behind her. She'd left a twenty dollar bill and a note on the kitchen counter, telling him to use the money to cover breakfast and lunch for himself. She'd have to go grocery shopping later, even though she knew she'd be dog tired by the time she was done with her shift.

Hell, she felt dog tired right now, even though she'd barely started her day. Yesterday had been draining, and Elise wished she could call in this morning, even though she needed the money. But she knew she was already going to be in trouble for calling in last night. She didn't dare miss her morning shift, too. As she locked the door behind her, she felt her phone buzzing in her pocket. She looked down to see a message from Holden on the screen.

I'll stop by and see Nick later this morning, if that's okay with you? I want to make sure he's doing alright.

Elise smiled, and texted back an *Okay*. It would be torture sticking to her decision to keep Holden at arm's distance from herself, but it was worth it for Nick's sake. Holden was going to be a good influence in Nick's life, and it had been too long since the boy had had a true friend.

* * *

Holden glanced at his watch and knocked on the apartment door again. It was half past ten. Surely, Nick was awake by now? Violet had warned him that he might be going too early, but he'd brushed off her concerns, saying that even preteens wouldn't sleep later than ten. Apparently, he'd been wrong. Holden frowned. He hated being wrong, especially when it meant that Violet was right. The two of them had a long-running competition over who could be right more often. At the moment, it felt like Violet was pulling hopelessly into the lead.

Holden glanced down at the box of donuts he'd brought, and was about to knock again, when he heard the lock on the door click. The door swung open a moment later, and Holden found himself staring at a very sleepy looking Nick. The boy's dark curly hair was a mess, sweaty and flattened against his scalp, and he still wore the plaid cotton pajama pants he'd put on before bed last night. Holden said a silent prayer of thanks that Violet was not here to witness this. She would have taken great pleasure in rubbing into his face the fact that Nick had just woken up.

"I brought donuts," Holden said, holding up the box and hoping that sugar was an acceptable peace offering for waking up a twelve-year-old.

Nick said nothing, but opened the door wider and started walking toward the kitchen. Holden followed, closing the door behind him and setting the box of donuts down on the dining room table. Nick went to the refrigerator and grabbed a carton of milk. He sat down at the table and grabbed a chocolate sprinkle donut from the box, wolfing it down in two bites and then drinking several swigs of milk directly from the carton. Holden eyed him with amusement, and Nick must have noticed because he finally spoke at that point.

"Don't tell my mom. She hates it when I don't use a glass."

Holden made a motion of zipping his lips shut and throwing away the key. "Your secret's safe with me," he said.

Nick's only response was to grab another donut, which he ate only slightly slower than the first. When he was done, he took another couple of swigs from the milk carton and then wiped his mouth with the back of his hand.

"Did Mom send you over here?" he asked, eyeing Holden with a bit of suspicion.

Holden leaned back in his chair. "No. I wanted to come over. You had a big day yesterday, and I wanted to see how you were feeling today?"

Nick wouldn't meet Holden's eyes. "I'm alright," he said. "Considering I just found out I'm a dragon."

"Hey, I might be a bit biased, but I think being a dragon is actually pretty cool."

"I'm not so sure," Nick said. "It seems like shifters do awful things. That's not the kind of life I want."

Holden frowned. "What makes you think shifters do awful things?" he asked. "Of course, shifters have great power. But you can control that power. I'll teach you how. You can use your talents for good."

"I've never seen a shifter do good things. Not until you, I guess," Nick said sullenly.

Holden felt the hair on the back of his neck prickle. He didn't have a lot of experience with preteens, as his too-early arrival showed. But he knew enough to realize that there was something Nick wasn't telling him right now.

"What do you mean, you've never seen a shifter do good things?" Holden asked. "How many shifters have you seen?"

Nick didn't answer him. Instead he grabbed another donut and turned so that his face was angled away from Holden.

"Nick, this is really important," Holden said, trying to keep his voice from betraying the dread he was starting to feel. "How many shifters have you seen?"

Nick shrugged, and didn't answer. Holden forced himself not to push the boy, but he had to figure out a way to make Nick talk. Something about the way Nick was acting made Holden think he hadn't been as innocent about the existence of shifters as he'd acted yesterday. While Holden was still mulling over what to say, Nick turned to face him, narrowing his eyes.

"Who sent you here?" he asked. "To Blackstone, I mean. And how did you know I was here?"

Holden's senses were all on high alert. There was *definitely* something Nick wasn't telling him. "No one sent me to you, Nick," Holden said, keeping his voice neutral. "I was sent to Blackstone to scout out some…disturbances in the shifter world. But I had no idea that you were here until I saw your eyes glowing and churning outside the diner the morning I rescued you from that big fight."

Nick stared at Holden, squinting his eyes as though trying to decide whether what the older man had said was true. And then, to Holden's great surprise, Nick burst into tears.

"I don't want to be a shifter! I don't want to be one of them! How did they do this to me? Did you have a part in it?"

Holden was taken completely off guard by the outburst. He reached across the table to try to grab Nick's hand, but the boy pulled away, flinging donut sprinkles across the table as he did. Holden suddenly had a sinking feeling in the pit of his stomach.

"Nick, you've seen shifters before yesterday, haven't you?"

Nick looked up at him and sniffed. He wiped away a few tears, then nodded.

"Where?"

"In the tunnel," Nick said. "I...I know I shouldn't have been there. I could tell it was dangerous. But everything was so strange. It was like a real life video game, and I couldn't stay away. My life here is so boring, and...and...I was so careful to keep them from seeing me. But they must have, somehow. And they turned me into one of them. And now I'm an awful dragon, and I'm going to do awful things. My mom works so hard to give me a good life and I've ruined it all."

Nick started wailing again. Holden slid over so that he was in the seat next to the boy, instead of across the table from him. He took Nick by the shoulders and gently shook him.

"Nick! Nick, listen to me. No one turned you into a shifter. I told you, it's genetic. You've been a shifter since the day you were born. It's just taken a while for you to realize it. But I need to know what this tunnel is. Who are these shifters you're talking about?"

Nick sniffed again, then turned to look at Holden. To Holden's relief, Nick seemed to finally focus on what Holden was saying. "There's an underground tunnel that goes from the caves outside of Blackstone all the way to some caves that are between here and Sandview. The tunnel is old and I don't think a lot of people know about it. I found it one day by accident when I was really young, and I've spent a lot of my childhood riding my bicycle back and forth between here and the Sandview caves."

"But Sandview is fifty miles away!" Holden said. "That's a really long bike ride."

Nick shook his head. "No, the Sandview caves are a lot closer than Sandview itself. It's probably about twenty miles from here? And I've always been pretty fast on a bike."

"Of course you have," Holden said, rubbing his forehead. "You're a shifter after all."

Holden was starting to feel sick to his stomach. If Nick knew about shifters because of some caves near Sandview, that could only mean one thing: Nick had inadvertently discovered Saul's hideout. Holden was about to ask Nick for more details, but the boy had started talking again of his own accord. It seemed that once Nick finally started confessing to his little tunnel trips, the words just came tumbling out.

"A few months ago, the Sandview caves, which had been empty for as long as I've known about them, were suddenly full of people. The first time I saw people there, I hid from them because I thought I'd get in trouble if anyone saw me and told mom that I'd been in the tunnel. But it didn't take long for me to realize that the real danger wasn't someone tattling on me. These people were strange, and not nice. They could change from human to animal form and back again. They brought people in and tortured them. I think they were people from Sandview, but I'm not sure. The animal people, uh, I guess you call them shifters, were very strong. They held the torture victims down and some other people used rings to hurt them. I didn't understand it at the time, but now I know the people with the rings were wizards, like Violet. Only they weren't nice like Violet. They used their magic to do mean things."

Holden sat back in his chair, stunned. "My god, Nick," he finally said. "You found Saul's hideout."

"Saul?" Nick asked.

Holden figured there was no point in keeping details from Nick any longer. He explained to the boy about the war that was raging between the good and evil shifters and wizards. He told Nick how Saul had been building an army of bat shifters near Sandview, and, as Nick had seen, torturing the townspeople. When Holden was finished speaking, Nick frowned and picked up another donut, munching it slowly.

"Yeah," Nick finally said. "They're not very nice. When I started to turn into a dragon myself—just an arm or a leg at the time—I resisted it as hard as I could. I thought they'd done something to turn me into one of them. Are you sure that's not the case?"

"I'm sure," Holden said. "Shifters are born, not created. But what probably happened is that being around other shifters made your inner dragon restless, and sped up the inevitable process of your dragon forcing its way out."

Nick considered this for a second. "I feel a lot better today than I have in a long time."

Holden nodded. "That's because you allowed yourself to shift. You won't ever feel as awful as you did before you shifted yesterday, as long as you keep shifting at regular intervals. But tell me, do Saul's soldiers know about the tunnel?"

Nick considered this for a moment. "I don't think so," he said. "They never mentioned it as far as I heard. And I never saw anyone come anywhere near the entrance. It's not that surprising. I think that tunnel is about a hundred years old. It must have been built with dynamite blasts way back in the day. Kaboom!"

Nick threw his hands up above his head to mimic the motion of an explosion, and Holden chuckled. It didn't matter what age boys were—they all seemed to love the idea of things getting blown to smithereens. But Holden didn't care much why the tunnel had been built, or how. He was just glad to hear that Saul's men seemed oblivious to its existence.

"And what about the wizards and shifters who were torturing people," Holden asked. "Can you remember anything of what they were saying? What kind of questions were they asking the people they were hurting?"

Nick furrowed his brow. "I don't really remember. It was hard to understand them, and I was more interested in the flashes of light from their rings, or in the way the shifters turned into animals and back again. Besides, I didn't dare get too close. I didn't want any of them to see me."

Holden shook his head in amazement. "Nick, you don't even realize how lucky you are you're a ghoster. If you'd been a normal shifter, or even just a normal human, those shifters would have smelled you coming from a mile away. They would have known you were there, even if you were quiet and stayed out of sight. I seriously can't believe your luck."

Nick, for his part, seemed unmoved by this observation. He shrugged, and continued munching on his donut, looking thoughtful. After finishing the sweet treat, he looked over at Holden with apprehension in his eyes.

"Are you sure that I won't do awful things, like those shifters I saw?" Nick asked. "I don't want to be a bad person."

Holden smiled at him. "You're a good kid, Nick, and you have a good heart. Being a shifter doesn't automatically make you good or bad, just like being a human doesn't automatically make you good or bad. You're going to be just fine, trust me. In fact, there might be a way you can help us win this war, thanks to your ghoster abilities and your knowledge of the tunnel."

"Really?" Nick asked, perking up. "That would be so cool."

Holden laughed. "Yes, really. But first I need to talk to Violet and let her know everything you've told me. And then we have to talk to your mom and see if she'll allow it."

Nick made a face. "If it's anything remotely dangerous, she's going to say no. She's horribly overprotective."

"Well, I'm not going behind her back. I promised her I'd take care of you. Chin up, though. I'm sure we'll be able to find a way for you to help the war effort, no matter how overprotective your mother is."

"I'm not so sure," Nick said glumly, slumping in his seat.

Holden said nothing, but, from what he'd seen of Elise so far, he had a feeling Nick's worries were justified. She was overly protective of her son. Not that Holden could blame her. The boy was all she had in the world. Still, he had to at least try to convince her that the plan he was formulating was a good one. If he couldn't, his only other option was going to be a big, bloody battle—one that might leave him and several other good shifters and wizards dead. And he couldn't protect Nick anymore if he was dead. Holden was surprised at how much this thought troubled him. He looked over at Nick and smiled, tousling the boy's hair. He'd meant it when he said Nick was a good kid. He could see great potential in the boy's wary green eyes. It was sad that the boy had never had a shifter father to guide him, but Holden knew he could make a big difference in Nick's life if he only had a little bit of time.

"We'll figure something out, kid. I promise," Holden said.

And Holden *would* figure out a way to involve Nick in the war effort safely, if it was the last thing he did. Dragons don't break promises, after all.

CHAPTER EIGHT

"Absolutely not!" Elise said, standing with her hands on her hips. "There is no way I'm letting you just waltz up to an army of evil shifters and wizards who torture and kill people with no remorse."

"I'm not walking right up to them. I'm sneaking up to them. They won't even know I'm there."

"The answer is no," Elise said, trying to keep her voice from shaking with emotion. She could hardly believe that her son was sitting there with a straight face, asking to walk right into the lions' den. Literally, the lions' den! There were lion shifters in Saul's army, after all. Or so she'd been told. Nick crossed his arms and gave her a defiant look—the same look he used to give her as a toddler when she told him he could not have ice-cream for dinner.

"I'm a dragon. I can do whatever I want," he declared.

Out of the corner of her eye, Elise saw Holden wince, then frantically shake his head "no" at the boy. Elise walked right up to her son, grabbed his left earlobe, and twisted it hard.

"Ow! Mom!" he protested, pulling away.

"Dragon or not, I am still your mother and you still live in my house. If you want me to continue to put a roof over your head and to feed that dragon appetite of yours, you will do as I say. Do you understand?"

Nick whimpered and nodded his head.

"Now go to your room. I want to have a word with Holden."

Nick scurried off to his room, suddenly happy for the chance to get away from his mother's presence. Elise turned her gaze sharply on Holden, who winced again.

"Elise," he said. But she held up her hand and shook her head.

"No. I'll do the talking. And let's go to my bedroom where we're out of Nick's earshot. I guarantee you he has his ear pressed up against his bedroom door right now to listen."

Holden followed Elise to her bedroom without another word, shutting the door behind him as Elise whirled to face him. The sight of him in her room, leaning easily against the closed door, took her breath away. For a moment, she forgot to be angry. His bicep muscles flexed slightly as he looked over at her with intense, searching eyes. Elise had a crazy impulse to rush across the room and throw her arms around him, kissing him with abandon. There was just something so sensual about having him in her bedroom. She should have known better than to bring him in here.

She pushed away her thoughts of romance and tried to remember that he was only in here because she needed to make it very clear to him that she was not okay with his putting ideas of grand adventures into her son's head. She was here to protect Nicky, not to think about how sexy Holden's muscles looked in the soft light of her bedroom.

"What were you thinking?" she asked, putting her hands on her hips again and trying to look as stern as possible. But she must not have made a very imposing figure, because she saw a mischievous twinkle in his eye.

"Oh, am I allowed to talk now?" he asked.

"No! Yes! I don't know!" Elise said, frustrated at how flustered she felt. "I just can't believe you would even put an idea like that in Nick's head."

Holden let out a measured breath, not responding right away. Elise balled her fingers into fists and tried not to cry. She'd never been much of a crier. As a single mother, tears had not been a luxury she could afford. She'd had to remain strong for her son. But this week had been too much for her, and she'd found herself constantly on the verge of breaking down.

"I'm sorry," Holden said. "I only thought that—"

"You didn't think. That's the problem," Elise interrupted. "You didn't think about the fact that you were asking my son, the only family I have, to put himself in harm's way."

"It's not exactly like that," Holden protested.

"No? Then what exactly is it like?"

Elise could feel herself losing control of her emotions. She knew it would be better for her sanity right now if she just told Holden to leave and spent a few hours alone, composing herself. But she was too angry and irrational to do the smart thing at the moment. As if it hadn't been a shock enough learning that her son was a dragon, and that there were evil dragons and wizards out there who would love nothing more than to kill off him and every other good shifter, Holden was actually suggesting that her son sneak up on Saul's army and spy on them.

Elise reached over to steady herself on the headboard of her bed. She'd felt sick to her stomach when she sat there and listened to Nick describe the secret tunnel he'd been playing in for years without her knowledge. The tunnel itself wasn't a big deal, but knowing that there was now a group of crazed, evil shifters and wizards on the other end of that tunnel was enough to make Elise's heart stop. Here she had been, working her ass off at the diner to make ends meet, not knowing that her son was spending hours in danger of being discovered by some very violent people. Elise knew she couldn't have known, and yet she felt like a failure as a mother.

And now, Holden, who had sworn he would protect Nick, was suggesting that the boy sneak back through the tunnel to spy on Saul's men. He wanted Nick to take pictures of Saul's operations, and to eavesdrop on what the soldiers were saying. As though asking a twelve-year-old boy to spy on coldblooded killers was no big deal.

"I'm sorry, Elise," Holden was saying again. "I wouldn't have asked you if I thought there was a high likelihood that he would be caught. He's a ghoster, so they can't smell him. Shifters 'see' with their noses more than their eyes. As long as he was careful, there's virtually no chance he'd be caught."

"Don't you get it, Holden?" Elise asked sitting down on her bed and putting her face in her hands. "He's twelve. You can't put that kind of responsibility on him. You can't ask him to walk into such a dangerous situation, no matter how small the chances that he'll be caught. He's too young. And you swore to protect him!"

Holden was silent for a long time. Finally, he walked over and sat on the bed next to Elise. He wrapped his arm around her shoulders and took in a deep breath, exhaling it slowly.

"You're right. I'm sorry," he said. "I should have thought it through more clearly, and I should have asked you before bringing it up with him. I got so excited about the possibility of getting the upper hand on Saul that I wasn't thinking straight."

Elise mumbled out something that sounded like "It's okay," but she was finding it hard to speak. Holden's arm around her was so warm and strong, and it made her feel so safe. She couldn't stay angry at him when he held her like that. She wanted to pull away, to tell him that she couldn't handle being this close to him, and that they couldn't have a future together. After all, hadn't he just proven to her that he didn't take her son's safety as seriously as she did? Why would she even consider a relationship with someone who might just leave, or might put her son in harm's way?

A little voice in her head told her that no one would ever take her son's safety as seriously as her, because she took it a little too seriously. And perhaps that was true. Perhaps she was overprotective. But Nicky was all she had, and just the thought of anything happening to him made it hard to breathe.

Elise stood up abruptly. This was all too much for her. Too many confusing, mixed emotions were swirling through her mind right now.

"I can't be with you like that," she said firmly, crossing her arms and giving Holden a defiant look. He wasn't looking for an argument, though.

"I'm sorry," he said in a weary tone. "I didn't mean to imply anything by putting my arm around you. I just wanted to comfort you, as a friend. I'm not exactly looking for romance, either, but I do care about you as a person. And about Nick, too. He's a shifter, and you're his mom. That makes you both my family, in a sense. We stand by each other in the shifter world, and we take care of each other."

Elise kept her arms crossed and frowned. Holden had spoken the perfect response. They were to remain friends, and that was it. He cared about her in a strictly platonic way, and wanted Nick to be taken care of. That's exactly what Elise wanted, so why did she feel a rush of disappointment at his words?

"You okay?" he asked.

She forced the frown away. "Yeah. Just a long day. Long week, really."

Holden nodded. "You've had a bit of an intense week, that's for sure. Do you work tonight?"

"No. Thank god I'm actually not on the schedule tonight. I'm so on edge right now that I'd probably lose it on the first customer who complained about something stupid like having to wait more than two seconds to get a refill on their drink."

Holden laughed. The sound filled Elise with warmth, and she couldn't help but smile.

"Why don't you go out to dinner with me?" Holden asked. "As friends of course. But I think you could benefit from a night where someone is refilling *your* drink rather than the other way around. You deserve a bit of a break."

"With Nick, too?" Elise asked.

"He can come if you want him to," Holden said. "But he could also go spend some time with Violet tonight, and you could have a real break for once. A real, adult dinner out. Violet's been working today on researching the location of the dragon ruby, and I bet Nick could help. It might make him feel a little better if he had a way to help out with the war effort. He really just wants to do something that matters, you know?"

Elise bit her lip, stalling for time. The thought of going to dinner with Holden alone sent a thrill through her whole body, which was exactly why she thought it was a bad idea to go. She didn't trust herself alone with him. How could she sit across from him for an entire dinner, looking into those soulful green eyes, and not feel any kind of desire? Her mind was screaming at her to say no, but her heart managed to get a hold of her mouth first, and she found herself saying, "That sounds great."

Which was how, an hour later, Elise found herself sitting in a booth across from Holden at Blackstone's only Italian restaurant. She peered at the sticky, laminated menu that had a bit of crusted pasta sauce on one corner, trying to figure out what she could order that wouldn't be too difficult to eat in a ladylike manner.

It's not a date, she told herself. But she still found herself opting for a chicken dish with bowtie pasta in a white lemon sauce. She wanted to steer clear of long spaghetti or red sauce, both of which would have made it difficult to eat without getting food all over her face or shirt. Holden seemed to have no such qualms, and ordered the spaghetti and meatballs. Elise felt another twinge of sadness as she reminded herself that they were only here as friends. What was wrong with her? She should be happy that they were both on the same page, and not interested in a romance.

Her phone buzzed on the table, mercifully distracting her with an incoming text from Nick.

"Sorry," Elise said. "I'm not trying to be rude by using my phone at the table, but I want to make sure I'm available if Nick needs me."

Holden waved his hand to tell her to go ahead, then reached for a slice of bread from the basket in the middle of the table. Elise was beginning to see that all dragon shifters had enormous appetites. She'd never met a man who could pack away food like Holden, and yet still maintain such a fit, muscular physique. Elise wanted to groan, thinking about how much Nick already ate—and he wasn't even an official teenager yet. Keeping the refrigerator stocked was a constant problem.

Elise unlocked her phone and glanced over the text message, then smiled. She should have known that Nick would be asking about food.

"He wants to know if he can order pizza," Elise said with a small laugh. "Apparently Violet said he has to get permission from me first before she'll let him have junk food for dinner."

Holden laughed. "That sounds like Violet. She's a big proponent of healthy eating. Gets mad at me anytime I stock the freezer with ice-cream."

Elise chuckled, but couldn't stop herself from feeling a bit jealous at the reminder that Holden and Violet lived together. He'd assured her they were only work colleagues, and, besides, Elise had no claim to Holden. But she still hated the thought of him potentially looking at another woman with desire.

"What's it like, living with a wizard?" Elise asked. She tried to keep her voice casual, and she tried to tell herself that she was genuinely curious about what life with a wizard was like. But if she was honest with herself, she knew she was just grasping for some sort of reassurance that Holden really did view Violet as just a friend.

Holden shrugged, oblivious to Elise's underlying reason for the question. "It's not that different from living with anyone else, I suppose. Occasionally she does stupid shit like use magic spells to make the coffee table levitate or stuff like that. And she'll cast invisibility spells on herself to try to hide and spook me when I don't know she's there, but I don't startle easily and now I half-expect her to jump out and yell 'boo' at any given time. She's kind of lost the element of surprise there."

Elise frowned. She wasn't sure how to take Holden's response. Did Violet joke around with Holden to flirt, or was it just friendly fun?

"You okay?" Holden asked, breaking into Elise's thoughts. "You're looking awfully serious over there."

Elise forced a smile onto her face. What was wrong with her? She was sitting here overanalyzing a man she had no intention of dating, anyway.

"I'm great," she said. "Still just winding down from the long week, I guess."

Holden seemed to accept this explanation at face value. "You know what you need? A nice big glass of wine?"

"Holden, no. It's fine, really." Truthfully, Elise would have loved to drink a glass or two of wine right about then. Her nerves could use a little bit of calming down. But she wasn't sure whether Holden was intending to pay for dinner or not, and she couldn't afford to buy a bottle of wine right now, even if they were splitting the cost. Tips had been a bit low this week, and she'd missed an entire shift the night she discovered that Nick was a dragon shifter.

"I insist," Holden said, raising his hand to flag down their server. And then, almost as though he knew the reason for Elise's hesitation, he winked at her and said. "My treat."

Elise's cheeks burned and she looked down at the napkin in her lap. She hated always feeling so strapped for cash. She worked so hard, but finances were always so tight.

"I can pay you back next week," she offered weakly, forcing herself to look up and meet Holden's eyes. He looked back at her like she'd lost her mind.

"My treat," he repeated. "That means I'm treating you to dinner as a gift. Don't offer to pay people back for gifts. That's rude. And silly. And besides after all the chaos I caused between you and Nick tonight, the least I could do is buy you some damn pasta and wine."

Elise sighed. "Thank you," she said quietly. "You really don't have to do that."

"And you don't have to continue being nice to me after I so irresponsibly suggested that your son go spy on an army of evil villains, but here we are. We all do things we don't have to do, Elise. It's called friendship. We're friends, right?"

"Right," Elise said, smiling over at him. The server arrived, then, and Holden turned his attention to ordering their wine. While he discussed with the server which Pinot Noirs were available, Elise let the word "friendship" roll around in her mind. It was such a happy word, and yet, she couldn't keep down the disappointment she felt at knowing that friendship was all she had with Holden.

She wanted more, but she couldn't. Not when Nick needed her to be strong. Elise set her face in determined line and reached for a piece of bread. Nick mattered more than anything, and she would always put him first. But she couldn't help it if her heart beat faster every time Holden looked up at her and smiled. All she could do was smile back at him and remind herself over and over that they were only here as friends.

When the bottle of wine arrived, Elise had never in her life been so glad to gulp down a glass of red.

CHAPTER NINE

"Violet just texted me. Nick fell asleep watching a movie," Elise said, then giggled. Then hiccupped. They'd been at the restaurant for close to three hours, now, and had shared two bottles of wine, along with a giant piece of tiramisu for dessert. Holden had finally, reluctantly, asked for the check five minutes ago. Their server had just dropped off the paid receipt, but Holden didn't want to sign it. He didn't want to leave the restaurant, and have this meal come to an end.

Holden loved seeing Elise like this—relaxing, and not worrying about Nick or work or whatever other dozens of things she seemed to constantly fret about. She was always beautiful, even when she was running around harried, working a shift at the diner. But right now...

Holden forced himself to look down at the receipt and grab the pen. He left the waiter a generous tip. After all, they'd been taking up his table for most of the dinner shift. After signing his name, Holden stood and held out his hand to Elise.

"Shall we?" he asked. She hiccupped again, and nodded. Holden was glad they had walked to the restaurant. Walking back would give them an excuse to spend a bit more time together. Besides, after sitting for three hours, it would feel good to stretch his legs and get some fresh air.

As they stepped out onto the sidewalk, he saw that there was a gas station about half a block away from the restaurant.

"Come on," he told Elise. "Let's get you a bottle of water. I'm already afraid that I'm going to be responsible for the wicked hangover you're going to have when you wake up tomorrow morning. The least I can do is make sure you stay hydrated."

Elise giggled in response, and Holden sighed, wrapping his arm around her shoulders as they walked, feeling somewhat guilty. He forgot sometimes that full humans didn't hold alcohol nearly as well as shifters. Elise was nicely toasted right now, and, although she seemed happy at the moment, Holden had a feeling she was going to be cursing him when her alarm went off for her morning shift at the diner.

After they bought the water, though, Elise downed it all in one long series of gulps. Not long after that, she seemed to sober up slightly. Perhaps it was the combination of the exercise, fresh air, and water. Whatever the case, Holden was glad that she seemed to already be recovering.

"So is Nick staying at my place tonight, then?" Holden asked.

Elise nodded. "Violet said he was snoring like he's dead to the world. She said it was fine if he stayed there, and I think it's probably best. Have you ever tried to wake up a sleeping preteen? It's damn near impossible."

Holden laughed, and so did Elise. He still had his arm around her, and he could feel her shoulders shaking slightly as she chuckled. She had steadied up quite a bit, and he could have moved his arm away without worrying about her falling over. And yet, he couldn't bring himself to pull away. She was so soft, so warm, and she felt like home.

Home, Holden thought. His own home in the Redwood forests of Northern California had been captured by Saul's army. Ever since the capture, Holden had felt adrift. Yet somehow, standing here in the middle of Blackstone with his arm around Elise, he felt anchored and safe. For the first time in quite some time, he felt like he belonged.

Elise was still talking about how much Nick liked to sleep, but Holden was having a hard time paying attention to what she was saying. He had just realized that the apartment he was walking Elise home to right now was empty. Nick was with Violet, and that meant that there was no one to spy on him as he dropped Elise off at her front door. There was no one who would see if he kissed her goodnight.

Holden's heart began to race in his chest. He knew better than to dwell on the thought of kissing Elise, but once the idea had entered his head, he couldn't stop thinking about how soft her lips were, or how beautiful she looked in the silvery moonlight. The more he tried to ignore his thumping heart, the louder it seemed to beat. How was he supposed to maintain his composure when he was about to be alone on the doorstep with the most beautiful girl he'd ever known.

Elise seemed to sense his mood, or perhaps she had also realized the implications of being alone with Holden, for she had gone quiet as well. Holden's arm felt heavy as he rested it on Elise's shoulders, as though the heaviness of the moment was weighing it down. He kept his arm around her as they climbed the steps to her second floor apartment, and made no move to let go once they finally stood in front of her door. They stood there, breathing raggedly for several moments. Holden's mind screamed at him to move, to say goodnight, and to leave. But, still, he remained. He felt like he was on the edge of a cliff, looking down into a beautiful pool of sparkling blue water. He wanted so badly to jump over the edge, to let the sweet cool waves ripple over him. But he could not quite find the courage to jump.

His whole life had been shaded by the loss of his parents at such a young age. He was terrified of losing any of his clanmates. How much worse would it be to lose a woman he loved?

Step away from the edge, he told himself, his heart pounding in his chest. *Step away from the edge. Tell her goodnight, and go home.*

He turned to face her, letting his arm slide off her shoulders.

"Elise," he said.

And then, he was gone. His heart betrayed him, overpowering the more sensible voice in his head. His hands reached up to her face, and he cradled her cheeks in his palms. His lips were on hers, drinking in their sweet softness. He felt her melting into him, moaning softly as his tongue slipped into her mouth. She reached into her small purse for her keys, never breaking their kiss as she pulled them out and jangled them around, finding her front door key by feel. She put it in the lock and turned it, then pushed the door open without ever opening her eyes or pulling away from him. Holden kicked the door shut behind him, then wrapped his arms around Elise's waist. He fell backwards onto her couch, pulling her along with him so that she lay on top of him. Her hair fell around his face in a cascade of fiery curls, appropriate since Holden's whole body felt like it was going up in flames.

He had never in his life felt this way about a woman. He'd been attracted to women, sure. But he'd never felt like he was burning up from the inside with desire. He could hardly breathe, and yet he'd never felt so alive. They kissed for several glorious minutes, his tongue dancing with hers, their hearts beating as one. He was lost in the moment, until he reached for the hem of her shirt and she stopped him. The motion seemed to have snapped her out of the trance they had been in, and she sat up and scooted away from him, clapping her hand over her mouth.

"I shouldn't be doing this," she said, her eyes wide.

Holden closed his eyes and rubbed his forehead. "I know," he said, although it killed him to say it. "I shouldn't, either. But if it's so wrong, why does it feel like it's meant to be?"

Elise didn't answer, so Holden opened his eyes to look at her. She was sitting by his feet on the couch, twisting a curl of hair so tightly around her finger that she looked like she might pull it right out of her head.

"It's late," she said, although there was no conviction in his words.

"I know," Holden replied, sounding even less convinced than she did. They remained suspended in that moment, staring into each other's eyes and struggling to do the smart thing, to walk away from each other. They might have stayed that way forever, had Holden's phone not dinged loudly in his pocket to alert him to an incoming text. Glad for the interruption, and a chance to breathe, Holden reached for the phone. He sat up to look at the screen, noticing that it was nearly eleven o' clock at this point. The text was from Violet.

"Violet says that Nick is still sleeping on the couch and that she's about to go to bed. She wanted to tell me to be quiet when I came in."

"You should go," Elise said, her voice sad. Holden nodded and stood. He made his way to the front door, each step making his heart feel heavier than the one before. Elise followed him, and he stopped with his hand on the doorknob to look at back at her.

"Thank you for such a lovely evening," he said.

"I should be thanking you," she replied. "It was your idea, and you sprang for the check."

"I wanted to take you out. You're working so hard, and you deserve a night of fun now and then."

Elise smiled at him and shrugged, as though she didn't really believe she deserved a night out. Holden waited for her to say something, but she didn't, so he finally admitted to himself that it was time to go. There were no more excuses, no more reasons to stall.

"Right then," he said. "Good night."

"Good night," she replied. And when she did, he saw her lip quiver with emotion. He wasn't sure what emotion it was, but the vulnerability of it reached straight to his heart, making him lose his senses all over again.

"I can't leave you," he said in a strained voice. Then he let go of the doorknob and pulled her into his arms. She didn't resist. In fact, she welcomed him, wrapping her arms around him as well, and tilting her face upward to meet his kiss. This time, Holden knew, there would be no hesitation. No holding back for either of them. They had both just jumped headfirst over the cliff.

Holden picked Elise up in his arms, never breaking their kiss as he carried her toward her bedroom. She shuddered, an excited breath rippling through her body as he stepped over the threshold of her room and kicked the door shut behind him. Even though they were alone in the house, he felt like closing the door was a wise idea, just in case. He didn't want to take any chances on any interruptions.

When he reached the bed, he dropped Elise on it, and immediately started pulling off his shirt. He felt an urgency that he had never felt before, and all he wanted to do was feel his skin against Elise's skin as soon as possible. Every second that went by where he could not feel her was one second too many. Happily, Elise seemed to feel the same way, because even as Holden tore off his own clothes, she was removing her shirt and pants. She wore black, lacy undergarments, but Holden barely had time to look at them before she'd torn them off and thrown them across the room. In less than a minute's time, they had both stripped completely naked in front of each other. There was a hunger between them that demanded to be satisfied.

Holden could feel his inner dragon, restless and demanding. A deep, primal instinct was urging him on, wanting more of Elise. His dick stood at attention between his legs, stiff and hard—and impressing Elise, if the wideness in her eyes when she looked at it was any indication of her feelings.

Holden joined Elise on the bed, pushing aside the pants she had wriggled out of and letting them fall to the floor. He marveled at the beauty of her body, tracing a fingertip around one of her nipples. The hard nub stiffened instantly at his touch, making a lovely contrast to the soft fullness of her breast. He closed his mouth over the other nipple, tasting the sweetness of her skin, and drinking in the lovely sound of her soft moan. Her body was exquisite, a perfect combination of hills and valleys, of curves and softness. He had never before seen anything so beautiful, and he was sure he would never after, either. She was everything, the epitome of beauty.

He traced a hand down the length of her torso, stopping to trace a small circle around her belly button. She shivered when he did this, and he smiled. He loved the way her whole body responded to his touch. He paused, and took the time to trace another little circle, delighting in the way she once again shivered. Then he let his fingers make their way down past the very bottom of her stomach, to the spot where her legs joined together. He buried his hand in the soft mound of hair just before her entrance, marveling at the fact that he was here with her, touching her in such an intimate way. She was still now, except for the rapid rise and fall of her chest as she tried to even out her breathing. A hopeless task—Holden knew—since he'd been trying and failing to do the same thing ever since he entered this bedroom with her.

He let his fingers slide even further down, finding her slick, wet entrance. She was dripping with anticipation for him, and feeling the juices of her desire sent a fresh wave of passion through Holden's whole body. He'd been intending to spend some time letting his fingers play inside of her, but, suddenly, he was filled with a nearly uncontrollable, burning hunger.

"Elise," he said, his breath feeling heavy in his own mouth. She understood that he was asking a question, and she answered it without breathing a word herself. Her hands reached down and found the sides of his upper arms. She tugged gently, trying to pull his face up toward hers. She was inviting him to position his body over hers: his face to her face and his dick to her sweet, wet entrance.

Holden did not wait for a second invitation. He pulled himself up and kissed her. The feeling of her lips against his, and her breasts against his chest, sent tingling heat through every fiber of his being. But the truly magnificent sensation was between his legs, where he could feel himself hardening with such force that he thought he might explode. He desperately needed relief, and he was about to find it, he knew.

Sliding into Elise felt like the most natural thing in the world. Holden let out a low moan of appreciation as her soft, wet warmth covered him. She moaned as well, arching her back and pushing her hips up against his, begging for more. Holden marveled at how tight she was. He could feel himself pushing against her inner walls, and every movement he made seemed to delight her further. She shuddered and shivered and moaned underneath him. Now and then, she even whispered his name, begging for more.

Holden could hardly hold back the pressure inside of him. His body was hungry, clawing for a release. But he kept his own pleasure in check, at least for the moment. First, he would take care of Elise. He moved his hips backward and forward, backward and forward, sliding against Elise's most sensitive places, and delighting in the way she squeezed her eyes shut tightly and moaned. He had never felt like as much of a man as he did at that moment, knowing that he was the one bringing this deep level of pleasure to the most beautiful girl in the world.

He moved with a slow, steady rhythm, and he could feel Elise growing hungrier and more desperate beneath him. He smiled as she dug her fingernails into his back, trying to pull him closer to her than he already was. This was an impossibility, of course. He was already as deep into her as he could be, and their sweaty bodies were pressed hard against each other.

She had been so hungry for this, Holden thought. As hungry for me as I was for her. Why had we been holding back? Out of fear, he knew. His fear of losing her, and her fear for her son. He didn't exactly understand all of her worries about her son, but he knew they had been her reason for holding back. But now, in this moment, all other fears and worries were forgotten. Everything else was pushed away but the need for each other. Holden felt Elise shudder beneath him again, and then, with a loud scream, she finally gave in and found her release.

The spasms that came from her body were intense, like nothing Holden had ever experienced. He felt her inner muscles clenching around his dick over and over, each tremor feeling hotter, wetter, and stronger than the one before. The sensation was overwhelming, and Holden barely had time to catch a breath before his own body was responding to hers. He felt his whole body stiffen, and then, with a roar, he came into her as she squeezed herself around him. He felt like a fire was being drawn up from every corner of his body, and being shot straight through his rock hard manhood into her body. He felt his dick pulsing, and he felt the tingling heat inside of him reaching its crescendo.

He roared as she moaned, and together, they reached the height of human ecstasy. He felt the fire in his body turning slowly from a tingling electricity to a sweet, steady heat. His core was warm, so warm. The trembling in his body slowly stopped, but the heat remained. Holden took a deep breath and slid off of Elise when he felt her body calming as well. But even when he was no longer inside of her or on top of her, the heat remained. He grabbed her hand and held it, lacing his fingers through hers and letting the realization of what had just happened wash over him.

He had made love to Elise, recklessly and with complete abandon. He had wanted nothing more than to be with her, to be as close to her as was humanly possible. And, in giving in to that desire, he had formed a lifemate bond. He'd heard enough about lifemate bonds over the years to recognize the heat in his core. He had bonded to Elise. He'd been so lost in passion that it had never occurred to him that maybe she was actually his lifemate. Or, perhaps, he had not let himself entertain the idea that she might belong to him. It would have been horrible to have hoped for something so wonderful only to have his hopes dashed.

Yet here he was, bonded to Elise. He was scared out of his mind, and happier than he'd ever been. And what more could you ask for in love than that? Holden looked over at Elise, and saw the same mixture of fear and joy in her eyes that he knew was in his. He reached his arm around her to pull her close to him. There would be plenty of time later to talk about their future together. The details would all work themselves out, somehow. They always did. Right now, Holden didn't want to think about anything except how lucky he was. For there, in his arms, lay perfect beauty in human form. Elise had let him make love to her, and he had bonded with her. Life had just changed forever, but for the better.

Yup, Holden thought as he kissed the top of Elise's head. Terrified and overjoyed pretty much summed up his feelings right now.

CHAPTER TEN

Elise's eyes flew open, and she sat straight up in bed, breathing heavily. Beside her, Holden turned over and opened his eyes, then sat up with concern when he saw the wild look on her face.

"What's wrong," he asked, instantly alert.

Elise blinked a few times, trying to make out his expression in the darkness. It felt strange to have him here. It had been ages since she'd had a man in her bed. She liked having him beside her, strong and warm. She could get used to this, but she wasn't sure yet that she dared to. There were still so many details to work out. And there was her son to consider. Elise wasn't sure she'd made the right decision by rushing into things with Holden right now, but she strangely felt no regret. Everything last night had felt like it was meant to be.

"Nothing's wrong," Elise said, shaking her head and looking sheepish. "Just a bad dream."

Holden reached up to caress the side of her cheek, then pulled her back down beside him. "It's alright. I'm here," he murmured. "Go back to sleep."

He himself promptly followed his own advice. A few moments later, Elise heard his breathing steady out beside her as he gave himself back over to his own dreams. She could not find sleep again so easily, however. She looked over at the alarm clock on her bedside table, its numbers softly glowing to tell her that it was just past three-thirty in the morning. Less than two hours until she needed to be awake for her shift at the diner, and yet she already knew she was going to waste most of those two hours lying awake and worrying.

It hadn't exactly been a bad dream that woke her, as she'd told Holden. In fact, she couldn't remember what she'd been dreaming, or whether she'd been dreaming at all. Rather, she had awoken from a bad feeling. She knew in her gut that something was wrong, but she couldn't say what. Why did she feel a sense of dread weighing down on her, and why did she feel like it had something to do with Nick?

Elise let out a long sigh and slowly lay back down against her pillow. She looked over at Holden, who was still breathing with the rapid rhythm of sleep. She was impressed by how quickly he had woken up when she sat up in bed, and equally impressed by how quickly he had fallen back asleep once he realized that all was well. Elise wished she had those kind of sleeping skills.

But was all well, really? Elise couldn't shake the bad feeling in her heart. She wrestled with whether or not to call Violet and ask if Nick was still there, and alright. She knew of no reason that he wouldn't be. After all, Violet was a wizard, and trained to do battle. The woman knew how to fight, and could, in all honesty, probably protect Nick better than Elise could.

In the end, Elise decided against calling Violet. She didn't want to look like a crazed, overprotective parent. Elise had learned over the years that mother's intuition was a real thing, but she couldn't imagine what could possibly be wrong with Nick when he was safe in an apartment guarded by a wizard. After an hour of tossing and turning, Elise finally forced herself to go back to sleep. She awoke shortly after to the sound of her alarm, which she switched off as quickly as she could. She winced as she felt Holden stirring beside her, and felt bad for waking him up. But he merely squinted one eye open, smiled at her, and then settled back down to sleep.

Elise shook her head in amusement. From the looks of it, Holden could give Nick some competition on who had better sleeping skills. Elise had always been a light sleeper, and she envied people like her son and Holden who could fall asleep easily and rest as much as they wanted. Elise remembered that Nick's father had been able to sleep a lot as well. She wondered if perhaps it was a dragon skill.

The thought of Nick once again niggled at Elise's nerves. As she took a quick shower, she couldn't keep from worrying that there was something wrong with him, but she made herself hold back from dialing Violet's number. She would call on her first morning break at the diner. By then, it would be after nine a.m., a more reasonable time to call. And, surely, when Elise called, Violet would assure her Nick was fine.

After her shower, Elise watched Holden as she quietly pulled on her work uniform. She studied his face in the gray light of dawn, and wondered what the hell she'd gotten herself into. Last night, buzzed by the wine and giddy from the fun of a night out on an actual date, it had been all too easy to fall into Holden's arms. But now that the light of day was coming, Elise was beginning to panic. Not because she thought she had made a mistake by sleeping with Holden, but because she was realizing that the morning was doing nothing to dim her feelings for him. She was falling in love with him, and that love was coming from more than just too much wine and a night out on the town. It was coming from somewhere deep within her. Her belly felt warm and tingly when she thought of Holden, and she had to bite her lip to hold her feelings in check she wanted nothing more than to climb back into bed next to Holden, waking him with a kiss and making love in the full light of day.

But we don't always get what we want, and Elise could not afford to be late for her shift at the diner. With a sigh, she blew Holden a silent kiss and then slipped out the door of the bedroom. She didn't bother leaving him a note. He knew where she was going, and that she didn't have a choice. He knew that she would much rather spend the day with him than serve eggs and coffee to grumpy restaurant customers. She didn't need to tell him that.

Elise grabbed a banana from the fruit bowl and made her way out the door. The sky was streaked with pink and orange now, and she smiled at its beauty. If there was one positive side to waking up so early in the morning, it was getting to see the sunrise almost every day. Nothing compared with the beauty of a day starting anew.

Elise drove to the diner on autopilot, not registering with her conscious mind where she was or what she was doing. She'd driven this route so many times that she almost could have done it with her eyes closed, especially this early in the morning when there was no other traffic on the road. She continued to move on autopilot when she got to work, making sure the cash register was ready and that hot coffee was brewed. The cooks were in the back of the kitchen already, busily prepping food for the morning rush. They whistled while they worked, but Elise didn't feel like whistling this morning.

She should have been over the moon with happiness. She'd found a man she loved, and she was pretty sure he loved her. Best of all, he knew how to take care of Nick in ways that Elise never could. So why was her stomach turned up in knots? Was it because she knew deep down that she could never trust a man? Not where Nick was concerned, anyway. Nick already felt deeply the loss of the father he'd never known. He didn't talk about it much, but Elise could see the pain in his eyes when other boys' dads showed up to sporting events and he had no one there. Elise tried to make it to as many events as she could, but she couldn't always get away from work. And besides, it wasn't the same as having a dad there. She knew that. And she could never bear the pain of watching Nick look to Holden as a father figure, only to have Holden leave. But hadn't Elise greatly increased the odds of Holden's leaving by allowing romance into their relationship? Romances were complicated, and Elise knew that if things went south between her and Holden, that would spell out the end of Nick's relationship with Holden as well.

"Hey, you alright?" a voice broke into Elise's thoughts. She looked up to see the head cook from the back standing beside her with a worried a look on his face. She smiled at him as warmly as she could.

"Yes, I'm great, just a bit distracted," she said. "How are you?"

He creased his eyebrow in an expression of worry. "I'm good. But I've asked you the same question three times and you've been staring out into space like you couldn't hear me at all. Are you sure you're alright?"

Elise felt foolish. She must have been really lost in thought. "Yeah, I'm good. Just thinking. I've got a lot on my mind these days with my son and all..." she trailed off. It wasn't exactly a lie that she was worried about Nick. Of course, her worries had more to do with Holden than just with Nick's general poor behavior lately. But the cook didn't need to know that detail.

Elise watched as an expression of sympathy crossed the man's face. "Don't worry, Elise. Boys all go through these rebellious phases. He'll come around."

"I know," Elise said, still smiling as widely as she could. The man had no idea what had caused Nick's rebellious phase, and that it had been anything but a typical boyhood stage. But Elise would never be foolish enough to confide in one of her coworkers about Nick's dragon side, no matter how nice they were to her. There were certain things that even her kind, open-minded coworkers would gawk at.

"Well, anyway," the cook said with a gentle smile. "I was just asking whether you were going to unlock the door. It's ten minutes past opening time."

"Oh, shit!" Elise said, looking at her watch and seeing that he was right. She'd been so caught up in her thoughts about Nick and Holden that she hadn't realized how late it had gotten. "I'll go open the door right now."

The cook chuckled at her. "You really are off in another world today," he said, then disappeared back into the kitchen.

Elise didn't bother calling after him with any sort of reply. She rushed to the door instead, flipping the sign in the window so that the side which read "We're Open" faced outward. She thanked her lucky stars that this was not one of the mornings where her boss showed up early to make sure that everything was in order right at opening time. He had a habit of doing that, and he would have been livid to find that Elise had not unlocked the door yet, even though there hadn't been any customers walking up to the door in the last ten minutes. Her boss was the kind of man who loved finding any reason to yell at her, or any of her coworkers. Elise took a deep breath to steady her rattled nerves, and then went to stand behind the counter and await their first customers of the morning.

Less than five minutes later, a group of older ladies from town walked in the door. They were early birds, and often the first ones at breakfast. Elise greeted them, and went to grab the coffee pot without being asked. She already knew that this crew liked their coffee strong, black, and plentiful. They would sit here most of the morning, downing mugs of caffeine long after the rest of the breakfast rush had left. Elise didn't mind. They were a friendly group, and, besides, they always left exceptionally generous tips.

While Elise was pouring coffee for the women, the waitress who would be working the morning shift with Elise arrived. Elise glanced up at her and smiled, then turned her attention back to filling mugs. The front door was already opening again, and two more tables of customers walked in the door. It was going to be a busy morning, as usual. Elise was grateful for that. She needed the tips, and, besides, as long as she stayed busy, she wouldn't have time to worry about Nick or Holden.

The morning flew by, and the diner was so busy that Elise didn't bother taking her normal fifteen minute break. She was in constant motion, scurrying about with her order pad, plates of food, and a pot of coffee. The pockets of her apron were filling up with cash from tips, and Elise had finally forgotten the feeling of dread that had hung over her like a cloud since the wee hours of the morning.

Around eleven, the breakfast rush finally slowed. Two waitresses arrived, ready to take over the diner for the lunch shift. Elise closed out her tabs and went happily to the back room to close out her till and balance all of her receipts. It had been a good morning, and she could hardly wait to count her tips. There were times, of course, that working for tips was not so great. But on days like today, when she'd been busy with generous customers all morning, she loved the thrill of seeing how much she'd made at the end of a shift. She always sorted her bills by order of descending denomination, then turned them so they all faced uniformly in the same direction. Only then would she finally allow herself to count them, her fingers flying as the smell of money filled her nose. She loved watching the bills flip through her fingers, knowing that each one meant security for Nick and her. Each dollar she earned allowed them to eat, to pay rent, and, occasionally, to buy some new clothes. Elise might not be proud of the way she'd never told Nick's father about him, but she was damn proud of the fact that she'd made it on her own all these years. No one had ever supported her but herself. She didn't owe anyone anything.

Elise had just finished sorting the bills and was about to count them out, when she heard her phone buzzing from inside her purse. Elise set down her money on the desk in the small back office, and reached up to the shelf above the desk where she always placed her purse while she worked. Her boss did not allow his employees to carry cell phones while they worked, so she always left hers in the office. Some of her coworkers tried to sneak theirs out in their apron pockets, but Elise never did. Her boss was always mad enough at her as it was. She didn't need to take a chance on giving him yet another reason to chew her out. Elise grabbed her purse and sat back down at the desk, then pulled her phone out. When she looked at the screen, her heart instantly dropped.

She had eleven missed calls and twice as many missed texts. No one except Nick ever called or texted her, and he knew better than to bug her with minor concerns while she was at work. Something was very wrong. With shaking fingers, Elise unlocked the phone and started to read the texts. The missed calls were all from Violet and Holden, as were the texts. The words "Nick" and "missing" jumped out at her through the tears that were starting to fill her eyes. How had she been so stupid? She had known that something was wrong this morning. Why had she ignored the feeling?

Elise immediately started stuffing her morning's tips into her purse, not caring that she was messing up the carefully sorted pile. What did it matter how well sorted her tips were, or how much money she'd made, when her son, the joy of her life, was missing? She ran toward the office door, ready to bolt for her car and drive like hell away from the diner. She didn't even know where she would go. Home? To Holden and Violet's apartment? To the police? She would figure it out on the way, when she called Holden back. All she knew right now was that she had to get away from the diner.

She had barely made it out of the office door, though, before she ran smack into a towering figure of a man. She knew before she even looked up that it was Holden. No one in town had a chest that muscular, or a scent that woodsy.

"Holden!" she yelped, looking up at him with wild eyes. She wasn't sure whether to be angry at him or to collapse into his arms in tears. "What's going on? I just saw your texts. What happened to Nick? How long has he been missing? Does anyone know where he went? And how did you get back here? My boss would kill me *and* you if he knew you were back here!"

"One of the cooks told me you were back here. And I'd like to see your boss try to kill me," Holden said. "He thinks he's such a badass, but he's never had to deal with a dragon before."

Holden's voice was strained, and Elise felt her heart clenching with fear as she looked up at his pale, drawn face.

"What's going on? Please tell me you know where Nicky is, and that he's going to be alright."

"I know where Nick is," Holden said, his voice breaking with emotion as he spoke. "And you're not going to like it."

CHAPTER ELEVEN

Holden reached a hand across the table to hold Elise's, but her expression didn't change. Her mind didn't even seem to register the fact that someone was touching her. Holden had never seen anyone's eyes as filled with fear as Elise's were right then, and he'd seen plenty of people scared shitless in his lifetime. His heart broke, and he felt terrible for the part he'd played in the heartache she was feeling right now. He had been the one who had planted the idea in Nick's head to sneak into Saul's camp and take pictures. And now, Nick was there, against his mother's wishes, placing himself in danger with no plan in place to call for help if needed.

"You're sure that's where he is?" Elise asked, her voice sounding hollow and empty. She looked down at the table as she spoke.

"That's what his note said," Violet replied, answering before Holden could. Holden studied Elise's face carefully, but her expression did not change. She kept looking down at the table without really seeing it, fear swirling in her eyes.

Holden picked up the note that had been left behind when Nick left Violet's apartment that morning. According to Violet, Nick had still been asleep on the couch when she went out to the living room at nine a.m. She'd gone to buy some donuts for him as a breakfast treat, but when she returned, Nick was gone with only a short note left in his place. The note was written in hurried, childish scrawl, but it was direct and to the point.

Dear Violet, I'm sorry to leave without telling you, but I need to go through the tunnel and see what Saul's army is doing. I know my mom does not want me to, but I'm the only one who can get through without his soldiers knowing I'm there. I want to do my part to help stop the evil dragons and wizards. Please tell my mom not to worry about me. I'll be back soon. Nick

Oh the naïveté of youth, Holden thought. Telling his mom not to worry was about as pointless as throwing a bird out of a tree and telling it not to fly. Some things were gut instincts that could not be overridden. That bird would flap its wings and fly, and Elise would worry about her son. That's just the way it was.

Holden wished he could take Nick by the shoulders and give him a good firm shake right about now, shaking some sense into him. Of course, that was impossible at the moment, too. They would all just have to wait things out. Holden had called Weston in a panic when he realized what was going on, hoping that his friend, the expert on ghosters, might have some advice on what to do. Weston did have advice, but Holden hadn't liked it. Neither had Elise. The best way to keep Nick safe was to stay as far away from Saul's soldiers as possible. If Holden went through the tunnel to try to rescue Nick or bring him back, Saul's soldiers would smell him, and know there was a shifter stalking them. This would blow Nick's cover, probably before Holden was even close enough to take Nick under his dragon wings and protect him.

So Holden waited, a constant stream of curses running through his head as he looked over at Elise. She had insisted at first that they needed to chase after Nick. It had been all Violet and Holden could do to convince her that they had to stay away to keep Nick safe. Holden could see the accusations in her eyes, even though she didn't give voice to them.

You dragged him into this war, and gave him visions of glory, her eyes seemed to say. *You put the idea of spying on the enemy in his head. This is all your fault.*

Holden stood and paced the room. He couldn't bear the weight of guilt on his shoulders right now. At least keeping his body in motion made him feel like he was doing something, even if he wasn't. He hated being cooped up in Elise's tiny apartment, staying still and silent while Nick ran straight into the enemy's camp. Part of Holden was angry with the boy, and part of him was just jealous that Nick was taking action—action that could very possibly make a difference in the war.

Holden resisted the urge to punch a wall in frustration. When he'd come up with the idea for Nick to sneak into Saul's camp and spy on the enemy's operations, he'd never intended to have Nick go in blindly. Holden had wanted to set up a video feed back to himself and Violet, so that he could see what was going on and know immediately if Nick was in trouble. Holden had also planned to give Nick a secret signal to use if he was in trouble. But now, Holden had nothing to go on except the hope that ghosting really was as effective as Weston believed it to be, and that Nick was smart enough not to be actually seen by any of Saul's soldiers. Holden had been holding out these hopes for the last four hours. He was trying to decide at what point he would need to stop waiting around and go rescue Nick. Finally, he told himself that if the boy wasn't back by six p.m. he was going to go find him, even if that meant potentially giving away Nick's position and ruining the spying mission for which Holden had been sent to Blackstone. He could only sit here so long, hoping that Nick wasn't already in the hands of Saul's men. Holden was trying to stay strong and appear calm for Elise's sake, but the truth was that it was killing him to wait. He cared deeply about Nick. He might not be able to understand what the depths of a mother's love felt like, but he did know that the thought of anything happening to Nick took his own breath away. He glanced helplessly at his watch, even though he'd already looked a hundred times in the last ten minutes. The time had just inched past two p.m. Four more hours to wait, if he was going to stick to his six p.m. deadline. God, he hoped Nick showed up at the apartment before then, laughing and oblivious to how worried everyone was about him, as children were wont to be.

Holden's pacing was interrupted when he saw Elise standing. The weary, frightened look on her face broke Holden's heart, and he longed to go to her and put his arms around her. But he wasn't sure how she would take it, and the last thing he wanted right now was to give her more cause for distress. So he stayed where he was, feet planted uneasily in the middle of her tiny living room, and waited to see what she was doing.

"I'm going to try to get some rest," she said in a shaky voice. "I have a feeling it's going to be a long night. Let me know right away if there's any word about Nicky."

"Of course," Violet said, reaching over to touch Elise's arm. Holden envied the fact that Violet could so easily reach out to comfort Elise, without worries that the gesture would be misconstrued. He wondered anew whether Elise would still want to talk to him when this was all said and done. She hadn't been openly hostile to him when he broke the news that Nick had gone to spy on Saul's soldiers, but that didn't necessarily mean much. She was in shock right now, and at some point she was going to come out of that shock enough to be angry at Holden.

He tried to think of something to say that would ease Elise's mind, but words seemed so futile right now. Before he could settle on what to say, she had disappeared into her bedroom, closing the door behind her with a gentle click. Holden stared at the closed door for several seconds, resisting the urge to run after her. Violet's voice finally pulled him back to the present, away from his internal struggles.

"Weston is coming," she said.

Holden whipped his head around to look at her. "What?!? Here?"

Violet nodded. "I didn't want to talk about it in front of Elise, because I'm afraid it will only worry her more. But he sent me a message several hours ago, right after he talked to you, letting me know he got permission to leave Falcon Cross and come to Blackstone. He was taking the next flight out, and should be here sometime this afternoon."

"Why didn't he tell *me* he was coming?" Holden asked. He felt his heart sinking. If Weston felt the need to come, that meant he was worried that something awful would happen to Nick. But if that was the case, why hadn't he said so on the phone? Holden felt a little hurt. Weston was his best friend. Why was he keeping secrets, and telling those secrets to Violet, no less.

"He didn't want to worry you," Violet said. "He knew if he told you that he was coming, that you'd freak out. And he was right—you did freak out. I can see it in your face."

"Well, hell, Violet. Maybe I am freaking out. But I think I should know if there's a reason to freak out, don't you? I've seen a lot of shit in my life, remember? My own parents were killed right in front of me. There's no need to shelter my delicate feelings from the harsh realities of war."

Violet kept a neutral expression on her face. "It's not about your feelings, Holden. It's about Elise. You two obviously have some sort of connection. If she saw you this upset, she'd be losing it."

Holden took a deep breath, and forced himself to listen to Violet and actually process what she was saying. He realized that Violet was more right than she knew. Holden and Elise did have a connection—a lifemate bond. Although, Holden wasn't sure how Elise would feel about spending the rest of her life with him after he'd inadvertently encouraged Nick to run off into enemy territory on his own. But he'd have to worry about that later. Right now, the important thing was getting Nick home safely.

"Fine, you didn't want to upset Elise," Holden said. "But now that Elise is in her room sleeping…at least I hope she's sleeping and not eavesdropping on us through the door—"

"Oh she's sleeping," Violet said. "I secretly put a sleeping spell on her as she walked toward her bedroom."

Holden managed his first genuine smile since he'd heard the news of Nick's disappearance. "You're a rascal, V, you know that? No wonder you and Weston get along so well."

He half-expected her to protest at his thinly veiled insinuation that she and Weston liked each other, but she didn't. She looked away for a moment and blushed, and Holden couldn't help but grin. He knew in that moment that, despite the fact that the reasons for Weston's impending visit weren't happy ones, Violet was looking forward to seeing him. The happy expression didn't last long on his face, however.

"So if Weston's coming, he must be worried about Nick's safety," Holden said. It was more of a question than a statement. He was fishing for information, wanting Violet to tell him what Weston's fears were. But Violet merely shrugged.

"He thinks the boy has a good chance of making it out okay. After all, Nick's been there several times before. Maybe not on a spying mission, exactly, but he's snuck around and watched Saul's soldiers, and he's lived to tell about it. Of course, there's a chance that things could go poorly, though. And if they do, Weston knows you're going to be heading toward Saul's camp as fast as you can. He knows you're not going to leave the boy alone in enemy territory, even if that means risking your own neck to get Nick back."

"Well, of course I'm going to fight for Nick. The whole reason he's there in the first place is that I put this stupid idea in his head. Besides, I care about him. I've never had a son, but if I did, I'd want him to be just like Nick. A little too fearless, a little too wild, and madly devoted to seeing good prevail in the world. We need more kids like Nick. He's had a rough time of it lately, sure. But it's not easy to discover you're a dragon, and he's handled the transition beautifully. You can see he has a good heart. And I'll be damned if I let Saul's men hurt him while there's still breath left in my own body."

Violet smiled at Holden. "I know. And Weston knows that, too. He knows I won't be able to hold you back very long, so he's on his way out here to help you. He's your ride or die, Holden, you know that. If you fight, you fight together. Of course, I'm still hoping it won't come to that."

Holden glanced at his watch. It was getting close to two-thirty now. "I hope so, too," he said. But every minute that passed was causing his stomach to tie itself up in tighter knots. Nick could already be in the hands of the enemy, for all he knew.

"So what do we do now?" Holden asked, beginning his helpless pacing once again.

Violet looked at him calmly from her seat at the dining room table. "Now we wait," she said. Holden gritted his teeth together, but did not answer Violet.

A dragon could only wait for so long.

CHAPTER TWELVE

The next hour felt torturous. Violet tried to distract Holden by discussing what the next steps in their Blackstone mission should be, but she might as well have been speaking Latin to him. Holden could not focus on anything she was saying well enough to comprehend it. His mind swam with thoughts of Elise and Nick, and he wished more than anything that Weston would hurry up and arrive. Maybe, once Weston was there, he'd agree to start heading towards Saul's camp on a rescue mission. Holden was beginning to feel like waiting until six o'clock was going to be an impossibility. The more time that went by, the more he felt like he was failing Elise. She was sleeping in the next room, blissfully unaware of the passing hours thanks to Violet's sleeping spell. But Violet would have to break the spell eventually. If Elise woke up and Nick wasn't back yet, she was going to jump to the conclusion that he'd been captured. And with every passing minute, that conclusion felt more and more like a real possibility.

A sharp knock at the door made both Violet and Holden jump in their seats a bit. They looked at each other, eyes wide with hope for a split second. But Violet shook her head slightly.

"That'll be Weston," she said. "Nick wouldn't knock on the door of the apartment where he lives."

Holden nodded. He would have preferred to have Nick reappear, but even Weston would be a welcome sight at this point. Having his clanmate nearby would make Holden feel a little less helpless. One dragon would have a difficult time stealing a prisoner away from Saul's men, but perhaps two dragons could manage a sneak attack together? The odds of success were better, at least, even if they still weren't good.

Holden and Violet stood in unison and went to the door. Violet got there a split-second before Holden and peered through the peephole.

"It's Weston," she confirmed, then reached for the doorknob and flung the door open.

"Wes!" she said, throwing her arms around him in greeting. She must have been too happy to see him to worry about whether her gesture would be interpreted as a romantic one. Holden's own heart felt encouraged at the sight of his best friend. As soon as Violet stepped aside reluctantly, Holden pulled the man into a big bear hug.

"You're a sight for sore eyes, brother," Holden said. "Thank you for coming."

"I wasn't about to leave you here to deal with this situation on your own," Weston said. "Coming here was the right thing to do. And besides, I can't complain about the chance to get away from the office for a bit. Dragons weren't meant to sit behind desks, doing research. My god, I was ready to poke my own eyes out if I had to spend one more day in front of a damn computer screen."

Holden smiled, feeling less discouraged by the moment. "Well, if you want some action, I think you've come to the right place. I told myself I was going to wait until six p.m. to go storm Saul's hideout, but now that you're here I'd be willing to leave now and go get Nick away from those bastards. What do you say?"

Weston shook his head no, and Holden felt his heart sinking. "I say that we're not going to be storming Saul's camp. Not tonight, anyway."

Holden's heart sank further, and he felt confusion and anger rising in his chest. Was Weston really going to refuse to fight? So much for being his ride or die. "Weston, Nick's been there for almost six hours. He should've been back by now. We need to go rescue him before Saul's men really hurt him!"

But Weston just shook his head again. "No, we don't need to go rescue him. Because he's already found his way home."

Holden blinked, confused. Violet furrowed her brow, looking just as confused.

"What are you talking about?" Holden asked. "We've been here the whole time, mate, and I can promise you that Nick has not shown up."

"Can you now?" Weston asked, a familiar, mischievous glint dancing in his eyes. Holden had seen that glint thousands of times before. It usually meant that Weston was playing a trick of some kind, but now wasn't the time for jokes or tricks. Not when the life of a twelve-year-old boy hung in the balance.

"Come on, Weston," Holden said. "Don't be an asshole. There's a boy's life at stake here, so don't play games."

"The boy is gonna be just fine, Holden," Weston said, then winked before looking over to his left. "Nick! You wanna come out?"

Holden's breath caught in his throat, and then, from around the corner, Nick suddenly appeared, looking sheepish but exhilarated. He was wearing a backpack, and had his fingers curled tightly around each of the arm straps.

"What the...where did he come from?" Holden asked, looking back and forth between Nick and the boy. He wasn't sure whether he wanted to hug or kill Nick and Weston both. When he looked up and saw the satisfied smirk on Weston's face, he definitely started leaning in the "kill" direction. Weston looked a little too pleased with himself.

"I found him on his way in," Weston said. "He was walking up to the apartment at the same time I was, and I knew right away who he was. He looked so guilty, and his eyes have an animal look to them, even though he doesn't smell like a shifter at all."

Weston reached over and tousled Nick's hair. Nick smiled nervously in response, his eyes darting back and forth between Holden and Violet. Holden could see that Nick hadn't been as enthusiastic about Weston's little trick as Weston had been. And no wonder. Weston might have thought it was funny to make the group wait a few more minutes to discover that Nick had returned safely, but Nick knew he was in deep shit with his mother. Elise wasn't going to care how valuable the information Nick recovered might be. She was only going to care that he left in direct defiance of her wishes, and nearly gave her a heart attack in the process.

"You're a piece of work," Holden said to Weston, shaking his head. "If I wasn't so relieved to see Nick alive and safe, I'd teach you a lesson about not making jokes that aren't funny."

Weston only laughed. "I'd like to see you try," he said.

Holden could have made another salty comeback, but he let it go. He was more interested in how Nick was doing at this point than in punishing Weston for being an insensitive asshole. There would be time later to get back at his friend for his actions.

"Nick, I hope you know how worried sick we've all been about you," Holden said, keeping as stern a look as possible on his face. "And how foolhardy it was for you to head off on your own like that. We had no way of knowing whether you needed help, and we couldn't come after you without risking someone smelling us and knowing there were shifter spies afoot."

Nick had the sense to look ashamed for a moment, but then he raised his chin defiantly. "Well, I wouldn't have been going at all if I'd told someone. Mom didn't want to let me go. But I proved that I could do it. All her fears were for nothing."

Holden heard Violet let out a long sigh. "I think it's time we woke Elise up," Violet said. "Whether or not her fears were for nothing, she'll want to know that her boy is home safe."

Holden nodded, and stepped away from the door to allow Nick and Weston to enter. Violet gave Nick a warm hug once he was inside, and Holden thought he saw the shimmer of tears on her eyelids. She'd been worried sick about the boy, too. How could she not be? She knew what Saul's army had done in the past, and that they were capable of inflicting awful pain on their prisoners. Holden didn't have to ask to know that, for the last several hours, she'd been playing over all the possible scenarios in her mind of what might happen to Nick if he was caught. Holden gave Nick a gentle cuff on the ears as the boy passed him.

"Don't ever scare us like this again, you hear?" he asked the boy.

Nick still had a bit of a defiant look in his eyes, but he nodded nevertheless. "I hear," he said. Then he slipped his backpack off and set it down on the dining room table, rifling through its contents while Violet went to wake Elise up. Holden sat in one of the dining room chairs and stared at the doorway to Elise's bedroom. Part of him wanted to go with Violet, and to be the one to greet Elise with the news that Nick had returned. But another part of him held back, worrying that the last person in the world Elise would want to see right now was the person who had given Nick the idea to go spy in the first place. The only person who was watching Elise's bedroom more nervously than Holden was Nick. The boy had had his reasons for doing what he did, Holden knew. But that wasn't going to stop his mother from chewing him out royally the moment she saw him, and his mother's wrath was probably the only thing that scared him more than Saul's army.

"Nicholas!" a shout came from the bedroom, moments before Elise's face appeared. Tears were already starting to stream down from her face as she ran toward her son. "Oh, thank god you're okay. I would have died if I lost you!"

She wrapped her arms around him and sobbed, her whole body shaking as the realization hit her that her boy was back, and unharmed. Nick patted her awkwardly on the back.

"It's alright, Mom," he said. "I'm fine. They never even knew I was there."

Nick's voice made some part of Elise's emotions snap. She pulled back and slapped him across the face, hard.

"It's not alright, Nicky! Do you hear me? It's not alright for you to leave me here worried sick about you, not knowing if I would ever see you again. There's a reason I told you not to go. Contrary to what you might think, I wasn't trying to spoil your fun. I was trying to keep you safe."

Nick's hand covered his face where his mother had just slapped him. He winced, but the defiant look never left his face. In fact, his defiance seemed to grow stronger at her words.

"That's the problem, Mom! You always try to keep me safe. Too safe! You never let me live my life. You act like taking the smallest possible risk is going to result in me dying or being horribly injured. I'm so tired of it! You can't keep me in a bubble my whole life."

Holden saw Weston and Violet exchange glances. Violet seemed to be telling Weston something using only the expression in her eyes, and, apparently, he understood her meaning.

"I, uh, need to go get my things unpacked," he said.

"I'll help," Violet said, standing and heading toward the door. "You'll need someone to show you where our apartment is, anyway."

As she stood, she gave Holden a meaningful look, and he realized that she was trying to get all of them to leave and give Elise some privacy. Part of him agreed that the mother and son probably needed some time alone to work through their angry feelings. But part of him didn't want to leave Elise. He wanted to stay and hear how Nick had fared in Saul's camp. And he wanted to make sure that Elise wasn't too angry at the part he, Holden, had played in today's events. But the look on Violet's face told him that he better get up and follow her—and fast. Reluctantly, he stood to his feet.

"Yeah," Holden said halfheartedly. "I'll come help out, too, Weston.

But Elise had other plans. She'd seemed to not even be paying attention to anyone in the room other than Nick. In fact, she'd given no indication that she'd even noticed that Weston, a newcomer, had arrived. The moment Holden stood to leave, however, she turned to him with flashing, angry eyes.

"Oh no you don't," she said. "The others can go. But you! You're the one who put all these crazy ideas in my boy's head. I want a word with you."

Holden looked at Violet and shrugged. He wasn't sure whether to feel relieved that he got to stay, or regretful that he couldn't escape with the others. But it didn't matter much what he felt. Elise's tone made it clear to him that he was staying, whether he wanted to or not. Violet shrugged back at him and then turned toward the door. Holden wasn't sure how much she had picked up on the relationship between him and Elise, but she would have needed to have been an idiot not to realize by now that *something* was happening. After all, Holden had never come home last night, and Violet had mentioned the "connection" between Holden and Elise. Holden glanced up at Weston, who was looking at him with a raised eyebrow. Weston must have caught on to the "connection," too, and Holden knew there would be a lot of explaining to do later. He just hoped that he would be explaining how Elise had forgiven him, and not that she had said she never wanted to see him again.

Violet pushed a curious Weston out the front door before he could ask any questions, and, for once, Holden was glad for the woman's bossy side. He did not want to have to answer any questions about Elise right in front of her, and he knew Weston would have no qualms about brazenly asking what was going on with Elise while she was right there in the room.

As soon as Violet and Weston were gone, Elise seemed to forget about Holden again, and turned her attention back to Nick.

"For your information, son, I try to keep you safe because I love you. You may think I'm a crazy old lady, but I've lived longer than you have, and I can understand dangers in the world that you're too young to understand."

Holden willed Nick to just apologize to his mother and soothe Elise's flaring temper, but Nick had a temper of his own. He was ready to match his mother blow for verbal blow.

"That's where you're wrong, Mom. I *do* understand the dangers I was facing. I know that if Saul's soldiers captured me it would have meant torture and quite possibly death. But I also knew that I was capable of outsmarting his men. I was willing to take the risk, and I wasn't being foolhardy. It was a calculated risk."

Holden was surprised that he couldn't see steam literally coming out of Elise's ears, given how angry her eyes looked right now. He shifted uncomfortably in his seat, feeling like he was an awkward eavesdropper even though Elise knew full well that he was there and had, in fact, insisted that he stay. His movement must have caught her attention, because she turned to look at him then, and unleashed her fury on him.

"Did you fill my son's head with these notions of calculated risks?" she asked. "I should have known better than to let my son hang out with a dragon. You promised to protect him! And instead you let him run off into the middle of a war!"

"Elise," Holden said, trying to keep his voice calm. He struggled for the right words to say, but finding them wasn't easy. He needed to apologize to Elise, but he also needed to make her understand that her son was a dragon, and dragons all had a bit of a wild side. "I'm sorry that I made the suggestion to Nick that he go back through the tunnel and spy on Saul's soldiers. In hindsight, I should have known that bringing up the idea would spark a fire in him that wouldn't be satisfied until he completed the spying mission, with or without permission."

"Yeah, you should have known," Elise said. Her voice dripped with frustrated anger, and Holden did his best to remind himself that she was still recovering from the shock of thinking she might lose her son.

"I'm sorry," Holden repeated again, gently. "I misread the situation. I never intended for Nick to go alone, without having a way of communicating with us and sending a signal if he got in trouble. I'm new to this whole preteen world. Perhaps it was plain to you that Nick would react the way he did, and go off on his own. But I didn't see it coming. All I can promise you is that I'll learn from the experience, and do better next time."

Holden paused, his heart in his throat. He was half expecting Elise to snap at him again, and tell him that there wouldn't be a next time. That she didn't want him in her life. But she said nothing. The anger in her eyes didn't soften, but at least she hadn't thrown him out the door yet. Holden took a deep breath, and then continued speaking, hoping that he wasn't going to push Elise away forever with the words he spoke next. Regardless of what happened between him and Elise, though, he had to say his piece about dragons, and about what having a dragon for a son would mean. Holden owed Nick that much. The boy had not had a father to guide him or temper his wild dragon side. The least Holden could do, as a fellow shifter, was to try to warn his mother of what was to come.

"The only other thing I have to say about all of this, Elise, is that while I may be new to the world of preteens, I'm not new to the world of dragons. I've known my whole life that I'm a dragon, and I grew up around dragons. You could say I'm something of an expert on dragon shifters, and here's what I know: that 'wild side' that you want to tame in your son will never truly be tamed. Dragons need to be free, to soar, and to spread their wings. The more you try to hold Nick back and keep him safe, the more resentful he'll become. I would never dream of telling you how to raise your son, but I wouldn't be able to live with myself if I didn't at least try to explain to you what lies ahead for you as the mother of a dragon. Dragons are fiercely loyal and unapologetically fierce. Your son will never hesitate to give his life for you, or for the causes he cares about. You can try to protect him, but you will never truly tame him. That's why he went to spy on Saul's soldiers today. He cares more about fighting for the side of good than he does for his own life. I know that, as a mother, that's a hard thing for you to accept. But if you want to maintain an open, honest relationship with your son, you'll need to accept that."

Holden fell silent, then, already feeling as though he'd said too much. Elise's eyes were unreadable at this point. He wished she would say something, anything, that would give him a clue as to what she was thinking right now. His heart had not stopped pounding in his chest since the moment she'd commanded him to stay behind when Violet and Weston left. He didn't want to take the focus away from Nick right now, but there was so much more Holden could have said about dragons and their loyalties.

The truth was, Holden was struggling with his own fierce inner dragon. Even though it scared Holden to death, he'd realized that he would always be loyal to Elise. He would always care for her, and fight fiercely for her. He'd been scared of love for so long, and that hadn't changed. He was terrified at the emotional rollercoaster that might lie ahead of him. But he knew deep down in his bones that Elise was his lifemate, and that he would never be able to stop loving her. He would risk his life for her, and, because Nick was her son and meant the world to her, he would risk his life for him, too. There's nothing Holden wouldn't do for this family. If only he could find the right words to say to make Elise understand that. But before Holden could find more words of his own to say, he heard Nick's voice speaking up. The boy's anger had dissolved somewhat, but his eyes were just as determined and fierce as they had been from the moment his mother had walked out of her bedroom.

"He's right, mom," Nick said, quietly but with conviction. "I know you love me deeply, and only want to keep me safe. But I have a wild heart. I may be young, but I already feel like I'm destined for great things. I've known all along that I was no ordinary boy. I didn't know until this week that it was because I was a dragon shifter, but I've always known there was something different about me. I think you knew it, too."

To Holden's surprise, a reluctant smile crossed Elise's face. "Yes," she said. "I've always known you were different. Special."

Nick took a deep breath. He looked over at Holden, as if searching for the encouragement he needed to continue. Holden gave a slight nod of his head, letting the boy know he should continue his speech. Nick turned back to his mother.

"Mom, don't blame Holden for what happened today. He told me very clearly not to do anything that you didn't approve of, and I didn't listen to him. My actions today were my own, and I take full responsibility for them. I should not have disobeyed you behind your back, and I deserve whatever punishment you decide to give me. But please, hear me out on this. I went today because I needed to fight for the side of good. There is a war going on, and many lives hang in the balance, not just mine. There was something I could do to make a real difference for the side of good, and I had to do it. My heart didn't give me a choice. You always tell me that it's important to be brave in the face of bullies, and that's what I did today. I was brave in the face of that big bully Saul. I'm sorry I scared you, but I'm not sorry I went. I know I can do great things, Mom, if I just had the chance. I wish you would believe in me a little more. Holden is right. I need to stretch my wings."

Holden held his breath as he waited for Elise's reply. He knew that Nick must have been holding his breath, too. Elise sat down at the table and put her face in her hands. She stayed that way for a long time, and finally Nick sat down next to her. When Elise finally raised her face, it was streaked with tears, and her eyes appeared red and puffy.

"I'm sorry, Nick," she said. "I should have trusted you more."

Nick's eyes widened, and he looked over at Holden as though he could hardly believe what his mother was saying to him.

"Don't get me wrong," she continued. "I don't approve of you going behind my back and disobeying me. But you're right. I do need to let you stretch your wings more. I've been overprotective of you since the day you were born. I think it's because, since the very first breaths of your life, I saw that you had a wild streak in you, like your father. Now I know why."

Elise glanced over at Holden, and, to his surprise, a small smile turned up the corners of her mouth. She looked back at Nick, and reached out to cover her son's hand with her own.

"It's going to take some getting used to, Nicky," she said. "But I mean it when I say I'm proud of you, and that I think you're special. So from now on, I'll do my best to trust you a little more. Just, please, don't run off without telling me. My heart couldn't handle it if something happened to you. Waiting here and wondering whether you were dead or alive was the worst kind of torture."

Nick looked truly contrite. "I'm sorry, Mom," he said. "I didn't realize everyone would be that worried."

Holden almost wanted to laugh. Nick might be strong, and have dragon blood in him, but he was still a child. And children could be so oblivious to the worries of the adult world.

Elise wiped away the last few tears from her eyes and smiled at him. "Of course we were worried. We love you. But I accept your apology. Don't think this means you won't be punished, though. No video games for a week, young man. And that's letting you off easy, considering what you did today."

Nick opened his mouth for a moment as though to protest, but he quickly shut it again. He nodded in acceptance, although he did let a long, sad sigh escape his lips. His mother reached over to hug him, then, and Holden sat awkwardly across the table from them, feeling like he was intruding on a very intimate moment. He wondered if Elise even remembered he was there at this point, but he got his answer a few moments later. She glanced at him over Nick's shoulder, and mouthed the words, "We'll talk later."

Holden didn't know whether to be excited or afraid of what that conversation would bring.

CHAPTER THIRTEEN

Elise gently nudged Nick, who was fast asleep on the couch, snoring slightly as his chest rose and fell.

"Nick," she said. He didn't move so she tried again, louder. "Nick!"

He grunted, and rolled over, but never opened his eyes.

Elise stood up straight and looked helplessly over at Holden. "I swear to god, he sleeps like the dead."

Elise saw Holden glance up from the kitchen, where he was rinsing off their dinner plates. Her heart did a happy little flip-flop at the sight of him. A man who did dishes? What more could any girl ask for? Perhaps a man who didn't entice her son into life-threatening situations, Elise thought wryly.

"I'll get him," Holden said, turning off the water and wiping his soapy hands on a nearby dish towel. Elise watched him cross the small apartment in a few giant strides, and then effortlessly scoop up her son in his arms. Nick was big for a boy of twelve, but Holden lifted him as easily as if he were lifting a feather pillow. Elise followed Holden into Nick's bedroom, where he laid the boy down gently on the bed and pulled the comforter up over him. Elise bent down to kiss Nick's forehead, but Nick did not so much as grunt again. Holden laughed.

"He really is dead to the world," he said. "I've never seen anyone sleep through being carried across a whole apartment."

Elise laughed. "You've never seen an almost-teenager sleeping, then."

"Fair enough," Holden said. Their eyes met over the top of Nick's sleeping body, and Elise felt suddenly shy. In some ways, Holden knew her more intimately than anyone else in the world right now. And in other ways, he felt like a stranger. Who was this man, this wild dragon shifter, who had swooped into her life and stolen her heart despite her determination not to fall in love until Nick had grown and moved away? Elise felt her heart pounding in her chest at the intensity of Holden's gaze, and she was the first to look away.

"We should let him rest," she said. "He's had a long day."

"As we all have," Holden said. Elise glanced back at him and noticed for the first time how tired his eyes looked. She realized with a start that he'd spent the day worried sick, just like her. Perhaps that should have been obvious, but she'd been so consumed with her own worry and anger that she'd never considered the fact that Holden cared about her son's wellbeing, too. The thought made her heart do another strange flip-flop in her chest, and she looked away quickly.

What more could she ask for than a man who does dishes, she thought, repeating the joke of a question she'd asked herself earlier. Only this time, she answered it sincerely. A man who fights for what is right and good in the world. A man who protects those weaker than him. A man who is strong and handsome, and whose green eyes remind her of emerald jewels. A man who loves Nick as though he were his own son, even if he doesn't always understand how to navigate the confusing ways of a preteen. A man who makes her laugh. A man who turns her on in bed. A man who is friendly and kind.

A man like Holden.

Elise's heart was pounding so violently now that she felt certain Holden must hear it. But when she turned to look at him, he gave no indication that he did. Instead, he followed her out of Nick's bedroom, and then stood uncertainly in the middle of the living room, running his fingers through his hair.

"I should go," he said, but it sounded more like a question than a statement.

Elise didn't reply right away. She looked at him, long and hard, trying to decide in that moment whether she was going to stick to her no-romance policy. Her mind screamed at her to be rational, but the pounding of her heartbeat was doing a pretty good job of drowning out that sound. He was the one who finally broke the silence.

"I'm really sorry, again, for whatever part I played in Nick taking off today."

Elise had been so angry at Holden earlier, but now, with her son sleeping safely in his bed, she was finding it hard to stir up any feelings of outrage toward Holden. Instead, she let out a long sigh. It felt like her thousandth sigh of the day, and perhaps it was.

"There's so much about dragons I don't understand," she said, as though that explained everything she was feeling. Maybe it did.

"I can help you understand, Elise," Holden said, his voice husky. "I can help Nick understand. I'm not perfect and I make mistakes, but I care deeply for you, and for your son. I don't say that lightly, either. I've avoided falling in love for so long because I didn't want to love someone and lose them. But I realized today that it's too late for me to avoid falling in love with you. When Nick was gone, I was terrified. The thought of losing him took my breath away. The thought of causing you pain, or losing you, makes my heart feel like it's twisting up inside of me."

Elise felt a thrill in her core at the sound of his words, then felt guilty. Was she really doing right by her son if she let Holden stay in their lives? Nick needed guidance on being a dragon, that was true. Holden could give him that, but Holden would also encourage Nick to take risks, to be wild. Could Elise handle that? She knew that deep down her son had an adventurer's heart, but how much should it be encouraged?

"I told myself I wasn't going to love another man until Nick was older, at least," Elise said, her voice shaking slightly as she forced herself to meet Holden's eyes. "I've messed up so many things in my life already, and my mistakes have caused a lot of pain for Nick. I don't want to see him get excited about having a father figure, only to lose that father because a romance didn't work out."

Holden looked at Elise with those emerald eyes of his, and she felt like he was looking right through her. She felt her hands trembling, but she wasn't sure exactly what emotion was causing it. Fear? Excitement? Anticipation?

"That's the only reason you have not to be with me?" Holden asked. "You're afraid I'm going to leave you and break Nick's heart?"

"It's a pretty significant reason, don't you think?" Elise asked.

Holden crossed the space between them and took Elise's face in his hands, tilting her head upward so that she was looking directly at him.

"I am not letting go of you, do you hear me?" he said. "Never. I don't care what you do or say, or what obstacles lie between us. I'm never letting go. I will always love you."

Elise's heart did another flip-flop at the word "love." Her face was on fire where Holden was touching it, and she found it hard to breathe. Did he mean it? Did he really love her?

"How can you say that?" she managed to ask. "How can you say you love me? You barely know me."

Holden's eyes started to swirl as he looked down at her. She could see the primal, animal instinct taking over. He wanted her, he craved her, he needed her. But was it true that he loved her? Could he really know that for sure? Elise herself felt like she loved him, but she thought she was being foolish and letting her emotions get away with her. How could two people who'd met less than a week ago truly be in love?

"In some ways, it's true that I barely know you," Holden said. His voice was deep, gravelly, and hungry. "But in other ways, I've known you my whole life."

Elise raised an eyebrow, confused. She waited for Holden to explain.

"You see, Elise, shifters believe in lifemates. You've probably never heard the term before?"

Elise shook her head no. She hadn't.

Holden nodded. "The best comparison I could make is that lifemates are sort of like soulmates. But even that comparison falls short. Lifemates are destined to be together from the moment they are born. We shifters believe that fate works your whole life to make sure that you and your lifemate cross paths. Sometimes that's easy. For example, a lot of people grow up in the same town as their lifemates. But sometimes, it's not so easy, and I guess that's how it was with you and me. It's quite a unique set of circumstances that brought us together, don't you think?"

Elise blinked. "You think we're lifemates?" she asked.

"Yes," Holden said without hesitation. "I know we are. You see, when you find your lifemate and make love to them, a bond is formed. The lifemate bond. It's unmistakable, and unbreakable. I felt it forming when we made love. It manifests itself physically as a hot sensation in your core, but it's more than just a physical feeling. It's a knowing, deep down, that you love that person and that they mean more to you than anyone else ever has."

Elise could not speak. She was floored by Holden's words, because she'd felt exactly that when they slept together. She'd been surprised by the warmth in her core after they'd made love, and by the feeling of home. That's what it had felt like to her—being home. She'd felt, for perhaps the first time in her life, that she loved a man. She'd cared deeply for Nick's father at one time, sure. But it had been different. There had never been a feeling that she couldn't live without him. Ever since she'd slept with Holden, though, she'd had this thought that she'd never be able to live without him. She'd struggled to push away the feeling, all in the name of doing what was best for Nick. But what if being with Holden *was* what was best for Nick? Elise had never felt so confused in her entire life, and yet, at the same time, she had never felt so sure that her heart had been completely captured.

"I...I felt something similar," she finally said. "But I don't know if I can ever truly love someone. I have my son to think about, you know? I have to protect him, and...and..."

"And you're worried I'm going to leave you, and leave him," Holden finished for her.

She looked up at him with tears in her eyes. Her nod was barely perceptible, but she knew he saw it. He pulled her gently into his arms, and kissed the top of her head lightly. She breathed in his woodsy smell, and wondered how he managed to still smell like the forest in the middle of this godforsaken desert town.

"I won't tell you not to worry, or not to be afraid," he said, his voice somewhat muffled by her hair. "God knows I have fears of my own. I think it's impossible to love without also feeling fear. I'm terrified of losing you, of something hurting you. I tried to resist falling in love for so long because of that, but I couldn't help falling in love with you. You're worth the pain, the fear that goes hand in hand with loving. I think that, every now and then in life, you find something that's so wonderful that it's worth embracing, despite the haunting 'what-ifs' that accompany it. I decided that you were one of those things, Elise. And I hope you'll decide for yourself that I'm worth the worry, and worth the fear. I promise you, I will never leave you or Nick. You'll have to decide for yourself whether my words are enough of a guarantee for you. I can tell you all day long that you can trust me, but, at the end of it all, you'll have to take my word for it. That's a decision only you can make."

Elise frowned, and bit her lip. What Holden said was true. Any time she'd ever loved someone, she'd felt a bit of fear along with that love. He'd given her his word that he wouldn't leave her, but still she felt afraid. She had to decide whether that fear, that risk, was worth the joy of being with Holden.

She let herself debate the matter for a few moments, but she knew in her heart that she had already made her decision. She would trust Holden, because she did love him, and she couldn't imagine a future without him. He was a good man, and a loyal dragon. He was exactly what she needed in her life. She'd been alone for so long, and she'd managed. She'd worked hard, and provided for Nick all on her own. What did she have left to prove? She was strong, but she was lonely. It was time to listen to her heart for once.

And her heart was pounding in her chest right now, telling her that she belonged with Holden Pars. She tilted her head upward once more, and felt a rush of happiness when Holden's green eyes met her own.

"Okay," she said. "I trust you. But if we're going to make this work, you come to me first from now on when you have ideas that put my son in mortal danger. Don't give him any more fuel for his wild side. He has enough as it is."

Holden grinned. "Fair enough," he said. "I'm just glad you didn't chop my head off today when he was missing."

"Oh, I thought about it," Elise said, putting her hands on her hips in a gesture of indignation. And it was true. She had. She'd been so angry at him earlier, but her anger had faded with the realization that her son was safe, and that Holden couldn't be truly held responsible for Nick's actions. Nick had dragon blood in him, and he would find ways to be reckless whether or not Holden put crazy ideas in his head. Elise realized that now, and she also realized that if she tried to put Nick in a bubble, she was going to lose her son's respect. She had to let him live. Maybe she didn't have to let him walk straight into enemy territory, but she had to allow him to take some calculated risks. He would be eighteen before she knew it, after all. The last thing she wanted was for him to rebel and go crazy as soon as he was out from under her roof. No, she needed to start allowing him more freedom now. She needed to let him learn to manage his wild side, while she was still around to guide him and help him. And while Holden was here to guide him and help him.

Elise's heart leapt at the realization that, just like that, she and Nick were no longer alone. Holden was here. Holden loved her, and had promised to protect her and her son. Elise let her hands drop to her side, losing the look of feigned indignation and smiling at Holden.

"I guess I'm glad I didn't chop off your head," she said. "After all, it's quite cute."

Holden laughed. "Why thank you. I'm not sure how I feel about being 'cute.' I'd prefer 'sexy' or 'dashingly handsome.' But if 'cute' is what kept me from losing my head, I guess I'll take it."

Elise laughed, and felt a flutter of excitement between her legs as Holden pulled her body tight against his. She could already feel his erection, stiff and eager as it pressed against her body through their clothes.

"Besides," Holden said, his voice dropping to a low, husky tone. "If you'd chopped off my head, I wouldn't have been able to do this."

And then, his lips were on hers. They were warm, and tasted faintly of pineapple thanks to the Hawaiian pizza they'd all shared for dinner. Elise felt the feeling of excitement between her legs growing. She was growing warm, and wet. And she was beginning to freak out about the fact that she was making out with Holden in the middle of her living room, with only one thin bedroom door separating them from Nick.

"Holden," she gasped, pulling away. "Nicky! He'll hear us."

Holden threw back his head and laughed. "Half an hour ago you were telling me that preteens sleep like the dead."

"Well they do," Elise said reluctantly. "But on the off chance he wakes up..."

"Come on, then," Holden said, and scooped her up into his arms in one smooth movement. "I don't want you focused on anything except me. Let's get you safely behind your own closed door."

Holden carried her into her bedroom, dropping her on the bed in much the same way he had the night before. Elise could hardly believe that it had only been about twenty-four hours since she and Holden had first been together in this room, making love. This day had felt like it stretched on for weeks. Perhaps that's why it didn't seem so strange to her that Holden could say he loved her, and that she felt as though she loved him. It seemed they had already lived quite a bit of life together, despite the short time they'd known each other. According to Holden, in fact, they'd known deep down that they were destined for each other before they'd even met.

Lifemates, Elise thought, letting the word roll around in her mind as she watched Holden stripping his shirt off. It was a beautiful word, with a beautiful meaning. She'd always rolled her eyes when someone talked about finding their soulmate, but she had to admit that, now that she'd found Holden, she understood a little bit better what it was like to feel like fate had brought two people together.

Holden had taken off his pants now, too, leaving him wearing nothing except his tight black briefs. Elise's breath caught in her throat as she looked over at him from her spot on the bed. His body was a wonder to behold. His erection was large and stiff, its outline plainly visible beneath the fabric of his briefs. His tanned skin seemed to accentuate the outline of his sculpted muscles, and Elise thought for perhaps the hundredth time that she'd never seen anyone as strong as Holden. He was smiling as she watched him from her vantage point on the bed. She'd propped herself up on her elbow, waiting for him to undress. He didn't remove his underwear yet, though. Instead, he slid onto the bed next to her and pulled her close to him. His arms were warm and steady around her, like anchors in the chaos that was her life. She marveled that someone could be so strong and tender all at the same time, and then let out a little sigh of happiness.

She felt his breath, hot against her neck. Somewhat ironically, the heat of it sent shivers up her spine. He must have felt her shudder, because he pulled her even closer and kissed the top of her head. Elise could feel his erection against her as their bodies pressed against each other, and a wave of pure, primal passion flooded through her. She felt as though she'd been over-thinking everything for the last half hour or so. She'd debated in her mind whether she could possibly love Holden, and whether he was worth the risk of loving. She'd wondered if lifemates could truly exist, and whether Holden was hers. She'd fretted and worried and tried to fit everything into a logical, sensible pattern. But now, all of her rational thoughts were fading away. Her physical body was taking over, fueled by a deep, primal need. The moisture between her legs was growing, and she felt a happy, familiar fluttering in her belly.

Holden was also feeling a physical, primal urge. She could tell by the way his hot breath grew rapid. He wanted her, needed her. The thought made Elise smile. It felt so good to be wanted and needed by a man. Her whole body felt like it was on fire now, and she wondered how she ever could have hesitated to give herself to this man.

Holden dipped his lips to hers, and the heat in her body centered on her tongue as it danced with his. Every flick of his tongue brought a fresh thrill, and she lost herself in the magic of his kiss. This was what she had been waiting for her whole life, without even knowing it.

She wasn't sure how long they kissed. It was easy to lose track of time when she was with Holden. Eventually, though, he broke his lips away from hers and reached for the hem of her shirt. The next minute was a tangle of fabric, arms, and legs, as Holden reached to undress her, and she returned the favor by tugging at his underwear. They laughed and kissed as they untangled their clothes from their bodies, then found each other's lips again. Holden's erection pressed against Elise's belly button, but she wanted it lower. She scooted up slightly, so that her hips were even with his, and his dick was now pressing against her dripping wet entrance. He moaned softly as he felt the juices of her desire covering him. He paused in his movements for a moment, as if to savor their togetherness. And then, with a deep, growling noise, he flipped her onto her back and positioned himself on top of her.

From that moment on, he took complete control. His alpha instincts seemed to be taking over, and Elise got the feeling that he was reacting to some sort of dragon instinct, claiming his mate.

She had never been so happy to be claimed.

He slid into her quickly and deliberately. Even though she'd slept with him just the night before, she still found herself shocked at how large he was. She imagined that it would take some time to get used to his size, and she wasn't going to complain about that. She hoped that she'd be spending quite a lot of time making love to Holden in the future. Now that he was inside of her, the thrills of pleasure she had been feeling intensified. She felt the heat and tingling in her body grow, and her warm wetness increased as he slid back and forth against her inner walls. He moved his hips with a gentle strength. She could feel his power, but he never hurt her. He held his body above hers in a way that put pressure on her without crushing her. She moaned and closed her eyes, drinking in the wonder of being so close to him. All her worries fell away, and she felt almost like she was dreaming. Her heart continued to pound rapidly in her chest, beating in rhythm with the thrusts of his hips. The pressure of passion built within her, until she finally could hold back no more.

She had to bite her lip to stifle a scream as her body exploded around his. She felt her muscles spasming and clenching around his dick, claiming him as hers, just as he had claimed her as his. He followed only moments after her, finding his release with a low growl and pulsing into her. Together, they lay there, entwined in each other and breathing heavily as their bodies throbbed in unison. Elise had never been much of a religious person, but this moment made her believe that heaven might actually exist.

She wasn't sure how long they lay like that, but she was in no rush to pull away from Holden. By the time he finally slid out of her and moved to lay next to her on the bed, she had nearly fallen asleep. His movement caused her to stir, though, and she found herself once again awake, reveling in the peaceful satisfaction that filled her heart and body. Holden wrapped his arm around her and fell asleep soon after that, but, now that Elise was awake, she lay that way for a long time.

The day had been long, but, now that it had taken a happy turn, she almost didn't want it to end. Once she'd made the decision to truly give her heart over to Holden, she'd been filled with a mixture of relief, peace, and joy unlike any emotion she'd felt before. She almost felt like she was living a fairy tale. And, perhaps, she was. She was in love with a dragon, and that dragon happened to be a strong, loyal man who also loved her son. Maybe it wasn't exactly the same as your traditional fairy tale, but that was alright.

If there's anything Elise had learned over the course of the last twelve years, it was that fairy tales didn't always look like fairy tales...but that didn't mean that life was any less magical. And even though things were still far from perfect, Elise felt like her life was pretty damn magical at the moment.

CHAPTER FOURTEEN

Holden woke up to the smell of coffee and the sound of Elise's humming. He smiled as he heard her buzzing about the kitchen, clanging pots and pans. Then he sat up suddenly, realizing that Elise should have been at work by now. She'd called in for the dinner shift yesterday, thanks to all the drama with Nick. But she'd told him after Nick was found that she'd have to cover the breakfast shift this morning to make up for it. So why was she still here?

He pulled on his t-shirt and jeans, and then made his way out to the small kitchen, where he found Elise cracking eggs over a skillet. She had her back to him, and hadn't heard him coming over the sound of her humming. For a few moments, he watched her while she was unaware. He smiled at the sight of her curvy hips swaying to the music of her own humming. But then she turned slightly, and saw him out of the corner of her eye. Sheepishly, she turned around and shrugged.

"I like to hum while I cook," she said.

"Don't stop on my account," Holden said, coming closer to give her a quick good morning kiss on the lips. She blushed and started to turn away, but before she had fully gone back to minding the skillet, he caught a glimpse of the redness that rimmed her eyes.

"Is something wrong?" he asked. Elise shook her head no, but she didn't turn back to look at him. Holden knew that wasn't a good sign. If she wasn't willing to meet his eyes, it was because something definitely *was* wrong. Holden reached for her arm and gently turned her back so that she was facing him once again. She looked down quickly, but not before he saw the glimmer of moisture in her eyes. She was on the verge of tears.

"I thought you were working this morning," he said.

The tears came then. One or two escaped at first, making their way down her cheek in silence, but soon, she could not hold back the dam, and her face was soon covered with salty, wet trails.

"My boss called me before I'd even left the apartment this morning and told me not to bother coming in ever again."

Holden blinked a few times as he processed what Elise had just told him. "He fired you?" he asked, incredulous. "But you're the best waitress he has."

Elise shrugged, looking heartbroken. "I know. And I've always taken so much pride in my work. But apparently being the best and working the hardest wasn't enough. He said I've called in too much and he needs someone more dedicated to their work. Never mind that I've only called in twice, and with good reason. And that I've only missed shifts a total of six times in all the years I've worked there. None of the other employees can say that. They call in every other shift, it seems. But he's been looking for an excuse to sack me ever since that morning the fight broke out. You know, the fight you rescued Nicky from?"

"I know the one," Holden said. How could he forget?

Elise shrugged again. "Yeah, well, thanks to that little incident, I'm jobless now.

I...I'm not sure what I'm going to do. This is a small town, and most of the restaurants are fully staffed. God, if I have to move again, Nick's going to be so upset. But I don't see how I'm going to make ends meet unless I replace my job in the next day or two. I'm barely surviving as it is."

Elise turned abruptly back toward the frying pan, trying once again to hide her tears. Holden reached for her arm and firmly pulled her back.

"Hey. It's okay. You don't have to be so damn strong all the time, you know? You've had a couple of hellish days. It's okay to shed a few tears. And don't worry about the job. Your boss was a dickhead, anyway. You'll find something else, and in the meantime I can help you. We're in this thing together now."

He felt Elise bristle slightly at his words.

"I don't want help. I didn't agree to date you just so I could mooch off of you. I've always taken care of Nick by myself. I don't need help."

Holden sighed. "You do need help, from what you just told me. And there's no shame in that. I know this whole relationship is new, but we're committed to each other for life. We talked about that already. We love each other, and we're a family. And families take care of each other. Lord knows there have been countless times in my life that I've needed help, and my clan has been there for me."

"I hate feeling like a damsel in distress," Elise said, still looking at the floor. Behind her, the white edges of the over easy egg she'd been cooking were starting to turn a crispy brown. Holden took the spatula from her and deftly removed the egg from the pan, sliding it onto a plate that was sitting next to the stove.

"Well you shouldn't feel that way, because you're not a damsel in distress. You're a damsel who has done a kickass job of taking care of herself, and now deserves a bit of a breather." Holden picked up the plate with the egg on it and pushed it toward Elise. "Go. Sit. Eat. I'll finish cooking. You've spent enough mornings lately serving people eggs."

Elise opened her mouth like she was going to protest, but then she clamped it shut again and went to sit at the table. She munched silently for a few moments while Holden cracked another egg into the pan. As soon as it hit the heat and started sizzling, he left it for a moment to go put a few slices of bread in the toaster. Then he grabbed two mugs from the mug tree that sat on the counter, filling them with coffee from the pot that Elise had already brewed up. He took one of the mugs to Elise before turning his attention back to the skillet. As soon as his back was turned to Elise, he started talking again. He wanted to give her a chance to think about what he was going to say without feeling pressure to react a certain way. But god, he hoped she was going to accept the offer he was about to make.

"I actually wanted to talk to you about quitting that job, anyway," he said, in a voice that he hoped was loud enough for her to hear over the sizzle of the pan. "Because there's about to be an opening for a job here in Blackstone that would be perfect for you."

Holden paused for a moment, letting his words sink in, and then continued. "Weston called me last night, long after you had fallen asleep. Miraculously, I managed to sneak out of your bedroom without waking you, and had a long chat with him. He and Violet had gone over the video footage and photos Nick took in Saul's camp yesterday. It looks like your son managed to capture quite a bit of vital information during his short stint as a spy. Peter and Knox, the leaders of the army I'm fighting with, are sending a group to Blackstone to attempt a sneak attack on Saul's camp. All of those wizards and shifters will be hungry, and they could use someone to take care of meals for them. I've been given authorization to hire someone, and, instead of bringing someone down from Falcon Cross for the job, I was hoping you might take it."

Holden waited a few beats, but then could hold his curiosity back no longer. He turned around to face Elise, hoping he would find eagerness on her face, or, at least, interest. Her expression, however, was pure confusion. She was biting her lip, which he had quickly learned was an indication that she was nervous or unsure about something. He forced himself to remain quiet and let her think for a moment, but it was not easy task. He wanted to rush over to her and tell her that this was a perfect solution. She would be great for the job, and it would allow them to work closely together. Instead of always running off to work double shifts for a bully boss, she'd be cooking for people who actually appreciated her.

"Weston is the guy who was here yesterday?" Elise finally asked.

"Yes. He's also a dragon shifter, and one of my best friends. Sorry, I didn't realize you were never actually introduced. I guess everything was a bit chaotic when Nick first got back."

"Yeah, it was," Elise said, her face tensing up a bit at the memory.

"I'll introduce you to him later. Actually, he wanted to show me what Nick found. If you're interested in seeing it, he could bring it over here to show us both. That would give you a good chance to meet him, too."

"I'm not sure I want to see what Nick was doing yesterday," Elise said with a wince.

Holden smiled at her. "You should take a look. I know you didn't want him to go, but your son may have just made a big difference in our war effort. He found pretty interesting stuff."

Elise shrugged. "Well, I'd like to meet Weston, at least. You can tell him to come over. I'm sure Nick wants to spend more time with the latest dragon in town, too."

Elise rolled her eyes, and Holden laughed before turning to remove the eggs he'd just cooked from the stove. He put them on a plate and took it to the table, then turned back to the kitchen to grab the toast.

"Help yourself to more eggs if you want," he said, as he started looking for a butter knife. When he'd found one, he started slathering butter and then jam onto the toast.

Elise grabbed another egg from the plate, and took a bite, chewing carefully before speaking again. "So, this job would be cooking for a big group? You know I didn't do much cooking at the restaurant, right? I was more of a server. Usually, the only thing I made was coffee."

"I know," Holden said. "But Nick tells me you're a fantastic cook. And besides, you understand how to run a kitchen. You'd be great for the job. It pays well, and it's honestly probably less work than you were being forced to do at that diner. It would also give you a chance to get to know some of my crew. And, you know, do your part for the cause of good."

Elise still hesitated. "Are you sure you're not doing this because you feel sorry for me for losing my job?"

Holden sighed. "I'm doing this because I think it's a perfect job for you. Honest. I was planning to ask you even before I knew you'd been fired. In fact, I was worried I wouldn't be able to convince you to leave your job. But now that your boss made that decision for you, I hope you'll take the job I'm offering and join me in this war. It's not just about a job as a cook. It's about doing something that will help stop a truly evil man from continuing on his path of destruction. I know we haven't been together that long, but I'm pretty sure I know you well enough to know that you'd support a cause like that."

Elise kept chewing her lip, and Holden was starting to worry that she was going to tell him no.

"It'd help you keep an eye on Nick, too," Holden said, giving her a mischievous grin.

Elise laughed at that. "Okay, okay. I'll take the job," she said. "It'll be nice to do something other than plain old waitressing for a while, anyway."

Holden let out a whoop, and pulled Elise up from her chair to spin her around. He planted a kiss on her lips just as Nick emerged from his bedroom, sleepy-eyed with hair sticking out in every direction. Elise pulled back from Holden like he was on fire, and her cheeks turned red. Holden had been so caught up in telling Elise about the job that he'd forgotten Nick was in the apartment. He and Elise hadn't spoken yet about how they would tell Nick that they were dating, but it looked like they were about to have the conversation whether they were ready for it or not.

Nick raised a sleepy eyebrow at the two of them as he walked over to the kitchen table. He plopped down in one of the chairs and reached for the plate of eggs Holden had just set down, apparently intending to eat the entire pile himself.

"So, are you guys like a thing now or what?" Nick asked just before sticking a giant forkful of food into his mouth.

"You mean are we dating?" Elise asked, her voice sounding unnaturally high. "Yes, we are. I'm sorry you found out in such a surprising manner. I'd intended to sit down and talk with you but I was just so excited right now about a job Holden told me about and—"

"So you're his girlfriend, then?" Nick asked, interrupting.

"Well, yes. I'm his girlfriend. We're dating," Elise replied.

Nick shrugged. "Cool," he said, in a mildly interested tone, just before shoving an entire egg into his mouth at once.

Holden caught Elise's eye. She smiled and shrugged, and he leaned over to give her a quick peck on the cheek. It looked like Holden's relationship with Elise was just fine with his new son. And that is what Holden considered Nick—a son. After all, they were family now. Holden smiled as he went back to start cooking more eggs.

Family.

He'd been so scared to have one of those for so long, but nothing had ever felt so right to him as this moment. As he cooked, he replayed over and over in his mind the smile that had crossed Elise's face when she'd realized he was serious about the job. God, he could look at that smile for the rest of his life and never get tired of seeing it. And, it looked like that was exactly what he was going to get to do.

Holden cracked another egg into the pan and started whistling. Today was already a good day, and he hadn't even had breakfast yet.

CHAPTER FIFTEEN

Elise was biting her lip again. She'd been trying to kick the habit, but the last few days had run her nerves ragged. Watching the video footage of Nick's little expedition into enemy territory was doing nothing to calm her down, and they were only five minutes in.

"There!" Weston said, pausing the video and pointing to a dark spot on the top right hand corner of the screen. He'd hooked his laptop up to Elise's television, and was using the TV monitor to play back the footage. Elise was impressed with how stealthily Nick had snuck through Saul's camp, but she also felt slightly sick thinking about how close her son had been to such violent people.

He's a dragon, remember. Let him spread his wings.

"Watch that spot," Weston said. "That's where you'll see that Saul is hiding the bats."

Elise watched closely as Weston hit play again. She could see why Holden considered Weston his best friend. Weston was smart, funny, and just as stubborn as Holden. Elise wondered if all dragons were that stubborn. Every one that she'd met so far certainly seemed to be, her own son included, of course. Holden seemed to sense her tense mood. He reached over and grabbed her hand, and she instantly relaxed. She relaxed even more when she remembered that she now had a job working with Holden's crew. She could hardly believe how lucky she was. She loved cooking, and now she was going to get paid to cook for Holden and his friends, instead of having to work for a boss who seemed to exist just to make her life miserable.

The black spot on the television screen grew closer, and Elise strained her eyes. One of Saul's soldiers, a wizard, it seemed, opened the door with a flourish of their magic ring. From the vantage point Nick had had with his camera, it was hard to see into the opening. But there was a lot of movement inside the darkness, and now and then a bat flew out of the opening.

"That seems to be the hub of the bat cloning operation," Holden said. "If we can destroy that, it'll be a devastating hit to Saul's power."

"When do the others get here?" Violet asked.

"Tomorrow morning," Holden replied. "We'll need a day or two to brief everyone, but then we should be ready to hit the ground running. While the rest of our army continues to search for the dragon ruby, we'll be hitting Saul with a surprise attack."

"You're sure this will work?" Elise asked. She tried not to sound nervous, but she knew she was failing miserably at that task. Holden gave her a reassuring smile.

"We're never sure of anything, Love," he said. "But thanks to Nick, we know exactly how Saul's camp is laid out, and how he runs his operations. We have a big advantage. I know you're not happy that Nick snuck off, but I do have to say, that boy of yours has skills. He just handed us the tools to seriously cripple Saul's army."

Elise looked over at Nick, who was pretending not to hear Saul's praise. The way her son's chest was puffed up with pride, though, gave him away. He knew he'd done well. Elise sighed. She was really going to have to work on not worrying constantly, but at least she knew Holden was looking out for Nick. Holden was strong, and would fight to the death to defend Nick. What more could she ask for, really?

She watched the rest of the video with Holden's hand in hers, and then listened as the group made plans on how to best show the soldiers who would be coming into town tomorrow everything they needed to know about Blackstone, the tunnels, and Saul's camp. They talked for hours, and eventually realized they were hungry.

"I'd offer to cook you something, but I still haven't managed to squeeze in a proper trip to the grocery store," Elise said.

"No worries," Holden replied, standing up and giving her a wink. "You're not starting your job until tomorrow, anyway, so why don't we let someone else do the cooking for once? Do you have a suggestion for a good restaurant in town?"

Elise laughed. "You're going to think I'm crazy, but we should go to the diner."

Holden gave her a look that said he most definitely thought she was crazy.

"I'm serious," Elise insisted. "The cooks there make excellent food, and, honestly, I want to go and prove to everyone that I'm fine. I'm not scared of my old boss, and I'm not going to hide away just because he fired me."

"You sure you want to give him the business?" Holden asked.

Elise shrugged. "Just this once, to rub my happiness in his face. Besides, the tips go to the servers. They're still my friends."

Holden grinned. "Alright. Let's go, then."

The group made their way to the diner, and, as Elise had thought, all eyes turned in surprise when she entered with her new crew. Luckily, Hannah, one of her favorite former coworkers was on shift today. Hannah grinned when she saw Elise.

"Sit anywhere you like," Hannah said.

Ignoring the stares, Elise led the group to one of the large round tables in the restaurant's far right corner. She sat between Holden and Nick, but didn't bother picking up a menu. She already knew by heart what the menu said, and she already knew she was going to order the chilaquiles. While the others looked over the options, Elise looked around at the place, still hardly able to believe she didn't work here anymore. A smile played at her lips as Holden reached out underneath the table to put his hand on Elise's knee. Elise realized she was happier than she'd been in a long time. She was sitting between Holden and Nick, her two favorite people, and she was about to enjoy a good meal at a place where she no longer had to put up with the rude boss. A few minutes later, Hannah came by with the coffee pot.

"Coffee for everyone?" she asked. "Except for Nick, I suppose?"

Nick made a face in the direction of the coffeepot. "I'll take a lemonade, please," he said.

"I'll grab that for you in just a minute, hun," Hannah said as she started to fill the mugs on the table. She looked over at Elise and lowered her voice. "How are you doing, Elise? It was awful how the boss fired you. No good reason! What an asshole."

"I'm good," Elise said with a smile. "He did me a favor. I don't have to deal with him anymore."

"Have you found another job yet?" Hannah asked, keeping her voice low. "I wouldn't worry if you haven't. I overheard the boss saying that he was going to try to hire you back. He'll make it sound like he's trying to be nice and do you a favor, but the truth is everything's going to shit around here without you. You were the best employee here."

Elise smiled, feeling gratified to know her absence was being felt. Before she could answer, though, Holden put his arm around her and kissed the top of her head.

"As a matter of fact," Holden said. "Elise has found another job. She won't be needing to work for that asshole anymore."

Hannah's eyes widened as she seemed to truly notice Holden for the first time. "Are you with this hunk, Elise?" she asked.

Elise smiled. "Yes. And I'll be working with him and some of his friends from now on. It's kind of top secret, but trust me when I say that it's a good cause. You'll be seeing more of him and his crew around these parts. Make sure you're nice to them. They're good people."

Hannah smiled. "Anything for you, Elise. And good on you for finding a man. Sometimes I thought you were never gonna date again, but it looks like you were just waiting for someone spectacular. I'd say you found him."

"I'd say I have," Elise replied with a smile. Holden's arm around her tightened, and from the corner of her eye she caught Nick smiling up at her. She felt warm, loved, and optimistic about the future with her dragons.

And for once, she wasn't biting her lip from nervousness, but rather from happiness.

BOOK EIGHT: FURY AND THE DRAGON

CHAPTER ONE

Weston Pars flew through the night sky, the outline of his dragon body barely visible in the darkness. The scent of sulfur and ash filled his nostrils, traces of the stream of fire he had breathed out less than a minute before. The fire that had, maddeningly, missed its mark.

Weston did not dwell on his frustration, though. There was no time to feel sorry for himself right now. He had prey to catch, and he must not fail. He inhaled deeply, letting the cold night air fill his lungs and rinse away the remaining tinges of fire breath. He flapped his dark green dragon wings harder, willing himself to move even faster through the air. He was doing his best, but success was still far from guaranteed.

Catching a wizard was never an easy task.

Nevertheless, he tried. And somewhere to his left, he knew Violet was trying, too. In some ways, she stood a better chance than he did. She was a wizard herself, after all. She could fly through the air just as quickly as the escaping wizards in front of them. Her body, leaning low on her broomstick to encourage a more aerodynamic airflow, would fly a good bit faster than his larger dragon form. And yet, she needed him. She needed his dragon strength, and his dragon fire. If only she could catch the two fleeing wizards and hold them long enough for him to get to them, then he could bring them down. He could put an end to them, and to the worry that they would relay to enemy headquarters what they had seen.

Weston cursed himself for breathing out fire moments before. He should have known the fleeing wizards weren't quite in range of his fire, but he had been too eager, and made an attempt to burn them anyway. All he had managed to do was slow himself down, and give his enemies a small moment of reprieve. Those bastards had been lucky for that, and he swore he would not let them be so lucky again.

Ahead of him, to his right, he caught a small glimpse of light. Then another. He realized with a start that Violet was somehow on his right now. She had pulled quite a distance in front of him, and Weston's heart leapt with relief as he realized that she was on the verge of catching the escaping wizards. Less than a minute, he suspected, and she would be within shooting range. If she could land an attack spell or two on them, this pursuit would be all but over.

Weston couldn't keep a wry smile from curling up the edges of his dragon lips. Of course, Violet was going to give him hell later about the fact that *she* had been the one to actually catch the wizards. Never mind that Weston had been the one to originally discover the two spies, or to have the presence of mind to quickly breathe fire on their radios, effectively cutting off all their communication with enemy headquarters. Violet would take as much credit as she could for this victory. And, Weston would take as much as he could. He and Violet loved to tease each other, and to sigh and moan about having to pick up slack for the other, but the truth was that neither one of them could have accomplished all they had on their own.

They worked better together, and they were about to prove it once more.

Weston slowed his pace slightly as he saw another flash of light just ahead. Violet was definitely firing off attack spells now, which meant she had caught up to the wizards. He needed to come in slow enough that she could see him and avoid hitting him with a spell. Dragon hides were tough, and could withstand many wizard spells. But they did have weak spots, and the last thing he wanted was to be accidentally stunned or wounded by a spell coming from Violet herself.

"*Magicae appugno! Magicae appugno!*"

As Weston slowed his flight, and the rush of wind in his ears lessened, he could hear the sound of Violet's voice ringing across the sky. She was furiously throwing attack spells at the other two wizards, doing her best to keep them from flying away. They, in turn, were trying to throw spells back at her. She did her best to dodge their spells, and also put a great deal of her magical energy into a magic shield, to keep her safe. She wouldn't be able to keep this delicate dance up very long, Weston knew. That was where he came in.

He let out a long, loud roar, and then went charging toward the fray with smoke billowing from his nostrils. He saw one of the enemy wizards looking up at him with wide eyes, registering his presence with just enough time to yell out "*Magicae arma!*" to throw a magic shield in front of Weston.

Weston's long, streaming fire breath hit the shield a split second after it went up. The wizard screamed, and then shut his eyes tightly in concentration, trying to hold the shield in place against the deadly heat of Weston's sulfurous dragon fire. The shield did its job, but it required all of the wizard's energy, and Weston knew that no wizard could hold such a strong energy shield in place indefinitely. Weston paused for a beat, and then let out another long stream of fire. Meanwhile, Violet focused all of her attention on the other enemy wizard, who had momentarily tried to make a break for it. Out of the corner of his eye, Weston saw her shoot a stunning spell at the fleeing wizard, and then close in for fresh round of attack spells.

The next few minutes were a blur to Weston. The heat of battle always felt hazy and distorted to him. It was a strange sensation. On the one hand, he was one of the best soldiers in his clan. His fighting skills, especially in aerial combat, were unrivaled. And yet, he always felt like he was on autopilot when he fought. He felt like everything was happening too quickly for him to comprehend it all, like his eyes couldn't keep up with the action around him. Somehow, he still managed to be an exceptional warrior. He supposed it came from years and years of practice. His clan leaders had always placed emphasis on fighting drills in the sky. For many years, Weston had thought the practice drills were a waste of time. Now, he was grateful. The world had never been in such desperate need of strong dragons who fought for the side of good.

Weston could see through the smoky, sulfur haze that the enemy wizards were slowly losing energy. Their shields were getting weaker, and their counterattacks were all but nonexistent at this point. The relief Weston felt was palpable. The last thing he needed was these two wizards running off to tell enemy headquarters everything they'd seen. He only hoped that they hadn't already sent information back before being caught.

Weston breathed in deeply, preparing to launch another stream of fire in the direction of the enemy wizards, when Violet's voice stopped him in his tracks.

"No!" she screamed, followed almost immediately by "*Magicae oblitero*" at the top of her lungs. Confused, Weston pulled back slightly. Was she telling him to stop? Was she hurt? His eyes strained through the smoky darkness, but he could not see what the problem was. And then, moments later, two giant explosions rang across the sky. Right in front of Weston, the two wizards he'd been struggling to attack had exploded. Pieces of broomstick, clothing, and other things he didn't want to think about started falling through the air like tiny falling stars.

"No, no, no!" Violet screamed again, whirling around in circles on her own broomstick as she watched them fall. Weston watched her point her magic ring at the flaming mess hurtling toward the earth. She let out a string of magic spells in such an urgent, hurried tone that it almost sounded like she was cursing. But whatever spells she was trying to cast had no effect. The flaming remains of the enemy wizards continued to fall toward the earth, fluttering almost beautifully against the night sky.

After about half a minute, Violet seemed to realize that her spells were useless. She pointed her broomstick downward, and sped at full speed toward the earth. Weston let out a smoky sigh, and followed her, descending at a much slower pace. They had been quite high up in the sky, so it took him a few minutes to reach the sandy desert floor. He felt grainy coolness between his toes, and he marveled at how rapidly the ground here could go from blazing hot in the day to blessedly cool at night. Violet had dismounted from her broomstick, and was walking around frantically amidst the burning remains of the two wizards. She was kicking at the little piles of burning debris, as though looking for something important. Weston sat on his dragon haunches and waited, watching her with glowing green eyes. Whatever she was looking for, she was unlikely to find in this mess. He still wasn't sure what, exactly, had caused the huge explosion in the sky—he had quite a few wizard friends these days, and he'd never seen any of them cast a spell quite so dramatic—but it didn't take a genius to see that there was nothing left of the wizards now except a pile of embers.

Violet finally seemed to accept this fact. She gave one of the larger piles of burning debris a powerful, frustrated kick, then looked up at Weston in resignation.

"We might as well go home," she said. "Nothing left to see here. Although, I suppose I should clean up this mess just in case, so there really is nothing left to see. We're in the middle of the desert, so it's unlikely anyone will come by here. Still, better to be safe than sorry."

Violet raised her magic ring and pointed it at one of the smoldering piles. "*Magicae eradico,*" she said. "*Magicae eradico. Magicae eradico.*"

She moved methodically back and forth, casting the obliteration spell over and over as she walked. Everywhere her magic ring pointed, the piles of debris turned instantly to dust. Weston continued to sit back and watch her. He could not speak while in dragon form, but it didn't matter much. He didn't have anything to say right now. He had realized, as Violet started destroying the evidence of their foes, why she was so upset: the enemies had not just been killed, they had been completely and utterly destroyed, which meant there was no possibility that any intelligence could be recovered from their bodies. A golden opportunity had been lost to do a little spying of their own.

Weston let out another long dragon sigh. It was not the first golden opportunity that had been lost during this war, and it certainly would not be the last. He hated to see Violet so upset, but she would get over it soon enough. The important thing was that the enemy wizards had not made it back to their headquarters, and Weston and Violet were both safe and uninjured.

Weston watched as Violet continued her cleanup efforts. A bit of wind was rushing across the dark desert right now, whipping her silky chestnut hair around her face. He could only see her silhouette, but that was all he needed to see to make his heart beat faster. He knew that nothing was guaranteed in war, but still, he had to believe that Violet was going to make it through every battle they faced. Allowing himself to think anything else would have filled him with a paralyzing feeling of despair.

And so, while Violet waved her magic ring around, cursing and ranting and casting obliteration spells, Weston breathed a silent prayer of thanks to whatever gods might be out there. In that moment, nothing sounded more musical to him than Violet's voice, angry though it was. He could not—would not—allow himself to think that they might not be so lucky in the next battle.

CHAPTER TWO

Violet Sanwick bit her lip to hold back a groan of agony as she climbed the stairs to the second floor apartment she shared with Weston. She would never have dreamed of letting on in front of him how much she ached right now, but damn, did her muscles ache.

She wasn't a soldier, not by training. But the last year had forced a lot of people who weren't exactly soldiers to fight like they were. Violet had gone to university for several years to become a Wizard Advocate. Advocates worked mostly in offices, handling a variety of research tasks around magical laws and making recommendations on how to discipline wizards who had used these laws in an improper manner. Occasionally, Advocates would be sent out to the field to deal with situations where full humans had accidentally encountered a magical object or the use of magic. Sometimes, these cases might require a memory wiping spell, or subduing a spooked human. But that was about as wild as Violet's life had been for the first several years of her career.

That all changed when Saul entered the picture. Saul, the evil dragon who also had wizard powers and was threatening to destroy everything Violet held dear. Violet had never been a soldier, true. Nevertheless she had jumped at the chance to join the dragon shifters out in the field, on a mission to find and destroy Saul's headquarters. She hadn't realized, though, when she signed up for this gig, that it was possible to feel as exhausted and sore as she did right now.

She'd been given a crash course in fighting right before leaving her hometown of Falcon Cross, and she'd thought she had the basics pretty well under control. But tonight had shown her that she still had quite a lot to learn. Lesson number one: nothing made your ass quite as sore as broomstick flying under threat of mortal danger. Violet winced despite her determination not to, and she reached back to rub her sore tailbone. Luckily, Weston seemed to have missed her expression of pain. He was too busy fumbling in his pockets for the keys to their apartment.

As she watched him, Violet considered, not for the first time, how strange it was to share an apartment with him. She would have been thrilled at this arrangement under normal circumstances. She'd had her eye on this handsome dragon for quite some time. But lately, with everyone so on edge, she was beginning to wonder if perhaps it would have been better if she'd ended up sharing an apartment with one of the female soldiers. Or heck, even with one of the other male soldiers, whom she wasn't attracted to. She found it somewhat maddening to be constantly in the same apartment with this man, but always acting like there was nothing between them.

There was *something* between them, of that she was sure. But neither of them would acknowledge it right now. Things were too tense, with a war raging around them, to pay much attention to romantic feelings. And so, they went to sleep in their separate bedrooms each night, never acknowledging that the growing tension in the air wasn't entirely due to Saul's evil army.

Weston had found his keys and opened the door, and Violet hobbled in after him. She collapsed on the couch, and, even though she didn't allow any expression of pain to cross her face, Weston seemed to know that she was aching.

"Where does it hurt?" he asked.

"Everywhere," Violet said, her voice coming out with a strange groaning sort of sound. She leaned her head back against the couch cushions and closed her eyes, willing the spinning sensation that had filled her to go away. She heard Weston bustling around in the kitchen, and a minute later, she felt her body shifting slightly as his weight depressed the couch cushion next to her. She opened one eye to peek, and saw him sitting beside her holding up a large glass of orange juice.

"Drink this," he said. "It'll make you feel better."

Violet couldn't keep from grinning. "Juice will help? What am I, a five year old? I was hoping for something more along the lines of some painkillers or something."

Weston cracked a small smile, but pushed the glass of juice closer. "I'm serious," he said. "You were flying around like crazy, heart pumping and adrenaline going through the roof. It wouldn't hurt you to replenish your blood sugar a bit."

Violet gave him a skeptical look, but took the juice from him anyway. "Since when are you a doctor?" she asked.

He ignored the question and asked one of his own. "Since when do you know how to do explosion spells?"

He kept his voice light, but there was a note of accusation in it. Violet sighed, and took a few moments to quickly drain the juice glass before answering him.

"It wasn't me," she said. "I don't, in fact, know how to do an explosion spell. Not like the one those two wizards did. What you saw tonight, my friend, was a powerful display of dark magic."

Weston looked confused. "They made themselves explode? Was it a spell gone wrong, then?"

"Oh no," Violet said, shaking her head back and forth. "That spell went exactly as planned. Your confusion comes from the fact that you think it was an explosion spell. A better name for what you saw would be a self-destruction spell."

There were a few beats of silence, and then a horrified look of understanding crossed Weston's face. "They...they self-destructed? Like some sort of kamikaze pilot or something?"

Violet nodded wearily. "It's a dark magic spell. Saul must have trained all his wizard soldiers on how to use it, and instructed them to make sure they were never taken alive. He doesn't want to take a chance on us interrogating any of his soldiers and getting inside information, I suppose. Of course, when those two self-destructed it also destroyed any kind of intelligence devices they might have been carrying on them as well. Essentially, any clues they had as to why they were spying or what they were looking for were destroyed. That's why I was so angry. We kept them from reporting back to Saul, sure. But we lost a chance to get some good intel as well."

Weston furrowed his brow for a moment, considering. "I see your point. But don't be too upset. The most important thing we had to do tonight was make sure those spies didn't have a chance to report back to enemy headquarters, and we did that."

Violet gave him a long, sideways look. His face was streaked with black soot, evidence of the fire he'd been breathing out while in dragon form. His hair looked like it hadn't been combed in a month, and there were dark circles under his eyes. She knew he was tired, and that, in some senses, his words were true. The most important task of the evening had indeed been accomplished, and they should be grateful for that. This war had been brutal, and they had to take joy in the victories they had instead of dwelling on the fights they lost. But still, Violet felt frustration rising in her chest. She was tired of struggling. Tired of always feeling like she and her fellow soldiers were hanging on by a thread. Tired of being so damn tired all the time.

Weston reached over and gave her upper arm a reassuring squeeze. The pressure on her sore muscles sent a fresh wave of achiness through her body, but it also made her stomach do a bit of a fluttering somersault. He was so handsome, even in this exhausted state. Why, oh why, had she not had the chance to meet him when life wasn't so chaotic? And perhaps, more to the point, why should she care that life was chaotic? Wasn't the midst of the chaos the best time to find comfort in someone else's arms?

Violet felt her cheeks turning pink with the heat of embarrassment, as though Weston must somehow be able to read her thoughts and know what she was thinking. But if that was the case, he didn't show it. Instead, he stretched and let out a long, weary yawn before standing up. Violet felt herself shifting slightly again as his weight left the couch beside her. The shift left her with a strangely empty feeling in the pit of her stomach. She wanted to beg him to sit down again, to let them both enjoy the warmth of a friend's company for a few moments longer. But she said nothing. She set her lips in a stiff line as she looked up at him, wondering how it was possible for a mere mortal to look as divine as Weston did.

"Don't stress so much, V," he said. "If there's one thing you have to learn about being a soldier, it's that the battles never go exactly like you want them to, even when you win. You just have to keep moving forward and do the best you can. Go get some rest. Things will look better in the morning, I promise."

Violet grunted noncommittally in response. She wasn't sure how she was going to sleep tonight, with her thoughts whirling around in such confusion in her head. Weston gave her a gentle cuff on the shoulder as he passed, heading toward his bedroom.

"Seriously, you should get some rest. Tomorrow's gonna be a long day. You know that."

Violet grunted again. "Night, Weston," was all she said in response.

She heard him exhale in frustration or amusement, she wasn't quite sure which. "Night, Violet," he said. She heard his bedroom door click shut behind him, but she didn't make a move to get up and go to her own bedroom. She knew he was right, and that the morning would bring a long, tiring day full of frustrations of its own. But still, she sat on the couch for a long time, staring at the pile of papers littering the coffee table and trying to forget the image that kept playing over and over in her mind's eye— the image of two wizards exploding from the inside out due to the strength of evil forces within them.

She knew Weston thought that her anger was only at the loss of an enemy to interrogate. She'd played up that part of her frustration to mislead him, because she couldn't find the strength right now to talk about what was truly bothering her. She'd seen, while she was locked in a frenzied battle with the two wizards, a medallion around one of their necks, glittering brilliantly in the light cast by the flames Weston had been breathing. She'd recognized the insignia on the medallion, and it'd caused her heart to drop the instant she'd seen it. It was the symbol of the Pine Bluff wizard clan. Violet had gone to summer camp with some wizards from the Pine Bluff clan as a young girl, and had spent many happy July afternoons swimming with them in lakes after practicing broomstick flying in sweaty summer fields. All of the kids she had played with had seemed so wonderful. How could any of them have grown up to be soldiers in Saul's army?

Violet worried that this war was going to get worse before it got better. If it ever did get better, that was. Lately, things seemed to be spiraling out of control more with every passing day. Saul was growing his army and taking over strategic hideouts for his evil purposes, while the good wizards and shifters merely sat around debating all of their options until they were blue in the face.

Violet stood with another long sigh, finally mustering up the energy to head to her room and sleep. She knew what she had to do tomorrow, when the leadership of her army met and asked for a report. She had to make the case for moving forward with attacks, and quickly. She knew Weston was going to caution against making quick, foolhardy moves, and she hated to disagree with him. But she could not in good conscience sit there and say that moving slowly and cautiously was a good idea.

When Violet finally crawled into bed and closed her eyes, the agonizing scene of two wizards self-destructing in front of her would not stop replaying in her mind, over and over. She willed herself to fall asleep, but it was a long time before she finally drifted off into uneasy slumber. She didn't know when, if ever, she would be able to sleep peacefully again, but she knew one thing for certain: the days of playing it safe were over.

CHAPTER THREE

Weston stood with Violet on the outskirts of the tiny town of Blackstone, Nevada, watching the first rays of dawn creeping over the horizon. Next to them stood Holden, Weston's best friend and clanmate, and a fellow dragon shifter. The three of them were waiting to greet the incoming group of wizards and shifters, who had traveled here for a special summit to discuss the next steps in the war effort. Weston had tried to dissuade everyone from choosing Blackstone as the location for the summit, but he had been overruled. Despite his protests that the town was too close to Saul's hideout, and therefore not a safe place for a meeting of VIPs, Peter had set Blackstone as the summit's location.

Weston should not have been surprised. Peter, the head wizard of the Falcon Cross clan of wizards, was something of a rebel. He was an old man, but energetic and full of spunk. Weston knew the old wizard wanted to see for himself the location which the evil Saul had chosen as his headquarters. Knox, the dragon shifter who led Weston's crew, had been equally eager to come scope out the lay of the land. And so, Weston had been forced to accept the fact that a large group of shifters and wizards would be flying into Blackstone, risking the ruin of the one thing the side of good had going for them right now: the element of surprise.

To be honest, Weston wasn't sure how much longer their operations in Blackstone were going to remain secret, anyway. One didn't have to look very far to notice that Saul was growing restless. The number of guards around Saul's headquarters had increased, and the spies that Weston and Violet had caught last night had certainly been sent to Blackstone for a reason. It looked like Saul was worried.

As he should be, Weston thought with a puff of bitter pride in his chest. *He hasn't beaten us yet. We still have some fight left in us. We just have to figure out how to get the upper hand on him.*

Weston's musings were interrupted by a single, softly spoken word coming from Violet's lips.

"Incoming," she said.

Weston followed her gaze up to the sky, but all he could see was an unremarkable gray sky with a few streaks of pink.

"How do you know?" Weston asked.

"I cast a magic-revealing spell when we first came out here," she answered. "My magic ring is vibrating like crazy now, indicating that heavy use of magic is nearby. I'd bet my firstborn child that it's because of the invisibility spells Peter cast over the group. You'll be seeing them soon enough."

"You don't have a firstborn child," Weston said, rolling his eyes. Violet shrugged.

"I might have one someday. Stop being a dumbass and watch the sky."

Weston, for once, did as Violet suggested instead of trying to come up with another comeback. He trained his eyes on the sky above them, trying to see any sort of disturbance in the color pattern that might give away the fact that someone up there was using invisibility shields. He saw nothing, though. Peter could cast the best invisibility shield of any wizard alive, and whatever shield he was using was doing its job well. The sky looked completely normal.

Until it didn't.

A sharp, dramatic pop filled the air, and then, suddenly, the invisibility shield Peter had been using disappeared. In the sky almost directly above where Weston was standing, he could suddenly see the group Violet's magic ring had been able to see well before he had. They were flying too fast now for even Peter's invisibility shield to keep up.

Peter and Knox were in the center of the group. Knox was in dragon form, of course, so that he could fly. It had been a while since Weston had seen his clan leader, let alone seen him in dragon form, and, oh, was it a sight to behold. Knox's dragon was giant, his iridescent scales shimmering in the early morning sun as his powerful wings sliced through the air. His mighty tail swished behind him like a rudder, and Weston felt pride puffing up his chest once again. Weston was proud to be part of such a magnificent clan of dragons, and seeing his leader majestically flying through the air buoyed his morale.

Beside Knox's dragon, Peter the high wizard flew. Even from the ground, Weston could see Peter's long white beard, which was outlined sharply by his dark black robe. Peter might have been an old man, but he maneuvered his broomstick with ease. His athleticism matched that of any man half his age, and he had no trouble keeping up with Knox's dragon.

Around the two leaders, an entire squadron of wizard soldiers flew, keeping their broomsticks in a tight formation to protect Peter and Knox. Weston kept his eyes on the group as they zoomed closer to the earth and closer to the spot where he, Violet, and Holden were standing. Less than a minute after they had first appeared in the sky, the wizard soldiers, Peter, and Knox were coming to a rapid landing just a few yards from Weston. As soon as their feet touched the ground, the wizards all began dismounting from their broomsticks. Knox immediately began to shift back into human form, and one of the wizards was waiting close by to give him a fresh set of clothes to put on.

"So this is Blackstone," Peter said. "Looks like a sleepy little town from above."

"It is sleepy," Weston said. "That's probably why Saul hasn't bothered that much with it before now. He's too focused on his operations in nearby Sandview."

Knox had finished dressing now, and came over to give Weston and Holden each a big bear hug.

"Good to see you boys," Knox said, a wide grin spreading across his face. "I hope you've been staying out of trouble?"

"You hope for too much," Weston said with a grin. Knox laughed and shook his head.

"Fair enough. I should know better by now. So, you guys ready to get down to business and make some plans about how we're going to win this war?"

Weston nodded, but the grin faded off his face as he did. He glanced over at Violet, whose face was looking equally serious now. They both knew that today's meeting was going to be anything but fun. Weston was still blissfully unaware, however, of just how hard it was going to turn out to be.

* * *

Three hours later, Weston kept his eyes carefully glued on Peter's and Knox's faces as Holden finished a presentation on the war effort in Blackstone. But their expressions gave nothing away. It was anyone's guess what they were thinking.

Weston was sitting with the others in one of the bedrooms in a small house on the outskirts of town. The house had been rented to house some of the wizard soldiers sent to Blackstone. This bedroom had been turned into a makeshift conference room, and all of the junior soldiers had been sent away for the time being so that the senior officers could discuss the situation uninterrupted.

Holden had done an excellent job of presenting. The information had been thorough but to the point. Holden had shown all of the reconnaissance videos and photographs that Holden's stepson, Nick, had managed to get of Saul's headquarters. Thanks to Nick's efforts, they had a pretty good idea at this point of how Saul's lair was laid out. That knowledge was, of course, a huge help. But Weston was convinced that this insider information still wasn't enough to guarantee victory in a battle against Saul. The videos and photographs didn't just show the layout—they also showed how heavily guarded Saul's headquarters were. Hundreds of wizard and shifter guards patrolled the premises, and the number of guards seemed to have nearly doubled in the last week. Any fight against them would not be an easy fight, and would require very careful planning. Which was why, when Knox looked over at Weston with eyes full of questions, Weston slowly shook his head no.

"I know you all sent us a large group of soldiers so that we could attack Saul's headquarters and cripple his operations. But what we have here is not enough. We'd be risking certain defeat if we attack now. I'm not one to cower away from a fight, but I'm also not one to take foolhardy chances. Especially when those chances are being taken with the lives of soldiers under my command."

Knox and Peter both furrowed their brows, thinking. Neither one of them looked pleased, and Weston didn't blame them. Just over a week ago, Peter had sent a large group of wizard soldiers to Blackstone with the intention of attacking and damaging Saul's operations. Weston himself had come just before that group, and had also been hopeful about the possibility of attacking Saul. It had seemed, at first, straightforward enough. Now, things weren't so clear.

No one knew why, exactly, Saul had chosen Sandview as the location for his headquarters, but Weston could take a couple good guesses. The town was large enough to have a decent amount of supplies, but still relatively small and off the beaten path. Saul could easily control the population of the town—and any unlucky tourists who happened to travel through on their way to visiting one of Nevada's state or national parks. From the spying Nick had done, Weston knew that Saul was regularly torturing citizens of Sandview, trying to pressure them into joining his side in this evil war. Weston shuddered at the thought. Shifters and wizards tried to stay away from full humans for the most part, keeping them oblivious to the existence of shapeshifters and magic. Saul, however, liked to shock humans by letting them see shifters and wizards in action. He seemed to get some sort of cruel satisfaction from watching humans cower in fear.

Another reason Saul liked Sandview was the nearby caves. Saul was using these caves to house all his wizard and shifter soldiers, and to hide his bat cloning operations. Saul had figured out, like several evil leaders before him, how to rapidly clone bat shifters. He was cloning bat shifters as fast as he could, trying to raise an army that would overwhelm the size of any other army by sheer numbers. Weston knew that this bat cloning operation needed to be stopped, and soon. But he also knew that the number of soldiers they had in Blackstone right now was not enough to take on Saul at his headquarters.

Blackstone itself was a small town, much smaller even than Sandview. Holden and

Violet had been the first ones to arrive here on a scouting mission. They had come to see whether Saul had any guards in Blackstone, which he didn't. Saul seemed to think that Blackstone wasn't worth his time, but that was a grave mistake on his part. Blackstone was the perfect place for the good wizards and shifters to hide out, preparing for a surprise attack on Saul. And, unbeknownst to Saul, Blackstone was also connected to Sandview by a secret underground tunnel. If Weston and a group from Blackstone could sneak through that tunnel, they would have a good chance of surprising Saul. The problem was that, even with the element of surprise on their side, Saul's army at his headquarters was too strong. It was too risky to attack without bringing in at least three times the number of soldiers currently residing in Blackstone.

Weston took a deep breath, and started to stand. Peter and Knox hadn't asked for his opinion yet, but Weston didn't care. Before they wasted too much time thinking about other possibilities, he wanted to make sure they understood the trickiness of the situation, and the weak position of the shifters and wizards in Blackstone. But before Weston could fully get to his feet, Violet was standing. She wore a grave expression on her face, and she was pointing up at the map of Blackstone and Sandview that was on the large projector screen behind Holden.

"We need to move quickly," she said. "Saul is getting more suspicious by the day, and is sending spies out to Blackstone now. Weston and I took down two of them last night, in fact. Luckily, we were able to catch them before they sent any information back to Saul, but there will be more spies coming. Saul is going to realize that the spies he sent never came back, and he's going to know that this doesn't bode well for him."

For perhaps the first time since he'd met Violet, Weston was truly annoyed with her. How could she just stand up there and say they should attack, without consulting him first. True, he hadn't actually told her his thoughts on the matter, but he'd hinted at the need for a bigger army. She should have at least checked with him before telling everyone it was time to make a move. She was acting like she was in charge, and she wasn't. If anything, he had more say in military matters than she did. She wasn't even a real soldier, after all. She was an Advocate, and had only been trained as a soldier in a rush because Falcon Cross was so desperate to shore up its army.

Weston was glaring at Violet, but it wasn't having much of an effect on her because she was refusing to look in his direction. That told him all he needed to know.

She knew I wouldn't like this idea! he thought. *That's why she didn't tell me what she was going to say, and why she's not looking at me right now. Well, hell, two can play this game.*

Weston stood to his feet abruptly, before Peter and Knox had a chance to respond to Violet's suggestions.

"Actually, I think attacking Saul right now would pretty much be a suicide mission," he said. Out of the corner of his eye, he saw Violet whip her head around to look at him. No doubt, she was glaring now, but he wasn't going to give her the satisfaction of looking at her. In front of him, he did see Holden rolling his eyes. His friend knew Weston and Violet well enough to know how stubborn they could both be when they had their minds set on something. This was not going to end well.

Peter and Knox were looking at him expectantly now, so Weston took a deep breath and spoke his mind.

"Saul has been building up his army. You can see from the surveillance that's been done that the numbers are growing by the day. We don't have enough soldiers here to take on all of his guards, let alone to fight off all the bat shifters that he's cloning. If those bats have already been trained to fight, then we're screwed. I can't in good conscience sit here and recommend that we send our people in to certain death."

"It's not certain death!" Violet exclaimed. "I'll admit, it's dangerous, but waiting is also dangerous. We have to strike now while we still can. The longer we wait, the stronger Saul gets and the more likely we are to lose our surprise advantage. It's now or never, Weston. No matter when we attack we're going to lose soldiers. That's the way war works. It sucks, but no one joins the army thinking their life is perfectly safe."

Weston turned so that he was standing directly in front of Violet. She was tall, but he still towered over her. He looked down at her and put his hands on his hips. "Violet, you know I'm the first one to rush into battle. I love a good fight. But you're not asking for a good fight, you're asking to wipe out all of our forces here. There's no way it'll work."

She glared up at him, her hands on her hips as well. Her face was flushed red with fury, and her violet eyes, for which she'd been named, were blazing like a purple fire. And in that moment, despite the fact that he was more annoyed with her than he'd ever been before, he could not help but notice how beautiful she was.

She was always beautiful, but there was something about passion, about anger, that made her even lovelier than normal. Her skin glowed, and almost didn't seem human. Perhaps it was because she wasn't fully human. She was a wizard after all, magical. And perfect, despite her faults.

Weston felt his stomach flip-flopping with pleasure. His heart rate was rising, and a telltale stiffening began between his legs. He turned away from Violet quickly. He could not allow himself to be turned on by her. Not here, not now. Not in front of everyone like this. He hated to lose the little staring contest he'd just started with her, but it was either that or risk a full blown erection. She was fired up, and she was hot.

Weston turned his attention back toward Peter and Knox, desperately trying to regain control of his emotions and think of words to say that would convince them that his view of the situation was the right one. Violet had the same idea, and they both started talking at once. But it didn't matter much what they were saying, because in that moment another voice suddenly joined the noise in the room. The door flew open and Nick stormed into the room, breathless and pale faced.

"Guys, we have a problem!" he said, and all eyes in the room turned to him.

CHAPTER FOUR

Violet's face felt hot, and she could feel beads of sweat starting to form on her forehead. She wasn't sure if her heart was beating so fast because of anger, or fear—or perhaps a mixture of both—but Nick's news had left her more convinced than ever that they needed to attack Saul, and quickly.

Weston, however, remained maddeningly unconvinced. "We don't have any solid information," he said. "We still need to use caution."

Violet gaped at him. "No solid information?" she asked. "Did you not hear anything Nick just said? We need to move, now!"

Nick, for his part, shifted uncomfortably from one foot to another as he looked back and forth between Violet and Weston. The boy was a dragon shifter, and was damn good at sneaking around thanks to the ability to completely mask his scent. But he was still a boy, and he didn't seem to know how to handle the fact that the two adults standing in front of him were on the verge of a full blown argument.

"I…I think the information is pretty solid, actually," Nick said timidly. Weston glared at him and he shrank back, but Violet looked around the room with a victorious expression on her face.

"You see?" she said. "Nick is sure of what he saw, and I can't imagine anyone denying that we're running out of time after hearing his report."

Unfortunately, Peter and Knox seemed less convinced than Violet that Nick's report necessitated an immediate offensive against Saul.

"Weston, Violet, sit down in your damn chairs!" Knox said. "I can't think over your noisy squabbling."

The tone in Knox's voice left no room for argument. Reluctantly, Violet sat down, but she made sure to shoot daggers at Weston with her eyes as she did. He glared right back, and she realized with a start how handsome he looked right now. His mouth was set in a firm line, accentuating his chiseled face and the hint of stubble that was visible on his cheek. Usually, he kept up a clean shaven look, but with last night's adventure and today's early wake up call, he'd let shaving slide for the day. Violet rather liked the stubble. It made him look even more masculine than he already did, which was saying something because he always looked like a man's man. It was hard not to, with a body as tall and muscular as his. Violet looked away quickly, frustrated with herself for thinking such vain thoughts. She was supposed to be angry with him right now, not pondering what a sexy body he had. Thankfully, Knox was speaking again, giving her something else to think about.

"Nick, slow down and start over. I had a hard time understanding you over your panting and Weston and Violet's interruptions."

Violet winced internally. Knox was pissed off at her and Weston, but what was she supposed to do? Sit there and let Weston make light of everything Nick had just said? The situation was anything but trivial.

Nick, still looking uncertain, took a long shuddering breath before starting to speak again. "I was doing some more surveillance this morning. Just very basic stuff, mind you. My mom doesn't want me to get too close to any of Saul's guards, and lately the guards seem to be multiplying like rabbits. I was actually pretty far away from the main area of headquarters, and didn't expect to see much of anything. Which is why I was so surprised when two shifters suddenly came around the corner. I had to scramble like mad to get out of the way. In fact, I'm lucky they were so deep in conversation. If they hadn't been so distracted, they probably would have seen me."

"Nick, you need to pay better attention," Holden said, interrupting. "You're mom will kill me if someone from Saul's army catches you running around out there."

Violet saw Nick's face turn even paler. He nodded at Holden, looking remorseful. Holden had started dating Nick's mother not long after Nick first discovered that he was a dragon shifter. Nick's mother was a full human, and had been relatively calm at the sudden discovery that shifters and wizards existed. The woman was still, however, quite overprotective of her son. Not that Violet blamed her. It was a dangerous world out there right now, with Saul's army growing by the day. If Violet had a son she probably would have wanted to keep him locked up safe at home, too.

"Anyway," Nick said, turning his gaze back toward Peter and Knox. "I hid out of sight and eavesdropped on what they were saying, and it doesn't sound like it's good for us. They were talking about how two wizard spies have gone missing, and Saul is really angry about it. Saul is suspicious that there might be Falcon Cross wizards around, and, of course, he's right. The guards I was listening to didn't seem to know exactly what Saul was planning, but it sounded like he was going to try to launch some sort of attack on Blackstone. Maybe he's going to try to send more spies and find us or something. I don't know. But it sounds like we aren't going to be able to keep ourselves secret from him for very much longer."

Violet was tempted to stand up again and start ranting about how the situation was urgent, but she forced herself to stay in her seat. She could tell by the expressions on Peter's and Knox's faces that the two men were not in the mood for any more dramatic arguments right now. Peter was stroking his long beard thoughtfully, as he always did when he wasn't quite sure what course of action to take. Knox was staring up at the map on the projector screen, as though the answer might suddenly appear there. And Weston was glaring at both of them with his arms crossed over his chest, looking admittedly quite handsome. Violet couldn't decide whether she wanted to yell at him or kiss him right now. Quickly, she looked away and stared at the map on the screen, just as Knox had been doing.

"I think Knox and I need to discuss things in private," Peter finally said. "Why don't you all take a break? Grab some food and stretch your legs, and meet back in this room in an hour."

Violet let out a small sigh, and started to stand. She wanted to scream at Peter and Knox that there was nothing to discuss. Saul was probably already putting a plan of attack in place, and the longer everyone sat around discussing things the more likely it was that he was going to strike first. But Violet had already said her piece, and she knew better than to try to push Peter and Knox too far. Acting hysterical would only make them more likely to listen to Weston instead of to her.

Violet did her best to avoid eye contact with Weston as she left the room. She rushed quickly through the main area of the house and toward the front door, intending to go as far away from here as she dared during their hour break. But she'd barely made it outside before she felt a strong hand on her upper arm.

"Violet, wait."

She tried to wriggle free from Weston's grip, but he held her firmly. Finally, she gave up and turned to face him.

"Let me go," she demanded, her eyes flashing.

"I will in a second, but first, listen to me," he said.

Violet narrowed her eyes at him. "I don't have to listen to you," she said. "You're wrong. I know you think you're protecting everyone by moving slowly, but you're wrong."

"Violet, we can't rush into things. These are people's lives we're talking about."

"I know!" Violet hissed. "You think I don't realize that we're talking about people's lives? That's exactly why we have to move quickly. If we don't, people are going to die because of it."

"Violet," Weston said again. But he stopped before saying anything else. His eyes widened, and then he was grabbing her even firmer than before, pushing her back toward the house.

"Weston, what in the world? Let go of me!"

"Get in the house, V! Get in there and tell Peter and Knox that we've got trouble!"

Confused, Violet turned to look behind her, following Weston's gaze. Her heart sank all the way to her toes when she saw what had troubled him. A giant black cloud was heading rapidly toward Blackstone. But the cloud wasn't your normal cloud. It was alive, and full of hundreds of flapping wings.

"Bats!" Violet yelped.

"Stop staring and go warn Peter and Knox!" Weston yelled. His voice snapped Violet into action. She turned back toward the front door of the house and started running. But before she could reach the front door, she was stopped by Weston's grip once more. She turned, eyes wide and questioning to see what he could possibly want now.

As she turned, he pulled her close against him into a strong, warm embrace. He kissed the top of her head, and then, with a voice muffled by her thick hair, he spoke words that sent a rush of heat through her whole being.

"No matter what happens, V, I love you. Don't ever forget that, okay?"

And then, he released her and started running across the front yard of the house. His clothes were already tearing to shreds as he ran, thanks to the fact that he was shifting into dragon form. Violet knew she needed to run inside to alert the others, but it took her a few seconds to tear her eyes away from Weston. She hoped with everything in her that this would not be the last time she ever saw him alive, but the dark cloud in the sky was growing ever closer, and things did not look promising.

Why did you wait until death was imminent to finally tell me you love me? she thought, tears pricking at her eyelids. She didn't have the luxury of indulging in a good cry right now, though. The attack she'd feared was now coming even sooner than she herself had predicted. She took one last, longing look at Weston's dragon, and then ran into the house.

CHAPTER FIVE

Weston could hardly tell which way was up or down anymore. He was completely surrounded by enemy bats, making the air around him so black that it might as well have been night. He'd lost count of how many battles he'd been in over the course of this war, but this one was by far the worst. He was beginning to fear that it might be his last. Occasionally, he would see an enemy wizard darting in and out of the sea of bats, shooting off attack spells with gusto. He guessed that they were attacking some of his fellow soldiers, although he couldn't see any familiar faces through the thickness of the bats. His heart was pumping hard with adrenaline, and he tried to focus all of his energy on attacking the bats around him. He tried not to think about Violet. Whenever her face appeared in his mind's eye, it filled him with a deep sense of worry. He could fight battles all day long and not fear for himself, but just the thought of losing Violet made it hard to breathe.

Weston darted in and out of the bats, breathing fire in every direction, taking down dozens of bats with each breath. He must have killed hundreds of the pesky bat shifters by now, but they still kept coming. They weren't very strong, and, on their own they almost wouldn't have been worth the effort to kill. But together, the multitudes of bats were overwhelming. Weston was beginning to feel as though he could hardly breathe. He kept fighting though, doing his best to hold them at bay and to keep his mind off of Violet.

He felt a deep sense of remorse when he realized how right Violet had been. She'd seen this coming, but he'd been too blind to acknowledge the writing on the wall. His heart had been in the right place. He'd merely wanted to keep his soldiers out of a battle that promised to be a massacre. But they were involved in a massacre now whether they wanted to be or not. Weston could only hope that Violet had warned everyone with enough time for them to not be taken completely by surprise.

As soon as Weston had seen the bats heading toward Blackstone, he'd shifted into dragon form and launched himself into the sky with a giant roar. He'd wanted to draw the army away from the city as best he could, so he'd been loud and obvious and obnoxious. He'd thought that this move was likely to result in his death, but he hadn't hesitated. He'd wanted to give his soldiers every chance to rally, and he'd wanted to keep the unsuspecting human citizens of Blackstone from getting caught in a wizard-shifter battle. He had no idea at the moment whether either goal had actually been accomplished, but he was pleasantly surprised to find himself still very much alive.

The bats had turned out to be easier to handle than he'd thought. At first, he'd been heartened by how quickly they fell from the sky. Now, however, he was starting to tire. Even the weak bats were soon going to be too much to handle. He could only hold off a sea of them for so long.

Weston told himself not to dwell on the morbid possibility of his own death. All he could do right now was to continue to fight and hope for the best. He continued to flap his wings with as much energy as he could muster, breathing stream after stream of fire into the air and thinking that, at the very least, each bat he took down was one less bat that his fellow soldiers would have to fight.

He continued this way for what felt like hours, telling himself to just continue on fighting the next bat and the next. In reality, it was probably only fifteen minutes of fighting like this, but time in the middle of a battle doesn't feel like normal time. Weston did the best he could on his own, and then, suddenly, he wasn't on his own any longer.

He heard them before he saw them. The dull drone of flapping bat wings was suddenly punctuated by the sharp hissing of magic attacks coming from wizard rings. For a moment, Weston worried that enemy wizards had found him. He knew he was too weak at this point to hold up very long against the attacks of dark wizards. Dark magic spells were significantly harder to deflect than weak bat bites. But before his heart could sink too much, he caught a glimpse of a familiar face to his right. One of the Falcon Cross wizards had flown up right beside him on her broomstick, and was sweeping her magic ring left and right with gusto, bringing down bats with every swipe of her hand.

After another few seconds had passed, Weston suddenly found himself completely surrounded by Falcon Cross wizards. A group of them had found him, and had flown into a circle formation around him, protecting him on all sides. The sight of his fellow soldiers, alive and well, gave him fresh hope and a fresh burst of energy. He let out a roar, and began attacking with renewed determination. The bats still came in thick droves, but he was no longer alone, and that made all the difference. And then, another very familiar face flew up beside him, and he felt his heart leap with relief.

Violet.

She was swerving left and right as she hovered in mid air, expertly avoiding the flurry of bats that tried to attack her. She maneuvered herself right up next to him, and gave him an encouraging smile. Weston thought his heart was going to melt right in his chest when he saw that smile. He didn't know how she felt about the fact that he'd said he loved her. He didn't know whether she was going to be raging mad at him later for trying to keep the Falcon Cross soldiers from fighting. But he did know one thing: right then, in that moment, they were one. They were together, on the same team, and fighting the same enemy. He'd worry later about the fallout from their argument. Now, they fought together. They'd always been an amazing team in the sky, and today would be no different.

Violet caught his eye, and nodded at his back. She wanted to ride his dragon, so that she could focus fully on attacking spells rather than on flying. He nodded his dragon head in agreement. He was only too happy to oblige her. She flew right over him and landed deftly on his back. He felt her set her broomstick down and attach it to his back with a sticking spell, and then, she was up on her knees on his back, ready to fight.

"*Magicae arma,*" she yelled into the chaos. Instantly a protective shield formed around both of them. Suddenly, the bats that had been constantly running up against Weston weren't able to reach him. The constant barrage of bites on his dragon hide stopped almost instantly, a welcome relief. The bat's teeth couldn't get through his thick dragon skin, but the relentless pricking, poking, and prodding had been driving him crazy.

With the protection of the shield around him, he was finally able to get his bearings. He could see that he was several miles away from Blackstone at this point. Whether or not the townspeople had noticed that there was a giant cloud of bats, dragons, and wizards in the distance was anyone's guess, but at least they weren't right in the heart of the city. Weston continued to fly away from Blackstone, hoping to at least lessen the chances of anyone in Blackstone seeing what was happening and freaking out.

Weston could hear Violet on his back, yelling out attack spells. He could see the slashing laser light from her ring swiping left and right across the sky, felling dozens of bats with each swoop. He breathed in deeply to breathe out fire, once again adding his own fury to the fight. The Falcon Cross wizards circling around him were taking down scores of bats as well, and Weston almost thought that the thickness of the bat cloud was starting to diminish. He felt his heart once again buoyed by hope, and he attacked with fresh energy.

A few minutes later, he was sure of it: the bats were definitely starting to lessen. Now, he could see a bit into the distance. A little ways off he saw Holden's dragon, also surrounded by Falcon Cross wizard soldiers. On his other side, he could see Knox's dragon, careening through the air like a fiery streak, leaving a trail of dead, falling bats behind him. And beyond Knox, was Peter, riding on his broomstick just as quickly as the younger wizards, launching attack after attack. Most of the Falcon Cross wizards were surrounding Peter, protecting him, but Weston knew that was probably due to everyone else's insistence rather than Peter's request. The old wizard had no concept of how old he was, or that he was supposed to be slowing down. He seemed to have missed the memo that old age required him to act like an old man, and he looked like he was almost having fun as he weaved in and out of the bats and enemy wizards, swiping his ring back and forth across the sky to hit the enemy where it hurt.

As the last of the bats began to die off, Weston and his fellow soldiers faced a new challenge. The enemy wizards, who had been, until now, just as blinded by the bats as everyone else, could see much better now. They began closing in on Weston and the others, ready to attack. Weston gritted his giant dragon teeth and flew forward to meet them at full speed. He was not in the mood to watch any of his soldiers die. He was going to fight his heart out to defend them, even if it cost him his own life. He knew Violet would feel the same way, a belief confirmed by the whoop of excitement he heard her let out as he picked up speed. Weston would have smiled, if not for the fact that he was flying too fast to really bother with details like that. He felt heartened knowing that Violet was with him in this fight, however it went. On the one hand, he hated to fly toward danger while she was with him. But, on the other hand, he knew that Violet would force herself into the heart of the battle whether anyone wanted her there or not. At least if she was with him, he could help protect her.

It turned out that she didn't need his protection all that much. She was in fine fighting form today, holding her magic shield steady while also shooting out attack after attack. She was taking down more enemy wizards than the rest of the Falcon Cross soldiers combined, and Weston felt pride as he watched her, even though he hadn't been the one to train her. Somehow, he'd come to think of Violet as 'his girl' in the last half hour, and he was proud to see her doing so well in battle.

Weston no longer felt stressed by the battle, or even afraid. He was easily handling all of the attacks that were being thrown at him, and the enemy forces were dwindling rapidly. To his left and right, he could see his fellow wizard soldiers and dragons as they fought. Somehow, miraculously, he had survived. They were going to come out of this battle victorious. This knowledge gave him yet another fresh burst of energy, and Violet must have felt similarly, because he heard her whooping again.

Then, almost as suddenly as the battle had begun, it was ending. Someone in the enemy army must have given a signal to retreat. Within seconds, all of the enemy wizards and the remaining bats were turning around as quickly as they could to fly back to Sandview. For a few minutes, Weston and his fellow soldiers chased them down. Eventually, though, Peter gave the signal to fall back. The battle was done, at least for the moment.

On his back, Weston heard Violet ending the sticking spell on her broomstick so she could pick it up once again. She climbed back on and then flew off his back, zooming in front of him to give him a quick wink before zooming off at full speed toward Blackstone.

Weston felt a thrill of pleasure in his chest at the sight of her, but he wasn't going to let himself get too excited yet. He might have finally confessed his love to her, but he wasn't sure whether she was going to admit to having similar feelings.

No matter, he thought as he started flying after her. If he had to convince her, then he would. He had always loved the thrill of the chase.

CHAPTER SIX

Violet was once again sore, dirty, and exhausted. But she was happy, and she was safe. The battle today had been tough, but it had been well-fought by all the Falcon Cross soldiers. The Redwood Dragons had done well, too, especially Weston. As much as she loved to tease Weston, making wisecracks about how he didn't know what he was doing, she had to admit that the boy knew how to fight.

There would be no admitting anything to his face tonight, though. Violet felt smug as she and Weston made their way up the stairs to their shared apartment. It was nearly midnight, and she knew they both needed rest. But she also knew she wouldn't be able to go to bed without at least a few words of "I told you so" aimed in Weston's direction. Rarely had she had the luck of such a clear cut case of being right when he was wrong, and she wasn't going to squander the moment.

To her dismay, though, Weston beat her to the punch line.

"I know, I know," he said, before the front door of the apartment was even fully shut behind them. "You called it. A battle with Saul's army and his stupid bats was inevitable. I'm sorry. You were right."

Violet felt a bit deflated. It wasn't as fun to be right when he was readily admitting to it before she could even say anything. Still, she was determined to enjoy the moment.

"I guess I'm a better soldier than you thought," she said, putting her hands on her hips.

Weston collapsed onto the couch and grinned up at her. "I never said you were a bad soldier," he said, then patted the seat next to him to indicate that Violet should sit down next to him. Reluctantly, she did.

"You didn't trust my judgment," Violet said, her voice slightly huffy.

Weston gave her a sideways glance and a maddeningly playful smile.

"Don't make fun of me!" Violet said. "This is supposed to be my chance to rub in your face the fact that you were wrong."

Weston kept smiling. "I was wrong. Once. Don't get used to it."

Violet rolled her eyes, and opened her mouth to make another dig at him. But before she could say anything, she was surprised to find his lips on hers. Her eyes flew to his face, and she pulled back in surprise. Weston raised an eyebrow at her.

"What?" he said. "You don't want a victory kiss?"

Violet's face felt hot. She was sure that her cheeks must be turning red, although she wasn't sure if she was feeling anger or embarrassment. "You're supposed to be groveling about how wrong you were! Not kissing me!"

Weston threw back his head and laughed. "Dragons don't grovel," he said.

"But..." Violet was at a loss for words. She wasn't sure how she had expected Weston to react, but she hadn't expected a kiss and laughter, almost as though he was making fun of her.

"What?" Weston asked, leaning in toward her again and then repeating his question. "You don't want a victory kiss?"

Violet blinked, confused. *Did* she want a victory kiss? She looked at Weston, who sat looking back at her, patiently waiting for a reply.

This day had been strange, to say the least. Weston had gone from angry at her in the meeting room, to confessing his love for her before battle, to fighting alongside her in the air, to now kissing her instead of letting her rub in the fact that she was right. Part of Violet wanted nothing more than to give in and kiss Weston, and part of her screamed that this wasn't the right time for romance. Sure, they had won the battle today, but the war raged on. And Saul was going to be angry about his losses today. He was going to regroup and attack again as soon as he was able. Whether that was tomorrow or a week from now or a month from now was anyone's guess. It seemed irresponsible to think about a future with a man when the future of the rest of the world hung so precariously in the balance. As much as it pained Violet to do it, she shook her head now and scooted away from Weston.

"I think we should save victory kisses for when we actually win the war. We've got a long ways to go still."

Weston's face fell. "Violet, I know I'm not always the best at showing it, but I really do care about you. When I told you today that I love you, I meant it. I honestly thought there was a good chance I was going to die today, and I didn't want to go to my grave without telling you how I feel about you. I thought I was going to go out into the heart of Saul's army and sacrifice my life to this war effort, and I wanted my last words to you to leave you with the knowledge that you mattered so much to me. But since I did survive, I feel as though I've been given a second chance at life. I want to spend that life with you, and I don't want to wait until this war is over to do that. It might be a long time before we see a final victory. Should we really be expected to put our entire lives on hold indefinitely? I mean, look at my clan. Over half of my clanmates have already found love during this war. Why can't we as well?"

Violet felt her heart wavering, and she knew she had to get away from Weston before she made a rash decision. Quickly, she stood to her feet, shaking her head.

"I'm sorry, Weston. I do care about you, but I can't fall in love right now."

Then, before he could say anything more to change her mind, she rushed toward her bedroom and closed the door behind her. The last thing she saw before blocking out the light of the living room was the expression on Weston's face. He looked shocked, and almost grief-stricken. It took all of her resolve not to rush back out there and rush into his arms. She leaned against the closed door instead, closing her eyes and cursing under her breath. She realized that she had just given up a chance to kiss Weston. She'd been wishing for the chance to be with him for almost as long as she'd known him, so why had she run in the other direction when he finally made a move?

She could tell herself until she was blue in the face that it was because it was better to wait until the war was over, when they had time to focus on things like love. But was that true? Or was it, perhaps, that she was so afraid of losing Weston in the war that she thought it was better not to acknowledge how much she cared for him?

Violet wasn't sure how to sort out her feelings, and so she pushed them all away. She did her best not think about Weston at all while she took a quick shower and got ready for bed. Of course, it wasn't an easy task, when every other thought that popped into her head seemed to involve him in some form or fashion. To keep her mind busy, she mentally ran through all of the information she had seen Holden present at the meeting today. She thought about the surveillance pictures and videos, and wondered how many bat shifters Saul had left after the battle today. They had killed so many, but the one thing no surveillance video had been able to show them was how many bat shifters there were, or how quickly, exactly, Saul was cloning new bats. This information could make a big difference in how long it would take Saul to regroup and attack again, but Violet couldn't see any realistic way to find it out. Finally, she gave up trying and let sleep take over her mind. She managed to fall asleep without pining too badly for Weston, although memories of riding on his dragon back kept pushing their way to the front of her thoughts. They made a good team in battle. Surely, romance would ruin that. Romance always complicated things, didn't it? That's what Violet's girlfriends always said. It had been so long since Violet had a serious boyfriend, though, that she herself had precious little experience with romantic complications.

When Violet did finally drift off to sleep, her mind betrayed her with strange dreams revolving around kissing Weston in the middle of battle. She tossed and turned, fretting and worrying as the troubles she'd tried to bury in her subconscious bubbled to the surface. At one point, she dreamed that Weston was in her room, shaking her and trying to get her attention. She tried to push him away, but the dream persisted. Violet tossed and turned, trying to drown out the sound of Weston's voice, but the more she turned away from him the more the voice persisted. Suddenly, she woke with a start and realized that it hadn't been a dream. Weston was actually standing there in her room, shaking her shoulders. Instantly, Violet sat upright.

"Weston! What in the world are you doing? What's wrong?" As the haze of sleep started to fade away, Violet felt fear gripping her heart. Had something terrible happened? Why was Weston insisting on waking her in the dead of night?

"I couldn't sleep," he said, his green dragon eyes glowing slightly in the darkness.

Violet's heartbeat slowly started returning to normal, and she blinked at him in annoyed disbelief. "Are you kidding me? You came in here to shake me awake in a frenzy just to tell me that you couldn't sleep?"

Weston sat down on the foot of Violet's bed, and, even in the darkness, she could see him running his fingers through his hair. He was bouncing his leg up and down rapidly as well, causing Violet's bed to shake slightly from the movement. It didn't take a genius to see that he was agitated. Violet sat up on her elbow and squinted at him in the darkness.

"What's wrong?" she asked.

"I think we should go to Saul's headquarters and destroy his bat cloning operations."

Violet flopped back down onto the bed and stared up at the blackness of the ceiling. "Really, Weston? You came in here and woke me up just to tell me that, like it's some sort of giant news flash? Doesn't everyone in our army think that? I mean, it's not like anyone is arguing to just let Saul keep his little bat cloning project."

"I know that," Weston said, sounding defensive. "I'm not just saying we should stop Saul's bat cloning in general. I'm saying we should go stop it right now."

Violet sat up on her elbow again. "Right now? As in, right now, in the middle of the night."

"Yes."

"Are you out of your mind?"

"Possibly."

Violet considered, slowly chewing her bottom lip. What Weston was suggesting sounded like a suicide mission, but she knew that he wasn't the type of man to run blindly to his death. He was brave, but not foolhardy. So if he was suggesting they rush into enemy territory in the middle of the night without any preplanning, then there must be a reason for it.

"Why now?" Violet asked.

Weston took a deep, shuddering breath, as though somewhat unsure of himself. Not a promising sign. But when he did finally speak, his voice did not waver.

"Saul knows now that we're here, which almost certainly means that he knows about our bat cloning operations. After today's battle, he is going to be focusing a lot of energy on boosting his guard around his headquarters in Sandview."

"Uh-huh," Violet agreed. No surprises there.

"But, as far as we know, today was the first time Saul realized how large and real the threat of our army is. Think about it. He wouldn't have sent his bats and wizards to attack today if he'd thought they were going to be defeated as soundly as they were. He underestimated us."

"Right," Violet said, still unsure of what point Weston was trying to make here. Everything he was saying seemed to be pretty much just stating the obvious.

"I'd say that Saul is as vulnerable right now as he'll ever be," Weston said. "His army took a huge hit that he wasn't expecting, and he's had less than twenty-four hours to figure out how he's going to deal with the loss of soldiers he suffered today. He hasn't had time to call in any reinforcements from his other far-off bases. And…"

Weston paused, as though he almost didn't want to say out loud what he was about to say. But Violet was tired and groggy and the suspense was getting on her nerves.

"And what?" she demanded.

"And, while he scrambles to figure out how to defend his headquarters, he's going to be preparing for an attack by a large army."

Violet blinked a few times in the darkness, trying to understand what Weston was getting at.

"So?"

"So, he's watching the sky for a big, dramatic invasion. The last thing he's expecting is for two lone soldiers to come sneaking quietly into his lair with no backup."

In an instant, everything Weston was suggesting became clear to Violet. Perhaps they had lost their overarching element of surprise, since Saul now knew that there was a small army of good shifters and wizards in Blackstone. But that didn't mean they couldn't still throw a few surprises Saul's way. If they acted in unexpected ways, they might still be able to gain some victories while Saul was trying to catch his breath from today's battle.

"What, exactly, are you suggesting we do?" Violet asked.

"We go to Saul's headquarters, using the underground tunnel. As far as we know, he's still unaware that the tunnel exists, so we should be able to get pretty close before he realizes we're coming. We'll have to use a masking scent so their shifter guards don't smell us approaching from a mile away. How effective that will be depends on how well trained his shifters are in detecting masking scents."

"Hopefully not very well," Violet said, sitting up straighter. Her heart was starting to pound with a mixture of fear and excitement. This mission sounded dangerous, but thrilling.

"Hopefully not, but we can't be too sure," Weston said. "All we can do is be as careful as possible and keep our fingers crossed for good luck. Once we get to enemy headquarters, we'll sneak in under the cover of an invisibility spell and head to the bat cave. Thanks to Nick's surveillance videos, we know exactly where it is."

"And once we find it, how do we destroy it?" Violet asked.

Weston shrugged. "Lots of dragon fire? Wizard laser beams? I'm sure we'll figure out something."

Violet shook her head, half in amusement and half in incredulity. "You're crazy."

"Maybe," Weston said. "But my crazy plan actually has a good chance of working. I'm told that bat cloning is dependent on having one master bat. The master bat is a genetically engineered bat that takes a bit of time and expertise to make. But once that master bat is made, you can clone rapidly from it. The catch is that the bat clones have to stay near the master bat for the first twenty-four hours of their lives, drawing on her energy, or they'll die. So the master bat is vital to any bat cloning operation."

"This all sounds pretty farfetched to me," Violet said, frowning.

Weston laughed at her. "Says the girl who does magic. Cloning is all based in science, you know. It has perfectly logical explanations, whereas this hocus pocus magic stuff you do does not. It's just weird shit."

Violet grinned sheepishly. "Fair enough, I guess. So your plan, I'm assuming, is to destroy the master bat."

Weston nodded. "If we can do that, Saul's bat cloning operation will come to a grinding halt. It will take quite some time and energy for him to get another master bat. Even if he does decide to try again, we'll have a period of time we're he'll be unprotected by his obnoxious little bat army."

Violet considered all of this. "I get what you're saying about now being a good time to catch Saul off-guard. But even so, this is still going to be really dangerous."

"I know," Weston said. "But it's a calculated risk. There's a good chance we'll be killed, but there's an equally good chance we'll pull it off."

"Have you told Knox and Peter about this plan?" Violet asked, even though she was pretty sure she already knew the answer.

"Um…" Weston said. Violet rolled her eyes. He had not.

"You know they're going to be furious with us if we go without telling anyone and get ourselves killed."

"So what? If we destroy the bats they will be happy enough that they'll get over being angry pretty quickly. And if we're dead then who really cares if they're angry at us."

Violet sighed. "You're out of your mind."

"I know," Weston said. "So what do you say? Are you coming with me?"

Violet peered at him through the darkness. She could only see his outline, but she didn't need to be able to see his face to know that it had a hopeful, mischievous expression on it right now. She took a deep breath, trying to figure out what the right thing to do here was. She knew that what Weston was suggesting was risky, but she also knew he wouldn't ask her to go if he didn't think she was up to the task.

She was still feeling badly about the way things between them had gone yesterday. She knew they had both just been standing up for the course of action that they each believed in, but she still didn't like the strain that had filled the air between them since yesterday. Perhaps this secret mission was a good way for them to get back on the same page. They worked well together in the heat of battle, and this had the potential to be their greatest battle yet—a secret battle, intended to take down those horrid bats that Saul seemed so intent on using in his disgusting, evil war.

Besides, Violet could not deny the way her heart beat faster whenever Weston was around. Even when she was angry with him, she couldn't hold back the desire to be with him. It was almost as if they were magnets, drawn toward each other. There was some sort of weird connection between them, a pull that Violet could not escape. She craved the sound of his voice, the casual touch of his hand on her skin, and the sight of his handsome face crinkling up in a smile. If he was going to face danger, she wanted to go with him. Perhaps she was a fool to agree to run straight into enemy territory, but if Weston was going, she sure as hell was going with him. In her heart, she knew that they could do anything together.

"Alright," Violet said, before she could change her mind. "I'll go."

Weston let out a whoop. "Yes!" he said. "I knew you wouldn't let me down. I know we've had our differences over the last couple days, but you and I make a pretty kickass team."

"Yes, we do," Violet said, a smile crossing her face at Weston's excitement. "So when are we leaving?"

"As soon as possible," Weston said. "Let's get dressed and then meet in the living room in ten minutes. We'll go over our plan and then get moving. It's already almost three in the morning, so we shouldn't dilly dally. The middle of the night, with its darkness, gives us an advantage for sneaking in. I don't want to wait too long and be caught in the light of day."

"Alright," Violet said, already pushing back the covers and swinging her legs over the side of the bed. "I'll get dressed and then come meet you for a powwow."

Her mind screamed at her that she was crazy, but she pushed the thought away. She was getting pretty good at doing that, considering all the crazy things she'd done lately. Love and war both required you to act in ways you normally didn't, and if Violet wasn't caught up in the middle of a battle these days, she was caught up in a confusing mess of emotions regarding Weston. There wasn't a whole lot of space in her mind left over for rational thought.

Perhaps that's why, when Weston leaned in to kiss her again before heading out of her bedroom, she didn't pull away. This time, in fact, she might have actually kissed him back.

Her lips tingled and her heart sang as she rushed to put on her military uniform. One way or another, she had a feeling that this was going to be a night to remember.

CHAPTER SEVEN

Weston couldn't remember the last time that he'd been this excited about a mission. Despite the danger he knew lay ahead of them, a smile curled up his lips as he crept through the dark tunnel. Occasionally, he glanced behind him to make sure that Violet was still alright. Every time he looked at her, she gave him a smile and a thumbs up signal. She seemed to be enjoying this almost as much as he was.

Weston was glad that Violet had agreed to work with him on this mission. He had hated the way he felt all mixed up inside when they argued. It had surprised him how much her unhappiness affected him. He wasn't used to caring so much about what anyone else thought, but Violet was special. She meant something to him. Something big.

He had said he loved her in such a fit of urgent passion, thinking he might be dead soon. But now that death was no longer imminent, he'd realized that his feelings were still the same. He loved Violet. He didn't care anymore if everyone teased him about being a softy. He didn't think there was anything soft about loving a woman and wanting to protect her, anyway. Heck, if anything in life was worth fighting for, it was the love of a woman.

These thoughts all rolled through Weston's head as he crept forward through the tunnel. In some ways, it didn't make sense to bring Violet along on this mission when he wanted nothing more than to keep her safe. This mission was going to be a dangerous one, after all. He couldn't guarantee that either or both of them would make it out alive. But everything was dangerous these days. One never knew when or where Saul's next attack would be. At least if Weston was with Violet, he could see if she was in danger and protect her.

They walked a few more minutes in darkness, until Weston felt Violet reach forward and touch his arm. He nodded and stopped, waiting for her to put a flying spell on her broomstick.

Weston hadn't wanted to fly at the very beginning of the tunnel. He'd wanted to walk for about half an hour, to make sure that there were no guards or surveillance cameras in here. He'd been carefully smelling the air, using his sharp dragon shifter nose to search for the smell of any enemy soldiers, or any masking scents. So far, he'd smelled nothing. His keen dragon eyes had roved back and forth across the walls and roof of the tunnel, looking for hidden cameras that might indicate the area was being watched. Again, nothing. It appeared that Saul was still unaware of the existence of this tunnel. If the evil dragon wizard had known it was there, he would have at least had guards or surveillance at the Blackstone entrance. But since Saul was unaware, the secret passageway between the outskirts of Blackstone and the far outskirts of Sandview would give Weston and Violet a way to sneak right up to Saul's headquarters unseen. Violet would still use an invisibility spell of course, but that wasn't a guarantee of anything these days. The dark magic that the wizards were using easily saw through many invisibility spells, but Violet still wanted to attempt to use one. At the very least, it might cause a delay in the ability of the enemy wizards to notice them. And, hopefully, the masking scent Weston was using would keep the enemy shifters from smelling them. Between the tunnel, the invisibility shield, and the masking scent, they might just pull this off.

Weston watched as Violet tested her broomstick. It was hovering a few feet above the ground now, buzzing with the energy of the flying spell she'd cast. Weston let his eyes run up and down her body appreciatively as she worked. She was wearing a slim-fitting, dark black military uniform. The Falcon Cross military insignia was embroidered over the left side of her chest in gold thread, and whenever the light from her magic ring hit the thread it glittered brilliantly. Weston loved how the sparkling uniform accented her curves and made her look almost like royalty. For a brief moment, he let himself think about how much he'd like to tear the uniform off of her, exposing the soft, smooth skin underneath. But only for a moment. If he thought for too long about taking Violet's clothes off, he was going to have a hard time concentrating on the mission at hand.

"We're good to go," Violet said, nodding at her buzzing, hovering broomstick. "You ready?"

Weston nodded. "I'm ready. I'm confident that the tunnel at least is safe. If the Blackstone entrance isn't guarded, the rest of the tunnel will be unguarded, too. That means we should be able to fly all the way to Sandview without worrying about running into enemy soldiers."

Violet shrugged mildly. "I hope you're right," she said. She didn't sound as confident as Weston, but she didn't sound concerned, either. Weston realized in that moment that she had put her trust in him completely for this mission. She was along for the ride with him, wherever that ride happened to take them. Weston felt his chest puff up with pride and happiness at the thought. It felt good to have Violet trust him, especially when he'd admittedly been the one in the wrong yesterday.

"Let's do this," Weston said. Violet smiled, and nodded.

"Hop on, Cowboy," she said. "I'm gonna take you for the ride of your life."

Violet swung her leg over the front of the broomstick, holding on tightly to its thick handle. Weston eyed the handle suspiciously, not sure how it was going to be able to support both of them while they flew. But he climbed on behind Violet without protest, trusting that she knew what she was doing, and knew the capabilities of the broomstick.

To his surprise, as he mounted the broomstick, he felt like he was sitting on a plush bicycle seat instead of merely a circular wooden rod.

"This isn't such a bad seat," he remarked as he wrapped his arms around Violet's stomach to hold on.

"It's the flying spell," she said. "When you cast it on the broomstick, it gives the broomstick more seating surface. You can't see it with your naked eye, but it's there."

Weston shook his head slightly in amazement. The things that wizards could do never ceased to amaze him. He'd thought that being a dragon gave him some special abilities—and it did, of course. But magic was another category entirely.

"Ready?" Violet asked, kicking up her heels. Weston kicked his heels up, too, and was surprised to find invisible stirrups beneath his feet. He should have known there would be magic footrests, too, he thought wryly.

"I'm ready," he said.

"Hold on tight," Violet said, even though he already was. He definitely wasn't complaining about having an excuse to wrap his arms around Violet's waist from behind. It was a strange role reversal to fly behind her instead of having her ride on his back while he flew in dragon form, and he was enjoying the change. His dragon was too large to fly through this tunnel, so Violet had suggested the broomstick. They'd had to do something to speed up their pace. Walking would take far too long, since the tunnel was about twenty miles long.

"Let's see what you got," Weston said, a challenge in his voice.

Violet accepted the challenge.

With another kick of her heels, the broomstick was suddenly in motion. Weston felt the wind whipping at his face almost instantly, and the walls of the tunnel became a blur. Violet had never been in this tunnel before, as far as Weston knew, but that didn't seem to slow her down. Despite the fact that the twists and turns were unfamiliar, she navigated them with ease. Weston felt slightly dizzy, and wholly impressed. This girl knew how to fly.

For the next several minutes, all Weston could do was hold on tightly as Violet flew. At first, he tried to lean left or right with her, to help move the broomstick in the direction it needed to go. But he gave that up after the first minute. He'd never been in this tunnel either, and, unlike Violet, he couldn't keep up with which way the path was going to curve to next.

His eyes stung as the wind whipped harder against them, and his heart pounded as the tunnel's wall frequently whizzed by only inches away from his face. Somehow, though, he knew they weren't going to crash. Violet had this under control. He pressed his chest against her back, wishing he could spend his whole life this close to her.

He lost track of time as they flew onward, and sooner than he expected he felt Violet starting to slow down. He knew this meant they were nearing the other side of the tunnel, where it opened into Sandview. Violet would want to go slowly to make her invisibility shield as effective as possible, and to make sure that they saw any trouble up ahead before it saw them. Weston sat up straighter, realizing for the first time how sweaty he had become. This surprised him, since the cave was relatively cool, but he supposed that the adrenaline pumping through his veins had caused his body to heat up a bit more than normal.

Finally, Violet came to a complete stop.

"*Lucis terminantur,*" she said softly, and the light beam emanating from her magic ring went out. The sudden darkness sent a shiver down Weston's spine, even though he was sweating. Anything could be hiding up ahead of them, but he was going to have to trust his belief that Saul didn't know about the tunnel yet. He hoped he wasn't wrong.

As Weston's eyes began to adjust to the darkness, he could barely make out the outline of Violet leaning her broomstick up against the wall. He realized that, although the darkness was thick, it wasn't complete. Their exit to the tunnel must not be too far ahead. How Violet had known this was beyond his comprehension. Now that they were stopped, he could smell just the hint of fresh air, but when they had been moving it had been too difficult to smell something so faint. Weston figured it must be another one of Violet's magic spells. It still amazed Weston how useful the wizards could be in a pinch.

"We'll be coming out to the opening soon," Violet said. "Are we still sticking with the original plan?"

Weston nodded. "Nice flying," he said, and squeezed Violet's arm as he passed her. It was hard to tell in the darkness, but he thought he saw her mouth turning up in a smile at his words. She didn't say anything, though. Neither one of them spoke as they moved forward, with Weston in the lead now. The less noise they made, the better. Even though the tunnel's entrance wasn't exactly in the heart of Saul's headquarters, it was close enough that there was always a risk that an enemy patrol might be close enough to hear or smell them.

Their plan was somewhat haphazard and foolhardy, but Weston thought it was just crazy enough to work. Thanks to Nick's surveillance, they knew exactly where the bat cloning cave was located. Their plan was to walk right up to it, go inside, and run straight toward the back, where the master bat was likely to be. When they found the master bat, they would destroy it, either with dragon fire or with a magic attack from Violet's ring. Perhaps both—Weston wasn't sure which one would be more effective against the bat.

At some point, the bats, wizards, and other shifters in Saul's headquarters were going to figure out that intruders had entered the camp. When that happened, all hell would break loose and Weston and Violet would be fully occupied with fighting off attackers. Weston's hope was that Saul's guards were weary after the big battle yesterday, and that the number of wizards and shifters available for guard duty was low. The further along in their mission they could get before being noticed, the better chance Weston and Violet stood of actually destroying the master bat and making it out of there alive. Weston thought their odds were good, or he wouldn't have come on this mission in the first place, let alone dragged Violet along. But one could never predict what would happen, and he and Violet had agreed to go forward with the mission no matter what. They were going to destroy that master bat or die trying. As soon as the master bat was destroyed, Weston and Violet would retreat. Not through the tunnel, though, unless that was literally their only possible escape route. If they could manage to keep Saul from learning of the tunnel's existence tonight, so much the better.

Weston felt the scent of outside air hitting his nose stronger than ever now, and, as soon as he rounded the next corner in the cave, he saw the flickering of stars. They'd made it to the exit. He breathed in deeply, searching for any scent of enemy wizards or shifters. He could make out the faint smell of strange wizards, and of various types of shifters. His nose detected, bears, lions, panthers, and, of course, bats. But the smells were all faint, and Weston knew that no enemies were close, at least not for the moment. Silent as shadows, he and Violet slipped out into the open desert night. They were on the outer edges of the caves of Sandview.

It felt strange to be here. Weston had a feeling of déjà vu, even though he himself had never walked through these rocks before. He'd watched Nick's surveillance videos so many times that he felt liked he'd been here a hundred times already. He looked around at the familiar rock formations, keeping a sharp eye out for any enemy soldiers. The night was quiet, though. Eerily so. Either he was missing something, or he'd been right about his assumption that enemy guards were in short supply tonight.

Weston looked back at Violet, who was much easier to see out here in the moonlight than she had been in the darkness of the tunnel. His breath caught in his throat at how beautiful she looked right now, her deep violet eyes shimmering like purple stars where the moonlight hit them. She smiled at him encouragingly, telling him to continue forward. All was well as far as she could see, too. He smiled back at her and then forced himself to turn around and creep onward. Why did he always feel the strongest for her when they were in the middle of a dangerous situation? He supposed that danger naturally heightened all emotions, including the ones that made him want to throw Violet down on the ground right then and there and make love to her. Perhaps one day soon, he could do just that, only without the worry of being caught by the enemy. Assuming of course, that he could convince her that he was a worthy mate. She'd seemed to avoid giving him any indication of how her true feelings might run, blaming her noncommittal attitude on the war. Weston frowned. There was no way in hell he wanted to wait for the war to be over before claiming Violet as his own. It could be years before Saul was finally defeated, and he couldn't spend years apart from Violet. Just the thought of days apart from her made his heart ache. She'd always done funny things to his feelings, but lately he couldn't think about anything but her. He was going completely over the edge for her. There was no turning back. He just had to figure out a way to bring her over the edge with him.

Weston forced his thoughts back to the present. Just because things were quiet tonight didn't mean he could let his attention slide. It would only take a moment of inattention for him to give the enemy the upper hand, and that could mean death for him or Violet or both. There was no way he could woo Violet and make her fall in love with him if he was dead. Weston gritted his teeth and moved forward with renewed determination. This goddamn mission was going to be a success. He was a dragon shifter, and a highly trained soldier, and he had a talented wizard at his side. He was here to teach Saul a lesson and he was going to do just that. There would be time to daydream about Violet later.

As Weston walked forward, the scent of enemy soldiers grew stronger. He and Violet stayed close to the walls of the caves, doing their best to stay out of sight of any passing guards. Violet still had an invisibility spell cast over them, but they had no idea how effective it would be. Weston hoped that the guards were too exhausted tonight to be constantly scanning for invisibility spells to thwart, but one never knew. Just in case, he and Violet were staying out of the way as much as they could. The closer they got to the heart of Saul's headquarters, the harder this was going to be. Neither one of them would have dreamed of turning back, though. The potential to destroy the master bat was too tempting. There might never be another opportunity as good as tonight's.

Less than a minute later, Weston nearly walked around the corner straight into a couple of wizard guards. They were moving so silently that he hadn't heard them coming, and it was hard for him at this point to judge where anyone was based on scent alone. There were too many different scents mingling in the air now. Weston's heart pounded at the near collision, berating himself for being so careless, even thought he knew that he couldn't be much more careful than he was being right now. He took a deep breath, trying to regain his cool, and then forced himself to continue forward. Pausing here longer wasn't going to make things any safer. He might as well keep moving, and hope that there were no more guards for at least a few more minutes, now that those two had passed.

Saul's headquarters were relatively large. They had to be, to house all of the shifter and wizard soldiers in his army. Luckily, however, the bat cave was located relatively close to the secret tunnel that Weston and Violet had just traveled through. Weston could see it now, in fact. The cave was dark and silent at the moment, but he knew from Nick's surveillance videos that this was the right one. Two sleepy looking shifter guards stood in front of it, looking bored and like they would rather be anywhere than where they were right then.

Weston looked over at Violet, who had crept up beside him then, and pointed at the cave, indicating that it was the bat cave. She nodded, but then she tapped him on the shoulder and pointed to her right. About a hundred feet away was another cave, this one more heavily guarded. Weston frowned as he strained to see what was in the cave. He didn't remember Nick's surveillance photos every showing any guarded caves where this one now stood, but whatever was in there must have been important to Saul, because he'd posted at least half a dozen guards there. Weston couldn't see much no matter how hard he squinted, but when he breathed in he could smell the very distinct smell of full humans. Weston looked at Violet in horror, wondering if she was thinking the same thing he was. She nodded at the question in his eyes.

"Prisoners," she whispered, her voice barely audible even though she leaned over to put her lips right next to his as she spoke the word.

Weston felt his stomach turn. He shouldn't have been surprised that Saul was holding full humans hostage. After all, it was no secret that Saul had been terrorizing the city of Sandview. Still, it was somewhat shocking to see a cave of prisoners, some of them full humans. Weston had no idea what Saul was doing with the prisoners, but he imagined it wasn't anything good. For a moment, he considered whether he and Violet should forget about the bats and try to save the humans instead. Apparently, she was thinking the same thing, because she tugged at his arm and pointed in the direction of the cave. For half a second, Weston thought she was right, and that they should go break out the prisoners. But then, he shook his head.

"Stick to the plan," he mouthed to Violet. She frowned, but nodded.

They'd promised each other that there would be no deviations from their plan. It was too dangerous to change course midstream, and even the knowledge that they'd found a cave of prisoners didn't change that. They didn't know how many more guards might be inside, or how well-bound the prisoners were. Without backup, Weston and Violet had slim hopes of saving the humans. They still had a good opportunity to take down the master bat, though. If they could do that, the ripple effect might make it easier to help the prisoners.

A screech high above his head caught Weston's attention. He looked up, and almost laughed when he saw what had caused the shriek. He nudged Violet, so that she would look, too. She followed his gaze, and together, they watched as bats flitted by in the moonlight. There weren't many of them here, but in the distance Weston could see a dark, moving cloud. He didn't know why it hadn't occurred to him before that bats were nocturnal, and preferred to be active during the evening hours. He would have been even more confident about this mission's success if he'd stop to think about that. The bat cave would be mostly empty except for the master bat, which Weston knew would not be allowed to leave the cave due to its importance. High above him, the bats flew back and forth across the sky. There hadn't been any above them when they first came out of the tunnel, but now the bats were slowly coming home from their hunting. Slowly was the key word. Most were still gone, so as long as he and Violet acted quickly, they could enter the bat cave and make a run for the master bat without having to also deal with hundreds upon hundreds of additional angry bat shifters.

Weston took another careful look at the guards in front of the bat cave. They still looked as bored and sleepy as ever. He glanced at the guards in front of the prisoners' cave. Those guards looked more alert, and they might come to assist the bat cave guards when it became apparent that Weston and Violet were after the master bat. But their response would probably not be instant. Weston and Violet could be successful if they worked extremely quickly and had a little bit of luck on their side. Weston took one last deep breath and looked over at Violet.

"Ready?" he mouthed at her, not wanting to actually speak out loud. She nodded at him. He paused for just a moment to appreciate how beautiful her face looked in the moonlight. If things went badly, and he was captured or she was killed, he always wanted to have the memory of her beauty to sustain him.

Weston held up his fingers to count. One, two, three. And then, he and Violet were off, running at full speed toward the bat cave.

CHAPTER EIGHT

Weston watched as Violet held her magic ring high, doing her best to hold protective and invisibility shields over them. The invisibility shield broke first. As they ran, the guards in front of the cave with prisoners seemed to sense that someone was out there. They called out a counterspell that cancelled out the invisibility spell just before Weston and Violet reached the mouth of the bat cave. The guards in front of the bat cave were shocked out of their sleepy stupor as Weston and Violet ran past them.

"Hey!" they called in unison, scrambling to their feet. Weston did not even bother turning his head to look at them. Now that he knew the invisibility shield was broken, it was time to shift into a dragon. He'd stayed in human form as long as possible so he would be smaller, making it easier for Violet to keep the invisibility shield over both of them. Now, all he wanted to do was be as big and fierce as possible. He felt a rush of excited energy as his soft human flesh gave way to thick dragon hide. His hands morphed into the clawed feet of a dragon as wings sprouted from his back. His head became a fierce dragon head, smoking and angry. He did turn then, to look at the guards who were chasing them, and he let out a long stream of fire. Still in a state of surprise, and unprepared to face the wrath of a dragon, the guards barely had time to register the fact that a wall of flames was coming at them before they were burned to a crisp.

Weston turned to continue to run forward. There would be more guards coming, who would be better prepared. But he would worry about them when they got here. For now, he focused on following Violet into the cave. A beam of bright light was emanating from her magic ring now, lighting the way for them as they ran deeper into the darkness. An occasional bat shifter flew at them, angry at the intrusion and crying out in rage. But one bat could not hope to do much against a dragon and a wizard, and Weston made quick work of taking down the pesky little creatures.

The way before them was clearer than they could have hoped for, and before they knew it they had traveled several minutes into the cave. Weston was surprised at how big this cave was. Most of the caves out here were nothing more than a small rocky shelter from the sun, but this cave seemed to actually have depth to it. They had reached a point now where the main path split off into two separate passageways. Weston looked over at Violet, smoke curling up from his dragon nostrils. She frowned, and shrugged.

"You take the left one, and I'll take the right?" she asked.

He nodded his giant dragon head in agreement. The left passageway was bigger, and would better accommodate his dragon form. He started running down it without another moment's hesitation. It was tougher going now, without the light of Violet's magic ring to guide him. He did his best to squint and see in the darkness, but it was tough for even his keen dragon eyes.

He felt like he'd been running a long time—too long—when the passageway suddenly came to an abrupt halt in what appeared to be a large room. Weston breathed a huge stream of fire into the air to light up the room, and that's when he saw it: the master bat.

The thing was huge—as big as a horse. It's ugly, yellow eyes watched him carefully, but nothing else on its body moved. Its wings were tense, its feet gripping tightly to the ceiling of the cave as it hung upside down and fixed a gaze of pure hatred onto Weston's face. Even in mighty dragon form, that gaze made him shudder.

The room went dark as Weston's stream of fire died down. He took a deep breath and then let out another long stream of fire, trying once again to get a glimpse of his enemy. This time, when his fire breath lit up the room, he saw that there were two wizard guards standing on either side of the bat. They had appeared seemingly out of nowhere, although Weston guessed they must have been in the room all along, perhaps under invisibility shields that they would have now shed in order to put all their magical energy into protective shields.

"Get out!" one of the wizards yelled. "I'm warning you, we are skilled in dark magic, and will make you wish you were dead if you don't leave now."

Weston ignored them. Instead of turning to flee, he raised his dragon head high and let out a long roar. He put all of his strength into that roar, and he hoped that it would be loud enough to echo across the passageways and make its way to Violet. She would know, if she heard it, that he had found the master bat and needed her help.

Weston had barely caught his breath from the roar, when the wizards attacked. They yelled out magic spells and started putting all the force of their power against him. He did his best to dodge the beams of deadly light that came from their magic rings, but they were too fast and he was too large. He could not dodge them completely. His dragon hide did protect him somewhat, but Weston was quickly realizing that these wizards were a step above the wizards he normally fought. Usually, wizard attacks bounced right off his dragon hide, unless they were lucky enough to land perfectly on one of his few vulnerable spots. These attacks were different, though. They were stronger, and instead of bouncing off of him, they seemed to burn right into his hide. They still weren't getting all the way through to truly hurt him, but he worried that if they hit the same spot multiple times they were going to do some serious damage. These wizards must have been especially well trained in the art of dark magic, and their extra training was helping them hold Weston back from the master bat, who still hung, glaring at him and hissing with rage.

Weston did his best to counter the wizards' attacks with streams of dragon fire, but their protective shields were holding better than most magic shields Weston had encountered in previous battles. The fire hit an invisible wall whenever Weston breathed out, and none of his attacks were doing much to hurt the wizards or hold them back. Weston let out another long, loud roar, hoping that Violet would hear him.

Moments later, his prayers were answered. She must have heard the first roar, because she burst into the room in a fury of magic attacks. She was waving her magic ring left and right, and yelling out attack spells at the top of her lungs. Weston's heart leapt in his chest. He was no longer alone. Violet was here, and he knew that even dark wizards would be hard pressed to hold up for long against the two of them fighting together.

The minutes that followed were a blur. Weston and Violet fought side by side, countering every attack that the dark wizards sent at them with an attack of their own. Violet knew several spells to break down protective shields, and she ran through all of them, trying her best to break down their enemy's defenses. Finally, mercifully, Weston heard her let out a shout of victory. He turned toward the wizard she'd been attacking, and immediately let out a long breath of fire. Before the wizard had time to renew his protective shield, Weston had taken him down. Now, there was only one more guard.

With Violet and Weston both focused solely on him, it didn't take long to break down his shield as well.

Weston saw, out of the corner of his eye, the master bat twitching nervously as the final wizard guard went up in flames. From behind him, Weston could hear the noise of distant shouting echoing down the cave's passageway. He knew more guards were coming, and he knew that destroying the master bat would become exponentially more difficult once they arrived. He roared loudly, gathering his energy, and then, he let out another stream of fire directly at the bat. He hadn't counted on the bat being as quick as it was, though.

In the blink of an eye, the bat had zoomed away from its perch at the back of the room, and was making its way toward the passageway that would lead out of the cave. Thankfully, Violet had already anticipated this move, and she pointed her ring at the mouth of the passageway.

"*Magicae murus!*" she yelled. The wall spell went into effect a split second before the bat would have made its escape. With a yelp of pain, the bat ran into the invisible wall and tumbled backward. It lay stunned for a second, but only a second. Weston tried to hit it with fire, and Violet tried to launch a magic laser, but both attacks hit the rocky ground instead of the bat. The creature was quick for its size, and had rolled out of the way in the nick of time. Now, it was flying around the room, flapping its wings angrily as it attempted to stay out of the way of Violet's magic ring and Weston's fire.

The roar from the passageway grew louder, deafening even. The enemy's reinforcements would be arriving soon, and Weston and Violet still had not managed to take down the bat. Weston redoubled his efforts, breathing out an almost constant stream of fire as he tried to follow the bat's path back and forth across the room. The bat shrieked as it flew, its angry yellow eyes darting back and forth between Weston and Violet. Weston grew frustrated as his fire breath missed its mark again and again. This bat flew quicker than any other bat he'd ever seen.

An angry pounding now joined the cacophony of sounds in the room. The enemy's reinforcements had arrived, but they couldn't get past the magic wall Violet had erected. Weston's dragon lips curled up into a smile. Violet's magic was saving the day right now. He felt a puff of pride fill his chest. He was fighting next to one of the best wizard soldiers around. Never mind that she didn't have much formal training in the ways of war. Thanks to her extensive training as a Wizard Advocate, she had a better grasp of magic spells than most. Her magic wall wouldn't hold forever, but it would hold long enough for Weston to make sure this master bat was never used to clone another bat shifter soldier.

Weston reached deep down into the depths of his energy, and took the deepest breath he possibly could, deeper than any breath he'd ever taken before. Then, with a roar, he let the breath out in one long, unending stream of fire. The master bat flitted back and forth across the room, screeching and desperately trying to escape Weston's attack. But Weston held the fire breath longer than he ever had before—long enough for the bat to make a mistake in its frantic flight pattern and fly straight through the flames. With a shriek, the bat tumbled to the ground, its wings burning as it tried to hobble away. Weston took another deep breath, ready to attack again, but it was Violet who finished off the bat.

"*Magicae appugno!*" Violet yelled, pointing her magic ring at the bat. The bat shrieked in pain as a beam of bright laser light shot out from Violet's raised ring and hit it square in the chest. Then, the bat was silent and still.

Weston looked over at Violet, his eyes wide with the thrill of victory. Her own eyes danced with happiness as she looked back at him. They had done it. They had destroyed the master bat, and brought Saul's bat cloning operation to an end for the foreseeable future. The joy of victory lasted only for a moment, though. Their task was not yet done. From behind the magic wall Violet had erected, shrieks of anger rose as Saul's soldiers realized that the master bat was dead. Weston turned his dragon head to look, and saw that the crowd of enemies by the front of the passageway had grown. Furious wizards were shooting spell after spell at the magic wall, and hundreds of bat shifters were hurling themselves toward it over and over.

"They're going to break through soon," Violet said, her whole body tensing up as she watched. Weston nudged her, and then looked at his back, indicating she should climb on. She understood what he meant immediately, and grinned at him.

"Alright then," she said. "Here goes nothing."

Weston crouched low to the ground so that Violet could easily swing herself up onto his back. She gripped his scales tightly and flattened herself against him as he slowly rose to his feet again, ready to fly like the wind to get them out of there. He hoped with all his heart that they would be able to make it out of this cave alive, but, even if they didn't, they were going to give these bastards one hell of a show.

"Steady," Violet said, her voice sounding strangely calm amidst the shrieking on the other side of the wall. "Steady…"

Weston backed himself up against the very back of the rocky room, directly across from where the passageway was located. Their way out.

"On my count," Violet said, and then, slowly and clearly, "One, two, three, go!"

Weston began running full speed directly toward the passageway. He did not flinch or slow down as he approached the magic wall. He was trusting Violet to time things correctly. And she did.

"*Murus terminantur!*" she yelled a split second before he would have made impact with the invisible wall. The wall spell ended, and Weston roared and let out a stream of fire as he rushed into the passageway. Behind him, startled wizards and shifters tumbled into the cave room. They hadn't been expecting the sudden disappearance of the magic wall. Ahead of him, though, Weston faced hundreds of additional bat shifters.

The bats must have realized something in the cave was amiss. Someone had sounded the alarm. Whether it was one of the wizard guards or some of the bat shifters themselves, Weston didn't know and didn't care. All he knew was that the hordes of Saul's bat shifter army had returned to the cave to defend the master bat. Running through them felt like trying to run through thick molasses, but Weston did his best. He just kept moving forward, and kept breathing out fire into the wall of bat shifters in front of him. He could hear Violet behind him, yelling out magic attacks from her perch across his dragon back.

Occasionally, the mass of bat shifters was broken up by an enemy wizard. Weston ignored the wizard guards completely, letting Violet deal with them using her powerful magic spells. Weston focused all of his energy on making progress toward the bat cave's exit. He felt like the passageway was much longer on the way out than it had been on the way in, but he knew this was due merely to how desperate the moment felt.

"Come on," he told himself. "If you can just make it to open air, you can make it out of here."

He pressed on, determined— and grateful for Violet's assistance in knocking out every wizard guard they came across. Just when he thought the passageway could not possibly have been this long on the way in, Weston suddenly found himself looking up at open sky. He blinked, surprised, and hesitated for a second from the sudden feeling of disorientation that the unexpected view gave him. The wall of bats had given way to open air. Bats still swirled around him, and out of the corner of his eye he could see more wizards and shifters running toward him. But he had made it out of the bat cave. He was no longer trapped in a long tunnel.

"Fly!" Violet screamed. "Fly, Weston!"

Weston snapped back into action at the sound of Violet's voice. He pumped his powerful wings, and started running again. A few moments later, he felt his body lifting into the air. Pesky bat shifters still nipped at him, but their teeth barely even scratched at his thick scales. Weston was free. There was open air ahead of him, and he was going to make it out of here alive. He could feel the adrenaline in his very bones as he rose higher and higher.

He could hear Violet on his back, still yelling out attack spells and taking down wizard after wizard. But everything sounded faraway to Weston's ears now, even Violet, who was in actuality only a few feet from his ears. All Weston could focus on was the open sky above him. He had to fly, faster and farther than the enemy wizards and bats. That's all he had to do: fly like the wind. If he could manage this one task, then he and Violet would survive, and their mission would be a complete success.

Weston pumped his wings harder than he ever had in his life. He straightened out his body into the shape of a bullet, and hurtled through the air as though he himself had indeed been shot out of some sort of giant gun. He breathed in the cool night air in giant greedy gulps. The fresh oxygen filled his lungs, giving him renewed energy. The wind whipped at his ears, blocking out all other sounds. He didn't look back and didn't slow down until he felt Violet wrapping her arms around his neck as he flew. This meant she had stopped launching magic attacks, which could only mean one thing...

Weston slowed and turned his head to look behind him. They were flying in clear air now. In the distance, he could see a cloud of bat shifters and wizards swirling above the desert sands. But none of them were following Weston and Violet anymore.

"We did it," Violet shouted, her voice filled with gleeful giddiness. "We slipped away. I managed to get up an invisibility shield they couldn't penetrate, and now they have no idea where we are."

Weston turned his giant dragon body so that he was looking at the enemy army they'd been flying away from. Even from this distance, it was evident how confused the enemy soldiers were. They turned in frantic circles, occasionally throwing out attacks in random directions as though they might by chance hit something. He wasn't sure how Violet had managed to give them the slip so completely, but she had. And together, he and Violet had just made a huge difference in the war effort for the side of good.

Weston felt Violet squeeze her arms tighter around his neck.

"Let's go home," she shouted. He smiled, and let out a puff of smoke as he turned around again. He flew back to Blackstone with a heart that felt much lighter than it had in months. He and Violet had done great things together as a team. He hoped that they could continue to find ways to work together, despite their occasional disagreements. Something deep down in his heart told him that they would, and that their next adventure wasn't too far off.

CHAPTER NINE

Violet blinked open her eyes, and, for a moment, could not remember where she was. In her head, she somehow thought she should have been back in her hometown of Falcon Cross, in her old familiar bedroom. Her mind, craving safety, had convinced her that she was home.

But as her eyes fully opened and the grogginess of sleep wore away, she saw that she was, of course, not in her old bedroom in Falcon Cross. She was still in Blackstone, in the small bedroom of the apartment she was sharing with Weston. The events of the previous day came back to her as she rolled over to look at the clock. It was just past six a.m. She'd been sleeping for over thirteen hours.

Violet sat up and stretched, surprised at how good she felt. She'd expected to be a bit more sore, but perhaps the long stretch of sleep had helped clear away the remaining aftereffects of the battle she'd fought. That was good, since she knew more battles would be coming. She groaned as she remembered the heated discussions she and Weston had had the day before with Peter and Knox.

Knox and Peter were, of course, thrilled at the news that the master bat had been killed off. This blow to Saul's army would ensure that the good wizards and shifters had some breathing room, which would allow them to focus their efforts fully on finding the dragon ruby. The dragon ruby was one of four dragon stones that held an incredible amount of ancient, supernatural power. Three of the stones—the dragon emerald, dragon sapphire, and dragon amethyst—had already been recovered by the side of good. But the remaining stone, the dragon ruby, was still missing, and it was rumored to be as powerful as all of the other stones combined. If Saul managed to get his hands on it first, this could spell disaster. Saul might be able to, with the power of that dragon ruby, overcome all of the forces of good. Violet shuddered. She did not want to even think about what the world would look like if someone as evil as Saul was in complete control.

The knowledge that Saul's forces in Sandview were crippled, though, was not enough to distract Peter and Knox from the fact that Weston and Violet had taken off on an unauthorized mission without telling anyone. Peter and Knox had been unhappy, to say the least. They had chewed Weston and Violet out in front of everyone, which, theoretically, should have made Violet feel upset and embarrassed. The strange thing was, she didn't really care.

She had still been on too much of an adrenaline high to worry about the fact that her superiors were upset with her. She could hardly believe that she and Weston had done what they'd done.

Now, in the darkness of her own bedroom, a broad smile crossed Violet's face as she remembered Peter telling her that a Wizard Advocate like her should know better than to participate in unauthorized missions. She'd made sure to keep a dutifully repentant look on her face while Peter reprimanded her, but on the inside, she'd been smiling just as broadly as she was now.

The truth was that she felt pretty badass. She'd spent her whole life coloring inside the lines and doing as she was told, but something about Weston and his adventurous spirit had encouraged her to go off into enemy territory in the middle of the night. It had been the best decision she'd ever made. She'd done something, *really* done something. She'd crippled the army of one of the most powerful forces of evil in the world today. No one could ever take that away from her.

Violet swung her legs over the side of the bed and made her way to the bedroom door. Thirteen hours of sleep had left her feeling quite hungry and thirsty, and she wanted to see what was available to eat in the kitchen. To her surprise, when she opened her bedroom door, she found Weston sitting on the living room couch. He had one lamp on, and looked up from the papers he'd been poring over as she entered the room.

"Hey," he said, his voice surprised. "I didn't even hear you stirring."

"I've only been up a few minutes," Violet said. "I think I woke up from hunger."

Weston smiled. "That would make sense. You've been sleeping for so long."

Violet padded over to the kitchen and opened the refrigerator. She pulled out a bottle of orange juice and a cup of yogurt. Grabbing a spoon and a glass, she went to sit at the dining room table. As she sipped her juice and ate her yogurt, she watched Weston intently. He was completely absorbed by the papers he was looking over, and didn't say much else to her until she couldn't stand the curiosity any longer.

"What are you looking at?" she asked.

He looked up in surprise, as though he'd already forgotten she was in the room, too.

"Oh," he said. "Maps I drew up of Saul's headquarters. I'm trying to figure out how we can get in there and get to those prisoners."

Violet raised an amused eyebrow. "You're not planning another secret mission, are you? Peter and Knox might have forgiven you for running off on your own once, but twice is asking for it, don't you think?"

Weston grinned at her. "Yeah, probably. Although I have a feeling you'd be down for another adventure if I asked you."

Violet tilted her head at him. "Perhaps. Are you going to ask me?"

Weston laughed. "Well, I think that in the interest of not getting kicked out of the Redwood Dragons clan, I'm at least going to run this by Peter and Knox first. I think I have a pretty solid plan for invading Saul's headquarters. He still has a lot of soldiers there, even with all the ones we've killed off in the last couple battles. But he's been weakened considerably, so our army might have a good chance of taking him if we use the tunnel to sneak in one last time."

"One last time?" Violet asked. "That sounds so final."

Weston nodded. "I think we can only get away with using it for a large army once before Saul's soldiers realize that we have access to this secret entrance. Besides, I think once we get the prisoners, we should all head back to Falcon Cross. It's safer there, and we've done all we can to destroy Saul's plans in Sandview. He wanted to clone bats out here, and we've put a stop to that. It's time to leave and get back to searching for the dragon ruby. We must find that before he does."

Violet nodded. "True enough. Do you think that Peter and Knox are going to agree with you?"

Weston shrugged. "Knox will. He chewed me out yesterday, but he's proud of me, I know. He's my clan leader, and he's known me for a long time. He trusts my judgment on things. I'm not so sure about Peter. The man is a bit of a wildcard. Sometimes he's willing to take big risks. Other times, he wants to play it ridiculously safe. I'm trying to make my plans as well thought-out and foolproof as possible before I go talk to them today. Maybe that'll appeal to Peter's cautious side."

"I hope you're right," Violet said. "Because I think we need to get those prisoners out of there. I'm not sure who they are or what Saul's doing with them, but it can't be anything good."

"Agreed," Weston said. "And since we're on the same page about this, do you think you'd be willing to look over my plans and see if I've made them as strong as I can? I want to be as prepared as possible before I go talk to Knox and Peter."

Violet grinned at Weston and then gasped in mock surprise. "Are you actually asking for my opinion on something, Mr. Weston Pars?"

Weston grinned right back at her. "I am. Don't get used to it."

Violet stood, and went to toss her empty yogurt cup in the trash. "I'll take a look, but do you mind if I shower first. I haven't had time to take a proper shower since our mission, and I feel disgusting. Plus, I could still use a little time for my brain to wake up."

"Sure, no problem," Weston said, already turning his attention back to the papers in front of him. "Take your time. I still have quite a few details to work out before I feel like this plan is complete."

Violet headed toward her bedroom and its attached bathroom, but she stopped in the doorway to turn for a minute and look at Weston. He didn't see her watching him, or, if he did, he pretended that he didn't. Things had been a bit strange between them since they got back from destroying the master bat. Neither one of them had mentioned the fact that they'd both admitted to having romantic feelings for each other. Violet supposed she couldn't blame him too much if he didn't want to try to make another move on her after he'd already told her he loved her only to have her reject his advances.

Violet turned away abruptly, forcing herself to tear her eyes from the handsome outline of his face. She'd made the right decision, hadn't she? They were at war, fighting battles every other day. There was no time to think about love or romance.

And yet, as she showered, Weston was all she thought about. Ever since she'd ridden out of that bat cave on his back, she'd felt different. She felt closer to him somehow. Perhaps it was the thrill of going on a secret mission together, or perhaps it was just that every passing day was one more day of living with the knowledge that her heart was yearning for Weston. Whatever the reason, her resolve to keep him at arm's length was slowly being whittled away. She could hardly look him in the eye now, for fear that the desire filling her would be evident on her face.

Violet stayed in the shower a long time, and took even longer getting ready. She felt like she needed more time to collect her thoughts before she went to talk to Weston again. She blow dried her hair until it was perfectly straight. She spent a long time choosing her clothes, as though it actually mattered what she wore today. She even put on makeup, which she almost never did, just as an excuse to spend more time hidden away in her bedroom.

Finally, though, she'd run out of reasons to stay behind her closed door, and she forced herself to walk back into the living room. Although she had no logical reason to think that this encounter with Weston would be anything special or different, she couldn't seem to slow the rapid pace of her breathing, or the pounding of her heart in her chest.

When she stepped out of her bedroom, Weston was no longer sitting on the couch. The papers he'd been looking over were all spread across the coffee table, but he was not there. It only took her a moment to find him, though, thanks to the sound of his voice.

"My god," he said from the kitchen, where he stood with a carton of milk in his hand. "You look beautiful."

Violet blushed. "Don't be ridiculous. I look the same as always."

Weston set the milk carton down on the kitchen counter, unopened, and started walking toward her bedroom door. "Well, you always look beautiful," he said.

Violet's heart continued to pound in her chest. Her breath grew more ragged with every step he took toward her. She had been right. Something was different between them now. Special. Violet felt drawn to Weston like a magnet. There was no escape. Her eyes locked on his, and she couldn't tear herself away. He felt the pull between them, too, she knew. He walked right up to her, until his face was mere inches from hers.

"Violet," he said, his voice husky. The only word he said was her name, and yet, somehow, he was saying so much more than that.

"Weston, we shouldn't," Violet said. But her voice didn't sound convincing.

"Shouldn't what?" he asked. He reached his right hand up and cupped the left side of her face with it. His palm was large and warm, easily covering both her cheek and her ear. His thumb reached to stroke gently at her lips.

Violet had no answer for him. She tried to put words together in her mind that made sense, but it was impossible to think with his hand on her face, and his thumb on her lips. Nothing on the outside had changed between them. After all, they'd been soldiers together in this war already. They'd fought battles together. But somehow, the mission to destroy the master bat had changed them. Violet knew that they had done something great together, and that they had only been able to do it because they trusted each other so completely. Sure, they argued about what the right course of action was at times, and they teased each other relentlessly about who was better at every little thing. But at the end of the day, all that mattered was that, in the heat of battle, they were always one. They fought together, they were willing to die together, and, so far, thankfully, they had always triumphed together.

Violet didn't know how to put into words what she was feeling, but she knew that her attraction to Weston was about so much more than just the way he looked. Oh, sure, he looked amazing. There was no denying that his muscular body, chiseled jawbone, and piercing green eyes were enough to send any woman's heart racing right out of her chest. But physical attraction was only the beginning. There was something about his soul, the very essence of who he was, that drew Violet's heart to his.

He was brave, loyal, and kind. He was fearless in battle, and willing to die to defend what was right and good in the world. He never wavered in his efforts to make the world a better place. He was, in short, a dragon. He had an old soul, a heart strengthened by the legacy of a thousand dragons before him. And somehow, miraculously, he was hers. She could not have told you how she knew this. She just did. Her heart leapt at the sight of him, and she knew that his heart did the same for her. He loved her. He had told her so. And in the middle of that tiny apartment in Blackstone, Violet finally fully admitted to herself what she had known since the moment she'd met him: she loved Weston Pars.

Before she could change her mind, or try to rationalize away the truth that was filling her heart, Violet tilted her head upward and found Weston's lips with her own. He tasted, strangely, like cinnamon. His lips were softer than she would have thought, and she closed her eyes as they pressed against hers, returning the kiss she had finally allowed herself to give him. For a moment, time stood still as they both came to the realization that they were finally letting themselves fall into each other.

And then, the softness of the moment ended, and was replaced by a sudden, heated urgency. Violet heard a low growl coming from Weston's chest. The sound was deep and primal, and it sent shivers of delight running down her spine. He broke his lips away from hers to lift her in his arms, then carried her over the threshold of her bedroom door. He lay her down on her back over the soft comforter of her bed, and reached for the buttons of her blouse even as he bent down to find her lips again. He slipped his tongue into her mouth as he fumbled with the buttons, and another deep growl rumbled from his chest. Violet reached her legs up and wrapped them around his hips, pulling him down toward her and making his button-removing task nearly impossible. She didn't care at the moment. There would be time to mess with buttons in a moment. All she knew right then was that she needed him close to her. She needed to have his body pressed up against her body, the same way her lungs needed oxygen. It was as though her life depended on it.

Weston let her pull him in, and Violet moaned as the weight of his body pressed across the top of hers. His tongue moved skillfully in her mouth, flicking back and forth against first her teeth, then her tongue, then the roof of her mouth. Every movement he made sent a wave of tingling pleasure emanating across her body. She felt the heat of it spreading to her furthest extremities, until even her toes were tingling. She could feel the space between her legs growing wet as her body's craving for him grew. With every passing second she wanted him more. With every passing second, the juices of her desire oozed out thicker than before. Her body beckoned to him, begged for him, prepared itself for him.

She lost track of everything in the room except him. She moaned as the stubble of his cheek brushed against her own smooth cheek. He hadn't shaved in the last twenty-four hours, and the shadow on his face made him seem more masculine than ever. She shivered as he pulled away from her kiss to finish his work of unbuttoning. He took her shirt off first, followed by her pants, then her bra and panties. The clothes she had spent so long in choosing this morning now lay on a crumpled heap on the floor. She was naked before him, her breasts rising and falling rapidly under the intensity of his gaze. The only thing remaining on her body now was the delicate gold chain around her neck, her favorite necklace from which a compass charm hung. Weston reached up and fingered the charm, holding it a few inches above her chest as he looked at it. Then, he let it fall, and he moved his fingers to her breasts. He circled her nipples carefully, his intense eyes drinking in the sight of her as he stroked the hard nubs that rose in response to his touch.

Violet trembled from the heat and pressure that filled her now. The comforter was growing wet below the point where her legs joined, as the wetness of her desire increased. She blushed, slightly embarrassed by how strongly her body was reacting to Weston. But she couldn't hold back. She had never wanted anyone the way she wanted Weston right now. She had never felt so intricately connected with another human being.

He traced his finger down to her navel, slowly circling her belly button before continuing on to lower, wetter spots. He raised his eyes to meet hers when he first felt the warm moisture that coated her slick entrance.

"You want me," he said. His voice was husky, pleased.

"I need...you," Violet panted out. "More. Now."

She was surprised at how difficult it was to speak. The heat that filled her body seemed to weigh down her tongue, making it impossible to form sentences. Weston understood, though. He smiled at her, warmly, then pulled back for a moment to stand next to the bed. He reached down to pull off his t-shirt, exposing his sculpted abs in all their perfection as he removed the garment in one swift movement. But, as lovely as his muscles were, it was not his stomach that caught Violet's eye. It was the space just below his stomach, where his erection was now pushing out insistently against his jeans. She sat up and let her legs hang off the side of the bed, with Weston standing in front of her. She reached for the button and zipper on his jeans, tugging, pulling and grunting with impatience as she struggled to remove the pants, which were so obnoxiously in the way right now. Weston let out a grunt of his own, bending slightly to kiss the top of her head. Finally, Violet managed to remove the jeans. She could see his outline clearly now, stiff and hard against his black briefs. She wanted to see it fully, with nothing between them but skin. In one smooth movement, she pushed off his underwear so that he stood naked in front of her. The sight turned the warmth in her body into a burning fire. How was it possible for a man to be as wonderful and perfect as Weston? He stood tall, muscular, and strong. His erection pointed straight at her, as though heralding her. She smiled, and reached to grab it with her hand. She wrapped her finger around his shaft, marveling. He felt like steel—hot steel. He was warm and throbbing beneath her touch, and she rubbed against his skin, hardly able to believe that she was lucky enough to share a moment this intimate with a man like Weston. She looked up at him, her face glowing with heat, passion, and desire.

"My dragon," she whispered.

"My lady," he answered.

And then he bent his knees just enough to position himself in front of the sweet spot where her legs joined her body. The bed was high, so he didn't have to work very hard to fit his tall frame perfectly in front of where she sat on the mattress. He slid into her and she gasped as he filled her. His thick shaft pressed against her inner walls and she could feel his heat as he slid back and forth. He reached down to wrap his arms around her back and then pressed into her, thrust after thrust, each one feeling deeper than the one before. She tilted her head back, her eyes closed as she drank in the wonderful sensations that filled her. Every movement of his body against hers increased the tingling pressure within her, until she felt that she was going to explode. Her breathing grew even more ragged than it had been as she felt her whole body reaching the point of explosion.

And then, her release came crashing over her. She let out a surprised moan as the intense shock waves rocked across her body. The heat and pleasure that filled her felt incredible, and she thought that she hadn't understood what true happiness and ecstasy were until that moment.

"Weston!" she cried out, needing to say something, but only able to gasp out his name.

He grunted in response and thrust harder, his impossibly stiff erection reaching into the deepest parts of her as he kept her pleasure going much longer than she would have ever thought possible. She probably would have fallen backward against the bed if he hadn't been holding her. She felt like she was floating and couldn't concentrate on minor details like holding her body upright. All she knew was that the tremors her body was experiencing right now made her feel more fulfilled than she ever had before.

Just as her own ecstasy began to slowly subside, Weston let out a roar and thrust into her one last time, long and hard. His shaft pulsed and throbbed, pressing against her inner walls as he found his own release and came into her. The feeling of him finding such pleasure inside of her set her off anew. She moaned with him, whimpering in happiness as her body once again quaked under his touch.

She wasn't sure how long she sat there, deliciously entwined with him as her body practically glowed from the aftereffects of their lovemaking. All she knew was that she was warmer and more at peace than she'd ever thought possible, and she wouldn't have traded that moment for anything. When at long last Weston pulled out of her, he didn't walk away. Instead, he sat on the bed next to her, then pulled her down with him so that they were lying at a funny diagonal angle across the mattress. He looked over at her and grinned, then leaned in to give her a quick kiss on the cheek.

"You're amazing," Violet said. It sounded like such a silly, juvenile thing to say, but she wasn't sure what other words to use to describe how he had made her feel. Words felt so inadequate right then. She looked at him in wonder, drinking in the sight of his tanned, stubbled cheeks and piercing green eyes. He crinkled up those beautiful eyes as his smile deepened.

"So are you," he said, then glanced over her shoulder at the alarm clock that sat on her bedside table. "It's already been the best day of my life, and it's not even nine a.m. yet. Who knows what wonderful things the rest of the day will bring."

"Who knows," Violet agreed. And although their conversation was somewhat joking and lighthearted, she had a feeling deep down that this day was indeed going to bring more amazing things. If only she had an idea what those things might be.

For now, though, she was at peace, basking in the beauty of this moment with her dragon. *Her* dragon. How had she been so lucky?

CHAPTER TEN

Violet had just finished taking her second shower of the day when Weston walked excitedly into her bathroom.

"Knox and Peter have agreed to an emergency meeting this afternoon!" he said. "They're going to let me present my plan to invade Saul's headquarters and rescue the prisoners."

Violet reached for a towel and stepped out of the shower, still dripping wet as she wrapped the fluffy cloth around herself.

"What, now you just waltz into my room like you own the place?" she teased.

Weston shrugged and grinned. "Well, I've already seen you fully naked. It's not like I'm going to see anything more than what I've already seen."

Violet gave him a playful punch in the arm, then grabbed a second towel to begin rubbing her hair dry. "How much time do we have before the meeting? I'm starving."

"Time enough to eat a quick bite," Weston said. "We're supposed to meet at headquarters in about an hour and a half from now."

Violet nodded as she turned toward her bedroom to find some fresh clothes to wear. She felt suddenly shy in front of Weston, and she avoided his eyes as she dressed. She knew he was watching her, taking in the curves of her body as she pulled her jeans on over them. Her nervousness must have shown, because he finally let out a small grunt and asked her about it.

"What's wrong, Violet. Having second thoughts about being together with me?"

Violet looked up at him in alarm. "Oh, no. Nothing like that. It's just that…"

What was it, exactly? she wondered as she took in the concern etched across his face. Perhaps it was her own fear of the future that made her want to put up a wall of protection around herself. She'd given herself to him completely, and she had fallen in a deeper love than she ever thought possible. She knew that he'd said he loved her first. Surely that meant he was serious about this. But what if he wasn't? What if he'd only said his words of love in the heat of the moment, and now that the threat of death or the intense passion they'd had in their moments of lovemaking was passed, he was having second thoughts.

"It's just what?" Weston asked. He wasn't going to let this go until he was satisfied that she'd told him the truth. She knew how stubborn he could be, and there was no use trying to pass off her emotions as nothing. Violet took a deep breath and decided to just be honest with him. She would lay all her cards on the table, and see how he responded. They were new at being lovers, but they had known each other for a while now. If she couldn't be honest and open with him in this moment, then they weren't ready for a future together. And Violet hoped more than anything that they were ready for a future together.

"It's just that I didn't expect to feel so strongly for you so quickly," Violet said, forcing herself to meet Weston's eyes.

"What do you mean?" he asked.

"Well, I've had feelings for you on some level for a long time. I don't think that's any secret," Violet said. "And I think I knew that I loved you, even before we slept together."

"Oh you admit you love me?" Weston teased. He tone was joking, but he looked happy.

"Yes," Violet said, holding his gaze. "I love you. And I have for a while. The same would go for the way you feel about me, it seems."

"Of course," Weston said, his voice turning soft and serious now. "I've loved you since pretty much the first moment I met you."

Violet felt her heart filling with warmth at his words. She told herself that he cared about her, and, even if he didn't agree with what she was about to say, she knew he would never mock her for it. This gave her the strength to continue, and to say what seemed like an absurd thing to say to someone after only admitting a few hours ago that you even wanted a romance with them at all.

"It isn't just that I love you, Weston," Violet said. "It's deeper than that. I love you so much that I want to spend the rest of my life with you. I know that probably sounds like a crazy thing to say so soon into our relationship. But I know deep within my bones that it's true. I can't exactly put it into words, but as soon as we made love I just knew. I've always been drawn to you, but after sleeping with you I feel connected. I don't even know if that makes sense, but it's how I feel. It's like we've been connected with some sort of bond that I know in my heart will never be broken. And it's how I can already stand here and tell you that, no matter what happens in the future, and no matter how you feel about our relationship, I know you are the only one for me. There will never be anyone else."

Violet felt like she was starting to ramble, so she paused to take a deep breath. She looked over at Weston expectantly, willing him to somehow understand the depth of what she was trying to convey. His green eyes looked at her with such intensity that they were practically glowing, although she couldn't quite read what kind of emotions were causing him to look at her that way.

"Violet," he said. His voice was husky, and her name on his lips sounded almost like a prayer. She gulped, and waited for him to say more.

"You have no idea how happy I am to hear you tell me everything you just did. You've just described exactly the way I feel, too. And, more importantly, you've described the lifemate bond."

"Lifemate bond?"

"Shifters believe in what is known as a lifemate bond," Weston explained. "We believe that every person has someone whom they are destined to be with, and that person is their lifemate. From the moment we are born, destiny works to bring us together with that person. It's similar to the human concept of a soul mate, although I'm not sure that wizards have any analogous beliefs."

"Well, I've heard people talk about soul mates," Violet said. "But I always just thought it was people being a bit overdramatic about falling in love."

Weston smiled. "Sometimes, it is. People tend to use the word soul mate somewhat lightly. But finding a lifemate is even more serious than finding a soul mate. Once a lifemate bond is formed, it's unbreakable. The only thing that can break it is death."

"And how is that bond formed?" Violet asked. "How do you know when it's happened?"

"It's formed the first time two destined lifemates make love," Weston said. "The act of making love seals the connection, and usually the two lifemates will feel a hot warmth in their core. They'll have the sensation that they're now 'connected,' as you said."

Violet could feel her heart thumping in her chest. "That's what I felt! I felt so hot, right in the very core of my stomach. And I just knew that I was connected to you. After we made love, I couldn't imagine ever being with anyone else. It felt like we were meant to be."

Weston walked over and pulled her into his arms. "It's because we are meant to be, Violet. You're my destiny. My lifemate."

Violet tilted her head up to look at him. Her heart was filled with a deep sense of wonder and gratitude. "How did I get so lucky? How did I end up as the destined lifemate of a mighty dragon, the most wonderful, handsome man I've ever met?"

But Weston shook his head at her.

"No," he said as he bent down to kiss her. "I'm the lucky one."

Violet wanted to argue that point, but she couldn't speak when his lips were covering hers. So she closed her eyes and melted into his kiss, the kiss of destiny.

* * *

Three hours later, Weston stood nervously in front of Knox, Peter, Violet, and Holden. He had just finished presenting his plan to break into Saul's headquarters and break out the large group of prisoners being held there. Violet and Holden were both looking at him with encouraging smiles, but Peter and Knox, as usual, did not allow their faces to reveal their thoughts. Their expressions were as stoic as ever, and for what felt like an eternity, neither one of them said anything. Then, finally, Peter spoke.

"How many prisoners do you think we're talking about here? I know you said it was impossible to tell, but can you at least give a rough estimate? A minimum number perhaps?"

"It's extremely hard to say," Weston said, earning him a frown from Peter. The old wizard wanted hard numbers, but Weston hadn't been able to see in the dark how deep the cave was, or how big the group inside it might have been. He could only tell Peter how many prisoners he had actually seen, so that's what he decided to do. "At a minimum, there were thirty prisoners. But keep in mind that's just what I could see. It's possible the number is much larger."

"I see," Peter said, leaning back in his chair and twirling the end of his long white beard around his right pointer finger. "I'm just worried that if there are too many of them, we won't be able to find a place to fit them all in Falcon Cross."

"We have to try, Peter," Violet said, speaking up for the first time since the meeting had started. Weston and Peter both looked over at her in surprise. Weston felt his heart filling with gratitude. Even though they had argued in the last meeting, she was supporting him now, when it really counted. He thought she had never looked so beautiful as when she stood up, the gold thread in her Falcon Cross uniform shimmering in the late afternoon sunlight that streamed in through the window.

"What makes you say that, Violet?" Peter asked, drumming his fingers together as he turned to face her. Weston held his breath and hoped that Violet's response would be persuasive to Peter. Weston thought the issue was clear, but he had long ago learned that wizards didn't think like dragons, and sometimes things that seemed obvious to him weren't so obvious to wizards.

"I know that Falcon Cross is stretched to the limit right now," Violet said. "We have most of the Redwood Dragons clan living there since their home has been captured by Saul's army. And everyone is on edge from the constant threat of an attack by Saul. But we cannot allow our discomforts or fears to keep us from reaching out to help those in need. These prisoners have no one else to help them. We don't know exactly what Saul's army is doing to them, but we know it isn't good. We are fighting this war to keep Saul's evil at bay. We can't turn a blind eye away from that evil when it's right in front of us. Falcon Cross is a safe haven in these times of uncertainty and distress. We should welcome the prisoners there, even if it's not the easiest thing to do. We should do it simply because it is the right thing to do. And who knows, those prisoners might have seen or heard things that will help us in our fight. You never know what inside information they might have. We're sitting here talking about whether to help them, when they very well might be the ones who end up helping us."

Weston watched as Peter pondered Violet's words. He continued to drum his fingers, his expression just as unreadable as before. Weston looked at Knox, who was also watching Peter intently. Knox's face remained unreadable, too, but Weston would have bet his life on the fact that Knox thought rescuing the prisoners was a good idea. Knox did not like to leave innocent people in the hands of evil men, and had often risked his life to protect others. But Knox was the leader of the Redwood Dragons, not Falcon Cross. Peter, as the head wizard in Falcon Cross, would have to be the one to make the final decision about whether to bring an undetermined number of prisoners there. Weston held his breath, waiting. He looked over at Violet for a moment, but she was too busy watching Peter to notice. Peter drummed his fingers together and thought about the situation for what felt like an hour. In reality, it was probably only two or three minutes. Finally, the old wizard stood and addressed the room.

"Violet speaks the truth," Peter said. "Falcon Cross has always prided itself on being a place of safety for all wizards. Now that the shifters are our allies, it should be a safe place for shifters as well. And, although it is unusual for us to welcome full humans into our city, we will welcome any humans who have been mistreated by Saul's army. It would be good for them to see that not all wizards and shifters are evil."

Weston felt like his heart was soaring in his chest. He had wished for a response like this, but he hadn't wanted to get his hopes up too high, just in case Peter or Knox disagreed with him. Now, though, all his hard work in preparing a plan was going to pay off. As if Peter could read Weston's mind, he continued speaking.

"And Weston," Peter said, a smile spreading across his face. "You deserve special thanks for putting together such a thorough plan of attack. The strategy you've presented is a sound one, and I think if our soldiers here follow it carefully, we will be able to strike down Saul's headquarters in Sandview completely, as well as free the prisoners."

"Thank you, sir," Weston said.

"How soon do you think our army here can be ready to attack?" Knox asked, speaking up for the first time. "I think the sooner we can attack, the better. Saul is vulnerable now, thanks to his losses in the last two battles. The longer we give him to recover, the harder our task will be, and the more time his anger will have had to fester."

"I agree," Weston said. "I think our armies could be ready by tomorrow night."

"Definitely by tomorrow night," Holden said in agreement. "If we start preparing everything now, we should be able to strike just over twenty-four hours from now."

"Alright then," Knox said, standing to his feet. "Let's get this ball rolling."

Weston grinned as he looked back and forth from Violet to Holden. He was about to launch the offensive of a lifetime with his lifemate and his best friend. There were always risks to battle, of course, but he felt confident that, with a group like this, their chances of failure were slim.

"Let's do this," Weston said. Holden nodded, and led the way out of the room. Weston followed, taking Violet's hand in his as he did. They hadn't made any sort of official announcement yet that they were together now, but this felt like as good a time as any to Weston to show the world that Violet was his. Feeling her palm against his made him feel like he could do anything. And maybe, just maybe, he could. It was time to find out.

CHAPTER ELEVEN

Early the following evening, while the town of Blackstone went about its normal business unaware, a group of three dragon shifters entered the secret tunnel on the outskirts of town. An army of wizards followed the dragon shifters into the cave, all holding broomsticks, which they would be using to zoom through the tunnel toward the outskirts of Sandview.

Weston was, of course, one of those dragons. On his right walked his clan leader Knox, and on his left, his best friend Holden. Behind him walked Violet and Peter, two of the most powerful wizards to currently walk the earth. Weston had never felt so alive. Adrenaline sent his blood racing through his body at record speed. This was going to be the biggest offensive attack that had been launched against Saul since the war had begun. Sure, there had been bigger battles, but they had all been instigated by Saul. Until now, the good shifters and wizards had been focusing mainly on defense, and on finding the dragon stones. Now, it was time for an all-out attack. Saul was about to get a taste of his own medicine, and to see just how fearsome the forces of good could be.

"Everyone ready?" Knox asked, looking back and forth among the group at the front of the battle lines. Weston nodded, along with the others. Knox nodded back at them, and then gestured to the two wizard soldiers who would be giving Knox and Holden a lift on their broomsticks. Weston would be riding with Violet, just as he had done last time he was in this cave. She would be leading the group, since she'd already successful navigated the tunnel at full speed. With her guidance, the wizard army would have no trouble making it to the other end safely.

"Mount your broomsticks!" Violet called out. A chorus of magic spells sounded off in the area as each of the wizard soldiers cast a flying spell on their broom. The brooms all hovered a few feet above the ground, and the wizards jumped on. Weston jumped on behind Violet, who looked over her shoulder to make sure the army was ready. As soon as the last stragglers were on their brooms, she turned forward again.

"Hold on, Weston," she said, even though he already had his arms wrapped tightly around her waist. He'd seen how fast she could fly, so he was making sure his grip was strong and secure. He felt her chest expand as she took a deep breath, and then, she was off. She zoomed full speed ahead into the tunnel, the rest of the army falling into place behind her.

Weston heard the now familiar sound of wind whipping against his ears as he flew. He rather liked the feeling of flying on a broomstick. Since he was usually in his giant dragon form when he flew, he almost felt like a feather when he was zooming forward so quickly in his comparably light human form.

Weston leaned close against Violet to keep their combined shape as aerodynamic as possible. As he had the last time, he began to lose track of time and space. When he wasn't the one actually flying, it was difficult for him to stay on top of where in the tunnel they were, or how long they'd been flying. He had to stay alert, though. Last time, he had known as soon as Violet decreased her speed that they were approaching the end of the tunnel. This time, however, there would be no slowing down as they neared the exit. Instead of worrying about going slowly and staying undetected for as long as possible—a difficult feat with an army this size—the soldiers were all going to continue flying at breakneck speed straight into Saul's camp. With any luck, they'd be able to do some damage before Saul's army knew what hit them. If they weren't so lucky and Saul's army was prepared for them, well, then they'd just have to deal with a rougher beginning to their mission.

Weston could feel his heart pounding in his chest. He loved the excitement that filled him on the cusp of battle. There was nothing quite like the moments right before two sides collided into a fight for the death. He knew some people thought he was crazy for being such an adrenaline junkie, but he couldn't help himself. The thirst for adventure was in his blood.

The tunnel seemed to go on forever, but finally, Weston thought he could smell the air getting fresher. He breathed in deeply, trying to see if he'd been imagining things, or whether he'd really smelled outside air. His next breath definitely did not smell like tunnel air, and Weston tightened his grip on Violet even more. In a minute or two, they'd be hurtling straight into Saul's headquarters.

Weston wondered whether Saul himself was there tonight. He knew the evil dragon wizard had been in and out of headquarters. One of Weston's clanmates had actually seen Saul flying above Sandview at one point, taunting the townspeople. But Saul himself seemed to stay far away from any battles. Weston thought this was a cowardly way to act. So what if Saul was the leader? Knox and Peter were the leaders of the good wizards and shifters, and they were always bravely flying on the front lines. They didn't ask their soldiers to go into battles that they themselves weren't willing to fight.

Weston's thoughts about Saul were cut short when he saw Violet raise her magic ring and send sparks flying into the air. This was her signal that the exit to the tunnel was less than thirty seconds away, and Weston knew that all the wizards behind him would be setting up sparks from their rings as well. All the way to the back of the army, each wizard would warn those behind him or her that the battle was beginning in mere seconds. Weston's heart thundered in his ears, and he prepared to shift into dragon form as soon as Violet was clear of the tunnel. He knew that right behind him, Holden and Knox would be shifting as well.

"Steady," Weston told himself. Keeping steady in the face of impending action had always been the hardest part of war for him, but he had to time this correctly. If he jumped the gun and started shifting too soon, his large dragon form would block up the tunnel's passageway. He might even get stuck. Weston forced himself to be patient, taking a few deep breaths to calm himself as the tunnel's exit became clearly visible in front of him.

"Steady, steady," Weston said through gritted teeth. And then, he yelled out "Now!"

He roared, and let his inner dragon begin to take over. He covered his head with his hands as he rolled off Violet's broomstick. She never slowed down, but his rapidly thickening dragon hide kept him safe from injury as he landed on the ground with a rolling thud. Knox and Holden landed beside him moments later, both of them in between dragon and human form, just as Weston was. Weston watched the rest of the wizard army zooming over him as his hands turned to dragon hands, his wings sprouted, and his body grew a tail and horns. He started running forward impatiently before his transformation was even fully complete. He didn't want to end up at the very back of the army. He wanted to be on the front lines, fighting alongside Violet.

When his wings had finally fully grown out, Weston began flapping them, and his dragon form rose high into the air. The wizards above him parted ranks to let him through, and then he flew a few yards above their heads as they all swarmed into Saul's headquarters. From his vantage point, Weston had a clear view of the chaos of battle.

It appeared that they had taken Saul's soldiers by surprise, much as they'd hoped they would. The moon was not very bright tonight, but torches were lit all over the place to give light to Saul's soldiers, and Weston could make out frantic enemy wizards running back and forth, waving their magic rings but unsure of even which direction they should be aiming their attacks. Enemy shifters were in the process of shifting into animal form, and several half-human half-animals were racing around in the frenzied army below as well.

Many of the Falcon Cross wizards had started to break off now, heading down to start attacking the enemy wizards and shifters. The scene below Weston quickly became a mass of colliding bodies, but Weston wasn't going to stop to fight until he reached the cave where the prisoners were held.

Up ahead of him, he could see Violet once again. He saw her veer downward and to the right, and he knew she must be right above the prisoner's cave. He strained his eyes to see it, but he wasn't able to quite yet. He could see the bat cave off to his left. A small cloud of bat shifters was rising from it, but the bat shifters didn't worry him much. He knew none of them had been trained to fight all that well yet, and besides, their numbers had been seriously decreased by the last two battles. And, of course, thanks to the master bat being destroyed, the number of bat shifters would continue to decrease. Saul wouldn't be able to clone new bats to replace the ones who were destroyed.

Weston adjusted his flight course slightly to the right, and then the prisoners' cave came into view. Violet was zooming above the guards on her broomstick, launching off magic attacks at them as quickly as she could. There were a lot of wizard guards, though, and they seemed to have strong protective shields in place. The lion shifters and bear shifters fell relatively quickly, but the wizards were clearly proving much harder to take down.

Weston dove toward the ground, already taking a deep breath as he zoomed toward the front of the cave. He breathed in as deeply as he possibly could, until he felt like his lungs were going to burst. He waited until he was swooping directly over the top of the wizard guards, and then let out the breath in one long streak of fire.

His fire met with quite a bit of resistance. The protective shields that the wizard guards had up did their jobs well, and Weston knew it would take quite a bit of firepower to get through them. He had expected this, though, and was not disheartened by it. He took another deep breath and swooped back in the direction he'd just come from, sending a second streak of flames at the enemy wizards.

He saw Knox and Holden fly up to join him, sending their own streams of fire across the group. And then, to his surprise, he saw a fourth dragon joining them. For a moment, Weston tensed up, thinking that somehow the enemy had recruited an evil dragon. Dragons were very hard to turn away from the side of good, but it could be done—as evidenced by the fact that Saul himself was a dragon. But then, Weston realized who the fourth dragon was, and his lips turned up in a smile. It was Nick, Holden's stepson. Nick was only twelve, and far too young to be on the battlefield. Nick's mother would have certainly told him not to come, but Nick, like many twelve year olds, didn't always listen to his mother. He must have snuck in at the tail end of the army, and now, here he was, joining in the fray.

So be it, Weston thought. Nick's dragon looked like it was strong and healthy, and the boy seemed to be holding his own in the battle. There was no sense in taking time out from fighting to try to convince the boy to go back. Weston took another deep breath and continued on with his fire attacks.

For what felt like a long time, not much seemed to change. The battle continued to rage on around them, and Weston and the other dragons kept their steady fire attacks going. The guards in front of the prisoners' cave were strong, and refused to back down. Weston could only hope that he and his fellow soldiers could outlast the evil wizards.

Weston hadn't been paying much attention to what was going on in the rest of the headquarters, but it seemed that his army was doing a good job of taking down Saul's soldiers, because at some point he realized that more and more of his own wizard soldiers were joining the fight at the front of the prisoners' cave. This meant that they had managed to beat back the enemy they had been fighting in other parts of Saul's lair.

Weston felt a fresh rush of adrenaline pumping through his veins as more and more good wizards joined him. He finally paused long enough to look around, and was happy to find that there were no bats visible anywhere. His army must have taken down the last of those pesky creatures. Weston flew even faster, breathing fire in a nearly constant stream. The noise of the battle had become deafening, but this also energized Weston. He knew that the rising noise was due to his soldiers growing excitement as they saw the battle slowly turning in their favor.

And then, suddenly, even the noise of battle was drowned out by the sound of a giant explosion. Weston slowed his flight path and turned his giant dragon head to look in the direction of the noise. About a hundred yards away, he could see a giant ball of fire rising into the sky. Several wizards were zooming around the fire on their broomsticks, shrieking. Weston could not tell from this distance whether the wizards were excited or angry, or even which side they were fighting for. Everything around the ball of fire was a chaotic mess. Time seemed to almost stand still as all of the soldiers, good and evil alike, turned to look at the fire in confusion. And then, to Weston's astonishment, he saw another dragon rising in the flames—a dragon he knew immediately was the infamous, evil Saul.

Saul's dragon was dark red, like the color of diseased blood. The light from the explosion's fire lit up his form as he flew, his translucent, scarred wings beating furiously against the night sky. Black spikes, almost like horns, extended from several points on his wings, and the same black spikes covered his enormous tail. One of his large dragon feet carried a wizard's wand. Weston shuddered. He knew already that Saul had been given wizard abilities through the use of dark magic, but seeing for himself the ugly, twisted dragon with a wand in his claws sent a chill through even Weston's boiling hot dragon blood. That chill only got worse when Saul turned his own dragon head to look back toward where Weston and the others were watching. Even though Weston was at least the length of a football field away from Saul, Weston could see that the evil dragon's eyes glowed red. For a few horrifying moments, time seemed to stand still, as Saul seemed to be looking straight at Weston. Weston could no longer hear the noise of the battle, or see anything except those horrible red eyes.

But then, the awful spell seemed to break as Saul turned his head away and started to fly as fast as he could away from the battle raging in his ruined headquarters. The noise, heat, and smell of the battle once again flooded Weston's senses, and he heard screaming all around him.

"Saul's retreating! He's leaving! He's abandoning headquarters!"

Weston couldn't be entirely sure whether the voices were happy or upset. He finally realized it was a mixture of both. Weston's own soldiers were overjoyed to see their greatest enemy on the run. Saul's soldiers, though, were in a state of panic. Weston knew in that moment that the battle was won for the side of good. All around him, the wizard guards were abandoning the prisoners' cave and taking off at full speed to fly after Saul. Weston's own soldiers started chasing after them, and they took a great number of them down as they attacked their retreating forms.

Weston didn't join in the pursuit. He would have loved nothing more than to take down Saul himself, but trying to do so without the help of one of the dragon stones would be a pointless exercise. Although Saul's lair was being destroyed, it didn't take an expert in magic to see that Saul himself was still surrounded by powerful protective shields. After all, he'd risen from a huge, powerful explosion without any wounds. Weston figured the dark dragon wizard must be concentrating all of his magic power on protecting himself. Saul had given up his headquarters as lost at this point, and with good reason. Weston could see that the majority of Saul's soldiers had fallen due to the attacks the good wizards and dragons were throwing at them.

Weston flapped his wings gently to hover in the air and watch as Saul's form grew smaller and smaller in the distance. Any of the evil soldiers that caught up to Saul seemed to be covered by his protective shield, because the good soldiers eventually were unable to attack them anymore. Soon, most of Weston's army was turning to fly back to where Weston waited, watching.

To his left, Violet was hovering on her broomstick and watching as well. Once it became clear there was nothing more worth seeing of Saul's retreat, Weston looked over at her. She looked back at him and smiled, her eyes dancing in the flickering light coming from the fires that seemed to be burning everywhere now. Weston smiled his best dragon smile at her, memorizing in that moment how beautiful she looked outlined against the chaos of battle. Then he slowly circled down to land right in front of the prisoners' cave. Violet followed him down, landing with a quick thud and hopping off her broomstick.

"Looks like we drove Saul out of his comfortable little lair," Violet said, her face lit up by a happy grin. "Serves him right, after he stole the Redwoods base away from you."

Weston huffed, sending two circles of smoke up from his nostrils as he did. It still hurt to think about how Saul had taken over the Redwoods Dragons home base. Sure, their little homes might only have been a group of cabins in the midst of the Redwoods, but those cabins were Weston's favorite place in the world. It turned his stomach to think of Saul's soldiers sitting around in them, acting like they had a right to be there. Weston, along with the other Redwood Dragons, had vowed to get the cabins back from Saul's men. But the dragons had to be patient. In the middle of this wretched war, other things took precedence over recovering the cabins. Like destroying the master bat, and searching for the dragon ruby. Weston sighed again, sending more smoke into the air. Violet must have sensed that his mood had dampened at the mention of the cabins, because she reached over and rubbed his neck.

"Hey, don't worry. We'll get your home back. And maybe, once we do, you'll find room in your cabin for your lifemate?"

Weston turned his dragon head to nuzzle Violet with his nose. His heart warmed at her words. He was still getting used to the idea that he wasn't alone in this world anymore. He had a lifemate! A beautiful, smart, brave lifemate. Violet was right. They would get the Redwoods base back eventually. And when they did, it would be even better than before, because she would be there with him.

Most of the wizard soldiers in Weston's army were back by now, all landing in the area around where Violet and Weston were standing. They looked expectantly at Violet and Weston, awaiting further instructions. Weston realized suddenly that he hadn't seen Knox, Holden, or Nick for quite some time. He looked around, worried, but his momentary fear was soon appeased. He saw them flying around, breathing fire into all of the caves Saul had been using for his operations. No weapons or supplies would be left behind for Saul to return to. The dragons were making sure of that.

Satisfied that his clan members were safe, Weston started scanning the crowd for Peter. He wasn't really worried about the old wizard. After all, Peter could cast the best protective spells of any wizard Weston knew. Still, Weston breathed a sigh of relief when he spotted the old wizard zooming above the crowd on his broomstick, heading toward Violet. Violet saluted Peter as he landed in front of her and dismounted.

"How are the prisoners?" Peter asked.

"We haven't checked yet," Violet said. "We were waiting to make sure Saul was really gone before we started talking to them."

Peter nodded. "Understood. Well, I guess I'll go in with you now, if you're ready?"

"I'm ready," Violet said. "Do you know what that explosion was, though? The one that seemed to drive Saul out of his hiding spot? I was surprised that anything could break through his dark magic shields."

Peter laughed. "Zoe, one of our younger wizard soldiers did that. She was actually attempting an attack spell but messed up the wording and set off a powerful explosive spell instead. It's one of the more dangerous spells, and can kill the wizard casting it when performed improperly. We don't teach it to our soldiers because of that, and Zoe is lucky to be alive. I'm going to keep an eye on her. That girl has more power than she even realizes."

Weston saw Violet's eyes widen. "The *Crepitus* Spell?" she asked.

Peter nodded. "Yes, that's the one. You know it?"

Violet nodded. "I know of it. They warned us about it in Advocacy school. I was told no one even uses it anymore because of the dangers. How in the world did this Zoe girl do it by accident?"

Peter shrugged. "You'll have to ask her. In any case, I'm glad she did, since she survived and the spell got Saul out of here. Should we go talk to the prisoners, who I suppose are no longer prisoners?"

Violet nodded, and looked over at Weston. "You coming?" she asked. He nodded his dragon head, and turned to follow her toward the mouth of the cave.

Inside, about one hundred bodies huddled, looking out at them with terror. Weston could easily see that the group was a mixture of humans, shifters, and wizards. The humans might have been from nearby Sandview, but he couldn't say where the shifters and wizards might have come from. He hoped that they would be willing to talk, and that the information they had might help in the fight against Saul. Peter, though, wisely realized that it was best to get the former prisoners out of the cave and to safety before attempting to grill them with questions.

"Good evening," Peter said. Holding his magic ring up to his face. He had a light spell on the ring, which made his face clearly visible. "I'm Peter, head wizard of the Falcon Cross clan of wizards. With me are some dragons from the Redwood Dragons clan of dragon shifters. Together, we are fighting against Saul, trying to bring an end to the evil he is doing in the world. We are here to help you."

"So it's true, then," one of the imprisoned shifters said with a gasp. "There *is* a resistance fighting against Saul. We'd heard rumors, but we didn't dare to believe."

Weston watched Violet stand a little taller next to him. She was proud of her clan, he knew. As she should be. He was proud of his clan. They were the resistance, and they were beating back Saul, slowly but surely.

"Well, it's time to believe," Peter said. "Because we're here, and you are all free. We will give anyone here who wants it safe passage and shelter in Falcon Cross. First, though, let's get all of you out of here. We have a safe house on the outskirts of

Blackstone. Our dragons will fly you there, and then we can sort out where everyone wants to go next. Is that alright with everyone? Flying with a dragon is very safe, I assure you."

Weston could see that a few of the prisoners were frightened at the thought of riding on a dragon, but they all nodded in agreement nonetheless. Weston looked around for his dragon clanmates. They were still flying around setting stuff on fire. At this point, they were just having fun burning things. Weston rolled his eyes, and then let out a roar, calling them over. They turned at the sound of his roar, and flew over to him.

"We're going to fly this group back," Violet said to them, gesturing toward the frightened faces inside the cave. Knox, Holden, and Nick nodded their dragon heads, then lined up next to Weston. All four dragons crouched low to the ground to make it easier for people to climb on. Even though dragons are large and can hold several people, it soon became apparent that not all of the prisoners would fit on the four dragon backs. Violet had a solution for that problem, though.

"Those of you who are wizards, are you willing to fly on the back of a broomstick with some of our wizards?" she asked.

The wizards who had been prisoners readily agreed. Weston had the feeling that they probably preferred riding with wizards instead of dragons anyway. Soon, all of the former prisoners, who were now refugees of sorts, were either loaded onto the dragons' backs or had climbed onto wizards' broomsticks. Violet herself climbed onto her broomstick, then looked back at Weston to make sure he was ready. He winked at her, and she winked back before starting to rise into the sky.

"Let's go, everyone!" she called out. "Time to go home and celebrate another resounding victory against evil."

Weston flapped his wings, rising quickly into the sky along with the other dragons and wizards. They turned toward Blackstone, tired but happy. They had shown Saul once again tonight that they were a force to be reckoned with.

CHAPTER TWELVE

The morning sun streamed through the windows and glowed against Violet's hair as she walked through the rows of refugees one last time, making sure that no one else still wanted more breakfast. She'd lost track of how many cartons of eggs and loaves of bread they had gone through. These poor people had been hungry. Saul's soldiers had only fed them the bare minimum to keep them alive. Some of them, who had been imprisoned for quite some time, had wasted away to skin and bones. Violet could not understand how anyone could treat fellow shifters, wizards, and humans so cruelly. She looked over at Weston and her heart overflowed with love for him. He had been the one to make sure these people were rescued. It was because of him, her dragon with a heart of gold, that the battle last night had even been fought in the first place.

Weston caught her staring, and walked over to plant a kiss on her lips.

"You should sit down and rest," he said. "You've barely taken a moment to catch your breath since you got up at five o'clock this morning."

Violet sighed as he wrapped her arms protectively around her. She loved how he felt strong and gentle all at the same time. "I just wanted to make sure everyone was taken care of," she murmured into his chest. "I can't imagine how scared these people must all have been, starving and at the mercy of Saul's awful soldiers."

"I know," Weston said. "But they're safe now. And well-fed. You should get off your feet for a minute."

Before Violet could respond, her moment with Weston was interrupted by Holden's voice. "Hey, you two lovebirds! Break it up and come to the meeting room. Peter and Knox want to powwow."

Violet blushed and tried to pull away from Weston, but Weston pulled her closer and gave her a big, showy kiss on the lips. Violet looked up just in time to see Holden rolling his eyes and turning around, but Weston just laughed.

"He's one to talk," Weston said. "He has a new lifemate of his own."

Violet smiled. It was true. Holden had found love when he met Nick's mother, Elise. The two of them had been nearly inseparable since they finally admitted to having feelings for each other. Elise was here now, but was busy in the kitchen cooking up a storm. She had worked in the restaurant industry before meeting Holden, so she was an old pro at making meals for large groups of people.

"Come on," Weston said, grabbing Violet's hand and pulling her toward the stairs. "We better head to the meeting room before Knox has to come looking for us. He doesn't like to have to ask twice to get people to show up to meetings."

Violet followed Weston to the meeting room on the second floor of the house. The whole house was overcrowded right now, since it had gained about a hundred new occupants overnight. But Peter and Knox had still managed to clear space in this room for a meeting location. Along with Peter, Knox, and Holden, several of the refugees sat at a long table that had been dragged up here. Violet had no idea where they'd found the table, but it fit quite well in the room. She sat down next to Weston and waited for Knox or Peter to begin the meeting.

Peter stood and gestured toward Violet and Weston. "I'm sure you all already know these two, but I'll introduce them, anyway. Weston here is a dragon shifter, and a member of the Redwood Dragons clan just like Knox and Holden. He's the one responsible for planning the attack last night, so you can all thank him for the fact that you're no longer captive to Saul's men."

The refugees all spoke words of heartfelt thanks before Peter continued with his introductions.

"And this here is Violet. She's one of the most talented wizards in Falcon Cross, and she helped Weston with the attack that destroyed the bat cloning operation. She's a great asset to our cause."

Violet felt her cheeks turn pink at Peter's praise, but he didn't seem to notice. He continued speaking, turning to introduce the refugees who sat in the room with them.

"We have here a representative from each group of refugees," Peter said. "There's Mark, a bear shifter. He's representing the shifters. Sid there is a wizard, here to represent the wizards. And Joseph is a full human."

Violet nodded hello to each of the men. "Nice to meet you," she said, then turned back to Peter. She knew the old wizard had a purpose for calling this meeting that went beyond just giving everyone the chance to get acquainted, and she was getting somewhat impatient to learn what that purpose might be. Peter did not keep her waiting for long.

"I've gathered all of you so that you can all hear what Mark, Sid, and Joseph have to say about their time as Saul's prisoners. I know that you've all worked very hard to bring an end to Saul's stronghold here, and I think you'll enjoy hearing what you've saved these people from. Who wants to go first?"

"I'll start," Joseph said. He stood and looked around at the group, making eye contact with everyone. "This has been quite a difficult time for me, and for many of the citizens of Sandview. As I suppose you know, Saul invaded our town. He tried to force all of us to join his evil army. Some did, out of fear. But many resisted. Saul captured all those who resisted. His power easily overcame us. How could mere humans hope to stand up to wizards and shifters? Of course, we were all shocked to discover that shifters and wizards existed. And until we met all of you, we thought they were all evil. I'm ashamed to say that we were even wary of the wizards and shifters who were being held as prisoners with us. Even though they were nice to us, we just couldn't bring ourselves to trust anyone who wasn't human when we'd been treated so poorly."

Violet sat up straighter, feeling a sudden sense of alarm. "But wait," she said. "If everyone in Sandview saw Saul, surely there must be humans there who are freaked out and trying to go to the police or government. That's going to cause problems for our war effort!"

Violet felt anger rising in the pit of her stomach. She couldn't understand how Saul was being so careless and exposing the world of shifters and wizards to humans. There was an unspoken agreement between all shifters and wizards, whether good or evil, that humans should not be allowed to see shifting or magic if it was at all possible to avoid it. Humans tended to freak out at these sorts of things, and this could make the lives of shifters or wizards difficult. When police or military witch hunts started, everyone suffered. But Saul had never respected these unspoken rules. Instead, he regularly recruited humans for his army, often using force to compel them to join.

"Well, the people in Sandview don't remember Saul anymore," Joseph said sadly.

Violet was even more horrified as the full implication of what Joseph was saying hit her. "You mean…"

Joseph nodded sadly. "Saul's wizards did memory wiping spells on everyone in town. They don't remember him at all. Of course, many of them don't remember who they are, or have forgotten big chunks of their lives. Some of them have straight up gone crazy."

Violet rubbed her forehead with her hands, fighting back tears. "Saul has to be stopped. He's so awful."

Murmurs of agreement filled the room. Violet shouldn't have been surprised that Saul had used memory wiping spells on an entire town. After all, Saul's dark magic and evil seemed to know no bounds. But she still sat in shock, thinking about how irresponsible and damaging such actions were. Memory wiping spells were dangerous. Falcon Cross only allowed their use in extreme cases, and even then their use had to be approved by a head council member. Such spells were highly intrusive and had the potential to go very wrong, as evidenced by the fact that many people in Sandview had now forgotten who they were or gone crazy.

"Saul's bad deeds didn't just extend to the humans of Sandview, though," said Mark, the bear shifter. "He trapped many shifters from across the country and kept us as prisoners to do scientific experiments on us. He was trying to figure out a way to clone other types of shifters besides bats. I've seen so many of my fellow shifters subjected to horrible experiments. These experiments never resulted in Saul being able to clone anyone, but they did result in a lot of deaths."

Violet shuddered again. She almost didn't want to hear what Sid, the wizard would say. But Sid was standing too, now, and Violet held her breath as he spoke.

"As for the wizards, we also suffered a great deal. Saul captured many of us and tried to force us to learn dark magic to join his army of dark wizards. If we refused, he would have his dark wizards use us to practice dark magic spells. Many wizards also died or were wounded."

Violet looked over at Peter and Knox, who both had grave expressions on their faces. And no wonder. Everything Violet had just heard was horrifying. She reached over and squeezed Weston's hand. He squeezed back and looked at her, his eyes wide and sad. She knew they were both thinking the same thing: they were so glad they had rescued these people. Their only regret was not doing so sooner.

Peter stood then, and looked at the three men who had just told of the horrors they had suffered at Saul's hands.

"We would again like to extend to all of you an invitation to come to Falcon Cross," Peter said. "Anyone who wants to join us in our wizard town will be given safe passage and protection in our town. I know it doesn't make up for what you have suffered, but hopefully it offers you the promise of a better future."

Violet watched the men look at each other, and then back at Peter. Sid, the wizard, spoke up first.

"We'd like for you to take the children, and any of the women who are willing to go," he said. But the rest of us have already decided to stay. We want to help the people in Sandview who are suffering after having memory-wiping spells used on them. We want to rebuild the city, and make it a stronghold against evil. If Saul tries to come back, we'll be prepared. He'll never take this town again."

Peter smiled. "I can't argue with that. If there's any help we can give you, let us know. And please let the children and woman know we'll be leaving for Falcon Cross tonight as soon as darkness falls. Anyone who wants to come with us is welcome."

"Thank you," Sid said, and Joseph and Mark murmured their thanks as well. Violet thought she saw the hint of a tear in Joseph's eyes, but he brushed it away quickly.

"What about Blackstone?" Weston asked. "Do you think any of the townspeople here saw what was going on?"

Knox spoke up. "We haven't heard anyone saying anything. We're hoping that because we're out on the edge of town and have tried to operate mostly at night, no one saw us. Or, perhaps, if they did see us, they think they're not seeing things correctly, and couldn't possibly have seen a dragon."

"We'll keep an eye on Blackstone," Sid said, "and make sure to let you know if any humans here get concerned."

"Well then," Peter said. "I guess that settles it. Everyone who's leaving, pack up your things. Tonight, we fly to Falcon Cross."

"Did you hear that, V?" Weston asked, looking over at Violet with a huge smile on his face. "You're going home. And, of course, I'm coming with you."

Violet's heart leapt in her chest. "I can't wait," she said. "Let's head to our apartment and pack our things."

The mission to Blackstone had been a life-changing experience, and Violet was grateful for it. But she had never been as excited to head home as she was right now.

CHAPTER THIRTEEN

As darkness fell over Blackstone that evening, a small group of humans, wizards, and other shifters rose into the night sky. The wizards rode on broomsticks, and the humans and shifters rode on the backs of the dragon shifters. They flew like the wind, and, in two days time, reached the wizarding city of Falcon Cross, where they received a hero's welcome.

Violet had never been so glad to be home. She was honored to have had the opportunity to serve on the mission to Blackstone, but there was nothing quite like being in your own bed. The first night, she slept for twelve hours. She had barely had time to wake up and sit down at her kitchen table with a mug of coffee when a knock sounded at her front door. A smile crossed her lips as she stood to go open the door. She already knew it was Weston. He'd gone to his own apartment in Falcon Cross the first night, so he could get some of his things. But he'd promised to come over as soon as possible today, and here he was. She saw him take in her bathrobe appreciatively.

"Not dressed yet, eh?" he said. "No complaints from me about that."

She rolled her eyes at him. "I haven't been awake that long. I slept twelve hours, if you can believe it!"

"I believe it," Weston said, walking into the house and shutting the door behind him. "I would probably still be sleeping if Knox hadn't dragged all of the Redwood Dragons out of bed for an emergency eight a.m. meeting."

"Eight a.m.? Really?" Violet asked. "What could possibly have been that urgent?"

"The dragon ruby," Weston said. "Knox wants to send a search party out for it. We have a few ideas of where it might be, and he thinks it's better to go out and look than to keep sitting around here researching and hoping something turns up."

"Wow," Violet said. "I guess that makes sense. It sounds like something Knox would want to do, anyway."

"Yeah," Weston said, cracking a smile. "None of us dragons really like to sit around in front of computers."

"So are you being sent on the mission?" Violet asked. Her stomach did a funny little flip flop. She wasn't sure if she could convince Peter to let her go on another mission right now, but she didn't want to watch Weston go off on a mission without her. Weston just shrugged.

"I'm not sure yet. Knox is going to talk to Peter and hammer out the details. Hopefully we'll have a more concrete plan by tonight. But in any case, don't worry. If I do go, I'm going to insist on taking you with me. I'm not leaving you again so soon after finally convincing you to admit you're in love with me."

Weston leaned over to give Violet a kiss, and she laughed. "I didn't take that much convincing, did I?"

Weston's face turned slightly serious. "You sort of did. I was afraid for a while there that you were seriously going to make me wait until the war was over for us to be together. Or that you were too mad at me for disagreeing with you in that one meeting to ever let me have a chance at dating you."

Violet grinned. "Maybe I was a little bit stubborn," she said.

Weston rolled his eyes. "Just a bit," he said. "But that's alright, everything worked out in the end. I got the girl of my dreams, and we're relatively safe from the war for the moment. I say we should celebrate."

With that, Weston lifted Violet up in his arms, and carried her toward her bedroom. She shrieked, and put up a bit of a struggle, but it was all just for show. She'd never been so happy to be carried by a man. His strong arms felt warm and secure, and his face looking down at her made her heart skip a beat. He was so wonderful, and so handsome. And he was hers. She was still in awe of the fact that he had chosen her, and that they belonged to each other.

Once they were in the bedroom, he set her down, then pushed her up against the wall with a kiss. She let herself melt into him, relishing the feel of his lips on hers. It didn't matter in that moment that the world around them was in turmoil, or that the dragon ruby was still missing. All that mattered was that they were here, together.

Violet had spent her whole life working hard. She'd poured her heart and soul into being a Wizard Advocate, and she loved her job. But it was nice to be able to forget about work for once. To just be at peace here in her home, with the man that loved her. She marveled again at how relaxed she felt when Weston's arms were around her. He centered her, like no one ever had.

His kiss was so sweet. It quenched her thirst, like rain on a dry desert. She hadn't realized how badly she'd wanted love until love had found her. She'd always been strong on her own, but it felt good to let Weston's strong arms hold her for a while, too.

Weston was in no hurry, and Violet loved that unhurried pace. He reached his hands up to hold the side of her face as he let his tongue dance with her tongue. Violet closed her eyes and let his heat wash over her. Her whole body tingled and trembled at his touch, and she could feel herself growing wet with anticipation. This was going to be a damn good morning.

Eventually, Weston pulled away from Violet just long enough to pull his t-shirt up and over his head. Violet bit her lip happily as she took in the sight of his bare chest. It was a work of art that she would never tire of admiring. She put her hands on his chest, and let them slide down, feeling his strong ribs and sculpted abs before stopping at the button of his jeans. She looked up at him coyly through her lashes as she unbuttoned and unzipped his jeans, then pushed them down so they fell around his ankles.

"Oops," she said, grinning.

He smiled, kicking off his shoes and then stepping out of his jeans. She loved the easy way he moved, like they'd been doing this forever. There was no awkwardness when they made love, just a sweet, sensual heat that slowly built, burning them both up in the best possible way.

Weston continued smiling as he reached down to untie Violet's robe. He pushed it off of her, letting it fall to the floor and leaving her naked underneath. His eyes roved over her whole body, and Violet could see his erection growing and stiffening beneath his tight briefs as he took in the sight of her.

"God, you're beautiful," he said. "I fell in love with you for your beautiful soul, but your body is gorgeous, too. There's no part of you I don't love."

Violet felt the tingling, trembling sensation within her increasing. Just the sound of his voice turned her on. It was so warm and comforting. She looked up at him, her eyes meeting his, and she marveled again at how at home she felt right now.

He had so quickly become her everything.

He leaned in to kiss her again, and she reached for the hem of his underwear as he did. She pushed it down and off, never breaking their kiss. His erection sprang free, poking against her stomach and causing the wetness between her legs to grow even more. She had enjoyed the slow pace at which Weston was moving until now. Now, she wanted him. She'd had enough waiting.

He had reached the same point, it seemed. With a low, hungry growl, he grabbed her two breasts in his palms and squeezed them tightly, using them as anchors to hold onto while he positioned his stiff dick right in front of her and pushed into her with another growl.

Violet's eyes closed again, and she let out a moan as the pressure and heat in her body became wonderfully unbearable. Her breasts throbbed beneath his touch, and she bit her lip in an effort to contain the building tingling sensation. The room felt like it was spinning. Even though she knew her back was securely against the wall and Weston had a secure grip on her, she couldn't keep from feeling a bit like she was floating. Or flying, perhaps. Whatever the sensation, Violet drank it in, wanting to relish every second of being here, safe and happy with Weston, filled with a passion like she'd never known before.

It didn't take long for him to push her over the edge. She tried to hold back, to drag out the buildup as long as she could. But it was impossible to resist the tremors trying to overtake her body. With a loud scream, Violet threw her head back and let her release come. She felt her inner muscles clenching around Weston, throbbing with the heat and moisture of her desire. Wonderful shivers of delight rushed up and down her spine, and she let herself collapse against Weston. It felt so good to fall into his arms while he was inside her. She felt loved, protected, and wanted. She could not have asked for more than this.

Weston held her tightly, and thrust deeper into her. His breath was hot in her ear as his hips moved with a greater urgency, searching for a release of his own. It didn't take him long to find it. With a roar, he came into her, pulsing and digging his fingers deeper into the soft skin of her back. He was probably going to leave a few red marks, but Violet didn't care. All she knew in that moment was that he wanted her so badly that his primal animal instincts were taking over. There was nothing in the world like being wanted on such a deep, honest level. Violet pressed her chest against his, and they stood together like that, breathing rapidly, until the tremors in each of their bodies had subsided.

Weston kissed her gently on the forehead and slid out of her, then reached down to grab her robe off the floor. Without a word, he gently held it up for her to slide her arms into, then tenderly retied the front sash for her.

"You're amazing," he whispered, winking at her as he pulled her into his arms again, still naked himself.

"I could say the same about you," Violet said. "You know that."

Weston's chest shook with laughter against Violet's face. "I'm glad you think so," he said. For a while there I thought you just thought of me as annoying."

"Oh that, too," Violet said, looking up and giving him a wink of her own. "But I guess amazing won out in the end."

Weston laughed again, the musical sound of it filling the room.

"In all seriousness, though," Violet said, wrapping her own arms tightly around Weston's broad back. "It's good that we can disagree with each other now and then. Knowing we can argue and still love each other and be on the same team makes us stronger."

"I agree," Weston said. "A life with no fireworks is a little boring, don't you think?"

Violet smiled. "So boring," she agreed. "And, anyway, I can't believe how wrong I was about waiting until the war was over to be with you. It doesn't make sense to put our entire lives on hold because the world is full of uncertainty. In fact, I feel better now that I have someone to hold on to during the times of uncertainty."

"You know things are probably about to get more uncertain, right?" Weston asked. "We gave Saul a big defeat this week, but the search for the dragon ruby is just heating up. We're going to all be working hard, possibly in some very dangerous situations."

"It's alright," Violet said. "The more uncertain things get, the tighter I'll hold on to you, my dragon."

Weston kissed the top of her head again. "We'll hold on to each other," he said. "Life lately has been one crazy, fury-filled ride. But we're taking that ride together, and that's all that matters."

Violet smiled and buried her face against his chest. He was right. All that mattered to her in the world was right here in her arms. The rest was just details, now that she'd found the love of a dragon.

BOOK NINE: COURAGE AND THE DRAGON

CHAPTER ONE

Boom! The sound, much louder than a normal thunderclap, made Zoe's brain feel like it was vibrating inside her head. Stunned for a moment, she gathered herself together and once again raised her magic ring high above her head.

"*Magicae superarma!*" she yelled, just as another boom blasted out and she was knocked backwards. She landed hard on her tailbone and winced. The force of the explosion had been incredible, and she hadn't been able to fully block it with her shield. But she had deflected the worst of it, and, other than a likely bruise on her backside, she'd remained unscathed.

She couldn't afford to rest on the ground for long, though. The wizard attacking her was circling her shield, looking for a weak spot and preparing to launch another blow. Zoe scrambled to her feet and watched the other wizard carefully, waiting until the split-second before he attacked again. With perfect timing, she yelled out, "*Superarma terminantur!*" and rolled out of the way. Her shield spell instantly ended, and the attack that had been intended to make a dent in the shield hit empty air instead. Zoe made her next move with lightning speed. She had to catch her opponent while his defenses were down, before he could gather his wits to launch another attack in place of the one he'd just wasted on her disappearing shield.

"*Magicae levitate! Magicae obstupefio! Magicae invado.*"

Zoe's spells hit her opponent before he could react, and he howled in pain as he flew high into the air, stunned and suddenly burning from the heat of the fire that had leapt from Zoe's magic ring and surrounded his body.

"That's enough!" a loud voice called on the other side of the room. "Zoe, let's end this session here."

Zoe nodded at Peter, the old wizard standing several dozen feet away from her. Then she turned back to the wizard she'd just attacked, and canceled all her spells.

"*Levitate terminantur. Obstupefio terminantur. Invado terminantur.*" She watched as the flames surrounding the other wizard instantly died out, and he fell to the ground, able to move once again. He was wearing a special suit of magic armor, which Peter had cast a protective spell on from across the room. Because of the armor, the spells Zoe had cast hadn't caused as much damage to her opponent as they might have under normal circumstances. Still, a group of wizard medics rushed toward him to check for damage and administer any necessary healing spells.

Zoe felt the beads of sweat that had formed on her forehead trickling down, catching on her eyebrows and trying to push their way through to her eyelids. She wiped at them with the back of her arm, and took deep, hungry breaths. Right now, her lungs felt like they would never again have enough air. She hadn't noticed the cramping in her side while the adrenaline of the moment had filled her, but now that the training exercise was done, the sharp pangs in her side demanded her attention. She wished she could sit down and rest for a moment, but she felt the pressure of dozens of judging eyes upon her. She had never been one to care much about the opinions of others, yet even she couldn't pretend that she didn't want the approval of the Falcon Cross High

Council. Not to mention, the approval of the Falcon Cross Military Commander, and the leaders of the Redwood Dragons shifter clan. This room was filled with VIPs whom Zoe could only have dreamed of meeting in person just a few weeks ago. Now, suddenly, she was something of a celebrity. And she wasn't exactly comfortable with the spotlight that had been thrust on her.

Zoe saw with relief that the wizard she'd been fighting was sitting up now. The medics had smiles on their faces and were laughing with him. That was a good sign. Zoe had been assured that, thanks to Peter's protection from the magic suit, the wizard would not suffer any serious harm. She'd been encouraged to throw attack spells at him with full force, so that the High Council could see what she was capable of. But despite their reassurances, Zoe couldn't stop herself from worrying. She'd fought in several large battles during her short time as a Falcon Cross soldier, so she was no stranger to killing people. But the idea of killing one of her own clan members, even by accident, was too much to take.

Peter started walking toward her then, followed by the two dragon shifters in the room. Peter was the head wizard of the Falcon Cross High Wizard Council, and he was the one who had decided to have Zoe go through these special training exercises. Not only was Peter the highest ranking wizard in Falcon Cross, but he was also one of the most powerful wizards in the world. His word was as good as law around these parts. The dragons next to him, Knox and Noah, were equally as powerful. Knox was the head of the Redwood Dragons Clan, and Noah was his second in command. Zoe felt her stomach doing nervous flip-flops as three of the most powerful men in the wizard and shifter world walked toward her.

She tried to stand a little straighter in her uniform. The dark black fabric, designed to offer ease of movement along with maximum protection from attack spells, fit her like a glove. The Falcon Cross military insignia was embroidered into the left chest of the uniform using gold thread, which gave the otherwise plain uniform a bit of glitz.

"Nice work," Peter said as he approached. He wiggled his white eyebrows, which matched his long white beard. He wore a dark purple robe today, and no wizard hat. Zoe rarely saw him outside of high court or official battles, where he always wore a hat. It was strange to be able to see the top of his head and the center part in his long white hair.

"Thank you, sir," Zoe said. She shifted her weight from foot to foot uncertainly, wondering if the heat in her cheeks was making them visibly pink. This whole situation made her unbearably uncomfortable.

"I've watched quite a few wizards in action by now," Noah piped in. "But I've never seen one move as fast as you did today. Peter was right. Your skills are exceptional."

Zoe felt the embarrassed heat in her cheeks growing as Noah spoke. She looked at her feet and mumbled out a thank you.

"Zoe, stop looking at the floor," Peter said. "That's not how Falcon Cross soldiers stand in the presence of high military officers."

Zoe forced her gaze up. She wished she could tell Peter that she'd just as soon not be in the presence of high military commanders, but she knew that would only make him angry. Peter expected his soldiers to treat all superiors with the utmost respect, and, certainly, Zoe should have been honored at the chance to be here. But she felt more confused than prideful at the moment.

A few weeks ago, in the midst of an intense battle against the greatest enemy of Falcon Cross—an evil dragon shifter wizard named Saul—Zoe had accidentally performed an attack spell so powerful that many wizards alive today didn't even know the spell existed. Zoe had considered her successful execution of the spell to be a fluke, but it had still caught Peter's eye. He'd pulled her aside soon after they got back to Falcon Cross, and told her that he suspected she had greater magic powers than many of her fellow wizards. He'd wanted to test how far her powers went, and to train her to perform several high level spells, if she was capable. Thus had begun the longest two weeks of Zoe's life.

Every day, Zoe had reported to this training room. It was a special room, magically insulated to withstand the severest of attacks. Training in here was by invitation only, and when you were invited, you didn't decline the invitation. Zoe had dutifully let the Master Wizards in Falcon Cross put her through a grueling regimen. They had seemed doubtful of her at first, looking skeptically at her short form as she walked in on the first day. But it hadn't taken them long to change their tune. After her first thirty minutes with the Masters, they had grown excited, and had started feverishly asking her to perform dozens of spells she had never heard of before. She'd managed each one perfectly, and the Masters had spent the last two weeks shaking their head in amazement and calling her a miracle. Zoe, never one to enjoy excess attention, had tried to downplay their unbridled admiration. But their excitement only grew as the days passed, and soon they were declaring that Peter and the rest of the High Council had to see what she could do.

Which was why Zoe had been asked to put on a show of sorts today for all of the Falcon Cross VIPs. She had no idea how the High Council was planning to use her skills in the fight against Saul, but she'd heard them refer to her several times as their "secret weapon." The terminology made her want to vomit. She didn't want to be a hero. She just wanted to be a good soldier, doing good work amongst the rest of the legions of soldiers in Falcon Cross. But the possibility of blending into the crowd was looking less and less likely as the days passed.

"Your speed is unlike anything I've ever seen," Peter was saying now. "Even though I've lived many years—too many, perhaps—I've never witnessed a wizard moving as quickly as you moved today."

Zoe forced her attention back to Peter, and silently reminded herself not to fidget. "Thank you, sir," she said. She resisted the temptation to brush off Peter's praise. Peter would not like to have his words contradicted.

"Now," Peter continued. "We've seen your speed and we've seen your attack skills. But I still haven't had the chance to witness your use of explosive spells. Can you show us the *Crepitus* spell?"

Zoe's eyes widened. "In here? Are you sure it won't destroy the training room? I know this place is reinforced with protective magic but still…the *Crepitus* spell is in a league of its own."

The *Crepitus* spell, in fact, was the spell Zoe had accidentally used during the battle in which she had initially impressed Peter. It was the most powerful explosive spell known to wizards, and even the master wizards who had trained her had warned her against using it in the training room. Peter, however, seemed unconcerned. He merely winked at her.

"This room will hold, don't worry. I'm protecting it with all of my magical energy. It might rock the walls a bit, but the building will hold."

Zoe blinked a few times. "Okay. If you're sure," she said. "But you should all probably step back as far as possible."

Peter nodded. "We will. Just aim the spell at the target on the wall over there, and let's see what you've got."

Zoe gave Peter a small salute, and watched the old wizard walk back to the opposite side of the room with the two dragon shifters. As soon as they were safely against the wall again, Zoe turned toward the target Peter had pointed out. Taking a deep, shaky breath, she raised her magic ring.

"*Magicae crepitus*" she yelled.

For the briefest of moments, nothing happened, and time seemed to stand still. And then, Zoe felt a powerful rush of energy shooting out from her ring. The force of the spell threw her backwards onto the ground, causing her to land on her sore tailbone once more. She winced, and tried to get her bearings amidst the sudden cloud of smoke that filled the air. The whole room was shaking with the reverberations from the spell, and everything around her was a fiery haze. Zoe glanced behind her to make sure that none of the wizard council or dragon shifters had been wounded in the explosion, but she couldn't see more than ten feet in front of her. She rubbed at the stinging in her eyes from the smoke, and startled a bit when several of the wizard training assistants ran toward the flames, already shouting out water spells so they could extinguish the blaze the *Crepitus* spell had caused.

Zoe stood slowly, wobbling a bit as she found her footing. And then, through the smoke, she heard the sound of cheers, and of her name being chanted. Zoe looked down at her magic ring and sighed. The spell must have gone off quite well, earning her even more praise from the group gathered in the room. Zoe should have been pleased, but she had a strange, uneasy feeling in her stomach.

This only meant more people would be singing her praises and taking notice of her. Zoe wished she could melt into the wall and disappear, but she knew that wasn't possible. Even she, with all her mysterious magical abilities, didn't know of a spell that would make people forget who she was and what she was capable of. She was just going to have to deal with the attention as graciously as she could.

CHAPTER TWO

Grayson Pars took half of his chocolate bar into his mouth with one bite. The chocolate caramel goodness, with a few nuts mixed in here and there, eased his hunger a bit the moment it touched his tongue. It must have been some sort of automatic reflex. As soon as he tasted the food, his brain sent a signal to his stomach that food was being consumed, and that it could ease up on the hunger pangs, already.

Hunger pangs weren't the only thing bothering Grayson right now, though. His scowl deepened as he walked down the long main hallway of Falcon Cross Military Headquarters. He had just come from a meeting with the top researchers from the team of wizards searching for the powerful dragon ruby, and he had presented them with information he'd found that pointed to a fresh lead on where the ruby might be. The information he'd discovered was something of a breakthrough, but no one had acknowledged that. They'd all just nodded blandly and thanked him for his time, then moved on to the next bullet point on their list.

Something about those blank stares and unenthusiastic nods had been the final straw for Grayson. He'd been working harder than anyone in his clan of dragon shifters, as far as he could tell. And yet no one seemed to notice him. He'd been passed over for all the good missions so far—missions to get the dragon amethyst, to scope out Saul's headquarters, and to destroy the bat shifter cloning operation that Saul had been running out of those same headquarters. Grayson had kept his head down and worked his ass off, but everyone else got all the glory.

Grayson took another, smaller bite of his chocolate bar as he continued to walk. His office was, of course, located at the very back of military headquarters. He'd been stuffed into the least prestigious part of the building and given a small desk that looked like it should have been retired thirty years ago. Still, Grayson had not complained. He'd been brought up to be loyal, and to be a tireless team player. He told himself that everything he was doing was for the good of the wizard and shifter communities at large, and not for the glory. Still, it would have been nice to be given a little recognition now and then. He would have appreciated the chance to go on an actual mission instead of being stuck on a never-ending research loop.

His clan's head dragon, Knox, was planning a mission to search for the dragon ruby, and Grayson desperately wanted to be the one chosen for it. Knox felt that the research on the stone had gone on long enough, and it was time to take action, and Grayson agreed. Four ancient dragon stones existed, and the Falcon Cross Wizards and Redwood Dragons had already recovered three of them—the dragon emerald, dragon sapphire, and dragon amethyst. But the final stone, the dragon ruby, was rumored to be the most powerful stone of all, possibly as powerful on its own as the other three stones combined. If Saul got a hold of the ruby before them, the war might be lost for the side of good. No one wanted to think about how awful that would be.

And yet, think about it they must. If they didn't take the danger seriously, Saul would swoop in and take over. Grayson's clan of dragons, along with the Falcon Cross wizards, were the only resistance standing in Saul's way. Grayson had never laid eyes on

Saul himself, but he'd been told the evil dragon wizard was an awful sight to behold. Grayson's whole body filled with rage whenever he thought of Saul, and Grayson wanted nothing more than to be the one chosen to go get the dragon ruby and seal Saul's defeat.

The odds of Grayson being chosen for the mission were slim, however. Rumors were already flying that his clanmates Holden and Weston, who had just returned from raiding Saul's headquarters, were going to be the chosen ones. Grayson, of course, loved his clanmates fiercely. But he was also fiercely jealous of them, and tired of them being the ones to get all the attention. His whole life, he'd been the one stuck with the less impressive missions. He'd been the one looked over for the most dangerous jobs. He never seemed able to grab his own share of the glory that all the other dragons in his clan had managed to secure.

He was, at the end of the day, unremarkable.

He was just as capable as the other dragons in his clan, but no one saw him that way. Grayson wasn't sure why. Perhaps it was because he'd always been the quietest one in the group. Sure, all of the Redwood Dragons liked to cut up and tease each other now and then. But Grayson was never as loud or obnoxious as the rest of them. And he was never as demanding as them when missions were being passed out. Perhaps it was time to change all of that, Grayson thought as he slowly chewed his chocolate bar. His strategy of being noticed on the merits of his hard work didn't seem to be working out too well for him.

Grayson's mood might have continued to spiral, had it not been for the sudden interruption of a giant explosion. Grayson stopped in his tracks, startled, as the hallway walls around him began to shake. For a moment, he stayed there, stunned. And then, instinct took over and he began to run—straight toward where the sound of the explosion had come from, of course. Dragons don't run away from danger, they run toward it. Especially when the source of that danger might be threatening their clanmates or allies.

The last bite of Grayson's chocolate bar fell from his hands as he ran, but he wasn't thinking about his hunger any more. He was thinking about what might have caused such a horrendous explosion, and whether it was actually possible that enemy soldiers had infiltrated the city of Falcon Cross without setting off an alarm from the guards who constantly patrolled the borders of the city. That didn't seem possible, and yet, there was no doubt that the explosion that had just rocked the ground he was standing on hadn't been an ordinary explosion. It had come from the direction of one of the training rooms, but there was no way that was some sort of practice spell. The training rooms were well insulated, and Grayson knew that wizards had cast incredibly powerful spells inside without so much as a picture rattling on the wall of the hallway outside. No, whatever explosion had just gone off was something different. Grayson's first instinct was that the city was under attack, and what better place to launch a secret attack than the middle of military headquarters?

With these thoughts running through his mind, Grayson sped toward the training room, preparing to shift into dragon form at a moment's notice if necessary. The door to the training room was being guarded by two sleepy looking wizards, who seemed unconcerned by the fact that smoke was seeping out from under the training room's door, and that the walls had just shaken as though an earthquake had hit them. Grayson didn't bother to stop and ask for permission to enter.

"Out of my way," he bellowed as he barreled toward the door. The guards both jumped, startled, and barely had time to register Grayson's huge form running toward them before he had pushed the door open.

"Hey!" one of the guards yelled. "We're not supposed to let anyone in there right now."

He was wasting his breath. Grayson didn't even hear him as he rushed into the training room. The door was protected by a fingerprint sensor, so most of the people in Falcon Cross would not have been able to simply open the door and get into the room. But, in a show of solidarity and trust, the high wizard Peter had give all ten of the Redwood Dragons free access to the entire city of Falcon Cross. Grayson's fingerprints would open any door in this building, even the ones that were restricted to those who had a top security clearance.

The only room in this building he cared about at the moment, however, was the training room he was standing in now. The entire room was filled with thick smoke, and the acrid smell of something burning tickled at his nose. Grayson came to a halt and assumed a defensive stance, his eyes straining to see through the smoke even as his hands were ready to launch out a volley of punches if necessary. His skin tensed up, feeling too tight for his body as he hovered on the edge of shifting into dragon form. He breathed in deeply despite the smoke, trying to detect whether there were any other smells in the air that would give away who was in this room. He wanted to know what sort of enemy he was facing.

For the space of an eternity—an eternity which in actuality only lasted about fifteen seconds—Grayson remained in this state of uncertainty, unable to see or smell anything that would show him what he was up against. He could hear shouts and people running around, but he couldn't make out what they were saying, and he had no way of knowing whether the voices belonged to friends or enemies. Grayson was just about to move forward into the unknown dangers of the smoke cloud, when he saw her.

Through the slowly clearing gray haze, his eyes landed on the silhouette of a short, curvy woman in a tight-fitting Falcon Cross Military uniform. He could see the Falcon Cross military insignia stitched into the left chest of her uniform. The insignia had been embroidered with standard gold thread, but the insignia didn't glitter like it normally did on the wizards' uniforms. It was too dark and gray in this room, like the smoke had sucked in all the light. There was no brightness for the gold thread to catch.

The woman appeared to be stunned. Grayson saw her eyes, which looked like the color of deep charcoal, as they fuzzily gazed over at him. He couldn't tell whether her eyes were actually dark gray, or whether the smoke was just making them appear that way. Her hair was pulled back into a tight bun, and the severity of the hairstyle accented the pale, drawn look on her face. She looked down at her magic ring, then back up at Grayson. Her face had an unreadable expression on it, but whatever she was feeling right now was definitely not happiness. She wobbled on her feet for a moment, but managed to steady herself and then looked back down at her ring.

Grayson went to her, moving as quickly as he dared. He didn't want to attract attention to himself if there were enemy soldiers around, and he didn't want to spook the woman. She had a deer-in-headlights look, like she might take off running in any direction at any moment. She watched him as he walked, her face scrunching up in confusion once he stood right in front of her face.

"Are you alright?" Grayson asked, keeping his voice low and soothing. Her face was streaked with soot and red scratches. She looked like she'd been in quite a fight today, although from a cursory glance she didn't seem to have any serious injuries.

"I'm fine," she said, although she wobbled unsteadily. Grayson reached out to steady her arm with one of his own strong hands.

"You look like you've taken a bit of a blow," he said, still soothing. "Can you tell me what happened?"

The woman's squint deepened. "You're not Knox or Noah," she said, ignoring his question.

Grayson frowned. It was a strange thing to say. Of course he wasn't Knox or Noah. Why were they everyone's favorite dragons? Sure, they were his clan leaders. But just because he wasn't a clan leader himself didn't mean he wasn't an exceptional dragon, too.

"I'm Grayson," he said. There was no flicker of recognition in her eyes, but she did lessen her squint a bit.

"I'm Zoe," she said, looking him up and down. "You weren't here before."

Grayson wasn't sure what she meant by saying he wasn't there before, but he decided to ignore it for the moment and focus on dealing with the danger of the present situation.

"Are you sure you're alright, Zoe? Can you tell me what happened here?"

Before Zoe could answer, a loud laugh rang out from somewhere to Grayson's right. He couldn't see anyone through the smoke, but he would have known that laugh anywhere. Knox. His clan leader was in here, and, if he was laughing, that meant that nothing was seriously wrong. In an instant, Grayson felt foolish. The explosion *had* just been a training exercise. Perhaps it had been a training exercise gone wrong, but still. There were no enemies in this room to defeat, yet Grayson had come rushing in like he was ready to do battle.

Grayson forced himself to turn sheepishly toward his right, where, to his horror, he saw that it wasn't just Knox walking toward him. It was Noah and Peter as well. All three of them had amused looks on their faces. Grayson didn't embarrass easily, but he was pretty sure his cheeks were turning red. He turned back toward Zoe merely so he wouldn't have to look at his clanmates and Peter for a moment. Hopefully, he could get his emotions under control and they wouldn't see how red-faced the moment had made him. He struggled to come up with a question to ask Zoe. He needed some sort of excuse for turning back toward her. As his brain scrambled to think of something, his eyes fell onto her uniform's name badge. Whitt.

"Whitt?" Grayson said before he could stop himself. Suddenly everything about the explosion was making perfect sense. "You're Zoe *Whitt?*"

Zoe did not look pleased by this question. She merely nodded, and set her lips in a tight line as though she were bracing for something unpleasant. Before either of them could say anything else, Noah spoke up, unnecessarily explaining what Grayson had already figured out.

"We've been testing Zoe's powers all morning," Noah said. "The explosion you heard was the *Crepitus* spell, not some sort of enemy attack. But it was quite noble of you to come rushing in to help."

"What else would I have done?" Grayson asked, the redness of embarrassment gone from his face and replaced with a deep, scowling glare. "If there's an attack on Falcon Cross, it's my duty as a dragon to defend the city."

Noah put his hands up in a gesture of surrender. "Dude, I was just explaining things. No need to get nasty. Do you have bees up your ass or something today?"

Grayson wished he could start a good old-fashioned fist fight with Noah right then and there, just to let off some steam. Back home in the Redwoods, that's exactly what he would have done. Grayson and his clanmates were always fighting. It was a good way to burn off energy or angry emotions. But here in Falcon Cross, things were different. There was an actual hierarchy here, and Noah was considered some sort of high-ranking officer. All of the wizards in the room would gasp at the scandal of a lower ranking dragon shifter attacking his superior. Back in the Redwoods, the dragons had all been brothers. Equals. Sure, Knox was technically in command and Noah was second in command. But no one had paid much attention to titles. When a leader was needed to make a decision, Knox stepped up. Otherwise, the dragons didn't spend much time worrying about showing appropriate respect to higher officers. Working with the Falcon Cross military had been quite a learning curve for Grayson.

Peter seemed to have already moved on from the amusement of seeing Grayson rush in as though an actual battle was taking place. The old wizard had turned his attention to Zoe, whose face still looked quite unhappy.

"Zoe, that was marvelous," Peter said. "You have an extraordinarily good command of the *Crepitus* spell. I've never seen anything like it. Just one more amazing thing our little secret weapon can do."

Peter smiled and put one of his hands on Zoe's right shoulder. Grayson saw Zoe stiffen, and she did not smile. But Peter didn't seem to notice her cool reception to his praise. Instead, he continued on with his analysis of what she had done well in her demonstration of magic skills that morning. Grayson wished more than anything that he had not rushed into the room when he heard the explosion. He was stuck here now, listening to Peter gush about Zoe's amazing fighting abilities, which, as far as Grayson knew, she'd acquired through sheer luck. He felt the scowl on his face growing deeper. No one ever praised his fighting abilities. Never mind the fact that he had worked damn hard to be the exceptional warrior that he was. He was just one of ten dragons, and the most quiet, ordinary of the ten at that.

Grayson could not escape from this moment, though. It would have been rude to interrupt Peter, and just as rude to walk off without saying anything. So he stood there, bitterly listening to all the wonderful things Peter had to say about Zoe. When Peter was done, Knox jumped in before Grayson even had the chance to realize that Peter had finished speaking. Thankfully, Noah had nothing to add to Peter's and Knox's long speeches, and Grayson thought he might be on the verge of being allowed to escape from this awkward situation. But then, Peter spoke up again, and his words made Grayson's blood boil.

"Zoe," the old wizard said, folding his hands serenely in front of him. "We're planning a mission to search for the dragon ruby, as you may know. We'd like to send you on that mission, if you're willing. The mission is likely to be dangerous, so whoever we send needs to be a smart, skilled wizard. You've proven that you definitely fit that description."

Grayson had to bite his tongue to keep from exclaiming that it wasn't right that someone who'd acquired their skills through luck was being offered a prime mission, while he, who had worked so hard for his abilities, was still stuck in an office, researching. For her part, Zoe did not seem thrilled by the idea. She smiled at Peter and stood tall as a soldier should. But there was no warmth in her smile, and her eyes betrayed a tired resignation.

"I'd be honored," she said. But Grayson caught the note of frustration in her voice.

She doesn't want to go, he thought. He couldn't believe it. He would have jumped at the chance to go search for the dragon ruby. But instead of accepting the mission with enthusiasm, Zoe was struggling to act excited. Her performance was not convincing, but if Peter noticed her hesitation, he did not say so.

Grayson felt the anger within him rising. If Zoe was so unenthused by a spot on the mission team for the dragon ruby, he would gladly take her place. Of course, he couldn't do magic spells like she could. But he could fight, and stand up for himself.

That's it, Grayson realized with sudden clarity. I haven't been standing up for myself. I've been working hard, thinking that hard work alone would get me the recognition I deserve. But I haven't tooted my own horn enough. The higher-ups don't notice anything unless it's a literal or figurative explosion in their faces. You have to be loud and insistent.

And in that moment, Grayson decided that loud and insistent was exactly what he was going to be. Normally, he wouldn't have bothered to tell Peter and Knox about the new lead to the dragon ruby that he'd just found. He would have figured that the people in charge of reporting research progress to the head wizard and head dragon would take care of updating them. But perhaps that had been his problem. He'd assumed that whoever was giving reports was giving credit where it was due. That might not be the case. Grayson's hard work might all be attributed to someone else, and he would never know. This time, Grayson wasn't going to let that happen.

"Speaking of the dragon ruby," Grayson said, standing up straighter and letting his voice take on a loud, booming quality. "I discovered this morning some records from Colorado indicating the ruby may be buried in a mountain near a small town out there called Shadowdale. The mountain is known as Red Point Mountain."

Grayson waited for a moment to make sure he had Peter's and Knox's full attention. The two men looked at him with mild curiosity, as did Noah and Zoe. Grayson would have liked them to show a bit more interest, but at least they were listening.

"There were actually several ancient records regarding the dragon ruby in some old bear shifter histories. No one thought to look there, but something else I saw in one of the dragon king's histories prompted me to look. I followed the rabbit trail, and it turns out I was right. There were several bear shifters hired to help escort the ruby to a new hiding place. The bears were used because the ancient dragon king thought they would be less conspicuous than dragon shifters. He must have been right, because as far as I can tell the ruby hasn't been moved since the bears escorted it to the mountain. I don't think Saul has figured out the mountain location, either. The records I found had not been accessed for decades, at least. Possibly longer."

Grayson stood proudly, waiting for Peter and Knox to process the news that they now had a location for the dragon ruby that was somewhat certain. But the two men still didn't seem as impressed as he thought they would. Despite the fact that Grayson had uncovered a huge lead, they both merely nodded in acknowledgement. There were no big exclamations of excitement. No big slaps on the back to show they were proud of him. Grayson felt deflated. What did he have to do to prove that he was an important part of this fight against evil?

Grayson opened his mouth to explain further. Perhaps Peter and Knox needed just a bit more explanation of how big this news really was. If they truly understood that Grayson might have just uncovered the actual location of the dragon ruby, then surely they would be a bit more enthusiastic. But before Grayson could say anything further, the group was interrupted by wizard medics, who had come over to check on Zoe.

"Any major damage?" one of the medics asked, pulling out a blood pressure cuff and attaching it to Zoe's arm. Peter and Knox seemed to take more of an interest in Zoe's medical exam than they had in Grayson's news about the dragon ruby. Grayson watched with irritation as they spoke to the medics about possible aftereffects from performing the *Crepitus* curse.

"God forbid anything happen to their precious little secret weapon," Grayson said.

He hadn't realized he'd spoken the words aloud until Noah gave him a slight shove in the arm.

"Dude, be a team player," Noah said.

"I always have been," Grayson said, scowling at Noah. "But it seems the coach likes to keep me on the bench and let the rest of the team play, when I'm the one who could make the winning shot."

"You'll get your chance," Noah said. Grayson would have told Noah that he'd like a chance right about now, thank you, but Peter and Knox were turning their attention back from Zoe.

"Sorry about that interruption," Peter said. "I just wanted to make sure Zoe was alright. We want to get the mission for the dragon ruby started as soon as possible. Great news on finding the location, by the way. Our research team had already briefed me that there was good news, but I'm glad to know just how good it is. Nice work."

Grayson stared at Peter blank-faced for a moment before remembering to mutter out a "Thank you, sir."

"Now," Peter continued. "If you wouldn't mind, Grayson, I'd like you to escort Zoe safely back to her quarters."

Before Grayson could speak up and say that he was a warrior, not some sort of nurse or chaperone, Zoe herself spoke up.

"I can walk back by myself just fine," she said, crossing her arms and looking at Grayson suspiciously, as though the suggestion to walk her to her room had been his idea.

"Be that as it may, Zoe, you need to rest," Peter said. "And if I send you by yourself, you're going to be mobbed like the little celebrity you are by everyone you come across. Grayson can act as a bodyguard and buffer, and get you back to your room with minimal delays."

Zoe started to protest again, and Grayson felt his own skin prickle with annoyance at being tasked with playing bodyguard to a Falcon Cross celebrity. But then he realized that all he really wanted at that moment was to get out of the training room and away from Peter and Knox. At least, if he took Zoe, he'd be making an escape. And with that realization, his mind was made up.

"Come on, Zoe," he said, grabbing her firmly by the upper arm and leading her toward the door of the training room. All around him, the smoke was clearing and he could see various wizard medics, assistants, and master wizard trainers scurrying about, cleaning and checking and discussing. Further into the room, he saw that the entire Wizard High Council was present. They were all huddling in a small circle, and glancing over at Zoe now and then. Grayson felt his stomach turn. He definitely had to get out of here.

"I can walk myself," Zoe said, trying to pull her arm away from Grayson.

"I'm sure you can," Grayson said in a voice that brooked no argument. "But I've been commanded to walk with you, so let's go."

Zoe pouted up at him for a moment, but after looking back at Peter and Knox, she relaxed her arm and stopped trying to pull away. Grayson got that feeling that she was just as eager as he was to get out of that training room. And so, together, they made their way quickly to the door. Grayson planned to get Zoe to her quarters as quickly as he could, and then get back to his office and shut the door behind him, not coming out for the rest of the day.

If he'd had any idea how much meeting Zoe was going to change his life, he might not have been in such a hurry to get away from her.

CHAPTER THREE

Zoe kept a frown on her face as she and Grayson exited the training room, but, truth be told, she was rather grateful for an arm to hang on to. She had been too nervous to eat much before going in for the demonstration this morning, and now she could feel her blood sugar dipping dangerously low. The hallway seemed to move in unnatural ways as Grayson led her toward the elevators, where she would be whisked up to the seventh floor of the military headquarters building. That's where rooms were located for soldiers who wanted to live in military housing. Almost no one lived there, so the rooms were mostly empty. People preferred to have their own apartments or houses, and, until recently, Zoe had as well. But these days, with everyone always swarming around her like she was some goddamn Oscar winning actress, Zoe preferred places that were mostly empty.

Frowning at the thought of being chased around like a celebrity, Zoe forgot to concentrate on walking, and stumbled forward. Grayson's strong arm kept her upright, and he gave her a suspicious sideways glance.

"You sure you're alright?"

"I'm fine," Zoe said, shrugging and then trying to pass off the stumble with a bit of self-deprecation. "I just tripped over my own two feet. I'm such a klutz."

Grayson raised an eyebrow. "From what I hear, you're the exact opposite of a klutz. No one can stop talking about how agile you are."

Zoe looked away. It wouldn't do any good to argue. Her agility and magical skills had been discussed ad nauseam by pretty much every citizen of Falcon Cross. Better to just let the matter drop and hope Grayson would do the same.

Grayson, it turned out, would not do the same. In fact, he seemed angry about something, like he almost welcomed an excuse to argue.

"Do you deny it then?" he asked. His voice had a sharp edge to it that made Zoe cringe a bit. "Do you deny that you're basically a goddess of a soldier and the self-proclaimed savior and secret weapon of Falcon Cross?"

Zoe looked back at him, stiffening slightly. "I don't deny that I'm a talented soldier. But I'm not the self-proclaimed anything of Falcon Cross. I hate the spotlight, and I've wished every day since I first did that cursed *Crepitus* spell and caught Peter's eye that I hadn't done it. It was an accident. I didn't know I had the abilities I have, and I wish every day that I didn't have them."

Grayson looked at her like she'd suddenly sprouted a third eye in the middle of her head. For a moment, he looked like he was trying to decide whether to chew her out or not. Zoe braced herself. She'd heard enough lectures already, from friends and military superiors, about how she had a duty to use her abilities to the fullest extent possible for the good of her people. Zoe had grown weary of being lectured. She was doing everything that was asked of her. She was going to all the special training the masters had arranged for her, and she would go on a mission for the dragon ruby, if that's what Peter wanted. But that didn't mean she had to be happy about having her calm, quiet life disrupted by sudden celebrity-dom.

Grayson must have decided not to lecture her in the end, though, because he snapped his mouth shut and just shook his head at her, an expression of deep disapproval on his face. He held her arm a bit more roughly than before, and started walking down the hallway at a brisker pace. Zoe was hit by the sudden realization that she wasn't sure which was the worse option—a lecture from Grayson, or his cold, disapproving silence.

Zoe's heart felt heavy as she let Grayson lead her down the last stretch of hallway toward the elevators. She had the uncomfortable thought that she actually cared about what Grayson thought of her. But why? She glanced over at him, trying to look at him without making it obvious that she was doing so. He had the same dark, reddish-brown hair that all the other Redwood Dragons had, as well as the same, piercing green eyes. Like most dragon shifters, his ears also had a slight, elfish curve to them, an indication of the fact that his breed of shifters had once possessed magical powers. Those magical powers had long ago faded out of the dragon shifter bloodline. The last of the great dragon kings had stored their powers in the dragon stones in an effort to preserve them, but other than the dragon stones there weren't many traces of dragon magic left on earth. Still, Zoe thought the elfish ears were adorable, especially on Grayson.

Although he looked somewhat similar to his clanmates, he wasn't an exact clone. There was something different about him. It wasn't just that he was tall or muscular— they all were. Or that he had a perfectly chiseled jawbone. Again, the other dragon shifters could boast of that feature as well. Zoe decided, as she looked over at Grayson's undeniably desirable body, that it was more than just his physical appearance that appealed to her. He had a certain expression in his eyes that marked him as different. It was as if she could see his very soul in those deep green eyes, and what a beautiful soul it was. Despite his hard exterior, there was something special about Grayson.

Zoe was so caught up in admiring Grayson's looks and soulful expression that she didn't notice the group of women running toward her until it was nearly too late. Luckily, Grayson had been paying slightly better attention.

"Shit," he said. "Stay close to me."

Zoe didn't have much of a choice in the matter, because in the next moment Grayson had wrapped his right arm tightly around her shoulders, pressing her whole side firmly against his. He held his left arm in front of them, forming something of a barrier between her and the women, who were now trying to dodge around Grayson's arm to touch Zoe. They all wore the uniforms that the administrative staff at military headquarters wore. They must have been employed as secretaries, or by the records department.

"Zoe! Zoe, oh my god I can't believe it's you!" one of the woman shrieked.

"We've been hoping to catch a glimpse of you," another one said. "I heard a rumor that the Masters were going to ask you to perform the *Crepitus* spell this morning. Is it true? Did you cast a *Crepitus* spell?"

Zoe ducked her head against Grayson's chest, squeezing her eyes shut and letting Grayson lead her blindly. This constant fangirling over her was ridiculous. She'd done nothing to deserve anyone's praise. She'd been born with a gift, and she was happy to use that gift to help her clan, but damn it all if she couldn't walk down the freaking hallway without grown woman shrieking at her like teenage girls at a boy band concert.

"Zoe's had a long morning, ladies," Grayson said. "Please back off and let us through so she can go get some rest."

His voice sounded deep and authoritative, and Zoe could feel the echoes of it against her face, which was now pressed up against his chest as hard as possible.

Grayson smelled like a mixture of woodsy pines and fresh soap, and Zoe found herself breathing in a little more deeply as he continued to command the women to get out of his way. They giggled and argued with him, and Zoe felt an occasional hand brush against her arm. But Grayson did a good job of moving her through the gaggle, certainly much better than she could have managed on her own. Zoe kept her eyes shut and tried to pretend that she was somewhere else, anywhere but here.

With her eyes closed, she became hyperaware of the way Grayson's arm felt around her. He was strong, which wasn't at all surprising. What did surprise her was the way that having that strong arm around her sent a thrill of pleasure up and down her spine. She felt safe and protected. She hadn't felt that way in a long time. In fact, she couldn't remember the last time she'd felt safe in someone's arms. Zoe drank the feeling in, forgetting for a brief moment even to worry about the women who were trying to fight against Grayson's outstretched hand. Zoe even forgot to listen to what Grayson was saying to the women, but whatever it was must have been effective, because a few moments later she heard a beep as the elevator arrived, and Grayson pulled her into the elevator with him. The door shut behind them, and suddenly everything was quiet. Zoe still didn't open her eyes, wanting to hold on to the beauty of being in Grayson's arms for just a moment longer.

"Floor seven, right?" Grayson asked, his voice once again echoing deeply in his chest.

"Yes, floor seven."

Zoe heard a beep a moment later, and then the elevator started rising. She had to open her eyes and pull away now. She'd pushed it as long as she could, but there was no longer any excuse for her to be in Grayson's arms. Holding back a sigh, she stepped back from Grayson and looked up at him.

"Thanks," she said, feeling a bit embarrassed. She could tell that he didn't like all the attention she got, but what could she do? It wasn't her fault that she got it. She hadn't asked for it. He only gave her a humph in response, then turned his eyes up to look at the digital numbers that indicated which floor the elevator was on. Right now, they were on four. Then five, six, seven.

When the elevator dinged and the door opened, Zoe realized that she hadn't been the one to push the button to get to the seventh floor. She looked over at Grayson with mild surprise.

"The seventh floor is fingerprint secured," she said. "You have access? Why? Did you live up here when you first arrived in Falcon Cross or something?"

Grayson looked down at her in silence. For a long moment, Zoe thought he wasn't going to answer her. There was something so strange about him. He was angry, but why? Surely it was more than just the fact that he didn't think she properly appreciated her exceptional magical powers. Something else was bothering him, something deeper. And for reasons Zoe couldn't quite put her finger on, she cared about his feelings. She wanted to say or do something to make him feel better, but that was hard to do when she didn't know what the actual problem was.

"I have access to every door in Falcon Cross," he finally said, eyeing her carefully. "All of the Redwood Dragons do. Peter made sure of it when we first arrived in Falcon Cross."

Zoe's surprise must have registered on her face, because Grayson laughed.

"What? Did you think you were the only special one in Falcon Cross?" he asked. His voice sounded kind now, almost jolly. Zoe had no idea what to make of him.

"Of course I don't think that," Zoe said. "I've just never heard of anyone having full access to the city except the high council members themselves. That's pretty cool.

I'd say you're the special one here."

Grayson rolled his eyes. "I'm not special. I'm one of ten dragon shifters. There's nothing special about being one of ten."

Zoe tilted her head at him. "If it makes you feel any better, I'd gladly trade places with you. I don't want to be the special one. I don't want to be noticed, and I don't want to go on the dragon ruby mission. I just want to be a normal soldier working hard and going home at the end of the day without any special recognition. And without being mobbed by fangirls."

Grayson's face darkened once again. "I can't believe how unfair this place is. I work so hard, and no one even notices me. You don't do any extra work, but you're lucky enough to have a rare talent, so you automatically get to go on the dragon ruby mission. But you don't even want to go. You don't want the adventure or excitement, or the glory. You just want to do the bare minimum and be left alone. And I, who would gladly go out and give my all—give my life, if necessary, for our cause, am stuck here behind a desk. I bleed for the side of good in whatever way I can, but I wish I was bleeding in battle instead of just getting bloody fingers from typing all damn day."

Zoe blinked a few times, trying to process the rush of angry emotions that filled her as Grayson spoke. She narrowed her eyes at him, losing patience.

"I never said I wanted to do the bare minimum. I do work hard. I just said I want to blend in with the rest of the soldiers, and be normal. I don't want or need special recognition. I love being part of this team, and I bleed for the side of good, too. I don't want to go on the dragon ruby mission because it's only going to add to the 'Zoe-mania' that seems to be sweeping this town. If I could go on an exciting mission and do good for our soldiers without it turning into a circus, I'd be happy to do that. But when people start pinning all their hopes on one individual, and when one individual gets caught up in chasing after recognition, things start to fall apart. War is a team sport, Grayson. Not a chance for individual soldiers to get their fame and glory fix."

Zoe had her hands on her hips, and her voice had raised several notches. She could feel bubbles of rage simmering just below the surface of her emotions, and she was desperately trying to keep calm. Grayson had no right to imply that she wasn't a hard worker, or that she wasn't giving her all for her clan. Just because she didn't want stardom didn't mean she didn't care about doing everything she could to help in the fight against Saul. But Grayson seemed unimpressed by her speech. He walked back toward the elevator and pushed the button to call it back. The elevator had gone off to some other floor by now, and as Grayson waited, he turned to glare at Zoe.

"It's easy for you to say you don't want fame or recognition, because you already have it. But me? I'm one of ten, and apparently the least noticeable of those ten. I don't ever get to go on any good missions. I work my ass off, and still I sit behind a desk. That's not what dragons were meant to do. If someone would just give me a chance, just *one* chance, on mission, then I could show them how much I'm really capable of. And once I had everyone's attention, I'd be able to go on more missions, and do more good. It's a self-perpetuating cycle. But no one wants to give me a chance, no matter how hard I work, to prove that I deserve a chance. Then you waltz in, and get all the chances in the world simply by dumb luck. And you have the audacity to sit there and complain about fame and recognition."

The elevator dinged then, and Zoe was saved the trouble of figuring out how to reply. Grayson stepped inside and out of her view as the door quickly closed behind him. Zoe stood in front of that elevator for a long time, her heart a mixture of strange, conflicting emotions. Grayson's words made her somewhat angry, and yet, she supposed he had a point. She had been given a lot, and he had been given nothing.

She'd seen Noah around a lot, working closely with Knox. And she remembered Vance, Myles, Finn, and Owen being recognized by the high council for their work in finding the dragon amethyst. Then, of course, Weston and Holden had destroyed Saul's bat cloning operation. But Grayson? Grayson had been in the shadows, blending in this whole time. She'd seen his face before, when the dragons all gathered together for high council meetings. But he was right. He was always one of ten. And he hadn't, as far as she knew, been given a chance to go on any missions or do any special work. He worked hard and kept his head down, but no one had noticed.

Zoe had noticed something, though. There was a fire in his eyes that was different from the other dragon shifters. Grayson was passionate and hungry unlike anyone she'd ever met. Perhaps his passion was slightly misplaced—Zoe didn't see any need for fame, but Grayson seemed to crave it. Still, he was eager to give his all to their cause. He had a lot of pent-up energy, and no one had given him a chance to use it. Perhaps, like Zoe, he was a secret weapon, too, just waiting to be discovered. Zoe brushed a stray strand of hair back from her face and frowned slightly as she looked at the shiny, gold-toned elevator door that had closed behind Grayson.

"Fine," she said, crossing her arms and looking at the door, as though Grayson were still standing right there. "If it's a chance you want, I'll give you a chance. Don't make me regret this."

CHAPTER FOUR

Grayson had barely left his office for three days. He arrived at work early and went straight there, bringing his own lunch with him in a paper sack so that he wouldn't have to leave again until he went home, which was usually long after most others in military headquarters had gone home. He threw himself into his work more than ever, working to finesse his latest discoveries on the dragon ruby's location. He managed, in three days, to write a rather extensive report. By four-thirty p.m. on the third day, the report was finished and edited, and Grayson sat back in his chair to let himself stare blankly at the ceiling. His brain was swirling, and needed a rest.

He hadn't done the report to try to gain recognition, or a chance at being asked on the dragon ruby mission. By now, he knew better than to get his hopes up. The team for the dragon ruby mission had already been chosen. No official announcement had been made, but rumors were flying that it would be Noah accompanying Zoe on the mission. Grayson was slightly surprised by this. Noah had thus far declined all missions, preferring to remain in Falcon Cross where he could help make leadership decisions as second in command of the Redwood Dragons. But that had been when Knox, their first in command, had been away in Texas. Knox had recently returned to Falcon Cross, which had likely made Noah feel free to take on a mission.

No, Grayson had no illusions that preparing a stellar report would somehow get him added to the dragon ruby mission. He knew that Peter wanted to limit the mission to two people, for secrecy's sake. It was easier for two soldiers to stay undercover than a large group, and, as far as anyone in Falcon Cross knew, Saul was clueless about the location for the dragon ruby that Grayson had found. Whoever went on this mission might be attacked, but they also might get the ruby and be back in Falcon Cross before Saul even realized what was going on. Better to bank on secrecy. But the limitation of two people, with Zoe already chosen for one of the slots, left little chance of Grayson being sent on the mission. One of his clanmates, who had already proven himself in battle or on a mission, would be chosen. If it wasn't, in fact, Noah, it still wouldn't be Grayson. Grayson had learned by now that hard work behind a desk was not enough to get sent on a mission.

He had worked his ass off to get the report done, anyway. For one thing, despite his anger at being constantly overlooked for missions, he was still a team player. He wanted his clanmates and the Falcon Cross wizards to be victorious. But for another thing, working like a madman kept his mind occupied. It kept him from constantly thinking about how angry he was at being virtually invisible behind this desk, and, perhaps more importantly, it kept him from constantly thinking about Zoe.

Zoe. Grayson rolled the name around in his head a few times, enjoying the sound of it. Now that he was done with his report, he couldn't keep his thoughts from heading straight back to her. He had wanted so badly to hate her. It would have made life so much easier. But once he'd met her, she'd been impossible to hate. Sure, he thought she was a bit ridiculous to actually say that she'd rather not go on the dragon ruby mission. But Grayson had to admit that her reluctance stemmed from honest reasons. She wasn't the pompous, haughty celebrity he'd thought she was before meeting her in person. Rather, she was a humble soldier, embarrassed by all the attention being heaped on her.

And she was beautiful. Good god, she was beautiful. Grayson had seen pictures of Zoe, and from the pictures it had been obvious that she was a beautiful woman. But her beauty was the kind that was impossible to capture in a photograph. Her gray eyes sparkled with so much life, and her face had glowed even in the smoky training room. She was something special, her sweet spirit matching her sweet eyes. In another life, Grayson might have kissed her up there by the elevator bank, when they were alone on the seventh floor. But despite Zoe's sweetness and beauty, she still represented everything he couldn't have. How could he kiss the woman who was going on the mission he wanted? The woman who had done nothing but be born with special abilities, and now was getting the recognition that Grayson's hard work had not been able to get for him. Logically, Grayson knew none of this was Zoe's fault, but he still felt bitter toward her. Kissing her felt like admitting defeat. He was determined not to become like one of Zoe's silly, giggling fans.

Grayson sat up in his chair and straightened the piles of papers on his desk. He'd printed several copies of his report to take to a meeting tomorrow morning. The dragon ruby mission was scheduled to begin that Saturday, so final preparations were in the works right now. Grayson's report would help tremendously, he knew. He'd finished it just in time, but he was already worried about what he was going to work on next. With the search for the dragon ruby underway, there wouldn't be much for him to do except sit around and wait. And sitting around and waiting was going to result in his constantly thinking about Zoe, which was going to make him grumpy. The next couple of weeks were going to feel long and weary.

Grayson stood and went to grab some folders from a small supply shelf in his office. He began arranging the copies of the report into individual folders. When he was done with that, he would leave for the day. He'd order pizza for dinner and find a movie to watch that would hopefully keep his mind off of everything going on in his real life.

Just as Grayson slipped the last pile of papers into a folder, a knock sounded at the door. Grayson looked up in surprise. No one ever bothered to come to his office, so far down the hallways of military headquarters. Half the time, the cleaning service didn't even bother coming to empty the small trash can under Grayson's desk, and he had to do it himself. So who was visiting him now?

"Come in," Grayson said in a loud voice as he sat down in his desk chair once again. The door opened, and Grayson's surprise only grew when he saw who his visitors were. Into his office stepped Peter, Knox, and Noah. The three men's figures completely filled the small open space in Grayson's office. Grayson stood to his feet quickly, then gestured toward the one open chair.

"Peter, please sit down," he said. "I'm sorry I don't have more chairs for the rest of you. One of you can take mine."

But Peter, Knox, and Noah all waved away his offer of a chair.

"We're not staying very long," Peter said. "But we have some news for you. We've been trying to call you for the last hour to ask you to come up to my office, but you haven't been answering your office phone. I was beginning to think that you'd gone home already, but you didn't answer your cell phone either so we had to walk down here to check."

"Oh, sorry," Grayson said, glancing over at his office phone and seeing for the first time that the bright red message indicator button was flashing bright red at him. "I turned all my ringers to silent so I could concentrate. No one ever calls me, anyway."

"No matter," Peter said. "We're here now, and I hope you're going to be pleased with the reason why."

Peter paused somewhat dramatically, and Grayson resisted the urge to roll his eyes. All of the wizards liked to do everything with a little bit of flair. Luckily, Peter did not hold his dramatic pause for long.

"Grayson, we'd like for you to join Zoe on the dragon ruby mission."

Grayson stared at Peter blankly for a moment, wondering if he had heard the old man correctly. This had been the last thing Grayson would have expected to come out of Peter's mouth.

"I'm sorry, what?" Grayson asked, not daring to hope that he had heard accurately. But Peter repeated the same thing with no hesitation.

"We'd like for you to join Zoe on the dragon ruby mission. If you're willing, of course."

Grayson's heart started pounding wildly in his chest. "Of course I'm willing! I would be honored. But I thought…"

Grayson looked over at Noah, searching his clanmate's face to see whether there was any sign of anger or jealousy. Grayson wanted to go on the dragon ruby mission more than he'd ever wanted anything before, but he did not want to take anything away from Noah. No mission was worth angering the second in command of his clan. But Noah merely smiled back at him.

"You thought I was going on the mission?" Noah asked. "Yeah, I've heard that rumor, too. I don't know who started it, but it's not true. You know I'm too busy here to take off on a mission right now. Knox just got here. I'm still trying to show him the ropes and pass off a lot of my leadership duties to him. If you want the mission, it's yours."

Grayson stood up straighter. "I would be honored," he said. "I'm quite surprised, though. I'd thought the mission had already been planned out completely. Has the start date changed? It seems a little late to be adding a new member to a mission that leaves in a few days."

Peter shook his head no. "The start date hasn't changed. Truth be told, we'd planned on another one of the dragon shifters for this mission. We were going to use one of the guys who has already gone on a mission and proven himself. I'm sure you understand."

Peter looked at Grayson brightly, waiting for Grayson to agree that, of course, he understood perfectly. But Grayson only blinked back at Peter warily. He didn't trust himself to keep his voice even while saying something about his clanmates and their supposedly superior abilities on missions. Grayson would rather hear Peter talk about why he had finally been chosen for a mission. It would be nice to hear someone say out loud for once how great his reports had been, or how his hard work had made a big difference in the Falcon Cross war effort. But when Peter spoke again, he didn't mention Grayson's work ethic or stellar research.

"Of course, one of the most important things to remember in choosing a mission team is that the mission members need to work well together. Zoe is a non-negotiable on this team. We definitely want her there, using her powers to protect and defend the team and the dragon ruby. And since she must go, we asked for her opinion on whom the second soldier should be."

Grayson felt like he had been punched in the stomach by Peter's words. Grayson realized what had happened before Peter finished his explanation, but Peter kept talking anyway.

"Zoe said that she had the most experience working with you. She said you two got along well and she thought you'd be a great asset to the team. She was quite insistent that the second team member be you, in fact. I hadn't realized that you two had worked together, but I guess you made quite an impression on her. So, congratulations. You've been chosen as the second member of the dragon ruby mission team."

Grayson could only stare at Peter. A sickening, sinking feeling filled his stomach. It hadn't been his hard work that got him this opportunity, after all. It had been Zoe's clout. Little Miss Secret Weapon got whatever she asked for, and she had asked for Grayson. But why? It wasn't true that they had experience working together. The only time they had spent together, in fact, had been when he walked her up to her quarters after running into the training room like an idiot a few days ago. Grayson realized that Peter was still looking at him, waiting for an acknowledgement that Zoe and Grayson were good partners. Grayson forced a smile onto his face.

"Of course. Zoe and I make a great team. It will be my honor to serve on the dragon ruby mission with her," Grayson said.

Peter nodded, satisfied. "Someone from mission control will be coming down to brief you first thing tomorrow morning. If you have any questions they can't answer, or you need anything else, feel free to reach out to one of us."

Peter swept his arm wide to include Knox and Noah in his offer of help. Grayson nodded stiffly and kept the forced smile on his face. With a satisfied nod, Peter turned to leave the room. Knox turned to follow him, but Noah remained behind.

"I'll catch up in a minute," Noah said to the others, then waited until they had gone before turning to Grayson.

"What's wrong?" Grayson asked, eyeing Noah carefully. "You know if you want the mission, it's yours. I wouldn't try to take something away from you, no matter how badly I want to go on a mission myself."

Noah smiled. "No, it's not that. The mission is yours, Grayson. I never wanted it, and I know you're well past due for a turn at some action."

"Well then, what is it?" Grayson asked.

Noah paused, giving Grayson a searching look for a moment before continuing. "Listen, I know that this isn't how you wanted your chance at a mission to come about. I know you've worked hard, and that you want recognition for that. You don't want to be awarded missions based on some pretty little wizard girl throwing your name out there."

Grayson set his lips in a stiff line and said nothing, so Noah continued.

"The truth is, things here in Falcon Cross work in strange ways. It's a lot more political than our clan in the Redwoods ever was. Missions aren't always awarded based on pure merit. My point is, you've been given the chance you wanted, even if you weren't given it in the way you would have wanted to be given it. So try to see past the fact that it was Zoe who recommended you for the mission. Go out there and kick ass. Show them what you're capable of. Unlike everyone here in Falcon Cross, I've seen you in action. And I know you're a damn good soldier. Make me proud. You always do."

And with that, Noah clapped Grayson on the shoulder and turned to leave. Grayson stood there for a long time, staring at the empty doorway and willing his racing heart to slow down. It was no use. Noah believed in him. He was going on the dragon ruby mission, even if the circumstances under which he'd been awarded the mission were a little unusual. And, strangely, the most exciting thought of all was that he was going to be spending a lot of time with Zoe over the next few weeks.

He sort of couldn't stand the thought of that, and he sort of thought that he'd never wanted anything more in his life.

CHAPTER FIVE

Grayson stood in the blue-gray light of early dawn, watching his breath briefly fog up the air in front of him each time he exhaled. It was August, still summer. But the mornings could be cold here in the Falcon Cross forest, and it was so early that you could barely even call this morning. Any earlier and it would have been more like the middle of the night.

Grayson tugged on the jacket of his Falcon Cross military uniform. Wearing a uniform felt strange to him. The Redwood Dragons had never bothered with details like uniforms. Their clothes were frequently ruined when they had to shift suddenly, so investing in uniforms would have been a waste of money. But the Falcon Cross soldiers wore their uniforms proudly, and Peter had given Grayson this new uniform for the trip to Shadowdale. It would have been rude to refuse it, and besides, Grayson had to admit that the uniforms were quite comfortable. And warm.

Grayson heard a rustling behind him, and turned to see Zoe walking toward him. She was wearing a military uniform as well, although that was nothing new for her. The fitted fabric hugged her curves, and Grayson let himself admire her silhouette as she slipped almost silently across the field. In her right hand, she carried a broomstick, which would be used to fly both of them out of Falcon Cross. Grayson would have preferred to shift into dragon form and do his own flying, rather than hanging onto the back of a broomstick. But Peter insisted that invisibility shields were much more effective when cast over smaller, human forms. Dragons were so large that even a powerful wizard like Zoe would have to work hard to keep an effective invisibility shield over him. And the stronger the invisibility shield, the better. Dark wizards were watching Falcon Cross with eagle eyes, and they had the ability to see through low quality invisibility shields. Reluctantly, Grayson had agreed to fly behind Zoe on the broomstick. At least she was pretty, and a woman. He would have been much less enthused about the arrangement if he'd been forced to ride behind a male wizard.

"Nice outfit," Zoe said as she approached, her voice light and teasing. Grayson loved the musical sound her words made when she spoke, but he wasn't in the mood to be teased about his uniform, so he ignored her jab.

"You're late," he pointed out. He'd been waiting five minutes for her, which wasn't a big deal in the grand scheme of things. But pointing it out was an excuse to change the subject away from his uniform.

"Hmm," Zoe said. She was distracted now, peering closely at the handle of her broomstick. "Peter wanted to talk to me before I left."

Grayson felt a stab of annoyance. "Just you? Does he realize I'm part of this mission, too?"

Zoe looked up at him and met his eyes for a moment. She opened her mouth like she was going to say something, then shut it again. She spent several more seconds looking over her broomstick before she spoke.

"I can't control what Peter does, Grayson. Don't take your anger at him out on me."

Grayson frowned. She was right, which only made him more angry. He watched her inspect her broomstick for another few moments before blurting out, "Don't think I owe you anything just because you put my name in for this mission. I didn't ask you for any favors, and I'm not going to put up with your holding it over my head."

Zoe looked up at Grayson in confusion. "I don't think you owe me anything. I put your name out there because I thought it was a win-win situation for us."

This surprised Grayson. "What do you mean? How do you win?"

Zoe carefully leaned her broomstick against the trunk of a nearby tree, and started tightening the straps on the large backpack she wore as she spoke. "Well, you wanted a chance to go on a mission, didn't you? Now you have that chance. And I wanted a chance to get away from everyone who wouldn't stop treating me like some sort of goddamn celebrity. It only took a few minutes of knowing you for me to realize that you're about as far from impressed with my magical abilities as anyone could possibly be. So I suggested you for this mission. You get to finally see some action, and I get to go on a mission without some idiot constantly yakking on about how amazing I am. Win-win."

Grayson frowned. "It was going to be a dragon shifter going with you, either way. None of the dragons would have treated you like some celebrity princess. It's not our style."

Zoe shrugged, giving her backpack straps one last tug before reaching to pick up her broomstick again. "I don't know that. I don't really know any of the dragons all that well, except Knox and Noah, who are always around Peter and always agreeing with him that I'm a fabulous secret weapon."

"Well, it *is* true that you have some kickass magical abilities," Grayson said. "And Knox and Noah mostly agree with Peter to appease the old wizard. Peter's a nice guy, a very good leader, and very kind. But he does seem to have a bit of an ego, if you ask me."

Zoe looked for a moment like she might disagree with Grayson, but then she shrugged. "Look, do you want to go on this mission or not? If you want to argue with me that there's a better dragon for the job, then, by all means name a name and I'll go tell Peter that I've changed my mind about who I want to accompany me. He wouldn't be happy about a last minute change, but he'd let me make it. He's convinced that the mission will fail without me."

Grayson felt his skin bristling with annoyance. He hated the fact that Zoe could so easily ask for anything she wanted and get it. But Zoe had already told him she didn't except anything in return from him for the chance to come on this mission, and, like Noah had said, Grayson had finally been given the opportunity he'd been waiting for. Who cared what the reasons for that opportunity were.

"Enough talk," Grayson said, gruffly. "We're already behind schedule. Let's get going."

Zoe grinned at him, nonplussed by the fact that he hadn't acknowledged her strange power to kick him off the mission if she wanted to. She pointed her magic ring at her broomstick and said, "*Magicae volant.*" Instantly, the broomstick started to buzz with energy, and it hovered next to Zoe, about four feet off the ground.

"Have you ever ridden on a broomstick?" Zoe asked, starting to climb onto the buzzing handle. Grayson shook his head no.

"It's really easy as a passenger," Zoe said. "All you need to do is hold on tight to me. Well, to my backpack, I guess. Don't bother trying to lean in the right direction to help me or anything like that. You'll likely do more harm than good. Just hold on tight and if for some reason there's an emergency that requires my attention, just tap me twice on the left shoulder. Got it?"

"Okay," Grayson said, eyeing the broomstick suspiciously. "But I don't understand how that little broom handle is going to hold up all of my weight."

Zoe winked at him. "It's a *magic* broomstick, remember? Trust me, it'll work. Just hop on and try it out."

Grayson gave Zoe a doubtful look, but heeded her advice to hop on. To his surprise, the surface of the broomstick felt more like a bike saddle than a thin rod. An invisible seat was holding him up, and his feet landed on invisible stirrups. He couldn't help but be impressed.

"Damn," he said. "That's a nice trick."

"Isn't it, though?" Zoe said. She sounded pleased. "Just let me cast a couple of protective spells and we can be on our way."

Grayson found a good spot to hold on tightly to Zoe's large backpack. He was surprised at how disappointed he felt over the fact that there was a backpack in between them. In his mind's eye, when he thought of riding with Zoe, he'd imagined his chest pressed up against her back, with his arms wrapped around her waist. But of course that was not the case. She needed her backpack of supplies, too. This might be a long mission. Grayson wondered why he had let his mind wander to places that involved his arms around Zoe, and why he was so keenly disappointed that those daydreams would not be realized.

To his relief, Zoe interrupted his somewhat troubled thoughts to let him know it was time to go.

"Hold on tight," she said, glancing over her shoulder to make sure Grayson was doing as he was told. He gave her a quick thumbs up sign, and she flashed him a brilliant smile before turning back around. She shouted out some sort of magic spell, then leaned back slightly to turn the front of the broomstick upward. The next thing Grayson knew, they were flying, ascending rapidly through the tree branches. Soon, Falcon Cross would be just a tiny dot below them.

Grayson peered into the early dawn sky, trying to see anything that would indicate enemy wizards were about. Everything looked perfectly normal, but he knew that didn't mean much. Saul's dark wizards were quite talented at remaining invisible, and they knew where Falcon Cross was located. No one in Falcon Cross tried to delude themselves into thinking that the city was not under constant surveillance by enemy wizards. Grayson could only hope that the invisibility shield Zoe had cast would work. In training, she had supposedly cast a shield so strong that even Peter had been unable to see through it, with all his powerful counterspells. Grayson hoped with all his heart that the dark wizards would be unable to see through it as well.

The whole mission departure had been planned to give Zoe and Grayson the highest possible chance of avoiding detection. They'd chosen early dawn because the light was still not good, but the dark wizards might not be watching as closely as they would have been in the dead of night. The dark wizards would expect any missions to leave under cover of full darkness, with as many hours of dark night left as possible to fly through. An early morning departure meant that any enemy spies around wouldn't have their suspicions up as high. That was the hope, at least.

Grayson wasn't that worried about being attacked at this particular moment. Peter had stationed several powerful wizard guards all around Falcon Cross airspace. If Zoe and Grayson got into any trouble, Zoe would send up an emergency signal from her magic ring, and the wizard guards would come to their assistance. And Zoe herself had set up powerful protective shields. The odds that any harm would come to Grayson and Zoe over the course of their flight were extremely low. But it wasn't an attack during their flight that Grayson was worried about.

Rather, Grayson worried that they would be followed. Having one of Saul's soldiers follow them and figure out that they knew where the dragon ruby was located would be devastating. The ruby could not fall into Saul's hands. It just couldn't. Grayson didn't want to think about the evil that Saul would do if it did. This mission must succeed. And besides, Grayson needed to prove himself on this mission. He needed to get that ruby and bring it back to Falcon Cross amidst a hero's welcome. Then everyone would see that he wasn't just one of ten dragons. He was a hero.

As they rose higher and higher, and began to fly away from Falcon·Cross, Grayson still saw no sign of anyone suspicious in the gray sky surrounding him. The blueness of early dawn was now giving way to a pinkish orange as the sun began to peek above the horizon, making its way upward bit by bit. If there were enemies out there, they either hadn't seen them or weren't going to attack right now. Grayson knew he wouldn't have attacked, if he'd been in their shoes. He would have waited to see where the mission was going. And he couldn't keep away an uneasy feeling that they were being followed.

Whether that feeling was a true gut instinct or just the product of an overactive imagination, Grayson couldn't tell. There wasn't much he could do about it at the moment, anyway. Zoe had cast all the spells she could to keep them safe and invisible, and they would be flying a zigzagging, indirect route to Shadowdale. Hopefully, if any enemy soldiers did spot them, Grayson and Zoe would be able to lose them along their purposefully confusing route.

As the sun rose higher in the sky, Grayson began to relax even more. The day wore on, and flying on the back of a broomstick over miles and miles of forest became somewhat boring after a while. Grayson did his best to pay attention to where they were, and to keep an eye out for potential trouble, but his eyes soon grew weary of scanning the horizon that always looked the same. He let his daydreams take over again, alternating between thoughts of being given a medal of honor in front of all of Falcon Cross, and of spending time with his arms around Zoe.

He thought for a long time about how she'd asked for him as a partner on this mission because he hadn't treated her like a celebrity, as everyone else had. He wondered if she would regret her choice if she knew that he was having crazy thoughts about wanting to put his arms around her and kiss her. Would she think he was just like the rest of them?

He wasn't just like the rest of them, though, he argued to himself. He wasn't interested in kissing her because of her magical abilities, or her status as the current VIP of the Falcon Cross army. He just thought her body was damn sexy. Did that make him more or less of an asshole?

Grayson scrunched his eyebrows up, confused. It didn't really matter, did it? He couldn't act on any of these feelings while he was on this mission with Zoe, anyway. It wouldn't be proper. And she'd likely freak out and be angry with him for taking advantage of their working relationship.

Wouldn't she? Or did she harbor similar secret feelings toward him? Grayson had caught the hint of a sparkle in her eye when she looked at him, but he didn't know her well enough yet to know if that sparkle was because of him, or if she always looked at people that way.

Grayson's thoughts continued to run along in this bewildering way. There wasn't much of interest to see on the long flight, and he was relieved when the shadows started to grow long and Zoe started to descend.

They would grab dinner and a motel room, and hopefully the interruption in the monotony of the day would help him get his thoughts out of the Zoe rut they'd become stuck in. Then again, maybe sitting across a dinner table from her would only make his sudden, crazy infatuation even worse.

CHAPTER SIX

"You've got to be kidding me," Grayson said. His expression was a mixture of amusement and annoyance, and Zoe wasn't sure which one was winning out at the moment.

"It'll only take about half an hour," Zoe said. "And you don't have to come with me. In fact, if you're that hungry, you can just go grab dinner without me. I'll grab takeout or something on my way back to the hotel room."

"I'm not sure splitting up for so long is a good idea, especially on the first night," Grayson said. "We could have been followed from Falcon Cross for all we know, and we haven't had time to sit still and see if someone is planning to attack once we're no longer in the air and no longer moving at such rapid speeds."

"You're so paranoid," Zoe said, huffing a bit. "I can take care of myself, in any case."

Oops. Those words were a mistake. She felt him bristle.

"I know you can," Grayson said. "I've only been reminded every five minutes for the last several weeks about how great Zoe Whitt is. The all-powerful, secret weapon, miracle wizard of Falcon Cross can indeed take care of herself. And, believe it or not, I can take care of myself, too, lowly dragon shifter that I am. But it's our job to be paranoid. Any opening we give to our enemies is a possible chance for them to derail this mission. We have to be vigilant."

Zoe stared at him skeptically. "And that means being together twenty-four seven? I think that's a little extreme."

Grayson frowned at her. "Two are stronger than one. This mission already needs more soldiers than it has, although I understand why Peter limited it for secrecy's sake. But let's not weaken our chances further by separating."

Zoe sighed, exasperated. She clearly wasn't going to change Grayson's mind about the two of them being in separate rooms, let alone letting her—gasp!—go sightseeing by herself. So she changed tactics from trying to convince him to let her go to trying to convince him to come.

"Well, I'm not going to visit the hometown of my favorite wizard poet and not go see the house he grew up in. So if you don't want to split up, then you better put your shoes on and come with me."

A murderous look crossed Grayson's face, and for a moment, Zoe worried that she'd pushed him too far. She considered backing away from her demands, but then, she didn't want to let him win their first disagreement on this mission. It would set a bad tone. She could already tell that Grayson was a stubborn man, and she wasn't about to give him reasons to think that she was a pushover. Zoe stood her ground, wondering if she was imagining it or if smoke was actually coming out of Grayson's ears. Did dragons send off smoke even while in human form? Zoe realized there was a lot she didn't know about dragons.

"Fine," Grayson finally said, grunting in a way that told her he wasn't amused by having to humor a little girl. "But let's at least eat first, then go sightseeing. I haven't eaten since breakfast, and I've got a dragon appetite to satisfy."

"But the Erich Shafer House closes at seven," Zoe protested. "That's in forty-five minutes. We don't have time to go to dinner first."

The murderous look was back. "You're a goddamn wizard, Zoe. And supposedly one of the best in the world, at that. Just cast a spell and unlock the door or something. It can't be that hard. Give yourself a private tour."

"That's trespassing!" Zoe protested.

Grayson shrugged. "I don't see the harm in it, as long as you don't break stuff or take anything from the house."

Zoe considered protesting again, but finally nodded. "Alright, fine," she said. She didn't exactly like the idea of using her magical powers to break into the Shafer House, but Grayson's mood was worsening by the second. She would enjoy her time looking at the house a lot more if she wasn't spending the whole time trying to appease an angry dragon.

Dinner was a strained affair. They ate at a small diner near their hotel, wolfing down food and not saying much to each other. Grayson didn't seem to be in much of a mood to talk, and Zoe followed his lead. She didn't want to push his patience further and have him decide that he didn't want to see the Shafer House after all.

Grayson seemed resigned to the idea, though. After they finished their food and paid their check, he gave her a longsuffering look and let out an overly exaggerated huff.

"Alright," he said. "Let's get this over with."

The Shafer House was at the edge of the small town they were in, about a two mile walk from their motel. They walked under the cover of an invisibility shield. Neither of them had seen anything suspicious, and they were hoping that they had actually made it out of Falcon Cross without being spotted by Saul's spies. Still, they needed to be extra careful, and walking across town to break into a tourist site was the kind of thing that had the potential to attract a lot of attention.

Zoe hadn't been the one to plan their zigzagging route to Shadowdale. Grayson had been the one to do that, meticulously detailing every stop and alternate routes along the way if they thought they needed to shake off anyone who might be following them. So it had been pure luck that their first stop was in the small town where Erich Shafer had lived. Zoe had been obsessed with Erich Shafer since she was a small girl. He had written the most beautiful poetry—sad, haunting verses that had been a source of comfort for her when her parents died several years ago. Zoe had always been fascinated by Erich Shafer's story, too. Most of the world only knew him as a great poet, famous in a way that poets rarely were. But the wizard world knew that he'd had a secret. The giant ruby ring he'd always worn wasn't just one of his strange quirks, as his human fans all thought. Rather, it was a magic ring. The man was a wizard, living secretly among humans in a way that few persons of magical ability could do. It wasn't easy to constantly be on guard against discovery. It took a lot of mental fortitude to remember not to perform magic spells in front of people, when performing magic spells was almost second nature for most wizards. But somehow, Erich Shafer had done it. He'd managed to maintain his image as a quirky but otherwise normal human, who wrote damn good poetry.

Zoe had always wanted to visit the sleepy little town where he'd lived and written his poetry. His house was supposedly simple but beautiful on the inside, a perfect setup for reading and writing. Zoe's main interest in the house wasn't to spy on Erich Shafer's interior decorating style, though. She just wanted to walk on the same ground she knew he'd walked on. Perhaps it was strange for someone who loathed fangirling so much in her own life to fangirl after a poet, but Zoe figured since the man was dead, it couldn't bother him that much. Besides, Shafer had actually done something worth fangirling about. He'd written beautiful poems, and shown an amazing talent for harnessing the written word. All Zoe had done was to be born lucky. She wasn't on the same level as Erich Shafer at all.

The air was quiet as they approached the house. The warm summer night was humid, and fireflies glowed intermittently in the small field which sat in front of the charming little house. A locked gate blocked the footpath to the front door, and a sign on the gate announced the opening hours and suggested donation of ten dollars for a tour. Zoe looked quickly away from the sign, already feeling guilty about breaking into one of her hero's homes. But again, he was dead. Surely he wouldn't mind? She felt for her purse, a small cross body satchel which was slung across her chest. She had some cash on her. She'd make sure to leave a nice donation behind for the upkeep of the house. That would ease her conscience a bit.

Grayson was looking at her impatiently, waiting for her to unlock the gate and get this show on the road. He was probably counting down the minutes until he could sink into bed and fall asleep. Zoe didn't feel overly guilty about dragging him out here, though. He didn't have to come, and, besides, she'd been the one actually flying all day. All he'd had to do was hold on. Still, there was no sense in delaying any longer than necessary. Zoe glanced around to make sure no one was there to see her breaking and entering. Even though she was under an invisibility shield, she still felt somewhat nervous. As far as she could tell, the only ones around to watch her little crime were the fireflies. Zoe took a deep breath and pointed her magic ring at the lock on the gate.

"*Magicae resero*," she said, her voice barely more than a whisper. Instantly, the lock popped open with a soft click. Zoe reached to remove the lock and then gently open the gate. Grayson followed her, and then she closed the gate behind them. The property really wasn't that secure. She and Grayson could have climbed over the fence relatively easily, but using magic to unlock the gate was just as easy.

The door to the small house was locked as well, of course, but Zoe unlocked it with the same spell and stepped inside, the floorboards creaking as she did.

"*Magicae lucis*," she said. Instantly, a flashlight-like beam streamed out from her magic ring. Zoe swept the light across the main room, taking in with reverence what had once been Shafer's living room. She didn't know what she had expected, but the room looked like pretty much any other living room she'd ever seen. The furniture was obviously high quality and must have cost a fortune, but it was of a simple, unremarkable design. Informational plaques were posted all over the place, giving more details on the furniture or the particulars of how Shafer lived his everyday life. Grayson went to one of the plaques and started reading, using his cell phone as a light since he didn't have a magic ring to turn into a flashlight.

Zoe, happy that he was entertained, made her way deeper into the house. She passed through the kitchen and the small dining room, and found the stairs that led to the second level. She climbed, not bothering to read all the information posted on the walls. She had glanced at a few of the plaques downstairs, but none of them told her anything that she didn't already know. She had read every book there was to read on Shafer's life. She knew his story like the back of her own hand. It was a bit silly, perhaps. But he had been one of her childhood heroes, and the nostalgia of that had carried into her adulthood. And he was a damn good poet, after all. There was no denying that. His poems of love lost, death, redemption, and love found all hit on deep, universal themes that had been appreciated by so many. Such a pity he'd died of cancer relatively young. Sixty-two years had not been enough for a man like Erich Shafer. A hundred wouldn't have been enough either, but it might have at least given Zoe a chance to meet him before he passed.

With a sad sigh, she looked into the bedroom which had once been Shafer's. A full sized bed and a simple four-drawer chest were the only pieces of furniture in the room. She moved on to the second bedroom, which had been Shafer's writing room. This room had large floor to ceiling windows through which the moonlight was now streaming. One wall was completely lined by bookshelves, with books stuffed into every available space and then piled on top as well. A small writing desk was up against the wall opposite the window, and a large, bearskin rug covered the open space in the middle of the room. Zoe went to sit on the rug.

"*Lucis terminantur*," she said. The light from her magic ring instantly disappeared, and the light in the room became softer now that it only consisted of moonbeams. Zoe looked around the room, feeling suddenly overwhelmed by the fact that she was there. She felt somehow at home and at peace here, like the spirit of Erich Shafer was somehow telling her that everything was going to be alright. Maybe she was crazy. Maybe it was all in her head. But she was going to enjoy the sensation as long as it lasted. It turned out it didn't last long. Grayson chose that moment to break into her reverie.

"I thought you hated people who chase after celebrities," he said.

She looked up at him, ready for a fight, but the look in his eyes wasn't challenging. It was soft, and slightly amused. She relaxed a bit.

"No I hate people who treat *me* like a celebrity, when I haven't done anything to deserve it," she said. Grayson seemed pleased by this answer. He crossed the room and sat next to her on the rug. The moonlight lit up the chiseled edges of his face in an enormously pleasing way, and Zoe had to remind herself not to stare. She forced herself to look up at the moon instead of at Grayson, whom she'd just decided was infinitely more beautiful than anything else in this room.

"This guy was really something, huh?" Grayson said.

"Shafer, you mean?"

"Yeah. I was reading all those plaques downstairs. He did a lot of shit."

Zoe laughed. "I'm not sure he'd appreciate you calling his work shit."

"You know what I mean," Grayson said.

Zoe glanced over at him, allowing herself another chance to look in his direction. He smiled at her, and she felt her stomach do a funny flip-flop. She looked away again, confused. She couldn't feel for him the things she was feeling right now. They were on a mission together, for crying out loud. She hadn't asked for him to come along because of his good looks. But here he was, sitting next to her with his undeniably good looks, and his smile creating little ripples of happiness in her chest. Her stomach. Lower.

Grayson didn't seem to notice the internal turmoil she was feeling. He continued to speak, oblivious to the pounding in her chest. "I think I misjudged you a bit."

Zoe looked back at him in surprise. He wasn't looking at her anymore. He was also staring up at the moon, perhaps dealing with a bit of inner turmoil of his own.

"Misjudged me?"

"Yeah. I thought you were just some silly girl who got lucky with your extraordinary ability to do magic. I thought there wasn't much more to you than someone who happened to be born the right way. But I was wrong. I can see now that you do work hard, and there is some depth to you. I mean, you have a favorite poet for crying out loud. Most of the girls I've dated probably didn't even read poetry."

Zoe was silent for a moment. Most of the girls he'd dated? Was he trying to say that he wanted to date her? The ripples of pleasure within her core intensified. She tried to think of what the appropriate thing to say would be in this moment.

"I don't think of myself as someone extra special. I just live my life the way that seems best to me. I work hard. I enjoy good poetry. I like good food. What else can I say? All this recognition and fanfare surrounding me lately has been tiring. I know I shouldn't complain. But I don't need to be treated like some sort of goddess. I don't need medals of honor, or extra stripes on my uniform. I just want to serve my clan and do what's best for my people."

Grayson frowned. "Recognition and medals can open doors for you though. The more people respect you, the more you have chances to do work that really matters."

Zoe shrugged. "All of it matters. Everything that every soldier in Falcon Cross does to stop Saul is important. All of it is helping to save people's lives and push back evil."

Grayson did not reply for a few moments. Finally, he looked over at her and smiled, then put his hand on her knee. Fire shot from his hand into her knee, spreading like an explosion through Zoe's whole body. Her heart pounded rapidly in her chest, and she struggled to keep her expression neutral.

"You're really something, Zoe. All this time, because of what everyone else in Falcon Cross says about you, I thought you were full of yourself. But it's actually the opposite. You don't realize yourself how special you are. How ironic is that?"

Zoe stared at Grayson, at a loss for words. He stared back at her, his green eyes twinkling with merriment and burning with passion at the same time. And then, he asked her a question that took her completely by surprise.

"Zoe, may I kiss you?"

Zoe's eyes widened. The ripples of happiness had turned into tidal waves, and her heart was beating so hard it might as well have been trying to force its way out of her chest. There was nothing in the world she would have liked more in that moment than for Grayson to kiss her. But she felt shy about straight up telling him yes.

"No one has ever asked for permission before kissing me," she said, her voice trembling despite her best efforts to calm it. "And you don't seem like the kind of person who asks for permission to do things."

"Normally, I don't. But I know you've been overrun with unwanted attention lately, and the last thing I want to do is to contribute to that. So I'm asking you, Zoe: is it okay to kiss you?"

Zoe still hesitated. "Here? In the middle of Shafer's writing room? It seems a little sacrilegious."

"Does it?" Grayson moved his face closer to hers. His nose was almost touching hers. His hand was still on her knee, sending waves of heat through her entire being.

"I mean…we're not even supposed to be in here," Zoe said weakly. "And it was his writing room. Where he worked. It seems a bit juvenile to make out in a place like this."

"*Au contraire*, Zoe," Grayson said. "I think it makes perfect sense to share a kiss in a place where such a great poet penned so many lines about love and passion. So, let me ask you again. May I kiss you? I'm still waiting on an answer."

Zoe looked into Grayson's eyes, and knew in that moment that she was lost. There was no resisting the heat, the energy, the soul in those perfect green orbs.

"Yes," she whispered.

And then his lips met with hers.

CHAPTER SEVEN

Zoe had completely lost track of time. It might have been five minutes since Grayson first kissed her, or it might have been fifty. All she knew for sure was that she had never felt more alive in her life. There was something exhilarating about being in a house she shouldn't have been in, taking off piece after piece of clothing even though there was always the possibility of being caught.

Zoe had looked around for security cameras when she first came in, but hadn't seen any. She was still under an invisibility spell, although Grayson had been moving around the house without her, so he would have shown up on any cameras that were around. Zoe was finding it hard to care anymore about being seen, though. Her thoughts had become fuzzy, and the only clear thing she could think was *Grayson wants me.*

There had been something between them since the start. She had tried to ignore it, but now that she was here, lying under him on the bearskin rug as he moved his tongue in a perfect symphony with her tongue, it was hard to deny that what she'd felt had been more than just a friendly interest. She had also given up trying to convince herself that making love in Shafer's house was a bad idea. If Grayson made a move, she would let him. And even though her mind screamed at her that she was crazy, she hoped with everything in her that Grayson would make a move.

Perhaps he could read her mind, because no sooner had this thought crossed it than Grayson sat up and reached to pull his t-shirt up and over his head. Neither of them was wearing their military uniforms anymore—to do so in the middle of a human town would have been far too conspicuous. Instead, they'd both changed into the nondescript outfits of t-shirts and jeans. And now, Grayson was missing the t-shirt portion of that outfit. Zoe couldn't keep from staring at the outline of his abs. His broad chest gave way to a perfectly sculpted six pack, and the v-shape of the muscles that disappeared below the hem of his jeans drew her eyes low.

She didn't have long to gaze at his half-naked body before he was reaching to make her body naked as well. He pulled her t-shirt off, and then reached behind her back to unclasp her bra. He slid it off her shoulders and tossed it aside, then moved his mouth to her nipples. Zoe was powerless to resist. She hoped that her invisibility spell was still working well, and that there were no security cameras in here. The thought of some sleepy security guard somewhere watching her and Grayson get hot and heavy made her cheeks burn red. But the potential of being caught only intensified the thrill she was feeling. Grayson nibbled at her nipples, taking each hard nub in his mouth to suck and bite with the perfect amount of pressure. He stopped just short of true pain, but the pressure he applied left no doubt that he was in control. She was his now. She'd agreed to a kiss, and he was stepping up to take more.

And she was letting him. She knew she could have told him to stop at any time and he would have, albeit reluctantly. Grayson might have a bit of a temper and a stubborn streak, but he was nothing if not a perfect gentleman. But Zoe didn't want him to stop. She wanted him to keep going, to move his tongue and teeth further down her body. She wanted his hands to continue caressing the curves of her stomach and hips as they

703

were doing right now. Her back pressed against the soft fur of the bearskin rug as she lay there, drinking in every touch and stroke that Grayson had to offer.

The ripples of happiness she'd felt had become a wetness that seeped out between her legs. Her body was preparing itself for him, begging for him to be inside her. Zoe could feel her simple beige panties growing more soaked by the moment. She almost wanted to laugh at the strangeness of the situation. She'd asked Grayson on this mission to avoid having anyone pay too much attention to her. She'd never expected the kind of attention she was getting right now. But she wasn't complaining.

It had been a long time since she'd felt such pure, primal passion. And that's what this was, after all. A physical need, a deep lust. She had no delusions that Grayson was in love with her. They barely knew each other, and Grayson was so rough around the edges. He wasn't the kind of man who easily let someone in, or fell head over heels for a girl. Especially not a girl whom everyone else was constantly fawning over. Grayson was the type of person who wanted to swim against the current. He would never have wanted to fall in love with the woman who was currently the most sought after person in Falcon Cross. Zoe knew enough of him to know that that just wasn't his style.

But, she supposed, passion was harder to resist than love. And there was definitely a spark of passion between her and Grayson. She'd tried to ignore that spark in the beginning, but now, that spark had turned into a blaze, and she was lost in the inferno. She gave in to the irresistible pull, closing her eyes and letting the sensations of Grayson's hands and lips on her bare skin take over her thoughts.

When he stopped for a moment, she opened her eyes again, worried that the moment was over. She didn't want this to end yet. She wanted to keep going, to give in to the overwhelming urge to let Grayson inside, and to give him her body completely. She needn't have worried. Grayson wasn't stopping. He was merely pausing to unzip his jeans, pushing them off so that only his underwear remained. His erection pushed against his dark black briefs, and Zoe's breath caught in her throat at the sight of how large he was. When he pushed his underwear off completely, and she could see his manhood on full display, she only became more breathless. Without a doubt, she had never seen anyone larger. His shaft was long and thick, and it pointed proudly toward her with the stiffness of a steel rod.

"Grayson," she murmured, unsure of what else to say.

His eyes blazed as he looked down at her, swirling with an otherworldly look. She'd heard that shifter eyes could do strange things, especially when a shifter male was turned on. But nothing could have prepared her for the intensity of Grayson's gaze right now. He was something other than human, that was certain.

He moved toward her slowly, like an animal after his prey. The hunger in his eyes made Zoe shudder with pleasure. With deft fingers, he unbuttoned and unzipped her jeans, then started tugging them down. Zoe wanted nothing more than to finish what they'd started, but the wetness of her underwear made her suddenly reach up and stop Grayson with a gasp. Sex was a messy affair, and, although Zoe had long since given up feeling that making out in Shafer's office was sacrilegious, she wasn't about to ruin his bearskin rug by making love on it.

"The rug," she gasped out to Grayson. "We'll make a mess."

Grayson furrowed his brow for a moment, then caught her meaning. He looked around for his t-shirt, grabbed it, and motioned to Zoe to move aside. When she did, he laid the shirt down, forming a barrier between them and the rug.

"Now," he grunted, his voice deep and husky. "Where were we?"

He pushed Zoe back down onto the rug, her ass directly over the middle of his t-shirt. This time, as he pulled off her jeans and underwear, she did not resist. Her shoes had already been kicked off at some point, although she couldn't for the life of her remember when. Everything was a blur.

A wonderful, burning, tingle-filled blur.

Grayson moved his naked body so that it was directly over hers. He'd been moving fairly slowly up to this point, but the sight of her completely naked seemed to be almost more than he could take. He wanted her, and he wanted her now. His chest brushed against her breasts, and she felt his stiff dick poking at the area below her navel, moving lower and lower, searching.

When he found what he was looking for, he slid right in. Zoe thought with some amusement how strange it was that he had asked her permission for a kiss, but had not so much as paused for a beat before putting his dick inside her. She supposed they'd long since passed the point of no return, and he knew it. If she was going to stop him, she'd had plenty of opportunities to do so before now. And he had the right of it: she had no interest in stopping him.

She closed her eyes and let him fill her. He pushed against her, touching places within her that she hadn't even known existed. She felt a burning in her very core, and she wondered how she could feel so hot without literally bursting into flames. She felt like a thousand fireworks were going off inside of her, and all of her worries and fears were burned away. There was nothing in the world except Grayson, moving inside of her, making her feel like a woman in ways no one ever had.

It didn't take long at all for his smooth thrusts to push her over the edge. The pressure that had been rapidly building since he first kissed her finally exploded, and Zoe threw back her head and screamed as her release came. She didn't care that they were in a forbidden place, and she didn't worry that someone might hear her. She had no space in her mind for thoughts like that. All she could think was that this was heaven. Grayson inside of her was the best feeling in the world, and she never wanted the moment to end.

Grayson must have had similar thoughts. He roared, a sound even louder than Zoe's scream had been. He thrust harder, and with a greater urgency. And then, he stiffened, and roared again as he came. His throbbing, and Zoe's pulsing muscles, continued for at least a full minute. Zoe hadn't thought such an intense feeling of ecstasy was possible. Perhaps it was the fact that she was making love with a dragon. Perhaps it was because she was here, in a room where so many poems about love had been written, and romance hung heavy in the air. Or perhaps, it was just the intoxication of knowing she was far, far away from anyone who would chase her down and treat her like someone who belonged on the cover of *People* magazine.

Whatever the reasons, that time she spent on the bearskin rug was the most extraordinary experience of Zoe's life. As she dressed, she thought wryly that insisting on having Grayson as her partner on this mission had been the best choice she could have possibly made. She hadn't realized why until now, of course. But damn if it didn't feel good to be away from the prying eyes that were everywhere in Falcon Cross, and to be a little naughty in the process, too.

Later, when she and Grayson had both dressed, and were slipping out of Shafer's house, Zoe dug into her wallet and found a crisp one hundred dollar bill to drop into the donation box by the door.

That had been one hell of a self-guided tour.

CHAPTER EIGHT

Grayson awoke to the sound of rain falling the next morning, and the rain did not stop falling again for all twelve hours that he and Zoe flew. The weather was so bad that they couldn't make it to the next town on their itinerary, and they were forced to stop short by about a hundred miles. Zoe spotted a campground and RV park from their aerial vantage point, and she made her way down through the storm to land about a half mile out.

"We have to walk in," she explained to Grayson, as though he didn't already know that. "Flying in and then suddenly appearing from under the cover of an invisibility shield has the potential to draw far too much attention."

Grayson hmphed in response. He was wet, cold, and tired, and not in the mood to have a conversation that merely stated the obvious. Without another word, he slipped his backpack off his back and started looking for street clothes. Not only would it not do to fly in to the campground, it also wouldn't do to walk in while wearing Falcon Cross military uniforms. That was certain to stir up some questions. Grayson imagined they already looked suspicious enough as it was, coming in on foot in the middle of the rain, in an area where people mostly drove to their destinations. But they had little choice in the matter, unless they wanted to continue flying through the rain in the darkness, trying to reach the next city. In this weather, that was bound to take quite a bit of time, and Grayson had had enough of flying for the day. Possibly for the week, or even the month. He was more than ready to get to the part of this mission where he actually got to do something. Sitting on the back of a broomstick and letting someone else steer wasn't his idea of a kickass mission. The more delays they faced on the way, the grumpier he was going to get.

Out of respect for Zoe, Grayson turned around as she undressed and changed. It seemed a bit silly, after what they'd done last night. But he wanted to be polite. And, besides, he was confused as hell over what to do about his feelings for her. Grayson had, quite unexpectedly, fallen in love.

The possibility of love had been far from his mind when he and Zoe got it on in the middle of Shafer's house last night. He hadn't thought what he felt for her was anything other than blinding passion. One minute, he'd been trudging up the stairs, annoyed that they had been in the house for so long. Really, it hadn't been that long at all, but he hadn't wanted to be there in the first place, so every passing second felt like an eternity. But the next minute, he'd been staring hopelessly at Zoe's perfect curves, which were illuminated by the moonlight streaming into Shafer's office.

He'd forgotten to be angry, and he admitted to himself that perhaps he was giving Zoe too hard of a time. He had been quite impressed with all of the information he'd learned about Erich Shafer, and with the fact that Zoe was the kind of person to know so much about poetry. Before he knew it, he'd let the little swirls of desire in his stomach get the better of him, and he'd asked to kiss Zoe. The rest had been history. As soon as his lips touched hers, he knew he was a lost cause. He'd never wanted anyone so badly in his entire life. For a while, he feared at every moment that Zoe was going to pull back, to stop him, to say she didn't want this. But she'd let him have her completely.

They had slept together in an act of pure lust. And damn, were they a good fit for each other in the physical department. Zoe made him feel stronger sensations than he'd ever thought possible, and, if her reactions to his touch were a reliable indication, he'd done the same for her. Zoe had made teasing remarks all last night and this morning about how fun it was to have a coworker with benefits, and Grayson had played along. But the truth was that it had only taken a few seconds of being inside of Zoe to know that she was more than just some sort of fling.

"We're going to have to change again as soon as we get to the campsite," Zoe complained. "It only took about a half second for my clothes to become drenched again."

Grayson took that as an indication that Zoe was done changing, and turned around. She was indeed changed, and now wore a pair of jeans and a fitted navy t-shirt, both of which were just as wet as if she'd just climbed out of a swimming pool.

"Come on," he said wearily. "There's nothing to be done about it but get to the campsite as quickly as possible, and hope that they have some sort of cabin open."

Grayson and Zoe didn't have a tent with them. They had packed as lightly as possible, and a tent had not made the final cut. They were supposed to be stopping at hotels along the way, and at their final destination in Shadowdale. If they did have to stop somewhere in the woods, they could sleep under the stars. It was summertime after all, and the weather was likely to be good.

So much for that, Grayson thought as a bolt of lightning flashed across the sky. He put his head down and told himself to just put one foot in front of the other. If he'd been able to shift into dragon form right now, things wouldn't have been nearly so unbearable. All this rainwater would have slid off his dragon hide, and his giant dragon wings could have easily cut through the windy skies. But there was no use wishing for what he could not have. Flying in dragon form would be much too dangerous, and the security of the mission was top priority. A much higher priority, to be sure, than being comfortable in the rain.

Grayson trudged along, doing his best to keep his thoughts off Zoe for the rest of the walk to the campsite. When they walked into the main office, a teenage boy with long stringy hair looked up in annoyance.

"Can I help you?" he asked, in a voice that indicated helping them was the last thing he felt like doing right then. In his hands he held a magazine that appeared to be about racecars, if the pictures could be trusted. Grayson wondered if the boy read it for the racecars, or for the pictures of women in skimpy clothing posing on the cars in the magazine's advertisements. Perhaps both. Well, whatever the reason, Grayson was probably just as keen to get out of this office as the boy was to get back to his cars and women. The sooner they could get a place for the night sorted out, the better. Zoe hung back by the door, standing on the weather mat in front of it. Grayson, however, walked right up to the counter, ignoring the fact that he was leaving a long wet trail behind him. It was just water. It would dry.

"We were wondering if you have any cabins available," Grayson said. "My friend and I got caught up in the rain, and we don't have a tent. I noticed you have some standalone cabins on your site."

The boy looked back and forth between Grayson and Zoe with a suspicious look in his eye. Grayson had the feeling that the boy hadn't missed the fact that he'd called Zoe his friend and not his girlfriend. And Grayson couldn't miss the way the boy's eyes roved up and down Zoe's curves with appreciation. The rain had caused all of her clothing to stick tightly to her skin, not leaving much about her shape to the imagination. Grayson found himself feeling overly defensive.

"You're too young for her, son," Grayson snapped. "Now can you tell me if you have a campsite available?"

The boy gave Grayson a sullen look, then sat up and reached for a giant three-ring binder. He flipped through several pages of spreadsheets, stopping when he came to one labeled "CABINS" in bold, capital letters across the top. He ran his fingers down the lines of scribbled handwriting on the spreadsheet, muttering under his breath. Grayson impatiently tried to see whether it looked like there were any openings. But he couldn't read very well upside down, especially not when the handwriting was this messy. Besides, he wasn't sure exactly what all the abbreviations on the page meant. Still, he tried. The boy took his time, almost as though he knew that doing so would annoy Grayson further. Finally, he looked up, his face still sullen.

"It's just the two of you?" he asked doubtfully, daring for a moment to steal another glance back at Zoe.

"Yes, just us," Grayson said, doing his best not to completely snap at the boy. Did the kid have pudding for brains?

"We only have one cabin left and it's an eight person cabin. It's big. Two bedrooms, with two bunk beds in each room. And a separate dining area and kitchen. It's a bit too big for two people, I'd say."

"How much is it?" Grayson asked. The cost didn't matter much. He and Zoe needed to rest, and if an eight person cabin was all this place had, they would take it.

"One hundred and twenty a night," the boy said, sounding almost apologetic. He winced a bit, as though he expected Grayson to yell at him about the exorbitant price.

Grayson wanted to laugh. Perhaps, as campsites went, one-twenty was on the pricey side. But it wasn't much more than he and Zoe would have spent on a hotel that night, and it was a dry place for them to stay.

"Do you take credit cards?" Grayson asked, already fishing in the front pocket of his backpack for his wallet. Visibly relieved that he wasn't going to be yelled at, the boy brightened and nodded.

A little more than five minutes later, Grayson was grabbing the key for their cabin from the boy's hand. When the boy took another glance at Zoe, Grayson felt a wave of possessiveness wash over him.

"She's mine," Grayson growled under his breath at the boy, hoping that Zoe was too distracted to hear him. "Go find someone your own age."

The boy frowned in confusion. "I thought you said she was your friend," he protested.

Grayson's scowl deepened. "It's complicated. But *you* stay away from her, you hear?"

The boy raised his hands in the universal gesture for surrender, then went back to his magazine with a huff. Grayson turned to see Zoe looking at him with amusement. As soon as they'd closed the office door behind them and stepped out into the rain again, she laughed.

"Touchy, touchy," she said. She sounded pleased. Grayson wasn't sure how much of his exchange with the boy she had actually heard, and he wasn't sure he wanted to know.

"Come on," he said, ignoring her jab. "We've got a bit of a walk. Our cabin is on the far end of the campground."

They bent their heads low against the wind and started walking through the rain again, making their way past the small tents, large RVs, and tiny cabins. The last row of cabins was slightly larger than the rest, and the very last cabin on that row was theirs.

"What a walk," Zoe said as they stumbled through the front door, bringing a large puddle of water with them.

"At least we're relatively secluded," Grayson said, already peeling off his soaking t-shirt. "Although I think it's a good walk back to the community bathrooms."

"Bummer," said Zoe. "I want to take a shower."

Grayson saw her look up at the sky with a doubtful frown.

"If you're waiting for a break in the rain," he said. "You're likely going to be waiting a while."

"I might just make a run for it, then. I want to take a shower. I'll find a trash bag or something to hold over my head on the way back to keep me dry."

Grayson just nodded. He thought Zoe was a bit crazy for wanting to take a shower, but he wasn't about to argue with her about it. He would welcome a few minutes away from her, in fact, and his sense of relief when she dashed out into the rain again was almost palpable. He needed to sort out his feelings for her, and quickly.

When he saw the boy in the office look at Zoe, the strength of Grayson's possessive feelings had surprised him. But perhaps they shouldn't have. Grayson was slowly coming to admit to himself what he had known in his heart since he and Zoe gave in to their passion on that bearskin rug last night: she was his lifemate.

It seemed an improbable match to him in many ways. He was a dragon, who freely admitted to his desire for fame and glory. And she was a wizard, who did her best to avoid the fame and glory she'd so unwillingly found. They wanted different things out of life, it seemed. So why had destiny brought them together?

It was hard to deny that it had been destiny that aligned their paths. All the things that had seemed like coincidences to Grayson now made perfect sense. His initial meeting of Zoe, and her subsequent request to have him accompany her on the mission, had all been part of fate's plan to bring them together. And once they were together, it hadn't taken long for the passion between them to simmer to a boiling point. After Grayson had acted on that passion, he'd felt the telltale burning in his core, the warmth of the lifemate bond.

Grayson rubbed his forehead and stared out the front window of the cabin, looking for Zoe. She was too far gone now. The rain was too thick to see more than ten feet in front of the cabin. Perhaps it was better that way. Less chance of anyone seeing them here and asking questions. He doubted that any of Saul's spies were around, but still. He preferred to keep to himself.

A glance at the clock on the wall told him it was just before seven. They would need to eat soon, and, while they had meal replacement bars in their bags, Grayson would rather save those for when there was quite literally no other option. He had seen a little general store near the front of the campsite, and he decided to make a run for it and see if there was anything edible there. Without bothering to put on another shirt, Grayson grabbed his wallet and ran out into the rain. The run to the store, with no backpack weighing him down, felt much quicker than the slow trudge out to the cabin had felt. In no time at all, Grayson had arrived at the general store, and tumbled through the doorway with a blast of wind and rain.

The inside was surprisingly large, and filled with everything from food to souvenirs to camping supplies. Grayson noticed that there were tents for sale. He and Zoe could have bought a tent for the night if they'd had to, although he didn't mind being in a cozy cabin instead in the midst of this storm. Grayson also noticed that the man behind the counter did not seem pleased to see him. The man eyed him up and down, pausing for an extra beat on the puddle forming around Grayson's feet. When he looked back up to meet Grayson's eyes, he frowned, then pointed to a sign above his head that read, "No shirt, no shoes, no service."

"You gotta have a shirt, mate," the man said, shrugging and turning back to look at whatever magazine he was holding in his hands. Grayson wanted to roll his eyes. Apparently all the employees at this place wanted to do was to sit around and read magazines.

"Come on, man," Grayson said. "Don't make me go back and get a shirt. I'm the only one in here, and I ran all the way over here in the pouring rain."

"I noticed," the man said sourly. "You're leaving a puddle all over my floor. Rules are rules."

He went back to his magazine again as though that settled it. Grayson scowled, narrowing his eyes as he looked around the store until his gaze landed on a display of souvenir t-shirts with "Woodlake Camp" written on them in big, gaudy letters. He chose a large, hot pink one just to make an additional statement that he didn't care what the man thought of him. Then he ripped the tags off and slipped the shirt on over his head. He marched up to the counter and threw the tags down.

"I'd like to buy this shirt," Grayson said. "And then I'd like to buy some food."

The man, whose nametag read "Ralph," scowled right back at him. "You don't own that shirt yet. I can't help you until you're wearing a shirt you actually own."

Grayson resisted the urge he had to punch the man just to see if he would bounce off the wall behind him. The people who worked here were the most unfriendly lot Grayson had ever met. If he were the type to write online reviews, he'd give this place zero stars. But Grayson wasn't the type to spend time writing reviews, and he needed food. So he just crossed his arms over his chest and gave Ralph a stern look.

"I can take the shirt off and leave, in which case you've got a ruined shirt and no sale. Or I can buy the shirt, along with a good amount of food and supplies. Doesn't look like you're doing any other business tonight."

Ralph looked like he would protest again for a moment, but finally he shrugged and rolled his eyes like he could care less what Grayson did. "Suit yourself."

Grayson didn't waste any more time on the man. He grabbed a hand basket and made his way to the grocery section, where he found steaks, potatoes, and salad fixings. He grabbed a bottle of wine as well, and cereal and milk for breakfast. A ripe bunch of bananas caught his eye, and he threw it in the basket as well. By that time, the basket was almost full, but he still managed to find room for a small umbrella. A box of chocolate chip cookies that looked homemade sat by the counter, and Grayson grabbed that as well. Ralph sighed and started ringing up the purchases like it was the greatest annoyance in the world. Grayson ignored him and started fishing his credit card out of his wallet. He was paying for everything with his Falcon Cross business credit card, and he'd been given the freedom to spend as much as he wanted, so the purchase was a fairly large one. Ralph should have been pleased.

"You want a bag?" Ralph asked as he finished ringing up the last of the purchases.

Grayson nodded, and Ralph huffed again, stuffing all of the purchases in one single bag until it was about to burst. Grayson handed over his credit card without even waiting to hear the total. He just wanted to get out of here at this point.

"Nice color on that shirt," Ralph said, raising an eyebrow at the hot pink shirt Grayson was wearing.

Grayson smiled and shrugged. "Real men wear pink."

He'd had a feeling Ralph was the type who wouldn't be able to resist making a comment on the shirt. Grayson had always been good at reading people, and Ralph was practically an open book: sour old man, with no ambition who looked for any reason to make other people feel small. But Grayson was a dragon. He couldn't be intimidated so easily. And he didn't have much patience for people like Ralph. There was a giant war going on between good and evil right now, for crying out loud. What did it matter what color shirt someone wore? But Ralph did not and could not know about the war, or about Saul and his army. Ralph was like many other sleepy men, going through life thinking they were better than everyone, when really, they had no idea how hard others had worked to keep them safe and free.

As Grayson turned to leave, he noticed a mop leaning against the door that must have led to the back storeroom of this place. He grabbed the mop, and quickly walked around the store, sopping up the wet trail he'd made as he shopped. Then he replaced the mop and turned to leave without another word. He could have left the mess for Ralph to clean up. The man had no shortage of time. But Grayson wanted to make one last, silent statement: I'm a better man than you.

Satisfied that he'd had the last word, Grayson turned to leave. The rain had lessened somewhat. It was still coming down steadily, but it no longer looked like a monsoon outside. He popped his new umbrella open and managed to get back to the cabin without getting his new t-shirt wet.

Zoe wasn't back yet, but Grayson decided to get changed into dry pants and get started on dinner. By the time he was done with everything, she would hopefully have returned. He was a bit surprised she wasn't back already, but he supposed that women took longer showers than men, and, besides, it probably felt good to stand under a steaming hot stream of water after flying all day, let alone flying in cold, rainy weather.

Grayson slipped into a pair of gray cotton sweatpants, but left on the t-shirt. He was curious to see Zoe's reaction when she saw the shirt. Besides, it was actually a fairly comfortable shirt, even if it was rather gaudy.

Grayson got to work on dinner, and in record time he'd placed oven roasted steaks, baked potatoes, and a colorful salad on the table in the small dining room, along with two glasses of red wine. He surveyed the spread and decided that being in an oversized cabin instead of a tent definitely had its perks. Then he suddenly thought that the meal looked quite romantic, and he panicked. Would Zoe think he was trying too hard? Not trying hard enough? Should he try to find some candles to add to the table? What was the appropriate thing to do when you had just slept with a woman in a rush of passion and then realized you were actually in love with her, but didn't know whether she loved you back? For a dragon who was always so sure of himself, Grayson felt entirely unprepared to deal with the intricacies of the dance of romance.

Before he could spend too much time worrying about what to do, though, the front door to the cabin opened, and Zoe was back. It was too late to change anything now, so he'd just have to go with things the way that they were.

The dining room and kitchen together formed the whole front room of the cabin, so when Zoe walked in she immediately saw the table. Her eyes widened and a smile lit up her face.

"Wow," she said, letting her bag slide to the floor. "This looks amazing."

"So do you," Grayson couldn't help but saying. It must have stopped raining completely by now, because Zoe didn't have a single drop of water on her from the walk back, as far as Grayson could tell. Her hair had been washed and blow-dried so that it hung in loose waves around her face. Grayson rarely saw it down, since she always pulled it back into a tight bun when working. Now, he couldn't stop staring. She'd put on a little bit of makeup, too, and had changed into a fresh pair of jeans and long-sleeved navy t-shirt. She looked incredible.

Zoe smiled over at him, her way of acknowledging his compliment. Then, she raised an eyebrow at him. "Nice shirt," she said.

Grayson looked down and laughed. "I was hoping to get a reaction from you by wearing pink, but I forgot all about what I was wearing when you came through the door."

Zoe laughed, too, and the sound of it instantly made Grayson relax. What was he worried about? He and Zoe were friends, and they worked well together. Yes, last night had changed things between them in ways neither one of them understood yet, but that didn't mean they couldn't sit down and enjoy a nice dinner together.

And that's exactly what they did. They sat down and ate, savoring the steak and baked potatoes, and completely polishing off the salad and the wine. They told stories about their lives before the war, and Zoe laughed heartily at all of Grayson's stories about his clanmates and their antics. They talked a little bit about their current mission, but not too much. There wasn't much to say. They had been delayed slightly by the rain, but they would try to make up the time as best they could. If they couldn't, well, a day or two wasn't likely to make much difference in the grand scheme of things. As far as they could tell, they had not been followed by anyone. There had been no signs of pursuit, and the Falcon Cross spies who were watching Saul's movements hadn't noticed anything unusual. Saul and his army appeared to be sitting as still as ever. Grayson hoped that this meant that Saul had no idea that he and Zoe were hot on the trail of the dragon ruby.

Well, Grayson hoped they were hot on the trail of the dragon ruby, at least. There was always the possibility that the ruby had been moved again, or that his research was not correct. There was no way to know, though, until they got to Shadowdale.

After a dessert of chocolate chip cookies, which were surprisingly delicious and tasted homemade, Grayson and Zoe decided to go to bed. It was after nine o'clock now, which wasn't terribly late—but they wanted to get as early a start as possible. Although there were two bedrooms, they both chose to sleep in the same one. Grayson took one of the bottom bunks, and Zoe took the other.

Grayson wanted so badly to be in the same bed as Zoe. He wanted to slip in beside her, slip her out of her soft cotton pajamas, and make love to her. Not just sleep with her out of pure passion as he'd done last night, although that had certainly been wonderful. No, he wanted to move in her slowly and tenderly, to truly make love to her. But for someone who was never frightened by anything, Grayson was admittedly frightened by how in love he felt. He felt panic rising in his chest once again, the same way it had right before Zoe had returned to see the somewhat elaborate dinner he'd made. Grayson didn't know how to handle the overwhelming feelings of affection he was feeling right now, so he decided to talk about something else in an effort to distract himself. There, in the darkness of the cabin, with the rain once again falling outside, he turned to look at the dark silhouette that was Zoe.

"Do you really not want any recognition for your powers, Zoe?" he asked. "Even if you only acquired them through luck, you *are* doing a lot for Falcon Cross. What's wrong with being recognized for that? If you're going to have to deal with being followed around like a celebrity all the time, you might as well get some perks and recognition for it too, don't you think?"

There was a long silence, and then a soft sigh from Zoe's bunk. Grayson strained to see in the darkness, but there was no moonlight tonight. It was impossible to see the expression on Zoe's face, but he imagined her brow was probably furrowed in concentration as she thought carefully about what to say.

"It doesn't matter to me that much who gets the glory," Zoe said. "People are more important than glory. The meaning of the mission is more important than who gets the praise."

"But someone is going to get recognition. Someone is going to get medals and awards. It might as well be you, don't you think? I care about people, and about the meaning of the mission. But I also know that being recognized means more chances to get exciting missions in the future. And heck, if I work hard, I deserve a little praise, don't you think?"

Another long pause.

"It's alright to enjoy recognition when you receive it, I think," Zoe said. "But chasing after it can be dangerous. It can make you lose sight of the important parts of the mission, of the people we are trying to help to protect. Better to focus on doing the best work you can for the sake of the people, and let recognition come if or when it does."

Grayson was silent now, thinking. He wasn't sure he entirely agreed with Zoe. She had noble intentions, sure. But he'd realized lately that the more you tried to let your work speak for itself, the quicker life passed you by, and others received the credit for work that you had done. He might be a good man and a hard worker, but if he didn't get some credit here and there, he would soon be forgotten amongst the ranks of hundreds of other soldiers. No, he needed to make sure that this mission to the dragon ruby counted. He needed to achieve their goal in such a spectacular way that everyone in Falcon Cross and in the Redwood Dragons clan would know that he, Grayson Pars, had been instrumental in winning this war, and that he had mattered.

Zoe had fallen silent, too. Grayson wondered if his comments about needing fame were building an invisible wall between them. She hadn't said anything about how they'd slept together last night. She'd been as courteous and friendly as ever, but there had been no indication that she felt a spark of love, like he did. She was so hard to read sometimes. Or perhaps she was waiting for him to say something, to step up and be a man. To be the first one to acknowledge that there were feelings between them that should be explored. Hadn't Grayson just told himself, after all, that he needed to go after the recognition he wanted? Was love any different? If he wanted Zoe to recognize him as a worthy lifemate, and someone to love, then he needed to make some moves, and be a bit aggressive. He at least needed to talk to her about how he felt.

Mustering up all his courage, Grayson peered over at Zoe's silhouette on the bunk across the room.

"Hey, Zoe?"

No answer.

"Zoe?"

Again, no response. Grayson was quiet for a moment, then, and could hear the soft rhythm of Zoe's breathing. She had fallen asleep. Grayson had missed his chance, at least for the night.

Sleep did not come so easily for him. He lay awake a long time, staring at the ceiling and trying to formulate the right thing to say to Zoe to make her realize that they belonged together. But dragons aren't so good with words. They're better at actions. Which is why Grayson finally stood up and walked across the room, slipping into Zoe's small bunk with her. His act of lying next to her would say so much more than his jumbled words ever could. When she woke up in the morning, she would surely realize how he deeply felt for her.

Or would she?

CHAPTER NINE

Zoe stood outside her cabin in the early morning light, running a pre-flight safety check on her broomstick for the tenth time. She'd already eaten a quick breakfast of cereal and sliced bananas, and had repacked her backpack after carefully drying all her soaked clothes with a drying spell. Now, she was out here under the guise of getting ready to leave, when really she just wanted to avoid speaking to Grayson.

She didn't know why it had freaked her out so much when she woke up to find him curled up next to her in bed, his arm gently draped over her as his chest rose and fell with his dreams. Perhaps it had been in that moment that she realized that what was happening between them amounted to more than just a quick fling. It was more than just a physical passion, more than just an itch to scratch.

She'd realized this the first night she and Grayson had given in to their desires on that bearskin rug. Her heart had warmed in ways she'd never felt before, and the next day she hadn't been able to tear her thoughts away from Grayson even for a second. She'd gone to take an obscenely long shower at the campsite just so she could get away from him. She spent the whole time convincing herself that he didn't have feelings for her beyond a purely physical passion, and she had come to peace with that. But walking in to their cabin and seeing that he'd cooked such an amazing dinner set her heart to racing once again. She thought that surely he was going to make another move on her after dinner, but he never did. Instead, he settled into a separate bunk, and proceeded to interrogate her—again!—about why she never wanted any special recognition for her exceptional work as a soldier.

Zoe knew then that she and Grayson couldn't work. They were too different, and besides, he hadn't even mentioned sleeping with her. It hadn't meant anything to him. She told herself once again that there was nothing there, and forced her mind to go quiet so she could sleep. Then, she'd woken up to find him in her bed and promptly freaked out.

She couldn't handle this up and down. She needed to take her own advice and focus on the important work of her mission, and only on the mission. She was here to find the dragon ruby, not to find a boyfriend. She was here to help the people of Falcon Cross, not to indulge in lovemaking and be distracted by a dragon shifter. Even if that dragon shifter was the most handsome man she'd ever met.

Zoe was running her safety check for the fourteenth time when Grayson emerged from the cabin, his expression neutral. He was dressed, and his backpack was already slung securely on to his back. He did not give any indication that he was surprised or disappointed by the fact that Zoe had already been gone from the bed when he woke up. He was going to be all business this morning, and so was she. They were both going to avoid talking about what they had done together at Shafer's house, or what it might mean.

Good, Zoe thought. Let's just focus on getting the ruby. She should have felt relieved, since she didn't want to talk to Grayson, anyway. So why did she feel so sad? Gritting her teeth, Zoe forced herself to smile brightly at Grayson.

"Morning. Ready to go?" she asked.

Grayson did not smile back, but he didn't scowl, either. He just looked at her with slightly narrowed eyes, and nodded. "I cleaned up inside the cabin. We can check out and then be on our way."

Zoe followed Grayson toward the main office in silence. She saw a few people give her curious looks, and she supposed that walking around with a broomstick must seem a bit odd. But unless someone knew about wizards, which was unlikely, they would just think she was a bit crazy. Last night, Zoe had put an invisibility spell on her broomstick as they walked into camp, but right now she was too worn out to care if anyone thought she was crazy. She needed to save her energy for flying and for casting invisibility and protective shields while she and Grayson were in the sky.

And not much later, they were preparing to launch into the sky. They hadn't spoken much during their walk to the office, and then to a spot that was about a half mile away from the campsite. And even then, it was only business talk.

"Do you think we can make it to Shadowdale today?" Grayson asked.

Zoe shrugged. "If winds are in our favor, it's a possibility. We have a lot of lost ground to make up from yesterday, though, and I don't want to push our speed too much and compromise our invisibility shields."

"No, definitely don't compromise our shields. Just do the best you can," Grayson said.

That had been the extent of their conversation. Zoe was flying as quickly as she dared, and the winds were indeed in their favor. But she still doubted they would make it all the way to Shadowdale tonight. They'd have to stop off again for the night somewhere. Grayson had made a list of alternate towns to stop in, just in case their schedule got off course. Zoe figured she'd see which of those towns was closest when later afternoon came, and they'd stop there. It would mean one extra night before they reached the dragon ruby, but so be it. There was no sense in rushing things too much and making rash mistakes that would lead to Saul's soldiers discovering their whereabouts. Saul had eyes in a lot of places. Zoe had carefully scanned the campsite last night for any sign of magic, which would indicate nearby wizards. And Grayson had used his keen dragon sense of smell to make sure no shifters were present. But Zoe and Grayson could not be constantly scanning and sniffing while they flew. They had to rely on their shields. If Zoe messed up those shields it would mean big trouble for them.

And so, Zoe flew slower than she wanted to. She wanted the flying portion of this trip to be over just as badly as Grayson did. She knew he didn't like sitting idly behind her for the journey. But she also didn't enjoy the mental stress of flying. She was good at it, sure. But it was far from her favorite task. Some soldiers loved nothing more than zooming around on their broomsticks. Zoe preferred to have two feet on the ground, where she could fight without having to worry about maintaining flying spells as well.

Nevertheless, flying was necessary. There was no sense in wasting time or energy complaining about it. Zoe flew on, flying straight through lunch as she usually did. She and Grayson would both be starving by dinner, but they hated stopping. They just wanted to get the journey over with.

As the shadows started lengthening, Zoe made the decision to stop in a town that was thirty miles outside of Shadowdale. She probably could have flown the last thirty miles tonight if she really pushed herself, but she was tired and would rather finish off the last tiny leg of the journey in the morning. She knew Grayson wouldn't be pleased with this decision, but he would just have to get over it. Zoe started circling downward, her mouth already watering in anticipation of the big meal she was planning on having. She hoped there was an Italian restaurant in this little town. She'd love a nice big plate of lasagna right now. She'd even settle for pizza.

She descended slowly. Shields were always harder to maintain while descending, and, although Zoe didn't think any enemy soldiers were around, it was ingrained into her to be careful when circling toward the earth. They were about a mile outside of the little town. Once they landed, they would walk in and find a hotel. And then food. Zoe could hardly wait.

She had completed about half the distance to the ground when she suddenly felt a lurch from the back of her broomstick, followed moments later by a yelp of pain. Her balance was thrown off, and it only took her a split second to realize that it was because somewhere between two hundred and two hundred and fifty pounds had dropped off from the back of her broomstick.

"Grayson!" she screamed, pulling the handle of the broomstick up to stop her descent, and swinging around to look for him. He was falling, away from her at what looked like an incredible speed.

"No!" she yelled, and started diving downward toward him, as fast as her broomstick would carry her. Shields be damned, she was going to rescue him. Someone had already broken through her shield, anyway, if they had managed to knock Grayson off. She knew he'd been attacked. There had been no mistaking the pain in his voice as he fell away from the broomstick, and, besides, he would never just fall off. Something had pushed him. Someone.

Someone Saul had sent, no doubt.

Zoe was flying so rapidly that she could hardly see. She kept her eyes trained on Grayson's falling form, not daring to look away for even a second lest she lose sight of him. They had several thousand feet until the ground, still, but she wasn't sure she'd be strong enough to pluck him out of thin air at the speed he was falling. She clenched her right fist, feeling the metal of her magic ring against her skin. She would hit him with a suspension spell that would hold him up in midair. Once he was no longer hurtling through the air, she'd pull him back onto the broomstick and release the spell.

Zoe felt her stomach turn nervously. It had been a long time since she'd done a suspension spell, and she hoped she could do it correctly. But surely, if she could handle the *Crepitus* spell, she could manage a suspension spell. She took a deep breath and was about to utter the spell, when she saw a burst of green tearing through the shirt of Grayson's military uniform. The green grew larger, and the rest of his clothes tore away as well. His backpack went hurtling toward the earth as his dragon emerged. The late afternoon sunlight caught his green scales and made them shimmer with hues of purple, blue, and even pink. His head became a large fearsome dragon head, his hands and feet became dragon hands and feet, ending in razor-sharp claws. A tail extended out from his huge dragon body, and then—wings. The wings were the last part of his dragon to emerge, and Grayson had fallen dangerously close to the ground by the time they did. But he was already flapping them before they had even fully finished growing out, and in a matter of seconds he had managed to stop his terrifying freefall toward the earth.

He roared, and soared upward, his giant dragon head swinging back and forth as he looked for Zoe. She pulled into an abrupt stop, and took a moment to let her heart settle back into her chest. She'd been afraid for a moment that she was going to lose him, and the thought had filled her with a sense of dread so sharp that her physical body felt like it had been wounded.

But no, he was fine. He was there, in dragon form, flying toward her as his powerful wings cut through the air. Zoe hovered in midair, watching him come, telling herself that everything was fine, even though she knew deep down that everything was not fine. Grayson might be alright, but everything was not fine.

Saul's soldiers had found them. But how? Their invisibility shields had been flawless. Zoe had been so careful about not flying too fast. And none of the Falcon Cross scouts had reported any suspicious activity from Saul's camps, which were being watched every second of every day.

Zoe didn't have much time to ponder where things had gone wrong, though. As Grayson flew toward her, she saw a blur cutting across the sky to his left.

"Grayson! On your left!" she shouted. She was already flying toward him, leaning into her broomstick. She was still too far away for her spells to do much good. Luckily, Grayson heard her and reacted before thinking. He swung his dragon head sharply to the left and let out a long stream of fire. The wizard that had been approaching him didn't have time to dodge the flames, but she did have a magic shield up. The flames slowed her, but didn't stop her completely. She veered sideways and threw an attack spell at Grayson. It bounced off his thick dragon hide as he turned to breathe another stream of fire at his attacker.

Zoe continued to fly toward him, but she never made it. Before she could reach firing range, another of Saul's wizards attacked her. Zoe pulled to an abrupt stop and returned his attack spell with one of her own. The wizard had a shield up, but not a very strong one. Zoe quickly adjusted her attack strategy and began beating back the wizard. Grayson was going to have to fend for himself, which was just fine. Now that he was in dragon form, he was more than capable of doing so.

Zoe focused all of her attention on the wizard in front of her. She kept her own protective shield strong while throwing out spell after spell. She let her invisibility shield go. There was no point in wasting magical energy on trying to stay invisible. Saul's soldiers had obviously broken through the invisibility shield she'd had up. She moved rapidly across the sky, zigzagging back and forth to avoid the spells the enemy wizard was throwing at her, and throwing back several attack spells of her own. It didn't take her very long to throw a knockout blow at her opponent. The wizard yelped in pain, and then fell off his broomstick, hurtling toward the earth.

Zoe glanced quickly up at Grayson, and saw that he was holding his own quite well against the wizard he was fighting. He was slowly wearing down the other wizard, and as soon as he got through her magic shield he'd be able to quickly defeat her. Zoe made a split-second decision, and decided to chase after the wizard she'd just knocked down. If she could catch the wizard before he hit the ground and died a sudden, violent death, she might be able to get more information about how these wizards had found them, or how many more were out there. As far as she could see, there were only the two enemy wizards out here right now. It surprised her that they had attacked her on their own. They were using dark magic, yes. But they weren't very good at it, and they didn't seem to be well-trained fighters. The whole situation felt strange.

Zoe dove after the falling wizard, leaning hard against her broomstick and picking up speed with each passing millisecond. Once she was within firing range, she pointed her ring at the wizard and shouted, *"Magicae suspendo."* She wasn't nervous about performing the spell, as she had been when she'd been trying to perform it on Grayson. Here, if she missed, she'd lose out on the chance to interrogate an enemy. That didn't even come close to the pain it would have caused her to lose Grayson.

She shouldn't have worried about her ability to perform the spell. She executed it perfectly. One second, the enemy wizard was falling to his death. The next, he had come to an abrupt stop, hanging in midair. Zoe slowed her flight slightly, but not by much. She could already see him holding his magic ring out at the invisible bonds that suspended him, trying to break free from the spell she'd cast. It was a suicide effort, to be sure. If he broke the suspension spell, he would be falling to his death once again, with not enough time to perform a saving spell of his own. Zoe had just saved his life, but he didn't want to be saved. He didn't want to be captured alive.

"Too bad, buddy," Zoe said. She pointed her ring at him again and said *"Magicae obstupefio."*

The stunning spell froze him in place immediately. The only thing he could move now was his head and neck. Zoe could hear him yelling at her as she approached, but she couldn't make out his words. No matter. Without the ability to move his hand, he couldn't perform magic spells properly. He was highly unlikely to break free from the prison Zoe had cast around him.

Zoe turned her attention back to Grayson, high above her. She looked just in time to see him finally break through the protective shield the other wizard had up. The enemy wizard was on fire a few moments later, as dragon breath consumed her. She went tumbling to the earth in a spectacular ball of flames. Grayson chased after her, and Zoe knew he was going to make sure that she was fully dead, and that she didn't catch the whole goddamn forest on fire.

Zoe turned her attention back to the frozen wizard.

"You're coming with me," she said. She flew right up to the wizard, grabbed him by one of his feet, and started flying toward the ground, dragging the wizard behind her. The wizard screamed out a stream of curses at her, but Zoe didn't care. He could curse all he wanted, but his words couldn't hurt her now. And if she had her way, she was going to find out in another minute what this wizard's deal was.

She had just landed on the forest floor with a soft thud when she heard the pounding of wings behind her. It was Grayson, coming in hot. He let out a roar as he landed, and the sound was not a happy one. For someone who had just escaped a brush with death, he didn't seem as joyful as he should have been.

"What's wrong?" Zoe asked, looking up from the captured wizard.

Grayson let out a grunt. He couldn't talk in human form, so he shifted back into human form in a burst of powerful energy. He had barely regained his human head when he was shouting, his voice more agitated than Zoe had ever heard it.

"There were three of them!"

Zoe frowned and looked up at the sky. She didn't see another wizard, but that didn't mean that there wasn't one there. Some of these dark wizards were exceptionally skilled at invisibility spells. Still, she didn't see why Grayson was quite so upset. If they had taken these two wizards individually, surely handling a third wizard together would be no problem. But Grayson was anything but calm right now.

"Help me find him!" he shouted. "I don't know where my backpack went. It had the map to the dragon ruby in it. It was in code, but still. Codes can be broken."

Zoe felt her blood go cold as understanding swept over her. The third wizard had seen Grayson's backpack fall and had abandoned the attack to chase the bag down. If the papers in Grayson's bag got into the wrong hands, this whole mission could be derailed. Grayson was right—codes could be broken. Zoe and Grayson were about to lose the head start they'd had in the race for the dragon ruby.

Zoe forgot about the wizard prisoner she'd taken and started running. Behind her, she could hear Grayson shifting back into dragon form. Less than a minute later, he was rising above her in the air, pounding his wings and roaring as he searched from up high for his backpack and the third wizard. Zoe had a sinking feeling in her stomach about this. They'd spent several long, long minutes fighting the other two wizards. That would have given a third wizard plenty of time to chase Grayson's backpack down and run off with the information. He could be miles from here by now. But if he wasn't…

"*Magicae clamo!*" Zoe yelled, holding her magic ring high above her head. She waited a moment, praying the spell would work, praying the wizard was still close by. It was an ancient spell, one that required a great deal of power. One of the master wizards had taught it to her, saying he was one of the only people left in the world who could perform it properly. He'd been pleased with her efforts, and told her that with a little bit more practice she might too master the spell. Zoe hadn't practiced since then, but she was practicing now—and praying it would work. She stood perfectly still and waited. To her immediate right, she heard the wizard she'd captured yelling out at the top of his lungs. But he was not the wizard she was looking for. Several seconds passed, and she was about to give up. Either she hadn't managed to do the spell properly, or the wizard was far away by now. But then, she heard it. A scream far off to her left.

She took off running again, heading in the direction the scream had come from as fast as her legs would carry her. Above her, she saw Grayson turning to fly in the direction of the scream. He'd heard it, too. He would beat her there. The best thing she could do was to help him locate the wizard by forcing the wizard to scream again. Zoe stopped running and once again raised her magic ring high above her head.

"*Magicae clamo,*" Zoe yelled. Again, the captured wizard to her right screamed first. Then, a few seconds later, another scream came, from her left. Zoe kept repeating the spell, watching the sky above her as Grayson circled, searching for the source of the scream.

Zoe was sweating from the effort of performing such a powerful spell over and over. But she would not stop until she knew that Grayson had found their enemy. The spell was on the very outer edges of what was considered acceptable magic. It forced any human being it hit to scream out at the top of their lungs, essentially drawing out their voice in full force against their will. Zoe had known that if she could do the spell correctly, and if their enemy was close enough, it would force him to reveal himself. It didn't matter how strong of a protective or invisibility shield the enemy wizard had up. Nothing was a match for a properly executed *Clamo* spell.

Zoe could feel herself growing weak, but she forced herself to continue. Reluctantly, she let the stunning and suspension spells she'd had on the first wizard end. She was risking an attack by him, and she was definitely losing her chance to interrogate him. But finding the third wizard, who might have Grayson's backpack, was more important. Zoe gave the search effort her all. She could hear now that the wizard whom she'd just freed was running away from her. At least he was not going to attack, although it was a great loss that he'd be able to go warn the rest of Saul's army that Zoe and Grayson were out here.

Zoe couldn't worry about that now. *Concentrate on the* Clamo *spell*, she told herself. She focused as much as she could, until finally, she saw Grayson stop circling and start to dive downward at full speed. She let herself relax, choking for air as she finally had a break from the strenuous undertaking that casting that spell had been. She knew that if Grayson was diving, it meant he'd found the wizard. She could rest for a moment.

After a minute to regain her strength, she started walking toward where she had seen Grayson dive. She could hear him roaring now and then, and she figured he must be fighting the third wizard. Zoe wasn't too worried. Grayson was a strong fighter, and probably didn't need her help. Even if he did need her help, she was going to need a few more minutes to recover before she'd have enough energy to do anything useful in battle. She moved along as quickly as she could without overexerting herself, listening carefully to Grayson's roars. If he sounded like he was truly in need of help, she'd make an effort to speed up, but right now he was beating his opponent soundly.

The roars continued, until Zoe had reached the small clearing where Grayson had found the wizard. She had to laugh. Grayson had the wizard pinned under his giant dragon arms. One arm held down the man's chest, and the other kept the wizard from moving the arm to which his hand with his magic ring was attached. The wizard was desperately trying to fight Grayson with spells, but without being able to move his ringed hand, it was difficult for him to properly cast any spells.

Grayson looked up when he heard Zoe approaching. He let out another roar, and Zoe realized that Grayson had continued to roar well after he'd pinned down this wizard. Grayson was angry. Furious, even. Smoke curled from his nostrils in circular wisps, and his eyes blazed a dark, swirling green.

"*Magicae obstupefio,*" Zoe said, pointing her ring at the wizard, careful not to aim anywhere near Grayson's dragon arm. Instantly, the wizard stopped struggling, frozen in place by Zoe's stunning spell. Grayson grunted, then stepped backward and began to shift into human form once more. Zoe watched while he transformed, keeping one eye on the wizard as well. She wasn't about to let this one get away, after she'd released her first prisoner in order to catch this guy.

Zoe noticed that Grayson's backpack was on the ground, the straps torn from where Grayson had shifted out of them. The rest of the backpack seemed to have escaped undamaged, but it was open, and the contents were strewn haphazardly around the clearing. Zoe hadn't seen the mess before, because Grayson's large dragon body had been blocking it. But now, she could clearly see the papers, clothes, food, and other supplies that had been thrown about in disorderly haste. Grayson was fully back in human form now, and was digging through the mess for some clothes to replace the ones he'd lost when he shifted.

"When I found this bastard, he was taking photographs of all our mission files. I don't know how many he had taken, or if he'd transmitted them to anyone yet. But it's quite possible we're screwed. We've definitely lost our element of secrecy."

Grayson's voice dripped with anger, and he still had smoke coming from his nostrils even though he was in human form once more. Zoe felt her own stomach dropping. How had they been found? They'd been so careful. And were there more dark wizards about?

Zoe turned and stormed over to the dark wizard, standing right above his stiff form and pointing her magic ring in his face.

"Are there more of you?" she yelled. "How many of you were chasing us? And how did you find us? I swear to god if you don't tell me, I'll use a *Calor* spell on you!"

"Zoe," Grayson said, his voice troubled. "We aren't authorized to use torture spells."

What he said was true. His own voice didn't sound that convinced though. Zoe knew he was just as eager as her to get the answers to the questions she'd asked. The *Calor* spell was a mild torture spell that made its victim unbearably hot. Zoe had never used it before, but she wasn't above trying it out for the first time on this guy. She could feel her own blood boiling, and if she was going to be hot with rage because of this guy, she saw no reason not to make him hot with pain.

But the wizard only laughed at her, shaking his head—the only part of his body he could move—in great amusement. "You don't have to torture me for me to tell you how I found you. I'll gladly tell you. You guys were idiots and walked around that campsite openly with a broomstick."

Zoe stepped back, bile rising in her throat. "But...there were no wizards or shifters at that campsite. I was sure of it."

The dark wizard laughed again. "Oh, no. There weren't any wizards or shifters. But there were plenty of humans. And Saul has a lot of human spies on his payroll. He's planted them all over the country, and is paying them exorbitant amounts of money to report any possible shifter or wizard activities. Someone walking around with a random broomstick is one of the things they've been trained to look for. My buddies and I were alerted to possible enemy activity in the area, and we worked hard all day searching for invisibility shields. Yours was hard to find but we finally managed to break through it. And ooooh boy. What a payoff for all our hard work. I don't know what papers you've got in those bags there, but they look mighty important. Saul will be pleased that we intercepted you."

Zoe stared at the dark wizard, the sick feeling inside of her rising. It had been her fault. She damn well knew better than to walk around with a broomstick, but she'd gotten careless about it. She didn't dare look over at Grayson. She was breaking out into a cold sweat just thinking of the disapproval that must be in his eyes right now.

"You didn't answer my other question," Zoe said, raising her voice and pointing her ring threateningly at the wizard. "How many of you were there?"

The wizard laughed at her. "Touchy, touchy," he said. "What's the matter? Feeling a little flustered that we found you? Or that I've scanned all those papers and sent them to Saul? I'm assuming, since they were in code, that you were not supposed to let them fall into the wrong hands, eh?"

"Just answer the question!" Zoe yelled, shaking her ring in his face.

He laughed again. "Oh, there were just the three of us. Don't worry, no one is going to be jumping out of the woodwork and attacking you. Not yet, anyway. But I'm sure Saul will be sending an army after you as soon as he sees the papers I sent. I might not be able to read everything that was in code, but I know enough to recognize a picture of the dragon ruby when I see it. As soon as the big boss sees that you were after the dragon ruby, he'll be sending reinforcements. And I can die with honor, knowing that I was the one who finally intercepted a Falcon Cross quest for the ruby."

"Die with honor?" Grayson asked in a puzzled voice. Zoe shared his confusion. The wizard didn't appear to be seriously wounded. But then, Zoe realized that the wizard's eyes were turning black, and everything made sudden sense.

"Turn around!" she yelled at Grayson, already turning around herself. "Turn around and run!"

He did as he was told without asking for an explanation. Which was a good thing, since it was only about five seconds later that the explosion came, knocking Grayson and Zoe both flat on their faces.

CHAPTER TEN

Zoe leaned down against her broomstick, pushing it to the upper limits of the speed it could handle. She ignored the throbbing pain on the left side of her head. She could feel the sticky warm wetness of blood where she'd landed hard against a rock, but she didn't dare raise a hand to wipe at the wound right now. She needed to concentrate all of her energy on flying.

Grayson was behind her, his chest pressed close against her back. The explosion had destroyed his backpack, so they'd rescued as much as they could of his things—which hadn't been much—and consolidated everything into Zoe's bag. Grayson now wore that bag on his back, meaning that now there was no bag separating him from Zoe as they flew. She rather liked the closeness of his body to hers, but she wished the chance to fly with their bodies against each other had come under happier circumstances. Even Grayson's arms circled around her waist could not lessen the terror Zoe felt right now.

The wizard in the clearing had self-destructed in a remarkably large explosion. Self-destruction was becoming a common problem amongst Saul's dark wizards. They had, it seemed, been taught to self-destruct rather than be taken captive. The wizard Grayson had caught must have realized he wasn't going to escape, and had set off a timed self-destruction spell before Zoe had frozen him with a stunning spell. Zoe was lucky she had realized what was happening. If she and Grayson hadn't started running away from the wizard when they did, they would have certainly been killed. Grayson had sustained worse injuries than Zoe. He had two huge gashes in his head, another large gash in his arm that probably should have been stitched up, and some sort of problem with his ankle. Zoe guessed it was sprained, but Grayson insisted it was nothing—even though he hadn't been able to keep from hobbling on it as they rushed around preparing to fly like the wind for the location up on Red Point Mountain where they hoped the dragon ruby was located.

Zoe kept giving herself the same mental pep talk over and over as she flew. Saul hadn't known until about half an hour ago that the dragon ruby's location had been discovered. He likely didn't have many soldiers out here in the middle of Colorado, just waiting and ready to go searching for a dragon ruby. If Zoe and Grayson flew quickly, they had a good chance of reaching the ruby's location before anyone Saul could send.

Zoe had abandoned all attempts to maintain invisibility or protective shields by flying slowly. She and Grayson had both agreed to screw the shields and focus on beating the forces of darkness to the ruby. This was why, not too much later, a dark wizard had no trouble spotting them zooming toward him across the sky. The dark wizard had been waiting for them, and he raised his magic ring to place an invisible magic wall right in front of Zoe.

She saw the wizard and realized what he had done. But she was flying so fast that, despite her attempts to come to a screeching halt before the wall, she still collided with it at an uncomfortably fast rate of speed. She raised her magic ring and prepared to attack the dark wizard, cursing under her breath. She'd been hoping to make it a little further without having to fight another battle with one of Saul's dark wizards, who seemed to be everywhere. Behind her, Zoe heard Grayson let out a low growl, and felt him tensing up. He was preparing to shift. Damn it, this meant their backpack was going to go flying to the earth again.

But before Zoe could launch an attack, or Grayson could begin shifting into dragon form, the dark wizard raised his hands above his head, showing a clear gesture of vulnerability and that he was not preparing another attack on them.

"Stop!" the dark wizard yelled. "I'm not here to attack you. I merely have a message from Saul."

Zoe paused, uncertain. Behind her, Grayson remained tense, but did not yet begin to shift.

"What's your message, then," Grayson yelled, his voice coming out in something representing a growl. Zoe tensed up quite a bit herself. She kept her hands firmly on the handle of the broomstick, hovering. She never took her eyes off the dark wizard. If he made one false move, she'd have her magic ring in the air, unleashing a destructive spell at him before he had time to complete any attack spells of his own. Zoe was the fastest wizard on the draw, and she felt confident that she could move faster than the wizard in front of her. He didn't look like much of a warrior. His appearance definitely fit that of a simple messenger or scout. Zoe felt herself relax just the tiniest bit. There were plenty of mortal threats out there, but this wizard was not one of them.

"What's your message?" Grayson yelled again. "Speak up now, or we'll make short work of destroying you and continuing on our way."

The dark wizard gave Grayson a withering look, which Zoe found somewhat amusing. Unless the wizard had backup somewhere that Zoe couldn't see, he didn't stand a chance in a fight against Grayson and Zoe. Part of Zoe wanted to go ahead and destroy him now. After all, he was an enemy soldier, and he was directly blocking their flight path to the dragon ruby. But another part of her wanted to hear whatever supposed message Saul had sent. She hoped there was some information in the message that would be helpful in determining whether Saul had any chance of actually reaching the dragon ruby before them.

She should have been more careful what she hoped for. She wanted reassurance that Saul was too far behind them to be able to stop them. But when the dark wizard finally spoke, his words were anything but reassuring.

"Saul would like to inform you that we've dispatched a large squadron of soldiers to the town of Shadowdale," the wizard said, his face twisting up into a wicked smile. "You must be familiar with Shadowdale, since it's the closest town to Red Point Mountain, where the dragon ruby is waiting for Saul's men to recover it."

Neither Zoe nor Grayson replied. The dark wizard was baiting them, trying to get an angry reaction by stating that Saul's soldiers would be the one to recover the dragon ruby. Zoe would not engage in petty arguments with this fool. She would let him finish his message, and then, he'd better hightail it out of there before she took him down with one strike from her magic ring.

The wizard's face looked a bit crestfallen at the lack of reaction from Zoe, but he pressed on in a haughty tone nonetheless. "Within the next half hour, our soldiers will have reached Shadowdale. We'll be holding the citizens hostage, and we'll be killing one every ten minutes unless you abandon your quest for the ruby."

Zoe felt her heart dropping. Saul knew all too well that the one way to disrupt the plans of the good shifters and wizards was to hurt innocent people. Unlike Saul's soldiers, the good soldiers cared about what happened to people. It's why they were fighting this war in the first place. Zoe knew that Saul would have no qualms about killing off an entire town of people if it served his purposes. Still, a small part of her wanted to believe that this wizard was bluffing. That there wasn't really an army on its way to Shadowdale. After all, Saul wouldn't have had time to organize something so quickly, would he have?

"You're lying," Zoe said, glaring at the other wizard. Behind her, Grayson let out a roar.

"Let's get rid of this fool now, and be done with it," Grayson said. But the dark wizard only laughed.

"Oh, I'm telling you the truth," he said. "Make no mistake about that. But if you want the blood of hundreds of innocent people on your hands, that's on you. We're still going to beat you to the dragon ruby. We had wizards close by, and they're flying even faster than you are to reach Red Point Mountain."

Zoe wished she was close enough to spit in the dark wizard's face. Where did he get off, telling them that the blood of innocent people would be on their hands? The dark soldiers were the ones actually doing the killing. Still, Zoe knew she would not be able to turn her back on a whole city of people in need of protection. And she could tell that the dark wizard was not, in fact, lying—as much as she wished he was. One of the things the Masters back in Falcon Cross had taught Zoe was how to spot a liar, and this dark wizard had none of the signs. He was a craven asshole, to be sure. But he was telling the truth. Saul was going to destroy Shadowdale. Zoe felt her heart dropping. She put a brave, determined expression on her face and yelled at the wizard.

"You can't stop us from getting the ruby!" Zoe yelled. "We'll get it first, and then we'll use it to destroy your army at Shadowdale, along with the rest of Saul's blasted army."

But the other wizard just laughed. "Yeah, good luck getting the ruby before us. Our soldiers are closer than you are to Red Point Mountain. You can't beat us there. And all you're doing by trying is giving us an excuse to destroy Shadowdale."

Before Zoe or Grayson could reply, the dark wizard had turned and zoomed away as quickly as his broomstick would carry him.

"Get him!" Grayson yelled, pointing after the wizard. But Zoe only shook her head!

"*Magicae murus terminantur,*" she said, pointing her ring at the invisible magic wall that the dark wizard had erected. The spell removed the wall, and Zoe could fly forward once again. But she didn't move very quickly. Instead, she slowly drifted, rubbing her forehead in frustration.

"Go!" Grayson yelled, his voice filled with frustration of his own. "Get him!"

Zoe shook her head. "Grayson, chasing after him would be a waste of our time. I think we need to adjust our course to head to Shadowdale."

Even though Grayson was behind Zoe and she couldn't see his face, she knew it would have an angry expression on it right about now.

"Zoe, are you out of your mind? There's no way we're abandoning our quest for the ruby to save a couple of random people in a town out in the middle of nowhere. Once we have the dragon ruby, we can use it to go back and drive back Saul's soldiers from Shadowdale."

"By then, people will have died. Also, we don't know how to use the ruby, and if we can't figure it out it won't do us much good in a battle."

"We'll figure it out between the two of us," Grayson said, his voice rising. "It can't be that hard."

"It might be," Zoe said. "I've heard the stones are pretty useless if you don't know how to use them right. Besides, we might not even be able to get to the ruby first. That wizard sounded pretty certain that Saul's soldiers were going to beat us there."

"Yeah, well, they *are* going to beat us there for sure, if you don't get moving. Jesus, Zoe, *fly*. If we don't get that ruby first, everything is ruined."

Zoe felt a strange chill run down her spine at Grayson's words. Something about his tone told her that this was about more than whether the wiser option was to save Shadowdale or get the ruby.

"Grayson," she said, in a suspicious tone. "We cannot let a whole town of people die. Not for a ruby that we don't know is even there, and which we probably won't beat Saul's men to, anyway. What's ruined if we save the town of Shadowdale instead of letting them die? Your chance at glory? At being famous as the dragon who recovered the dragon ruby?"

Grayson's stony silence was all the answer Zoe needed.

"Grayson, you should be ashamed of yourself! This mission isn't about fame or about proving that you're the coolest dragon around. It's about saving lives. And right now, the only way to do that is to go to Shadowdale and fight for its people."

"Oh come on, Zoe," Grayson countered, the tone of his voice bordering on all-out rage. "You're in no position to talk about things not being about fame, when fame just fell in your lap. It's easy for *you* to say that it doesn't matter. And besides, you're wrong. We can let a whole town of people die. I don't care if our chances of reaching the dragon ruby before Saul are slim. I have to try. The dragon ruby is too important to just let it go without a fight."

"Grayson. The *people*. They're going to die."

"I don't care," he said. His voice sounded strangely cold and emotionless now. "Are you going to fly to the dragon ruby, or do I have to fly there myself?"

Zoe felt herself growing hot with a mixture of anger, disbelief, and disappointment. "Fly yourself," she spat out. "If you're going to abandon a whole town of people to their death in a futile attempt at glory, then I can't stop you. But I want no part in it."

"It's not about glory," Grayson said. But his empty words didn't convince Zoe.

"If you're going, then go," she said. "I have some lives to save."

"So do I," Grayson spat back. "That's what capturing the dragon ruby is all about. Saving lives. Here, take this."

He handed Zoe the backpack he'd been wearing. She grabbed it with one hand, not saying a word to him. A few seconds later, he jumped from the broomstick, already letting out a roar. Zoe watched him falling away from her toward the earth, already morphing into dragon form. She watched as wings sprouted a few seconds later, and he flapped them vigorously to bring a halt to his freefall. He turned his giant dragon body toward Red Point Mountain, flying at top speed.

Zoe hovered in the air, watching him go for several minutes with an empty feeling in her heart. She'd been such an idiot, she realized. She'd let herself fall for a man who cared more about fame than about people. And wasn't fame the thing she hated more than anything? It was so stupid, so arbitrary. What had she been thinking, letting herself give in to an attraction to Grayson? He was obsessed with fame. Obsessed with the thing she hated. Why had she ever assumed things between them could work?

Still, she couldn't deny she cared for him, as angry as she was right now. It hurt to watch him fly away toward the dragon ruby, more than anything in her life had ever hurt before. She wouldn't go after him, though. She knew in her gut that they were not going to beat Saul to the dragon ruby. She knew Grayson would think she was being ridiculous if she told him she just had a feeling that it wasn't going to work out. He would have laughed at her, and told her that dragons rely on facts, not feelings.

Zoe took a deep breath and rallied the last bit of her strength. She didn't have time to sit here and pine after Grayson, or mourn the loss of the man she thought he was—

the man who would have placed the well-being of a town of people high above a losing quest for glory.

Sadly, Zoe turned her broomstick in the direction of Shadowdale and bent low against its handle, once again picking up speed until she was flying like the wind.

CHAPTER ELEVEN

Grayson never bothered to look back at Zoe. He knew she wouldn't be following him. She was going to go save Shadowdale. Try to save it, anyway. Although Zoe was more talented than your average wizard, he still wasn't sure one wizard could do much against a whole squadron of Saul's soldiers. He should have admired her willingness to try, but, right now, he was too angry at her for abandoning the dragon ruby to feel anything but frustration toward her. The dragon ruby was their mission. Not saving Shadowdale. She had no business changing course mid-mission.

Even as Grayson fumed, he had to push away the little voice within his head telling him that Zoe had been perfectly within her rights to change course for Shadowdale. There was a well-understood rule that any mission could be adjusted at any time if necessary to save the lives of innocent people. A threat like the one the dark wizard had just made against Shadowdale certainly qualified as something from which innocent people needed to be saved. But Grayson could not bring himself to give up on the dragon ruby. If he botched this mission, he might never get another good one. This was his chance of a lifetime, and he wasn't about to blow it.

Grayson pumped his wings harder, ignoring the burning sensation of overworked muscles. He was pushing himself too hard, he knew. At this rate, he wasn't going to have any strength left if he needed to fight Saul's soldiers to get the ruby. He was placing his bets on beating everyone else to the ruby. He had no idea how much of a gamble that really was. The dark wizard claimed that Saul's soldiers would beat Grayson there, but there was no proof. Grayson flew faster still, giving all his energy over to this one quest.

This mission must not fail. The fate of the world hung in the balance. Grayson had sworn he would come back with the dragon ruby, and, if he didn't, he might as well not go back at all. He and Zoe had already screwed up by walking through the campsite with a broomstick in full view. He would not pin the blame for that solely on Zoe. He could have told her to hide it, but he didn't. They were both culpable. They both should have known better. And that one tiny mistake might have cost them the dragon ruby, the war, and Grayson's chance at glory. Funny how, if we're not careful, the tiny, seemingly unimportant mistakes we make can turn into huge ripples that wash away what truly matters to us. No mistake is without its consequences.

Grayson tried not to dwell on these negative thoughts as he pressed forward. He wasn't that far from Red Point Mountain now. He could see it rising in the distance. Off to the right of the mountain, he saw in the valley the cluster of buildings that he knew was Shadowdale. He couldn't see any wizards, but that didn't mean they weren't there. If Saul's soldiers were indeed heading for Shadowdale, they would be flying under invisibility shields. Grayson felt a pang of fear, thinking of Zoe flying straight into the heart of an enemy squadron, but he pushed the fear away. He was not responsible for protecting her. She was a big girl, and she was making her own choices. She was well aware of what the consequences might be, and he wasn't going to let himself worry about how things would turn out for her. Not when the dragon ruby was so close at hand.

The wind whipped at Grayson's dragon ears, the steady buzz of it blocking out all other sounds. He breathed in deeply, filling his lungs with the fresh, cool air that he was sharing with the clouds, and he willed that fresh air to keep him going longer than he should have been able to. If ever there was a time to give something your all, this was it.

Grayson lost track of time. He flew on, intent only on getting to the dragon ruby as soon as possible. At some point, he saw a curl of smoke rising from the direction of Shadowdale. When he looked over, he saw a huge triangle of orange and yellow glowing beneath the smoke. Fire. Shadowdale was burning. Saul's soldiers had arrived.

Grayson turned his gaze away, trying and failing at an attempt not to think about Zoe. The dragon ruby is all that matters, he told himself, over and over. But each time he repeated the phrase, he was less certain that it was true. His heart felt like a heavy weight in his chest, pulling him downward, urging him to leave the ruby quest and go help Zoe. He ignored his heart, which he should have known by now was never the right thing to do.

The smoke above Shadowdale was thickening as Grayson neared Red Point Mountain. He was so close to the ruby now that he could taste the fame and glory that would come with bringing that deep red stone safely back to Falcon Cross. And yet, he was close enough now to not only see the rising fire in Shadowdale, but to hear the screaming. The city was in chaos, with wizards, shifters, and humans all scrambling in different directions. Grayson could make out their sprinting forms, some running for their lives, others attacking to kill. The stomach-turning aroma of burning flesh filled his nostrils, and his wings slowed slightly.

Uncertainty was taking hold of him. He looked up at the mountain, looming in front of him, the guardian of the ruby. He only had another ten minutes to go, if that. He could reach the ruby. He could change the course of history. He could be the hero spoken of in all the history books, sung about in all the songs.

But even as these thoughts filled Grayson's mind, his heart still pulled him down toward Shadowdale. Zoe was somewhere in that mess. He couldn't see her, but he knew she was there. The more time that passed, the more he felt an uneasy stirring deep in his core.

She was his lifemate. He could not deny that. They had bonded, and he was forever connected to her. And right now, deep in his very soul, he could feel that his lifemate was in trouble. She needed him. How could he ignore her? As angry as her decision to go to Shadowdale had made him, he could not let Saul's soldiers kill her off. He would not let them.

Grayson adjusted his course mid-flight. He expected to be filled with great sadness as he gave up his quest for the dragon ruby, but then, a funny thing happened. His heart, which had felt like a leaden weight in his chest, suddenly lightened. He knew in that moment that he was doing the right thing. He picked up his pace again, flying full-speed toward Shadowdale. And the closer he got, the louder the anguished cries became. They filled his ears, a terrifying symphony, even as the acrid smell of smoke and fire filled his nose.

Grayson felt ashamed of himself. Zoe had been right. These people needed help. They were being tortured and killed for the sole crime of happening to live near the dragon ruby. Grayson had let himself stoop almost to the level of Saul's soldiers, only caring about himself, fame, and glory. He'd forgotten that the single most important thing in this war was protecting innocent lives.

Well, now he'd remembered. He was going to give Saul's soldiers hell. Sure, he wasn't going to win any medals of honor for something as basic as defending a bunch of humans under attack. But he was doing what he knew in his heart was the right thing, and that was more important. He wished Zoe was with him now, so he could tell her how sorry he was. She'd spoken truth to him, and he'd scorned her for it. He only hoped she could forgive him. That she would survive this battle to be able to forgive him. The thought of losing her filled his heart with a terrible fear, and he pumped his wings even harder. He was nearly above Shadowdale itself now. His eyes scanned back and forth, trying to see anyone that might resemble Zoe. But everything was such a mess. He wasn't even sure where to start, so he decided the best thing to do was just start somewhere. He took a deep breath, and prepared to dive into the fray.

Before he could manage to begin his descent, however, a long, loud, and inhuman laugh filled the air. Grayson felt his blood going cold in his veins, an odd sensation for someone in dragon form. Usually, he felt like his entire dragon was boiling hot. But the evil in the laughter was just that awful.

Grayson swung his head around, and his eyes landed on the most awful sight he'd ever seen. In the distance, another dragon was flying through the air as well. This dragon was blood red, and even from this far away Grayson could see the scars criss-crossing the dragon's translucent wings. Black, spikes covered the red dragon's tail and the tips of his wings. Fire came spewing out of his mouth in an unnatural blood red color.

Saul.

The evil dragon wizard himself had come to Red Point Mountain. Grayson shouldn't have been surprised. The dragon ruby was Saul's last chance at achieving his quest to take over the world with evil. He wouldn't have wanted to trust his soldiers alone to make sure the ruby was recovered. After all, his soldiers had already failed him in their attempts to capture the other dragon stones.

Saul had not failed this time. As the evil dragon flew, the fading sunlight caught the glint of two things. First, the blood red stone that was affixed to Saul's wizard wand, a long staff that he carried in his left dragon foot. And second, the blood red stone that he held in his right dragon foot.

The dragon ruby. The shimmering stone was larger than Grayson had thought it would be. It must have been about the size of a basketball, and Saul's claws were spread wide to hold it. Grayson felt like he was watching the hopes of his entire clan fly away as Saul turned to fly toward the west, his chilling laugh once again filling the air as he flew. An army of wizard soldiers surrounded him on their broomsticks, not even bothering with invisibility shields. Saul didn't want to be invisible right now, Grayson realized. He wanted anyone from the side of good who happened to be around to see him, to know that he'd captured the ruby.

In one sense, seeing him with the ruby validated for Grayson that he'd made the right decision in turning toward Shadowdale. If Saul was already flying away with the ruby, then his men had reached it long before Grayson would have. No matter how fast he'd been flying, Grayson never would have reached the stone before his enemies. Helping Shadowdale had indeed been the better choice, for more reasons than one.

And yet, that small validation didn't do much to ease the sense of despair rising in Grayson's chest. Saul had the dragon ruby. The air seemed darker now, and the candle of hope that had been burning for the armies of good was flickering low.

Grayson tore his eyes away from Saul, and back toward Shadowdale. There was no sense in chasing after the ruby anymore, or wasting energy lamenting its capture. There were hundreds of people right below him who needed his help, and Zoe, his destined lifemate, was one of them.

Grayson took a deep breath, and began to dive full-speed toward the earth below.

CHAPTER TWELVE

The world was colored in shades of gray. Smoke hung so thickly in every corner of Shadowdale that no matter which way you turned, your eyes stung and your lungs felt like they would never be clean again.

Grayson ignored the pain. Smoke and fire were not enough to stop a dragon. Dragons lived for smoke and fire. Grayson ran through the city, roaring and swiping at every enemy shifter and wizard he found, taking them down with his razor claws. His aim was good, and he rarely missed. But if he did, he breathed a stream of fire at the enemy soldier to stop them in their tracks. He didn't want to do anything to add fuel to the fires already blazing throughout the city, but he figured that, on balance, eliminating another enemy soldier was more important than worrying about a little extra fire.

Grayson had been searching for Zoe for what felt like an eternity. He was beginning to wonder whether he was going in circles, because all the buildings looked the same in this gray haze, and he felt like he should have found her by now. She was still alive, and close by. He could tell that much from the way his insides were twisting up in agony. The lifemate bond was still going strong, and it was letting him know that Zoe was here and in trouble.

Grayson continued running through the streets, doing his best to save as many of the townspeople as he could. Many of them were running around frantically, panicking in the same way that a squirrel caught in the middle of a highway might panic. They ran back and forth, in this direction and that, often straight into the oncoming traffic of evil soldiers. Grayson wanted to yell at all of them to run into their homes and hide, taking shelter as best they could until this all was over. But Grayson couldn't talk while in human form, so he had to content himself with taking out as many evil soldiers as he could, hoping that he was saving several lives in the process.

The devastation in Shadowdale was unfathomable. Saul's soldiers were having a heyday, treating their attempted annihilation of this city like some sort of afterparty for recovering the dragon ruby. Grayson could not contain his anger or disgust. He let himself fully vent his rage on all of Saul's soldiers, all the while searching for any sign of Zoe.

He heard her long before he saw her. Roars of pain, explosions, and shrieks of terror filled the air like a devil's symphony. In between the louder, more troubling sounds, Grayson could occasionally make out the words of a magic spell, spoken by Zoe's determined voice. He raced toward the sound as fast as his dragon legs could run. He no longer stopped to try to kill every enemy he came across. He'd found Zoe. She was all that mattered now.

In less than a minute, he'd reached the city center. He came to a screeching halt just in time to avoid skidding into the middle of another giant explosion as it filled the square. He swung his gaze left and right, taking in the view with a mixture of horror and pride. On one side of the square, about a hundred dark wizards and shifters were gathered. They had formed ranks, and were launching attack after attack at the opposite side of the square.

And on the very edge of the opposite side of the square stood what appeared to be half the people of Shadowdale. Men, women, and children all cowered in fear, their eyes glued to the enemy army that stood across from them. In between these two groups stood Zoe.

Her military uniform was torn in several places, and blood oozed from below several of the torn shreds of fabric. Her hair, which had been in a tight bun earlier in the day as she flew away from him, now hung free in a tangled, glorious mess. She had put some sort of shield around the group of townspeople, but she herself did not seem to have a shield around her. Every blow that the enemy wizards managed to hit her with tore further at her skin. She was sacrificing herself, Grayson realized, to put the maximum amount of magical energy into a shield for the citizens of Shadowdale.

Luckily, she was still fast, even though she was severely wounded. For a few brief moments, Grayson stood on the edge of the city center, transfixed by her speed. She turned and bent and somersaulted through the volley of wizard attacks being thrown her way. She repeatedly shot repelling spells out at the shifters that tried to charge at her. Her movements were impossibly graceful. She was a beautiful ballerina, twirling placidly through the midst of a war zone.

There was nothing placid about her next attack, though. Just as Grayson started to move forward, he saw her raise her magic ring high above her head and bring it down rapidly, pointing it straight at the enemy lines.

"*Magicae crepitus!*" she roared. Grayson immediately started backing away from the city center. The last thing he wanted was to be caught in the midst of a *Crepitus* explosion. He'd seen firsthand in the training room how powerful that spell could be. He felt a rush of energy hit him and he lost his footing as the spell filled the air in town square. There were roars of pain, and more screaming from the townspeople as flames shot up into the air. The buildings surrounding the square shook in their foundations, and one of them crumbled. Grayson started running back toward the scene, hoping that the spell had worked as well as it did in the training rooms.

Town square had plunged into complete chaos. The shield that had been surrounding the townspeople had vanished, and most of them were running in scared circles, just like the rest of the scared townspeople Grayson had encountered in the city. To his right piles of dead enemy soldiers littered the ground. Most of the enemy wizards and shifters had died in the explosion. But several dozen seemed to have survived and were slowly stirring to their feet. Grayson looked around frantically for Zoe. It didn't take him long to find her. She had fallen to the ground in the middle of town square, her hand with its magic ring stretched out in front of her, frozen in place. All around her, people, wizards, and shifters were running and screaming, but she did not move. She wasn't dead, at least not yet. Grayson knew that much from the fact that the lifemate bond still burned within him. His core was going crazy now, telling him that Zoe was in mortal danger. But he didn't need the lifemate bond to tell him that. He could see it plainly with his own eyes.

In the seconds it had taken Grayson to survey the scene, the enemy soldiers who had staggered to their feet had started running toward Zoe. He heard one of them whoop and raise his magic ring, preparing to launch an attack that would likely kill Zoe, who lay defenseless on the ground.

"Oh, no you don't!" Grayson yelled. With one giant leap, he jumped through the air and landed right in front of Zoe. The attack the wizard had launched hit his dragon hide instead, as did several other attacks that the other wizards had launched a split second after the first wizard's attack. Luckily for Grayson, his dragon hide was thick enough to repel most wizard attacks. He turned with a roar and breathed out a long

731

stream of fire at the wizards who had attacked Zoe. They screamed in pain, and fell to the ground in burning heaps.

The next few minutes were a repetition of the same scene, over and over. Enemy wizards and shifters came rushing forward to attack, and Grayson beat them all back. He stood directly over Zoe, turning in giant circles, breathing fire and swishing his giant tail back and forth. Now and then, he swiped with his claws, taking out as many enemy soldiers with each blow as he could. All around him, people were screaming, wizards were yelling out spells, and shifters were roaring. But Grayson ignored the noise. His sole focus was protecting Zoe.

At last the enemy soldiers seemed to realize that they weren't going to win against this giant of a dragon. They called out some sort of signal to retreat, and suddenly the whole sky filled with wizards. The remaining shifters and wizards started hightailing it away from Shadowdale as quickly as they could. Those that had still been scattered throughout the city left their attacks on the townspeople and followed the retreating crowd. Grayson roared after them, a menace in his tone that told them he'd be only too happy to finish them off if they dared to come back.

He would have loved to have followed them, but he would not leave Zoe's side. Not when she was unable to defend herself. Ignoring the terrified screams of the townspeople that still rang out around him, Grayson swung his head around to nudge Zoe's face gently with his warm dragon nose. She stirred slightly, then opened her eyes for a moment. When her gaze focused on him, a tired smile crossed her lips.

"You came," she said. "You finally came."

Grayson stepped a few feet back and left out a huff of smoke. Then, with a roar, he shifted back into human form. He ignored the gaping stares of the townspeople. They would just have to get over the fact that the dragon in their midst had just turned into a large, naked man. It's not as though they hadn't seen enough strange things already today.

"Of course I came," Grayson said, his voice catching in his throat as he knelt beside Zoe once again. She smiled up at him, and opened her mouth as though she were going to say something else. But the words never came. Instead, she closed her eyes and went limp against the ground.

Frantically, Grayson jumped to his feet, looking around at the dozens of curious and terrified townspeople who still milled about.

"Doctor!" he shouted. "I need a doctor! Is anyone here a doctor?"

When Zoe's heart stopped, Grayson felt like his did, too.

CHAPTER THIRTEEN

Zoe blinked her eyes open, trying to focus on something, anything. The sky above her was different. It was the wrong color. No longer was it a blue-gray mixture of smoke and open air. Instead it was a strange, swirling white. And the ground was no longer hard and stony. Instead it felt soft, like feathers.

Before Zoe could process what all of this meant, a smiling face appeared directly above her own face. The sudden change in view to that of a woman with dark brown hair, bright blue eyes, and perfect red lips shocked Zoe somewhat. It took her a moment to realize who the face belonged to.

"Izzy?" Zoe asked.

Izzy's smile deepened. "Welcome back, Zoe. How are you feeling?"

"Uh…" Zoe took a moment to consider. The last thing she remembered was casting a *Crepitus* spell on the army attacking Shadowdale. She'd been thrown backwards, blacked out, then regained consciousness just long enough to see that Grayson was there. Zoe smiled at the memory. Grayson had come for her. Zoe wriggled her arms, legs and neck, expecting to find spots of extreme pain. But everything felt relatively normal. Slowly, she sat up. That's when she realized that, of course, she wasn't still outside in the middle of Shadowdale's town square. She was in a hospital room. The softness beneath her was a feather bed. The white above her was the room's ceiling.

"I feel pretty good, actually," Zoe said, reaching for a bottle of water that stood on the bedside table next to the large hospital bed. "How long have I been out."

"About a week," Izzy said.

Zoe choked on the water she'd just swallowed. "A *week?*"

Izzy nodded, then sat in a chair next to the bed, her easy manner soothing Zoe's nerves. Zoe liked Izzy. Izzy was one of the best doctors in Falcon Cross, and had been assigned to do medical checks on Zoe before and during the special training exercises Zoe had participated in. Izzy had always been down to earth, and had never looked at her in that annoying, googly-eyed way that so many other wizards had after they discovered Zoe's special powers.

Zoe looked around again, taking the room in. This was some sort of room for long term hospital residents, she could see now. It was large, with several chairs for visitors and its own private bathroom. A large table across the room was loaded down with dozens of huge bouquets, cards, and teddy bears. On the wall above the table, hung two framed pictures of the city of Falcon Cross.

Zoe glanced back at Izzy, a thousand questions filling her mind. She started with the easiest one.

"Am I back in Falcon Cross?"

Izzy nodded. "Yup. You've been back for almost the entire week."

"What happened?" Zoe asked. "I mean, I remember casting a *Crepitus* spell, and Grayson coming over. But that's it. Everything else after that goes completely black."

Izzy sat up a bit straighter. "Yeah, you cast a *Crepitus* spell. From what Grayson has told us, and what we figured out by doing an exam on you, you're lucky to be alive right now. You were quite weak already by the time you cast the spell, and you were expending the majority of your magic energy on a shield to protect the people of Shadowdale. The spell was too much for you. It wasn't even a full *Crepitus* spell. You didn't have enough energy for that. But, at least, the spell you did manage to cast knocked out enough enemies for Grayson to step in and finish off the rest."

"Grayson," Zoe said softly, savoring the sound of the name. "Where is he?"

"He's around here somewhere, and I have no doubt he'll be back soon," Izzy said. "He's barely left your side, but I made him go get some food and go home to take a shower. I purposely waited until he wasn't here to bring you out of sedation."

"Sedation?" Zoe asked.

"Yeah, we've kept you nicely sedated for most of the time you were here. Early on, you were quite, um, spirited. Thrashing about and trying to fight us like we ourselves were Saul's soldiers. Like I said, the *Crepitus* spell did a number on you when you cast it. Any weaker wizard would have died instantly. Even you, as strong as you are, had to be resuscitated. Your heart stopped for a minute there."

"*What?*"

Izzy nodded serenely. "Right after you woke up and saw Grayson, you passed out again. Your heart stopped, but luckily there was an emergency room doctor nearby who knew how to resuscitate you. I'm not clear on the exact details, because Grayson was a bit too distraught to take note of exactly how everything went down. But, in short, you got emergency medical attention, your heart was restarted, and as soon as you were stable you were transferred to Falcon Cross. You've been under my care ever since."

Zoe blinked a few times. "Wow."

Izzy laughed. "Yeah, 'wow' about sums it up."

"And Shadowdale?" Zoe asked. "Are the people there okay?"

"We've sent an emergency team to help clean up the city and provide trauma support. A team of Advocates who specialize in wizard-human relations is there to explain the world of shifters and wizards, and to explain any questions they might have about the whole ordeal. They lost a few citizens, but overall the town is alright. Or will be alright, I should say. You and Grayson have pretty much been heralded as heroes for what you did for them."

"Great," Zoe groaned. "Just what I need. More hero worship."

Izzy laughed. "Well, you were pretty incredible out there, you know? You were willing to sacrifice your own life for the people of Shadowdale. And Grayson…without Grayson all of your sacrifices would have been for nothing. The dark soldiers that were left after the *Crepitus* spell would have killed you, and then killed the rest of the townspeople."

Zoe shrugged. "We just did what any soldier would have done," she said. Even as she said it, she wondered what had changed Grayson's mind. He hadn't been willing to come to Shadowdale in the beginning. Perhaps what they'd done wasn't just what any other soldier would have done. But that was a conversation she'd have to have with Grayson, not Izzy.

"And the dragon ruby?" Zoe asked, her eyes dropping to her lap. She wasn't expecting any good news here.

"Saul has it," Izzy said grimly.

Zoe nodded, unexpected tears pricking at her eyes. "I messed up. I let one of his informants see my broom."

Izzy shrugged. "Well, we had a spy in Falcon Cross. The informants only knew to be on the lookout for you because someone in the Falcon Cross military had leaked to

Saul's people that you and Grayson would be flying along that general path. If not for that, no one would have been paying so much attention. It wasn't entirely your fault."

"A spy? Inside Falcon Cross?" Zoe asked. "But how?"

Izzy shrugged. "Saul was getting a bit desperate for information, I guess. He apparently paid a lot of money to this soldier for information. She told us everything, in exchange for a lighter punishment."

Zoe rubbed her forehead. "So what now?"

"Now," Izzy said, standing to her feet. "You get some rest. You've made a good recovery, but it would still behoove you to take it easy. I'll keep you in the hospital for another day before sending you home, just to make sure you're completely recovered."

"I meant what happens now with the dragon ruby, and with Saul's army," Zoe said. "Are there plans to try to steal the ruby back?"

Izzy paused for a moment. Zoe got the impression that she knew, but was holding back the information on purpose.

"Just tell me, Izzy," Zoe said. "If you don't, then Grayson will."

"Fine," Izzy said. "But don't go getting all riled up and wanting to run down to Military Headquarters to help out. You need to rest first."

Zoe said nothing. She wasn't making any promises, and Izzy knew it. Izzy sighed.

"Right now, the other three dragon stones are on their way to Falcon Cross from safekeeping in Texas. Plans are in the works to use the power of those three stones to fight Saul and recover the dragon ruby."

"But the dragon ruby is as strong as the other three stones combined," Zoe said.

Izzy shrugged. "So it should be a fair fight. Now, that's all I know. You get some rest. I know you're going to want to be part of the army that goes after the ruby, but until I clear you to fight you won't be allowed back on the battlefield. So you best do as I say."

Zoe frowned, but settled back into the bed as Izzy left. The better she listened to Izzy, the sooner Izzy would let her out of here. And the sooner she was out of here, the better.

But Zoe wasn't tired. For hours, she tossed and turned and tried to remember as much of the fight in Shadowdale as she could. All her memories kept coming back to one single point: Grayson. She wished more than anything she could talk to him right now. Her feelings were so jumbled inside of her about so many things, but mostly about him. She needed to see him, to talk to him, to sort things out.

She was about to get her wish.

CHAPTER FOURTEEN

The door creaked open, and Grayson tiptoed in. He had the impressive ability to move as silently as a little cat, despite being nearly twice the size of most normal men. Zoe watched him as he slowly closed the door behind him, the latch barely clicking. He was trying to be quiet for her sake, not realizing that she had woken up already.

"Zoe!" he said when he turned and saw her sitting up with eyes wide open. He dropped the messenger bag he'd been holding and ran to her bedside, wrapping his arms around her neck and holding on tightly, as though he might lose her if he wasn't hanging on for dear life.

"Hi, Grayson," Zoe said, her voice soft and muffled in the fabric of his t-shirt. Being pressed against him like that reminded her of how her face had been pressed against his chest the first day they met, when he protected her from the fangirls who had found her in the hallway of military headquarters.

"Izzy told me you weren't sedated anymore, but she said she'd left you sleeping," Grayson said.

Zoe's shoulders shook slightly with laughter. "No, she left me with orders to sleep. It's not quite the same thing."

Grayson laughed, too. "No, not quite," he said, leaning away from Zoe slightly so he could look into her eyes. "And how are you feeling?"

"Good," Zoe said. "A little stiff. I got up and took a shower. I can tell that my legs haven't been used for a week, but they should be back to normal soon enough, I suppose."

"You got up and took a shower?" Grayson said. "Did Izzy approve that?"

"No, but she didn't forbid it. And besides housekeeping came in to change the linens on the bed, so I had to get up anyway."

Grayson shook his head. "You're quite stubborn when you want to be."

Zoe gave him a suspicious look. "Like when I insist on abandoning the dragon ruby quest to save a town of people?"

She held her breath, waiting for his reply. They hadn't spoken since she stormed off on him. Not unless you counted the one brief moment she'd woken up on the ground in the middle of Shadowdale's town square. Zoe wasn't quite sure what to expect, and she was afraid to broach the subject with him. But it had to be done. The elephant in the room had to be dealt with.

To her relief, Grayson's heartbroken gaze contained no animosity. "I'm so sorry, Zoe. You were right. Saving the people of Shadowdale was more important than anything else in that moment. I got caught up in the need for honor and fame, and I lost sight of what was truly important. I should have listened to you from the beginning."

"What changed your mind?" Zoe said, reaching over to hold one of Grayson's hands in her own.

"I saw the city burning, and heard the people screaming. I realized that you were down there with them. I just came to my senses, I guess. I realized that the dragon ruby didn't matter if I let myself stoop to the level of Saul's soldiers, of caring more about fame and riches and things like that than I did about people. So I switched course and I came to help you. In the end, it was the best choice, anyway. Almost as soon as I'd turned away from the mountain, Saul came flying out of it holding the dragon ruby. He would have beaten me to it no matter what. I've made peace with the situation. I'm just sad that the mission was a failure."

Zoe squeezed his hand. "The mission wasn't a failure. The mission was always about people. It just turned out that helping people meant letting the dragon ruby go in this case. Like you said, we wouldn't have been able to get to the ruby first, anyway. I'm proud of you. You did the right thing. We kept our own honor and integrity, and we saved lives. That's the most important thing."

Grayson squeezed her hand back, and looked directly into her eyes. "Does that mean you forgive me?" he asked.

Zoe smiled. "Of course I forgive you. As long as I still have rights to say 'I told you so' on this one."

Grayson laughed. "I guess I can live with that. I can live with a lot of things, actually. What I wouldn't have been able to live with is losing you. God, I was so scared out there when your heart stopped. I felt like my whole life was coming to a grinding halt along with yours."

"It's weird for me to hear about," Zoe said slowly. "I don't remember any of it. I just remember seeing you, and thinking I was so relieved that you were there. Then everything went black and the next thing I know I was waking up in this hospital bed with Izzy hovering over me."

"It's probably better that you don't remember it," Grayson said softly. "It was one of the scariest moments of my life. And believe me, I've seen some scary shit."

Zoe sat up a little more. "But you were that scared of losing me?"

The question held so many questions within it—questions that Zoe wanted so desperately to ask, but couldn't bring herself to say out loud. Did Grayson feel more for her than just a passing physical attraction? Had he also started to fall in love? Could they see eye to eye on enough things to be able to make a future together?

Luckily, Grayson seemed as eager to discuss their future as she did. "Yes, I was that scared of losing you. I know this might sound crazy, but I realized after we slept together in Shafer's house that I felt more for you than just physical passion. Don't get me wrong, the physical part is pretty damn good. I mean, look at you. You're the most beautiful creature I've ever laid eyes on."

Zoe blushed and looked down at her hands.

"But it's more than that," Grayson continued. "I'm attracted to your soul. Your spirit. The very essence of you. You're a beautiful person, Zoe. You make me a better man. If it had been anyone else on that mission with me, I would have kept going toward the ruby, and I would have regretted not saving the people of Shadowdale for the rest of my life. You remind me of what's truly important."

Zoe's heart was pounding in her chest. She wanted to say so many things to Grayson. She wanted to tell him that she believed in him. That he was brave, loyal, and a true friend. That, even though he had his faults—and don't we all?—there was so much more to him than just good looks, too. She wanted to tell him that she had fallen in love with him. But the words stuck in her throat. She felt nervous in a way that she hadn't for a long, long time. Grayson had all sorts of strange effects on her. He got to her in a way that no one else did. And she wouldn't have wanted it any other way.

"Scoot over," Grayson said, and Zoe did, making room for him on the hospital bed. It was easy to do. The bed was surprisingly large, and feather soft. Zoe imagined that it was one of the better rooms in the hospital. She supposed there were at least a few perks to being a celebrity, and getting the posh hospital suite must have been one of them. She'd take it.

Grayson snuggled in next to her, reaching to hold her hand once again. For a few moments, they were silent, just enjoying the feeling of being pressed up against each other. But Grayson didn't let the silence linger for too long. It seemed he had a lot on his mind, and wanted to clear the air between them just as much as Zoe did.

"Have you ever heard of lifemates, Zoe?" Grayson asked.

Zoe scrunched her brow. Her hand felt warm and safe inside of Grayson's. "No. I've heard of soulmates, but not lifemates. Is it sort of the same thing?"

"Not exactly," Grayson said. "Lifemates are more serious than soulmates. You see, we shifters believe that each of us is born with a destined lifemate. This lifemate is someone we are fated to be with for life. From the moment we are born, fate is working to bring us together with this person. Once lifemates find each other and sleep together, the lifemate bond is formed. This bond is unbreakable. It ties lifemates together for the remainder of their days, and makes their hearts beat as one. When one lifemate is in danger, the other lifemate can sense it. When you are near your lifemate, especially when you are being intimate with them, you can feel the bond as a deep heat in your very core."

Zoe looked at Grayson with widened eyes. "Grayson...when we were in Shafer's house...I..."

"I know," Grayson said, his voice dropping to a low, husky tone. "I felt it, too. The warmth. The connection. The lifemate bond. I honestly didn't expect it. Don't get me wrong, I think you're a wonderful girl, and that's just the problem. It never occurred to me that I would be lucky enough to have someone so wonderful as my lifemate. Once I realized that we were destined to be together, I freaked out a bit. I wasn't sure how to process all of my feelings. Then, when we argued over the dragon ruby mission, I tried to tell myself that I hadn't really felt what I felt for you. That I had only imagined the lifemate bond."

"But you didn't imagine it," Zoe said quietly. She already knew, from the way she herself felt deep down inside, that she and Grayson were meant for each other.

"I didn't imagine it," Grayson agreed. "When you were in trouble in Shadowdale, I knew it. And I was terrified that I was going to lose you. And now that I haven't lost you, now that you're here next to me, safe and healthy, I don't want to let another moment go by without telling you how I feel."

Zoe took an emotional, shuddering breath as Grayson reached to grab both of her hands in both of his. She bit back tears as she looked into his eyes and saw how intense his feelings were.

"Zoe," he said, squeezing her hands. "I love you. I can't imagine a life without you, and I know in my heart of hearts that you're my lifemate. I want to spend the rest of my days protecting you and caring for you. I know things are so uncertain right now, especially since we lost the dragon ruby to Saul. But no matter what the future brings, I know one thing for sure: I want to spend that future with you. Please tell me you feel the same."

The tears did spill over then. Zoe smiled and nodded, reaching to wrap her arms around Grayson. "I love you, too, Grayson. I can't think of anything that would make me happier than spending my entire future with you."

Grayson let out a long breath, and Zoe realized he'd been nervous about her reaction. That thought made her laugh. The very idea of rejecting Grayson seemed preposterous to her. He leaned his face back to look at her.

"What's so funny?" he asked.

Instead of answering, Zoe put her lips on Grayson's. The heat that rushed through her body burned away any lingering doubts. Grayson was her lifemate. Her destiny.

And then, despite the fact that they were in a hospital room, where any doctor or nurse might walk in at any moment, Zoe and Grayson could not hold back their passion for each other. As Grayson undressed her, then undressed himself, Zoe figured that it was late, and Izzy had left her with orders to sleep. They weren't likely to be disturbed. Besides, the possibility of getting caught only added to the excitement of the moment.

Grayson threw his clothes and Zoe's hospital gown into a pile on the floor next to them, then crawled under the thick hospital comforter with her. The scent of fresh laundry from the comforter mixed with that heady, woodsy smell that always clung to Grayson, and Zoe closed her eyes to breathe in the wonder of having her dragon right here next to her. There was no sound in the room except for the soft hum of the hospital machines, and the ragged breathing coming from both her and Grayson as they explored each other's bodies.

Warm and safe under the comforter, Zoe gave herself over completely to enjoying Grayson's hands on her body. After he spent plenty of time kissing her lips, their tongues dancing together, he moved on to her breasts. He took his time there as well, circling each nipple with his pointer finger, then massaging with his tongue and nibbling with his teeth. He was hovering over her, and the whole time he was sending tingling ripples of pleasure through her breasts, she could feel his stiff erection pushing against her leg. She moaned softly as the symphony of his lips, his hands, and his erection touching her skin filled her with overwhelming heat and pleasure. She closed her eyes and drank in the wonder of him, of his body against hers, of the juices of her desire flowing from between her legs. She was ready for him, and she wanted him now. But at the same time, she never wanted this moment to end.

Grayson must have felt the same. He was in no hurry to leave her breasts, and he gave Zoe's nipples such pleasure that, by the time he did pull his mouth away, she was on the verge of coming just from his tongue and teeth.

But Grayson wanted more than just her breasts. He wanted all of her, and now, in the still hum of this dimly lit room, he was going to take her. And she was going to give herself to him. He shifted his body so that he was directly above the sweet spot between her legs, and then, quietly and gently, he slid into her.

The movement set off a thousand fireworks inside of Zoe. She felt hot electricity spreading from his body to hers, and the pressure of his shaft pushing against her inner walls caused the pressure building in her core to reach its breaking point. Grayson had barely begun to thrust against her when she felt her release come.

The sweet, burning heat intensified with each spasm of her inner muscles. She felt her inner walls squeezing his dick over and over, wanting more and more of him, never satisfied. His hips pressed against her hips as he pushed deeper and deeper inside of her, every thrust renewing the intensity of her own body's pleasure. And then, moments later, he found his release, too. She felt him, throbbing and pulsing inside of her, giving himself completely over to her. There, in that moment, they were one. The wonder of that truth washed over Zoe, and she felt happier than she could ever remember feeling.

Grayson stayed inside her long after both of their bodies had stopped trembling. When he did finally slip out to lie next to her, he wrapped Zoe in his arms and then let out a long, satisfied sigh. Zoe thought to herself how different being with him had been this time. Before, they had both been overcome by a fit of primal passion. This time, they had been overcome by a need to make love—truly make love—to each other. It had been sweet and meaningful.

But both times had been wonderful, and Zoe had a feeling that they had only scratched the surface of the good times they would have together, both in and out of the bedroom. With a happy sigh, she snuggled closer to her dragon. Perhaps they had lost the dragon ruby, but their mission together had still been successful, in more ways than one.

CHAPTER FIFTEEN

Grayson blinked at the bright sunlight that shone directly into his eyes, but he did not turn his head. He stared proudly straight ahead at the crowd gathered below the stage and listened as Peter, the highest ranking wizard in Falcon Cross, continued to praise the work that Zoe and Grayson had done.

"These two displayed what we try to teach all our soldiers from the very first day of training: the most important mission is to protect innocent lives. They showed tremendous presence of mind when they flew directly to Shadowdale and saved that city from danger. Thanks to their selfless bravery, hundreds of lives were saved, and we were able to avoid permanent harm in wizard-human relations. Today, we honor their work, and give them the recognition they deserve."

The crowd cheered as Peter stepped away from his podium and walked over to where Grayson and Zoe stood. Zoe was wearing wizard dress robes in a rich, velvet purple. Her wizard hat was deep purple with golden threads interwoven throughout. Grayson thought she had never looked more beautiful than now, her clothing and her face alike shimmering in the sunlight. As for Grayson, he wore a fresh Falcon Cross military dress uniform. The gold thread in the black uniform shimmered as well, and he stood tall and proud as Peter took a medal from a box that an assistant held out for the old wizard.

"Zoe Whitt, for your part in rescuing the people of Shadowdale, I now present you with the Falcon Cross Medal of Courage, a high honor bestowed on those who go above and beyond to save the lives of innocent people."

The crowd went wild as Peter placed the medal around Zoe's neck. Peter took a second medal from the box and turned to Grayson.

"And Grayson Pars, for your part in rescuing the people of Shadowdale, I now present you with the Falcon Cross Medal of Courage, a high honor bestowed on those who go above and beyond to save the lives of innocent people."

Again, the crowd roared. Grayson bent his head low so that Peter could place the heavy golden medal around his neck. When Grayson looked up again, he took in the view before him. On the front row of the crowd, he saw his own Redwood Dragons clan, all cheering him on. Knox, his clan leader, was whooping loudest of all. Behind his clan, the crowd stretched on and on, and Grayson realized that he'd gotten what he so desperately wanted after all: fame, glory, and recognition. The funny thing was that, now that he had these things, he realized they didn't matter as much to him as he thought they would.

He'd realized what the important things in life were: love, honor, loyalty, and, yes, courage. He still regretted not getting the dragon ruby, but he knew there would be another chance. Saul's day was coming, and all of the Falcon Cross wizards and Redwood Dragons would work together to make sure Saul's evil plans were stopped. That was what true courage was, after all. Not seeking after glory, but seeking to help the cause of good wherever and however you could, to the best of your ability.

Grayson looked over at Zoe then. She looked back at him, beaming, then took his hand. Grayson felt his heart warming at the gesture.

"Looks like you got your medal of courage, after all," she said to him with a wink.

"It doesn't matter anymore what medals I get," Grayson said. "I got something far better out of our mission. I got you."

And then, with everyone watching, Grayson leaned over and placed a kiss on Zoe's lips. The whooping from the crowd instantly reached a deafening level, but Grayson didn't notice. He'd found someone who made him much happier than a cheering crowd, and he was never letting her go.

BOOK TEN: VICTORY AND THE DRAGON

CHAPTER ONE

Izzy had never been so short on both sleep and caffeine, but her utter exhaustion didn't stop her from bounding to her feet the moment the red-alert sirens went off. The sirens filled her with dread and energy all at once, and she sprinted from her office toward the command central room, not even bothering to put on the shoes she'd kicked off under her desk. In stocking feet, she ran, her heart pounding in time with the whirring of the alarms. She had known this moment would come soon. Had expected it. And yet, the fact that she had known it was coming did not lessen the fear she felt.

The dragon stones were in trouble. That was the only reason the red-alert sirens would be sounded. It was three o'clock in the afternoon, and the sun was shining brightly outside, but everything felt dark to Izzy. She darted around the panicked faces that filled the hallways of Falcon Cross Military Headquarters, and took the stairs in lieu of the elevator. The elevators would be stopping on every floor right now, picking up anxious wizards who were trying to get to the main entrance to hear what was going on. Izzy didn't have time for their wide-eyed gawking. She needed to get to command central.

A few minutes later, huffing and puffing from her dash up several flights of stairs, Izzy burst into the room where many of the VIPs of Falcon Cross were already gathered. Knox, the leader of the Redwood Dragons dragon shifter clan, had already arrived, along with Grayson and Myles, two of his dragons. MacKenzie, better known as Mac, had already taken her place in a seat near the head of the table. She was the lead commander of the wizard army in Falcon Cross. Several more important wizards and dragon shifters filtered into the room, most of them talking in excited tones and already scrolling through the screens on their tablets, trying to see if there was an update on why the sirens had gone off. Izzy hadn't bothered to bring her military-issued tablet to this meeting. There was no point. There would be no information sent across the main computer network—that much she knew. With all of the hacking and spying issues Falcon Cross had dealt with, electronic communications were being kept to an absolute minimum.

Izzy quietly took her seat, trying to steady her breathing amidst the hubbub and chaos around her. No one seemed to notice her, which was just fine with her. She wanted a moment to collect her thoughts without needing to respond to questions. But she didn't have very much time to breathe before the last two VIPs stepped into the room. Noah, the second-in-command of the dragon shifter clan, came bolting into the room. His hair was a mess and his clothes were wrinkled. He was still rubbing sleep from his eyes, and Izzy had to bite back her laughter. Looks like she wasn't the only one feeling the pain of too little sleep. She'd been tempted to catch a nap at her desk herself quite a few times in the last few weeks. Noah took the only empty chair, which was next to Izzy. He plopped down hard with a grunt, and didn't bother to greet her or anyone else. Izzy didn't mind. In fact, she appreciated his silence. Nothing annoyed her more in tense situations than unnecessary small talk.

After Noah came Peter, the head wizard in Falcon Cross. Peter, as always, looked immaculately put-together. His long wizard robes and high wizard hat were perfectly straight and clean, and not a hair was out of place on his long white beard or hair. Izzy sometimes wondered if he knew a magic spell for replacing energy that he wasn't sharing with them. Peter never seemed tired, no matter how bad things got in this goddamn war.

Peter shut the door firmly behind him, and silence fell over the room as the talking ceased and the alarms were blocked out. There were no siren bells or flashing red lights in this room, and the door had been designed to be completely soundproof. The head wizards had wanted a room where they could speak freely without fear of eavesdroppers, and so the only alarm that could be heard in here was the alarm signifying a breach of the city's magic shield.

"What's the news?" Knox asked, the first to speak up. His face was set in a tense line, and he drummed his fingers impatiently on the table. Knox had three of his clan members out on the battlefield with the dragon stones, and Izzy could see the worry etched into his expression. He remained calm enough, but his face could not completely hide his concern. Izzy chanced a sideways glance at Noah, who had similar worry lines crossing his face.

"All our men are safe, at least for the moment," Peter said. "Let's call roll and then we'll discuss the situation further."

Beside her, Izzy heard Noah give a slight groan. The dragon shifters had little patience for the formalities of the wizarding world. The dragons were the type to act first and think later, but wizards always wanted everything in order. Izzy had worked on several missions that combined the talents of dragons and wizards, and she had seen firsthand the annoyance the dragons felt toward the wizards' overly-structured ways. Izzy herself was a wizard, though, and admittedly favored a structured approach. She wasn't originally from Falcon Cross, but she did appreciate the orderly way the Falcon Cross leadership conducted their affairs.

"Isabelle Torres?" The sound of Peter's voice calling her name broke into Izzy's thoughts.

"Here," she said. It always sounded strange to her when her full name was used. No one had actually called her Isabelle except her mother, who had long since passed away. To the entire world, she was now "Izzy," but, still, the roll call was done with full and proper names. Izzy bit back a wry smile. Perhaps the wizards were just a tad too uptight, after all.

Roll call was quickly completed, and Peter wasted no time in explaining the situation at hand.

"Saul has managed to locate our troops who are traveling with the dragon stones. This is unfortunate, since they were less than two days from making it safely to Falcon Cross. Now, all bets are off. Our commanders in the field have notified me that they are being followed by a large army. Scouts have been sent to survey the danger, and they believe that Saul is bringing up the rear of the army. This also means it is likely that the dragon ruby is with the pursuing army."

Peter paused for a moment to let this news sink in. Izzy could feel the mood in the room grow even darker. Saul, their evil nemesis, had captured the dragon ruby several weeks ago, and everyone in Falcon Cross had been holding their breath, knowing that he might use the powers of the ruby to launch a deadly attack at any moment. So far, things had been quiet, and hopes had been high that the other three dragon stones—an emerald, a sapphire, and an amethyst—would make it safely to Falcon Cross before Saul realized they were being transported. Now, those hopes were dashed. The other three stones were out in the open with a small army, not safely behind the magic shields of Falcon Cross, protected by the entire, huge wizard army.

"Any chance our men could still beat Saul to Falcon Cross?" Noah asked. Izzy looked over at him as he spoke, noting that the stubble on his face and neck was thick. He hadn't shaved in several days, from the looks of it. His shimmering green eyes were tired, but intense. The dragons always seemed able to think clearly, even when exhausted. Izzy envied them that. The more tired she became, the more her logical reasoning skills seemed to disappear. And, to add insult to injury, she was pretty sure she didn't look nearly as sexy when tired as Noah did right now. She'd spent a good deal of time around the man, in various official meetings, but she had never been quite so close to him. She was startled to realize that he looked even better up close than he did from far away. Her cheeks grew warm at the thought, and she forced herself to look away from him, and back toward Peter, who was stroking his beard as he slowly answered Noah's question.

"It doesn't look likely," Peter said. "Saul's army is moving much faster than ours. I'm not sure how, since it's so big, and our army isn't exactly slow. I suspect he's using some sort of dark magic to speed things up."

Another groan from Noah. This time, Izzy shared his frustration. Saul was infamous for using dark magic to gain an advantage in the war. Even though dark magic eventually destroyed the soul of whoever used it—resulting in death—it took a long time for that destruction to occur. Dark wizards could cause a great deal of damage before their evil ways did them in.

"Our men have to change course, then," Knox said. His words were followed by silence. Everyone in the room knew that he spoke the truth, but no one could quite bring themselves to agree out loud. If the dragon ruby was as powerful as they believed it to be, then even with the dragon stones, the Falcon Cross Wizards and Redwood Dragons would be obliterated on an open field in a fight against Saul. They needed the safety and reinforcements that the city of Falcon Cross provided.

"But, our soldiers," Mac finally said, weakly.

Peter shook his head. "We all have people we care about out there in that army, but we cannot risk the entire city of Falcon Cross. There are women and children here. If there isn't time for the army to make it safely back behind the magic shields before Saul catches up with them, then they'll just have to change course."

Izzy felt her stomach doing nervous flip-flops. For the Falcon Cross army to reenter the city, the magic shields would have to be temporarily disabled. The army was far too large to get back in otherwise. But, of course, lowering the magic shields when Saul was nearby would be ludicrous. That would allow the entire dark army into the city.

Izzy looked around at the frowning faces in the room. This situation was not a surprise to anyone. Open battle had always been a possibility, but no one had ever admitted it to themselves. The prospect of losing so many people they loved, or, worse, losing the war, hung heavy in the room.

"We all should go," Mac said quietly. "We might not be able to get our dragon stone army back into Falcon Cross, but we can get our army in here out to them before Saul gets here."

"But that leaves the entire city of Falcon Cross virtually unprotected," Myles protested.

Mac shrugged. "It's our only chance. If our army out in the field is defeated and the other dragon stones are taken, then it won't matter whether we have soldiers watching Falcon Cross or not. Saul will have won the war. Leaving to help the dragon stone army is the only thing we can do."

Izzy felt her stomach turning even more. The prospect of meeting Saul again made her physically ill. She was the only VIP in Falcon Cross who had actually met and spoken directly with Saul, and the experience had scarred her deeply. Izzy had been a prisoner of Saul's when her wizard clan had been attacked by his dark wizards. She'd only had a brief encounter with Saul before being transferred to another outpost under one of Saul's minions, but that brief encounter had been more than enough for Izzy to know that she never wanted to see Saul's face again.

Izzy looked down at her hands, which were folded in her lap. She hoped that the shame washing over her was not evident in her face right now, but she couldn't be sure. Lately, she'd been experiencing such a constant mixture of emotions that she found it difficult to maintain a poker face. How could she admit to this group that she was scared, though?

She had been on so many missions, and had managed to keep a brave front up throughout it all. But the truth was that she was no soldier. She was a doctor, which was why they sent her on missions in the first place. In times like these, it was always helpful to have a trained medical professional around. But she had taken on the part of soldier and played it well, to convince them all that she was capable of playing with the big dogs, and of being in the VIP meetings. Now, she could feel her façade beginning to crumble. If she did get sent out to the battlefield, there was a good possibility that she would meet Saul again. She hated herself for the dread and anguish that filled her at this thought, but she couldn't keep from biting her lip, hard, wishing that she was anywhere but here. She wished her own clan had never been invaded, and that she had never been caught up in this war. She had felt so proud over the last several months to be part of the Falcon Cross elite—the dragons and wizards standing alone against the threat of the evil trying to take over the world. But in this moment right now, she felt small and panicked. She should never have acted like she was brave enough for the big leagues. Right now, she was terrified, and there was no way out of this except to admit to being a total coward.

Beside her, she felt Noah shift in his seat. She glanced over at him again, wishing that she could be half as brave as he was—as all the dragon shifters were. Right now, Noah was stroking his chin thoughtfully, as though he were contemplating his next move in a simple game of chess. There was no fear in his deep green eyes, and his handsome face betrayed no emotion. He was in complete control of whatever emotions he might feel, and, in that moment, Izzy both admired and loathed him for that. He opened his mouth to speak, and Izzy waited for him to proclaim bravely that he was ready to rush into battle against Saul. But he didn't say what she thought he would, and, for the first time since she'd walked into this room, Izzy felt hopeful that there might actually be a way to avoid facing Saul. Noah's words gave her the chance for which she was so desperately grasping.

CHAPTER TWO

"It's time to win back the Redwood Dragons' home base."

Noah's words hung in the air, and even the stoic dragons had trouble not raising their eyebrows in surprise.

"Are you crazy?" Myles finally asked. "I mean, don't get me wrong—I want to win our home back, too. But we can't focus on that until we've got the dragon ruby. Otherwise, any success we might have in getting our cabins back would be temporary."

Izzy watched as Noah sat up a little straighter. Despite his messy hair and wrinkled clothes, he made an imposing figure in that moment. The air of authority that surrounded him was so thick that she felt like she could reach out and touch it.

"I'm not crazy," Noah said. "Think about it. We're overlooking a major source of power in this war. We dragons have been collecting powerful ancient artifacts for years. These artifacts all hold a great deal of power. Sure, each one individually is nothing compared to even one single dragon stone. But if we get back the redwoods base, we can unlock the vaults with those artifacts and arm hundreds of our wizard soldiers with an extra boost in power. That might be enough to push us over the edge, so that we are more powerful than Saul and his dragon ruby."

Everyone continued to stare at Noah as though he'd suddenly sprouted a third head. Everyone except for Izzy. She was quickly realizing that a mission to the Redwood Dragons' Base would allow her to stay away from Saul. Whether or not Noah's idea was crazy, it was a way for Izzy to go somewhere, anywhere, other than straight toward the enemy she feared the most. She should have cared more about winning the war than avoiding Saul, but her fear was too great right now to allow her to think clearly. She could see her chance slipping away as the doubt on everyone else's faces increased, and she spoke up without taking time to really consider what she was saying.

"I think it's a great idea. In fact, I'll go with Noah."

All eyes in the room swung toward her now, and she did her best to appear calm. She hardly ever spoke up in strategy meetings. Medicine was her forte, not battle-planning. But surely, Noah wasn't a complete idiot. He was second-in-command of the dragon shifter crew, after all. If he thought going to the redwoods now was a good idea, then Izzy would trust him. Her only other choice was to go along with the rest of the crew and head out to Saul. She realized that everyone was waiting for her to further explain why she was siding with Noah, so she forced herself to stammer out a few words.

"It's just that we need all the help we can get," Izzy said, and then, in a sudden burst of inspiration, she continued, "And, besides, with everyone focused on the imminent clash between the two armies who have the dragon stones, it's unlikely that there will be many guards at the redwoods. It's the perfect time to get that base back. We don't need many people. We can take them by surprise."

"She's right," Noah said, perking up even more now that he had support. "I'd guess I could almost get the place back myself. Saul doesn't know the extent of powerful artifacts hidden there, so he probably isn't being too careful about guarding the place right now. He's much more interested in the dragon stones that our army is transporting."

Izzy held her breath as she watched the faces in the room slowly change from incredulity, to thoughtfulness, to acceptance. Peter was the first to speak.

"There is some truth in what Noah is saying," Peter said. Izzy resisted the urge to point out that she was the one who'd brought up the point about the redwoods being lightly guarded. Now wasn't the time to fight over credit for a good idea. It was time to keep her fingers crossed that she would be chosen to go with Noah to the redwoods. She saw Peter glance at Knox, who was leaning back in his chair, pondering. Since the redwoods base belonged to Knox, he would be the one to make the final call on whether or not to go fight for it at this time. Falcon Cross had promised to help the dragons win back their home, but everyone had thought that a battle for the redwoods would have to wait until after the dragon ruby was recovered.

Come on, Izzy pleaded silently with Knox. *Send me to the redwoods with Noah. I've been through enough shit with Saul. Just give me this one small chance to do something other than come face to face with that monster again.*

"I can't deny that I love the idea of winning back the Redwoods Base," Knox said. "And what Noah and Izzy are saying does make a lot of sense."

Izzy silently thanked Knox for including her in the praise. At least the dragons knew how to give credit where credit was due. But Knox was still hesitating, and for several awful seconds, Izzy thought he was going to deny the request to fight for the redwoods. Her heart pounded in her chest as Knox began speaking again.

"It's just that we can't spare a lot of soldiers right now, and we have no idea what the situation at the Redwoods Base actually looks like. We haven't had any scouts look at the place for quite some time, since we've been so busy with everything else. We can speculate that the place would be easily taken, but no one really knows."

Knox gave Noah a pointed look, and Izzy got the feeling that the two men were practically capable of reading each other's minds. Noah stuck his chin out defiantly at whatever message he saw in his leader's eyes.

"It's worth a shot," Noah said. "If I'm right, and the place is so sparsely guarded that I can take it back by myself, then we'd be idiots to ignore this chance. We can win our home back, and get our powerful artifacts back. I can't think of any idea that has better potential to swing the war in our favor right now."

Izzy felt her heart drop a little when Noah talked about going by himself. The wizards abhorred solo missions, and always tried to work at least in pairs. But the dragons were different. They often preferred to work alone. Since this mission covered dragon territory, Knox might actually send Noah off on his own. Izzy frantically tried to think of something to say to convince Knox that she was needed on this mission as well, but, thankfully, Peter stepped in before she could.

"My advice would be to send two scouts out together," Peter said. "Noah can take a wizard along—perhaps Izzy would be willing to go since she also spoke up on behalf of the mission."

Izzy tried not to look too eager as she nodded her assent in Peter's direction.

"If Noah can indeed take the place back by himself, then all the better that he has the additional help of a wizard," Peter continued. "And given the current instability in this war, I'd rather have at least two people out there who can report back. If one soldier is…indisposed somehow…at least there's one more chance at us knowing what's going on."

A shiver went down Izzy's back at Peter's words. His meaning was clear. He half-expected that a scouting expedition to the redwoods might end in someone's death. He hoped that if he sent two soldiers, at least one of them would survive to report back.

"I don't need help," Noah insisted. "An extra person will only slow me down."

Izzy didn't look at Noah. She didn't want to see whatever scowl might be on his face right now. She half-felt that she deserved whatever anger he was feeling. He didn't know it, of course, but her motivation to go on the mission was from fear, not from noble intentions. Izzy suspected that Noah would react with disgust if she admitted her angst. To her relief, she saw Knox frowning at Noah.

"I have no doubt you can do things on your own, buddy, but in this case I think taking a wizard with you is a good idea. You might find magical help useful, especially when it comes to opening the vaults. Bree cast some pretty strong protective spells over each vault. It wouldn't hurt to have someone along who knows how to cancel the spells, just in case."

Izzy dared to look at Noah. She saw his angry scowl slowly relax into acceptance at Knox's words, and he shrugged.

"Fine. But don't say I didn't warn you if things go slower than you'd like."

Knox merely smiled. Then he turned to look at Izzy. "Izzy, if you're willing to go with Noah, I think you'd make a great partner for him on this mission. Bree can brief you on the spells she cast, to be sure you know how to cancel them if necessary."

Izzy nodded enthusiastically, no longer able to completely hide her excitement. Not only was she going to go on a mission that did not involve direct contact with Saul, she was also going to get to spend one-on-one time with Bree. Bree was Knox's lifemate, but, more importantly in Izzy's mind, she was the wizard who had bravely defied the high wizard council to bring to everyone's attention the importance of finding the dragon stones. Bree's actions had united the wizards and dragon shifters, and she was hailed as a hero by wizards and shifters alike.

"Well, that's settled, then," Peter said, impatience in his tone. Izzy knew the old wizard would be eager to move on to planning how to send the rest of the Falcon Cross army out to the army that was currently transporting the dragon stones. Noah picked up on Peter's impatience and quickly smoothed over the rough moment.

"Yes, all settled," Noah said. "Izzy and I will work out the details of our scouting mission after this meeting."

Peter nodded, and then turned back to discussing plans for the Falcon Cross armies. Izzy had trouble paying attention, and barely heard as the old wizard discussed the best flight path to lead Saul away from Falcon Cross while still staying close enough that the army leaving Falcon Cross could quickly catch up with the army in the field. The most likely scenario was that Saul's army would catch up with the dragon stone army in about four days. Izzy swallowed hard. That also meant that, if she and Noah were going to take back the Redwoods Base Camp in time for it to do any good, they would have to hurry. There wouldn't be a lot of time for planning. No wonder Noah was so concerned about an extra person slowing him down.

When the meeting adjourned, Izzy stayed in her seat next to Noah while the rest of the VIPs filtered out of the room. The red-alert sirens had stopped now, but the general feeling of unrest still hung heavy in the air. Izzy knew that, out in the many hallways and offices of military headquarters, hundreds of soldiers would already be preparing to take flight. The automatic response to a red-alert siren was to prepare to head straight to battle. Odds were good that the vast majority of the soldiers still in Falcon Cross would be flying out to join the dragon stone army this very night.

Izzy looked expectantly over at Noah. She had a feeling that he already knew how he wanted to conduct this mission, so she would let him take the lead on planning.

Unfortunately, she was a little too right about his knowing how he wanted to conduct the mission. He stood up, turning to face her with his arms crossed. He towered above her, and she couldn't help but feel intimidated. He was already taller than the average man, and with her sitting down, he looked like a giant. An angry giant.

"Listen," he said, his voice low and tense. "This is how things are going to go. I'm in charge of this mission. You do what I say, and you do it right away. I don't want you slowing things down on me. We have one shot at this, and if we blow it because of you, so help me god I will personally make sure you never work in this army again."

Izzy felt anger rising in her chest. She stood, too, and crossed her arms just like his. She still wasn't nearly as tall as him, but at least she felt a little less beneath him.

"Don't you dare threaten me," she said. "I'm a good soldier, and, besides, I stood up for you. Everyone thought your idea was crazy, but I took your side in that meeting. You should be thanking me, not threatening me."

Noah snorted in laughter, then turned to walk toward the door. "Nice try, Izzy. I know you only stood up for me because you want any excuse not to go on the mission to Saul's army. You're not taking my side. You're afraid, and you're avoiding the things you're scared of."

Izzy's jaw dropped slightly. How did he know? Had she been that obvious? Had he seen the fear in her eyes? She'd tried so hard to hide it. Shame and guilt washed over her anew as Noah grabbed the door handle to exit the room.

"Be ready to leave tomorrow at six a.m., sharp," he said over his shoulder. And then, he turned, pausing before he left to scrutinize her up and down. He smiled as if he could read her mind, and could see the questions forming about how he had known her true motivations. Then he spoke four words that chilled her anew.

"Dragons can smell fear."

CHAPTER THREE

Despite his annoyance at being forced to take along a partner, and his disdain for her timidity, Noah had to admit that, on the whole, Izzy was a capable soldier. She could keep up with him on a hike at least.

They had agreed not to fly in to the Redwoods Base Camp directly—even though Noah could easily fly when in dragon form, and Izzy was as talented as any wizard at broomstick flying. With so much uncertainty surrounding the camp, it was better to land far out and come in slowly, on foot. That way they could take their time assessing what they were up against. But this slow approach meant a half day of hiking, and Noah wasn't happy about the wasted time. With Saul's army closing the gap between himself and the other dragon stones, there wasn't much time to spare. Noah only wished he'd thought of invading the Redwoods Camp earlier. He might have convinced Knox to let him come here, even before the threat of Saul and the dragon ruby was imminent. Then Noah would have had more time to plan how he would overtake whatever enemy awaited him in the redwoods.

But there was no use dwelling on alternate possibilities now. The reality of his situation remained unchanged, no matter how much he regretted not acting sooner. He was traipsing as fast as he dared through thick forest, trying to outpace Izzy and failing. He had wanted to prove to her that she couldn't keep up, but she seemed just as determined to prove that she could. And, right now at least, she was doing a damn good job of matching his pace. This only served to annoy him even more. He'd wanted to come on this mission alone, like the good old days when the Redwood Dragons were always sent on solo missions to recover ancient artifacts. This war had resulted in far too much socializing, if you asked Noah.

But no one had asked Noah, so he kept marching forward through the redwoods, gritting his teeth and glancing back every now and then with a grudging look to make sure Izzy was still keeping up. She always was.

He tried to push her out of his mind and focus on enjoying the trees around him. The city of Falcon Cross was located in the middle of a beautiful forest, but it was still too much of a city for Noah's liking. There were houses and cars and big government buildings—and people everywhere. So many people. Noah was glad for the space that surrounded him now. He and Izzy were likely the only humans out here for miles and miles. There was something intoxicating about being alone. Or, almost alone. Noah frowned, and tried not to let his anger at Izzy bubble to the surface too much. Focus on the trees, he told himself.

And what magnificent trees they were. The trees near Falcon Cross were nice enough, but they had nothing on the redwoods. The ancient giants towered above him, their impossibly wide trunks taking up large footprints on the forest floor. The reddish brown bark smelled like home to him, and the green canopy of their leaves offered plentiful shade from the bright midday sun. Noah smiled, and took in a long, deep breath.

He'd spent most of his life in these woods. He and the other Redwood Dragons had been rescued as young children, when the last great war orphaned them. They'd grown up together, as brothers. Noah could hardly wait for the day when they would return here together as brothers, to live in their cabins once again. His heart beat faster at the thought. Things had changed, sure. All of the dragons except him had found lifemates now. Life in the redwoods would be different. Busier. But that wouldn't be all bad. Noah wouldn't deny that there were several ways in which a woman's touch would improve their little camp. He imagined little gardens behind each cabin, lovingly tended. His stomach rumbled at the thought of home-cooked food. A smile crossed his face as he wondered which of his clanmates would be the first to father a new baby dragon. Noah had no particular desire to settle down with a woman and have a family himself, but he liked the idea of having a bunch of nieces and nephews to spoil.

Uncle Noah, he thought, trying out the title in his head as he walked. It sounded good. If this damn war would just hurry up and be over, they could all get down to the business of actually living. He missed good times with his clan brothers, hanging out around the barbeque and just shooting the breeze. Unconsciously, he quickened his step. The sooner he got to base camp and regained possession of it, the sooner he could help out the soldiers in the field. And the sooner Saul would be defeated. Noah would not allow himself to think about the possibility of losing this war to Saul. Defeat was simply not an option. They must win. They would win.

"We should stop for lunch," Izzy called out from behind him. Noah turned and scowled, annoyed at having his thoughts interrupted.

"We don't have time to waste on lunch," Noah said, even though he knew what he was saying was ridiculous. He was feeling belligerent, though, and would have argued with just about any suggestion that Izzy made at that point. Before Izzy could even reply, Noah's stomach betrayed him by letting out a long, hungry growl. Izzy raised an eyebrow.

"I think your stomach disagrees with you," she said. "It's half past two, and if we want to keep up this pace, it's better that we eat. Stopping for fifteen minutes isn't going to make much difference in the grand scheme of this hike, but whether or not we nourish ourselves matters."

Noah wanted to argue more, but his stomach growled loudly again. He *was* quite hungry.

"Fine," he said. "But only fifteen minutes."

Izzy looked like she might roll her eyes at him, but in the end she merely let out a small sigh before sitting down and removing her large hiking backpack. She began digging in its depths for her food stash, not deigning to look at Noah while she did. He huffed and sat down himself. Quickly, he pulled out a peanut butter and jelly sandwich that had become rather smashed, and a bottle of water. Izzy was still digging in her pack as he unwrapped his sandwich and took a bite. The bread was slightly soggy, but it would do. At least he had quickly found his food, he thought, feeling superior. Izzy must not be as organized as the other wizards, if she hadn't packed things well enough to find them right away.

Noah took another bite and continued to watch Izzy as she began pulling a few packages out of her pack. He'd never really looked closely at her before, and her perfect curves, outlined by her snug-fitting military uniform, sent an unexpected rush of warm blood through his body—a rush that seemed to center right between his legs. He turned his head away, trying desperately to think of something else. The trees, that oddly shaped rock over there, the war…anything to get his mind off of Izzy's body and stop the stiffening between his legs from giving him away. What the hell was wrong with him? He didn't even want to be friends with Izzy. He just wanted to be alone on this mission. And he definitely didn't want to be thinking about her in any sort of romantic or lustful way. All his clanmates had managed to get themselves tangled up in a relationship when they were out on missions, but not him. He wasn't here to play games. He was here to win this war so life could get back to normal.

"Are you really not going to talk to me for this whole mission?" Izzy asked.

With a sigh, Noah turned to look at her. He was startled to realize that she had quite an elaborate spread of food in front of her. She was holding what looked like a turkey and cheese sandwich on a baguette, and in front of her was a selection of nuts, cheeses, grapes, and berries. Forgetting to answer her question, he snorted with laughter.

"What the hell is all this?" he asked. "Did you pack for a hike to a war zone, or for a five course picnic in the south of France?"

Izzy glared. "For your information, the food I packed offers quite a bit more nourishment than that measly sandwich you have over there. Laugh all you want to, but these nuts and fruits will keep me going much better than a tiny bit of bread and jelly."

"Bread, jelly, *and* peanut butter," Noah corrected. "I'm eating nuts, too, just in a different form."

Izzy rolled her eyes at him, and Noah winced a bit when he realized the gesture somewhat turned him on. He always had liked a bit of sass in his women. Not that he'd had much time for women over the years. His missions hadn't usually left him any free hours for chasing after girls. Desperate for a way to smooth over the fresh rush of attraction he felt for Izzy, he decided to press the issue of her fear. He knew this would make her angry, but that was a good thing. It would keep her too distracted to notice that he couldn't stop staring at her, and it would remind him that he didn't want to be associated with a coward.

"So, Izzy," Noah said. "Why did you decide to become a soldier if you're afraid of fighting? Seems like there are a lot of other honorable careers out there that would better suit you, if battle makes you so fearful."

Izzy didn't look up from her food, but Noah could see her furrowing her eyebrows angrily. "I did have another career. I'm a doctor, remember? And besides, no one can say I haven't been brave. I helped Myles and Harlow escape from one of Saul's camps. And I've done my part to fight on many missions since then."

"But you only came on this mission because you're afraid of meeting Saul. Don't try to deny it," Noah said. He knew he was poking the bear, and making her angry. But he couldn't help himself. He was angry, too. He wasn't happy about having Izzy along. She was a distraction, in more ways than one.

"This mission is just as important as going to fight Saul directly," Izzy said, sticking out her chin defiantly. "And now, if you don't mind, I'm going to start packing up. I believe it's been fifteen minutes already, and that's all the time you wanted to allot to eating."

Izzy started carefully folding up her packages of food and putting them back in her backpack. Noah realized as he watched her that she hadn't taken a long time to get her food out because she didn't know where it was—she had just gone slowly to make sure she didn't get things out of order. She was quite organized, after all.

Noah stood to his feet. He crumpled up the tin foil that had surrounded his own sandwich and shoved it into his backpack with unnecessary force. He didn't need fancy food and packing methods to stay energized on this hike. Over thinking things always holds people back. Let Izzy feel proud about her little picnic. When it came down to it, he was the one who would be ready to fight at a moment's notice.

He would be the one to save the Redwoods Camp.

CHAPTER FOUR

Noah hiked the rest of the way in silence. Izzy was apparently giving him the cold shoulder, which was just fine with him. He didn't really care if she was angry with him, and he was happy to not have to talk.

His thoughts swirled in dozens of different directions as he walked. He wondered how things were going with the rest of the dragons and wizards. Because there had been so much spy and hacker activity lately, Noah and Izzy had agreed that they would not have any contact with Falcon Cross unless it was an absolute emergency. Status updates were an unnecessary risk. If intercepted, simple updates would alert Saul's army to Noah and Izzy's mission. This whole mission, like so many in this war, relied on the element of surprise. Saul might have a large army, and more powerful magic. But the good wizards and dragons had so far managed to outsmart him at every turn. Well, almost every turn. He'd captured the dragon ruby, which had been a devastating blow to the side of good. But Noah believed in his heart that good would win out in the end. It always did. Evil was not a solid enough foundation to stand the test of time. Truth and right would prevail one day, even if that day turned out to be further away than Noah hoped.

By the time Noah began recognizing familiar trees, the sky had turned black as night. There was an almost full moon up there somewhere, but thick clouds had blocked out its light completely. Noah was glad for his keen dragon eyesight. Even in the near darkness, he could see several feet in front of him. Izzy was not so lucky. He heard her stumbling behind him several times, and it made him feel triumphant that his ability to walk through blackness so thoroughly trumped hers.

He felt a little bit guilty for thinking this. After all, he and Izzy were on the same side. It wouldn't hurt him to be a bit more gracious to her. But Noah wasn't feeling particularly gracious at the moment, and, besides, there wasn't much he could do to help Izzy. Turning on any sort of light was out of the question at the moment. They were far too close to the Redwoods Base Camp to risk being seen. Izzy had supposedly put up an invisibility shield around them, but Noah didn't put much faith in invisibility shields these days. Saul's men had shown over and over again that their dark magic was capable of breaking through even the heartiest of invisibility shields. Noah wasn't sure why the wizards even bothered with such shields anymore.

Noah was trying to rely on old fashioned methods of staying invisible: moving slowly and silently, and blending into the dark trees and brush as much as possible—that sort of thing. Of course, this effort was somewhat hampered by Izzy's constant stumbling. Noah gritted his teeth and kept moving forward. If they were ambushed because of her carelessness, he was never going to let her hear the end of it.

And yet, the possibility of ambush didn't seem likely. Things were quiet here. Too quiet. Eerily quiet. Noah breathed in deeply, trying to pick up on the scent of shifters or wizards. Or even humans. But even as they crept closer and closer to base camp, all he could smell were the scents of the forest. He breathed in the aroma of bark, of leaves, of dirt, and of stones. But nothing living. The silence weighed heavier.

Noah told himself that he should relax a little. There was nothing here to fear. Perhaps Saul had completely abandoned the Redwoods Base Camp, deeming protecting it an unnecessary nuisance. After all, the dragon stones were all accounted for, and Saul knew that none of those stones were here in the redwoods.

And yet, the uneasy feeling Noah had persisted. It continued for the next half hour of slow, steady hiking, until he reached the small clearing in the redwoods that was just a short distance away from the Redwood Dragons' cabins. This clearing had previously been used as a landing area. When Noah or his clanmates flew into their camp in dragon form, they would land here and shift back into human form for the short walk to the cabins. Noah knew that, if Saul still had wizards and shifters guarding this camp, they would have been watching this spot. But there was still no scent or sound of anyone out here other than Izzy and himself.

Nevertheless, Noah's nerves were on edge, and his hair was standing on end. Something wasn't right here. He looked back at Izzy, raising an eyebrow at her, questioning. He wasn't sure if she could see his face in the darkness, but she seemed to understand why he was turning around. She shrugged, and shook her head in a way that implied that she had no idea what was going on here, either. Noah took a step toward her, until their bodies were only inches apart. She smelled like a mixture of sweat and soap, and he felt another involuntary rush of arousal. Her breathing was slightly labored, and, against his better judgment, he allowed himself for one split second to imagine what it would feel like if he was the cause of her breathlessness. The stiffening between his legs returned, and he quickly forced his thoughts back to the present situation. He reminded himself that he was mad at her, that she was a coward, and that he was only tolerating her. He could not allow himself to think about her as anything other than a nuisance. Any kind feelings toward her would take him down a slippery slope, he knew. So he was all business as he whispered in her ear.

"It sounds and smells abandoned, but I have a feeling that there's something here we're missing. Walk close behind me, as quietly as possible. And be ready to fight at a moment's notice."

Izzy nodded, a few loose wisps of her dark brown hair brushing against Noah's face as she did. He resisted the urge to close his eyes and enjoy the feeling of her hair against his face. Instead, he turned and started creeping along the old familiar path to the cabins.

He could have made this walk with his eyes closed. He had traveled this same path thousands of times. But he kept his eyes wide open, peering into the dark brush and expecting something to jump out at him at any moment. Nothing did, however. He made it to the edge of the small trail without seeing or smelling another soul, and found himself peering out at the cabins where he had grown up.

In this clearing, here in the heart of the redwoods, stood eleven cabins. They were lined up in two rows, with a large open space between them. The fire pit and barbeque still stood in the open space, although the logs were missing that he and his clanmates had once used as benches to sit around the fire pit. The cabins themselves seemed to have suffered a great deal of damage. It was difficult to see the full extent of destruction in the darkness, but Noah could tell that whoever had lived here had taken pleasure in tearing up random portions of the old cabins. A wave of anger washed over Noah's heart. He would make Saul's men pay for treating his beloved home this way. Who did they think they were, coming in here and treating this sacred ground like trash?

Noah took a tentative step forward into the clearing. Still, things were silent. He was beginning to truly believe that there was no one here. He kept his ears alert and he breathed in deeply. No smells. No sounds. He took another step.

"Noah, wait," Izzy whispered from behind him. Her voice sounded worried, and Noah rolled his eyes. Of course she would be afraid. She was a pretty girl, and she might be a good doctor, but she would never be a true soldier. Not when she made all her decisions based on fear. Let her stay in the trees, hiding. He was going to go look at his old cabin up close, and see what repairs his home would need.

Confidently, Noah took another step into the clearing, holding his head high. That's when he smelled it. The awful stench hit his nose with such force that he physically doubled over for a moment. He forced himself to stand, covering his nose and looking around for the source. It smelled like death. How had he not caught wind of it before? The smell was too strong to have appeared so suddenly. Noah gagged and peered ahead of him, thinking there must be a pile of dead bodies up ahead that he'd somehow missed. Perhaps that was why this place was deserted. Someone, or something, had beaten him here, and had already killed of Saul's soldiers.

"Noah! No-ahhhhh!"

Noah's name, screamed from Izzy's lips, sent a chill down his spine. He whirled around, instantly ready to shift and fight. The uneasy feeling was back, and stronger than ever. But before he could even turn a complete one-eighty, something struck him in the side and knocked him to the ground.

For a moment, he lay there stunned. It was the sound of Izzy's screams, which were now yelling out magic attack spells, that roused him. He let out a roar, and began to shift. His skin thickened and began to turn into dragon scales. His legs and arms began to grow and morph into the legs and arms of a dragon. He felt his fingernails becoming sharp claws. Less than a minute more, and he'd be a full dragon, ready to fight whatever enemy it had been that had knocked him over.

But then, suddenly, a fresh wave of the awful death stench hit him, and he found himself unable to breathe. His roar was cut off, and he gasped for breath. Noah saw a large hairy hand, covered in slime, reach down to grab him. The hand itself was as big as a man, and it easily wrapped around Noah's entire body. Noah struggled to get away, but the smell of the creature was so bad that he could only gasp for air and do his best not to vomit.

Noah found himself raised into the air, and staring into two eerie yellow eyes, each eye the size of a man's head. The creature looked like some sort of cross between an ape and a man, with perhaps a little bit of abominable snowman thrown in. Its hair was gray, and covered everywhere with the thick slime that Noah could now tell was the source of the awful smell. The slime oozed from the creatures nose, mouth, ears and eyes, and ran in slow trails down its whole body. Its fingers were long and ended in sharp claws, and Noah struggled fruitlessly against the creature's grip.

Noah tried to concentrate on breathing. He could not finish shifting if he couldn't breathe. But the smell of this monster, its slime just inches from Noah's nose, made breathing itself a nearly impossible task. The creature held Noah suspended in midair, somewhere between his human and dragon forms.

For a moment, Noah stopped struggling and tried to get a better look at the thing, whatever it was. It eyed him back, curiously, and then, seeming to decide that Noah was most definitely a threat, it bared its teeth at him with a huge roar. Noah was not easily frightened, and could handle the sight of the long, sharp teeth—each one as big as a man's arm. But the smell of the creature's breath was another matter. That alone was enough to nearly cause Noah to pass out. Noah struggled to stay conscious, trying to focus his breathing. For a brief moment, he thought that this might actually be how he died. What an awful way to go, he thought, done in by the stench of some sickening beast.

But Noah had forgotten one tiny detail: he was not alone in this fight. As his vision blurred and his limbs started to go weak, Noah heard Izzy's voice shouting out spell after spell. Somehow, in the midst of this horror, her voice came into sharp focus, and he clung to it. She was his only salvation.

"*Magicae invado. Magicae appugno. Magicae invado.*"

Her voice was angry and authoritative, but it sounded like the sweetest music in Noah's ears. At first, the creature holding Noah seemed impervious to Izzy's attacks. But she must have worn him down, or finally found an attack that worked, because in an instant, everything changed. Noah felt the slimy fingers that had been holding him go lax as a stench-filled roar of pain escaped from the monster's lips.

Then Noah was falling several feet to the ground. He landed on his back with a thud that nearly knocked him out. Luckily, his back had already thickened into dragon scales, which lessened the blow somewhat and kept him from what probably would have been a broken spine if he'd been in full human form. Noah lay there for a brief moment, shocked to find that he was alive and out of immediate danger. Once again, it was the sound of Izzy's voice that snapped him back to reality.

He turned his head to look over at her. Even with his dragon sight, she wasn't easy to see in the darkness. Her black uniform blended into the black night. But every few seconds, a burst of light would shoot out from her magic ring, illuminating both her and the awful ape-man monster, which was now focusing its full anger on her. Izzy fought bravely, Noah had to admit. He had judged her to be a complete coward, but as he watched her parrying the monster's attack, he had to admit that she had courage. In this moment, when it really counted, she was brave. She was fighting with everything in her, and not shrinking back. She had saved his life.

This realization hit Noah right in the gut. He had given Izzy nothing but grief over the fact that she had come along on this mission. And yet, if she hadn't been here, he would very likely be dead right now. Noah had never felt so humbled. With every ounce of strength he had, Noah pushed his half-dragon, half-human form up from the ground. He brushed off the remnants of slime as best he could and stuck his nose straight up toward the sky, searching for fresh air. He took a deep breath, and felt clean air filling his lungs. With it, his strength rapidly returned. He took another breath, and another, and then let out a loud roar.

He began once again to shift. His body grew, larger and larger. The scales that had covered his back continued to thicken and cover the rest of his body. His head morphed into a dragon head, and he sprouted wings and a tail. The last tattered pieces of his human clothing fell away, and he stood in the clearing of his old home, a full dragon against the backdrop of magnificent redwoods.

The monstrous creature was still attacking Izzy, and she was still fighting it with all her might. Neither one of them seemed to have noticed that Noah had risen, and had finished his transformation into a fearsome dragon. The slime-covered creature seemed hell-bent on killing Izzy.

Oh no you don't, Noah thought. *Not on my watch.*

With another giant roar, Noah bounded across the clearing toward the slimy monster. He took in a deep breath without slowing his pace, preparing to unleash a stream of fire at this strange enemy. Izzy looked up and saw him coming, then quickly turned to run out of the way. She'd been around dragons long enough to know what was coming next.

With a burning, sulfurous blast, Noah let loose his rage. He had hoped that this creature would be vulnerable to fire, and he was not disappointed. Despite its ability to defend itself rather well against Izzy's magic attacks, it was no match for the inferno of a dragon's rage. It screeched in pain when the first blast of fire hit it. Then, it crumpled to the ground, writhing in pain. Noah continued to send fiery streaks at the monster long after he was sure it was dead. He was filled with rage, and was taking it out on this now-expired monster.

"Noah!"

Once again, Izzy's voice centered him. He ceased his fire-breathing and looked up at her, his big dragon eyes slowly focusing on her silhouette. She stepped forward, between him and the burning heap. Her black uniform once again showed off her perfect curves, this time against the backdrop of orange flames. She took another step forward, and put one of her hands on his giant dragon chest. He trembled at her touch.

"Noah, it's done," she said. "It's dead."

Noah nodded his giant dragon head and quickly took several steps backwards. He took in a deep breath, then let it out with a roar, shifting back into human form. When his transformation was complete, he stood there, sweating and gasping for breath, and unable to keep himself from staring at the burning pile of monster that had very nearly defeated them. Izzy walked quietly over to the pile, raised her magic ring, and said, "*Magicae aqua.*"

Water spouted from her ring, and Izzy waved her ring back and forth like a hose until the fire was completely out, leaving only a sizzling, steaming pile of ashes.

"*Aqua terminantur,*" she said quietly, ending the water spell. Then they both stood there for several long moments, staring at the wet black circle that covered a good portion of the ground in front of them.

Eventually, Izzy looked up at him with an expression of mild shock. She was panting heavily, and little streams of sweat were running down her face. Noah could see the veins in her forehead pulsing. She was undoubtedly coming down from a heady adrenaline rush, just like him.

"I almost died," she finally said, struggling to get the words out.

"So did I," Noah said. Blood pounded in his chest, in his ears…in his groin.

Without pausing to think, he crossed the few feet between Izzy and him and put his lips on hers. She tasted salty, like the sweat of battle.

She tasted like the warrior she was.

CHAPTER FIVE

Izzy laughed as Noah winced.

"I thought you were Mr. Tough Guy," she said. "Looks like you can't even handle a bit of rubbing alcohol."

"That was more than a bit," Noah protested. "I think you dumped half the bottle on that gauze strip."

"Oh, stop your whining and hold still," Izzy said. "All you men are the same. Tough as nails until you have a little boo-boo, or, worse, a man cold. And god forbid one of you gets the flu. You'd think the entire world was ending."

Noah glared at her, but Izzy just laughed. She wasn't easily intimidated when she was in doctor mode. Here, tending to Noah's many minor wounds, she was confident and in control. She was the expert now. Her skills as a soldier might not be world class, but no one could tell her that she wasn't a talented doctor.

"Sit still!" Izzy commanded again. Noah huffed but did as he was told. Izzy worked for several more minutes in silence, forcing herself to concentrate on her work instead of how gorgeous Noah's eyes were as they looked up at her. He'd shaved before they left on their mission, so his face was smoother than it had been in the VIP meeting room a day ago. But already, a hint of dark stubble was starting to reappear. Izzy resisted the urge to lift a palm and run it across his cheek.

Things had changed between them, in ways that would have seemed impossible just a few hours ago. They had started out this mission on shaky ground, and then they had saved each other's lives. They had survived, together, and everything was different now. Izzy bit her lip gently remembering for a brief moment how Noah's lips had felt on hers.

Had his kiss meant something, or had it been just a byproduct of the adrenaline-drenched moment they'd both been caught up in? Izzy wanted to ask, but she was afraid of the answer. She wasn't even sure which answer she wanted. She hadn't been looking for love. She'd only been trying to make it through this war in one piece. And yes, she'd been a bit of a coward, shying away from Saul. But, in the end, her cowardice had saved Noah's life, so he couldn't be too angry about that anymore, could he?

"All done," she said briskly, standing straight up a little too quickly. Her back, a bit sore from the fight, sent little shivers of pain across her left side in protest of her rapid movements. She rubbed at the worst spot on her lower spine, doing her best not to wince. It wouldn't do to show pain when she'd just teased Noah for the very same thing. She gave him a smile that she hoped was convincing, but faltered a little when she noticed that he was staring at her. They were in one of the cabins now—the one that had been least damaged by Saul's army. According to Noah this cabin used to belong to Grayson. It was small but cozy, and something about the setting felt a little too intimate, especially with Noah looking at her like he could see right through her.

"What?" she asked. The intensity in his emerald eyes unnerved her. His hair was mussed up after battle in the same way it had been during the red-alert meeting. That meeting felt like another lifetime now.

761

"Nothing," Noah said finally, looking away. "We should eat something."

He stood slowly and crossed the room, reaching for his backpack, which now had tattered straps since he'd been wearing it while he shifted. He dug in and pulled out a meal replacement bar. He frowned at the bar, then let out a resigned sigh and sat down at the small kitchen table to eat it. Izzy felt her heart go out to him a bit. She knew he was now regretting his choice to pack in a hurry and only take along simple food like meal bars and stale peanut butter and jelly sandwiches. It would serve him right if she spread out all her carefully packed, delicious food and ate it up without offering him any. A few hours ago, that's probably what she would have done. But, as she'd already realized, things were different between them now. He owed her his life, and she owed him hers. She couldn't very well sit here and feast without inviting him to join.

Silently, she stood and went to her own bag. She carried it to the table and slowly pulled out packages of food. She arranged the grapes, cheeses, and berries in neat rows, using the paper they'd been wrapped in as a sort of makeshift tablecloth. She pulled out a package of gourmet crackers, and another small package of mixed nuts. Then she pulled out her last sandwich, a deluxe ham and cheese on a baguette. She could feel Noah's eyes on her as she tore the sandwich in two, then held one of the halves out to him like a peace offering.

"Here. Eat. And help yourself to all of this, too," she said, sweeping her hand in a wide gesture to indicate the food spread across the table.

Noah looked hungrily at the sandwich, but didn't reach for it right away. "You don't have to share just because we had a battle together, you know."

"Stop being a stubborn male for three goddamn seconds and take the sandwich," Izzy replied, exasperated.

Noah shrugged and gave her a sheepish grin, but then reached out to take the sandwich. For a few minutes, silence hung over the room as they both ate greedily. Izzy spoke first.

"Should we risk a transmission to Falcon Cross now?" she asked. Noah didn't answer right away. He drummed his fingers on the table, considering. Finally, he shook his head no.

"We should wait at least until morning," he said. "I want to make sure there isn't anyone else, or anything else, hiding out here. If there are more enemies nearby, they'll likely attack tonight, under cover of darkness. We'll sleep in shifts for the rest of the night. If morning comes and we still haven't been attacked, we'll take another look around. As long as we don't see anything else suspicious, then I'd say we're pretty much home free. We can tell Falcon Cross that the Redwoods Base Camp has been recovered."

Izzy nodded. She would have liked to send word back to Falcon Cross right away, but Noah was right. Better to wait until they knew for sure that things here were safe and secure. The message they sent to Falcon Cross would be short and cryptic, in case it got intercepted. All it would be was a code word, letting the wizards and dragons back home know that the Redwoods Base Camp was recovered. As soon as Falcon Cross got word of this, an army of wizards would start heading here to gather up the ancient artifacts that the Redwood Dragons Clan had been stockpiling over the years. Izzy and Noah could not send word until they were certain that it was safe for the Falcon Cross soldiers to come.

They had looked around as best they could in the darkness, before coming into this cabin to clean up their wounds. As far as they could tell, the place had been deserted, except for the strange creature they'd unwittingly disturbed when they walked into the camp. The cabins were all damaged in some shape or fashion, some worse than others.

But all of them had clearly been abandoned for weeks. Layers of dust covered every surface, and what little food remained in the fridges was rotting and moldy.

"Any idea what that creature was?" Noah asked as he reached for a handful of crackers and several slices of cheese. Now that he'd gotten over his initial hesitation about sharing Izzy's food, he wasn't at all shy about helping himself. She was glad for that. She'd brought plenty, and the berries and cheese were better eaten fresh. They could probably forage for more food tomorrow, provided the area did prove to be free of enemy soldiers. Besides, it gave her heart an undeniably warm, happy feeling to see Noah enjoying himself so much.

"I'm pretty sure it was a shifter altered by dark magic," Izzy said. She felt her stomach turn at the thought of the creature, and she reached for her water bottle to take a long sip. The cool liquid didn't calm her nerves as much as she would have hoped, however.

Noah looked over at her in confusion, pausing with a cheese and cracker sandwich held in mid-air. "What does that mean?" he asked.

Izzy shuddered. "It's…disturbing, just to warn you. But I suppose nothing is more disturbing than seeing a monster like that in real life. There are dark magic spells that allow wizards to turn any shifter into a state of being permanently between animal and human form. Except, as I'm sure you saw tonight, it's not a normal animal or human form. It's some sort of deranged human mixed with a monstrous beast. The spells were created centuries ago during one of the great shifter-wizard wars. Wizards were scared that shifters were going to take over and destroy wizards completely, so some of them created these spells. They wanted to create these inhuman shifter monsters out of captured shifter prisoners, and use the monsters to fight against attacking shifters. The spells were quickly outlawed, because the high wizard councils ruled that they fell squarely under the category of dark magic—"

"I can't imagine why," Noah interrupted.

"Right," Izzy said. "It doesn't take a genius to see that turning someone into one of these monster creatures is evil in the purest sense. But, as we know, Saul has no qualms about using all sorts of different dark magic. I'm sure this was his work. What I wonder is whether he created that monster and left it here to guard the place *after* moving his soldiers out, or whether he just let the monster loose and it killed off all the soldiers."

Noah looked up at her in horror. "Why would Saul allow his own soldiers to be killed?"

"Why would he do any of the awful things he does?" Izzy asked.

Noah sighed. "True enough. It's just still hard for me to believe that anyone could be so awful. The man has no soul."

"Well, you're actually more right about that than you know," Izzy said, shuddering. "I'm sure you've been briefed on how dark magic works. Each dark magic spell requires a bit of the soul of the person casting the spell. Someone like Saul, who has been doing these deep dives into the world of dark magic, likely doesn't have much of a soul left to speak of."

Noah frowned as he slowly chewed a mouthful of cheese and crackers.

"Why did the, uh, monster, smell so awful?" he asked. "Was it because he killed people? And why didn't I smell him until he was right on top of me?"

Izzy made a face. "He would have smelled like that whether or not he'd killed anyone. It's a hallmark of those creatures. They produce this slime as a byproduct of the dark magic, and that's what smells so bad. They can emit pheromones to mask their scent when they're sneaking up on someone, though. That enables them to take enemies by surprise. Once they have their enemies in their grasp, they let their awful stench come back through. As you know well by now, that smell is enough to suffocate a person. The creatures are dangerous, but also kind of dumb. They do whatever their creator tells them to do without really questioning anything, and if they don't get orders they wander around aimlessly destroying things."

"You know an awful lot about these monsters."

"Yeah, well, growing up as a wizard we were constantly warned about the dangers of dark magic. Monsters like this were always used as examples of what awful things evil magic was capable of. As wary as wizards might have been of shifters, we still have morals. We didn't want to be part of anything that would turn human beings into these awful shells of themselves. I hate to even use the word monster, because it's referring to someone who used to be a person. It almost seems disrespectful to call them a monster. But, then again, the creatures are quite monstrous, and they don't really bear any resemblance anymore to who they used to be."

"I know what you mean," Noah said sadly. "I feel awful that I killed a shifter. But he wasn't really a shifter anymore, was he?"

"No, he wasn't."

Izzy and Noah sat in silence for a few minutes, chewing on their food and lost in their own thoughts. Izzy was wondering just how far Saul would be able to take his dark magic when Noah spoke up.

"Why are you so afraid of him?"

Izzy didn't have to ask to know that Noah was talking about Saul. She tensed up a bit, but there was no animosity in Noah's tone this time. He sounded genuinely curious. Concerned, almost. Still, she felt ashamed to admit to her fear. She looked into the emerald pools of Noah's eyes, wondering whether she could really trust him. They had shared an intimate moment out by the corpse of the monster, true. But did that single instance really make that much difference?

Izzy didn't know Noah well. She had no idea what his personality was really like, and his actions over the last day, on the whole, had not left a very favorable impression. But what did she really have to lose by giving him a second chance? He already knew she was a coward, so telling him about Saul wasn't going to make things worse between them. If, by some chance, he actually listened to what she said, then maybe he would soften his attitude toward her. Maybe he would realize that courage isn't always a black and white attribute. Izzy took a deep breath, and decided to talk about Saul. She hadn't really done so since she'd helped Myles and Harlow escape from one of Saul's minions, and she found her voice shaking slightly as she began to speak.

"I guess you could say that, before this war, I'd lived a fairly sheltered life. I grew up in a small clan on the east coast, where life was pretty rosy and calm. I had heard tales of old wars, of course, but all of that seemed like distant history. I thought dark magic and evil shifters and wizards were things of the past. That all changed the day that Saul invaded my clan's little town."

Izzy paused to steady her breathing. Her palms were growing sweaty and she could feel her heart pounding in her chest at the memories, but she had said too much to stop talking now.

"I was out with friends when Saul and his army came. One minute I was sitting there at a restaurant, laughing over beers and loaded nachos, and the next I was being pulled to the ground and everyone around me was screaming. Saul's dark wizards came flying through the town, shooting off random attack spells and laughing at the terrified chaos they were causing. After several minutes of this, Saul flew overhead, in dragon form. He started yelling at all of us that we had to join his army or die. I had never seen a shifter before, and just the sight of a dragon flying overhead was enough to horrify me."

"What did you do?"

"Well, the dark wizards rounded everyone up in the center of town. There, each person was brought before Saul one by one. He gave us each the chance to either join his army or die. I watched as my clanmates refused, one after the other. People I had known my whole life—friends, relatives, neighbors—were all killed in an instant when they spat in Saul's face and told him they would never join his cause. I stood there, shaking, waiting for my turn to die. And then, I had a thought. What good did it do me to die? I couldn't help push back the forces of evil if I was dead. But maybe, just maybe, if I pretended to side with Saul, I could do something to harm his cause from the inside. I had no idea what I might be able to do, but I decided that it was worth a shot. When my turn came to stand before Saul, I told him I would join his cause. I was terrified that he might be able to somehow read my mind and see that I wasn't actually intending to help him, but I guess even dark magic has its limits. Saul took me at my word, and seemed pleased to have recruited a new soldier."

"What did he do with you then?" Noah asked.

"He had his wizards put me through all sorts of tests to see what I was capable of. I didn't tell him I was a doctor. I didn't want to have to use my medical skills to help any soldiers of his who might be wounded. Unfortunately, though, I don't have many talents outside of being a doctor. I'm horrible at one-on-one combat, I don't have much endurance, and I'm not very strong. With each passing test, Saul grew angrier and angrier. When I didn't live up to his expectations, he would slice my stomach with one of his claws. I was already weak and tired. Losing so much blood from the wounds he was creating made it nearly impossible to perform any of the physical tasks he was asking of me. I thought he was going to kill me, and I began to regret not just spitting in his face and dying quickly. Finally, though, he asked me to show him my broomstick flying skills. That's something I'm actually really good at, and, mercifully, he seemed impressed after watching me fly. He sent me to an outpost in northern Montana, where I served as a guard and waited for a chance to help the side of good. The dark wizard in charge of that outpost often tortured me, presumably at Saul's command, but I held on to hope that things wouldn't be that way forever. I'd heard rumblings that there was a resistance force, and when Harlow was captured I knew I had to help her. Thankfully, after helping her and Myles, Peter agreed to take me in as a member of the Falcon Cross Clan."

Izzy met Noah's eyes as she finished her story, but she couldn't tell what he was thinking. Once again, in true dragon style, he was doing a damn good job of hiding his emotions. She could feel her hands trembling, and she kept them hidden under the table in her lap. She already felt vulnerable enough after telling him about her experiences with Saul. She didn't want him to see her shaking, too. Izzy knew that many did not agree with her choice to pretend to join Saul's army. There were plenty of wizards who thought that doing so had been cowardly. They thought she should have died honorably instead of acting like she was willing to help the side of evil. But Izzy felt deep down that her choice had been a good one, even if it had been cowardly. After all, Myles and Harlow might very well have died without her help, and then the dragon amethyst would not have been recovered. Izzy stuck her chin defiantly out in front of her, almost daring Noah to tell her once again that she had no spine and would never be a true soldier. But when Noah finally spoke, his voice was as tender as she'd ever heard it.

"I was wrong about you, Izzy. I'm sorry."

Izzy blinked at him, not quite sure how to interpret the statement. Luckily, he kept talking and explained things further.

"Maybe you aren't brave in the traditional sense. You're not rushing eagerly into battle and wanting to meet Saul head-on. But you're brave when it counts. In that moment when the monster had me in its claws, you came through for me. I know you never asked for this, Izzy. You just wanted to live your calm, settled life and be a doctor. And it sounds like Saul and his minions tortured you something awful. Despite everything you've been through, you're still standing tall and still helping the side of good, even when your head is telling you that you should be scared out of your mind. You're following your heart, and I think your heart tells you that you have what it takes to make a difference."

Izzy blinked again, this time to blink back tears. Hearing Noah say those things filled her with a rush of emotion. She wasn't sure exactly how to label that emotion, but if the warmth spreading through her core was any indication, she was feeling something dangerously close to desire. When Noah leaned across the table to put his lips on hers, that warmth turned into a burning hot fire.

He tasted like the berries he'd been eating a few minutes before. His lips were sweet, and surprisingly soft. Izzy's mind screamed at her that she still didn't know Noah well, and that kissing him was a foolish idea. But her heart told her that this was right, and that there was something special about him. And, as Noah had already observed, Izzy was pretty good at following her heart.

Her heart felt pretty disappointed when Noah pulled abruptly away from the kiss and started cleaning up the remnants of their dinner. Still, Izzy couldn't help but smile when she licked her lips and tasted the sweet berry flavor that lingered there from Noah's lips. She had a feeling that the fire between them had only just begun to burn. More heat was in her future.

CHAPTER SIX

Izzy awoke the next morning to bright sunlight and the sound of birds chirping in the trees. Beside her, Noah was still sleeping. They had shared a bed last night, but hadn't touched each other again after their post-dinner kiss. Noah had decided that guard shifts were unnecessary, but had insisted that they should sleep near each other in case of an attack. If they had to fight at a moment's notice, it was better for them to be together instead of in separate rooms, or, worse, separate cabins.

Izzy had been happy enough to agree to this sleeping arrangement, although she'd half-expected Noah to make some sort of move on her in the middle of the night. She didn't know whether to feel relieved or disappointed that he hadn't, and she didn't want to think too deeply about it. If she sat here any longer, staring at Noah's gorgeous face as he slept, she was going to give in to the temptation to make a move on him. With a barely perceptible sigh, she slipped quietly from the bed and crept out to the front room of the cabin.

She peered out the front window, scanning the landscape for any sign of enemies. Everything was still, however. The leaves on the trees occasionally rustled in the wind, but other than that, nothing moved. In the morning light, Izzy could see that the damage to the cabins was even worse than it had seemed last night. Most of the windows were shattered, and several cabins were missing doors. Here and there, the walls of the cabins themselves looked like someone had randomly taken an axe to them. Izzy shook her head in disgust. She'd been forced to work with several of Saul's soldiers up in Montana, and she knew all too well how they loved to destroy things just for the sake of destroying them. She couldn't understand how people could take pleasure in ruining perfectly good cabins, but then, there were quite a few things in this war that she didn't understand.

Satisfied that, at least for the moment, no enemies were around, Izzy turned to the kitchen to search for a way to make coffee. She found a coffeepot in the cabinet under the sink, and, after a bit more searching, she found a bag of coffee grounds. The grounds were likely a bit stale, but she couldn't exactly hop down to the local market and get more. This camp was in the middle of nowhere.

Tentatively, she reached to turn on the tap, and was relieved to see water coming out. At least the pipes had remained intact. She filled the coffeepot with water and grounds and pushed the brew button. The power was still working as well, at least in this cabin. Out here, the electricity came from the solar panels on the roofs of the cabins. Many of the cabins had suffered severe damage to their roofs, but this one seemed to have survived quite well.

Before the coffee had even finished brewing, Noah was sticking his head out of the bedroom. "Mmm, smells good," he said. "I could use some caffeine."

Izzy smiled. "Me too. I've just woken up and I already feel tired."

"Agreed. We have a long day ahead of us, though. We need to do one more check for enemies, go check the artifact vaults to make sure they haven't been disturbed, and then send a message to Falcon Cross if all is well."

Izzy nodded. "The sooner we get going, the better. Let's eat a quick breakfast and then head out."

After munching on the remaining cheese and crackers, and finishing the whole pot of coffee between the two of them, Izzy and Noah made their way out to inspect the Redwoods Base Camp. It didn't take long for them to determine that the place was completely deserted. Saul had only cared enough about the place to leave the monster behind to guard things, it seemed.

"Let's check the vaults," Noah said. "Either Saul raided them already and that's why he abandoned this post, or he wasn't able to find them and gave up. I'm really hoping for the latter option."

Izzy followed Noah without comment as he started walking into the woods. She knew from various mission briefings that there were five vaults near the Redwood Base Camp, all containing powerful artifacts that would assist in the war effort. The vaults were protected by state-of-the art fingerprint sensors, as well as protective magic spells. They were also supposedly quite hard to find if you didn't know what you were looking for.

Noah knew what he was looking for.

They spent the next several hours looking through vaults that contained hundreds, if not thousands, of old spears, jewels, swords, helmets, and armor. Everything glittered and shone when the vault doors were opened and the sunshine streamed in. Izzy could have stood and stared at the treasures for hours, but Noah wasn't wasting time on sightseeing. After the first three vaults, he was satisfied that Saul had not been able to find the old artifacts.

"Let's get back to the cabins and tell Falcon Cross to send over some wizards," he said, his voice laced with excitement. Izzy felt excited, too. Their mission had been a resounding success. Now if only the rest of the wizards could get here in time to arm themselves for the imminent battle with Saul.

Noah and Izzy didn't waste time walking back to camp. They flew, he in dragon form and she on her broomstick. Izzy felt free and happy as the wind whipped across her face. She admired Noah's dragon form as she flew behind him, forgetting for a few brief moments that there was a war going on, and just enjoying the open air and spectacular view. For as far as she could see, the earth was filled with gently sloping hills of redwoods, and the sky was blue and cloudless. Despite the circumstances, life felt pretty good in that moment.

All too soon the flight came to an end, and Noah shifted back into human form in front of the cabin where they'd stayed the night before. Izzy looked shyly away from his nakedness. She'd seen plenty of naked dragon shifters, since every time they shifted back into human form they had no clothes on. But somehow, looking at Noah now felt different. They'd kissed. They'd shared a life or death experience together. There was some sort of chemistry in the air between them. Izzy didn't dare to look at Noah's naked body. She felt she might explode with desire if she did. She knew it was ridiculous to be thinking about things like that right now, but she couldn't help herself. Noah had kindled a fire in her that refused to be quenched.

"You alright?" Noah asked, breaking into Izzy's confused thoughts. She looked up at him, startled, and nodded. Who knows what kind of crazy expression she'd had on her face, or how long she'd been standing there frowning like an idiot. Noah was fully dressed now, and was standing in the doorway of the cabin, his military-issued handheld computer in hand.

"I'm good," Izzy said. "Just, uh, a lot on my mind."

Noah stared at her in that way that was becoming so familiar—that way that made

Izzy feel like his intense green eyes were seeing straight into her soul. She wanted to look away, but she couldn't. He was holding her captive. Drawing her in. She took a deep, shuddering breath, and wished that she could think of something clever to say right then to break the moment. But she was at a loss for words, and Noah was the one to speak next.

"We're in agreement, then, that it's safe to send the transmission?" he asked, his voice suddenly businesslike.

Izzy nodded, grateful for the chance to focus on something other than her flip-flopping stomach. "Yes. There aren't any enemies here as far as I can see, and the vaults appear to be untouched. The protective spells on each of the vaults we checked were holding up well. I'd say we're ready to bring in the army."

Noah smiled. "Good. I'll send the transmission now."

He powered on the small tablet, and furrowed his brow as he swiped at the screen several times. A small series of beeps erupted from the tablet, and then all was silent. Noah powered off the device.

"Alright," he said. "That's done. Now we wait."

"Now we wait," Izzy agreed. "It'll take them a half day to get here, at least. Maybe more, depending on where they are right now."

Noah grinned. "Enough time for me to show you some of my favorite places around here. Come on."

Izzy was surprised at how boyish his face appeared. He looked so happy in that moment that it made her heart hurt. She knew he'd grown up here, and, for a brief moment, she imagined him as a young boy, running through the forests, climbing trees, and causing havoc with his clanmates. Then she let her mind run further, wondering what it would be like to have a young dragon shifter son of her own running through these woods. She coughed loudly, startled by the thought and worried that somehow Noah would guess what she was thinking. What the hell was wrong with her? She was here to work, and so far their mission had been wildly successful. She needed to keep focusing on the tasks at hand and not on Noah.

The only problem, of course, was that there wasn't exactly an urgent task at hand. Noah was right: the only thing to do at the moment was wait. And it was hard not to fantasize about a life with Noah when he was standing right in front of her, smiling from ear to ear with sunshine lighting up his hair and face. Izzy had all but forgotten how angrily he'd scowled at her just a day ago. He seemed to have forgotten his anger as well. Now, he held out his hand to her, a gorgeous gentleman wanting to take her on an adventure. Izzy reached out and grabbed his hand.

Soon, she forgot to feel guilty or guarded. She laughed along with Noah as they ran through the forest, which felt downright magical. He showed her the best spots to find banana slugs, and where the deer liked to hide. He took her to a giant, hollowed-out tree trunk that was big enough for ten grown man to stand inside. She looked up in awe at the trees that had been standing there for thousands of years, silently watching as countless generations of men came and went. And she squealed with laughter and ran away when he threatened to toss her into his favorite swimming hole, clothes and all. Much too soon, the shadows grew long, and Noah glanced up at the sky with a concerned expression.

"We should head back," he said. "I'm almost certain these woods are deserted right now, but on the off chance that they aren't..."

"It's better for us to be safely in a cabin than out in the open," Izzy said, finishing his thought for him.

He nodded, and they both reluctantly turned back toward the cabins. Izzy's disappointment was mollified somewhat by the fact that, as they fell into step next to each other, Noah once again reached over to grab her hand.

CHAPTER SEVEN

Noah laughed along with Izzy at whatever story she'd just told. He couldn't have told you the punch line of the joke if his life depended on it. She'd been saying something about the time a visiting wizard in her old village had mistaken her for an animal doctor instead of a human doctor. One thing had led to another and Izzy had apparently ended up agreeing to stitch up an old hound's foot.

Noah should have been paying better attention. He wanted to know everything that there possibly was to know about Izzy, and she was sitting here freely regaling him with tales from her various life adventures. But despite his curiosity, he found it hard to concentrate on the words coming out of her lips when what he really wanted to do was kiss those lips.

Noah was beginning to understand why his clanmates had been so willing to settle down with a lifemate. Izzy could have asked him for anything in that moment and he would have given it to her, including a promise to spend the rest of his life with her. She was a drug he couldn't resist. He had no idea how she'd gotten past his defenses, but she had. He knew it was too late to resist. He was already gone. There was no turning back for him. The only question now was how long to hold off before showing her how deep his feelings were.

If he said something right now, would she think he was crazy? *Was* he crazy? They hadn't spent much time together, and half of that time he'd been acting like a total jerk to her. He winced, thinking of how he'd called her a coward and told her she was unfit to be a soldier. He'd acted like an asshole, and he felt ashamed of himself. She was brave, deep down. And how could he blame her for not wanting to see Saul again? After being tortured by Saul and watching the evil dragon murder everyone she knew, one could hardly expect her to jump for joy at the prospect of facing off with the evil dragon.

"What's wrong?" Izzy asked.

Noah quickly smoothed out his features, realizing that he'd allowed his face to show his emotions a bit too clearly. He smiled at Izzy, trying to give off an air of nonchalance.

"Nothing. Just a bit tired I suppose."

Izzy glanced up at the clock on the wall, which had been stuck in the three o'clock position for who knew how long. But a clock wasn't needed to know that it was late. Outside the cabin, the sky was a deep, velvet black. Tonight, there were no clouds, and hundreds of glittering stars were sprinkled across that velvet, along with one very bright full moon. That moonlight was all that lit up the leftover bits of their dinner on the table, and yet everything was easy to see in the dazzling silver light.

"We should go to sleep," Izzy said, standing to start cleaning up the table. "With any luck, the Falcon Cross Wizards will arrive very early tomorrow morning."

Noah nodded his agreement and stood to help Izzy clean, although sleep was the furthest thing from his mind right now. He wasn't quite sure how he was going to manage to lie in bed next to Izzy tonight without kissing her. He considered sleeping on

771

the couch, but he felt that trying to do so after insisting on being in the same bed last night would be inescapably awkward. So it was that, fifteen minutes later, he was lying in bed next to Izzy, desperately trying to regulate his breathing and willing her to fall asleep quickly so he could stop worrying that he was going to end up with a ridiculously obvious erection.

The room felt like it was full of static electricity. Noah could practically hear the air crackling, and he found it impossible to believe that Izzy couldn't hear it, too. But when he chanced a look over at her, she seemed completely calm. She had her face turned slightly away from him so that she could look out the bedroom window. The window was facing directly toward the brilliant moon, and Noah allowed himself to admire for a moment how beautiful Izzy's face was in its silver light. He felt a stiffening between his legs and quickly looked away, trying to think of something, anything, that would slow the flow of blood to his rapidly hardening dick.

His efforts were futile, however. Izzy must have sensed that he was looking at her, because she turned then, and her honey brown eyes met his gaze. She smiled at him, and then glanced down at where his erection was poking up against the blanket, forming an unmistakable peak. There was no denying it. His body betrayed the hunger in his heart. He wanted Izzy with a desperation unlike anything he'd known before. He held his breath, waiting for her to react. Would she pull away from him? Act disgusted that he'd so far overstepped the bounds of their professional relationship? Kissing her had been risky enough, but letting himself lie in bed next to her fully aroused was a whole different level.

She didn't pull away. Far from it, in fact. Instead she slid her hands underneath the blanket, and reached across the bed to close one of her palms around his thick shaft. He closed his eyes and let out a small moan. Shivers ran up and down his spine, despite the warmth of the night and the blanket. He hated the fabric of his cotton pajama pants, which was the only thing separating the skin of her hand from the skin of his erection. She rubbed her thumb up and down, while the rest of her fingers kept a firm, steady grip. Every slight movement she made felt like it was leaving a trail of fire on his body. He felt himself trembling, something he'd never done at a woman's touch before. But he could already tell that Izzy wasn't just another woman. She was special. The real deal. His.

He couldn't keep himself from letting out a low, guttural growl. Feelings of possessiveness surged unexpectedly through his body. Izzy was his. He knew that as surely as he knew his own name. And he was going to show her tonight how desperately he wanted to take care of her, and how completely he would love her.

He should have been frightened by the word love. But somehow, when it popped into his head, it just felt right. He wouldn't say it aloud. Not yet. But he felt a peace, knowing deep down that he loved the woman lying next to him.

He also felt horrible for treating her the way that he had. He was usually an understanding man. He tried to give others grace and show them that he cared. But he had let himself get caught up in the stress and uncertainty of the war, and he had acted in ways that were not fitting for a noble dragon like himself. He couldn't take back all the cruel things he'd said to Izzy, but he could apologize. He could man up and let her know that, at the very least, he recognized that what he'd done was wrong.

Noah sat up on his elbow, turning toward Izzy. She let her hand slip away from his shaft, and looked up at him with wide, questioning eyes. The silver light of the moon outlined her hair, making her look truly magical. He supposed that was fitting for a beautiful wizard like her. Her face was flushed with the passion of the moment, and her lips parted in an invitation to kiss her. He would kiss her soon enough. He would be happy to spend all night kissing her. But first, he had to clear the air between them.

"Izzy," he said, his voice husky and catching with emotion. "I'm so sorry. I should never have said the things I said to you. You're no coward, and, for someone with hardly any formal training, you make a damn good soldier."

Izzy's face softened into a smile. "You already said you were sorry. You don't have to apologize again, Noah. All that's in the past now."

"But I do have to apologize," he insisted. "You've saved a lot of lives in this war. I had no right to criticize you just because you show your bravery in a different way than I do. Will you forgive me, Izzy? Will you give me a fresh chance to show you just how special I think you are?"

Izzy nodded, with moisture glistening in the corners of her eyes. "Of course," she said. "I've already forgiven you."

Noah bent his head to kiss her lips softly. Then he pulled back to look into her eyes, searching her face to see if there was anything there that would indicate that she was feeling something as strong as he was. He had never fallen like this before, and he felt his chest tightening up with anxiety, like he might die if she wasn't falling, too.

She met his eyes with an unflinching gaze of her own. "This is crazy," she whispered.

"I know," he said. He didn't have to say what he knew they both were thinking. Crazy or not, tonight they would give themselves to each other. Perhaps they were crazy, but at least they would be happy. And happiness had become so hard to find these days. The war had taken much of the zest out of life. Noah was about to put a little bit of it back.

He put his lips on hers again, this time with force and urgency. He slipped his tongue into her mouth as he slid toward her under the blanket. She was lightly dressed in cotton shorts and a simple white t-shirt, but even that was far too much clothing. He wasn't wearing a shirt, and he wanted to feel the bare skin of his chest against hers.

He told himself to be patient. He'd been waiting his whole life for this moment, it seemed. Surely, he could wait a few minutes more. He closed his eyes and let the sweetness of her kiss overwhelm him. Izzy seemed to melt into him, and he put his hands on the back of her head, running his fingers through her hair while his tongue danced with hers. Everything else faded away. There was only her, here in this moment.

When he couldn't stand it any longer, he reached to pull her shirt up and over her head. She wasn't wearing a bra, and he found himself with his mouth right in front of her bare nipple. He seized the opportunity to pull the hard nub into his mouth, chewing and sucking and relishing the taste of her. She arched her back, pressing her chest harder against his mouth. He welcomed the pressure, drinking her in. Between his legs, he was now stiff as a rod. His erection poked against the fabric of his pants, searching for a way out, and a way into her.

After several minutes of teasing Izzy's breasts, Noah pulled himself up and threw the blanket back, intending to pull off the rest of Izzy's clothes as well as his own. He quickly kicked out of his pants, and made quick work of pulling off Izzy's shorts and underwear. Finally, they were both naked. Noah felt jolts of electricity every time his skin brushed against Izzy's. He felt a deep, primal hunger overtaking him. His erection was throbbing now, and he knew he couldn't hold back much longer. He pushed Izzy onto her back, and moved to hover over her.

Then, he stopped short at what he saw, feeling as though he'd been punched in the gut. He looked down at Izzy, and felt as though his heart might break for her. There, cutting across her perfect stomach, were at least a dozen long silvery-white scars. The lines were long, stretching completely from ribcage to hip and back again. The lines made Xs and other tangled marks, like pathways to nowhere. Noah felt anger burning in his heart as the full realization of what he was seeing hit him. Izzy must have mistaken his expression as some sort of judgment on the way she looked, because her cheeks flushed red and she reached to pull the blanket over her stomach.

"I know it looks awful," she said, her voice thick with tears. "I don't think I'll ever wear a bikini again."

With strong, forceful hands, Noah pulled the blanket away. "It doesn't look awful," he said, in a tone that said he would not let her argue. "You. are. perfect."

He emphasized each word, looking deep into her eyes so that she would know that he damn well meant what he was saying. The tears that had been threatening her eyes did spill over then, leaving two wet trails down the sides of her face before disappearing into her hair. She took a deep breath, and shuddered. He could tell she was fighting hard to regain control of her emotions—and losing.

"Listen to me, Izzy. You are so brave. I never should have told you otherwise. And that bastard Saul might have been able to torture you and scar your body, but he can never take away from you the fact that you've fought for the side of good, and saved lives. You're beautiful, and perfect. I mean that. And I swear to you, if it's the last thing I do, I will kill Saul for how he hurt you. Not just for the physical scars, but for the emotional ones, too. As long as there is breath left in my body, I will fight to avenge you, and to protect you."

Noah could feel himself shaking with rage. He couldn't believe that anyone could have hurt Izzy like this. She deserved so much better. He'd had a bit of a rough start in his relationship with her, but he determined in that moment that, if she would let him, he would spend the rest of his life showing her how well she deserved to be treated.

Tenderly, he bent his head down to kiss her scars. He covered each scar with a trail of kisses, pressing on even when he felt her body shaking with tears.

"It's alright, Baby," he said. "You're safe with me. I'll take care of you. You're beautiful, and perfect, and I'll never let anyone treat you as less than the princess you are."

Noah had never called anyone Baby before, let alone princess. But he'd also never felt desire this strong. He gave in fully to the emotion. Why would he have wanted to fight this feeling, anyway? It was the most wonderful, intoxicating feeling he'd ever had. He had a sneaking suspicion that it was, indeed, love.

"I feel so small," Izzy choked out, her voice hardly more than a whisper. "I used to feel like I was an expert at what I did, and in control of my life. Now, I feel lost, and like I don't fit anywhere. Falcon Cross has never felt like home, and, as hard as I try, it's true that I'm not a very good soldier. I want you so badly, Noah, but I'm terrified that you're going to realize that I'm not good enough for you."

Noah slid up so that his face was right above Izzy's. "You're too good for me. And it isn't true that you don't fit anywhere. You fit with me. You're braver than you know. You're better than anyone has given you credit for being. Even I judged you too harshly, but I won't make that mistake again. If you want a home, then stay with me. I'll be your home. Your anchor. Your safe space."

Noah could hardly believe the words that were coming out of his mouth. He'd never been good at the whole romance thing, so it surprised him that such sweet, romantic words came so easily when he was talking to Izzy. Maybe he'd just never found the right person before. Now that he had, it was easy to give her his whole heart. He wasn't trying to come up with something swoon-worthy to say. He was merely giving voice to the deep emotions that filled him. He'd never thought of romance as a very manly thing, but he was surprised to find that he'd never felt like more of a man than he did in that moment. He figured that he might as well keep talking, as long as his heart was still giving him the right words to say.

"Izzy," he whispered to her, his whole body tense as it hovered right above hers. "I want to make love to you."

He watched her eyes as they found his once again. And then, she smiled, and he knew that she wanted him as badly as he wanted her. Without another word between them, he slid into her.

He groaned as her warm wetness enveloped him. Her inner walls were tight on his erection, and he loved how wet she was for him. Her heat felt like heaven on his dick, and he felt the pressure between his legs instantly ratcheting up to a nearly unbearable level. He forced himself to hold back, though. He must be patient, and pleasure her first. Although, damn, was it going to be hard to do that. He felt like he would explode if he moved even one centimeter against her perfect heat.

Before he could overthink things too much, instinct took over. He thrust himself deeper into her, squeezing his eyes closed in concentration to keep the fire within him from bursting forth. He rocked his hips against hers, thrusting in and out and listening to the sweet, sweet sounds of her moans as he brought her to the very edge of ecstasy. Her breathing grew rapid and labored as he continued to push deeper and deeper into her. His whole body burned and tingled with the effort of holding back his own release, but he refused to give in until he knew she was coming with him.

She didn't make him wait long. After less than a minute of that delicious, tortuous pressure, she suddenly gasped and cried out his name. In the next instant, he felt her inner muscles clamping down hard around him. After that he could not have held back even if he'd wanted to. Her spasms drew him in, causing his own body to give in, pulsing and spasming into her. Fire rushed through his veins, starting from his extremities and running like hot lava through his bloodstream. The heat centered between his legs and came bursting out of him as he came into her, giving himself fully over to her.

The room was still only lit by the silvery moonlight, and yet everything appeared to Noah like it was drenched in full color. The air around him sparked, and he trembled as he finally collapsed against Izzy's body. The sweat that glistened on both of their bodies intermingled, and he could feel her pounding heart beating against his chest in the same way that his heart beat against hers. Noah had been through a lot of highs and lows in his life, and had felt plenty of adrenaline rushes before. But he had never felt quite this alive. He pulled his head up to look at her, brushing back a strand of hair that was plastered across her sweaty forehead.

"This is crazy," he whispered, unable to find any other words to describe how he felt.

"It is," she whispered back. "The best kind of crazy."

Noah wasn't going to argue with that.

CHAPTER EIGHT

The next time Noah opened his eyes, the dark, black velvet of the night sky had given way to the soft gray of dawn. The first thought that crossed his mind was *Izzy*. He looked over at her and smiled. She slept peacefully, on her stomach with one arm draping off the side of the bed. Slowly, Noah sat up, peering out the window at the deep green of the treetops, thinking how beautiful the color looked against the early morning sky.

And then, his eyes widened and he bolted out of bed.

"Izzy!" he yelped, already reaching to pull on his pants from the day before, which he'd carelessly thrown onto the floor. "They're here."

Izzy groaned and rolled over, clearly unhappy at the idea of leaving sleep behind. Noah went over and shook her by the shoulders.

"Wake up, Izzy! The wizards are here."

This time, his words seemed to register with Izzy. She sat straight up and swung her head to look out the window. Noah looked out as well. In the distance, hundreds of black dots were approaching through the sky. The wizards were flying at top speed, not bothering with invisibility shields. He knew they were from Falcon Cross because, even from this distance, he could see the giant Falcon Cross military banner they were carrying, rippling behind one of the wizards on the front lines.

"Shit," Izzy said. "I need to get dressed." She bounded out of bed, completely naked, and started scrambling around the room looking for her clothes. Her bare breasts bounced invitingly against her chest as she moved, and Noah had to look away. As much as he would have loved to throw her back down on the bed and do a repeat performance of their romp from last night, he would have to wait. The Falcon Cross Wizards would be here in mere minutes, at the speed they were traveling. They would want to arm themselves with the artifacts and start heading for the battle with Saul.

Noah felt a shiver of adrenaline run down his spine as he pulled on his shirt. Depending on how far away Saul's army was from here, the final showdown with Saul might take place today, even. After spending so much time searching for dragon stones and trying to thwart Saul's plans, it felt strange to realize that today might bring an end to this war, one way or another.

Noah looked over at Izzy, who was now dressed in her Falcon Cross uniform and was pulling her hair into a tight bun. He felt his heart tighten with fear, a strange emotion for a dragon like himself, and certainly not a feeling he would have wanted to admit he had. After all, he'd given Izzy such a great deal of grief over how afraid she'd been of meeting Saul. But this was different. His fear wasn't for his own life, but for Izzy's. He'd only just discovered that he loved her. He couldn't bear the thought of losing her, but he knew there wasn't much he could do to protect her in the battle that was coming. Things would be chaotic, and life-or-death situations were sure to be the norm. Noah clenched his fists. He realized, with searing clarity, that his life would not be worth living without her in it.

He crossed the room slowly, and pulled her into his arms from behind. With her back pressed against his chest, he buried his nose into the top of her hair, slightly messing up the bun she'd so carefully made.

"Noah!" she said in protest. But she didn't pull away from him, and he tightened his hold on her. His arms fit perfectly around her, and, for just a moment, he closed his eyes and tried to memorize the way she felt.

"Noah," she said after a few more seconds, trying to wriggle free. "We need to get out there. The wizards will be here in minutes."

"What's the matter?" Noah teased. "Are you embarrassed to be caught with me like this?"

Izzy let out a longsuffering sigh. "No. If anything, I'm proud to be seen with you. Quite honestly, I'd like to shout from the rooftops that I've found a man like you. But there's a war going on, in case you've forgotten. And we need to get weapons in these wizards' hands as soon as possible."

"I know. But before we go out there, I need to tell you something."

Izzy didn't reply, but Noah could feel her breathing accelerate. He took a deep breath himself and then plunged forward with the words he was burning to say. He knew it was a risk to try to explain his feelings to Izzy right now, with only minutes to spare before they would be surrounded by hundreds of other people. He wasn't sure how she'd react, and he worried that she would think he was crazy for saying what he was about to say when they'd only just discovered their passion for each other. But he knew that there were no guarantees beyond this moment. It might very well be now or never. Noah held Izzy tighter, and whispered into her ear.

"I love you, Izzy."

One small, almost imperceptible tremor passed through her body. Noah wasn't sure if that was a good or bad sign, but he had no choice but to keep plunging forward.

"I've watched all my clanmates find love, and, quite frankly, I thought they were crazy. I didn't understand how they could get distracted by a woman in the midst of the war. Now I understand, because you're not just any woman, Izzy. You're my lifemate."

"Lifemate?"

"It's something we shifters believe in. Sort of like a soulmate, but deeper than that. Every shifter has a lifemate out there—someone they're destined to be with. From the moment we're born, fate works to bring that person across our path."

"And…you think I'm that person for you?"

"I know it, Izzy. When you make love with your lifemate, a lifemate bond is formed. I felt that bond last night. I felt a burning in my core, a warmth that told me that I was home. That I'd finally found you, my lifemate."

Izzy sucked in her breath and turned around to face Noah. "I…I felt a warmth, too. It was so strange, unlike anything I've felt before. Is that the lifemate bond?"

Noah hadn't even realized he'd been holding his breath, but now he exhaled. His heart began pounding with excitement. Izzy was confirming for him that they were meant to be together, and that made him slightly dizzy from happiness. His heart warmed as he looked deep into her eyes. "Yes. That's the lifemate bond. It's unbreakable. At least, for shifters it is. You'll have to make your own decisions about what you want, Izzy, but for me, there will never be anyone other than you now. I will spend the rest of my life, however long that might be, protecting you and loving you. I need you to know that before all the other wizards get here and we head off to fight for the dragon ruby. I don't know if we'll make it through the battle alive. God, I hope we do. I hope we have decades ahead of us, for me to love you and treasure you and spoil you. But just in case this is the end, I had to tell you how I felt. I had to say I love you. I know it's sudden, and a complete change from the things I was saying when we first left

Falcon Cross yesterday. But it's true. I love you. With everything in me, I love you."

Izzy's eyes misted. "I love you, too. I can hardly believe I'm saying that. I thought I hated you at first—"

"I probably deserved to be hated."

Izzy grinned. "No comment on that. All I'll say is I've seen past your rough exterior, and to your heart. To who you really are. And I love who you are. I love you. You make me a better person. A braver person. I hope with everything in me that we make it through this battle and this war, because I want to spend the rest of my life showing you how much I care for you."

Noah bent his head to kiss away her tears, and then kissed her lips. "If I do have to die today, at least I'll die a happy man."

"Don't say things like that," Izzy said, her voice catching in her throat.

Noah sighed. "There are no guarantees. You know that. But I'm going to do the best I can to make it through this. For you. For us."

"For us," Izzy repeated. Noah kissed her again, and then, through the window, he saw the first of the Falcon Cross Wizards landing in the clearing outside. His moment alone with Izzy was over. It was time to equip the soldiers for war.

Noah reluctantly pulled away from Izzy, and turned to leave the window. Izzy followed him without a word, and together they went outside. They stood tall and proud, watching the wizards fly in.

The Falcon Cross army had grown over the last several months. The incoming soldiers only accounted for about half of the army's total numbers, and yet, there were still enough soldiers here to make an impressive showing. They flew in to land without slowing down, the gold threads in their black uniforms glittering in the slowly rising morning sun. Noah felt a rush of pride in his chest. He was part of this. He had helped build and train this army. The wizard-dragon shifter alliance had been a good one, and he still had hope that this alliance would be enough to defeat Saul. As the wizards continued to fly in on their sleek, military broomsticks, Noah suddenly saw a familiar face.

"Raven!" he said, waving her over. Izzy whipped her head around at the sound of Raven's name, then went running toward the wizard commander. Raven was one of the top military officers in the Falcon Cross army, and was also the lifemate of Noah's clanmate, Owen. Noah was happy to see a familiar face in the sea of soldiers, and he hoped that Raven had some good news about the battle against Saul. As Raven approached, though, her face looked grim. She embraced both Noah and Izzy warmly, but her voice was strained when she spoke.

"I can't tell you how glad we were to get your message yesterday. Things aren't looking good for us at the moment. The army with the dragon stones is barely ahead of Saul's army. At this point, it looks like Saul will overtake them tonight. And his army is strong. Our scouts have brought back word that hundreds of dark wizards are flying with shifters behind them on their broomsticks. Saul has been demonstrating the ruby's power just for fun, it seems, and every time he does his army cheers and gets more riled up."

"And?" Noah asked. Raven knew right away what he meant by the question.

"And, the rumors about the ruby appear to be true. It holds an incredible amount of power, more than the other dragon stones combined. If we manage to win this war, it will be thanks to the artifacts from the redwood dragon vaults. Your insistence on recovering this base camp might just save us."

Ordinarily, Noah would have felt a puff of pride at knowing that his work might be the determining factor in a victory. Now, though, he felt sick to his stomach. The war was coming to a head, and success was far from guaranteed for the side of good. There was nothing left to do, though, except keep moving forward. Noah watched as the last of the wizards landed. They didn't all fit into the clearing, and scores of wizards had moved back into the forest so that there was enough room for everyone to land.

"Was this place unguarded, then?" Raven asked. Noah glanced over at her, but she was also looking out at the army and didn't meet his eyes.

"It was guarded," Izzy said before he could speak. "By a monster created from a *Monstrum* spell."

Raven turned with wide eyes. "You're kidding me."

"No," Izzy said shaking her head. "I wish I was. I just hope there aren't any more of those monsters with Saul now."

Raven sighed. "There's only one way to find out. Let's get this army loaded up with artifacts and get going. If we hurry, we can reach the rest of our army just before Saul gets to them. They're going to need our help."

Noah took charge then. He felt adrenaline pumping through his veins as he began yelling out orders. Izzy stepped up to help as well, and they began quickly organizing the soldiers into groups. For the next several hours, Noah led the groups to the different vaults, arming them with the powerful ancient artifacts hidden away in the vaults. Wizard soldiers donned jewels, swords, helmets, and other armor that hadn't seen the light of day in decades. Noah stole glances at Izzy every chance he got, admiring the way her cheeks glowed from the exertion of organizing and arming such a large group. He wished he could take her back to the cabin where they'd been last night, and shut out the rest of the world. He wished he could kiss her and make love to her like there was no tomorrow.

Because, he realized as the last of the wizard soldiers was armed, there might not be a tomorrow.

CHAPTER NINE

Wind and rain whipped at Izzy's face as she flew, but she would not allow herself to slow down. If there was a weak link in this army today, it would not be her. Izzy bent low against her broomstick and kept her squinted eyes trained on Noah's dragon form, which sliced through the air in front of her. In front of him, Raven flew, leading the way to where Saul's army would be overtaking the rest of the Falcon Cross army. The hundreds of Falcon Cross soldiers that were now armed with ancient artifacts leaned in on their broomsticks, flying behind and around Izzy. The group was strong, and well-armed: three of the five Redwood Dragons' vaults had been completely emptied, and the treasures that had been hidden within were now worn by the Falcon Cross Wizards. Even still, would this group be strong enough? Would their strength, joined with the rest of the Falcon Cross army and Redwood Dragons, be enough to push back Saul?

Izzy did her best to squelch the sick feeling she got in her stomach every time she thought of Saul. Despite Noah's apologies for all of the cruel things he'd said, she knew there was truth to at least one aspect of his words. She was a coward. Perhaps not a total coward. After all, she'd stepped up in battles before, and she had managed to save Noah's life when the monster attacked him in the redwoods. But that didn't change the fact that thinking about Saul made her feel like she was going to hurl. She knew the odds of her coming face to face with him in battle weren't too high, but that didn't matter. Just the fact that there was a slight chance she'd see that evil dragon's face again filled her with fear.

The rain wasn't helping her mood. It had been sunny in the redwoods, but as Izzy and the rest of the army started flying northeast, clouds began to gather. By the time darkness fell, those clouds had started to spew rain in sheets. Izzy had never flown through rain quite so thick, and she couldn't shake the feeling that the weather was some sort of ominous, foreboding sign. It was looking like the battle of the century was going to take place at the same time as the storm of the century. Izzy tried her best to make her mind go blank, to only focus on flying and not on the destruction she knew waited ahead of her. But it was impossible to completely block out the terror slowly rising in her chest.

She saw the flashes of light well before she heard any of the battle noise. At first, she thought she was seeing lightning, but after a few seconds, she realized she was seeing the bursts of light that always accompanied wizard attacks. Mixed in with these flashes were frequent red-orange streaks, indicating that one of the dragons was breathing out fire. Izzy swallowed hard. The battle was in full swing.

Izzy knew that Raven and Noah would have seen the fight up ahead, but neither one of them slowed, sped up, or given any other indication that anything had changed. They continued flying at a steady, rapid pace, heading right for the heart of the storm. Izzy wished she could talk to Noah somehow. She wished they could slow their flight for long enough for her to grab his dragon face in her hands and tell him that she loved him. But the time for declarations of love was past. Noah and Izzy had both spoken their feelings to each other. He knew how she felt, and telling him one more time would not make any difference. Izzy needed to stop focusing on what she could not do and could not have. She needed to save her mental strength for the battle ahead.

The closer they flew, the clearer Izzy could see the scene in front of her. Wizards swooped through the air in a hundred different directions at once, constantly shooting attacks from their magic rings. Dragons flew back and forth spewing fire from their mouths, and, although Izzy couldn't tell which Redwoods Dragon was which while they were in dragon form, she was relieved at least to see that all of the dragons in her view were from the Redwoods clan. She knew Saul was out here somewhere on this dark battlefield, but the longer she could go without seeing him, the better. As long as she didn't have to look at him, she could manage not to panic.

By now, Izzy could also hear the noise of the battle. Roars of anger filled the air, mixing with awful shrieks of panic. Soldiers yelled, but the words they spoke were unintelligible. There was too much noise, too much chaos, for Izzy to be able to understand what words they were actually speaking. She did her best to block out the cacophony, and to focus only on staying as close to Noah as she could. As they neared the outer edges of the fighting, Noah finally slowed just enough to turn and look back at her. She raised her hand in a small wave, acknowledging that she was still there. She was still flying, and still acting brave. A flash of lighting streaked across the sky just then, and by its light Izzy could see Noah's dragon lips turning upward in a smile. If she had known what would happen next, she would have tried a little harder to savor that smile.

But she hadn't known, and nothing could have prepared her for it. One moment she was flying steadily, with one hand on her broomstick and one hand raised to wave at Noah and his smiling face, and the next, she was inexplicably hurtling through the air, colliding with soldier after soldier from the force of what felt like a giant wall of wind.

Somehow, in the midst of all of this, Izzy managed to hold onto her broomstick. It must have been sheer instinct that caused her to automatically tighten the grip her one hand had on the handle the moment she felt herself losing her balance. She had never been a strong fighter, but her flying skills had always been exceptional. She was thankful for that, at least. After several seconds of tumbling through the air, she managed to right herself on her broomstick. Taking a wild look around, she saw that many of her fellow soldiers had not had reflexes as quick as hers. Below her, screaming in terror, many of them were falling to certain death, having lost hold of their broomsticks completely. Izzy's eyes widened, and she did the only thing she could think of. She began flying downward like a madwoman.

She pointed her magic ring at wizard after wizard, shouting out, *"Magicae suspendo!"* over and over. The suspension spell stopped the falling wizards in midair, although it did leave them rather helpless and stuck. A few of them with better presence of mind started casting magnet spells to draw their broomsticks back toward themselves. Luckily, as soon as the stunned wizards saw their fellow soldiers doing this, they followed suit. Izzy saw many of the wizards grabbing hold of broomsticks once again, but she didn't cancel the suspension spells. Not yet. She was too busy still zooming downward, trying to stop the descent of as many falling wizards as possible. A few of the other Falcon Cross soldiers who had managed to stay on their broomsticks caught on to what she was doing, and started casting suspension spells with her. Together, they managed to save hundreds of lives. Izzy didn't allow herself to think about the ones they hadn't managed to save. If she started grieving over every soldier they lost, she would never make it through this night.

When it was clear that she'd saved all the wizards she possibly could, and that every suspended wizard had recovered his or her broomstick, Izzy shouted out *"Suspendo*

781

terminantur." Instantly, all of the spells she'd cast to suspend the wizards ended. The wizards started falling again, but, this time, they had their broomsticks. They were able to quickly recast their flying spells and head back into the battle. Izzy took a precious moment to pause and just breathe, trying to regain her senses after the sudden chaos of the last few minutes. Before she started moving forward again, she saw Raven zooming toward her through the rain.

"Thank god you're alright," Raven said as she approached Izzy. Her voice was raised so that Izzy could hear it over the fierce storm.

"Same to you," Izzy said as she tried to wipe the blurring rainwater from her eyes. It was useless, of course. The rain was coming down so heavily that it was impossible to keep it away. She strained through the darkness to try to see Noah, looking for the unique pattern of spikes on his dragon tail. But she couldn't see any outlines of dragons anywhere near her. She felt herself starting to panic, and Raven must have noticed and guessed that Izzy's concern was due to Noah. Even though Noah and Izzy hadn't said anything about being lifemates, their newfound affection for each other must have been obvious.

"Noah's fine," Raven said. "At least, he was fine when I flew away from him three minutes ago. He's heading toward the front lines with the rest of the dragons. They're going to try to make a fire wall of sorts to hold back the dark wizards."

Izzy simultaneously felt relieved and panicked. She was happy to hear that Noah had survived the blast, but she didn't like the idea of his being on the front lines. She had no choice but to swallow back her fears, however. No matter how scared she was for Noah's life, she knew he had a job to do. And Noah would never shy away from battle. Dragon blood ran through his veins, and dragon blood amounted to no less than liquid bravery. Noah and the other Redwood Dragons did not have even the tiniest shred of cowardice in their bodies. Izzy took another deep, steadying breath and looked around for a moment before turning back to Raven. She and Raven were nearly at the back of the Falcon Cross army by this point. The last of the wizards were rushing by them, heading towards the heart of the battle up ahead. Izzy could see bursts of light from wizard rings, the occasional rush of fire, and the constant flashing of lightning. Everything looked like a normal enough battle, but Izzy had an even greater feeling of uneasiness than normal.

"What was that burst of power that knocked us all off our broomsticks?" Izzy asked.

"A warning shot," Raven said grimly. When Izzy gave her a confused look, Raven explained further.

"It was a blast of power from the dragon ruby," Raven said. "Saul was showing off just a tiny bit of what the dragon ruby is capable of. He wants us to know that he has unbelievable strength due to the ruby. If he uses its full force, it's going to be much worse than that. The good news is that our soldiers who are holding the other dragon stones are now on high alert. They didn't expect Saul to use the ruby so quickly, so they weren't fully prepared to counteract its effects, but now they know that all bets are off. They'll fight back with the other dragon stones if necessary. I just hope that the other stones, and the artifacts, are enough."

Izzy nodded, feeling a fresh tingle of fear. So the use of the dragon stones had already begun. This battle wasn't going to be pretty, that was certain. But there was nothing left to do except fight. Raven knew this, too, and was already turning her broomstick to head back toward the front lines.

"I'm glad you're okay, Izzy. Don't feel badly about hanging back a little alright? You've got nothing to prove out here. We all know you're a good soldier, and I have a feeling we're going to need your medical expertise much more than your fighting skills before all of this is over."

Before Izzy could reply, Raven was zooming off. For a few moments, Izzy hovered alone in the dark, rainy sky. The last of the soldiers had passed her by now, and she felt horribly alone. Part of her would have loved to do as Raven said and hang back. But another part of her knew she could never live with herself if she did that. She at least needed to catch up with the stragglers, and fight toward the back of the battle lines. She might not be the bravest soldier out here, but she wasn't a total coward. Besides, she was possessed by an overwhelming urge to be near Noah and see that he was alright. She realized this was a bit absurd. After all, if he was in trouble, she was the least likely person to be able to help him. But she wanted to be closer to him nonetheless. Gritting her teeth, she turned her broomstick and started flying toward the battle.

No sooner had she reached the outer edges of the fight than she felt another boom of power. Saul was using the dragon ruby again, and the force of it felt even stronger this time. But the wizards were better prepared. Everyone had been keeping a tight grip on their broomsticks, and, as far as Izzy could tell, no one near her had gone flying toward the ground. The boom of power was followed almost immediately by an answering boom, presumably from the dragon stones that the Falcon Cross army held. The night sky lit up with a new kind of light—a strange explosion of green, blue, purple and red light. Izzy had never seen the dragon stones in action before, but she knew without a doubt that what she was seeing was the dragon stones' power. Roars of pain sounded out across the dark lines of the armies, but Izzy couldn't tell whether the sounds were coming from friends or enemies.

In the next few minutes, the noise grew even worse. Blast after blast of power shot forth from the dragon stones, each one more powerful than the one before. Saul seemed to increasing the strength of his attack with each blow, and the Falcon Cross army did their best to follow suit. The booms from the dragon stone were joined by the buzz of power from the ancient artifacts many of the Falcon Cross soldiers were wearing. The artifacts now seemed to come alive with energy, and Izzy could vaguely tell that the tides of battle were turning ever so slightly in their favor.

Saul must have felt this shift as well, because he increased the use of the dragon ruby. Izzy found herself in the midst of constant blasts of powerful energy. She forced herself to focus her mind on the task at hand, instead of on the fear building in her core. She set her lips in a hard line and leaned into her broomstick, flying forward toward the front lines. She might not be the bravest soldier out here, but, damn it, if she died today she would die fighting as close to the front lines as she could get. Somehow, she felt that she was proving herself to Noah by making this decision, even though he had no way of knowing about her sudden display of courage. He was occupied somewhere ahead of her, doing his best to hold back the dark wizards. At least, Izzy *hoped* he was still ahead of her. The further she went, the more the fighting intensified, and she couldn't help but think that even a dragon would have difficulty dodging the attacks that seemed to come from every direction.

No longer was Izzy surrounded completely by Falcon Cross soldiers. Here, in the thick of things, she was surrounded by a constant stream of dark wizards as well. They launched dark magic attacks, while the shifters riding on the backs of their broomsticks lashed out with claws, swords, and other various razor-sharp weapons. Izzy moved on autopilot, slashing her magic ring through the air in large arcs, and shouting out different shield and attack spells. Her real saving grace, however, was her ability to outfly everyone else. She swooped up and down, and zigzagged left and right, avoiding attacks by her sheer speed.

She wasn't sure how long things went on this way. It felt like hours, but she didn't trust her sense of time to be accurate right now. She kept flying, dodging and attacking in turn, and holding onto her broomstick tightly to ward off the jolts from the constant rushes of power caused by the dragon ruby.

Izzy still hadn't seen Noah. In fact, she hadn't seen Raven, or any other familiar faces, since she'd started flying toward the front lines. Izzy tried her best not to think about what that might mean. She told herself that the armies were too big for her to be able to keep track of people she knew, and she kept fighting. She felt like she was in some sort of strange dream. She could feel herself moving, and she could hear the battle noise surrounding her, but she felt strangely removed from it. Her mind felt like it was shutting down, refusing to believe that she was actually here in the middle of such an intense fight.

And then, miraculously, Izzy started to notice fewer and fewer dark wizards. Even though she was still flying toward the front lines, the mass of soldiers seemed to be growing thinner rather than thicker. She realized that the soldiers around her were mostly Falcon Cross soldiers, and the attacks against her were lessening. Her heart leapt with hope, even as another blast of destructive power from the dragon ruby tried to knock her off her broomstick. The other Falcon Cross soldiers around her seemed to have notice the change, as well. One of them even let out an excited whoop.

Izzy's breath caught in her throat. Was it possible they were going to win this war after all? She'd been too worried to be optimistic about the future, but now, she allowed thoughts of a peaceful life, of lazy days with Noah, to fill her mind. She couldn't help but smile, and that smile only widened when she saw Raven zooming toward her, looking triumphant.

"We're doing it!" Raven shouted, not addressing anyone in particular. Her words were intended to buoy the spirits of any Falcon Cross soldier within earshot. "We're driving them back, slowly but surely. The dragon ruby is powerful, and Saul is still fighting with all his might, but he's falling short. With the other three dragon stones, and all the Redwood Dragons' artifacts on our side, we're managing to push them back."

Excited whoops broke out from the Falcon Cross soldiers, but Izzy didn't pause to join in. Instead, she started flying forward, as quickly as she could, to the front lines, where she knew Noah would be. She only wanted to see him, and know that he was alright. She knew the fight wasn't over yet, but it was getting close, and she wanted to celebrate their victory with him by her side. This moment had been so long in coming. She wanted to enjoy it to the fullest.

As she flew closer to the front lines, the blasts from the dragon ruby began to feel stronger. She wasn't sure whether this was due to her being closer to their source, or whether Saul was, in desperation, pushing the ruby to the absolute limits of its power. Whatever the case, the Falcon Cross army was continuing to push back the forces of darkness. The soldiers in charge of the dragon emerald, dragon sapphire, and dragon amethyst were responding with all-out attacks of their own, and the rest of the Falcon Cross army was gathering strength from the realization that they were winning. The air crackled with excitement as Izzy flew, and she felt her own excitement rising as she drew nearer to where she hoped to find Noah.

She could see blasts of fire now, and she followed them. Those flames would lead her to the dragon shifters, and to Noah. She admired the reddish-orange glow of fire that lit up the sky so fully. The dragons were fighting harder than ever, and she felt a puff of pride in her chest knowing that one of those dragons was hers. Soon she would be with him. As she drew closer, shooting down the occasional dark wizard who came at her, Izzy finally caught sight of Noah. A deep smile crossed her face as she locked her eyes on his form.

"I'm coming," she whispered under her breath. "I'm coming to fight by your side." She was so excited in that moment, that she even forgot about her fear of Saul. But it only took one glimpse of the evil dragon to remind her.

He appeared seemingly out of nowhere. His dark, spiked dragon form glowed a sickening red, even in the pouring rain. When lightning lit up the sky, Izzy could see that Saul held his magic wand in one dragon foot, and the dragon ruby in the other dragon foot. A thousand horrible memories came rushing back to Izzy's head as Saul's glowing red eyes turned toward her. She pulled up short on her broomstick, all of her courage draining away in an instant. But Saul wasn't looking at her directly. He was looking past her, at the vast Falcon Cross army behind her. His own army had dwindled, but he refused to give up. Izzy watched in horror as he raised the ruby high, and then brought it down with a mighty roar.

It was the heaviest blow yet. Izzy managed to hold on to her broomstick, but she was pushed backward several dozen feet by the force. Little shockwaves of pain echoed through her body, and she yelped in anguish before she could stop herself. All around her, she heard similar cries of pain.

But then, the answering blow came from the Falcon Cross army. Flashes of green, blue, and purple light echoed across the sky, and seemed to all hit Saul at once. The evil dragon roared in pain, and was himself pushed backward. He started to fall, and Izzy felt her hope returning once again. It looked like he was going down, possibly for good. The rest of the soldiers on the field, both good and bad, seemed to feel the same, because there were yells of joy and terror. One army was watching its leader go down while the other army was watching their evil nemesis suffer his last blow—or so they thought.

Izzy started moving forward toward Noah again. He turned to face her, and a smile of recognition curled up his dragon lips when he saw her. She smiled back, but then, as she flew toward him, she saw his smile turn to a gasp of pain. Izzy's own mouth dropped in horror.

Saul, on his way down, had somehow used his tail to reach up and pull down the first soldier he could catch. And Noah's dragon just so happened to be in the perfect spot for Saul to grab. Izzy screamed as she saw Saul falling away, with Noah struggling but unable to escape as the dragon ruby glowed red. Izzy dimly realized that Saul was somehow using the dragon ruby to keep a firm hold on Noah. Saul's face was twisted in an awful, evil expression, and he laughed with a chilling, haunting sound as he and Noah both fell toward the earth.

"No!" Izzy screamed. Without stopping to remember that she was more afraid of Saul than anything else in the world, Izzy pointed her broomstick downward to rush after Noah. But when she tried to fly, she couldn't move forward. She screamed again, and struggled to fly, but she was stuck. Helpless, she watched as Noah's dragon fell further and further away from her, and Saul's taunting laughs grew more and more distant.

CHAPTER TEN

"Izzy, stop! You have to calm down!"

Izzy stopped struggling for one brief second to glare at Peter, and then continued to struggle. It was useless to try to break the *Stabit* spell Peter had cast on her, and she knew it. But she couldn't force herself to calm down. Not when the love her life was in the hands of that awful wretch.

"Izzy," another voice said. Izzy turned to see Mac, the head commander of the Falcon Cross military, hovering near her on a broomstick. Mac's voice was gentler than Peter's, and even sounded a bit choked up.

"We have to save him!" Izzy yelled, this time in Mac's direction.

All around Izzy, Falcon Cross soldiers were cheering. The enemy soldiers had fled once they saw their leader fall. Dark wizards flew away as quickly as their broomsticks would carry them, while terrified evil shifters roared behind them. Some of the Falcon Cross soldiers had given chase to the fleeing soldiers, but just as many were now flying in circles through the still-pouring rain, drunk on the knowledge that, at long last, Saul himself had been defeated.

"Izzy! Izzy, listen to me!"

Izzy turned her head sharply, surprised to hear Grayson's voice. Grayson was one of the Redwood Dragons, but he had been in dragon form only minutes before. None of the Redwood Dragons could talk while in dragon form—talking while in animal form required dark magic, and the Redwood Dragons stayed far, far away from that. But Grayson had shifted back into human form, and was riding on the back of his lifemate Zoe's broomstick. The realization that not even the dragons themselves were going after their clanmate filled Izzy with terror. The dragons would give their lives to save Noah if they thought there was even a one percent chance of helping him. If they were not pursuing him, that meant things really were hopeless. Izzy stopped fighting against the *Stabit* spell that held her back, and started to cry. Her sobs were quiet things she tried to hold back, but she couldn't completely stop them.

"We have to help him," she said weakly.

"Izzy," Grayson said, his own voice sounding like it was thick with tears. "That's what Saul wants. For us to go after Noah. He's running out of power himself. He's sold too much of his own soul to dark magic, and he's having trouble using the ruby to its fullest extent. He thinks that if he draws several good wizards and shifters in, he can draw energy from their souls and make one more push with the dragon ruby. Noah is dead, whether we go after him or not. Saul was already trying to pull from his soul as they fell. That's why Noah's cries were so anguished."

Izzy felt her body going numb with shock. "Dark wizards can use *other people's souls* to perform dark magic?"

She'd known that dark magic required the person using it to give up a piece of their soul for each spell performed. But she'd had no idea that a dark wizard could draw from someone else's soul to perform evil spells. Izzy looked over at Peter in confusion. The old wizard nodded sadly in confirmation.

786

"It's not easy to do, but it is possible for wizards to use other people's souls to perform dark magic. It requires a very advanced use of dark magic, and the magic is weaker so you have to have dozens of souls at once, unlike when you use your own soul and only need yourself. But if anyone could do it, Saul could. He's been doing nothing but practicing dark magic for most of his life, as far as we can tell."

Izzy felt bile rising in her throat. "We can't just leave Noah, though!" she said again. But again, everyone shook their heads sadly at her.

"Izzy," Mac said. "This is war, and unfortunately there are casualties. We've lost many soldiers, and Noah happens to be one of them. He wouldn't want us to come after him. He'd know the risk of Saul performing a counterattack would be too great. The risk of our frail victory falling through is too great. The best thing we can do now is wait Saul out. Saul is dying, and as long as he has no good, pure souls to reenergize his dark magic, he'll be gone soon. Noah knows this. He'll be proud to die as a martyr for the cause."

Mac was keeping her voice as gentle as possible, but the words still felt like swords in Izzy's heart. The war was all but won, but what did it matter? If Noah was dead, then Izzy had no reason to live. The happy cheers of the Falcon Cross soldiers near Izzy felt empty. There would be no victory celebrations for her. There would only be mourning. Mourning that she had barely found her lifemate before losing him.

Peter seemed to sense that Izzy had given up her struggling. As she sat dejectedly on her broomstick, hunched over with silent sobs, she heard him say, "*Stabit terminantur.*" She felt a small rush of cool air as the *Stabit* spell around her was cancelled. She could move freely again, but what did it matter? There was no saving Noah. She felt like she never wanted to move again.

The rain was starting to subside now, and Izzy felt betrayed by it, too. How could the sky dare to stop crying, when she had just lost everything?

"Come on, Izzy," Peter said. "Let's all head down to camp. You can get a warm meal and get some rest."

Izzy was pretty sure she would never eat again, but she didn't say that. Instead, she silently turned to follow Peter as he made his way down toward the earth below, where a supply squadron would already be on the way with tents and food. Around Izzy, the dragons and other wizards flew. Many of the Falcon Cross soldiers were still cheering and swooping happily through the sky, but the soldiers closest to Izzy, the VIPs, were somber. The dragon shifters still in dragon form seemed to have no life left in their wings as they flew, and the faces of the wizards were strained.

This isn't right, Izzy thought as she descended. *I don't care if it puts all of us at risk. I cannot just let Noah die. And besides, the ruby needs to be rescued. We can't leave it there for god only knows who to find. What if someone truly evil gets to it before us, once Saul is dead?*

Izzy's heart thumped in her chest as she flew. A burning in her core, which she now recognized as the lifemate bond, was growing hotter and hotter. Her connection to Noah was telling her that he was in trouble. She dreaded the moment that the heat started to subside. She would know, then, that Noah was dead. She'd rather have this searing heat burning her from the inside out than know that Noah was gone. Didn't Peter or the other dragons understand how the lifemate bond burned within her? How it urged her to risk everything for Noah's sake, for her lifemate who was in mortal danger?

With sudden clarity, Izzy realized that this was the problem. The others didn't realize how her very core burned for Noah. They didn't realize that she and Noah were lifemates, and that she could not turn her back on Noah, no matter what the consequences. The lifemate bond was born of deep, pure love. Love that would sacrifice everything. Love that would rescue Noah or die trying.

Izzy looked around at the wizards surrounding her. Peter could cast strong spells, so if she wanted to get away she'd have to fly out of his range with lightning speed—before he realized what she was doing. The only wizard who could fly faster than her was Zoe, but Zoe was carrying Grayson on her broomstick at the moment, which might just slow her down enough to give Izzy a real shot at flying away. Izzy felt a cold sweat breaking out on her forehead as she considered her options. Was she really going to do this? Was she really going to defy the head wizards and dragons, and risk her own soul, just to go confront Saul? Saul, the evil dragon whom she was more terrified of than any other living thing in existence? Izzy didn't have to ponder the question. She already knew the answer. Her lifemate was in danger. Fears be damned. The high wizards and dragons be damned. She was going to try to save Noah, even if it was the last thing she did. Which, she realized, it very well might be the last thing she did.

Izzy slowed her speed ever so slightly, just enough to let Peter and the others pull imperceptibly ahead of her. She fell back as far as she dared—any more and suspicions would rise about what she was about to do. Taking one more deep breath, Izzy bit her lip in determination and then, as quickly and silently as possible, she turned and flew in the opposite direction of Peter and the rest of the crew.

She didn't dare look back. She knew they would be chasing her in a matter of seconds, and she didn't want to slow her speed just to see what she already knew. She bent low against her broomstick and put every ounce of her energy into the effort of flying.

In less than five seconds, she heard shouts from behind her. They had realized what she was doing. She kept flying, praying that her tiny head start was enough. She didn't know how long it took Peter to realize what was going on, but it must have been long enough for her to zoom out of his range. She heard him start to yell stopping spells, and she braced herself for impact, but nothing happened. Her heart leapt with joy. Now, if she could just stay ahead of Zoe, she was home free.

Izzy flew and prayed, and prayed and flew, panting hard and hoping against hope that she could make it away from the others before they could stop her. For a moment, she thought Zoe's shouts were growing louder, but then they started to fade away again. It was several minutes later before Izzy finally dared to look over her shoulder. No one was following her anymore. She could see the outlines of the dragons and wizards far behind her, hovering in midair. They were letting her go. Zoe had been too slow with Grayson as a passenger, and the others knew this meant that Izzy would get away. They were likely giving her up as lost at this point, too.

Izzy swallowed hard, a fresh lump of fear in her throat. She hoped with all her heart that they were wrong to think that no one would be able to challenge Saul right now while still keeping his or her soul intact. The idea of Saul using her to perform dark magic was a terrible one, but more terrible still was the thought of Noah dying at the mercy of a crazed, evil dragon wizard.

"Hang on, Noah," Izzy said as she faced forward and headed toward the spot where she'd seen Saul and Noah falling toward the earth. "I'm coming for you."

CHAPTER ELEVEN

Noah groaned as another jolt of painful, electric energy flowed through his dragon body. Saul, also in dragon form, let out an awful laugh. In some ways, the sound of that laugh was worse than the physical pain of each jolt from the dragon ruby.

Noah did his best to act as though Saul's little performance with the dragon ruby was not affecting him, but that was getting harder and harder to do. Noah knew what Saul was doing. Peter had briefed all of the dragons on the fact that it was possible for someone as advanced in dark magic as Saul was to use someone else's soul to power dark magic spells. All of the dragons had agreed that, because of this, they would not attempt a rescue should one of them be captured. It was better to let one dragon fall than to risk giving Saul access to all the dragons. If rescue attempts went poorly and the dragons were captured, Saul would have ten dragon souls at his disposal. That might be enough for him to power through some seriously destructive spells.

Noah's body twisted in pain again, followed moments later by another horrid laugh from Saul. At least this time Noah had managed not to groan. He tried to focus all his thoughts on Izzy. He'd seen her, right before Saul had taken him down. Izzy had been sitting proudly on her broomstick, a brilliant smile on her face. Noah's greatest consolation in this moment was that the war was over, and Izzy was safe. At least he could die knowing this had not all been for nothing.

Saul's large dragon form sauntered proudly back and forth across the large room they were in, and Noah couldn't keep from staring. The evil dragon was a terrible sight to behold. His hide was blood red, with swirls of black color here and there. His whole body was covered with deep, angry scars, and his head, wings, and tail all sported black spikes. His eyes were an unnatural red color, and seemed to have no pupils. Noah shivered. He wondered if Saul had always looked this awful in dragon form, or if the evil had twisted him into something especially ugly. Noah had a feeling it was the latter option.

"You fools think you've won the war," Saul said now, his voice sounding raspy and hoarse. "But I know how loyal you all are to each other. Your little friends will come rescue you, and when they do, I'll have enough soul power to launch a counterattack. This fight isn't over yet, my friend."

Noah couldn't answer while in dragon form, but he didn't want to dignify Saul's comments with a response, anyway. Someone as evil as Saul would never understand what loyalty actually meant. Noah closed his eyes so he wouldn't have to see Saul's disgusting form, and focused instead on the picture of Izzy he held in his mind's eye. The pain he felt at knowing he would never see her again weighed heavily on his heart, and he tried to recall the brief happy times they'd had instead of thinking about what her life would be like lived out without him. He wondered if destiny would send her a new lifemate. Sometimes, when a lifemate was lost to death, fate saw fit to bring a new lifemate across your path. As hard as it was to imagine Izzy with another man, Noah hoped she would find love again. He just wanted her to be happy.

Another jolt of pain, another laugh from Saul. Noah could feel his strength beginning to fade. He wondered if this gentle ebbing away of strength was what losing your soul felt like. Or perhaps this was just physical exhaustion. After all, Saul was unlikely to waste much soul power just to irritate Noah. Saul would want to save every last ounce of power for whatever final blow he had planned. Noah smiled at the thought that Saul would never get to make his final stand. No one was coming for Noah, and that was that.

A sudden chorus of loud roars rose from behind the door of the room where Saul had been torturing Noah. Noah's eyes slid open to see that even Saul seemed startled by the noise at first. But the brief moment of confusion on Saul's dragon face was quickly replaced by a happy expression.

"They're coming," Saul said. "You're friends are here for you. Too bad they're never going to take you alive. Or, should I say, they're never going to take you with your soul intact."

More evil laughter. Noah frowned, shudders of horror running through him anew at the sound of Saul's human voice coming from dragon lips. But his frown was about more than just Saul's voice. His frown was at the thought that one of his dragon clanmates had come after him.

No, Noah thought, frustration rising from his core. *We agreed not to perform any rescue operations. Go back. Don't let Saul have access to your souls.*

Another chorus of loud roars sounded from behind the door, and then, suddenly, Noah felt a hot, burning sensation in his core. The lifemate bond. Izzy was in trouble.

In the split-second before he heard her scream, Noah realized that it hadn't been one of the dragons to come for him. It had been Izzy. He was shocked, touched, and horrified by this fact. Shocked because he knew how afraid Izzy was of Saul. Touched because Izzy had come for him despite that fear. And horrified because he doubted that Izzy stood much of a chance of winning in a one-on-one fight against Saul, especially when Saul still held the dragon ruby.

Saul, still laughing, went to fling open the giant door of the large room in which they sat. Noah had been too wracked with pain to pay much attention when Saul dragged him into this building, which seemed to be some sort of hideout for the evil dragon. But now, with his presence of mind somewhat recovered, Noah could see that the door of the room led into a large, arched hallway. And in that hallway were dozens more of the same awful-looking, awful-smelling monster creature that Noah and Izzy had encountered at the Redwood Dragons Base. Noah's stomach turned at the smell, then turned again in fear when he saw that Izzy was in the hallway, too, surrounded by the awful, bloodthirsty things.

Her yells, he realized now, had been magic spells. She was yelling out attack spell after attack spell, spinning in constant circles to keep the monsters at bay. Noah groaned and tried to raise his head to help her, but he couldn't move very well. He seemed to be under some sort of spell himself, one that kept him exhausted and glued to the floor. Saul saw Noah's movement out of the corner of his eye, and turned toward him for a moment.

"*Magicae illido,*" Saul said, pointing his wizard wand at Noah. Instantly, searing pain flooded Noah's body, and a large gash appeared on the side of his left side. Hot red blood flowed down his dragon hide, and Noah could not hold back a roar of pain.

He saw Izzy look up for a moment at the sound of his roar. She never stopped circling and yelling out spells, but he saw the anxiety filling her face. She knew this was not going to be an easy rescue, if a rescue was even possible at all. Noah wished he could help her, but when he tried to stand again, despite his wounds and pain, Saul once again yelled a dark magic spell in his direction, resulting in a second gash across Noah's left side.

Izzy roared in anger herself then, and seemed to find renewed gusto. She took out several of the monsters in a row, until Saul bellowed out "Stop!" This was followed by a long string of Latin sounding words from Saul's lips. Noah wasn't sure what Saul had said, but it seemed to have the effect of calling off the monsters. They roared angrily and then ran past Izzy toward what Noah presumed was the exit. Noah dimly saw Izzy's face registering horror as she was forced to look Saul squarely in the eyes.

Noah thought for a moment that Izzy might turn and run in terror. He wished that she would. He wanted to scream at her to run, and to save herself. But he could not speak in dragon form, and he felt too weak to shift. He could feel himself bleeding out on the floor, and he wanted to weep at the thought that now not only was he going to die, but Izzy would die as well. Why had she chosen this moment to be brave? Where had she suddenly found the courage to face Saul? And why hadn't any of the other dragons or wizards stopped her, dammit!

None of that mattered now. All that mattered was finding a way to stand up, to regain his strength, and to breathe fire on Saul before Saul destroyed Izzy. But no matter how hard Noah concentrated on moving, he could not lift even one claw. He watched helplessly as Izzy stepped into the room.

Her Falcon Cross military uniform was torn in several places, and her hair was coming wildly loose from its bun. Her face was smeared with dirt and blood, and she had a rather angry gash across her left cheek.

But she had never looked more beautiful. Her eyes sparked with anger as she glared at Saul. Gone was the timid, fearful Izzy who had volunteered to go on a mission with Noah just to avoid facing Saul. This version of Izzy was out for blood—the blood of the evil dragon standing in front of her. Noah had the fleeting thought that he'd never been so turned on in his life, and that if by some miracle they both made it out of this, he was going to make love to her until she was too sore to stand properly. With a frustrated sigh, he once again strained to lift his head, but he still couldn't move. Saul's evil laugh rang out once again.

It looked like today was not going to be a day of miracles.

"Step away from the dragon!" Izzy yelled, suddenly charging into the room. Noah groaned, wishing he could somehow convince Izzy to leave. But Izzy was walking forward into the room with her eyes flashing and her magic ring raised high. She had no intention of backing down.

Saul laughed at her. "Or what? You'll zing me with that puny ring of yours? In case you haven't noticed, I've got the freaking dragon ruby on my side. Not to mention I know dark magic spells. You don't stand a chance against me."

"Good always stands a chance against evil," Izzy declared. She was still holding her ring high, but Noah heard the slight tremor in her voice as she spoke. She *was* terrified. She was doing her best to hide it, but she couldn't completely mask the way she felt. Noah was starting to catch the scent of fear coming from Izzy's direction. He wondered if Saul could smell it, too. But Saul seemed too caught up in waving the dragon ruby around to notice any smells. Noah continued struggling, but all he succeeded in doing was widening the gashes on his side. He couldn't move, and now blood was flowing out in fresh currents.

The room grew blurry. Noah stopped trying to stand, and focused all of his energy on staying conscious. Dimly, he watched as Saul and Izzy started sparring. Saul's haughty laughter rang through the air as the evil dragon flapped his wings to hover in midair, then raised both his wand and the dragon ruby. A rush of red light and electric energy surged toward Izzy, and Noah winced, thinking he was about to see Izzy die.

But she was not going to be taken down so easily.

In a flash, she had ducked and rolled to the opposite side of the room. Noah's eyes widened. He had never seen anyone move so quickly. Saul was apparently surprised by this, too, because his haughty laughter turned into an angry roar. The evil dragon raised his wand and the ruby once more, and unleashed another attack. Izzy ducked and rolled again, then responded by launching an attack from her own magic ring.

"*Magicae appugno!*" Izzy yelled out. The attack spell hit Saul square in the chest, but it had no effect. Dragon hide was thick enough to ward off most magic spells, unless you managed to hit them in a particularly vulnerable spot—and it was going to be hard for Izzy to hit Saul in a weak spot. With all of her ducking and rolling, she had to shoot off whatever attacks she could, without worrying too much about aiming.

Noah watched in despair as Saul and Izzy went round and round in circles in the large room. She avoided every attack from his wand, and threw up shield after shield when he used the ruby to attack. Noah wasn't sure how the ruby worked, but he could tell that Saul wasn't using even close to the full extent of its power right now. Noah guessed that this was because a full attack in a room this small would probably kill all of them at once. Saul was a twisted, pathetic soul at this point, but he still thought he deserved to live while others were killed off.

On and on Saul and Izzy went. The dueling pair seemed to have forgotten that Noah was even in the room. They yelled and roared and attacked. Eventually, Saul began breathing fire, but Izzy's shields were able to counter that as well. Noah wanted to scream at her to run, but all he could do was pray silently to whatever gods might be out there listening that somehow Izzy would make it through this.

Her uniform was even more tattered now, and she had several new gashes on her body. She didn't pay any attention to her wounds, though. Her eyes focused only on Saul. Noah could practically feel the hatred radiating from Izzy toward the evil dragon. The scent of fear was gone. Fear had been swallowed up by action. Noah knew the look on Izzy's face well. He'd seen it in battles dozens of times before. A soldier might be afraid for a little while, but eventually, the intensity of fighting made you forget to be afraid. Everything in you focused only on killing your opponent. Worrying about your own life was a luxury that no one had time for in the heat of battle.

Izzy fought well, but Noah could tell she was fading. Her movements were growing slower bit by bit, while Saul's speed remained steady. It wouldn't be long now before Saul managed to take her down. Noah felt adrenaline rushing through his own veins. He tried over and over to stand up, but the spell Saul had cast on him held him down. Frustrated, Noah even tried whipping his tail around to strike Saul with its spikes. But his tail was weighed down by dark magic as well. Noah felt his strength seeping out of him, and, if not for the primal urge he felt to protect Izzy, he would have been happy to just give up and die. He could not give up, though. Not while Izzy still lived. He would break through this spell and help Izzy, or he would die trying. He was not going down without a struggle.

He strained his neck upward again just in time to see Saul finally hit Izzy with a spell from his wand. The scene unfolded before Noah as if he was watching it in slow motion. Izzy's forward motion was stopped with sudden force. She looked like she had just run into a wall. Her eyes widened in pain and shock, and Noah saw her starting to tumble to the ground. Saul's evil laughter rang out once again when he realized he'd hit his mark. The laughter grew louder as Izzy crumpled to the ground like a rag doll, her eyes still wide in shock. Noah's heart twisted in his chest when he saw a small river of dark red blood beginning to flow from Izzy's side. He struggled harder than ever to raise himself up, but his efforts were just as useless as before.

Saul stepped closer to Izzy, laughing and twirling his wand in his disgusting black claws. He raised it to hit Izzy with another spell, one that would likely be the final death blow to the woman Noah loved. Saul seemed to have forgotten all about keeping Izzy alive to save her soul for his dark magic. The twisted dragon had become deranged and bloodthirsty in the heat of battle.

No! Noah thought. From deep within him, words he had spoken to Izzy in the Redwoods came rushing back to him. *I swear to you, Izzy, if it's the last thing I do, I will kill Saul for how he hurt you... As long as there is breath left in my body, I will fight to avenge you, and to protect you.*

Noah still had breath left in his body, and it was past time to avenge Izzy. He had not come this far and fought this hard only to watch the woman he loved die before dying himself. In desperation, he focused all of his energy only on his spiked tail. He squeezed his eyes shut and concentrated on lifting his tail and hurling it in Saul's direction. If only he could hit Saul somewhere it would count. Somewhere that would cause the evil dragon intense pain.

Noah focused and struggled, but his tail didn't budge. He was about to give up when he heard a soft, pathetic whimper. He opened his eyes and saw that Izzy, barely conscious, was trying to shield her face from Saul's raised wand, as though her hands alone could somehow stop whatever spell he was about to throw at her. A feeling of protective rage surged through Noah, giving him just the energy boost he needed to get his tail off the ground. He swung toward Saul's eyes, knowing he would only have one shot. He had to hit something that mattered.

Saul turned his head slightly, sensing the movement behind him. Noah missed Saul's eyes because of this, but managed to lodge a spike deep into one of Saul's ears. Saul yelped in pain, heaving his giant dragon body upward in surprise and hitting his head on the ceiling. When his head collided with the ceiling, Saul lost his grip on the dragon ruby. The ruby slipped from his fingers and clattered across the floor, stopping just inches from Noah's front right dragon claw.

Hardly daring to believe his good luck, Noah grasped for the ruby. When his claws closed around the cool hard stone, he felt a surge of hope. He was not alone or defenseless anymore. He had no clue how to use the ruby, but at least he had it in his grasp. Saul would be significantly weaker without it.

Saul realized then what had happened, and roared with anger at the sight of Noah holding the ruby. Saul raised his magic wand and pointed it directly at Noah's head. From somewhere behind Saul, Noah heard Izzy screaming in terror.

Noah had no time to think, or to wonder how the dragon ruby worked. He raised it in front of him like a shield, surprised to find that he could move a bit easier now. The ruby was giving him power, even though he was still under Saul's spell. Saul yelled out another attack spell, and Noah, in desperation, yelled out to the ruby.

"Kill him!" Noah screamed, right before a fresh wave of pain washed over his body from Saul's attack spell. Noah squeezed his eyes shut, sure for the dozenth time tonight that he was about to die. But he didn't die. Instead, he heard an anguished roar coming from Saul's lips.

Noah opened his eyes again to find that Saul was covered in red electricity and was swaying back and forth. The evil dragon's red eyes twisted in pain, and he pawed at the air as though looking for some relief. Foam started coming from his mouth, and then, with a sudden lurch, he fell to the ground.

Noah blinked in surprise, looking from the lifeless dragon to his own hand, where he still clutched the dragon ruby.

"It listened to me," he said in amazement. "The ruby listened to me. I told it to kill

Saul, and it did."

A moan from across the room snapped Noah out of his brief reverie. He looked over to see Izzy holding her side, and gasping in pain. Noah quickly stood and started walking over to her, then realized with a start that he could move again. The spell Saul had cast over him had disappeared as soon as Saul had died. Noah gave Saul a tentative shove with his dragon nose as he passed. The evil dragon did not move. His face was frozen in a twisted expression of horror, and his wide, empty eyes were fixed lifelessly on the ceiling above them. The evil dragon, who had caused so much pain for so many, was indeed dead.

Noah turned his dragon head to look at Izzy, but it was hard to assess her injuries while he was in dragon form. With a grunt, he closed his eyes and began shifting back into a human. When his transformation was complete, he was horrified to see how deep the wounds in his side were. The wounds had been irritated by his shifting, and blood flowed anew from his sides. He needed medical attention, and soon. But he couldn't focus on his own needs until he knew that Izzy was alright. Limping, he made his way over to kneel beside her. She blinked her eyes open, staring up at him with a dazed look. She had deep gashes in her side, too, and had lost a tremendous amount of blood. Noah did his best not to panic. He had no idea how they were going to get out of here together and find medical care, wounded as they were. But he had to believe that they had not come this far just to die themselves.

"Saul...dead?" Izzy asked, unable to find the strength to form even a complete sentence.

Noah nodded. "He's dead. He won't be hurting anyone else."

Izzy closed her eyes and sighed, and Noah bit back tears.

"Stay with me, Izzy. I'm going to get you help. We're going to be okay."

"Too...late...for me," Izzy said, then coughed and sputtered blood from her mouth.

"No!" Noah said. "No, it's not too late. We just need a doctor to stitch you up and you'll be good as new in a few days."

Izzy made no reply, other than to sigh again. Noah pulled her head against his chest, unable to stop a few tears from squeezing past his eyelids. Izzy was right. Unless a doctor miraculously appeared out of thin air within the next few minutes, she wasn't going to make it. He choked on his sobs, trying to hold them back and to stay strong for her sake.

"Shhh. It's all going to be okay," he whispered in her ear, even though he knew it wasn't.

And then, as if to make things worse, he heard shouting in the hallway, along with the pounding of boots. More dark wizards, he thought. Can't they leave us alone? Saul is dead, and we're as good as dead. Just let us die in peace.

When the door to the room flung open, Noah looked up wearily and readied himself to once again shift into dragon form and fight. But then he stopped, his eyes widening at what he saw. A large group of men, all dragon shifters from the scent of them, had barged through the open doorway and were looking from him to Saul to Izzy. They all started talking at once, but Noah didn't have the strength to tell them to speak one at a time. He didn't have the strength to ask them who they were or where they'd come from. All he knew was that the sight of these dragons, with their pure eyes, clearly unsullied by Saul's evil ways, was the most beautiful thing he'd seen in a long time—other than Izzy, of course.

"Doctor," he choked out, looking up at the men and using his last strength to ask for help. He held Izzy's limp hand tightly as he spoke. "Need…doctor."

And then, his world went black.

CHAPTER TWELVE

Izzy blinked her eyes open and was startled to see sunbeams dancing on the green nylon roof of the tent she was lying in. The last thing she remembered thinking was that death was only minutes away for her, but she must have been wrong. She didn't have strong views on whether there was an afterlife or not, but she was pretty sure that whatever heaven might be out there was unlikely to be populated with green nylon tents.

Not to mention the dull, throbbing pain she could feel in her left side. Her hand went to the spot under her t-shirt from where the pain seemed to emanate, and she felt the prickly, plastic feel of stitches. No, she definitely wasn't in heaven. She was pretty sure that once you got to heaven, any major injuries were healed up for you.

Slowly, wincing, Izzy sat up. She was wearing a pair of loose black sweatpants in addition to her white t-shirt. Her feet were bare, and she bit back a gasp at the sight of them. They were black and blue with bruises, and on her right foot her big toe had been bandaged up. She tried to wriggle it, then quickly stopped when the movement instantly caused needlelike pain to shoot into her foot and up her leg.

Izzy stretched out her arms in front of her and saw that they were also bruised and scratched. She put her hands to her face and felt long, scabbed wounds there as well. She decided it might be a good thing that tents didn't usually have mirrors. If her face looked anything like her feet and arms, she'd rather not look at it right now.

Izzy crawled stiffly toward the entrance of her tent and unzipped it. When she peered out, she was greeted by the sight of dozens of other tents. Here and there, hiking backpacks were propped up against trees or large stones, and several dozen yards away from her tent, she could see groups of people milling about, all wearing Falcon Cross military uniforms. Izzy strained to see a familiar face among the clusters of soldiers, but none of them looked familiar. The face she really wanted to see was Noah's.

With a sigh, Izzy crawled completely out of the tent and stood to her full height. She paused for a few moments, feeling dizzy at the change in position even though her movements had all been slow and careful. Before she could get her bearings again, she heard a voice that made her heart leap and sent a rush of warm happiness through every last cell in her body.

"Izzy! You're up."

She turned to look behind her tent. There was a spot there for a large campfire, although no flames burned at the moment. Dozens of log benches surrounded the spot, and Noah was rising from one of the benches. Dimly, she realized that many of the other Falcon Cross VIPs were sitting on the benches, too. The dragon shifters, the wizard military officers, Peter, and some other tall men who looked important but whom Izzy didn't recognize. She didn't care that much who was here, though. Noah was the only one who mattered, and he was running toward her now. She tried to run, too, but only managed a slight hobble.

When he reached her, he threw his arms around her. She didn't care that the movement jabbed at her stitched up side in the wrong way, sending a searing pain through her body. All she cared about was that Noah was alive. He was safe, and his arms were around her. And then, his lips were on her lips. He pressed a long, firm kiss onto her mouth, which resulted in a chorus of teasing whoops rising up behind him. He ignored them, pulling away to look into Izzy's eyes.

"Are you alright? How do you feel?"

"I'm okay, I guess," Izzy replied. "My side hurts, but it seems you found someone to stitch it up nicely."

"Yeah. They stitched me up, too." Noah raised his t-shirt to reveal long, red marks which ran angrily down both his left and right sides.

Izzy gasped. "I should be asking you if *you're* okay."

Noah shrugged. "I'm fine. Dragons heal quickly. I was more worried about you, but you seem to be recovering nicely. It's a long story, but a group of dragon shifters had been imprisoned in Saul's hideout, and they were set free when Saul died. Luckily, one of them had medical training."

Izzy looked at the group of unfamiliar men on the logs near the VIPs. "Are those guys the dragons from Saul's hideout?"

Noah nodded. "Yup. Guess it's not that hard to tell when someone is a dragon, once you know what to look for."

"So Saul is really dead?" Izzy asked, still looking over at the new group of dragons.

"Yup. We killed him together. You were one hell of a warrior in there. Really made me eat my words about you being a coward."

Izzy looked up at Noah's green eyes that she loved so much. "I think I'm still a coward. I still felt terrified. But I couldn't leave you there alone." Izzy glanced over at Peter, who was deep in conversation with Raven at the moment. "I directly defied the head wizard," she said, feeling a rush of guilt at the memory. "He must be furious with me."

Noah laughed and bent to kiss her nose. "I wouldn't worry too much about that. Because of you, Saul is dead and we recovered the dragon ruby. I think you'll find that these victories put Peter in quite the forgiving mood."

Izzy smiled. "Victory," she said. "Such a sweet word."

"Agreed."

"But if we won, then why are we all still camped out here? Why not head back to Falcon Cross?"

"We were waiting for you to wake up and feel well enough to travel. There's no rush, but as soon as you're up to it, we'll be heading back. Most of the army has been packing up to head out tonight, but a small squadron will stay behind while you heal."

"I can leave tonight," Izzy said, standing up straighter as though that would prove she was well enough to travel.

"Are you sure? There's really no rush."

"I'm sure. I'm ready to be home."

* * *

The trip home was mercifully uneventful. Riding on a broomstick wasn't easy for Izzy in her weakened state, but she managed. As soon as they entered Falcon Cross airspace, Izzy knew she'd made the right choice in coming straight home. The mood in the city was nothing short of jubilant. News of the final victory over Saul had already spread, and people were dancing in the streets. Celebration festivals were already in full swing, and Izzy felt energized by the happiness in the air.

With the chance to sleep in her own bed, in safety and peace, Izzy made a quick recovery. Noah visited her often, but he was also quite busy with official business. He had dived right back into work, although now work was much more fun than it had been before. There were official celebrations to be planned, and award ceremonies to be attended. For two solid weeks, there was at least one victory party every day. Izzy attended as many of them as she could. She was awarded a medal at one of the ceremonies in recognition of her help in recovering the dragon ruby. Izzy didn't feel that she needed any special recognition, but she was quite glad that Peter had so easily pardoned her for her defiance of his orders. He knew as well as she did that things could have gone quite badly if her rescue attempt had been unsuccessful, but he didn't hold this against her. Peter had never been the vindictive type.

Two and half weeks after arriving home, Izzy found herself sitting next to Noah in the VIP meeting room, in the very same chair where she'd sat at their last meeting, when she'd been so afraid of Saul. It had been less than a month, but that day felt like a lifetime ago.

The mood in the room was quite different this time, too. Instead of strained worry, there was laughter and joy. And instead of Noah being merely an acquaintance, he was Izzy's lifemate and lover. He reached to hold her knee under the table, and Izzy couldn't stop a silly grin from spreading across her face.

"Alright, alright everyone!" Peter yelled above the din of conversation. "Let's get this meeting started. We have quite a few things to cover."

It took several more tries before Peter managed to quiet everyone down. When he did, he started briskly going through his long agenda. There were several items that related to how the Falcon Cross military would be reorganized for peacetime. There were also a few more official celebrations remaining, and Peter asked for volunteers for various tasks. The most pressing matter, however, was what to do with the prisoners of war. After she returned to Falcon Cross, Izzy had learned that many of Saul's dark wizards and evil shifters had been captured. Many were too far gone to help, having lost too much of their soul to dark magic. Those wizards had been placed in prison cells here in Falcon Cross to live out the rest of their lives, however short that time might be. Most wizards didn't last very long when they'd been practicing as much dark magic as these ones had. Some of the wizards, however, had been new enough to Saul's army that Peter believed they could be rehabilitated to become good citizens of the wizard and shifter communities.

Izzy found her mind wandering while Peter spoke. She wasn't sure what part she was going to play in the efforts to rebuild after the war. She hoped there would be some way for her to work as a doctor again, instead of as some sort of military officer. Surely, there was a place for a doctor to be useful in the post-war world. She missed doing the work that she knew she did best. And, from the sound of it, there was a lot of work for everyone to do. Peter was now talking about the monsters, many of which had escaped from Saul's hideout the night Izzy had stormed in to rescue Noah.

"We don't know how many there are, unfortunately. We searched Saul's headquarters and it seems he did not keep a record of how many shifters he changed into monsters. Our best guess, based on the food supplies left in the rooms that had housed the monsters, is that there were about fifty monsters total. We have a team trying to track them down, but it isn't easy. They tend to find places deep in the forest to hide, only coming out when they are in the mood to kill."

"Um, how often are they in the mood to kill?" Grayson asked, sounding somewhat alarmed.

Peter shrugged. "No one can say. They are inherently unstable creatures, thanks to the dark magic used to create them. Saul appears to have used them as guards. That's why he left one at the Redwoods Base. But they are relatively easy to take down if you are prepared to meet them. Our wizards will track them down and kill them, even if it takes a while. Some of the dragons Saul had imprisoned want to help with the search effort, too. They are eager for a chance to do anything to destroy what Saul had built."

Izzy perked up at the mention of the dragons. "Where did Saul find those dragons?" she asked. She'd been meaning to ask Noah for more information about the dragons, but he had been so busy and there had been so many other things to catch up on as well. Izzy had, at least, had the opportunity to meet with the dragon who had stitched up her and Noah, saving their lives. There had been a lot of life-saving going on in the last week of the war, it seemed.

Knox was the one to answer her question. "Saul found the dragons all over the place. Most of them were in normal human towns, trying to live as normal humans and keep their dragon shifter side a secret. But Saul had scouts specially trained to find dragons. Once the scouts found the dragons, they took them unaware. The dragons had no idea there was any kind of war going on, so they were easy to take by surprise. Saul imprisoned them and was trying to convince them to join his army. We think he was intending to use their souls for dark magic spells if they didn't agree soon. But, thanks to you and Noah, Saul got distracted and never got that far."

Izzy felt a puff of pride in her chest. Even though she'd defied Peter and the others, it seems she'd done the right thing after all. "And now?" she asked. "What will those dragons do now?"

Knox shrugged. "Well, like Peter said, some of them will help track down the monsters. The remaining majority will find new homes, probably in shifter or wizard communities. A few will head back to where they lived before the war, but most of them don't want to go back to their human towns now. They didn't like being caught off guard by what was going on in the shifter and wizard worlds. We think they'll become good allies for us in holding back evil forces and making sure evil doesn't rise again like it did with Saul."

Izzy nodded. "It seems, then, that everyone is settling down again after the war."

"That's true," Noah said, squeezing Izzy's hand again under the table as he started speaking. "And I think that means it's time for the Redwood Dragons to go home, too."

Izzy felt her heart sinking. She had known, of course, that this day would come. The dragons had only come to Falcon Cross because of the war. But now, the war was over, and their home had been reclaimed. They would want to go back and repair the damage to their cabins, restock the artifact vaults, and get back to life as a clan of their own. Izzy wasn't sure that there would be a place for her in the Redwoods, though. She knew Noah would want her to come. They were lifemates, after all. But what would she do for work out in the middle of nowhere, with a group of ten dragons and their lifemates? Before Izzy could twist her mind up too much in worry, Knox was speaking again.

"Noah's right. It's time for the dragons to go home. We have a lot to do back in the redwoods—including building new cabins."

"New cabins?" Peter inquired with mild interest. "You mean you're not going to just repair the ones that were damaged? Do you think they're too messed up to fix?"

Knox shook his head no. "We'll fix the damaged cabins. But we'll need to build new cabins, too. You see, our clan has voted, and we've decided to open our home base up to any shifters who have been left homeless by the war. We know there are many who need homes, and we want to do our part to help. This war has also made us realize that our clan is too isolated. Being here in Falcon Cross, and being part of the wonderful city you wizards have built here, has made us realize that we would benefit from building up our clan into a larger village."

"Knox, that's wonderful!" Peter said, sitting up and clapping his hands twice in excitement. "There are so many shifter refugees that will be thrilled to hear that."

Izzy felt her own heart pounding with excitement. Surely, if the Redwoods base was going to be built up into an actual city, then there would be something for her to do there. The town would need doctors wouldn't it?

Noah had already anticipated Izzy's question. He was looking at her now, his lips stretched into a wide grin and his eyes sparkling. "We're gonna need a town doctor. What do you say, Izzy? Would you be willing to come out to the Redwoods and help establish our first official clinic?"

A grin just as wide as Noah's spread across Izzy's face. "I'd love to," she said. And then she leaned over to give him a hug and a firm kiss on the lips. She didn't care that they were in front of all of the Redwood Dragons and Falcon Cross VIPs. She was overcome with love for Noah in that moment.

And, for the first time since she'd been pulled into this war, she felt like she was anchored to something. She was going home—to her new home.

CHAPTER THIRTEEN

Izzy spent the rest of the week on a cloud, happily packing up her few belongings and making plans for her trip to the Redwoods. But when all of her packing was done, and she found herself sitting in an apartment full of boxes with nothing to do except think about the move she was about to make, she came tumbling down off that cloud.

She started to panic, and couldn't stop herself from worrying about every single thing that could possibly go wrong. Noah had promised to come over after work that day, and by the time he arrived at five forty-five p.m., Izzy was pacing like a wild animal and desperately trying to hold back tears. She felt like an idiot for being so overcome by worry, but it was too late to act like everything was fine. She hadn't heard Noah letting himself in, and he saw the distress in her face before she had time to hide it.

"Izzy? What's wrong?" He set down the bag of takeout he'd brought with him and crossed the room in three quick strides, hopping over a small pile of packing tape and bubble wrap to pull her into his arms. "You look like you've had a horrible day."

"It's nothing," Izzy said, refusing to look into his eyes. She felt like if she met his gaze, always so warm and intense, that she might crack. Her heart felt fragile, like she'd been holding it together through sheer will during the entire war, and, now that peace was finally here, she had no strength left to keep the fractures from splitting completely open.

"It's not nothing," Noah said, putting a finger under her chin and forcing her to look up. She tried to smile bravely, but it was no use. The tears came then, warm and salty and unrelenting. Noah pulled her in close and wrapped his arms around her.

"Hey, it's ok. You're safe here. Tell me what's wrong."

Izzy sniffed and desperately tried to get enough control of her emotions to speak. "That's the problem," she said. "I'm not sure that I'm safe. I'm not sure I'll ever be safe again. And now that the reality of once again starting over somewhere new is setting in, I'm terrified. I've only just gotten used to Falcon Cross, and now I'm leaving. My life feels like one constant change after another, and I'm tired of it. I'm tired of always being the new person, and of not truly fitting in."

Izzy felt a deep grunt coming from Noah's chest. She blinked rapidly at the tears still escaping down her face, and for a moment marveled at how blurry all of the boxes looked through her water-filled eyes. Noah didn't say anything yet. He merely stroked her hair and sighed again. Izzy wasn't quite sure how to interpret his sigh, so she kept talking.

"I want to be brave, but I feel like I used up all of my bravery facing down Saul. I'm tired, and spent. I feel like I packed up everything here while on some sort of post-war high, but now I've come crashing down. I feel cold, and alone, like I'll never truly be safe again. Sure, the war is over. But what's to stop another evil man from rising? What's to stop some other catastrophe that will force me to move homes again? What if I don't fit in at the redwoods? What if the shifters don't like me, once they get to know me? What if—"

"Izzy, stop," Noah said, cutting in. "You're working yourself up for no reason. I have no doubt that everyone in the redwoods will love you, but even if they don't, it doesn't matter. *I* love you. I can't guarantee that there will never be another war or another evil villain. No one can guarantee that. But I can guarantee that I will always fight for you. As long as I'm alive, you'll never be alone. And with my arms around you, you'll never be cold."

Izzy sniffed in response, still trying to stem the flow of tears.

"I don't foresee us ever having to move away from the Redwoods," Noah said. "But even if we do, moving physical locations shouldn't make you feel unstable. All this stuff isn't your home."

Noah paused to sweep one of his arms wide, indicating all of the cardboard moving boxes.

"Your home is in my heart," Noah said. "As long as we are together, it doesn't matter where we are. We're safe, and warm, and home."

Izzy sniffed again, and Noah gently pushed her chin up.

"Look at me, Izzy," he said, his voice urgent. "I need you to hear me. I need you to understand this. We're together now. Your days of being alone and without security are over. It's okay to be nostalgic or sad about leaving behind the places where you used to live, but don't feel like you're just drifting. You're settling down into a brand new family. Our family. I love you, and you love me. That's enough. Together, we make a family."

Izzy took a deep breath and let it out slowly. Noah's words were finally starting to reach her and calm her. She gave him a weak smile, and he smiled back. The sight of his grin stirred up a familiar warm feeling in her core. She took another breath, and her own smile grew a bit stronger.

"Thank you for believing in me, Noah," she said. "I know sometimes I'm too nervous and not so easy to deal with. But I promise I'm working on things. And knowing that you're here with me helps a lot."

Noah bent to kiss her nose, not caring that it was wet from crying. "Don't apologize. You're perfect just the way you are. You've proven over and over again that you're brave when it counts. And you aren't afraid to admit it when you feel weak. That in itself takes a lot of guts and strength."

Izzy wiped at the last of her tears, feeling much better. The panic that had risen in her chest over the last several hours finally started to subside. She knew there would be challenging days ahead, as the Redwoods Base was rebuilt and as she and Noah figured out how to best build their own life together. But what fun was life without a little challenge?

Her life had been completely turned upside down by this war, but a lot of good had come of that, too. After all, she had Noah. She had a new clan thanks to the Redwood Dragons. And, even though it was true that nothing could ever be guaranteed, the future looked like it would be full of times of peace and happiness. Izzy took one more deep breath and let it out in a happy sigh.

"Feel better?" Noah asked.

"Much. Thanks for the pep talk."

He laughed. "Anytime. Now, are you ready to eat? I got us Thai takeout, and we should eat it up before it gets too cold."

"I'm starving. Packing is hungry work."

Noah laughed, and over the next hour Izzy shared noodles and a bottle of wine with him. When they'd polished off the last of the food. Izzy sat back against the wall with a satisfied grunt.

"I wish my TV wasn't packed away already," she said. "I'd give anything to sit my butt on the couch and watch a movie right now. I deserve it after working so hard to get all this packing done."

"Are you finished packing up, then?" Noah asked, looking around. Izzy also gazed around the room.

"Pretty much. I have some toiletries left in the bathroom and some blankets left on the bed, but that's about it. The truck for donations comes at noon tomorrow, so I had to be done by then at the latest."

Noah nodded, still looking at the boxes. "Will you miss your stuff?" he asked. He sounded slightly guilty.

Izzy laughed. "No, not really. It was all new stuff that I wasn't attached to yet, anyway."

It was true, she thought as she glanced at the box directly to her right. Like the vast majority of the boxes, she had written "To Donate" on it in bold, permanent marker letters. Since she'd be living in a small cabin out in the redwoods, she couldn't take much with her. All of her furniture would be donated, along with almost all of her household goods. But she'd only owned these things for a short time, while she'd been living in Falcon Cross. Everything she had owned in her former life, before Saul invaded her clan's village, was long gone by now. In some ways, though, it was nice to have a fresh start. There was nothing holding her back from being exactly who she wanted to be.

"Well, we could always go back to my place to watch TV if you want," Noah said. "My apartment was pre-furnished so all of the furniture is staying behind when I leave. But if you want to stay here, I could think of other ways we could entertain ourselves."

Noah's voice dropped to a low, husky tone as he spoke this last sentence, and Izzy felt a ripple of desire rush through her body. She didn't have to ask Noah what kind of entertainment he had in mind. His eyes told her everything she needed to know.

"I think I'd rather stay here," she said, her own voice sounding low and thick.

Noah smiled, and then leaned over to push her onto her back, smashing her against the plush carpet with both his body and his kiss. Izzy loved having the weight of him on top of her. He was more muscular than any man she'd ever seen, and yet, he held himself over her in a way that kept her from being truly squashed.

The pressure of his body on hers intoxicated her. They'd made love dozens of times since that first night, stealing away any time they could to enjoy each other's bodies. But tonight, the heat between them felt hotter than ever. Perhaps it was the fact that this was the last time they would be together in Izzy's apartment here. Their intense kiss felt like a goodbye toast. They were raising a glass to Falcon Cross, the place that had brought them together.

Izzy felt the wondrous, familiar feeling of melting into Noah. His tongue slipped into her mouth, and she closed her eyes to focus fully on savoring his taste. He ran his hands up and down her body, feeling her curves underneath the soft cotton of her t-shirt and sweatpants. She had dressed for packing today, not for impressing a man. She was keenly aware that her face was streaked with dust and sweat, and that her hair was held up in a messy bun that pushed the limits of the word "messy." But Noah didn't care. He loved her just the way she was, as evidenced by the way he pulled back to look at her and whisper, "God, you're beautiful."

Another ripple of pleasure radiated through Izzy at his words. She felt herself growing wet between her legs, already dripping with the anticipation of what she knew was coming. If there's one thing she'd learned about her dragon in the last several weeks, it was that he was truly a beast in bed. Even when he was being tender in his lovemaking, there was a certain authority and power in his movements that made her truly feel like she was experiencing the fire of a dragon.

And she wouldn't have wanted it any other way.

He was on fire now, this dragon of hers. He was kissing her again, with renewed intensity, while already reaching down for the hem of her t-shirt. He was hungry today, Izzy could tell. He wasn't going to be spending a lot of time on any preliminary mating dances. He was going to take her, and take her with a vengeance. She shivered in delight at the thought.

Their arms and legs became a tangle of limbs as he pulled back to pull off her shirt, then yanked her bra off without even bothering to unclasp it. She heard the hook snap as it broke, and she giggled.

"Hey! Bras are expensive, mister," she teased.

"I'll buy you a new one," he growled. Then he was tearing off more clothes—his own shirt, her pants, his pants, their underwear. Everything was a blur of cotton and skin, until they were both naked on the carpet in a valley between mountains of cardboard boxes. Izzy could smell the thick papery scent of cardboard mixed with the woodsy smell that always clung to Noah, and she breathed in deeply as the fire in her belly turned into an inferno.

There was nothing quite like the moment Noah slid into her. His stiff, thick shaft slipped into her hot, wet entrance like a steel rod. A thousand fireworks went off within her, and she moaned at the pleasure that came from his large girth pressing insistently against her inner walls, making room. He must have felt a similar rush of pleasure, because he let out a long moan as their bodies connected.

"You're so wet," he said.

"For you," Izzy whimpered.

"I love that I do this to you."

And then he was thrusting. The fireworks intensified, and the pressure within her built. She squeezed her eyes shut and let the wonder of it overtake her. She felt like she was on the very edge of a cliff, suspended in time as she waited to fall over the edge into the magnificence that lay beyond.

And then, she fell.

She fell into the sweet release he gave her. Her body trembled and spasmed as heat rushed through her. Wave after wave of ecstasy washed over her, until she could hardly breathe from delight. She heard Noah growl, and felt him thrusting harder and faster. Within moments, he had joined her in jumping over the edge, pulsing into her as he found his own release. Their bodies throbbed together for several long, rapturous moments, until finally their breathing steadied and their bodies settled into a sweet, satisfied calmness.

Noah slid out of her and lay beside her amidst the boxes, reaching over to interlace his fingers with Izzy's. She smiled, and then laughed.

"What?" he asked, turning his head sideways to look at her.

"It's just funny that my bed hasn't been hauled away yet but we still made love on the floor."

Noah raised his shoulders in a slight shrug. "I couldn't be bothered to pause to get up and go to the bedroom. Besides, I think you and I like to do things a bit differently, wouldn't you say?"

Izzy smiled. "I suppose we do. But that's not all that surprising, is it? After all, our lives have been anything but normal."

Noah squeezed her hand in response. Izzy closed her eyes and enjoyed the feeling of the soft carpet against her back, and Noah's warm hand around hers. Her life hadn't been normal, and, many times, it had been almost unbearably hard. Yet, somehow, she'd come out on the other side of the war better than before. She was a work in progress, but she was braver, stronger, and wiser than the woman she had been the day her clan had been killed off by Saul. She would move forward in her new life with a better sense of what it meant to truly live.

And she would move forward with the love of her life beside her. Her dragon, her everything. Together, they had found victory. Together, they would forge this new trail. Together, they were stronger.

CHAPTER FOURTEEN

*** *Epilogue: Three Years Later* ***

"Hey! Are you guys gonna actually cook any meat, or are you just gonna stand there and drink beer all day?" Knox yelled.

Noah laughed, then looked over at Myles and rolled his eyes. Myles burst out laughing, probably more due to the number of beers he'd had than to his amusement at Noah's facial expressions.

"I'm not kidding," Knox said. "Vance is going to die of starvation if you don't get him some brats soon! Look at the poor man. He's wasting away!"

Vance was, in fact, stuffing his face with mashed potatoes at that very moment. Beside him, Grayson, Owen, and Weston were similarly occupied. Noah laughed again, but then turned his attention momentarily to adding more brats and burgers to the giant grill in front of him. He glanced up again once the meat was sizzling, and took in more of the scene in front of him. Holden and Finn were playing catch with some of the youngest boys in the Redwood Dragons Clan. The boys were actually bear shifters instead of dragons. In fact, the Redwood Dragons Clan was now made up of just about every type of shifter you could imagine, but the name "Redwood Dragons" had stuck, anyway.

Today was the three year anniversary of the day the Redwood Dragons had returned to the redwood forests to rebuild after the war. In honor of that momentous occasion, this day had been designated an official clan holiday. Last year the tradition of a celebratory barbeque had begun, and this year, that tradition was being continued with an even bigger barbeque. The clan had a lot to celebrate.

After the war ended, the dragons and many other shifter refugees had not only rebuilt the original redwoods cabins, but also built several dozen new houses. A general store was added, and a school, along with a town center and a city hall. Slowly but surely, the place began to resemble an actual village, albeit a small one. Noah had worried that he wouldn't like living in a village as opposed to a small camp of ten bachelors, but the change had been a good one. The dragon stones were kept here now, in the vaults, so it was nice to have plenty of men to guard the place. Besides, Noah's life was richer thanks to all of his new friends, and he had to admit that living in a community had its perks. Everyone here had different talents, and they all pitched in to make life in the redwoods the best, fullest life it could be. Of course, Noah was proudest of Izzy and her little medical clinic. She had done a great job of keeping everyone here healthy.

"Unkie Nowah. Unkie Nowah! More!"

Noah looked down to see the source of the little voice drifting up to him, then smiled. Lucas, Knox and Bree's son who was just over two years old, was in search of another burger. Noah smiled down at the boy and took a small burger from the pile of meat that was already cooked.

"Here you go, buddy. Uncle Noah has a burger here just for you! If you want ketchup go ask your uncles at the picnic table. They've got some over there."

Noah placed the burger on the boy's paper plate, and the toddler proudly waddled off toward the picnic table where many of the other dragon shifters were sitting. Bree intercepted him on the way, admonishing him to hold the plate more carefully lest his burger fall to the ground.

"Dirt builds the immune system!" Noah called out to her. Bree glared back at him and then turned her attention back to her son.

Noah only laughed, then focused his attention on turning the meat. When he looked up again, his eye caught a blue streak that he knew was his own son, Jacob, as the boy ran across the lawn, squealing with laughter as his Auntie Elise chased him. Noah's heart filled with pride as he watched the boy, who was younger than Lucas by a month. Noah had thought he'd be the last one of the dragons to have kids, but he'd very nearly been the first. What could he say? He couldn't keep his hands off Izzy, so they'd had plenty of opportunities to make a baby. In fact, they were well on their way to having a second baby.

Noah's gaze turned to where Izzy was standing now, munching on a hamburger while talking to Zeke, Mac, and Raven. Zeke was rubbing Mac's belly, which was swollen in its ninth month of pregnancy. Izzy was not far behind, with an only slightly smaller seven month belly. Raven, who hadn't yet jumped on the baby train, would be taking over for Mac in heading up the wizard-shifter military alliance while Mac was on maternity leave. All of the wizards who'd joined up with the Redwood Dragons had found new jobs to do here that allowed them to live with their dragons while continuing their work. The ties between Falcon Cross and the Redwood Dragons were unbreakable now, and Noah knew this meant that the peace that the shifters and wizards had enjoyed for the last three years was very likely to continue. Evil could not easily rise against such a tremendous alliance for good.

Izzy turned then, and saw Noah staring in her direction. She smiled and blew a kiss at him, which he returned by blowing a kiss of his own in her direction. She was always lovely, but now, glowing with his baby on the way, and with a mini-me already here and running around, she was impossibly breathtaking. He would never dream of calling her a coward anymore. Motherhood took a special kind of bravery that even he, a mighty dragon would never have.

Still, he was glad that she'd been frightened three years ago on the cusp of that last great battle against Saul. That fear had driven her into his arms, and made them both stronger. And now, they were living out their happily ever after. As a wizard, she was magical, but the true magic was in the joining of their hearts.

Even a tough dragon like Noah could appreciate a fairytale ending. Looking around at his clanmates as they happily enjoyed the celebration with their lifemates, he had a feeling that they could, too.

ABOUT THE AUTHOR

Bestselling author Sloane Meyers writes steamy paranormal romance that will keep you turning pages well past bedtime!

Sloane thinks we could all use a little escape in our lives. And what better way to shake up the ordinary than to transport yourself to the mysterious worlds beyond our world? Sloane brings you hot alpha males and spunky, spirited heroines—always with happily ever afters!

When she's not busy writing, Sloane spends her time reading, hiking, or just hanging out with family and friends.

Want more interaction? Visit Sloane on her website at www.sloanemeyers.com.

Printed by Amazon Italia Logistica S.r.l.
Torrazza Piemonte (TO), Italy

13203128R00465